La Regenta

LEOPOLDO ALAS

LA REGENTA

TRANSLATED WITH AN INTRODUCTION
BY JOHN RUTHERFORD

The University of Georgia Press
Athens

The University of Georgia Press
Athens, Georgia 30602

First published 1884–85
This translation first published 1984

Copyright © John Rutherford, 1984

ISBN 0-8203-0700-9

Set in Palatino
Filmset, printed and bound in Great Britain by
Hazell Watson & Viney Ltd, Aylesbury, Bucks

CONTENTS

INTRODUCTION

La Regenta

Towards the end of 1884, at the age of thirty-two, Leopoldo Alas, a professor of Roman law at the University of Oviedo in the north of Spain, finished volume one of his first novel, *La Regenta*. He had previously published some short stories and would later write another novel, *Su único hijo* (1891). By April 1885 the second, final volume of *La Regenta* was complete. Alas's speed of composition was remarkable, especially since he had little time to devote to his novel. For he was not only a teacher (and a dedicated one). This job being badly paid, he needed another source of income and had become well known as the feared and hated literary critic 'Clarín' (bugle) who in regular articles in the national newspapers poured witty scorn on the multitude of dilettante poets and other scribblers who plagued the Spain of his time. He made so many enemies that his own literary effort stood little chance of receiving objective appraisal. It was attacked as an obscene irreligious monstrosity and a plagiarism of Flaubert's *Madame Bovary*. Prominent citizens of Oviedo (the capital of the province of Asturias) were shocked to find that the Vetusta of the novel was unmistakably their own town. Some saw unflattering and even libellous depictions of themselves in the novel, although nobody noticed that the grotesque Don Saturnino Bermúdez is to a large extent a self-portrait. Only a few critics attempted a sober assessment of the work, and even they did not know what to make of it. They offered vague and muted praise of its descriptions and some of its characterization, but expressed concern at what they regarded as the dubious morality of its forthright attacks on the Church and frank treatment of sexual matters. The eminent Catholic critic Marcelino Menéndez y Pelayo informed Alas that he liked the novel's style and the picturesque quality of some of the minor characters, but found the major characters too complicated and some of the subject-matter distasteful.

La Regenta was soon forgotten. Leopoldo Alas died in 1901. His novel remained in relative obscurity until about twenty years ago, but such has been the recent reversal of opinion that there are now few Spanish-speaking critics or novelists who do not recognize it as one of the Spanish classics. It was, then, a novel in advance of its own times and, therefore, rejected by them, which society has only become capable of appreciating many years later. It is still little known outside Spain, however, and this is the first English translation.

7

Although Alas was influenced by the theories of his eminent French contemporary, Émile Zola, *La Regenta* is a realistic novel rather than a naturalistic one. Unlike Zola, Alas was not impressed by the scientific discoveries of his time. The only extensive reference in his novel to nineteenth-century scientific materialism is a mocking one, when we learn of Don Alvaro Mesía's course of reading:

Nevertheless, it would be a good idea to acquire some culture, to make a foundation for that materialism which accorded so well with his other ideas about the world and how to exploit it. He asked a friend for books which would prove materialism in a few words. What he first learned was that there was no longer any such thing as metaphysics, an excellent idea which did away with a number of puzzling problems. He read Büchner's *Force and Matter*, and some books by Flammarion, but these upset him, for they spoke ill of the Church and well of heaven, God, the soul – and what he wanted was the precise opposite. Flammarion wasn't *chic*. He also read Moleschott, Virchow and Vogt, in translation, bound in saffron-yellow paper covers. He did not understand much of what they said, but he got the gist of it: everything was grey matter – splendid, that was just what he wanted to be told. His principal requirement was that there should be no hell.

The realistic novelist differs from his naturalistic counterpart in that he does not try to confirm theories but to explore experience. For the naturalist, the novel is an illustration of the validity of the scientific approach to knowledge; for the realist it is another kind of knowledge. Despite what naturalists such as Zola claimed, the realistic novel is both more objective than the naturalistic novel and more likely to stand the test of time; this is precisely because it is less influenced by the scientific ideas of its own period, which must, sooner or later, be superseded by others. So the novels of the naturalists are interesting in proportion as they wriggle free from the clutches of their own theory. So, also, the realistic novelist can make discoveries which psychologists only make many years later.

This is, I believe, what makes it possible for so much of the psychology of *La Regenta* to seem strikingly modern. I am thinking now, for example, of the descriptions of the symptoms of neurosis in general and hysteria in particular, in Ana's inner monologues, particularly in Chapters III and XXVII; and of the accuracy with which many of the inner monologues recapture the rapidity and illogicality of associative trains of thought (the last paragraphs of Chapter XV offer one of many examples). I am thinking, too, of the presence of sex as a principal (although often subconscious) motivator of action. *La Regenta* gives a detailed account of what psychologists call sublimation (in Ana, of course, but also in such minor characters as Visita, who sucks sweets as a substitute for sex), of the importance of the childhood trauma (the events after Ana's night on the ferry-boat with Germán, rather than the night itself), and of various sexual aberrations in inappropriate contexts, such as the latent foot-fetishism, sado-masochism and lesbianism of the procession on Good Friday in Chapter XXVI. The use of multiple perspectives for characterization makes the novel interesting from the standpoint of what is now called the psychology of interpersonal behaviour. In the book of that title by Michael Argyle (Penguin Books, 1967, especially Chapter 7), many of the essential features of characterization in *La Regenta* are presented (without any reference to prose fiction, of course) as recent discoveries about human behaviour – for instance our creation of images of ourselves and our subsequent modifications of these images on the basis of what we think other people think of us; and our modelling of ourselves on our fellows and on ideal fictional figures. The chains of imitation in *La Regenta* are many and complex: for example, Paco Vegallana and Pepe Ronzal model themselves on Alvaro Mesía, who models himself on the Don Juan figure of Spanish literature and on the Parisian gentleman of his times; and lesser men in turn model themselves on Paco and Pepe. When I talk about the modern psychology of *La Regenta* I am also thinking of dreams and their interpretation, especially Ana's dreams in Chapter XIX and her interpretation of them in Chapter XXI, with its revealing blind spots: her suppressed wish for a sexual relationship with Canon De Pas is embodied in disguised form in her dreams, and still suppressed as she remembers them afterwards. There is also the functioning of memory, in Chapters III and IV, as Ana thinks about her childhood, and wonders about the validity of her remembrances: are they memories of events, or memories of memories, or memories of memories of memories? Personal relationships in *La Regenta* have all the intense complexity which we often associate with more modern writing, consisting, on both sides, of positive and negative feelings: attraction, admiration, love, goodwill, and at the same time repulsion, envy, hatred, malice (for example the relationships between Mesía and Ronzal, and between De Pas and Don Custodio). One especially striking feature of this novel is the non-verbal communication, both deliberate and unintentional, which takes place throughout. Here is a scene between Ana, her husband Víctor Quintanar, and their friend Alvaro Mesía, at the beginning of Chapter XXIX, which also shows characters occupied in one of their favourite activities, manipulating and playing games with each other:

At dessert the master of the house became thoughtful. With furtive glances he followed Petra's comings and goings as she waited at table. After coffee Don Alvaro could see that his friend was impatient. Since the summer, when they had both stayed in the hotel in La Costa, Don Víctor had acquired the habit of having Don Alvaro as his table companion. He found him more talkative and agreeable at table than anywhere else, and often invited him to luncheon. But on other occasions, after chatting for as long as he felt like chatting, Quintanar would leave the table, walk around the garden, and go to dress, singing all the time – and thus leave Anita and his friend alone together for half an hour or more. And now – no, he wasn't moving. Ana and Alvaro looked at each other, and their looks asked what could be the reason for this novelty.

Ana bent down to retrieve a napkin from the floor, and Don Víctor made Mesía a sign which said, 'She's in the way. If she left, we could talk.'

Mesía shrugged.

Ana raised her head smiling at Don Alvaro and he, without Quintanar seeing, indicated the door with one movement of his eyes.

Ana left.

'Thank God!' said her husband, with a deep breath. 'I thought the girl was never going.'

He did not remember that he was always the one who went.

'Now we can talk.'

'I'm listening,' replied Alvaro in a calm voice, puffing on his Havana so as to obscure his face; it being his habit to put up smoke-screens when it suited him.

If Alas had been much influenced by the psychological theories of his time, they would only have narrowed his vision and prevented his depiction of human behaviour from being as perceptive as it was. I am sure that only chronology has saved us from a shelf-ful of theses on 'Leopoldo Alas's debt to Freud'. Such theses would have made specific reference to Alas's treatment of that Spanish archetype Don Juan (and, by extension, of the whole ethos of machismo). For *La Regenta* was the first critical examination of Don Juan as a man whose valour, vigour and virility are far from what they seem to be, and so it anticipates the Freudian analyses of Don Juan by twentieth-century Spanish writers who have seen him as a man whose inability to love one woman alone is a result not of manliness but of its opposite.

La Regenta is also notable for the intensive and subtle use of many of the techniques developed by the realistic novelists of the nineteenth century. Alas identified one of them in his perceptive review of *La desheredada*, the novel written in 1881 by Benito Pérez Galdós under the influence of Zola's naturalistic theories. 'Another procedure employed by Galdós,' wrote Alas, 'and now with more insistence and success than ever, is one also used by Flaubert and Zola with very impressive results: replacing the observations which the author often makes in his own voice about a character's situation by the character's own observations, using the latter's style – not, however, in the manner of a monologue, but as if the author were inside the character, and the novel were being created inside the character's brain.' So Galdós's novel brought the expressive possibilities of *sympathetic projection* to Alas's notice, and he used this technique in *La Regenta* much more insistently and for a far wider range of characters than did Galdós or Zola or even Flaubert. In my *Critical Guide to La Regenta* (Grant & Cutler, 1974) I have discussed Alas's skilful handling of this device, which he also called 'the underground speaking of a consciousness' and *'estilo latente'*. Many years later, French critics of Flaubert were to give it the name by which it is now commonly known, *style indirect libre* (and to create the myth that Flaubert invented it). *Estilo latente* made it possible for Alas both to give a panoramic view of a society and to explore the inner lives of its individuals. But it involves a frequent switching of viewpoint. In the following passage, for example, only a responsive reader will follow the movement of the point of view:

> Ana's attack of nerves was, as on the previous evening, melting into tears, into an impulsive pious determination always to be faithful to her husband. In spite of his infernal machines, Quintanar was her duty; and the canon theologian would be her aegis and protect her from all the formidable blows of temptation. But Quintanar knew nothing of this. The theatre had left him feeling awfully sleepy – he had not slept a wink the night before! – and full of lyrico-dramatic enthusiasm.

The subtleties of *estilo latente* were lost on readers accustomed to third-rate tales of adventure and romance, and bad translations of foreign novels (the Spanish novel was just beginning to be revived, after centuries of neglect). The principal difficulty of *estilo latente* is that it has no formal or grammatical identifying marks to distinguish it from authorial statement. In the passage I have just quoted, the reader has to make his own decisions about questions of style to attribute the first sentence to the (detached) narrator, the second to Ana, the third (as far as the end of the parenthesis) to Quintanar, and the last five words to the (now ironical) narrator. But judgements about style can seldom be definitive. We *could* attribute the whole passage to the narrator's voice, if we thought that this narrator speaks with an uncontrolled hotchpotch of styles and interrupts his story every so often to inform us of its future course ('and the canon theologian would be . . .'). The essential ambiguity of free indirect style has been exploited by many novelists. Jane Austen makes much use of it to report the thoughts of her credulous heroines in such a way that the reader is at liberty to take them for omniscient authorial pronouncements:

> Harriet certainly was not clever, but she had a sweet, docile, grateful disposition; was totally free from conceit; and only desiring to be guided by any one she looked up to (*Emma*, Chapter 4).

Yet in *La Regenta* we often find free indirect style complicated by a device the main effect of which is to destroy its ambiguity and thus (when a character's thoughts are being reported) to increase the illusion of projection: enclosing it within speech-marks. This can at first seem strange, ungrammatical and confusing to modern readers:

> When, close to nightfall, as the horses dragged their coach uphill, the new presiding magistrate asked Ana if he was fortunate enough, perchance, to be

the first man whom she had loved, she bowed her head and said, with a melancholy which sounded to him like sensual self-abandonment:

'Yes, yes, the first, the only one.'

'No, she didn't love him; but she would try to love him.'

The inverted commas around the last sentence force the reader to regard it as an account of Ana's thoughts, just as in the following extract from *Emma* (Chapter 25), the inverted commas make it clear that the enclosed words report what the Coles say, not necessarily the 'truth':

The Coles expressed themselves so properly – there was so much real attraction in the manner of it – so much consideration for her father. 'They would have solicited the honour earlier, but had been waiting the arrival of a folding-screen from London, which they hoped might keep Mr Woodhouse from any draught of air, and therefore induce him the more readily to give them the honour of his company.'

(The first sentence of this extract is another example of ambiguous free indirect speech.)

The reader of *La Regenta* faces the problems of a bouncing narrative not only over point of view. Here is a description of the bank clerk's wife Visitación and the young widow Obdulia:

When Don Alvaro was in the company of close friends he spoke of Visitación with disdain and grimaced with ill-concealed disgust. He affirmed that she had pretty feet and that her calves were much more handsome than one might suspect, but her shoes were shoddy, and her petticoats and stockings left a great deal to be desired – his listeners knew what he meant. And he wiped his lips with his pocket-handkerchief.

Paco Vegallana swore that the woman used garters made of red tape and that he had once discovered her wearing one made of string. All this was to be mentioned only in the company of men, of course, and they were to be discreet about it.

Obdulia's underclothes, on the other hand, were irreproachable; unlike her behaviour. But this was such common knowledge that nobody talked about it any more. To each successive lover, Obdulia herself denied all her previous affairs, except her affair with Alvaro Mesía. It was her pride and joy. The man had fascinated her, why deny it? But only him. She was a widow who never remembered her husband; it was as if she were really Alvarito's widow. 'She had no past but Alvaro!'

That afternoon both women were looking very pretty, one had to admit it. At least the ingenuous Paco Vegallana admitted it.

Even the longer passages of 'the underground speaking of a consciousness' are studded with interruptions as the outside world impinges on the attention of the character and redirects his train of thoughts. In this way, inner monologues become lively dialectics between the subjective and objective worlds.

Some of the features of Alas's restless writing are probably disconcerting to any reader. It is strange, for example – especially in a nineteenth-century novel – to find time handled with such freedom, to find that events are seldom related in chronological order, but that, instead, there are abrupt jumps forward, flashbacks, flashbacks within flashbacks. . . . In some places, tenses can seem disordered, particularly when the narrator switches between the viewpoints of a contemporary witness and a subsequent historian, between present and past tenses. Such disturbing qualities of *La Regenta* have caused some critics to find parts of it, at least, confused and cluttered. I think that this criticism is, on the whole, mistaken (and I have, therefore, not taken it upon myself to tidy up *La Regenta* in any major way while translating it). Such attacks rest upon the assumption that a novel should, in its form and style at least, present the fewest possible problems to its readers, should be readily consumable (it is strange, incidentally, that many critics who welcome disturbing content reject disturbing form). It appears more likely to me that, on the contrary, it is one of the most important functions of literature to play games with the reader, frustrate his expectations, puzzle him and so invite him to re-examine his assumptions. *La Regenta* certainly does this. Restoration Spain, however, was not prepared to be ruffled.

The smug parochial society of Alas's Spain was quite unable, too, to appreciate the novel's deflating, satirical humour. *La Regenta* abounds in angry sarcasm, expressing Alas's exasperation at the mediocrity all around him:

> Don Robustiano had never read Voltaire, but his admiration for Voltaire was as intense as the abhorrence felt by Gloucester, who had never read Voltaire either.

But the novel also contains irony of a quieter kind: the turn of phrase which has something disturbing about it, the word which seems somehow odd or inappropriate, and to which the reader responds by wondering whether all is as it seems to be, whether an alternative ironical interpretation is necessary. Indeed the very first sentence, with its abrupt bathos and jingly rhythm after an apparently grandiose start, invites us to read the whole novel ironically.

La Regenta, rich in wit and humour, is also a work of intense moral seriousness. But Alas's audience, the Spanish middle and upper classes, was composed in the main of the same kind of shallow, frivolous, complacent people as *La Regenta* portrays. A novel which poses searching questions about our ability to control our destiny and find self-fulfilment, and about God's interest in our activities – and which suggests gloomy answers to these questions – could not be accepted in such an atmosphere.

The subject-matter of *La Regenta*, the life of a shabby Spanish provincial town in the late nineteenth century, might make it seem dated and parochial. But thanks to its universal themes, psychological insight and technical boldness it has proved itself to be worthy of the attention of modern men and women. *La Regenta* is ambitious – astonishingly so for a man of thirty-two writing his first novel. It is a big, rich novel in the nineteenth-century tradition – not just a long novel but an all-embracing one of many styles and moods, from broad humour to the most intense feeling, kept from degenerating into sentimentalism by Alas's controlling irony.

Restoration Spain

The action of *La Regenta* starts in the late 1870s and occupies exactly three years. The first fifteen chapters, constituting Volume One in the two editions prepared by the author (1884–5, Barcelona, and 1901, Madrid), take place on St Francis of Assisi's Day (4 October) and the two days preceding it, probably – to judge from passing references to the Russo-Turkish War in Chapters VI and XIX – in the year 1877. But such a calculation is unimportant, since the action is not given an exact date by any obvious allusions to contemporary events (although the *days* on which the action occurs are usually defined, by reference to the Christian calendar). It is clear, however, that *La Regenta* is set in the early years of the Restoration.

In Spain the nineteenth century had been a period of decline and unrest. Between 1810 and 1820 most of Spain's American empire had been liberated, leaving only Cuba and Puerto Rico in her possession. Her hold on these remnants was insecure, and was to be broken in 1898. Throughout the nineteenth century, however, lower-class Spaniards – especially those from the north – continued to emigrate to Cuba, and some of them returned with fortunes. In Spain there had been a series of rebellions and civil wars as conservatives and liberals failed to find peaceful ways to resolve their differences. When Fernando VII died in 1833, the conservatives supported his brother Carlos's claim to the throne, but the liberals declared them-selves in favour of the regency of Fernando's widow, María Cristina, during the minority of their daughter, Isabel; and the First Carlist War, between Carlistas and Cristinos, broke out. This lasted until 1839, when the Carlists were defeated. Isabel was declared of age in 1843, when she was thirteen, and reigned for twenty-five uncertain years at the end of which the 'Glorious Revolution' of September 1868, the first revolution directed against the Bourbon dynasty, toppled her from power. Six years of confusion ensued. Parliament, reassembled in 1869, decided in favour of a non-Bourbon monarch, but could not think of one. At last Prince Amadeus of Savoy was elected king in November 1870, only to abdicate in February 1873 after a reign which never had any chance of being effective. After a short period of anarchic republicanism, Alfonso, Isabel's son, was proclaimed king of Spain in December 1874. After just six years the Bourbons had been restored to the throne.

The failure of the anti-monarchical liberal revolution of 1868 and of the extreme conservatives, the Carlists (now supporting the claims to the throne of Carlos's grandson, Carlos María), in the Third Carlist War of 1874, put the moderate conservatives, led by Cánovas del Castillo, in a dominant position. The moderate liberals – known as the Dynastic Liberal Party – agreed to work within the limits imposed by the new regime. The preservation of an ordered society was the common interest of both 'dynastic conservatives' and 'dynastic liberals'. This was achieved for twenty-five years thanks to the system known as the *turno pacífico*, the peaceful alternation in power, whereby the conservatives governed most of the time, but guaranteed the liberals a reasonable presence in parliament and occasionally allowed them into office. Elections were rigged to achieve this end, although the appearance of a parliamentary democracy was maintained. Local power was handed to *caciques*, provincial political bosses. And Restoration Spain did enjoy peace and economic growth, thanks to a political system which embraced all parties except the extreme right, the Carlists, and the extreme left, the Republicans. The *turno pacífico* is satirized at the beginning of Chapter VIII of *La Regenta*.

La Regenta is about conservative times and a conservative society – the wealthy classes of a proud, ancient, backward-looking provincial town (the Spanish adjective *vetusto* – feminine *vetusta* – means 'ancient', and is itself an archaic word). No sector of Spanish society was more resolutely reactionary than the Church, where the Carlist cause was cherished. The Church took every advantage of the propitious political circumstances to regain the power and wealth which it had lost under liberal governments. As a result of the 1851 Concordat the Spanish Church was more dependent upon the state than it liked, for the Ministry of Grace and Justice remained in control of ecclesiastical economics. Despite this handicap, the Restoration was a period of expansion for the Church.

In *La Regenta*, Canon Fermín De Pas is a characteristic priest of his times and, being a man of formidable talent, he enjoys great success. Although he is not a church dignitary but only a simple prebendary he has, to the envy of colleagues superior to him in the hierarchy, been appointed by the bishop not only canon theologian but also vicar-general. His two special positions in the cathedral chapter are complementary. They give him respectively prestige and power, which together mean domination of Vetusta. As canon theologian – the canon appointed to deliver sermons on special occasions – he basks in the admiration of the public, and in particular of wealthy pious ladies, his spiritual daughters. As vicar-general of an ineffective bishop he works behind the scenes in the diocesan curia to gain great power and amass a fortune.

It is not only in its description of the Church that *La Regenta* gives a penetrating account of its times. The depiction of the industrial working classes in *La Regenta* is of great interest. Seen from the protagonists' aristocratic viewpoint, they are a mysterious, menacing presence in the background, alive with a rough vitality of which the aristocrats are privately both afraid and envious. But most of the time Alas shows in vivid and telling detail the absurd, unchanging world of mediocrity, pretence, hypocrisy, boredom and quirkiness of decadent provincial society. Against such a backcloth Fermín De Pas and Ana Ozores stand out as powerful protagonists. The canon theologian and the judge's wife are, in Spanish, *el magistral* and *la regenta*, words with incidental yet inescapable suggestions, impossible to recapture in translation, of 'the man who is the master' and 'the woman who rules'.

This translation

I have translated from the excellent edition by Gonzalo Sobejano (Editorial Noguer, Barcelona, 1976 – now out of print, but an even better version is now available in Clásicos Castalia, 1981), also referring to the two editions prepared by Alas himself. Like Sobejano I have found it necessary to include a rather large number of explanatory notes. This is because *La Regenta* contains many references to the Bible, subsequent Christian works, classical culture, Spanish history and literature, contemporary European literature and science, painting, philosophy, the law, and music, especially the opera. I have not annotated every cultural reference but, on the whole, only offered comments where they can add to an understanding of the text.

A few words about Spanish names and titles, which cannot sensibly be translated (although I have modified one or two names in an attempt to reproduce puns made on them). The normal courtesy-title for a man of social standing is *Don* (or *Señor Don*), always used with the Christian name; the feminine equivalents are *Doña* and *Señora Doña*. *Señor* and *Señora* are normally used with the surname alone (sometimes, though, they can be used as courtesy-titles with Christian names, for people of some social position but not enough for *Don/Doña* – such as rich villagers). *Ilustrísimo* and *Excelentísimo* are official titles given to men of considerable eminence. A Spanish woman does not lose her maiden name on marrying, so Doña Ana Ozores, after her marriage to Don Víctor Quintanar, is called either Doña Ana Ozores or Doña Ana Ozores de Quintanar. Affectionate diminutives are formed in various ways: Ana–Anita, Anunciación–Anuncita, Visitación–Vista, Fermín–Fermo, Francisco–Paco–Paquito, Alvaro–Alvarín, Alvaro–Alvarico, Ronzal–Ronzalillo.

Translation is a strange business, which sensible people no doubt avoid. By my calculation I have spent at least five times as many hours writing this English rendering of it as Alas spent writing *La Regenta*. To what extent this is a consequence of Alas's natural gifts as a novelist, or of my lack of natural gifts as a translator, or of the peculiar problems of translation itself, I do not know. I only hope that, at the end of it all, I have done some justice to this marvellous novel. If I have not, it is not for lack of good advice, nor, of course, is it any fault of those many colleagues, pupils and other friends who have helped me so generously and in so many ways. I cannot mention them all. I want in particular to thank the distinguished children's novelist Peter Carter for showing me the life, complexity and elegance of the English sentence (I wish I had been quicker to learn), and the eminent critic Gonzalo Sobejano, for his patient and detailed replies to all my inquiries about *La Regenta*. Among all the others I particularly remember the late Cyril Jones, without whose encouragement I would not have undertaken the translation, and Hugo Donnelly, Luis Miravalles, Peter Russell, Rosa Rutherford and Ron Truman. I have been lucky that such a skilled and patient person as Patricia Lloyd typed and retyped the successive versions of the translation, and I am grateful for sabbatical leave and travel grants from both my college and my university.

The Queen's College, Oxford, October 1980

VOLUME ONE

I

The city of heroes was having a nap. The south wind, warm and languid, was coaxing grey-white clouds through the sky and breaking them up as they drifted along. The streets of the city were silent, except for the rasping whispers of whirls of dust, rags, straw and paper on their way from gutter to gutter, pavement to pavement, street corner to street corner, now hovering, now chasing after one another, like butterflies which the air envelops in its invisible folds, draws together, and pulls apart. This miscellany of left-overs, remnants of refuse, would come together like throngs of gutter urchins, stay still for a moment as if half asleep, and then jump up and scatter in alarm, scaling walls as far as the loose panes of street lamps or the posters daubed up at street corners; and a feather might reach a third floor, and a grain of sand be stuck for days, or for years, in a shop window, embedded in lead.

Vetusta, that most noble and loyal city, the capital of the nation once long ago, was digesting its boiled bacon and its chick-pea stew, and relaxing as, half asleep, it listened to the familiar monotonous drone of the hour-bell high in the graceful tower of the Holy Cathedral Church. The tower, a romantic poem in stone, a delicate hymn, with its gentle lines of silent eternal beauty, was a sixteenth-century work (although begun earlier) in the Gothic style – but a Gothic tempered, it could be said, by an instinctive sense of prudence and harmony which curbed the vulgar excesses of such architecture. One could gaze at that stone finger, which showed the way to heaven, for hours on end without tiring. It was not one of those towers with spires so delicate that they seem to be on the point of snapping, spindly rather than slender, and full of affectation like overdressed young ladies who lace their corsets too tightly. This tower was a solid one, but no less charged with spiritual grandeur for all that; it rose like a mighty castle to its upper gallery, adorned with elegant balustrades, from which it launched itself upwards in the shape of a graceful, tapering pyramid, inimitable in its measurements and proportions. Like a mass of muscle and sinew, stone, wreathing around stone, climbed skywards, balancing acrobatically in mid-air; and, as if by some marvellous feat of juggling, a great gilded bronze sphere stood upon the tip of the limestone pyramid, seemingly held there by magnetism, and on top of this sphere was another smaller one and on this a cross of iron surmounted by a lightning-conductor.

When, on important occasions, the cathedral chapter had the tower illuminated with Chinese lanterns and coloured glasses, this romantic

21

pile looked well enough, shining amid the gloom; but such finery diminished the ineffable elegance of its profile, making it look like an enormous champagne bottle. It was better to contemplate the tower on a clear moonlit night, gathered into pleats of light and shadow, silhouetted against an immaculate sky, and surrounded by a halo of stars: a ghostly giant watching over the small black city sleeping at his feet.

Bismarck, an illustrious Vetustan urchin, so nicknamed by the other urchins for some unknown reason, was gripping the well-worn rope attached to the huge clapper of Wamba,[1] the great bell used for summoning to the divine office the very venerable canons who formed the cathedral chapter, of superior qualities and privileges.

Bismarck was by trade a postilion, or 'whipster', as those of his station were called in Vetusta. But belfries attracted him, and by delegation from a certain churchman, Celedonio – an acolyte performing the duties of bell-ringer, although no more in permanent possession of that post than Bismarck – this illustrious whipster-statesman sometimes enjoyed the honour of awakening the venerable chapter from its beatific siesta and convoking it to the prayers and canticles of its peculiar incumbence.

Bismarck was normally cheerful, mischievous, and full of fun, but he took charge of Wamba's striker with all the seriousness of an inspired soothsayer. When he sounded the hours (as the expression was), the postilion experienced something of the dignity and responsibility of a clock.

Celedonio, a filthy, black, threadbare cassock clinging to his body, was sitting astride a window-sill and leaning out, spitting disdainfully through his teeth into the square below. If the fancy took him, he threw pebbles at one of the rare passers-by, whom he considered to be of the size and importance of mice. Height went to the two urchins' heads and excited in them a profound scorn for earthly things.

'Look, there goes Chiripa. He says he's a better fighter than me!' said the acolyte, spitting out the words; and he hurled half a rotten baked potato at a canon in the street, safe in the knowledge that it would miss him.

'No, he isn't!' replied Bismarck, who fawned upon Celedonio so long as they were in the belfry, and tyrannized him outside, tearing the keys from him by brute force in order to climb the tower and ring to prayers. 'You can beat all the post-boys – but you can't beat me.'

'That's only because you trip me up, big head. Anyway, you're older than me. Hey Bismarck, here comes the canon theologian. Want me to cop him one?'

'Can you see it's him from here?'

'Of course I can, you fool. I know him by the way he waves his cloak about. Look – don't you see how he flaps it out in front and behind as he walks along? That shows what a lot he thinks of himself. You know Don Custodio the beneficiary? Well the other day I heard him say to Don Pedro the bell-ringer, "That fellow Don Fermín's as proud as Lucifer himself," and Don Pedro had a good laugh. As soon as Don Fermín had gone past Don Custodio said, "Come, come, my fine young fellow, anyone can see you've been rouging your cheeks again!" What about that, then? He paints his face!'

Bismarck refused to believe it. The truth was, the beneficiary was jealous. If Bismarck were a canon and a dignitary (as he thought Don Fermín was), instead of a post-boy with a nickname taken from matchboxes, he would act even grander than the second driver on a coach. Of course he would! And if he were a real bell-ringer, like Don Pedro, then, by God, he wouldn't talk to anyone at all, except the bishop and Señor Roque, the mail-coach driver!

'You don't know what you're on about,' said Celedonio. 'The beneficiary said that in the Church you must be humble, climb down to people, give in, and put up with a slap in the face if you've got to. If you don't, the Pope will be after you, and he's – what did he call him? – sort of, the servant of all servants.'

'They just say that,' replied Bismarck. 'Look, the Pope's got even more power than the King. I saw a painting of him once – a great big picture. He was sitting in his coach, but it looked more like an armchair, and instead of mules there was a team of Holy Joes' (Bismarck's expression for priests) 'drawing it, and they were scaring away the flies with an umbrella. It looked like a show in the theatre. I know all about the Pope, mate.'

The debate became heated. Celedonio defended the simple ways of the primitive Church; Bismarck stood for all the later splendours of the cult. Celedonio threatened the acting bell-ringer with a request for his resignation; the whipster made covert allusions to certain probable thumps as soon as they were downstairs. But a bell clanking on a cathedral roof called them to order.

'The lauds bell!' shouted Celedonio. 'Come on, that's the signal.' Bismarck grasped the rope and pounded metal with the huge clapper.

The air trembled and the post-boy shut his eyes, while Celedonio put on a display of imperturbable serenity, listening to the deep, powerful tones of the bell as if it were a couple of leagues away. The wind bore the vibrations from the tower, carrying them over Vetusta to the nearby sierra and the ranging fields which shone in the distance in a hundred shades of green.

It was early autumn. The meadows were springing back to life, the grass was growing fresh and vigorous after the recent September rains. Chestnut, oak and apple groves, spreading over the broad valley in hollows and on hillsides, stood out in dark tones against meadows and maize-patches and amid so much greenery a few fields of wheat showed yellow. Dotted over valley and sierra, the white farm homesteads and a few summer villas of the same colour reflected the light like mirrors. The resplendent green landscape, marked by gold and silver iridescences, faded away in the sierra, as though the slopes and peaks of those hills were covered by the shadow of an invisible cloud; where there were bald patches among the vegetation, which was less vigorous and varied than in the valley, tints of red appeared. The sierra was to the north-west; to the south the horizon fell away and was marked only by the faint outlines of mountains which the mist, as dazzling as some incandescent dust-cloud, almost hid from view. To the north, beyond the perfect arc of the horizon, the sea could be divined beneath a clear sky through which sailed, like distant ships, small clouds of palest gold. The moon, floating among them in the milky blue, looked like a shred of one of the tiniest clouds.

On the outskirts of the city a more intensive and conscientious system of farming than that of the valley and sierra, with better fertilizers and a greater variety of crops, had given rise to colours with no precise names, sketched out against the dark brown backcloth of regularly ploughed and well-irrigated earth.

Somebody was coming upstairs. The two youngsters looked at each other in amazement. Who on earth could have such cheek?

'Maybe it's Chancer,' suggested Celedonio, caught between anger and fear.

'No, it's a Holy Joe. Can't you hear his cloak?'

Bismarck was right. There was a hiss-hiss of cloth brushing against stone, like a soft voice demanding silence. Then the cloak was before them. It belonged to Don Fermín De Pas, the canon theologian of that holy cathedral church and the bishop's vicar-general. The post-boy shuddered, thinking, 'Has he come to belt us?'

Don Fermín had no reason to do so. But that didn't matter. Bismarck was used to being slapped and kicked for no clear cause. He assumed that all men of authority (and he considered Don Fermín to be a real nob) used and abused their right to hand out beatings. He did not challenge the legitimacy of this prerogative, but merely kept out of the way of the great of the earth, among whom sextons and constables figured prominently. It was a law which enjoyed his full support, although he did his best to avoid its consequences. If he were someone important, like a gentleman, a mayor, a canon, a plumber, a keeper of the botanical gardens, a box-office clerk, or a night-watchman, he would do exactly the same – kick everyone around! But he was just Bismarck, a postilion, and he knew his role in life: keeping out of the way of the nobs of Vetusta.

But this time there was no escape. Either throw himself out of the window, or await the coming storm. The entrance to the spiral stairway was blocked by the canon. Bismarck could only curl himself into a ball, hidden on a beam behind Wamba, and await developments.

Celedonio was not surprised by this visit. He had often seen the canon theologian going up the tower in the afternoon, before or after the divine office.

Why had this highly respectable gentleman come here? This was the question the post-boy's eyes fired at the eyes of the acolyte. Celedonio knew the answer to this, too, but he smiled and said nothing, taking pleasure in his friend's fear.

The altar-boy's arrogant bearing had changed into an attitude of humility. Suddenly he wore his official expression. Celedonio was twelve or thirteen years old, and he already knew how to adapt the muscles of his pug face to the demands of the liturgy. His eyes were large, of a dirty chestnut colour, and when he considered himself to be on ecclesiastical duty he moved them affectedly, first up, then down, imitating many priests and devout ladies of his acquaintance. But, without realizing it, he thereby imparted a suggestion of wantonness and cynicism to his look, like a side-street harlot who proclaims her unhappy trade through her eyes, so that the police can do nothing to uphold the rights of public morality. His mouth, agape and lacking many teeth, followed as best it could the eyes' contortions. In putting on a show of beatific humility Celedonio turned from a tolerably ugly boy into a disgustingly ugly one.

Just as in girls of his age the graceful contours of their sex are presaged by incipient curves, so in the unordained acolyte a perversion of natural instincts, whose seeds had been sown by the aberrations of a devious upbringing, could be foreseen in the near future. When, under his wax-stained cassock, Celedonio tried to imitate the rhythmic, flowing movements of Don Anacleto, the bishop's familiar (believing this to be the way to manifest his vocation), he moved and gesticulated like some cheap brazen barracks siren. This had been noted by a lay worker in the cathedral, nicknamed Turtle-dove, a dog-catcher, as his position was called in vulgar parlance. But Turtle-dove had not dared communicate his suspicions to his superiors, in accordance with the principle by which, with dignity and prestige, he had discharged his complex duties of vigilance and sanitation for thirty uninterrupted years.

In the presence of the canon theologian, Celedonio, after dismounting from the window, had crossed his arms and bowed his head. Down in the Calle de la Rúa Don Fermín had looked like a beetle, but now how huge he appeared to the altar-boy's lowered eyes and to the terrified eyes of his companion! Celedonio was waist-high to the canon. He saw before him a spotless soutane, with true, symmetrical, sculptural creases – an autumn soutane, of the best fine flannel – and flowing over it a voluminous silken cloak, with numerous folds and flares.

Bismarck, behind Wamba, could see no more of the canon than his lower legs, and was admiring them. This was real class! Not one stain! The feet were like a lady's; the hose was purple, like a bishop's; and each shoe was a work of painstaking craftsmanship in the finest leather, displaying a simple yet elegant silver buckle which looked very splendid against the colour of the stocking.

If the rascals had dared to look at Don Fermín face to face, they would have seen him serious and frowning as he entered the belfry; somewhat disconcerted when he became aware of the presence of the bell-ringers; but immediately full of smiles – slippery softness in his gaze, practised righteousness on his lips. The post-boy was right, De Pas did not use cosmetics. His face, with its white sheen, looked more as if it were stuccoed. In his cheeks, which were just prominent enough to give his face strength and character without making it ugly, there was a tinge of red, with an occasional tendency towards the colour of his bands and his hose. It was not cosmetics, or the rosy colour of good health, or a sign of drinking; it was the red which rises to the cheeks in the warmth of loving or shameful words, attracting like magnets the blood's iron. Such a flush might also, of course, be caused by a sudden rush of thoughts of the same type. The most striking feature about the canon theologian's eyes, which were green with speckles that looked like grains of snuff, was that they seemed as soft, smooth and clammy as lichen; but sometimes a piercing gleam would shoot out from them – an unpleasant surprise, like finding a needle in a feather pillow. Few people could bear that look. Some were frightened by it, others were disgusted; but if anyone were bold enough to withstand it, the canon lowered his eyes, and veiled them with their broad, heavy lids, which were as meaningless as flabby flesh always is. There was too much flesh, too, towards the tip of his long straight nose, which was neither well-proportioned nor distinguished, and drooped like a tree under the weight of an excess of fruit. The nose was a mere superstructure upon such an expressive face, although whatever that face did express must have been written there in Greek, for it was no easy task to read and translate what the canon felt and thought. His lips, long, thin, pale and delicate, seemed to be under constant pressure from his chin, which had an upward tendency, and threatened, in a still-distant old age, to join forces with the overhanging tip of his nose. As yet this defect did not give his face an appearance of age but an expression of prudence verging on cowardly hypocrisy and revealing a cold and calculating egotism. It could be avowed with confidence that those lips guarded like a treasure the supreme word, that word which is never spoken. The canon's pointed levantine jowl was like a clasp securing this treasure. His head, small and well formed, with its short, thick, black hair, was set upon a firmly muscled neck, strong and white. The neck was that of an athlete, as were the body and limbs of this robust canon who, back in his native village, would have been the best skittles-player and the most marriageable lad, or, in the streets of Vetusta, dressed in a fashioned frock-coat, the sprucest gadabout in town.

The canon theologian greeted Celedonio as if the acolyte were a great personage, making him a gracious bow and holding out the taper fingers of his elegant white right hand, on which no greater care could have been lavished had it belonged to the finest of fine ladies. Celedonio replied with the genuflexion which he used at mass.

Bismarck watched in horror from his hiding-place as De Pas took a tube, which seemed to be made of gold, from an inside pocket of his cassock. He saw the tube being stretched out as if it were made of rubber, and then converted into two tubes, then three, all stuck together end to end. It must be a small cannon, enough to finish off an insignificant post-boy like him. No, it was a rifle, for the canon theologian was holding it up to his face and aiming. Bismarck breathed again – the shot wasn't meant for his humble person, for the Holy Joe was leaning out of a window and aiming towards the street. Celedonio had tiptoed up behind the vicar-general and was trying to see where the telescope was pointing. Celedonio was a sophisticated altar-boy, an intimate in the best houses of Vetusta, and had he known that Bismarck took a spyglass for a rifle he would have burst out laughing.

Climbing was one of Don Fermín De Pas's solitary pastimes. He was a highlander, and his instincts led him to mountain peaks and church belfries. In every country he had visited he had climbed the highest mountain or, if there were none, the loftiest tower. He felt ignorant about anything of which he had not had a bird's-eye view, taking it all in from above. When he went with the bishop on his visits to country parishes, he always had to make a trip on foot or on horseback, however he could, to the local high spots. All over the province of which Vetusta was the capital there were numerous mountains whose peaks were lost in the clouds, and the canon climbed the highest and most difficult of them, outstripping the stoutest walker, the most expert mountaineer. The higher he climbed the stronger was his urge to continue climbing, feeling not fatigue but a fever which lent his legs a steely vigour and put the power of a blacksmith's bellows into his lungs. To gain an eminence was a voluptuous triumph for him. To see many leagues of country, to descry the distant sea, to contemplate towns and villages at his feet as if they were playthings, to think of men as microbes, to watch an eagle or perhaps a kite glide past under his gaze, showing him its sun-gilt back, to look down upon clouds – all these were intense pleasures for his lofty spirit, and he procured them whenever he could. And then fires glowed in his cheeks and darts shot from his eyes. In Vetusta he could not satisfy this passion, and had to be content with occasional trips up the cathedral tower. He usually went in the morning, before the divine office, but sometimes it suited him better to go in the afternoon.

Celedonio had peeped once or twice through the canon's spyglass when its master had left it behind, and he knew that it was a powerful device: from the tower's upper gallery, which was far above the belfry, he had once had a clear view of the judge's wife, a very pretty lady, as she walked, reading a book, in her back garden, known as Ozores Park. Yes, he'd seen her close enough to touch, even though her house was in the corner of the Plaza Nueva, quite a long way from the cathedral tower, with the cathedral square and two streets besides – the Calle de la Rúa and the Calle de San Pelayo – in between. What else? Through that spyglass you could see part of the billiards room in the Gentlemen's Club, next to St Mary's Church; and he, Celedonio, had seen the ivory balls rolling over the table. But without the spyglass, pooh, the window looked like the door of a cricket's cage! While the acolyte whispered all this to Bismarck, who had ventured forth, convinced that he was not in danger, the canon surveyed the city, scrutinizing all its corners, lifting roofs in his imagination, oblivious of the bell-ringers, engrossed in this minute inspection, like a naturalist studying a tiny section of an organism under a powerful microscope. He did not look towards the fields, or contemplate the backcloth of mountains and clouds. His gaze did not leave the city.

Vetusta was his passion and his prey. Although others thought of him as a wise theologian, philosopher and lawyer, he himself prized above all other branches of knowledge his knowledge of Vetusta. He knew it inch by inch, inside and out, soul and body; he had examined the corners of consciences and the corners of houses. What he felt in the presence of the heroic city was gluttony; he explored its anatomy not like the physiologist whose only concern is to study, but like the gastronome who searches out the tastiest morsels; rather than a scalpel he wielded a carving knife.

Still, it was quite an act of resignation to content himself, for the time being, with Vetusta. De Pas had dreamed of better positions, and he had not lost all hope of gaining them. Brilliant scenes, which ambition had painted in his imagination, were stored in his memory like recollections of some heroic poem read with enthusiasm as a youth. He had seen himself officiating in pontificals in Toledo, and at a conclave of cardinals in Rome: even the tiara itself had not seemed excessive. There was nothing that could not be acquired along the way, the important thing was to keep moving onwards. But, as time passed, these dreams had become hazier and hazier, as if they were retreating into the distance. 'Such are the perspectives of hope,' thought the canon. 'The closer we come to the goal of our ambition, the more distant does this desired object appear, for it lies not in the future, but in the past; before us there is only a mirror reflecting the chimerical vision which has remained behind, at the far-off moment when we dreamed it.' He had not abandoned the climb, the attempt to get as near as he could to the top, but as time passed those vague long-term ambitions of his adolescence concerned him less and less. He was thirty-five years old now, and his greed for power was stronger and less idealistic: he was satisfied with less, but desired it more intensely, needed it nearer at hand. His was the hunger which will not wait, the burning thirst in the desert which is sated in a dirty puddle without waiting to discover the distant hidden spring.

Sometimes, with a shudder, he sensed – although without admitting it – lapses in his will and his faith in himself. At such moments he thought that perhaps he would never reach any of the places to which he had aspired, that maybe his career would take him no further than his present position or – and this would be sheer mockery – an inferior bishopric in his old age. Whenever he was troubled by such ideas he would, in order to overcome and forget them, throw himself into the frenzied enjoyment of immediate pleasures – of the power he wielded – and then he devoured his prey, churchly Vetusta, as a lion in a cage devours the miserable scraps of meat tossed to it by its keeper.

At such times his ambition, concentrated on something concrete and tangible, was much more intense; in the entire diocese there was no obstacle capable of resisting his resolute will. He was the master's master: he held the bishop in an iron grip, a voluntary prisoner who did not even notice his shackles. In such moods the vicar-general was an ecclesiastical hurricane, a biblical punishment, the Scourge of God, sanctioned by His Lordship.

These crises of morale were usually provoked by staff news: the appointment of a young bishop, for instance. Then De Pas would do his sums: he had fallen far back, he could never reach certain important positions in the hierarchy. Yet the beneficiary Don Custodio's principal reason for hating him was that he had been made canon theologian at the age of thirty.[2]

Don Fermín gazed down upon the city. Others wanted to wrest this prey from him, but he alone was going to devour it all. What? Was even this wretched empire to be snatched from his grasp? No; it belonged to him. He had won it in fair combat. Why did they persist in their foolish pretension? Height went to the canon theologian's head, too; like the urchins, he looked upon Vetustans as beetles. The dingy squat old dwellings regarded by their vain owners as palaces were in reality no more than burrows, holes in the ground, heaps of earth, the work of moles. . . . What had ever been achieved by the owners of those ancient, decrepit residences in the cathedral quarter, La Encimada, down there at his feet? Yes, what had they done? They had inherited. And he, what had he done? He had conquered. When

Don Fermín's adolescent ambition crackled in his soul, Vetusta seemed too cramped a place for him; he, who had preached in Rome, who had for a short time savoured the incense of praise in the highest places, thought of Vetusta cathedral as a backwater in which he had been abandoned. But on other, more frequent, occasions the memory which assailed him was that of his dreams as a precociously ambitious child; and then he saw in this city, humbled all around him at his feet, the culmination of his wildest desires. What De Pas felt when he compared his childhood illusions with present reality was, he thought, a physical pleasure. As a youth he had dreamed of much higher things; but now his power seemed like the promised land of the musings of his childhood during lonely melancholy afternoons in mountain pastures. The canon was beginning to feel some contempt for his adolescence; the dreams of those years sometimes seemed rather ridiculous, and his conscience took no pleasure from going back over his deeds during that time of intense passions which had found infrequent and inadequate satisfaction. He preferred to refresh his spirit in the contemplation of scenes in the remotest corners of his memory. While his childhood moved him, his adolescence displeased him, like the thought of a woman once deeply loved who made us commit a thousand foolish deeds and who now seems worthy only of oblivion and contempt. But that puerile physical pleasure was a consolation for his soul during the frequent failures of his morale.

Fermín De Pas had been a cowherd in the mountain passes of Tarsa – and he, the very same, was now in command of all Vetusta! In this leap of the imagination the canon theologian found the essence of that intense, infantile, physical pleasure, which he enjoyed as if it were a sin of the flesh.

How often, standing in the pulpit, wearing a lordly mozetta and under it a crimped white rochet which followed the lines of his strong yet graceful body, and seeing admiration and delight on the faces of the faithful below him, had he been forced to still his soaring eloquence, choking and speechless from the sheer joy of it all! Hardly breathing, the congregation had waited in silence for the speaker's religious fervour to allow him to continue, and he had heard, in an ecstasy of self-worship, the sputtering of wax-candles and lamps; inhaled, with strange voluptuousness, the air made fragrant by the incense from the chancel mingling with the warm, aromatic emanations rising all around him from the ladies below; listened to the restrained rustling of silk and the fluttering of fans, like the whispering of a breeze amidst leaves in a forest. And in that expectant, attentive, enraptured hush he had well understood the speechless admiration which he savoured, as it rose to him, sure that the thoughts of the faithful were for the elegant, well-graced preacher, melodious of voice and distinguished in manner, not for the God about whom he was speaking. And then he would be visited by vivid memories, which refused to be banished, of his childhood in mountain passes, of those afternoons in his early life as a melancholy, pensive cowherd. . . . He spent hours and hours, until darkness fell, day-dreaming on some high crag, as he heard the cows, scattered over the rocky hillside, clanking their bells – and what were his dreams? Dreams of an enormous city, a hundred times bigger than Tarsa village – down there, in the wide world, far, far away; a city called Vetusta, much bigger even than San Gil de la Llana, the local market town, which, like Vetusta itself, he had never seen. In the great city he located marvels which gratified his senses and filled the solitude of his restless spirit. Between that ignorant, visionary childhood and the present moment of self-contemplation there was no interval in the preacher's mind; he saw himself as a boy and as the canon theologian; the present was the childhood dream come true, and in this he rejoiced.

Feelings of this sort engaged De Pas's soul as his telescope, reflecting the sun in brilliant gleams, moved slowly from roof to roof, from window to window, from garden to garden.

Close around the cathedral lay old Vetusta. This was the quarter known as La Encimada, and it dominated the city, which had spread out towards the north-west and the south-east. From the tower one could distinguish, in inner courts and private gardens of old, half-ruined houses, remains of the ancient city walls, serving here as a terrace, there to separate a vegetable plot from a chicken yard. La Encimada was both the noble quarter and the poor quarter. Vetusta's most aristocratic inhabitants lived there, next to its most ragged; the former in comfort, the latter packed together like seeds in a pine-cone. La Encimada was where the true Vetustan dwelled. There were people foolish enough to hold in the highest esteem the possession of a house, however wretched, in this elevated part of the city – in the shadow of the cathedral, or of St Mary Major's or St Peter's, the two ancient parish churches which shared the noble territory of La Encimada. The canon looked down upon this aristocratic quarter, composed of large houses with palatial airs, convents and monasteries the size of villages, and hovels in which were heaped together those plebeians who were too poor to live in the new suburb, El Campo del Sol, to the south-east, where a workers' town had grown up around the majestic chimneys of the Old Factory. Nearly all the streets in La Encimada were narrow, crooked, damp and sunless, and grass grew in some. Those streets with a preponderance of residents who were of the nobility, or had noble pretensions, were clean with a sad, almost squalid cleanliness, like that of a dismal workhouse kitchen; the municipal broom and the broom of the fastidious nobility seemed to have left in those small squares and narrow lanes the kind of marks that a brush leaves on threadbare cloth. There were few shops, and those were not impressive. From the tower one could witness the history of the privileged classes, and above all of the Church, told in the stone and the mud bricks of old Vetusta. Religious houses occupied about one-half of the terrain; St Dominic's alone took up a fifth of La Encimada; the next largest was the Convent of the Recollects, where, during the September Revolution,[3] two communities had come together, making ten nuns in all, whose convent and gardens occupied one-sixth of La Encimada. It was true, though, that St Vincent's had been turned into a barracks, and that its walls echoed to the indiscreet voice of the bugle, a constant profanation of the sacred silence of the centuries; that the state had turned the spacious, plateresque convent of the Poor Clares into an office block; and that St Benedict's was now a gloomy, insecure prison. All this was sad enough; but as, with bitterness on his lips, the canon witnessed such despoliation vividly depicted in his telescope he could, at least, open his breast to consolation and hope by looking away from the noble quarter and towards the north-west, at the graphic signs of reborn faith on the outskirts of Vetusta. For there the pious were building new abodes for religious life, more luxurious and elegant than the old, if not so solid or large. The Revolution had destroyed, it had stolen; but the Restoration, which could not give anything back, did encourage the spirit of reconstruction. Already, the Little Sisters of the Poor had completed their own building, a shining new pin near the Mall, to the west, not far from the great houses and chalets of La Colonia. This was the new residential area, inhabited by men who had emigrated to Latin America and returned with a fortune, and by home-grown merchants. To the north, among velvety pastures of a dark, intense green, a white edifice was rising, being built at immense cost by the Salesian Sisters, who, for the present, were huddled in a corner of Vetusta in an old house with a wretched little oratory for a chapel, close by the sewage outlet from La Encimada – in fact, almost buried in the sewer itself. There dwelled, as in niches, the heiresses of many wealthy and noble families: girls who, for the sake of the Crucified, had left the luxury of spacious, comfortable mansions near the cathedral for the insalubrious confines of that pigsty, while their parents, brothers, sisters and other relatives indulged their idle bodies in the luxurious expanses of the sad but huge houses of La Encimada. For it was not only the Church that could stretch its arms and legs in upper Vetusta. The inheritors of parchments and ancestral homes had also appropriated yards, gardens and orchards like forests, in relation to the city's total size. These plots were indeed rather hyperbolically known as parks when they were as large as those behind the Ozores's or the Vegallanas' houses. And while not only convents and great houses but even trees were allowed all the room they needed to stretch and spread as they liked, the unhappy plebeians, unable in their poverty to avoid being elbowed aside by the egotism of nobility and Church, were packed into houses of mud which they were required by the municipal corporation to cover with a layer of whitewash. It was a sight to behold that great heap of hovels crowding over and into each other, roofs poking into eyes: into windows, that is to say. They looked like a herd of playful cows jammed together on a narrow road, each one jumping on to the back of the beast in front.

In spite of the distributive injustice[4] which lay, without vexing him, beneath Don Fermín's eyes, this worthy canon loved more than anything else the cathedral quarter, the great church's favourite child. La Encimada was Don Fermín's natural empire, the metropolis of the spiritual power which he exercised. The smoke and the whistling from the factory made him throw hostile glances towards El Campo del Sol. It was there that the rebels lived, the grimy workers, whose skin was blackened by the paste which coal and iron make when mixed with sweat: the workers, who listened open-mouthed to hotheads preaching equality, federalism, redistribution of wealth, and a thousand other absurdities, yet who would not listen when he talked of celestial rewards and compensations beyond the grave. It was not that he was without influence among the workers, but he influenced only a minority. Certainly, when the one true creed, the Catholic faith, did take root among them, the roots were firm, like iron chains. But each time a good, believing worker died, two or three more were born who would never hear of resignation, loyalty, faith and obedience. The canon theologian did not entertain any illusions. El Campo del Sol was slipping from the Church's grasp. The last ditch of the faith was being defended there by women. A short time before the day on which De Pas meditated in this manner, several women from the workers' suburb had stoned a stranger who said he was a Protestant pastor; but such excesses, paroxysms of a dying religion, saddened the canon more than they pleased him. No, that factory smoke was not the smoke of incense. It rose towards the sky, but it did not reach heaven. The whistling of the machines was a mocking whistle, a satirical whistle, the whistle of a whip. Those tall, slender chimneys were monuments of idolatry, and they even seemed to parody church steeples.

The canon turned his telescope back to the north-west. There stood La Colonia, modern Vetusta, mapped out in straight lines, dazzling with vivid colours and steely reflections, like some bird from a South American jungle, or a savage Amerindian woman adorned with feathers and ribbons of clashing colours. Geometrical regularity; chromatic irregularity, indeed anarchy. On the roof-tops all the colours of the rainbow, as on the walls of Persian Ecbatana;[5] glassed balconies protruding on every side, depriving the houses of whatever graces they might otherwise have possessed; inopportune displays of stone; sham solidity, vociferous luxury. The city of an emigrant's dreams, combined with the city of a money-lender or draper or flour merchant who stays at home and builds while wide awake. Scrimped walls, inviting pneumonia; ridiculous ostentation, assuring discomfort. But it matters not, the canon theologian pays no attention to such things, all he sees there is wealth: a miniature Peru, of which he intends to be the spiritual Pizarro. And he has already made a start. The 'Americans' in La Colonia, who heard very few masses in the New World, return, in Vetusta, to the faith of their forefathers, as to their homeland: the religion whose forms they learnt as children is one of the sweet promises of that Spain which they saw in their dreams. What is more, they refuse to tolerate anything which is not in good taste or smacks of the plebeian, or indeed any reminder whatsoever of the humble origins of their stock. The only unbelievers in Vetusta are half a dozen mischief-makers who have not a penny in the world to call their own; for all men of substance are practising Christians, as people say nowadays. Páez, Don Frutos Redondo, the Jacas, Antolínez, the Argumosas and many, many other illustrious Amerigo Vespuccis[6] of La Colonia meticulously follow, in so far as they are able, and despite their humble surnames, the distinguished customs of the noble families of La Encimada, such as the Corujedos, Vegallanas, Membibres, Ozoreses and Carraspiques, who pride themselves on being deeply devout Christians with ancient, unblemished pedigrees. And even if Páez, Redondo and the other Americans had not done so of their own accord, their respective wives, daughters and other relatives of the weaker sex would have made them imitate in religion, as in everything else, the behaviour, ideas and words of the envied aristocracy. For all these reasons it is with more covetousness than distaste that the vicar-general looks at the suburb to the north-west. Although there are many souls that he has not yet sounded and much terrain still to be discovered in that little America, nevertheless all the explorations which have been carried out so far, and all the *trading-posts* which have been established, have given excellent returns. Don Fermín does not doubt that he will bear the light of pure faith – and with it, naturally enough, his own influence – into every corner of La Colonia's well-regimented houses, all of an exactly identical height, as established by the municipal corporation.

Lovingly De Pas returned his spyglass to his own favourite, the noble and venerable La Encimada, huddled in the shadow of the magnificent tower. Below him stood, one to the east and the other to the west, like a guard of honour for the cathedral, the two ancient churches, St Mary Major's and St Peter's, which may have witnessed her birth, and certainly saw her progress to a grandeur and splendour never achieved by them. Their history is written in the chronicles of the Reconquest, and now, overcome by damp and pulverized by the centuries, they are rotting away in glory. All about St Mary's and St Peter's, in narrow streets and small squares, there are ancestral homes whose greatest distinction would be to be able to proclaim themselves contemporaries of the two ruinous churches. But they cannot, for their relative youth is betrayed by their architecture, which shows the heavy, decadent, over-elaborate bad taste of much later periods. All these buildings have been blackened by the inclement weather which allows no object in Vetusta to remain white or unsullied for very long.

Don Saturnino Bermúdez, who swore he possessed documents proving to anyone who knew about heraldry that his surname derived from King Bermudo himself,[7] was the expert in the field of relating the history of each of these large houses, which he considered to be national glories. Whenever some radical city council started to demolish some pile of ruins, or even made plans to do so, or to expropriate some ancient mansion as a public utility, Don Saturnino created a great fuss and published in *El Lábaro*, the organ of Vetusta's Catholic right, long articles which no one read and which the lord mayor himself would not have understood, had he read them. In them he praised to the skies the historical merits of each and every partition wall, and showed any load-bearing wall to be a veritable monument. There is no doubt that Señor Don Saturnino was not a little given to falsehood, and to making somewhat free with the Romanesque and Moorish styles – although it was all for the sake of Art. For him everything was Romanesque that was not Moorish, and on more than one occasion he dated to King Fruela's time[8] the foundations of a wall put up by some modest stone-cutter who was still alive. But these lapses did not harm the scholar's reputation, for the few people who were capable of noticing them regarded them as pious exaggerations, praiseworthy anachronisms, and no one else in Vetusta read that sort of thing. But this did not induce the savant to desist from his displays of rhetoric, in which he firmly believed. He paraded bold images and powerful figures, among which the most daring sort of personification, and epanadiplosis[9] of the most delicately cadenced kind, were outstanding: walls would speak like books, and declare, 'A-quiver is my bedrock, my merlons are a-quiver'; and there was a *porte-cochère* that brought tears to the eyes with the pathos of its monologues (for which reason it often concluded the antiquarian's articles, saying, 'In fine, gentlemen of the Committee of Works, *sunt lacrymae rerum!*').[10]

The canon theologian spent more than half an hour at his observation post that afternoon. Tired of looking, or unable to find what he was looking for – over towards the Plaza Nueva, in which direction he had repeatedly turned his spyglass – he stepped back from the window, closed the instrument, put it with great care in his pocket and, with a gesture of hand and head to the bell-ringers, descended the stone spiral with the same majestic step as before. As soon as he opened the door at the bottom, and found himself in the north aisle of the cathedral, his face recovered the fixed smile which was its habitual expression, he crossed his hands in front of him, he gave his finely sculptured head a slight forward inclination, with a certain half-mystical half-romantic languor, and he glided rather than walked over the great draughts-board of the black-and-white marble floor. Through the high pointed windows and the three rose windows in the west wall came shafts of many-coloured light which imitated sections of the rainbow in the nave and aisles. The canon's cloak swung to the rhythm of his smooth swaying gait, and as it floated over the floor its voluminous folds took on the iridescent hues of a pheasant's feathers, at times even looking like a peacock's tail. A few bands of light found their way up to the canon's face, colouring it at one moment pale green like a plant of the shade, at another giving it the viscous appearance of an underwater plant or the pallor of a corpse.

In the nave there were very few of the faithful, scattered well apart; in the side-chapels, built into thick walls and sunk in shadow, groups of women were scarcely visible, kneeling around confessional boxes. Here and there a low murmur could be heard: the secret conversation of a priest and a devout lady in the tribunal of penance. In the second chapel on the north side, the darkest chapel, Don Fermín could make out two ladies who were whispering to each other. He walked on. They wanted to follow, call out, but they did not dare. They had been waiting for him, searching for him, and in the end they had to go without him.

'He's going to the choir,' said one of the ladies. And they sat down on the low platform surrounding the confessional, engulfed in gloom. It was the canon theologian's chapel. On the altar there were two empty brass candlesticks secured by small iron chains. In front of the reredos was a wooden figure of Jesus the Nazarene. Its sad glass eyes shone in the dark with gleams that gave them the appearance of something cold and damp. Its face was that of a man suffering from anaemia. Its mannered look bespoke some obsession petrified in those delicate lips and sharp cheekbones, which had been worn to that shape, it seemed, by the friction of devout kisses.

Don Fermín passed, without a pause, by the side-door of the choir and reached the crossing, but the barrier from the choir to the altar-rails was closed. The canon, who was on his way to the sacristy, walked round the apsidal retrochoir, which was flanked by another succession of chapels. Opposite each chapel a cluster of columns projected from the inner wall, and between these clusters confessional boxes lurked, visible only from directly in front. This was the place used by the beneficiaries for the sorting and settling of sins. As the vicar-general walked through the retrochoir, the beneficiary Don Custodio emerged from one of the hiding-holes like a partridge roused by dogs. His face was pale, except his cheeks, which were aflame in a

livid purple colour. He was sweating like a damp wall. The vicar-
general looked, unsmiling, at the beneficiary. He seemed to pierce
the man with needles hidden in his soft, dull eyes. Don Custodio
lowered his gaze and walked past him towards the choir, bewildered
and nonplussed, his head bowed. He was plump and dainty, and had
the airs of some French commission-agent in neat, elegant clerical
dress. Beneath his voluminous cloak his finely turned body was girt
in a rochet which looked like a woman's garment, upon which he
displayed the light silk mozetta of his benefice. Don Custodio was an
enemy within the camp, a beneficiary for the opposition. He believed,
or at least he divulged, all the offensive rumours with which it was
hoped to overthrow the vicar-general, and envied him for however
much truth all these calumnies might contain. The canon theologian
despised the beneficiary; this wretched priest's envy was a mirror in
which to contemplate his own merits. The beneficiary admired the
canon theologian and believed in his future; he envisaged him as a
bishop, a cardinal, a favourite at court, with influence in ministries
and salons, pampered by fine ladies and great men. The beneficiary's
envy dreamed greater glories for Don Fermín than he himself ever
saw in his best hopes. Don Fermín's look darted along the floor to the
confessional-box from which his envious enemy had emerged. He
saw a pale-faced young woman in Carmelite garb[11] kneeling at one
of the gratings.

She was not a lady – presumably she was a servant girl, or
seamstress, or something like that, thought the canon. Her eyes were
full of malicious curiosity, more aroused than satisfied. She made the
sign of the cross on herself, savouring the final protracted meeting of
lips and thumb, and knelt back on her heels to relish the details of her
confession, without leaving her place close to Don Custodio's confessional-box, which was still pervaded by his warmth and odour.

The canon walked on, rounded the apse, and entered the sacristy.
This was a chapel in the shape of a Latin cross, large and cold, with
four high vaults. Along all the walls there were chestnut-wood
wardrobes in which vestments and articles of worship were kept.
Above the wardrobes hung pictures, most of which were old and
mediocre, although there were a few passable copies of works by
good painters. Between the pictures there were small, ancient mirrors
with large, ornate, gilt frames. Because of dust and flies, they reflected
little light. In the middle of the sacristy much space was taken up by
a table of local black marble. Two young acolytes in red robes were
putting chasubles and copes away in the wardrobe. Turtle-dove, in a
filthy cassock, sagging open at the neck, and with an enormous wig
on the back of his head, had just finished sweeping up the dirt left in
a corner by a certain cat which entered the cathedral (nobody knew
how) and profaned everything. The dog-catcher was furious. The
acolytes pretended not to notice, but he, without looking at them,

alluded to them with threats of terrible if hypothetical punishments, most of which were designed to turn the stomach. The canon walked on, pretending not to pay any heed to these vulgar trivialities, so foreign to the sanctity of the cult. He approached a group of people whispering together at the other end of the sacristy in the subdued tones of the profane conversation which wishes to respect a sacred place. There were two ladies and two gentlemen. The faces of all four were upturned. They were contemplating a picture. The only light came in through narrow windows high in the vault, which deflected and enfeebled it before it could reach the paintings. The picture they were examining was in almost complete darkness and looked like a large, dull, black stain on the wall. The only distinguishable features in any other colour were the frontal bone of a skull and the tarsus of a bare, fleshless foot. Nevertheless, Don Saturnino Bermúdez had already devoted five minutes to the explication of the painting's merits to the ladies and the gentleman, who were listening to the antiquarian full of faith and with mouths agape. The canon theologian came across Don Saturnino occupied in this way almost daily.

As soon as a stranger of any importance arrived in Vetusta, he sought everywhere for someone who would ask Bermúdez to be so kind as to take him to see the antiquities of the cathedral and of La Encimada. Don Saturnino was very busy all day long, but from three until half past four he was always at the disposal of any persons of gentility, as he called them, who might wish to put his historical knowledge and unwavering amiability to the test. For he believed himself to be not only the province's foremost antiquarian but also – and in this he was correct – the best-mannered and most courteous man in all Spain. He was not a priest but an amphibian. His immaculate clothes, black from head to toe, indicated something which Frillity, a Darwinist whom we shall meet later, called adaptation to the cassock, the influence of the environment, and so on; by which he meant that if Don Saturnino were to make so bold as to decide to engender another Bermúdez, it would be born, at the very least, a deacon, according to Frillity. Don Saturn (for that was what people called him) was short; he wore his hair cropped close, like a brush with black bristles, combing it back to accentuate the way it receded at the temples; it was plain to see that premature baldness would have been not a little pleasing to him. He was not old – 'The age of Our Lord Jesus Christ,' he would say, in the belief that he was venturing a respectful yet somewhat worldly quip. It was not his intention, but a law of nature, that he should resemble a priest. After losing certain illusions in the course of a serious adventure in which he was taken for a priest, he grew a beard, which was as black as Indian ink, but he kept it as closely clipped as the box-tree in his garden. His mouth was large, and his ingratiating smile stretched his lips from ear to ear. No one knew why, but it was that smile, more than anything else, which revealed that Bermúdez did not complain without reason when he grumbled about his confounded stomach, bad indigestion and, above all, perpetual constipation. His smile was a furrowed smile – it was more like a grimace caused by a pain in the bowels – and with its aid Bermúdez hoped to be accepted as the most *spirituel* man in Vetusta, the man most capable of understanding a profound, intricate passion. For his serious reading (chronicles and other old books) took its place in his ambitious spirit alongside the most subtle and psychological novels being written at that time in Paris. It was altogether in spite of himself that he resembled a priest. He ordered the most fashionable machine-knitted frock-coats, exactly like those worn by all the young fops, but the tailor saw, to his astonishment, that Don Saturn's donning such a garment and its turning into a cassock were all one. Don Saturn always seemed to be in mourning, even when he was not. His hat was seldom without its black crape, however, for he considered himself to be related to the entire nobility of Vetusta, and as soon as an aristocrat died he hurried off on his errands of condolence.

Deep in his heart he believed himself born to love; his passion for history was to be regarded as a kind of succedaneum. Upon reading in the most reputable French and Spanish novels that personages in the best society felt more or less the same urges which he suffered, he came to the conclusion that all he had lacked had been a suitable theatre. The unmarried young ladies of Vetusta were incapable of understanding him, and when alone he had to confess to himself that he would never dare approach such a young lady in order to say anything of moment on the subject of love.

Perhaps married women, or some of them at least, might understand him better. The first time he had this thought, his remorse lasted a week. But the tempting idea came back and, inasmuch as it nearly always happened in the novels which he relished that the heroines were married women – sinners indeed, but finally redeemed by love and great faith – he did, therefore, determine and declare that it was quite proper to love a married woman and even tell her of one's love, so long as it was all kept within the limits of the purest idealism. And Don Saturn did fall in love with a married lady, but the same thing happened with her as with the unmarried ones: he could not bring himself to tell her of his love. He tried to convey it with his eyes, and even with certain parables and allegories from the Bible and other oriental books, but the lady of his love took no notice of his eyes, and did not understand the allegories or the parables. Her only response was to say, behind Bermúdez's back, 'I just can't see how that fellow Don Saturn knows so much; he seems such a nincompoop.'

This lady, known in Vetusta as the judge's wife, because her husband, now retired, had reached the eminent position of chief stipendiary magistrate in the provincial court, never knew of the antiquarian's burning passion. The sentimental young lover of knowledge grew weary of consuming his unique passion in silence, and cultivated a fickle, distraught air instead – which posed him no great problems, for there never was a more distraught man than he, as soon as a woman took it into her head to harass him with a glance or two. For four years now he had not missed a single ball, party, theatrical performance or promenade, and still all the ladies, whenever they saw him dancing a rigadoon[12] (his boldness did not reach to waltzes or polkas), kept saying, 'But old Bermúdez's quite unrecognizable!'

Absolutely everyone had decided that Don Saturnino was a recluse! It drove him to distraction. True, he had never tasted the gross material delights of carnal love, but was this public knowledge? True, he was no more likely to miss eight o'clock mass than was the sun to fail to rise each morning, but his devotion, and his taking Holy Communion twice a month, was neither let nor hindrance (his own words) to the title of Man of the World which he claimed for himself. And if people only knew! Who was the muffled figure that, late at night, at the maidservants' hour, as they call it in Vetusta, crept out into the Calle del Rosario, turned amid shadows into the Calle de Quintana and, stalking from one street to another, reached the arcades in the Plaza del Pan, left La Encimada, and ventured into La Colonia, deserted at this hour? Why, it was Don Saturnino Bermúdez, Doctor of Theology, Doctor of both Civil and Canon Law, Master of Arts and Bachelor of Science: the author, no less, of *Vetusta in Roman Times*, *Vetusta in the Times of the Goths*, *Vetusta in Feudal Times*, *Vetusta in Christian Times*, and *Vetusta in Times of Change*, one Vetusta per volume. That's who it was, disguised in a cloak and a soft felt hat. There was no risk of anybody recognizing him dressed like that. And where was he going? To fight against temptation in the open air, to weary the flesh with interminable walks, and also, in part, to catch a whiff of vice, of crime as he conceived it – crime that he was certain he would not commit, less because of the striving of virtue than because of the invincible power of the fear which never allowed him to take the final decisive step into the abyss. He reached its brink every night: a dirty, black, rickety door in the shadows of some filthy side-street. Sometimes temptation called out from the depths of the aforementioned abyss. Then the scholar turned all the more urgently on his heel, regained lost ground, went back to where the streets were broad, and, with delight, breathed pure air, air as pure as his body; and, the sooner to reach those ideal regions which were his proper milieu, sang 'Casta diva'[13] or 'Spirto gentil'[14] or 'Santo fuerte',[15] while thinking of his boyhood loves or the heroine of one of his favourite novels.

Oh, the joy of these victories for virtue! How clear, how evident was the concept of Providence during such moments! The ecstasy of the mystics must have been something like this! And Don Saturn, quickening his step, returned home intoxicated with idealism, moistening the upturned lapels of his cloak with the tears which he wept after that bath in the waters of ideality, as he called it. His tender emotions were eminently pious, especially on moonlit nights.

Back at home, closeted in his study after supper, he either wrote verses by the light of the paraffin lamp, or pored over his tomes. At length he retired to his bed, satisfied with himself, pleased with life, happy in his much-maligned world where, whatever people may say, there are some virtuous men, some strong spirits. Don Saturn's good works gave him a feeling of voluptuous idealism which, as it mingled with the pleasurable warmth of his soft, soothing bed, turned him by slow degrees into a different man; and then began the imagined adventures of romantic love in Paris, which was the land of his dreams, as Man of the World. The judge's wife usually appeared in these bedtime stories, and he would join with her, or with other no less pretty ladies, in sparkling dialogues, in which he opposed the wit of the female to his own serious and manly wit. In the course of these exchanges, which were all on a spiritual plane and never went further than vague promises of future favours, the antiquarian would start to feel sleepy; and then logic would begin to work in crazy ways and morality itself would become perverted as the fortress of that fear which a little earlier had saved the Doctor of Theology came tumbling down.

Next morning Don Saturn would awake in a bad mood and with stomach-ache, his soul full of despairing pessimism and his body full of wind. 'Memento homo,'[16] said the unfortunate man, forcing his sluggish body out of bed, and trying to persuade some reaction from his spirit with an acute and terrible remorse and a determination to engage in good works, which he encouraged by pouring cold water down the back of his neck and washing himself with large sponges. It may well be that cleanliness, the great virtue advocated with such insistence by Mahomet, was the only virtue which the illustrious author of *Vetusta in Times of Change* possessed to any positive degree. After a good wash he always went to mass, to search for the *new man*[17] that the Gospel demands. The new man would come, by little and little; and in his vanity, or his faith, this devotee of the Sacred Heart of Jesus believed in his regeneration every morning. This was why it was incorrect to say that the soul grows older:[18] for it was not the soul but the stomach, poor Don Saturn's confounded stomach, that refused to heed his fervent contrition. And to think that he had been assured that matter is not vile and base!

That morning, before luncheon, he had received a perfumed note from his friend, the young widow Obdulia Fandiño. What a thrill! He delayed opening the mysterious letter until after he had taken his soup. Why not dream a little? What could it be? 'O.F.' said two letters, intertwined like snakes, in the crest on the envelope. 'From Doña Obdulia,' the servant had said. As all Vestuta knew, this lady was very free and easy, perhaps excessively so – even capricious. And so, perhaps – why not? – a rendezvous. After all, they did have an understanding, not of the sort that some people suspected, but an understanding none the less. She would gaze at him in church, and sigh. Once she said to him that he must know even more than the proverbial Tostado,[19] praise whose full value he was able to appreciate, having read the works of the illustrious theologian of Avila. On another occasion she dropped her pocket-handkerchief, scented with the same perfume as the letter, and he picked it up, and when he gave it back to her their fingers touched, and she said, 'Thank you, Saturn.' Just 'Saturn', without the formal 'Don'.

One evening, during one of the gatherings held by Doña Visitación Olías de Cuervo, Obdulia had touched his leg with her knee. He had not withdrawn his leg, nor Obdulia her knee; then he had touched the beautiful lady's foot with his, and she had not withdrawn it . . . A spoonful of soup went down the wrong way. He drank wine and opened the letter.

It said:

'Dearest Saturn, Will you be a sweet, kind man and come over here at three o'clock this afternoon? I shall be awaiting you with . . .'

'With impatience,' he thought. He turned the sheet of paper over. The letter went on, '. . . with some friends from Palomares who would like to visit the cathedral in the company of a knowledgeable person . . .'. Don Saturn blushed as if he had made a fool of himself in front of an entire assembly.

'No matter,' he said to himself. 'This visit to the cathedral is a mere pretext.'

He added, 'The Lord knows how deeply I regret the profanation in which I am being invited to participate.'

He dressed as correctly as he was able, and after seeing himself in the mirror as a Lovelace[20] with history as a hobby, he left for Doña Obdulia's house.

This, then, was the personage who was explaining to two ladies and one gentleman the merits of a black painting, in which an olive-coloured skull and the heel of a fleshless foot could just be distinguished. The picture represented St Paul the first hermit; the artist was a Vetustan of the seventeenth century, known only to specialists in the antiquities of Vetusta and its province. It was for this reason that the picture and the painter were so notable in Bermúdez's eyes.

The gentleman from Palomares wore an extremely long raisin-coloured summer coat, and in his right hand he held a panama hat, which was inappropriate at this time of year, but which, in view of its being a four- or five-dollar hat (its price in Havana), he considered right to wear throughout the autumn. Señor Hidalgo believed it to be his responsibility to show a better appreciation of the scholar's artistic raptures than the ladies, whose natural ignorance was some excuse for their failure to be struck with wonder by a picture which they could not see. He searched for some opportune expressions and came provisionally upon:

'Ah! Indeed! Of course! Quite so!'

Then he bent his head over his chest, as if to meditate, but in point of actual fact, as Bermúdez would say, to rest in reaction to the uncomfortable position in which the scholar had kept him for a quarter of an hour. He finally exclaimed:

'I feel, Señor Bermúdez, that this most famous picture by the illustrious . . .'

'Cenceño.'

'Yes, by the most illustrious Cenceño, might look a trifle better if . . .'

'If you could see it,' interrupted Señor Hidalgo's wife. The former shot out a terrible glare of conjugal repression and said, by way of correction:

'It might look better, if it weren't so smoky. Perhaps the candles – the incense . . .'

'No, my good sir; smoky indeed!' replied the scholar, smiling from ear to ear. 'That which you attribute to smoke is *patina*; precisely what gives old pictures their charm.'

'Patina!' exclaimed the countryman, convinced. 'Yes, most likely.' And he promised himself that, as soon as he was back in Palomares, he would look into the dictionary to find out what patina was.

At that moment the canon theologian was approaching, to greet Don Saturn. He recognized Obdulia and bowed with a smile, but less of a smile than when he greeted Bermúdez. Then he inclined his head and part of his body towards the couple from Palomares, introduced to him by the scholar:

'Señor Don Fermín De Pas, Canon Theologian and Vicar-General of the Diocese.'

'Ah! Ah! Yes! Yes!' exclaimed Hidalgo, who had been admiring the canon from a distance for some time. His wife manifested a desire to kiss the vicar-general's hand, but a second glare from her husband restrained her, and she limited herself to an unsteady curtsey. The canon theologian spoke aloud, and his words echoed about the vault; his example gave the others courage to shout as well. Soon Obdulia Fandiño's laughter, like fresh, dewy pearls (as Don Saturn would say), filled the air, which had already been profaned by the worldly perfume with which she had saturated it from the moment she had entered the sacristy: the perfume of her letter, the perfume of her pocket-handkerchief, the perfume of Obdulia, about which the scholar sometimes dreamed. Combined with the perfume of candles and incense, it was like a taste of heaven for the antiquarian, whose ideal was to bring together in this way mystical and erotic scents in a kind of harmony or compromise, which was what he thought must be, in another, better world, the reward for those who had on earth succeeded in resisting all kinds of temptation.

Obdulia could ill conceal her boredom during all the talk of pictures, ogees, stilted arches, voussoirs and other such nonsense that she had never understood, but she came back to life with the arrival of the canon, her spiritual father in spite of all his efforts to pass her on to Don Custodio, who was hungry for this kind of prey. The woman set Don Fermín's nerves on edge; she was a walking scandal. One only had to observe the clothes which she wore to the cathedral. 'Such women throw discredit upon religion.' She sported a bonnet of crimson velvet, from under which, like a cascade of gold coins, flowed a profusion of ringlets of an artificial, metallic, sullied blond colour. A week earlier the canon had seen that hair, through the grating of his confessional, jet black! About the lady's skirt, which was of black satin, there was nothing exceptional, so long as she remained motionless. What was really objectionable was something which looked like a doublet of scarlet silk – quite alarming, even. The doublet was stretched over some kind of breastplate (nothing less substantial could have stood the strain), which had the shape of a woman excessively endowed by nature with the attributes of her sex. What arms! What a bust! And it all looked as if it were on the point of bursting! This sight entranced Don Saturn, while it annoyed the canon, who did not want such scandals in church. That lady understood religion after a fashion which might be acceptable elsewhere, in a great city like Madrid, Paris or Rome; but not in Vetusta. She confessed the most appalling sins in a confidential tone, just as she might gossip about them to some like-minded friend in her boudoir. She was much given to quoting her friends the Patriarch of the Indies and the jovial Bishop of Nauplia; she proposed Catholic raffles, wanted to organize exclusive charity balls, novenas and jubilees for people of quality – a thousand absurdities! The canon tried, whenever possible, to keep her under control, but it was not always possible. In spite of his virtually absolute authority he could not subdue her: like a ball of quicksilver she kept slipping from his grasp. This Doña Obdulita was a nuisance and a burden to him. And to think that she was trying to seduce him, and make him her own, as she had already done with the Bishop of Nauplia, that sleek prelate who never left her side when they lived in adjacent rooms in the Hotel de la Paix, in Madrid! The most ardent, the darkest looks of those large, dark, burning eyes were for De Pas; and the widow's worshippers knew it, and envied him. Yet he cursed her blockade.

'Does the foolish woman really think that I can be conquered like Don Saturn?'

In spite of this cordial dislike, he was always affable and courteous to the widow, for in this matter he made no distinction between friends and enemies. It was not until someone was crushed beneath his foot that Don Fermín stopped being irreproachably polite to him. Urbanity was a dogma for the canon theologian as it was for Bermúdez, but they put it to very different uses.

While the party spoke of all the good things in the cathedral, and the countryman showed his admiration and his wife echoed his exclamations, Obdulia looked at herself, as best she could, in the little decorative mirrors high on the wall.

The canon took his leave. It was not possible for him to accompany the ladies – he was extremely sorry, but he had to obey the call of duty – the divine office. Everyone bowed.

'First things first,' said the gentleman from Palomares, alluding to the Deity and performing a genuflexion (though whether meant for the Deity or for the vicar-general is uncertain).

Luckily, as Don Fermín affirmed, he could in his ignorance be of no use to them anyway, while Bermúdez was a living chronicle of the antiquities of Vetusta.

Don Saturn arched his eyebrows and signalled a wish to kiss the ground, and then he fixed Obdulia with a serious gaze, as piercing as a drill, as if to say, 'You heard that. I, who declare myself your slave, am the foremost antiquarian in all Vetusta, in the opinion of its finest theologian.' All this was what he meant his look to convey to Obdulia, but she seemed not to have received the communication, for as she said goodbye to the canon she left her soul, conducted by her eyes, among the voluminous, rhythmic folds of his cloak. Don Fermín walked to a wardrobe, removed his cloak, and with great gravity donned his close-fitting rochet, his lordly mozetta and his choir-cope.

'Isn't he handsome!' said Doña Obdulia from a distance, while the visitors admired, in blind faith, another picture being praised by Don Saturnino.

They walked round the sacristy. Near the door were some new pictures, quite well-executed copies of works by famous painters. Señora Hidalgo appeared to like them better than Cenceño's marvels, doubtless because they were more visible. But her prudent husband, seeing that Bermúdez proceeded with affected disdain past the fresh, vivid colours, nudged her to make her understand that this part of the sacristy was to be passed through without any agitation. Among these pictures there was a copy, quite faithful and neatly done, of the famous Murillo, *St John of God,* in the Hospital of Incurables at Seville. The attention of the lady from the country was caught by the saint's head, which once seen can never be forgotten.

'Oh, how lovely!' she exclaimed, unable to restrain herself.

Don Saturn looked up with a smile full of compassion and said, 'Yes, it's a pretty little thing; but terribly well known.'

And he turned his back on St John carrying the sick beggar on his back, in the gloom.

Señor Hidalgo pinched his wife; his face fired up, and he muttered this remonstrance: 'You always have to show me up. Can't you see it hasn't got any – patina?'

They left the sacristy.

'This way,' said Bermúdez, pointing to the right; and they crossed the transept, not without scandalizing some devout ladies, who interrupted their prayers in order to pick Obdulia's fiery doublet to pieces. The widow's satin skirt, unremarkable so long as it was stationary, was the most subversive part of her costume as soon as she began to walk. It was such a close fit that it looked like a tight pair of trousers, clinging to statuesque forms which, thus displayed, were unsuited to these hallowed precincts.

'Now, ladies and gentlemen, we shall behold the Pantheon of the Kings,' spoke the antiquary, in a hushed voice, preparing the appropriate sections of *Vetusta in the Times of the Goths* and *Vetusta in Christian Times*. And if the truth is to be told it must be said that he did not know which king to turn to – that is to say, that he mixed and confused them, the cause of such confusion being Obdulia's skirt. For the scholar could not help admiring this most daring invention, new to Vetusta, which enabled the graceful and meaningful undulations that he had only seen in his dreams to appear before his eyes. The devout antiquarian was beginning to realize, with a heavy heart, that the incongruity between the insinuations of Obdulia's skirt and the holiness of this place, instead of extinguishing the fire within him, only fed the flames which he so deeply regretted, as if paraffin were being thrown on to a bonfire.

They entered the chapel which contained the Pantheon. It was large, dark, cold and of rough construction, but of an imposing and majestic simplicity. The disrespectful clatter of the bronze-coloured imperial boots which Obdulia displayed under her tight, ankle-length skirt, the rustle of silk on petticoats, the crackle of starched underskirts of snowy foam (which was how they were imagined by Don Saturn, who had caught glimpses of them on occasions), all this would have been enough to rouse from their sleep of centuries the kings buried there – always supposing that the antiquarian was correct in what he said about the eternal rest of these highly respectable gentlemen:

'Here, ever since the eighth century, have lain the Kings . . .,' and he pronounced the names of six or seven sovereigns – changing some of the vowel-sounds, in the opinion of the countryman, who always put modern-sounding equivalents in the place of archaic diphthongs.

The countryman was full of wonder at Don Saturnino's wisdom and eloquence.

Within a crypt-like opening cut into one of the walls there was a great stone sepulchre covered with reliefs and illegible inscriptions.

Between the sepulchre and the wall was a narrow passage, a foot wide, and on the outer side, at the same distance, an iron railing. In the passage there was total darkness. The visitors from the country remained by the railing. Bermúdez, with Obdulia in his wake, disappeared into the gloom-filled passage. After Don Saturnino's enumeration of kings there was a solemn silence. The scholar had coughed. He was about to speak.

'Pray light a match, Señor Hidalgo,' said Obdulia.

'I haven't got any on me. But we could ask for a candle.'

'No, sir, there is no need. I know the inscriptions by heart – and, in any case, they cannot be read.'

'They're in Latin?' Señora Hidalgo ventured to suggest.

'No, madam, they are effaced.'

And there was no light.

The antiquarian spoke for about a quarter of an hour. He recited, slyly pretending to be improvising, chapters one, two, three and four of one of his *Vetustas*, and he was about to conclude with the epilogue, which we shall copy word for word, when Obdulia interrupted, saying, 'My God! Are there mice here? I think I can feel . . .'

And she screamed, and clung to Don Saturn who, encouraged by the gloom, felt bold enough to grasp between his hands the hand which pressed his shoulder. After soothing Obdulia with an energetic squeeze, he concluded:

'These were the far-famed paragons who, with the guerdon of rich treasures, enviable privileges and pious foundations, regaled this Holy Cathedral Church of Vetusta, which accorded their mortal remains a perennial ultra-telluric mansion; with the majesty of which deposition its renown so grew that it found itself betimes to be a great emporium, and indeed to enjoy hegemony, as one might say, over the no less Holy Churches of Tuy, Dumio, Braga, Iria, Coimbra, Vizeu, Lamego, Celeres, Aguas Cálidas, *et sic de coeteris*.'

'Amen!' exclaimed the countrywoman, unable to restrain herself, while Obdulia congratulated Bermúdez by pressing his hand in the dark.

II

The divine office was over: the venerable canons' task of praising the Lord between yawns was done for the day. They filed into the sacristy with the air of boredom of functionaries who always perform their official duties in the same mechanical way, with no belief in the usefulness of the effort by which they earn their daily bread. These honourable priests' spirits had been worn threadbare by the ceaseless rub of canonical canticles, like most of the rochets, mozettas and copes which they removed before putting on their cloaks again. What is common in many corporations could be observed in the Vetustan chapter: some prebendaries did not speak to each other, others did not even exchange salutations. Yet an outsider could not easily notice this disharmony: prudence covered up the rough edges, and in general there reigned the greatest and most jovial concord. There were handshakes, pats on the back, age-old jests, jokes, laughter, whispered confidences. But some priests took a taciturn and hurried leave before departing from the cathedral; and there were those who left without even saying goodbye.

When the canon theologian entered the sacristy, the Ilustrísimo Señor Don Cayetano Ripamilán, an Aragonese from Calatayud, had one hand resting on the marble table, because his elbows did not reach such heights, and was declaiming, after sniffing several times like a dog following a trail:

> 'Aha! Methinks I can catch
> A whiff of . . .'[1]

The entrance of the vicar-general restrained the archpriest, who cut short his quotation and added: 'It would appear that there have been petticoats among us, Señor De Pas?'

And without awaiting a reply he made various waggish allusions, courteous yet a trifle risqué, to the young widow's resplendent beauty.

Don Cayetano was a little old man of seventy-six, sprightly, cheerful, thin, spare, the colour of old leather, and as wrinkled as scorched parchment. His small person, seen as a whole, was reminiscent – no one knew exactly why – of the silhouette of a life-sized eagle; though according to other opinions the resemblance was rather to a magpie or a hunched-up and dishevelled thrush. To be sure, there was a bird-like air about his figure and his gestures, which was all the more marked in his shadow. He was angular and spiky, and wore an old-fashioned shovel hat, long and narrow, with both sides of the brim furled, like Don Basilio's in *The Barber of Seville;* since he always wore it on the back of his head, it seemed as if he were surmounted by a telescope. He was short-sighted, and corrected this defect with gold-rimmed eyeglasses sitting on his long, hooked nose. Behind the lenses shone two small, restless eyes, which were very black and very round. He often wore his cloak with its skirts gathered up and thrown over one shoulder, as university students do; he liked to stick his arms akimbo; and he had the habit, when involved in a conversation on a theological or canonical subject, of extending his right hand and forming a circle with his thumb and first finger. In order to see his interlocutor's face, he would twist his head to one side and look up with one eye, as domestic fowls often do. Although Don Cayetano was a canon and an important dignitary – an archpriest, no less, with the honour of sitting on the right of the bishop in the choir – he considered himself to be worthy of respect and even of admiration not because of these humdrum distinctions, nor because of the insignia which gave him the title of Ilustrísimo, but rather because of his inestimable gifts as a bucolic and epigrammatic poet. His gods were Garcilaso and that illustrious fellow Aragonese, Martial. He also held Meléndez Valdés in high esteem, and had considerable regard for Inarco Celenio.[2] He had come to Vetusta as a beneficiary at the age of forty, had attended divine office in the cathedral for thirty-six years, and could consider himself as much a Vetustan as the next man. Indeed, many people did not know that he was from another province. Apart from poetry he had two worldly passions: women and shot-guns. He had renounced the latter, but not the former, whom he still worshipped with the same chaste and innocent veneration as when he was thirty. Not a single Vetustan, even counting the group of free-thinkers who met in a certain restaurant every Good Friday to eat meat, would have dared entertain doubts about Don Cayetano's age-long chastity. That was not his way. His adoration of women had nothing to do with sexual requirements. Woman was the burthen of poesy, as he said; for he took pride in speaking like the poets of better times, and said 'burthen' instead of 'subject'. Ever since his youth he had felt the irresistible need to be gallant with ladies, to frequent their company and to compose for them madrigals which were as innocent in their intention as they were mischievous and spicy in their execution. In the history of the chapter there had been periods of black intransigence when Ripamilán's foible was persecuted as if it were a crime, and when there was talk of scandal and of burning a book of poems which he had published at the expense of the Marquis de Corujedo, the great protector of letters. At that time there was also a move to excommunicate Don Pompeyo Guimarán, a character whom we shall meet later.

The gale of fanaticism blew itself out, Ripamilán – who was not yet an archpriest – having drifted on through it with his cargo of bucolic ingenuousness, well liked by all (except wild rabbits and partridges). But how far distant were those times now! Who now remembered Meléndez Valdés, or the *Eclogues and Canzoni by a Pastor of Bilbilis*,[3] in other words by Don Cayetano Ripamilán? Romanticism and liberalism had made havoc of it all. And Romanticism itself had gone out of fashion; but the pastoral genre had not come back, nor did epigrams, however mischievous they might be, have any effect. Don Cayetano was not just one more of the canons *laudatores temporis acti*,[4] as he called them; he did not praise the past as a simple matter of course, but as far as poesy was concerned one had to say that the Revolution had not achieved anything worth while.

'We live in a hypocritical, sad and boorish society,' he would tell the young gentlemen of Vetusta, who loved him. 'For example, none of you know how to dance. Where, now, could you have come across the idea that it is good form to grip a young lady by her waist and press her against your chest?'

He was under the impression that the intimate polka which he had seen performed years before, on the occasion of a certain curious journey to Madrid, was what people danced in salons.

'In my time we used to dance differently.'

The archpriest spoke in good faith, forgetting that he had only ever danced with the occasional chair. Once however, as a seminarist, he had been a fine player of the flute and solitary dancer. And now, imagining, with the aid of the abundant poetic fantasy which God had given him, the rigadoons in which he had displayed his fine figure and graceful bearing, he would, *en petit comité* (as he said) sling the end of his cloak over his shoulder, thrust his shovel hat under his arm, hoist his cassock an inch or two, and perform intricate and witty solos, full of pirouettes, genuflexions and even entrechats.

The youngsters would laugh heartily; and the good archpriest would be in his glory, achieving with his feet triumphs which his pen could no longer attain in those prosaic times.

Such dancing displays were usually given at parties, which the old man never missed, for ever since his doctors had forbidden him to write or even read after dark, he could not be without lively and gallant company in the evening. Card-games bored him, and conventicles of canons and frock-coated bishops, as he described them, saddened him. 'He was neither a liberal nor a Carlist. He was a priest.' He was attracted to youth, and he preferred its company to that of the most eminent Vetustan brains. Local amateur poets and journalists had in him a canny and guileful critic, although always a courteous and affable one. He would come upon Trifón Cármenes in the street, for example – Cármenes was Vetusta's most assiduous poet, the eternal victor in bloodless bardic jousts – beckon him to his side, bring his hooked nose close to the poet's large ear, and say:

'I've seen your latest piece. It's not bad, but you mustn't forget the precept, *versate manu*.[5] The classics, Trifón my boy, the classics! Where will you find anything to rival the simplicity of, "Once I saw a little thrush settling on a basil-bush"?'[6] And he would recite Villegas's tender poem to its last line, his eyes full of tears and his lips moist, too.

Most of the chapter absolved the archpriest of his indecorousness on condition that he be considered in his dotage. 'All the same,' said a certain burly canon, new to Vetusta and to his officer, and a relative of the Minister of Grace and Justice, 'all the same, the imprudence with which he speaks on every subject cannot be taken so calmly. He lets his tongue run away with him, makes hurried judgements, and employs words and allusions which are unbecoming in a dignitary.'

This canon had sometimes taken the archpriest to task by making insinuations about the spiciness of his epigrams, but the archpriest had reduced him to silence:

'Come, come! Let me quote what my beloved fellow-countryman, the poet Martial, wrote about cases of this sort, to wit – *Lasciva est nobis pagina, vita proba est.*[7]

With which words he indicated that – as was true enough – his ribaldry was confined to his tongue, while others, no less canons than he, kept their ribaldry in another place. And Don Cayetano's chastity was not a recent development: he had always been loose-tongued about this subject – but never more than loose-tongued. Such was his free rendering of the quotation from Martial.

The archpriest was in a talkative mood that afternoon. Obdulia's visit to the cathedral had aroused his anaphroditous instincts, his disinterested passion for women or, more accurately, for ladies. Don Cayetano could still catch that smell of Obdulia, which nobody else noticed any more.

The canon theologian answered him with non-committal smiles. But he did not go away. He had something to say to him. De Pas was not one of those priests who made a habit of staying behind for the *coterie*, as the juicy conversations in the sacristy after the divine office were called. If it was fine, the *coterieans* would take a stroll together along some country road, or walk to the Mall. If it was raining or threatening rain, they prolonged their chatter in the sacristy until Turtle-dove gave the cathedral keys a discreet tinkle, and then each canon took himself home. This should not be taken to mean that the chatterers were close friends. No indeed, for the general law of gossip applied there. They would all backbite those who were absent, as if they themselves were faultless, had struck the happy medium in all things, and were never to be parted. But when one of them did depart, the rest would maintain a certain respect towards him only for a few minutes; and as soon as this foolhardy man was assumed to have arrived home, one of those remaining behind would suddenly declare:

'He's just the same.'

Everyone knew that gesture towards the door and those words to mean: 'Rapid fire!'

And *he* was shot to pieces.

The archpriest was by no means the least of the gossipers. Indeed, it was he who had given the archdeacon, Don Restituto Mourelo, the nickname which he bore unawares like a cloth tail pinned to his back by a joker. No member of the chapter called him Mourelo, or Archdeacon; they all called him Gloucester. Don Restituto's right shoulder was a little out of line – although otherwise he was a fine figure of a man, almost as tall as the minister's relative – and since this incurable defect was an obstacle to the aspirations to elegance which he had always entertained, he thought out the plan of making the best of a bad bargain, as they say: in other words, of turning the blemish with which he was marked to his own advantage, as a personal distinction. Instead of concealing his physical defect, therefore, he accentuated it, twisting himself more and more to the right, leaning over like a weeping-willow tree. The effect of this strange posture was that Mourelo looked like a man always lying in wait, in anticipation of rumours; his own advance guard for gathering news, searching out hidden motives, and even listening at keyholes. The archdeacon had not read Darwin, but he found a certain mysterious and perhaps cabbalistic relationship between the *F* shape of his own body and the qualities of sagacity, astuteness, duplicity and discreet malice – and even the canonical Machiavellianism which was what most concerned him. He believed that his smile, a partial copy of the smile which the canon theologian used, fooled everybody. Indeed, it was true that Don Restituto enjoyed the benefit of two faces: he ran with the hare and hunted with the hounds; he hid his envy behind a sticky amiability, and feigned perplexity (which was never, of course, a failing of his). None the less, said the archpriest, neither does his amiability deceive everyone, nor is he as Machiavellian as he supposes, however crafty a self-seeker he may be.

Whenever he could, the archdeacon would whisper into his listener's ear, winking alternate eyes. He took delight in using expressions with one, or even two, hidden meanings, like a nest of Chinese boxes. He was a hypocrite who simulated a certain carelessness about the external forms of worship, to make his piety look simple and spontaneous. Everything became a secret with him. He told anyone who would listen that he was opening his heart for the very first time.

'I know well enough that "the fish's mouth is its death". I am not the man to forget that "the closed mouth catches no flies"; but with you I do not mind being frank and outspoken, possibly for the very first time in my life. Well, this is the secret.'

And he would tell it. He spoke in a soft, mysterious voice. He often entered the sacristy muttering in a scarcely audible whisper, 'Pleasant weather, gentlemen! Let us hope it lasts!'

Ripamilán, who years before had made occasional clandestine visits to the theatre, lurking in the shadows of the proscenium box, or 'pocket' as it was usually called, saw Bretón de los Herreros's adaptation of Delavigne's *Les Enfants d'Édouard*[8] one night. As soon as Gloucester, the hunchbacked, twisted, malicious regent, came on to the stage, Ripamilán exclaimed: 'Here comes the archdeacon!'

The expression prospered, and Don Restituto Mourelo was from then onwards Gloucester for all cultured Vetusta. And there he stood listening with feigned enjoyment to the roguish jokes being told by the archpriest, whose tongue he feared both in its presence and in its absence. Whenever Don Cayetano turned his back – for he never stopped swinging about on his heels while he was talking–Gloucester would wink at the dean and drill his own forehead with a finger. He was referring to the bucolic poet's madness. The poet continued:

'No, gentlemen, this is no mere idle gossip! I know all about the widow's life in Madrid, because she was on close terms with the Bishop of Nauplia, and I was then a good friend of his. Once, at a hostelry in the Calle del Arenal, I was given the opportunity to become well acquainted with our Obdulia; before that I hardly used to give her good-day here in Vetusta, in spite of our both belonging to the Vegallana coterie. Now we are great friends. She's an epicurist. She doesn't believe in the sixth commandment.'9

This produced a burst of laughter. But the vicar-general restricted himself to smiling, inclining his head, and assuming the look of a saint who suffers such aural scandal for the love of God. The archdeacon laughed a listless laugh.

The history of Obdulia Fandiño profaned the sacristy, as a little earlier her laughter, her costume, and her perfume had profaned it.

The archpriest narrated the lady's adventures as Martial would have done, the Latin apart.

'Gentlemen: young Joaquín Orgaz has told me that the clothes displayed by that lady in the Mall . . .'

'Are most scandalous . . .' said the dean.

'But very select,' observed the minister's relative.

'And numerous. She never wears a costume twice, every day a new piece of frippery,' added the archdeacon. 'I do not know where she obtains them, for she is not wealthy; in spite of her pretensions to nobility, neither is she in fact noble nor has she anything more than a miserable income and a paltry widow's pension . . .'

'That's what I mean,' interrupted Don Cayetano in triumph. 'The Orgaz boy, who concluded his medical studies at San Carlos Hospital, has told me that during recent years Obdulia was working in Madrid for her cousin Tarsila Fandiño, the famous mistress of the famous . . .'

'Yes, yes, what did he say?'

'That she worked for her as a go-between, so to speak. Well, not exactly that; but, don't you know, she accompanied her, and her cousin is naturally grateful, and sends her the clothes she leaves off. And since they are still new when she does so, and she has so many of them, and they are so select . . .'

The chapter, pretending to hear the archpriest out of courtesy alone, was in fact engrossed in his story. Ripamilán himself was savouring the ribald gossip only for its pleasantry. The rest began to feel embarrassed listening to such chatter in each other's company. The archpriest had his penetrating little dark eyes fixed upon the canon theologian, Obdulia's confessor; he seemed to be calling for his testimony.

The vicar-general was only there for a private talk with Don Cayetano, and endured his impertinent remarks with patience, for he had a high regard for the old man, and forgave him his innocent displays of rhetorical eroticism because he knew his conduct to be irreproachable, and his heart to be of gold. They were good friends, and Ripamilán was Don Fermín's most determined and enthusiastic supporter in the struggles which took place within the chapter. Others were his followers out of self-interest, and many out of fear, but Don Cayetano was incapable of fearing anyone and helped and loved Don Fermín because, in his opinion, he was the only outstanding man in the cathedral. The bishop was a saintly old soul, Gloucester was a sly dog with more malice than talent, but the canon theologian was a scholar, an orator, a politician, a man of letters, and, most important of all, Ripamilán believed, a man of the world. When there was talk of the vicar-general's alleged venality, of his tyranny, of his sordid trafficking, the old man became indignant and roundly denied even the most probable cases of simony. But if the topic of his amorous adventures – no more than a collection of anonymous rumours, without the support of any factual evidence – was brought up, the archpriest smiled as he made his denials, as if to say that it was all quite possible, but of less moment.

'The truth is that Don Fermín is a strapping young fellow, and if devout ladies fall in love with him when they see him up in the pulpit looking so handsome, smart, and elegant, and speaking like a Chrysostom, he is not to blame nor is it against the wise laws of nature.'

The canon theologian knew everything that Ripamilán thought about him, and considered the old man to be his most faithful supporter. That was why he was still in the sacristy. He had to ask the archpriest certain questions which could be dangerous put to anyone else. Gloucester had scented something in the wind.

'Why didn't the canon theologian go away? Why was he subjecting himself to this ordeal? No, *he* was not going to abandon his post either.' Gloucester was the vicar-general's most cordial enemy. The archdeacon's most refined Machiavellian effort consisted in appearing to maintain a good relationship with 'the despot', passing for one of his followers, while undermining him in secret, preparing for him a fall which would make even that of Don Rodrigo Calderón[10] pale in comparison. Gloucester's plans were on a vast scale, full of twists and turns, ambushes and labyrinths, traps, petards, and even infernal machines. Don Custodio the beneficiary was his lieutenant. That afternoon he had passed on to Gloucester the news that the judge's wife was in the canon theologian's chapel, awaiting him for confession. A stupendous occurrence. The judge's wife, a most eminent lady, was married to Don Víctor Quintanar, who had been a stipendiary magistrate in various provincial courts and finally in that of

Vetusta, where he had retired on the pretext of preventing gossip about certain dubious disqualifying circumstances, but in reality because he was weary and could leave active service and still live in comfort. His wife had continued to be known as the judge's wife. Quintanar's successor was a bachelor, and so there had not been any conflict. But a year later another chief stipendiary magistrate had come, with a wife, and then the trouble had started. In Vetusta the judge's wife was for ever to be Quintanar's wife, one of the illustrious Vetustan Ozoreses. As far as the *newcomer* was concerned, she had to be forbearing, and make do with being with the *other* judge's wife. Besides, the conflict would not last long: the term 'President' was now beginning to be used, and there would soon be a name for each lady. In the meantime the judge's wife was Ana Ozores. She had always been Don Cayetano's spiritual daughter; but having for some time only confessed a few hand-picked friends of high social standing, nearly all of them ladies, he had now tired of even this light load, which was a heavy one for a man of his years. Determined to withdraw from the confessional, he had asked his spiritual daughters to free him from his task, and had even indicated successors for such a grave and interesting ministry, each lady being assigned a priest to suit her. This inheritance or, more accurately, succession *inter vivos*, was coveted by the members of the chapter and their subordinates among the cathedral clergy. Before the religious reaction which in Vetusta, as in the whole of Spain, had been provoked by the excesses of free-thinkers extemporized in taverns, coffee-houses and congresses, the archpriest had been the confessor to the cream of La Encimada, because he was easy-going about certain matters. But now fashions had changed and a warier path was trodden in matters of immorality; so the canon theologian, who picked his steps with care, was preferred. Nevertheless, a few ladies – some out of habit, others in order not to snub Don Cayetano, and others because they were still content with his easy-going system – had continued to attend the latitudinarian's confessional, until he himself grew tired and politely began to brush the flies away.

Don Custodio, a young man of ardent desires, had excessive faith in the miracles of fortune performed by auricular confession and, for no good reason, attributed the canon theologian's progress to them; so he kept watch on the archpriest's succession with greater avarice than anyone and with imprudent passion. He had ascertained that Doña Olvido, the haughty only daughter of Páez, one of the wealthiest returned emigrants in La Colonia, had gone over, some time earlier, from Ripamilán's confessional to that of Don Fermín. This was a choice enough titbit. But what a scandal now! Now (Don Custodio had found out about it by listening behind a door) the stupid old bucolic poet was leaving the canon theologian the most desirable of his penitential jewels, in other words Don Víctor Quintanar's worthy, virtuous and lovely wife. Don Custodio felt the proverbial slaver of envy dribbling from his lips! After meeting the vicar-general in the retrochoir he had gone on into the nave, and in *that fellow's* chapel he had, with a side glance, seen two ladies, who must be new, since they were not aware that Don Fermín did not *sit* that afternoon. He had retraced his steps, he had taken another furtive but more careful look, and he had seen, in spite of the shadows in the chapel, that one of the ladies was the judge's wife in person.

He went into the choir, and told Gloucester, who was an aspirant to this particular succession, believing the honour of confessing Doña Ana Ozores to belong to him because he was a dignitary. 'The bishop was out of the running. The dean was an old dotard who was only capable of eating and trembling; once, during a penitential procession, half a dozen drunkards had given him a fright, from which only his stomach had recovered; his digestion worked well enough, but not his mind; his thinking was confined to what was necessary for him to continue vegetating and attending choir; he was out of the running as well. The archpriest was renouncing the judge's wife: well, who was the next dignitary? He was. He, as archdeacon, was designated by hierarchy. This, then, was an outrage, an injustice which cried out to heaven – and he could not even cry out to the bishop, for the bishop was Don Fermín's slave.' Don Custodio agreed with Gloucester, for although the beneficiary was not so pretentious as to claim such a fine morsel for himself, he wanted, at the very least, to prevent his enemy from enjoying it. He flattered Gloucester and encouraged him to fight for the just cause of his rights. Gloucester, gratified, and as red as a beetroot, said into his confidant's ear, 'Do you think that it is the lady's own free choice?' And moving away a little in order to observe the effects of his shrewd comment, he looked at the beneficiary with his eyes full of sly malice, while his puffed-out scarlet cheeks betrayed a sac of laughter, on the point of spilling out through the corners of his mouth.

'Possibly so,' replied Don Custodio, emphasizing the words in order to show himself aware of the question's hidden implications.

While the archpriest was profaning the four limbs of the cross – the sacristy – with the worldly story of the life and miracles of Obdulia Fandiño, the smiling Gloucester pondered on the canon theologian's motives for listening to Don Cayetano instead of hurrying to the confessional at whose foot awaited him the most penitent in Vetusta the noble.

The Machiavelli of the Vetustan chapter swore to himself not to abandon his post before discovering with what he had to reckon.

The canon theologian had resolved not to go that day into the chapel which people called his. To hear confession that afternoon would have been an exception, sufficient in itself to set tongues wagging. Would those ladies still be there? On descending the tower and walking along the aisle he had seen and recognized them: the judge's wife and Visitación, he was certain of it. Why had they come without warning? Don Cayetano must know. When an eminent lady, like the judge's wife, wanted to become the canon theologian's spiritual daughter, she warned him in good time, she asked for an appointment. People he did not know, common women, did not make so bold; the few women of that class whom he did confess came in a crowd to the dark chapel whose secrets Don Custodio envied, and there those anonymous penitents awaited their turn. Such humble devotees knew which were the canon's days of rest. This was one of them, and the chapel had been empty until the two ladies arrived. Visitación attended for confession once every two or three months, and she was not sure which days he was on duty and which days off – she had no idea when he sat and when he did not. This was the judge's wife's first attendance. 'Why hadn't she warned him? The event was solemn enough, and would ring out loudly enough, to merit more ceremonious preliminaries. Was it pride? Was it that the lady thought he would move heaven and earth to discover when she was going to honour him with her visit? Or was it humility? Was it that, with great delicacy and with a Christian good taste which was not common among the ladies of Vetusta, she wished to be lost in a crowd of common people, confess anonymously, be one among many?' This hypothesis pleased the canon theologian. It seemed a poetic and sincerely religious gesture. 'He was tired of Obdulias and Visitacións. The stupidity of these and other ladies made them irreverent and coarse, yes, coarse, in their attitudes towards the sacrament and the cult in general. They took liberties that were profanations, and assumed an importunate familiarity which gave rise to the calumnies of fools and knaves.

'He was no Don Custodio – a man ignorant of the ways of the world, lost in day-dreams, and ambitious for a certain kind of ecclesiastical tinsel which could, perhaps, be acquired in the confessional – to be gratified by imprudent revelations, the only effect of which was to flood his soul with tedium. He was waiting for something new, something more refined, something select.' He had heard the rumour that the archpriest had advised the judge's wife to go to the canon theologian's chapel on the grounds that he himself was retiring from the confessional. But Don Cayetano had told him nothing. Furthermore, since good priests are silent about confessional matters, Don Cayetano, who could be serious when dealing with serious subjects, had never spoken to the canon theologian about the judge's wife from the point of view of one judging her from that sacred tribunal. De Pas hoped to discover something that afternoon. But Gloucester did not go away. The talk was no longer about Obdulia or her cousin from Madrid, her model, it was about the weather. And still Gloucester did not move. By now all the other canons had taken their leave, in ones and twos. Only the three of them remained, with Turtle-dove, who was noisily opening and closing drawers and muttering to himself – curses, no doubt.

Don Cayetano stemmed the flow of his chatter, realizing that the canon theologian wanted to say something to him and that Gloucester was in the way. He remembered that he wanted to speak to De Pas and, not being one to hold his tongue in such situations, cut the conversation short.

'Oh, my wretched memory! Don Fermín, a word with you, by the archdeacon's leave – actually not just a word, we have to speak at length. It's a spiritual concern.'

Gloucester bit his lips, gave a twisted bow, turning himself into the arch of a bridge, and departed from the sacristy muttering into his white and purple stock, 'One day I'll make the ill-mannered old idiot pay for all this!'

It was the habit of the archpriest to employ incongruous remarks, broad hints and other such stratagems to make a mockery of all the archdeacon's diplomacy and Machiavellianism.

'If everyone were like me, Gloucester wouldn't know what to do with all his cunning and hypocrisy. What would become of foxes if there weren't any chickens?'

Gloucester always left by the cloister door, at the end of the north transept, that being his quickest way home, but today he decided to leave by the tower door, since this route took him past the canon theologian's chapel. He looked in: nobody. He paused, eagerly looked in again, and took a step into the chapel. There was certainly nobody there. 'So the ladies had departed without confessing; so the canon theologian had permitted himself the luxury of slighting no less a personage than the judge's wife!' The archdeacon envisaged the world of intrigue which might be founded upon this lapse. He took holy water from a large black marble stoup and, as he crossed himself and bowed to the altar in front of the rood-screen, he muttered, 'This will be your Achilles' heel. For I shall see that you pay dearly for this slight.'

And he left the cathedral, using his fingers to make calculations, which soon turned into traps, cabals, intrigues, espionage, and even secret doors and underground stairways.

The archpriest's mouth fell open when De Pas informed him that the judge's wife was, he had been told, in the cathedral and that he had not hurried to greet and confess her, if this was the purpose of her visit, as was to be supposed.

'But what must that angel of goodness be thinking?' cried Don Cayetano, aghast at this news. He called to Turtle-dove.

'Hey, Rodríguez, hurry to the canon theologian's chapel, and if you see a lady there . . .'

It was useless. Celedonio the acolyte was entering the sacristy, and he broke into the conversation.

'They have gone, sir. It was Doña Visita and the judge's wife. They have gone. I spoke to them. I told them that the canon theologian did not sit today. Doña Visita had wanted to leave earlier anyway and she took Doña Ana by the arm and led her off.'

'What were they talking about?' asked Don Cayetano.

'Doña Ana didn't say anything. Doña Visita was put out because Doña Ana had insisted on coming without sending a message first. I think they went for a walk, because Doña Visita said something about the Mall.'

'To the Mall!' cried Ripamilán, grasping the canon theologian's arm in one hand, and his own shovel hat in the other. 'To the Mall!'

'But Don Cayetano. . . !'

'It is a question of honour; in a sense I am to blame for this slight.'

'But it was not a slight,' the vicar-general repeated, as he let himself be taken along, his face beautified by something akin to a holy light of happiness which suffused it.

'Yes, sir, it was a slight. In any case, I wish to offer my dear friend an explanation. To the Mall! We can speak on the way. I want you to know that woman well – know her psychologically, in the language of these modern pedants. She is a fine woman, an angel of goodness as I have just said, an angel who does not deserve a snub.'

'But there was no snub. I can explain everything. I was not aware . . .'

They spoke in whispers, for they were now walking along the south aisle of the cathedral, towards the door. The last chapel on this side was the Chapel of St Clementine. It was large, and built in the seventeenth century, hundreds of years after the other chapels. In the centre there were four altars standing back to back. The chapel's walls were adorned with a profusion of foliage, arabesques and other decorations characteristic of the decadent style in which it was built.

The canon theologian and the archpriest heard voices in the chapel. The former paid no attention to them, but the latter stopped, sniffed, and stretched his neck, in his listening position.

'Good Heavens, it's them!' he said in astonishment.

'Who?'

'Them; Don Saturn and the young widow. I know that tuneless cricket when I hear it!'

And the archpriest, who seconds earlier had been in such a hurry to leave the cathedral, insisted on going into St Clementine's Chapel. The canon theologian followed him, in order not to reveal that he wanted to reach the Mall as soon as possible.

Indeed, it was *them*.

In the middle of the chapel, Don Saturnino, perspiring copiously, his frock-coat covered with cobwebs and smudged with whitewash, his face red, his ears scarlet, was haranguing his audience, with one arm extended towards the vaulting. He was indignant, it seemed, and was communicating his indignation, willy-nilly, to the Hidalgos.

'Ladies and gentlemen,' he was exclaiming, 'you can see for yourselves: this chapel is the blemish, the ugly blemish, or rather the flaw, in this Gothic jewel. You have seen the Pantheon, with its severe Romanesque architecture, sublime in its bareness; you have seen the cloisters, in a pure Ogival style; you have walked along the triforia, sober, unmannered Gothic; you have visited the crypt known as the Holy Chapel of Relics, and there you have seen a likeness of the primitive Christian churches; in the choir you have savoured wonders of the relief-work not, maybe, of a Berruguete,[11] but of a Palma Artela, an unknown yet sublime artificer; on the reredos behind the main altar you have admired and delighted in the genial – yes, I may say genial – verve of the chisel of a Grijalte; and, to reassume, throughout this Holy Cathedral Church you have been able to corroborate the fact that this temple is a work of pure, simple, severe, delicate art. This notwithstanding, ladies and gentleman, one must admit that in this chapel unrestrained bad taste, bombast and redundancy have joined forces to carve these stones in which affectation goes hand in hand with excess, extravagance with deformity. St Clementine (I speak of her chapel) is a disgrace to Art, the ignominy of Vetusta Cathedral.'

He remained silent for a moment in order to wipe the perspiration from his forehead and the back of his neck with Obdulia's perfumed pocket-handkerchief, for his own had for some time been soaking in liquefied eloquence.

The Hidalgos were sweating, too. Pandemonium had broken out in Señor Hidalgo's head. He had been listening for an hour and a half to a peripatetic course of lectures (standing or walking the whole time!) on archaeology and architecture, and another course on pragmatic history. By now the poor man had the caliphs of Cordova and the columns of its mosque jumbled together in his mind, and he no longer knew whether it was the caliphs or the columns that numbered more than eight hundred; the Doric, Ionian and Corinthian orders were mixed up with the Alphonsos, Kings of Castille, and he was not sure whether the foundation of Vetusta was due to a discalced friar or to the semi-circular arch. To reassume, as the scholar said, he was attacked by an overpowering nausea, and he could hardly even hear what the gentleman was saying, for he was more concerned with his efforts to contain impulses of his stomach whose release would have been irreverent.

'If we were aboard a ship, it wouldn't be so out of place,' he thought. 'But in a cathedral!'

Indeed, the Hidalgo did feel as if he were on the high seas, and every time he heard talk of this aisle and that aisle and the great nave he imagined himself in charge of a navy, and found that Don

Saturnino smelt of tar. Nevertheless, the unfortunate countryman continued assenting to everything he was told.

'Quite so, the whole thing was a profanation. How ponderous indeed, were all those canopies and niches! Ah yes, how ponderous! For he was fearful that they were all going to fall on top of him: they were swaying, without any doubt! But good God!' he continued, 'if the plateresque style is cloying and ponderous wherever could anything more plateresque be found than this man Don Saturnino?'

The thought crossed the Hidalgo's mind that maybe the historian was making fun of them because they came from a fishing town. But no, that was not the face of a liar. He was telling the truth, that business about King Veremundo[12] and the emigration of the Persian pineapple to Arabic columns must be correct; but of what interest was it all to him, an electoral delegate?

The Hidalgo's worthy consort was also tired, bored and footsore, but she still had her wits about her. For more than an hour now she hadn't listened to a single word spoken by that charlatan, shyster, libertine. Oh, if it weren't for her husband, who considered whatever she did to be inappropriate and ill-mannered! If it weren't for the fact that they were in the house of God! She was shocked and furious. Fine figures she and her perfect fool of a husband were cutting! She had made signs to him, but it was no good. He thought she was referring to all that talk about architecture, and pretended not to notice. And what about that young Doña Obdulia? She seemed to be a real expert at this sort of hanky-panky. They hadn't let a single chance go begging. And that (of course!) was why she and her husband had been dragged hither and thither through attics and cellars, tired to death. As soon as it was dark (of course!) they held hands. Señora Hidalgo had seen it happen once, and assumed it to be happening the rest of the time. And he pressed his foot on hers, and they were always close together, and wherever there was any narrow opening they made to go through together, and through they went, such wantonness! But how had her husband come to be friendly with that female? The noble countrywoman was even beginning to feel jealous. She did not utter a single word; and if Obdulia and Bermúdez had been less concerned with the Renaissance, they would have noticed the scowls and the surliness of the formerly amiable and courteous country lady. Don Saturn resumed his discourse. He was going to prove the truth of his injurious assertions.

'Or else,' he continued, 'just regard what is evident to the eyes (I refer to the eyes of the soul) of any person of taste. Accursed the most worthy Bishop (with all due respect), accursed the most worthy Bishop Don García Madrejón, who consented to this jumbled agglomerate of decoration and foliage, the quintessence of the baroque, of prodigal profusion, and of falsity! Cartouches, medallions, niches' (pointing to each in turn), 'capitals, broken pediments, festoons, canopies, frondescence, arabesques, pullulating in the ornamentation of doors, windows, skylights and pendentives: in the name of art, of the sacred concept of sobriety, and of the no less immaculate concept of harmony, I condemn you to the malediction of history!'

'Well, you listen here,' Señora Hidalgo ventured to retort, without looking towards her husband: 'You can say what you like, but I think this chapel is ever so nice; and I also think that it is very nasty of you to profane this temple, blaspheming God and his holy saints like that!'

So there! She had had enough! She wished to do battle with the libertine and had chosen, with evident propriety, the neutral ground of pure, disinterested art. What was more, she really did like the chapel – and she was not going to beat about the bush any longer.

Señor Hidalgo believed that his wife had gone out of her mind.

'*She* must be feeling ill, too.' He tried to speak, but he could not manage it. Obdulia let loose a peal of laughter, which was heard outside by Don Cayetano. Don Saturn, abashed, and with a fair suspicion of the motives for this unexpected opposition, was fain to bow in the manner of the canon theologian and screw up his mouth and his eyebrows in a way he himself had invented while standing before his looking-glass. All this meant that a Bermúdez did not argue with ladies. He only replied:

'Madam, I am profaning nothing. Art . . .'

'Yes, you are profaning!'

'But, dear heart! But Carolina!'

'Oh, let her be, my good sir. I respect all opinions.'

And, afraid lest the countrywoman might be gaining the upper hand in the argument about his alleged profanation, Don Saturnino hastened to add:

'Quite apart from all that, as you will understand, my dear friend, I am simply following the canons of classical beauty in energetically condemning baroque taste. This is plateresque . . .'

'Churrigueresque!'[13] exclaimed the electoral delegate, with the intention of thereby making amends for his wife's preposterous protest.

'Churrigueresque!' he repeated. 'I find it quite sickening!' – and it was plain that he did.

'Churrigueresque!' he managed to whisper once more.

'Rococo!' concluded Obdulia.

At that moment the archpriest was greeting her with a bow, as if to kiss her bronze-coloured boots.

They all walked out of the cathedral together.

Don Saturn took his leave in a hurry. His cheeks were aflame. He was not wearing his cloak, and he felt cold. The warm wind smacked of a chill northerly to him.

'I fear I may catch pneumonia!' he said, as he made his escape, buttoning up his frock-coat.

He needed to be alone, to savour that afternoon's emotions.

'He was in love, and believed himself loved.'

III

That afternoon the judge's wife and the canon theologian conversed while they were taking their promenade. The archpriest arranged their meeting, using his familiarity with the judge's wife to bring about the interview.

The beautiful lady and the vicar-general had rarely exchanged words, and their conversations had never gone further than the commonplaces required by social intercourse.

Doña Ana Ozores did not belong to any religious guild. She paid her monthly subscriptions to the adult Sunday school, but she attended neither lectures nor classes; she was outside the circle in which the canon theologian reigned. He paid few visits to those who could not, or would not, be of service to him in his propaganda work. When Señor Don Víctor Quintanar was the chief magistrate of Vetusta, the canon theologian had visited him on every ceremonial occasion on which local custom demanded this act of courtesy; and Señor Quintanar, after Don Saturnino Bermúdez the best-mannered gentleman in the city, had returned such visits with the punctiliousness which he always observed in such matters. The canon's courtesies had become scarcer after Don Víctor's retirement – it was never known why – until they had finally ceased altogether. Don Víctor and Don Fermín sometimes conversed when they met out of doors, in the Mall, and they always greeted each other with the greatest amiability. They held each other in high esteem. The calumnies with which scandalmongers persecuted De Pas came up against an insulator in Don Víctor. Indeed, not only did he refuse to be a conductor for their propagation, but he even made it his task to dissipate their pernicious power. Doña Ana, however, had never spoken alone with the canon theologian, and after his visits ceased she seldom saw him at close quarters. Not, at least, so far as she could remember. Don Cayetano, who was aware of all this, made a tactful pretence of introducing them to each other, in that half-jocular half-serious tone of voice which he never relinquished. The judge's wife and the canon theologian did not speak much; Ripamilán did most of the talking, and Visitación, who was with Ana, had her say. Doña Ana soon went home. She retired early that night.

Of that afternoon's brief conversation she remembered only this: that the next day, after the divine office, the canon theologian would await her in his chapel. He had suggested – insinuated, rather – that it was appropriate, on changing confessors, to make a general confession.

He had spoken in an affable, mellifluous voice, but he had said little; there had been a certain coldness in his manner, and he had seemed rather inattentive. She had not been able to see his eyes, only his eyelids, heavy with white flesh. Yet she had observed a singular gleam beneath his eyelashes.

At her bedside, upon her knees, the judge's wife prayed.

Then she sat in a rocking-chair near the dressing-table in her boudoir, at some distance from her bed so as not to fall into the temptation of lying down, and spent a quarter of an hour reading a pious book which treated of the sacrament of penance by questions and answers. She did not turn the page. She stopped reading. Her look was fixed upon the words: *If you have eaten meat.*

Mechanically, she repeated those five words, devoid of all meaning for her; she repeated them in her mind as if they were in an unknown language.

As her thoughts emerged from she knew not what black pit, she took notice of what she was reading. She left the book upon the dressing-table and clasped her hands upon her lap. Her full-flowing brown tresses tumbled in waves over her shoulders to the seat of the rocking-chair, and spread around on to her lap; a few strands were caught between her interlocked fingers. She shuddered, and was surprised to find her teeth clenched so tightly that they ached. She passed a hand over her forehead, felt her pulse, and held both hands open in front of her eyes, to test whether her sight was failing. She rested assured. It was nothing. Best not to think about it.

'General confession!' Yes, that was what the priest had intimated. The book which she had just put aside was no help in such a weighty matter. It would be better to go to bed. The previous day she had completed her examination of conscience for recent sins. She could make the examination for the general confession in her bed. She went into her bedroom, which was large, stuccoed, with a high coffered ceiling. It was separated from the boudoir by elegant drapery of garnet-red sateen hanging between two columns. Ana slept in a commonplace double bed, gilt, with a white canopy. On the carpet at the foot of the bed there was a real tiger-skin. There was no holy image other than an ivory crucifix, hanging above the headboard, which, as it leaned over the bed, seemed to be looking down through the canopy of white tulle.

Obdulia, that indiscreet widow, had several times invited herself into this bedroom.

'Anita – what a strange woman she was!'

'She was clean, no one could deny that, as clean as ermine; you had to admit this was a merit – and a reproach to many Vetustan ladies.'

But Obdulia added:

'Apart from her being clean and tidy, there aren't any signs there of a woman of elegance. A tiger-skin – has that got any *cachet*? Well, I don't know, I'm sure. It strikes me as an expensive and eccentric whim, quite unfeminine, if you think about it. Her bed is atrocious! Just the thing for the Mayor of Palomares's wife. A double bed! And what a bed! Pure vulgarity! And as for the rest? Absolutely nothing worth while. There's no sex there. Leaving its tidiness aside, it's just the same as a student's room. Not a single *objet d'art*. Not one wretched *bibelot*. None of the things demanded by good taste and *confort*. Just as the style is the man, so the bedroom is the woman. You know a woman by the bed she sleeps in. And what about the religious side? Piety is represented there by a commonplace crucifix placed in a manner quite contrary to all good form.

'It's such a pity,' concluded Obdulia, feeling no pity whatsoever, 'that such a precious *bijou* should be kept in such a miserable jewel-box!'

'Ah, but she did have to admit that the bedclothes were worthy of a princess! What sheets! What pillow-cases! She had run her hands all over them, how smooth they were! The sateen of that delectable little body wouldn't feel any coarseness in the touch of those sheets.'

Obdulia sincerely admired Ana's figure and complexion and, at heart, she envied her the tiger-skin. There were no tigers in Vetusta; the widow could not demand them from her lovers as proof of their affection. All she had at the foot of her own bed was a lion-hunt – printed on a miserable imitation tapestry!

Ana closed the garnet-red drapery with great care, as if someone might see her from the boudoir. Absently, she slipped off her blue dressing-gown with its cream-coloured lace, and stood there, white, as Don Saturn often saw her just before he fell asleep, but much more beautiful than he was capable of imagining her. After leaving aside the garments which she did not wear in bed she stood upon the tiger-skin, burying her bare feet, small and plump, in the fur with its brown markings. One naked arm rested on her head, which was slightly tilted, the other hung alongside her body, following the strong hip's graceful curve. She looked like some immodest model, transported by the sensuousness of the academic pose which an artist had told her to strike. Neither the archpriest nor any of her other confessors had ever prohibited the delight of stretching her torpid limbs, or of feeling the touch of cool air over her body, alone at bedtime. She had never thought such relaxation to be a matter for confession.

Ana drew back the bedclothes. Without moving her feet, she let herself fall face downwards, arms outspread, upon the silky softness of the sheets. She rested her cheek on the bed, keeping her eyes wide open. She took great delight in that tactile pleasure, which ran from her waist to her temples.

'General confession!' she was thinking. 'That is the story of a whole life.' Tears came to her blue eyes, and trickled down to moisten the sheet.

She remembered that she had never known her mother. Maybe her greatest sins sprang from this misfortune.

'No mother and no children.'

She had retained the habit of caressing the sheet with her cheek ever since her childhood. Then, a curt, thin, cold, formal woman had made her go to bed every night before she felt sleepy. The woman had turned out the light and gone away. Ana would weep on her pillow, and then jump out of bed; but she did not dare walk about in the dark, and continued to weep, kneeling by her bed and resting upon it face downwards, just as she was now, with her cheek caressing the sheet, which her tears used to moisten then, too. There had never been anything warm and maternal in her life, only the yielding softness of a feather mattress; the poor girl had known no other kind of tenderness. At that time, according to her vague remembrance, she must have been four years old. Twenty-three more had gone by, and still that grief moved her. Since then, for most of her life, she had suffered much trouble and vexation, but now she scorned its memory; a lot of fools had conspired against her, and it was repugnant to remember all this. Her sufferings as a young girl, though, the injustice of being put to bed without feeling sleepy, without a story, without caresses, without light, still aroused her indignation and inspired the sweetest feelings of self-pity. Just as one who is roused from her bed before she has rested as long as she needs feels a strange sensation which could be called a nostalgia for softness and for the warmth of her sleep, so Ana had felt all her life a sensation of nostalgia for a mother's lap. Her young head had never been pressed to a soft warm breast, and the girl had searched everywhere for something similar. She vaguely remembered a noble, black, long-haired dog, probably a Newfoundland – what could have become of it? The dog used to stretch out in the sun, its nose between its fore-paws, and she would lie down by its side, her cheek upon its curly back, almost hiding her face in smooth, warm hair. Out in the meadows she would throw herself down upon heaps of new-mown grass. Since there was nobody to comfort her when she was crying herself to sleep, she sought comfort from within, telling herself stories which were all light and caresses. She had a mamma who gave her everything she wanted, who held her to her breast, and who sent her to sleep singing by her ear:

> On Saturday, Saturday, my pretty maid,
> The little bird got himself taken inside,
> In irons and in fetters he's chained and he's tied. . . .

and:

The speckled bird was perching
In the shade of a lemon green. . . .

These were songs which she heard poor women singing in a big square as they put their little children to sleep.

And so she too would fall asleep, making believe that the pillow was the breast of the mother of her dreams, and that she could really hear the songs which sounded within her brain. Little by little she had become accustomed to having no pure and tender pleasures other than those of the imagination.

As the judge's wife thought about the girl that she had once been she began to admire her, and to feel that her own life had been divided into two parts, one of which belonged to the little angel whom she now believed dead. The girl who used to jump out of bed in the dark had been more vigorous than this Anita of the present; she had possessed an extraordinary inner strength for withstanding unhumiliated the demands and the injustices of the curt, cold, capricious people in charge of her.

'What a way to make an examination of conscience!' thought Doña Ana, somewhat ashamed.

She went barefoot into her boudoir, took up the book on her dressing-table, and ran back to her bed. She lay down, brought the light close and began to read, her head half-buried in the pillows. *If you have eaten meat,* her sleepy eyes saw again, but she read on. One, two, three leaves – she went on, unaware of what she was reading. At length she stopped at a line which said:

'The places where you have been . . .'

She could understand that. While turning over the pages she had been thinking, not knowing why, about Don Alvaro Mesía, the president of the Gentlemen's Club of Vetusta and the leader of the Dynastic Liberal Party in the town. But on reading 'The places where you have been' her thoughts suddenly returned to far-off times. As a girl – one old enough to confess – she used, whenever the book said 'Pass your mind over all the places which you have frequented', to remember, unintentionally, the ferry-boat at Trébol, that great sin which she had committed unawares, the night she had spent in the boat with that boy, Germán, her friend. . . . The wretches! The judge's wife felt abashed and angry as she remembered that calumny. She left her book open on the bedside table (yet another commonplace piece of furniture which irritated Obdulia's good taste), turned out the light, and found herself in the ferry-boat at Trébol, at midnight, by the side of Germán, a blond-haired boy of twelve, two years older than she. With great care he was wrapping her in the canvas sack they had found in the bottom of the boat. She asked him to wrap himself up as well. The two children lay under the sack, as if it were a counterpane, on the boards of the boat, whose dark sides prevented them from seeing the fields around them. They could only see the clouds above moving across the face of the moon.

'Are you cold?' Germán was asking.

And Ana replied, her eyes wide open and fixed on the moon as it moved behind the clouds:

'No!'

'Are you afraid?'

'Of course not!'

'We're married,' said he.

'I'm a mamma!'

And she heard beneath her head a gentle murmuring, sweetly lulling, as if to send her to sleep; it was the murmuring of the tide.

They told each other many stories. He also told her the story of his life. He had a papa in Colondres and a mamma too.

'What was a mamma like?'

Germán explained as best he could.

'Do mammas give lots of kisses?'

'Yes.'

'And do they sing?'

'Yes, I've got a little sister she sings to. I'm too big for that.'

'And I'm a mamma!'

Then it was her turn to tell the story of her life. She lived in Loreto, a little village, quite far from that part of the estuary, but next to the sea, over there, by the sands. She lived with a lady called Governess and Doña Camila. Anita didn't like her. The governess had servants and maids and a gentleman who came at night-time and kissed her. Doña Camila slapped him and said, 'Not in front of the girl, she's an artful little creature.'

She was told that she had a papa who loved her very much and that it was he who sent her all her clothes and money and everything. But he could not come home, because he was away killing Moors. She was often punished, but not beaten. Instead, she was locked in her room, made to go without meals and, the worst punishment of all, sent to bed early. She would escape through the garden gate and run weeping towards the sea, for she wanted to climb into a boat and sail away to the land of the Moors and look for her papa. A sailor would find her weeping and pat her. She would suggest the voyage to him, he would laugh and agree, and pick her up, but then she would find that the cheat had taken her back to the governess's house, to be locked in her room again. One afternoon she had escaped along another path, but still she could not find the sea. She had gone by a water-mill. When she had tried to cross the canal by a bridge made out of the hollow trunk of a chestnut-tree, a dog had blocked her way. Ana had lain down on the trunk because she became dizzy looking at the white water angry beneath her like the barking dog before her. But the dog had scrabbled over Anita without trying to bite her. From the other bank she had called to it and said, 'Hush! Here you are, this is for you.'

It was her tea, which she was carrying in her pocket, a piece of bread and butter, moistened with tears.

She nearly always ate her tea-time bread salted with tears. When she was alone she wept of grief; but in front of the governess, the servants and the man she wept with rage. After the water-mill she had come to a wood and she had run through it singing, even though her eyes were still full of tears; but she was singing out of fear. She had walked out of the wood and seen a meadow of very tall, very green grass. . . .

'And I was there, wasn't I?' cried Germán.

'That's right.'

'And I asked you if you wanted to go aboard the ferry-boat at Trébol, because the boatman had been my servant, and I was from Colondres, on the other side of the estuary.'

'That's right.'

The judge's wife remembered it all as it is written, even the conversation; but she believed that what she really remembered was not the actual words which had been spoken, but, rather, a subsequent recollection of them, when she had re-created, as in a novel, the events of that night.

Then they slept. It was daytime when they were awoken by a voice shouting from the Colondres bank. It was the boatman, who could see his boat on a little island left in the middle of the estuary by the ebbing tide. The boatman gave them a good scolding. One of his sons was to take her to Loreto, but on the way one of the governess's servants met them. They were looking for Anita everywhere. They thought she had fallen into the sea. Doña Camila was ill in bed from the fright. The man who kissed the governess took Ana by the arm and squeezed it until it bled. But she did not cry.

They asked her where she had spent the night and she would not answer, for fear that they would punish Germán. They shut her up, they gave her no food all day, but still she said nothing. Next morning the governess summoned the boatman from Trébol. According to him, the children had made careful plans to spend the night together on the ferry-boat. Who would have thought it? Ana finally confessed that they had both slept in the boat, but without meaning to do so. Their idea had been to become the masters of the boat for one evening, even if they were to be scolded at home, cross from one bank to the other by themselves, pulling on the rope, and then return, he to Colondres, she to Loreto. But the water in the estuary had gone away, the boat had hit the stones on the bottom, half-way across, and however hard they had tried they had not been able to move it. And so they had lain down and gone to sleep. If they had been able to break the rope holding the boat they would have sailed to the land of the Moors, for Germán knew the way across the sea. She would have looked for her papa and Germán would have killed lots of Moors. But the rope was very strong. They could not break it and instead had lain down to tell each other bedtime stories.

This was what Germán had told the boatman, too, but he did not believe the story.

What a scandal! Doña Camila seized Anita by the throat and almost throttled her. Then she quoted an obscene proverb, insulting both Ana and her mother – as Ana realized much later, because at the time she did not understand it.

Doña Camila blamed the man who kissed her for the girl's wicked ways.

'You have opened her eyes with your indiscreet behaviour.'

Anita did not understand, and the governess's gentleman merely laughed.

From that day on the man would look at her with eyes ablaze, smile and, as soon as the governess left the room, ask her for kisses; but she never gave him any.

A priest came and shut himself up with Ana in her bedroom, and asked her questions which she did not understand (later, after thinking hard, she understood some part of it all – they wanted to convince her that she had committed a great sin). They took her to the village church and made her confess. She could not answer the priest, and he declared to the governess that the girl was not yet ready, because out of either ignorance or artfulness she made a secret of her transgressions. Boys in the street looked at her in the same way as did the man who kissed Doña Camila; they took her by the arm and tried to make her go with them. She did not leave home again without the governess. She never saw Germán again.

'I have written to your father telling him all about you. As soon as you are eleven you are going to a Recollect school.'

This was just one of Doña Camila's empty threats; but Ana would not have been sorry to leave Loreto and go anywhere else on earth.

From then onwards she was treated as a precocious animal. Without fully understanding what she heard, she realized that the sins which were attributed to her were imputed to her mother's faults.

When the judge's wife reached this point in her recollections she felt herself suffocating, her cheeks aflame. She turned on the light and pushed the heavy counterpane aside; her form, of a modern Venus, provocative and voluptuous, was both revealed and exaggerated by the coloured blanket of fine-spun wool, drawn close about her. The counterpane lay crumpled at her feet.

Those remembrances of childhood receded, but the anger which they had awoken, its cause now so distant, did not disappear with them.

'What a stupid life!' thought Ana, passing to considerations of a different kind.

Her bad temper increased with the awareness that she was about to experience a quarter of an hour of rebellion. She believed that she had sacrificed herself to self-imposed duties. Sometimes she saw these duties as a poetic mission which explained the meaning of life, and then she thought:

'The monotony and dullness of this existence is only apparent, for in truth my days are taken up by matters of moment; this sacrifice, this struggle, is greater than any adventure in the world.'

At other times, such as this one, her subdued passions rebelled as her ego protested, called her crazy, romantic, foolish, and said, 'What a stupid life!'

How exasperating to be made aware in such a way of the uprisings of one's own spirit! She wanted to placate them but only became more irritated. It was as if there were thistles in her soul. When she felt like this she loved nobody, pitied nobody. Now she wanted to hear music; no other sound would be appropriate. And – she did not know how it happened, nor did she intend it to happen – the Royal Theatre in Madrid came before her eyes, and she saw none other than Don Alvaro Mesía, the president of the Gentlemen's Club, wrapped in a high-collared scarlet cape, singing under Rosina's balcony:

'Ecco ridente in cielo . . .'[1]

The judge's wife was breathing deep and fast, her nostrils were pulsating, her eyes, flaring as in a fever, and fixed upon the wall, were staring at the sinuous shadow of her body, swathed in her coloured blanket.

She wanted to think about all this, about Lindoro, about the Barber, in order to assuage that asperity of soul which so tormented her.

'If I had a child – here – now, kissing it, singing to it!'

The vague image of the baby receded, and the well-built figure of Don Alvaro presented itself again, but now in a close-fitting white top-coat, greeting her as King Amadeus used to greet people.

And he lowered his love-sick gaze before her imposing, imperious eyes.

Ana felt her spirits flagging. The aridity and tension which were tormenting her turned gradually into disconsolate grief.

She had stopped being wicked, now she felt as she wished to feel, as the idea of her sacrifice returned to her; but great, sublime now, like a flow of tenderness capable of flooding the world. By degrees the image of Don Alvaro was disappearing, too, like a dissolving view in a magic-lantern show; now only the white top-coat was visible, and, behind it, as if some special trick were being played with light, the details began to appear of a tartan dressing-gown, a green smoking-cap of velvet with gold braid and a tassel, a white moustache and a white goatee, two bushy grizzled eyebrows; and, at last, upon a black background, there shone out in its entirety the respectable and familiar figure of her own Don Víctor Quintanar, with a nimbus of light all around him. That was the burthen of her sacrifice, as Don Cayetano Ripamilán would have said. Ana Ozores deposited a chaste kiss upon the gentleman's forehead.

She was overwhelmed by a vehement desire to see him and kiss him in reality, as she had kissed the dissolving view.

But that, evidently, was not a good moment.

Fortune, however, favoured the chaste wife's desire. She felt her pulse, looked at her hands, could only see the blurred outline of her fingers, her pulse was violent; behind her eyelids little stars were exploding, like sparkling fireworks, yes, yes, she was ill, she was about to have one of her attacks – she had better ring. She seized the bell-rope, she rang. Two minutes passed. Couldn't they hear? Again she tugged on the rope. She heard hurrying footsteps. As her startled maid, Petra, almost naked, entered through a side-door, the garnet-red drapery was drawn aside and the dissolving view appeared – the man in the tartan dressing-gown and the green smoking-cap, with a candlestick in his hand.

'What is the matter, my child?' cried Don Víctor, approaching the bed.

'It was one of her attacks, although she couldn't be certain that it was going to be accompanied by all the usual nervous disturbances; but the symptoms were the same: she could not see, sparks from a brazier were bursting behind her eyelids and in her brain, her hands were growing cold, and felt so heavy that they did not seem to belong to her.' Petra ran to the kitchen without awaiting orders, already knowing what was needed: linden tea.

Don Víctor relaxed. 'He was accustomed to his beloved wife's attacks. The poor dear suffered, but it was nothing grave.'

'Do not think about it; you know that is best.'

'Yes, you're quite right. Come near, talk to me, sit down here.'

Don Víctor sat on the bed and deposited a paternal kiss upon his good wife's brow. She pressed his head to her breast and shed a few tears. Having duly taken note of them, Don Víctor exclaimed:

'Do you not see? You are weeping now; a good sign. The tempest of nerves is dissipated in a torrent of tears. The attack has been averted and will not continue, as you will see.'

Indeed, Ana did start to feel better. They talked. She displayed an affectionate attitude, for which he was duly grateful. Petra returned with the tea.

Don Víctor observed that the servant girl had not repaired the disarray in her dress, which was no dress at all, for it was composed of a chemise, a short woollen shawl thrown over her shoulders, and a skirt which, carelessly fastened around her body, allowed the girl's charms to be divined – always supposing that they were charms, for Don Víctor did not enter into such inquiries; although he did, without intending to do so, venture to himself the hypothesis that her flesh must be very white, inasmuch as her hair was saffron-blonde.

The tea made Ana calm. She took a deep breath, feeling a sense of well-being which filled her soul with optimism.

'How obliging was Petra! And her dear Víctor – what a good man!'

'And there was no doubt that he had once been handsome. True, his fifty-odd years looked more like sixty, but sixty years of enviable robustness. His white moustache, his white goatee and his grey eyebrows all gave him the venerable and even heroic aspect of a brigadier or perhaps a general. He did not look like a retired provincial magistrate but rather an illustrious military leader off active service.'

Petra, shivering, with her arms crossed – sheer-white well-turned arms – discreetly left the room, but she remained in the next, awaiting orders.

Ana insisted that Quintanar, as she nearly always addressed him, should drink the small amount of linden tea left in the cup.

But Don Víctor did not believe in nerves! He was quite calm! Half-asleep, but tranquil.

'Never mind that. It was just a whim of hers. He didn't realize it, but he'd had a fright.'

'But not at all, my child; I swear . . .'

'Yes, yes, come on.'

Don Víctor drank linden tea, and at once gave an energetic yawn.

'Are you cold?'

'What, me cold?'

And he remembered that in three hours' time, before daybreak, he would be leaving, in the utmost secrecy, through the gate out of Ozores Park (their back garden). Then it would be cold, particularly when he and his beloved Frillity, his cynegetic Pylades[2] as he called him, reached Montico Hill. They were going to hunt – an activity forbidden by the judge's wife at such an hour. Ana did not release Víctor as soon as he would have liked. His darling little wife was in a most talkative mood, recalling hundreds of episodes in their married life, which had always been tranquil and harmonious.

'Wouldn't you like to have a child, Víctor?' asked the wife, nestling her head in her husband's bosom.

'With all my heart,' replied the ex-magistrate, searching within it for the fibre of paternal love. He did not find it, and in order to imagine something similar, he thought about his decoy-partridge, a choice present which Frillity had given him.

'If my wife knew that I only have two and a half hours of rest at my disposal, she would allow me to return to my bed.'

But the poor dear knew nothing about all that, and indeed she must know nothing. The judge's wife took more than half an hour to

tire of her nervous loquacity. So many plans! So many rosy horizons!
And Víctor and she would always, always be together.

'We will, won't we?'

'Yes, my dear child, yes; but now you should rest. Talking over-
excites you.'

'You're right, I feel tired and peaceful. I shall go to sleep.'

He bent down to kiss her forehead, but she, throwing her arms
around his neck and her head backwards, received his kiss on her
lips. Don Víctor coloured a little, he felt his blood boil. But he did not
dare . . . Furthermore, within three hours he must be on his way to
Montico Hill with his shot-gun over his shoulder. If he remained with
his wife, he could say goodbye to the hunt. And his friend Tomás,
alias Frillity, was inexorable in such matters. He could forgive anything except failing to appear or being late for an early-morning
excursion of this sort.

'Let principles be upheld,' thought the huntsman. 'Good-night, my
dove!'

And he remembered the doves in his aviary.

After depositing another kiss, on his own initiative, upon Ana's
brow, he departed from her bedchamber bearing the candlestick in
his right hand, while with his left hand he raised the garnet-red
drapery. He turned around, smiled good-night to his wife and, with
a majestic step (despite the embroidered carpet slippers he wore),
made his way towards his own bedchamber, at the other end of
Ozores Mansion.

He crossed a large room known as the withdrawing-room, walked
along broad corridors, came to a windowed gallery, and there
hesitated for a moment. He turned back, retraced his steps along all
the passages, and tapped discreetly on a door.

Petra appeared. She had not put her clothes in order.

'What's wrong? Has she got worse?'

'It is not that, my girl,' replied Don Víctor.

'Such brazenness! Did that young woman not consider that she
was almost naked?'

'It is – it is merely that, in case Anselmo falls asleep and fails to
hear Don Tomás's signal . . . Anselmo is such a lout. I want you to call
me if you hear the three barks – you know – Don Tomás . . .'

'Yes, I know. Don't you worry, sir. Just as soon as Don Tomás barks
I'll go and call you. Is there anything else?' added the saffron-blonde
servant girl, with provocative eyes.

'Nothing else. And now go to bed, for you are very lightly dressed
and it is extremely cold.'

She feigned an embarrassment which she was far from feeling and
turned her almost naked back. Then Don Víctor raised his eyes and
was able to appreciate that those were, indeed, charms which the girl
did not properly veil.

Petra's door closed, and Don Víctor resumed his majestic progress along the passages.

But before entering his bedchamber he said to himself, 'Well now; since I am up I shall take a look at my little people.'

At one end of the windowed gallery there was a door. He eased it open and entered the house of his birds, who were sleeping the sleep of the just.

He shaded the candle with his free hand, and tiptoed to the canary-cage. All was as usual. His inopportune visit went unnoticed, except by two or three canary-birds, that fluttered their wings and hid their heads among their feathers. He walked on. The turtle-doves were sleeping, too; there were some murmurs of disapproval, which caused Don Víctor to move away, as he did not wish to be indiscreet. He approached the cage of, 'without any exaggeration, the most philharmonic song-thrush in the province'. The thrush was sitting erect upon a perch, his head sunk between his shoulders; but he was not asleep. His impertinent eyes stared at those of his master, but he refused to show any recognition of him. The little creature could have stared like that all night, in defiance, without lowering his gaze; 'he knew him well; he was a real stubborn Aragonese. And so like Ripamilán!' Don Víctor walked on. He went to look at the quail, but this African savage jumped in alarm, striking his head again and again on the linen padding tied inside the top of his squat, round cage, and Don Víctor moved on to allow him to calm down. Before the decoy-partridge he fell into raptures. If, perchance, some impure thought had besmirched his conscience a little earlier, the contemplation of the partridge, that masterpiece of nature, restored to him all the loftiness of purpose and grandeur of spirit which befitted the foremost ornithologist and unrivalled huntsman of Vetusta.

With his heart at ease again, Don Víctor returned to the warmth of his sheets.

In that room, years before, he and Anita, loving spouses, used to sleep together in her gilt bed. But by little and little they had come up with the same idea.

He vexed her by rising so early to go hunting; she vexed him because she forced him to make the sacrifice of rising less early than he should, so as not to awaken her. The birds, moreover, were in a kind of exile, far from their master. But it would be cruel to bring them near while Ana was there, as they would not allow her to sleep through the morning. Yet with what delight he would have savoured the song-thrush's first note, the voluptuous cooing of the turtle-doves, the quail's monotonous rhythm, and the unsociable partridge's cacophonous cackling, so sweet to the huntsman's ears!

Neither of them remembers which one it was, but he believes that it was Anita who ventured to manifest the desire for a separation with regard to the connubial bed – *quo ad thorum*. Her timid proposition was accepted with ill-concealed jubilation, and the most harmonious couple in the world divided their bedchamber. She went to the other end of the house, which was warmer because it faced south, and he remained in his own room. Henceforth, Ana could sleep through the morning, with no one to interrupt this pleasure, and Quintanar could rise with the dawn and delight his ear with the nearby matutinal concerts of quails, thrushes, partridges, doves and canary-birds. If anything had been wanting for the couple's complete harmony, their domestic bliss was now perfect, in so far as concord was concerned.

Apropos of this matter Don Víctor would say, recalling his magistracy:

'The liberty of each individual extends as far as the limit where the liberty of others commences. By bearing this in mind I have always been happy in my marriage.'

He attempted to sleep for the short time which remained, but could not. As soon as he was slumbering he dreamed that he heard Frillity's three barks.

How peculiar! On other occasions this did not happen. He always slept like a log and awoke at the correct moment.

It must have been the linden tea! He lit the lamp again. He took up the only book on his bedside table. It was a bulky tome. 'Calderón de la Barca,' said the gilt letters on the spine. He read.

He had always been fond of acting, and he particularly enjoyed the theatre of the seventeenth century. He was enthralled by the customs of those times when people knew what honour was and knew how to uphold it. According to Don Víctor, nobody was as knowledgeable as Don Pedro Calderón de la Barca about matters concerning nice points of honour, nor did anyone deliver in such an opportune manner the sword-thrusts which cleanse reputations, nor could any author hold a candle to him in subtle discussions about what is and is not love. In the taking of just and sweet vengeance by offended husbands, the divine Don Pedro had been more inventive than anyone else, and without denying to *Justice Without Revenge*[3] and other marvels by Lope de Vega the merit which they possessed, Don Víctor found nothing to match *The Physician of His Own Honour*.[4]

'If', he would say to Frillity, 'my wife were capable of being so wanton as to merit punishment . . .'

'Which it is absurd even to suppose . . .'

'Very well, but supposing such an absurdity – I, too, would have her bled to death.'

He even named the quack whom he would summon and blindfold, and summarized all the rest of the story of the play. The idea of setting fire to his own house and thus taking secret revenge for his wife's supposed adultery did not seem to be an unacceptable one, either. If such a circumstance arose, which of course it would not, he did not intend to break into a tirade of fine poetry, because neither was he a poet nor did he wish to roast in the heat of his burning home. But in all other respects he would, if such a circumstance arose, be no less rigorous than those gentlemen and many other similar ones who had lived in that Spain of happier days.

Frillity was of opinion that such things were all very well in plays but that it was not up to a husband in real life to amuse the public with strong emotions, and that what he should do in such an awkward situation was to prosecute the seducer in the courts of justice and try to get his wife into a convent.

'Absurd! Absurd!' Don Víctor would shout. 'Nothing of the sort was ever done in the glorious years of those illustrious poets.'

'Fortunately,' he added, calming down, 'I shall never find myself in the grievous extremity of having to devise a means of avenging such offences – but I swear to God that, were the circumstance to arise, my atrocities would be worthy of Calderonian *décimas*.'[5]

And he meant what he said.

Every night, before sleeping, he gorged himself on old-fashioned honour, as he called it; honour which spoke both with the sword and with the prudent tongue. Quintanar was versed in the use of the foil, the rapier and the dagger. This hobby had arisen out of his passion for the theatre. While *treading the boards* as an amateur he had become convinced of the importance of fencing, in the course of the numerous duels in which he took part on stage. He took to it with such ardour, and showed such a natural disposition for it, that he came to be little short of a master. Of course, he had no intention of killing anybody: he was a lyrical swordsman. But his greatest skill was his handling of the pistol. He could light a match with a bullet at twenty-five paces, he could kill a gnat at thirty, and he excelled at other exercises of the same type. But he was not boastful. Indeed, he thought so little of his ability that hardly anyone knew of it. What was important was to possess the sublime idea of honour, so suitable for *redondillas* and even sonnets. He was a peaceable man; he had never struck anybody. The sentences of death to which he had put his signature as a judge had always made him lose his appetite and given him headaches, in spite of the fact that he did not consider himself to be responsible.

Don Víctor was, then, tirelessly reading Calderón, and he was about to see how two valiant gentlemen who were paying court to the same lady transfixed each other with their respective *quintillas*, when he heard three distant barks. 'It was Frillity!'

Doña Ana was long in falling asleep as well, but her vigil was not now an impatient, disagreeable one. Her spirit had been refreshed by the new turn which her thoughts had taken. That noble husband to whom she owed her dignity and her independence fully deserved the constant abnegation on which she had determined. She had sacrificed her youth to him: why not continue the sacrifice? Now she did not think about those years of calumny which could have corrupted the purest innocence, instead she thought about the present. Maybe the adventure of the ferry-boat at Trébol had been providential. Because she was then so young, she had not at first derived any lessons from the unjust calumnies which had persecuted her. But later, and thanks to this very persecution, she had learned to keep up appearances. Remembering the past, she had realized that there is no virtue in the world's eyes but that which is ostensible and conspicuous. Her soul rejoiced in the imaginative contemplation of the offering of respect and admiration made to her as a virtuous and beautiful woman. In Vetusta, to say the judge's wife was to say the perfect wife. Anita did not now recall the *stupid existence* of a little earlier. She remembered that she was known as the mother of the poor. Although she was not sanctimonious, she was considered to be a good Catholic, even by Vetusta's most ardent female zealots. The most forward Don Juans, famous for their temerity, lowered their gaze before her, and adored her beauty in silence. Perhaps many men loved her, but none told her of his love. Don Alvaro himself, who had a reputation for never flinching from an adventure and for never failing in one, loved her, adored her, without any doubt, of that she was certain – she had known it for more than two years, but he had never said anything, except with his eyes, where she pretended not to notice a passion which was a crime.

It was true that these last few months, particularly during recent weeks, he had been more audacious – and even somewhat imprudent, he who was prudence itself, and who for this reason alone merited her not being outraged by his infamous enterprise – but she would know how to restrain him when the time came. Yes, she would put him back into line, freezing him with a look. And so, pondering on her conversion of Don Alvaro Mesía into an icicle while he insisted upon being of fire, she slipped sweetly into sleep.

At that moment, Don Víctor, pale and heavy-eyed, as if he were emerging from an orgy, was standing in the garden below and looking up at the closed balcony-window of his wife's boudoir. He was stamping his feet to shake off the cold, and saying to his friend Frillity: 'Poor dear! How remote she must be, in her serene sleep, from the idea that her husband deceives her and leaves home two hours before she thinks he does!'

Frillity smiled in the manner of a philosopher and set off. He was neither tall nor short, but square. He wore a brown woollen shooting-jacket, a black hunting-cap with ear-flaps and, instead of a topcoat, an immense checked muffler which went a dozen times around his neck. The rest was hunting equipment and accessories – all of it unostentatious, like that of a Nimrod.[6]

As Don Víctor arrived at the park gate, he looked back at the balcony, full of remorse.

'Come on, come on, it's getting late,' muttered Frillity.

Day had not yet dawned.

IV

The Ozores family was one of the oldest families in Vetusta. Many counts and marquises bore the name, and there were few members of the city's nobility who were not related to this illustrious lineage through some connection or other.

Ana's father, Don Carlos, was the eldest child of a younger son of the Count of Ozores. Don Carlos had two sisters, Anunciación and Agueda, who lived for many years with their father in the ancestral mansion in Vetusta. The family's principal branch, that of the count himself, had long resided abroad.

Don Carlos, not content to be merely the inheritor of a few farms, a handful of rural leases and a large town house suffering from a leaky roof, decided to follow a career. He became a military engineer. He performed brave actions, in many battles he displayed an extensive knowledge of Vauban's art,[1] he built enduring and well-positioned fortresses on various coasts, and soon he was a colonel and the commander of the Corps of Engineers. Tired of casemates, curtains, parallels and castles, he found employment in Madrid and began to lose his military interests, retaining only his scientific ones: he preferred pure physics and mathematics to their practical application, science to art, and with each day that passed he became less of a warrior. But at the same time he indulged in the delights of Capua,[2] and at length, after many amours, he fell in love with all the passion of a scholar (or someone similar) who is no longer young.

Don Carlos Ozores, madly in love, was married at the age of thirty-five to a humble Italian dressmaker, who lived a poor and honourable life in the midst of countless allurements. She died in giving birth to Ana.

'Just as well!' thought Don Carlos's sisters in their great house in Vetusta.

The colonel's marriage had brought about a rupture with his family. Two curt letters were written and there was no further contact.

'If my father were alive,' thought Ozores, 'he would surely have pardoned this unequal marriage.'

'If father were alive the shock would have killed him,' said the implacable old maids.

The two ladies regarded the hapless confinement of the Italian dressmaker, their unworthy sister-in-law, as a divine punishment, and the entire Vetustan nobility approved of their action.

Ozores Mansion belonged to Don Carlos, as his sisters told him in another cold, laconic letter.

'They were prepared to quit it, if he so required. They only requested that he consider how that precious relic of such a noble past was to be preserved.'

The colonel replied 'that for God's and all his Holy Saints' sakes they stay where they had been born. He beseeched them to do so for the good of the property itself, which would surely go to pieces if they left.'

The old maids, without replying or making any concessions in the matter of their brother's marriage, remained in the house, to stop it from falling down.

It grieved Don Carlos that he was not even asked about his daughter. The nobility of Vetusta was of opinion that although the dog be dead, the biting should not cease: that the dressmaker's providential death was not a sufficient motive for making peace with the infamous Don Carlos or even for inquiring about his daughter's fortunes.

There would be time enough for the Ozores sisters to extend their protection to the girl without any loss of dignity if, as was to be expected, her father's insane conduct dragged her into destitution. Furthermore, word went around Vetusta that Don Carlos had become a freemason and a republican – and, therefore, an atheist. His sisters dressed themselves in black and, in the great chamber, the withdrawing-room, they received the condolences of the entire Vetustan aristocracy.

The room was in almost total darkness. Through the large balcony windows only a single ray of light was permitted to pass. Little was said, there was a great deal of sighing, and the fluttering of fans could be heard.

'How much better it would have been had he gone mad!' exclaimed the Marquis de Vegallana, the leader of the Conservative Party of Vetusta.

'Mad!' replied one of the sisters, Doña Anunciación. 'One would rather say, my lord: "Would that he had been called to meet his Maker, rather than see him come to this." '

Unanimous approval was signalled. Many heads were languidly bowed, and there was renewed sighing. No further comment was needed on the subject of republicanism.

Don Carlos had, indeed, become a liberal of the most radical kind, and from his physico-mathematical studies he had moved on to philosophical studies. As a result, he was now a man who only believed in what he could touch – with the sole exception of Liberty, which he was never able to touch, but in which he believed for many years. In those times the life of an active liberal was not a tranquil one. Don Carlos dedicated himself to being a philosopher and a conspirator, to which end he believed it opportune to request his discharge from the army.

'As a military engineer I could never conspire' (he believed in *esprit de corps*). 'As a civilian I can work for the country's salvation by the most adequate means.'

It should not be thought that Don Carlos was a fool, for he was a good mathematician, and quite well informed about various subjects. He had managed to accumulate a moderate library, in which there were not a few books condemned in the Index. He had an ardent love for literature and he was, at that time, quite as romantic as one had to be to conspire with progressives.

Whatever there may have been that was false or contradictory in Don Carlos's character was the work of his times. He was not lacking in talent and he was enthusiastic; he quickly understood an idea and assimilated it without difficulty; but he was distinguished neither by originality nor by prudence. His self-esteem as a free-thinker had not reached the order in the hierarchy of pride where one only admits that which one creates for oneself. But at all events, he was a pleasant enough man.

His daughter was the victim of his weaknesses. Having wept at some length for the death of his wife, Don Carlos turned his mind back to matters which he considered important, such as propagating free thought among a select group of Spaniards, and working for the triumph of full proportional representation. Entertaining such projects amounted to dedicating oneself to the life of a lone highwayman, always on the run. A conspirator cannot be accompanied by a young motherless girl. There was talk of schools, but Don Carlos abhorred them. He took a governess, a Spanish Englishwoman,[3] who in no way resembled the Cervantine one, for she had no moral charms and put her physical charms, always supposing that she had any of those, to ill use. Don Carlos, who appointed the governess because she was said to be a liberal Catholic, was unaware of all this. He had been told:

'She is a cultured woman, although she is Spanish, for she was brought up in England, where she learnt the noble spirit of tolerance.'

And, moreover, she cured children's hearts and minds with pills which she compounded from the Bible, and with lozenges which she concocted from English novels for family use. She was, in short, one of those fine hypocrites who know that men like women to be neither zealots nor unbelievers, but rather a discreet medium – men themselves not knowing where this medium is to be found. Doña Camila's hypocrisy extended even so far as to form part of her constitution, for while her appearance was that of an anaphroditous statue, a sexless being, her ruling passion was lust, satisfied in the English manner –

lust which could be called Methodistical if it were not a profanation to do so.

Don Carlos was forced to emigrate and Ana remained in the custody of Doña Camila who, through his unforgivable imprudence, found herself disposing almost at will of most of her master's revenues, which became smaller and smaller, since conspiracies cost a great deal of money.

Doctors ordered sea and country air for the girl, and the governess wrote to Don Carlos to tell him that a friend of his, Iriarte – the man who had recommended her – was offering for sale in the north of Spain, just outside Vetusta province, a villa in a picturesque little town, a seaport which was salubrious in all weathers. Don Carlos gave orders that what little property in the province of Vetusta he had not already squandered be sold at any price, and devoted one-half of the product of this alienation to the purchase of his friend Iriarte's villa. The other half was allotted to the succour of more or less authentic patriots. His only remaining property in Vetusta was his house, in which the spinsters lived rent-free. The country villa and its surrounding land were worth much less than the conspirator might have supposed, had he judged by what they cost him. But he paid no heed to such matters. He, like his country, was going to ruin, but while the civil list grieved him as much as if he paid all of it himself, it was of small concern to him that others were playing fast and loose with his possessions. It would not, however, be true to say that Don Carlos was acting out of pure disinterestedness. He envisaged patriotic compensations in the distant future, but, although they were included in his party's programme, they never came his way.

Anita, the governess, and the domestics went off to Don Carlos's new property, and after them went *the man*, as the girl always called the personage who disturbed the sleep of her innocence more than once. He was Iriarte, Doña Camila's lover, and the villa's former owner.

The governess had tried to seduce Don Carlos. She knew that his late wife had been a humble dressmaker, and she, Doña Camila Portocarrero, who believed herself to be descended from nobility, could well aspire to succeed the Italian woman. She thought that Don Carlos had married out of necessity and that he was the kind of man who marries servants. She knew his type, and she knew how to deal with such a man. But it was to no avail. In the short time at her disposal for putting her shrewd and complex system of seduction to the test, Don Carlos did not even notice that a love-net was being extended before him. At that time he was almost a Saint-Simonian.[4] Soon he had to go into exile. Doña Camila swore eternal hatred of the ingrate and, with the patience of the English Dissenters, consecrated a cult of posthumous envy to the Italian dressmaker who had succeeded in marrying that lump of stucco. Anita paid for both of them.

The governess asserted on all sides, between breathed interjections, that the upbringing of that four-year-old young lady demanded very special care. With sly, vague allusions, wrapped in mystery, to the Italian woman's social condition, she intimated that the science of education expected no good to come from that product of meridional concupiscence. The governess whispered that 'perhaps Anita's mother had been a dancer before she became a dressmaker'.

At all events, Doña Camila surrounded herself with pedagogical precautions and constructed a veritable gymnasium of English morality for Ana Ozores's childhood. When this tender shoot began to peep out above the earth it found that it already had a stake by its side to ensure upright growth. The governess asserted that Anita needed this stick by her, and to be firmly tied to it: the stick was Doña Camila. Locking the child up and depriving it of food were her disciplines.

From the age of four, Ana, who never found any joy, laughter or kisses in life, took to dreaming about all such things. When she was locked up she would at first despair, but her tears soon dried in the heat of her fantasy, which fired her mind and her cheeks. The child would imagine miraculous escapes from these confinements, which were like death to her, and conjure up impossible flights.

'I've got wings and I'm flying over the rooftops,' she would say to herself. 'I'm escaping like those butterflies.' And no sooner said than done; she was no longer in her room, she was flying through the blueness which she could see above her.

If Doña Camila came to the door to listen through the keyhole, she heard nothing. The girl, with her eyes wide open and shining, and her cheeks flushed, would spend hours and hours wandering through spaces which she herself created, full of confused reveries, yet illuminated by a diffuse light which flashed in her brain.

She never begged forgiveness; she felt no need to do so. She came forth pensive, haughty, silent from her confinements; she was still dreaming; fasting gave her new strength to dream. The heroine of the novels which she made up at that time was a mother. At the age of six she composed a poem in her tawny-curled head. The poem was compounded from the tears shed by this ill-treated, motherless girl in her moments of deepest misery, and fragments of stories which she heard from the shepherds of Loreto and the domestics. She escaped from the house whenever she could; she ran alone through meadows and went into the huts of the shepherds, who knew her, and patted her, and whose big dogs gently pawed her; she often ate with the shepherds. From her excursions into the country-side she returned with material for her poem, like a bee with the essence of flowers. Just as Poussin[5] picked grasses in the meadows in order to make a study of nature before transferring it to canvas, so when Anita came back to civilization after her escapades, her eyes and her imagination were full of treasures, the finest things which she ever enjoyed. At twenty-seven Ana Ozores could have recited that poem from beginning to end, even though she had added another part to it at each new stage in her life. In the first part there was an enchanted dove with a black pin in its head. It was the Queen of the Moors: Ana's mother, who never came. All doves with black head-markings could be mothers, according to Ana's poetic logic.

The idea of the book as a spring from which beautiful falsehoods flowed was the greatest revelation of her entire childhood. To be able to read! This ambition was her first passion. Ana forgave Doña Camila with all her heart for the grief which she inflicted before she succeeded in making her learn the syllables. At length Ana did learn to read, but the books which came into her hands did not speak of the things about which she dreamed. No matter; she would make them say whatever she wanted them to say.

She was taught geography. Where there were tedious lists of rivers and mountains, Ana saw crystal-clear running waters and the sierra with its tall, tall pines and their magnificent trunks. She never forgot the definition of an island, because she imagined a garden with the sea all around it, and that was sheer joy. Sacred history was manna to her imagination in the wilderness of Doña Camila's lessons. Her poem took on a firm shape, losing its nebulousness, and in the tents of the Israelites, which she embroidered with coloured stripes, she imagined armies of valiant sailors from Loreto, with their bare legs, muscular and hairy, their knitted pixie-caps, their sad, kind, weather-beaten faces, their bushy, frizzly beards, and their dark eyes.

Epic poetry predominates in the infancy of individuals as well as in that of nations. Henceforth, most of Ana's dreams were of battles: an Iliad or, more accurately, a Ramayana[6] without a plot. She needed a hero and in Germán, the boy from Colondres, she found one. Not suspecting the perilous adventures in which his friend was involving him, he basked in her admiration and was happy to come to the meetings which she arranged in the ferry-boat at Trébol.

She said nothing about the great battles which she made him win in the Far East, and in which she, in the role of Queen Consort, assisted him with Amazonian sallies. Sometimes, whispering into his ear, she proposed perilous trips to remote countries of which he had never even heard, but he accepted without hesitation and was quite prepared to turn himself into a stage-coach if Ana took the role of mule, or vice versa. But that wasn't what Ana wanted. She wanted to make a real trip to the land of the Moors and either kill infidels or convert them, whichever Germán preferred. Germán preferred to kill them. No sooner said than done; they would jump into the boat while the boatman slept in the shade of an awning on the river bank and, at the cost of much toil, they would achieve a slight rocking of the great ship they were manning, and see themselves speeding at full sail through unnavigated seas.

Germán would shout: 'Luff the helm! Starboard! Port the helm! Man overboard! A shark!'

But that was not what Anita wanted either. She wanted to really go away – far, far away, fleeing from Doña Camila. The only occasion on which Germán lived up to the ideal which Anita had created from his character and qualities was when he agreed to the nocturnal escapade to stare at the moon together in the ferry-boat and tell each other stories. This project seemed more viable to him than going off to the land of the Moors, and it was carried out. We know how the gross, lascivious Doña Camila interpreted the children's adventure. This woman's wickedness was such that she considered whatever vexations the incident might occasion her, because of the responsibilities which she held, to be well worth while, so long as her predictions were seen to be confirmed by the facts.

'Just like her mother!' she would say to acquaintances. 'Improper, improper!' she would add, in English. 'It is just as I said! Instinct – blood – there is little that education can do in opposition to nature.'

Henceforward she educated the girl without any hope of saving her, as if she were cultivating a flower which was already rotting after a grub-bite. She had no hopes, but she did her duty. Loreto was a small village and since Doña Camila recounted the adventure to anyone who would listen to her – the unfortunate woman would weep the while, overcome by her burden of responsibility, for she had little power against nature – the scandal flew from mouth to mouth, and even the gentlemen in their club knew all about the confession which the accused had been forced to make. There was a physiological discussion of the case. Factions were formed; some gentlemen said that it was perfectly possible, and a variety of examples of similar precocity were cited.

'Believe you me,' said Doña Camila's lover, 'man is wicked by nature, and so is woman.'

Others denied at least the verisimilitude of the event.

'If you put it in a book, nobody would believe it.'

Ana was an object of general curiosity. Everyone wished to see her and scrutinize her face and her gestures to see if there were any visible signs. . . .

'She's certainly well enough developed, very well developed indeed, for her age,' said Doña Camila's lover, savouring a foretaste of future lechery.

'Indeed she's a regular little woman.'

And she was devoured by men's eyes; there was a desire for a miraculous, instantaneous growth of charms which existed not in the girl but in the imaginations of the members of the Gentlemen's Club.

Germán, who was never again seen in Loreto, was said to be fifteen years old. 'He posed no problems.'

Doña Camila believed herself to be under an obligation of conscience to say something to the family. Not to the father, of course, the shock would be enough to kill him. Instead she wrote to the aunts in Vetusta.

'This was the final blow! The good name of Ozores, dishonoured! For, after all, the girl was an Ozores, even though she was unworthy of the name.'

Doña Anuncia, the elder sister, wrote to Don Carlos, because the matter was an urgent one. She did not give an exhaustive account of the affair of dishonour, because neither did she know exactly what had happened, nor was it decent to recount such scandals to a father; and in any case, an unmarried lady, even though more than forty years of age, could not descend to certain details. The letter to Don Carlos, therefore, said no more than this: that it was imperative that he take Ana away with him, because if the child did not live by her father's side, the family's honour was exposed to grave perils, if not actually placed in imminent danger. But at that time Don Carlos could not restore himself to the fatherland, as he put it.

Years passed, there arose an opportunity, which he accepted, to receive amnesty, and he returned, a disillusioned man. Doña Camila and Ana moved to Madrid, and there the three lived for part of the year, although they spent their summers and autumns in the villa at Loreto.

The calumny with which the governess had attempted to stain Ana's virginal purity for ever faded away little by little, and the world forgot that absurdity. By the time the girl reached the age of fourteen, nobody remembered the cruel, base fabrication, with the exception of the governess, her gentleman friend (who was still waiting), the aunts in Vetusta, and Ana herself, who remembered it all the time. In the beginning the calumny had done her little harm, had been just one more of Doña Camila's many injustices. But a suspicion gradually found its way into her mind, and with incredible intensity she applied all her powers to the enigma which exercised such an influence over her life and made it necessary for the governess to take so many precautions. Ana wanted to know what was the sin of which she was accused. The perversity and ill-concealed turpitude of Doña Camila's own life sharpened the girl's shrewdness, so that she began to understand what it meant to possess honour and what it meant to lose it – and, since everybody gave her to believe that her adventure in the ferry-boat at Trébol had been a shameful one, her ignorance provided confirmation of her sinfulness. By the time Ana's innocence had shed its last veil and she was able to see clearly, that period of her life was far distant; she had a vague remembrance of her friendship with the boy from Colondres, but all she could really make out was the memory of a memory, and she doubted and doubted whether she had been guilty of all those sins. When no one else thought of such matters any longer, Ana still thought of them and, confusing innocent acts with blameworthy ones, took to mistrusting everything. She came to believe in a great injustice which was the law of the world, because God so wished it. And she was so afraid of what people thought of everything she did that, denying her own strong instincts, she turned her life into a perpetual schooling in dissimulation and suppressed all her happy impulses. Ana – formerly so haughty, capable of opposing the whole world – declared herself defeated, and followed the moral conduct imposed upon her, without arguing, blindly, lacking any faith in it, but never playing false.

Such was her condition when her father returned from exile. He was not satisfied with the character that he found.

Had he not been told that the child was a danger to the honour of the family? Well, what he saw, on the contrary, was a girl who was all too shy and reserved, and excessively prudent for her age. He now regretted having delivered his daughter up to English prudery which, in his opinion, was unsuitable for the Latin race. He was very Latin at the time of his return from his stay abroad. Fortunately he was there now, to correct her defective upbringing. He dismissed Doña Camila and took personal charge of his daughter's education. While he was away, Don Carlos had become more philosophical and less political. There was no saving Spain. It was an exhausted country. What was more, America was swallowing Europe. He was extremely worried about the canned meat which was imported from the United States.

'They are consuming us, consuming us. We are poor, very poor – miserable wretches whose only aptitude is for taking the sun.'

He himself was certainly poor, and poorer with each day that passed, but he placed the blame for his penury upon general decadence, the lack of blood in the race, and other such absurdities. He still had his library, which he had improved, and his friends – all new ones, of course.

Every day, over coffee, in Ana's presence, the divinity of Christ was discussed. Some called Him the first democrat. Others said that He was a symbol of the sun and that the apostles were the constellations of the zodiac.

Ana would contrive to retire as soon as she could do so without offending the susceptibilities of her free-thinking father. What sorrow it gave the girl to consider, without wanting to, that her father's friends were indelicate people, reckless prattlers! And her papa himself – this was worst of all, and had to be borne in mind as well – her beloved papa, a talented man who was capable of inventing gunpowder, the clock, the telegraph, anything at all, was being sent mad by all his philosophizing, and had no idea how he should behave with his daughter, whose understanding of religious matters was already greater than his own.

Ana's outward submissiveness, the sacrifice which she was making to the world's prejudices and injustices of her day-to-day life and relationships, was not hypocrisy on her part – was not a mask for pride. But it was impossible to tell from outward appearances what was happening inside her. Just as in girlhood she would take refuge within her own fantasies to escape from Doña Camila's mindless, prosaic persecution, so, now that she was an adolescent, she shut herself into her own mind, in order to find some compensation for the humiliation and unhappiness which her spirit suffered. She no longer dared oppose her impulses to what she held to be a conspiracy by all the fools in the world; but when she was alone she made up for all her suffering. The enemy was stronger, but she kept control of that impregnable fastness, her inner being.

Nobody had ever made her see religion as a source of comfort. Doña Camila regarded Christianity as she did geography, or sewing, or ironing – as an embellishing subject, or a domestic necessity. She said nothing to Ana which ran contrary to dogma, yet she never attempted to explain the tenderness of Jesus with a motherly kiss. Holy Mary was, indeed, the Mother of God, but once when Ana returned home from the fields saying she knew that the Virgin washed Baby Jesus's swaddling clothes in the river, Doña Camila exclaimed, full of indignation: 'Improper! Who can be responsible for inculcating such vulgar nonsense into the child?'

On this point Don Carlos approved of Doña Camila's attitude, for he himself believed that the Mystery of the Incarnation was comparable to the golden rain which Jupiter caused to fall, and, going still further back in time, by virtue of comparative mythology, he found similar dogmas in Indian religions.

Ana had few religious works at her disposal in her father's house. But she knew a great deal of mythology, with and without veils.

Don Carlos kept from his daughter only that which the most elementary sense of modesty demands must be kept back. She could, and should, know all about everything else. Why not? And, with a multiplicity of quotations, Ozores would explain and advocate an *omnilateral and harmonic education*,[7] as he understood it.

'It is my desire', he would conclude, 'that my daughter should know both good and evil, so that she may freely choose the good, for otherwise what merit would her deeds possess?'

None the less, if his daughter had been a tightrope-walker on a high wire Don Carlos would have placed a safety net below her, even though the exercise might thereby have lost some merit.

There were some modern novels which he did not allow her to read, but whenever it was a question of Classical Art, of 'true art', there were no veils whatever, she could read everything. Ozores the Romantic was now Classical, in the aftermath of his Italian tour.

'Art is sexless!' he would cry. 'Look here, I let my daughter see prints that reproduce the Art of the Ancients, revealing the full beauty of the nude, which we moderns seek, in vain, to imitate. The nude is no more!' And he sighed.

Anita learned about mythology as in her early childhood she had learned about the history of Israel.

'*Honni soit qui mal y pense!*' Don Carlos would repeat; and the other saying, '*Oh, procul, procul estote profani!*'[8]

He took no other precautions.

It was fortunate that the strongest impression made on Ana's spirit by the Art of the Ancients and by Greek fables was a purely aesthetic one. Her imagination, above all, was excited, and it was thanks to her imagination, not to Don Carlos, that this inopportune study of the classical nude did not play havoc with the girl.

She envied Homer's gods, who lived as she had dreamed that one should live, in the open air, with light and adventures in plenty, and unmenaced by the ferule of a half-English governess.

Ana also envied the shepherds of Theocritus, Bion and Moschus;[9] she dreamed of the enamoured Cyclops' fresh, shady grotto; and she took great pleasure, mingled with a certain melancholy, in transferring herself and her illusions to that burning Sicily which she imagined as a nest of love. But since it was as a result of abandoning herself to her instincts, dreams and chimeras that she had met with the nebulous adventure of the ferry-boat at Trébol, which still filled her with shame, she regarded all talk of relationships between men and women with suspicion and even moral repugnance if they gave any pleasure, however ideal it might be. The confusion, compounded from guile and innocence, in which Ana had been immersed by the governess's calumnies and by other people's gross comments, made her cold, surly, evasive in all matters concerning love, as she imagined it to be. She had been systematically kept away from any close relationship with men, as inflammable material is kept away from fire. Doña Camila had regarded her as a barrel of gunpowder that a spark might ignite. 'Her natural girlish instincts had gone astray, and her relationship with Germán had been sinful, however incredible that might seem. It would be best to shun all men. She didn't want any more humiliation.' Circumstances favoured this aberration of her spirit. Don Carlos's few friends were all solitary troglodytes – philosophasters and conspirators, gentlemen who must have been alone in the world: if they had wives and children, they never introduced them or talked about them. Anita had no friends. Furthermore, Don Carlos treated her as if she were Art, and therefore sexless. Hers was a neuter education. Although Ozores cried out for women's emancipation, and cheered whenever a lady in Paris burned her lover's face with vitriol, at heart he regarded woman as an inferior being, an agreeable pet animal. He did not stop to consider what Ana's needs might be. He had loved her mother dearly, had even kissed her bare feet during their honeymoon, which had been full of such excesses. But, without realizing it, he, too, had come by degrees to see the former dressmaker in her, and had behaved towards her, in the end, like a good, gentle, satisfied master. Whatever his reasons may have been, he believed that he was doing his duty by Ana in taking her to the art gallery, the military museum, occasionally to the fair-ground and, most often, for walks with a few friends of his, free-thinkers who stopped every ten steps for an argument. They belonged to the class of men who have hardly ever talked with women. This breed might seem rare, but it is more abundant than one might think. The man who never talks with women can usually be recognized in that he talks a great deal about Woman. Ozores's cronies, however, did not even do this; they were solitary northern pines, and they did not sigh for the palm-trees of the south.

Although Ana had reached the age at which a girl begins to acquire womanly charms, she excited no notice and nobody had fallen in love with her. Doña Camila and Don Carlos, between them, had faded the roses in her cheeks; that changing and filling out of her figure which had once drawn sparks from the eyes of the governess's lover had come to a stop. Anita was about to become a woman, yet she still seemed very far from this crisis, for she was pale, thin, weak, a graceless fifteen. At ten she had looked thirteen, and now at fifteen she still seemed thirteen.

Since it has not yet been decided to support philosophers at public expense, Don Carlos, whose only occupation was putting the world in order and condemning it in its present state, soon found himself in a precarious economic situation.

'He was tired; he had done enough fighting,' in his opinion, and it did not occur to him to look for work, for he was unwilling to work any more than he already had. He preferred to retire to his villa in Loreto, in response to the pleas which Ana made him with her hands clasped together. The unhappy girl suffered from acute boredom in Madrid. While her imagination was dispatched to Greece, Olympus, and the art gallery, she herself, the Ana Ozores of flesh and blood, had to live in a narrow, dark street, in a wretched mezzanine which seemed to press in on her from every side. Some of the neighbours invited her to go for strolls with them, or to social gatherings, or to the back-street theatres which such young ladies frequented. In Madrid, poverty is either resigned or ridiculous. Those neighbours were ridiculous. Anita could not bear them; she was disgusted by them, by their parties, and by their theatres. They had soon dismissed her as a little prig, as proud as a dog with two tails. Her half-year in the country was much more pleasant, even though that was the scene of her confinements and of the adventure in the ferry-boat and the subsequent calumny. But of all the people who might remind her of her disgrace, she only saw Señor Iriarte, the governess's man-friend, who came to visit Don Carlos, and looked at the girl with the eyes of a farmer who is getting ready to gather in his harvest.

When Don Carlos decided to live in Loreto throughout the year, for the sake of economy, Anita kissed him on the eyes and mouth and was, for a whole day, the expansive, joyful girl she had been before her transplantation to Doña Camila's pedagogic glass-house.

In previous years an occasional boxful of books had been taken to Loreto, but this time the entire library, Don Carlos's legitimate pride, was sent there with the muleteer.

One sunny May morning, one of the first days of Ana's new life in Loreto, she was happily singing as she cleaned the library shelves, dusted books and put them up in the order indicated in the catalogue compiled by Don Carlos.

She came across a French book, bound in yellow pasteboard. She thought that it was one of those novels which her father forbade her to read and was about to put it away when she read on its spine: *Confessions of St Augustine.*

What was St Augustine doing there?

Don Carlos was a free-thinker who did not read books by saints, priests or ultras, as he called them. But St Augustine was one of the few exceptions. Don Carlos thought him quite a good philosopher.

Ana was seized by an irresistible impulse to read the book. She knew that St Augustine had been a pagan and a libertine, converted by heavenly voices thanks to the tears shed by his mother, St Monica. But that was all she knew. She dropped the feather duster and stood, her small, curly head and the open book bathed in sunlight, reading the first few pages. Don Carlos was away from home; so with the book under her arm, Ana walked out into the garden and entered the arbour, with its dense covering of perennial creepers. The shadows cast by the leaves in the green vaulting played upon the pages of the book, which shone out in white and black; near by, behind her, she could hear the cool discreet murmur of water flowing lazily along an irrigation channel in the sunlight; outside the garden the branches of tall poplar-trees rustled bright new leaves which glittered like steel lances.

Ana read on, her soul caught in the grip of the letters. As she finished one page, in spirit she was half-way through the next. This was new indeed. All mythology was madness, according to the saint. And love – that love – just as she had thought, a sin, a petty trifle, an error, blindness. She had been right to stay on her guard. She remembered that, in Madrid, two students had written her letters to which she had not replied. This had been her only

adventure of that kind since the shameful incident in the ferry-
boat at Trébol. The saint said that children are evil by instinct and
that what makes those who love them enjoy them and laugh at
them is this innate perversity; but their drollery is a fault, they are
moved by egotism, anger, vanity.

'It's true, it's true,' she thought, repentant.

But in that case she needed something else. Was that emptiness in
her heart going to be filled? Was that life of indifference, black in the
past and in the future, futile, and beset with vexation and stupidity,
going to come to an end? She heard within her head the explosion
of a tremendous 'yes' which shattered into brilliant sparks in her
brain. All this happened as she read, and she was still bewildered,
frightened almost, by that voice which she had heard within herself,
when she came to the passage where the saint relates how, while he,
too, was walking in a garden, he heard a voice which said *'Tolle,
lege'*[10] and hurried to the sacred text and read a verse of the Bible.
Ana cried out as a tremor ran over the whole surface of her body and
into the roots of her hair, like a breath which made it stand on end
and left it erect for many seconds.

She had a sudden fear of the supernatural. She thought that some
apparition was about to take shape before her. But her moment of
panic passed, and the motherless child felt a gentle flow inside her
which rose to her brimming eyes and calmed her heart. The welling
tears clouded her vision.

And she wept over St Augustine's *Confessions*, as over a mother's
breast. In that moment her soul grew towards womanhood.

During the afternoon she finished the book. She left the last few
chapters unread, because she did not understand them.

That evening, in the library, Don Carlos was arguing with a priest
from Loreto and various other gentlemen with a taste for philosophy
and good cider, which the impoverished Ozores dispensed in
abundance so as to ensure a supply of opponents. He often said that
to think alone was to think by halves. He needed opposition. The
priest wished to keep the flag of the Church flying high and to have
an agreeable way of spending the evenings, which were eternal in
Loreto, even in the spring.

Ana was sitting some way off, sunk almost out of sight in a great
leather-cloth easy chair with huge wings, in which she had often
day-dreamed. Her eyes were wide open and motionless, and she was
day-dreaming now, too, about St Augustine, whom she imagined in
a great golden mitre and a cope of satin and gold, crossing the desert
in an Africa populated with wild beasts and palm-trees which rose to
the clouds. It was delicious to let her imagination wander, just as it
had been in her childhood; it made another canto for her poem. On
remembering St Augustine's gentleness when he was reconciled in
his pulpit with an estranged friend who came to hear him, Ana felt

an ineffable tenderness which made her love the whole universe in the person of the bishop.

Don Carlos was swearing that Christianity was an importation from Bactria.

He was not certain that the word which he had read was Bactria, but in his village disputations he was not very scrupulous about historical data, being able to count upon the ignorance of his audience.

The priest did not know what Bactria was, and it therefore seemed to him that the idea of bringing Christianity from there was quite the funniest and most ridiculous blunder imaginable.

And, dying with laughter, he said:

'Lord-a-mercy! *Bagtrees,* a likely story. Where can Señor Ozores have read all this?'

'This priest is no St Augustine,' thought Anita. 'No, for St Augustine would not drink cider or be so bad at refuting arguments like those of my father.' No matter, the priest was right, and that was enough: he spoke great truths without realizing it. At that moment Don Carlos began to defend the Manichaeans.

'It seems to me less absurd to believe in a good God and a bad God than to believe in Yahweh-Elohim, who was a despot, a dictator, a tyrant.'

'Her father a Manichaean! St Augustine, who had also once believed such errors, had some fine things to say about Manichaeans!' But conversion would come to her father one day, just as it had come to her, filling her heart with love for everybody and with faith in God and in the saintly Bishop of Hippo.

Some time later, searching in the library, she found *The Genius of Christianity,*[11] which was a revelation. To prove religion through beauty seemed the most felicitous idea in the world. If her reason resisted Chateaubriand's arguments, her imagination, and with it her will, soon surrendered.

'Señor Chateaubriand was a fine jackanapes, according to Don Carlos. He possessed his works only because his style was not too bad.' Everyone was speaking ill of Chateaubriand at that time.

Ana next read *The Martyrs.*[12] She would have been happy to be Cymodocée, and her father could pass muster as Demodocus, particularly after his trip to Italy, which had turned him into a pagan. But what about Eudore? Where was Eudore? She thought of Germán. What could have become of him?

It was not easy to find among her father's books any others which spoke favourably about religion. One volume of the *Spanish Parnassus*[13] was devoted to religious poetry. Most of the poems were dull and obscure, but among them she found some which made a better impression on her than Chateaubriand himself. There were *quintillas* by Fray Luis de León which began thus:

If thou shouldst wish, some of these days,
To praise a lady's silken hair,
'Tis Mary's hair that thou must praise,
More golden far, more bright, more fair
Than noontime sun's most brilliant rays.

The poet-ecclesiastic, who forgot about other heads of hair in order to praise Mary's, seemed sublime in his tenderness, and these five lines aroused in Ana's heart what might be called the *sensation of the Virgin*, for it resembles no other sensation. As Ana experienced it, she was in ecstasies of religious love.

Mary was not only the Heavenly Queen but a Mother, the Mother of the afflicted. Even had Mary appeared before her, Ana would not have been afraid. Devotion to the Virgin surged with more force into the heart of the girl who was becoming a woman than devotion to St Augustine or Chateaubriand. The Ave Maria and the Salve Regina acquired new meaning for her. She never stopped praying. But that was not enough, she wanted more: she wanted to compose prayers herself.

Don Carlos also possessed the Song of Songs, in the poetic version by St John of the Cross.[14] It was one of the books which Anita was not permitted to read.

'They can't fool me,' Don Carlos would say, winking. 'This "beloved" might be the Church, but – I'm not so sure, I'm not so sure.'

He would babble on and on in this way, for although he was incapable of slandering his equals, he thought that slander was by no means amiss when he was talking about saints and priests.

After Ana had read St John's poem, she felt that she herself might be capable of improvising prayers. She would speak them, in verse, during her solitary walks on Loreto Hill, which smelt of thyme and dropped precipitously into the sea.

Poems after the manner of St John, as she called them, bubbled out of her soul, all of a piece, simple, tender, and impassioned. In this way she spoke to the Virgin.

The excited, nervous Anita perceived – and she felt a strange pain in her head as she did so – a mysterious analogy between St John's verses and the fragrance released by the wild thyme which she trod underfoot as she climbed the hill.

Indeed, Ana's mind had recently been seeking and discovering such secret correspondences, quite without her consent. They inspired her with a melancholy affection which, by degrees, became a severe headache.

One autumn afternoon, after drinking a glass of kümmel which her father made her take after coffee, Anita went out alone, planning to begin to write a book, up in the Pine Hollow, a place she knew well.

It was a work for which the idea had come to her days earlier: a collection of poems 'To the Virgin'.

Don Carlos allowed Ana to go by herself for walks on condition that she left through the garden gate and climbed the hill where the wild thyme grew, for nobody could see her up there, and no one else climbed the hill except to collect firewood.

That day her walk was longer than usual. The hill was an arduous one, and the path was like a goat-track. On her right, fearsome cliffs fell sheer into the ocean, which exhausted its rage far below in foam and roars that reached these high places like an underground murmur. On her left the wild thyme accompanied the path up the hill, which was crowned by pine-trees in whose branches the wind echoed the ocean's inextinguishable lament. Anita strode on upwards. The effort of climbing the hill excited her, made her feverish. In her cheeks, which were usually ice-cold, fires were burning, as they had often burned in former times. She climbed with an impassioned urgency, as if the path were taking her to Heaven.

After a sharp turn a new panorama confronted her. Loreto was out of sight. Before her was the ocean, until now heard but unseen, more vast than it looked from the harbour, and more peaceful, more solemn. From here its waves did not resemble the violent convulsions of a caged beast, but rather the rhythms of a sublime song, the vibrations of great resounding bars, equal, symmetrical, stretching from east to west. Far to the west there was an amphitheatre of mountains like a giants' stairway ascending to Heaven, where clouds and mountain-tops mingled in confusion, reflecting colours on to each other. At the highest point of this cumulus of blue stone Ana descried a minute speck; she knew it was a chapel. The Virgin was there. The clouds in the west were breaking up and pouring light from deep within themselves to form an aureola for the Mother of God, whose temple stood upon that peak. The sunset was a magnificent finale. The sails of the small fishing-boats of Loreto, buried deep in the shadow cast by the hill, looked like doves flying over the waters.

At length Ana reached the Pine Hollow. It was a dell between two low hillocks crowned by bushes, where there were also some magnificent specimens of the tree which gave it its name. In the middle of the dell, the dried-up course of a mountain stream displayed its bed of grey-white stone, and a bird, which the girl imagined to be a nightingale, sang its song in its hiding-place among the bushes on the western hillock. Ana sat upon a rock by the dry river-bed. She imagined herself to be in the wilderness. No noises there reminded her of man. The sea, now out of sight, again sounded like an underground murmur; the pine-trees sounded like the sea; and the bird like a nightingale. She was assured of her solitude. She opened a common place-book, placed it in her lap, and wrote in pencil upon the first page: 'To the Virgin'.

She meditated, awaiting divine inspiration.

Before she wrote, she allowed her thoughts to speak.

When her pencil began to write the first line, the whole of the first stanza was already complete in her soul. Her pencil hurried on over the paper, but her soul was always ahead of it. One line gave birth to many more, as one kiss calls forth a hundred kisses; and from each amorous, rhythmic concept, clusters of poetic ideas sprang into life already clothed in all the colours and perfumes of that simple, noble, impassioned poetic expression.

Her mind was still pouring forth words, when her hand had to decline to follow it because the pencil could write no more. Ana's eyes saw neither letters nor paper, they were full of tears. She felt the lash of a whip on her temples, and on her throat an iron hand, squeezing.

She rose to her feet, she tried to speak, she screamed, and her voice resounded through the dell. The nightingale stopped singing, and Ana's verses, recited like a prayer amidst tears, came forth into the breeze, and were repeated by the echoing hillsides. With words of fire she called upon her Mother in Heaven. She was enraptured by her own voice, she shuddered, and she could speak no more. Her legs gave way, she rested her forehead on the earth. A mystical terror overcame her for a moment. She did not dare raise her eyes, fearing that she might be surrounded by the supernatural. A light which was stronger than the light of the sun pierced her eyelids. She heard a noise near by, she cried out, and in terror she lifted her head. There could be no doubt, a bramble on the hillock in front of her was moving. With her eyes open wide before the miracle, Ana saw a dark-hued bird fly from the thicket and brush over her brow.

V

Señorita Doña Anunciación Ozores had entered her forty-seventh year without ever having set foot outside the province of Vetusta. So it was most inconvenient, perhaps even dangerous, for her to venture along the coastal road to Loreto on a stage-coach journey of some twenty hours' duration. She was accompanied by Don Cayetano Ripamilán, a canon whose years and social standing made him respectable, and by an old family maidservant.

Don Carlos had died suddenly, at night, unconfessed, without the sacraments. The doctor spoke of a haemorrhage, a blood vessel . . . Pure materialism. Doña Anuncia could see the hand of God, who chastises with no common stick or stone. But this did not prevent her, dressed in deep mourning, from manifesting during the journey a grief hardly mitigated by Christian resignation.

'Ana, the dressmaker's daughter, was prostrate in her bed. The child was alone, in the hands of domestics: there was no alternative but to go and fetch her. In the face of that demise, family differences came to an end.'

'Dead dogs bite not,' a Vetustan nobleman had said.

When Doña Anuncia and Don Cayetano reached Loreto, Ana was at death's door. It was a nervous fever – a terrible crisis, the doctor said, for the illness had coincided with certain transformations proper to her age. Proper, maybe – but they should not have been explained in front of ladies with the clarity and detail employed by the doctor. Don Cayetano could hear it all, but Doña Anuncia would have much preferred metaphor and periphrasis. 'Repressed development', 'the critical and mysterious metamorphosis', 'the chrysalis bursting open' – all this was acceptable, but the doctor added details which Doña Anuncia did not hesitate to describe as coarse.

'The people my brother associated with!' she exclaimed, showing the whites of her eyes.

The poor girl, orphaned and ailing, had been alone, in the hands of domestics, for two weeks, because Doña Anunciación did not resolve to undertake the twenty-hour journey until this act of charity was begged of her in the name of her niece, who was by now close to death. Ana was already ill when the catastrophe overtook her. Her illness was melancholic; she felt a sadness which she could not explain. At first the loss of her father frightened her more than it grieved her. She did not cry; she spent her days shivering with cold, deep in a somnolency peopled with wild thoughts. The girl was possessed by a horrible, remorseful self-concern. She was afflicted more by her own forsakenness, which terrified her, than by her father's death. All her courage vanished, and she felt herself to be everybody's slave. The fortitude which silent suffering inspires was not enough, nor was it sufficient for her to shelter in her own inner life: she needed a refuge in the world. She knew that she was very poor. A few months before his death her father had sold the mansion in Vetusta to his sisters at a wretched price. This had been the last vestige of his inheritance. The proceeds of this disadvantageous sale had been used to pay off old debts. But others remained. The villa itself was mortgaged, and it was not worth enough to keep anyone's head above water. In the philosopher's hands it had become more and more dilapidated.

'In other words, I'm very nearly destitute.'

It would be some time before she could collect her orphan's allowance which, she was told, would be a derisory sum, in fact hardly anything at all; and, in any case, she had nobody to tell her how and where to apply for it. She was alone, utterly alone. What was to become of her? The philosopher's friends were of no use whatsoever. They only knew how to argue. The priest never came back to the house, Don Carlos's sudden death having had a somewhat sulphurous smell about it.

One morning, three or four days after her father's burial, Ana could not get up when she tried to do so. Her bed was holding her down with invisible arms. The night before, she had fallen asleep with her teeth clenched, shivering with cold. She had attempted to write to her aunts in Vetusta, but she had not been able to put the words together, and had even doubted her spelling.

She had nightmares, and although she tried not to reveal that she was unwell, her illness was too much for her. The doctor spoke of fever, of the need for the utmost care, and asked questions which she could not answer and did not want to answer. She was alone and it was absurd. The doctor said that there was no one with whom he could discuss matters, and cursed the domestics' negligence.

'They're going to let you die, my girl.'

Ana cried out, she felt scared and faint-hearted. Weeping, and clasping her hands, she begged that a call be sent to her aunts, her father's sisters, who lived in Vetusta, and whom she understood to be very good Christians.

The aunts felt some vague remorse about the purchase of the house. They realized that it was worth more, much more, than they had paid their brother for it, taking unfair advantage of his straitened circumstances and his rash disregard of his own financial interests. And to think that he had abjured the faith of the Ozores 'so as not to be the victim of a mystification'!

Now the opportunity was being offered to soothe their consciences by succouring the unfortunate daughter of that bothersome brother of theirs.

Doña Anuncia was better able to apprize the greatness of her good deed when she saw that Anita was 'living in beggary, almost'. The villa which she and her sister had believed to be worthy of an Ozores – although an erring one – was a mere cottage, painted in bright colours but of no value, with a moderately productive kitchen-garden. What was more, it was bound up in a debt which its total value would be hardly sufficient to settle. A pretty pickle Ana was in! That wretched atheist had not even been capable of getting rich. Losing both soul and body, heaven and earth! A profitable deal, indeed! But still, one must now face the music.

Doña Anuncia had taken a very heavy load on to her shoulders: but who does not have her cross to bear?

It was a month before Ana left her bed.

But Doña Anuncia was bored in Loreto, where there was no society; and the date of their return to Vetusta was brought forward, against the advice of that uncouth little doctor fellow, who made free with the most transparent medical terms.

As soon as they were in Vetusta the orphan girl suffered 'a set-back to her convalescence', according to the family doctor, who was prudent and did not call things by their right names.

The set-back was another fever which put Ana's life in danger once again.

The judgement which the Señoritas Ozores and the nobility of Vetusta were to pass upon the daughter of Don Carlos and the Italian dressmaker was suspended until such time as they could assemble sufficient evidence. While the girl hovered between life and death, Doña Anuncia found her conduct irreproachable.

To tell the truth, one could not complain about her manners or her character. She made an excellent patient: she never asked for anything and she took everything she was given. If she was questioned – 'How are you feeling, Anita?' – 'A little better, ma'am,' she would reply, whenever she could.

On other occasions she did not reply, lacking the strength to speak. And sometimes she did not even hear.

During her second convalescence she was not impertinent, either.

She never complained, everything was just right for her. She did not indulge in any excesses.

In the aristocratic circle of Vetusta, to which the Señoritas Ozores naturally belonged, nobody spoke about anything other than the saintly ladies' self-abnegation.

Gloucester (Don Restituto Mourelo), at that time a simple canon, declared in a mellifluous, mysterious voice at the Marquis de Vegallana's coterie:

'This, ladies and gentlemen, is old-fashioned virtue, not false, garrulous modern philanthropy. The Señoritas Ozores are putting into practice a charitable work, a close analysis of which would yield a long series of good deeds. It is not just a question of taking up the enormous burden of providing maintenance and, as I am given to believe, even clothing and footwear for a person who will, in all probability, survive them – a burden which is therefore taken on for life, in other words perpetual – but, what is more, the girl stands for an abdication which I refrain from qualifying, an abdication by a father . . .'

'An abominable abdication,' ventured a penniless baron.

'Abominable,' repeated Gloucester with a bow. 'She also stands for an ill-starred alliance in which the manifestly blue blood of the Ozoreses was mixed, in an evil hour, with plebeian blood. And, what is even worse, as we all know, the girl stands for the negligence in matters of morality of her mother, the unhappy . . .'

'Yes, of course,' interrupted the Marchioness de Vegallana, who could not abide Gloucester's speeches, 'yes, of course, the mother was a trollop – fair enough, but the lass herself seems agreeable, according to her aunts – docile and quiet.'

'Of course she keeps quiet, she cannot speak yet out of sheer weakness.'

This was the doctor to the aristocracy, Don Robustiano, who attended Anita.

That night, it was agreed by the coterie to accept Don Carlos's daughter as an Ozores, descended from the best nobility. On no account was her mother to be mentioned; this was forbidden, but Ana would be held in estimation as the niece of ladies who were deserving of such high praise.

Great was the consolation for Doña Anuncia and Doña Agueda upon being informed by the doctor of the Vetustan nobility's decision.

Ana spent many hours alone. Her aunts were in the habit of working – knitting and quilting – in the dining-room, and their niece's bedroom was at the other end of the house.

Furthermore, these illustrious ladies spent long hours away from their sad ancestral mansion. They were on visiting terms with the best people in Vetusta and with the Blessed Sacrament, before which they watched once a week. They attended every novena, every sermon, every meeting of the religious guilds, and every refined coterie. They went out for luncheon two or three times a week. Most of their time was spent returning visits. This was the occupation to which they gave most importance among all the occupations in their busy lives. Not to return a visit from a person of *quality* seemed to them to be the greatest crime which could be committed in a civilized society. They loved religion, because it was a stamp of their nobility, but they were not very devout. Deep in their hearts their principal cult was the cult of *quality*; and if a visit to the Guild of the Court of Our Lady had been incompatible with a visit to the Vegallana coterie, the Blessed Virgin, in her immense goodness, would have had to excuse them – for they would have gone to the coterie.

Etiquette, as it was understood in Vetusta, was the law by which the world was governed. Even celestial harmony depended upon etiquette.

If etiquette were abolished, the stars would collide, and probably collapse. What did their young niece know of such matters? That was the question. The looks which Doña Agueda – who was somewhat stouter, younger and kinder than her sister – shot at Anita, as she gave her a bowl of broth, were fraught with such inquiries.

The orphan always smiled, always said thank you. She was compliant in all matters. But her condition remained unchanged, and this made her aunts impatient. She neither recovered full strength nor relapsed; there were no signs of a definitive outcome. Furthermore, her true character could not be discovered while she remained in this state. Her total submission might be caused by her illness. Don Robustiano, the doctor, said that it was.

One afternoon, in the belief, perhaps, that their young niece was asleep, or forgetful of her presence close by, the two sisters talked in the boudoir adjoining her bedroom about a very important subject.

'I'm all of a tremble – I don't suppose you can imagine why?' said Doña Anuncia.

'I wonder if it's the same thing that's worrying me.'

'What's that?'

'Whether the girl . . .'

'Whether the disgraceful . . .'

'That's right!'

'Do you remember the governess's letter?'

'Of course – I've still got it.'

'The child was thirteen or fourteen then, wasn't she?'

'A little younger, but that makes it even worse.'

'And you think that . . .'

'Psha! Of course.'

'Might she be another Obdulita?'

'Or another Tarsilita. Do you remember Tarsila, who was involved in that episode with a cadet, and then had some kind of affair with Alvarito Mesía?'

'All quite innocent, so people said – the numskulls!'

'Innocent my eye. I'm to believe she's got that many lovers in Madrid' (opening and closing both hands with fingers outstretched)

'It's clear enough. A leopard never changes its spots.'

'If there isn't a solid foundation . . .'

'As if one didn't know!'

'And what about Obdulita? You know what people said last year. Then it was all denied, and declared to be a calumny.'

'Fancy coming with tales like that to an old soldier like me!'

'As if one didn't know!'

'If one had so desired!'

This Señorita Ozores sighed. Her sister sighed as well.

Ana, who had been resting, fully dressed, on her humble bed, jumped to her feet at the first words of the conversation. As pale as death, with two frozen tears in her eyes, and her thin hands clasped together, she heard her aunts' entire dialogue.

When they were alone they did not talk as they talked in front of *persons of quality*: they were not prudent, they were not discreet, they did not choose their words with fastidious care. Doña Anuncia uttered expressions which would have scandalized her upon other lips. It was some time before the conversation returned to the subject of Ana's sin and the disgrace to which Doña Camila's letter had referred. The orphan in her bedroom heard stories which outraged her sense of decency and revealed a thousand secrets

which she had not seen in any books of mythology. But the two
old women had forgotten all about her by now. Tarsila, Obdulia,
Visitación, another young woman who used to escape from her
balcony with her sweetheart, the Marchioness de Vegallana herself,
her daughters, her nieces from the country, indeed all Vetusta,
including its inhabitants of quality, were put to shame during that
act of solitary vengeance by the two unmarriageable Señoritas
Ozores. In that world of weakness and scandal, who now remembered their sickly young niece's adventure – which, after all, had
never attracted much attention?

At length the old maids returned, however, to their point of
departure. According to them, the affair had to do with a sailor who
had taken advantage of the girl's innocence, or precocity. There was
a discussion, as there had been in the Gentlemen's Club in Loreto,
about the likelihood of the crime from the physiological point of
view. The two ladies talked like fully qualified midwives. Such a
wealth of data! Such well-documented empiricism! Doña Anuncia's
mouth was watering. She made repeated use of the porcelain
receptacle at the foot of her easy chair.

'As far as morality was concerned, the case was not a grave one,
because nobody in Vetusta was likely to know anything about it. It
would be bad if the girl had continued to lead such a dissolute life,
but there was no reason for thinking that she had. They possessed no
other condemnatory information about her. And, at all events, time
would tell.'

Ana, who found courage to listen until the very last words of the
conversation, discovered that her aunts could forgive everything
except letting down appearances – that so long as, in future, she was
as they were, the past, whatever it might contain, would be forgotten.
How they were – this was something which she was only now
beginning to discover. But she would study further.

There had been a few moments of silence.

Doña Agueda broke it –

'And I think the girl's going to be pretty, if she gets better.'

'I believe she used to be somewhat rickety – at least, not very well
developed.'

'That's beside the point. I used to be like that, too, and after . . .'
(Ana felt her cheeks burning) 'I began to put on weight, and to eat
well, and I was soon as fat as butter.'

Doña Agueda sighed again, remembering the butter-pat which she
had once been.

Doña Anuncia had had a good reason for not putting on weight:
rabid romantic love. Of that love there remained various songs to the
moon, in a kind of plainchant which she accompanied on the guitar.
One of the songs began with the words:

Yonder moon shining bright in the heavens
Melancholic'ly me doth inspire.
'Tis the last dying chord of my lyre,
Which shall send forth its strains nevermore.

It was all about a condemned man.

Doña Anuncia's perfect ideal had always been a journey to Venice with a lover. But now that everything was *commercialized*, and girls no longer knew anything about falling in love, she wished, if possible, to put Ana's beauty to good use – because if Ana ate well she would be handsome, like her father and all the family, for it ran in the blood. Yes, it was vital to feed her, to plump her up. And then a young man would be found for her. A difficult enterprise, but not an impossible one. No thoughts could be entertained of an aristocrat. Aristocratic young gentlemen were very urbane and gallant towards ladies of their own rank, but if these ladies were without dowries the young aristocrats married the daughters of returned emigrants and of wealthy merchants. The sisters knew as much from a painful personal experience. The *ignoble* young men of Vetusta, as they might be called, were not good prospects, but even had the sisters been prepared to stomach ('to stomach' was the verb used by Doña Agueda in the bosom of her family) some awful lawyer fellow, no such numskull would dare pay court to an Ozores, even though he be dying for her. The only hope was an American. These returned emigrants had a keener desire for nobility and were more forward – they had faith in the prestige of their money. An American would therefore be sought. But first the girl must get well and put on weight.

So Ana realized that her first obligation was to get well quickly.

Her convalescence was becoming impertinent. She employed all her will-power to secure good health as soon as possible.

From the day when the doctor said that it was time for her to eat her fill, Ana, with tears in her eyes, ate as much as she could. Had the poor girl not overheard her aunts' conversation, she would not have dared eat much, even if she had wanted to eat, so as not to make their burden – herself – any heavier. But now she knew what she must make up her mind to. They wanted to fatten her up, like a cow for market. It was her duty to devour, even though swallowing the mouthfuls of food might cost her a few tears at first.

Nature soon came to the aid of this terrible effort of her will. Ana desired strength, health, colour, flesh, beauty, she desired to free her aunts of her presence. Taking great care of herself, feeding in abundance, appeared to be her supreme duty. Her spirit, in its present state, offered no resistance to these plans.

The accesses of religiosity, which she had believed to be a providential revelation of her true vocation, had ceased. They had been the cause of the violent crisis which had endangered Ana's life, but when health returned they did not return with it. New blood did not bring them back.

During Ana's attacks of insomnia and nervous exaltation, so intense that it almost made her delirious, her mystical visions, powerful intuitions of faith and sudden surges of compassion had consoled her on some occasions and tormented her on others. She had realized, with sorrow, that her faith was too vague. Although a fervent believer, she did not know in what she believed. Her greatest misfortune – the death of her father – had not been met by as strong a consolation as she had expected to find in the piety which she had thought so firm and profound, even though so new. Religion was of some service to her when she missed her father and needed to believe that she would see him again in another world, but it was of little use as a consolation for her immediate troubles, as a remedy for the anguish caused by a terrified ego and by all the afflictions which assail those who are poor and lonely. Her panic-stricken feeling of forsakenness, the feeling which overwhelmed all others, was not cured by faith.

'The Virgin is with me,' Ana would think in her bed, in Loreto. And she would weep and pray, and her head would be caressed by the invisible hand of God. But then she would suffer a nervous attack, and feel the pangs of loneliness, of the cold all around, of being left in an eternal silence; at such times no mystical images came to her. She needed visible protection. So she thought of her aunts, whom she did not know and of whom she had heard little good – but she desired their presence, believed in the power of blood and of family ties.

While Ana was convalescing after her first fever, her brain used its returning powers to imagine epics, novels, plays and lyric poems. This constant composition, the unremitting activity of her mind, began as an agreeable diversion and, moreover, gratified her vanity. But it was torment in the end. Everything she created in her imagination seemed excellent; as she contemplated the beauty which she had made, her admiration was such that she wept tender tears, just as when she thought of the love of Baby Jesus and His Holy Mother. But in moments of serene reflection she examined, with some distress, the similarity between the two feelings. Her emotion was just as profound and sincere when she contemplated the artistic beauty which she had made as when she contemplated the beauty of the idea of God. Might both feelings be religious? Or did her tenderness spring from vanity and egotism? At all events her suffering was great. It seemed as if all the life there was in her had risen to her head; as if her stomach were a machine which had stopped working, and her brain a furnace in which her entire being was aflame. Thinking – unintentionally, indeed unwillingly – of anything complex, original, delicate or exquisite gave her nausea, and it occurred to her to envy animals, plants, stones.

During her convalescence after her second attack of fever in Vetusta, she was afflicted once more by her mind's indomitable activity; but a little after forcing herself to eat again she found that the wheels inside her skull were turning more slowly, with a harmonious movement. She invented fewer heroes and heroines, and those which remained in her head were less fantastic, their sentiments were less exquisite. Now she took pleasure in describing their physical beauty, placed them in delightful and picturesque surroundings, and made all their adventures end in scenes of love or in great battles.

When Anita awoke each morning she surprised a smile in her soul and placid lethargy in her body. Her aunts permitted her to rise late, and she relished these early hours. Ana's bed was not then in that ancestral mansion, or in Vetusta, or indeed anywhere on earth; it was floating through the air, she knew not whither. She would abandon herself to the swaying of that soft little boat, as her day-dreams took her sailing through the sky ... And while the characters of her fantasy spoke fond words to each other, she prepared for them a succulent repast in a garden full of the purest penetrating fragrancies. With voluptuous pleasure Ana inhaled the ideal aromas of her grand visions.

On occasion, unfortunately, the Russian prince dressed in fine furs, or the Scottish noble displaying a well-turned, robust calf in a bright tartan stocking, suddenly turned into a pale, thin, liverish man in a panama hat, who took his leave of his lady-love with the words 'So long. Be seeing you!' and the swaying of a hammock in the vowels. This was the returned emigrant whom Ana and her aunts could see in the distance.

Doña Agueda was an excellent cook. Not only did she have a thorough empirical knowledge of the art of cookery, but it was, for her, one of the fundamental principles of life. She had memorized *The European Cook*, a work which explains the art of preparing all the dishes in English, French, Italian, Spanish and various other national cuisines. But cooking the *European* way cost the earth, according to Doña Agueda. Whenever there was a great luncheon or dinner for the aristocracy, she directed operations in the Marquis de Vegallana's kitchen, and then she had recourse to the *European*. But in her own house money was scarce, and she contented herself with recipes inherited from her ancestors. So Anita ate the choicest delicacies and marvels of home cooking, as soon as her stomach could take them. Doña Agueda gazed in raptures at the convalescent, with eyes large and sugary to no avail (for no man had wanted them for himself). Ana was plumping out visibly from day to day, according to the Ozores sisters. While the girl savoured those morsels, paying a tribute of praise to the cook with each mouthful, Doña Agueda, satisfied to the very roots of her vanity, passed her small, plump hand, with fingers like sausages bound with rings, through the wavy, chestnut

hair of that little imp of a niece of hers, as she called her. The artist
and her work exchanged smiles between one dish and the next.

Doña Anuncia did not cook, but she went shopping with the
maidservant, and brought home the best that little money could buy.
She was aided in her judicious shopping by an emeritus professor of
psychology, logic and ethics, a devotee of the Scottish school[1] and of
home-made sausages. He had no great faith either in the evidence of
his senses or in the black puddings sold at market. He was Doña
Anuncia's close friend, and he helped her to bargain.

After market, the old maid would make a round of visits to the
houses of the nobility in order to proclaim the extraordinary charity
with which she and her sister were giving an example to the world.

'If only you could see her now,' she would say. 'She's unrecognizable. One can actually see her plumping out. She's like a balloon,
being inflated little by little. Mind you, my dear Agueda is an absolute
wizard. Well, you all know my sister's cooking from your own
experience. I don't know what I wouldn't do for the girl. There are no
half-measures in our house, where charity is concerned. You see poor
relations taken in every day – but why? To save a manservant's or a
parlourmaid's wages: they're tossed a crust of bread, and get no pay.
But we understand charity after a different fashion. Anyway, you'll
see the girl for yourselves. And she's going to be pretty, to be sure.
You'll see.'

And, indeed, the nobility flocked in pilgrimage to see the prodigy
– to see the girl plumping out.

The masculine element was much quicker than the feminine to
notice Ana's extraordinary beauty. Only a few months after her fevers
she had grown miraculously, and her form had acquired a harmonious
amplitude which filled the Vetustan nobility with pride. The fact was
that the aristocratic type was never lost, whatever the rabble, who
would like there to be no such thing as class, might say. And so as
soon as the girl had been taken away from a vulgar life in the power
of a wrong-headed, wild liberal of a father, and had been well fed,
she had regained the racial type. It was resolved, by a unanimous
vote, that she was extremely beautiful. The lower class shared the
nobility's belief, and the middle class was of the same opinion. Her
fame as a beautiful woman was soon firmly established: Anita Ozores
was, by acclamation, the prettiest girl in town. When a stranger came
to Vetusta he was shown the cathedral tower, the Summer Promenade
and, if possible, the niece of the Ozores sisters. These were the three
wonders of the city.

Doña Agueda was grateful for this triumph in much the same way
as Pheidias might have felt grateful for the tribute of admiration
which the world paid to his Minerva.

'She's a regular Greek statue!' was the pronouncement of the
Marchioness de Vegallana, whose vision of Greek statues had been

shaped many years previously by one of her worshippers, a lover of ample forms.

'She's a Venus of Melons!' said a well-born young blade named Ronzal, alias the Student, in raptures.

'Rather than the Venus of Melos, the Venus of Medici,' corrected the youthful and already wise Saturnino Bermúdez, who knew what he meant, more or less.

'She is a Pheidias!' exclaimed the Marquis de Vegallana, who had travelled, and remembered that one said 'a Zurbarán', 'a Murillo', and so on and so forth, when talking about paintings.

And Bermúdez ventured to correct once more:

'In my opinion, she more closely resembles a work by Praxiteles.'

The marquis shrugged.

'A Praxiteles, then.'

The ladies were the ones who could judge best, for many of them had contrived to see Anita as one sees statues. They did not know whether she was a Pheidias or a Praxiteles, but they did know that she was a fine figure of a girl; a *bijou*, said the penniless baroness, who had spent a week at the Paris Exhibition.

The orphan girl's beauty was her salvation. She was admitted without reserve into the ranks of *persons of quality*, into the fellowship of the *classes*, on the grounds of her beauty. Nobody remembered the Italian dressmaker. Nor must Ana even mention her, by express command of the aunts. Everything had been forgotten, even her father's republicanism; everything; it was a general pardon. Ana was *of quality*; she honoured the classes with her beauty as a pure-blooded, silk-skinned horse honours the stables and even the house of a potentate.

The young ladies of the nobility were not very envious of Anita, however, because she was poor. For them beauty was a secondary matter. They placed a higher value on a dowry and clothes, and they believed that any *prospect* – any acceptable suitor – would do likewise. They knew what to expect. At coteries, balls and country outings, *the niece* would not lack worshippers, for most of the aristocratic young men were libertines – some of them being furtive about it and others more open – and would be attracted by Ana's beauty; but they would not marry her. The only care an aristocratic girl need take was to forbid her formal suitor – her future husband – to *pay court* to the orphan girl, at least in front of his future wife. If Anita were not careful, thought the heiresses, she might compromise herself to no avail. It was not probable that she would marry within the ranks of the nobility. Rich noblemen looked for rich aristocratic young ladies, their equals; poor noblemen looked for a comfortable settlement in the new part of Vetusta, in the Colony of Indians, as the aristocrats called the suburb of the returned emigrants. A plebeian emigrant, or *Vespucci*[2] – as the nobles also nicknamed them – paid dearly for the pleasure of being father-in-law to a title, or to a high-born gentleman.

The aunts' calculations about Ana's marriage had not undergone any modifications, in spite of her great beauty. Being pretty would not get her married to a noble. They would have to renounce any such idea and allow her to marry some rich commoner. Meanwhile, what was needed was to exercise great vigilance and to ensure that the girl was forewarned.

'In Vetustan high society,' Doña Anuncia often said, 'one needs to know how to trim with the times – something very hard to learn.'

Although the explanation of this balancing, or trimming with the times, was a little awkward, and even more so for an unmarried lady, who officially should know nothing about such things – as was the case with Doña Anuncia – the two sisters agreed that it was indispensable to give the girl some instructions.

Ana seldom allowed herself to reveal her desires, tastes or aversions – least of all her aversions – if they encroached on the area of her aunts' preferences, but one evening, on her return from the Vegallanas' select coterie, she could not restrain herself.

'Have you had an enjoyable time?' asked Doña Anuncia, who had remained in the dining-room, by the great fireplace, reading the *feuilleton* in *Las Novedades*.[3] (She was a liberal as regards *feuilletons*.)

'No, ma'am, I have not had an enjoyable time. And I would prefer not to return unless accompanied by one of you. When I go alone . . .'

'What?' exclaimed Doña Anuncia, suggesting with the harsh tone of the monosyllable that her niece would be wise not to utter a single word of censure of her own favourite coterie.

'When I go alone – I find those young gentlemen all too much of a bore.'

This was not what Ana had intended to say. Her aunt was well aware of the fact, but she wanted a clearer explanation and she retorted:

'Bore! Bore! Pray explain yourself, young lady. Do you mean to say that you consider Vetustan society to lack refinement?'

In the 'pray' and the irony, Ana noted that Doña Anuncia was displeased.

'It's not that, Aunt. I mean that some of them are very forward – I don't know what they take me for. You don't want me to be retiring, solemn, unsociable . . .'

'Of course not.'

'Well, *they* shouldn't be so forward. Even if Obdulia consents to certain things – I won't, I won't.'

'I will not have you comparing yourself to Obdulia. She is a nobody – I do not know how she was ever admitted into the coterie – and, so as to be able to put on airs and say that she is a close friend of the marchioness and her daughters, she tolerates absolutely anything. But you are a person of quality.'

'But it's not only Obdulia who tolerates – what I will not tolerate. Even Emma, Pilar and Lola allow liberties . . .'

'Don't you dare bring the marquis's daughters into this!' shouted the aunt, rising to her feet and dropping *Werther*[4] upon the threadbare carpet.

'I'm an ass,' Ana thought. 'I should have kept quiet.' Each time she failed in her resolution not to contradict her aunts she felt a kind of remorse, like the remorse of the artist who has made a mistake.

Doña Agueda came in. She had overheard the conversation from the parlour. The two sisters exchanged glances. The moment had come to explain that matter of trimming with the times.

'Anita, listen,' said the perfect cook, in a mellifluous voice. 'You are a young girl, and although we know little of the world, we do have some experience based on what one can observe.'

'Quite so. What we observe in others.'

'In the world into which you have entered, and to which you belong by right, one needs a special knack of – trimming with the times.'

'Yes, trimming with the times.'

'Above all, in one's dealings with men. You will have noticed that, in public, persons of quality never fail to observe the strictest and most meticulous – yes, decency.'

'Which is what matters most,' said Doña Anuncia, in the manner of one reciting the Decalogue.

'You can never have seen Manolito, or Paquito, or the young baron, or the viscount, or Mesía – who is not a noble, but who mixes with them – going one whit too far, in public. But when in the company of close friends, persons of quality exclusively, things are different.'

'Very different indeed,' said Doña Anuncia, realizing that, since she was the elder sister, it was her duty to continue the explanation of trimming with the times.

'Since we're all related in some way with each other,' she went on, 'we behave accordingly. And if young gentlemen come up very close when they speak to you, or make playful and witty allusions to the beauty of your shoulders, or to the fine turn of that tiny, tiny fraction of your leg which they glimpsed as you descended from your coach, none of this, or even a little more, so long as it is not too much more, should alarm you, or shock you, or make you take umbrage.'

'Not in the least,' added Doña Agueda, by way of support.

'To do otherwise is to betray a knowingness which you should not possess. Your innocence fits you to tolerate all such things.'

'That is the way of Pilar, Emma and Lola.'

'But . . .'

'But, my dear girl . . .'

'But if – as is not at all to be expected . . .'

'Not in the least . . .'

'If any man were to carry things too far, really too far, in particular if he were to take matters in earnest, and press his suit' (an expression popular in the times of Doña Anuncia's youth), 'press his suit in a proper manner, then you must be on your guard; let him say his piece, but don't let him touch you. From someone who proposes a formal relationship, you should not tolerate any pinches, or indeed anything that is not inoffensive. Taking umbrage is ridiculous, it's like not knowing what piece of cutlery to eat something with.'

'It's considered bad manners by persons of quality.'

'And tolerating too much is risky. You won't be marrying any of them.'

'I haven't the slightest wish to do so, Aunt,' said Anita, again unable to restrain herself, and at once regretting having spoken.

Doña Agueda smiled.

'You can keep your wishes to yourself,' exclaimed Doña Anuncia, on her feet again and dropping *Werther* back on to the floor. 'You are a very bumptious girl,' she added.

'Leave her be, she's just putting a good face on an ill game.'

'You're quite right; sour grapes, said the fox. But the important thing is that you should not forget what I'm telling you. Before setting foot in the marchioness's house you must leave aside those peevish airs and that curt tone of voice of yours – for that is sheer impertinence. What is correct, perfectly correct – and you can see that you receive all due praise for your good points – is that in public you should maintain the severe mien which merits no fewer eulogies than your pretty face and fine figure.'

'Yes, my dear girl,' interrupted Doña Agueda. 'It is vital to make the best of the gifts which the Lord has heaped so prodigiously upon you.'

Ana was dying of shame. Such praise was her greatest torment. She felt as if she were being put up to public auction. First Doña Agueda and then her sister dealt at great length with the question of the probable value of Ana's beauty, which they regarded as their own work. For Doña Agueda her beauty was like some superb sausage: she was proud of that face, just as she might have been proud of a black pudding. Everything else, in particular her slim waist, was the achievement of race, said Doña Anuncia, who prided herself on being slim, because she was thin.

When the two spinsters aired such matters the characteristics of the society procuress, who differs from other procuresses only in that she is noiseless, became discernible in them; and, as if presaging a witch-like old age, the blazing fire cast the ladies' distorted silhouettes on to the wall, where the movement of flames together with the movement of gestures formed an embryonic coven in the shadows.

What men, particularly returned emigrants, were like, the things which displeased them, how to fluster them, what had to be conceded at first and what should not be tolerated afterwards; all this was discussed at length, always concluding with the protestation that such great wisdom was born of the observation of others.

'Besides, neither your Aunt Agueda nor I ever had any leanings towards matrimony.'

Thus it was that the orphan girl had the subject of trimming with the times explained to her.

That night Anita wept in bed as she had often wept when in the power of Doña Camila. But she had enjoyed an excellent supper, and when she awoke next day she felt the delightful lethargy which was almost her only pleasure in life. There was no reason now why she should not get up at the normal time, and her housework summoned her at an early hour; but she always tried to be awake long before she had to leave her bed, to be able to savour her dreams, while snuggled in the sheets' gentle warmth.

In her dreams Ana disdained, one by one, all the praises sung to her beauty by the noble young gentlemen and the lawyerlings of Vetusta, and, indeed, by all who beheld her; but when she awoke, the sensuous dawning of her soul was enveloped in those honeyed praises, all condensed into one, as if they formed a cloud of sweet-smelling incense; and Ana savoured this perfume with delight. Since, as Tacitus commands, history should make bold to tell all, it must be stated that Anita, whose chastity depended upon her strength of character, found exquisite pleasure in verifying the justness of all this praise. It was true: she was beautiful. She could understand the fervour intimated by all the young men in Vetusta, some in looks, others in mysterious words. But was this love? No, love was in a still-distant future. Love must be too great, too beautiful to be so close to this wretched life which was suffocating her with the stupidity and the pettiness all around. Maybe love would never come, but she preferred going without it to profaning it. All Ana's apparent resignation was, deep inside her, an invincible pessimism. She had persuaded herself that she was condemned to live among fools; she believed in the superior strength of that general stupidity; she was right, in the face of them all, but she was under them, the loser. Besides, her poverty and her forsakenness were what most preoccupied her. She thought only of freeing her aunts of their burden, of that charitable work which every day was proclaimed with more solemnity by the old women.

She wanted to liberate herself, but how? She could not work for her living – the Ozores sisters would sooner kill her than allow that to happen – and so there was no decorous way out, other than marriage or the convent.

But Ana's devotion had already been judged and condemned by

the proper authorities. Her aunts, who knew something of her transient mysticism, had made cruel fun of it. Besides, the girl's false piety was complicated by the greatest and most ridiculous defect which a young lady could have in Vetusta: literature. This was the only serious vice which the aunts had discovered in the girl, and it had already been rooted out.

When Doña Anuncia came across a notebook full of poems, an inkwell and a pen on Ana's bedside table, she displayed no less astonishment than if she had found a pack of playing-cards, a bottle of spirits or a revolver. That was a mannish thing, indeed a vice of vulgar, plebeian men. If Ana had smoked cigars the old maid's stupefaction would not have been greater. 'A bluestocking in the family!'

'That was where the Italian dressmaker showed her colours. Ana's mother must have been a dancer, as Doña Camila had insinuated in her famous letter.'

The notebook full of poems was presented before the grave fathers of the aristocracy and of the cathedral chapter.

The Marquis de Vegallana, whose travels gave him a reputation as a cultured man, declared that the verses were free.

Doña Anuncia was beside herself with rage.

'So they are indecent, free? Who would have believed it? The dancing-girl . . .'

'No, Anuncita, don't upset yourself. Free means blank – they don't rhyme. You don't understand such things. Apart from all that, it's not bad poetry. But it's better for her not to write it. I've never met a bluestocking who was a respectable woman.'

This opinion was shared by the penniless baron, who had, for a period in Madrid, been kept by a poetess who translated *feuilletons*.

Señor Ripamilán, the old canon, said that the verses were quite fair, possibly good, but after a romantic-religious school which he found cloying.

'They are an imitation of Lamartine, in a pseudo-classical style. I don't like them, although they do reveal great ability in Anita. Besides, women should occupy themselves in gentler tasks. The Muses don't write, they inspire.'

The Marchioness de Vegallana, who read scandalous books with singular pleasure, found the verses guilty of sanctimoniousness. 'She wouldn't have the human and the divine mixed together. In church, hats off; in literature, anything goes.' Besides, she didn't like poetry, she preferred novels, with everything depicted in a lifelike manner and as it really is. 'There wasn't much she didn't know about the ways of the world. As far as *the niece* was concerned, there was no doubt but that those outbursts of false, novelesque piety must be eliminated. And, in any case, you needed a great deal of talent to be a bluestocking. She would have been one, if she had lived in a different atmosphere. The things those eyes of hers had seen!' She remembered some *Adventures of a Courtesan* which she had planned to write, back in her tender years, so rich in experience.

The protest of the *great world* of Vetusta against Ana's literary efforts was so general and so animated that she, too, came to believe that she had made a fool of herself and had been deluded by vanity.

Sometimes at night, alone in her bedroom, when tormented by sadness, Ana would again write verses, but she would tear them up at once and throw the paper out of the window so that her aunts should not discover the *corpus delicti*. Anita was subjected to such extremes of persecution, and her desire to express in writing her ideas and sorrows caused her so much vexation, that in the end she had to relinquish the pen altogether, swearing to herself that she would not be a bluestocking, that abominable hybrid being of which Vetustans spoke as they spoke of repulsive, hideous monsters.

Her young lady-friends, who had got wind of all this, and had never before found anything to criticize in Anita, took advantage of this weakness to try to *take her down a peg* in front of men – and they were sometimes successful. Nobody knew (though there was a belief that it was Obdulia) who had given Anita her nickname, but her lady-friends, and the young men whom she had slighted, called her George Sand.

Long after she had abandoned all her poetic pretensions, people still talked in front of her, with malicious enjoyment, of bluestockings. Ana would become flustered, as if the talk were of some crime of hers which had been discovered.

'In a beautiful woman, writing is an unpardonable vice,' said the little baron, fixing his gaze upon Anita in the belief that he was making himself agreeable to her.

'And who wants to marry a bluestocking?' Vegallana would say, in all innocence. 'I should not like to have a wife more talented than myself.'

The marchioness shrugged. It was her firm belief that her husband was an idiot. 'What queer ideas some husbands have about talent,' she thought, feeling well pleased about the past.

'I don't want my wife to wear the trousers,' added the effeminate little baron. And the marchioness, taking vengeance on him for her husband's remark, said:

'In that case, dear boy, yours must be a sansculotte household.'

Apart from the marchioness's mild defence, opinion was unanimous: a bluestocking was a living absurdity.

'On that point, the fools were not mistaken. She wouldn't write any more.' But she avenged herself for all the taunts by scorning them and spurning the advances of men whom her pride held to be no more than aristocratic apes. She accepted the homage which was paid to her beauty but, like some haughty eminences, rejected, one by one, the faithful who prostrated themselves before their idol. For her, the idea of love was irreconcilable with any of those nobles, formerly so audacious and now abject cowards in the face of her supreme disdain. She was too credulous in the vain, repugnant matters of the world in which she lived, and so she preferred Doña Anuncia's advice to her own judgement. At first she had imagined that she could, with the aid of a little cunning, have conquered any of those wealthy noblemen who dallied with all the girls and married the ones with the largest dowries. But such an idea seemed despicable and loathsome, and not once did she attempt to put her resourcefulness to the test, preferring to believe her aunt: those self-seeking aristocrats were not potential husbands. She became accustomed to this idea and regarded her friends and relations as she did fashion-plates in tailors' shops. Indeed, she found them so feeble in spirit that she thought of them as being made of drawing-paper.

In the end the young blades of the aristocracy had to confess that Ana was an exception; either she was even shrewder than her aunts or she was a genuinely virtuous woman.

'Hang it all, there was bound to be one such, somewhere!'

Middle-class seducers, always eager to worm their way into the aristocracy, made the same declaration: 'Ana is invulnerable.'

'She must be waiting for some Russian prince,' said Alvarito Mesía, whose life was led between commoners and nobles. Alvarito had never even said 'what pretty eyes you have' to Anita. Here was a pair of parallel prides.

Mesía went away to Madrid, to shake provincialism from his heels for a time. In Vetusta he left many victims of his good looks and amatory art, but he intended to make the greatest ravages on his return.

On the afternoon when Alvaro caught the stage-coach, Ana had gone with her aunts for a walk along the Madrid road. They met the coach. Alvaro, sitting in the front compartment, saw them and waved. His eyes met Ana's. They looked at each other as if they had never properly seen each other until that moment.

'What pretty eyes,' thought the Don Juan; 'I'd never really tasted them, until now.'

And he continued thinking:

'She must be one of my first.'

For more than an hour he could see that cloud of dust which looked like light and, in the midst of it, the niece's eyes.

And the niece carried the image of Don Alvaro home in her mind's eye.

She thought:

'He must be one of the least dreadful of them all. He seemed more distinguished and he wasn't a bore, there was a certain dignity about him – he was self-controlled – coldly elegant – the least stupid of the lot of them, no doubt.'

And her pessimism made her repeat for many days on end: The least stupid man in Vetusta has gone away.'

But after a month Ana no longer remembered Don Alvaro, nor did Don Alvaro remember Ana once he reached Madrid.

'Oh! the convent, the convent. That is the most natural and decorous solution. Either the convent or the emigrant.'

Ana's confessor, Ripamilán, refused to listen to her idea.

'Tut, tut! Tut, tut!' he exclaimed, forgetting that he was in church. 'Brides of Christ aren't made of what you're made of, my daughter. Bring happiness to a man – you can easily do that. Forget about makeshift vocations. It's all the fault of Romanticism, with its scandalous plays about pretty young nuns escaping in the arms of plumed troubadours and bandit chiefs.[5] I ought to tell you, Anita, that I've found you a suitor – a man from Aragon, like me. Go back home now, and I shall soon be there to tell you all about him. It would be a profanation here.'

Ripamilán's candidate was a magistrate, a native of Saragossa, young for a judge and somewhat mature, although not excessively so, for a suitor. Señorita Doña Ana Ozores was then nineteen years of age, and Señor Don Víctor Quintanar was over forty. But he was very well preserved. Ana begged Don Cayetano to say nothing to her aunts until she had known Quintanar for some time. If Doña Anuncia suspected that there was a suitor she would make her marry him without further consideration.

'That's fair enough. I, too, believe that such matters are better decided by the heart. Moratín, my beloved Moratín, gives us a splendid demonstration of the fact in his immortal comedy, *Maidens Choosing*.'[6]

So that was settled.

If only Doña Anuncia had known that the long dreamt-of suitor, who was beginning to be rather slow in making his appearance, passed daily by their side in the Mall (the Winter Promenade), or on the Madrid road, with its borders of tall poplars converging in the distance!

Ana had noticed that every afternoon they met Don Tomás Crespo, an intimate in their home, with a gentleman who devoured her with his eyes. Don Tomás was one of the few people whom she esteemed, because in him she found moral qualities rare in Vetusta: tolerance, expansive cheerfulness and an unprejudiced attitude towards superstitious belief.

While Don Tomás stopped to greet them, the other gentleman would look at them from a distance. He was Quintanar, the magistrate. It was true that he was not badly preserved. He had tidy clothes and an agreeable aspect.

For the Señoritas Ozores, 'who had not yet seen him in any of *their* houses, he was an *outsider'* – a word with a special meaning in Vetusta.

'He is a magistrate,' Crespo had told them one day. 'A good, honest, brave Aragonese gentleman – a fine huntsman, most honourable, and very fond of the theatre. He acts like Carlos Latorre.[7] You should see him, particularly in the theatre of the old school.'

This was all the aunts knew about the suitor who was being prepared for them behind their backs.

Crespo discovered that the girl had some notion of what was happening. One afternoon, acting on the spur of the moment, he stopped the Ozores sisters on the Madrid road and introduced them to a magistrate, Señor Don Víctor Quintanar. The two gentlemen accompanied the ladies during their promenade, leaving them in the gloomy porch of Ozores Mansion. Doña Anuncia made the ritual declaration that her house was always open to Don Víctor. He assumed that the aunts knew of his honourable pretensions and, on the following day, in black frock-coat and trousers, he visited the noble ladies. Ana was very amiable towards him. He seemed most agreeable.

The only person to whom she dared say anything about what was happening inside her was Don Tomás Crespo, who claimed that he was not prejudiced in any way, not even in favour of being unprejudiced, which was one of the silliest prejudices there was.

Ana was very observant. She believed herself to be superior to those around her, and thought that somewhere there must be a society in which people lived as she wanted to live and shared her ideas. But in the meantime, Vetusta was her prison, its mindless routine was a sea of ice which held her fast. Her aunts, aristocratic young ladies, female pharisees – all of this was stronger than she. She could not fight back, and surrendered unconditionally, reserving the right to despise her tyrant, and to live on dreams.

But Crespo was an exception, a true friend who could read between the lines what her aunts, the baron and all the rest would not have understood in tomes as big as houses.

Don Tomás was nicknamed Frillity because if he was told about one of those lapses which small towns are wont to punish with hypocritical and exaggerated displays of outraged morality, he would shrug his shoulders, moved to do so not by indifference but by philosophy, and exclaim with a smile: 'What do you expect? That's just human *frillity*, as someone once said.' Meaning frailty. That was Don Tomás's motto: man is frail.

He himself had been frail. He had once had an excessive belief in the laws of adaptation to the environment. But this will be spoken of in due course. Eight years later, his noble mania for forgiving everything shone out in its full splendour.

He had a keen scent for goodness in human souls, and had divined spiritual treasures in Anita.

'Look here, Don Víctor,' he would say to his friend, 'that girl is worthy of a king or, at least, a lawyer who will soon be a chief stipendiary magistrate, like yourself, for example. Imagine a gold-mine in a country where nobody knows how to work gold-mines; there you have Anita in my beloved Vetusta. The best things in Vetusta are the trees.'

'Leave the flora be, Don Tomás.'

'You're right, I was wandering. I was saying that Anita is a first-rate woman. Can you picture that lovely body of hers, that's made butter and cheese of you? Well when you see her soul you will melt like that same butter in the sun. I should point out that for me a good soul is simply a healthy soul; goodness is born of health.'

'You are something of a materialist, but I shall not grow angry about that. You were saying that the girl . . .'

'I am the blazes, my dear sir! begging your pardon. Don't hang labels on me. I detest all systems. What I am saying is that I only believe in the goodness given by nature. Health must enter a tree through its roots. Well, the soul is just the same.'

And he continued philosophizing, to reach the conclusion that Anita was the finest girl in all Vetusta.

He added that he had taken the girl aside one day, of his own accord, and recommended Señor Quintanar to her.

'He was the only suitor worthy of her. Like trees which last for centuries, he was, at forty-odd, in his youth, his early youth. A ten-year-old dog is older than a hundred-year-old crow, if it's true that crows last for centuries.'

Ana held all Frillity's advice in high esteem. She had consented to receive Quintanar, but without any obligation, and on the same conditions as she had imposed upon Don Cayetano: the aunts were to know nothing. Don Víctor agreed to this style of suitorship.

'Look here,' said Frillity, 'a little secrecy is the spice of such affairs, so the girl will take the bait all the sooner – you'll see.'

Ana did not notice the time slipping by when she was at Quintanar's side.

'He had ideas which were pure, noble, lofty, and even poetic.'

He did not dye his grey hairs, he was straightforward, although his language was rather declamatory and high-flown. This defect was due to the many verses by Lope de Vega and Calderón which he knew by heart. It was hard for him not to speak like Sancho Ortiz and Don Gutierre Alonso.[8]

But, when alone, Ana would say to herself: 'Isn't it folly to marry without being in love? Didn't they say that her religious vocation was false, that she wouldn't be a good bride for Christ, because she didn't love Him enough? Well, if she didn't love Don Víctor either, she should not marry him.'

Ripamilán, when consulted, replied that 'between a magistrate – who was not even a presiding magistrate – and the Saviour of the world there was a great difference. Did not Anita confess that Don Víctor was to her liking? Yes. Well, she would find him more attractive every day. In the convent, on the other hand, she who begins without love ends in despair.'

Don Cayetano, who could be serious when necessary, tried to convince his young friend that her piety, although it was sufficient for the life in the world of an honourable woman, was not strong enough for the sacrifices of the cloister.

'All she had told him about having wept with love as she read St Augustine and St John of the Cross meant nothing. It had been an effect of the critical age through which she was passing at the time. As for Chateaubriand – she should take no notice of him. That business about taking the veil without any vocation was all very well in the theatre, but in the world there were no Manriques or Tenorios[9] climbing into convents, thank God. True piety consisted in bringing happiness to such a perfect and enamoured gentleman as Señor Quintanar, his fellow-Aragonese friend.'

Ana gradually relinquished the idea of being a nun. Her conscience cried out to her that this was not a sacrifice which she could make. The cloister was probably the same as Vetusta. It would not be with Jesus that she would live, but with sisters who, she was sure, would be more like her aunts than St Augustine and St Teresa. The nobility got wind of Ana's 'mystical whims', and the ladies who had called her George Sand spoke their minds again, criticizing her latest caprice with even greater cruelty.

That she was virtuous, in so far as nothing *shady* was known of her, was generally confessed; but this was a poor reason for thinking that one had a vocation to sainthood.

'Were the rest of them, perchance, some crowd of hussies?'

'She is pretty, but over-proud,' said the penniless baroness, whose husband and son were both in love with the young niece, but in vain.

Contrary to Frillity's expectations, Ana was in no hurry to make up her mind. But her aunts made it up for her by discovering another suitor. The latest wooer was the longed-for and feared American, Don Frutos Redondo, ex-Matanzas[10] with a cargo of millions of dollars. He had come back determined to build the best villa in Vetusta, own the best carriages in Vetusta, be a deputy for Vetusta, and marry the prettiest woman in Vetusta. He saw Anita, was told that she was the beauty of the town, and felt the prick of love's arrows. He was warned that his dollars were not sufficient for the conquest of this fortress, and this made him fall much more deeply in love. He had himself introduced in the Ozores household, and asked Doña Anuncia for the niece's hand.

Doña Anuncia shut herself in the dining-room with Doña Agueda, and at the termination of the conference Anita was summoned. Doña Anuncia rose to her feet by the pseudo-feudal fireplace, dropping to the carpet *Ethelwina*,[11] a novel which had been the delight of her youth, and exclaiming:

'Young lady – my dear girl, the moment has arrived which could be decisive in your existence.' (This was the style of *Ethelwina*.) 'Your aunt and I have made every kind of sacrifice for you. Not even our great poverty, concealed from the world with the utmost difficulty, has prevented us from surrounding you with every desirable comfort. Charity is inexhaustible, but not our resources. We have never reminded you of what you owe us' (they reminded her every day at luncheon and at dinner), 'we have forgiven you your origins, that is to say those of your unfortunate mother; all, all has here been forgotten. Well then, you would be repaying all this with the darkest ingratitude, with the most criminal ingratitude, if, to the proposition which we are about to put to you, you were to reply with a refusal which would be – indescribable.'

'Indescribable,' repeated Doña Agueda. 'But I don't think there's any need for a sermon,' she added, 'for the girl will jump with joy when she knows what it's all about.'

'That is what I wish to know; in what way I can be of service to you both, to whom I owe so much.'

'Everything.'

'Yes, everything, dear Aunt.'

'As I suppose', Doña Anuncia went on, 'that you no longer even remember that crazy idea of becoming a nun . . .'

'No, ma'am . . .'

'In that case,' interrupted Doña Agueda, 'since you can't want to be left alone in the world when we are no longer here . . .'

'Nor can you be involved in a secret flirtation, for that would be indecent . . .'

'And since we have done all we can . . .'

'And since it is your duty to accept the happiness that is being offered you . . .'

'You will die with delight to know that Don Frutos Redondo, the richest man in La Colonia, has this very day asked for your hand.'

Against the express command of her aunts, Ana did not die with delight. She remained silent, not daring to meet the offer with a flat refusal.

But Doña Anuncia needed no more to let loose the basilisk of fury which she carried in her bowels. Her shadow, amidst all the other shadows on the wall, at times resembled that of a gigantic witch; at other times, multiplied by the flickering of the flames and the old woman's jerks and contortions, it represented all hell let loose. There were moments when Doña Anuncia's shadow had three heads on the wall and three or four others on the ceiling, and it seemed that screams and shrieks were coming from all of them, so strident were her vociferations.

Even Doña Agueda was horrified.

After that scene, the niece spent nine days confined to her bedroom. When the novena of her confinement, which was rather like being detained in custody, was complete, Doña Anuncia appeared, calm, dignified, severe, to pronounce sentence. 'The dancer's daughter – who could now doubt that the dressmaker had been a dancer? – the dancer's daughter would not be denied a bed in the ancestral mansion; but they, the aunts, had no food left to put upon the table, the girl had eaten it all.'

Ana wrote to Frillity.

And on the following day Don Víctor Quintanar, dressed up to the nines, as on the occasion of his first visit, entered the Ozoreses' withdrawing-room. He had come to ask for the hand of Ana, 'who was not, he believed, altogether indifferent to him'.

'He was taking this step earlier than he had intended, because he had recently been promoted. He was to depart for Granada with the position of presiding magistrate, and he wished to take his wife with him, if his ardent desire was fulfilled. He had his salary, and some vineyards and not a few flocks in La Almunia de Don Godino.[12] He would never have ventured to solicit the hand of such an eximious, illustrious and beautiful young lady if he were not able to offer her, not opulence but at least an *aurea mediocritas*,[13] as the Latin poet had said.'

Doña Anuncia was bedazzled. Don Godino – *mediocritas* – the Cross of Isabella the Catholic! It was a great temptation.

Frillity had informed Don Víctor, as he pinned the cross to his chest, that Doña Anuncia was enamoured of speeches which she did not understand, and of decorations.

As Don Víctor spoke, he believed he was making a fool of himself. But the old woman was fascinated.

'Don Frutos,' she thought, 'had pounded clods in the suburbs of Vetusta, twelve years previously; she remembered having seen him in shirt-sleeves.'

Señorita Ozores replied that 'she could not dispose of her niece's hand, even if the girl were agreeable, without consultation, without the consent of the nobility, of persons of quality'.

The Gentlemen of the Robe, the lawyers of the Royal Provincial Court, were the secondary aristocracy in Vetusta, although they did not cut such a dash now as in former times.

But justice was respected with a superstitious terror, inherited through the centuries. The hottest-headed liberals, who ranted about anarchy and burning everything, would tremble at the voice of an usher in the criminal court shouting at a witness who had crossed his legs: 'Order in court!'

The aristocracy – the primary aristocracy – was of opinion that it would be a foolish marriage for Ana to make.

She made it.

Don Frutos went back to Matanzas, promising to return avenged, that is to say with many more millions of dollars. He kept his promise.

A month later, Ana Ozores de Quintanar, together with her chivalrous husband, left Vetusta by the Madrid road in the front compartment of the same stage-coach in which she had seen Don Alvaro Mesía departing.

All Vetusta went to bid them farewell: both the nobility and the middle classes. Frillity had tears in his eyes.

'As soon as you can return, you must,' he said, with one foot on the step and his head inside the coach. 'Then you will be the First Lady of Vetusta, Anita – the Judge's Wife!'

'The law does not permit it, because of her aunts,'[14] replied Don Víctor.

'Bah! A way would soon be found round that. You will be the Judge's Wife.'

Don Cayetano also tried to climb on to the footboard, but he could not manage it.

Doña Anuncia and Doña Agueda had remained in their withdraw-ing-room, in almost complete darkness, sighing, surrounded by a few gentlemen-friends and lady-friends, perhaps the same ones who, on another occasion, had come with their condolences for the civil death of Don Carlos.

'And she is happy to be leaving,' said the baron.

'Psha! I am sure she is.'

'Youth knows no gratitude.'

'Step aside there, we're setting off,' shouted the stage-coach lad.

And the coach departed. Don Víctor pressed between his hands the hands of the wife whom an entire town envied him.

A 'goodbye!' filled the air in the Plaza Nueva. It was a sad goodbye, a farewell to the wonder of the town. All Vetusta witnessed the departure of the new presiding magistrate's wife as it might have witnessed the cathedral tower, another wonder, being borne away.

Meanwhile, Ana was thinking that in the throng standing in admiration of her beauty there was perhaps no one more worthy of possessing it than this man Don Víctor, in spite of his forty-odd years – the 'odd' being something of a mystery.

When, close to nightfall, as the horses dragged their coach uphill, the new presiding magistrate asked Ana if he was fortunate enough, perchance, to be the first man whom she had loved, she bowed her head and said, with a melancholy which sounded to him like sensual self-abandonment:

'Yes, yes, the first, the only one.'

'No, she didn't love him; but she would try to love him.'

Night fell. Ana, her head resting against the shabby cushions in the old carriage, closed her eyes, pretending to sleep, and listened to the jumbled, thunderous noises of the glass, iron and wood of the ramshackle stage-coach; in the din she seemed to hear the last farewell cries.

Not a single one of the men below her back there had ever spoken to her of love, nor had any inspired her with love. Going back over all the years of her aimless youth, she remembered, as the greatest amatory delight for which she could, perhaps, be called to account, an occasional glance from some stranger during one of those prom-enades along roads bordered with trees full of sparrows and gold-finches.

Between Ana and the young men of the society in which she lived, her pride and their stupidity had soon erected a wall of ice.

'They would not marry her, Doña Anuncia had said, because she was poor. But Ana had forestalled them, scorning them for their fatuity and mediocrity.'

If any man had attempted to behave towards her as towards Obdulia, he had soon encountered a haughty disdain and a cruel irony which could have frozen a burning ember.

'Perhaps, although it was by no means certain, there might be, among those men who admired her from a distance, devouring her with their eyes, someone worthy of being loved – but her aunts had ensured that distances were kept, as good tone demanded. And the poor young lawyers, or whatever, who were perhaps democrats in theory, respected such prejudices and participated in them in spite of themselves. They kept away.' All those men who had made some effect – although never a great one – on Ana, as they spoke with their eyes, were anything but prospects. In Vetusta, the unmoneyed young are unable to earn a living – they earn a pittance at the most. Young men and girls drink each other in with their eyes, they love each other, they even tell each other of their love – but then they *break off*: he has no position; the girls lose their beauty and finish up haunting churches; the men put aside their shiny top hats, muffle themselves in cloaks, and become gamblers.

All those who want to prosper leave the town. The only rich people there are those who have inherited wealth and those who have made a fortune far from sleepy Vetusta.

'She could have had a choice between returned emigrants, rich merchants, and fatuous, uncouth, grotesque firstlings,' Ana went on thinking. 'Don Frutos Redondo could speak to that. But, besides, why deceive herself? It was not in Vetusta, it could not be in that miserable corner, that she would find the reality of her dreams, the hero of her poem, who had first been called Germán, then St Augustine the Bishop of Hippo, then Chateaubriand, and then a hundred and one other names, and who was all grandeur and splendour, and sensitive, rare, choice gentleness.

'And now she was married. Now it was a crime – a real crime, unlike the incident of the ferry-boat at Trébol – to think about men. Don Víctor was the great wall of China to her dreams. To imagine anything in excess of the five feet and various inches of the man by her side was a sin. It was all over – without ever having started.'

Ana opened her eyes and looked at her Don Víctor who, by the light of a travelling lamp, a silk cap pulled down to his ears, his brow furrowed, sat calmly reading *Jealousy the Greatest Monster, or the Tetrarch of Jerusalem*,[15] by the immortal Calderón de la Barca.

VI

The Gentlemen's Club of Vetusta occupied a large, solitary building, its stonework blackened by the ravages of damp, in a little square, dirty and dismal, near St Peter's, the ancient church close by the cathedral. The younger members wanted to move, but a change of address would be the death of the society, according to the serious, longer-established element. The Gentlemen's Club did not move, and it continued patching up its leaks and other ancestral ailments as best it could. Three generations had yawned in those dark, narrow rooms, and the solemnity of inherited boredom was not to be exchanged for the hazards of a dubious future in the new part of town, La Colonia. Moreover, said the elders, if the club ceased to reside in La Encimada, that would be the end of the club. The club was an aristocrat.

Generally, the ballroom was shown to outsiders with pride, while the remainder of the building was admitted to be of little interest.

The servants at this establishment wore uniforms like those of the urban police. The outsider who summoned a servant, not being used to this state of affairs, might think that he was about to be arrested. All the servants had bad manners, inherited like their uniforms. Indeed, they had been provided with uniforms so that there should be some way of telling that they were the servants.

In the hall two porters sat by a pine table. It had been a long-established custom that these gentlemen did not greet members on their way in or out. But now that Pepe Ronzal, who had observed other usage during his short journeys, was on the committee, the porters nodded when an ordinary member went by, and even emitted a low growl which a lively imagination might interpret as a word of greeting; if it was a committee member they rose about half a hand's-breadth from their chairs; if it was Ronzal, they rose a full hand's-breadth; and if Don Alvaro Mesía, the president of the club, passed by, they jumped to their feet and stood to attention like recruits.

Beyond the hall there were three or four passages converted into rooms for waiting in, resting in, conversing in, playing dominoes in – all haphazardly mixed up together. Further on there was another, more luxurious room, with large hearths which consumed a great deal of firewood, but not as much as the servants claimed. The firewood gave rise to serious polemics at annual general meetings in December. From this room the strident domino had been outlawed, and it was the meeting-place of the gravest and most important personages in Vetusta. There must be no disturbance in this room because at its eastern end, behind a majestic *portière* of crimson velvet, was the ombre-room,[1] known as the red parlour. Silence must reign here and in the next room as well, if possible. Ombre had previously been next to billiards, but the noise of cues and balls annoyed the ombre-players, who betook themselves to the red parlour, which was the reading-room at that time. The reading-room went away to join the billiards. The ombre-room never saw the light of day: it was always sunk in murky shadow, which made the candles' dismal flames seem palpable, like miners' lamps in the bowels of the earth.

Don Pompeyo Guimarán, a philosopher who hated ombre, called the occupants of the red parlour 'the counterfeiters'. He imagined that no lawful activities could ever take place in that den, which one entered in mysterious silence and where all joyfulness, all expansion of the spirit was repressed. On entry into the red parlour, the most boisterous youngsters took on a premature seriousness, like young priests of some strange religious cult. Entering there was the equivalent in Vetusta of putting aside the *toga praetexta* and assuming the *toga virilis*.[2] There was always some pallid youth playing or watching the play, deep in concentration, affecting a disdain for the vain pleasures of the world (perhaps out of satiety) and a preference for the serious preoccupations of the *codille* and *sans prendre*. To examine with some care the habitual priests of this ceremonious and circumspect cult of the spade and the club is to make the acquaintance of intellectual Vetusta in one of its characteristic aspects.

Indeed, although the Director of Public Works asserted that all Vetustans were fluky card-players, this was merely a pretext to go on upstairs to the gaming-room, the *chamber of crime*,[3] in search of more substantial and rapid gains, for ombre was played in the Gentlemen's Club of Vetusta with a perfection which was now famous. There were some inexpert players, and indeed there had to be some, for, otherwise, who would beat whom? But the facts protested against the Director of Public Works's assertion. From Vetusta, and only from Vetusta, emanated those illustrious ombre-players who, once they reached higher spheres, took flight and occupied eminent posts in state administration, owing it all to the science of trumping.

There is a table in each of the four corners of the room, and four more tables in the middle. Half of the tables are occupied. All around, seated or standing, are various onlookers, most of them the slaves of their vice. Little is said. Usually a request for a cigarette. Little advice is proffered. It is not required, or it would be pointless. Basilio Méndez, who works for the municipal corporation, is the stoutest champion among those present. He is pale and thin. No one can tell whether his clothes are those of a workman or a respectable person, as they say in Vetusta. His earnings are not sufficient for his needs, for he has a wife and five children; ombre is a help to him; he is respected. He plays like a man with a joyless job of work to do, always in a bad humour, brusque, seldom replying if he is spoken to. He is minding his own business: a three-storey house which he is building, at ombre's expense, near the Mall. At his side is Don Matías, the solicitor; he plays at ombre in order to keep away from monte.[4] When fortune does not smile on him *upstairs*, he comes down and provides himself with the opportunity of winning at ombre as much as he can and of losing very little – because if he starts losing he stops playing. The man who is out of the play at the moment, because he has just finished dealing, is the goose that lays the golden eggs for the solicitor and Don Basilio. They are killing him – of consumption. He is the eldest son, the heir in tail, of a rich village family, and he is nicknamed Herring-tail. Once he used to come to town at fair-time, to play at ombre; then he became a provincial deputy, in order to play at ombre; and in the end he took up residence in Vetusta so as never to be far from those champions whom he so admires while, unawares, he makes them rich. The ombre played in his village gives him no pleasure. Herring-tail plays from three o'clock in the afternoon until two in the morning, with no break other than that which is necessary for a rough-and-ready supper. Don Basilio and the solicitor take charge of plucking him by turns, relieving each other, although sometimes they both pluck him at the same time. The fourth card-player could be anybody. At the other tables the games are more even. There are many outsiders playing, most of them office clerks.

It is an axiom that good breeding is revealed at the gambling-table. There are many well-bred people in the room but, since the greatest confidence reigns among them, expressions such as the following can often be heard:

'I tell you that you did give me it.'

'I tell you that I did not.'

'I tell you that you did.'

'You are lying, then.'

'You are monstrous polite, sir.'

'Politer than you, sir.'

It was all about a counterfeit five-peseta piece.

In order that harmony might subsist, thanks to a kind of equilibrium established by nature among the gamblers' personalities, some ombre-players were blusterers with devilish tempers, and others, for example Herring-tail, were as peaceful as lambs and as timid as doves.

Don Basilio would assert that the young man's play was not as correct as it should be. Herring-tail would defend the rights of his dignity, and then the council-worker would shout: 'I'm not taking insolence from anybody!' And he would strike the table with his fist.

Herring-bone would keep quiet and go on being given codille.

These disputes, which were infrequent, broke the silence for a few instants, but calm was soon restored and the place was once again a temple, never to be defiled by rivers of blood.[5]

The reading-room, which also did duty for a library, was narrow and not very long. In the middle there was an oblong table covered with green baize and surrounded by armchairs upholstered in utrecht velvet. The library itself was a walnut-wood bookcase of no great size, built into the wall. The wisdom of the society was there represented by the Royal Academy's *Dictionary* and *Grammar*. The purchase of these books had been motivated by the recurrent disputes between members who disagreed about the meaning and even the spelling of certain words. There was also an incomplete set of the *Revue des deux mondes,* and other sets of various illustrated magazines. *L'Illustration* had been discontinued in an outburst of patriotism, because of a print in which some unidentified Spanish kings were shown fighting bulls. On the occasion of this radical and patriotic step many excellent speeches were made at the annual general meeting, with timely references to the heroes of Sagunto, the heroes of Covadonga and, finally, the heroes of 1808.[6] In the bottom drawers of the bookcase there were works which provided more substantial instruction, but the key to that section had been lost.

When a member asked for one of these books, the porter, with a bad grace, came up to the asker and made him repeat his request.

'Yes, sir, the *Chronicle of Vetusta.'*

'But are you sure it is there?'

'Yes, sir, it is.'

'The fact is,' and *sir* – the porter – scratched an ear, 'since it is not customary . . .'

'What is not customary?'

'Very well, then, I will see if I can find the key.'

The porter turned and walked away at tortoise-pace.

The member, who must of course be a new one to entertain such pretensions, could amuse himself in the meantime by looking at the map of Russia and Turkey, and the paternoster in pictures, which decorated the walls of this centre for recreation and instruction. Back came the porter with his hands in his pockets and a malicious smile on his lips.

'It is just as I thought, my dear sir. The key has been mislaid.'

Members of longer standing regarded the book-shelves as if they were painted on the wall.

More use was made of newspapers and illustrated magazines. So much so, that the former disappeared almost every night and any prints of merit were carefully torn out of the latter. The theft of newspapers was one of the difficult questions to be resolved at meetings. What was to be done? Chain the papers up? The members would tear the pages out or carry off both paper and chain. In the end, it was resolved to leave the newspapers unfettered, but to exercise the utmost vigilance. It was to no avail. Don Frutos Redondo, the richest of the Americans, could not sleep at night without first reading the Club's copy of *El Imparcial* in bed. And he was not going to transfer his bed to the reading-room. He took the newspaper away with him. The five céntimos which he saved in this way smacked of glory. With regard to the writing-paper, which also kept disappearing, and was more expensive, it was resolved to give one sheet to any member who made an urgent request for it – and he could consider himself lucky to get even that. The porter had acquired the attitude of a prison warder in these dealings. He regarded members who were fond of reading as people of dubious probity, and treated them with scant respect. He did not always come when he was called, and he often refused to replace rusty pens.

There was room for twelve around the table. It did not often happen that there were as many readers as that, except at the post-hour. The majority of the lovers of knowledge among the members only read the news.

Among the subscribers to the reading-room the most worthy of consideration was an apoplectic gentleman who had exported cereals to England and believed himself duty-bound to read the foreign press. He arrived each evening at nine o'clock without fail, picked up *Le Figaro,* and then *The Times,* which he placed on top of it, donned his gold-rimmed spectacles and, lulled by the faint whistling sound emitted by the gas-burners, fell into a gentle sleep over the world's leading newspaper. It was a right which nobody disputed. Shortly after this gentleman died, of apoplexy, over *The Times,* it was discovered that he knew no English. Another assiduous reader was a young aspirant to vacancies in tax and registry offices, who devoured *La Graceta Oficial* from cover to cover, omitting not so much as a single auction-notice. He was a one-volume Alcubilla:[7] he knew by heart everything that has been done, undone, made good and destroyed again by our public administration.

By his side there usually sat a gentleman with a secret vice: writing letters to Madrid newspapers conveying the most contradictory pieces of news. He signed his letters *Your Correspondent*, and whenever a Madrid newspaper spoke of 'The Latest Events in Vetusta' it was all his work. On the following day he would deny his own story in another paper, and it emerged that 'The Latest Events in Vetusta' had not taken place. In this way he had become an out-and-out sceptic on the subject of the press. 'He knew only too well how newspapers were put together!' When the French and the Germans came to blows, *Your Correspondent* had his doubts about the war: perhaps it was something invented by speculators. He was not convinced that anything was really the matter until the capitulation of Metz.[8]

The poet Trifón Cármenes was another member who never failed to be on hand when the mail arrived. He would scan various newspapers with feverish anxiety and disappear carrying one more disappointment in his soul: for 'they had not printed it' – 'it' being a poem or fantastic tale which he had sent to some newspaper and which the editors somehow never brought themselves to publish. Cármenes, who in competitions held in Vetusta carried off all the rose-garlands, could not manage to find a place for his verses upon the printing-presses of Madrid – in spite of his use of all the refined good manners in the world in the letters which he sent recommending his compositions. His customary formula was as follows: 'My dear and most highly esteemed sir, Pray find enclosed some verses which, if perchance you should deem them worthy of such a signal honour, you might like to bring to public light in the columns of your distinguished newspaper. Written without pretension. . . .' But it was to no avail; they never appeared. A year later he asked for their return. But 'Manuscripts could not be returned'. He made use of the draft and published the thing in *El Lábaro*, Vetusta's reactionary newspaper.

Another constant reader was a feeble-minded old fogy who never went to bed without reading the leaders of all the papers available in the club. He took singular delight in the ponderous prose of a newspaper with a reputation for sagacity and circumspection. Concepts were wrapped in such euphemisms, preteritions and circumlocutions, and were themselves, because of their fine-spun subtlety, so fragile, that the old fellow was always left in the dark.

'What sagacity!' he would say, not understanding a word.

This was why he believed in the said sagacity; for if he were ever to catch sight of it, it would thereupon cease to exist.

One night this reader of editorials awoke his wife with the words:

'Hey, Paca, I can't sleep, you know. Let's see if you understand something I read in the paper today. "We cannot avoid avoiding the conclusion that it is reprehensible that . . ." Do you understand it, Paca? Do they think it's reprehensible or don't they? I shan't be able to get any sleep until I settle the matter.'

These and other assiduous readers hand the newspapers around in silence, devouring reports which they read over and again in eight or ten dailies. Such is the nourishment of these cultured spirits. By eleven o'clock at night, they have all retired, satisfied, to their beds, convinced that the cashier in this or that establishment has indeed absconded with the funds. They have read it in eight or ten different sources. These gentlemen, all respectable and worthy of esteem, are the servile slaves of Madrid newsmongers. The greater part of their perishable stock of knowledge consists of cuttings from *La Correspondencia*, which in the offices of the poorer newspapers is passed on, like the ball in a game of catch, from one pair of scissors to the next.

It often happened, when in the midst of a library silence it almost seemed that one could hear the sapient readers' brains working, that the clamour of an earthquake suddenly shook the floor and the windows. Old members took no notice and did not even raise their eyes; new ones looked up in terror at the ceiling and the walls, expecting to see the building collapse. That was not what was happening; it was merely that the gentlemen playing billiards were banging the floor with the butts of their cues. The members' ingenious good humour was proverbial.

By eleven o'clock at night no one was left in the reading-room. The porter, half-asleep, would fold up the newspapers, turn down the gas, and leave the room in almost complete darkness, going back to his own quarters to sleep.

Now was the time for the arrival of Don Amadeo Bedoya, a captain in the artillery, in civilian dress, muffled in a broad-caped box coat. He looked all around: there was nobody there, and darkness was his ally. With supreme caution he approached the bookcase. From his pocket he took a key, he opened the bottom drawer, picked up a book, put in its place another book hidden under his cape, tucked the first book into the folds of his box coat and locked the drawer. After taking a deep breath he approached the table, whistled the national anthem, and pretended to glance through the newspapers. He, bothering with newspapers! To keep up pretences he stayed there for five minutes, and then departed in triumph. He was not a thief; he was a bibliophile. Bedoya's key was the one which had been lost by the porter. Don Amadeo was the Don Saturnino Bermúdez of the military. He had once been a valiant soldier, but then he had had the honour of being elected president of an infantry athenaeum, and had been obliged to prepare and pronounce a speech, finding, to his great surprise, that he was an excellent orator in his own opinion and in that of his superiors. One thing leading to another, he had ended up as a man of letters, to the extent of solemnly swearing to himself, with all the vigour that is so becoming in defenders of the fatherland, to become a scholar. Vetustans had begun to take notice of the military man who knew more about letters than many civilians, and Bedoya himself, amused by what he regarded as a contrast between artillery and literature, had warmed to the task. In time he had become either a corresponding or full member of many scientific, artistic and literary societies. He excelled at history and botany, especially the latter in its relationships with horticulture. He was a specialist in the diseases of the potato and had produced a treatise on the subject which had somehow not yet been awarded a government prize. He also had a gift for military biography. He knew of various lieutenant-generals who had been veritable Farneses or Spinolas[9] without the world's suspecting it, and had brought to light the life of a certain brigadier who, not having been in command of the action on a certain field, would, if he had been, have conquered the glory of a Napoleon, instead of losing his positions – as the inept general had done.

The sources for this kind of biography, of people who could have been important, were to be found in books such as those in the bottom drawer of the bookcase in the club. There must have been other copies about the world, but nobody knew of them, and Bedoya belonged to that class of scholars who find merit in reproducing what no one else has seen fit to read. As soon as he saw upon his own paper the paragraphs which he copied in the neat, graceful copper-plate hand that God had given him, he considered them to be all his own work. But antiques were his forte. An *objet d'art* had no merit in his eyes, even though it dated from the time of Noah, unless it was his. Whereas Bermúdez loved antiquity for itself, dust for dust's sake, Bedoya was more subjective, as he put it – he needed the cherished object to belong to him. 'If only he could talk! He would make Bermúdez, the canon theologian, and all the rest of them look pretty small.' But he could not talk. He would probably go to prison if he talked. 'Well, between ourselves, he owned' (and he glanced from side to side as he spoke), 'he owned a superb manuscript in the hand of Philip II, a political document of great importance.' He had stolen it from the National Archives at Simancas. How? That was his proud secret. So Bedoya, certain of his superiority, looked down his nose at other antiquarians, and was silent. He was silent for fear of prison.

The *chamber of crime* – the room where games of chance, to be exact roulette and monte, were played – was on the second floor. It was reached after traversing many dark, narrow passages. The authorities had never disturbed the calm of this hidden and secluded refuge of the aleatory arts – not even in times of greatest public morality. At the request of authors of articles in the local press, and in particular the chief contributor to El Lábaro, prostitution was cruelly persecuted, but the persecution of gaming was not possible. Yet how could 'those contemptibles who trafficked with their bodies' (as Cármenes called them writing El Lábaro's leaders incognito) escape persecution, when incitements worded in such powerful language were being published daily in the local press?

Almost every morning an article would appear, entitled, for example, 'And What of Those Cooing Doves?', or 'Open Fire on Them!', and on one occasion Don Saturnino Bermúdez, no less, wrote his own piece called simply 'Meretrices', ending with the words 'of the shameless *scortum*'.

To return to the subject of gaming: whenever some energetic provincial governor had threatened to give the members of the club a fright, influential gamesters had prophesied his dismissal. It was more normal for a blind eye to be turned, and from time to time subventions were duly provided, in the most decorous form possible, as the contracting parties put it. The gamesters of Vetusta had one virtue: they did not play all through the night. They were busy men who had to rise early. There was a doctor who retired at ten, having lost his day's earnings. He rose at six next morning, tramped all through the town amidst puddles and mud, defied snow, hail, cold and wind, and after his arduous toil he returned, as with an offering for the altar, to lay upon the green baize the pesetas he had earned. Barristers, solicitors, clerks, merchants, industrialists, office-workers, landlords, all did likewise. In the ombre-room, the reading-room, the billiards-room, the conversation-room, the dominoes-room and the chess-room the same faces were always to be seen; but the *chamber of crime* was the centre of reunion for all occupations, all ages, all opinions, all tastes, all temperaments.

It was not without reason that Vetusta was said to be distinguished by its unimpeachable patriotism, its religiosity and its fondness for forbidden games. Its religiosity and its patriotism were explained by history; its fondness for gaming by the great amount of rain which fell there. What were members to do if they could not take their daily walk? For this reason Don Pompeyo Guimarán, the philosopher, proposed that the cathedral be made into a covered promenade. 'Risum teneatis!'[10] was Cámenes's reply in an article in *El Lábaro*.

Religiosity, in the lamentable form, however, of superstition, was displayed in the vice of gaming itself. Prodigious stories were told in the club about the credulity of the most famous gamesters. One merchant, who was a liberal and by no means over-pious, kept a pair of old shoes by the door of this place of recreation. He would arrive at the club, put on the shoes with holes in the bottoms and go upstairs to try his luck. He swore that fortune had never smiled on him when he was wearing new boots. He was, as it were, a gamester of a discalced order. The combination of his faith and a certain cunning, born of experience, brought him certain winnings. One year he offered a splendid novena to St Francis, attended by all *edified Vetusta*, to use Bermúdez's expression.

After Bedoya left the club, unseen by the porters, who were sweetly sleeping, the only members remaining were eight or ten sworn night-birds. Few of them, and always the same ones. Some were time-worn personages who had contracted the habit of staying up all night in Madrid; others were Vetustan rakes and dandies who imitated them. But of this late-night coterie we shall have to speak later, because characters of importance in this story attended it.

It was half past three in the afternoon. It was raining. The room next to the red parlour was occupied by the usual members, those who did not play any games and the six who played chess. The latter had placed their boards by a balcony window, to be more in the light. At the other end of the room it seemed as if night were about to fall. Over a marble table the flame of a burner which was used to light cigars shone out in the midst of dense tobacco-smoke, like a star on a foggy night. In a corner, hidden in shadows, all around the table – some sprawling on a divan, others in straw-bottomed rocking chairs – were half a dozen founder-members, who from time immemorial had arrived at three o'clock every afternoon to take coffee and brandy. They were men of few words. None of them ever permitted himself to venture an assertion which could not be unanimously accepted. Men and events of the day were judged there, but without passion. Every innovator, anyone who had done anything out of the ordinary, was condemned, but not insulted. Praise was bestowed, without any great enthusiasm, upon those citizens who knew how to behave in a restrained and courteous manner – without going to extremes in any respect. Better tell falsehoods than go to extremes. Don Saturnino Bermúdez had on more than one occasion received a homage of prudent admiration from this circle of respectable gentlemen. But they usually preferred to talk about animals – about, for example, the instincts of some of them, like the dog and the elephant, although always, of course, denying them any intelligence – 'the beaver constructs its lodge today just as it did in Adam's time; it is not intelligence, but instinct'. They also spoke of the usefulness of other dumb animals: the pig, every single part of which can be eaten, the cow, the cat, and so on, and so forth. And they found conversation about inanimate objects even more interesting. They took delight in those parts of civil law which deal with kinship and inheritance. If a member walked by and one of these founder-members did not know him, he asked:

'Who is that?'

'That is the son of — who was the grandson of — who married — who was the sister of . . .'

And most of the inhabitants of Vetusta would be drawn out, like cherries from a basket, hooked on to each other by kinship. Such conversations always ended with the same sentence: 'When one comes to think about it, we are all related in some way with one another.'

Meteorology was another subject which was never missing from the list of topics for discussion. Whatever wind was blowing was always of grave concern to these worthy members. The present winter was always colder than all others which they could remember, save one.

At times, too, they gossiped a little, but in the most restrained way, especially if the talk was of priests, ladies or persons in authority.

In spite of the agreeableness of such conversations this group of venerable greybeards, among whom there was but one young man (and he was bald), preferred silence to the pleasantest tittle-tattle; and it was to silence that this species of siesta taken awake was principally dedicated. They were nearly always silent.

Not far from them, and causing them at times no small annoyance, there were two or three groups of rowdies, and in the distance could be heard the disagreeable clatter of the domino, exiled by the venerables from their room. The domino-players were nearly always the same people: a professor, two civil engineers and a magistrate. They laughed and shouted a great deal, and they insulted each other, but always in jest. These four friends, united by the double six, would have sold scholarship, justice and public works to save a fellow domino-player. In the ballroom, where games-playing and coffee-drinking were not allowed, the Gentlemen of the Robe took their daily promenade together with other personages, such as the Marquis de Vegallana, on rainy days when he could not go on his outings.

All animation was confined to the aforementioned groups of rowdies.

'They have no respect for anything or anyone,' muttered the old men in the corner. Although the two groups were no more than a couple of paces apart, their conversations seldom intermingled. The elders would keep silence and then pass judgement.

'Such indiscretion!' whispered one venerable.

'You may observe', came the reply, 'that they rarely talk about any of the true interests of the province.'

'Except when Señor Mesía is present.'

'Oh, but Señor Mesía is a different class of person altogether.'

'Yes, a man of calibre. He knows all about finance and that business which people call Political Economy.'

'I am a believer in Political Economy, too.'

'I am not, but I do have a great respect for the memory of Flórez Estrada,[11] whom I knew personally.'

Anything but argue. At the slightest sign of an argument, the matter was hushed at once by tacit common consent.

At the table in front of them sat a vociferating gentleman who had been a liberal lord mayor and was a money-lender within all political systems. He was a cunning man, and an enemy of priests, for he believed that this was the way to give proof of his liberalism without expending much effort.

'Let's see, now,' he was saying, 'who has assured you that the canon theologian has refused to confess the judge's wife?'

'I have been informed by the person who with his own two eyes saw Doña Anita entering Don Fermín's chapel, and Don Fermín leaving without greeting her.'

'Well, I saw them greeting each other and talking together in the Mall.'

'That's right,' shouted a third, 'I saw them too. De Pas was with the archpriest, and the judge's wife was with Visitación. What's more, De Pas blushed.'

'Come, come!' exclaimed the ex-mayor, pretending to be shocked.

'Well I know more than the lot of you,' yelled a youth who copied Zamacois, Luján, the younger Romea,[12] and indeed all the comic actors in Madrid, where he had just graduated in medicine.

He lowered his voice and made a gesture of secrecy. The whole circle closed in. Placing his hand, like a screen, by his mouth, and leaning forward on the chair upon which he sat astride until its back rested against the table, he said:

'Paquito Vegallana told me that the archpriest, the famous Don Cayetano, has asked Anita to change confessors because . . .'

'Come, come! How can you know why?' interrupted the enemy of the clergy. 'The seal of the confessional!'

'Yes, yes! I have it on the best authority. Paquito told me.' He lowered his voice still more. 'Alvaro Mesía is making passes at the judge's wife.'

General scandal. Mutters in the dark corner.

'That was going too far.'

'It was permissible to gossip, to indulge in idle chatter, but not to that extent. The canon theologian and the seal of the confessional – one could let all that pass, but bringing the judge's wife into it! There could be no doubt but that this milksop was most imprudent.'

'Gentlemen, I'm not saying that the judge's wife is responding to the passes, but that Alvaro is making them, which is something quite different.'

Everyone denied the probability of his claim.

'Come now, the judge's wife – that's going a bit far!'

The youth shrugged.

'He was quite sure of it. The marquis's son, Mesía's intimate, had told him so.'

'Let's see now,' said Señor Foja, the ex-mayor; 'what have these passes that Mesía is supposed to be making at the judge's wife got to do with the canon theologian and auricular confession?'

He was unwilling to abandon his prey. It was not always that one could speak ill of priests at the club.

'Well they've got plenty to do with both of them, because the archpriest has asked De Pas for help. He wants to foist on to him the burden of her conscience.'

'My boy, my boy, you're on a slippery slope,' warned the scandal-monger's father, for this gentleman was present, admiring his son's effrontery, which had been acquired in Madrid without any possible doubt and at the father's own great expense.

'I mean Anita's very pernickety, as we all know,' and the boy continued to lower his voice, and the rest to come closer, forming a cluster of heads worthy of a second *Bell of Huesca*.[13] 'She's very pernickety, and she might perhaps have noticed how he looks at her – and all the rest, what? And I suppose she thinks that prevention is better than cure – and the archpriest is in no state for complicated cases of conscience, and the canon theologian knows plenty about all that.'

The ring of faces could not help smiling approval.

The prattler's papa was as pleased as Punch, and he winked to a friend. There could be no doubt that Madrid was the place to send youngsters who wanted their wits sharpening. It cost a lot of money, but in the end you saw results.

The boy's pertness often gave rise to protests, but they were soon overcome by the eloquence of his mischievous epigrams and of his showy, jangling gestures and accent.

At that time, the so-called Flamenco style was coming into fashion in some of Madrid's artistic quarters and in certain social circles. The young doctor wore tight-fitting trousers and combined with great skill the ringlets which were then worn on the forehead with the locks which bullfighters comb over their temples. His hair looked like a fretwork wig.

His name was Joaquín Orgaz and he *made eyes* at all the marriageable girls in town, which is to say that he leered at these young women and had the pleasure of being looked at by them. He had completed his studies earlier in the year and his intention was to marry a wealthy young lady as soon as possible. She would contribute her dowry and he would contribute his fine figure, the title of Doctor, and his Flamenco skills. He was not a fool, but his enslavement to fashion made him seem more mediocre than perhaps he was. In Madrid he had been one among many, but in Vetusta he only had to fear five or six rivals who had imported similar manners. He had spent his vacations trying to establish relationships with wealthy or noble Vetustan families. He had become Paquito Vegallana's close friend; and so some of the splendour radiating from the famous Mesía, the pick of the Vetustan beaux, was reflected on to him, although from a distance. Joaquín Orgaz called Mesía by his Christian name because Mesía and Paco were so very close and because Orgaz, in turn, was friendly with Paco, too – or so he said.

Joaquín, encouraged by the success of his comments, went on to uphold the view that the respect and admiration excited by the judge's wife reflected a ridiculous naivety.

'She's a beautiful woman, an extremely beautiful woman; a woman of talent if you like, worthy of another theatre, of moving in higher circles. If you press me I'll even say she's a superior woman, if such women exist, but when all's said and done she's a woman, *et nihil humani* . . .'[14]

He did not know what the Latin saying meant, or how it ended, or who had said it, but he came out with it whenever the talk was about possible human failings.

The other members burst out laughing.

'The little blighter can even swear in Latin!' thought his father, even more satisfied about the sacrifices which he had had to make for the young scoundrel.

Joaquinito, bright red with pleasure, and to some extent from the anisette which he had drunk, now thought it suitable to cap his triumph by singing something new. He rose to his feet, stretched out one leg, swung around on his heel and sang, or *warbled*, to use his own word:

'Open up the door, girl,
The wicket in your gate . . .'

'These popular prejudices should be done away with. The judge's wife! Was she made of anything other than flesh and blood? And Alvaro had always been irresistible . . .' The younger Orgaz interrupted the dance which he had begun while making these observations. In the next room footsteps had sounded, shaking the floor.

'Here comes the Englishman,' the Flamenco singer muttered, paling a little.

Indeed, it was Ronzal.

Pepe Ronzal – otherwise known as Blunderbuss, although nobody knows why – was a native of Pernueces, a village in the province. As the son of a wealthy cattle-farmer, he had been in a position to continue his studies (it will soon be seen what sort of studies they were) in the provincial capital. His youthful fondness for monte being as great as that of Herring-tail for ombre, he had been unwilling to return to Pernueces even during vacations, anxious not to miss so much as a single run of court-cards. He had been unable to complete his studies. Even the professors' traditional benevolence had not sufficed to enable Blunderbuss to become a Bachelor of Both Laws.

He had once been asked in an examination:

'What does testament mean, my boy?'

'Testament – it speaks for itself, it's something made by the dead.'

As well as Blunderbuss, he had been called the Student, an ironical antonomasia which he did not understand.

Time had passed by and the cattle-farmer had died. Pepe Ronzal had ceased to be the Student, had sold land, moved to the provincial capital and begun to be a political man – no one knows exactly how or why.

The fact is that from the presiding committee of a local electoral college he had moved on to the town hall, and from being a councillor he had moved on to be the provincial deputy for Pernueces. Although he was never able to shake off his pristine ignorance, he did achieve gradual progress in his manner of walking, of dressing and even of greeting people. One had to have lived in Vetusta for a long time to remember how rustic the man had once been. From the year of the Restoration onwards, Ronzal was regarded as a man of initiative, successful in love-affairs of a certain type and as an agent for young men who wanted to buy themselves out of military service. He was a determined supporter of established institutions. He combed his hair after the models which he found on postage stamps and one-peseta coins, and his footwear was of the sturdiest – indeed it was armour-plated. He believed that this gave him the look of an English nobleman.

'I am very English in all respects,' he would say with deliberation, 'particularly in boots.'

He 'campaigned' in the most reactionary of the parties which took turns in power.

'Give me a Saxon people,' he would say, 'and I will become a liberal.'

He later became a liberal without being given a Saxon people but something quite different which has no place in this history.

Ronzal was tall, corpulent and not badly built. He had a small round head, a low forehead and the expressionless frightened eyes of a wild animal, which he did not move whenever he wished, but whenever he could. To talk with an excited and loquacious Ronzal, to hear him blurting his nonsense with energy and enthusiasm, and to observe that his eyes did not move or express any part of what he was saying, but stared out with all the stupefaction and suspicion of the beasts of the forest, brought shudders to the spine.

His colour was a deep healthy brown, and he had well-shaped legs. Where he was in advance of his times was in his trousers, which were rather short. He always wore gloves, whether it was hot or cold, and regardless of whether or not they were appropriate: for Ronzal the glove had always been a badge of refinement (as he said) and of gentlemanliness (as he also said). Moreover, he had sweaty hands.

He hated anything that smacked of the plebeian. *Those wretched republicans* had a formidable enemy in him. One St Francis's Day the porter did not hang any drapery from the club's balconies, and Ronzal, who was a committee-member by that time, was on the point of hurling the poor man from one of them.

'But, sir,' cried the porter, 'today is only St Francis of Paola's Day!'
'What difference does that make, you oaf?' replied Blunderbuss in fury. 'Don't you come powlering me! When it's St Francis's Day it's a gala day and the balconies are draped!'

He believed that this was the way to serve Institutions.

As a result of exploits of this sort he grew little by little to be respected. That is, nobody laughed at him to his face any more.

He was not so lacking in perspicacity that he did not realize that the world sets great store by appearances, and that in the club those who shouted most, who were most obstinate and who read most newspapers were held to be the wisest. And he said to himself:

'A fellow needs to be wise, as well. I shall be wise. Luckily, I've got energy' (he had a good pair of fists), 'no one beats me at stubbornness, and I am blessed with lungs as strong as monologues' (monoliths, of course). 'This, and reading *La Correspondencia*, is all I need to make me the Hippocrates of the Province.'

Hippocrates was Plato's teacher, whom Blunderbuss never called Socrates – nor had he any need to do so.

Thenceforth, he read newspapers, and novels by Pigault-Lebrun and Paul de Kock,[15] the only books at which he could look without falling asleep. He paid careful attention to wise-sounding conversations, and, above all, he endeavoured to assert himself by often shouting and always having his own way.

If another man's arguments were causing Ronzal some difficulty he would settle matters by striking into his opponent's heart the fear of what cannot be called God, for it was a rattan, which he brandished as he yelled:

'And let it be understood that I shall maintain this, at any place you like to choose! At any place you like to choose!'

He would repeat the expression about the choice of place five or six times, so that his opponent should pay attention to the trope and to the cudgel, and give in.

He realized that in the club the least compromising conversations were those concerned with the most important subjects and with remote affairs, and so foreign policy became his forte. The more distant the country whose interests were under discussion the better it suited him. In these cases the peril lay in geographical lapses. He kept confusing countries with generals in command of invading armies. In the course of one unfortunate polemic he was forced to come to blows with Captain Bedoya, who denied the existence of General Sebastopol.

Ronzal believed that his reputation as a man of parts would be better established if he showed his strength at chess, and he applied much energy to this game. One afternoon, when he was playing in the presence of various members and had already lost many pieces, he saw his salvation in making a pawn into a queen.

'This one's going to be a queen!' he exclaimed, fixing his eyes on those of his opponent.

'That is impossible.'

'What do you mean, impossible?'

And his opponent instinctively withdrew a man which was in the way of the pawn which was going to become a queen.

'It's going to be a queen, and I'm making it a personal matter,' Blunderbuss added, emboldened and beating his fist upon his breast.

His opponent, not knowing what he was doing, left another square free.

And so, moving on from one square to another, and taking his life into his hands with each move, the energetic provincial deputy for Pernueces did make the pawn into a queen, and won the game.

VII

Such qualities, among others, distinguished Pepe Ronzal, of whom Joaquinito Orgaz was much afraid. Perhaps the man from Pernueces knew that Joaquín did a perfect imitation of the nonsense he spoke and the way he spoke it. Moreover, Ronzal loathed Don Alvaro Mesía and all those who praised him and were friendly with him. Joaquín was hand and glove with the Young Marquis – as the Marquis de Vegallana's son was often called – and the latter was Don Alvaro's close friend.

'Good afternoon, gentlemen,' said Ronzal, taking a place in the circle.

He put his gloves on the table, ordered coffee, and proceeded to survey Joaquín, who would have liked to become invisible, from top to toe.

'Who are we gossiping about today, my lad?' asked the deputy, slapping the milksop's not very impressive thigh.

Ronzal's legs were legs to be proud of. He stretched them out alongside those of the youngster, so that the other gentlemen could make the comparison.

Joaquín replied:

'Nobody.'

And he shrugged.

'I don't believe it. These whipper-snappers from Madrid have always got something to say about us poor provincials.'

'You are quite right,' said Foja, the ex-mayor. 'Your friend the vicar-general was today's victim.'

Ronzal became serious.

'Aha!' said he, 'a *nespy four*, eh?' (a strong-minded person, in Blunderbuss's French).

'It is,' added Foja, 'a question of the passes to which a certain hitherto highly respected lady does or does not respond, and of the spiritual reinforcement which her afflicted innocence does or does not seek in the moral direction of Don Fermín. Hee, hee!'

Ronzal did not understand.

'Look here! I demand plain speech.'

Joaquinito looked towards his father as if to implore help.

Señor Orgaz ventured to murmur:

'Come now, as for demanding . . .'

'Yes sir. I demand it. And I'm making it a personal matter!'

'But what is it that you're demanding?' asked the youth, with a display of energy which used up all his courage.

'I'm demanding what I've got every right to demand, that's what. And I repeat, I'm making it a personal matter.'

'But what matter?'

'The matter under discussion!'

Joaquinito, as pale as death, shrugged again. He realized that, in these circumstances, having right on one's side was the least important consideration. By now sparks were shooting from Ronzal's animal eyes. He had worked himself into a tangle, and nothing irritated him so much as to make the sad discovery that he had lost his thread.

'Yes sir, *that* matter. And I want plain talk.'

Ronzal himself did not know what he was demanding.

Foja took it upon himself to clarify the subject.

'Señor Ronzal wishes it to be explained to him whether it is thought that he is the person who is making the passes to which the lady does or does not respond.'

'That's right!' said Ronzal, who was thinking of no such thing but felt flattered by the supposition.

'I want to know,' he added, 'whether anyone thinks I'm capable of casting doubt upon the virtue of such a highly respectable lady.'

'But which lady?'

'The lady I'm talking about, Don Joaquinito – that lady! And nobody makes fun of me!'

The argument grew heated. So serious did the incident become that the venerable gentlemen in the dark corner were fain to intervene. They were unanimous in taking Señor Ronzal's side, although they recognized that he had allowed himself to become too angry. They explained the whole affair to him, for he had still not permitted anyone to put him in the picture. 'Ronzal had not been the subject of discussion. What had been stated, with somewhat questionable prudence, was that the canon theologian was henceforth to be the confessor of Señora Doña Ana Ozores de Quintanar, because this illustrious and highly virtuous lady, fleeing from the snares laid by a beau – who was not Señor Ronzal . . .'

'It's Mesía,' interrupted Joaquín.

'Whoever says that is a liar,' yelled Blunderbuss, incensed by this news. 'And that Don Juan fellow can go knocking at another door, because the judge's wife is an impregnable fortress. And as for the person who comes with such stories to a public establishment . . .'

'The club is not a public establishment,' interrupted Foja.

'And this was a private discussion among friends,' added Orgaz senior.

'And why don't you go and repeat what you said about "that Don Juan fellow" to Mesía himself?' shouted Orgaz junior, from the doorway, ready to flee should the taunt make the barbarian from Pernueces fly into a rage.

It did not. Blunderbuss coloured like a tomato, but he did not move. Instead, he blurted –

'I'm not scared of Mesías, or of Messiahs either, for that matter! And whatever I've got to say, I say it face to face and in front of everybody, *turby and torby*[1] (to the city and to the world, in Ronzalesque Latin). 'Anyone would think that Don Alvarito eats live babies for breakfast and that every woman he meets . . .' and he added an outrageous expression which scandalized the gentlemen in the dark corner.

'Silence!' Joaquinito, still in the doorway, ventured to whisper.

'What do you mean, silence? No one says that to me, my young sir!'

A sonorous, booming laugh rang out. Fiery Ronzal's blood froze. There could be no doubt about it – that was Mesía's laugh. Mesía was talking to the domino-playing gentlemen in the next room. Paco Vegallana and Don Frutos Redondo were with him. The three of them approached Ronzal, who had again seated himself and was complaining that his coffee was cold. He had made a signal to the others in the circle, to indicate that he was holding his tongue merely out of discretion.

Don Alvaro Mesía was taller than Ronzal and of much finer build. He bought his clothes in Paris and went there in person to be measured. Ronzal ordered his clothes from Madrid. For each suit he was charged the price of three, his frock-coats never fitted, and he was always dressed in the latest fashion but one. Mesía made frequent trips to Madrid and abroad. Although he was a Vetustan he did not speak with the regional accent. Yet when Ronzal tried to speak correct Castilian he sounded like some peasant from the farthest wilds of Galicia. Mesía spoke French, Italian and a little English. The deputy for Pernueces was most envious of the president of the Gentlemen's Club.

Ronzal believed that no Vetustan could beat his mother's son for bravery, elegance, success with women, or political prestige – except Don Alvaro. Blunderbuss had to admit that he was inferior to Mesía, his perfect ideal. In Blunderbuss's imagination the president of the

Gentlemen's Club was every inch a man from the pages of a novel or even a poem. He believed him to be braver than the Cid and more skilful in the use of arms than the Zouave.[2] His figure was a faultless fashion-plate, his clothes were the very model of clothes. As for the reputation which Don Alvaro enjoyed as a daring and irresistible lady-killer, Ronzal considered it to be well grounded, and indeed the most enviable possession that a man who liked to enjoy himself in this dashed world could possibly covet. Although Ronzal spent his life spreading malicious rumours about the origins of the moderate fortune attributed to Mesía, he did not believe that a single céntimo had been acquired by dishonest means.

Ronzal was a reactionary within the Restoration establishment. Mesía, who also adhered to the Restoration, figured as the head of the Liberal Party of Vetusta, which respected institutions. Wherever Ronzal looked, there was Mesía, in triumphant opposition to him. Ronzal's men were in command in the province, and he was on the standing committee, which managed all provincial affairs, yet whenever Don Alvaro walked into the council offices, Ronzal was overshadowed. Don Alvaro was nothing in the council, having only a tiny minority, yet everyone from the hall porter to the president doffed his hat to him, and it was Don Alvaro here, and Don Alvaro there; and never was there a mayor of Don Alvaro's making who failed to get his accounts approved by the council, or any of Don Alvaro's younger followers whom the council would not certify to be mortally ill when they were called up for military service, or, in short, any official transaction of his which was not settled at a stroke.

But there was one thing even more extraordinary than all of this: Mesía and women!

Often in the theatre, when the entire audience was giving its attention to the stage, the eyes of one spectator in the proscenium box, Ronzal, would be fixed on the elegant Mesía, that pale, blond man of men, with those grey-brown eyes of his, usually cold, but full of fire if there was a woman to be charmed. That inimitable shirt-front, or *plaster-on*[3] (as Ronzal called it), with its sheen which no Vetustan laundress could bring out and no shirts from Madrid ever displayed, attracted the provincial deputy's gaze as light attracts moths. He superstitiously attributed a major part in his enemy's amorous conquests to that *plaster-on*.

Ronzal also made much show of his shirt-front, but he had an unconscious tendency towards high-buttoned waistcoats and large starched neckties. But then he would see Mesía's shirt-front again, and revert to open waistcoats. In the theatre Ronzal would watch Mesía and if his hated model applauded he applauded too, with deliberation and making no sound, like his model. But Don Alvaro would lean his elbows on the rail in front of his box and cross his hands and turn to talk with friends in a singular manner which Blunderbuss was never able to imitate. If Mesía scanned the boxes and stalls with his opera-glasses Ronzal followed their movements, thinking of them as two cannon loaded with deadly shrapnel: unhappy the woman at whom that destroyer of hearts took aim! Regardless of whether she was single or married, Ronzal believed that she must already be dying of love, or dishonoured at the very least.

Ronzal knew better than anyone else who were the Vetustan Don Juan's victims. He spied on him, followed not only his looks but even his footsteps, interpreted his smiles, and more than once (he would sooner die than admit it, though), more than once he had waited as long as it took Mesía to tire of a lady in order to attempt to catch her in the coarse nets of Ronzalesque seduction.

On such occasions he usually found that Paco Vegallana, the Young Marquis, was enjoying these left-overs.

But Blunderbuss did not tell anyone of what he knew.

He denied Mesía's conquests.

'He's past his prime,' he would declare. 'I'm not saying that back in those times sunk in iniquity, thanks to the Revolution – I'm not saying that he might not have had a few affairs then. But nowadays, at the present historical moment' (the man from Pernueces swelled with self-importance as he said this), 'the moral fibre of our families is the best shield against his attacks.'

Such conversations were repeated every day. The objects of the gossip varied little, the comments less, and the key phrases not at all. It would almost have been possible to announce what each gossip was going to say and when he was going to say it.

Mesía noticed that his presence had brought the conversation to a halt. This was nothing new. He was aware of the hatred which the man from Pernueces felt for him and of the admiration which accompanied this hatred. The hostility of Ronzal, the great propagator of the legend which had Mesía as its hero, both amused and suited him, and the legend itself was useful in many ways. Mesía was also aware of the Student's grotesque imitation – he still called Ronzal by this nickname – and he enjoyed watching him, as if looking at himself in a distorting mirror in a fair-ground. Mesía did not bear Ronzal any ill-will. He would even have done him a good turn, so long as it was not any trouble. Perhaps he had already done Ronzal some good turns, unbeknown to the man.

The conversation returned to the subject of married women, although without any further allusions to the judge's wife.

Ronzal, as always, took as his general thesis the defence of present-day morality, which was what it was thanks to the Restoration.

'Come now, you, Ronzalillo, in these times of morality . . .?' asked the ex-mayor, with his usual cunning.

Blunderbuss smiled for an instant, but recovering his composure exclaimed:

'Neither I nor anyone else – believe me! There's no encouragement for vice in the life of Vetusta. I'm not saying that all is virtue, but the opportunity for vice never arises. And the good influence of the clergy, particularly the cathedral clergy, is very important. We've got a bishop who's a saint, a canon theologian . . .'

'What, the canon theologian! Don't come to me with those stories. If I were to talk . . . What's more, as you all know . . .'

The speaker making these insinuations was Foja.

'The canon theologian,' said Mesía, addressing the group for the first time, 'is hardly what one would call a mystic, but I do not take him for a philanderer.'

'What's that?' asked Joaquinito Orgaz.

Foja explained.

There was a discussion about whether the canon theologian was one. Ronzal, Orgaz senior, the Young Marquis, Mesía and four others said that he was not; Foja, Joaquinito and two others said that he was.

The vote having been gained, the president of the club, in order to keep the minority happy, made the impartial pronouncement that 'the vicar-general's true sin was simony'.

The Young Marquis, a bachelor of civil and canon law, was made to explain this difficult word.

According to Don Alvaro, ambition and avarice were the canon theologian's cardinal sins – avarice especially. Apart from that, he was a scholar, perhaps the only scholar in Vetusta, and an incomparably better orator than the bishop.

'He is no saint,' he added, 'but none of what is said about Doña Obdulia and him is to be believed, or about him and Visitación for that matter; and, as regards his relationship with the Páez family, I am Don Manuel Páez's bosom friend and have known his daughter Olvidito since she was so high' (half a yard) 'and I protest against all such slanderous aspersions.'

(Ronzal made a note of the word; he had always thought that one said 'nasturtiums'.)

'What aspersions?' asked the Young Marquis, who was present for that purpose.

'Don't you know? Well, it is said that Olvidito is a slave of Don Fermín's will; that she is not getting married, nor will she ever marry, because he wants to turn her into a nun, and that Don Manuel consents to all this, and . . .'

'And I swear that it is all true, Señor Don Alvaro,' shouted Foja.

'But do you also believe that the canon theologian is spooning the girl?'

'That's what I don't know.'

'No more than you know about all the rest,' said Ronzal.

Mesía regarded him with an approving nod and an affable smile.

'Gentlemen,' added Blunderbuss, warming to his subject, 'this is scandalous. Everything gets turned into politics here. The canon theologian is a very worthy person in every respect.'

'Says you!'

'Yes I do say so!'

'Just as if the cat had said it.'

There was a pause. The ex-mayor was no Joaquinito Orgaz.

The mention of the cat demanded vengeance, Ronzal was sure of that, but he did not know how to reply to the insolent liberal.

At length he said:

'You are an ill-mannered lout.'

Foja, who was good at insulting people, but who could also forgive those who insulted him, did not take offence.

'What I say I can prove,' he replied. 'The canon theologian is the scourge of the province. The bishop's besotted by him, he's got the clergy under his thumb, he's become a millionaire in the five or six years he's been vicar-general, and the diocesan curia isn't an ecclesiastical court at all, but an extension of the Montes de Toledo.[4] About the confessional I prefer not to speak; about the Society of St Vincent de Paul I shall also keep silent; about the young girls who go to him for instruction – not a word, it's better to avoid the subject; about women's guilds like the Court of Our Lady – we'd better move on to something else. In short, he's like a fox in a henhouse. This is the truth, the simple truth. And as soon as there's even a moderately liberal government in Spain that man will slink away with his cassock between his legs. That's all I have to say.'

This was how the ex-mayor understood liberty. It was a question of whether or not the clergy was persecuted. Such persecution, and freedom of trade, were the essentials. Freedom of trade boiled down to freedom of the interest-rate. Foja was even more of a usurer than a priest-hater.

Although he was a gossip, he did not usually dare insult priests in such a barefaced way, and his speech caused some amazement.

How had that sly old wheedler, who was always on his guard, allowed himself to be carried away in this outburst? The truth was that no such thing had happened. He was perfectly composed. He knew his part. His intention was to please Don Alvaro, for reasons best known to himself. Even though the president of the club might pretend to support the canon theologian, Foja knew that he did not take kindly to him.

'Señor Foja,' replied Mesía, in the certainty that everyone was expecting him to speak, 'there is, to say the least, a considerable degree of exaggeration in what you have just said.'

'*Vox populi* . . .'

'The people are fools,' shouted Ronzal. 'The people crucified Our Lord Jesus Christ, the people gave the hemlock to Hippocrates.'

'To Socrates,' corrected Orgaz junior in revenge for earlier events, his safety being now assured by Don Alvaro's presence.

'The people', continued Ronzal, taking no notice of Joaquinito, 'killed Louis XVI . . .'

'Oh God! he's off again,' interrupted Foja.

And picking up his hat he added:

'Au revoir, gentlemen. Where wise men speak, we ignoramuses are out of place.'

He walked to the door.

'By the way, talking about wise men,' said Don Frutos Redondo, the American, who had not spoken until then, 'we've got a wager pending, Señor Ronzal. Surely you remember – that tricky word.'

'Which one?'

'Sentry. You said it's spelt with a *c*.'

'I stand by what I said – and I'm making it a personal matter.'

'No, no, don't you start trying to evade the issue; you wagered a tripe-and-onion supper.'

'That is the wager.'

'All right, then. Ha! ha! ha! Let the dictionary be brought from the library.'

'Let it be brought!'

A servant came with the dictionary. Such consultations were frequent occurrences.

'First look it up under *c*,' said Ronzal in a thunderous voice to Joaquinito who, with great pleasure, had taken upon himself the task of crushing the man from Pernueces.

Don Frutos was beside himself with gloating glee. He would have given one of his many millions for such a victory. Now they would see which one was more uncouth. He winked at everybody, he laughed in satisfaction, he rubbed his hands together.

'Oh, what a feast of tripe! What a feast!'

Orgaz solemnly looked for sentry under *c*. It was not there.

'You must be looking for it under *sc*. Look it up under *c* alone.'

'It's no use, Señor Ronzal, it's not there.'

'Now look it up under *s*!' exclaimed Don Frutos, solemn now, determined to assume a dignified mien at the moment of victory.

Ronzal was as red as a tomato. He looked at Mesía, who feigned inattention.

Finally, staking his all, Blunderbuss jumped to his feet in the middle of the room and snatched the dictionary from Orgaz, who thought that the wild man from Pernueces was going to hurl it at his head. No, he threw it down on a divan and shouted:

'Gentlemen, whatever that wretched old book may claim, I assure you, on my word of honour, that the dictionary I've got at home spells sentry with a *c*.'

Don Frutos was about to protest, but Ronzal did not give him any time to do so, for he added:

'Anyone who denies it calls me a liar, casts doubts upon my honour, flings down the gauntlet, and I believe he knows where I am to be found. We all know how such affairs are settled.'

Don Frutos's mouth fell open.

From the doorway, Foja ventured:

'Señor Ronzal, I can't believe that Señor Redondo, or anybody else, would dare to doubt your word. If you have a dictionary in which a sentry has a *c*, that's your look-out. I even think I can guess which dictionary it is. It must be the *Dictionary of Authorities*.'⁵

'Yes sir, the government dictionary.'

'Well, that's the dictionary which lays down the law; and you are right, and Don Frutos is getting his sentries mixed up with Central America, where he made his fortune.'

Don Frutos felt well satisfied. He had understood the joke about the seeing sentry who was Ronzal's look-out, and pretended to consider himself defeated.

'Gentlemen,' he said; 'all right, let there be no further discussion of the matter. I shall pay for the tripe.'

In the club he was nearly always considered to be the most ignorant member, and it gave him great joy to see Ronzal made the object of general mockery.

It was agreed that everyone in the group would have supper that evening at Don Frutos's expense. Unusual generosity indeed, in a spirit so enamoured of economy! Ronzal believed that he had asserted himself yet again, by dint of his energy; and this time in front of Don Alvaro! He accepted the invitation to supper and the role of victor, certain though he was that he had no dictionary at home. Still, if Foja said so . . .

It had stopped raining. The meeting broke up and everyone said goodbye until the evening. They were, apart from Orgaz senior, the usual night-birds.

It was to be a late supper. Mesía offered to attend, in spite of the many demands on his time.

How Ronzal envied this expression! He knew that everybody had interpreted those 'demands' as he had. Oh! they were lovers' meetings. 'Possibly with the judge's wife,' thought the man from Pernueces, making himself a promise to keep watch over them.

Don Alvaro Mesía, Paco Vegallana and Joaquín Orgaz left together. The Young Marquis realized that Orgaz's presence was an embarrassment to Don Alvaro.

'Hey, Joaquín, now that I remember, there's something you should know.'

'What is it?'

'That you have a redoubtable rival.'

'In which arena?'

'Of course – I was forgetting what a busy campaigner you are. It has to do with Obdulia.'

'Hallo!' said Mesía, smiling out of sheer compassion. 'So Joaquín is laying siege to our young widow?'

'Yes,' said Paco, 'it's the Great Siege of Vienna.'[6]

Joaquín, for all his Flamenco brashness, was disconcerted, caught between shame and pride. He knew that Don Alvaro had been Obdulia's lover, because she had confessed as much to him. But Joaquín suspected that Paco had inherited her favours. Obdulia swore that he had not.

'Well, your rival is Don Saturnino Bermúdez, the descendant of a hundred kings. You know, my cousin, according to him. I hear there was a scandal yesterday in the cathedral, that Turtle-dove more or less had to kick them out. What did you think, then – that Obdulia only had rendezvous in coal-holes? Well, she uses palaces and temples, too: *pauperum tabernas, regumque turris.*'[7]

With a feeble pretence of good humour, Joaquinito asked:

'But how do you know all this?'

'Very simple. Señora Hidalgo – Alvaro here knows who she is . . .'

'Yes,' said Mesía, 'that woman from Palomares.'

'That's right. She visited the cathedral with Obdulia, Don Saturn went with them, and I'm to believe that in the Chapel of Relics, in the crypts, in the galleries, everywhere, they were giving each other such – hugs and squeezes. Mother nearly died laughing when the Hidalgo woman told her; *she* was furious. Mother, just for a little fun (you know how the poor dear enjoys such pranks), wanted to bring Obdulia and Don Saturn together today, at home, to see the looks on their faces when she mentioned what happened yesterday. Mother sent for Obdulia, but she said she couldn't come because she had to spend the afternoon in Visitación's house, making some pies for tea – you know, one of those tea-parties Visitación puts on for her friends.'

'Yes, I know.'

'So there you have them, with their sleeves rolled up, and – well, as you might say, the cakes are all ready for eating.'

'I must admit,' observed Mesía, 'that the widow is appetizing in such circumstances. I have seen her in Paco's house, in her big white apron, with her underskirt clinging to her body, a little bit of her legs showing, and her arms fully exposed, in a fine high colour, all worked up.'

The Flamenco artist swallowed hard.

'She's some woman,' he could not help saying. 'What about *him*?' he added.

'Who?'

'The old know-all.'

'Ah! Don Saturnino? Well he didn't accept mother's invitation either. He replied with great courtesy, in a perfumed note, which you'd think was from some sacristy cocotte, like all the notes he sends . . .'

'What did it say?'

'That he was ill in bed and would mother be so kind as to send him the recipe for that very effective purgative she told him about. Poor Bermúdez would be a happy man, always supposing that he succeeds in supplanting you, if it weren't for those irregularities in his digestive tract.'

After talking for a few minutes more about the marchioness's pranks, Joaquín took his leave.

'Poor devil!' said Mesía.

'He's such a bore.'

They fell silent. Now and again Vegallana glanced at his companion out of the corner of his eye. Don Alvaro was in a thoughtful mood. This was one of those silences which precede the exchange of interesting confidences between two close friends.

Their friendship was like that of a young father and a son who regards him as a comrade, wiser and worthy of respect. In addition, however, Paco saw Mesía as a hero. Neither being the heir to the most enviable title in Vetusta, nor having such a fine figure, nor enjoying such success with women made Paco feel as proud as did his close friendship with Don Alvaro. The president of the Gentlemen's Club was somewhat over forty years old, and the future marquis twenty-five or twenty-six; but in spite of the difference in their ages they understood each other and had the same tastes and ideas, if only because Paco attempted to imitate his idol in these things. Paco did not, however, imitate Don Alvaro's dress or manner, because as soon as the older man had observed in the younger a propensity to do so, he had discreetly given him to understand that this kind of imitation was vulgar and ridiculous. By making fun of Blunderbuss he had guided Paco, who had an instinctive sense of elegance, away from such tendencies. And as a result the Young Marquis dressed in an original and fashionable style – as fashion was understood by his tailor in Madrid, who took him seriously and looked after him as an intelligent and meritorious customer. Paco did not go to extremes, his clothes being neither too close-fitting nor too loose; nor were his shirt-collars excessively pointed, or the brims of his hats too broad.

He cultivated his own style in dress so as not to look like any ordinary dandy. He did not believe in the tailors of Vetusta, and would not buy so much as a trouser-buckle there. Nobody was a tailor in his own country. In summer Paco had a preference for white hats, light-coloured waistcoats and bright neckties. The essence of dressing lay in being neat and correct, and the danger in vulgar exaggeration. His complexion was pale, with a rosy tinge, but there was no effeminacy about him, for he had fine skin, good blood and excellent health. Women praised, in particular, his mouth (including his teeth), his hands and his feet. Even those parts where most men lose all their charm, being duty-bound to do so, won him some victories, and he was not a little proud of the fact. He was disdainful towards mistresses won in fair combat, and considerate, even affectionate, towards those who cost him money. His reading was limited to the *History of Prostitution*,[8] by Dufour, and *The Lady of the Camellias*[9] and its derivatives, together with some other fictional panegyrics on the fallen woman. He believed in the hearts of gold of those ladies whom Bermúdez called *meretrices*, and in the absolute corruptness of the upper classes. He was certain that unless there was another invasion of Barbarians the world would soon be rotten to the core. He lamented the fact but found it all terribly amusing.

Furthermore, he believed that a man needed to have had many adventures to be a good husband. He was destined to marry a certain heiress who was as scrawny as she was virtuous, and had laid down as a condition for promising his hand that he be allowed many years of freedom, during which he would make himself ready to be a good husband.

The doubt which tormented him, and about which he often consulted Mesía, was:

'Should I marry soon, so as not to find that my wife is an old woman by the time she comes to my arms? Or should I delay taking her until she is old, and be longer free to enjoy other young creatures?'

Needless to say, he did not intend to abstain from adulterous love when he was married; but then there would always be the inconvenience, and one would always be on the run, hiding like some criminal.

He preferred to continue making himself ready to be a good husband.

There were few seducers, apart from Mesía, as fortunate as the Young Marquis. Vanity often helped him in his conquests, as not a few women yielded to the future Marquis de Vegallana; but on other occasions (and this was what he preferred), the victory was won by his blue eyes, soft and amorous, and by his particular understanding of pleasurable activities.

'For a really good time,' he would say, 'give me women in their thirties. At that age they're experienced and knowledgeable, and love one for one's own personal qualities.'

Just as an elegant and wealthy lady lets her servant girls have left-off clothes which are almost new, so Mesía more than once left scarcely used mistresses in Paco's arms. And, Mesía being Mesía, Paco was happy to take them. So great was his admiration for his hero.

Paco was of medium build, but arm in arm with his friend he looked short, for Mesía was even taller than Ranzal, the strapping young man from Pernueces.

'Where shall we go?' asked Vegallana, hoping that this might prompt Alvaro to make the confidence which he was awaiting.

Don Alvaro shrugged.

'Maybe she's at my place,' added Paco.

'Whom do you mean?'

'Anita, of course!'

Don Alvaro looked upon Paco with fatherly affection, and smiled.

He placed his hands on the younger man's shoulders and drew him forward, as he said:

'My lad, you're an *enfant terrible.* Such ingenuity! But who has been telling you . . .?'

'These two witnesses here.'

And Paco placed a finger over each of his eyes.

'What have you noticed? No, it's impossible. I'm certain I haven't been indiscreet.'

'But what about *her*?'

'I'm not even sure she knows I like her.'

'Bah! I'm sure enough. And what's more, I'm sure she likes you, too.'

One of Mesía's hands trembled a little on Vegallana's shoulder.

The Young Marquis felt it and noticed on his friend's face signs of great efforts to hide his joy. The dandy's cold eyes brightened. He drew on his cigar and puffed out the smoke as a cover for his feelings.

They walked a few steps further in silence.

'What have you noticed – about her?'

'Aha! I'd say she's beginning to bite at the bait.'

'Indeed she is! But exactly where do you think she's biting?'

Vegallana turned to look at Mesía.

The Don Juan, with a gesture which was half serious, half jocular, pointed to his own heart.

'Phew!' Paco shaped the sound with his lips.

'Do you doubt it?'

'I refuse to believe it.'

'Don't be such a fool. Don't you think it's possible for a man to fall in love?'

'I fall in love without the slightest difficulty.'

'It's not that kind of love.'

'Are you blushing?'

'Yes, I'm rather embarrassed. I can't help it. It must be because I'm getting old.'

'Come on, though: what does it feel like?'

Mesía explained to Paco what it felt like. He deceived him in the same way as he often deceived certain women with upbringings and sentiments similar to those of the Young Marquis. Paco's imagination, his habits, and the special perverseness of his moral principles made his soul an effeminate one, in the sense that he resembled countless married and unmarried ladies who are sound in wind and limb, idle, hearty eaters, and brought up to lives of leisure and plenty in the midst of ready, everyday vice.

He was prone to a vague sentimentalism which, like such women, he regarded as exquisite sensibility, very nearly a virtue. But this kind of virtue for the use of fine ladies is ruled by the laws of a privileged morality which is much less severe than the disagreeably dour morality of the common people. Without thinking much about it, and not thinking at all clearly, Paco still hoped for some pure, great love, like love in books and plays. Although he realized that it was ridiculous to go searching for such love, and was a declared sceptic on the subject, deep down in the regions of his spirit into which he seldom ventured he could glimpse something better than everyday flirting, something more serious than the satisfaction of carnal appetites and of vanity. For all this to come to the surface, and for Paco to become aware of it, he needed an imagination more powerful than his own to set his mind working; Mesía's insinuating, corrosive eloquence was the most effective stimulant. In a quarter of an hour spent walking through streets and squares, Don Alvaro made Paco experience those undefinable 'somethings' of dosimetric love,[10] which was the highest ideal reached by the Young Marquis's spirit.

'Yes, it was perfectly pure. True, she was a married woman. But ideal love, the love of elegant, select souls, sticks at nothing. In Paris, and even in Madrid, married ladies are loved without any trouble at all. In this respect there is no difference between love which is pure and the ordinary kind.'

The leader of the Dynastic Liberal Party of Vetusta was most concerned that his young friend should believe him to be enamoured in this subtle, refined way. If Paquito was convinced of the purity and strength of Mesía's passion, he would be a great help. The friendship between the Vegallanas and the judge's wife was a close one. Paco had never uttered a single word of love to his friend Anita, and she held him in high esteem. Indeed, she displayed some candour in her behaviour towards him, which was more than she had ever done with other men. Moreover, in the marquis's house Mesía could often see her, while in other houses the opportunity seldom arose. If Mesía wanted to achieve anything, Paquito was indispensable. Supposing Ana agreed to talk with him alone, where could they talk? In the judge's house? Impossible, thought the seducer; that would be a formal betrayal of the sort which alarmed women more than anything else, and the judge's wife would not countenance any such complications – to begin with, at least. Paco's house was neutral ground and, therefore, the most suitable place to lay siege in a right and proper way, and await developments. Don Alvaro had learned this from experience. He had won his most heroic amorous victories in Vegallana's house. His pride advised him not to make for Ana Ozores an exception which all Vetusta would imagine to be indispensable.

This was why he wanted his triumph to take place at the Vegallanas' place: so that everyone should see.

It would be in the Yellow Salon, the famous Yellow Salon. What did Vetustans know of such things? The judge's wife was a woman like any other, why did everyone insist on regarding her as invulnerable? What armour protected her heart? With what singular, miraculous ointment did she make frail flesh fireproof? Mesía did not believe in the possibility of absolute virtue in a woman, and it was this disbelief, he thought, which gave him the superiority acknowledged by everyone. A handsome man (which he undoubtedly was) who had such ideas was bound to be irresistible.

'I believe in myself and I do not believe in women.' This was his motto.

The effect of the superstitious respect which the judge's wife inspired in Vetusta was, as he well knew, to excite his desire, to increase his determination that what he was telling his young friend about falling in love should come to be not far short of the truth.

'He was, above all, a political man: a political man who used love and other passions for his own personal gain.' This had been his dogma for more than six years now. Previously he had conquered for the sake of conquering. But now it was always with an eye to the possible returns – for some good reason and to some good end. At this very moment he had in hand a vast project in which a prominent role was played by the wife of a political personage whom he had met by the seaside, at Palomares. She was another fortress of virtue, a bomb-proof fortress. And she was in society. Well, he had begun to undermine the fortress. This was a major project indeed! He was hopeful of success, but he was not hurrying himself. He never hurried himself when engaged in difficult enterprises. He, the Alexander of seducers, who had conquered the chastity of a robust village girl after two hours' fighting, who had broken up a wedding in one night and taken the bridegroom's place – he, the extempore Don Juan, proceeded, in serious cases, with the patience of a timid student whose love is purely platonic. There were women who succumbed only in this way – unless frequent opportunities for sudden attack, with secrecy assured, presented themselves, for this expedited the capitulation. The wife of the personage from Madrid was one of those women who took years. But victory in this case would assure him of great advancement in his career, and this was the main consideration for Mesía, the political man. People were beginning to talk in Vetusta about whether he had his eye on the judge's wife. It made him feel ashamed to admit it to himself! For two years now she must have believed him to be enamoured of her sterling qualities! Yes, he had already devoted two years to the external worship of the judge's wife – worship which was prudent and discreet and nearly always silent, its only eloquence being the eloquence of looks, of certain comings and goings, and of attitudes – now sorrowful, now impatient, perhaps even desperate. And, what was even more embarrassing, the same two years had also been employed by the poet Trifón Cármenes, the lyrical lover of the judge's wife, in ingratiating himself with her. Don Alvaro had become well aware of the fact and, although he did not regard his rival as a redoubtable one, it was ridiculous to coincide with such a character in both the timing of the operations and the system of attack. But it could not be helped, at the beginning; it was necessary to proceed in this way. The poet had been left far behind, of course. He had not advanced beyond this unpromising situation: the judge's wife still did not know that he was in love with her. Sometimes she would notice his stares and think:

'That little poet who writes for *El Lábaro* is such a dreamy fellow! He must be worried about his rhymes.' And would immediately forget all about Trifón Cármenes. So the only witness to the poet's grief was Mesía; Mesía was the only person in the world who understood the deep, hidden meaning of his amatory verses. Trifón's elegies were like charades, and only Don Alvaro, who held their key, could decipher them. This, which the well-favoured Mesía saw as the ridiculous aspect of his enterprise, sometimes infuriated him and sometimes put him in an excellent mood. It was droll! He, Trifón's rival! An assault would have to be made. Enough had been done, surely, to prepare the ground. The ground was the heart of the judge's wife.

The president of the Gentlemen's Club apprized cultural progress by the speed or slowness with which such matters proceeded. Vetusta was a primitive place – what was happening to him with Anita Ozores proved that. True, in the course of those two years he had conquered other fortresses, but none of these adventures had made much noise in the world. The judge's wife could not have any sure knowledge of them, and her discreet adorer's love and constancy must be, for her, little short of certain fact. Prudence and secrecy were Don Alvaro's most positive qualities in such affairs. Few people knew about his current adventures, and those which everyone talked about and he himself would even recount were all old ones. This, together with the natural vanity which always makes a woman believe that a man really loves her, might induce the judge's wife, if she were interested in him, to think that the Don Juan of Vetusta had stopped being a Don Juan and had turned into a true, constant and platonic lover of her charm. This was what he wanted to find out for certain. Would she trust him? Would she be prepared to sacrifice the tranquillity of her conscience and other comforts which she enjoyed in her honoured home?

Certain possibly rash insinuations had lost him some ground, and this set-back had coincided with her change of confessors.

'All might be lost now,' Don Alvaro had thought. 'Religion would be a more fearsome rival than Trifón Cármenes, and the canon theologian a guardian more worthy of respect than my good friend Don Víctor Quintanar.'

He had no alternative but to stake everything on a complete victory. The time had come to reap the harvest: was he going to gather nothing but thistles? He did not think so. All the signs were promising, but, although he attempted to hide the fact from himself, he still had his doubts. He was all the more irritated by Vetusta's superstitious faith in the lady's virtue because, much against his will, he shared that stupid faith.

'And yet I have information which argues against it,' he thought, 'and there are certain symptoms. What's more, I refuse to believe in feminine virtue. Lord above, even the Bible says it! *Who can find a virtuous woman?*'[11]

If Paco Vegallana had known these thoughts, which showed that his friend's love was false, he would have denied him his able assistance in the attack on the judge's wife. Strong, invincible love alone could excuse everything. That, at least, was what Paco's morality asserted. If Don Alvaro's love was as great and sincere as he said, it would be nothing out of the way for the judge's wife to love him back. A married woman sins less than an unmarried one when she does something wrong because, clearly, the married woman doesn't compromise herself.

'This is positive morality!' the Young Marquis would say, in all seriousness, whenever somebody opposed his arguments. 'Yes, sir, this is modern, scientific morality, and that business they call Positivism preaches precisely this: immoral acts are those which do some positive harm to someone. What harm is done to a husband who knows nothing about it?'

Paco believed that this was the message of the latest fashionable philosophy, which he considered to be excellent for such purposes, although, as a good conservative, he wanted none of it in the universities.

'Why not? Because it is not for boys to know such things.'

When they reached the porch of the Vegallanas' mansion its future owner had tears in his eyes. His heart had been softened so by Mesía's eloquence! How great was his hero Don Alvaro now! Much greater than ever. So inside the out-and-out sceptic, the man of ice, the disillusioned dandy, there was another man? Who would have thought it? And how well the colours of the two men matched (their subtle shadings, Paco meant). What a fine contrast between his apparent indifference and elegant pessimism, and his hidden erotic fervour, with just a hint of the romantic about it! If instead of the *History of Prostitution* Paquito had read certain fashionable novels he would have realized that Don Alvaro was only imitating the heroes of these elegant books – and imitating them badly, for he was above all a political man. Paco did find in his reading someone who resembled Mesía: he was a Marguerite Gautier[12] of the male sex, a man who could be redeemed by love. It was necessary at all costs to redeem him, to help him.

'And Don Víctor, a man incapable of being sceptical, cold and prosaic on the outside, but romantic and tender within, would have to forgive him.'

As the two men climbed the stairs, Paco Vegallana, the most popular young man in town among the women of the same, was resolved:

1. To favour as much as he could the love of the judge's wife and Mesía, which he regarded as being beyond dispute.

And

2. To seek, for his own use, a neo-romantic arrangement, a true passion compatible with his fondness for voluminous forms and hyperbolical protuberances – which is not, needless to say, what Paco called them.

'Is there anybody at home?' he asked a manservant, certain that the judge's wife would be there, because he had a hunch about it.

'Two ladies.'

'Who are they?'

The servant pondered.

'I believe that one of them is Doña Visita, although I did not see them; but she can be heard from a distance. I do not know who the other lady is.'

'Very well,' said Paco, turning to Mesía. 'It's them. These last few days Visita hasn't left Ana's side.'

Mesía's legs trembled a little, much against his will.

'Listen,' he said, 'let's go to your room first. I want you to tell me the truth – nothing but the truth, and as solemnly as if it were your dying confession – of whatever you have noticed about her that could be favourable to me.'

'All right, let's go upstairs.'

Paco was a little alarmed. The truth of what he had noticed was not much to speak of. But, pooh! with the aid of a little imagination – and, as it happened, he was so worked up just now!

The Young Marquis's rooms were on the second floor. When the two men reached the first-floor landing they heard loud guffaws, coming from the kitchen. It was Visita's eternal laughter.

'They're in the kitchen!' said Mesía, astonished, recalling former times.

'Hey,' added Paco, 'wasn't Visita waiting for Obdulia at her place, to make pies and other such stuff?'

'That's what she said.'

'In that case, what's she doing here?'

'And why are they in the kitchen?'

A beautiful female head wearing a fancy white hat appeared at a window on the other side of the courtyard around which the house was built. Beneath the white hat floated abundant, graceful black curls, a fresh happy mouth was smiling and large, busy eyes were speaking volumes. Two robust, well-turned arms, white and firm-fleshed, with the hands of a china doll, held up above the hat a plucked chicken, still quivering in its death-throes, blood dripping from its beak.

Obdulia, turning towards the speechless gentlemen, made to twist her victim's neck, and cried in triumph:

'All by myself! I did it all by myself! That's what I do to all the men!'

'It was Obdulia! Obdulia! So *she* wasn't there.'

VIII

The Marquis de Vegallana was the leader in Vetusta of the most reactionary of the parties which adhered to the Restoration, but he had no liking for politics and was more of a figurehead than anything else. There was always some favourite of his who was the real leader. His current favourite (to the shame and scandal of that free play so essential to the smooth working of institutions in general and of Restoration politics in particular!) was none other than Mesía, the leader of the Dynastic Liberal Party. The reactionary leader believed that he settled his own affairs, but in fact he followed Mesía's promptings. But Mesía did not abuse his secret power. Like a man playing himself at chess and taking as much interest in the white pieces as in the black, Don Alvaro looked after the commercial concerns of conservatives as much as those of liberals. He scratched the marquis's back, and the marquis scratched his. If the marquis's faction was in power, Don Alvaro would distribute hunting permits, commissions, licences to sell tobacco, and often more succulent morsels still, just as if his own men were in command. Then the liberals would come into office, yet, thanks to Don Alvaro, the marquis did not cease to be the arbiter of elections, and now it was he who handed out tobacconists' licences, situations, and even sinecures.

This was how the political system worked in Vetusta, in spite of all the surface appearances of bitter dissent. The so-called rank and file cudgelled each other in the villages of the province, while their leaders had a private understanding and, indeed, were hand in glove. The shrewdest of their supporters had some suspicion of what was happening, but they did not complain about it. Rather, they tried to make the most of the secret, and get two slices of cake.

Vegallana had a great passion: 'swallowing up the miles' – in other words going for long walks.

Local political intrigues bored him. He was an honorary leader, the real leader was his right-hand man, Mesía. Don Alvaro was to the marquis in politics what he was to the younger Vegallana in love: his Mentor, his nymph Egeria.[1] Father and son both considered themselves to be incapable of thought on these topics without the aid of their Pythoness.[2] This was the secret, known to few, of Vegallana the politician.

As men came away from a meeting in the room in his house known as the 'Antiques Gallery', they would exclaim:

'What a mind! The marquis was born to manage elections, to handle people!'

'And he doesn't let his age get him down, he never seems to change at all!'

And everything they were praising was Mesía's work.

When Don Alvaro wanted to punish one of his followers he put him up against a reactionary candidate who had to be allowed to win. The marquis was grateful to Don Alvaro for his self-denial and repaid him by saying, for example:

'Look, my supporter, old so-and-so, is putting up at – what's the name of the place? – but the man gets on my nerves, you can let the liberal candidate win.' And Mesía would reward the services of some faithful follower.

What would Ronzal have said had he known that he owed his place on the standing committee to one of these skilful manoeuvres!

The marquis often said that 'fate had led him to be an activist in a conservative party – his birth, his obligations to his own class – but in temperament he was a liberal'. He had great 'personal friends' in villages and hamlets, and he distributed embraces throughout the district for many leagues around. During elections, when many people, nearly everyone in fact, believed that he was manipulating the complex machinery of personal influence, the only positive, direct service he was giving was that of an electoral agent. He would ask Mesía for a handful of candidates and distribute them among the electoral parishes which, like the Wandering Jew,[3] he visited on his excursions.

Whenever he went for a walk along a route which he did not know, he would count his steps – even when official measurements were available, for he had no faith in governmental kilometres. He counted his steps, and recorded the thousands with small stones which he put into his coat pockets. When he arrived home he would empty these bulging sacks on to a table and count the milliary stones with even greater satisfaction than he had the first time. The talk at the gathering in the Vegallanas' house on such an evening would be, for the most part, about the marquis's walk.

'Where are you off to today, my lord?' a friend, coming across him in the country, would ask.

'Cardona, via La Carbayeda, one thousand one hundred and one, one thousand one hundred and two, three, four . . .' And the marquis continued counting his steps, leaning on a knotted, charred walking-stick, of the same kind as the local villagers used.

His stick, his plain coat and his wide-brimmed hat of soft felt assured his popularity in the villages. He shared all the pride and prejudice of the other Vetustan nobles, but he affected a straightforwardness which delighted simple souls.

He had another mania, the corollary of his pacing: a mania for weights and measures. He knew, to several decimal places, the capacity of all the theatres, parliament-houses, churches, stock exchanges, circuses and other notable edifices in Europe. 'Covent Garden is so many metres wide by so many long and so many high,' and he would calculate its cubic content in the twinkling of an eye. 'The Royal Theatre in Madrid is so many cubic metres smaller than the Paris Opera House.' He often told falsehoods in order to dazzle his audience, but he could be precise, astonishingly precise, when he wanted. 'Give me facts, data, figures,' he would say; 'all the rest is mere German philosophy.'[4]

He was deeply concerned about architectural proportions. To achieve a proper proportion between the cathedral and the square in front of it the cathedral should be moved back three or four metres – and he would have been happy to propose such a move. He was Don Saturnino Bermúdez's natural enemy in matters concerning historical monuments and public ornamentation. He wanted everything to be in straight lines. He dreamed about the streets of New York (which he had never seen), and if this argument was put to him, 'But the nobility, of its very essence, opposes all such egalitarian ideas,' he would reply: 'My dear sir, *distingue tempora*'[5] (this was not what he meant), 'let's have no misrepresentation, now, no irrelevances, *post hoc ergo propter hoc*'[6] (nor was this what he meant). 'True inequality is a question of blood, but all buildings should be of identical height. That is the way of America, a country which is far ahead of us.'

The houses of La Colonia, the new part of Vetusta, were, thanks to the marquis's powerful influence, of identical height.

No roof was above another.

There were protests from returned emigrants who wanted to build mansions eight storeys high in order to be able to see the church-towers of their native villages from their attic windows, but the municipal council, under pressure from the marquis, levelled all roofs, 'leaving for other spheres of life the natural inequalities of the society in which we live', as the marquis said in an anonymous article which he published in *El Lábaro.*

The marchioness regarded her husband as a perfect fool, a condition which she believed to be almost universal in husbands. She was a real liberal. Very pious, but very liberal, for one thing did not exclude the other. Her piety consisted in presiding over numerous religious guilds, demanding alms at church-doors as she clanked a twenty-five-peseta piece in the collection plate, presenting canons with sweetmeats, inviting them to lunch, and sending capons to the bishop and fruit to nuns who made preserves. Liberty, according to this lady, was a principle applicable above all to the sixth commandment.[7] 'She had been neither wicked nor perfectly virtuous, but just like any other woman who is not altogether wicked. One virtue which she did possess was the most ample tolerance. She was of opinion that the only thing left for aristocrats to do nowadays was to amuse themselves. They were unable to imitate the virtues of the nobility of former times? Well then, let them imitate their vices.' As far as the marchioness was concerned, there were only two things in life worth bothering about: Regency[8] and Louis XV. The furniture in her Yellow Salon and the fireplace in her boudoir were modelled on those in a room at Versailles, so the upholsterer and the architect had said, but the marchioness's love of soft cushions and padded upholstery had, over the years, brought about great modifications in the Regency Salon.

Captain Bedoya, the eminent antiquarian, made this salon the target of his gossip:

'The marchioness insists that it's in the Regency style. The only Regency I can see there is that of Espartero.'[9] The chairs and settees were luxurious, but they bore the marks of careless handling and, what was worse from the historical point of view, had all been turned into flagrant anachronisms.

The marchioness had subjected them to various alterations, all with yellow as their basis. First she had covered them with damask, then with brocaded silk, and finally with quilted satin, or *capitonné*, as she called it, forming small rounded protuberances which Don Saturnino considered indecent. The upholsterer had duly protested: *capitonné* work did not suit the salon, according to his dogma, but the marchioness laughed at such official impositions. The rest of the salon's furnishings – mirrors, console tables, drapery and so on – had developed from what the furniture-maker had believed to be Regency into the most scandalous hotchpotch, in accordance with the marchioness's whims and ideas of comfort. If anyone mentioned bad taste, she replied that the modern fashion was all for *confort* and freedom. The old paintings, of Cenceño's[10] school no doubt, but all venerable family heirlooms, had been banished to the second floor, and their places filled by cheerful water-colours of bullfighters and their mantilla'd young ladies, and roguish-looking friars. To the scandal of Bedoya and Bermúdez, she had even put up some coloured prints which were somewhat immodest and not at all artistic. Among the furnishings in the adjacent boudoir, where the marchioness spent the day, anarchy was complete, but again everything was comfortable. Almost all the pieces of furniture were for lying on: chaises-longues, rocking-chairs, ottomans, couches, footstools – it was like a conspiracy against action, and anyone entering that room felt tempted to stretch himself out. The sofa, with its broad, bulging belly and its buttons buried in satin like the pistils of yellow roses, was a wordless anacreontic song,[11] accompanied by the tantalizing aromas of the hundred and one perfumes which the marchioness scattered to the four winds.

The Excelentísima Señora Doña Rufina de Robledo, the Marchioness de Vegallana, rose every day at twelve o'clock, took her breakfast, and sat or lay in one of the chairs in her boudoir, reading novels or crocheting until luncheon-time. The great hearth was lit between October and May. In the evening Doña Rufina went to the theatre whenever there was a performance, even though it be snowing or thunderbolts be falling. That was why one kept carriages. If there was nothing on at the theatre – and this was a frequent occurrence in Vetusta – she remained in her boudoir, where she received any of her lady- and gentleman-friends who wanted to have a chat among themselves while she read novels, magazines and satirical newspapers full of cartoons. She would only intervene in the conversation to make some comment in the style of the epigrams for which her good friend the archpriest was renowned. During these brief interruptions, Doña Rufina displayed a profound knowledge of the world and a tasteful pessimism on the subject of virtue. In her opinion there was but one mortal sin: hypocrisy. She branded as hypocrites all those who did not betray any erotic inclinations; that they might not feel them was a possibility she did not admit. Whenever anybody guaranteed some other person's virtue, the marchioness, without lifting her eyes from the cartoons, would shake her head and mutter between her false teeth, as if to ruminate denials. Sometimes she would speak up:

'Don't you come with those tales to an old soldier like me!'

She had never been a soldier, but what she meant to convey was that she had been more faithful to Regency manners than to Regency furniture. Her historical references were usually to the mistresses of Henry VIII and Louis XIV.

If not many people had come, the Yellow Salon remained in

discreet darkness. But when there was an attendance of half a dozen or more, a cut-glass chandelier hanging in the middle of the salon was lit. It was quite high, and the only person who could reach the gas tap was Mesía, the tallest of all the men. The other men complained. It wasn't fair.

'Why must the chandelier be so high?' they would demand, in deep dudgeon.

Doña Rufina would shrug her shoulders.

'One of his whims,' she would reply, referring to her husband.

The marquis was not himself very scrupulous in the matter of private morality. But one night he had been feeling his way along the wall of the Yellow Salon on his way to his wife's boudoir, the door of which was ajar, when his hand had brushed against a nose, he had heard a woman's cry (he was sure of it) and then the sound of creaking chairs and footsteps muffled by the carpet. Discretion had obliged him not to mention the incident, but he had told the servants to put the chandelier up higher. That would stop people from dimming it or turning it out. But the result was an exasperating inequality, for Mesía, by going on tiptoes, could still reach the gas tap.

Of the marquis's three daughters, two, Pilar and Lola, had married and were living in Madrid. Emma, the second-born, had died of consumption. The small vigilance which the marchioness had felt obliged to observe while her daughters were still living with her had now gone with the wind. For Doña Rufina, in her solitude, had but one consolation. Each year, at fair-time, she summoned one of her many nieces who were dispersed throughout Vetusta province. These high-born village girls longed for fair-time to come around, because it might be their turn to go away to Vetusta. Ever since early childhood they had become accustomed to regard as a time of special pleasure the period spent with their aunt among the very best people of the provincial capital. There were a few prudish parents who raised objections derived from that private morality which did not concern the marquis, but in the end vanity always triumphed, and the marchioness was never without a niece at fair-time. The niece used the rooms of the absent daughters; Emma's room had not been slept in again but it was entered whenever necessary. For a few weeks the niece would enliven with the sounds of happier days all those sitting-rooms and corridors, bedchambers and boudoirs, which were so large and sad when empty. In the evenings, however, there was never any lack of animation on the first floor, whether a niece was in residence or not. On the second floor, adventures were always taking place, by day and by night, but these were silent adventures. Paquito was one of their regular protagonists. In moments of serenity he would swear that there was nothing worse than chasing after serving-women in one's own house, but he could not control himself. *Videor meliora*,[12] said Don Saturn, but Paco did not understand. Whether a niece was present or not, most of the people who went to visit the marchioness were young. Daughters of the most distinguished parents often went to provide company for the unfortunate lady who had lost her own three daughters. Either they arranged to meet their young gentlemen before going, or they went alone and awaited developments. Romantic relationships were often improvised in the Vegallanas' house, and from the Yellow Salon had issued many marriages *in extremis*,[13] as Paquito called them, in the belief that *in extremis* meant something very amusing. But the Yellow Salon more often provided material for scandalmongers. The marquis's house was respected, but the people who went there were picked to pieces. When the story was told of some escapade it almost always concluded with the words:

'The most hateful thing about it all is that those little hussies should have chosen such a respectable, worthy house for their fun and games.' Progressive liberals, however, who did not believe in half-measures, maintained that the house was the worst feature of the whole business.

Yet the backbiters did their best to be introduced into that house where so many adventures took place.

Although there had been a certain relaxation of customs, and the circle of *persons of quality* was not as exclusive as it had been in the times of Doña Anuncia and Doña Agueda (R.I.P.), it was not everybody who was allowed to the intimate gatherings at the Vegallanas' house. The guests themselves tried to keep the doors closed to outsiders partly because by doing so they could give themselves airs and partly because it did not suit them to have witnesses present. 'They were better off *en petit comité*.' The marchioness had infected her friends with her spirit of tolerance. People did not spy on each other; everyone minded his or her own business. Since the lady of the house was a more than sufficient guarantee of the respectability of the gathering, mammas who had nothing more to expect from the vanities of the world allowed their daughters to go alone. Furthermore, there were always some married ladies present who were still concerned to protect the honour of their offspring, or to have a good time on their own account. And who could doubt but these ladies would command respect? Visitación, for example. There were some mothers who would not countenance such a state of affairs, but they were ridiculous fussers, like the fathers who behaved in a similar way. Sometimes a canon would, with his presence, give greater guarantees of morality, although it is true that this did not happen often, nor did the canon stay long, for the cathedral clergy preferred to visit the marchioness by day. People with scruples were hypocrites – that was all there was to say about it.

The marchioness knew that in her house young people fell in love with some enthusiasm. At times, as she read, she would notice that somebody was opening a door with great care, trying not to make any noise, so as not to disturb her; she would look up – a boy was missing, very well. A little later she would notice the same thing happening, she would look up again, a girl was missing, very well, so what? She continued reading. And she thought, 'They are all of good family, they are all aware of the regard which is due to this house, and as for peccadilloes – that's up to them.' This was the criterion which she had applied when her daughters were living with her. And she continued thinking, 'They're good girls, and if any man goes too far, I know them well, they'll warn me with a good slap. All the rest is just innocent fun and games; so long as there aren't any warnings, it can only be that.' After all, her own daughters had married, and they hadn't been returned with complaints of serious damage. If anything had happened to them it must have been fun and games, too. And the other girl had died because that had been the will of God. Consumption – the fashionable disease. Whenever she had spotted a danger signal in her daughters she had applied the appropriate remedy, in a frank and expert way, without making any scandal, but without beating about the bush, either.

But with her young friends, the girls who went to keep her company in the evening, she took no such precautions. 'They've got mothers of their own,' she would say, or: 'It's their own look-out.' And she always added her other saying:

'So long as they are not found wanting in the respect which they owe to this house.'

One of the men who had most benefited from the ideas of the marchioness and her friends was Alvaro Mesía.

'But one could forgive that man for absolutely anything. Such tact! Such prudence! Such discretion!'

'He could live in a nunnery without fear of scandal.'

A hundred times she had advised Paco, her beloved Paco, to take as his model the expertise and circumspection of Mesía – whenever she had surprised her darling boy in the arms of some seamstress, laundress or serving-girl.

Her Paco was so gauche, so ignorant.

'Look, my lad, it's indecent for me to catch you sowing your wild oats. Wait until you can reach the table before you start trying to eat meat. First learn to be careful, and after that – what you choose to do is your own affair.'

And, feeling that she had been too indulgent, she would add:

'What's more, such adventures shouldn't take place at home. Just ask Mesía.' She was the one who had initiated the Young Marquis into his cult of the Vetustan Don Juan.

But realizing that her son was incorrigible, the marchioness made a point of coughing and talking in a loud voice whenever she went up to the second floor.

When her nieces were in Vetusta there were concerts, luncheon parties and trips into the country, as well as the gatherings at home; it was just like the good old days. Gaiety scampered through the house once again, not a single nook provided safe refuge from the audacity of close friends, and in boudoirs, and even in bedrooms, where the virginal beds of the Vegallana daughters still stood, laughter and suppressed cries would sometimes be heard, betraying the revels of which life in that homely Arcady was composed.

Don Alvaro looked upon this Arcady with loving eyes, for it was the theatre of his greatest triumphs. Each piece of furniture had a secret story to tell him: those plump-bellied chairs and those solemn sofas with arms like the arms of oriental idols had an air of trustworthiness, a guarantee of the eternal silence which was their strongest recommendation. The wood with its fine film of white varnish seemed to declare: Fear not: no one will say a word. In the Yellow Salon the lover could see a whole volume of reminiscences – reminiscences 'so tender and happy' not just 'when God willed it', but now and always. The 'pleasant favours for his joy discover'd'[14] were the discreet tapestries, and the silken stuff which covered the chairs – quilted, distended, yielding, silent – and the thick carpet, which resembled Mesía himself in the way it muffled any sound which might betray the secrets of love.

The marquis tolerated it all. Just his wife's whims.

'He hadn't managed to moralize her, so there was little chance oi his moralizing her guests.' He lived on the second floor.

He had realized that, over the years, the Yellow Salon had lost the austerity proper to a drawing-room, and he had decided to convert the large room on the second floor, immediately over it, into a reception-room.

The marchioness never went up to this new drawing-room. She received all her guests downstairs, whoever they might be. Any guest of the marquis on a formal visit was made to die of cold in his 'Antiques Gallery'. This, together with the marquis's study, constituted what was, according to him, 'the serious part of the house'. In his study all was unpolished oak; there was no gilt whatsoever; it was all wood, nothing but wood. Vegallana set great store by the austerity of his study; there was nothing, in such circumstances, so serious as oak. The 'sobriety of his furnishings' bordered on poverty.

'It's my cell!' he would say, with affection.

It was a cold place into which to venture, and Vegallana seldom ventured there. On the walls of the 'Antiques Gallery' hung tapestries of dubious authenticity but undisputed age.

They were the only objects which Captain Bedoya considered to be worthy of respect in that Museum of Forgeries (to use his expression). The marquis vainly thought that his money could make him into an antiquarian, but the truth was that he paid through the nose for what turned out to be the work of *truqueurs* (the captain's word). The implacable Bedoya, one of the marchioness's most assiduous guests, both pitied and despised her husband. Having no desire to upset him, however, he had refrained from providing him with unequivocal proof of the sad fact that the marquis himself was older than the Henry II furniture[15] in his 'Antiques Gallery'. He thought that it was authentic, that it had come into the world at the same time as the son of the horse-riding king[16] – he had bought it all himself in Paris! But whenever anyone adduced this argument in the Vegallanas' house in Bedoya's presence he would call that person aside and, taking care not to be seen, would take him upstairs to the second floor, creep into the 'Antiques Gallery', lock the door and, with all the thievish furtiveness of his book-borrowing visits to the Gentlemen's Club, advance upon a Henry II chair, turn it upside-down, and search for a hidden section of the foot where he had made various little holes with a pen-knife and filled them with wax the same colour as the chair; he would remove the wax with his pen-knife, scratch the wood and – this was the moment of triumph! – it did not crumble into powder; it broke up into tiny splinters, but not powder.

'Do you see?' said Bedoya.

'See what?'

'This is new wood; if it belonged to the period the marquis supposes, it would crumble into powder. Old wood always gives off the powder made by woodworm. This is a fact known to us experts, but not to amateurs who are gifted only with money and credulity. All this is *truquage*, mere *truquage*!'

He would replace the wax in the holes, leave the chair in its place, and descend the stairs in triumph, saying, 'So now you know what I mean! But of course the poor marquis must not be told a word of all this.'

At first Paco Vegallana regretted finding Obdulia in his house that afternoon. He was in no mood for frivolity. Don Alvaro's confidences had moved him, and his spirit was soaring in an ideal atmosphere. He had been blown by a breath of romantic air which made him tingle inside with a pleasure the very uncommonness of which increased its intensity. Being in this frame of mind was an unusual experience for him.

Obdulia and Visitación, laughing like madwomen in the kitchen window overlooking the courtyard, shouted to the two men.

'Up here, up here! Everyone's got to lend a hand!' screamed Visitación, sucking her fingers, which were covered with syrup.

'But what's this, ladies? Weren't you in Visita's house, getting tea ready?'

Visita coloured a little.

They all laughed at the thought of Joaquinito Orgaz's frustration at the end of his hunt after Obdulia.

Obdulia explained everything. Visita did not have the moulds for a certain caramel-cream dish, the invention of the late Doña Agueda Ozores; furthermore, her oven was not as large as the marchioness's; and her kitchen was wanting in other technical specifications, which the men would not understand. In short, they could not make the caramel cream or the syrups or even the sandwiches in Visita's kitchen and, without as much as a word of warning, had moved their camp to the Vegallanas' house.

It had seemed a very amusing idea to Obdulia and Visita. They had surprised the marchioness having her afternoon nap in her boudoir. She had approved of everything except being woken up. Without stirring from her chair, she had issued orders for the chef and his assistants.

'Tell Pedro, Colás and the girls to help these young ladies and to go and get whatever they need.'

Turning to the ladies, she had said with a smile:

'Come on, away with you, you mad creatures, away to the kitchen, and leave me in peace.'

And she had buried herself in Dumas's *The Mohicans*.[17]

Visita often made such incursions into friends' houses. That was what friends were for. And her own kitchen was hell! Smoke came back down the chimney, you couldn't go in without suffocating, or into her dining-room, which was next to the kitchen. Few Vetustans could boast of having seen either Visita's dining-room or her kitchen, in spite of the fact that she regularly invited friends to her house to play at charades and run along the corridors. But she kept certain doors closed, to stop the smoke from getting out, and, pointing towards the dark narrow passages, she would say:

'You can run about down there as much as you like, you mad young things, but nobody's to open that door.'

Her generosity, as a lady receiving visits from close friends, ran to making old worsted dresses and kerchiefs available for imaginative young blades to dress up as women or as Turks. The garments were placed in a room containing a truckle-bed which lacked both bedclothes and mattress, so that it showed all its springs (or, rather, its rope netting). This was the dressing-room for the actors and actresses of charades. They all changed together, for they wore their fancy dress over their ordinary clothes. Anyway, Visita did not light the room – why should she? People in the sitting-room would suddenly hear voices behind the green taffeta curtains:

'Pepe, stop it or I'll slap you.'

'Hullo! That wasn't on the programme.'

'Come now boys and girls, behave yourselves.'

'Why don't you give them a lamp, Visita?'

'Because the mad things are capable of burning the house down.'

'Visita's right, quite right,' the cry would come from Joaquinito Orgaz or from the Pepe who had been threatened with a slap.

It was in other people's houses that Visita displayed her great familiarity with friends, her frankness and her straightforward, unpretentious behaviour. In other people's houses Visita went crazy.

She talked incessantly, at the top of her voice, with a dozen laughs to each sentence. At fifteen she had been much praised for her amusing scatter-brained ways; but now she was nearly thirty-five, and still in a whirl. She was a cascade of gaiety, as the poet Cármenes said in her album. She was more like a cataract of bad manners according to Doña Paula, the vicar-general's mother, who would never return her visits. But whether she was a cataract, a cascade, or a whirlpool, it was always with an eye to the main chance. Her giddiness was the result of close, profound study. While she was being giddy her watchful eye would be searching out the prey – some trinket, or a sweet, anything except money. She believed – or rather pretended to believe – that objects have no value, that only money is wealth.

'I owe you the five céntimos you put in the collection-box for me the other day.'

'Forget it, Visita, such a small sum. Pray don't put me to shame.'

'But of course! Here you are. My, what a pretty pin-box!'

'A worthless bauble.'

'It's lovely!'

'It's yours, if you want it.'

'You'd better not say that again!'

'It's yours, if you want it – a great treasure, I'm sure!'

'Really? In that case I'll have it. What a magpie I am!'

Indeed she was a magpie, for that was what Doña Paula called her: the thieving magpie.

Her greatest ravages were wrought among eatables.

She would enter a neighbour's house, in fits of laughter.

'Do you know what's happened? We've looked everywhere, and there aren't any signs of it, we've lost the cupboard key – and so here I am, dying of hunger. Come on, come on, give me some food, you cunning little vixen, if I don't have something to eat I shall faint from hunger.'

Games of lotto or dice were played in her house twice a week. On such occasions a fund would be set aside for a picnic in the country and a committee appointed to prepare the food. Its members were always Visita and a certain young man, a cousin of hers. For reasons of economy, and because the pastry-cooks and confectioners of Vetusta filled her with disgust, Visita took personal charge of making the pastry, the syrups, and indeed everything which could be made in her kitchen. But then it turned out that nothing could be made in her kitchen. That wretched smoke! That landlord of hers, who refused to have the oven enlarged! In the name of the devil, the Lord forgive her!

Caught in this predicament, Visitación turned to the Vegallanas' kitchen, or to a kitchen in some other fine house, but usually to the former. The whole operation was carried out there. Visita had the marquis's servants at her disposal, and obtained Pedro the chef's permission to take provisions from the larder. But she sent the servants to the grocer's for sugar, raisins, pepper, salt: the chef – in the name of the devil! – insisted on keeping all the cupboard-drawers locked, so they'd just have to go out and buy all the other things she needed. 'Money? Don't you worry about that, I've got an account there.' But in the end it was all put on to the marquis's account. Mistakes will happen. After all, it had been his servants who had done the shopping. At the next evening gathering in Visita's house after the picnic her friends would comment upon it.

'What's the position, Visita? Are we deeply in debt?'

'Not much – just a tiny bit.'

'Come on then, let's all pay up.'

'Yes, that's only fair.'

'We'd better go shares.'

'Stop it – be quiet, will you? I refuse to discuss the matter, it isn't worth it.'

This provided Visita's household with the main course of their meals for several weeks, and with the sweet for months. Her husband was a humble bank clerk, but he came from a very good family and was related to persons of title. If Visita didn't use her ingenuity how could they keep up the appearances of respectability, as they must if they wanted to continue being related to the nobility?

Before Visita's marriage there had been talk (but then, who is not subject to such gossip?) about whether she had jumped from a balcony – not because of a fire, but because of a gentleman-friend whom some people presumed to have been Mesía. It had all been conjecture, nothing was certain. But, then, she was rather flighty, and she did not save appearances. . . .

Nobody now remembered that gossip. She was as scatter-brained as ever, notorious for her sweet tooth and her sponging – to use the expression favoured by Vetustans as by everyone else – but for nothing worse than that. Her untimely merriment made her unbearable, but in grave matters, where there is no room for trivialities, nobody made any accusations, in public at least. Of course this or that little slip doesn't count.

She was tall, slim, blonde and attractive, but not as attractive as she thought. In her small eyes, which she had the habit of screwing up until they disappeared, there was a certain malice, but not the spicy and voluptuous charm she imagined there. The hand which touched

Visita's ungloved hand felt the clammy traces of some sweetmeat which she had just eaten.

When Don Alvaro was in the company of close friends he spoke of Visitación with disdain and grimaced with ill-concealed disgust. He affirmed that she had pretty feet and that her calves were much more handsome than one might suspect, but her shoes were shoddy, and her petticoats and stockings left a great deal to be desired – his listeners knew what he meant. And he wiped his lips with his pocket-handkerchief.

Paco Vegallana swore that the woman used garters made of red tape and that he had once discovered her wearing one made of string. All this was to be mentioned only in the company of men, of course, and they were to be discreet about it.

Obdulia's underclothes, on the other hand, were irreproachable; unlike her behaviour. But this was such common knowledge that nobody talked about it any more. To each successive lover Obdulia herself denied all her previous affairs, except her affair with Alvaro Mesía. It was her pride and joy. The man had fascinated her, why deny it? But only him. She was a widow who never remembered her husband; it was as if she were really Alvarito's widow. 'She had no past but Alvaro!'

That afternoon both women were looking very pretty, one had to admit it. At least the ingenuous Paco Vegallana admitted it. And although he did not renounce the idea of devoting the rest of the day to idealism, so opportunely awakened by his friend's revelations, he agreed to go up to the kitchen to smell the dishes which the ladies were cooking.

The Vegallanas' positive grandeur was reflected in their kitchen. These were no impoverished aristocrats: abundance, cleanliness, comfort, diligence, and refinement in the culinary arts, all this and more besides was apparent upon entering that kitchen.

When Pedro the chef and Colás the kitchen-boy cooked an everyday meal it seemed as if they were preparing a banquet. The marquis's dominions were scattered all over the province in the form of rented rural properties. In addition to the rent, which was small, because never raising the rent is a luxury which an aristocratic landlord can enjoy, each tenant paid Vegallana the tribute of the finest produce of his farmyard, the nearby river and his hunting expeditions. Hares, rabbits, partridges, woodcocks, salmon, trout, capons, hens, all made their unwilling way to the marquis's kitchen, as if they had been summoned to another Noah's Ark in the face of a second universal flood. At every hour of the day and night, supplies for Vegallana's table were being procured somewhere in the province; one could be sure of it.

At midnight, when all the ovens in Vegallana's kitchen were cold, and Pedro was asleep, and his master was asleep, and nobody had any thoughts for food, a poor villager was wide awake in a wretched little half-rotten, leaky boat on the River Celonio, a couple of leagues from Vetusta. Under a sombre crag, which like a leaning tower threatened to fall into the fast-flowing stream and which darkened the darkness of the backwater, the villager kept watch for salmon, grasping a bundle of burning straw whose flame was reflected in the rippling river as if the boat had a wake of fire. The salmon caught by the magnate's tenant in the light of a portable bonfire now lay bleeding in slices upon a spotless white pine table, awaiting its turn to go to the gridiron.

By night, too, a little before dawn, a man set out on his expedition into the wilds; he was a tenant who prized himself on bringing his master the first woodcocks, the finest partridges. Now the partridges, too, lay upon the board of pine, their dull brown feathers contrasting with the silver and red of the mutilated salmon. Near by, in the larder, there were hens, pigeons, monstrous eels, monumental hams, white puddings and black puddings, dark purple spiced sausages, all in apparent disorder, some lying piled on top of each other, others hanging from great iron hooks. That larder devoured the most exquisite specimens of the edible flora and fauna of the province. The vivid colours of the largest and ripest fruit enlivened the picture, which would have been a somewhat melancholy one had it been composed only of the dull tones of life stilled and either made into sausages or salted. Yellow pears, red pears, apples of gold and scarlet, piles of walnuts, hazelnuts and chestnuts, all brightened and gave variety and harmonious proportions of light and shadow to the scene, a succulent sight; and the pungent odours of culinary chemistry mingled with the discreet, mellow aromas of oranges, lemons, apples and hay – the soft bed upon which the fruit rested.

All this had been movement, light, life, sound: singing in woods and flying through blue skies, snaking through fresh waters, gleaming on sunlit boughs with all the colours of the rainbow, alive in valleys, pastures, moors and rivers. 'There's no doubt that Vegallana's got what it takes to be a great lord!' Visita thought, with a sigh. She often dreamed, dying of envy, about that larder, a permanent exhibition of all the most appetizing fare in the province of Vetusta.

The marquis smiled whenever someone spoke to him of extending the vote. 'Who cares? Aren't nearly all of them my own tenants? Don't they present me with all their best produce? Are men who give me their most delicious morsels likely to refuse me something as unsubstantial as a vote, a mere *flatus vocis*?'[18]

An opulent, ostentatious multiplicity of pots and pans, worthy of the larder, shone down from every wall upon range, tables and chests. Pedro, haughty and bad-tempered, commanded over it all with an imperious voice, ruling the kitchen as a tyrant. He ate all the best food, he upheld all the traditions of kitchen discipline, and he even kept watch, from a distance, over the service in the dining-room – for he was no vulgar cook, no mere protector of saucepans and casseroles, but a captain-general of chefs, both exposed to fire and heedful of developments around the table. Pedro was still quite young. He was forty years of age – forty well-nursed years. He was an amorous man and, when he took off his apron and donned the clothes of a gentleman, he regarded himself as a dandy within the circles in which, as a chef, he moved. Colás was a kitchen-hand with a decided vocation for his work, a ruddy-faced, lively man with a busy pair of hands and a cunning look in his eyes.

These two personages, together with Visita's servant, a robust highland girl, helped the two ladies. Pedro gave them his expert assistance without neglecting his principal concern, dinner for his master and mistress. At first, he had merely tolerated the tea-making irruption. There was enough room in the kitchen for both operations and, since the tea was of no consequence, the chef had granted his indispensable permission with ill-concealed disdain. By degrees, however, his attitude had changed from one of tolerance to one of protection. First he deigned to give the highland girl some words of advice, then he gave her a pinch. The scene became livelier.

'Colás, place yourself at the disposal of these ladies,' said Pedro in solemn tones.

The marchioness's command was not sufficient; the kitchen-boy obeyed Pedro, and Pedro obeyed the dictates of his duty. Had the marchioness demanded that he perform some action contrary to his artistic convictions she would have succeeded only in obliging him to tender his resignation. This was Pedro's language. He read newspapers before rolling them up into cornets.

As soon as Obdulia, provoked by the haughty chef's coldness, attempted to seduce him with involuntary collisions and looks lasting half a minute, Pedro surrendered, and every so often bestowed masterly touches upon Visita's tea.

He went even further than this. In order to captivate Doña Obdulia with demonstrations of his skill, he came to her aid whenever a theoretical problem or a practical difficulty presented itself.

'What should I add next?'

'What should I toast first?'

'How many times should these eggs be turned?'

'How do you fasten the pastry around this filling?'

'Should I add pepper or shouldn't I?'

'Would it be indiscreet to add some cinnamon?'

'Is this syrup ready yet?'

'How do you beat these egg-whites?'

To all these questions Pedro's skill and intelligence provided a complete answer. When an explanation was not enough he took personal charge and settled everything in a trice.

Obdulia, who had learnt in Madrid from her cousin Tarsila how to bestow rewards upon celebrated geniuses, illustrious men of the arts and the sciences, now determined, just as on the previous afternoon she had driven Señor Bermúdez out of his mind with voluptuous pleasure as a prize for his historical erudition, to grant the Vegallanas' chef fortuitous and surreptitious favours: an ardent look, seemingly involuntary, as she listened to a luminous theory about pork fat, and a squeeze of the hand, apparently accidental, as the two kneaded the same lump of dough or both poked a finger into the same saucepan. The chef almost fell flat on his back from pure delight when, in order to ascertain the amount of boiling required by the peach preserve, Obdulia came up to him and, with a smile, slipped into his mouth the same spoon which had just been caressed by her ruby lips (the 'ruby' is the chef's).

This aproned personage could already see, in the distance, the conquest of Obdulia as his final reward for an entire life devoted to seasoning the food of so many ladies and gentlemen whose progress towards the sweet yet substantial comforts of love he had thus both smoothed and stimulated.

Pedro even went to the extraordinary length of permitting the servant girls to participate in the activities surrounding the black iron casseroles. He loved Woman – he loved all women – but he did not believe in women's culinary skills. The fair sex was destined for other things. Cooking and women were antithetical – a word he had learnt from his newspaper cornets. Liberty and government were antithetical, he had read in a radical newspaper, and he applied the expression to cooking and women. Pedro thought of female cooks what all Vetusta thought of bluestockings: he called them Amazons.

If someone alleged that chefs were expensive and extravagant, he replied:

'Look here, people who aren't rich had better go without eating.'

In all other matters, however, he was a socialist.

When the young gentlemen came into the kitchen, Pedro reverted to his habitual manner – to the cantankerous demeanour which he assumed with servant girls and with tenants bringing supplies from distant villages. The cooking-range was a god, Pedro its sovereign pontiff; people came to make sacrifices upon the range's various altars and Pedro officiated in mysterious silence. He reverted to his disdainful air when the young gentlemen came in because this was how he showed respect. He hardly replied when they spoke to him. It was not long before he could see with his own two eyes that *la donna è mobile*,[19] as he had so often sung, for as soon as the two gentlemen came in Obdulia forgot all about him. Just as she had earlier forgotten all about Don Saturnino, who was now lying upon his sick-bed with a lard poultice on each temple, given over to the pleasure of ruminating on the sweet memories of that historic afternoon!

The conversation about erotic metaphysics in which Mesía and Paco had recently been engaged did not allow them, at first, to participate in the ladies' gastronomic and culinary enthusiasm. True, it was almost dinner-time, and those kitchen smells whetted the appetite. But ideals do not eat. Mesía possessed the supreme art of coming out of coal-holes, kitchens and mills untouched by smut, grease or flour. In the marquis's kitchen, as in the Yellow Salon, he was thoroughly at home and never bumped into anything. He had distributed kisses in that kitchen during many different and now remote periods of his life. There was, perhaps, not a single corner of that house which did not harbour similar memories for Mesía. It goes without saying that the same was true of Paquito. His first love had been a servant girl who had slept in what was now the larder. The Young Marquis was an expert at crawling about the kitchen in the dark; once he had measured, with his curled-up body, the coal-hole by the side of the range.

In spite of the young gentlemen's ideals, it was not long before they were taking a more active part in the joyful, expansive enthusiasm of those kitchen-artists. They too were painters.[20] And, in spite of the kitchen-hand's jokes, which bordered on impudence, and in spite of Pedro's insulting smile, the two gentlemen set about testing their skills, and poked their fingers into pastries, syrups and indeed everything the women were making. Soon Paco was spattered with food, but Mesía was as immaculate as ever, even while labouring as a kitchen-hand.

Obdulia had already bumped into the Young Marquis dozens of times; their arms, their knees, above all their hands were in contact for long minutes and they pretended not to notice. Obdulia, who was wearing an ankle-length dress, drawn close about her body by the strings of her white apron, made a sudden movement which revealed a part, a large part, of a new style of tartan stocking. The young aristocrat had always considered the fact that he liked feminine forms which were veiled better than completely naked ones to be one of the antinomies of love.[21] Why did veils excite him more than flesh? He could not understand it. He would see the calf, plump and naked, of some barefooted village girl, and it had no effect at all, but, if he glimpsed a stocking a couple of hand's-breadths above the ankle, all his idealism vanished! And so it was this time. Furthermore, if Obdulia's stocking had not been a tartan one, it is probable that his idealistic tranquillity would not have been disturbed, but that red, black and green check, with its stripes of other colours, brought him back down to crude, gross reality, and Obdulia soon realized that she was going to achieve what she wanted. For one of the most subtle pleasures in Obdulia's life was a happy 'session' with a former lover. It was so delightful not to have to go through all the preliminaries! And memories were so magical! To savour a memory as something present! What greater happiness could there be? Paco had been her lover. She would have preferred a session with Alvaro, who had also been her lover, and belonged to a much earlier period of her life; but Alvaro was acting like a beast. He was behaving towards her as Don Saturnino had behaved before he got bolder, with all the courtesy in the world, looking at her with cold correct indifference, just like the bishop. She was certain that her presence never aroused the slightest carnal desire in either Alvaro or the bishop. Alvaro was such a surly creature. So was the bishop. Yet she had been faithful to him (to Alvaro, that is), God in heaven knew that; and, in a way, she still loved him. She would always have preferred him to all the other men. But he didn't want to . . . All that was over and done with, now.

They had tired of playing at cooks. Visita was the only one who still derived pleasure from inspecting casseroles and rummaging through cupboards, dressers and shelves. Whenever she spoke it was evident that there was a sweet in her mouth. Pedro noticed that the thieving magpie was pocketing lumps of sugar and even sachets of saffron, the sight of which aroused uncontrollable envy in her. She also tucked away among her skirts a packet of the best tea.

Each of these thefts was accompanied by a guffaw and by humorous explanations which no longer made anyone laugh. Everybody knew that this was Doña Visita's special vice.

The ladies left the preparation of the tea to the servants and went to wash their hands and tidy their clothes and hair. They knew that as a powder-room they could use the bedchamber in which the marchioness's second daughter had died. But nobody thought of that now. The bed was still there, but of the poor girl not a single belonging, not one memory remained.

Mesía and Paco went in with the ladies, why not? They all knew each other too well to pretend to have any scruples about it. And besides, 'they weren't going to let the men see anything', as Obdulia said. Paco and the widow washed their hands in the same bowl, fingers twining around fingers in the water. This was a particularly piquant pleasure, according to Obdulia. It reminded her of better days. The rays of the setting sun came into the room as far as the foot of the bed, haloing the two scapegraces. The work in the kitchen, the heat from the cooking-range and the jokes had kindled glowing embers in Obdulia's cheeks, and one of her ears was aflame. She felt excited, she wanted something and she did not know what it was. Not something to eat, to be sure, because she had sampled a hundred and one different kinds of sweets and even, just for a little fun, some of the marquis's dinner.

Visitación and Mesía, in a more tranquil mood, were conversing on the balcony, leaning against the cold iron of the handrail. They wouldn't turn round, she was sure of that.' Among those comrades certain tacit pacts were never broken.

Suddenly the Young Marquis guffawed.

'What are you laughing at?' asked Obdulia.

'At the thought of Joaquinito Orgaz, our Flamenco friend, searching everywhere for you. It's droll, isn't it?'

Obdulia thought for a moment and burst out laughing. 'It was droll, indeed.' The widow had seated herself on the dead girl's bed, and her feet were swinging back and forth like pendulums. The tartan stocking became visible again. A moment later, two stockings were visible. Obdulia sighed. They talked about the past. 'Actually, they had never stopped loving each other; there was *something* uniting them, in spite of themselves. Relationships break up, because absolute constancy is out of the question and anyway it becomes an utter bore in the end – a long-lasting affair is ridiculous. This was a fact which they had both learnt in Madrid. Wives and husbands should be bored with each other after a couple of years, at the most; affairs could last a bit longer, but not much.'

'Yet don't you think', said Obdulia, making herself look her prettiest, 'that coming together like this from time to time is rather like a nice sunny day in the middle of winter, in this wretched land of rain and fog?'

'How magnificent!' exclaimed Paco. 'You're quite right, I had a funny feeling I didn't understand – and that's what it was.'

Since this sentiment seemed subtle and poetic to Paco he devoted himself to winning the widow's heart that evening.

This was what she called 'savouring memories'.

Visitación's cheeks, too, were glowing like embers. Her small eyes had been made more attractive by the heat of the kitchen and all the boisterous tomfoolery there, and sparks of feigned passion shot from them. Tangled locks of curly brown hair tumbled down over her forehead. She and Don Alvaro talked to each other with affection, like brother and sister. He had been her first real love, that is to say the first one who had made her behave indiscreetly – had made her jump from a balcony at night, for instance. But it was all so far distant now! Life had put all its prosaic worries between Visitación and those long-ago times.

The constant need to come up with ways of staunching the wounds of credit and averting bankruptcy had converted that madcap's spirit to vulgar positivism and checked the erotic excesses of her adolescent imagination.

She made a very good wife, in people's opinion; that is, she attended to her property and her household chores with care and diligence.

In the winter of their love Mesía and Visita did not enjoy any of the sunny days of which Obdulia had spoken. But when they were alone together and one of them had some worry or care, grave enough to call for confidants and counsellors, they told each other everything, or nearly everything; they would sit close together and speak in low voices, with intimate familiarity, just as they had in the past. They looked like a husband and wife, still on good terms although time had destroyed their love.

'Bah!' said Visitación, with a degree of real sadness, which added interest to her declining beauty. 'Bah! You've really fallen this time, I can see that, but just let me tell you something, my dear: you're going to have to work for it.'

Mesía was franker with Visita on the subject of the judge's wife than with Paco. It was necessary to follow a different policy. The Young Marquis had to be told of pure love, for the reasons already mentioned; Visita, of one more conquest. Don Alvaro realized that Visitación wanted to push the judge's wife into the black pit into which she and so many other women had fallen. Visita had been friendly with Ana ever since she had come to Vetusta with her aunt Doña Anunciación and Ripamilán, now the archpriest. Visita admired Ana, praised her beauty and virtue. But secretly she was annoyed, as were all the other women, by Ana's beauty; and Ana's virtue infuriated her. She wanted to see that little ermine sunk in mud. She was wearied by so much praise. The whole of Vetusta saying, 'The judge's wife, the judge's wife is invincible!' That eternal refrain became tiresome after a while. Even the name people had given her was stupid. The judge's wife! Why? Weren't there any others? Ana had been a judge's wife only for a short while in Vetusta. Her husband had quit his office soon after their arrival. The judge's wife here, the judge's wife there – what was it all in aid of? The bank clerk's wife had little time to dedicate to these malicious passions of her imagination, for her attention was constantly claimed by the difficult prose of daily existence. But she needed some outlet: well then, this was it – making sure that Ana turned out, in the end, to be just the same as all the other women. She stayed with Ana as much as she could, and although Ana seldom left home they went together to church, to the promenade, to the theatre. Ever since the bank clerk's wife had discovered that her friend was interested in Don Alvaro and that he wanted to conquer that fortress of virtue, she had thought only of hastening what was, in her view, inevitable anyway. She did not believe that any woman was capable of resisting her former lover.

Whenever Visita was alone with him they talked about this matter.

Alvaro denied that there was any love on his part. It was just a stubborn whim which the very difficulty of the enterprise had caused to take root in him.

Visita pretended to wish that it were a true passion and concealed the profound pleasure which Mesía's assertions gave her.

'Loving isn't for people of all ages, Visita – you know that well enough.'

'Don't let's talk about that now.'

'You fall in love just once, and when it's over – you rub along as best you can.'

As Mesía said this he shrugged his shoulders in a gesture of humorous despair, which in his eyes and in those of the ladies who adored him was most attractive, even Byronic (if the ladies had heard of Byron).

'And she's lovely, Alvarín – lovely, lovely, I swear she is.'

'Yes, anyone can see that.'

'You can't see everything, you know, my dear. And since Ana doesn't follow *her* example' – pointing over her shoulder with her thumb to where Paco and Obdulia could be heard whispering – 'since Ana never tightens her petticoats and her skirt around her waist with tapes and pulleys, or stuffs herself into her clothes . . . If only you could see her!'

'I can imagine . . .'

'That's not the same.'

There was a pause. Visita went on:

'Can you picture that sweet, peaceful face, where the only hint of passion is in the eyes? And even there it seems to be repressed, in the shadow of her eyelashes, you could say.'

'Frillity's right, isn't he?'

'What does that old sleep-walker say?'

'That the judge's wife looks just like the Madonna of the Chair.'[22]

'It's true; her face, certainly . . .'

'And her expression, and the way she bows her head when she's lost in thought: it's as if she were caressing a baby with that perfect rounded chin of hers.'

'Aha! aha! There speaks the artist!'

The sparks in the ageing beauty's eyes shot out as from a fire being fanned.

'He says he's not in love and then he compares her to the Virgin!'

'I believe the poor thing is very sad because she hasn't any children.'

Visita shrugged and, after swallowing something bitter lodged in her throat, she said in a hoarse, hurried voice:

'She'd better get herself some, then.'

Mesía concealed the repugnance which these words provoked in him.

'But oh, Alvarín! if you could see her in her room, especially when she's having one of those attacks that make her twist and turn! How she writhes about on her bed! She's a different woman. And then, I don't know why, I can understand that caprice of hers, the tiger-skin they say an American gave her. Do you remember the extravaganza which that comic-opera company danced at the theatre last year?'

'Yes, what about it?'

'Do you remember the Dance of the Bacchantes? Well, it's like that, only better. She's like a real Bacchante, if they ever existed, in those far-off lands. That's what she looks like, when she twists and turns. How she laughs when she's having an attack! Her eyes fill with tears, and she puckers her lips in the most enticing way, and from that lovely, lovely throat of hers come such sounds, such cries, like underground laments – it's as if Love, always kept down and in chains, were moaning away in there, I don't know I'm sure! She sighs, she hugs the pillows! And then she goes all languid and curls herself up! During her attacks you'd think she was having nightmares, and going mad with desire, or dying of love. That idiot Don Víctor with his birds and his plays, and with his precious Frillity grafting combs on to cockerels – he isn't a man at all. It's all so unfair, life shouldn't be like that, and it isn't like that, all this farce is just an invention of you men.'

She was silent for a moment, for she had lost the thread of her argument, and then added:

'I know well enough what I mean.'

When she had calmed down, she returned to her subject.

'If only you could see her! She's not just any ordinary beauty. Look, I'll tell you. She's got a pair of arms that . . .'

And she went on to give a minute description, with all the wealth of detail to which she could refer when talking to a man who had been her lover and was now her confidant, of Ana's rotundities, her sculpturesque perfection, and her veiled charms, to use Trifón Cármenes's expressions in *El Lábaro*. But Visita called them by their right names, and when they had none, or she did not know them, she used whimsical diminutives, invented in former times by Alvaro in the enthusiasm of their sweetest intimacies. These girlish words were fixed in Visita's memory as if branded there; but they only came to her lips when she was talking to Alvaro, and even then were seldom uttered. They smacked of glory to the bank clerk's wife, but left a bitter after-taste. 'All that was as if it had never existed. Her husband, the children, the shopping, the servants, the landlord – in the name of the devil!'

Without intending to flirt, without even thinking about what she was doing, carried away by her own enthusiasm, Visita pointed out on her own body the corresponding parts of the judge's wife; when she had finished her description, she said, pointing over her shoulder:

'*She* piques herself on her fine forms. There's no comparison!'

The reference was a wise and opportune one. Visitación assumed that Don Alvaro knew what *her* body was like; and indeed there was no comparison!

Now the president of the Gentlemen's Club was the one who swallowed hard. He was as red as a poppy. His eyes, usually expressionless, reflected the sparks shooting from Visita's eyes.

'But you're going to have to work for it.'

'Maybe not,' said Mesía, losing some of his self-control.

'True, she's swallowed the hook.'

'Do you think so?'

'I'm sure of it. But don't you get too confident just because of that, my dear. You might only land a piece of flesh, and leave the fish in the water.'

'If I just see the moment to strike . . .'

'You've been a long time thinking it over.'

'Who said so?'

'These witnesses.' She placed a finger over each eye.

'And how do you know how *she* feels?'

'Aren't we inquisitive! And he says he isn't in love!'

'In love? Out of the question. But naturally enough I want to know what sort of state she's in, so that I can make my calculations.'

'She's pretty ruffled, that's for certain. And I'm sure she's keeping most of her feelings to herself. She has nervous attacks all the time – when she got married they stopped, as you know, then they came back again, but they've never been as frequent as they are now. Her mood is uneven, she judges others much more severely than ever, everything bores her. She shuts herself up in her room for hours at a stretch!'

'Tut, tut! That doesn't signify.'

'It signifies a great deal.'

'Nothing to my advantage.'

'How can you tell? Look, if anyone speaks to her about you, either she pales or she colours like a tomato, goes dumb, and changes the subject as soon as she's capable of talking again. At the theatre the very moment you turn your head away she fixes her gaze on you and then, when the audience is paying most attention to the stage and she thinks nobody's watching her, she fixes her opera-glasses on you. But I watch her – just out of curiosity, of course, for when all's said and done what's it to me? Her life's her own affair.'

'Aren't you her close friend?'

'Her friend, yes. But close? She's close only to whatever's going on inside her own head. It's one of her little weaknesses – she's very pensive, and keeps everything to herself. What she says will never tell me anything about what she thinks.'

A moment of silence.

'Unless she goes and spills the beans to the canon theologian. I suppose you know she's taken him as her confessor.'

'So they say. I believe it's the archpriest's doing, because he's tired of the confessional.'

'No, it's her own doing, she's got those mystical projects on her mind again.'

Visita applied the word 'mystical' to any kind of devotion unlike her own – which was no devotion at all.

'I've found out that as a girl in Loreto Ana had these fits, as if she'd gone mad – and saw visions: disorders of one kind or another. Now she's having them again, but this time for a different reason,' and she pointed to her heart. 'She's in love, Alvarico, don't you doubt it.'

Don Alvaro was filled with tender, profound gratitude. Those words gave him such faith in himself!

He did not want to hear any more. He realized that Visita had nothing positive to add.

In her face he could see bitterness betrayed by certain muscles, while others fought to erase the expression. There was a slight tremor in her voice. She was a sorry sight. At least Mesía felt sorry for her.

'Forget about all that now,' he said, coming closer. 'Let's not talk about other people, let's talk about ourselves. You're looking most extraordinarily pretty today.'

'You're wasting your time trying those tricks on me now.' She seemed to be speaking with a tongue of metal.

'Silly! Don't be so suspicious.'

'What's all this in aid of now?' demanded the lips and tongue of steel plate.

'Now? *Now*, you say, you ungrateful girl?'

Don Alvaro brought his face close to the face of the sweet-toothed lady. There was nobody in the street. It was one of the most deserted streets in town; indeed, grass grew between its cobble-stones. It was filled with a silence which Don Saturnino Bermúdez called 'solemn' and 'aristocratic'.

Obdulia and Paco, behind them, could see nothing, Don Alvaro was certain of it. He came closer to Visita.

The sound of a slap rang out, followed by the clamorous laughter of the bank clerk's wife, as she stepped back to evade Don Alvaro.

'You idiot!' Mesía groaned, wiping his cheek, which was damp and sticky to his touch.

'Just try me again, my dear! Fancy trying those tricks on an old soldier like me, as the marchioness would say!'

The lady, perfectly calm, and smiling, popped a sugar-lump into her mouth.

This was her system. Her distrust had led her to prohibit herself from enjoying the fraudulent delights of love; and she substituted sweetmeats, which 'thickened the blood'.

With sadness and remorse, Mesía remembered the night when that woman had jumped from a balcony, full of faith and deeply in love.

At one of the corners of the street, at the cathedral end, a woman appeared and was recognized at once by the couple in the balcony. It was the judge's wife, dressed in black and wearing a mantilla. Her maid, Petra, was with her. The two women were soon under the balcony. Ana was clearly lost in thought, for she did not raise her head.

'Anita, Anita,' shouted Visitación.

And then Mesía was able to see Ana's face as she smiled and waved. He had never seen her so beautiful. Although she was by nature pale, her cheeks were rosy now, and she looked as if she had been standing close to a cooking-stove, like Visita and Obdulia. In her eyes there was a gleam, a sparkle of happiness, and its reflections were diffused throughout her face, the face of a woman smiling at her own ideas.

In addition to all this, Mesía realized that she had looked at him unmoved, unperturbed, just as she had looked at Visita. Even in the way she had greeted him, more open and expansive than on other occasions, he had spotted a kind of rebuff, the expression of an indifference which irritated him. It was as if she had said to him, 'You're just a little puppy-dog whose bark is worse than its bite. I'm not afraid of you.' They would soon see about that. But that affability of hers was a form of contempt. What had happened in the cathedral? What sort of man was Don Fermín, who had brought about such changes in the woman, in the course of a single conversation?

All this passed through Mesía's mind in a moment. He was irritated and yearned to resolve his doubts and misgivings, but none of this showed on his face. He greeted Ana in his usual grave manner, that manner of an English gentleman which filled Blunderbuss, his admirer and mortal foe, with such envy.

'Have you been to confession?' asked Visita.

'Yes.'

'With the canon theologian, of course?'

'Yes.'

'What was it like? He's very good, don't you think? What did I tell you? Aren't you coming up?'

'No, I can't, not now.'

Obdulia heard Ana's voice and ran to the balcony without bothering to repair the disorder of her dress and hair.

'Come on up, Ana, don't be silly!' shouted the widow as she devoured her with her eyes.

For Obdulia, other women were merely dressmakers' dummies. Women were for clothes, men for all the rest.

Ana excused herself once more. She had work to do. She took her leave with a graceful smile, and walked on. Her eyes had met Mesía's for a moment but they had not hidden themselves or even betrayed any embarrassment as on other occasions. They had looked at him with an air of abstraction, and had not attempted to avoid contact with his eyes, in spite of the mixture of lust and irritated self-love with which they were charged.

Everyone on the balcony was silent as the judge's wife disappeared down the deserted street. All eyes followed her until she turned the corner. Obdulia, trying to affect a disdainful tone, said:

'She's very plainly dressed.'

And she went back to the marchioness's boudoir.

'You just gobble her up, my dear!' shouted Visita into Alvaro's ear, in a voice tinged with mockery. And she added, very serious now:

'But beware of the canon theologian: he knows a thing or two – and not just about theology!'

IX

In a corner of the Plaza Nueva, for ever sunk in gloom, stands Ozores Mansion, its elaborate, ostentatious, inelegant façade built of great blocks of stone blackened, like those of the Gentlemen's Club, by the damp which crawls up the walls to the roof.

When Ana reached the porch she stopped, shivering, as though feeling cold. She looked towards the street which entered the square by the side of her house; a resplendent panorama extended before her. The Calle del Aguila ran down a steep hill and it gave a view of the distant sierra and the meadows, green and gleaming, on its slopes. Across the square and over the roof-tops, restless chattering swallows flew, coming and going as if they were making farewell visits before their imminent winter travels.

'Don't ring, Petra, let's go for a walk.'

'The two of us alone?'

'Yes, us two. Through fields, across country.'

'But the fields will be very wet, ma'am.'

'Along some path – out of the way – where there won't be any people. You come from those parts, you know them well – can't you think of somewhere we can go without meeting anybody?'

'But it will all be so damp.'

'Not now, the sun must have dried things out. I'm wearing a good pair of shoes. Come on, let's go, Petra!'

Ana appealed to Petra in the voice of a capricious child; her face had the expression of a mystic seeking celestial favours.

Petra looked at her mistress in astonishment. She had never seen her like this. What had happened to that habitual coldness of hers, that tranquillity which seemed like a mask for distrust and suspicion?

Ana's maid was a little over twenty-five years old, had saffron-blond hair, pale skin, and perfect features: a beauty appealing more to lust than to love. Because of her concern to avoid the disagreeable regional accent she spoke with intolerable affectation. Having served in many important houses, she was good at almost anything, and was bored in Quintanar's house, where neither she nor anybody else ever had any adventures. Master, mistress and servants were all like lumps of stucco. Don Víctor was an old man with a weakness, perhaps, for easy love, but with her he had never ventured beyond the occasional insistent sticky stare and a few complimentary remarks made in roundabout terms which did not compromise him. Her mistress was a silent, pensive woman, who either had nothing to hide or hid it well. But Petra had become convinced that she, too, was bored stiff. The maid always took full advantage of the few opportunities she was given to enter into the confidence of the judge's wife. Her behaviour was solicitous and discreet, and she affected humility, in her opinion the most difficult of all the virtues.

The prospect of a walk across country, after confession, all by themselves, on a damp afternoon, gave Petra much food for thought. There was nothing she would have liked better, but she maintained her opposition, to test the strength of her mistress's caprice. After all, this was how other women had started . . .

They walked down the Calle del Aguila. Where this street ended it was crossed at right angles by the Madrid road.

'Not that way,' said Petra's mistress. 'Down here; let's go to the spring of Mari-Pepa.'

'Yes, at this time of day there won't be anyone there, and the ground will be dry, the sun's shining. Look, ma'am, there's the spring.'

Petra pointed into the fertile valley below them towards a ring of poplars which was so caught at that moment by the oblique rays of the setting sun that it looked as if it were made of gold and silver. The path to it was narrow, but firm and level, and on either side there were meadows of tall thick grass and fields of vegetables. These fields and meadows, irrigated by water from the city, are more fertile than the land elsewhere; the meadows, dark green with iridescences of a blue so deep that it almost seems black, look like thick velvet and give off dazzling reflections of the westerly sun. Thus they shone that afternoon. Ana half-closed her eyes as she basked in the light filtered through the freshness rising from the ground.

Hedges of bramble and honeysuckle lined the path, and here and there an elm-tree rose from their midst, stocky, sturdy, with an enormous head, shaped like an Indian club. A few shoots grew out of its bald top – thin weak twigs shaken by the breeze and rattling the solitary leaves on their tips like castanets.

'Look, ma'am, how funny! There aren't any leaves left on any of those branches, except one right at the top, on the very tip.'

After this observation and others like it, Petra stopped to pick flowers in the hedgerows, laughing and shouting as she pricked her fingers and caught her skirt in the brambles. Alone with her mistress in the middle of the countryside, on solitary, ill-famed paths which knew so many things about her that were better kept quiet, she was beginning to behave in a more familiar manner.

Petra found her mistress's sudden piety hard to credit.

'A confession lasting more than an hour! Her face all lit up when she came to her feet, once she'd been given absolution. And now this walk through fields – and laughing – and allowing me these liberties. I've got my doubts; let's wait and see.'

Ana's maid was inclined to take her calculations and fantasies to extremes. She could already see, in the distance, gratuities in ringing gold coins. But that religious slant which the affair was taking – for she assumed that something was up – brought with it complications which were new in the experience even of Petra, who had seen what was known only to herself, and to God, and to those solitary paths and others like them.

They reached the spring of Mari-Pepa, which lay in the shade of sturdy chestnut-trees, their bark furrowed with initials and names. The ring of poplars which could be seen from afar acted as a rampart, further secluding the spot, and shading it at sundown; to the east stood a hillock which also sheltered the peaceful retreat created by nature around the spring. Although the spring was in a hollow there was a magnificent view from it. The land to the west rose and fell like a billowing green sea, and one could gaze along the troughs into the distance and there descry Mount Corfín, shrouded in mist, its peaks hidden in the clouds and its slopes plunging into unseen valleys behind the intervening hills. The sun's rays slanted through the air, which seemed to have luminous dust floating in it; beyond loomed the violet bulk of Corfín.

Ana sat on the exposed roots of one of the chestnut-trees shading the spring. She gazed at the mountainside, which looked as if it were illuminated with bengal lights, and, already half-asleep, heard the discreet murmur of the spring by her side and of the brook as it hurried away to refresh the meadows. Sparrows and chaffinches hopped to and fro on the branches of the chestnut-tree, never keeping quiet for a moment yet never managing to sing properly, their attention caught by the smallest trifle, restless, mischievous and vainly talkative. From time to time dead leaves dropped from the branches into the pool, where they floated in slow eddies, drawing closer and closer to the narrow channel through which the water flowed, gliding away at speed and disappearing in the stream, where the glassy surface of the pool turned into crinkled silver. A wagtail (for Vetustans a 'washer-woman') was pecking at the ground and hopping about at Ana's feet, unafraid, trusting in the agility of its wings. It turned here and there, sweeping the dust with its tail, going to the water to drink, then, in one leap, reaching the hedge, hiding there for a moment among the lowest brambles and appearing again, out of sheer curiosity, always cheerful and sprightly. It remained motionless for a moment, as if deliberating, and suddenly, without the slightest motive, but as if something had frightened it, flew away, its flight fast and straight at first, then undulating and unhurried, as it disappeared into the sky tinged purple by the oblique rays of the sun. Ana watched the wagtail until it was out of sight. 'These little creatures', she thought, 'have feelings, desires, even thoughts. That bird had a sudden idea; it tired of the shade and went off in search of light, warmth, space. Lucky fellow! Getting tired – such a natural thing!' She herself, the judge's wife, was tired enough of the shade in which she had spent her whole life. Could it be that what the canon theologian had promised her was something new and worthy of her love? When she had told him that during her adolescence she had experienced mystical impulses, and that afterwards her aunts and all her friends in Vetusta had made her disparage such vain piety, what had been his answer? She could remember it well; her ears were still humming with that sweet voice which had come in pieces through the squares in the grating, as if passing through a sieve. In an eloquent sentence which she could not repeat word for word he had said something like this: 'My daughter: neither were your aspirations to find God, before you knew Him, pure piety, nor was the disdain with which those aspirations were maltreated the least bit prudent.' She was certain that he had said 'the least bit'. The canon theologian's eloquence in the confessional was unlike his eloquence in the pulpit; she realized that now. In the confessional he had used familiar words to express, in such a vivid way, ideas never to be found in rhetoric-laden books. And he had made a comparison: 'If, my daughter, you go to bathe in a river and, as you splash about in the water, for fun, as we often do, you find in the sand a tiny nugget of gold, worth less than a peseta, do you therefore think that your discovery is going to make you wealthy? That you are already a millionairess? That the river is going to devote all its energies to bringing you twenty-five-peseta coins bearing our dear king's head? That would be absurd. But is this going to make you cast the nugget away in disdain, and continue frolicking in the water, waving your arms and splashing the stream with your legs, never giving another thought to the speck of gold which you found in the sand?' It was a good comparison. Ana had pictured herself in her sleeveless bathing-suit, swimming in the river, in the shade of hazel bushes and walnut-trees, and on the bank was the canon theologian, in his pure white rochet, upon his knees, his hands clasped, imploring her not to throw the piece of gold away. That was the secret of eloquence – speaking in such a way that what was said could be seen. That flow of gentle, new words, words of heavenly joy, had filled her with enthusiasm, and she had opened her heart before that deep hole with its criss-cross laths, using words which she had never spoken before. The canon theologian, sitting behind his grille, had remained silent, and when she had finished, the voice inside the confessional had trembled. 'My daughter, this history of your sad times, of your day-dreams, of your fears, is worthy of a great deal of thought on my part. You have a noble soul, and it is only because I cannot eulogize a penitent in this place that I abstain from indicating where the gold is to be found in you, and where the dross . . . and from showing you that there is more gold than might appear. None the less, you are unwell. Every soul that comes to this place is unwell. I cannot understand how anybody can speak ill of confession, for apart from its status as a divine institution, regarding it from the point of view of its human utility, can you not understand, could anyone fail to understand, that this hospital for souls is necessary for those who are sick in spirit?' The canon theologian had spoken of the advice columns for the elucidation of matters of conscience in the pages of Protestant newspapers. 'Protestant ladies, who have no spiritual fathers, go with their problems to the press. Isn't that ridiculous?' There had been a smile in his voice.

He had continued: 'She should not attend the confessional merely to ask for the absolution of her sins. The soul, like the body, has its own therapeutics and its own hygiene, and the confessor is a hygienist; but just as the sick person who does not take her medicine or who conceals her illness, and the healthy one who does not follow the diet prescribed for her in order to conserve her health, only do themselves harm, and deceive themselves, so likewise the sinner harms and deceives herself who conceals her sins or does not confess them precisely as they are, or who examines them in a hurry, without due care, or who fails to observe the spiritual regimen which she has been ordered to follow. A single conversation is not sufficient to cure a soul; and to come to the confessional with old, neglected illnesses is not indicative of a real desire to be healed. From all of this it can be deduced rationally, quite apart from any religious precepts, that regular confession is vital. It is not a question of following a formula; confessing has nothing to do with that. When one has to undergo treatment it is essential to choose a confessor with care, but once he has been chosen he must be regarded as what, in effect, he is – a spiritual father, and also – leaving the religious aspect aside for a moment – as an elder brother, a soul brother, for unburdening one's sorrows, and talking about one's desires, and reassuring oneself about one's hopes, and dissipating one's doubts. Even if all this were not laid down by religion it would be required by common sense. Religion is reason, from the highest dogma to the least important detail of ceremony.'

This congruity between faith and reason delighted the judge's wife. How could it be that, at twenty-seven years of age, she had never heard of such a thing? She had not dared ask the canon theologian this question, but there would be time later.

A sparrow with a grain of wheat in its beak stood before the judge's wife and gave her a bold insolent stare. She remembered the archpriest, who had a talent for resembling birds.

'Ripamilán was a kind man, but what a way to hear a confession! A routine which had never taught her anything. She had derived nothing, except her marriage, from her confessions with him. The poor man would say that he knew her sins by heart, and interrupt her with his eternal "Yes, yes, carry on: anything else? Carry on. Say three Our Fathers and one Salve Regina and give alms." What a strange man! When had Don Cayetano ever talked about whether she possessed this or that kind of temperament? But the canon theologian had, at once: he had said that hers was a special temperament, that this and other considerations would have to be borne in mind. It was all completely new to her.'

Furthermore, she had been flattered to find Don Fermín speaking to her as to a cultured person, a man of letters, quoting various authors and taking for granted that she knew them; and he had used technical terms without hesitation and without explaining them.

'And what elevation! What was virtue? What was saintliness? That had been the best part. Virtue was the beauty of the soul, its cleanliness – the easiest thing in the world for noble, pure souls. For people who are indolent, and have an aversion to water and to freshly laundered clothes, cleanliness is a torture, an impossibility; yet for a respectable person' (yes, those had been his words) 'it is one of the most imperious necessities in life. Religion only presents the path of virtue as an arduous one to those who are sunk in sin; but the new man[1] is always ready within us, one only has to say the word, and he comes. Virtue commences with an effort which is not great, even though it goes against the grain, and the next day the effort is even less demanding, and its efficacy even greater, because of the momentum gained, because of the inertia of goodness. This is mechanical' (yes, that was what Señor De Pas had said). 'Virtue could be defined as the stable equilibrium of the soul. Furthermore, it was a joyful thing, a fine sunny day, gusts of fresh, scented air. The virtuous soul was like a birdcage in which the gifts of the Holy Spirit sang happy songs to cheer one's heart in the sad moments of life. That melancholy of which Ana complained was a nostalgia for the virtue she would most certainly achieve, the virtue for which her spirit sighed as for its homeland. Virtue was a question of skill, of ability, and was not only to be gained by fasting and asceticism. This was a very saintly path, but there were others. In the bustle of our cities it is still possible to aspire to perfection.' (At that moment the judge's wife imagined Vetusta, which had always seemed so small, dull and dismal, as some kind of Babylon.) 'She had read St Augustine – did she not remember that the saintly bishop enjoyed religious music, not because it delighted his senses, but because it elevated his soul? Well, in the same way, all the arts, the contemplation of nature, the reading of historical and philosophical works – so long as they were pure – could elevate her soul and put it, in the diapason of saintliness, in unison with virtue. Yes, why not? Ah! and then, when one reached higher regions, and was sure of oneself, when one feared temptation only with prudent fear, many entertainments which had previously been fraught with peril were found to be edifying. And so, for example, the reading of forbidden books, poison for the weak, was a purge for the strong. The person who achieves a certain degree of strength finds that the presence of evil uplifts him, in a sense, because of the contrast which it provides.' The canon theologian had not said whether *he* was as strong as all that; but she supposed he was. At all events, virtue and piety were quite different from what she had been taught by her aunts and by the commonplace religion (this was what she privately called it) which she had learnt as a mere routine. Yes, true religion was certainly more like her adolescent day-dreams, her visions on Loreto hill, than the dull, stupid discipline which she had been taught as the only serious, genuine piety. And the canon had promised her so many more lessons on other days! How many new things was she going to learn, and going to feel! And how fortunate she was to have an elder brother, a soul brother, to whom she could talk about such subjects – without a shadow of doubt the most interesting and elevated subjects there were!

About the personal question – that is to say Ana's sins – little had been said. The canon had turned back to generalities as soon as this subject had threatened to emerge. 'He did not have sufficient data, first he needed to know her personally.'

As Ana remembered this, she was troubled by scruples of conscience. He had absolved her of her sins, yet she had said nothing about her inclination towards Don Alvaro. 'Yes, her inclination. Now that she believed she had overcome her sinful impulse, she wished to face up to it. She did feel an inclination. There must be no disguising her weaknesses. She had spoken in vague terms of evil thoughts, but she had considered it indecorous, unfair to herself, and even coarse and vulgar, to personify those temptations, to say that they concerned one man with certain attractive qualities, and to specify the dangers that she faced. But should she not have done so? Maybe. Wouldn't that, however, have made Don Víctor look ridiculous for no good reason and to no good purpose, since she was faithful to him in body and in mind, and would remain so for ever? But still, she should have been more specific in that part of her confession. Was she fully absolved? Could she take the communion on the following day with a clear conscience? No, certainly not. She would not receive the communion. In the morning she would stay in bed pretending she had a migraine, in the afternoon she would go to complete her confession, and the next day she would take the sacrament. That was the best plan. Her decision not to take the communion on the following morning gave her a girlish joy. It was like a day's holiday from school. She could spend the night thinking about religion and virtue in general in terms of this new system, and not worry about the need to receive the Lord in a proper fashion. It was a deferment, a breathing-space. And it no longer seemed wrong to give free rein to her happiness – that happiness caused purely by moral forces; the dawn, maybe, of the resplendent day of virtue.

'How happy the canon theologian must be, basking in the light of virtuous joy, his soul full of birds singing to him like choirs of angels in his heart! That was why he wore that eternal smile, and promenaded with such poise along the Mall amid people with lazy souls, amid petty spirits and – amid Vetustans. And what a healthy colour he had!

'Vetusta, Vetusta contained that treasure! Why hadn't he been made a bishop? Who could say! Why was she herself, although worthy of a better theatre, no more than the wife of a man who had once been a magistrate in Vetusta? The setting was the least important consideration; variety, beauty, was in the soul. That little bird has no soul, and it flies on feathered wings; I have a soul and I shall fly on the invisible wings of the heart through the pure radiant atmosphere of virtue.'

She shivered with cold and came back down to earth. The whole place was in shadow. Behind the curtain of poplars, the sun was hiding the last traces of its light, like a purple rag, among thick grey clouds. The cold and the shadows had come suddenly. From a pool in a nearby meadow, a strident choir of frogs bade the sun farewell; their croaking sounded like a hymn sung by pagan savages to the darkness approaching from the east. The judge's wife remembered the rattles[2] which children play in church in Holy Week when the last candle upon a mysterious triangle goes out and, with a hair-raising racket, the floodgates of youthful enthusiasm burst open.

'Petra! Petra!' she cried.

She was alone. Where had her maid gone?

A toad was squatting only a few inches from her dress on a thick tree-root which stuck out of the ground like a claw, and gazing at her. She cried out in fear. She fancied that the toad had been listening to her thoughts and was mocking her illusions.

'Petra! Petra!'

The maid did not reply. The toad's impertinent gaze filled Ana with disgust and foolish dread.

Petra appeared. She was bright red, perspiring, and panting. Small golden locks tumbled down over her eyes. Seeing her mistress so engrossed in her own thoughts she had gone to her cousin Antonio's mill, which was but a stone's throw from the spring.

Ana fixed her eyes on those of her maid, who defied the inquisitorial stare. Petra's cousin, Antonio the miller, was in love with her, and her mistress knew it. Petra intended to marry him – later, when he was richer and she was older. From time to time she went to see him, to keep alive the fire upon which she was relying to warm her in her old age. Petra regarded the mill as a bank in which she was accumulating her amatory savings. Ana felt annoyed, without knowing why. 'What sort of love could there be between Petra and the miller? But what did it matter to her?' As Ana stared at Petra, scrutinizing the details of her dishevelled clothes, taking note of her ill-concealed fatigue, her perspiration, the colour of her cheeks, she displayed a curiosity which she tried, in vain, to hide. 'What had the woman been doing in the mill?' Much against Ana's will, this trivial thought, this stupid obsession which was almost a pain, absorbed all her attention.

'Come on, come on, it is late.'

'Yes ma'am, it's late all right. By the time we get home the street lights will be on.'

'Not as late as all that.'

'You'll see.'

'If you had not stopped so long in your cousin's forge . . .'

'Forge? It's a mill, ma'am.'

Petra regarded Ana's mistake as a piece of malicious cunning.

By the time they reached the first houses night was falling. The yellow light of the gas-lamps shone out at intervals beside the dusty branches of the stunted acacias decorating the Boulevard, as the street by which they were entering the city was popularly known.

'Why have you brought me this way?'

'What difference does it make?'

Petra shrugged. Instead of climbing the Calle del Aguila they had made a detour and were walking into Vetusta along one of its few new streets, lined with three-storey buildings, all identical and covered with glazed galleries of gaudy discordant colours. The pavement, three metres wide – a hyperbolical pavement for Vetusta – was bordered with a row of street lamps on iron columns, painted green, and with a row of trees imprisoned in small wooden tubs which were also painted green. This was why the Calle del Triunfo de 1836[3] was known as the Boulevard. At nightfall, when the working day came to an end, the pavement was turned into a promenade along which it was difficult to walk without being brought to a halt every three paces. Seamstresses, waistcoat-makers, ironers, shoe-binders, cigar-makers, match-makers and other working girls would gather under the acacias with gunsmiths, shoemakers, tailors, carpenters, and even bricklayers and stonemasons and many other types of labouring men, and promenade there for an hour, dragging their feet over the paving-stones with a raucous clatter.

This evening walk had begun as a kind of parody, when working-class girls had started to imitate the manners, accents, and conversations of young ladies, and young working men had pretended to be gentlemen, taking each other by the arm and affecting a haughty, strutting gait. By slow degrees, however, the joke had turned into a habit, and now the city, sad and empty by day, became lively as night commenced, with an elated joy, as if all the plebs, as they were called in the Vegallana coterie, were infected with nervous excitement. Here was the power contained in workshops surging forth into the open air: muscles moving of their own accord and as they liked, free from the monotony of routine tasks. And although these men and women were not conscious of it, they all felt the satisfaction of having done something useful, of having worked. The girls were laughing for the sake of laughing, thronging together, pinching each other, jostling each other. When bunches of men passed by the noisy merriment increased: there were slaps on backs, peals of roguish laughter and shrieks of feigned indignation and mock modesty – uttered not out of hypocrisy but in the spirit of a comic sketch. The girls' prudery was a pretence, but any man who went too far ran the risk of ending up with his cheeks smarting. Every virtuous girl there knew how to defend her virtue with a good slap. There was a certain degree of order in the crowd's movements, in that one section of the pavement was for coming, and another for going. Some young gentlemen mingled with the groups of working men. The girls usually approved of a flirtatious compliment from a student or a shop assistant, but their feigned indignation was greater when a *toff* overstepped the mark, and then the protests of outraged modesty were accompanied by sarcasm. Young women who could not always be sure of a meal when they went back home would insult the *toff* who said that they were beautiful by suggesting that he was no more than a *poor hungry devil*. At the most they would admit that he might eat birdseed. Old hands were not disconcerted by these conventional insults, which were a mark of refinement in the Boulevard, but persisted in their advances and finally reaped their harvest if there was a harvest to be reaped. Virtue and vice rubbed shoulders without qualms, both dressed in the same untidy way. Although some of these daughters of toil and sweat were well scrubbed, in a throng they emitted an acrid smell which the regular passer-by did not even notice but which was unpleasant and sad: the stench of slovenly, resigned poverty. Many beautiful women gave off that aroma of rags; some were strong and willowy, others were delicate and gentle, but all of them were badly dressed, most of them unwashed, and a few uncombed. The hubbub was infernal; they were all talking at the top of their voices, they were all laughing, some were whistling, others were singing.

Girls of fourteen with angelic faces did not bat an eyelid as they heard oaths and obscenities which every now and then even made them laugh like lunatics. Everybody there was young: the elderly worker has none of this joviality. Of the men, perhaps none was thirty, for the labouring man soon grows taciturn and loses his expansive, motiveless joy. There are not many old blades in the ranks of the proletariat.

Without realizing what was happening, Ana found herself hemmed in by the throng. There was no escape from the pavement, for the road was full of mud, and carts and carriages were passing in a continuous procession: the mail train was due, and this was the road to the station.

The groups of people split up to allow the judge's wife through. The most daring young lads drew their faces close to hers with a certain insolence, but the benevolent beauty of her features – those features of a madonna – commanded admiration and respect even from them.

The needlewomen stopped murmuring and laughing as Ana passed by.

'It's the judge's wife!'

'Isn't she pretty!'

This comment came from both women and men. It was spontaneous, disinterested praise.

'*Olé*, my beauty! Good for your mother!' an Andalusian lad with a northern accent[4] ventured to shout.

His enthusiasm provoked a friend who was more respectful to 'fetch him a crack' (strike him on the head).

'You ignorant brute, can't you see it's the judge's wife!'

Her beauty enjoyed great popularity.

The youths were telling Petra that she was an archangel, which pleased her considerably. Ana smiled and walked faster.

'This is a fine place in which to end up.'

'What does it matter? Nobody's going to eat you, you can see that. Lots of young ladies could learn manners from these ragamuffins.'

The judge's wife had come this way once or twice before at nightfall. But it was only now that she thought she could see and sense in this mass of dirty clothes – even in the acrid smell of the riff-raff, in the hubbub made by the rabble – a manifestation of the delights of love: love which was, it seemed, a universal necessity. Here, too, in the midst of this racket, secrets were whispered into ears; and there were languid looks, frowns on jealous lovers' faces, glances like lightning-flashes of passion. In the apparent cynicism of these conversations, these sudden contacts, this insolent jostling, this bragging brutishness, there were delicate flowers, pure illusions, true modesty, dreams of love living even here, oblivious to the miasmas of poverty.

For a moment Ana was a part of this ragged sensuality. She thought about herself, about her life devoted to sacrifice and to an absolute prohibition of pleasure, and felt the profound self-pity of egotism aroused by its own misfortune. 'I am poorer than any of these girls. My maid has her miller who whispers into her ear words which set her face alight; and here I am listening to these guffaws of pleasure which give rise to emotions I have never experienced.'

They had to stop in the midst of the throng. A drama was being enacted on the pavement. A tall dark-skinned young man with curly black hair, dressed in blue overalls, was shouting:

'I'll kill her! I'll kill her! Let go of me, I'm going to kill her.'

His companions were holding him back and trying to pull him away. Fire was shooting from the youth's eyes.

'What's up?' asked Petra.

'Oh, nothing,' a man replied. 'Just jealousy.'

'Yes,' shouted a girl, 'but if she's not careful he'll strangle her.'

'It's all she deserves, she's a little tart.'

The young man was forced to leave the promenade, dragged away by his friends. As he passed the judge's wife he looked at her, face to face, with an abstracted gaze, thinking of his revenge; she felt those eyes on her own, making violent contact. *Just jealousy!* So that was the look of jealousy! The beauty of those eyes was an infernal beauty, no doubt, but how powerful it was, how human!

At length the lady and her maid left the Boulevard and entered the Calle del Comercio. From the shops all along this street came beams of light which reached the wet, muddy stones of the gutter. At the window of a new cake-shop, the most luxurious one in Vetusta, a group of urchins between eight and twelve years old were discussing the quality and the names of those sweetmeats which were not for them, and the merits of which they could only conjecture.

The smallest boy, with his eyes closed, was licking the glass in ecstasies of delight.

'That one's called a *putty shoe*,'[5] a lad said in dogmatic tones.

'Come off it! It's a Swiss roll. *I* should know.'

This scene moved the judge's wife, too. She always felt a tightening in her throat and tears in her eyes when she saw poor children admiring cakes or toys in shop windows. They were not for them, and this seemed the most terrible of all the cruelties wrought by injustice. But what was more, Ana – without knowing why – regarded these ragamuffins, arguing about the names of morsels which they would never eat, as companions in misfortune, as younger brothers. She wanted to go home. Being moved like this by all she saw was something which alarmed her. 'She feared an attack, she was feeling very nervous.'

'Hurry up, hurry up, Petra,' she pleaded in a feeble voice.

'Wait a minute, ma'am. Over there – I think they're making signs at us, yes, the signs are meant for us. Ah yes, it's them.'

'Who?'

'Paco and Don Alvaro.'

Petra noticed that her mistress trembled a little and paled.

'Where are they? Can't we escape, before . . .?'

It was too late, Don Alvaro and Paco were before them. The Young Marquis halted them with an exaggerated bow, which was one of his ways of showing *esprit*, as even Ronzal now called it. Mesía made a correct greeting.

Light streamed from the new cake-shop, dazzling the Vetustans, who were not accustomed to such extravagant use of gas. Don Alvaro saw the judge's wife bathed in this footlight flare – and his first glance told him that she was no longer the dreamy woman he had seen an hour or so earlier. For some unknown reason that placid, tranquil, open look had dispirited him; and now – for no better reason – this look, timid, fleeting, frightened, seemed like a new hope; Ana's submission, his triumph. 'Not as much as all that, perhaps, but he was pleased to find this encouragement. Without faith in himself he would not make a move. And he had to make many moves – and fast.'

In Vetusta it rains nearly the whole year round, and people make the most of the few fine days to breathe fresh air. The promenades, however, are crowded only on fiesta-days, because poor young ladies – who form the majority – cannot resign themselves to displaying the same dress every afternoon, year in year out. But night changes everything. The ladies leave home in their ordinary clothes and stroll through the new part of town, the Calle del Comercio, and the Plaza del Pan, where there is an arcade, albeit a narrow one; and go to the Boulevard a little later, once the *riff-raff* is asleep. Shopping is the excuse. So many things are needed in a house! And so the Calle del Comercio is the nucleus of these disguised nocturnal promenades. Nevertheless, although the ladies enter the shops, they do not purchase much. Gentlemen come and go along the broad pavement, looking, in a more or less brazen manner, at the ladies seated by the shop-counters who, with one eye on the season's latest fashions and the other on the shop-door, haggle about prices and receive all the compliments and signals from the street. The shop assistants are mostly Catalans, but they speak reasonably correct Spanish. They are amiable, and most of them are handsome. Beards trimmed in the style of Christ's beard; black, syrupy eyes; rosy cheeks. They bow their heads with a languor which is half romantic, half phlegmatic: a gesture which could equally mean 'Madam, I harbour a secret passion, which . . .' or 'Madam – Job himself wouldn't have had the patience – but *I* shall'.

'Oh dear, you must be finding me so very tiresome!' says Visitación to a fair-haired young man in a sailor-collar, who has already had to go and fetch at least fifty rolls of calico for her.

'Ah, not at all, madam! It is my duty – and besides, I am only too willing. . . .' 'A shop assistant must be tireless, that is his job.'

Visitación is always about to make her maid a pinafore, but she can never bring herself to do it. On other nights *she* is the one who hasn't a thing to wear.

'Winter's coming, and I shan't have a stitch on my body.'

The shop assistant gives her an amiable smile, happy to imagine the slim but well-formed lady shivering in her night-dress in the rigours of a snowstorm.

'Don't be naughty! Don't be so physical!' she chides, looking as embarrassed as a scatter-brained schoolgirl who suspects that she has been indiscreet; and she fixes her smiling, screwed-up eyes – which, she believes, give off sparks – on the shop assistant. The Catalan pretends to be seduced by her eyes, and brings the price down by five céntimos each time she makes a pass at him.

Visitación triumphs. But what she does not know is that the same calico has been sold earlier to Obdulia by the same smiling shop assistant with the Jewish beard, with reductions of ten céntimos – and that even then the profit was greater than had been expected.

The fair ladies of Vetusta, as the columnist in *El Lábaro* calls them, cannot tear themselves away from fashion-shops. They look at everything, they turn everything over and they still have time to beguile the shop assistants and enjoy the sideways passes – Joaquinito Orgaz's expression – made at them by the young gentlemen who promenade along the pavement arguing in loud voices in order to announce their presence. A rumbustious gaiety reigns here: motive-less gaiety, which is the most expansive and pleasurable kind. And – who would have thought it? – not only the younger components of both sexes (from *El Lábaro*) but serious people too, such as magistrates, professors, officials, lawyers, and even priests, look forward all day long, without realizing it, to shopping time, when the weather is fine and ladies can 'decorously' pick up a mantilla and go out into the street. It is a time for coming together upon which the Vetustans have unconsciously agreed, in order to satisfy their need to see each other, rub shoulders with each other and hear human noise. It should be noted that Vetustans both love and hate, both need and despise one another. The Vetustan speaks ill of his fellow citizens as individuals, but he defends the character of the town *en masse*, and if he is taken away from it he sighs for his return. The nocturnal promenade, which has a suggestion of subreption about it (at least that is what Don Saturnino Bermúdez says), is made all the more attractive by the opportunities it offers to the imagination. Gas is not something to be squandered by a debt-ridden municipal corporation, and one street lamp here, with another fifty paces away (if the moon is not shining, for on romantic nights the lamps are not lit), does not dazzle anyone or rob the night of its mystery. People see what is not there. Each individual, according to his own imagination, attributes whatever appearance he pleases to those who pass by.

'They don't look like the same girls at all,' say the young blades.

Vetustans enjoy the illusion of believing themselves to be somewhere else without having to leave town. All around them are new faces which turn out not to be new, after all.

'Who are those girls, over there?' And those girls are found to be the Mínguez girls, the eternal Mínguez girls, yesterday's and the day before yesterday's Mínguez girls, the Mínguez girls of every day. But while the illusion lasts . . .! In towns where free shows are seldom staged, mutual contemplation becomes such a show, more interesting than most. The occasion (taken by the forelock) of a promenade gives a delicate yet intense pleasure, savoured with ineffable delight by the workers of the honourable Spanish middle class.

A student retires to his bed satisfied with half a dozen looks gathered here and there in his walk up and down the Mall and the Calle del Comercio; and a girl of marrying age has enough to keep her mind occupied for a week with some loving words which she pretended to disdain because of their impertinence but which she savours while she embroiders carpet-slippers for seven endless days alone behind a window lashed by the untiring rain. Such is the explanation of all these comings and goings in and out of shops and of this willingness to laugh at anything and be amused by every sentence uttered by a shop assistant, even by the mischievous remarks of the student who pokes his head through an open shop window. All is movement, laughter, happy noise. These are the same people who, silent, grave and stiff, make their appearance at formal promenades and, bowing their heads full of repentance and pious unction (from *El Lábaro*), attend sermons, novenas, Holy Week services, and even the Miserere.

Ana thought she could see the flame of poetry upon every face. Vetustan women seemed more attractive, more elegant, more seductive than on other days; and in the men she found a distinguished air, resolute expressions, a romantic cut. In her imagination she paired off the men and women as they passed by, and started to fancy that she lived in a city in which servant girls, sempstresses and young ladies loved and were loved by millers, industrial workers, students and army reservists.

She alone was loveless; she and the poor children licking the glass panes of cake-shops were the paupers of Vetusta. A wave of rebelliousness rolled through her blood towards her brain. Again she feared an attack.

'What was happening, Lord, what was happening?' Why, on such a day, when her spirit had just started out on a new life, the life of a victim – not, however, one of sterile unwitnessed self-sacrifice, but encouraged by the ever-present voice of a soul brother – why on such an untimely occasion should that longing in her very bowels, which she attributed to her nerves, come to torment her, to bellow a war-cry inside her head, and to turn everything upside-down? Hadn't she just been sitting by the spring of Mari-Pepa, with all her thoughts devoted to the hope of future virtue? Weren't new horizons being opened up before her soul? Wasn't she going to have something to live for in the future? Oh, if only the canon theologian would appear before her! Her hand came into brief contact with a man's hand and she felt a gentle warmth, a sticky touch. It wasn't the canon theologian, it was Don Alvaro, who was walking by her side, talking about something or other. She could hardly hear him, and she did not want to attribute to his presence that change in her moral temperature which, in her heart, she regretted, as she watched the young women and the not-so-young women of Vetusta flirting on the pavement and inside the blazing shops.

Don Alvaro was of the opposite opinion, being convinced that his presence and his contact were indeed sufficient to accelerate the course of events. To form some idea of Mesía's opinion about the prestige of his *physical attraction* it is necessary to imagine an electrical machine which is aware of the fact that it is capable of giving off sparks. Mesía thought of himself as an electrical machine of love. It was simply a matter of making sure that the machine was tuned. Yes, his conceit went to such lengths, but let it be said in his favour that nobody knew this, and that he could cite numerous facts which gave him grounds for his monstrous vanity. He considered himself to be a man of talent ('he was principally a politician'). He had faith in his experience as a man of the world and a skilled Don Juan, but to himself he humbly declared that all this was nothing in comparison with the prestige which his physical beauty gave him. 'For the seduction of pleasure-worn women with jaded palates, pampered, and sated with love, perhaps looks are not enough, or even the most important thing; but honourable virgins' (he knew another kind) 'and decent married women surrender only to the man who is handsome.'

'I do not know of any seducers who are hunchbacks, or dwarfs,' he would say, shrugging his shoulders, on the few occasions when he spoke with close friends about such matters. This was usually after a hearty supper. 'Aberrations of taste? They're the exception. Nobody can want to be among lovers what asafoetida is among smells; and yet, when Rome was declining, women . . .'

At this point Paco Vegallana would chime in with evidence from his readings in technical pornography, and would describe all the aberrations of feminine sexuality in ancient times, in the Middle Ages, and in the modern period. There was nothing new under the sun. 'All the things done by the most perverted Parisian women were known and done by the prostitutes of ancient Babylon and Harridan.'

Paco was subject to confusion when he delved into ancient history. Harridan was Hamadan,[6] but that was what he called it, by mistake, no doubt. He knew in his own mind which city he meant. It was one which had been surrounded by a number of walls of different colours, one he had read about in the *History of Prostitution* – not Dufour's history, but another which he knew. Paco was a scholar.

'I have read,' Don Alvaro would add during such conversations, 'of princesses and queens besotted by monkeys, and sleeping with them – with monkeys, mind you.'

'Yes, that's right,' Paco would chime in again, 'Victor Hugo says so in a novel called *L'Homme qui rit.*'

'But apart from that, which is an exception,' Mesía would continue, 'let's not deceive ourselves: what women want is *physical attraction.*'

'That's what I think, too,' Pepe Ronzal would affirm, 'woman is the same *turby and torby*' (everywhere, in Blunderbuss's Latin).

Furthermore, Don Alvaro was profoundly materialistic, and this was something which he admitted to nobody. Since the politician was uppermost in him he tolerated the faith of Paco's forefathers and scoffed at the idea of separating Church and state. Moreover, he considered it to be vulgar to contradict bona fide Catholics. In 1867, in Paris, at the Exhibition, he had learnt that it was *chic* to have the faith of a little child. Sport and Catholicism, this was the fashion, and it reigned yet. But of course, having faith merely meant saying that one had faith. He had none whatsoever, 'and he had no blessed need of it', except when the fear of death came over him. Whenever he fell ill and found himself in his hotel alone and unloved, all his rich experience of life could not stop him from feeling truly sorry that he was not a sincere Christian. But he recovered and said, 'Bah! it was all caused by physical weakness.' Nevertheless, it would be a good idea to acquire some culture, to make a foundation for that materialism which accorded so well with his other ideas about the world and how to exploit it. He asked a friend for books which would prove materialism in a few words. What he first learned was that there was no longer any such thing as metaphysics, an excellent idea which did away with a number of puzzling problems. He read Büchner's *Force and Matter*,[7] and some books by Flammarion,[8] but these upset him, for they spoke ill of the Church and well of heaven, God, the soul – and what he wanted was the precise opposite. Flammarion wasn't *chic*. He also read Moleschott, Virchow and Vogt,[9] in translation, bound in saffron-yellow paper covers. He did not understand much of what they said, but he got the gist of it: everything was grey matter – splendid, that was just what he wanted to be told. His principal requirement was that there should be no hell. He began reading a French translation of Lucretius's poem *De rerum natura*[10] but abandoned it half-way through. There were some good things in it, but it was very long. Mesía was soon seeing atoms everywhere, and his fine figure was a happy combination of hook-shaped molecules for fastening on to all the pretty women who appeared before him. Such were Mesía's inmost beliefs, but not even Paco, who was a good Catholic, according to Mesía, had penetrated into these subterranean depths. All this was for Mesía alone, so long as he was in Vetusta. On his trips to Paris, the false bottom of his trunk came out, and so did his materialism. He tried to imbue his mistresses – the ones who were not too sanctimonious and who were very much in love – with his ideas about the atom and force. Mesía's materialism was easy to understand. He explained it in two lectures. Once a woman was convinced of the non-existence of metaphysics, things took a much smoother course for Don Alvaro.

When he remembered one of the women whom he had converted to epicureanism he would exclaim, his eyes wide open and burning: 'What a creature she was!' And he would sigh. That creature was never a Vetustan. Vetustan women did not believe in metaphysics, either: they had never heard of it. But they did not go along with certain things.

Don Alvaro walked by Ana's side, convinced that his presence was enough to produce deleterious effects on that virtue in which he himself believed. Words were, at that early stage, and without prejudice, what least mattered. He could speak with eloquence too – to the soul, of course – in other circumstances, however, later on.

Paco, behind them, did not disdain to talk to Petra, who was all airs and graces as she replied to the Young Marquis. Where love was concerned the servant girl did not believe in class distinctions, and could well imagine a nobleman getting infatuated with her and even marrying her. She was not assuming, by any manner of means, that this was the case with Don Paquito; yet he was praising her golden hair and her white skin, and there had to be a beginning to everything.

'You must get very bored in Vetusta, Ana,' Don Alvaro said.

He was searching, in vain, for a natural way of bringing their conversation around to a point analogous, at least, to the one on which he intended to speak with her at length, as soon as a suitable occasion should arise.

'Yes, sometimes I am bored. It rains so much!'

'Even when it is not raining. You never go anywhere.'

'Obviously you do not notice me. I go out often enough.'

Ana had hardly finished speaking these words when she realized that they were imprudent. Was it she who had uttered them? That was how Obdulia spoke to men; but she, Ana!

Don Alvaro was in a quandary. What did the woman want? Did she want to talk about their relationship – which, in reality, was nothing much to talk about? Should he have been surprised by her blunder? He did not notice her! Was this just vulgar coquetry or something more complicated which he did not understand? Was she trying to deny what both of them were well aware of – their meetings without any explicit arrangement to meet, in a church, at the theatre, at the promenade? Was she trying to disown the long, intense looks which she sometimes bestowed upon him like precious celestial favours not to be squandered?

In fact, Ana had been driven by an involuntary impulse.

She had spoken like someone repeating a meaningless formula, but then she had thought that her reply might discourage Mesía, giving him to understand that she had not been a party to their silent pact. But this itself was untimely. It was denying too much, denying what was evident.

Don Alvaro was afraid to risk very much that night, and thought that the least ridiculous course of action was to 'turn on the charm', in the manner of the men of Vetusta. So he said, in tones of forced, commonplace gallantry:

'Madam, you cannot fail to attract the attention of even the most indifferent of men.'

Since this speech seemed cheap and indeed rather ambiguous, he added some other words, which were no less cold and commonplace.

He did not realize yet that turning on the charm, although it would have been ridiculous with other women, was his best weapon against the judge's wife. Ana immediately forgot everything else, thinking about the pain she felt as she heard his words. 'Might I have been imagining things? Might this man never have looked at me with love in his eyes? Might seeing him everywhere have been a simple coincidence? Might the eyes which gazed at me have done so in mere indifference? Those fits of melancholy, those ill-concealed outbursts of impatience and despair, which I watched out of the corner of my eye (oh! yes, indeed, out of the corner of my eye!) – might they have been illusions, just illusions? But that's impossible!' Such thoughts made her shudder and perspire. Never, never would she consent to satisfy the longings to which his looks bore mute yet eloquent witness. She would always be virtuous, and she would consummate her sacrifice: Don Víctor and nothing else – and that made a sum total of nothing; but then, precisely nothing had been her love dowry. But to renounce temptation! That was too much. Temptation belonged to her – it was her only pleasure. She was doing quite enough if she avoided being conquered; but she did want to be tempted!

The idea that Mesía expected nothing from her, and asked for nothing, gave her the sensation that a black pit had opened in her heart and was being filled with nothingness. 'No, no; temptation belonged to her, and it was her only pleasure. What would she do if she had nothing to struggle against? And besides,' came the unavoidable thought, 'she should not, she could not love; but why should she not be loved? Oh, what a terrible ending for that day which had seemed so happy, the day on which she had found a soul companion, the canon theologian, the confessor who told her that virtue was so easy! Yes, virtue was easy, she knew that, but if she was deprived of temptation virtue would have no merit, it would be something prosaic, something Vetustan, all that she most despised.'

Although Don Alvaro was not as good a politician as he imagined himself to be, he did know a little about the diplomacy of flirtation, and he realized that here, quite by accident, he had hit the target.

In Ana's voice and confused words he noticed that she had been affected by the dryness of his banal compliment. 'Was she expecting a declaration of love? Already? But tomorrow she's going to take the communion! What sort of a woman is this? A woman of great beauty!' added the materialist as he glanced at Ana walking by his side with fire in her eyes and crimson in her cheeks.

They reached the porch of Ozores Mansion and stopped there. The gilt lamp hanging from the ceiling hardly shed any light into that broad space. Neither had spoken for some time.

'Where's Petra? Where's Paco?' asked the judge's wife, taking fright.

'Here they come, they're turning the corner now.'

Anita's mouth was dry, in order to speak she had to moisten her lips with her tongue. Mesía noticed this action, one which he adored, and, unable to restrain himself, departing from his plan, *natura naturans*,[11] he exclaimed:

'How lovely! how lovely!'

But he said it in a hoarse, hushed voice, hardly aware that he was speaking, and without showing any disrespect. It was an escape of passion, and therefore of more consequence than any insipid compliment, and not impertinent. It could be taken for a declaration of love, for the foolish blunder of a man whose blood had been stirred, for anything except a shameless piece of effrontery – of which a perfect gentleman could never be guilty.

Ana pretended not to hear, but her eyes betrayed her. Shining in the shadows, searching for Don Alvaro, who had stepped back in the darkness, they repaid with interest the delight which his words had poured into her soul like a beneficial shower of rain.

'She's mine,' thought Don Alvaro with a pleasure even greater than that which he had anticipated he would feel on the day of triumph.

'Would you like to come up and rest awhile?' the lady asked the two gentlemen, when she saw Paco approaching.

'No thanks. Anyway, I'll soon be coming back for you with mamma.'

'For me?'

'Yes; hasn't Alvaro here told you? You're coming with us to the theatre this evening. It's a first night, that is to say the first performance this year of a play by Don Pedro Calderón de la Barca, your husband's idol. Didn't you know? An actor has come from Madrid – Perales, a good friend of mine – who does an excellent imitation of Calvo.[12] Today they're performing *Life is a Dream*.[13] But of course you must come! Really! Mamma insists. She's already dressed and waiting.'

'My dear child, I have to take the communion tomorrow.'

'What does that matter?'

'Of course it matters!'

'You can put it off until another day. Well, you'll have to settle things with mamma, because she's coming for you.'

Without waiting for a reply the scatter-brained Young Marquis marched out of the porch.

Petra was already in the courtyard, pretending not to hear. 'Now she knew what to make herself ready for: him. Well, he was a beginning. The Young Marquis had been keeping her amused so as to leave the other two alone. You could tell that from his coldness. He hadn't given her so much as one miserable hug in the dark.' She listened. She could hear Don Alvaro taking his leave in a humble, trembling voice.

'Won't you be going to the theatre?'

'No, certainly not,' replied the judge's wife, shutting the door behind her and walking into the courtyard.

X

At eight o'clock the marchioness's berlin was rolling through the streets of La Encimada, its wheels striking sparks from their uneven surface. It reached the Plaza Nueva and stopped outside the old mansion in the corner.

The marchioness, in blue and gold, her dress revealing a suggestion of what had once been charms, but were now languishing hillocks,[1] her grey hair dyed black and the dye powdered white, threw doors open as she swept into Ana's dining-room, followed by her son.

'What? What's this? You aren't dressed?'

'What a stubborn thing you are!' exclaimed Paquito.

Don Víctor bowed his head and shrugged his shoulders, thereby giving to understand that he was not responsible for his wife's stubbornness.

'*He* was ready.' Indeed he was buttoning up his gloves and was already wearing his close-fitting, machine-knitted frock-coat.

Ana smiled at the marchioness.

'But this is madness. Why have you gone to such trouble?'

'Madness? You're getting dressed directly. Since I've gone to such trouble, as you say, it's not going to be in vain. Come on! Upstairs with you, otherwise I'll comb your hair and put your shoes on, and dress you, right here, here in front of these two gentlemen.'

'That's right,' said Paco, 'we'll dress you, comb your hair . . .'

Don Víctor, too, urged Ana to accompany them to the theatre.

'*Life is a Dream*, my child, is the portent of all dramatic portents. It is symbolical, philosophical.'

'Yes, I know, Quintanar.'

'And Perales, who recites it so well, my friend Perales . . .'

'And there'll be such a crowd,' added the marchioness.

'Please, my lady, I should be delighted to go, if it weren't for . . . Surely I go often enough! But tomorrow I have to take the communion!'

'Tut, tut! What's that got to do with it? Does anyone know? Are you going to the theatre to commit some sin?'

'Art is a religion!' Don Víctor pointed out, looking at his watch in fear of missing 'Wild hippogryph, that flyest with the wind . . .'[2]. He later discovered that this part was being omitted. 'How scandalous.'

'My child,' he continued, 'we are being greatly honoured by the marchioness.'

'Honoured – fiddlesticks! But she's coming.'

'No, it is useless for you to insist.'

They argued for some time, but in the end Doña Rufina, who also wanted to see the beginning of the play, relented and took Don Víctor away, once he had made his formal protest:

'Since she is so stubborn, I too shall remain behind.'

'That's out of the question!' exclaimed the judge's wife in dismay. 'You go alone on other evenings, don't you?'

Don Víctor insisted a little longer upon staying behind and missing that drama among dramas.

But finally Ana found herself alone in the dining-room, by the Churrigueresque fireplace with its great chimney-piece swarming with plaster reliefs and painted in lizard colours; by the fireplace in whose warmth so many *feuilletons* had been read in former days by Señorita Doña Anunciación Ozores, who was now resting in peace. No fire burned there now; the uncovered fire-basket was a gaping hole of sadness.

Petra cleared away the coffee-service. Her movements were torpid. She wandered in and out, several times, but Ana did not even see her, so intently was she staring at the cold, black fire-basket. The maid was devouring her mistress with her eyes. 'She isn't going to the theatre! Something's up. Am I in her way? Or does she need me?'

'Will madam be needing anything?' she asked.

Startled, the judge's wife replied:

'Me? What? No, nothing, you may go.'

'It had been silly of her to snub the marchioness, having already decided not to receive the communion tomorrow. But why shouldn't she receive the communion? Was she some sanctimonious prude, stuffed with ridiculous scruples? Of what could she accuse herself? What sins had she committed? All Vetusta was enjoying itself, with noise, light, music, happiness; and here was she alone, alone, in the cold, dark, sad dining-room – with all its odious, stupid memories – shunning the opportunity to encourage a passion which would have flattered the vainest of women. Was this sinful? She wasn't responsible for Don Alvaro. He could be as enamoured as he pleased, but she would never concede even the most insignificant favour to him. Indeed, she wouldn't even look at him. She had made up her mind. What was there for her to confess? Nothing. Why then go back for a further confession? For no good reason whatsoever. She could take the communion without qualms; yes, she would get up early and go to mass. But enough! For God's sake enough of thinking about all that! She was going mad. It was agony to be always examining her own mind, and spying on herself, and accusing herself of having evil thoughts when they were in fact perfectly innocent ones: agony piled on top of all the other agony which life had brought her and was still bringing her, although she had never looked for it. Yet what could a woman like her do, except brood? How could she amuse herself? Hunt with birdlime or a decoy-bird, like her husband? Plant eucalyptus-trees where they didn't want to grow, like Frillity?'

She pictured all the Vetustans happy in their own way, some given over to vice, others to their manias, but all of them pleased with life. She alone was in a kind of exile. 'But she was an exile who had no homeland to return to, or to sigh for. She had lived in Granada, in Saragossa, in Granada again, and then in Valladolid, with Don Víctor always by her side. What had she left on the banks of the Ebro, the troubadour's river, or on the banks of the Genil or the Darro?[3] Nothing; or at the most, the beginnings of some ridiculous adventure. She remembered the Englishman who owned a villa near the Alhambra, the one who had fallen in love with her and given her the skin of a tiger caught by his servants in India. She had subsequently learned that this Englishman (who had written swearing that he would hang himself from a historic tree in the gardens of the Generalife, 'by the founts of eternal poetry and voluptuous coolness'), poor Mr Brooke, had married a gipsy girl from the Albaicín.[4] The best of luck to him. Anyway, it had been a stupid adventure. She had destroyed his letter, but still possessed the tiger-skin – because of the tiger, not because of the Englishman.' Obdulia was not very well informed on this subject, thinking that the man had been an American, because this was what Visitación had told her.

'Why hadn't she gone to the theatre? There, perhaps, she could have dispersed these miserable ideas which were sticking into her brain like pins into a pincushion. She was being silly. Why shouldn't she behave like all the other women?' Ana's thoughts were founded on the assumption that there were no other virtuous women in all the town. She stood up, impatient, almost angry, and looked at the flame of the lamp hanging over the table. The light offended her. She walked out of the dining-room and into her boudoir, opened her balcony window and leaned her elbows on the iron handrail and her chin upon her hands. A crescent moon shone before her, above the proud eucalyptus-trees in the park, planted there by Frillity. The south wind still blew, soft, warm, languid; from time to time a lively gust would shake the drying leaves and make them sound like jingles on tambourines. It was as if nature were shivering before she fell into her winter sleep.

Ana could hear confused sounds from the city, with prolonged, melancholy resonances: shouts, snatches of distant songs, barking, all dissipated through the air, like the white light reflected by the fine mist which was hovering over Vetusta as if it were the soft, warm body of the wind. She looked up at the sky, at the great light in front of her, not knowing at what she was looking; there was silvery dust in her eyes and threads of silver descended from the heavens into them, like spiders' webs. Her tears were refracting the rays of moonlight.

'Why was she crying? What was wrong now? She was such a stupid woman. She felt afraid of these attacks of tenderness which did nobody any good.'

The moon looked down at her with one eye, the other being sunk in the abyss of the heavens. Frillity's eucalyptus-trees leaned towards each other with slight, majestic bows, telling each other in discreet whispers what they thought of that lunatic, that woman without a mother, without children, without love, who had sworn eternal fidelity to a man who preferred a good male partridge to all the conjugal caresses in the world.

'That man Frillity, the planter of the eucalyptus-trees, was the culprit. He had talked her into accepting Quintanar. Eight years had elapsed since then, yet Ana still thought of his underhand trick as if it had been an insult suffered but the day before. And what if she had married Don Frutos Redondo? Perhaps she would have been unfaithful to him. But Quintanar was so kind, so gentlemanly! He was like a father to her, and even leaving aside the faithfulness which she had sworn him it would be ungrateful and despicable to deceive him. With Don Frutos everything would have been different. She would have had no option. He would have been so brutish, so coarse. Then Don Alvaro would have abducted her, oh yes, and by now they would be at the end of the world together. And if this had vexed Redondo he would have had to fight a duel with Mesía.' Ana pictured Don

Frutos, the wretched man stretched out upon the sand, drowning in a pool of blood, like the blood she had seen at bull fights, black blood, thick and foaming.

'How awful!' She was nauseated by this image and by the ideas which had brought it into her mind.

'How wretched I become when I lose heart like this! What heinous crimes I'm imagining!' She was suffocating on the balcony. She wanted to go down into the park. Without calling for a lamp or looking for one herself, but by the light of the moon, she walked through several rooms in the direction of the stairs which led down into the garden. As she was passing Quintanar's study, however, she changed her mind and said to herself: 'I'll go in. He's bound to have some matches on the table. I'll write to the canon theologian and tell him to expect me tomorrow afternoon, for I need to make another confession, I can't receive the communion in this state. Tomorrow I'll tell him everything, everything inside me – and everything deeper down inside me, as well.'

The study was in darkness; the moonlight did not enter there. Ana felt her way forward along the walls. At each step she bumped into a piece of furniture. Now she regretted having ventured without a lamp into that room where not a single square foot was free of obstacles. But it was pointless to turn back now. She took a step forward, away from the wall, and continued in the same direction with her arms outstretched to avoid a collision.

'My God! Who's that? Who is it? Who's holding me?' she cried in horror.

Her hand had touched a cold metallic object which had yielded to its pressure; she had heard a crack and felt two blows on her arm, which was imprisoned in inflexible pincers tight upon her flesh. With the strength lent her by fear she shook her arm to try to free it from its imprisonment, all the while shouting:

'Petra, bring a light! Who is it?'

The pincers did not release their victim. Instead, they followed her movements, and she felt their weight on her arm and heard the noise of glass breaking as it crashed to the floor together with other resounding objects. Ana could not bring herself to use her other hand to grasp the pincers as they tightened on her flesh, but however much she shook her arm she could not free it. As she tried to find the door she blundered into a thousand objects, her progress marked by a continuous sound of things breaking or rolling noisily over the floor. Petra arrived with a light.

'Oh, madam, madam! What's this? Burglars!'

'No, be quiet! Come here and remove this contraption – fastened on to me like a pair of pincers.'

Ana was red with shame and rage. Her wrath was as great as that of Achilles, the son of Peleus.[5]

Petra attempted to pull from her mistress's arm the trap into which she had fallen.

It was a device which, according to Frillity and Quintanar, its inventors, was going to be used to catch foxes in hen-houses, as soon as certain mechanical difficulties, which were retarding the contrivance's application, were overcome.

The animal's snout had to touch a certain spot; if it did, a metal bar immediately fell upon its head, while an identical bar held it under its lower jaw. The spring was not strong enough to kill the farmyard thief, but it was sufficient to detain him, with the aid of certain skilfully fashioned, harmless hooks. Neither Frillity nor Quintanar wanted bloodshed; they only sought to catch the offender *in fraganti* and hold him fast. If the inventors had not succeeded in harmonizing the interests of industry with the statutes of the Society for the Protection of Animals, the judge's wife would have had a bad time of it that evening. Fortunately Quintanar was a reformer – he was for the correction of the guilty party, not his destruction, and the foxes which he caught would survive. For the machine to be perfect, only one thing was required: that the hen-robbers should, like Ana, happen to knock against the knob which released the devilish spring.

Neither Petra nor her mistress knew the purpose of the contrivance, which they had to destroy, at the cost of no little toil, in order to disengage the bruised arm.

Petra could hardly contain her laughter, but was content to exclaim: 'What a *mess*!' as she pointed at the pieces of pottery, glass and other indeterminate materials on the floor. 'If it had been me, Don Víctor would have given me the sack. Oh, madam, you've broken three of those new flower-pots! And the butterfly-picture is all smashed into little bits! And one of the herbariums is broken! And . . .'

'That is enough! Leave the lamp there and go away,' interrupted the judge's wife.

Petra persisted, enjoying her mistress's suppressed anger:

'Do you want me to bring some arnica, ma'am? Look, your arm's going all blue – of course, a diabolical guillotine like that mustn't half give you a bite. But what can it be? Do you know?'

'I – no – no – leave me alone. Bring me a little water.'

'Of course, and linden-tea, too, you're as pale as death. But why were you walking around in the dark, ma'am? What a fright! What a fright! What the devil can it be? Well it's not for catching sparrows, that's for sure. And now we've broken it, look – but there was nothing else we could have done.'

Petra left the room and returned with some arnica, which the judge's wife refused. Then she came with linden-tea, and collected the remains from the floor and placed them upon tables and cupboards as if they were holy relics. She experienced a singular joy on seeing in ruins those objects which she was obliged to consider as sacred vessels of an unknown cult.

'If it had been me!' she kept muttering to herself as, squatting on her heels, she gathered together the last fragments.

From her standpoint of blamelessness she was revelling in the catastrophe.

Ana went down into the garden, having forgotten all about the letter which she had intended to write. Her arm was hurting – hurting with the moral sting of the slap in the face which brings dishonour. The whole affair seemed shameful, a ridiculous degradation. She was furious. 'Her precious Don Víctor! That idiot! Yes, idiot! At that moment she would not take it back. What must Petra be thinking? What sort of a husband was that, who caught his own wife in a trap?' She looked up at the moon and saw it pulling faces at her, making fun of her adventure. The trees were still whispering with all their leaves into each other's ears, commenting with ironical smiles on the incident of the guillotine, as Petra had called it.

'What a beautiful night! But who was she to be admiring the serene night?[6] What had all that melancholic poetry of sky and earth to do with what was happening to her?

'Does Quintanar think that woman is made of steel and that she can, without falling into temptation, put up with the manias of a husband who invents absurd machines for bruising his wife's arms? Her husband was a botanist, an ornithologist, a floriculturist, an arboriculturist, a huntsman, a dramatic critic, an actor, a lawyer: everything, in short, but a husband. He loved Frillity more than his own wife. And what was Frillity? A madman, likeable enough years earlier, but now quite out of his mind. A man with a mania for acclimatization, who wanted to harmonize, mix and confuse everything, who grafted pear-trees on to apple-trees and believed that all was one and the same and claimed that the important thing was to "adapt oneself to the environment". A man who in his orgy of absurdities had reached the extreme of grafting English cockerels on to Spanish cockerels – she had seen them herself! Poor creatures, with their combs cut open and on them, held in place with pieces of rag, stumps of raw, bleeding flesh – how nauseating! Frillity was a modern Herod; and this Herod was her husband's Pylades.[7] For three years now she had been living with that pair of sleep-walkers, with nobody else close to her. Enough, enough! She couldn't take any more, what had just happened was the last straw – getting caught in a trap set by one's husband in his study as if it were the open country! The height of absurdity!'

The intemperance of Ana's unreasonable, puerile anger made her aware of her mistake. '*She* was ridiculous, to be sure. Getting so irritated about a petty, insignificant incident!' And she turned all her scorn against herself. 'How can he be blamed if I go into his study at an unreasonable hour, in the dark? Had she any rational motive for complaint? No. Oh! there was no excuse, no excuse at all, for ingratitude.

'But that wasn't the point. She was dying of boredom. She was twenty-seven years old, her youth was slipping away, for twenty-seven years, in a woman, were the threshold of old age, and she was already knocking at the door. Not once had she enjoyed those delights of love about which everyone talks, which are the subject of plays, novels and even history. Love is the only thing worth living for, she had often heard and read. But what love? Where was this love? She had never experienced it. And she remembered, half in shame half in anger, that her honeymoon had meant no more than futile arousal, a false alarm for sensuality, a cruel practical joke. Yes, yes, why try to keep the fact hidden from herself when her memory was shouting it at her? On the first night, when she awoke in the bridal bed and became aware of a magistrate breathing at her side, it seemed absurd and impertinent that if Señor Quintanar was in there with her he was not wearing his long machine-knitted frock-coat and his black flannel trousers. She remembered that the inevitable physical pleasure had been an embarrassment, a mockery and a source of bewilderment: lying with that man, against her will, reminded her of the phrase spoken on Ash Wednesday, *quia pulvis es* – thou art ashes, you are mere matter – but at the same time it threw light on the meaning of all those things she had read in her books of mythology and overheard in the mischievous whispering of servants and shepherds. To think of what it could have meant – and what it had meant! And in that prison of chastity she was not even left with the consolation of being considered a martyr and a heroine. She remembered, too, the envious words and curious looks directed at her by Doña Agueda (R.I.P.) during the first few days after the marriage; she remembered that although she had never spoken disrespectfully to her aunts she had needed to make a great effort not to scream "Idiot!" when she saw her aunt looking at her in that way. And life had gone on and on in the same manner. She had suffered the same existence in Granada, in Saragossa, in Granada again, and then in Valladolid. And nobody even felt sorry for her. No question of children. True, Don Víctor did not pester her. He had soon tired of playing the beau and had by degrees adopted the role of greybeard, for which he was better suited. Oh, as a father, certainly, he was lovable! She could not go to bed at night without his kiss on her forehead. But spring would come around, and she would try to make him kiss her on the mouth; for it filled her with remorse not to love him as a husband, not to desire his caresses and, furthermore, she was afraid of senses aroused in vain. All this was a great injustice and she did not know who was responsible for it, an incurable pain which did not even have the attractions of poetic suffering, a shameful pain, like the illnesses she had seen named in advertisements on lamps painted green and red, in Madrid. How was she going to confess all this – above all in this way, as it was in her mind? For confessing it meant just that.

'And youth was slipping away, like those little clouds of crinkled silver passing in front of the moon on speedy wings. They were silvery now, but they went rushing on, flying on, away from that bath of light, falling into the dark abyss of old age, miserable old age, where there was no hope of love. Behind these silver fleeces crossing the sky like flocks of birds, loomed a great black cloud which extended to the horizon. And then the images were reversed, and it was the moon which was rushing on, to fall into the black chasm, and put out its light in that sea of darkness.

'She was just the same. Like the moon, she was rushing through life alone, to plunge into the abyss of old age; into the darkness of the soul, where there was no love, no hope of love – oh no, no, not that!'

She felt cries of protest in her very bowels, cries which seemed to call upon her with supreme eloquence, cries inspired by justice, by the rights of the flesh, by the rights of her beauty. And the moon rushed onwards, falling, falling into the abyss of the black cloud which, like a sea of bitumen, was going to swallow it. Ana, almost delirious by now, could see her own destiny in the night sky: she was the moon, and the cloud was old age, terrible old age, where there was no hope of being loved. She held out her hands towards the sky and ran along the paths in the park as if attempting to fly away and change the course of the star of eternal romanticism. But the moon plunged into the dense vapours of the atmosphere, and Vetusta was enveloped in shadow. The cathedral tower, whose spiritual outline had stood out in the light of a clear night – surrounded by stars, like paintings of the Virgin; the sky beyond showing through its lace-like open work – was now, in the dark, just a ghost with a pointed shape, one more shadow.

Languid and faint-hearted, Ana rested her head against the cold bars of the great iron gate at the entrance to the park from the Calle de Traslacerca. She remained thus for a long time, staring at the darkness outside, engrossed in her own suffering, giving free rein to her will and to her thoughts, which were coming and going, whither she did not know, at the mercy of impulses of which she was not conscious.

Almost brushing against Ana's forehead as it protruded between two bars, a shape passed along the solitary street, close to the garden wall.

'It's him!' she thought, recognizing Don Alvaro even though his appearance had been so brief, and stepping back in alarm. She was uncertain whether he had passed through the street or through her brain.

It was indeed Don Alvaro. He had been at the theatre, but during an interval it had occurred to him to go out and satisfy an intense curiosity he had been feeling. 'If, by any chance, she were in her balcony . . . She won't be, that's almost certain, but supposing she were?' Wasn't his life full of happy accidents of that kind? Didn't he owe to good fortune, to *la chance* as he said, a great part of his success? Me, and opportunity![8] That was one of his mottoes. Oh! if he saw her he would speak to her, tell her that he couldn't continue living without her, that he had come to walk up and down outside her house like a twenty-year-old platonic, romantic lover, content to gaze upon paradise from without. Yes, he'd tell her all this nonsense, with the eloquence which would come to his lips in due course. All he needed was for her, by chance, to be in her balcony. He left the theatre and walked up the Calle de Roma, across the Plaza del Pan and into the Calle del Aguila. When he reached the Plaza Nueva he stopped and looked across the square into the corner – there wasn't anybody in the balcony. Just as he'd supposed. Hunches aren't always right. Never mind. He walked a few times around the square, which was deserted at that hour. Nothing up there, not even a cat. 'Now he was here, why not continue his romantic siege?' He laughed at himself. What a long way he had to go back into the history of his love-affairs to come up with walks of this kind! In spite of his amusement, and in spite of all the inevitable mud awaiting him in the uncobbled Calle de Traslacerca, he walked under an arch and down an alley-way, and from this into another one, and finally came to the street behind Ozores Park. Here there were no houses, no pavements, no lamps. It was a street only because people called it a street; for it was, in reality, merely a rough track with an uneven muddy surface between two high walls, one belonging to the prison and the other to the Ozores's garden. As Mesía approached the gate, keeping close to the garden wall to avoid the mud, he felt what he believed was one of his genuine hunches. He thought of them in such terms because they seemed a sort of instantaneous divination or second sight. His greatest triumphs of every kind had come like this, after genuine hunches, which gave him, a little before the victory, a sudden unaccustomed bravery, an absolute certainty: throbbing in his temples, blood in his cheeks, an uneasy, oppressive feeling in his throat. He stopped. 'The judge's wife was there, in the garden. Everything he was feeling told him so. What was he going to do if his feelings were not deceiving him? What he always did in such cases: stake his all! Beg her, on his knees in the mud, to open the gate and, if she refused, climb it; that was little short of impossible – but he would climb it. If only the moon would shine again! But no, it wasn't going to shine, the cloud was a huge, thick one and it would be half an hour before it was light again.'

He reached the gate, and saw the judge's wife before she saw him.

And he recognized her, or rather sensed who she was, before she recognized him.

'She's yours!' the demon of seduction shouted at him. 'She adores you, she's waiting for you!'

But he could not speak, he could not stop. He felt frightened of his victim. He realized now that he too was affected by the Vetustan superstition about Ana's virtue. It could perhaps drive the enemy away even after its death, as the Cid had done.[9] He – running away! Something he had never done before! He was afraid – for the very first time!

He walked on. Three, four more steps, without making up his mind to turn back, however much the demon of seduction might cling to his arms, pulling him towards the gate and mocking him with words of fire in his ear: 'Coward, seducer of prostitutes! Come on, let's see your courage in the face of real virtue. Now or never!'

'Now, now!' shouted Mesía with all the courage left in him. Ten paces past the gate, he turned on his heel and ran back in fury, crying: 'Ana! Ana!'

He was answered by silence. In the darkness of the park he saw only the shadowy forms of the eucalyptuses, acacias and horse-chestnuts, and in the distance, like a black pyramid, the outline of the Washingtonia, Frillity's only true love – he had planted it and watched over the growth of its trunk, its branches, its leaves.

Mesía waited, in vain.

'Ana, Ana,' he repeated, softly, very softly; the only reply now was the rustling of dry leaves swept by the gentle breeze over the sandy pathways.

Ana had fled. Seeing, so close to her, that temptation which she loved, she had been assailed by fear and by her panic-stricken sense of rectitude. She had run to hide in her bedroom, shutting doors behind her, as if that bold libertine were capable of walking through the garden wall and following her. It was as if Don Alvaro could filter through walls and even into souls. Everything in the house was pervaded by him, and she was afraid she might suddenly see him appear again, as he had appeared by the park gate.

'Might it be the devil who brings about these coincidences?' thought Ana (who was not superstitious) in all seriousness.

She was terrified. She regarded her virtue and her home as being under blockade, and she had just seen the enemy mounting a breach in the ramparts. The nearness of crime had awoken her ingrained sense of virtue; but the nearness of love had left an overpowering perfume in her soul.

'How easy crime was! The gate – the night – the darkness. Everything had become an accomplice. But she would resist. Oh, yes! That powerful temptation, which promised such delights, such unknown pleasures, was an enemy worthy of her. That was how she preferred to fight. She was tired of the commonplace struggles of ordinary life, the everyday battles with boredom, with absurdity, with the prose of existence; they were like a war in a muddy tunnel. But to fight against a handsome man, who stalks one, suddenly appears like a spectre or a thought, calls out from the shadows, and is surrounded by a kind of aureola, a perfume of love – this was something different, this was worthy of her. She would fight.'

Don Víctor returned from the theatre and directed his steps unto his wife's boudoir. She threw herself into his arms, threw her own arms around his head, and wept abundant tears upon the lapels of his machine-knitted frock-coat.

As on the previous evening, Ana's attack of nerves was melting into tears, into an impulsive, pious determination always to be faithful to her husband. In spite of his infernal machines, Quintanar was her duty; and the canon theologian would be her aegis and protect her from all the formidable blows of temptation. But Quintanar knew nothing of this. The theatre had left him feeling awfully sleepy – he had not slept a wink the night before! – and full of lyrico-dramatic enthusiasm. Frankly, in his view, these periodical fits of sentimentality were excessive and tiresome. 'What the devil was wrong with his wife?'

'What is the matter, my child? You are ill.'

'No, Víctor, no, please let me be as I am. Don't you know I'm a nervous woman? This is what I need – to love you very much and caress you; and I need you to love me in the same way, too.'

'My dear darling, with all my heart! But – this is not natural – that is to say, it is perfectly in order, of course, but at this hour – I mean – at this time of night. Well, it is merely that . . . And if we had been engaged in an argument – it would have been more understandable, but in this manner, without any warning . . . I love you deeply, as you well know; but you are ill, and that is why you find yourself in this state. Yes, my child, these excesses . . .'

'They aren't excesses, Quintanar,' sobbed Ana, making a supreme effort to idealize her husband as he stood there with his tie under one ear.

'All right, my dear, maybe they are not; but you are unwell. Yesterday there was the threat of an attack, you became rather agitated. Today look what a state you are in. There is something wrong with you.'

Ana shook her head.

'Yes, my child. The marchioness, the doctor and I have been discussing this matter at the theatre. Don Robustiano is of opinion that the life you are leading is not a healthy one, that you should diversify your cerebral activity and take some exercise – that means recreation, walks. The marchioness says that you are too serious-minded, too virtuous, that you need to get some fresh air, to go about visiting people. I am of the same opinion, and I am resolved' – he said this with much energy – 'I am resolved that this solitary existence shall come to an end. You are indifferent to everything; you live in your dreams. Enough, my child, you have dreamed enough. Do you remember what happened in Granada? Months on end without ever going to the theatre, or on visits, or anywhere at all except on solitary excursions to the Alhambra and the Generalife, where you spent hour after hour reading and day-dreaming. The result was that you fell ill, and had I not been transferred to Valladolid I would have had a dead wife on my hands. And what happened in Valladolid? You regained your health, thanks to the strength which you derived from good food, but your ill-concealed melancholy persisted, those nerves again, on and on and on. Then we return to Vetusta, almost breaking the law to do so,[10] and as soon as we arrive we have to go into mourning for your poor Aunt Agueda, gone to join her sister, and you make that the excuse to shut yourself up in this old mansion, and for a whole year nobody is capable of inducing you to go out into the sunlight. Reading and toiling away as if you were some piece-worker . . . Do not interrupt me. I seldom scold you, as you are aware, but now that the time has come, I shall say everything I have to say, yes, everything. Frillity never stops telling me, over and over, "Anita is not happy." '

'What does he know about it?'

'You are well aware that he loves you, that he is our best friend.'

'But why does he say I'm not happy? How can he tell?'

'I do not know. I had not noticed anything, I must confess, but now I feel more and more inclined towards his opinion. These scenes at night . . .'

'Just nerves, Quintanar.'

'In that case let us make war on nerves, upon my soul!'

'Yes . . .'

'Not one word more. You have been found guilty of the charges brought by this court and it is now my duty to pass sentence. You must be made to change your ways, as of tomorrow. We shall go everywhere and, if you push me, I shall send Paco or even Mesía, that Don Juan, our charming Don Juan, to woo you.'

'What an outrageous idea!'

'Here is the programme!' cried Don Víctor. 'The theatre twice a week, at least; the marchioness's coterie every five or six days; the Mall every fine afternoon; the private parties in the Gentlemen's Club as soon as they are inaugurated; the marchioness's tea-parties, all the excursions of the high society of Vetusta, and the cathedral whenever Don Fermín is preaching and the bells are rung loud. Ah! and in the summer, Palomares, for bathing and wearing loose shifts to let the sea air through to your body. There! now you know all about your future life. And this is not a governmental programme: every part of it will be carried out. The marchioness, Don Robustiano and Paco have promised to assist me, and Visitación, who was in Páez's box this evening, also informed me that I can count upon her to make you come out of your shell. Yes, ma'am, we are coming out of our shells. I do not want any more of these nerves, I do not want to hear Frillity saying that you are unhappy . . .'

'What does *he* know about it?'

'I do not want any more of this crying, robbing me of my sleep. When you weep without knowing why, my child, I have such an uneasy feeling, a superstitious fear. You seem to be heralding some misfortune.'

Ana shivered, shuddered.

'Do you see? You are shivering. To bed, to bed, my angel, let us all be off to bed. I, myself, am ready to drop.'

Don Víctor yawned and departed from the boudoir, after depositing a chaste kiss upon his wife's forehead.

He entered his study, in a bad humour. 'This mysterious illness of Anita's – for that was what it was, an illness, he was sure of it – both worried and annoyed him. He had no mind to pour oil on troubled waters. He had a profound dislike for nerves. All this grief, without known cause, did not awaken any feelings of sympathy in him, but merely irritated him. He regarded it as one of the vagaries of a sick woman. Although he loved his wife dearly, he hated nerves. What was more he had been engaged in a heated argument at the theatre. Some fool, a milksop who was studying in Madrid, had said that modern dramatists should not imitate the theatre of Lope de Vega and Calderón, that verse was unnatural on stage, and that prose was more suitable for the contemporary drama. The idiot! Verse unnatural, indeed! What could be more natural than for all of us, without distinction of classes, to break into sonorous *quintillas* upon being insulted! Poetry will always be the language of enthusiasm, as the illustrious Jovellanos[11] says. Let us suppose that I am Benavides and that Carvajal[12] is seeking to deprive me of my honour,

> In darkness prowling, creeping,
> Like a thief of infamous deserts;

then what could be more natural than for me to feel put out, and to exclaim with Tirso de Molina' (acting the part):

> 'To vindicate my wrongéd fame
> Which thou hast stolen, come I hence.
> A roaring lion's mine honour's shame:
> A lion mine ensign represents,
> And Benavides is his name.
> He shall avenge mine heart, stung sore

By foul embraces, and provide
Mine issue's emblem ever more:
A noble lion, crimson-dyed
With two base traitors' bloody gore?'

Don Víctor glared at a side-table, which was playing the part of Carvajal, and was about to allow him to speak, and say by way of excuse:

'Now we are brothers in the law,
Thy words can give me no offence . . .'

when, to his horror, he saw upon the table the remains of his herbarium, his flowerpots, his collection of butterflies, and dozens of delicate pieces of apparatus which he used in his diverse industries as a manufacturer of birdcages and cricket-cages, marquetry-inlayer, botanical and entomological collector, and in other industries no less respectable.

'My God! What is this!' he cried, in cultured prose. 'Who has been the cause of this devastation? Petra! Anselmo!' And he tugged on the bell-rope.

Petra entered, smiling.

'What is the meaning of all this?'

'It wasn't me, sir. Maybe the cats got in.'

'The cats! What am I being taken for?'

Don Víctor seldom made a fuss, but if anyone touched anything in his museum, as he called that permanent exhibition of manias, he was transformed into a Segismundo.[13] And, indeed, without realizing what he was doing, he began to parody Perales, whom he had just seen on stage kicking and screaming like a madman.

'Call Anselmo! Bring Anselmo to me – I shall throw him from the balcony if he does not furnish me with a satisfactory explanation.'

Anselmo was ushered into Don Víctor's presence. 'It wasn't him, either.'

In the midst of his wrath, Quintanar saw his fox-trap in a corner of the room, shattered, useless.

'This, too! Good God! Just when I was about to put Frillity's nose out of joint. But who on earth has been messing in here?'

Ana arrived, having heard the row from her room.

She explained everything.

'But Petra,' she added, 'why did you not tell your master the truth?'

'I – didn't know if I should, ma'am.'

'If you should what?' asked Don Víctor, with a puzzled look.

'If I should . . .'

'You are never to hide anything from your master,' said the judge's wife, riveting haughty eyes on her maid.

Petra gave a twisted smile and bowed her head.

Don Víctor looked around with wrinkled brow, like a man suffering from temporary imbecility.

Soon he was left alone in his study, meditating upon the ruins of his inventions, machines and collections.

'My God! Might the poor dear be mad?' sighed Quintanar, with his head in his hands. He retired to bed resolved upon serious consultation about *that business* of his wife's.

Soon everyone in the house was resting except Petra, who, in the middle of a corridor, with a candlestick in her hand, was spying on the silence of the honoured home with looks fraught with questions.

'She had seen a deal of things during her life as a servant. Something was going to happen in that house. What could her mistress have been up to in the garden? Hadn't she heard a voice over towards the garden gate? Probably just her imagination – but something was afoot. What role would they have for her? Would they bring her into it at all? God help them if they didn't!'

And, with unhealthy delight, the sensual blonde scented the dishonour of that house, as she listened to Anselmo snoring in the distance – 'another idiot who had never come for her in the secrecy of night'.

XI

The canon theologian was an early riser. His life was so full of activities of the most varied kinds that his only chances to study came in the early morning and late at night, leaving little time for sleep. His twofold mission as an administrator in the diocese and a scholar in the cathedral gave him an overwhelming amount of work. Furthermore, he was a clergyman of the world, which meant that he received and returned numerous visits; and this occupation, one of the most tedious but also one of the most important, took up a great deal of his time. In the morning he studied philosophy and theology, read Jesuit journals, and wrote his sermons and other literary pieces. He was working on a *History of the Diocese of Vetusta*, a serious, original book which would throw light upon certain obscure aspects of the ecclesiastical annals of Spain. When, after a hearty meal, Don Saturnino Bermúdez was a little merry, he made unkind comments about this book, which he had not read. He whispered, in confidence, that 'the canon theologian was worthy to be called a scholar, but hardly an historian; nobody could be good at everything'.

Don Fermín was writing by the thin white light of the dawn. It was a cool morning and from time to time he took a rest, blowing his fingers and thinking. His feet were wrapped in one of his mother's old shawls and on his head was a threadbare black velvet cap. His cassock, embroidered with darns, was going brown with age, and the sleeves of the jacket which he wore under it shone with the sad sheen of worn cloth. These squalid clothes, such a contrast to the neatness, elegance and splendour which the canon displayed to the world, disappeared as soon as his work was done and the hour approached when visits were likely. Then he would don a fine, flowing robe, comfortable, brand-new and well-cut, and hide his selvage carpet-slippers and his grimy cap in a corner of his bedroom; and the shoes so admired by Bismarck, the postilion, and a skull-cap which glowed like a black sun would cover either end of this important personage. In his study he only received those whom he wished to dazzle with his wisdom, but in Vetusta and its province hardly anyone was dazzled by wisdom, so most of his visitors were shown into the drawing-room next to the study.

Few people could boast of knowing the vicar-general's house from top to bottom; hardly anyone had seen more than the hall, the stairs, the passage, the ante-room, and the drawing-room with its green curtains and chairs with grey cloth covers, which, being kept in near darkness, was only half visible. One of the arguments employed by those who defended the vicar-general's honesty against his detractors consisted in reminding them of the modesty of his furnishings and his domestic life.

This had been the subject of discussion the previous afternoon in the Mall among a group of gossips, both priests and laymen.

'It is unlikely that he and his mother, between them, spend as much as three thousand pesetas[1] a year,' said Ripamilán, the venerable archpriest, in a serious voice. 'True, he dresses well, indeed with elegance, luxuriously even, but he keeps his clothes for a long time, cares for them, and ensures that they're well brushed – so this is an insignificant item on his budget. Just remember, gentlemen, how long a shovel-hat used to last us in those ominous times when the government refused to pay us.[2] And what can they spend on other things? Doña Paula, with her black habit of St Rita[3] – no more than a piece of serge – her shawl pulled tight about her shoulders, and her silk scarf drawn over her temples, has clothes to last her a whole year. Their food? I have not seen them eating, but there's a way to find out about everything. The Professor of Psychology, Logic and Ethics, a good friend of mine as you know – even though he is a follower of some devilish Scottish school[4] – spends his life in the covered market, as if it were the Stoa or the Academy,[5] and he says that he has never seen the vicar-general's servant girl buying salmon, and that she only buys sea-bream when it is very cheap indeed. And what about his house? You all know that his house is but a cottage kept spotlessly clean – the house of a true Christian priest. The best part of it is the part we all know, the drawing-room, and, good heavens, what a drawing-room it is! The style is perfectly prehistoric: sober and tidy, to be sure, but how many ruses that darkness conceals! Who is to say that the insides are not hanging out of the green damask chairs? Have you ever seen them without their covers? And what of that ancient, bulging console table, which was once gilt; and what of that musical-box on top of it, with neither music nor spring? Gentlemen, I'll brook no contradiction: the canon theologian is a poor man, and all the gossip about subornation and simony is infamous slander.'

'That's all true enough,' retorted Foja, the money-lender and ex-mayor, and an assiduous participator in all conversations of this kind. He seemed to have been born to gossip. 'It can't be denied that they live like paupers, but so does Señor Carraspique, and he's a millionaire. All misers are rich. A penny saved is a penny gained. Doña Paula keeps her pile well hidden – and what a pile it is! And what about all the houses the canon theologian buys in the villages? And what about the villas Doña Paula has bought in Matalerejo, in Toraces, in Cañedo, in Somieda? And what about her shares in the bank?'

'Calumny, pure calumny! You haven't seen the deeds, you haven't seen the papers, you haven't seen anything . . .'

'But I know who has.'

'Who?'

'Everybody!' shouted Don Santos Barinaga, who was always present to speak ill of his mortal enemy the vicar-general. 'Everybody! I – I – If I were to speak . . .! But one day I shall speak!'

'Tut, tut, Don Santos, you can't be judge or witness in this trial.'

'Why not?'

'Because you hate the canon theologian.'

'Of course I do.' He raised clenched fists. 'And I'll make him pay for it!'

'But you only hate him because two of a trade can never agree, as they say. You sell articles of worship: chalices, patens, cruets, lamps, tabernacles, chasubles, candles, and even wafers.'

'Yes, sir, and proud of it, too.'

'I know, but you sell all such things, and . . .'

'Hullo! hullo!' interrupted Foja. 'What a fine thing to confess! What a fine piece of information! Don Cayetano confesses that Don Santos and Don Fermín are enemies because they practise the same trade. So our eminent Señor Ripamilán admits the truth of what everybody is saying: that the canon theologian, breaking both divine and human law, is a tradesman – that he's the owner, the real owner, of La Cruz Roja, the bazaar for articles of worship, to which, by hook or by crook, all the priests of all the parishes in the diocese are forced to go, willy-nilly, to buy what they need and what they don't need.'

'One moment, Señor Foja, or Señor Devil . . .'

'And then, of course, people imagine the worst, and since it just so happens that La Cruz Roja is on the ground floor of the house next door to the vicar-general's, and since it also just so happens that we all know there's a door connecting the basements of the two houses . . .'

'Come, now, don't be such a trouble-maker, don't tell falsehoods.'

'Take care, Sir Canon, I am not a trouble-maker, nor do I lie, nor am I an obscurantist, nor do I take lip from anybody, especially a priest.'

'Maybe you are not an obscurantist, but your brain-box is shut tight to everything but roguery. Of what consequence is it that Señor Barinaga, our good Don Santos here, has taken it into his head that his ironmongery is on the decline because of the competition which he thinks the vicar-general wages against him? Of what consequence is this, you dunderhead, to the question whether the Cruz Roja bazaar, as you call it, has a basement and whether the canon theologian owns a shop even though this is prohibited by both canon and commercial law? Be a liberal if you like, for that is not offensive to God, but do not be a slanderer – be more careful about what you say.'

'Listen here Don Cayetano, neither being old nor being Aragonese gives you the right to be insolent.'

'Don't bellow so, Sir Fierabras,⁶ don't bellow so!' retorted the canon, gathering up the skirts of his cloak and flinging them over his shoulder.

It is to be noted that the jesting tone in which these strong words were spoken emptied them of all importance and offensiveness. In Vetusta good humour consists in exchanging banter and taunts the whole year round, as if it were always carnival-time. Anyone who takes offence not only strikes a jarring note, but is considered to be ill-mannered.

'Well,' cried the ex-mayor, 'I could kill a canon as I'd kill a mosquito.'

'I'm sure you could – with calumny. Look here, you little viper of a free-thinker, you Voltaire in a cloth-cap, you Luther with a rattling tail: according to that absurd way of thinking employed by Your Excellency, we can also accept what people say about the loans made by the canon theologian at a rate of interest of twenty per cent.'

'*Non capisco*,' replied the ex-mayor, who knew operatic Italian.

'You do understand me, but I shall speak more plainly. With your wagging tongue and busy feet – which I'd like to cut off – you're just one more of the walking calumnies who devote themselves to sacrificing the canon theologian's honour. So if Don Santos attacks the canon because he takes custom away from his ironmongery, you must hate him because of the little matter of usury: "two of a trade . . .".'

'Be careful, Señor Ripamilán, you're going to make me explode.'

'That would not be difficult – there's nothing but hot air inside you.'

'You called me a usurer!'

'Yes, exactly.'

'I employ my capital honourably, and I assist both the employer and the worker; I am one of the agents of industry and I naturally collect my earnings. That's as plain as the nose on your face. If these time-serving priests, who are the fashion nowadays, knew anything about anything they would know that political economy authorizes me to charge for the advance of money, for the risk, and, if need be, for the insurance premium.'

'You're the one who needs insuring – against loss of reason, you fiddle-faddle economist.'

'I contribute to the circulation of wealth . . .'

'As a sponge contributes to the circulation of water.'

'And priests are the drones in the social beehive.'

'Well, now, if we are to start talking about drones . . .'

'Priests are the dunces . . .'

'And if we are to start talking about dunces, I knew a certain mayor during the Glorious Revolution . . .'

'What have you got to say against the Revolution? I seem to remember that it gave you the title of Ilustrísimo.'

'The blazes it did! I acquired the title by my own merits, by my works, by my . . . Sir Simpleton!'

'Keep your insults to yourself, and explain why I should be the vicar-general's personal enemy. Do I loan villagers money at thirty per cent interest? And does the money which I lend proceed from endowments of which I am the trustee, without authorization to make a personal profit from the interest on those endowments? Does my income proceed from the poor, simple-minded Christians who get involved in the affairs of the diocesan curia? Do I go thieving in those Montes de Toledo[7] which people call the Bishop's Palace?'

'Let me tell you this: if you are going to blabber such nonsense, and to look for real trouble, I shall leave you to prattle away to yourself.'

'What I have to say isn't directed at you, Don Cayetano or Don Hothead. You may be a bit of an old rake, but you aren't a – a canon theologian – a vicar-general – the Luis Candelas[8] of the Church.'

Everyone, except Don Santos, agreed that this was going too far:

'Come now, Luis Candelas . . .!'

But Don Santos shouted:

'No, gentlemen, he isn't a Luis Candelas, because that paragon of chivalrous robbers was a very generous man, and he risked his life whenever he went stealing.' What was more, he stole from the rich and gave to the poor.

'Yes, he robbed Peter to pay Paul.'

'Well the vicar-general robs both Peter and Paul to pay himself. He's a scoundrel, you have the word of Santos Barinaga for that: a scoundrel, and I know what sort of an end he's going to come to.'

Barinaga smelt of alcohol: the smell of his spleen.

Don Cayetano shrugged his shoulders and turned on his heel. As he walked away he said:

'And these are the liberals who would make us all happy. Now they're annoyed because they aren't allowed to say these outrageous things in the press.'

Conversations of this kind were held every day in Vetusta: at the promenade, in the streets, in the Gentlemen's Club, even in the cathedral sacristy.

De Pas knew all about the gossip, for he had several spies, veritable cassocked henchmen. The most active, shrewd and secretive of them was the deputy organist in the cathedral, who had previously been an informer in the seminary: he used to go into the gallery at the theatre in order to surprise apprentice-priests who were devotees of Thalia,[9] or whoever it might be. He was a young, pug-nosed clergyman, the favourite of the vicar-general's mother, and his name was Campillo.

Whatever people might be saying about him did not worry Don Fermín very much, but he did like to know the details of the gossip, and how far the insults went.

However, the canon theologian was not thinking about such matters on that cold October morning as he blew his fingers, deep in thought.

What De Pas should have been thinking about and what, uncontrollably, he was thinking about, were two quite different things. He wanted to search within himself for religious fervour, pure faith which would provide the inspiration for a sonorous, rounded and eloquent paragraph to be written with the force of conviction. But his will refused to obey him and instead his thoughts remained with the memories which were assailing him. His delicate aristocratic hand drew short parallel lines in the margin of a sheet of paper and then other lines crossing them. It looked like a grating. Behind this grating he imagined a black cloak, and behind the cloak two sparks, two eyes gleaming in the dark. And if only the eyes had been all!

'But that voice! That voice, transformed by religious emotion, by a woman's special sense of modesty as she bares herself in all her purity, without compunction yet not without shame, before a confessional!

'What kind of woman was she? Could it be true that this treasury of spiritual graces, this prize reserved for the Church, was here, in Vetusta – and that he, the spiritual master of the entire province, had not known anything about it?'

Poor Don Cayetano was a man of some talent for certain things – for matters of mere form, for the superficialities of the life of the world – but what did he know about being the director of such a soul as this?

Don Fermín could not forgive Ripamilán for having taken so long to pass on to him such a precious jewel, whose true value the archpriest was incapable of appreciating. And it was only through laziness that the old man had finally decided to leave him that treasure.

Don Cayetano had spoken about the judge's wife in a tone of great gravity.

'Don Fermín,' he had said, 'you are the only man capable of coming to an understanding with this beloved child of mine, who would have sent me out of my mind had she gone on telling me about her moral scruples much longer. I am too old for that kind of to-do. I do not even understand her. I ask her if she accuses herself of any sins and she says it isn't that. Why worry, then? And, none the less, on and on she goes. Well, I am no good at that sort of thing. So I am handing her over to you. As soon as I indicated that it would be advisable for her to confess with you she accepted my suggestion, realizing that I cannot cope any longer. It's true, I cannot cope. I understand religion and morality after my own fashion – a very straightforward fashion indeed. I don't regard piety as some kind of Chinese puzzle. In short, Anita is something of a romantic – you know that she used to write poetry. That does not prevent her from being a saint, but she wants to bring romanticism into religion, and at this point I think it's best for me to leave well alone – I haven't the strength to free her from that danger. It will be easy for you.'

The archpriest had come up closer to the vicar-general and, on tiptoe and stretching his neck as if trying, in vain, to speak into his ear, he had added:

'She saw visions, pseudo-mystical visions, in Loreto – at that critical age – something to do with the blood – when she was turning into a woman and suffered that fever, and her aunt Doña Anuncia and I went to fetch her. Then she recovered from all that, and became a bluestocking. You'll soon see what she's like. She isn't just another fine Vetustan lady. She is a tenacious woman. She may seem as meek as a lamb, but under all that she's a different person altogether. What I mean to say is that she consents to everything, but in her heart of hearts she is always objecting. In confession she has spoken of this, saying she realizes that it is all pride. Empty fears. It is not pride, but the outcome of it all is that she is feeling wretched, although nobody suspects it. You'll soon see what she's like. Don Víctor is as God made him. He has no insight into these complicated matters, and nor have I. And since we had better not go in search of a lover for her, so that she can let off steam with him' – at this point Don Cayetano laughed again – 'the best course will be for you two to come to some kind of understanding.'

As the canon recalled these words, he also remembered that he had turned the colour of a poppy.

'The best course will be for you two to come to some kind of understanding!' In this sentence, uttered by Don Cayetano in all innocence, Don Fermín found cause to meditate for hours on end.

He had spent the whole night thinking about it. Would they reach an understanding one day? Would Doña Ana be willing to open her heart to him?

The canon theologian knew a kind of underground Vetusta: the hidden city of consciences. He knew the inside of every important house and of every soul that could be useful to him. Shrewder than any other Vetustan, priest or layman, he had found a way to draw to his confessional all the most important believers of this pious city. Ladies with certain pretensions had come to regard him as the only confessor *comme il faut*. But he chose his spiritual sons and daughters with care, and possessed a singular talent for turning tiresome people away without offending them; he confessed whom he wished, when he wished.

He had a prodigious memory for the sins of others. He could remember the lives and weaknesses of even those dilatory people who took six months or a year to come to the tribunal of penance. He related one confession to another, and by degrees he had drawn up a spiritual map of Vetusta – of Vetusta the noble, for he scorned plebeians unless they were rich and powerful, in other words noble in their own way. La Encimada was all his, and La Colonia he was conquering little by little. Just as meteorologists forecast cyclones the canon theologian could have forecast many storms in Vetusta – family dramas, scandals and adventures of every kind. He knew that the devout woman, unless she is very discreet, reveals the weaknesses of all those close to her when she confesses.

And so the canon knew all about the lapses, the manias, the vices and even, occasionally, the crimes of many Vetustan gentlemen who did not confess with him – who maybe did not confess with anybody.

There was more than one liberal denouncer of auricular confession whom De Pas could have told how many times he had been drunk, the amounts of money he had lost at the gambling-table, whether he had soiled his hands in some shady affair, and whether he ill-treated his wife, together with other, more intimate secrets. Often, in houses where he was received as a close friend, he would listen to family quarrels in silence, his gaze set discreetly on the floor; and while his expression suggested that none of all this concerned him or indeed was understood by him, in fact he was perhaps the only person present who was in the secret, the only one who could unravel this tangled skein of discord. Deep in his heart he despised the Vetustans. 'They were nothing but a muck-heap.' In consequence, however, excellent fertilizer. He used it on his farm; and all that manure which he was stirring brought him a splendid, plentiful harvest.

And now he saw the judge's wife as a treasure discovered in one of his own fields.¹⁰ This treasure was his, rightly his. Who would dare dispute his claim to it?

Minute by minute he relived that hour – and somewhat more – of confession with the judge's wife.

'An hour and more!' The cathedral chapter would talk of nothing else that morning when, after the divine office, the canons belonging to the sacristy coterie assembled.

Don Custodio, the beneficiary, had been on tenterhooks all the previous afternoon, at first because of his concern to witness the arrival at the cathedral of the judge's wife and, after that, with his efforts to spy on the confession, which went on, and on, 'scandalously'. Pretending to have various jobs to do, he scuttled to and fro along the north aisle, passing the canon theologian's chapel, sometimes close by it and sometimes at a distance. First he had seen other women at the grating, and Doña Ana praying by the altar. On going past again he had seen that it was now the judge's wife whose head, covered by her mantilla, was resting against the confessional. Past the chapel again, and she had not budged; and again – and always she was there, the same scene always.

'Don Custodio,' said Gloucester, the illustrious archdeacon, who had been observing his comings and goings, 'what is new? Has the lady arrived?'

'An hour! An hour!'

'A general confession, as you can see.'

A little later:

'What is new?'

'An hour and a half!'

'She must be telling him about the sins of all her ancestors, starting with Adam.'

Gloucester stayed in the sacristy, awaiting 'the conclusion of that scandal'.

The archdeacon and the beneficiary saw the judge's wife leaving the cathedral and went off together, talking about the event, to spread such an extraordinary piece of news throughout the city.

'They were not going to add any comments. The facts, the simple facts. Two hours!'

Indeed, it had been a long confession. The canon theologian had not noticed the minutes passing, and nor had Ana. Her story had taken some time to relate. Furthermore, they had talked about so many things! Don Fermín felt pleased with his eloquence, certain that it had produced an effect upon her. Doña Ana had never heard anyone speak like that.

'The longing he had felt, before his secret conversation with Ana, had been an intimation of what really was going to happen. Yes, yes, this was something new, something new for his spirit, a spirit weary of living only for its own ambition and for another's cupidity, that of his mother. His soul needed tenderness, gentleness of heart, to compensate for so much asperity. Was everything in life to be pretence, hatred, domination, conquest, deceit?'

He remembered his years as a theological student at San Marcos College in León when, full of pure faith, he had been preparing himself to join the Company of Jesus. 'There, for a time, he had felt the beating of a gentle heart in his breast, he had prayed with fervour, he had meditated with loving enthusiasm, ready to sacrifice himself *in Jesus*. All that was so far distant! He did not seem to be the same man. Might not all those sensations which he thought he had experienced since the previous afternoon be something of the same sort? Might not the fibres which had throbbed within him in the past, on the banks of the Bernesga,[11] be the same ones which were throbbing now, like placid music for his soul? A bitter smile spread over the canon's lips. 'Even if it should all be an illusion, a dream, why not dream a little? And who can tell whether this ambition which is devouring me is not a perverted form of another nobler passion? Could this fire not burn for a higher kind of affection, one worthier of my soul? Could I not be consumed in a purer flame than the flame of my ambition? My ambition! How base it is, how wretched! Would the conquest of this lady's soul not be of more value than the battle for a bishop's mitre, a cardinal's hat, even the tiara itself?'

The canon theologian found that he was drawing a tiara in the margin of the paper.

He sighed, throwing the pen aside as if it were to blame for his thoughts – which he was already beginning to regard as vain ones – and with a shake of his head he took up another pen.

The previous paragraph read:

'The event so long awaited by the Catholic world, the definition of the dogma of papal infallibility, had finally arrived on the glorious day of eternal memory, the 18th of July 1870: *haec dies quam fecit Dominus.*'

The canon theologian continued:

'Thus, at long last, was solemnly confirmed the doctrine of the Fourth Council of Constantinople, which said: *Primum salus est rectae fidei regulam custodire*; thus was confirmed the doctrine professed by the Greeks with the approval of the Second Council of Lyons; and thus, likewise, was it declared and defined, *sacro approbante Concilio*, that the Roman Pontiff, *quum ex cathedra loquitur*, is in full possession, *per assistentiam divinam*, of the infallibility which the Divine Redeemer has bestowed upon His Church.'

Don Fermín put his pen down and leaned his chin upon his hands.

'He did not know what was wrong with him, but he could not write. Was it the subject? Perhaps he was not in the right frame of mind that morning to deal with such a sublime matter. Infallibility!

A terrible yet most courageous dogma, a formidable act of defiance by a Faith beset by the incredulity of a jeering world. It was like being in the Roman circus amid wild beasts, and calling them forward, urging them on, goading them. So much the better! That was the right attitude!' Ever since the beginning of the battle, the canon theologian had been an enthusiastic supporter of the declaration. 'It represented courage, energetic will-power, an affirmation of authority, a theological adventure, like the adventures of Alexander the Great in war and of Columbus on the ocean.'

He had defended this heroic dogma from the pulpit in Rome with an eloquence which at that time had been spontaneous – with warmth, as if he himself were the infallible one. He had called Dupanloup[12] a coward. In Madrid he had attracted a great deal of attention preaching in Las Calatravas church on his return from Rome with the worthy Bishop of Vetusta. His theme then had been infallibility, too. The newspapers had compared him with the best contemporary Catholic orators: with Monescillo and Manterola, both ecclesiastics like himself, and with the laymen Nocedal, Vinader and Estrada.

And it had all come to naught; he was a nobody. 'That is the way of the Church,' thought De Pas, with his chin in his hands and his elbows on the table, forgetting all about the infallible Pope. 'The Church proclaims humility, and indeed it is humble as an abstract, collective entity, as a hierarchy; in order to contain the impatience of the ambition waiting below. I cut a figure in Rome, I filled the faithful with admiration in Madrid, I dazzle the Vetustans – and I shall be made a bishop when I am sixty. And then it will be my turn to act humble and refuse such alms. Intriguers prosper; cronies, sycophants, hangers-on, all thrive with no need of sermons; but those of us whose chances of promotion depend on our own apostolic merit are not allowed to be impatient and must wait in an appropriate attitude of submission and respect. It's a farce, one great farce. Oh, if I were just to spread my money about . . .! But my money belongs to my mother and, anyway, I will not buy something which is my due, something I deserve because of my brains, not because of my money-bags. Hadn't we decided that I was a luminary? Wasn't it said that I was a firm pillar of the Christian Church? Well if I am a pillar why don't you give me my proper share of weight? Am I a pillar or a toothpick, Sir Cardinal, what *have* we decided?'

The canon theologian, who was alone, and sure of it, banged the table with his fist.

'Coming, master,' called a sweet fresh voice from an adjacent room.

The canon did not hear it. A twenty-year-old girl came in. She was pale, tall and slim, but full enough for her figure to be shaped as womanly beauty requires. Her skin was soft and delicate in tone, making a fine contrast with her sloe-black eyes, large, dreamy, yet restless; eyes which seemed to be doing gymnastics, committed day and night to the mystical contortions of a mechanical piety which was in large part artificial and counterfeit. Her features came close to the Greek model, and the gentle severity of her look matched them well. The girl was tall but not graceless, spiritual but not thin, solemn and hieratic. Everything about her was expressionless except her eyes and that gentleness which was like an eloquent perfume emanating from her entire body.

She was Doña Paula's servant, Teresina, but her bedroom was near the master's bedroom and study. This proximity was something upon which Doña Paula had always insisted. She lived at her ease on the second floor, for she did not want to be bothered with the sound of priests and monks coming and going, but she was not prepared to allow her son, her poor Fermín – for her, now and always, a child who needed to be looked after with great care – to sleep far from all Christian creatures. The servant girl's bed must be near the master in case he called, so that she could tell his mother, who would then come down immediately.

At home the canon theologian was the *master*. The mistress of the house referred to him thus when talking to the servants, and thus they addressed him – and were obliged to address him. Doña Paula had not always been a *mistress* and she liked the sound of *master* even better than 'reverend sir'.

All Doña Paula's servant girls came from her own home village. She picked them herself on her summer trips to the country and kept them for a long time. The condition that they must sleep near the master, in case he called, was imposed on them as something perfectly natural, indeed Edenic, and neither the girls nor the canon had ever taken the slightest objection to the arrangement. Doña Paula's light blue, expressionless, wide-open eyes removed every possibility of suspicion, making it clear that she would not tolerate any doubts about the purity of her son's habits and the innocence of his bed. Indeed, she would not have allowed even her son himself a single word of protest or the slightest objection on the grounds of what people might say. What could they say? In that house the chastity of Doña Paula, the widow, and that of her son, the priest, were indisputable, absolutely obvious facts, above discussion. 'Don Fermín was still a boy who would never grow up to a knowledge of certain matters.' It was a dogma in that house. Doña Paula demanded that everyone should believe that she believed in her son's perfect purity. But always in silence.

Teresina walked into the room, doing up the topmost fasteners on the bodice of her black Servite habit and then tying a black silk scarf, which crossed her chest, behind her back.

'What did you want, master? Are you feeling ill? Shall I bring your coffee?'

'Me? No, my child – I did not call.'

Teresina smiled. She passed a slender, delicate hand across her eyes, half-suppressed a yawn, and added:

'I could have sworn that I heard . . .'

'No, not me. What is the time?'

Teresina glanced at the clock above the canon theologian's head. She told him the time and again offered him coffee, smiling in a somewhat coquettish manner checked by the expression of piety which was the livery of that household.

'My mother . . . ?'

'She is asleep. She went to bed very late last night. Now that they are busy with the quarterly accounts . . .'

'Very well, bring me some coffee, my child.'

Before leaving the room Teresina put the furniture in order, even though it could hardly have been accused of insurrection for it remained as she had left it the previous day. She ran her hands over the books on the writing-table but she did not dare touch the books lying on the chairs and the floor. They were not to be interfered with. While Teresina was in the canon's study he followed her with impatient eyes, frowning, as if waiting for her to go away so that he could continue to work and meditate.

It was not until the coffee was before him that he remembered that it was part of his job to say mass; that he was a priest. Was there a mass to be said today? Had he promised to say one? He could not resolve his doubts. But the certainty with which Teresina went about her chores put his mind at ease.

Neither Doña Paula nor Teresina ever forgot about such details. It was their responsibility to hear the hour-bell, to make a note of all the masses to be said, and to concern themselves with everything connected with church ritual. De Pas fulfilled these routine duties, but he had to be reminded about them. He had so many other things on his mind! He was forgetful only at home; away from it he prided himself on being the most faithful observer of all the synod's decisions, and his diligence was a frequent lesson to the master of the ceremonies himself.

He drank the coffee and stood up to pace his study, trying to turn his mind in another direction, to free it from the irksome thoughts which prevented him from making any progress with his work.

Teresina was entering and leaving the study without a 'by your leave', but she made not the slightest sound. She was silence incarnate. She took the coffee-service away and came back for the pewter pot and the bucket from the wash-stand, which she returned together with a clean towel. She went into the bedroom, leaving the glazed doors open, and set about *making up* the bed, an operation which consisted in shaking the pillows and the two mattresses, folding the sheets and the counterpane and putting them away between the mattresses, spreading a blanket over the bed and putting the pillows back in their place, one on top of the other, without their pillow-slips. The canon sometimes took a siesta, and Doña Paula had his bed made ready for him in this manner, for the sake of economy. To make it properly would have meant an extravagant amount of laundering and ironing.

Don Fermín returned to his armchair. The rapid movements of Teresina's black skirt caught his glance as she pressed her thighs against the bed, gaining leverage to lift the heavy mattresses. As she pounded their woollen surface, each blow made her skirt jump, revealing the hems of her immaculate embroidered petticoats, and a little of her legs. The canon's thoughts were far away as he followed the details of the domestic chore. In one of her movements, lying almost flat with arms outspread, Teresina exposed most of her calves and a great deal of white cloth. De Pas felt that expanse of whiteness on his retina as if he had looked at a lightning-flash. Discreetly he rose and recommenced pacing his study. The servant girl, panting, with one arm hidden inside a folded mattress, suddenly turned over, almost lying back on the bed. She was smiling and there was a rosy tinge in her cheeks.

'Is the noise bothering you, master?'

The canon looked down at his servant, the beautiful devotee, on whose face there was at that moment no trace of hypocrisy. Resting one hand on the lintel of the bedroom door and smiling back at his maid the master said:

'To tell you the truth, Teresina – my work today is very important. If it's all the same to you, come back later and finish tidying up when I have gone.'

'Very well, master, very well,' replied the servant girl in a grave nasal voice and a plainsong tone.

And sending the bedclothes flying almost up to the ceiling she hastily finished making up the bed and left her master's rooms.

He paced up and down for three or four minutes between the books lying on the floor, along the paths left by these flower-beds of theology and canon law. After smoking three cigarettes he sat down again, and wrote without stopping until ten o'clock. When the sun's rays reached the nib of his pen he lifted his head, satisfied with his work.

He looked out of the window, and saw a cheering, cloudless sky. In Vetusta good weather is valued all the more because of its rarity. The canon caressed one hand with the other, well pleased. While he had been writing, in an almost mechanical way, an improvised defence of infallibility for a certain Catholic journal read only by convinced Catholics, he had been maturing his plan of attack.

His thoughts were similar to those of the judge's wife: he believed that he had made a great discovery, that he was going to have a soul sister.

The canon, who read enemy authors as well as those on his own side, recalled a poetic narration by the impious Renan[13] whose protagonists were a monk from Sweden, or Norway, or thereabouts and a devout young woman who was German, if his memory did not deceive him. At all events, they were two Christian souls who loved each other in Jesus, in spite of the great distance between them. There was no false, pseudo-religious sentimentalism in the relationship, it was pure affection, nothing like the love of a Luther or even an Abelard,[14] but the severe, noble, immaculate truth of mystical, sexless love, of which it was unthinkable that it could ever have been defiled by corrupt flesh. 'Why should he be remembering this pious novelesque legend? What had he to do with that monk, romantic and fanatical, mystical and passionate, medieval – and Swedish? He was the canon theologian of Vetusta, a priest of the nineteenth century, an ultra, an obscurantist, a drone in the social beehive, as Foja the money-lender said.'

When these thoughts came into De Pas's mind as he washed himself and combed his hair in front of the mirror, he smiled a bitter smile, mitigated by the traces of optimism left by his earlier thoughts.

He was naked from the waist up. His powerful neck seemed even more powerful now, because of the strain put upon it by his tensed position as he leaned over the white marble wash-basin. His arms, like his broad, powerful chest, were covered with fine black curly hair; they were the arms of an athlete. The canon looked sadly at his muscles of steel, charged with useless power. His complexion was pale and delicate, the slightest emotion tinging it rose-colour. On the advice of Don Robustiano, the doctor, De Pas exercised with heavy weights; he was a Hercules. One evening during the Revolution a patriot had challenged him on the outskirts of the city, and had then tried to run him through with his bayonet for refusing to surrender unconditionally. De Pas had smashed the war-hardened sentry's musket over his shoulders. Nobody knew about this feat, not even Don Santos Barinaga, who was always in search of anything, whether slanderous or true, being said at the expense of La Cruz Roja, Don Santos's collective nickname for the vicar-general and his mother. The militiaman, for his part, had kept quiet about the incident, swearing eternal hatred of the clergy and of flintlock muskets. He was one of those men who, when gossiping about the canon theologian, would add: 'If I were to talk . . .'

As Don Fermín washed, he recalled his prowess at skittles, back in his home village, where he had always made the most of the opportunities offered by holidays from the seminary to go half savage, running through rocky scrub in the high hills. The brawny, hairy young fellow before him in the mirror somehow seemed like a lost *alter ego* which had stayed behind in those hills – naked, as hairy as the King of Babylon,[15] yet free, happy. He was alarmed by this sight, which carried his thoughts far away, and he dressed hurriedly. As soon as the canon had buttoned up his collar he was once again the image of Christian meekness, strong yet spiritual and humble, still well-built, of course, but no longer formidable. He was a little like his beloved cathedral tower, also powerful, well-proportioned, well-built and elegant and mystical; but made of stone.

It was good to know that there was a strong body hidden beneath his epicene cloak and his flowing, sculptural cassock.

As he was leaving, Teresina appeared in the doorway, gravely gazing at the floor with the expression of a saint on a picture postcard.

'What is it?'

'A young woman is asking if she can see you, master.'

'See me?' Don Fermín shrugged. 'Who is she?'

'Petra, the judge's wife's housemaid.'

As Teresina said this she fearlessly looked her master in the eyes.

'Doesn't she say why she has come?'

'She didn't say anything about that.'

'Let her in.'

Petra came into the study alone. She wore black, her straight saffron-coloured hair was drawn across her forehead, her eyes were lowered and a sweet innocent smile played on her lips.

The canon recognized her. She was a young woman who had made up her mind to confess with him and who, by dint of patience and tenacity, had achieved what she wanted; but later he had been obliged to rebuff her several times to stop her pestering him. She was one of those unhappy women who believe the absurdities spread by scandalmongers to discredit priests. She confessed sins of her bedroom and bared herself before the grating amid tears of false repentance. She was beautiful and provocative, but the canon had sent her packing, just as he would send Obdulia packing if social requirements did not prevent it.

Petra entered as if she were a stranger, as if such an insignificant creature must have been obliterated from the memory of such a lofty personage. In other circumstances, perhaps, she would not have been well received, but on being told that she had come on behalf of Doña Ana, the priest was filled with gentle pity, and suddenly forgave the wayward creature all the vain and perverse insinuations she had once made. He pretended not to recognize her.

Teresina was spying on them from the shadows in the passage. The canon assumed she was and spoke as he would have spoken before witnesses.

'Are you Señora de Quintanar's servant?'

'Yes, Father, her housemaid.'

'Have you come on her behalf?'

'Yes, Reverend Sir, I have brought a letter for you.'

The 'Reverend Sir' brought a smile to De Pas's face. He considered the expression to be most opportune.

'And is that all?'

'Yes, Father.'

'In that case . . .'

'Madam told me to hand this letter to you personally, Reverend Sir. She said that it was urgent and that your servants might lose it – or take a long time to give it to you.'

There was a rustling in the passage. De Pas heard it and said:

'In my house letters are not mislaid. If you come again with a written message you can hand it in at the front door with complete confidence.'

Petra smiled what she thought was a discreet smile and wrung a corner of her apron.

'Please forgive me, Reverend Sir,' she said in a tremulous voice, blushing.

'Do not mention it, my child. I thank you for your concern.'

Don Fermín was thinking that this woman might prove useful to him, he did not know when, or how, or to what end. He felt an urge to win her over to his side, without knowing why this should be of any interest to him. He also thought that he should tell the judge's wife that the girl's conduct was unedifying. But all this was premature. For the time being he did no more than bid her a gentlemanly and courteous, but cold, goodbye. As Petra was about to go through the doorway it was filled by a woman who was almost as tall as the canon and who seemed even broader-shouldered. She was a rough-hewn figure, and her clothes hung on her as on a clothes-horse. This was Doña Paula, the canon's mother. She was sixty years of age but she looked little older than fifty. A black silk scarf, tied under her chin, covered her head, and beneath it thick plaits of a dirty, lustrous light grey were visible. Her forehead was narrow and bony, and pale, like the rest of her face; and her eyes, of the lightest blue, were expressionless – the only sensation they communicated was that of a chilling touch. Nobody would discover anything about that woman from her eyes. Her nose, mouth and chin were identical to those of her son. A black merino shawl, gathered tight around her angular shoulders, hung in graceless creases over her habit of black serge with white edges. Doña Paula, with such clothes and such a face, looked like a shrouded corpse.

Petra greeted her, a little flustered. Doña Paula openly surveyed the servant girl from top to toe.

'What do you want?' she asked. So stony was her voice that the question might have come from one of the walls.

Petra composed herself and replied in an almost haughty manner:

'I brought a message for the canon.'

And she left the study.

At the door at the top of the stairs, Teresina received her with an affable smile and they took their leave of each other, exchanging kisses on the cheek in the manner of the young ladies of Vetusta. They were friends, both being aristocrats among servants, and they respected each other without prejudice to their mutual envy. Petra envied Teresina her height, her eyes and her job in the canon theologian's house. Teresina envied Petra her nerve, her comeliness and her knowledge of fine manners and of city life.

'What does that woman want with you?' asked Doña Paula, as soon as she found herself alone with her son.

'I don't know, I haven't opened her letter yet.'

'Her letter?'

'Yes, there it is.'

Don Fermín wished his mother a hundred leagues away. He could not hide his impatience, in spite of the self-control which was one of his greatest strengths, for he longed to read the letter but was afraid he might blush in front of his mother. 'Blush?' yes, without reason, without knowing why; but he was certain that if he opened the letter in Doña Paula's presence his face would turn the colour of a cherry. It was just nerves. But his mother was his mother.

Doña Paula sat down on the edge of a chair, leaned her elbows on the writing-table – an imposing secretaire – and began the difficult task of rolling a cigarette as thick as a finger. For Doña Paula smoked, but 'now they'd got the cathedral job' she only smoked in secret, in front of the family and close friends.

The canon theologian strolled twice around the study, slipping the letter into an inside pocket, under his soutane.

'Goodbye, Mother. I must go and congratulate Señor Carraspique. It's his name-day.'

'So early?'

'Yes. Later the place will be full of people visiting him, and I have to speak to him alone.'

'Aren't you going to read it?'

'Read what?'

'That letter.'

'Later, outside, it can't be urgent.'

'Read it here, just in case. You may have to reply directly or leave a message, don't you think?'

De Pas made a gesture of indifference and read the letter.

He read it aloud. To do otherwise would arouse suspicion. His mother was not used to being kept in the dark about anything. In any case, what could the judge's wife have written? Nothing of importance.

My dear friend, I could not receive the communion today; I need to see you first; I need to confess again. Do not think that it is a question of scruples, of the kind against which you warned me. I believe it to be a serious matter. If you were so kind as to consent to see me for a moment this afternoon, this, your obedient child and affectionate friend, would be most grateful,

ANA OZORES DE QUINTANAR

'Good God, what a letter!' exclaimed Doña Paula, her eyes riveted on her son.

'What's wrong with it?' asked the canon, turning his back.

'Do you think that's a proper way to write to your confessor? It's the sort of thing you'd expect from Doña Obdulita. Didn't you say the judge's wife is so discreet? The woman who wrote that letter is either stupid or mad.'

'She is neither stupid nor mad, Mother. It's just that she doesn't know about such matters yet. She writes to me as she would write to any other friend.'

'In short she's a pagan who wants to be converted.'

The canon theologian fell silent. He never argued with his mother.

'Yesterday afternoon you didn't go and see Señor Ronzal.'

'I forgot all about our appointment.'

'Yes, I know. You spent two and a half hours in the confessional and Señor Ronzal got tired of waiting and couldn't give Señor Pablo a reply, and *he* went back to his village thinking that you and Ronzal and I are a bunch of humbugs and jackanapes – that when we need him we know all about how to use him yet when *he* needs *us* we leave him in the lurch.'

'But there's time enough, Mother. The lad is still in the barracks here, the recruits haven't been moved away yet; they don't leave for Valladolid until Saturday. There's still time.'

'Yes, time for him to rot in gaol. And what can Ronzal be saying? If you, the one with most interest in the matter, forget all about it, what do you expect him to do?'

'But duty comes first.'

'Duty is keeping faith with people, Fermo. And why has that old pest Don Cayetano taken it into his head to foist such an inheritance off on to you?'

'What inheritance?'

De Pas was showing his anxiousness to leave as, leaning against the door-frame, he turned his open-brimmed shovel hat round and round in his hands.

'What inheritance?' he repeated.

'That woman. The woman who wrote that letter, the woman who seems to think my son's got nothing better to do than be with her.'

'Mother, you're being unfair.'

'Fermo, I know very well what I'm saying. You're too good-natured. You go all lordly, and that stops you from seeing or understanding anything.'

Doña Paula thought that 'lordly' meant 'with one's thoughts elevated to things divine'.

'Thanks to the archdeacon and Don Custodio,' she went on, 'your little session was the talk of that hussy Doña Visitación's coterie last night. Yes sir, your little session with that woman – whether it had or had not gone on for two hours ...'

The canon crossed himself and said:

'Are they gossiping already? The wretches!'

'Yes, they are! And that's why I'm speaking up. Things like this must be nipped in the bud. Do you remember the brigadier's wife? Do you remember the trouble that miserable calumny gave me, all because you're so noble and trusting? Fermo, I've told you this a thousand times, being virtuous isn't enough, you've got to know how to look virtuous, too.'

'I feel only scorn for calumny, Mother.'

'I don't, son.'

'Don't you see how I trample over the lot of them, in spite of all their filthy prating?'

'Yes, so far, but who can be sure it's going to last? The pitcher goes so often to the well. Don Fortunato is a babe in arms, true enough, he isn't a bishop, he's just a puny little lamb, but . . .'

'I've got him eating out of my hand!'

'Yes, I know, and I've got him eating out of mine, too, but you know well enough that once he gets something into his head he's blind to all reason. If His Lordship Punchinello ever again gets obsessed by the notion that your slanderers might be telling the truth, you're dished.'

'Don Fortunato does nothing without an order from me.'

'Don't you be so sure. It's only because he thinks you're infallible, but the day they make him see all your scandals . . .'

'How could he ever *see* such a thing, Mother?'

'You know what I mean: if he believes what he's told about them – for him that's the same as seeing them. On that day we're dished. The babe, the lamb, the Punchinello will turn into a tiger and he'll fling you out of the vicar-generalship and into priests' prison.'

'Mother, you're upset – you're imagining things.'

'All right, all right, I know what I mean.'

Doña Paula stood up and tossed the stained cigarette-end, which could not have been shorter, to the floor.

She continued:

'I want no more of these sweet letters, I want no more conferences in the cathedral. If Madam Judge's Wife wants good advice let her go to your sermons, that's when you speak to all Christians – let her go and listen to your sermons and leave me in peace.'

'So Gloucester . . . ?'

'Yes, and Don Custodio.'

'Who told you?'

'The Pug.'

'Campillo?'

'The same.'

'But what can they have seen? What can those wretches be saying? How can such matters be discussed at a ladies' coterie? What understanding do those people have of the respect due to things sacred?'

'Pooh, pooh! Envy, just envy. Respect? God grant it to them. The archdeacon wanted to be her confessor, and that's natural enough – he's very fond of putting on airs, and of having people say . . . God forgive me! but I do believe he enjoys being gossiped about, and having people wonder whether or not he makes passes at devout ladies. He's a peacock – and a villain!'

'Mother, you're exaggerating, how could a priest . . .?'

'You're so easily taken in, Fermo. The world is in a mess, that's why everyone always imagines the worst and why you've got to keep your wits about you. You've got to pretend to be more virtuous than you really are – even if you're an angel. Didn't you know that people are saying thousands of spiteful things about us? Gloucester, Don Custodio, Foja, Don Santos and even Don Alvaro Mesía himself, with all his diplomacy – they all devote their lives to discrediting you. We're coining money here in the palace, so they say.' Doña Paula began to check off the points on her fingers. 'We're bleeding the diocese; we were penniless when we took the vicar-generalship over and now we're the bank's biggest shareholders; you make money out of this, that, and the other; our henchmen go around like sponges sucking up a sea of wealth, and then they come and pour it all into our water-tanks; the bishop is a puppet in our hands; we sell candles, we sell altar-slabs; you ordered the altar-slabs in all the parishes in the bishopric to be changed, because the new ones would have to be bought from you; Don Santos is going to the dogs not because of drink but because of us; you rob the people who go to you for dispensations; you swallow up endowments; I collect tithes and first-fruits[16] all over the diocese; we . . .'

'Enough, Mother, enough for God's sake!'

'And, to cap it all, your love-affairs, the way you take advantage of being a spiritual counsellor. You,' checking off on her fingers again, but now tapping the floor with her foot as well, as if beating time, 'you've made half the town into fanatics; it's your fault that the Carraspique girls are nuns, and it's your fault, too, that one of them is dying of consumption, as if you were the damp and the filth in that pigsty; it's your fault that the Páez girl, the richest millionairess in Vetusta, won't get married, because she can't find a suitor to her liking – and even that's your fault, too.'

'Mother . . .'

'And what else? They even take it amiss that you teach young girls Christian doctrine at the Holy Mission for Catechesis.'

'The wretches!'

'Yes – wretches, but there's beginning to be rather a lot of wretches, and when we least expect it they're going to sink us.'

'Oh, no they're not, Mother!' shouted the canon theologian, losing his temper, his cheeks purple and his glare as sharp as if there were steel pins in his eyes, erect to repel an attack. 'Oh, no they're not. I've got them all under my heel and I can crush them whenever I want. I'm the strongest one here. Every one of them, every one without exception, is a fool; they're good for nothing – not even for being spiteful.'

Doña Paula smiled, taking care that her son should not see her. 'That's my boy,' she thought, and continued:

'But the only weak point they'll be able to find is this one, Fermo. You know that well enough – remember what happened the last time.'

'She was a – loose woman.'

'But she tricked you, didn't she?'

'No, Mother, she did not trick me. What do you know about it?'

Doña Paula's eyes were like two inquisitors. She had never managed to sort out that business of the brigadier's wife. All she knew – to her cost – was that it had been a scandal which she had only just managed to stifle in time. De Pas was repelled by such memories, the follies of youth. How stupid to fear that he might be careless again, at thirty-five years of age! At that time, when he had become involved with the brigadier's wife, he had been an inexperienced youngster, easily gratified by vainglory and seduced by the heady incense of flattery.

'If Mother could see into the depths of my soul, she would entertain none of these fears with which she is tormenting me.'

Doña Paula persisted in describing all the dangers of calumny; she knew that she was hurting her son's very soul but she regarded it as a necessary pain – because she feared for him a fall like the fall of Solomon.[17]

Don Fermín's mother believed in the omnipotence of woman. She herself was a good example. She was not afraid that the other canons' intriguing could do much harm to the prestige of her Fermín, who was the instrument which she used to squeeze the bishopric. Fermín was ambition, the need to dominate; his mother was cupidity, the need to possess. Doña Paula pictured the diocese as a cider-press like the ones in her village. Her son provided strength – the cross-beam and the platten which pressed the fruit, squeezing, coming lower and lower; she was the screw, tightening. The steel spindle of her will ran through her son's will, made of wax (the spindle went through the nut, as was only natural). 'It was mechanical,' as Don Fermín so often said when he talked about religion. 'But set a woman to catch a woman,' thought the screw. 'Her son was still young, he could still be seduced – they'd already tried it once, and maybe they'd succeeded.' She believed in the influence of woman but not in her virtue. 'The judge's wife, the judge's wife! She's said to be incapable of sinning, but who's to be so sure of that?' Doña Paula had heard some of the gossip. She was friendly with certain of those devout ladies who have one foot in church and the other in the world: the ladies who know everything, even when, as sometimes happens, there is nothing to know. They had told her – without Flamenco frills – more or less what Orgaz had said in the Gentlemen's Club two days before: that Don Alvaro was in love with the judge's wife, or at least wanted to make her fall in love with him, as he had done with so many other women. 'That man Don Alvaro was one of her son's enemies. She knew he was.' Don Fermín himself did not regard Mesía as his enemy, even though on occasions he had conjectured that he was a rival for the control of Vetusta. But Doña Paula had superior instincts and could see further than anybody else where her son's power was concerned. 'That man Don Alvaro was another good-looking fellow, bright, too, elegant, a man of the world. His love-affairs gave him prestige, and he'd got the wives of several Vetustan personages on his side – and sometimes the personages themselves, thanks to their wives. He was a party leader, and the Vegallanas' right hand, maybe even their head; he could challenge Fermín, perhaps from a position of equal strength, for the domination of Vetusta, that Vetusta which always needed a master and, when it had none, complained about the lack of character of its leading citizens. And why shouldn't Mesía be making his challenge already? Wasn't it within the bounds of possibility that that holy saint the judge's wife and precious Don Alvarito had come to some kind of understanding, and were trying to catch Fermo in a trap?' Doña Paula was always ready to dream up such machinations, however complicated and subtle they might be, because her own life was devoted to similar intrigues. Of all these suspicions she only passed on to her son what was necessary to warn him against the judge's wife and her two-hour-long confessions. She did not name Mesía. A question played upon her lips: 'But what the devil did you talk about, for two whole hours?'

She did not dare go that far. 'After all, her son was a priest, and she was a Christian.'

To ask that question would be irreverent, indeed it would be a sacrilege which would make Fermo furious – and there was no need for that.

'Goodbye, Mother,' said Don Fermín, when Doña Paula fell silent because she did not dare ask the sacrilegious question.

He had already reached the stairs when he heard his mother saying: 'So you aren't going to prayers today, either?'

'They must be over by now.'

'Very well, very well!' she was left muttering to herself. 'We aren't that rich we can afford to pay fines.'

At last the canon theologian found himself in the street, as happy as a boy escaping from the rod of an implacable schoolmaster.

A brilliant sun was approaching the zenith. Not a cloud was over Vetusta: an Andalusian sky.

Yes, but the canon's humour was overcast, his mother had made him nervous and angry – although he did not know with whom he was angry.

'She was his tyrant: a dear, beloved, deeply beloved tyrant, but sometimes an overpowering one. And how could he break his chains? He owed everything to her. Without her perseverance, without her iron will-power, which went straight to its goal, breaking through everything in its path, what would he be now? A cowherd in the mountains or a hewer of coal in the mines. He was abler than all the rest of them, but his mother was abler still. Doña Paula's instincts were superior to all reasoning. Without her he would have been routed more than once in the struggle of life. In particular, when his feet were enmeshed in the fine nets put in his path by his enemies, who pulled them free? His mother. She was his aegis. Yes, mother before everything else. Her despotism was his salvation; her yoke was a beneficent yoke. And, further- more, an inner voice told him that his filial affection and respect were the best part of his soul. At times when he felt only contempt for himself, he needed, in order to find something pure in his soul which would stop self-contempt from turning into despair, to remember this: he was a good son, humble, docile, a boy: a boy who would never turn into a man. He, whom the world saw as a man who often turned into a lion!

'But now there was rebellion in his soul. His mother's suspicions were unfounded. All Vetusta believed in the virtue of the judge's wife; and indeed she was an angel. He was not worthy to kiss the ground *she* trod on – not the other way about. Which of them should feel afraid of the other?'

Now he discovered the cause of his sudden ill-humour. 'His mother had spoken of the calumnies with which people were trying to ruin him – of the excesses of ambition, pride and sordid cupidity imputed to him, of the pernicious influence which he was accused of wielding over the lives of many families – but was it really all a calumny? Oh, if the judge's wife knew him she would not have confided the secrets of her heart to him. By an act of faith that lady had scorned all the abuse with which his enemies persecuted him, she had refused to believe any of it, and she had come to his confessional to beg for light in the darkness of her conscience, to beg for a saving thread in the abysses which opened before her at every step of her journey through life. If he had been an honourable man he would have said to her there and then, "Hush! be silent! I am not worthy to welcome the majesty of your secret into my wretched dwelling; I am a man who has learned to say half a dozen words of consolation to weak-willed sinners and half a dozen words of terror to the poor in spirit whom I have turned into fanatics; I am as sweet as honey with people who are taking the bait and as bitter as gall with those who have taken it; sugar is the lure I offer, aloes the food I give my prisoners. I am full of ambition and, what is worse, a thousand times worse, infinitely worse, I am avaricious; I hoard ill-gotten riches, yes, ill-gotten riches; I am a despot, not a shepherd; I sell Divine Grace, I trade like a Jew with the religion of the Saviour who cast the buyers and sellers out of the temple. I am a wretch, madam; I am not worthy to be your confidant, your spiritual director. My eloquence yesterday was false, it did not come from the soul, I am not the *vir bonus*,[18] I am what the world says I am, what my detractors say I am." '

But this was going rather too far, and the canon theologian was aware of a reaction in his conscience, in defence of his own good name.

'Let us do ourselves more justice,' he thought, unintentionally, prompted by the instinct of self-preservation with which self-love is endowed.

And then he remembered that it was his mother who pushed him into all those acts of avarice which were bringing colour to his cheeks.

'His mother was the one who hoarded. It was for her – to whom he owed everything – that he handled and even chewed the filth of their unscrupulous sordid trafficking. His own passion, the passion which spontaneously played havoc with him, was the ambition to dominate; but was this not noble at bottom, and, in reality, was it not just? Did he not deserve to be in charge of the diocese? Wasn't the bishop happy to recognize his moral superiority? Indeed it was a considerable act of resignation to content himself, for the time being, with ruling only Vetusta. Oh, he was sure that if some day his friendship with Ana Ozores reached the point where he could confess to her and tell her about his ambition, she, who had a generous soul, would absolve him of the sins which he had committed. His mother's sins, the sins into which he had been dragged by his mother's cupidity, were the sins for which there was no excuse – the ugly shameful sins which could not be confessed.'

While such thoughts in turn tormented and consoled the canon theologian, he was walking along the narrow, worn pavements flanking the streets, tortuous and almost deserted, of La Encimada, his cheeks aflame, his eyes lowered, his head a little on one side, as was his custom, his graceful body held upright, his step majestic and rhythmical, his voluminous cloak, without the suspicion of a stain, flowing behind him.

He replied to greetings as if he were putting heart and soul into his replies, bending at the waist and baring his head as to a king, yet sometimes he could not even see the person he was greeting.

Such pretence was second nature with him. He had the gift of speaking with great tact while his thoughts were far way.

Doña Paula had gone back into her son's study. She inspected the bedroom with its made-up bed, stiff and fresh – it had not one crease, nothing to tell her. She walked out of the bedroom and into the study and there examined the blue rep sofa, the easy chairs, the correct lines of books piled up on chairs and shelves on every side; she scrutinized the disposition of the table, the armchair, all the other chairs. She seemed to be smelling something out with her eyes. She called Teresina and asked her a question, excavating the girl's face with her look, like someone prospecting for a mine, and plunging into the very folds of her clothes, which were in perfect order, like the chairs, the books, everything. She made her speak so as to gauge the tone of her voice, as one gauges a coin by its ring, and then dismissed her.

'Oh,' she spoke again. 'No, nothing, you can go.'

She shrugged.

'It's impossible,' she muttered under her breath. 'There's no way to find anything out.'

As she left the study, she said:

'Men – what capricious creatures!'

And, climbing the stairs to the second floor, she added:

'He's the same as the rest of them, just the same: all day long away from home!'

XII

Don Francisco de Assisi Carraspique was one of the most influential members of the Carlist junta of Vetusta, the member who had made the largest pecuniary sacrifices at the right time. He was a politician because he had been convinced that the cause of religion would not prosper unless good Christians got into government. He was dominated by his wife, an ardent fanatic who hated liberals because during the war before last the Cristinos had hanged her father from a tree without giving him time to confess. Carraspique, who was nearly sixty years of age, was notable neither for personal courage nor for political flair. He was notable for money. He was the province's leading contributor to the surreptitious sovereignty of Don Carlos VII. His religiosity – Carraspique's – was sincere, profound and blind (obviously a virtue); but the feebleness of his character and his brain, and the malevolence of the people who surrounded him, turned his piety into a source of constant trouble for him, for his family, and for many others.

Dona Lucía, his wife, confessed with the canon theologian, who was the infallible pontiff in their honourable home. The Carraspiques had four daughters. They had all made their first confessions with Don Fermín, and they had all been educated in the convent school chosen by Don Fermín. The eldest two had taken the vows, one with the Salesian Sisters and the other with the Poor Clares.

Carraspique had bought his palace cheaply on the occasion of the bankruptcy of a liberal aristocrat who had, in consequence, died of a broken heart. It faced the mansion of the Ozores in the ancient, mouldering square called the Plaza Nueva.

The canon theologian was ushered into the drawing-room by a housemaid in her sixties who barked like a vicious dog at poor people, but would have been happy to lick the feet of priests.

'Wait a minute, sir, pray be seated, the master is in there, he will be coming out directly.' And in a mysterious, bitter voice: 'He is with the doctor – that dreadful man, madam's cousin.'

'Yes, I know – Don Robustiano. What is new, Fulgencia?'

'I believe that Sister Teresa is a little worse – but that's no reason to alarm my poor master and mistress so. The poor girl is not seriously ill, is she, sir?'

'I do not think so, Fulgencia, but what does the doctor say? Has he been to the convent today?'

'Yes sir, he has, and he has been shouting and screaming at the master. He is furious – he's a madman. I don't know why they call him in. It must be because he's a relative.'

The drawing-room was rectangular, spacious, fitted out in a severe style without any luxury, but given a certain elegance by its venerable antiquity, its exquisite cleanliness, its sobriety and its very austerity. The only new piece of furniture was an Érard grand piano.[1]

Don Robustiano came into the room and Fulgencia left, muttering under her breath.

The doctor was a tall man of powerful build with a long white beard. He dressed with the arrogant luxury of certain provincial personages who want their appearance to reveal their social standing. He was a handsome figure, still successfully resisting the ravages of time. Don Robustiano had been the doctor to the nobility for many years. Although in politics he passed for a reactionary and mocked all progressives, in religion he was regarded as a Voltairian, or what he and other Vetustans understood by that term. Don Robustiano had never read Voltaire, but his admiration for Voltaire was as intense as the abhorrence felt by Gloucester, who had never read Voltaire either. As far as his reading was concerned, including his reading in his own subject, Don Robustiano could hardly claim to be a Triton among the minnows – among the more modern Vetustan doctors, youngsters dying of hunger there. He had not studied much, but he had made a great deal of money. He was a doctor of the world, a doctor who had a way with people. Years before, flatulence had been his explanation for everything, but now it was all a question of nerves. Encouraging words were his medicine; he never told a patient that he or she was going to die. He treated friends without payment, but if the illness worsened withdrew his services and told the family that he would not feel offended if they summoned another doctor. 'He couldn't bring himself to see a dear friend dying.'

When with his patients he was always joking.

'And so, Señor, you're at death's door, are you? Well now, by God, we'll soon see about that . . .'

This was a ritual expression, and Don Robustiano had many others. They had made him rich. He did not use many technical terms because, according to him, one should not alarm laymen with Greek and Latin. Although not a pedant, whenever he found himself in difficulties or contradicted he would invoke the sacrosanct name of science, as if he were calling in the police superintendent. 'Science orders this; science orders that.'

Nobody was allowed to answer him back.

Leaving science aside, for science was not his forte, Don Robustiano was anyone's match at being genial, happy, amiable and, indeed, full of common sense and not at all lacking in perspicacity. He was, however, over-talkative.

He hated the canon theologian, but he feared his influence in aristocratic houses and treated him with feigned frankness and false amiability.

De Pas regarded Don Robustiano as a great fool, but he was always polite to him, as indeed he was to everyone, without making any distinction between fools and men of talent.

'Oh, Señor Don Fermín, how good it is to see you! You have arrived just in time, my friend. My cousin is inconsolable. What a fine name-day for him! I have told him the truth, the whole truth, and now that the case is beyond hope, he's becoming desperate, of course. That is to say, I think there still may be some hope – but these extreme ideas which . . . well, one can speak frankly to you, because you are a person of culture.'

'What is new, Don Robustiano? Have you been to the Salesian convent?'

'Yes sir, I have been in that pigsty.'

'How is Rosita?'

'Rosita? Rosita is no more! Rosita's done for. She's Sister Teresa now, without any roses in her name or her cheeks.'

Don Robustiano came close to the canon, looked around, scrutinizing all the corners and doors in the room; and, shielding his mouth with his hand, he said:

'The end isn't far away.'

The canon felt a shudder running through his body.

'Do you think so?'

'Yes, I believe a catastrophe is imminent. That is to say, I make a distinction, a distinction in the name of science. As Robustiano Somoza I cannot hope for any improvement. As a man of science I have to declare, first, that if the girl remains in that environment, she is beyond saving, but if she is taken away, perhaps there is some hope for her; secondly, that it is a crime, a crime against humanity, not to make use of the means recommended by science. Do you, sir, a person of culture, believe that religion consists in letting oneself die by the side of a sewer? For that convent is one big latrine, yes, indeed, an open drain.'

'You know that it is a temporary residence. The Salesian Sisters are having their new convent built, as you know, near the gunpowder factory.'

'Yes, I know. But by the time the convent is built and the women can move into it, our Rosita will be dead.'

'Doctor Somoza, your affection is perhaps making you see the danger as greater than it really is.'

'Greater you say, Señor De Pas? Would you know more than science? I have already given you the opinion of science; secondly, that it is a crime against humanity . . . Oh! If I could lay my hands on the priestling who's to blame for all this! For there's a priest mixed up in this affair, my dear canon theologian, I am sure of it. You must excuse me – but, as you know, I make a distinction between priests and priests. If they were all like you . . . I am sure our good Señor Don Fermín would not advise a father with four daughters as pretty as a picture to turn them all one by one into nuns, as if they were Panurge's sheep.'[2]

The canon could not help smiling, as the thought crossed his mind that Panurge's sheep had been neither nuns nor even monks. But Don Robustiano repeated the remark about Panurge's sheep, not knowing what animals these were, just as he did not know a great many other things. He did not read books – he did not have the time.

Don Fermín was thinking, 'Is the fool trying to insinuate something with all this nonsense?'

'I suspect,' continued the doctor, 'that poor Carraspique is subject to the will of some fanatic – for instance the Rector of the Seminary. Don't you agree that it might be Señor Escosura, that Torquemada *pour rire*, who has brought such misfortune upon this house?'

'No, sir, I do not believe that it is he, nor indeed that this house is as full of misfortune as you say.'

'Two girls have gone to their graves already.'

'What do you mean, to their graves?'

'Or to the convent – it comes to the same thing.'

'The convent is not death, and, as you know, this is a matter about which I am in no position to offer an opinion.'

'Yes, yes, I know. Pray forgive me. If there have to be convents, though, let them be hygienic ones. If I were the government I would close all those which had not been subjected to scientific inspection. Public hygiene prescribes . . .'

Doctor Somoza expounded at length various commonplace notions about the renovation of the air, heating, aero-therapeutics and other subjects taken from the pages of semi-scientific *feuilletons*. Then he returned to the misfortune of that house.

'Four daughters and two of them nuns already! This is absurd.'

'No sir, not absurd, because they themselves are the ones who freely chose . . .'

'Freely! Freely! You, my dear Canon Theologian, a person of such culture, can laugh, yes laugh at this alleged freedom. Can there be freedom where there is no choice? Can there be choice where only one of the terms of which the choice consists is known?'

Don Robustiano spoke almost like a philosopher when he became heated.

'Oh, they can't deceive me,' he continued, 'I know all about this farce. Don't you realize, my dear sir, that I saw all those girls being born, I watched them growing up, I have followed all the vicissitudes of their existence? Now I'll tell you how the system works.'

Don Robustiano sat down and continued:

'Until they are fifteen or sixteen years of age my cousin's daughters see nothing of the world. At ten or eleven they are sent to the convent school, and God only knows what happens to them there. They cannot tell anyone because their letters are dictated by the nuns and always cast in the same mould – "the school is paradise". At fifteen they come back home. By then they possess no will of their own, having left that faculty of the soul, or whatever it is, in the convent like a piece of junk. In order to satisfy the world, as a sop to public opinion, when they are between the ages of fifteen and eighteen or nineteen the farce is performed of making them see life – through a keyhole. This way of seeing the world is a most amusing one, my dear Don Fermín. Do you remember the story about the fox and the stork?[3] Well, this is just the same. The girls can see the world inside the flagon but they can't taste it. Dances? God forbid. The theatre? An abomination. Novenas, sermons! And once in a blue moon a little walk with mamma along the Mall or the Summer Promenade, eyes fixed on the ground, not a word to a soul, then straight home. And next comes the great test: the trip to Madrid. They go to see the animals in the Retiro Park, the Royal Picture Gallery, the Naval Museum and the Military Museum. No theatres or dances, for they are even more dangerous in Madrid than in Vetusta: no, for them it's tramping the streets all day long, seeing lots of strangers and getting sore feet, then back home. The girls make the return journey saying in all sincerity that they were bored in Madrid – oh for their beloved convent school, how much more they used to enjoy themselves there with the sisters and their schoolmates! Back to Vetusta. A lad falls in love with one of them. *Vade retro!*⁴ He's soon sent packing. At home all the canonical hours are recited without fail, matins, vespers . . . and then the rosary on their beads and an Our Father to every saint in the celestial court; fasts, vigils; and no walking out on to the balcony, no parties, no friends – for friends are dangerous. Oh, yes, they can play the piano if they wish, and sew away to their heart's content. As a special treat the girls are allowed to laugh as much as they like at the jokes told by the archdeacon, the diplomatic Señor Mourelo, alias Gloucester. Our handsome friend with a twisted back comes out with one of his slobbery witticisms, the girls laugh, papa drools with delight too, the wretch! – and *tutti contenti*. But no, the archdeacon isn't the priest lurking in these particular shadows, he represents the other side, the devil or the world. But, naturally enough, the attractions of the world, reduced to the witticisms of Mourelo, seem pretty paltry to the girls; while on the other hand the cloister offers pure pleasures and a certain liberty – yes sir, a certain liberty, compared to the arch-monastic life of what I call the Order of Doña Lucía, my dear cousin. Oh, what an easy victory for the Church, Señor De Pas! Seeing that life in Vetusta means plodding from church to church with lowered eyes, life in Madrid means stumbling on aching feet from museum to museum, and life in their own home means being confined to a barracks for mystics with a priest's jokes as their sole entertainment, the girls *freely* decide to become nuns, so as to enjoy a little autonomy, to use the word of those wild liberals who want to give us a liberty rather like that which is enjoyed by Señor Carraspique's daughters.'

The canon theologian listened patiently to the doctor's discourse, and then, for the sake of saying something, said:

'You cannot deny the frankness and joviality which characterize the behaviour of everyone here; these good people are very far from being sanctimonious.'

'Another farce! I don't know who the devil has taught my cousin to play that little game. Anyone who comes here dismisses as calumny all he has heard about the monastic strictness of this honourable but dull home. Appearances are deceptive. All this happiness for no apparent reason, all this holy humour (if you'll forgive me), and all this purely formal, external tolerance – it's sheer pretence, to keep outsiders' mouths closed.'

The canon theologian was looking at the doctor with great curiosity and considerable astonishment. 'How could such a dim-wit reason in this manner? Did Somoza know that it was he who was the *hidden priest,* the spiritual leader in that house? If he did know, why did he speak like that? Did fools, too, possess the art of dissimulation?'

Carraspique came into the drawing-room. His eyes were moist from recent tears. He embraced the canon and fervently begged him to go to the Salesian Convent to see how his daughter was, for he did not have the heart to go himself. Don Fermín promised to go that very day.

Somoza again described the lack of *hygienic conditions* in the convent.

'But what do you expect me to do, Cousin?'

'Nothing, my boy, I don't expect you to do anything, because I know what you people are like. But what I say is this: the girl is very sick, and it isn't her fault; there are no flaws in her constitution, and she used to be a strong girl. But now she never sees the sun, and she's being devoured by damp; she needs warmth, and has none; light, and there's no light in that place; clean air, and she breathes nothing but putrefaction; exercise, and there's no room for her to move a finger; entertainment, and such a thing doesn't exist there; nourishment, and she's given bad food and little of it – but it doesn't matter, apparently God is satisfied. What is perfection? Life between two sewers. The world has gone to the dogs? Well, then, let's go and live inside a – convenience.'

This word seemed a refined one to Somoza, but it did not express what he wanted to say, but quite the opposite, so he added:

'Inside a convenience – which is the antithesis of a convenience.'

'In short, gentlemen,' he went on, 'you are defending an absurdity, and my patience does not extend that far. To resume: science can restore Rosita's health with fresh air, in the country, by the seaside; with a happy life, good food, above all, meat and milk. If not – I cannot be held responsible for the outcome.'

He picked up his hat and his gold-knobbed walking-stick, nodded goodbye to the canon and walked way, muttering:

'St Simon Stylites himself had better living conditions, on top of a pillar, and it wasn't a pillar of that order; it wasn't a dung-heap.'

Doña Lucía appeared in the room and with a surly grimace she gave her reply to her cousin's words, which she had heard from a distance:

'He's a madman, pay no attention to him.'

'But he loves us deeply,' Carraspique pointed out.

'He's a madman – giving him the benefit of the doubt.'

The canon theologian said, in smooth words, what amounted to the same thing. 'They should not heed Somoza, he was a sectarian. True, the Salesian Sisters' provisional convent was not ideal accommodation. It was in a low district of the town, at the foot of a hill, a sunless spot, where the badly constructed sewers of a large part of La Encimada discharged their contents; and in some cells damp did indeed seep through the walls, in which there were a few cracks. It could not be denied that the smell was sometimes insufferable, and such miasmas could not be healthy. But this state of affairs would not last much longer, and Rosita was not as unwell as the doctor claimed. The nuns' doctor had affirmed as much, and had said that to take her away, separating her from her beloved fellow nuns and from her regular life, would kill her.'

Next, Don Fermín considered the question from the religious point of view. 'The body was not everything. Such purely human, worldly arguments as those with which Somoza and others like him could be countered were the least important consideration. What was vital was to decide whether hurrying into steps which would alarm opinion might not give scandal. With any such steps, any excessive affection, any inordinate solicitude, they might set malicious tongues wagging. Was this not precisely what the enemies of the Church wanted? It would be said that the Salesian Convent was a slaughterhouse; that the Christian religion led blossoming youth to that latrine and let it rot there. So much would be said! No, it was not possible to take any radical steps yet. It was necessary to wait. Morever, he would go and see Sister Teresa . . .'

'Yes, Don Fermín, for God's holy sake!' exclaimed Doña Lucía, pressing her hands together. 'I am quite sure that the dear girl will recover her health if you take the consolation of your word to her.'

Doña Lucía did not dare call the girl her daughter. She believed that the girl belonged to God, to Him alone.

They turned to another subject. There had never been any discussion of the matter, but it had been tacitly agreed that the two youngest girls would not take the veil unless they had a vocation superior to all prudent and moderate resistance. This implicit agreement had been imposed by conscience, or by a fear of public opinion. The elder of the two girls had a suitor. The canon theologian had come to ensure that he was rejected. 'He was a godless man.'

'Ronzal a godless man? Your friend?' Carraspique made bold to say.

'Yes, Don Francisco – my friend; but there are other more important considerations. I sacrifice my friend where your daughter's happiness is at stake.'

A tear – one of the few tears in her – rolled down the face of the mistress of the house. It would have been more aesthetic and symmetrical had there been two tears, yet there was but one – the other tear must have been so small that it was swallowed up in the eternal aridity of the eyelids before it could emerge.

It was a tear of gratitude. 'The canon theologian was sacrificing, for them, the name and even the interests of a friend, a great friend, his defender, his supporter – none other than Ronzal, the provincial deputy. She was wise to entrust the keys of her heart and of her conscience to such a man – to such a saint, rather.'

Ronzal, alias Blunderbuss, aspired to the hand of a Carraspique girl – either girl would do – because of increasing expenditure and decreasing income: Don Francisco de Assisi was a millionaire with very well brought-up daughters. But the canon theologian had other plans.

'Ronzal a godless man?' repeated Carraspique, aghast.

'Yes, godless – relatively speaking. It is not enough for a person to have religion on his lips, it is not enough for him to respect the Church and even protect it. In politics and social intercourse one often has to be content with this, in these sad times in which we live, but that is a different matter. Ronzal, compared with some others – Mesía, for example – is a good Christian. Even Mesía himself, who has not, after all, separated himself from the Church, is a Catholic, a religious man – compared with the atheist Don Pompeyo Guimarán. But neither Mesía nor Ronzal is a godly man, and they are both far from being sufficiently pious. Would you give a daughter to Don Alvaro Mesía?'

'I would sooner die.'

'Well, although Ronzal calls himself a conservative and is in favour of Catholic unity and other principles contained in our programme, he is not a good Christian – not to the degree necessary for the husband of a Carraspique.'

The warmth with which Don Fermín defended the family's spiritual interests deeply moved the master and mistress of the house.

Ronzal was rejected.

The canon turned to other matters. He had to call on the Carraspiques for further donations: generous alms for Rome; alms for the Little Sisters of the Poor, who intended to buy a house; alms for the Holy Mission for Catechesis; alms for the Novena of the Immaculate Conception, because it would be necessary to pay a Jesuit preacher handsomely to come from afar. He was asking for a great deal, indeed, but if those good Catholics who still had some money left did not make sacrifices, what would become of the Faith? If only others were in a position to do so!'

Doña Lucía sighed as she heard this. She understood. The canon theologian meant that if he were rich all his wealth would be for Rome and for pious institutions. 'And to think that there were people who slandered that saint, claiming that he was made of money!'

Before leaving this house, in which his dominion was limitless, Don Fermín again promised to visit the Salesian Convent.

'But there was no need to become alarmed, or to lose patience.'

'If the worst comes to the worst,' he ventured to say when he considered it at last opportune to do so, 'God's will be done. If it is necessary for the good of the Faith that we suffer a terrible trial, we shall know how to suffer it, because being a Christian requires this and much more of us.'

In this house Don Fermín never said that virtue was easy. It was little short of impossible. Salvation was achieved at the expense of much suffering, and very few people achieved it. When the canon theologian preached terror his voice was no less mellifluous than when the ideas which he was expressing were pleasant. His discourses on salvation sounded as sweetly as the strains of a pan-pipe; and when he said 'God is merciful but he is just' his tongue imitated the whispering of the breeze amidst flowers.

He never spoke to the Carraspiques about the flames of hell. Torment of the conscience was what he offered them if, as was probable, they did not achieve salvation in spite of all their tribulations.

Doña Lucía found Don Fermín to be rather out of form that morning. He was not speaking with his usual sublime unction, but seemed to be forcing his pious pessimism from his lips. The good lady noticed that her spiritual director was talking like a man with his mind on something else.

The canon departed.

Finding himself alone in the entrance hall, and unable to control himself, he struck his clenched fist on the marble banisters of the sumptuous staircase.

'It can't be helped, it can't be helped!' he muttered, 'I can't start a new life now. I'll have to go on being the same man.'

On leaving this house on other occasions he had experienced the intense, piquant pleasure given by the gratification of his pride; to dominate souls, something which he did there in an absolute manner, was sweet satisfaction for his self-love. But now there was none of this. He did not feel pleased with himself. He had contrived to shorten his visit by omitting some parts of his holy harangues.

'That idiot Don Robustiano had put him in a bad mood. It must be that.'

'He needed to throw off his mask, give rein to his bad temper, trample on something in rage.' He bent his steps towards the palace.

This was the name given, by way of ellipsis, to the Bishop's Palace. Adjoining the cathedral, and overshadowed by it, this building occupied one side of the small, damp square called La Corralada. Of the same age as the tower, it was in worse taste, having often been patched up in the course of the previous two centuries. With its whitewash sticking-plasters and its mud poultices, it was like an architectural invalid; and its renovated main façade, overladen with Churrigueresque ornamentation, especially around the door and the balcony above, gave it the grotesque look of an old man primped up to please the ladies.

The canon walked through the entrance hall, which was large, cold, bare and not very clean, crossed a square courtyard where there were a few scrawny acacias and some flower-beds containing wilted plants, climbed a staircase, the bottom flight of stone and the rest of half-rotten chestnut, and at the end of a corridor enclosed with rubble-work and narrow windows came to an ante-room in which the bishop's familiars were playing at cards. The arrival of the vicar-general interrupted their game. The familiars stood up and one of them, a handsome blond man whose movements were smooth and undulating, and whose vesture was immaculate and perfumed, opened a door covered with cherry-coloured damask. The walls of the chamber which now became visible, and through which De Pas passed without a pause, were lined with the same material.

'Where can I find him, Don Anacleto?'

'I believe he has visitors,' replied the familiar. 'Ladies.'

'What ladies?'

Don Anacleto's answer was a graceful shrug of the shoulders and a smile.

Don Fermín hesitated for a moment and took a step back, but immediately stepped forward again and opened a side-door, through which he disappeared.

After traversing various other chambers and corridors he reached the Bright Room, as the room where the bishop received personal visitors was known in the palace. It was rectangular, thirty feet by twenty, with a high ceiling heavy with plateresque coffers in dark walnut. Its walls, painted brilliant white and decorated with narrow gilt mouldings forming squares, reflected the torrents of light which streamed through the balcony windows, open wide to this joyful scene. The furniture, upholstered in yellow damask, its woodwork painted white like the walls, its luxury an old-fashioned, kindly, pleasant luxury, was laughing, laughing with a writhing of contorted wood: bulging curves, wreathed columns. The easy chairs looked as if they had their arms akimbo; the feet of the console tables made pirouettes. The floor was bare, except for one moquette carpet which paid homage to the sofa; it depicted a basket of red, green and blue roses, and was His Lordship's personal favourite. On the north wall there was a painting by Cenceño and on the south wall another, both of them touched up with glorious garish colours. The other two walls were decorated with four large English engravings in ebony frames: Judith, Esther, Delilah and Rebecca at the critical moments of their careers.[5] An ivory carving of Christ on the cross stood on a console table before a mirror which reflected the back of the crucifix; Christ gazed across the room at his Holy Mother, twice his size, carved in marble, standing on another console table. There were no other saints or indeed anything else to suggest that this was a bishop's room.

The Ilustrísimo Señor Don Fortunato Camoirán, the Bishop of Vetusta, allowed his vicar-general to govern the diocese as he pleased, but the vicar-general was not to interfere with anything in this room. And so it had been of little use for Don Fermín to admonish Fortunato not to adorn the balconies with simple but joyful birdcages in which goldfinches and canaries hopped to and fro, overwhelming everyone with their racket. In truth, they seemed quite mad.

'You ought to be thankful that I don't take my birds with me to the cathedral to sing the Gloria when I say mass in my pontificals. When I was the parish priest of Las Veguellinas, goldfinches and larks and even linnets used to sing and whistle in the chancel, and it was lovely to hear them.'

Fortunato was a joyful saint who could not see any irreverence where one of God's works was to be admired and loved.

Gloucester 'was of opinion (this was his little secret) that the bishop was not up to his job'.

'It is not sufficient to be virtuous to govern a diocese,' he would say. 'Neither do poets make good politicians nor do mystics make good bishops.'

This was the general opinion among the clergy in the bishopric. The members of the Carlist junta shared its view. They had never been able to rely upon the bishop for any help whatsoever!

One consequence of this excessive piety was that His Lordship left himself in his vicar-general's hands in all matters concerning ecclesiastical government. Some people regarded this as the ruination of the clergy and of the Faith, others as a great stroke of luck; but everyone agreed that the good Camoirán had no will of his own.

He had only accepted the mitre on condition that he be allowed his own choice of a man whom he could trust to take care of the government of the diocese, rather than have someone with friends in high places imposed upon him. The canon theologian was, without doubt, the most talented man he had ever known. More to the point, when De Pas was still a humble seminarist, his mother, Doña Paula, was employed by Camoirán, then a canon in Astorga, as his housekeeper. Ever since then the iron woman had dominated the poor saint of wax. De Pas, aided by his mother, maintained the tyranny and, as they said, 'they had him feeding out of their hands'. Fortunato was delighted that it should be so.

How had such a man become a bishop? At a time of wire-pulled appointments, of palace politics, a search was made for a saint to whom a mitre could be given in order to allay the complaints of public opinion, and Canon Camoirán was found.

He came to Vetusta showering blessings upon the people and receiving blessings from them. To the great scandal of his simple, humble heart, prodigious tales were told about his virtue and near-miracles were attributed to him. Once when he was visiting remote parishes in the heart of the mountains, riding a donkey through snow along the edge of a precipice, a desperate mother came before him with her child in her arms. It had been bitten by a viper.

'Save it, save it!' cried the mother, on her knees, blocking the donkey's way.

'I can't! I can't!' cried the desperate bishop, fearful for the little angel's life.

'Yes, yes – a saint like you!' howled the mother.

'A cautery! A cautery! but I can't . . .'

'A miracle! A miracle!' repeated the mother.

Fortunato's life was filled with four all-absorbing preoccupations: the cult of the Virgin, the poor, the pulpit and the confessional.

He was fifty years old and his hair was as white as snow, but his heart was still aflame with love for Holy Mary. Ever since his days in the seminary – and much water had passed under the bridge since then – his life had been an ode devoted to the praise of the Mother of God. He knew his theology, but his favourite study was the doctrine of the mysteries of the Woman *sine labe concepta*. He could repeat by memory everything said by the Holy Fathers and the Mystics in honour of the Virgin. He could praise her in an oriental style, with metaphors taken from the desert, the sea, flowered valleys and cedar forests; in a romantic style, which irritated the archpriest; and in a familiar style, with expressions of fatherly, brotherly and filial love.

He had written five books, which had at first been sold at one peseta each and were later given away. Their titles were: *The Rose-Bush of Mary* (in verse), *Flowers of Mary*, *The Devotion of the Immaculate Virgin*, *The Ballad-Book of Our Lady*, *The Virgin and Dogma*.

The Heavenly Queen had never appeared before him, but she brought him solace in plenty, flooding his spirit with a light and joy which could not be darkened or troubled by all the misfortune in the world – or at least not by the sort of misfortune he had suffered.

Nearly all the money which the government paid him, and much of what he had inherited, went on alms. But woe betide his tailor if he tried to cheat him by charging too much for patching his trousers! Didn't Fortunato know all about patching clothes? Hadn't His Lordship darned his own clothes and sewn buttons on to them often enough? And his cobbler, who was one of the humblest cobblers in town, had to keep all his wits about him so as to ensure that the soles and patches with which he mended the bishop's shoes were not too visible.

'But you are asking for a miracle, sir,' his housekeeper, Doña Ursula, who had inherited Doña Paula's position, would cry. 'How can you expect the stitching not to be seen? For God's sake do the proper thing and buy some new shoes.'

'And who has informed you, Madam Know-all, that God wants us to buy new shoes when our neighbour has no shoes? If that cobbler knew his job these would be a glorious sight to behold.'

He had his reasons for insisting that his shoes must be mended invisibly. The vicar-general gave the bishop a daily inspection as if he were a recruit in the army, surveying him from top to toe when he thought that his attention was distracted; and if the vicar-general spotted any carelessness in his dress which betrayed a poverty unworthy of a bishop he gave him an acrimonious reprimand.

'This is preposterous,' De Pas would say. 'Are you aspiring to act like the bishop in *Les Misérables*,⁶ a bishop in a forbidden book? Are you doing it to spite the rest of us who dress like respectable people and as the decorum of the Church requires? Do you believe that if we all sported patched trousers, like knife-grinders or chimney-sweeps, the Church would ever rule in the regions of power?'

'It isn't that, my son, it isn't that,' the bishop would reply, abashed, and wishing the earth would swallow him. 'It's glorious to see you all dressed up in new clothes, that's only right and proper, I know that. Do you think I don't love to see you and Don Custodio and the minister's cousin all looking so fine and handsome, so dashing and fashionable in your plush shovel-hats with their short, broad brims? Of course I do – you're a blessed sight to see, that's only right and proper. But do you know Rosendo? He's a great scoundrel who wants three pesetas to sole a pair of shoes, and then doesn't even patch a tiny hole in the upper. These are new shoes, I give you my word of honour they are, it's just that they're yawning a little – what can I do about it if they're feeling sleepy?'

For a few years Fortunato had been the fashionable preacher in Vetusta. The bishop preceding him had seldom gone up into the pulpit; and seeing Fortunato there almost every day awoke first the curiosity and then the interest and even the enthusiasm of the faithful. His was a spontaneous, burning eloquence; for he was an improviser, a true orator, better in the pulpit, in the heat of the moment, than on paper. His speech was rapid, and as flames of mystical love rose from his heart to his brain the pulpit became an incense-burner exuding perfumes of devout poetry which filled the cathedral and permeated souls. Without realizing it, Fortunato possessed the supreme art of making people shiver: such was the effect of his words of eloquent, holy unction. When he spoke, charity became the supreme necessity, the greatest beauty, the highest joy. As he descended from the pulpit wishing everyone glory for ever and ever his unction ran through the cathedral like magnetic induction – if people touched each other, it seemed, sparks of electrical charity would fly. Enthusiasm and conversion could be read in looks and smiles; and at such moments the idea that they were all brothers was taken seriously by the Vetustans.

But that had been at the beginning. Then the public began to tire of the bishop. They said that *he was too fond of making an exhibition of himself.* 'The canon theologian did not believe in making an exhibition of himself.'

'His sermons are better prepared,' said some.

'He may be less ardent, but he's more profound.'

'And he expresses himself more elegantly.'

'And he cuts a better figure in the pulpit.'

'The old man may be an apostle, but the canon theologian is an artist.'

Gloucester had long been unable to comprehend the bishop's popularity as a preacher. 'He had to confess that he did not understand those sermons. They were too florid.' All that talk about burning with love for one's neighbour was, for Gloucester, no more than *mere rhetoric.* 'It rang hollow.'

'And what about dogma? What about controversy? The bishop never spoke ill of anyone. He preached as if there were no such thing as gross materialism, or the Hydra of revolution, or the satanic *non serviam*[7] of the free-thinker.'

In Gloucester's opinion, Camoirán had begun to bring discredit upon himself in the Judges' Sermons. Every Friday in Lent the Royal Provincial Court paid for a sermon which some Vetustan notable of the pulpit preached in the ancient church of St Mary's, and they listened to it with religious attentiveness or mystical somnolence.

'Well now,' Gloucester would say, 'on such occasions one cannot speak just for the sake of speaking, or blurt out the first thing that comes into one's head. It is not sufficient on such occasions to burn with divine fire; no, it is necessary to do better than that, so as not to offend the gentlemen's intelligence. One is speaking, my dear sir, before jurisconsults, before scholars, and one must make sure of being well drilled before setting foot in the pulpit.' But the bishop had spoken to the Gentlemen of the Robe, to the provincial court, just as he spoke to the ordinary faithful.

The chief magistrate – not then Quintanar – had said to one of the other magistrates, in confidence, that the sermon lacked substance. The magistrate had spread this piece of news and the public prosecutor had ventured to add that the bishop never came to the point.

Gloucester was a man who did believe in coming to the point. The same year that Fortunato had performed so badly, in the opinion of the magistrates, the sinuous archdeacon had distinguished himself in his own Friday sermon. He had been prophesying this triumph for many days before.

'You cannot say, gentlemen, that you have not been warned. I must be read between the lines. I do not preach for housemaids and soldiers, I preach for people capable of – as I said, reading between the lines.'

Irony was Gloucester's muse. On that memorable Friday he

appeared in the pulpit with a smile upon his face, as usual (the bishop had brought discredit upon himself on the previous Friday). Gloucester bowed to the altar, bowed to the magistrates, and even deigned to bow to the Catholic congregation. His eyes scrutinized every corner of the church to see if, as he had been informed, some free-thinking character, one of those fellows who went to study in Madrid and came back rotten to the core, was present. He spotted two or three known to him, and thought, 'Good, now I'll show you.'

The chief magistrate, wearing a wrinkled brow and an unwrinkled gown, sat in a velvet-and-gold armchair placed in the middle of the nave; and as he contemplated the preacher he prepared to separate the wheat from the chaff, in the supposition that the sermon would turn out to be a mixture of the two. Other magistrates, less inclined towards criticism, prepared themselves for a quiet sleep with the aid of resources furnished by their experience on the bench.

Gloucester soon came to the point. Antiphrasis, euphemism, allusion, sarcasm and all the other missiles in the arsenal of his rhetoric, which he considered to be sly and subtle, were hurled at the impious Arouet, as he always called Voltaire. Mourelo was still taken up with poor Voltaire, for he did not know much about contemporary unbelievers – just a little about Renan and one or two Spanish apostates, but that was all. Hardly any proper names: gross materialism, foul sensualism, the swine in the sties of Epicurus, and other generalizations of the same type did the job well enough; but there was no mention of Strauss, or of the exegetical disputes in Tübingen and Göttingen:[8] oh, no, that was the canon theologian's province, much envied by Gloucester.

Voltaire, and sometimes the crazy Genevan philosopher,[9] were made to pay for that. This was not all, however, for the archdeacon had another hobby-horse: paganism, the idolatry of the ancients. On that Friday he spoke most wittily at the expense of the Egyptians. The chief magistrate could hardly contain the laughter which Gloucester was doing his best to excite in him.

Those filthy pigs who worshipped cats, leeks and onions were, for the sacred orator, highly amusing. 'He flashed his gab all right, pulling the Egyptians' legs,' according to Joaquinito Orgaz, who was religious because it was fashionable to be religious, and who sincerely believed that idolatry was ridiculous.

'Yes, Excelentísimo Señor, yes, my good Catholic people, those inhabitants of the banks of the Nile, those blind heathens whose wisdom impious authors tell us to admire, adored leeks, garlic, onions. *Risum teneatis! Risum teneatis!*'[10] he repeated, squaring up to St Roch's dog, which stood open-mouthed upon the altar in front of him. But the dog was not laughing.

He spent some thirty minutes confounding the Pharaohs and their subjects with jokes of this sort. 'Men who worshipped such rubbish

must surely have been off their heads.' Two months later Blunderbuss, an admirer of the sermon, was still pressing Gloucester's
references into service in arguments in the club, and declaring:

'Gentlemen, what I maintain here and at any place you like to
choose is that if we proclaim freedom of worship and civil marriage
we shall soon go back to idolatry and be like the ancient Egyptians,
worshippers of Isis and Iris, a she-cat and a dog, I believe.'

The chief magistrate, together with the entire provincial court, was
of opinion that Señor Mourelo, the archdeacon, had been a cut above
the bishop. This news spread through coteries, gossiping sessions
and promenades, and every Vetustan who aspired to pass for an
educated person lamented that there was so little substance in the
prelate's sermons, that he did not prepare them more adequately,
and that he was so fond of making an exhibition of himself.

In the end, opinion declared the following (but this time without
Gloucester's approval):

'One should not deceive oneself any longer; Vetusta's real preacher
is the canon theologian.'

This opinion soon became a commonplace, a conventional expression, and the bishop's reputation as an orator was irremissibly lost.
In Vetusta, once something was said as a matter of course, it was
impossible for a contrary idea to prevail.

And so it was in vain that Fortunato made a sublime description of
the death of Christ during one Easter-week sermon.

It was in the large, austere parish church of St Isidore. The place
was in near darkness, a darkness which seemed to be reflected and
multiplied by the black cloth covering altars, pillars and walls. The
only candles, long, thin ones on the tabernacle, gave out pale light,
their flames almost licking Christ's feet, which dripped blood. The
sweat painted upon His figure reflected the light in sad tones. The
bishop, buried in the shadow which filled the pulpit, spoke in a voice
of distant thunder. All that could be seen of him, from time to time,
was a purple blur and a hand outstretched over the congregation. He
described the creaking of the bones in Our Lord's chest when the
executioners bent His legs to force His feet to the place where they
were to be nailed. Jesus hunched Himself up, His whole body seemed
to be trying to climb, but the executioners wrestled with it; for they
were going to have their way. 'My God! My God!' exclaimed the Sun
of Righteousness as His dislocated body broke with muffled cracks.
The executioners were growing annoyed at their own clumsiness;
they had still not managed to nail down His feet. They panted and
sweated and swore. Their breath besmirched the face of Jesus. 'And
He was God, the only God, their God, our God, everyone's God! He
was God!' cried Fortunato in horror, his hands tensed, stepping back
against the cold stone of the pillar, trembling before a vision, as if he
could feel the executioners' breath on his own forehead, as if the

Cross and Christ were there in front of him, hanging over the congregation amid the shadows in the nave. At that moment Fortunato suffered the immense sorrow, the infinite horror of the ingratitude of man, who killed God: that absurdity of evil. He suffered with ineffable sadness, as if a universe of grief weighed upon his heart, and his gestures, his voice, his words contrived to express the inexpressible: his sorrow. He himself realized – as if from a distance, however, as if the preacher were someone else – that his sermon was sublime, but then this notion disappeared like a lightning-flash. He forgot about himself, and there was nobody left in the church who understood or felt the apostle's eloquence, except one or two children with powerful, fresh imaginations who were hearing the description of the scene on Mount Calvary for the first time.

The strength of the bishop's feeling forced him to make eloquent pauses charged with pathos, which were answered below by the obligatory sobs of the pious women, humble villagers, who formed the greater part of the congregation: the indispensable Passiontide sobs, the same sobs as would be exhaled during any village priest's sermon, in part sighs, in part belches caused by the Lenten diet.

The few ladies present were not sighing, they were looking at their books of devotion, open on their laps, and even turning the pages. Intelligent members of the congregation were of opinion that the prelate 'had upset himself' and perhaps got carried away. 'Trying to put the fear of God into people like that!' That wasn't what preaching was all about. Gloucester, lurking in a corner, was scandalized. 'But what a comedian it is!' he thought; and he intended to repeat the words as soon as he was out of church. He believed that he had found a clever turn of phrase: 'But what a comedian it is!'

The canon theologian was not a comedian, or a tragedian, or even a reciter of epics. 'He did not try to put the fear of God into people.' In general, he managed without the Christian epopee in his sermons, and he seldom preached during Holy Week. 'He shunned commonplaces,' according to Don Saturnino Bermúdez. The fact was that De Pas's imagination lacked the creative power needed to paint New Testament scenes with originality and vigour. Whenever he had to repeat 'And the Word was made flesh' he saw in his mind's eye not the manger and Baby Jesus but the sentence from the Gospel according to St John painted in red on a piece of wood in the middle of an altar: Et Verbum caro factum est.

During one period of his youth, doubt had so often tormented him with pangs of conscience when he had thought about these matters and tried to picture the life of Jesus that he had begun to feel afraid of such images. And he had avoided them, not wanting any more headaches. 'There was enough on his mind as it was.' At heart he was an iconoclast. He had no appreciation of the plastic arts and, although he did not dare say so, he believed that paintings, even ones by great artists, profaned churches. The part of dogma which he preferred was pure theology, abstraction; and he liked morality better than dogma. His vocation for theological philosophy and his love of controversy had been born at the seminary. His spirit had been steeped there in sectarianism, which is often a substitute for the enthusiasm of true faith. His experience of life had given rise to his liking for moral studies. Reading La Bruyère's *The Characters*[11] gave him great pleasure; of Balmes's books he only admired *The Art of Thinking*;[12] and – what would Señor Carraspique have said! – in novels, sometimes forbidden ones, by contemporary authors, he studied customs and temperaments and looked for observations about life, comparing his own experience with that of others.

How often the canon theologian smiled with a kind of pity as he read an impious author's account of the imaginary adventures of a priest! 'Such scruples! Such tortuosities! Such roundabout routes to sin! And afterwards such remorse! These liberals don't even know how to be spiteful. Their priests are as much like the priests I know as kings in plays are like kings in real life.'

Don Fermín's sermons were nearly always about the struggle against modern impiety, or the controversy of the day, or the vices and the virtues and their consequences. He preferred the latter subject. From time to time, so as to preserve the reputation as a scholar which he enjoyed among persons of culture, he would pick a fight with infidels and heretics. But he did not go back to the Egyptians, or even to Voltaire. The heretics torn to pieces by the canon theologian were fresh ones. He attacked Protestants, making witty fun of their disputes and skilfully searching out the weak points in their doctrines and their ecclesiastical discipline. Sometimes when he was describing the consistories of Berlin he made his audience think: 'But those poor devils are out of their minds.'

He did not paint the enemy as criminals wallowing in sinful error, but as thick-headed fools. The preacher's vanity communicated with the vanity of his listeners and the two fused into one; cordial enthusiasm developed, the magnetism of two vanities in agreement. 'What a pity that so many millions and millions of men living in the shadows of idolatry, heresy, and so on, lacked the natural talent of the Vetustans huddled together in the cathedral crossing around the pulpit! Otherwise the salvation of the world would be a reality.'

In the pulpit, the canon theologian's intention was always to demonstrate 'mathematically' the truth of Catholic dogma. 'Let us for a moment do without the assistance of faith, let us make use of our reason alone. Reason suffices to prove . . .' He was anxious indeed that reason should suffice! 'True, reason cannot explain the sacred mysteries, but it can explain why they cannot be explained.' 'It's mechanical,' he would repeat, happy to come back down to the popular style. At such moments his eloquence was sincere. When he was set upon expounding an argument, striving to demonstrate an article of faith with the aid of his theologico-rational *a* plus *b* system, he spoke with warmth, with enthusiasm. Then, and only then, he became a little agitated. He stopped making his rhythmic, smooth, academic gestures, he bent his knees, he crouched like a huntsman, as if lying in wait to fire upon the opposing argument, he delivered rapid irregular slaps upon the pulpit, a frown appeared on his face, the steel needles in his eyes stood on end, his voice became a harsh raucous trumpet. But oh! he was being carried away. *His* public did not understand such things – and De Pas became himself again, stood erect, folded away the needles of steel and continued raining references upon the bemused Vetustans, who walked out of the cathedral at the end of the service with aching heads, saying: 'What a man! What wisdom! When can he find the time to learn so much? The day must last forty-eight hours for him!'

Although the ladies also admired all that talk about how Renan copied the Germans, and how the only genuine scholars were Father Secchi and five or six other Jesuits, and all the other stuff about Tübingen and Göttingen, and the orientalist Oppert, and so on and so forth, they preferred to hear the canon theologian preaching his sermons of manners; and he preferred to please the ladies.

When dealing with dogma he sought the aid of sound reason, but in moral matters he always had recourse to utility. Salvation was a transaction – the great transaction of life. He was the Bastiat[13] of the pulpit. 'Self-interest and charity are one and the same thing. To be virtuous you merely have to remember where charity begins.' The many returned emigrants listening to the canon smiled with pleasure at these formulae for salvation.

'Who would have believed it! Having made their fortunes in South America they could now, back in the old country, and without even needing to leave home, easily win themselves a place in heaven. They had been born under a lucky star!' According to De Pas, wicked people were like heretics: they were simply fools. That, too, was mechanical, and could also be demonstrated with his *a* plus *b* logic. Sometimes he painted, in strokes worthy of a Molière or a Balzac, the figure of the miser, the drunkard, the liar, the gambler, the proud man, the envious man; and after the vicissitudes of a wretched existence it always turned out that they themselves had the worst of it all.

His most perfect portrait was that of the young man who gives himself over to lust. First De Pas would show him with a fresh and ruddy countenance, happy, in his bloom, graceful, full of grand dreams, the hope of his family and of his country; and then dried-up, cold, satiated, withered, useless.

De Pas nearly always forgot to mention the trouble awaiting the victims of vice in the next life. Ladies and returned emigrants could understand this utilitarian morality perfectly. In their hearts they summarized it thus: 'Steer clear!'

'How right he is!' thought many ladies as they heard him talking about adultery. Most of them were honourable women who had not committed adultery – who had gone no further than to fool about a little, like all the others. Sometimes Don Fermín's devotees had the feeling that he was imprudently recounting in the pulpit what they had told him in the confessional.

The vicar-general had also routed his bishop in the tribunal of penance.

When Camoirán came to Vetusta he found himself beset by the fair sex, of all social classes. At first, all the women wanted the bishop to be their spiritual father, but he brought discredit upon himself in the confessional even sooner than in the pulpit. He was so humdrum! And not at all broad-minded or agreeable. He only asked a few questions and they were silly ones. He talked a great deal and said almost exactly the same thing to each woman. What was more, he got up too early, and had no consideration even for delicate ladies. As soon as day dawned he was in his confessional.

By little and little the ladies left him. It was not very amusing to have to rub shoulders, in the chapel of Mary Magdalen behind the high altar, with a mass of servant girls and other sanctimonious poor women, and, furthermore, the bishop made everyone, without exception, wait her turn, as at the hairdresser's, without taking into account whether she was a lady or a servant. He took playing the apostle too far. They left him.

He soon found himself surrounded only by the early risers of the lower classes. Carlist stonemasons, bricklayers, shoemakers and gunsmiths, poor pious women, housemaids affected by a more or less authentic mysticism, waistcoat-makers and shoe-binders; soon this was his flock of penitents. 'That was why he complained, full of sorrow, about the wicked ways of the world and about the many illegitimate children that must, by his reckoning, be coming into it. Now if he had dealings with young ladies . . .!'

Once he went so far as to say to the civil governor of the Province: 'Please, haven't you got the authority to put an end to that promenade of the canvas-shoed?'

The bishop was alluding to the working-class promenade at nightfall in the Boulevard.

He believed that Vetusta's growing corruption originated in this promenade and in the cheap dances held in the theatre.

This, then, was the good Fortunato Camoirán, the prelate of the exempt diocese[14] of Vetusta, the noble former capital of the nation; this was the humble bishop whom his vicar-general reprimanded with a glare like a thunderbolt as he entered the room.

The bishop was sitting in an armchair and there were two ladies on the sofa.

The ladies were Visita, the bank clerk's wife, and Olvido, the daughter of Páez the returned emigrant and second richest millionaire in La Colonia.

When the bishop saw the canon theologian he coloured like a seminarist caught by his betters puffing at his first cigarette.

'What is the meaning of this?' demanded the glare from the canon, who then greeted the ladies with a graceful and innocently coquettish bow. 'Ladies with the bishop! And no gentleman accompanying them! This has never happened before.'

It was one of Visitación's bright ideas, an attempt to seduce His Lordship into honouring with his presence a solemn prize-giving for champions of virtue organized by a certain philanthropic society. It was called the Free Fraternity, an ugly un-Spanish name with an odour which was far from being one of sanctity. This society had a committee of gentlemen and a subcommittee of Lady Patronesses (to use the grammar of the president of the society).

The Free Fraternity had been founded as an institution with pretensions to being *independent of the yoke of religion*, and its first president had been Don Pompeyo Guimarán, who had avoided excommunication only by some miracle and who never took the communion anyway.

The society was a rival to the Little Sisters of the Poor, the Holy Mission for Catechesis and the Sunday School, and other similar organizations. War was immediately declared upon it by the entire religious sector, and within a few months there was not a pauper in the municipality of Vetusta who would accept the Free Fraternity's charity, prizes or education.

The girls from the Sunday School and the boys from the Mission for Catechesis, who did not sing profane ditties as they walked along the street, but 'Holy God, Holy and Mighty,/Holy and Immortal,'[15] and 'O come and let us all go hence/With flowers for Holy Mary,'[16] composed a song attacking the society: 'The children of the poor won't err/To the Free Fraternity,/The children of the poor prefer/Pure Christian charity.'

The 'pure Christian charity' and the perfection of the rhyme revealed the style of Don Custodio the beneficiary, who was – such heights had he reached – the director of the Sunday School for poor girls.

The Free Fraternity would have died of consumption had it not been for its president's valiant self-sacrifice. Señor Guimarán realized that the time was not yet ripe for the secularization of charity and of primary education and he presented his resignation 'sacrificing himself', he said, 'not to the false imputations of fanaticism but to the welfare of abandoned children'. With the resignation of Don Pompeyo and the happy idea of creating the subcommittee of Lady Patronesses, the charitable society improved its reputation a little, and total war was no longer waged against it. But it had still not been cleansed of the original sin which it carried in its very name. The vicar-general despised this society.

Visitación was the first lady to be made a member of the subcommittee, because of her eagerness to be a member of everything. Indeed, she was the treasurer of the Lady Patronesses.

What now had to be done was to erase the last vestiges of heresy or whatever it was, by establishing a good relationship with the cathedral chapter and asking the bishop to take the chair at the solemn prize-giving that year. 'But who was the woman to bell the cat? – Visitación, the bank clerk's wife.' Who could there be more suitable for such an audacious feat? She requested that, for the sake of appearances, she be accompanied on her visit by another lady of family. None of them wanted to go with her – they did not dare – so a vote was taken and Olvido Páez was elected, because of her papa's standing and because she was so well liked in the palace.

'Yes,' said Visitación at the meeting, 'Olvido must come. That will stop the canon theologian from imagining that all this is aimed at him personally – he can't bear the sight of me.'

It was true, De Pas despised the bank clerk's wife; indeed he regarded her as a wretch beneath contempt. She was one of the few ladies who helped the archdeacon with his conspiracy. Yet Visita sometimes confessed with Don Fermín, in spite of his rebuffs. 'He knew what that little shrew was after, but he made sure that she drew a blank – he kept to the ten commandments and that was that.'

'Anything else? Carry on; anything else? Ripamilán-style. Gloucester's talebearer would have no success with him.'

Fortunato had already given his word of honour that he would attend the Free Fraternity's solemn session. The vicar-general's ill humour was aggravated by this, and by the sight of the Páez girl, his most faithful devotee, there with Visitación. It was not easy for him to be polite and gracious now, and he only succeeded because of his habit of controlling himself and dissembling. Visitación was happily imagining the vicar-general's wrath, and harassing him with her jokes and with the dizzy behaviour 'which turned his stomach'.

'But my dear ladies,' said De Pas, 'let us speak seriously for a moment.'

'What? What can you mean by that? Do you want to back out of an agreement, have His Lordship go back on his word?'

'I believe . . .'

'Say no more, say no more! One's word is one's word. We're off, we're off, keep talking, my dear – I can't hear a thing, gentlemen. Let's go, Olvido. I can't hear a thing, can't hear a thing.'

By some kind of acoustic miracle each word uttered by Visitación sounded like seven, as if the whole subcommittee of Lady Patronesses were perorating there.

She stood up and walked to the door, towing the Páez girl behind her.

The canon protested in vain. 'That society had been founded by an atheist, it was against the Church . . .'

'Not at all,' cried Visita from the door. 'If that were true we wouldn't figure as members of the ladies' subcommittee.'

'I am a member,' the Páez girl explained, 'because Visita here insisted, and persuaded papa.'

'But look here, gentlemen, the Free Fraternity has changed its tune now, ever since we've been members all the chat about freedom and hocus-pocus like that has stopped.'

'She's right,' the bishop, who was still taken in by Visita's affected giddiness, ventured to say. 'The mad young thing is right.'

'No she's not!' shouted the vicar-general, losing at least a little of his temper. 'No she is not right, and this has been – most imprudent of you.'

Visita looked back and poked out her tongue. 'What a way to treat him!' she thought, full of envy for a man who dared call the bishop imprudent.

The ladies departed. His Lordship was embarrassed and, after suggesting to the canon that he might accompany the ladies through the narrow, maze-like corridors of the palace, he made good his escape, shutting himself away in his oratory to avoid having to give an explanation of his actions.

But the canon had no thought of going to search him out.

The Páez girl walked along with her head bowed, also fearing a reprimand. Taking advantage of a moment when Visita stopped to greet a family for which she had spoken a good word to the bishop, De Pas whispered into the girl's ear in a tone of paternal authority:

'It was wrong, very wrong of you to come here with that – madwoman.'

'But they all voted for me.'

'If you had not become a member of that committee . . .'

'Papa expects you for lunch today. I was going to write myself. Please consider yourself invited.'

'Come, come. Can't you bear to hear the truth?'

'I am just saying that papa . . .'

'Well, I cannot go to your house today – for lunch at least. I was invited to lunch days ago, by another Francisco who . . . but we can meet in your house in an hour's time, as soon as I have hurried through my work here.'

They took their leave of each other. The ladies went out into the street and the vicar-general swept through corridors, galleries and halls into the offices of ecclesiastical government, the diocesan curia.

He walked into his room and, not bothering to greet the people who were waiting for him there, sat on an armchair of crimson velvet behind a secretaire covered with papers tied up with red tape. He rested his elbows upon the desk and buried his head in his hands. Of course he knew that people were waiting there to talk to him, but he pretended not to know. This was one of his ways of making others feel the weight of his tyranny. In this manner he humiliated his subordinates, scorning them to the point of not seeing them even when they stood before him. His bad temper came first. A pitch-black bad temper. He could taste his bile on his teeth. Why? For no reason. No one had done anything to make him so angry. But many little things all coming together had spoilt this day which had promised to be a joyful one as he had looked up at the brilliant sun and happily washed in front of the mirror. First his mother treating him like a little boy, and reminding him of the calumnies with which he was persecuted; then the doctor's alarming news and foolish jokes; then that woman Visitación, the Free Fraternity, Olvidito violating discipline; and then that devil of a bishop confounding him with his humility, reminding him by his mere presence – the presence of a frightened hare – of an entire history of holiness, of spiritual grandeur, compared with his own history, which – why try to hide it from himself? – was not an edifying one. That eternal parallel which Fortunato drew without realizing it irritated the canon theologian. And now it irritated him more than ever. Now he thought that the vicar-general's intellectual superiority was nothing compared to the moral grandeur of the bishop. He was the only person who could fully appreciate Fortunato's worth. How poetic, how noble, how spiritual the other man's virtue, eloquence and romantic cult of the Virgin seemed now! And his own abilities – how wretched, how prosaic! His powerful, dominating character – how ridiculous in reality! 'Whom did he dominate? Beetles!'

'What do you want?' he shouted in a bitter voice, looking up at the beetles before him.

They were a priest who looked like a layman and a layman who looked like a priest. Both of them were ill-shaven, especially the cleric, whose face was covered with rough black bristles, and both were in mufti, in the style of village priests. The cleric's stock was white, stained with red wine and greasy sweat; the other man's shirt collar also looked like a clerical stock, but he wore a black bow-tie fastened behind his neck.

Don Carlos Peláez, an ecclesiastical notary who had another two or three jobs in the palace, not altogether compatible with each other, prided himself on being one of the people with most influence in the diocesan curia and even in the heart of the vicar-general. He was going to give clear proof of it now by interceding with his good offices to snatch the wretched parish priest of

Contracayes, a village in the mountains, out of the clutches of discipline. Some envious people had been telling tales, and the vicar-general knew that the priest from Contracayes had a weakness for converting the confessional-box into a school for seduction. At first, De Pas had wanted to bring the full weight of ecclesiastical censure and the severest penalties to bear upon the priest from the mountains. Thanks to the notary's pleas, however, he had consented to interview him before initiating proceedings, promising that if he found any signs of genuine repentance he would be content with an unpublicized punishment which would not harm the priest's reputation. He was a loyal voter and a reliable supporter of the good cause.

'What is it?' repeated De Pas, directing a mechanical smile at the notary.

Peláez gestured towards the man by his side, who was burly and swarthy, with bushy eyebrows, a scowling expression, fiery hazel eyes, a large mouth, pointed ears, a powerful neck and a protruding Adam's apple. He seemed to be covered with grime, although he was not; there was as much of the coal-man as of the cleric about him. It seemed as though the colour made by those black bristles set into his purple cheeks must extend all over his body. Never before had he found himself face to face with the vicar-general, whom he feared because of the thunderbolts which he wielded – but only to the extent to which a savage giant can fear someone whom he could, if necessary, flatten with a punch. Don Fermín noticed that the priest was more confused than afraid. The priest greeted the vicar-general with a grunt; the vicar-general did not reply.

The notary was all sugar and honey. He sat himself down sideways on a chair to show that he was quite at home, spoke in the most familiar language possible without being irreverent, ventured jokes, and was even about to declare that solicitation was not one of the worst sins and that the affair could be hushed up without difficulty. But since the canon frowned Peláez changed the subject and spoke, feigning abstraction, about the latest elections, going so far as to allude to the exploits of a certain priest from the mountains, an acquaintance of his, who had made a couple of civil guards shake in their shoes. The priest from Contracayes grinned like a bear.

The canon theologian was wondering how that brute set about soliciting his penitents. There was a moment of silence. Not a word had been spoken about the business in hand, and even Peláez himself realized that the thorny question would have to be broached.

Don Fermín, suddenly remembering his bad temper and all the contretemps which he had suffered, sprang to his feet, confronted the parish priest – who also stood up as if about to be attacked – and rasped:

'I know everything, my man, and I regret to have to inform you that the settlement of this affair of yours will not be pleasant for you. The Council of Trent considers the sin which you have committed to be akin to heresy. I do not know if you are aware of the fact that the Constitution *Universi Domini* of 1622, made by His Holiness Gregory XV, calls you and all others of your type execrable traitors, and that the punishment which it prescribes for the crime of soliciting penitents *ad turpia* is of the severest. And, furthermore, it ordains that you be degraded and delivered to the secular arm.'

The priest opened his eyes wide and stared in consternation at the notary, who, behind Don Fermín's back, winked at him.

'Benedict XIV', continued the canon theologian, 'confirmed the punishments imposed for solicitation by Sixtus V and Gregory XV; and, in short, however one looks at the matter, your position is a hopeless one.'

'I thought . . .'

'You thought wrongly, my man! And if you doubt my word, over there on that shelf you will find Giraldi's *Expositio juris pontificii*, which deals with the matter in volume two, part one, with a great profusion of data.'

Señor Peláez was used to the vicar-general's style. He was never more erudite than when sinking his claws into a victim.

'Sir,' the priest from Contracayes ventured to say, for he was by now a little riled and had lost much of his fear, 'your word's good enough for me, and anyway I'm not complaining about the sacred canons but about my bad luck, which made me slip and fall where many, very many others I know slip and don't fall.'

The canon spun around as if he had been bitten on the back.

'Get out of here, you insolent creature, and do not sleep in Vetusta this night!' he screamed.

'But, sir . . .'

'Be silent I tell you! Be silent and do as you are told or you will spend the night in priests' prison!'

And the canon dealt his secretaire a formidable blow with his clenched fist.

'Well, that's a fine favour you've done me!' bawled the priest, no less furious than the canon, turning towards the dismayed Peláez, who had not foreseen this clash between two hot tempers.

'Please, gentlemen, calm yourselves.'

'Get out of here, you knave!' cried the canon, slinging the end of his cloak over his shoulder and thus, against his custom, revealing how furious he was. 'You had better prepare for the worst! You can give yourself up for lost, you rogue-priest!'

'But what have I said, sir?' exclaimed the priest, somewhat frightened by the attitude of the man in whom he recognized the moral superiority of a Jupiter of the Church.

As soon as De Pas saw that his authority was being heeded he began to calm the stormy waves of his wrath. Finally, his face pale, but in a serene voice:

'Go away,' he said, pointing to the door, 'go away. You are going free only because you are mad. But do not remain in this city for so long as two more hours, or speak to a single soul about what has happened here. As regards your execrable crime, I shall come to an agreement with Señor Peláez without any need to see you again, and he will inform you of our decision.'

The priest made to humble himself, to beg forgiveness.

'Go away this very moment.'

He went.

Peláez, livid-faced and trembling, ventured:

'I am so sorry, Canon De Pas, sir!'

'There is no need for you to be sorry. You came at a bad moment. I am feeling nervous. I wanted to frighten him, terrify him into respect – and I failed to take account of my bad temper. I became over-heated, I allowed myself to be carried away by my anger.'

'Oh no, not at all! He's a real brute, an animal.'

'Yes, he is an animal – and for that very reason I should have dealt with him differently.'

'What I cannot condone is all this unpleasantness.'

'Let it be, let it be. We shall talk about the scoundrel – another day. Today I cannot; today – it would be impossible for me to promise to temper the rigours of the law, which is categorical in such matters.'

'Yes, I know. But since it is never enforced . . .'

'Only because there is no proof – as there is in this case. And a beginning has to be made sometime. Well, as I say, we can speak about it later. I need to be alone now.'

Peláez, too, went away, and De Pas, alone with his thoughts, allowed the blood which his shame had been accumulating inside him to rise to his face.

'How degrading!' he thought, and he began to pace his room as a wild beast paces its cage.

When he felt calmer he rang a bell. A tall young man appeared, tonsured, pale and lugubrious, probably consumptive. He was a cousin of the canon theologian's who acted as his secretary.

'Did you fellows hear anything?'

'Shouts, nothing much.'

'The priest of Contracayes, an animal.'

'Yes, I know.'

'What business is there?'

'Nothing urgent.'

'I can go, then? You don't need me?'

'No, not today.'

'In that case I shall go. I have a headache. I am not fit for anything.

But don't tell my mother. If she knows I left the office so early, she will think I am ill.'

'Yes, yes, she will.'

'Just a minute – has the permit for the Páezes' oratory come through yet?'

'Yes.'

'Has it been validated, can I take it along with me now?'

'You'll find it in that portfolio over there.'

'Is it all in order? Will the curate of Parves be able to say the two masses?'

'It's all in order.'

'This is Don Saturnino Bermúdez's card. What did he come for?'

'For the usual thing, to ask us not to heed poor Don Segundo, of Tamaza, who is claiming for all the requiem masses which Don Saturn has had him say.'

'And for which he will not pay.'

'It's his custom. He's in debt to the entire clergy. He's saved half the souls in purgatory,' the tonsured youth coughed violently as he tried to contain his laughter, 'half the souls in purgatory, at his creditors' expense.'

'The priest of Tamaza is a loud-mouthed nuisance.'

'But he's only asking for what's due to him.'

'But there's nothing to be done about it. Do you want me to get into the bad books of the little frock-coated bishop?'

'Certainly not. He would make us pay for it in *El Lábaro*, which is treating you very well at the moment. Talking about newspapers – in yesterday's edition of *La Caridad*, from Madrid, there was a report from Vetusta and, if I am not greatly deceived, Gloucester had a hand in it.'

'What does it say?'

'Stupid nonsense: that the Carlists have taken control of certain dioceses in which men have been illegally made vicars-general – men who are only allowed to occupy that office temporarily and by special dispensation – and that, because of certain services to the cause of the Pretender, their superiors are turning a blind eye to it all.'

'So I can't be vicar-general?'

'It seems you can't, because among these exceptional cases the article refers to "holders of simple prebends" and brings up some papal dispensation or other.'

'Yes, I know. A brief of Paul V and two or three of Gregory XV. The fools! It will be a miracle if they don't come up with the business about "being a native of the diocese" too. The idiots! These false Catholics have no practical common sense whatsoever! Gloucester must be that rag's correspondent – such blundering cleverness can only have come from him. Pah! what enemies I have, Lord, what enemies! Animals, simply animals!'

The canon theologian was taking deep breaths, as if suffocating in that atmosphere of stupidity.

He wanted to go away, without seeing any of the clerics or laymen waiting in the ante-room and the office next to it; but he had no defence against invasions. Señor Carraspique poked his nose around a door.

'May I come in?'

'It was Carraspique!' Yes, pray do, he had to say.

Carraspique had come to request that a certain application to the General Dispensation Agency[17] be made as soon as possible, and that various matters to do with benefices be dealt with. Registers would have to be looked into, clerks consulted. The canon, forgetting himself, ventured out from his room into the office and found that he was surrounded by litigants and aspirants to various positions, nearly all of them clean-shaven, and all dressed in black, either in cassocks or in frock-coats which looked like cassocks. The office did not display the luxury of the canon's room or anything like it. Large, cold and dirty, it was not furnished as one might have expected such an office to be furnished, and had the odour of a sacristy mixed with the peculiar smell of a guardhouse. The clerks were pale with the pallor caused by abstinence and contemplation, but in their case it was the result of the moral miasmas of petty bureaucracy – wretched, sordid, and noxious – complicated by the jaundice endemic among minor church officials.

There was a table in each corner, and gathered around each table were priests and laymen, talking, gesticulating, coming and going, insisting on what they were asking for and fearing that they would be snubbed. The clerks, in a calmer state, were smoking, writing, replying in monosyllables, sometimes giving no reply at all. It was an office like any other, a little less bad-mannered than most, a little more impassively, cruelly hypocritical.

As the vicar-general entered, the noise died down. Most of those present turned towards him, but the *chief* merely held a hand up in front of his face as if to repel all these pests, and went to a table to ask about a submission concerning church lands. 'Just as he had thought, there was no answer from the Public Treasury Offices; all the submissions were sleeping the sleep that knows no waking, buried in dust.'

Señor Carraspique was beating his foot upon the floor.

'These liberals!' he muttered, close by the canon theologian. 'What kind of Restoration do you call that? It's the same pack of dogs wearing different collars.'

'Yes, my dear sir, the state is playing with the Church, that is evident, the Concordat might as well not exist. Promises in plenty, but nothing is done.'

Two priests approached the vicar-general, humbly. They were

village priests, and they, too, wanted to know whether the submissions . . .

'No, no, no, gentlemen. Listen,' said the vicar-general in a loud
voice so that all those present should hear, and stop bothering him.
'The reply from the government offices is that the submissions will
be dealt with individually, because there is no generally applicable
criterion – which is to say that the precious submissions will never be
dealt with.'

De Pas found himself caught up in the daily round of canonico-
bureaucratic chores. Without realizing it, and much against his own
intentions, he had become bogged down, as he did every day, in the
complicated questions of his ecclesiastical rule, in which his own
interests and those of his mother were so intimately involved. A
hundred and one terms of ecclesiastical discipline, many of which
had, in the primitive Church, stood for pure, poetic aspects of
worship and the priesthood, were used now to disguise the eternal
question of money: *commenda, fructos intercalares,* annates, foundations, emoluments, endowments, stole-fees, stipends, licences, dispensations, dues, funeral rights and dozens of other words were
bandied about, combined with one another, repeated and substituted
for each other; they always had a metallic ring, and the vicar-general's
profits – his mother's profits – were always bound up with them.
Doña Paula had never set foot in this singular market-place, the
diocesan curia, but her spirit seemed to preside over it. She was the
invisible general in command of these daily battles; her son was her
able instrument.

On that morning, as usual, tangled questions came before the
vicar-general and he dealt with them, as usual, in a mechanical way,
using his own gain as his criterion, with astonishing skill,
absolute formal correctness, and apparently exquisite delicacy. More
than once, however, his spirit faltered as he decided upon an
injustice, an extortion, an expedient act of cruelty (he was feeling
nervous, he did not know what had got into him), but the thought of
his mother, together with the presence of those daily witnesses of his
firm, able defence of his own interests – and in great part, too, the
force of inertia, of habit – kept him at his post; and he was the same
vicar-general they all knew, he settled all matters in his usual way,
and no one had cause to wonder if he had gone mad nor did he need
to make up any stories to deceive his mother about what had
happened. 'Doña Paula could feel well-pleased with her son; yes, her
son, not the foolish hare-brained dreamer who earlier in the morning
had been embarrassed to read an insignificant letter and who had felt
happy without any obvious reason at the sight of a resplendent
sun in a clear sky. The sun! The sky! What did they matter to the
vicar-general of Vetusta? He was a curial officer, wasn't he? A curial
officer making himself into a millionaire so as to pay off sacred debts

to his mother and to slake with cupidity the thirst of frustrated ambition.

'Yes, yes, that was what he was, and he should not entertain any illusions or go in search of a new life. He ought to be feeling satisfied – and he was.

'An hour and a half in the office!' he said to himself as he left the palace, half ashamed, half pleased, 'and it only seemed like twenty minutes!'

When De Pas found himself once more in the open air, in La Corralada square, he took a deep breath. Coming out of the palace was like emerging from a cave. So much talking in there had left him with a dry, bitter taste in his mouth – he even thought he could detect a tang of copper. He sensed the air of the counterfeiter about himself. He hurried away from the little square in the shadow of the grey cathedral and escaped in the direction of broad streets, leaving behind him La Encimada with its echoing pavements, narrow and worn, its sad, solemn solitude, its grass growing between cobbles, its large old smoke-blackened houses, its convex iron gratings. He walked towards La Colonia along the Plaza del Pan, the Calle del Comercio and the Boulevard, where the small trees were shedding dead leaves upon broad flagstones. His cloak attracted the leaves, drawing them along over the stone in its wake, with the endless rhythmical swish of the breaking of the waves of the sea.

Now he could see a good expanse of sky, completely blue, and before him the outline of Corfín mountain, of the same colour. That was happiness, life. 'Endowments, bulls, annates, reservations! What did all this have to do with the world, the beautiful, wide world? Did that stone giant, the grave, majestic, tranquil Corfín know what agencies were? Did it know that there was an agency for obtaining dispensations? Did it know why licences to do anything cost money?'

The canon theologian walked along the Boulevard, greeting people right and left, dismayed that such ideas – the ideas of some religious bucolic – should have found their way into his head. He had always been an enemy of ecclesiastical Arcadies, professing a kind of prosaic positivism concerning the Church's temporal needs. Was he ill? Was he going mad? While the cool air (the wind had changed from the south to the north-west) filled his lungs with a voluptuous tingling, his imagination went on herborizing – he could not stop it, it would not take any notice of objections and orders – and rooted itself in the first centuries of the Church's existence; and he could see himself going from door to door with a basket under his arm to collect the luscious fruit which Páez, Don Frutos Redondo and the other Vespuccis in La Colonia were picking in the gardens now beginning to appear on either side behind gilt railings and dazzling foliage full of the murmur of the wind and the twitter of birds.

Páez's villa was the first of the six which adorned the high street on

its southern side. It was an enormous cube which looked like one of
the watch-towers to be found all along the coast of Vetusta province
– relics, it is said, of the defence against the Normans.

Señor Páez did not fear a landing of pirates, for the sea was several
leagues from his palace, but he believed that 'solid elegance consisted
in building thick walls, making lavish use of marble and, in short,
Cyclopican construction'. At the highest point of the façade, instead
of a coat of arms, something which Señor Páez did not possess, there
was a great black marble semicircle and in the middle of it in letters
of gold this eloquent inscription: '1868', which indicated the date of
the Cyclopean construction. The roof-terrace was surrounded by a
great balustrade which crowned the castle, and at each of its four
corners an iron eagle painted green was attempting to take off.
According to Señor Páez these eagles matched the two others in the
carpet in his study. The worthy Don Francisco was not the richest
American in La Colonia; Don Frutos had a few millions more, but the
eagle-loving Vespucci 'let neither the precious Don Frutos nor anyone
else get the better of him as far as putting on a show was concerned',
and he was the only Vetustan who visited in a coach and had lackeys
wearing braided livery every day of the year, even though he never
managed to make these lackeys dress with the care, correctness
and gravity which he had observed in their metropolitan counterparts.

Páez had spent twenty-five years in Cuba without ever hearing
mass, and the only religious book he had brought back with him was
the *People's Gospel* by Señor Henao y Muñoz,[18] not because Páez was
a democrat – God forbid! – but because he liked a succinct style. It
was his steadfast belief that God was an invention of priests. On the
island, at least, there was no God. Páez had lived in Vetusta for a few
years without modifying these ideas, although he had refrained from
making them public; but his daughter and the canon theologian had
convinced him by slow degrees that religion was both a brake on
socialism and an infallible sign of refinement. In the end, Páez became
the most fervent supporter of the religion of his forefathers. 'Undoubtedly,' he would say, 'a mother-country ought to be religious.' And he
went religious. He gave the Church all the money for which he was
asked, and although he often prattled at the expense of Catholic
dogma, he was always ready to take such absurdities back and replace
them with inoffensive ones.

Religion, in the form of a canon theologian, had succeeded in
penetrating the granite fortress of that free-thinking spirit through
two breaches: his love for his daughter and his mania for refinement.

Olvido would say in a sharp voice and a tone of reprehension:
'Papa, that is common.' And Don Francisco would abominate what
had previously seemed excellent to him.

The canon dominated Olvido, and Olvido controlled her papa thanks to the power of love and to her understanding of what, there at least, was known as refinement.

Olvido was a tall pale thin young woman with proud grey-brown eyes. Having no mother, she led the life of a little idol – supposing the idol to have movement and consciousness. She was waited on by Negroes and Negresses and one white man, her father, who was her most faithful slave. Not a single caprice of hers had gone unsatisfied. At the age of eighteen she had conceived the idea that she wanted to be wretched, like the heroines of the novels she read, and had invented for herself a torment both romantic and amusing: imagining that she was a kind of King Midas of love, that nobody could love her for herself, but only for her money – which is indeed a wretched situation for any young lady. To all the elegant young men – whether men in prominent positions, aristocrats, or men of talent – who had ventured to declare their love to Olvido she had given the fatal cold shoulder which she had sworn to give to all men, with an invariable formula: 'Love was not her lot,' she did not believe in love. By slow degrees this farce had gained control of her spirit, and she had taken her role as Queen Midas seriously, renouncing love without ever having discovered what love was, and dedicating herself, heart and soul, to luxury. She had become a lover of art for art's sake, the lady who made the greatest display of wealth at promenades, balls and the theatre. Dress had become a religion for her. Olvido would never display the same clothes twice. She used to arrive late at the promenade, walk up and down three or four times and, once she felt herself to be sufficiently envied, return home without deigning to glance at any marriageable member of the sterner sex. Vetustan men had come to regard her as a dressmaker's dummy laden with fashionable clothes, amusing only for other young ladies. 'She was a marvellous prospect', but they might as well forget all about her.

'Olvido is waiting for a Russian prince,' was the time-honoured expression. Whenever an unwary outsider ventured to try his luck with her he was ironically known as 'the Russian prince' until he received his rebuff.

Later, though, the Páez girl, weary of a heart full of nothing but fine clothes, had taken it into her head to go religious. She had sought out the canon theologian in a civil way, as the canon theologian liked to be sought out; and she had found him. They had come to an understanding. For Don Fermín this thin, dry, cold girl was merely the way to the heart of Don Francisco, a man who used his millions to buy influence. But Olvido had also conceived the unwise idea of falling mystically in love (as she put it to herself) with the canon. He pretended not to notice and took advantage of this, the girl's latest folly, to win her father over all the sooner. Since it was clear to him that the capricious little American girl's imaginary passion was not dangerous, he had not turned her away, as he had done with other women who were less timid and offered greater temptation to the flesh. De Pas had a plan: to marry Olvido to whomever he chose, something he was confident of achieving. There was as yet no candidate: this *prospect* was to be the prize for some great service rendered him, he did not yet know how or in what straits.

On that morning, as always, he was received in Villa Páez in state, to use Don Francisco's expression.

As the canon theologian trod those carpets, looked at himself in those mirrors as large as the doors, let his body sensually sink into the yielding softness of that ostentatious luxury, openly extravagant and overwhelming, he felt himself transported to regions which he believed to be appropriate for his lofty spirit. Surely, he thought with pride, he had been born for such surroundings; but his mother's avarice, the inadequacy of his own fortune to attain such splendour, his position as a priest, and the need to present a façade of modesty, even of poverty, kept him away from this, his natural environment. When the canon entered these rooms and halls his suave manner became still more suave, he manipulated his cloak and folded down his soutane with easy elegance, and moved his hands, eyes and head with a worldly distinction which never degenerated, however, into the brazenness of the priest who renounces the modesty of his habit when he sets foot in the palaces of high society (or their substitutes). De Pas never stopped being the canon theologian, but he knew how to demonstrate, with a gesture, a smile, or a look, that a prebendary can take his place in society as well as anyone else. This gift, together with the physical qualities with which he was endowed, and his reputation as an eloquent speaker and a man of great influence and talent, made him, as the Marchioness de Vegallana said, 'a very presentable priest'.

Don Francisco Páez and his daughter begged Don Fermín to have luncheon with them – nobody else was coming, it would be a family meal, just the three of them.

'Just the three of us!' said Olvido, melting for a moment.

The canon theologian, standing in a doorway, his fair hand holding a velvet curtain and drawing it into creases, made a graceful bow, smiled, and shook his small, finely modelled head, with a certain epicene coquetry.

'Go on, Papa! Grab hold of him,' said Olvido in an imploring tone, drawling the words, which seemed to come out of her nose.

'I cannot stay.'

'He's very stubborn, my child, let him be. He doesn't want us to show him our gratitude for the licence to have a private oratory and for Don Anselmo's permit to say mass twice the same day.'

'You must thank His Holiness for that.'

'Yes, yes, His Holiness likes the look of me and that's why he's granting me these favours, I'm sure.'

The canon smiled, ready to escape should they try to seize him.

'But let us have a reason, give us a reason,' cried Olvido, her normal icy self again.

The canon coloured a little.

He had to tell a lie.

'Another Francisco invited me, three days ago, to take luncheon with him today. I cannot fail to attend, it would be taken as a snub. You know what these small towns are like – tongues would start wagging.'

No such thing had happened. Nobody had invited him to luncheon. His mother expected him home as on any other day.

Nevertheless, when he declined the spontaneous, cordial invitation, which on any other occasion would have gratified him, he was acting on a presentiment. He did not know why he imagined that he would be invited to luncheon at the Vegallanas' house, the last one he intended to visit that morning. Why should they invite him? What was more, luncheon there was taken very late, in the French style, although Doña Rufina kept changing the times of meals and lunching when she felt like it. In any case, they did not usually celebrate Paquito Vegallana's name-day with a party, nor had they invited him, nor . . . but, nevertheless, he had left that visit until last. And why should he prefer the marquis's table to that of Páez, which was no less splendid? Although he tried to avoid the answer to this captious question, his conscience provided him with it, like something bursting in his ears, before he had time to prepare a lie. 'The judge's wife sometimes has luncheon with the Vegallanas, especially on days like this, because they regard her as one of the family.'

'But what did the family, or the judge's wife, or the Vegallanas' luncheon matter to him?'

After visiting two more important Pacos and a devout Paca, the canon theologian, with something of an appetite, a healthy appetite, walked through the arcades of the Plaza Nueva into the Calle de los Canónigos, crossed the Calle de los Recoletos and reached the Calle de la Rúa, and in a tremulous voice asked the Marquis de Vegallana's doorman, a dwarf dressed in whimsical livery:

'Is the marquis's son at home?'

The courtyard door crashed open and peals of laughter came out. The canon recognized Visita's voice, shrieking:

'No, sir! They are not blue.'

'Yes they are, madam – blue with white stripes,' Paco retorted, clapping his hands.

'Do you want to bet on it?'

'You silly thing,' said another, softer voice from a first-floor window, 'don't you believe him, nobody saw a thing. I was even lower and I didn't see anything.'

This voice was the voice of Ana Ozores.

The canon's ears buzzed. He walked into the courtyard.

XIII

Sunlight poured into the Yellow Salon and into the marchioness's boudoir through the great balcony windows, opened wide, for the sun was one of the guests, and so was the breeze, which was indiscreetly stirring the fringes around the satin pelmets, the prisms of the chandeliers and the pages of the books scattered over the occasional table and the console tables. Floods of light and fresh air were flowing in and torrents of gaiety were streaming out – bursts of laughter whose echoes would die away in the deserted streets of La Encimada, and the sounds of skirts, starched petticoats, the rustling cloaks of the clergy, chairs being fetched and carried, fluttering fans. Salon and boudoir were filled with all the best people in Vetusta. Doña Rufina, in electric blue, her hair powdered and adorned with fresh flowers which, for some unknown reason, looked like artificial ones, reigned but did not govern in this society, so much to her liking, where canons laughed, fatuous aristocrats played the peacock, young girls flirted, mature women displayed firm, white flesh, provincial deputies solved the region's problems and itinerant dandies imitated the affected manners of their counterparts in Madrid.

The marchioness lay on a sateen-upholstered chaise-longue by her boudoir windows, delightedly inhaling fresh air. People were arguing in loud voices. Near her, standing triumphant, his right hand voluptuously waving a fan inlaid with mother-of-pearl, Gloucester was displaying his handsome twisted figure. Over his other hand, as if it were a picture-nail, hung his cloak, which fell in graceful folds towards the floor but came to a halt in a gleaming mound of black cloth upon the cherry-coloured skirt of the ever-showy Obdulia Fandiño. Obdulia was seated on an ancient stool (stolen from the marquis's Antiques Gallery) at the feet of the marchioness and of the archdeacon and was leaning over the lap of her noble friend in a position more winsome than modest or decorous. These three formed a group in the windowed balcony, while in the boudoir itself various people sitting and standing here and there listened to Gloucester: three other canons, the Vegallanas' personal chaplain Don Aniceto, three noble ladies, the civil governor's wife, Joaquinito Orgaz, and two other Vetustan youths, students in Madrid.

In loud voices, between guffaws of laughter, jokes repeated from generation to generation and from town to town, and ancient formulae, they were arguing whether woman can serve God as well in the world as in the cloister; and whether more virtue is needed to confront the temptations which assail a good mother and faithful wife living in the world than to shut oneself away in a convent.

All the ladies except one – tall, corpulent, wearing Carmelite garb, a lady who looked like a friar – maintained that the good wife living in the world possesses greater merit than the bride of Christ.

The governor's wife grew excited, tapping the archdeacon's head with her closed fan as she spoke and calling him *my dear sir*.

Gloucester defended the cause of the cloister but, out of gallantry, finally beat a retreat, smiling and fanning himself.

In the salon the talk was about local politics. A great conflict had been created for the government, in the opinion of everyone present, by the lord mayor and the widow of the Marquis de Corujedo, who had both demanded the same tobacconist's licence, the licence for the important stall in the Mall, for their respective protégés.

The financial secretary was telling his listeners that he had said it was a problem for the civil governor to settle. The civil governor had consulted the government by telegram (his wife had just said so) and the government now had to decide between snubbing the conservative lady who controlled the most votes in Vetusta and snubbing one of the firmest supporters of the cause of law and order, the lord mayor. Opinion was divided. The Marquis de Vegallana and Ripamilán, who was in the middle of the group, turning this way and that, declared that if they were the government they would give the licence to the widow. 'Ladies must come first!'

Blunderbuss – Pepe Ronzal, the member of the provincial standing committee – believed, together with the majority of those present, the financial secretary included, that for reasons of state the mayor's claim should be preferred, even though it was rumoured that he wanted the licence for a cast-off mistress.

'As you can see, it's a scandal!' said the marquis, all of whose illegitimate children lived in remote country villages. 'The man has no idea of what it means to be discreet.'

'I don't mind so much about that,' said the archpriest. 'There's nothing wrong with wanting to pay off sacred debts. What is wrong is having contracted them in the first place. But his rival is a lady!'

While the occupants of the salon and the boudoir argued in this way, and in many others, joyful, boisterous races were being run through the inner rooms on the first floor, through the dining-room, through corridors, and up and down the stairway which led to the courtyard and the garden, by Paco Vegallana, who was celebrating his name-day, Visitación, Edelmira (the marchioness's niece, a girl of fifteen who looked twenty), Don Saturnino Bermúdez and Señor Quintanar. The judge's wife and Don Alvaro Mesía were witnessing these innocent games from a dining-room window which overlooked the courtyard.

Quintanar had asked Paco for a smoking-jacket to wear instead of his machine-knitted frock-coat, in which he kept entangling his legs. The smoking-jacket was both too short and too loose for him. It was made of palest alpaca.

On the stairs the canon theologian found Visitación and Quintanar, who were searching every nook and cranny for the ex-magistrate's cigar-case, hidden by Paco and Edelmira. Don Saturnino, pale and with rings around his eyes, smiling a courteous smile from ear to ear, was behind them, alone, also acting the fool, in the most unfortunate way imaginable. It was sad to see him enjoying himself thus, jumping about, imitating the others' rowdy gaiety. But there, it was his duty! As a relative, an intimate in that house and one of those who were going to stay for luncheon, he had to do as all the others did – run around, join in the hubbub, even pinch the ladies if the ladies came to hand. But he was always alone. Whenever he wanted to say something to the judge's wife, Visitación or Edelmira, they left him talking to the air, their attention irresistibly straying elsewhere. It was not that they did not know better; it was just that Bermúdez's sentences were so complicated and consisted of so many main clauses and subordinate clauses that to hear out a whole paragraph of them would have been too much of an ordeal. When he saw the canon theologian he saw his chance to escape; now he had an excuse to recover his decorum. He greeted De Pas with 'the politeness which characterized him' and prepared to walk with him to the salon. Paco, from a distance, had met the canon with a curt, hurried greeting, because at that moment he was making off with Quintanar's cigar-case to hide it in the garden, pursued by Edelmira, his plumpest, bounciest and ruddiest girl-cousin.

'The boy goes mad when he starts his tomfoolery,' said Bermúdez, excusing his relation's conduct and receiving the canon in the character of a member of the family.

Don Fermín looked out of the corner of his eye at the judge's wife and Don Alvaro as they talked to each other in the dining-room window. He pretended not to see them and, his cheeks flushed, was ushered by Don Saturnino into the salon.

The grave gentlemen there received him with the most flattering demonstrations of respect and esteem.

'My dear Canon Theologian!'

'How good it is to see you!'

'The Antonelli of Vetusta!'[1]

The marquis gave him an embrace which was envied by a small priest, the marquis's personal chaplain.

Ripamilán shook Don Fermín's hand with effusive affection, and they walked together into the boudoir.

The three canons came to their feet and the lady who looked like a friar smiled with satisfaction and murmured:

'Oh, my dear Vicar-General!'

'Thanks be to God, you lost soul,' cried the marchioness, as she sat up a little and held out a hand which, thanks to his height, the canon was able to take in his own, arching his body with elegant ease over the appealing form of the cherry-attired Obdulia, who, from where she sat, seemed to be trying to swallow the handsome priest down into the depths of her large black eyes. The archdeacon remained with his fan open and motionless, like the sail of a windmill on a still day. He suddenly realized that he had been supplanted. He was no longer prima donna but a mere member of the chorus and, indeed, his discourse, to which priests and ladies had been listening with delight, died away without anybody missing it. Such was the eclipse of Gloucester that he even thought he felt cold, as if the sun had suddenly disappeared.

'That was what always happened; he had good reason to hate that man.' Nevertheless, Mourelo, who was a clergyman of the world, hid his feelings yet again, held out his hand to his enemy, and accompanied this gesture with a torrent of guttural cries signifying his immense joy. 'Greetings, dear fellow, greetings!' and he slapped the other man's back.

The canon theologian could not savour this ordinary and commonplace triumph at his ease, because he found himself thinking about the couple in the dining-room window. As he gave his modest, discreet replies to all these friends, his imagination was out in the courtyard. The minutes were slipping by and the two people in the dining-room still had not come.

'Was Anita going to have luncheon in the marchioness's house? If she was, she would not go to confess that afternoon, as she had said in her letter.'

The apparent cordiality and expansive happiness of all those present concealed an undercurrent of rancour and envy. The ladies, clergymen and gentlemen were divided into two hostile camps: the envious and the envied, in other words, those few who had been invited to lunch and all those who had not. Although there was a great deal of talking about a great many things, the thought obsessing everyone was the invitation. No one referred to it, yet no one thought of anything else. People started to make their farewells, and those who were leaving dissembled their indignation and shame, considering themselves humiliated, ridiculed almost. Some young men blurted out their goodbyes and slunk away. The ladies were the least successful at pretending to be untroubled and indifferent, and some of them even blushed as they left. Gloucester was one of those who had not been invited. The doubt which tormented him was: 'What about *him*? Has De Pas been invited?' Gloucester did not know the answer and was unwilling to depart without discovering it. Since it was getting late and the boudoir and the salon were emptying little by little, the canon theologian felt that he too should leave. He approached the marchioness but could not bring himself to say goodbye and instead spoke about the first thing that came into his head. At that moment Visitación entered the boudoir, eyes and cheeks aflame, and 'by the gentlemen's leave' had private words with the marchioness and Obdulia. The three ladies surrounded the canon theologian and by the gentlemen's leave (the gentlemen being by now reduced to the archdeacon and two insignificant Vetustan youths) a private confabulation took place, with bursts of laughter, and protests from the canon – protests as endearing as they were elegant, to judge from the facial expressions which accompanied them. In the ladies' low voices there was pleading in the form of complaints, coquetry void of sex, and coquetry full of it, although expressed with due modesty. Gloucester pretended to listen to the dull young men as he devoured the other group with the corner of his eye. 'There could be no doubt about it, they were imploring him to stay for luncheon.' The confabulation came to an end, Obdulia and Visitación ran noisily from the room, making a show of the familiarity with which they treated the Vegallanas, and the young men took their leave. The marchioness, the canon theologian and Gloucester were left in the boudoir. There was a moment of silence. The archdeacon allowed himself one minute more, to see if the other man took his leave as well. In the salon voices could be heard saying goodbye to the marquis. Only the people invited to lunch remained in the house. Gloucester, gathering strength from despair, rose to his feet, held out his hand to Doña Rufina and left the room, joking and bowing and with many a forced laugh. He was blind with mortification and fury. 'Inviting that man to luncheon – a holder of a simple prebend – and snubbing *him*, a senior dignitary! The enemy triumphant, always! But he'd make him pay for it, one day.'

In the porch, as Gloucester threw his cloak around his shoulders (even though it was a hot day), he thought: 'This marchioness woman is nothing but a – go-between, a bawd! She's set her mind on that young woman's ruin! She's set her mind on *forcing him down her throat!*' He walked away thinking savage thoughts and searching for a *decorous* way of communicating these thoughts to others.

The guests for luncheon were Quintanar and his wife, Obdulia Fandiño, Visitación, Doña Petronila Rianzares (the lady who looked like a friar), Ripamilán, Alvaro Mesía, Saturnino Bermúdez and Joaquín Orgaz. In addition, the canon theologian and a few other illustrious Vetustans, for instance Doctor Somoza, were invited at the last moment. Edelmira counted as one of the family because she was a guest in the house.

Paco's name-day was usually celebrated away from home rather than in this way. On this occasion, however, a private party had been improvised and luncheon was to be taken, for once, at the normal Spanish hour, so as to leave time in the afternoon to drive in the family carriages to the estate known as El Vivero, where the marquis owned a house surrounded by forests, and a tannery set up in the old style. They were going to inspect the hunting dogs and a St Bernard which Paco had bought a few days before. They were his pride and joy. After prostitutes, the Young Marquis's greatest admiration was for tame animals, in particular dogs and horses.

Inviting the canon theologian had been a plot hatched by Quintanar, Paco and Visitación, who had conceived the idea. It was a joke she wanted to play on Mesía. She wanted to see the confessor and the devil – the tempter – face to face. Quintanar was told that De Pas was being invited so that they could watch Obdulia flirting with him and poor love-stricken Bermúdez raging in silence. The idea seemed a good one to Quintanar, but he said that 'he washed his hands of the matter, because the plan had a certain irreverence about it, in spite of the fact that, as they well knew, he considered priests to be no different from other men'.

'In another way,' added the ex-magistrate, 'I am glad that Don Fermín will have luncheon with us, for that will take the blessed idea of going to confess this afternoon out of my wife's head. I want to accustom her to seeing her new confessor at close quarters, so as to convince her that he is no different from other men. That is to say – and with all due respect – perhaps you could attempt to get him drunk for me.'

Paco did not want to prejudice Mesía's plans, which were, perhaps, to some extent responsible for the party, but it struck him that upsetting the canon theologian would be great fun and most piquant if, as Visitación suspected, it really did vex this illustrious priest to see the judge's wife delivered to the secular arm of Mesía.

Visitación had told Paco straightaway that she knew everything, that Alvaro did not keep any secrets from her, either.

'But what about Ana? Has she told you anything?'

'Ana? Never once. She's a good one she is. But just you wait.'

'Of course, this is only a – spiritual thing.'

'Oh, yes, highly spiritual.'

'Because otherwise we – we wouldn't lend ourselves . . . As you can see – poor Don Víctor . . .'

'I can see well enough! Fun and games, just fun and games, but you'll soon see them sticking in our precious canon's throat.' This was how Visitación spoke to close friends.

'He'll have comfort from Obdulia. She's laying siege to him, and she likes him better than Don Saturn or the bishop or my good friend Joaquín.'

'But he hates her. She's always causing scandal. He doesn't like that sort of woman.'

'You hate him, that's for sure.'

'I just can't stand hypocrites. And listen to me: it's a good thing for you if the canon does stay for lunch.'

'Why?'

'Because then Obdulia will leave you alone and you'll be able to concentrate on your young cousin. That's something I really wouldn't forgive you for! I'm a protector of innocence. I shall be watching you.'

'Don't be so silly. The mere fact that she's a guest in my house is enough to make me behave myself.'

'Oh yes! That's a good one, such a well-behaved young gentleman! Well I don't trust you an inch.'

Edelmira interrupted their dialogue and without further ado it was agreed to ask the marchioness to invite the canon theologian to luncheon and, if necessary, to beg him to stay.

Visita arranged everything in a trice.

As she always did. If Visitación was in the company nobody else was allowed to do a thing. Her whole life was devoted to her passion for managing other people's affairs, sucking other people's sweets and eating in other people's houses. In her own house sat her modest husband, the humble bank clerk, a small man with the face of an aged angel, stroking his little grey moustache and caring for the children. Visitación demanded that much of him. She wasn't going to do everything. Who managed the household? Who rescued it when it was in difficulties? Who warded off threats of dismissal from the bank? Who overcame all the problems of the family budget? Who was the family's financial wizard? Visitación. Well then, they must allow her to go out and enjoy herself, they couldn't expect her to stay at home all day long. And she was such a fast worker that everything was ready for the day, the house clean and lunch prepared, before other women had even started their sweeping or lit their fires. The house was not perhaps quite as clean as it might be, but the bank clerk's wife, always on active service everywhere, had a clear conscience as she left home to hunt for news, gossip, lumps of sugar and favour in high places.

Her latest campaign, perhaps the most important one she had ever waged, she called *forcing him down her throat*. The 'her' was Anita. Ever since Visita's conversation with Mesía the previous afternoon she had thought of nothing else. That very morning she had gone to Quintanar's house and found him pacing his study in his shirt-sleeves. His embroidered braces, which in fine brightly coloured silk represented every incident in the hunting of a fabulous stag with horns of improbable size, hung at his sides. Don Víctor, engaged in fastening a collar-stud, was biting his lower lip and stretching his head upwards as if to implore supernatural assistance from on high. Visitación walked into the study by mistake.

'Oh! forgive me,' she said, 'am I intruding?'

'No, my child, no, you have come at precisely the right moment. This blessed collar-stud . . .'

While the lady, without removing her gloves, fastened the collar-stud for Don Víctor, he began to give her an account of his irrevocable plans for the entertainment of his wife.

'This is my programme.'

He expounded it from A to Z.

Visitación approved every section. They went to Ana's boudoir, where Ana seemed to be trying to hide as she hastily sealed the letter which a little later Don Fermín would read to his mother.

Almost by main force, Visitación and Quintanar made Ana dress 'decently' and go out with them. Visita left them in the cathedral square and went to see the bishop about the Free Fraternity. They would meet again in the Vegallanas' house, for the marchioness had written early that morning to the Quintanars asking them to luncheon and announcing the day's programme. Ana had an argument with her husband. She wanted to go to confess, she had said so in a letter to the vicar-general, and he wasn't a man to be sent scurrying here and there on false errands. 'Never mind about that! Don Víctor was prepared to be inflexible.'

'You can go to confess, if you feel able to do so, after luncheon with the Vegallanas; and you will have to be quick about it, so that we can proceed immediately to El Vivero. On that I am firm!'

And off they went to congratulate various Franciscos and Franciscas. At a quarter past one they were at the marquis's house.

The first thing to meet Ana's eyes was Don Alvaro.

As she replied to his courteous greeting her fear was that she would blush and her voice tremble. She looked towards her husband in some alarm but he was shaking Don Alvaro by the hand with affectionate effusiveness. Quintanar found Mesía a very agreeable fellow and, although they did not often meet, every time they spoke they tightened the bonds of an incipient friendship which threatened to become an intimate and lasting one. In Quintanar's eyes Don Alvaro possessed the rare merit of not being stubborn. In Vetusta, according to the worthy Aragonese ex-magistrate, everyone was stubborn, but that paragon of gentlemanly excellence never insisted on upholding an absurd opinion – he always ended by granting that Quintanar was right. Quintanar would say, behind his handsome friend's back: 'If he went to Madrid he would get on wonderfully – with that fine figure of his, and that air about him, and his way with people! Oh, he is going to do great things!'

Ana suddenly decided to control herself, to treat Don Alvaro like any other man, without suspicious reserve, remembering that, after all, there were no ties between them – there could and indeed must be no ties between them.

A few minutes later, Mesía was skilfully cornering the judge's wife by a dining-room window while Víctor went with Paco to his rooms to don the short loose smoking-jacket. In order to remain cool and calm, Ana had to keep telling herself that there had never been any serious ties between them, and that the looks with which she might have emboldened him were not commitments for which a man of the world could call her to account. Ana's ideas about men of the world were derived from what she had read in novels, since she had never met them on this test-ground.

Don Alvaro avoided any reference to their brief encounter in the park the previous night, but he spoke with greater familiarity, in an intimate tone which he had never used with her before. They had seldom spoken to each other and had never done so alone. Ana was on speaking terms with everyone in Vetusta, but most of her relationships with men were distant ones, and her only close gentlemen-friends were Paco and Frillity. She was not an expansive person and her invariable amiability did not draw people out but, on the contrary, inhibited them. Visita declared that there was no door into that little heart of hers or if there was, Visita had never found the key to it.

Don Alvaro talked well and at length in a candid, natural way, attempting to please the judge's wife with wholesome sentiments rather than with brilliant original ideas. It was plain to see that he was in search of friendliness and cordiality and that he was presenting himself as a straightforward man with his heart in the right place. He laughed in a frank and jovial manner, opening his mouth wide and displaying a perfect set of teeth. Ana considered the way in which Mesía handled this strange situation to be in excellent taste. But whenever he was silent she was revisited by her fears, imagining that he, too, was thinking about the ties between them – about his appearance, his fiendish appearance, the night before, about their walk through the streets together and about all their other meetings, which he in mysterious ways had sought, requested, pursued, and to which she had implicitly assented like a coward and a criminal.

Don Víctor was not much taller than Ana; but Don Alvaro had to lean over as he spoke, to make his breath brush against her small graceful head. He was like a protective shadow, a shelter, a support; it was good to be near that fortress of a man. As she listened to her handsome companion, her head bowed, looking down at the flag-stones in the courtyard, all she could glimpse, out of the corner of her eye, was his immaculate, light-coloured top-coat. Whenever Don Alvaro made any vigorous movement he left in the air a perfume which was delicious the first time she noticed it, but afterwards fearsome; it was a perfume which must go to one's head very quickly;

she did not know what it was, but it must be good tobacco and other purely masculine things which only elegant men possessed. Sometimes his hand came to rest upon the window-sill; and then, unable to prevent it, Ana saw long, slender fingers, white skin, blue veins, oval finger-nails polished and neatly trimmed. And, if she lowered her eyes still further so that he should not think that she was admiring his hands, she saw trousers which fell away in an elegant curve to long slender feet in a pair of shoes far smarter than any others in Vetusta. It could not be at all sinful to acknowledge that this was a pleasant sight, and furthermore that it was only right and proper that it should be so.

Ana could hear vague sounds from the kitchen – where Pedro shouted his words of command as he organized the preparations for lunch – mingling with the murmur of the fountains in the courtyard and the laughter and cries of her husband, Visita, Edelmira and Paco as they rushed to and fro up and down stairs, along passages, around the garden, throughout the house.

She had not noticed the arrival of the vicar-general. Visita came and whispered in her ear:

'You can have your confession here and now if you like, my dear, because your father-in-God's turned up. He'll be having lunch with you today.'

Ana shivered and walked away from Mesía without looking at him again.

'Hullo hullo hullo,' said Don Víctor, entering the room with robust, ruddy-faced Edelmira on his arm. 'So, my dear wife, you are having a little tête-à-tête with this gentleman, are you? Well, here am I with my own partner, yes indeed, in just revenge for your infidelity.'

Only Edelmira laughed at this witticism, a new one for her. They all walked to the salon, where the other guests were gathered. Obdulia was talking to the canon theologian and Joaquinito Orgaz, while the marquis was arguing with Bermúdez, who was tilting his head to the right, opening his mouth in a smile from ear to ear, and calling in question the magnate's assertions with the greatest courtesy imaginable.

'Yes indeed, I would be quite happy to have St Peter's Church demolished and the market built . . .'

'Oh, come, your Lordship! I do not think that you would really go so far. Your political tenets . . .'

'My tenets are quite another matter. The fruit and vegetable market cannot continue to be held in the open air, exposed to the elements.'

'But St Peter's is a great monument and a glorious inheritance from the past.'

'It's a ruin.'

'That is perhaps something of an exaggeration.'

The canon intervened, so as to escape from Obdulia, who

was already laying siege to him, as Paco and Visita had foreseen.

When the judge's wife walked into the room De Pas involuntarily
cut short a measured, elegant phrase and bowed a somewhat guarded
greeting.

Behind Ana appeared Mesía. His left cheek was aglow and he was
stroking his silky blond moustache. He walked in looking straight
ahead like a man who could see what was in his thoughts rather than
what lay before him. De Pas held out a hand and Mesía shook it,
saying:

'My dear Canon Theologian. This is a great pleasure.'

On the rare occasions when these two gentlemen conversed they
did so with extreme formality. Ana saw them standing side by side,
both of them tall, but Mesía a little taller, both of them well-built and
good-looking, but each in his own way: Don Fermín of more powerful
build, Don Alvaro's body of nobler proportions; the priest's expression
and looks indicative of superior intelligence, the dandy's features
closer to perfection.

Don Alvaro was already beginning to distrust and even fear the
vicar-general. But the vicar-general did not suspect that Don Alvaro
might be the enemy who was tempting the judge's wife. If he did not
like the man it was because he considered his influence in Vetusta to
be a danger to his own influence there and because he knew that,
although he was not a declared or outspoken adversary of the Church,
neither was he on the Church's side. Yet when Don Fermín saw Don
Alvaro by the dining-room window deep in conversation with Anita,
and saw both of them so oblivious to everybody else, he was seized
by an anxiety which grew while he waited for them to appear in the
salon.

Ana smiled at the canon. In her smile there was a mixture of open,
noble tenderness and chaste humility signalled by a fleeting blush –
an involuntary reference to the secrets she had confessed the previous
afternoon. She remembered everything they had said to each other;
and she also remembered that she had spoken to him as she had
never spoken before, her ears and her heart rejoicing at his words of
hope and consolation, at his promises of light and poetry and of a life
full of meaning, a life dedicated to something good, great and worthy
of what she felt within herself, of all that lay in the depths of her soul.
She had occasionally read something of the sort in books, but where
was the Vetustan who knew how to speak like that? Furthermore,
reading such good and beautiful ideas in books was very different
from hearing them from a man of flesh and blood with gentle warmth
in his voice, soft music in his speech, and honeyed sweetness in his
words and gestures. Ana recalled the letter she had written a few
hours earlier, and this was another delightful, mysterious link
between them, which sent a tingle through her body. The letter was

an innocent one, anybody could read it, and yet it was a letter about which she could talk to a man who was not her husband, a letter which this man might be carrying somewhere close to his body – and about which he, too, perhaps, was thinking.

Ana did not try to understand how this mildly sensual feeling could be reconciled with the clear conception she had of the kind of friendship which was growing between her and the canon. What she knew for certain was that in Don Fermín lay salvation – the promise of a virtuous life without boredom, replete with noble, poetic pursuits which demanded effort and sacrifice but which, for that very reason, lent dignity and grandeur to the dull, animal-like, unbearable existence of Vetusta. And now, being so certain that she could save herself from the frankly criminal temptation of Don Alvaro by giving herself to Don Fermín, she wished to defy the danger; and she allowed her eyes to come into contact with Don Alvaro's eyes, of an indeterminate grey, transparent, almost always cold, but sometimes flaring like beacons, their flames saying shameless things about which she had no right to complain. If, in alarm, Ana sought protection in the canon's eyes she only found veils of white flesh, those blank eyelids which were not even expressive of discretion as they were lowered at the precise moment prescribed by priestly modesty.

Don Fermín was not reluctant to look at women when he conversed with them. He looked at the judge's wife, too, when he conversed with her, because then his eyes were no more than a kind of punctuation for his speech: there was no feeling in them, only intelligence and orthography. But in silence and face to face he did not look at ladies, at least not if there were witnesses present.

Don Alvaro noticed that, although most of the guests were chatting together as they stood in the salon waiting to be called to table, Ana had sidled up to the canon and was talking to him in a low voice. She seemed somewhat agitated and was smiling and blushing.

Mesía recalled what Visitación had said the previous afternoon: *beware of the canon theologian, he knows a thing or two, and not just about theology.* But Mesía did not need any encouragement to think obscene thoughts about priests and women. He did not believe in virtue. The version of materialism which was his religion led him to believe that nobody was capable of resisting natural impulses, that all priests were therefore hypocrites, and that ill-contained lust gushed out of them however and whenever it could. Don Alvaro was well able to present himself as a character from a sentimental, idealistic novel when circumstances demanded; but in the sanctuary of his conscience, to use the language of *El Lábaro*, he was a systematic cynic. He both envied and feared the priests to whom his mistresses confessed and indeed, whenever he exercised sufficient influence over a woman, he forbade her to confess. 'He knew all about such matters.' During the moments of unrestrained passion into which he dragged *a female* whenever he could, he forced his victim to bare her soul and contemplated her self-degradation, achieving the profound enjoyment of a new experience as the aberrations of her senses rose to her tongue and between absurd caresses and ridiculous kisses shameful confessions poured forth – womanly secrets which Mesía savoured, and stored in his memory. Like a bad priest who abuses the confessional, Don Alvaro knew all about the comical or disgusting weaknesses of many husbands and lovers, his predecessors; and in the chronicles of scandal which constituted his store of obscenities, an important section was formed by the lascivious pretensions of *soliciting priests* and their perversions, sometimes pitiful, more often repugnant and odious. Proud of his knowledge, Mesía drew general conclusions from it. He believed himself to be on firm ground, supported by 'facts repeated times without number', when he affirmed that woman looked to the priest for the secret pleasure and spiritual voluptuousness of temptation, while the priest, without exception, abused the advantages offered to him by an institution 'whose sacred character Don Alvaro did not question' in public, but which he denied when he privately turned back into a French materialist in octavo, a *commis voyageur materialist*.

He did not believe, God forbid, that the canon theologian looked to his new spiritual daughter for the satisfaction of gross, base appetites. De Pas would not dare to go as far as that and, anyway, it just was not possible to attempt such an outrage against a lady of her standing. But 'insinuatingly, insinuatingly' (he repeated the word as he mused on the matter) 'it's more likely than not that in the end he'll try to seduce this beautiful woman, in the flower of her youth, with nothing to do and no one to love her. Yes, this priest is after what I'm after, but he's using a different system and all the resources available to him as a priest and confessor. I should have come sooner, to prevent it, but I can't do anything about it for the moment, I haven't enough authority over her yet for that.' These thoughts, and others like them, left Mesía in a bad mood and furious with the canon theologian, whose influence in Vetusta, especially over the weak, devout sex, had been annoying him for a long time.

'So now I can't come this afternoon?' Ana was saying in a soft, humble, tremulous voice.

'Certainly not,' replied the canon, his voice like a breeze amidst flowers. 'It is of paramount importance to obey Don Víctor's wishes and even anticipate them whenever possible. This afternoon must be devoted to enjoyment, pure enjoyment. You can confess early tomorrow morning.'

'But you will have to put yourself to trouble – you are not in the habit of going to the cathedral at such an hour.'

'No matter, tomorrow I shall, it is my duty – and a great satisfaction to be of service to you, dear friend.'

The ineffable tenderness which Ana found in what she heard was not contained in the words themselves, words of commonplace gallantry, but in the voice, in the gestures, in a perfume of *spiritual incense* which seemed to reach down into her very soul.

They agreed that early the next morning Don Fermín would wait for her in his side-chapel to hear her confession.

'And in the meantime, no thoughts of serious matters. Enjoy yourself, run about, go on the rampage, as Señor Quintanar commands, for in doing so he not only has right but also sound reason on his side. It is most probable that your – sad feelings, those preoccupations of yours' – the canon coloured slightly and his voice trembled a little because he was alluding to the confidences of the previous afternoon – 'that anguish of which you complain and accuse yourself has a great deal to do with your nerves and can be cured – physically at least – by this new life which you are being advised and indeed required to adopt. Yes, yes, and why should it not be so? When, my daughter, we know each other better, when you know my ideas on the subject of *worldly pleasures*, you will understand that, for a firm, well-nourished soul, they can be an innocent pastime, even an insipid, insignificant one; a useful distraction from which we can benefit as from a tasteless but efficacious medicine.'

Ana understood perfectly. 'What the canon meant was that when she became capable of enjoying the delights of virtue, she would regard all those entertainments in which people seek a sense of physical well-being as commonplace, childish, dull games, the only purpose of which was to provide her with some relaxation. Yes, she understood. It was all rather like that already. She derived so little amusement from balls, theatrical performances, promenades, banquets!'

Quintanar approached them, and when he heard Don Fermín say that exercise was hygienic, and a happy carefree life very healthy, he applauded with enthusiasm. His satisfaction grew still greater when he discovered that Ana no longer intended to go to confession that afternoon.

'It would be absurd!' said Don Fermín. 'This afternoon you are off to the country, to El Vivero.'

'Luncheon, come to luncheon!' cried the marchioness from the salon door.

'Sacred word!' exclaimed the marquis.

Everyone said something in honour of the announcement and, all happily talking and gesticulating, 'without ceremony', for there was no standing on ceremony in Doña Rufina's house, they made their way to the dining-room. The marquis and marchioness knew well enough how to behave towards guests according to all the rules of the provincial aristocracy's cloying etiquette; but in these parties of close friends, from which aristocratic relatives who did not approve of certain liberties were excluded, they behaved as any rich plebeian might behave – although without losing, even when at their most expansive, certain innate airs of distinction and of Vetustan nobility. The marquis possessed the art of showing himself to be a gentleman while acting as plain as a pikestaff, as he said in the humblest prose ever spoken by an aristocrat.

'The luncheon was an informal one, they all knew that.' This meant that, although their guests would be treated like kings, the marquis and the marchioness did not intend to forgo their gastronomical whims and manias in deference to them. At that table informality did not mean scarcity or slovenliness. Livery was laid aside, as were tiresome ceremonies (together with the silver dinner-service inherited from a Vegallana who had been a high official in Mexico), but not the exquisite wines, aperitifs and hors-d'œuvres for which that table was renowned, or, in short, any of the finest products of the flora and fauna of the province from land, air and water. Other aristocrats might contest Vegallana's supremacy as regards nobility or wealth, but not one of them would dare deny that the marquis's kitchen and cellar were the finest in Vetusta.

The marchioness usually had girls of some twenty summers to wait on her: girls fresh and fair and as clean as new pennies.

'No doubt it's in bad taste,' she would say, 'the sort of thing poor people do, but my guests are always happy to be served by waitresses.'

'For I've observed', she would add, 'that as a general rule ladies don't like menservants at table; they don't take any notice of them. But a man always likes a pretty girl – men like girls with everything.'

Paquito had welcomed his mamma's innovation: 'That's right! Having girls to wait on one seems to cheer one up. It reminds me of the refreshment-stalls and some of the cafés at the Exhibition.' The marquis was indifferent to the change. He did not sin at home or indeed anywhere else in town.

The dining-room was square, with views of the garden and the courtyard through four long windows which almost reached the low ceiling. In each window the marchioness had piled flowers in pots, jardinières and Japanese vases of dubious authenticity. The bright metallic colours of this flower-show contrasted with the sombre matt tones of the walnut coffered ceiling and the moulding and panels of the great glass-fronted cupboard which ran around the dining-room, interrupted only by doors, windows and a large sofa standing against one of the walls. These were decorated with pictures – wherever there was any room for them – in poor taste, even though they all depicted the many activities connected with good eating. There was one of a hunt set in times that Vegallana fancied to be feudal: the lady of the castle upon her palfrey, the page at her feet with the hawk on his fist raised above his head, the heron up in the clouds, the colour of egg-yolk, and behind them the lord of the forests, of the castle on the cliffs, and of the town just visible in the distance. . . . Facing it was a scene from a novel by Feuillet,[2] also a hunt, but without heron or hawk or feudal lord; a corner of a wood, a lady mounted side-saddle and a horseman riding after her, ready – to judge from appearances – to kiss her hand as soon as he could grab it. Elsewhere was a table in disorder; further on an eating house, the realism of which made it intolerable after meals. And finally, up on the ceiling, staring down from a medallion on the pendant in the middle of the room, was Don Jaime Balmes,[3] nobody knows why or wherefore. What is the Catalan philosopher doing up there? The marquis has never been prepared to explain it to anybody. Bermúdez considers it to be an absurdity; Ronzal says that it is 'an anachronism'; but in spite of such murmuring the leader of the conservative party of Vetusta keeps Balmes on his medallion and refuses to give any explanations.

The marchioness thinks that this is one of her husband's least tiresome follies.

The guests sat down. The only earmarked places were those on either side of the marchioness and the marquis. On the right of Doña Rufina sat Ripamilán, and on her left the canon theologian; on the right of the marquis sat Doña Petronila Rianzares, and on his left Don Víctor Quintanar. All the other guests sat wherever they liked, or wherever they could. Paco sat between Edelmira and Visitación, the judge's wife between Ripamilán and Don Alvaro, Obdulia between the canon theologian and Joaquín Orgaz, Don Saturnino Bermúdez between Doña Petronila and the Vegallanas' chaplain. On Don Víctor's left was Don Robustiano Somoza, the dashing doctor to the aristocracy, who tied his napkin around his neck with an elegant knot.

Before the others had their soup the marquis helped himself to a great plateful of fried pilchards while he talked to Doña Petronila Rianzares about the demolition of St Peter's Church, an idea which she considered to be ignominious. Meanwhile, the guests made themselves busy with the choice, varied, delicious hors-d'œuvres. It was an informal meal, they all knew that, and customs of which they were all aware had to be respected. Vegallana always started with his pilchards; he would devour a few dozen and then rise from the table and discreetly disappear from the room. Following long-established usage, everyone pretended not to notice the marquis's absence, and meanwhile the soup arrived and was served. When the master of the house returned to his place he was a little pale, and perspiring.

'All right?' muttered the marchioness, formulating the question more with her look than with her lips.

Her husband replied with a nod which meant: 'Perfectly!' And helped himself to a generous bowlful of turtle soup. The pilchards were no longer inside him.

Another mystery, like Balmes on the ceiling.

The marchioness liked to concoct her own singular hodgepodges, to which, again, nobody any longer paid attention. She ate lettuce with almost every dish and sprinkled vinegar or spread mustard over everything. Her neighbours at table knew about her whims and looked after her solicitously, showing their long experience in the preparation of her vinegary mixtures. While Ripamilán, who was on his feet and jerking his head to and fro as if it were mounted on a spring, held a heated argument with his dear friend Don Víctor, he mixed the marchioness's third salad with all the dexterity of a smooth-running machine; and the lady let the diminutive canon proceed with his task, trusting him yet not taking her eyes off his hands, though certain of his complete success.

'My dear sir!' cried Ripamilán as he dissolved salt in oil and vinegar on Doña Rufina's plate by beating it all with the point of a knife. 'My dear sir, it's my belief that Señor Carraspique had every right to do so, and I don't know where you pick up these subversive ideas, ideas I have never heard from your lips in all these forty years we have known each other.'

'Pray listen to me, you rogue-priest!' exclaimed Quintanar, who was in excellent spirits and beginning to feel rejuvenated. 'I am perfectly certain of what I am saying, and neither you nor any other eighty-year-old ladies' man like you can give me lessons in morality. But, as a liberal . . .'

'Twiddle-twaddle!'

'More of a liberal today than yesterday, and tomorrow more than today.'

'Bravo! Bravo!' shouted Paco and Edelmira, who were also feeling youthful, and they made Don Víctor clink glasses with them.

It was all in jest. Neither was Don Víctor more of a liberal today than yesterday nor did he use formal words like 'pray' when talking to Ripamilán or consider him to be a ladies' man. It was just his way of expressing the cheerfulness imparted to everyone by the clear wine gleaming in fine glass, glinting gold, shining with the mysterious iridescence of a magic grotto – the amaranth and deep violet hues of the claret in which the most venturesome rays of the sun bathed after filtering through the green foliage which curtained the windows on the courtyard side. Why not be merry? Why not laugh and play the fool? All was contentment. Out in the garden were the sounds of water and trees swaying in the wind, and the frenzied singing of garrulous birds; from the courtyard windows came perfumes carried by the breeze, which had set all the leaves jingling. The fountains were an orchestra accompanying the boisterous banquet. Pepa and Rosa – one blonde and the other as dark as a mulatto, both wearing brightly coloured but well-cut, close-fitting dresses, cheerful, jaunty, as clean as an ermine, and sinuous and rustling as they walked – waited at table with grace, speed, good humour and skill, showing the men teeth like pearls and bending over with the dishes with coquettish humility. According to Ripamilán, such a luncheon served in such a way was pure milk and honey.

All the people sitting around the table responded to the cheerfulness in the air. They laughed, shouted, lavished attention on each other, complimented each other by means of discreet antiphrastic gibes. They all knew that an insolent attack meant its very opposite: it was shameless flattery.

The gaiety in the dining-room was echoed in the kitchen. When Pepa and Rosa returned there with the dirty plates they were still smiling at the scene which they had just left. In the whole house there was but one completely serious personage: Pedro the cook. His turn to enjoy himself would come later, but for now he thought only about his responsibility. He was coming and going, directing operations as if in a battle, and from time to time he looked in at the dining-room door and corrected minor mistakes in the service with magnetic looks which Pepa and Rosa obeyed like automata, well-disciplined like old soldiers in the midst of all the expansiveness and hubbub.

After Pedro, the least boisterous people in the house were the judge's wife and the canon theologian. From time to time they looked and smiled at each other. De Pas said a word to Anita now and again, leaning over behind the marchioness so that Anita could hear him, and at such moments Don Alvaro would observe them, silent, frowning, unaware that Visitación, seated by his side, was watching him. With a discreet touch of her foot the bank clerk's wife brought him out of his reverie.

'Things are getting hot, eh?' said Visita.

'What, what?' asked the marchioness, who was eating without a pause, happy in the midst of the racket. 'What's hot?'

'The peppers, my lady.'

Don Alvaro was grateful to Visitación for her warning and immersed himself once more in the general chit-chat, hiding as best he could his boredom, which he described in his own mind as 'sovereign'.

'What a strange thing! He was touching the dress and at times even feeling one of the knees of the judge's wife, the woman he desired – and when would another opportunity like this present itself? – yet he was bored. He believed he was wasting his time and he was certain that the luncheon would not further his plans and that the judge's wife was not a woman who became merry on such occasions. At least not yet.'

'It would be most imprudent to make any more moves. Were I to take advantage of the state of excitement induced by the meal, I should be in her bad books for ages. I am sure that she's feeling a little worked up, too, that she's thinking about my knees and elbows, as I am about hers; but the time is not yet ripe to turn such physiological advantages to account. This opportunity is no opportunity at all. We'll wait and see what happens at El Vivero, but here there's nothing to be done – however strong the urge.' And his behaviour towards Ana became more courteous; he paid his attentions to her in the distinguished style which he could assume when it suited him, but he went no further than that. Visitación could not believe her eyes. 'What was happening?' When nobody was looking, she stared at Mesía in astonishment, opening her eyes wide and puffing out her cheeks, a gesture which meant: 'You milksop – I'm flabbergasted to see you acting like a little mouse after I sat you next to her with the best of intentions.'

Mesía's sole answer was to move closer to the bank clerk's wife and press his foot on hers, but she received him with kicks, giving him to understand that 'she was an old soldier' and was standing by the principle implicit in the slap she had administered the previous afternoon.

Paco did not dare press his *latest cousin*'s foot, but he had her under his spell with the jokes he was telling her, the jokes of a well-bred young gentleman who had lived, and indeed *lived it up*, in Madrid. What was more, he smelt so nice, smelt of such fresh things, such elegant, refined things, too! In her village Edelmira had thought a great deal about the Young Marquis, whom she had seen two or three times when she was still a little girl and he was an adolescent. Now it was a different Paco she was seeing, and he far surpassed everything she had dreamed and imagined; for he was better-looking, rosier-faced, more cheerful, fleshier. That afternoon the Young Marquis was wearing a suit of fine alpaca, the colour of pease-pudding, a piqué waistcoat of the same colour, and a pair of summer slippers which Edelmira considered to be the height of elegance, although they would have suited Turkish feet better. Her cousin's trinkets, his coloured shirt, his necktie, his magnificent showy rings, his hands, which looked like the hands of a young lady – they all captivated Edelmira, who was, like Paco, very fond of everything clean and healthy.

Little by little Paco had been bringing one of his knees closer to the girl's skirt, until he finally felt something solid yet yielding; he was about to withdraw but the girl remained so calm that he left his leg there as if he had forgotten it. In her innocence Edelmira was so hard to shock that Paco could have gone so far as to press his foot upon hers and she would not have complained unless it hurt. 'Besides,' thought the girl, 'it's the custom here.' Tradition recounted much greater marvels about the house of her uncle and auntie.

Obdulia, sitting opposite, directed occasional languid looks at the lively couple. She remembered the winter sun of the previous afternoon. Paco had already forgotten it! He only had thoughts for that fresh young beauty, smelling of grass and rosemary, brought from her village to gratify his senses. But after devoting a moment of wistful reflection to her follies of the previous day, the widow turned back, provocative and suggestive, to the canon theologian. She was trying to turn his head with her perfumes, with her drop-curtain glances and, indeed, with all those resources at her disposal which could be employed against such a man and in such circumstances. De Pas responded to Obdulia's coquetry with ill-concealed indifference and did not even feel grateful for the burnt offering which she was making, for his sake, of Joaquín Orgaz's attentions, received by her with obvious disdain.

Joaquinito was seething with indignation. 'That woman is a . . .' and he thought of a Flamenco word. 'Well she's making passes at the vicar-general, isn't she?' The other guests either did not notice or pretended not to notice these goings-on, but Joaquinito, who had a deep personal interest, paid them his closest attention. He did not surrender, however, and persisted in flirting with the widow and turning a blind eye to what was happening between her and the canon. Usually Obdulia and Joaquinito got along well together. 'Lord! he'd even had a date with her in a coal-hole once! True, he couldn't boast of having taken that stronghold, that dismantled stronghold. He hadn't enjoyed her supreme favours – yet, but still, advances, pledges, or whatever you liked to call them – he'd had those all right. Ah! if he achieved complete victory, as he expected to, he'd make her pay for all her flighty disdain, her changes of mood, the humiliation of being put in second place behind a Holy Joe!'

The man bereft of all hope, overwhelmed by disillusionment and dying of sorrow, was Don Saturnino Bermúdez. After the events in the cathedral, where he had thought that he had taken such long strides forward (at the great expense of his conscience), he had not seen Obdulia again until that morning. But when he had approached her to tell her how great had been his sufferings in her absence (without mentioning, however, the constipation which had obsessed him and kept him in bed), when he had made to recite into her ear the short speech which he had prepared – in the style of a novel written by Feuillet in a sacristy – she had turned her back on him not once but three or four times, making it clear that *non erat his locus*,[4] that he would only be tolerated in church.

'Such was Woman! Such, in particular, was this woman! Wherefore love women? Wherefore pursue the ideal of love? Or rather, wherefore love real women, women of flesh and blood? Better far to dream – to continue dreaming.' Thus thought the melancholy Bermúdez, a man always sad in his cups, while he replied in a cold absent manner to Doña Petronila Rianzares, who was busy delivering a whispered panegyric on her idol the canon theologian. From time to time Bermúdez gazed at the judge's wife, whom he had loved in secret, and from time to time he gazed at Visitación, whom he had also loved, as an adolescent, during the period when she was rumoured to have climbed from a balcony together with a gentleman-friend. Not even Visitación had ever heeded him in the slightest; not once had she screwed up her small eyes at him in the way which, she believed, captivated men. It was not that the ladies of Vetusta scorned Bermúdez, it was just that they saw him as a sage and a saint, but not a man. Obdulia had discovered the man in him but had immediately disparaged her discovery.

The canon theologian, Ripamilán, Don Víctor, Don Alvaro, the marquis and the doctor were the principal participants in the conversation. Vegallana and the canon tended towards serious subjects, but Ripamilán and Don Víctor gave each discussion a festive slant and, in the end, everyone took it in fun. Once the marquis felt fortified, thanks to the wise gastric equilibrium of liquids and solids which, with great precision, he had established inside himself, he returned to his root-and-branch reformism. 'Now then! He wanted to demolish St Peter's and there was to be no talk about his tenets. Apart from the fact that he was not a fanatic, and that the conservative party was not to be identified with certain ultramontane doctrines, apart from all that, religion was one thing and local problems were quite another, and a covered fruit and vegetable market was an absolute necessity. The site? There was only one possibility, he would have no arguing about it, St Peter's square. But how? Where? By means of the demolition of that ruinous church.'

Doña Petronila protested, invoking the authority of the canon theologian. He supported Doña Petronila, but did not insist on his arguments. Ripamilán, his small eyes gleaming like glass beads, cried:

'Away with that iconoclast! Vegetables, vegetables! Does this mean that Your Grace puts a radish before religion, art and history?'

'Bravo, there speaks a true Aragonese!' shouted Don Víctor, standing with a glass of champagne in his hand.

'You people won't be serious, it's impossible to argue with you,' said the marquis. 'Quintanar here is applauding Ripamilán and a moment ago he was calling himself a liberal.'

'But what has that got to do with it?'

'You don't want to have the church demolished, yet you want to make Carraspique's daughters leave the cloister.'

'A simple matter of secularization.'

'Víctor, Víctor, don't say such silly things,' ventured the judge's wife with a smile.

'It is just a joke,' the canon theologian remarked.

'A joke?' cried the doctor. 'Upon my word, if Don Víctor attacks my cousin Carraspique for a joke, I'll take up my sword and attack him in sober truth – and what began in jest will end in earnest. Gentlemen, that girl is rotting away.'

The argument came to an end for no reason at all or, rather by reason of the fumes of the wine which the protagonists had drunk. Everyone was talking. Paco was another who wanted to secularize nuns, and Joaquinito Orgaz began to tell Flamenco jokes to the great amusement of the marchioness and Edelmira. Visitación even rose from the table to rap with her open fan anyone who expressed unorthodox ideas. Pepa and Rosa and the other serving-girls smiled discreetly, not daring to participate in the disorder, but a little less disciplined than at the beginning of the meal. Pedro had stopped coming to the door. Two glasses had been broken. The birds in the garden were perching on the climbing plants around the windows to see what all the fuss was about, and were adding their loud, shrill twitter to the general din.

'Serve the coffee in the arbour!' ordered the marchioness.

'Good, good!' cried Don Víctor and Edelmira; and, to the strains of the national anthem (the ex-magistrate's choice of words), played by Visitación somewhere indoors on an out-of-tune piano, they marched arm in arm into the garden, followed by Paco, intent on crowning Don Víctor's grey head with a wreath of orange-blossom. He had found it in a wardrobe in his late sister Emma's bedroom, which was Edelmira's bedroom now. They all went out into the garden, an extensive one surrounded, like Ozores Park, by tall, thick trees which concealed a large part of it from the gaze of neighbours. Don Víctor, Paco and Edelmira ran along distant paths among the trees. The marchioness was on Don Alvaro's arm while in front of them, held back by the marchioness's conversation, walked Anita, chewing leaves from the box-trees in the flower-beds, her head bowed, her eyes shining and her cheeks aflame. The canon theologian had remained behind, the prisoner of Doña Petronila Rianzares, who was speaking to him about a serious matter: the house of the Little Sisters of the Poor which was being built near the Mall on land presented by Doña Petronila, to the admiration and applause of all Catholic Vetusta. Señora de Rianzares was the widow of a former intendant in Havana, who had left her one of the most respectable fortunes in the province. She employed a large portion of her income in the service of the Church, above all in providing would-be nuns with dowries, building convents, and protecting the cause of Don Carlos while his party was under arms. She believed herself to be little less than a female pope, and she would even have gone so far as to pronounce provisional excommunication on a sinner, certain that the Pope would ratify her act. She treated the bishop in the manner of one great power dealing with another. Ripamilán, who could not abide her because he thought her an Amazon, called her Constantine the Great, an allusion to the emperor who bestowed his protection on the Church. 'The good woman thinks that just because she has succeeded in wearing her widow's weeds with decorum and has put up buildings for pious causes she is a saint, virtually the archbishop.' The archpriest was right. Doña Petronila had thoughts only for her protection of the Catholic faith and believed that everybody else should spend his or her life praising Doña Petronila's munificence and widowly chastity.

Among the entire Vetustan clergy she recognized no superior except the canon theologian, whom she esteemed much more highly than the bishop. 'He was in every respect a great man who out of sheer humility had accepted a life utterly unworthy of him.' The canon treated Señora de Rianzares like a queen, or as if she were the mother bishop, according to the archpriest; she, in turn, was grateful, and repaid De Pas by being his most eloquent advocate everywhere. If she was present, there was to be no gossip about the canon theologian. She did not allow it.

When they reached the arbour, where coffee was served, Señora de Rianzares lowered her head, the head of a corpulent friar, until it was close to the canon's shoulder and, showing the whites of her eyes, said in a honeyed voice:

'Come! My dear friend! I beg it of you – accompany me to El Vivero. Be kind to me, out of charity.'

The canon theologian, not a whit less unctious than his friend, savoured this incense, behind which he could divine so many money-bags.

'Madam, I should be more than delighted – if I could. But – I have work to do, at seven o'clock I have to be . . .'

'Oh no, I will not allow any excuses. Help me, my lady, help me persuade this scoundrel.'

The marchioness helped her, but to no avail. Don Fermín had decided not to go to El Vivero that afternoon. Everybody present was an intimate in that house, except him, and he had only accepted the invitation to luncheon because he had not been able to restrain himself – in a moment of weakness, and he wanted no more weakness. What role could he play on that trip? He knew that all those madcaps – Visitación, Obdulia, Paco, Mesía – went to El Vivero to disport themselves with excessive abandon, to copy children's games with much enthusiasm. Ripamilán had told him so several times. Ripamilán did not scruple to go there, but everyone knew that the archpriest was the archpriest; he, De Pas, should not witness those scenes which, without being exactly scandalous, were not for the eyes of a serious canon. No, he must not make an exhibition of himself. He had always managed to accomplish that feat of balancing, being a sociable priest without degenerating into a worldly one; he knew how to uphold his good reputation. Excessive intimacy, a too familiar relationship, would damage his prestige. He was not going to El Vivero. Though he certainly wanted to go, because that Mesía fellow was breathing down the neck of the judge's wife again. Don

Fermín was beginning to suspect the celebrated Vetustan Don Juan of intentions which were *non sanctos.*

The marchioness called Ana to her side – it was an innocent action, as all the marchioness's actions were – and said to her:

'Come here, come here, let's see if this disobliging gentleman takes more notice of you than of us.'

'What is the matter?'

'Don Fermín refuses to come to El Vivero.'

And Don Fermín, whose cheeks were already flushed from drinking more than usual, turned the colour of a cherry when the judge's wife looked him in the eyes and said with heartfelt sorrow:

'Oh, please, don't be like that, you'll make us all so sad, you know. Come with us, Don Fermín.'

In the look on her face anyone could see (as both De Pas and Don Alvaro certainly saw) a sincere expression of sadness – the marchioness's news had upset her.

A searing sensation passed through Don Alvaro's soul and, knowing all about such matters, he immediately identified it as jealousy. To be feeling jealous was something which angered him. 'That meant that he was more seriously affected by the woman than he had thought; and there were obstacles – what obstacles! A priest! A handsome priest, one had to confess it.' The normally lifeless eyes of the elegant Mesía flashed as he riveted them on the canon, who felt the impact of the glare and resisted it with a glare of his own darting as sharp as a needle from under those soft, fleshy lids. Don Fermín was alarmed by the impression which Ana's look, more than her words, made on him; for he felt a tender thankfulness and, deep inside his body, a warmth which was new to him; and this was not a simple question of the pleasurable gratification of his vanity but something which affected the very fibres of his heart and made them ring in some strange and unknown way. 'What the devil is this?' thought De Pas. It was at this moment that he met Don Alvaro's look, a look which, as it hit him, became a challenge – the kind of look which slaps a man in the face. Nobody noticed it but the judge's wife and the two gentlemen. There they stood, side by side, both handsome and well built; Mesía's close-fitting frock-coat, sober and formal, displaying its correctness in lines no less dignified and elegant than those of the priest's voluminous, hieratic cloak, which gleamed in the sunlight as it flowed to the ground.

'They were both handsome and attractive, rather like St Michael and the Devil, but the Devil when he was still Lucifer: Lucifer, the Archangel-Devil. Both of them were thinking about her, she was certain of that; Don Fermín as a protective friend, the man by his side as an enemy of her honour, though a lover of her beauty. She was going to grant victory to the one who deserved it, to the good angel, who wasn't quite so tall, who hadn't got a moustache (a moustache always looked good on a man), but who was debonair and elegant in his own way, in so far as a man can be debonair and elegant in a cassock. She had to confess – the thought was in her mind only for an instant, though – that it was agreeable to have so dashing and well-graced a saviour; such a distinguished man, as Obdulia always said, and she was right about this, at least. And above all to see those two men glare at each other like that just because of her, each claiming victory – the conquest of her will – but for different purposes, of course. At last, here was something which interrupted the monotony of Vetustan life, something to arouse her interest, something which might turn out to be dramatic and which was, indeed, already beginning to be dramatic. Honour, that riddle which kept cropping up in the verses recited by her husband, was safe. That sort of thing was out of the question, of course she knew that. But it would be good to have such an intelligent man as the canon theologian to defend her against the attacks, however innocuous they might be, of the handsome Mesía, who was no fool, either, and who was displaying great tact and prudence and, what was worse, a genuine interest in her. Yes, she had become convinced of it, Don Alvaro wanted to conquer her not out of mere caprice or vanity but because of true love – he would, most certainly, have preferred her to be unmarried. In fact, Don Víctor was a hindrance – worthy of the utmost respect, of course. But she loved him, she was certain she did, she loved him with filial affection mixed with conjugal familiarity, which was as valid in its way as a passion of another kind. And besides, if it weren't for Don Víctor, the canon would have no cause to defend her, and there wouldn't be any need for the struggle which had just started between these two distinguished men. She mustn't forget that Don Fermín didn't, and couldn't, want her for himself, but for Don Víctor.'

While Ana was lost in these thoughts, and others like them, Obdulia was heard screaming for help. The occupants of the arbour, who had been quietly drinking coffee, hurried to the end of the garden.

'Where are they? Where are they?' asked the marchioness in alarm.

'On the swing! On the swing!' said the doctor, Don Robustiano.

It was a wooden swing, like those erected for the people of Madrid during the great annual fiestas of St Isidore, but more elegant, of more careful construction. On one of the seats, inside an imitation of the basket under a hot-air balloon, Don Saturnino Bermúdez crouched motionless, pale and smiling, about a yard from the ground, making the most ridiculous sight imaginable, as he knew only too well. His efforts to disguise his situation, attempting the impossible task of making it appear a normal one, merely made him look still more ridiculous. Opposite him, in the other basket, which had caught on a piece of wood protruding from a wall, the remains of recently

dismantled scaffolding, Obdulia Fandiño was displaying her exuberant person and the gaudy colours of her skirts as she clung to the
swing-boat like a castaway of the air, terrified, but showy and
coquettish in her terror and what she imagined to be her peril.

'Do not move, do not move,' Don Víctor was crying with theatrical
gestures under the swing-boat, probably seeing what Obdulia was
not very concerned to hide, in her present predicament at least.

'Don't move, don't move, if you fall you'll kill yourself,' Paco was
saying as he searched for something with which to release the swing.

'Three and a half metres,' said the marquis, who had arrived in
time to measure – by eye, as he made all his geometrical calculations
– the distance which Obdulia might plunge.

The fact was that neither Don Víctor nor Paco nor Orgaz was able,
by his own efforts, to devise a means of reaching the piece of wood
stuck in the wall and releasing Obdulia.

'It was all Paco's fault,' said Visitación, whose legs were bound
with a length of string over her dress. 'He pushed too hard, to try and
make Saturn fall out, and whoosh! up went the swing, and when it
came down again, it got caught on that bit of wood.'

Obdulia was sitting as still as a statue, but she was screaming
ceaselessly.

'Don't shout, my child,' said the marchioness, who had stopped
looking up at her because of the awkward craning position into
which such an action put her head. 'They'll soon have you down
again.'

The marquis climbed a small ladder, used by the gardener to trim
the pillar-like box-trees and the tops of the bushes. But even when he
stood on the highest rung he was not close enough to the swing-boat
to be able to lift it off its hook.

'Call Diego – I mean Bautista,' said the marchioness.

'Yes, yes, get Bautista!' cried Obdulia, remembering the coachman's
power.

'It would be pointless,' the marquis said. 'Bautista is a strong man,
but he would not be able to reach the swing, for he is no taller than
I. All we can do is look for another ladder.'

'There isn't another ladder in the garden.'

'Heaven only knows where we'll find one.'

'For God's sake! For God's sake! I'm feeling dizzy, I'm going to fall,
out of sheer fright!'

And then Don Alvaro, at whom Ana had directed a look both
imploring and encouraging, made up his mind. The thought had
already occurred to him that, thanks to his height, he could easily
take hold of the swing and pull it free from its ties. But what did
Obdulia matter to him? He might expose himself to ridicule, dirty his
frock-coat. Ana's look sent him bounding to the ladder. Luckily, he
was an agile man. In the eyes of the judge's wife he looked as smart,

dashing and elegant perched up there like a lamplighter as when he promenaded along the Mall.

'Bravo! bravo!' cried Edelmira and Paco when they saw the arms of the well-built Mesía appearing between the poles of the swing-boat.

'Don't push me out, Alvarito, don't push me out!' screamed Obdulia as she felt her former lover's hands under her legs. Visita gave Edelmira, with whom she was already on intimate terms, a little pinch. The girl understood the meaning of the pinch, for she had noticed how Obdulia had addressed Mesía.

'Pray be calm, madam, this will not put you in danger,' replied Don Alvaro, already repentant of having yielded to Anita's tacit plea.

He made lengthy preparations to position his arms so that he would be able to apply sufficient force to the swing to lift it above him. As he made his first effort, which from the beginning he knew would be in vain, he imagined the look on the canon theologian's face.

'Heave ho!' cried Visitación beneath him, to add to his ignominy.

'You can't do it, you can't do it! Don't shift it, you'll just make things worse! I'm going to get killed!' screeched the widow.

The others said nothing.

'Can't you keep still?' muttered Don Alvaro in a hoarse, furious voice; he would have been happy to see her fall head first.

He made his second unavailing effort.

The thing would not budge. He was sweating, more from shame than from fatigue. He should have been able to lift that weight.

'Leave it be, leave it be, let's see if Bautista . . .' said the marchioness. 'Damned youngsters!'

'Bautista isn't tall enough,' the marquis observed once again. 'Another ladder – someone try the coach-houses. There must be one there.'

Don Alvaro gave his third push. Useless. He looked down, as if searching for a way to shed some part of the weight. In the other basket, under his nose, in a ridiculous humble posture, crouched Don Saturnino, motionless, forgotten by everyone. Mesía could not help smiling, even though he was seething with fury. He felt like spitting as he looked down at Bermúdez, who beamed endlessly back at him. In tones of forced tranquillity Mesía said:

'Well now! that's a fine thing, isn't it? So there you are, are you? Do you suppose that I am practising weight-lifting and need you to sit yourself down there to test my strength?'

General laughter.

'Yes that's right, you all laugh,' cried Obdulia, 'this is all highly amusing, I must say.'

'I – I,' stammered Bermúdez, 'pray forgive me – since nobody said anything to me – I thought that I was out of the way down here – and furthermore – I believed that if I descended – I might worsen the lady's plight – by shaking the swing.'

'Oh no no! Don't get off!' cried the terrified widow.

'What do you mean "don't get off"?' roared Don Alvaro in fury. 'Do you expect me to lift this monstrosity above my head with both of you on it?'

'It is – merely that – I cannot quite see how – if someone does not come to my assistance – I am so far from the ground.'

'Hardly a yard,' the marquis observed.

Paco took Don Saturn in his arms and lifted him out of his hateful box.

'Now,' he said, 'we'll help you by pushing from below.'

'It would be pointless,' observed the canon theologian in a gentle voice. 'Since the piece of wood is caught between those two poles on the side of the swing-boat, if one man does not lift the whole thing above his head, it will not be possible to free it.'

'Of course,' bellowed the man above him, and he tried his strength once more.

But apparently Bermúdez did not weigh very much, for Don Alvaro still could not budge the cumbersome contraption.

The dandy imagined himself stuck up on a pillory in disgrace. With a leap, which he tried to make an elegant one, he returned to the ground. Brushing dirt from his hands and wiping his brow he said:

'Can't be done! Better go and look for another ladder.'

'We could have found one by now.'

'If I could reach it . . .' the canon theologian suggested, his voice and face radiating modesty.

'Of course,' said the marchioness, 'you're a tall man, too.'

'Yes, he'll reach it, he'll reach it,' cried Paco, who wanted to see the priest make a fool of himself.

'Yes, you will be able to reach the swing,' concluded the marquis. 'If you are strong enough . . . And nobody can see you here.'

The problem was how to climb the ladder without looking a sorry sight in his priestly garb.

'Take your cloak off,' suggested Ripamilán.

'There is no need for that,' replied De Pas, horrified at the idea of being seen in his cassock.

And without losing an ounce of his dignity, gravity or grace he tripped like a squirrel to the highest rung, his cloak flowing behind him.

'So far so good,' he said, as he inserted his arms into the place where moments earlier Mesía had put his.

Applause from the multitude. Obdulia repressed an indecorous shriek.

Doña Petronila, open-mouthed with ecstasy, exclaimed in a low voice:

'What a man! What a luminary!'

Without any apparent effort, with agility, even with elegance, the canon theologian held aloft the swing-boat, which, free again, and restrained in its descent by the same force which had raised it, swung down in majesty. Somoza, Paco and Joaquín Orgaz helped Obdulia out of her hateful box. The canon theologian received a clamorous ovation. Paco admired him in silence, for muscular strength inspired Paco with a kind of religious terror. He had wasted his own strength in battles of love and, although there was flesh enough on him, it was flabby flesh. It was not easy for Don Alvaro to hide his shame. 'The whole thing was so puerile! But still he felt ashamed.' What was more he, who had always regarded priests as feeble women, a special variety of the weaker sex, because of their clerical garb and the lenity imposed on them by canon law, had just seen the canon theologian as an athlete, as a man perfectly capable of killing him with a single blow, if the unlikely occasion for it were to arise. Mesía recalled that he had often said (in particular during village elections), 'Well, you just let your priest know he'd better not play any tricks, he'd better not try to take advantage of his skirts, because if he rubs me up the wrong way I'll grab hold of his cassock and fling him from this balcony.' Never having given the matter much thought, he had always imagined that once a man had rid himself of respect for religion he could give a priest a pummelling with impunity; for he assumed that priests had no courage, no strength, no blood in their veins. 'And now, this canon, who was perhaps some sort of rival, had given him that little lesson in gymnastics, which could well serve as a healthy warning.'

Obdulia's gratitude knew no bounds, but the canon considered it necessary to control it by assuming a cold austerity of manner and giving it to understand that 'he had not done it for her sake'. The widow, undaunted, insisted that she owed him her life.

'Most certainly,' Doña Petronila confirmed, not suspecting how Obdulia intended to repay the canon for the life which she said she owed him.

Ana silently admired her spiritual father's strength, in which she saw only a physical symbol of the fortitude of his soul: a fortitude which undoubtedly provided her with a solid and indeed impregnable defence against the temptations which were already beginning to assail her.

Visita climbed into the swing-boat, her legs still tied together with string, as she did not want her petticoats to be seen.

Obdulia protested:

'What? Could you see anything? That's not fair! Why didn't someone warn me? That was a dirty trick.'

'The lady is right,' said Don Víctor. 'Equality before the law. Off with the string.'

Edelmira climbed into the other boat, stringless. There was no need to take any precautions, nobody could see anything.

Don Víctor and Ripamilán had a turn on the swing, too, but it made them dizzy.

'The coaches are ready,' cried the marchioness from a distance, and everyone ran to the courtyard.

The marchioness, Doña Petronila, the judge's wife and Ripamilán climbed into the open calash, a luxurious carriage which had once been a model of its kind but was now old-fashioned and cumbersome. The team of black horses was worthy of the king. The other guests settled into an old travelling-carriage, solid but unsightly, drawn by four horses. It was the carriage used by the marquis on his trips about the province, sometimes for fetching and carrying electors, sometimes perhaps for hunting on forbidden ground. So many things were said about this travelling-carriage! It looked like the ancient post-chaises which still carry the mail from the central post office to the various railway stations in Madrid. It was known as the Gondola, as the Family-Coach, and by other nicknames.

The canon theologian was squeezed between Ripamilán and Anita, having been given the solemn promise that he would be dropped at the Mall, where he had to meet someone. He did not have to meet anyone, it was a pretext to enable him to fulfil his intention not to go to El Vivero.

'Let's kidnap him,' Obdulia had said.

'Yes, yes, kidnap him, that's what we must do, we won't let him go,' agreed Doña Petronila.

'No, I must object – in that case I shall not join you.'

He joined them. The calash set off, striking sparks from sharp-edged cobble-stones on its way through the narrow streets of La Encimada. It was followed by the Gondola, which deafened the neighbourhood with a terrifying racket of jangling bells, cracking whips, rattling windows, and shouting and laughing.

The sun was still warm, and the ladies in the calash used their parasols to improvise a gaily coloured hood which also sheltered the canon theologian and the archpriest. Ripamilán, half-hidden among the skirts of Doña Petronila, who was facing him, was in the seventh heaven; not because of his contact with Constantine the Great, but because he was sitting among ladies, beneath their parasols, inhaling their perfumes, and feeling the air from their fans. A trip to the country with ladies! A courtly pastoral, almost! The perfect ideal of the old poet, of the eternal platonic lover of Phyllis and Amaryllis in silk bodices, was being realized.

The canon theologian was a little embarrassed. In a way he regretted, and in another way did not regret, the coincidence, or whatever it was, which had brought him into contact with Ana. Only just into contact, of course. They were both sitting still. He was uneasy, but she was not, for she was content to be by his side, still thinking of him as her strong, well-fashioned shield. She was protecting him from the sun and he was defending her against Don Alvaro. 'If Don Fermín were to come to El Vivero, perhaps that man wouldn't have the courage to approach me. But otherwise, he will – he will pluck up courage, naturally, since everyone there goes his own way, and Víctor is perfectly capable of running off with Paco and Edelmira to act like a fool, like a child. No, I certainly shan't let that man know I'm afraid of him. So, if he does approach me – I shan't run away. But if only *he* would come!'

'Don Fermín,' she said, as they neared the Mall, in a humble voice and with the gentle, quiet respect with which she always spoke to him. 'Don Fermín, why don't you come with us? It would be little more than an hour. I believe we're to return earlier today. Please come, please come!'

De Pas felt the most delightful tingling sensation all over his body when he heard these words and, not thinking what he was doing, he leaned towards Ana as if attracted to her by magnetism. It was fortunate that the other ladies and the archpriest were engrossed in an agreeable conversation the object of which was to flay poor Obdulia. Ripamilán was referring, as he usually did when he discussed this matter, to the Bishop of Nauplia, the hostelry in Madrid, the dresses of her courtesan cousin, and so on. It cannot be denied that the canon's resolution was at the breaking-point, but he considered that it would be unworthy to display so little will-power and, what was more, was afraid of what might happen at El Vivero. He couldn't go about behaving like some lovesick adolescent. If Don Alvaro wanted revenge for his defeat at the swing and challenged him to some other kind of exercise, he, with his cloak and cassock, labouring under the burden of being a canon, was liable to be made to look a fool. No, he would not go. And as he confirmed his intentions he experienced an intense, profound, voluptuous thrill: the thrill of pride satisfied. He well knew how strong he had to be to resist the temptation of those lips – lips all the more seductive for their innocence – and this made him even more appreciative of his own energy, of the fortitude of his soul, which 'had undoubtedly come into the world for more important missions than the struggle with obscure Vetustans'.

He turned his soft eyes to his friend and, putting a new tone into his voice, an affectionate familiar tone which, she noticed, was rather like the tone of Mesía's voice in the dining-room window, he murmured:

'It wouldn't be right for me to go with you.'

The indescribable look on his face gave her to understand that he was sorry, but since he was a priest, and she had confessed to him, and Paco and Obdulia and Visita were rather wild, and in Vetusta people with nothing to do (that is to say nearly everybody) gossiped about the most innocent event . . .

All this was what the judge's wife read in the look, even though it might not have been intended to convey these meanings; and she resigned herself to coping with Mesía once more without the protection of the vicar-general.

They did not speak again. The carriage stopped, the canon rose and bade the ladies farewell. The judge's wife smiled at him as she would often have smiled at her mother, had she known her. De Pas was not capable of smiling like that, his soft eyes were not equipped for such crises, and in the glance with which he responded there were sparks of which he remained unaware – and so did Ana.

They were at the end of the Mall, Priests' Promenade by an old name. Don Fermín stepped down from the carriage to the lamentations of Doña Petronila.

'You're a very disagreeable fellow,' said the marchioness, permitting herself the use of the familiar tone of voice in which she spoke to all the canons, except Don Fermín.

And she even went so far as to rap him on the knuckles with her closed fan. She meant by this to indicate her desire to tighten the bonds of the rather distant friendship between the vicar-general and the Vegallanas. De Pas understood, and was grateful. Being closer to the Vegallanas meant being closer to Don Víctor and his wife, he knew that well enough; for they were always together – at the theatre, at the promenade, everywhere – and the judge's wife often ate at the marquis's house. And if he wanted to see her, that was a much better place than the cathedral. All this went through the canon's mind in the short time he needed to climb down from the footboard, stand back, and bid the ladies his last farewell.

'Carry on, Bautista!' cried the marchioness, and the calash continued its progress, exciting the attention of priests, ladies and gentlemen promenading along the Mall, children playing in a nearby field, and workmen labouring in the open air.

The canon watched the carriage out of sight. The judge's wife was smiling at him from afar with the same sweet, chaste expression, and making a discreet timid gesture with her fan. Finally, all that could be seen was Ripamilán's angular outline, with arms waving like the sails of a toy windmill.

The other coach passed by like a flash of lightning. De Pas saw a gloved hand waving to him from a window. The hand belonged to Obdulia, the eternally grateful widow. She did not wave with both hands because the other one was being given gentle, furtive squeezes by Joaquinito Orgaz, who never turned up his nose at left-over dishes so long as they were succulent.

XIV

The Mall was a narrow, treeless promenade, sheltered from the northwesterly winds – the coldest winds in Vetusta – by a wall, not very high, but solid and well-preserved, at either end of which there was a miniature architectural display in the form of a monumental fountain of dark stone whose origins were revealed in the ablative absolute *Rege Carolo III*[1] engraved in the middle of the pile, as if it were the work of the water trickling over the limestone for years and years on end. Opposite the wall, the promenade's boundary was marked by a row of long benches, also of stone. The Mall possessed no other embellishment or attraction except the sun which, if it shone all afternoon, warmed the sad wall. From time immemorial this wall had provided shelter for the promenade of the many clergymen who have always been the principal ornaments of Vetusta, this former capital of the nation. In winter they promenaded from two until four or five o'clock, and in summer from a little before sunset until nightfall. As well as being sheltered, the Mall had once been secluded and tucked-away, to use the common Vetustan expression. But that was before La Colonia came into existence. The best part of town, Vetusta's new development, had spread in this direction and, although the Mall and the area immediately around it were respected, a few paces away began the life, the noise and the bustle of the villas which were being built – of the Colonial suburb which was rising up as if by magic, according to *El Lábaro*, for which newspaper ten or twelve years were, it seemed, a mere moment.

It should be stated that although the Vetustan clergy was famous for its intransigence in matters concerning dogma, morality, even discipline and, perhaps, politics, it had never looked askance at the proximity of urban progress. Indeed it was happy to see Vetusta *being transformed from one day to the next* in such a way that within twenty years *nobody would recognize it*; which just goes to prove that civilization itself, in the proper sense of the word, was rejected by neither the parochial nor the cathedral clergy of Bermúdez's *Vetusta in Christian Times*.

But that is not the end of the story. By tradition, the Mall was the patrimony of priests, melancholy magistrates, and families in mourning, but ever since certain ladies had noticed that Priests' Promenade was warmer than the other promenades, they had begun, in coteries and guild meetings, to discuss the question whether the winter promenade should be transferred there. Don Robustiano Somoza, who was above all a public hygienist, shouted on every side:

'It stares you in the face! It's what I've been saying for donkeys' years, but there's no fighting prejudice and fanaticism in this town. Back in the times when these priests lived on the fat of the land –

knowing what's what, and using solitude and seclusion as their excuses – they grabbed the best place of recreation, the most sheltered and hygienic place.'

In short, certain upper-crust ladies made so bold as to break tradition, and from October until Easter they promenaded, with great effrontery, in the Mall. Other ladies made bold to follow them; the *young blades* noticed that Priests' Promenade was shorter and narrower than the open esplanade, and this suited their purposes, as well; and within a year the Mall, the attractive Mall, had become the Winter Promenade, suffering partial secularization.

Some clergymen objected. Most of these were either old or poor. But in the end they abandoned *their* Mall and scattered over the roads which led out of town.

'The world, the mad world, had cast them out of their solitary place of recreation! The world was invading everything!' And they retreated along the Castile road and other dusty highways which ran between interminable lines of poplars and oaks.

But the younger element, which formed the majority of the canons and beneficiaries – the priests whose dress was neatest and most elegant, and who wore the latest model of broad, foreshortened, open-brimmed shovel-hat – resigned itself to this invasion by Vetustan high society. These priests had no objections to rubbing shoulders with ladies and gentlemen, or if they had they did not show it. After all, *they* had not gone off in search of the crowds and the bustle of the world; they were still in their own home, in their own domains, pretending not to notice the presence of intruders.

Perhaps this new custom in Vetustan life was responsible in part for the meticulous care which, in recent years, had been noticeable in the dress of many priests. What can well be called the gilded youth of the city clergy (so envied by their colleagues up in the mountains, who themselves admitted that each day they were more like animals) was, without fail, present in the Mall every fine autumn and winter afternoon. There they were, relucent, like a collection of black diamonds. Without giving any cause for comment they watched the comings and goings of the elegant young ladies; and observant people could spot signs of love and coquetry in certain gestures, movements, laughs, looks and blushes. But no more than signs.

Yet the rector of the seminary, an excessively sanctimonious man, according to the Marchioness de Vegallana, would not acquiesce to that jumble of priests and women promenading together in an area which was not a stone's throw in length and hardly five yards wide.

'No, my Lord,' he would say to the bishop, 'I do *not* see that it is innocent and inoffensive for a priest to bump into the elbows of all the pretty young ladies in town.' The bishop believed that young ladies were incapable of such bumping. 'Now if you were talking

about those incorrigible lasses in the Boulevard, the waistcoat-
makers . . .'

The protests of the rector of the seminary were soon forgotten.

'Who takes any notice of him?' said Visitación, the bank clerk's
wife. 'A boor – saintly, yes, but uncouth. In short, a man who threw
me out of St Dominic's sacristy – me, the treasurer to the Guild of the
Sacred Heart of Jesus!'

'A man like that', declared Obdulia, 'ought to spend his life on top
of a pillar.'

'Like St Simeon the Stylist,' added Blunderbuss.

From Easter until the autumnal equinox, approximately, the priests
were left almost by themselves in the Mall, but October saw the return
of certain ladies who were afraid of the damp and of *the effects of
the trees* in the Summer Promenade. On the afternoon that the
Vegallanas' carriage left the canon theologian at the end of the Mall,
many clergymen and not a few laymen of years and respectability
were promenading there, but few ladies. There were, however,
enough of them to comment with an abundance of scholia and
footnotes on the extraordinary fact that the canon theologian had
alighted from the Vegallanas' calash, in which all of them, every
single one of them, with her own two eyes, had seen him sitting by
the side of the judge's wife. 'Talk of the devil,' many people had said
when they saw the calash. To tell the truth, the priests themselves
were also talking about this inopinate event, as the archdeacon called
it. The ex-mayor Foja was promenading between the archdeacon (the
illustrious Gloucester) and the beneficiary, Don Custodio, the most
honeyed priest in Vetusta. The liberal money-lender was not usually
to be found in the company of cassocks, but that afternoon the
importance of events had brought together these three enemies of the
canon theologian.

'What cheek!' Foja was saying.

'It is most unwise of him, he has no notion of diplomacy, of
dissimulation,' observed Mourelo.

'And I wouldn't believe you when you told me that he had stayed
to lunch with the Vegallanas.'

'Well now you can see for yourself!' exclaimed Gloucester in
triumph.

'And where are the rest of them off to?'

'To El Vivero, no doubt. As you can imagine – to jump and prance
about like young colts.'

'That's the conservative classes for you!'

'No, sir, they are the exception.'

'And coming in an open carriage . . .'

'And by her side . . .'

'And alighting in the Mall,' the beneficiary ventured to put in.

'Yes, Custodio here is right – alighting in the Mall . . .'

'My dear Archdeacon, permit me to say that your colleague is tempting providence.'

'I agree! I agree! And it pains me. But the bishop, the blessed man . . . Well, what can you expect?' Gloucester hinted, and leered.

A clever turn of phrase came to his mind and in order to pronounce it with all due solemnity he halted, extended a hand as if to keep the other two men at arm's length and, leaning over towards Foja, shouted into his ear:

'It takes all kinds, my dear friend, to make God's Holy Church!'

Gloucester's companions burst out laughing and it was not until the canon theologian was close that they stopped. The two priests greeted him with great courtesy and Gloucester stepped up to him and gave him a familiar caressing pat on the back.

Gloucester was consumed by envy, but he was not going to stop dissembling because of that. He was a diplomatic man, regardless of the situation.

The canon theologian restricted himself to inwardly spitting upon him.

He walked up and down a few times alone, greeting people right and left in his usual amiable way, but mechanically, and hardly seeing the people whom he greeted. He was holding the folds of his cloak across his paunch, which was beginning to be noticeable; and with one hand placed over the other – he had beautiful hands – he promenaded for a quarter of an hour at a slow pace (which it was no easy job for him to maintain, for he would have been happy to break into a run – after the marquis's coaches), in humble defiance of all the looks directed at him, certain that everybody or nearly everybody was talking about him and about the two- or three- or four-hour-long confession. 'God only knew how long it would have become by now! Gloucester and his henchman Don Custodio would have been careful to set the ball rolling. The things his enemies must be saying! But what did it matter to him? All he regretted was not having gone on to El Vivero. The wretches would gossip whatever he did! And as for respectable people, the people who mattered, they would not think ill of him just because he, like Ripamilán and other priests, went to the marquis's country estate.'

A few of his true friends – or at least avowed supporters – were promenading along the Mall, but they did not dare approach the illustrious vicar-general, for he had a sullen air, in spite of the sweet smile fixed on his face ever since he had stepped from the coach. Just as light makes people with weak eyes wrinkle up their eyelids, so it made Don Fermín smile that smile which the public always saw him wearing, as though it were a strange effect of the light on the muscles of his face.

But those people who knew him well – most of them to their cost – were not deceived by this smile. The first person who dared make to approach him was the dean, who had just arrived. De Pas went to meet him. The dean seldom spoke, and he was at his most silent while promenading. As they walked, Don Fermín continued as if he were alone. Later the canon who was a minister's relative approached them and it became necessary to talk, and soon after that a frock-coated bishop (to use an expression then much in vogue) joined them and the conversation became livelier. The talk was of politics, ecclesiastical intrigues and a hundred and one other matters which the canon theologian regarded as nonsense, gossip unworthy of priests. 'What about himself, though? What about his own thoughts? They were puerile indeed, ridiculous, even sinful. For hadn't he started noticing – because his head was bowed – his colleagues' cloaks and cassocks, and his own, and thinking that priestly garb was absurd, that priests didn't look like men, that there was a certain carnival effeminacy about their attire? And a thousand other crazy thoughts! He was ashamed to be wearing long skirts and the soutane which at other times he displayed with such majestic grace. If it had an opening at the side, like certain tunics . . . but then people would see his legs – how terrible! – his black trousers, the shamefaced man inside the priest.'

'And what do *you* think about it?' the lay bishop asked, coming to a halt and placing himself in front of the canon to show that he expected a reply.

De Pas had no idea what they were talking about. Thinking of the openings in the soutane had driven all else out of his mind.

'The fact of the matter', he said, 'is that it – merits careful consideration.'

'Well, that's just what I say!' the lay bishop cried in triumph; and he allowed De Pas to continue walking.

'Do you see? The vicar-general is of the same opinion as I. He says that the matter merits close study, that it is an arduous one – and it most certainly is!'

The canon theologian took a deep breath. Before he could be exposed to another inopinate question, as Mourelo would call it, he took his leave of the gentlemen, saying that he had work to do in the palace.

He could not stand it any longer; that afternoon he was suffocated by his colleagues' company, overwhelmed by all that hanging black cloth; and he might blurt out the most absurd nonsense if he stayed. He strode away. His last look was into the distance along the road to El Vivero where he had seen the coaches disappear in clouds of dust.

'A fine state we're in!' he thought as he walked along. 'He was not fond of giving things names, especially things which were not easy to christen. What was happening to him? It had no name. It was not love. He did not believe in a special passion, a pure and noble feeling which could be called love – that was something which existed only in novels and poems. Sinful hypocrisy had resorted to that sanctifying word in order to disguise many of the hundreds of forms assumed by lust. What he was feeling was not lust, either, for his conscience was not troubling him. He was convinced that it was something new. Might he be ill? Might it be his nerves? Somoza would certainly have said that it was.'

'At all events it had been stupid, and maybe ill-mannered, to refuse to accompany the ladies. What would they be saying about him at El Vivero?'

He had reached La Encimada and was walking up its lower streets. He passed the door of the civil governor's offices and inside, in the courtyard, he saw a well which he knew was blocked. He remembered that Ripamilán had spoken to him several times of a dry well at El Vivero. Paco Vegallana, Obdulia, Visita and other madcaps – the archpriest had said – amuse themselves cutting ferns, grass and branches and hurling it all into the well, and when the greenery has nearly reached the top – whoosh! they hurl themselves in, first one, then another, and sometimes two or three at once. They had even made Ripamilán go down into the pit in spite of all his respectability; and indeed a rope had been needed to haul him out. The canon theologian had never seen the well, but he could see it now in his mind's eye, and he imagined Mesía inside it, on top of the branches and the grass, his arms outspread awaiting the sweet burden of Ana's mortal body. Would she sink as low as that? Would she agree to throw herself into the well? Don Fermín was on tenterhooks. What did it matter to him? But he was on tenterhooks.

He wandered along, not knowing where to go, until he found himself at his own front door. He turned on his heel and, certain that no one had seen him, hurried away down a side-street leading to La Corralada, the little square in front of the bishop's palace.

'Mother!' he thought. He had not remembered her all afternoon.

He had lunched out without warning her! She regarded this type of domestic indiscipline as a major sin. Her son seldom committed such sins, and this made them all the more remarkable for her.

'Why didn't I think of sending her a message? But who would have gone with it? Wouldn't it have been ridiculous to say to the marchioness, "My lady, I must inform my mother that I shall not be having luncheon with her today"? That happy servitude in which he lived his life – yes, happy, it did not humiliate him – was not, however, something about which he wanted people to know. But why hadn't he stayed at home now? He had been away for long enough – why not turn back, defy his mother's ill humour? No, he did not dare, he was in no state for dramatic confrontations, he was horrified by the prospect of a harangue disguised as something else, as all his mother's harangues were, and of a discourse on utilitarian morality. She would tell him all about the nonsense she had heard in the course of the morning. And if he said "I have lunched with the judge's wife in the marquis's house", what a scene there would be! But Lord, how soon the rabble, the wretched rabble of Vetusta, had begun to gossip about their friendship! In the space of just two days so many rumours, his mother with her ears full of calumny and evil gossip, and her soul full of suspicion, fear and apprehension! Yet what was it all about? Nothing, nothing whatsoever, a lady who had made a general confession and who by now was probably down a well crammed full of dry grass in the company of the most handsome man in town. What did all that have to do with him – with him, the vicar-general of the diocese? Oh yes! he would go back home to assert himself, and tell his mother that it was indecorous to suspect him and attempt to hide the truth and disguise appearances, as she persisted in doing – what for? He had nothing to hide, he wasn't a child, he felt only scorn for calumny . . .'

He went into the palace.

The shadow of the cathedral, spreading over the bishop's dismal, ailing old house, engulfed it in darkness. The rays of the setting sun cast a purple glow over the background and fired many of the houses in La Encimada. The flames were reflected in their windows.

The canon theologian walked into a study where the bishop was correcting the proofs of a pastoral letter.

Fortunato raised his head and smiled:

'Hullo, so it's you.'

Don Fermín sat down on a sofa. He was dizzy, his head ached, there was a burning sensation and a sticky dryness in his throat: he was suffocating in that narrow closed chamber. Drinking had upset him. He did not take liqueurs, but that afternoon, in an unguarded moment, without realizing what he was doing, he had gulped down the glass of chartreuse or whatever it was that the marchioness had offered him.

As Fortunato read through his proofs he continued smiling. He seemed to have lost his fear of the canon, yet only a few hours earlier he had avoided being left alone with him, fearing a reprimand for those attentions to the Lady-Patronesses of the Free Fraternity. Don Fermín noticed the change.

'Will you be so kind as to read these smudgy letters here for me? I can't make them out.'

De Pas went to his side and read.

'You smell to high heaven, my boy! What have you been drinking?'

Don Fermín, taken by surprise, raised his head and frowned at the bishop.

'I smell?'

'You smell of drink. I don't know what drink – rum – something like that.'

De Pas shrugged, giving the bishop to understand that the observation was both impertinent and petty. He walked away from the table.

'By the way – why didn't you tell your mother?'

'Tell her what?'

'That you were lunching out.'

'But do you know . . . ?'

'I should think I know, my son. Teresina has been here twice, sent by Paula. Where was the master, had he lunched here? No my child, he has not – I had to go out and tell her so myself. And half an hour later here she was again. Had something happened to the master? Madam was alarmed, I must know something . . .'

The canon was pacing the study, stamping his feet. He could barely conceal his impatience and bad temper, though perhaps he was not even trying.

'I told her not to worry,' Fortunato continued, 'you must have lunched in Carraspique's house, or in Páez's, since it's their nameday – and that's what's happened, isn't it? You had luncheon with Carraspique?'

'No, my Lord!'

'With Páez?'

'No, my Lord! My mother – my mother treats me like a child!'

'The poor woman loves you so.'

'This is too much.'

'But Fermín!' The bishop looked up from his proofs. 'So you still haven't been home?'

The canon did not reply. He was already in the corridor. From the study door he had shouted 'Good-day!', shutting it behind him with more force than was necessary.

'The boy is right,' thought the bishop, who treated the canon theologian as a weak father treats a spoilt son. 'Paula manipulates us all like puppets.'

And he went back to his pastoral letter.

De Pas retraced his steps up the side-street, but when he was near his house he stopped. He did not know what to do. The chartreuse, or whatever it had been – might it have been brandy? – was still making him feel uncomfortable and now he too realized that his breath smelt.

'If Gloucester were to approach me now, tomorrow all Vetusta would know that I am a drunkard.'

'No, no, I'm not going up. What a state mother must be in! And I'm in no condition to listen to sermons, or put up with gibes, or interpret hints. Even Teresa's involved! Twice she's been to the palace! The lost child! This is insufferable!'

The cathedral clock slowly struck the hour. First four high-pitched notes, then several low, hoarse, vibrant ones.

As if his will depended upon the mechanism of the clock, De Pas suddenly made up his mind and turned right, down the street to the Mall.

He forgot about the brandy, the bishop, his mother, Teresina. His only thought was for the marquis's coaches, surely on their way back by now.

The vicar-general of Vetusta paced along the road which led to El Vivero, having left the tortuous streets of La Encimada behind him. By the time he reached the Mall it was deserted and the lamps were lit. It did not occur to him that he was acting like a madman, that all these comings and goings were unworthy of the vicar-general of the diocese. That occurred to him later. Now he was obsessed by one idea: 'Have they come back? No, they can't have come yet, there hasn't been time, but they must be getting near by now.'

'Anyway, this evening breeze will refresh me, clear my head, assuage my thirst.' The waters in the monumental fountains were murmuring their melancholy monotone in the silence of the sad and solitary promenade. When De Pas reached the westerly fountain he was tempted to put his lips to the iron tube which a stone lion grasped between its teeth, and satiate his burning thirst in the tempting, gushing stream. But this he did not dare to do, and he turned away and continued his lonely walk. He reached the other fountain. The same burning, the same temptation. Another turn; back again. He walked up and down for half an hour. His thirst seared his throat – why didn't he go home? Because he didn't want them to pass by and not see them – not see the carriages. Ana would come back in the open calash, of course, and as it passed a street lamp he would see her without being seen, or, at least, without being recognized. His thirst could wait. The university clock chimed thrice. Three-quarters of an hour! It must be fast. No – the cathedral, which was the chronometric authority in Vetusta, ratified the university's affirmation; and, for what it was worth, the town-hall clock, which had not succeeded in secularizing time, confirmed its colleagues' laconic statements, expressing its opinion in the shrill tones of a vulgar cattle-bell.

'But what can those people be doing?' asked the canon; adding, for the satisfaction of his conscience, that, of course, it did not matter to him.

Until that moment he had not noticed a group of boys of ten to twelve years of age, street arabs, who were playing near by, around one of the lamp-posts which, in the spaces between the stone benches, marked the boundary between the promenade and the road. Among these young rascals there was a girl, who was the mother. They were playing at 'Bash 'em on the Brain-Box' – a popular game within the reach of all, rich or poor. The mother was sitting at the foot of the lamp-post, on the pedestal supporting the iron pillar. A filthy headscarf with a magnificent knot in the middle converting it into a whip was the 'banger', which stood for coercive power. The ragged girl held one end of the piece of cloth and the other end was passed from hand to hand around the circle of children.

'Something beginning with C!' the mother cried.

'Conkey,' replied a blond-haired boy, the strongest in the group, who always took first place, by right of conquest.

The headscarf went to the next boy.

'Something beginning with C.'

'Conk.'

'No. Now you. Something beginning with C.'

'Crown-piece.'

'Hey, bighead, what's a crown-piece?' yelled the Samson of the group, approaching his dear friend and thrusting an elbow in his nose.

'A crown-piece's a sort of peseta, by Christ!'

'What do you mean a peseta?'

'Just what I say!'

'I'll smash your . . . if you weren't such a little rat. I'd smash your teeth in – for putting it on.'

'So what? That's not it,' said the girl, making peace. 'Come on, you're next. Something beginning with C.'

'Christina.' No. None of them guessed the word.

'Round the ring again.'

'Give us a clue, skinny!' The dictator spat the words more than he spoke them.

Separating his legs and crouching ready to pursue his companions with the whip, he gave it a turn around his hand and added:

'Give us a clue I can understand or I'll smash you in two!'

And he pulled the headscarf as if to tear it from the mother's grasp.

'Here's a clue. Bet you don't get it.'

'Bet I do.'

'Stop pulling.'

'Well, give us the clue then.'

'It's something that tastes very nice! very nice! very nice!'

'Something you can eat?'

'Of course – seeing it tastes nice.'

'Where can you find it?'

'Ladies and gentlemen eat it.'

'That isn't fair, skinny! How should I know what ladies and gentlemen eat?'

'Well, you might have seen it sometimes.'

'What colour is it?'

'Yellow, yellow.'

'Cockles, by Christ!' howled the young urchin as he tugged on the headscarf, getting ready to set about his companions with it.

'You're pulling my arm off, you pig. Anyway, that isn't the word!'

The other youngsters had already made good their escape and were running along the road and the Mall.

'Come back! Come back! That isn't the word!' shouted the mother.

'It is! It is! Crikey! I'll smash your . . . cockles are yellow, aren't they? And they taste good, don't they?'

'But *you* eat cockles, too.'

'Of course I do – when I can pinch them from Señora Jeroma's stall.'

'Well, that's not the word. Your turn next. Something beginning with C.'

A thin, pale, nearly naked boy touched the end of the headscarf; his eyes gleamed, his voice trembled, and with a timid look in the direction of the cockles boy he whispered:

'Custard!'

'Bash 'em on the brain-box!' cried the mother with enthusiasm. '*Bash 'em on the brain-box!*'

And they all ran away as the victor followed them on wavering legs without any great desire to flog his friends, pleased with his triumph but not anxious for revenge.

Blondie would not run. He was protesting.

'For Christ's sake! What's custard?' he screamed as he held his hand up in front of his face while the Mouse made simulated attacks on him.

And Blondie added, in fury:

'Shout "paxies", skinny, or I'll beat you to pulp!'

'Paxies! paxies!'

The Mouse found himself besieged by his companions.

'Bash 'em on the brain-box!' the mother cried again, and the urchins scattered once more.

At that moment the canon theologian approached the girl.

The mother cried out in fear. She thought it was her father coming to slap and kick her home, as usual.

'Tell me, my child – have you seen two carriages going by?'

'Where to?' she replied, coming to her feet.

'Up the hill – one of them drawn by two horses and the other by four with bells. Not long ago.'

'No, Father, I don't think so. Wait à minute, Your Reverence, maybe the boys . . . Paxies! paxies!' she cried, and the flock of night-owls came back to the lamp-post, followed by the Mouse. On seeing the vicar-general all of them except Blondie surrounded him, those wearing caps bared their heads, and they kissed his hand by turns which were not at all pacific.[2] Some of them wiped their mouths and noses first.

'Have you seen two coaches going up the hill?'

'Yes.'

'No.'
'Two.'
'Three.'
'Down the hill.'
'You're lying, big head. I'll flatten . . .! Up the hill, Your Reverence.'
'It was a wagonette.'
'It was a coach, show-off!'
'It was two carriages, big head.'
'I'll smash . . . !'
'I'll flatten . . . !'

The canon could discover nothing. He was inclined to believe that the coaches had passed by. But he did not leave the promenade, and continued walking up and down, wiping the hand kissed by the rabble. Its clamminess discomforted him and he washed his fingers in one of the fountain-basins.

The street arabs dispersed. Don Fermín was left alone with a bat which was flying to and fro over his head, almost touching him with its devilish wings. The bat, too, began to make him feel uncomfortable. Hardly had it flown past when it came back again, the orbit of its flight getting smaller and smaller.

'There must be two of them,' he thought, feeling a chill in the roots of his hair each time he saw the creature above him.

It was a beautiful evening. The last pale dusk-light had faded away. Over the sierra, the outline of which was marked by a faint luminous band of mist, shone the Plough, the Great Bear; and, almost brushing against Corfín, which was the highest point of the dark mountain range, Aldebaran glimmered alone in a deserted region of the sky. The breeze was dying away and the whistling of toads, like a hymn of some fatalistic religion of resignation, filled the countryside with drowsy sadness. Muffled sounds came from the city on the hill, with intervals of deep silence. In La Colonia, nearer to the Mall, there was no sound at all.

Don Fermín was not in the habit of contemplating the serene night,[3] although he had been at one time, long ago, in the Jesuits' College, in the seminary, and during the first years of his life as a priest, when his health had been delicate and he had been prey to that sadness and those scruples which used to eat away at his soul. Later, life had made a man of him and he had followed in the footsteps of his mother, a peasant woman who could see in the countryside nothing but the exploitation of the land. That which in books was called poetry had died in him years ago – oh yes, many years ago! The stars! How seldom had he contemplated them since he had become a canon! De Pas stopped, bared his head, wiped the perspiration from his forehead, and stood looking at the stars shining above him, buried in the abyss of the heavens. 'Pythagoras was right, they did seem to be singing.' In the silence he could hear the pulsing of the blood in his head – and he thought he could hear another noise, too, like bells jingling in the distance. Was it them? Was it the carriages coming back? There were no bells on the calash, but the horses drawing the Gondola wore them. Or was it cicadas, crickets – frogs – any of those creatures which sing in the fields, accompanying the silence of the night? No, no, it was horse-bells, now he was sure – it sounded nearer now, and there was a rhythm to it – nearer and nearer and nearer.

'It must be them! How late they are!' he said aloud, as he walked over to the side of the road, into the shadow thrown by one of the lamps in the promenade.

He waited there for a few moments, inclining his head towards El Vivero and spying on every sound. He saw two lights in the distant darkness, then four – yes it was them, the two carriages. The rhythmical jingling of the horse-bells became clear, strident; at times it mingled with other noises which sounded like shouts, snatches of songs.

'The crazy people, they're singing!'

He could hear the wheels' dull rumble, which sounded almost subterranean; the fiery breathing of the tired steeds; and finally the thin reedy voice of Ripamilán. The occupants of the large coach were quiet now. The calash was about to pass close to the canon, who pressed himself up against the iron pillar so as not to be seen. The calash went by at a fast trot. De Pas was all eyes. In Ripamilán's place he saw Don Víctor Quintanar, and in the place of the judge's wife he saw Ripamilán, yes, he could see them clearly. The judge's wife was not in the open carriage! She was with the others! And her husband had been bundled into the calash with the old canon, the marchioness, and Doña Petronila! So Don Alvaro and she were travelling together – and maybe they were all drunk, or merry at least!

'It's indecent!' he thought, his indignation sticking in his throat.

And unaware that he was parodying Gloucester he added:

'They're determined to throw her into his arms! That Vegallana woman is nothing but an amateur procuress!'

'And they were singing!'

The carriages receded into the distance. Discreetly silent now, they went up the main street of La Colonia, their lanterns swaying, disappearing and coming back into view, becoming smaller and smaller.

'Now they're quiet!' thought Don Fermín. 'That's even worse – much worse!'

Once more the horse-bells sounded like the distant song of crickets and cicadas on a summer night.

The canon had forgotten all about the stars. He left the Mall and strode up the main street of La Colonia after the Vegallanas' coaches.

Only his sense of shame prevented him from running up the hill.

'But what would he achieve by that? Nothing, it would just be an outlet for his ill-humour and a way of consuming the energy that he could feel in his muscles and in his useless soul – an annoying feeling, like an attack of pins and needles.'

As he walked past Páez's front garden the gaslight shining from a white glass globe through the iron filigree-work of the railings cast his shadow, the grotesque shadow of a priest, upon the dusty road.

Don Fermín, the witness of his own follies, was struck with shame. He slowed his pace.

'I must be drunk. That must be what's wrong. Bah! that crowns it all. I've always known how to control myself – and now I have to go and start behaving like an idiot.'

He remembered his arrangement to meet the judge's wife, and this gave him some relief from his repressed fury. 'Tomorrow will soon come. By eight o'clock I shall know – yes, I shall know, because I shall ask her everything. Why not? I'll find a way to ask her. I have the right.'

He reached the Boulevard, which was empty – the working people's promenade had finished – and walked up the Calle del Comercio and through the Plaza del Pan. When he reached the Plaza Nueva he peered into the dark corner; the only light he could see in Ozores Mansion was the one in the porch.

'Haven't they been left at their house? Are all those people still together?' Not thinking what he was doing, he walked on to the Calle de la Rúa, following the route which he had taken at midday. The balcony windows of the marquis's house were open now, too, but light was not streaming in through them, it was streaming out and cutting through the darkness in the narrow street, on which the feeble glow of distant gas-lamps made little impression. De Pas heard cries, laughter, and the harsh metallic notes of an out-of-tune piano.

'The fun and games aren't over yet!' he said, biting his lips. 'But what am I doing here? What does it all matter to me? If she is the same as all the other women, I'll know tomorrow. I'm mad! I'm drunk! If mother could see me now!' The balcony windows projected great rectangles of light on to the black wall of the house opposite, and across these patches of garish, impudent brilliance shadowy forms passed, as in a magic-lantern show. Sometimes there was the figure of a woman, sometimes an enormous hand, or a moustache like a watering-hose. That was what De Pas saw opposite the boudoir windows; opposite the salon windows the shadows on the wall were smaller, but numerous and indistinct, thronging together and making his head swim.

'They aren't dancing,' he thought. But that was no consolation.

Beyond the boudoir there was another balcony, with closed windows. It belonged to the bedroom in which the marquis's daughter had died. The canon theologian remembered having knelt there, holding a great wax candle, while the poor girl received the Lord – many years before. Suddenly the balcony window was flung open. De Pas saw the figure of a woman pressing up against the iron railing and leaning over it, as if she were about to hurl herself into the street. He could just make out a pair of arms tight around the woman's waist; she was struggling to free herself. 'Who was it?' It was impossible to tell. She seemed to be tall and well built; it might be Obdulia or it might be the judge's wife. 'But no, it couldn't possibly be the judge's wife, quite out of the question! And the arms, whose were they? Why didn't the man come out on to the balcony?' De Pas was sure that he himself could not be seen where he stood in a doorway opposite, in total darkness. There was nobody else in the street, yet somebody might come – and what would a passer-by think if he saw the canon theologian spying on the marquis's guests? He ought to go away – yes, but until those figures left the balcony he could not move. The anonymous lady, with her back towards the street now, her head leaning towards the invisible man, was speaking in a calm voice and carrying out a mechanical self-defence with light feline blows on hands which every so often tried to grasp her shoulders.

'They're in the dark! There's no light in the room. How scandalous!' thought Don Fermín, not moving a finger.

The woman on the balcony continued talking, but in such quiet tones that he could not recognize her voice. It was simply a sibilant murmur, completely anonymous.

'Of course it can't be her,' thought the priest in the porch.

In spite of these reflections, which could not have been more rational, De Pas felt uneasy. The darkness in the balcony was like a vacuum – it was stifling him. The shadowy woman's head disappeared for a moment. There was solemn silence and then the clear ringing smack of a bilateral kiss and a shriek like Rosina's shriek in the first act of *The Barber of Seville*.

The canon theologian breathed again. 'It isn't her, it's Obdulia.' There was nobody on the balcony now and Don Fermín left the porch and hurried away, hugging the wall. 'It wasn't her, it certainly wasn't her,' he was thinking. 'It was that other woman.'

XV

At the top of the stairs, on the first-floor landing, Doña Paula, with a candlestick in one hand and the string for opening the front door in the other, watched in silence, motionless, as her son slowly climbed towards her, his head bowed, his face hidden beneath his broad-brimmed hat.

She had opened the door herself without bothering to ask who it was, certain that it must be him. When she saw him, not a word. The son climbed the stairs, the mother did not move; she seemed to be making ready to block his way as she stood stiffly in the middle of the landing like a tall, black, angular ghost.

When De Pas reached the last steps Doña Paula left her post and stalked into the study. Now that she could not see him he looked up at her.

On her temples he saw two poultices plastered with lard: huge, ostentatious poultices.

'She knows everything,' he thought. Wearing lard poultices and not speaking was his mother's way of indicating that she could not be more angry, that she was furious. As he passed the dining-room door he noticed that there were two places laid at table. It was too early for dinner. On other nights the table-cloth was not brought out until half past nine. The clock had just struck nine.

Doña Paula went to the desk and lit the oil-lamp under which her son worked by night.

He sat on the sofa, put his hat down by his side, and wiped his forehead with his pocket-handkerchief. He looked at Doña Paula.

'Have you a headache, Mother?'

'I have had a headache. Teresina!'

'Yes, ma'am.'

'Dinner!'

And she stalked out of the study. The vicar-general made a gesture of forbearance and followed her. 'It wasn't dinner time yet, dinner time was more than forty minutes away – but just try telling her so!'

Doña Paula perched herself sideways on her chair, like a second-rate comedian in the theatre. At Don Fermín's place there was a toothpick-holder and a cruet-stand containing salt, oil and vinegar. His table-napkin was ringed, his mother's was not.

Teresina came with the first course, salad. She was gazing gravely at the floor.

'Aren't you going to sit down?' said Doña Paula to her son.

'I don't feel hungry – but I am very thirsty.'

'Are you ill?'

'No, madam – no.'

'Are you going to have your dinner later?'

'No, madam, no.'

The canon theologian sat in his place opposite Doña Paula, who helped herself to salad in silence.

With his elbow on the table and his head on his hand De Pas contemplated his mother, who was eating quickly, abstractedly. She looked even paler than usual, and her large, cold, light-blue eyes were riveted on some thought which she appeared to be able to see on the floor.

Teresina came and went in silence, like a well-trained cat. She took the salad to the master.

'I've already said I'm not having any dinner.'

'Let him be, he isn't having any dinner. She didn't hear you, you know.'

And she caressed the servant girl with her eyes.

Silence again.

De Pas would have preferred to have the argument without delay. Anything rather than poultices and silence. He was suffering from nausea but did not dare ask for a cup of tea, was dying of thirst but afraid to drink water.

Doña Paula talked to Teresina more than usual and with an amiability rare in her.

She was treating her servant as if she had to be consoled for some misfortune for which Doña Paula was in part to blame. This at least was what the canon thought.

Something which should have been on the table was still on the sideboard, and the mistress herself rose from her place to fetch it.

Don Fermín asked for sugar to put into his glass of water and his mother said:

'The sugar-bowl is upstairs in my room. No, I'll go and get it.'

'But Mother . . .'

'No, I'll go.'

Teresina was left alone with her master and, as she filled his glass, raising the jug high so that the water splashed down into it, she breathed a discreet sigh.

De Pas looked at her in surprise. She looked very pretty, like a wax Virgin. She did not raise her eyes. Anyway, he did not like her. His mother was spoiling her, and one should always keep a tight rein on servants.

Doña Paula came back downstairs and, when Teresina had gone out of the room, said, as she looked towards the door:

'I don't know how the poor girl can have any strength left in her body.'

'Why?' asked Don Fermín. He had just heard the first thunderclap.

His mother, standing by his side and stirring the sugar and water in his glass, looked down at him with an indignant glare.

'Why? She's gone twice this afternoon to the palace, once to the archpriest's house, to Carraspique's, to Páez's, to the Pug's, twice to the cathedral, twice to the Holy Mission, to the Society of St Vincent, to the . . . I don't know where else! The poor girl's dead beat.'

'Why did she go?' replied De Pas to the second thunderclap.

A solemn pause. Doña Paula sat herself down again and with a display of patience which would have put Job himself into the shade, with great calm, weighing her words, she said:

'She went to look for you, Fermo – that's what she went for.'

'That was wrong, Mother. I am not a little boy who needs people to go from house to house looking for him. What must Carraspique have said, what must Páez have said? This is preposterous.'

'Teresina isn't to blame, she does what she's told to do. If it was wrong I'm the one to scold.'

'A son does not scold his mother.'

'No, but he worries her to death, he puts her in danger, he puts the household – fortune, honour, position, everything in danger, all because of a . . . because of a . . . Where, pray, did you have lunch today?'

It was useless, apart from being shameful, to lie. His mother knew everything. The Pug must have told her, having no doubt seen him alighting from the calash in the Mall.

'I had luncheon with the Marquis de Vegallana. It is Paco's name-day and they insisted. It could not be helped, and I did not send you a message – because it would have been ridiculous, because I do not know them well enough for that.'

'Who else had lunch there?'

'Dozens of people, I cannot say exactly.'

'Stop it, Fermo, stop shamming!' shouted the poulticed lady in a hoarse voice. She rose to her feet, shut the door and, standing at a distance from him, continued:

'You went there to look for that – woman, you had lunch sitting by her side, you had a ride with her in an open carriage, all Vetusta saw you, you got off in the Mall. We've another brigadier's wife on our hands. You seem to need scandal, to want to ruin me.'

'Mother! Mother!'

'Don't you start mothering me! Have you had a single thought for your mother all day long? Didn't you leave your mother to have her lunch alone – or rather not to have it? Did it bother you that your mother was getting alarmed, naturally enough? And what have you been up to after that, until ten o'clock at night?'

'Mother, Mother, for God's sake! I am not a little boy.'

'No you aren't a little boy, it doesn't grieve you that your mother's being eaten away by impatience, dying of doubt. Your mother's just a piece of furniture, someone to look after your property for you, like a dog. Your mother gives you her blood, gouges out her eyes for you, damns herself to hell for you – but no, you aren't a little boy, and you go and give your blood and your eyes and your chances of salvation – for a hussy.'

'Mother!'

'For a wicked woman!'

'Madam!'

'A hundred times, a thousand times worse than the ones who tickle Don Saturn's fancy, because they take their money and leave the man who came for them in peace. But these fine ladies suck away at your life, your honour, they destroy in a month what it took me twenty years to build. Fermo – you're an ungrateful son, you're crazy!'

She sat down, wearied by her harangue, removing her headscarf and winding it like a bandage round her temples.

'My head's about to burst!'

'Mother, for God's sake calm yourself! I have never seen you in this state before. But what is going on? What's going on? It's all calumny – and how quick they've been to hatch it! Another brigadier's wife, another fine lady! It isn't like that – I swear it isn't like that – it's not like that at all!'

'You're heartless, Fermo, heartless.'

'Madam, you are imagining things. I assure you . . .'

'What have you been up to until ten o'clock at night? Hanging about that monster's house, for sure.'

'For God's sake, madam! That is unworthy of you. You are insulting an honourable, innocent, virtuous woman. I have not spoken to her more than a couple of times. She is a saint.'

'She's a woman like all the others.'

'Like what others?'

'Like the others.'

'Madam! If people could hear you!'

'Tut, tut! If people could hear me I wouldn't be talking. Fermo – few words are best. Look, Fermo, you don't remember, but I do, I'm the woman who bore you, do you see? And I know you – and I know the world – and I know I've got to take everything into account, everything. But these are things that you and I can't talk about, not even alone – you know what I mean – but I've put up with quite enough, I've held my tongue quite enough, I've seen quite enough.'

'You have not seen anything.'

'True. I haven't seen – but I've understood all right and, well, I've never spoken to you about these filthy things, but now you seem to delight in being seen – you're straying from the beaten path.'

'Mother, you have just said so yourself – it is absurd, it is indecorous for you and me to talk about certain things, even if we do veil our words.'

'I know, Fermo – but you've left me no choice. What happened today was scandalous.'

'But I swear it isn't like that, this isn't the slightest bit like all those other calumnies years ago.'

'That makes it worse, much worse. And what I fear most is that *he* might find out, that Camoirán might believe all these things people are saying already.'

'The things they're saying already! Within two days!'

'Yes, in two days, or in half a day – or in an hour. Can't you see they're after your blood? That this is just adding fuel to the fire? Two days? Well they'll say it's been two months, two years, whatever they like. It's all beginning now? Well, they'll say it's now that it's coming out into the open. They know the bishop, they know that's the only way to get at you. They can tell Camoirán you've stolen the pyx if they like – he won't believe that. But this he would believe – remember the brigadier's wife!'

'The brigadier's wife! You seem to be obsessed by her, Mother! We cannot talk about such things, but – if I could explain . . .'

'I don't need any explaining. I understand everything. I know everything, in my own way. Fermo, has it done you good to be guided all your life by your mother in the wretched affairs of this workaday world? Has it done you good?'

'Yes, Mother, yes!'

'Did I or did I not drag you out of poverty?'

'You did, dear Mother!'

'Didn't your poor father leave us starving and up to our ears in debt, everything distrained, everything gone?'

'Yes, madam, yes – and I shall eternally . . .'

'Leave eternity out of it. I don't want words, I want you to carry on believing what I tell you. I know what I'm doing. You preach and beguile everyone with fine words and fine manners – and meanwhile I play my own game. If that's the way it's always been, Fermo, why are you going astray now? Why are you trying to break loose?'

'I'm doing no such thing, Mother.'

'Yes you are, Fermo. You aren't a little boy, you say – you're right, but it's worse if you're a fool. Yes, a fool, with all your learning. Are you any good at stabbing a man's honour in the back? Well just take a look at the archdeacon – with his twisted body and all, he does it like a master. There's an ignoramus for you who knows more than you do.'

Doña Paula tore her bandage and her poultices from her temples, and her thick light-grey plaits fell on to her shoulders and down her back. Her eyes, usually lifeless, flashed fire. This rough-hewn woman had become a rustic statue of experienced, eloquent prudence.

The tempest had dissipated in a torrent of words and advice. They were no longer quarrelling, they were discussing their differences with warmth but without anger. The memories evoked by Doña Paula had moved Fermo, even though she had not intended to appeal to his emotions. They were mother and son again, and the danger that words might turn into thunderbolts had disappeared.

Doña Paula possessed the advantage of never being moved by anything. She called caresses tomfoolery, but she was very fond of her son in her way, from a distance. Her love for him was an oppressive, tyrannical love. Fermo, as well as being her son, was her investment, her mint. She had made a man of him through self-sacrifice, shameful deeds, half of which he knew nothing about, sleepless nights, sweat, calculation, patience, astuteness, energy and sordid sins. She was not, then, asking for too much if she asked the result of all her efforts, the vicar-general of Vetusta, for her interest. The world belonged to her son, because he was the most talented man of them all, the most eloquent, the shrewdest, the wisest, the handsomest; but her son belonged to her, she had a right to charge interest on her capital. And if the mint stopped working or broke down it was her prerogative to claim for damages; she had a right to demand that Fermo should maintain production.

In Matalerejo, her native village, Paula Raíces lived for many years by the coal-mines which provided work for her father, a poor farmer who tilled an infertile field of maize and potatoes and also worked as a day-labourer down the mines. The men who emerged from those caves, black, sweating coal, with swollen eyes, surly, swearing like demons, handled more money with their grimy fingers than the peasants who scratched the surface of the earth in the fields and mowed the grass and made heaps of it in fresh flowery meadows. Money was in the bowels of the earth, one had to dig deep to get it out. Cupidity reigns over Matalerejo and all its valley. The blond, sallow boys and girls, swarming on the banks of the black river which winds down the slopes of mountains covered with chestnut-trees and ferns, are like children of dreams of avarice. When Paula was a girl her hair was as yellow as a cob of maize, her eyes so pale that they were almost white. Ever since she had been capable of thinking for herself, all the cupidity in her village had been concentrated in her soul. In the mines, and the factories surrounding them, there is work for a child as soon as it can carry a basket of earth on its head. The farthings which poor children earn in this way are the seeds of avarice cast into their tender hearts: metal seeds which become rooted deep in their bodies and are never dislodged. Every day Paula lived with the wretched poverty in her home: if there was bread for one meal there was none for the other, for her father spent in the bar and at the gambling-table what he earned down the mine.

By slow degrees the girl learned the value of money, observing the grief with which those around her lamented its absence. By the age of nine Paula was like a sun-scorched ear of maize, dry and lank. She no longer laughed, she pinched her friends as hard as she could, she worked hard, and she hid coins in a hole in the yard. Cupidity turned her into a woman before her time, giving her a premature seriousness and a cold, inflexible mind.

She spoke little and observed a great deal. She despised the poverty of her home and was possessed by the idea of soaring, soaring above all that wretchedness. But how? The wings would have to be made of gold. Where was the gold? She could not go down the mine.

Being an observant girl, she soon realized that the Church offered a seam which was less dark and dismal than the seams in the earth below. 'The priest didn't work yet he was richer than her father and the other miners. If she were a man she wouldn't give up until she was a priest. But she could become a priest's housekeeper, like Señora Rita.' She began to frequent the church, missed not a novena, not a rogation, not a mission, not a rosary, and was always the last to leave. The inhabitants of Matalerejo had buried the piety of former times with the coal; they were indifferent to religion and in the nearby villages even had the reputation of being heretics; so Señora Rita soon noticed Paula's religiosity. 'The daughter of Antón Raíces', she said to the priest, 'is turning out to be a saint, she's never out of church.' The priest spoke to the girl and assured Rita that she was indeed a budding St Teresa of Jesus. The housekeeper fell ill and the priest asked Antón Raíces for his daughter as a replacement. Rita recovered, but Paula did not leave the presbytery. The days of trudging to and fro with a basket of earth on her head were over. She dressed in black and gave up father and mother for Christ's sake.[1] Two years later, Señora Rita left the presbytery shaking her fist at Paula and carrying a box which contained twenty years' savings. The priest died of old age and his successor, a man of thirty, accepted the daughter of Antón Raíces as an integral part of the presbytery. Paula was a tall young woman, fresh, white, firm-fleshed and smooth-skinned, but ill-formed. One night, at twelve o'clock, by the light of the moon, she walked out of the presbytery, which was towards the top of a hillock surrounded by chestnut-trees and acacias, a hundred paces below the church. She was carrying a black scarf in which white clothes were wrapped. After her came a shadow in a sleeping-cap and shirt-sleeves. When Paula saw that she was being followed she started running down the lane which led into the valley. The man in the sleeping-cap caught up with her, grasped her serge skirt, and forced her to stop. They spoke, he spread his arms wide, placed his hands upon his heart, made two fingers into a cross and kissed it; she shook her head. After an argument lasting half an hour, they returned to the presbytery together. He went in, she followed him and bolted the door after saying to a barking dog:

'Hush, it's only the master!'

From that night onwards, and without any detriment to her honour, Paula was the priest's tyrant. A moment of weakness in the empty night cost him many years of slavery without even satisfying his desire. He had the reputation of a saint. He was a young man who preached morality and chastity, especially to the other priests in the district, and he practised what he preached. But as he ate his supper one evening he noticed that Paula was an unshapely woman, and those angles of flesh and bone, those ungainly hips, those long strong legs which must have been like a man's legs, awakened a blind, savage, irresistible lust for her. To his first abrupt suggestion, made with looks more than words, his housekeeper replied with a grunt, pretending not to understand what he wanted; to his second attempt, the clumsy, brutal attack of a pure man maddened in a moment by lust, Paula responded with a leap and a kick. Without a word she went up to her room, made some clothes into a bundle – merely a symbol of her departure, for she had many trunks full of clothes and other possessions – and walked out, shouting from the stairs:

'I'm going to sleep in my father's house, Your Reverence!'

The price of the compact which the priest made with Paula was total abdication, being humbled in the dust. Thenceforth, they lived in peace, but he always regarded her as his absolute master, who held his honour in her hands – who could ruin him. She did not ruin him. But one evening when he was having a late supper after studying, Paula approached him and asked him to hear her confession.

'At this time of night, my child?'

'Yes, Father, I've got the courage now – and I can't say for certain that I'll ever have the courage again.'

She confessed that she was pregnant.

Francisco De Pas, a discharged gunner and distant relation of the priest who often came to the presbytery, had begged for her love and she had replied by slapping his face – the priest coloured, remembering the kick which he had received – but the ex-sailor had stubbornly persisted in courting her and had given his word that he would marry her as soon as he was granted the tobacconist's licence which he had been promised by the government. She had felt reassured by this, and the suspect warship had been granted a parley. Following local usage the gunner would go at midnight to talk to Paula not at the grating of a window, for windows do not have gratings in Matalerejo, but from the balustraded platform running around the granary, a wooden construction supported two or three yards from the ground by thick pillars. In the summer she used to sleep inside the granary. One night Francisco had broken their agreement, audaciously entering the granary itself. Paula had struggled, struggled until overcome – she swore it before a crucifix – overcome by the gunner's strength. After that she had taken a dislike to him; but she wanted to marry him. The outcome, perhaps, of that betrayal of her trust, Fermín was born two months after the good priest had united Paula and Francisco with indissoluble bonds. Everybody in Matalerejo said that Fermín's true father was the priest, who gave his housekeeper plenty of doubloons as a dowry. Francisco De Pas was not, in fact, a mercenary man. He had always intended to marry Paula, but people had filled his heart with suspicion and anxiety and he, determined that a priest should not make fun of an ex-gunner, had done what he had done. But the terrible battle in the dark of the night had convinced him of the priest's innocence and of Paula's virtue. That was not something which could be shammed; the gunner knew all about the ruses of the world, he knew all about false virgins, but he returned home at dawn convinced that, by fair means or foul, he had vanquished a true virtue.

And he renewed his plans to marry the priest's housekeeper. He swore so, on his knees before her, as he had seen actors swear in theatres, out in the wide world. 'Tomorrow I'm going to ask your parents and the priest for your hand.' 'No,' she said, 'not yet.' And they continued to meet. When Paula was certain that the betrayal of her trust, or the subsequent concessions, had yielded fruit, she said to her sweetheart, 'Now I'm going to tell the master. When he calls for you, refuse to marry me, say that people are saying you aren't the only one – that, well . . .' 'Yes, yes, I understand.' 'All those things you were thinking about me, you animal!' 'Yes, I know.' 'Well tell him all that.' 'And then what?' 'Then let the priest make you an offer. And don't say yes to his first promise, wait for the price to rise. Don't say yes the second time, either. The third time, give in.'

And so it was. At one swoop Paula tore from the poor parish priest of Matalerejo, the most chaste priest in the deanery, all the rest of the price which she had put on her silence. With what fervour the good man preached unwavering chastity after that! 'Oh sinner! One moment of weakness and you are undone, just one moment is enough! A desire, a desire which you do not even satisfy, costs you your salvation' (and all your savings, and the peace of your home, and the tranquillity of your entire life, he added to himself).

Paula bought large consignments of wine and sold it to the barkeepers of Matalerejo. The business began well, thanks to her intelligence and industry. She worked for both of them. Francisco was a man who had his fancies, according to his wife. He liked to recount his exploits, and even his amorous adventures – these in secret – as he enjoyed a drink with a customer after setting up a few skins of the deep red wine of Toro. He was a generous man, and in the warmth of friendships improvised in bars he allowed the barkeepers vast credits. This gave rise to tragic battles at home: chairs flying through the air, knives ending up stuck in a pine table, muttered threats, and reconciliations – expressive ones on the gunner's part, but dry, cold and insincere on the part of his wife. The mania for giving wine on credit became a vice and a passion for the spendthrift ex-sailor. He liked to give himself the airs of a wealthy man and made a great show of disparaging money. 'The countries he had seen! The women he had seduced, far, far away!' His friends the barkeepers, who had seen no other river than that of their homeland,[2] were tricking him by the time he was drinking his second glass of wine. While he became lost in his memories and his dreams of the past, dreams which he believed to have materialized, his cronies interrupted him and between words of admiration and praise extracted skin after skin of wine, all to be paid for in due course. 'He didn't want to hear any talk of payment.' 'Man is honourable,' the gunner would say; adding, 'If I have five pesetas, for example, and a friend needs – for the sake of argument – those five pesetas – and just as I say five pesetas I could say ten firkins of wine, for instance . . .' So, although the business had been prosperous at the beginning, De Pas only needed a few years to bring it close to bankruptcy. One customer ventured not to pay, and after him others, and in the end hardly anybody paid. Paula had dominated two priests and she was ready to dominate the world, but she could not control her own husband. 'Just as you please, you're quite right,' he would say, and half an hour later would be back into his old ways. If she grew annoyed, what he called his patience was soon exhausted, and in physical contests the gunner was always victorious. Paula was built like an oak-tree, but Francisco had been the lustiest lad in the Spanish navy and he had the muscles of a bear. Born high in the hills, he had worked in mountain passes looking after cattle until he was twenty. When poverty knocked at the door and Paula decided to give the business up, De Pas decreed that what little money remained should be devoted to cattle-farming. He came to an agreement with a cattle-breeder to look after some animals for him and went back to his home village with his wife and son to make his living herding cows on precipitous mountainsides. Here Fermín spent his childhood and reached adolescence. His mother wanted to make him into a priest. 'A cowherd and a cattle-dealer he'll be, like his father and his grandfather before him,' shouted the ex-sailor each time his wife spoke of sending the lad to study Latin with the priest in Matalerejo. The cattle business fared no better than the wine trade had. Francisco took it into his head that he had always been a fine shot. He devoted himself to hunting, pursued roebucks and boars, and would even make bold to face up to a bear on the few occasions when he came across one. One winter afternoon Paula saw four men arrive in the village carrying her husband's broken body on their shoulders, on a stretcher improvised out of oak-branches. He had fallen from the top of a high rock in the arms of the wounded she-bear which the cowherds had been trying to catch for a week. The gunner died in glory, but his widow found herself overwhelmed by old debts and bills and – fate's little joke at her expense – in possession of countless IOUs which would never be paid. She returned to Matalerejo, having lost everything by distraint. With her she took the useless pieces of paper and the son who was going to be a priest. Fermín was already a strapping young lad, built like a fortress. He was fifteen, although he looked twenty, but Paula could handle him better than his father and, indeed, did what she liked with him. She made him study Latin with the priest, the same priest who had given the dowry squandered by the dead man. There was lost time to be made up for, and Fermín made up for it. He worked like a Trojan at his studies, and also did odd jobs about the presbytery and looked after the garden, thus paying for his meals and his education. He slept in the hut which his mother had knocked together at a pit-head to set up a bar. The expenses of her new business, which did not amount to much, had been met by the priest, whose generosity was now motivated more by charity than by fear. He was no longer afraid of what Paula might say, nor did she herself believe in the power of that weapon with which once, cold, cruel and sinister, she had threatened him.

The bar prospered. The miners found it waiting for them when they emerged into the light of day, and without having to take a step further they satisfied their thirst and their hunger and the passion for gambling which possessed nearly all of them. During interminable winter evenings, behind a wooden partition which did nothing to exclude the sounds of oaths and coins, the boy sat studying – the priest's son, as the miners cynically called him in front of his mother, but not in the presence of Fermín himself, who had shown many of them that studying had not weakened the muscles of his arms. The spectacle of ignorance, vice and degradation nauseated him, and he plunged into sincere, fervent piety, devouring his books and longing for exactly what his mother wanted for him: the seminary and the soutane – the robe of the free man, the robe that could tear him away from the slavery to which he would be condemned together with all the wretches around him, if his efforts did not carry him to another, better life, a life worthy of his soaring ambition and of the instincts which were awaking in his spirit. Paula suffered a great deal during this period. Her profits were guaranteed, and much larger than anyone might imagine who had not seen her exploiting the blind, brutal, undiscriminating appetites of the mob from the mines. But her occupation exposed her to the dangers faced by a lion-tamer; every day, every night there were fights in the bar, knives glittered, benches flew through the air. Paula applied herself to calm that stormy sea of brutal passions and, with greater insistence, to make any man who broke something pay for it at a good price. She added what could be called 'damages for scandal' to the bill. Sometimes Fermín wanted to help her and intervene with his fists in the tragic scenes in the bar, but his mother would not allow it:

'You get on with your studying, you're going to be a priest and you shouldn't get involved in fights. If people see you in this pack of thieves they'll think you're one of them.'

Fermín obeyed his mother, out of respect and out of disgust, and when the racket was at its most horrific he would cover his ears and try to bury himself in his work so as to forget what was happening behind the boards, in the bar. There were other things, apart from the fights between customers, which Paula kept hidden from her son. Although she was no longer a young woman, her strong body, her smooth white skin, her powerful arms and her broad hips aroused the lust of those wretches who lived in darkness. 'The Corpse is a bit of all right,' they said down the mines. She was known as the Corpse because of the pallor of her skin. In the belief that she was easy game, drunkards would hurl themselves upon her as upon a prey. Paula would receive them with her fists, her feet, her cudgel; and more than once she broke a glass over the head of one of these cave-dwelling beasts and was bold enough to charge him for it. These attacks of animal lust usually took place late at night. The love-stricken savage would linger upon his bench, waiting for the moment when he was left alone with her. Fermín would be studying or sleeping. Paula would shut the street door, because the law required her to do so. She did not throw the drunkard out, even though she knew what his intentions were, because while he was there he was spending money, Paula's supreme aspiration. And then the struggle began. She defended herself in silence. Even if the man shouted, Fermín did not come, thinking that it was just another fight between miners. Moreover, since some of them feared him because of his strength, and others because he was her son, they tried to have their way without letting him know. But they never had their way. At the most a furtive embrace, a kiss which was more like a scratch – nothing. Paula scorned their slobber; she was more nauseated by having to sweep up the filth which those bears from caves left behind them.

She did it all for her son, to earn enough money to pay for his studies; for she wanted him to be a theologian, not just a run-of-the-mill parish priest. She was there to sweep out into the street all that muck which came in every day through the bar-door. It sullied her, but not him, for he was inside with God and the saints, drinking out of his books the knowledge which was going to turn him into a gentleman, while his mother was out in the bar with her hands in the filth from which, farthing by farthing, she was gathering her son's future – her own future, too, for she was certain that she was going to be a lady one day. Up in the mountains, as soon as Fermín had learnt to read and write, she had made him teach her his learning. Now she could both read and write. In the bar, in the midst of the oaths and screams of drunkards and gamblers, she devoured books which she borrowed from the priest.

The civil guard had to pay her more than one visit and every so often she went to town to give evidence in a case of assault and battery or larceny.

The priest, Fermín and even the civil guards, who respected her integrity, had often advised her to give up that repugnant trade. Wasn't she tired of spending her life among drunkards and gamblers who so often turned into murderers?

'No, no, no!' People must let her be. She was making her pile, without anybody suspecting it. In any other occupation open to a woman with her scant resources she would not have been able to earn the tenth part of what she was earning there. The miners emerged from the darkness thirsty, hungry and with full pockets.

They paid good money, they spent it freely, and they ate and drank cheap poison, believing it to be good, expensive wine and food. In Paula's bar everything was adulterated; she bought the worst that money could buy, and the drunkards ate and drank it without knowing what they were swallowing, and the gamblers took it without even glancing at it, devoted heart and soul to their cards.

Sales were large and the profit on each article was considerable. This was the only reason why she had not set fire long ago to the bar with the whole pack of thieves inside it.

She did not give this trade up until Fermín's studies and age made it necessary. They had to leave the district and, as a result of a good word put in for her by the priest of Matalerejo, Paula went to be housekeeper to the priest of the Sanctuary of Our Lady of the Way, a league from León on an open, barren plain. Also thanks to the priest of Matalerejo's influence, and to that of the priest of the sanctuary, Fermín entered San Marcos College in León, which the Jesuits had established a few years earlier on the banks of the Bernesga. The boy stood up to all the tests to which the fathers submitted him; he soon showed great talent, sagacity and vocation, and the rector even went so far as to say that he had been born a Jesuit. Paula kept her own counsel, but she was determined to take her son away from the Jesuits when the time came – as soon as she could assure him of a future outside their holy house. She did not want him to be a Jesuit. She wanted him to be a canon, a bishop – who knew what else? He would speak to her of missions to the East, of tribes, of the martyrs of Japan, of emulating their example. His eyes shining with enthusiasm, he would read reports in newspapers of the dangers faced by Father Sevillano, a member of the Company, in a land of savages far away. Paula would smile and say nothing. A fine thing it would be, after all those sacrifices, for her son to go and get himself martyred! There was to be no foolishness now, not even the foolishness of the Cross.[3] In the Sanctuary of Our Lady of the Way a great deal of money is handled on the day when the collection-box is opened, in the presence of the civil authorities; but the priest is poor. Paula saw the five-peseta and one-peseta pieces running through his hands, but it was like sea-water to the thirsty; all that rummaging about in the Miraculous Image's brass and silver – there was nothing in it for her. Her reputation as a perfect housekeeper for a priest spread throughout the province. The sanctuary priest was unwise enough to praise her culinary talent, efficiency, integrity, cleanliness, piety, and other qualities one day at table in front of other priests, after eating well and drinking even better. Paula's reputation spread still further, and a canon in Astorga snatched her from the sanctuary priest. It was an act of treachery, and Paula's behaviour showed ingratitude. But the canon was a saint, and there was no treachery on his part. Indeed Don Fortunato Camoirán was incapable of treachery. A housekeeper was suggested to him and he accepted her, not suspecting that within a few months he would be her slave.

Nothing suited Paula so well as a master who was a saint. Within a year she was boasting of having saved Canon Camoirán from bankruptcy several times. Why, if it hadn't been for her, he'd have poured all his money down the drain: it would all have gone to the paupers and the rascals and the loafers who had been using charity as a picklock to pillage his house. Paula put everything in order. Camoirán was grateful for her intervention and continued giving alms in secret, but not many – only what he could pilfer from his housekeeper. The canon was incapable of attending to the pressing requirements of everyday life. He understood not a whit about worldly interests, and soon realized that Paula was his eyes, his hands, his ears, even his common sense. If it had not been for Paula he might, perhaps, have been sent to an asylum as a pauper and a lunatic.

This rule was the most tyrannical one ever exercised by the housekeeper. She made use of it to advance Fermín's career. The canon came to realize that he had to regard the boy as his own, for if Paula was devoting her life to Fortunato, then he should devote his attention and his money and his influence to Paula's son. Besides, the boy had stolen his heart; he was as discreet and sagacious as his mother but his manner was more amiable and more gentle. Paula asserted that he had to be taken away from San Marcos College. Not only did the boy himself want to leave, but his broken health made it essential. The apprentice Jesuit was taken away and went into the seminary to complete his theological studies. He was ordained and made the administrator of one of the fatter void benefices; and he was called to preach in St Isidore's Church in León, in Astorga, in Villafranca and wherever Canon Camoirán, by now famous for his piety, had any influence. When Fortunato was offered the bishopric of Vetusta he hesitated – or rather, he decided to go down on his knees and beg to be left in peace; but Paula threatened to leave him. 'That was preposterous!' He would not survive alone. 'Not for your own sake, Father, but for the boy's sake you must accept.' 'Maybe she was right.' Camoirán accepted, for the boy's sake, and they all went to Vetusta. In Vetusta another housekeeper was found for the bishop, and Paula continued to discharge her duties as chief supervisor from her own house. Fermín's career advanced by leaps and bounds. He was an able young man, but his mother was abler still. It was she who had made a man – that is to say a priest – of him, she who had turned him into the pampered child of a bishop, she who had pushed him up to where he was now; and she earned her money and wielded her power – and he was an ungrateful son!

This was the conclusion reached by the canon theologian that night when, after a long talk with his mother, he shut himself in his study to ponder over the sacrifices which that strong woman had undertaken and performed for his sake, so that he might rise in the world, so that he might dominate and gain wealth and honour.

'Yes, he was an ungrateful, ungrateful son!' and filial love drew from his eyes two tears of fire which he wiped away, surprised to feel moisture in those founts, dry for so many years.

'Why was he weeping? How strange! Might the tears have been caused by drink? Perhaps. Or by what had happened in the course of the day? Maybe it was a combination of the two. But his love for his mother was also tender, profound and worthy, and it raised him in his own good opinion.'

He opened the balcony windows wide. The moon was up, and seemed to be rolling along the roof of the house opposite. The street was empty, the night was cool, the air was good to breathe, the pale moonbeams and the gentle breeze were like caresses. 'What new things or, rather, what old, old, forgotten things he was feeling! Oh no, it was nothing new to feel his chest tightening as he looked up at the moon and listened to the silence of the night. That was how he had started to sicken in the Jesuit College; but then his aspirations had been vague ones and now they weren't; now he was longing for – but he didn't dare clarify and define his yearnings now, either. But now it wasn't mystical melancholy – the anxiety of a philosopher-cum-theologian – which afflicted him with that sweet pain which was like a languid stretching of his deepest fibres.' The smile of the judge's wife came before him on the mouth, the cheeks, the eyes which gave it life; he remembered, one by one, all the smiles which he had received from her. In books this was called platonic love, but he did not believe in words. No, he was certain that it was not love. It was gross of everyone – and of his mother with all the rest of them – to call their innocent friendship sinful. 'He should know what was good and what was evil! His mother loved him deeply, he owed everything to her, of course – but she wasn't capable of gentle feelings, she didn't know about tender, sublime affection. She had to be forgiven for that. Yes, but he needed a love sweeter than hers – a closer relationship, a more communicative one, with age, education, tastes in common. Although he lived with his dear mother he had no home, no home of his own, and that must be the supreme joy for serious spirits, spirits aspiring to greatness. What he lacked was company – there was no doubt about it.'

From the open balcony window of another house in the street came the sweet, languid, lethargic notes of a violin played by an expert: melodies from the third act of *Faust*. The canon did not know the music, and could not associate it with the scenes to which it belonged, but he realized that it spoke of love. Listening with delight, as he was, to that suggestive music was a form of self-indulgence – of dangerous sensual pleasure – but that violin expressed so well the strange things he was feeling!

He suddenly remembered that he had lived for thirty-five sterile years – thirty-five years rich only in trepidation and remorse, which became less painful as time passed by, but more deadening to his soul. He was overcome by tender self-pity; and while the violin lamented,

> 'Dammi ancor, dammi ancor, contemplar il tuo viso,
> al pallido chiaror
> che vien da gli astri d'or . . .'4

he wept, looking up at the moon through spiders' webs made by the tears which were flooding his eyes. He was looking at the moon exactly as Trifón Cármenes said he looked at it in *El Lábaro* every Thursday and Sunday, the days when the literary supplement was published.

'That's a fine state to be in!' thought Don Fermín as this odd idea came into his head. And it occurred to him again that the glass of brandy, or whatever it had been, must be playing a large part in this nocturnal sentimentalism.

Downstairs the takings were being counted. Every few days Doña Paula checked the accounts of the worthy Froilán Zapico, the proprietor of La Cruz Roja in the eyes of the public and of commercial law. Froilán was Doña Paula's slave, for he owed everything to her, including not having gone to prison. She had him, as she said, on a string, and this was why she could allow him to figure as the owner of the shop, without fear of betrayal. She called him 'Hey, you!' and often 'You crook' or 'You animal'. He would smile, puff on the pipe which was always stuck between his teeth, and say with the calm of a cynical philosopher, 'Just the mistress's way.' He wore a frock-coat and even – in processions – black gloves. He had to look like a gentleman to lend an air of verisimilitude to his proprietorship of La Cruz Roja, the most prosperous shop in Vetusta, and the only one of its kind since the wretched Don Santos Barinaga had gone to ruin.

Doña Paula had married Froilán to one of the servant girls acquired in her village, one of the girls who had preceded Teresa in her duties as a housemaid close to the master. Juana had slept, as Teresa slept now, a few paces from the canon theologian's bed.

This marriage had been Juana's reward. Zapico had listened to his mistress's proposition with a sly look on his face, understanding her perfectly. He was a man who took a philosophical view of life, and was not concerned about certain requirements which weighed on other men's minds. While his mistress suggested the marriage she thought, 'It's a lot to ask, but God help him if he tries to play me up!' Froilán did not play her up. Juana was a fine figure of a girl and she knew how to look after a man. On the day after the wedding Doña

Paula observed the bridegroom out of the corner of her eye, a little repentant, perhaps, for having 'tightened the screws a bit too much'. Yet he was looking delighted, behaving amiably towards her, and as sweet as honey with his wife.

'You'd put up with anything, Froilán, you've got some guts,' she thought, both admiring and despising him.

And he smiled a slyer smile than ever.

'What a let-down for the mistress, if she only knew,' he thought, puffing on his pipe. But of course he never told his mistress the secret of that night of surprises very different from the ones which she had thought were in store for him.

This was the only secret separating the mistress and her slave. It was the only time she had tried to play him false. And since the outcome had not been an unpleasant one, but, on the contrary, to Zapico's great benefit, he continued to esteem Doña Paula. Seeing him so pleased with himself, and not showing any resentment, she longed to ask; he, happy with his mistress's trick, which had turned out so well for him, longed to tell; but neither said anything. They would sometimes surprise a certain look on each other's face: the eyes of each digging into the face of the other in search of the secret. But not a word would they utter. Doña Paula would shrug her shoulders and Froilán would chuckle, rubbing the back of his hand across the porcupine-bristles under his clean-shaven chin.

What really mattered was money. Clear, accurate accounts always. Froilán was faithful out of self-interest and out of fear. The counting of the takings was a cult. Ever since his childhood, Fermín had been accustomed to see money matters treated with religious seriousness, and gold and silver handled with superstitious respect. Downstairs, in the back room of La Cruz Roja, which was reached from the canon theologian's house not through cellars, as gossip had it, but through a wide door in the party-wall on the ground floor, Doña Paula stood at a green desk upon a platform, scrutinizing the books and counting and re-counting the gold, silver, copper and brass in esparto panniers and greasy bags handed to her by Froilán, who was perched on the steps which led up to the platform. It was as if she were the priestess and he an acolyte of plutolatry. Don Fermín himself felt a vague, superstitious respect whenever he was present at these ceremonies, particularly if he contemplated his mother's face, even paler than usual, like the face of an ivory statue: a yellow Minerva, the Pallas Athene of chrysology.[5]

That night the canon was unwilling to oblige his mother by going down to the back room. The idea disgusted him; he imagined that room as a great centre of infection, a cistern full of filthy stagnant water. He could hear the faint, remote clink of the old copper three-céntimo pieces and the clear ring of the silver and gold; the sounds, softened by distance, floated up the stairs in the profound silence of the house. Again the violin pierced the silence outside with tremulous notes which seemed to flicker like the stars. It did not speak now of Faust's amorous yearning for Marguerite's look, chaste and pure; no, the violinist was caressing from the strings the lamentations of *la Traviata* moments before her death.

The canon saw a human shape appear at the corner of the street and approach on unsteady legs, walking at times on the pavement and at times in the gutter. It was Don Santos Barinaga on his way home. His house was three doors away, on the other side of the street. De Pas did not recognize him until he was beneath the balcony. Barinaga was talking to himself; but as he passed the house in which the violin was being played he came to a halt and fell silent. He removed his hat, a green one with the shape of a truncated cone, raised his head, and listened with the air of a connoisseur. From time to time he signalled his approval. 'He knew that piece, it was *La Traviata*, or the Miserere from *Il Trovatore*: good music, anyway.'

'Quite right too,' he said. 'I con – gratulate you, Agustinito, that's the way – cultivate the arts – not commerce – in this land of robbers, what?'

'It's the chandler's boy,' he added, looking to one side, towards the ground, as if he were imparting this information to another, shorter man standing next to him. The music stopped and Don Santos spun on his heel seemed to be looking for the notes. Immediately in front of him, and illuminated by a street lamp, he saw a shop sign with gilt letters which said: La Cruz Roja.

Barinaga replaced his green hat upon his head, slapped it down and, extending one arm as he stood swaying in the gutter, cried, 'Robbers! Yes sir,' and, lowering his voice, 'I won't take back a single word. Robbers – your mother and you too, Vicar-General – robbers!'

Although Barinaga was talking to the shop sign, the canon felt his cheeks burning. Before his neighbour could notice him, he sneaked back indoors and, taking care not to make the slightest sound, closed the windows until only a chink was left through which to watch and listen without being seen. So as to be safer still he turned down the oil-lamp and took it into his bedroom. He returned to the balcony window to spy on the words and actions of the drunkard whom he scorned every day of the year but who now, for some strange reason, alarmed and irritated him. On other occasions, at the same hour, as he had worked into the night, he had heard the wretched man muttering curses out there, but he had never bothered to go and listen to his nonsense. The canon knew that Barinaga blamed his mother and himself for the ruin of the ironmongery which had been his livelihood, but who was going to take any notice of a wretched victim of drink?

Barinaga continued:

'Yes, Vicar-General, you're a robber and a simonist, as Señor Foja says. He's a liberal – yes, indeed, a proven liberal.'

Since La Cruz Roja did not reply, Don Santos turned to his own shadow, which was rising to meet his face as he lurched towards the closed shop door, and taking it for Señor De Pas he said:

'You obscurantist! You darkness-pedlar! You've ruined my family – you've made me into a heretic – a mason, yes sir, now I'm a mason – to avenge myself – to – down with the clergy!'

His voice was loud enough to be heard by the night-watch as he came around the corner. The drunkard felt upon his eyes the powerful, impertinent glare of a light-beam from the lantern of his good friend Pepe.

Pepe recognized Don Santos and strolled up to him. Don Santos continued:

'Good evening, my friend, you're an honourable man, and I like you – but this black-coat here, this wafer-eater, this candle-filcher, this accursed tyrant of the Church, this vicar-general – is a robber, and I'll always maintain it. Here, have a cigarette.'

Pepe took the cigarette, hid his lantern, leaned his pike against the wall, and said in a serious voice:

'Don Santos, it's bedtime. Would you like me to open the door for you?'

'What door?'

'Your own front door – the door into your house.'

'I haven't got a house any more. I'm just a beggar – can't you see? Can't you see my trousers, my coat? And my daughter – she's a bitch – the priests have stolen her from me too – not this priest, though. This one's stolen my customers – he's ruined me – and Don Custodio's stealing my daughter's love. I haven't got a family – I haven't got a home – I haven't even got a cooking-pot on the fire. And then they say I drink! What am I supposed to do, Pepe? If it weren't for you – you and brandy – what would become of this poor old man?'

'Come on, Don Santos, come on home.'

'I'm telling you I haven't got a home. Leave me alone. There's something I've got to do here. Go on, you go away. It's a secret – they think nobody knows – but I know – I spy on them – I listen to them. Go away – don't ask – go away.'

'But you mustn't make such a noise, Don Santos, the neighbours have been complaining, and I – what can I do?'

'Yes, you – of course – since I'm a pauper. Go away, leave me alone with these damned bandits or I'll smash your pike over your head.'

The night-watch sang the hour and continued on his way.

Don Santos sometimes stood him a drink – so what else could he do? Besides, the old fellow didn't usually make too much noise.

Barinaga was left alone in the street. The canon theologian, behind the chink between his balcony windows, had his eyes riveted on the man whom he was beginning to regard as his victim.

Don Santos resumed his monologue, interrupted by difficulties with his stomach and his tongue.

'Wretches!' he said in a pathetic, deep bass voice. 'Wretches! Minister of God! Minister of my eye! The real minister's me, me, Santos Barinaga, an honourable tradesman who doesn't put the screws on anybody – who doesn't steal anybody's bread – who doesn't make all the priests in the diocese – yes, yes, come to his shop to buy chalices, patens, cruets, chasubles, lamps' (he was checking off these articles on his fingers, which he had difficulty in finding) 'and so on, and other items too – like altar-slabs. Yes, let even the deaf hear us, Canon Theologian, you ordered the altar-slabs in all the churches in the diocese to be changed – and I found out – and I bought a big consignment of them – because I thought you were – a respectable person – a Christian. A fine Christian you are! Jesus – who was a great liberal, like Señor Foja – that's right – a republican – didn't sell altar-slabs – and he cast the merchants out of the temple. In short, everything's gone to creditors, distrainers, burglars – and you sold hundreds of altar-slabs at the price you chose. People know every-thing, everything, you darkness-pedlar – Don Simon Magus – Torquemada – Calomarde![6] Can you all see this holy hypocrite? Well he even sells wafers – and candles – he's ruined the chandler too. And wallpaper. He ordered the Sanctuary at Palomares to be papered – just ask the Sea-Traders' Guild there – he's a robber – as I said – a robber, a Philip II.[7] Listen here, you scoundrel! I haven't got anything for supper tonight, there won't be any fire in my kitchen. I'll ask for a cup of tea – and my daughter will give me a rosary. You're wretches, all of you!' (A pause.) 'The Age of Enlightenment!' (pointing to the street light). 'Don't make me laugh! What do I want street lamps for if not for hanging robbers? Thunder and lightning! What about the revolution? Petrol! Let's have some petrol!'

The drunkard was silent for a moment. He stumbled to the door of La Cruz Roja, put his ear to the keyhole and, after listening attentively, laughed what is known in plays as a sardonic laugh.

'Ha, ha, ha!' was what came out of his throat and his nose. 'They're running their fingers through it now! I can hear you in there, you wretches, don't try and hide. I can hear you sharing out my money, you robbers; that gold belongs to me, that silver belongs to the chandler. Give me my money, Señora Doña Paula – give me my money, Señor De Pas, you fine gentleman, either we behave like gentlemen or we don't – my money belongs to me! At least, to my mind. Give me it then!'

Once again he fell silent and put his ear to the keyhole.

The canon theologian eased the balcony window open and leaned over the handrail to peer at Don Santos.

'Can he hear anything? It doesn't seem possible.'

Turning his head back into his dark, silent house he, too, listened with all his attention. Yes, he could hear something. It was the chink of coins, but it was a faint sound – one might recognize it if one already knew that money was being counted, but from outside nothing could be heard, surely. Impossible. But the idea that the drunkard's hallucination had coincided with reality disturbed De Pas even more, filling him with superstitious fear.

'Those wretches have got all the money in the diocese in there! And it all belongs to me and the chandler. Robbers! Hey there, canon theologian, you fine gentleman, I'll make myself clear: you preach a religion of peace – well then, that money is mine.'

Don Santos stood up, gave the crown of his green hat another slap and, holding out one hand and stepping back, exclaimed:

'No violence now. Open up to the law! In the name of justice, bring down that door!'

'Señor Don Santos, it's time for bed!' said the night-watch, returning to the scene. 'I can't allow you to continue making such a disturbance.'

'Open that door, knock it down, Señor Pepe. You represent the law. Well then – they're counting my money in there.'

'Come, come, Don Santos, enough of that nonsense.'

Pepe took hold of Barinaga's arm to pull him away.

'Just because I'm a pauper – you ungrateful creature!' said Barinaga, struck by profound dejection.

He allowed himself to be pulled away.

The canon, hidden in the darkness behind his balcony window, holding his breath, followed the two men with his gaze, oblivious of everybody in the world but that wretch Don Santos Barinaga who had been throwing mud at his face as he wallowed in the puddle of his pitiful drunkenness.

Don Fermín was like a man terrified. His very soul hung on the drunkard's lurches and on the words which he belched as he was dragged away. 'Could a glass of brandy, a somewhat heavy luncheon, a little claret have caused that irritation in his conscience, in his brain, or wherever it was?' He did not know, but never before had the presence of one of his victims given him those shudders of sorrow which were running all over his body. He imagined the empty shop, the bare shelves revealing chocolate-coloured backs like niches made ready to receive corpses. And he imagined the cold hearth, with not a spark among the ashes. If only he could have sent the poor old man the cup of tea for which he sighed in his delirium, or hot broth – or any of the things which help the sick and aged through their bad spells!

At length Don Santos and the night-watch reached the door of the ironmongery, which also gave access to the house. The canon theologian heard the resounding blows of the pike on the wooden door. It was not opened. The canon was on tenterhooks. 'Has that sanctimonious little prig gone to sleep?' he thought.

The words of the night-watch and Barinaga had a metallic ring and were jumbled together as if the two men were speaking in a foreign language.

Pepe knocked again, and after a couple of minutes a balcony window was opened and a bitter voice muttered:

'Here's the key!'

The window was slammed shut. Don Santos entered his shop, which was as the canon had pictured it, and, his way lit by the night-watch, plodded across the mournful room, where his steps echoed as if beneath high vaulting, and up the stairs, gasping for breath. The night-watch handed the keys over to the master of the house and left the shop. He shut the front door and went on up the street. Darkness and silence. The canon opened his balcony windows wide and leaned over the handrail towards Barinaga's house, listening.

At first he thought that what he heard was simply his own fears – sounds inside his own brain. But then, when light appeared in the windows, he knew that people were indeed quarrelling in that room, and that objects were being thrown and falling on the wooden floor.

Celestina, Barinaga's daughter, was a viperous zealot who confessed with Don Custodio. She treated her father as if he were a repulsive leper. The faction led by the archdeacon and the beneficiary had tried to take the utmost advantage of poor Don Santos's situation to combat the canon theologian, and to this end they had conquered Celestina; but Celestina could not conquer her father. Señor Barinaga was a drinker; so the vicar-general could not be blamed for his poverty. 'Of course,' Don Fermín's supporters would be bound to say, 'he spends it all on drink, he's always tipsy and he frightens his customers away. How can you expect priests to buy from a man given over to vice – who is a heretic into the bargain?' This was another unfortunate little irony. In spite of all his daughter's scolding and ill-treatment, Barinaga refused to go over to her side. Indeed he had become a free-thinker and repudiated the faith and the clergy in their entirety. 'No, no,' he would repeat, 'they're all the same, it's just as Don Pompeyo Guimarán says: the very roots are diseased, the roots must be burnt! Down with the clergy!' And the drunker he was the deeper he wanted to cut into the roots. It was in vain that his daughter tried to convert him by means of domestic torture. All she achieved was to make him weep in desperation like poor King Lear, or be overcome by fury and throw something at her head. She was taken for a martyr, but the real martyr was her father.

As Don Santos had suspected, Celestina would not give him any tea. She would not give him anything. There was nothing in the house, the fire was out, and this wasn't the time to . . . Shouting, weeping, objects flying. In the silence of the night the canon could hear faint sounds of the quarrel, which went on and on, as if there were no such thing as sleep. His eyes kept closing, but some strange force was holding him in the balcony.

During these moments he felt deep hatred for Celestina. He recalled that she was the young woman whom he had seen one afternoon a few days earlier at Don Custodio's feet by a confessional-box in the retrochoir. He had not recognized her then: she had looked like one more of those wretches who infest sacristies.

The sounds continued. From time to time De Pas could hear the crack of a sharp blow. Every so often a dark figure passed across the lighted window.

In the distance the night-watch sang the hour: twelve o'clock.

A little later the muffled, confused sounds of shouting died away.

The canon waited. The sounds did not return. 'They had stopped quarrelling.'

The light in the window disappeared.

The canon continued spying on the silence. Nothing there, no shouts, no light.

The night-watch sang the hour again, further in the distance.

De Pas took a deep breath and muttered:

'The drink must have sent him to sleep, at last.'

And a discreet click was heard, the click of a balcony window being closed by someone afraid of disturbing the silence of the night.

Don Fermín tiptoed into his bedroom.

He heard the rustling of the maize leaves in the mattress on which Teresa slept behind the partition, and then a noisy sigh.

He shrugged his shoulders and sat on his bed.

'Twelve o'clock, the night-watch had said, it was tomorrow already! That is, it was already today, in eight hours' time the judge's wife would be kneeling at his feet confessing her sins again.'

'Her sins!' murmured the vicar-general, his eyes fixed on the flame of the oil-lamp. 'If I had to confess my sins to her . . . ! How they would disgust her!'

And inside his brain, ringing like hammer-blows, he could hear the cries of Don Santos:

'Robber – robber – candle-filcher!'

VOLUME TWO

XVI

For the Vetustans, the end of October means the beginning of bad weather. Towards the middle of November the sun often shows itself for a week, but it is like a different sun, hurrying about on farewell visits with the preparations for its winter journey weighing on its mind. What is known as St Martin's summer is, it could be said, a travesty of fine weather. Vetustans do not trust such blandishments of light and warmth and they muffle themselves up, each looking for his or her own way of swimming through the hateful season which lasts until about the end of April. They are amphibians preparing to live under water during the period when their destiny condemns them to this element. Every year some of them complain, pretending that the change comes as a surprise. 'Look what awful weather we're having!' Others, being more philosophical, find consolation in the thought that the abundance of rain is responsible for the fertility and beauty of the land. 'Either green grass or blue skies, you can't have everything.'

Ana Ozores was not one of the Vetustans who resigned themselves. Every year, as she heard the doleful tolling of the bells on the afternoon of All Saints' Day, she suffered a nervous anguish which fed on external phenomena and, above all, on the prospect of yet another damp, monotonous, interminable winter, heralded by the clangour of those bells.

This year Ana started to feel miserable at the usual time.

She was alone in the dining-room. Upon the table stood the pewter coffee-pot and the cup and the glass from which Don Víctor, who was by now in the Gentlemen's Club playing chess, had drunk his coffee and his anisette. On the saucer lay a half-smoked cigar, its ash forming a repulsive paste with the slopped-over cold coffee. The judge's wife contemplated it all with profound sorrow, as if she were examining the ruins of a world. Her very soul was rent by the insignificance of those objects; she saw them as a symbol of the universe – ashes, coldness, a cigar left half-smoked because the smoker is tired of it. And she thought of her husband, unable to go through with either the smoking of a cigar or the loving of a woman. She, too, was like the cigar – something which had proved not to be of use to one man and could no longer be of use to any other.

Ana was thinking all these wild thoughts unintentionally, but in great earnest. The bells began to ring, making the terrible promise not to stop all afternoon and all evening. Ana shuddered. Those hammer-blows were meant for her; the unpunishable, irresponsible,

mechanical wickedness of all that bell-metal, echoing with an infuriating tenacity, for no reason and to no purpose other than the
universal purpose of causing annoyance – she believed that it was
directed at her own head. The tolling of the bells was not a funereal
lament, as Trifón Cármenes called it in his verses in that day's copy
of *El Lábaro*, which her maid had just placed upon her lap. It was not
a funereal lament, because it spoke not of the dead but of the misery
of the living, of the lethargy everywhere. Dong, dong, dong! So many
chimes! So many chimes! And so many more chimes yet to come!
What were the chimes telling? Maybe the drops of rain which were
going to fall that winter – yet another winter.

In search of diversion, some way of forgetting the bells' inexorable
din, Ana looked down at *El Lábaro*. Its pages were edged with black.
Not knowing what she was doing, she began to read the editorial,
which was about the brevity of existence and the pure Catholic
sentiments of the editorial staff. 'What were the pleasures of this
world? What was glory, wealth, love?' In the opinion of the writer,
nothing: words, words, words, as Shakespeare had said. Virtue
alone was solid. In this world one should not look for happiness: most decidedly, the earth was not the centre of the soul.[1] In
view of all of which the best thing to do was to die. So the writer,
having begun by lamenting *how lonely do remain the dead*,[2] concluded
by envying them their good fortune. *They* knew what awaited in the
great beyond, they had resolved Hamlet's great problem: *to be or not to
be*. What was the great beyond? A mystery. Be that as it may, the
writer wished the dead peace and eternal glory. And he signed 'Trifón
Cármenes'. All this nonsense strung together on platitudes, this stale
rhetoric without a spark of sincerity, increased Ana's gloom. It was
worse than the bells, more mechanical, more fateful – it was the
fatefulness of stupidity. How sad, too, it was to see ideas which were
great and perhaps true, phrases which had originally been sublime
ones, pawed over and trodden on and sullied by fools and, by some
miracle of stupidity, turned into trivial nonsense, the mire of inanity!
'That, too, was a symbol of the world. The great things in life, the
pure, beautiful ideas, were jumbled up with the prosaic, the false, the
wicked, and there was no way to separate them!' Trifón Cármenes
later turned up at the cemetery and sang a three-column elegy in a
combination of tercets and *silvas* of all things.[3] Ana looked at the
irregular lines as if they were written in Chinese. She did not know
why, but she could not read, she did not understand any of it. Even
though inertia kept her passing her eyes over it, her attention strayed
elsewhere, and she read the first five lines three times without
discovering what they meant. Suddenly she remembered that she
had once written poetry and that it might have been very bad poetry
too. 'Had she been a *Trifona*? Probably, and how painful it was to
have to direct at herself the scorn which her efforts deserved! With

what enthusiasm she had written many of those mystical poems which she now regarded as mannered and servile imitations of Fray Luis de León and St John of the Cross! What was worst of all was not that her verses had been bad, insignificant, commonplace, vacuous – what of the feelings which had inspired them? What of that lyrical piety? Had that been of any value? Not much, seeing that now, in spite of all the efforts which she was making to find the consolation of religion again . . . Might she be, at heart, nothing more than a shamefaced bluestocking, even though she no longer wrote either poetry or prose? Yes, yes, she still had the false, twisted spirit of the poetess, which down-to-earth common sense had its good reasons for scorning!'

As on other occasions, Ana went so far in her self-accusation that she had to react against it, and then she did not stop until she had blamed Vetusta, her aunts, Don Víctor and Frillity for all her woes. In the end, she was full of that tender, profound self-pity which often made her so indulgent towards her own defects and sins.

She went to the balcony. The inhabitants of La Encimada were walking through the square towards the cemetery, which was on a hill to the west, beyond the Mall. The Vetustans were wearing their Sunday best. Servant girls, wet-nurses, soldiers and swarms of young children formed the majority of the passers-by. They were shouting to each other and making happy gestures; it was clear that they were not thinking about the dead. Poor women and children were also walking past, loaded with cheap wreaths, thin candles and other decorations for graves. From time to time a liveried manservant or a porter would cross the square bowed down under the weight of a colossal wreath of immortelles, candles as big as columns, or a portable catafalque. This was the official mourning of the wealthy who, having neither the desire nor the time to visit their dead, sent them these greetings-cards. Respectable people did not walk all the way to the cemetery. Well-dressed young ladies could not bring themselves to go into that place and so stayed behind in the Mall, promenading and displaying their clothes and their persons as on any other day of the year. They were not thinking about the dead either, but they tried to conceal the fact: their dresses were dark-coloured, their conversations less noisy than usual, their faces somewhat more composed. People were behaving in the Mall as on a visit of condolence during the moments when no near relative of the deceased is present – with a kind of discreet, restrained gaiety. If any thoughts at all were devoted to the solemnity of the day, they concerned the positive advantages of not being dead. The philosophical Vetustan remembered that we are all made of clay, that many of those who were promenading so calmly would have been gathered to their fathers by the same time next year – any of them, that is, except himself.

That afternoon Ana hated the Vetustans even more than usual. Those traditional customs which they observed without any awareness of what they were doing, without any faith or enthusiasm, and to which they returned with a regularity as mechanical as a madman's rhythmical repetition of phrases and gestures; that atmosphere of gloom about which there was no grandeur, and which did not have to do with the uncertain fate of the dead but rather with the certain boredom of the living – it all weighed upon her heart. She even imagined that she could feel the air thick with tedium, an inescapable, eternal tedium. If she told any Vetustan what she was feeling she would be called a romantic, and she must certainly not mention her grief to her husband, for he would immediately become agitated and talk about diets, programmes and changing her way of life. Anything but take pity on her nerves or whatever it was.

The famous programme of diversions and entertainments drawn up by Quintanar and Visitación had begun to fall into disuse within a few days, and by now hardly any of its sections were observed. At first Ana had consented to be taken to the promenade, to all the promenades, to the theatre, to the Vegallana coterie and on trips to the country, but she soon declared herself to be tired and put up a passive resistance which Don Víctor and the bank clerk's wife could not overcome.

Visita shrugged her shoulders. 'It was beyond all understanding. Ana – what a woman! She was sure that Alvaro had taken Ana's fancy, he was pursuing her with great skill, she had seen he was, she herself was helping him, Paquito was helping him, Don Víctor was helping him too, the dupe, not knowing what he was doing – and still nothing happened. Mesía was worried, gloomy and ill-tempered, revealing – although he tried not to – that he wasn't making the slightest progress. Had the canon theologian got a finger in the pie?' Visita imposed upon herself the obligation to spy on the canon theologian's chapel. She found out which were the afternoons when he attended the confessional and she took a stroll around the cathedral on those afternoons, peering furtively through the grille to see if *she* was there. Visita later discovered that Ana had been seen confessing at seven o'clock in the morning. 'Hullo! Here was something fishy.' The bank clerk's wife was not imagining the enormities which had gone through Mesía's mind. She was not thinking, God forbid, that Ana was capable of falling in love with a priest, like that scandalous Obdulia or the Páez girl, a foolish, eccentric creature who scorned all the best prospects and as a child had eaten earth. Ana, too, was a romantic – all behaviour unlike her own was classed by Visita as romanticism – but in a different way. No, there was no fear, so early in the day at least, of a sacrilegious passion, but what Visita did fear was that in order to make war on the other man (it did not occur to her that people might have straightforward moral motives) the vicar-general might use his enormous talent to convert the judge's wife and turn her into a religious fanatic. How frightful! It must be prevented. Visita refused to renounce the pleasure of seeing her friend fall where she herself had fallen, or at least seeing her tormented by temptation. The bank clerk's wife had never imagined that this sight could be a source of secret pleasures, intense and alive like a powerful passion, but now that she had discovered this new sweetmeat she was determined to enjoy its strange, pungent flavours to the full. Whenever Visita watched Mesía lying in wait, hunting in Quintanar's preserves, or at least laying his traps there, she could feel her throat muscles tightening, her mouth becoming dry, her eyes burning like candles, fire in her cheeks, acridity on her lips. 'I don't care what he says, she's bowled him over,' she would think with a secret ache which had at its root the same kind of voluptuous thrill as is induced by a potent perfume. That pricking of her pride and of another more intimate part of her, deeper in her bowels, was something which she needed now, as the addict needs the vice which harms her while she is enjoying it, and which finally destroys her. Indeed, this was the only intense pleasure which Visita allowed herself in a life which had grown so stale, so humdrum, so full of repeated emotions. She was not cloyed with sweetmeats, but they no longer had a particularly sweet taste for her. This new passion was more vehement. She desired to see the judge's wife, the impeccable judge's wife, in Don Alvaro's arms, but she also enjoyed seeing Don Alvaro humiliated, in spite of wanting him to triumph – not for his sake, but so that Ana should fall. Visitación devised ways of causing them to meet and talk without making any plans to do so, or at least without Ana making any such plans. Paco, who had none of Visita's malevolence, was nevertheless a great help to her in this venture. Although Don Alvaro had taken the first chance which he had been offered to make Quintanar invite him to call at Ozores Mansion whenever he liked, and had already ventured a few visits, he realized that for the time being this could not be his theatre of operations. So he made his advances – consisting of looks and other ineffectual artifices – in the Mall, in Vegallana's house and, with a trifle more audacity but as little success, on trips to El Vivero. Ana devoted all her will-power to showing Don Alvaro that she was not afraid of him. She was always ready for him, she defied all his trickery, and in her quiet way she gave him to understand that she regarded him as inoffensive.

There had been frequent trips to El Vivero throughout October. Ana would watch as Edelmira and Obdulia, who had declared herself the mentor of the powerful, ruddy-faced lass, ran with joyful abandon through the wood of ancient oaks, chased by Paco Vegallana, Joaquín Orgaz and other *intimates*; she would watch as they hurled themselves intrepidly into the disused well stuffed with dry grass; and in these and other scenes from some piquant bucolic poem, full of gaiety, mysterious cries, surprises, scares, leaps and touches, she found only the crudest form of temptation, powerful when it came close and brushed against her, but repulsive when she observed it in cold blood from a distance. Don Alvaro had noticed that there was as yet little progress to be made with the judge's wife along this path.

For Vetustans there was nothing more ridiculous than romanticism. Everything that was not humdrum, pedestrian, prosaic and commonplace was called romantic. Visita was the pope of this anti-romantic dogma. Looking at the moon for half a minute was pure romanticism; contemplating a sunset in silence – ditto; enjoying scented country air when the breeze is blowing – ditto; saying anything about the stars – ditto; finding an expression of love in a look, without any need of words – ditto; feeling sorry for poor children – ditto; eating little – oh! that was the height of romanticism.

'The Páez girl won't eat potatoes,' said Visita, 'because eating potatoes isn't romantic.'

Ana's repugnance to the wild games played at El Vivero was sheer romanticism, Alvaro could take Visita's word for that.

'Look, my dear, that's just playing the fool, the bluestocking, the superior woman, the platonist. If I stay on my guard and keep my distance from all those snotty-nosed schoolboys who go off afterwards to the Gentlemen's Club to brag about their cheek, that's only to be expected, because – well, I have my reasons. But *she* hasn't got any cause to get the wind up – neither Paco nor Joaquín is going to dare lay a finger on *her*. It's just romanticism, but she can't fool me – as we all know, *pulvy says*.'[4]

On this Mesía was relying, on Visita's *pulvy says*, but Ana's romanticism was making him impatient. He was convinced that 'there was only one kind of love – physical, sensual love. Things would therefore turn his way sooner or later, but he was afraid that it might be later rather than sooner; the judge's wife was a fickle creature, and he could not venture so much as to brush his foot against hers, under pain of ruining everything.'

'Besides,' thought Don Alvaro, 'when, with the ground properly prepared, I do venture an open, personal attack' (this was the technical term in his lady-killing vocabulary), 'it won't be in the country, even though that might seem to be the most suitable place. I've noticed that in the face of nature, the starry vault of heaven, distant mountains and all that – in short, in the open air – the woman goes as solemn as an owl, falls silent, and becomes *sublimized*, all wrapped up in her own thoughts. She's extremely beautiful at such times, but not to be touched.' On more than one occasion, alone in the middle of the wood at El Vivero with Ana, Don Alvaro had felt a fool, guessing that this woman, who liked him in the marchioness's salon – he was certain of it – disdained him out here. He would see her survey him from top to toe and then lift her eyes to the crowns of the ancient oaks, and he would say to himself, 'The woman's measuring me up, she's comparing me with the trees and finding me small. I'll bet she is!'

What Don Alvaro did not know, although in his vanity he sometimes conjectured that certain favourable symptoms might indicate it, was that the judge's wife dreamed about him almost every night. She was vexed by the persistence of these dreams. What was the good of resisting when she was awake, fighting with all her strength and courage throughout the day, beginning to feel superior to this sinful obsession and almost to scorn temptation, if her nature was so weak that as soon as the spirit left it to its own devices it surrendered unconditionally and became an inert mass in the hands of the enemy? Whenever Ana awoke from her nightmares with the sour after-taste left by the satisfaction of evil passions she rebelled against laws unknown to her and, bitter and disheartened, she thought about the futility of her efforts and about the contradictions inside herself. At such times she imagined humanity as an accidental composition serving as a plaything for a hidden deity which mocked it like a demon. She soon recovered the faith which she strove to preserve and even to strengthen – pressed by the terror of being left alone in the dark if ever she lost it – and again demolished the turret of proud rationalism, nipped off the diseased shoot which re-sprouted time and time again in that spirit which had been brought up in the absence of any healthy religious discipline. Ana bowed to God's will, but this did not make her stop feeling annoyed with herself or help her regain the courage to continue fighting. Her nocturnal lapses were a check on the progress of her piety, which the canon theologian was attempting to awaken with the utmost prudence, fearful that if he took a false step he would lose in a day all the ground which he had gained.

Neither on the morning when Ana rectified her first confession with her new spiritual father, before receiving the communion, nor when she returned to his confessional a week later, nor in any of the subsequent early-morning conversations during which she told him about her doubts, fears, scruples and woes, did she say what she had proposed to say when she made the decision to rectify that first confession: she did not talk about the great temptation which had been pushing her towards adultery – that was its name – for such a long time.

She resorted to subterfuge to avoid confessing it and even deceived herself. The canon only discovered that she was separated *de facto* from her husband, *quo ad thorum*, as regards the marriage-bed, not because of a quarrel or for any other shameful reason, but because of her husband's lack of initiative and her own lack of love. This she did confess – she did not love Don Víctor as a woman should love the man whom she had chosen, or whom others had chosen, as her companion. There was something else: she was being assailed, more and more often, by formidable cries from nature, which were dragging her down towards dark, unknown abysses, abysses into which she did not want to fall. And she was assailed by capricious yet profound gloom; tenderness without any known object; ineffable anguish; aridity in her soul – bitter, prickly aridity, attacking it without warning. And it was all driving her mad, she was frightened but she did not know what was frightening her, and she needed the assistance of religion in her struggle against the perils of her condition. This was all the canon could discover; she did not make any concrete self-accusations. He, for his part, did not dare ask the judge's wife what, in the case of any other woman, would have been a necessary part of his skilful interrogation. Even though his curiosity was burning into his very bowels he contained it and contented himself with his conjectures; it was essential not to try to discover by force what she was unwilling to tell him spontaneously – it was essential to show himself to be discreet, dispassionate and superior to the humdrum shortcomings of the rest of mankind.

'In these first conversations,' the canon said to himself, 'my aim should not be to carry out a profound study of Ana, but to make myself agreeable to her, reveal the nobility of my soul and so command her respect. I must make her mine through the workings of the spirit and then, in due course, she will speak – and I shall know what happened at El Vivero. I have not been making a mountain out of a molehill, I think.'

In the conversations which De Pas held with his friend outside the cathedral he tried to discover what had happened during the trip on St Francis's Day and during subsequent excursions, but inside the confessional there was no decorous way to ask a woman like Ana about certain details.

The judge's wife was grateful to the canon for his prudence and discretion. She was pleased to see that this holy man was more concerned to prepare a virtuous life for her by means of his spiritual hygiene than to scrutinize her past history and present worries with microscopic questions, as he had called them when speaking of such matters.

'It was essential to avoid using force on Ana's undisciplined spirit. She had to be made to climb the hill of penitence without noticing it at first, go up a slope so imperceptible that it would look like a flat road; and to do this she would have to proceed in zigzags and curves, walk a long way to ascend only a little – but it could not be helped. Later, higher, things would be different, and then she could be made to go up the steep way.' Thus, in terms of geometrical metaphors, the canon theologian pondered over the matter – for him a very important one, because the idea that this penitent, this friend, might run away filled him with fear.

One morning Ana at last spoke of her dreams. Every word was veiled, but the canon did not need many of them to understand. He interrupted her, saving her the trouble of searching out the few polite expressions in the rich Spanish language for referring to scabrous topics, and so it was possible for their conversation that day to be as idealistic and delicate in form as their previous conversations. But afterwards, as De Pas entered the choir, he was less tranquil than usual. Lounging back in his high stall, fingering the lubricous reliefs on the arms of the chair as the choirboys raised their voices to the heights of the heavens, he pondered over Ana's revelations.

'She dreamed! The fortress of her waking hours crumbled during the night, and without being able to do anything about it she was tormented by importunate visions and sensations which would most certainly be sinful, if she were in any way responsible for them. In plain language, Doña Ana dreamed about a man.' Don Fermín could not sit still in his stall; the hard seat felt as though it were covered with thorns and fiery coals. As he rubbed the index finger of his right hand over two small round protuberances on the artistic bas-relief, representing Lot's daughters[5] in a passage from the Bible – without thinking about them, of course – he struggled to wrest from the darkness of his ignorance the secret which was so important for him: who was the subject of her dreams? Was it any one man in particular? And turning as red as a poppy in his stall, in a shadowy corner high in the choir, he thought: Me?

His ears buzzed and he could not hear the grave voices of the vicar choral and the choristers, or the hebdomadary's reluctant mumbling and grunting as he recited the Latin phrases of the Office of Prime somewhere below.

'No, he would not fall into the temptation of turning the tender friendship which was growing between them, and which promised so many new, exquisite feelings, into a vulgar scandal of base passions, of the sort which his enemies had sometimes imputed to him. True, it was flattering to think that he might be the object of the dreams which the judge's wife had confessed, he could not deny that, how could he deceive himself? – he could hardly manage to stay seated upon the hard boards of his stall! But this delightful feeling of vanity satisfied did not affect his firm intention to look to Ana not for the gross satiation of his senses but for the worthy employment of the busy activity of his heart and will, which was being destroyed by its involvement with such a wretched business as the struggle with indomitable Vetustans. Yes, what he wanted was a powerful, ardent, living interest capable of overcoming his ambition – which now seemed ridiculous – to become the undisputed master of the diocese.

He was already the master, even though a disputed one, and that ought to be enough for him.

'Why aspire to the impossible goal of absolute domination? Besides, he wanted his interest in Doña Ana to take the privileged place in his soul of all those other urges to soar higher still, to be a bishop, the head of the Spanish Church, perhaps even the Vicar of Christ. This transitory ambition, absurd and puerile – a wild idea which went away but kept returning – was something he wanted to overcome, so as not to suffer as he did, so as to be more resigned to life, so as not to find the world such an unpleasant and gloomy place. Only a noble, ideal passion, which a sublime soul would be able to understand and a base wretched malicious Vetustan alone could regard as sinful – only such a passion would enable him to succeed in this noble and praiseworthy effort. Yes, yes,' concluded the canon theologian, 'I am saving her and, although she does not know it, she is saving me.'

The occupants of the lower choir-stalls were singing: 'Deus, in adjutorium meum intende.'[6]

On the afternoon of All Saints' Day Ana believed that she would lose all the ground gained in her return to moral good health. That aridity of soul of which she had complained to Don Fermín and which he, quoting St Alphonsus Liguori, had shown to be a common weakness occurring even in saints, and a general affliction of mystics; that aridity, which seemed interminable when she experienced it, enveloped her spirit that afternoon, as fog envelops a ship at sea, shutting out every ray of light from heaven.

'And those bells ringing on and on and on!' She was beginning to imagine that they were inside her own brain – or that what she could hear was not the bells but the knocking of the neuralgia which wanted to take possession of that wretched head of hers, full, it sometimes seemed, of angry wasps.

Through no effort of her own, remembrances of her childhood came into her mind, fragments of the conversations of her father, the philosopher – the maxims of a sceptic, the paradoxes of a pessimist, which in the distant times when she had heard them had contained no clear meaning for her, but which now seemed worthy of her attention.

'The fact of which she was convinced was that she was suffocating in Vetusta. Perhaps the whole world might not be as unbearable as gloomy philosophers and poets said, but Vetusta was, without a shadow of doubt, the very worst town it was possible to imagine.' A month earlier she had thought that the canon theologian would help her to escape from this tedium and take her, without leaving the cathedral, to higher regions, full of light. 'And he was surely capable of doing as he said, because he had great talent and many things to tell her. It was she who fell back to earth, unexpectedly – back to tedium, to the aridity which was drying up her soul.'

There was nobody in the Plaza Nueva now, no servants, no priests, no children, no poor women. They must all have been in the cemetery or the Mall.

Under the arch leading into the Calle del Pan – the street which runs between the Plaza del Pan and the Plaza Nueva – Ana saw Don Alvaro Mesía, riding a magnificent white stallion, its coat gleaming, its mane luxuriant and wavy, its neck broad, its withers powerful, its tail long and thick: a Spanish thoroughbred. With a masterly use of his hands and spurs Mesía was making it paw the ground, prance and pirouette, as if it were showing impatience of its own accord and not because of its rider's hidden manoeuvres. Mesía greeted the judge's wife and rode up to the corner of the square until he was beneath her balcony.

The clatter of hoofs over the cobble-stones, the horse's graceful movements and the handsome figure of the rider suddenly filled the square with life and happiness. Ana felt a breath of fresh air in her soul. What an opportune moment for this fine fellow to appear! He sensed that he might have come at the right time when he saw in Ana's eyes and on her lips a sweet, open, lingering smile.

She did not deny him the delight of basking in her gaze, nor did she attempt to conceal the effect which his gaze had on her. They talked about the horse, the cemetery, the sadness of that afternoon, the stupidity of people agreeing to get bored together for a day, the uninhabitableness of Vetusta. Ana was in a talkative mood, and she even ventured some words of praise which, although directed in the first instance at the horse, included its rider.

Don Alvaro was amazed, and had he not known from experience that this fortress was protected by many different types of walls, and that the following day he might well find what now looked like a breach to be the most impregnable part of its defences, he would have believed that the time had come to make the personal attack, as he called the most brutal and direct type of advance. But he did not even dare try to get into her house – something which would in any case have been very difficult, for he could hardly leave his horse out in the square. What he did was to come as close as he could to her balcony, stand in his stirrups, crane his neck and speak in a quiet voice to make Ana lean over the handrail if she wanted to hear him, as she certainly did that afternoon.

How extraordinary! They agreed about everything. After so many conversations she now discovered that they had many tastes in common. At one stage of their dialogue they recalled the day on which Mesía was leaving Vetusta by coach when he met Anita and her aunts on the Castile road on their way home after a walk. They discussed the probability that she was sitting in the same seat in the same coach when, a little later, she left for Granada with her husband.

Ana felt as though she were falling into a well as she gazed deeper and deeper into the eyes of the man below her; it was as if all her blood were rushing to her head, as if all her ideas were mingling together in utter confusion, as if her notions of morality were becoming dulled and her will were losing all its power. And although she realized that it was dangerous and, of course, imprudent to talk like this to Don Alvaro, to gaze at him with unconcealed delight, to praise him, and to open to him the secret coffer of her pleasures and desires, she was not repentant, and she let herself slip, enjoying the fall, as if this pleasure were a revenge for old social injustices, for the cruel tricks played on her by fate and, above all, for the stupidity of the Vetustans, who condemned everyone who did not lead the dull, foolish, monotonous life of the dreary inhabitants of La Encimada and La Colonia. Ana could feel the ice melting inside her, the aridity being slaked. The crisis was passing, but this time everything was different – it was not going to dissolve in tears of abstract, ideal tenderness, in resolutions to live a holy life, in a longing for abnegation and sacrifice. What was coming now to help her out of the desert of cold, arid, vapid, barren thoughts was not the more or less imaginary strength that came at other times – it was something new, a relaxation of all her being, which overcame and destroyed her will-power and sent thrills of delight deep into her body, like a fresh breeze blowing through her veins and the marrow of her bones. 'If this man weren't riding a horse and could come up here now and throw himself at my feet, he'd make me his – he'd make me his,' she thought, and almost said as much with her eyes. Her mouth was dry and she ran her tongue over her lips. As if this action of the lady in the balcony had excited the horse, it pranced and beat the cobble-stones with its iron shoes. The looks of its rider were rockets shooting up to the rail upon which rested the strong, shapely bosom of the judge's wife.

After saying so much, they fell silent. Not a word of love had been spoken, of course, and Don Alvaro had not ventured a single flirtatious compliment, but this did not prevent either of them from being convinced that by means of invisible signs, emanations, mind-reading or something of the sort they were telling each other everything. Ana knew that Don Alvaro was being burnt alive by passion down there – that, sensing she admired and maybe even loved him, he was being consumed by a sweet and tender gratitude and by his own love, intensified by this gratitude and by the beguiling opportunity before him. Likewise, Mesía sensed and understood what was happening inside Ana – her self-abandonment, the limp-ness of her spirit. 'What a shame', thought he, 'that this critical moment has to catch me so far from her, and on horseback, and unable decorously to dismount.' His own coarse term for this moment was the *quarter of an hour.*

But it was not a quarter of an hour – not, at least, one of the kind to which the elegant materialist referred.

All Vetusta was bored that afternoon – at least that was what Ana had imagined. It had seemed that the world must be coming to its end, not with water or fire but with tedium, with the great sin of human stupidity. And then Mesía rode into the square, gay and dashing, and interrupted the cold, ashen sadness with a touch of colour, grace and strength. The appearance of that proud figure of horse and horseman all of a piece, restless and noisy, suddenly filling the square, was a resurrection of her spirits, her feelings and her imagination. It was a ray of sunlight in the midst of a black fog, a living revindication of her rights, a joyous, resounding protest against conventional apathy, against the deadly silence of the streets and against the idiotic noise of the belfries.

So Ana, standing faint-hearted in her balcony, saw Don Alvaro's appearance as a castaway alone on a rock in the middle of the ocean sees the ship which comes to save her, although she did not know why she reacted in this way. Thoughts and feelings imprisoned inside her like dangerous enemies broke their bonds; it was a delightful sensation, a general mutiny of her soul, which would have horrified the canon theologian.

Don Alvaro had not even remembered that this was the day celebrated by the Church as All Saints' Day. He had gone out for a ride because he liked the Vetustan countryside in the autumn and because he was worried and depressed, and knew that he would feel better after galloping his horse and bathing in air which left him breathless as he sped along.

'How right he was! Indifferent to religion, concerned only with his own pleasure, with nature, with the open air, he stood for rational reality, life taking delight in itself. All the rest of them, ringing bells and mechanically *commemorating* the dead whom they had long since forgotten, were no more than a train of mules, the eternal Vetusta which had crushed her entire existence under the weight of absurd prejudices, the Vetusta which had made her miserable. Oh yes, but she was still in time! She was rebelling, and she wanted her dead aunts to know it, she wanted her husband to know it, she wanted the town's hypocritical aristocracy, the Vegallanas, the Corujedos, all *persons of quality* to know it – she was rebelling.' This was Anita's *quarter of an hour*, not as it was imagined by Don Alvaro who, as he talked on, careful never to overstep the mark, was wondering where he could leave his horse for a moment. But it could not be done, he could not find an excuse to go up into Ana's house without embarrassing her and maybe ruining everything.

It was a profound satisfaction for Don Víctor Quintanar, on his return from the Gentlemen's Club, to see his wife happily conversing with the charming and chivalrous Don Alvaro, for whom he was beginning to feel an affection with which, in his own words, 'he was not wont to make free'.

'I am on the point of declaring', he would declare, 'that after Frillity, Ripamilán and Vegallana, Don Alvaro is now the local resident for whom I feel the most esteem.'

Unable to give his friend the pats on the shoulder with which he always greeted him, he administered them to the haunches of his horse, which deigned to look back and down at the humble infantry-man.

'Hullo, wild hippogryph that flyest with the wind,'[7] said Don Víctor, who often manifested his good humour by reciting verses by the Prince of poets or some other of the stars of greater magnitude.

'Talking of the theatre, Don Alvaro, it would appear that the good Perales is giving *Don Juan Tenorio*[8] tonight, after all. A few religious fanatics had been intriguing to prevent the performance. So absurd! The theatre is perfectly moral – so long as it is not immoral, of course – and besides, tradition ... custom ...' Don Víctor spoke at some length about morality in art, stepping back now and again from the wild hippogryph, which was becoming impatient with the academic dissertation.

Don Alvaro grasped the first opportunity with which he was presented to beg Quintanar to make his wife go and see *Don Juan Tenorio*.

'Say no more, my friend. I am ashamed to admit it, but it is the truth: my beloved consort, by one of those extraordinary contingen-cies ... has never seen or read *Don Juan Tenorio*! She knows a few lines here and there, as do all Spaniards, but she does not know the whole drama – or comedy, or whatever it is; for, begging Zorrilla's pardon, I do not know whether ... Damned animal, sticking its tail in my eyes!'

'I should step back a little – this creature can't keep still for a moment. But you were saying that Anita has never seen *Don Juan Tenorio*. That's unforgivable!'

Although Don Alvaro considered Zorrilla's play to be immoral, contrived, absurd, very bad, and always said that Molière's *Don Juan* (which he had not read) was far better, it suited his purposes to praise this popular work and so he did, using the phrases which a grateful hack might have used.

Quintanar could not forgive Zorrilla for the extraordinary notion of having Mejía's hands tied behind his back, and all in all he considered the adventure of Don Juan with Doña Ana de Pantoja to be unworthy of a gentleman. 'Anyone could conquer a woman in that manner.' But leaving this flaw aside he judged Zorrilla's work to be a *beautiful creation* – although there were better plays in the modern Spanish theatre. Don Alvaro felt that the expedient of tying Don Luis up and entering Doña Ana's house in the guise of her betrothed was a very realistic and ingenious and timely one. He had had adventures of that sort, which he had brought to a happy conclusion, and that didn't make him feel dishonoured. Love didn't waste its time on the rules of chivalry and, besides, going in search of pleasure was one thing and going in search of vainglory quite another; where the latter was concerned both he and Don Juan were perfectly capable of proceeding precisely as the point of honour demands. But the leader of the Dynastic Liberal Party of Vetusta kept this opinion to himself, too, and, like Don Víctor, begged Ana to go to the theatre that evening.

'She is an indolent woman. She refuses to leave the house. She has fallen back into her old ways, shutting herself into her room, and – but – there is no escape for you today, dear wife!'

The two men were so insistent that in the end Ana, with her eyes fixed on Mesía's eyes, made a solemn promise to go to the theatre.

And she went.

At a quarter past eight (the performance had begun at eight) she entered the Vegallanas' box with the marchioness, Edelmira, Paco and Quintanar.

The theatre – *our own Coliseum in the Plaza del Pan* as, in an elegant periphrasis, the reporter and critic of *El Lábaro* called it – was an ancient playhouse which threatened to fall into ruins and admitted free of charge all the winds on the compass. If there was a north wind and snow, a few flakes drifted in through the skylight above the chandelier. When the curtain was raised, the thoughts of the prudent spectators turned to pneumonia, and some of the occupants of the stalls dispensed with their manners and muffled themselves up. It was an axiom among the Vetustans that one had to wear warm clothes to the theatre. The most distinguished young ladies, who in the Esplanade and the Mall displayed throughout the year clothes of the brightest colours – white, red, blue – wore only grey and black and an infinity of shades of brown to their own Coliseum in the Plaza del Pan on all but the most formal occasions. Actors in their coats of mail shivered and shivered on the stage, and dancers, with chattering teeth, came out in shades of blue and purple under their rice-powder.

With the passing of the years the scenery had deteriorated, and the municipal corporation, on which there was a majority of enemies of art, did not intend to replace it. As in the play which the characters of *A Midsummer Night's Dream* perform in the woods, the spectators' imagination had to compensate for the deficiencies of canvas and cardboard in the theatre of Vetusta. The only remaining top-borders were those of the *royal hall* – a ceiling with gold and silver coffers painted in skilful perspective – and those depicting a serene blue sky. But most modern Spanish plays require a *respectably furnished living-room*, without coffers or anything of the sort. Producers confronted by this dilemma usually settled for the blue sky. Sometimes the back-cloths and the wings refused to budge, or came down too soon. On one occasion the worthy Diego Marsilla, bound hand and foot to a tree, suddenly found himself in Doña Isabel de Segura's[9] boudoir – which deprived the play of all its verisimilitude. The forest scenery had collapsed.

By now Vetustans were used to these anachronisms, as Ronzal called them, and tolerated all such occurrences. This was true in particular of the *respectable persons* in their boxes in the first and second tiers, who went to the theatre not to see the performance but to look each other over and tear each other to pieces from a distance. The ladies of Vetusta refuse to sit in the stalls, which, indeed, are not fit for ladies or even fit to be called stalls; only poor women with social pretensions, and an occasional country woman who has come to town for the fair, stoop so low. Elegant young blades, too, avoid the parterre, or the pit, as it is still called. They disperse themselves in the various boxes where, making little pretence of keeping the proprieties, they smoke, laugh, talk in loud voices, and interrupt the performance – all because it is the height of fashion to do so, a faithful imitation of what they have seen in theatres in Madrid. Those mammas who have lost all their illusions snooze at the back of their boxes, while those who still are, or still consider themselves to be, worthy of display accompany the younger women in the serious occupation of showing off their charms and their dark clothes while with their eyes and their tongues they pick the clothes of other women into small pieces. The Vetustan lady, in the main, is of opinion that dramatic art is an excuse to spend three hours every other evening examining what her female friends and neighbours are wearing and what they are up to. She does not hear, she does not see, she does not understand what is happening on stage. Only when the actors make a great deal of noise – either with firearms or with the howling which follows those anagnorises in which everyone turns out to be the parent and the child of everyone else, and in love with his or her closest relative – only then does the worthy lady of Vetusta turn her head; to see if there has been a real catastrophe on stage. The rest of the educated audience of this cultured city is not much more attentive or impressionable. Where nearly all its members agree is in the conviction that comic operas are superior to plays without music and, indeed, statistics prove that all companies which come to Vetusta to perform legitimate drama go bankrupt and disband. Most of the bit-actors stay in town, and they are easily recognized, because winter always surprises them wearing summer clothes, which are usually an extremely tight fit. Some of them take up their residence in Vetusta and devote themselves to being endemic chorus-singers in all the operas, both grand and comic, to be sung; others are granted benefits in which they take the main parts, perform meaty plays with the help of young amateurs, earn a few pesetas, and then leave for another province, where they go bankrupt again. These serious actors sometimes finish up in prison, too, according to the government at the helm of the ship of state. The impresario is usually to blame, refusing to pay them and then insulting them for being poor and hungry. Consideration of the bad fortune of dramatic companies in Vetusta might lead one to think that its inhabitants are not fond of the theatre, and this, in the main, is true; but there are entire groups within its society, shop assistants for example, and typesetters, who cultivate in household theatres the difficult art of Thalia with splendid results, according to *El Lábaro* and other local newspapers.

As Ana Ozores took her seat in Vegallana's box – the place of honour, which the marchioness never took for herself – there was a bustling and a whispering in the other boxes. The reputation which Ana enjoyed as a beautiful woman and her infrequent appearances at the theatre explained some part of the general curiosity. But people had been talking a great deal about the judge's wife for several weeks, commenting on her change of confessor – which, it was worth noting, had coincided with Señor Quintanar's determination to take her out everywhere with him. There had been discussions about whether the canon theologian would win her over to his side, and whether he would eventually dominate Don Víctor through his wife, repeating what he had done with the Carraspiques. Some people, more audacious, more malicious and believing themselves to be better informed, had whispered into their *intimates'* ears about an unnamed person who was trying to counteract the vicar-general's influence. Visitación and Paco Vegallana, the people who could speak with some authority, had maintained a prudent reserve. It was Obdulia who had given herself the air of a woman in the picture; her picture, however, was a false one.

'The judge's wife! Bah! – I'm quite sure the judge's wife is the same as other women. The rest of us are just as good as her – but she's cold by nature, she's hardly got any friends, and she's all puffed-up with pride because she thinks she's faultless, so she's less expansive than other women, and that's why nobody dares gossip about her. But there are plenty of women as good as her.'

Obdulia's innuendoes were still received with scepticism in most quarters. But condemning her for her evil tongue entailed circulating all the vague and cowardly hints which proceeded from it. Obdulia never gave much thought to what she said, but prattled away in a reckless, mechanical manner, thinking about something else. She fuelled the calumny unawares. Besides, the worst sin which the judge's wife could have committed was to have followed the stream of fashion – and Obdulia did not believe that she could possibly have gone that far. 'In Madrid and abroad this sort of thing is their daily bread and butter, but the women of Vetusta pretend to be scandalized by certain fashionable liberties – and then these same women go and take them all on the quiet, in fear and trembling, without any style, in the drab way everything is done in this place. But what can you expect from women who never take a bath, who never even touch a sponge unless it be to bathe their babies!' Whenever Obdulia spoke to outsiders she vented her scorn by describing the out-of-date hypocrisy and the dirtiness of the women of Vetusta.

'Believe you me,' she would repeat, 'their bodies don't know what a sponge is, they wash themselves like cats, and they do the dirty on their husbands just like women used to back in the days of the dinosaurs. What filth, what ignorance!'

Accustomed for many years to the public's cold, curious and insistent gaze, Ana seldom noticed the effects of her appearances in church, at the promenade, and at the theatre. But on the evening of All Saints' Day she received the spontaneous tribute of admiration as if it were sweet-smelling incense. She did not find any stupid curiosity, envy, or malice in it, as she did on other occasions. After Don Alvaro's appearance in the square her mood had changed, transporting her from aridity and cold black tedium to a region of light and warmth which bathed and permeated everything. Superstitiously, she attributed these sudden fluctuations in her spirits to a superior will directing the development of events and, like a skilful playwright, preparing them as the fate of each individual required. She was not fully confident that this idea was applicable to other people, but she believed its validity to be evident in her own case; for she was certain that God sent her messages from time to time, and presented her with coincidences in order that she might take the opportunities which He gave her, and might listen to His teaching and advice. Perhaps this was the profoundest part of Ana's religious faith. She believed in God's direct, manifest and singular attention to her actions, her sorrows and joys, her destiny. Without this belief she could not have borne the vexations of her sad, dull, random, useless existence. Those eight years spent with a man whom she considered to be humdrum, virtuous in the most annoying way imaginable, eccentric and shallow; those eight years of youth without love, without the fire of passion, without any attractions whatsoever except passing temptations, rejected as soon as they appeared – she believed she would have been incapable of surviving those years were it not for the thought that God had sent them to test the temper of her soul and to have a firm basis for the predilection with which He regarded her. In her moments of egotistic faith she believed herself to be admired by the invisible Eye of Providence. He Who sees all, and Who saw her, was satisfied. Her vanity needed this conviction if she was not to be carried away by other instincts, by other voices which tore her from her abstract thoughts and conjured up powerful images of worldly things, lovable and full of light and warmth.

When Ana found in the canon theologian's confessional a soul brother, a *supra-vetustan* spirit capable of taking her along a path of flowers and stars to the lucent region[10] of virtue, she believed that she owed this discovery, too, to God, and she decided to make good use of this message from heaven.

But then, on experiencing a sudden revolution deep inside herself in the presence of the noble horseman who had come with the curvets of his mount to shatter the sad silence of a day of stagnation, she did not hesitate to believe what inner voices told her about independence, love, joy and pure, beautiful voluptuousness, worthy of sublime souls. Her periods of rebellion had never lasted so long. Since the afternoon she had not stopped thinking that it was preposterous to let life slip by like a living death, that love was a right of youth, that Vetusta was a quagmire of triviality; and that her husband was in reality a guardian much to be respected, to whom she owed only the honour of her body but not the depths of her spirit, which were a sort of subsoil whose existence he did not so much as suspect. She did not have to render him any account of what, following the doctor Don Robustiano Somoza's example, he called her nerves – in reality the very essence of her being, where she was most herself: in short what she was. 'I will love, I will love everything, I will weep with love, I will dream as I wish and about whom I wish; my body will not sin but I will submerge my soul in the pleasure of these feelings, forbidden me by people who are incapable of understanding them.' These thoughts flew around Ana's mind like a whirlwind which she was powerless to stop, as if someone else's shouts were echoing in there; they filled her with a terror which was delightful. If something inside Ana suspected deception and noticed the sophistry in that chattering mob of rebellious ideas reclaiming supposed rights, she tried to suppress it. Her will, deceiving itself, took the cowardly and selfish decision to 'let itself go'.

This was Ana's frame of mind as she entered the theatre. She had yielded to the pleas of Don Alvaro and Don Víctor almost unconsciously – fearing that she was giving a rendezvous and making a promise, nevertheless saying that she would go. When she found herself alone in front of the mirror in her boudoir, she imagined that the Ana before her was demanding an explanation and, formulating her thoughts in complete sentences within her brain, she said:

'Yes, I'm going, but of course I make my honour the solemn promise not to allow that man to establish any claims on me. I don't know what will happen at the theatre, I don't know how much I'm going to be affected by this surge of freedom which is flooding the aridity inside me, but my going to the theatre is itself proof that I will not be party to any indecorous pact. I will not leave the theatre with less honour than I have now.'

Having pondered the subject and reached her decision, she dressed, combed her hair as best she could, and stopped bothering her head with points of honour, dangers and compromising situations, of the sort which Don Víctor so enjoyed in the verses of Calderón and Moreto.

Vegallana's box was in the first tier, next to the proscenium. It was the box known in Vetusta as the 'pocket', being separated from the others by a partition which secluded and half-concealed it. The box opposite, on the actors' left, belonged to Mesía and other elegant members of the Gentlemen's Club: bankers, a title and two 'Americans', the principal one being, without any doubt, Don Frutos Redondo. Don Frutos never missed a performance. He preferred the legitimate drama – 'there's no play like a straight play' was his saying – and, backed by the authority of his millions of dollars, he declared himself to be a first-rate connoisseur of the theatre, both serious and comic. 'I don't see where that's supposed to get me,' Don Frutos would say, using an expression neither refined nor intelligible which he had gleaned from the editorials of a serious newspaper. 'I don't see where that's supposed to get me,' he would say, referring to some comedy which did not embody a moral message or, at least, did not embody one within Redondo's grasp. And if he did not see where it was supposed to get him, he condemned the author and even said that he was cheating the audience, making it waste precious time. Don Frutos wanted to extract a profit from everything, and the proof of this is that he would declare, for example:

'So Manrique[11] falls in love with Leonor and the Count falls in love with her too and they fight over her and she and that good-for-nothing poet guy and the gipsy girl too all peg out, so what? What does that teach us? What do we learn from that? What do I profit from that? Nothing.'

In spite of Don Frutos and his disputatious drama criticism, Don Alvaro's box – as everybody called it – was the most *distinguished* box, the one with most power to attract the gaze of mammas and their daughters and those young blades who could not aspire to the honour of a place in that elegant, aristocratic corner where men of the world (in Vetusta the world was soon assimilated) gathered together, with the leader of the Dynastic Liberal Party in the chair. Most of these men had lived in Madrid, and they still imitated the habits, manners and gestures which they had observed there. And so, like the members of a Madrid club, they would hold shouted conversations in their box, talk to the actors, make flattering or shameless remarks to the chorus-girls and the ballerinas, and mock the great romantic ideals which appeared on stage, badly dressed but deeply poetic. These men were sceptics on the subject of conjugal morality. With the sole exception of Don Frutos, whose beliefs were still fresh, they did not believe that any woman could be virtuous; and they scorned love, devoting themselves with all their souls – or rather with all their bodies – to love-affairs. They were of opinion that a man of the world cannot live without a mistress, and each kept one, as cheaply as he could. Actresses were their favourite bait with which to swallow the hook of lust, dressed, however, as vanity: the vanity of imitating the corrupt customs of large cities. Cast-off ballerinas, disabled singers, melodramatic matrons who had been too sentimental in their distant youth, were pursued, cajoled, wooed and even wearied by these shabby seducers, most of them incapable of embarking on such an adventure without the assistance of their purses, or of the herpes suffered by the pursued lady, or of whatever physical or moral disorder made her easy to win and easy to manage.

The only serious lady-killer in the box was Don Alvaro, and the others envied him for that as much as they admired him for his fortune and handsome looks. But nobody envied or admired him as much as Pepe Ronzal, alias Blunderbuss and formerly the Student, who had a seat in the opposite box, the one next to Vegallana's. Blunderbuss was the nucleus of what was known as 'the other box', and he had attempted to rival Mesía's men for elegance and being *sans façon* and a man of the world. But his box was visited by *heterogeneous elements*, many of whom ruined everything. These men were not sceptics but brazen cynics, not equivocal seducers but out-and-out purchasers of female flesh. The seats in the other box belonged to: Ronzal, Foja, Páez (who had a separate box for his daughter), Bedoya, a clerk (famous for his lust, which cost him a great deal of money, for his knack of discovering virgins in villages and for his excellent relationships with all the bawds in town), a sculptor (whom nobody understood, whose statues nobody bought and who devoted himself to underhand archaeological ventures), the judge of first instance (who divided himself into two entities, (1) the judge, incorruptible, sullen, ill-mannered, a veritable porcupine, and (2) the man of society, the pursuer of married women with bad reputations, who provided a ready shoulder for any woman disillusioned by unhappy love to weep upon), and three or four ageing lady-killers of the Conservative Party (town councillors who made politics out of everything). These were the men who paid for the box, but it was also visited by all those members of the Gentlemen's Club who were friendly with any of them. Ronzal had complained several times. 'Gentlemen, this is looking like the gods!' he had often protested, but in vain. Joaquinito Orgaz went there, together with all the milksops from Madrid who passed through Vetusta, and even some who had been born and brought up in Vetusta and only had the varnish of the capital. And since people respected that man's box, and only men of considerable position dared visit it, Ronzal was furious. Coins were even thrown on to the stage from his own box, to draw still more attention to the boorishness of its occupants. Some insolent fellows there smoked in full view of the audience and dropped pieces of paper screwed up into balls upon respectable bald pates in the orchestra. From time to time they were called to order from the gallery or the stalls, but they scorned the masses and glared defiance at them. They talked to their friends in the second-tier boxes and made conspicuous and by no means seemly signs at certain vulgar women who never married and lived an eternal youth, always happy, always noisy, always scornful of people's prejudices about feminine modesty. There were few such women, however. Most of the women of Vetusta were, quite on the contrary, guilty of an excess of insipid staidness, which caused them to assume the expressions and postures of Egyptian statues of the first period as soon as they found themselves in the public gaze.

Whenever there was a first performance of a drama or comedy which had been applauded in Madrid, the occupants of Ronzal's box argued at the tops of their voices and a criterion of unalloyed provincialism prevailed among them, this seeming the most natural line to take in art. Vetusta had never produced an illustrious playwright, so Vetustans nursed a grudge against playwrights from elsewhere. Madrid trying to impose itself in all spheres was something which would not be tolerated in Ronzal's box. There were times when it was even said that a comedy had been hooted in Vetusta because it had been applauded in Madrid, and 'Vetustans would not be imposed upon by anybody', they did not accept second-hand judgements. Opera, opera was the delight of those clerks and councillors; they would pay a fortune to listen to a quartet which they imagined 'must have been hired in heaven' but which made a noise like chairs and tables being scraped across the floor during a spring-cleaning.

'Do you remember Pallavicini? The voice of an archangel!' said Foja, sarcastic and sceptical about everything else, but a fanatical believer in the music of cheap operatic quartets.

'Oh, I have never heard anything to match Battistini, the baritone!' replied the clerk, who liked baritones better than tenors or basses because baritones had more virile voices.

'A bass voice is more virile,' said Foja.

'Don't you be so sure. What do you say, Ronzal?'

'No – I make a distinction. If the bass sings the melody . . . But don't you come to me with your music. Do you know what I always say? That "music is the noise that bothers me least".[12] Ha! ha! ha! Besides, if you want a tenor, what about Castelar?[13] Ha! ha! ha!'

The clerk also laughed at the joke and the councillors smiled, not at the joke but at the malice it expressed.

Although the marquis's box was next to Ronzal's, the men in the latter seldom dared strike up a conversation with the Vegallanas or their guests. This was not only because the partition made conversation difficult. Most people would not presume in practice to ignore the existence of a class difference which was mocked in theory by many of them.

'We are all equal,' the members of the bourgeoisie would say;

'nobles are nobodies nowadays, what counts now is money, ability, merit. . . .' But in spite of all the fuss they made it could be seen even in their false disdain itself that most of them supported from below the prejudices maintained by the aristocracy from above.

The occupants of Don Alvaro's box, on the other hand, signalled greetings to the Vegallanas, smiled at the marchioness, aimed their opera-glasses at Edelmira and made signs to the marquis and Paco, both of whom often came over to Don Alvaro's corner, which was so *comme il faut*.

This, too, was envied by Ronzal. He was Vegallana's political ally yet he seldom spoke to the marchioness.

'He's such a dunce!' Doña Rufina would say whenever Blunderbuss was mentioned, and she kept him at a distance by treating him with ceremonious coolness.

Ronzal avenged himself by saying that the marchioness was a republican and wrote for the Barcelona revolutionary magazine *La Flaca*, and that as a young woman she had been no better than she should. These calumnies allowed him to let off steam. If he was asked why he so disliked the marchioness he replied, 'My duty, gentlemen, is to the cause which I defend, and it is with sadness, with great, profound sadness, that I see that lady, the marchioness, Doña Rufina, in a word, discrediting the Dynastic Conservative Party of Vetusta.'

After savouring the public's tribute of admiration, Ana looked towards Mesía's box. There he sat, gleaming, armed with that stiff pure white shirt-front, the object of Blunderbuss's profoundest envy. At that moment Don Juan Tenorio was tearing the mask from his venerable father's face, and Ana had to look at the stage, because Don Juan's extraordinary temerity had produced a good effect on the gallery, which was applauding with enthusiasm. Perales, the imitator of Calvo, was giving a modest bow, somewhat surprised to be cheered in one of the scenes in which he did not have to work very hard.

'That's the people for you!' said one of the councillors in the other box, turning to Foja, the liberal ex-mayor.

'What's wrong with the people?'

'They're fools! They applaud an act of treachery, unmasking a man . . .'

'Who turns out to be his father,' added Ronzal, 'an aggravating circumstance.'

'Man abandoned to his instincts is naturally immoral, and since the people are uneducated . . .'

The judge of first instance nodded his assent, without removing his eyes from the opera-glasses which he was aiming at Obdulia, dressed in red and black and sitting upon three cushions in the box next to Mesía's.

Ana began to take notice of the play at the moment when Perales said, with graceful and elegant disdain:

'To these scoldings from my father
I have never paid attention . . .'

The actor was tall, blond (this evening), willowy, elegant, agile, and had a fine pair of legs. His costume, fantastic but with historical pretensions, clung to his slim figure and suited him down to the ground. Don Víctor was enamoured of Perales; he had never seen Calvo, and regarded Calvo's imitator as an excellent performer of the cloak-and-dagger drama. He had heard him speak, with musical emphasis, the *décimas* of *Life is a Dream*, and had admired him in *Disdain's Reward Disdain*,[14] declaiming with fluency and much movement of arms and legs the subtle reasoning which starts:

'Tis wrong, as I shall make you see,
That any man should ever say
That to love is to honour: nay,
I'll tell you of love; now hear me . . .

and ends:

All love's labours have but one end:
Love's own delight, content and ease;
'Tis simple, then, to comprehend
That love, nor response to love's pleas,
Can any gratitude pretend.

And so Don Víctor regarded Perales as a very fine actor indeed. After tireless efforts he succeeded in being introduced to him, and would even have invited him to his house had his wife been a different woman. In general, Don Víctor envied any man who displayed the shape of a sword under a cloak of scarlet, even though it be on stage and in the evenings only. The worthy Quintanar realized that it gave Ana pleasure to contemplate Don Juan's gestures and figure, and in a voice trembling with emotion he whispered into her ear:

'He is a handsome fellow, is he not, my child? And such artistic movements of the arms and legs! People say that it is artificial, that men do not really walk in that way. But men should! And no doubt we Spaniards did walk and gesticulate in that way in the Golden Age, when we were masters of the world.' (Here he raised his voice so that the others should hear him.) 'But now that we are on the point of losing Cuba, all that remains of our former grandeur, it would be a fine thing for us to stride about and give ourselves such lordly airs.'

Ana did not hear her husband's words. She was beginning to take a real interest in the play, and when the curtain dropped she was left with a keen curiosity about the result of the wager between Don Juan and Mejía.

During the first interval Don Alvaro did not move from his place. He looked at the judge's wife now and again, but with great discretion and prudence, which she noticed and for which she was grateful. They smiled to each other two or three times, and the last time they ventured to do so the communication was interrupted by Pepe Ronzal, who, as usual, was keeping track of the telegraphic signals sent out by his admired and hated model.

Blunderbuss determined to redouble his attention, to keep his eye on Mesía, and to be as secret as the grave, as silent as a corpse. 'This is serious, very serious!' He was being eaten up by envy.

The second act started and Don Alvaro noted that he had a powerful rival that evening: the play. Ana began to appreciate the artistic worth of Zorrilla's enterprising, foolhardy, brave, wily Don Juan. She was fascinated by him, as were Doña Ana de Pantoja's maid and the go-between, Brígida, who offered him the love of the novice Doña Inés like a piece of merchandise. The dark, narrow lane, the corner under Doña Ana's grated window, Ciutti's diligence; Don Juan's schemes; Mejía's arrogance; the adventurer's first, *provisional* seduction, in which he did not have to give any proof of his valour; the fiendish preparations for the great adventure – the attack on the convent – it all moved the judge's wife to her very soul with its fresh, dramatic vigour which many people cannot appreciate, either because they were introduced to the play before they had the critical powers to enjoy it, and as a result are immune to its beauty, or because they do not know chalk from cheese. Ana marvelled at the poetry in those lanes of canvas, which she saw as transformed into solid constructions of another age – and marvelled no less at the scorn with which it was viewed and heard in boxes and stalls. The gallery, joyful and enthusiastic, seemed much more intelligent and cultured than the high society of Vetusta.

Ana felt herself transported to the times of Don Juan, which she imagined as vague historical romanticism would have that they were. Her sentimental egotism returned and she began to regret not having been born four or five centuries earlier. 'Perhaps in those times life in Vetusta was enjoyable, with its convents full of fair and noble ladies, its daring lovers and its troubadours serenading in the lanes beneath shuttered windows. The small, sad, dirty squares and streets might have looked as ugly as they do now, but they must have been full of the poetry of those times. And the façades blackened by damp, the iron gratings, the shadowy colonnades, the murky corners on moonlit nights, the fanaticism of the inhabitants, the vendettas, must all have been dramatic, worthy of the verses of a Zorrilla – not the heap of filth, prose, naked ugliness that it all is now.' To compare those Middle Ages of her dreams – it was Perales's fault that she located Don Juan Tenorio in the Middle Ages – with the spectators sitting around her was a sad awakening. Cloaks black and brown, top hats hideous and absurd – all sad, all dark, all clumsy and expressionless – cold. Even Don Alvaro seemed to be a part of the dull prose all about her. How much more she would have admired him in the tippet, cap, jerkin and knitted breeches sported by Perales! From that moment onwards she dressed her adorer in the costume of the actor and, as soon as the actor returned to the stage, she gave him her adorer's face and features without depriving him of his walk, his sweet melodious voice, or any of his other artistic qualities.

The third act was a revelation of passionate poetry. Ana shuddered when she saw Doña Inés in her cell. The novice looked so like her! As Ana noticed the resemblance so did the audience – there was a murmur of admiration, and many spectators ventured to take a furtive look at Vegallana's box.

Love had turned González into an actress. She had fallen in love with Perales, who had abducted her, and they had married in secret. Together, they toured all the provinces, and to help with the conjugal budget the love-smitten young woman decided to tread the boards, although she came from a very wealthy family. She imitated whichever actress Perales told her to imitate, but on occasions she made bold to be original, and was excellent in the role of an enamoured virgin. She was very pretty, and in the white novice's habit – her head imprisoned in a stiff wimple, her cheeks bright red, her eyes shining, her lips aflame, her hands poised in a hieratic position, and her whole figure radiating the most limpid modesty and chastity – she was a captivating sight. She spoke Doña Inés's lines in a trembling, crystalline voice, and in moments of rapture she allowed herself to be carried away by true passion – since she was performing with her husband – and achieved a poetic realism whose full worth neither Perales nor the greater part of the audience was capable of appreciating.

But Ana was. With her eyes riveted on the novice, oblivious of everything but what was happening on stage, she feasted on the poetry of that chaste cell into which love was filtering through the walls. 'But this is divine!' she said, turning to her husband, as she ran her tongue over her dry lips. Don Juan's letter, hidden in the book of devotion, read at first in a trembling voice and then with superstitious fear, as Brígida the go-between holds a candle close to the piece of paper; his almost supernatural nearness; the terror which his supposed sorcery awakes in the novice, who already thinks she can feel its effects; everything, everything Ana saw and imagined was poetic magic to her, and it was with difficulty that she held back the tears which were pressing at her eyes.

'Oh! yes, that was love: a philtre, fire, mystical madness. It was impossible to run away from it, impossible to enjoy greater fortune than to savour it, poisonous as it was. Ana compared herself with the novice. Ozores Mansion was her convent, her husband the rigid order of boredom and coldness in which she had professed a full eight years before; and Don Juan – Don Juan was Mesía, who also filtered through walls, made miraculous appearances and filled the air with his presence!'

In the interval between the third and fourth acts Don Alvaro came to the marquis's box.

As Ana held out her hand she was afraid that he might venture to squeeze it, but he did not – he gave it his usual energetic tug, following the fashion which was then beginning in Madrid, but he did not squeeze. He did sit down by her side, though, and they were soon talking together, apart from the general conversation.

Don Víctor had gone out into the corridor to smoke and to argue with some Vetustan youngsters who disparaged romanticism and quoted Dumas and Sardou,[15] repeating what they had heard in Madrid.

Giving Don Alvaro no time to develop the conversation as he wanted, Ana poured upon his prosaic imagination the torrent of poetry which had flowed into her from the noble play, fresh and full of beauty and colour, by the great Zorrilla.

Poor Ana spoke with impassioned eloquence, imagining that the leader of the Dynastic Liberal Party understood her – that he was not like all the other Vetustans, as stolid as stone walls, who even went so far as to smile with pity as they heard those verses, 'pretty and nice-sounding, but lacking in substance', as Don Frutos affirmed in the marchioness's box.

Mesía was surprised and even upset by Ana's enthusiasm. Talking about *Don Juan Tenorio* as if it were a brand-new play! Really, by now Zorrilla's *Don Juan* was only good for parodying! It was impossible to get her on to any suitable subject, and so the Don Juan of Vetusta attempted to chime in with his friend's vagaries and play the part of the secret sentimentalist like the ones in Feuillet's plays and novels – a great deal of *esprit* concealing a heart of gold, which keeps itself hidden for fear of the thorns of reality. That was the height of distinction as understood by Don Alvaro, and that was how he tried to present himself to the judge's wife, 'seeing that one clearly had to work for all one was worth to get her to fall in love'.

Ana did not try to stop the seducer from devouring her with his grey eyes, and she returned his look with a sweet, impassioned, unblinking gaze. In her exaltation she could not notice that his borrowed idealism was affected and false through and through. Indeed she spoke so incessantly that she could hardly hear him, and she thought that what he was saying agreed with her own ideas. That mirage of visionary enthusiasm, which often appears at such moments, came to Don Alvaro's aid that evening. His noble, virile good looks, heightened by his excited passion, were also a great help. His fine-featured face bore a look of spiritual melancholy, which was purely apparent, a combination of line and shadow and, in part, the marks of a life wasted in vice and love.

When the fourth act began, Ana placed a finger over her mouth and said with a smile:

'Be quiet now! We have talked quite enough. Now let me listen.'

'I – I don't know whether I shouldn't take my leave.'

'No, no – why?' she replied, immediately regretting her words.

'I don't know that I'm not in the way – whether there's room . . .'

'There's room enough, because Quintanar is in your box. Look.'

It was true, there he was, arguing with Don Frutos, who was insisting that *Don Juan Tenorio* lacked substance.

Don Alvaro stayed with the judge's wife.

He could see her neck, strong yet smooth and delicate, white and tempting with its black frizzy down and the provocative place from which her hair rose taut, convergent and graceful into her bun. Don Alvaro wondered whether, in this situation, he should venture to come a little closer to her than usual. He could feel her skirt brushing against his knees, he could conjecture where her foot was beneath her skirt and now and then he touched her foot for an instant. 'That evening she was – at simmering point' (a symbolical expression in Mesía's thought), but in spite of everything he did not dare come any closer to her – even though no horse hindered him there. 'The dear woman had become so sublimized! And, to keep up with her and gratify her, he had played the romantic too, the spiritual man, the mystic – so how the devil could he risk a pedestrian, personal attack now! What a diabolical *imbroglio* it had all become!' And, worst of all, he was unlikely to be able to bring the judge's wife to heel for a long while yet. How could he say to her 'Come back down to earth, my friend, you're only flying through imaginary spaces'? These facts, which to Don Alvaro seemed shameful and indeed ridiculous, induced him to resist his vehement desire to press Ana's foot or touch her leg with his knees.

Which was what Paquito was doing to his cousin Edelmira. The robust village-virgin was as red as a coal of fire and while Don Juan, upon his bended knees before Doña Inés, inquired whether the air was not better to breathe on that remote river bank, Edelmira choked and swallowed as she felt her cousin's fumbling feet and heard words whispered into her ear which were like sparks from a forge. Although not ill, she had dark rings around her eyes. She fanned herself incessantly, also using her fan to cover her mouth when, in the middle of scenes of high drama, she was attacked by the urge to burst out laughing at the Young Marquis's quips – he said such funny things!

Ana could not find any similarities between the fourth act and her own life – she hadn't come to the fourth act yet. 'Did it depict the future? Would she succumb like Doña Inés, would she fall maddened by love into the arms of Don Juan? She didn't think so. She believed she had the strength never to surrender her body, that miserable body which was, without any doubt, the property of Don Víctor. But, apart from all that, what a poetic fourth act! The Guadalquivir below, Seville in the distance – Don Juan's villa, the boat under the balcony, the declaration of love by the light of the moon . . . If that was romanticism, then romanticism was eternal!' Doña Inés was saying:

'Don Juan, Don Juan, I thee implore,
I call on thy nobility . . .'[16]

These lines – which foolish prosaism has tried to make ridiculous and vulgar, running them thousands upon thousands of times over its slimy lips, as slimy as the belly of a toad – sounded that evening in Ana's ears like the sublime expression of a pure, innocent love surrendering with a faith in the beloved natural in any great passion. And then Ana could control herself no longer. She wept, wept, with infinite pity for Inés. What was being enacted on stage was not now a love scene; it was somehow religious, and Ana's soul leapt on towards the highest ideals, towards the pure, perfect sentiment of universal charity – she didn't know exactly what it was, all she knew was that she was almost fainting from such intense emotion.

Nobody noticed Ana's tears. Don Alvaro only observed that her bosom was moving more rapidly and rising higher as she breathed. The man of the world made a mistake: he thought that the emotion betrayed by her violent breathing was caused by his own elegant and close presence, he believed in a *purely physiological influence,* and he almost ruined everything. He felt for Ana's foot at the instant when her thoughts, tripping on, had brought her to the concept of God, the pure, ideal, universal love which unites the Creator and His creatures. It was fortunate for Mesía that he was unsuccessful in his quest for one of Ana's feet in that pile of leaves, her petticoats. She had just placed them both on a rung of Edelmira's chair.

The quarrel between Don Juan and the Commander of Ulloa brought the judge's wife back to reality and made her notice the worthy Ulloa's extraordinary obstinacy. Since her excited imagination insisted on comparing Seville with Vetusta, she felt a superstitious fear when she saw the disastrous outcome of the Andalusian libertine's adventures. The pistol shot with which Don Juan settled accounts with the commander made her shudder; it was a terrible presentiment. As in a flash of lightning, Ana saw Don Víctor in jerkin and tippet of black velvet lying face upwards bathed in blood, and Don Alvaro standing over the corpse with a pistol in his hand.

When the curtain fell the marchioness declared that she could not take any more of Don Juan Tenorio.

'I'm off, my children, I don't like to see cemeteries and skeletons. There'll be more than enough time for all that later on. Goodbye. You stay if you like. God! half past eleven, come two o'clock it still won't have finished.'

Don Víctor provided Ana with a summary of the rest of the play. She decided to preserve intact the enchanting impression of the first part, and left with the marchioness and Mesía.

Edelmira stayed behind, with Don Víctor and Paco.

'I shall take the girl home, my Lady. Would you drop Ana off?' said Quintanar.

Mesía accompanied the ladies to the coach and took his leave. And then he did squeeze Anita's hand a little. She drew it back in alarm.

Mesía returned to the marquis's box to keep Don Víctor occupied in conversation. He had a back-scratching arrangement with Paco, who needed someone to distract Don Víctor's attention so as to be left alone with Edelmira. Mesía, who had so often been rendered similar services by the Young Marquis, knew his duty.

Moreover, he always seized any opportunity he was offered to tighten the bonds of his friendship with the pleasant Aragonese gentleman who was going to be his victim in due course – if he was half the man he thought he was.

Don Víctor welcomed his handsome friend with all his heart, and expounded his ideas on the subject of dramatic literature. As always, he concluded with his theory of honour as understood in the Golden Age, when the sun never set on the Spanish Empire.

'Look here,' said Don Víctor, to whom Don Alvaro was listening with interest, 'look here, I am ordinarily a highly pacific person. Nobody can say that I, an ex-magistrate of the Royal Provincial Court – of whom it can very nearly be said that I retired in order not to put my signature to any more death sentences – nobody, I repeat, can say that I am affected by that finical point of honour, so cherished by our forefathers, which those youngsters down there say is unrealistic. Even so, I am certain – my heart tells me so – that if my wife were to fail in her duty to me (an absurd hypothesis, of course) – I have told Tomás Crespo so, many times – I would bleed her to death.'

('You animal!' thought Don Alvaro.)

'And as for her accomplice – ah! as for him, for a start, I handle the sword and the pistol like a master. When I was fond of performing in the amateur theatre (that is to say, when my age and my social position permitted me to perform, for I have never ceased to be fond of it), realizing that it was most ridiculous not to fight in a proper manner on the stage, I took a fencing master and, as it happened, I soon revealed a great aptitude for the steel. I am a peaceful person, true, nobody has ever given me cause so much as to scratch him. But just imagine – the day when . . . Well, I can say the same and much more about the pistol. I am a dead shot. As I was saying, I would transfix her accomplice, yes, that is what I prefer. The pistol pertains to the modern drama, it is prosaic, so I would employ cold steel to kill him. But to return to my thesis. My thesis was . . . what was it? do you remember?'

Don Alvaro did not remember, but the proposed use of cold steel to kill the accomplice had alarmed him a little.

When, at nearly three o'clock, back at his hotel after a visit to the Gentlemen's Club, Mesía was trying to induce sleep by imagining himself in sensuous scenes of love by the side of their heroine the judge's wife – scenes which promised to materialize before very long – suddenly, as he was about to fall asleep, he saw the humdrum good-natured figure of Don Víctor. He saw him, at the absurd beginning of a dream, wearing cap and gown and grasping a sword. It was the sword with an enormous cross-guard brandished by Perales in *Don Juan Tenorio*.

When Ana awoke next morning she did not remember having dreamed about Don Alvaro. She had slept soundly, and did not awake until nearly ten o'clock. Petra, her sly blonde housemaid, was standing by her side with a discreet smile on her face.

'I have been sleeping for a long time, why didn't you wake me earlier?'

'Madam has had such a bad night . . .'

'A bad night? Me?'

'Yes, madam was dreaming aloud, shouting . . .'

'Me?'

'Yes, it must have been a nightmare.'

'And – did you hear me from . . . ?'

'Yes, ma'am, I was still up, I stayed up to wait for the master, because Anselmo's such a lout he always falls asleep. The master came home at two o'clock.'

'And I cried out . . .'

'A little after the master came home. He didn't hear anything, he didn't come in for fear of waking madam up. I returned to see if madam was asleep, or required anything – and I thought it must be a nightmare, but I didn't dare wake madam up.'

Ana felt tired. She had a bad taste in her mouth and was afraid that she might be feeling the first symptoms of migraine.

'A nightmare! But I don't remember suffering . . .'

'Oh no, it can't have been a very – bad nightmare, because madam was smiling – tossing and turning . . .'

'And – and – what was I saying?'

'Oh, what was madam saying! I couldn't make it out too well. Odd words. Names.'

'What names?' Ana blushed as she asked the question. 'What names?' she repeated.

'Madam was calling for the master.'

'The master?'

'Yes – yes. Madam was saying "Víctor! Víctor!" '

Ana knew that Petra was lying. She nearly always called her husband 'Quintanar'.

Her housemaid's undisguised smile only added to her suspicions. She fell silent and tried to hide her confusion.

Coming closer to the bed and lowering her voice Petra said, serious again:

'This has come for madam.'

'A letter? Who from?' asked Ana in a trembling voice, tearing the paper from Petra's hands.

'Could that madman have had the audacity . . .? It was preposterous.'

Having observed the expression of dismay which appeared on her mistress's face, Petra added:

'It must be from the canon theologian, because Teresina, Doña Paula's maid, brought it.'

Ana nodded as she read.

Petra left the room noiselessly, like a cat. She was smiling to her thoughts.

The canon's letter, written on lightly perfumed paper with a purple cross above the date, said:

My dear friend, You will find me in the chapel between five o'clock and half past five this afternoon. You will not have to wait, because you are the only person who will be confessing. As you know, today is not one of the days on which I normally hear confessions, but I thought it wise to ask you to come this afternoon for reasons which I shall explain to you. Your affectionate friend and servant,

FERMÍN DE PAS.

Not 'Canon Fermín De Pas.'

'How strange! Since the previous afternoon she had forgotten all about the canon theologian. Not once since Don Alvaro's appearance on horseback had the grave, graceful image of her respected, esteemed and admired spiritual father passed through her mind. And now he had suddenly come to frighten her, as if he had caught her committing the sin of infidelity. For the first time Ana was ashamed of her imprudent behaviour. What the presence of Don Víctor had not been able to awake in her was awoken now by the image of Don Fermín. Now she considered herself to have been unfaithful in thought. But how strange! Unfaithful to a man to whom she did not, and could not, owe any fidelity.'

'Of course,' she thought, 'we had agreed that I would go to confession early tomorrow morning – and I had forgotten all about it! And now he's bringing the confession forward. He wants me to go this afternoon. I can't! I'm not ready for it. With these ideas in my head, this rebellion in my soul, I can't go!'

She dressed as fast as she could. She took up a piece of paper perfumed like the canon's letter, but more strongly, and, in some agitation, as if she were committing treason, wrote him a tender letter in a trembling hand. She was deceiving him, telling him that she felt unwell, that she had suffered a migraine, and asking him to excuse her, she would let him know . . .'

She handed the lying letter to Petra and told her to deliver it at once, without telling the master.

Don Víctor had often manifested his nonconformity, as he called it, to Ana's frequent recourse to the sacrament of confession. Since he was afraid of being considered to lack resolution, and was indeed irresolute in his own house, he made a great deal of noise whenever he became angry.

So as to avoid the noise, which was bothersome, even though of no consequence, Ana tried to prevent him from finding out about her frequent visits to the cathedral.

'Her worthy husband could not imagine that they were for his own good!'

Ana had taken Petra as her confidante and accomplice in these innocent subterfuges. But the servant girl, while pretending to believe the motives claimed by her mistress for concealing her devotion, had horrible suspicions.

As she walked to the canon's house with the letter, she was thinking:

'Just as I feared, in pairs, they come in pairs – one a devil, the other a saint. *On earth as it is in heaven!*'

Ana was uneasy and annoyed with herself all day long. It was not that she repented of having imperilled her honour, of having given Don Alvaro's amorous audacity wings on which to fly – for they were wings of the very flimsiest gauze. Nor was she sorry to be deceiving poor Quintanar, for she was keeping her body, his legitimate property, for him. But to think that not once throughout the whole of the previous evening had she given a thought to the canon theologian, in spite of so many sublime thoughts and feelings!

'And now, to cap it all, she was deceiving him, telling him that she was unwell so as to avoid seeing him. She was afraid of him! Even the tender, almost loving style of her letter was treacherous. It was all so unworthy of her! Her body she had to keep for Quintanar; but shouldn't she keep her soul for the canon theologian?'

XVII

As twilight gathered on All Souls' Day Petra informed the judge's wife, who was strolling in her garden among Frillity's eucalyptus-trees, that the canon theologian had called.

'Light the lamp in my boudoir – but first ask him into the garden,' said Ana, surprised and a little alarmed.

The canon walked through the courtyard into the park. Ana was sitting in the arbour, waiting for him. 'It was a beautiful evening, just like a September evening; the fine weather was not going to last very long, though, it would soon be raining cats and dogs in Vetusta.'

Thus their conversation started. Ana became embarrassed when the canon ventured to ask about her migraine.

'She had forgotten all about her lie!' She explained as best she could why she was in the garden despite her migraine.

The canon's suspicions were confirmed. His sweet friend had deceived him.

The priest was pale, his voice trembled and he swayed ceaselessly in the rocking-chair in which Ana had invited him to sit.

They were still talking about trifles and Ana was waiting in fear for Don Fermín to mention the reason for his extraordinary visit.

The fact was that the reason could not be mentioned. It had been a fit of bad temper, a blunder which he was already beginning to regret and the causes of which he certainly could not explain to the lady.

The Pug – the priest who acted as bailiff to Doña Paula – was addicted to going to the theatre in disguise. He had acquired this hobby as a spy in the seminary, where the rector had sent him into the gods to denounce the seminarists whom he saw there, but now the Pug went to the theatre of his own accord. He had gone to the theatre the previous evening and seen the judge's wife there. Next morning he informed Doña Paula, and she contrived to slip this piece of news into her conversation over luncheon with Fermín.

'I do not believe that lady can have gone to the theatre yesterday.'

'Well, I know she did because someone who saw her there told me so.'

The canon felt wounded: it hurt his self-esteem to find himself ridiculed because of his new friend. Pious people in Vetusta, indeed the entire *devout world* of the town, considered the theatre to be a forbidden recreation throughout Lent and on certain other days, among them All Saints' Day. Many ladies had left their boxes empty the previous evening, not allowing anybody into them so as to make their protest a more forceful one. The Páez girl had not gone, and although Doña Petronila, or Constantine the Great, never went, she did have a box for her four nieces and had not allowed them to go, either.

'And Ana, who was supposed to be his favourite spiritual daughter, who was supposed to be a fervent and active Catholic, had turned up at the theatre on a day when it was forbidden, throwing all care to the winds, giving a display of unconcern for pious scruples – and she, in particular, was a woman who did not frequent that place. And on that evening, too.'

The canon theologian had left home in an angry mood. 'He was not worried for the moment whether she did or did not go to the theatre – the time would come when things would change. But people were going to gossip. Don Custodio, the archdeacon, all his enemies would make fun of him, say how little influence he exercised over his penitents. He feared ridicule. He himself was to blame, taking too long to tighten the screws of devotion on her.'

He entered the sacristy and found the archpriest, the illustrious Ripamilán, arguing as if he were fencing – making grand gestures and slapping the air. His opponent was the archdeacon, the smiling Señor Mourelo, who maintained, with more composure, that if the judge's wife was a genuinely pious woman she should not have gone to the theatre on All Saints' Day.

Ripamilán shouted:

'Social duties, my dear sir, are above everything else.'

The dean was horrified.

'Oh, oh!' he said, 'not so, my dear archpriest. Religious duties – religious – yes . . .'

And with a quivering hand he took a pinch of snuff from his mother-of-pearl snuff-box. This was how he always concluded complicated sentences.

'Social duties are indeed worthy of respect,' said a young canon, a cousin of the Minister of Grace and Justice. Ripamilán's statement seemed to lend weight to the claims of the Crown against those of the Church, and therefore to be worthy of his approval as the minister's relative.

'Social duties,' replied Gloucester, with honeyed words, calm, deliberate and emphatic, 'social duties, if you will allow me to say so, are most respectable, but God in his infinite goodness wishes them always to be in harmony with religious duties.'

'Absurd!' exclaimed Ripamilán with a jump.

'Absurd!' said the dean, punching shut his mother-of-pearl snuff-box.

'Absurd!' affirmed the royalist canon.

'One's several duties, gentlemen, cannot be in contradiction with one another; and one's social duty, precisely because it is one's social duty, cannot, therefore, be opposed to one's religious duty. Taparelli,[1] a highly respectable writer, says as much.'

'Tapper what?' asked the dean. 'Don't you come to me with those German fellows. Mourelo here has always been a heretic.'

'We're off the subject, gentlemen,' cried Ripamilán, 'the fact is . . .'

'We are not off the subject,' insisted Gloucester, not wishing, in the presence of the canon theologian, to continue upholding his thesis about the judge's wife's meagre religiosity.

Artfully he led the argument on to *philosophical ground*, and from there to theology, which was equivalent to throwing water on a fire. These venerable dignitaries professed for that sacred science a singular respect which consisted in never being willing to discuss *such lofty matters*.

What Don Fermín heard as he entered the sacristy was enough to make him realize that there had been talk about the theatre. His ill humour increased. 'All Vetusta knew about it, his moral influence had lost credit – and the perpetrator of it all was cruel enough to refuse to see him.' He had made the appointment with her to say that in future she should confess not in the morning but in the afternoon, because this would prevent them from attracting the exclusive attention of an audience of pious ladies. 'You should confess with the rest of the women, and, in addition, on some other days when nobody knows that I hear confessions. I shall let you know in advance and then we will be able to talk at greater length.' This was what he had planned to tell her, and she replied that 'she had a migraine'! In Páez's house he had also heard all about the scandal at the theatre. 'Various ladies who had promised not to go had been there, and even Ana Ozores, who never went to the theatre, had gone.'

The canon theologian was seething with rage when he left Páez's house. The mocking smile of Olvido, who was already jealous, had filled him with fury.

Not thinking what he was doing, he had walked straight to the Plaza Nueva, hastened to the dark corner and knocked at Ana's door. And there he was.

But how could he explain that these were his reasons for calling?

When Don Fermín realized that Ana had lied to him, that she was not ill and had resorted to trickery in order not to keep her appointment, his bad temper was on the point of turning back into rage, and he needed all the strength of habit to control himself and continue smiling.

'What rights had he over this woman? None at all. How could he dominate her if she wanted to rebel? Impossible. With religious terror? Out of the question. For this lady, religion could never mean terror. With persuasion, with affection, with love? He could not boast of having persuaded her or aroused affection in her, still less love – the spiritual love to which he aspired.'

Diplomacy was the only way. 'Humble yourself, in due course you'll rise again' was his maxim, which had nothing to do with the promise in the gospels.[2]

It looked as if the small talk was going to be spun out for ever, so the canon, who did not want to leave without achieving something, put an end to their chatter with a long pause and a profound, sorrowful gaze at the starry vault of heaven (fortunately, he was sitting in the entrance of the arbour).

It was now night-time but it was not cold; or at least they did not feel cold. On being informed by Petra that the lamp in the boudoir was lit Ana had replied:

'Very well, we shall go indoors.'

The canon had said that if she now felt well again it would do no harm to remain outside.

Don Fermín's silence and his gaze at the stars gave Ana to believe that a grave matter was about to be broached.

It was. The canon said:

'I have still not explained why I wanted you to go to the cathedral this afternoon. I wished to tell you – and this is why I have come now, apart from being anxious to inquire after your health – I wished to tell you that I do not consider it advisable for you to confess in the morning.'

Ana directed a questioning look at him.

'There are various reasons. You have told me that Don Víctor does not like you to frequent the cathedral, especially if you rise early to do so, and he will be less alarmed if you go in the afternoon – perhaps he will often not even know that you have gone. There is no deceit in this. If he asks, one should tell him the truth, but if he does not say anything, one need not say anything, either. Since it is all perfectly innocent, it does not involve any deceit or dissimulation whatsoever.'

'You are right.'

'Another reason is that I seldom hear confessions in the morning, and this exception is causing my enemies, of which there are many, and of an infinite range of types, to gossip.'

'You have enemies?'

'Oh, my dear friend! Can you count the stars?' – and he pointed heavenwards – 'the number of my enemies is infinite, like the stars.'

The canon smiled like a martyr amidst flames.

Doña Ana was assailed by terrible remorse for having deceived and forgotten that holy man who was being persecuted for his virtues[3] and did not even complain. His smile and his talk of the stars had touched her heart-strings. 'He has enemies!' she thought, feeling a vehement desire to defend him against them.

'Furthermore,' continued Don Fermín, 'there are ladies who consider themselves to be very devout, and gentlemen who think that they are very religious, who amuse themselves in the cathedral by observing people on their way in and out of the chapels. They like to notice who confesses often, who is negligent, how long the confessions last – and my enemies also take advantage of all this gossip.'

The judge's wife coloured, without knowing for certain why she did so.

'Therefore, my dear friend,' continued De Pas, deeming it inopportune to dwell upon this last point, 'it will be better if you come at the ordinary time, with the other ladies. And occasionally, when you have a great deal to tell me, you can warn me in advance and I shall suggest a time on a day when I do not normally hear confessions. Nobody will know about it, because I do not think people are going to be so wretched as to watch every move we make.'

Ana thought that the arrangement about special days was extremely hazardous, but she did not wish to oppose the saintly Don Fermín in any way.

'Father, I shall do everything you say, I shall confess whenever you say, I place all my confidence in you. You are the only person in the world to whom I have opened my heart, you know everything I think and feel; in you I place all my hopes for light in the darkness which so often engulfs me.'

As Ana said this she noticed that her language was becoming bombastic and unseemly, and she stopped. The metaphors were bad ones, but she did not know any other way to express her desires without speaking with excessive clarity.

The canon theologian was not thinking about Ana's rhetoric. It comforted him to hear his friend speak in this way.

This was an encouragement – and he spoke of the matter which was tormenting him.

'Now, my daughter, to use – or perhaps abuse – these discretionary powers which you have given me' (a smile and a lowering of the head), 'I am going to allow myself to scold you a little.'

A new smile and a sustained gaze, one of the few which he permitted himself.

Ana was assailed by a childish fear which much increased her beauty, as De Pas duly observed.

'Yesterday you went to the theatre.'

The judge's wife opened her eyes wide as if making the thoughtless reply: 'So what?'

'You well know that, in the main, I am an enemy of the prejudices which many mean spirits take for religion. It is not only permissible for you to attend such spectacles – it is desirable. You need diversions and your worthy husband is absolutely right in asking it of you; but yesterday – yesterday was one of those days when people should not go to the theatre.'

'I didn't remember. And I didn't think that . . . In truth – it didn't seem . . .'

'Of course, Anita, of course. But that isn't the point. Yesterday the theatre was, for you, as innocent a spectacle as it is all the rest of the year. But the fact is that the religious sphere in Vetustan society – which is, after all, our own sphere, the one which, although perhaps it takes certain ideas to extremes, comes closest to our way of seeing things – this respectable part of society regards the infringement of certain pious customs as a scandal.'

Ana shrugged her shoulders. 'She didn't understand. A scandal! Yet in the theatre her mind had gone tripping on from one lofty idea to another until she had experienced that artistic and religious enthusiasm which had so edified her!'

The canon saw at a glance that his client ('he was a doctor of the spirit') was refusing to take the medicine. Remembering the allegory of the hill, he thought: 'She's unwilling to climb such a steep slope, let's make it look like level ground.'

'The evil, my daughter, doesn't consist in *your* having lost anything, *your* virtue is not in danger, not in the slightest, because of what you have done. But' (back to the festive tone of voice) 'what about my pride as a doctor? A patient who rebels against me – just fancy! People have gossiped and said that the canon theologian's spiritual daughters can't be very frightened of his iron rod if they go to watch *Don Juan Tenorio* instead of praying for the dead.'

'People have been talking about that?'

'Bah! – at the Society of St Vincent de Paul, at Doña Petronila's house (she defended you, though) and even in the cathedral. Señor Mourelo had his doubts about the piety of Doña Ana Ozores de Quintanar.'

'So I have been imprudent – I have made you look ridiculous?'

'Good God! my child, far from it! That imagination of yours, Anita, that imagination! When shall we have it under control? Ridiculous! Imprudent! The only acts which can make me look ridiculous are the ones for which I am responsible. That is the only way I can conceive ridicule. You have not been imprudent, you have merely been naïve, you have forgotten about all those idle tongues. It is of no significance whatever, and you can imagine how much notice I take of such prattle. That was just my little joke – to bring us to a more important point affecting a subject which is of interest to us both, the healing of your spirit, in so far as its moral aspects are concerned – for as you know, I believe that a good doctor (not precisely Señor Somoza, although he is an excellent person and a very fair doctor) could be of great help to me.'

A pause. The canon theologian stopped gazing at the stars, brought his rocking-chair a little closer to the judge's wife, and continued:

'Anita: although, for very weighty reasons, of which you are well aware, I venture to speak to you in the confessional as a doctor of the soul rather than just as a priest who sorts and settles your sins; in spite of the fact that in the confessional I have by now acquired a reasonably accurate knowledge of what is happening inside you – nevertheless I believe' (his voice trembled, he was afraid that he might be risking too much), 'I believe – that the efficacy of our conversations would be greater if we sometimes discussed matters outside the cathedral.'

Anita, sitting in the dark, felt her cheeks burning, and for the first time since she had known the canon theologian she thought of him as a man – a handsome, powerful man, a man who, among certain evil-minded people, had the reputation of a brazen lady-killer. In the silence which followed his words he could hear his friend's fitful breathing.

)on Fermín calmly continued:

'In church there is something which obliges one to be reserved, which prevents one from analysing many interesting points. We are always in a hurry, and I cannot, without failing in my duty, set aside my role as judge. You yourself do not speak in the confessional with sufficient freedom or at sufficient length for me to be able to reach a full understanding of your meaning. In church, moreover, it seems idle to talk about anything but that which is sinful or which, at least, could lead to sin. To analyse your good qualities, for instance, would almost be a profanation – it isn't what we are there for – and yet for our own special purposes, it is indispensable, too. You have read a great deal and you know very well that many of the priests who have written about the customs and the character of the women of their own times have emphasized the shadows, painting a completely black picture, because they were talking about woman in the confessional-box, woman recounting her misdeeds, exaggerating them rather than concealing them, and keeping quiet, as is natural, about her virtues, her noble side. As examples of this, without going outside Spain, we have the famous Archpriest of Hita, and Tirso de Molina,[4] and many others.'

Ana listened with her lips slightly parted. She was enchanted by this gentleman whose speech was as smooth as a stream flowing between banks of fine sand and fields of flowers. No longer was she thinking about the coarse slanders of the canon theologian's enemies. She had already forgotten that he was a man, and would not have been afraid even to sit on his knees, as she had heard that ladies sat on gentlemen's knees in trams in New York.

'Well, then,' Don Fermín continued, 'we need the whole truth; not just the ugly part of the truth but the beautiful part as well. Why should we try to cure what is healthy? Why amputate a useful limb? I have noticed that there are many things which you do not dare to say in the cathedral and which I am sure you would not have any objection to saying here, for example – and such friendly, familiar confidences are what I miss. Besides, you need not only to be censured and corrected, but also to be encouraged – to be praised sincerely and nobly for the very many good aspects of certain ideas and actions which you believe to be wicked through and through. And in the confessional one does not have excessive recourse to this type of analysis, which is just but, strictly speaking, foreign to the tribunal of penance. Enough of my arguments, you have understood me perfectly from the first. But now that I remember it, here is my last argument: by speaking about our affairs in the way I suggest, outside church, it will not be necessary for you to confess very often and nobody will be able to chatter about whether you do or do not make too frequent use of this sacrament. What is more, on those days when you do confess we shall be able to settle the account of your sins and your peccadilloes with greater dispatch.'

The canon was astonished by his own audacity. Suggesting this plan, which he had not devised in advance – which had been merely a vague idea rejected dozens of times for its foolhardiness – was a reckless and audacious move, caused by passion, and might well frighten the judge's wife and make her suspicious of his intentions. The canon trembled as he awaited her reaction.

The ingenuous Anita, full of enthusiasm for the project and convinced by the arguments in its favour, let loose one of her floods of words and with the warmth of her poetic ideas gave extra force to the motives which her friend had adduced.

Oh yes, that would be the best thing to do, she would not give up the good work begun in the cathedral, rendering unto God the things that were God's, but she accepted the pious friendship which offered to listen to her confidences and advise and comfort her in the aridity of soul which so often tormented her.

The canon withdrew into a contemplative silence as he listened. His head, hidden in the shadows, was resting upon one of the iron bars which formed the frame of the arbour and around which jasmine and honeysuckle twined. Ana's loquacity was like a taste of heaven; her expansive words, the words of a woman elated as she spoke of her sorrows in the hope of consolation, poured from her heart into his soul like a flow of perfumed water; the dryness was disappearing, the tautness yielding, softening. 'Speak, speak on,' said the priest to himself, 'blessed be thy lips!'

Nothing could be heard but Ana's sweet voice and, from time to time, the rustle of leaves as they fell to the ground, or as the barely perceptible breeze brushed them over the sandy paths.

Neither the canon theologian nor the judge's wife had any thoughts for the time.

'Yes, you are absolutely right,' she said, 'I do so need a word of friendship and advice on those frequent days when I am prey to that bitterness which tears all my good ideas out of my mind and leaves only sorrow and despair.'

'Oh no, not that, Anita. Despair! What a terrible word!'

'You can't imagine the state I was in yesterday afternoon.'

'So bored, weren't you? Those bells . . . ?'

The canon smiled.

'Please don't laugh. No doubt it's all nerves, as Quintanar says, or something of the sort, but I was overcome by a horrible tedium, which would have been a great sin, I'm sure – if there had been anything I could have done about it.'

'One should not say that,' the canon interrupted, giving his voice the smoothest timbre of which it was capable. 'Your being able to do something about your tedium would not have made it into a sin. It would have been a sin had you not wanted to do anything about it, but, thanks be to God, we can and we will cure it. And that is our task now, my dear friend.'

Anita was intoxicated by confessions when she knew that her confidant understood everything, or nearly everything, she was trying to say. She decided to tell the canon *all the rest of it*, the things which had happened after the tedium – only concealing what she considered to be a purely incidental cause. She said nothing of Don Alvaro and his white horse.

'At other times,' she said, 'the dryness turns into tears, a desire for self-sacrifice, a determination to seek self-denial – as you know. But yesterday my elation took me off in a different direction. I can't – I can't explain it very well. If I tell you in the only way I know . . . taken literally it's a sin, a rebellion, it's horrible – but not how I felt it.'

And the canon heard what had happened in his friend's soul during those hours of rebellion, which she already regarded as famous in the history of her solitary spirit. Although she did not give a precise description of her feelings and thoughts, he understood perfectly.

It was more difficult for him to understand how Don Juan Tenorio could have made Ana think about God and feel tender, profound piety.

'She said that maybe she was mad, but it wasn't the first time such a thing had happened. Often, during spectacles which were not at all religious, she had fallen under the spell of consoling piety, tears of love for God, infinite hope, limitless charity and self-evident faith. One day, after giving a poor child a peseta to buy a balloon like those which the other children were sharing out, she had had to hide her face so as not to be seen weeping. Her tears, bitter at first, had been sweetened by the ideas which had sprung up in her brain, and God had manifested himself in her soul as a powerful voice and a hand caressing away all the asperity there. It was beyond her. She couldn't explain it.' And she begged the canon to understand her. 'Something similar happened when she saw the unfortunate novice, Doña Inés, fall into Don Juan's arms – hardly a very religious situation, as the canon could see – but she was so sorry for that innocent, impassioned girl and, as her thoughts went tripping on, she thought about God, loved God, felt God close to her – exactly as on the day when she had given a poor child a coloured balloon. What was it? She knew only too well that it wasn't true piety, that such raptures were of no merit in God's eyes – but mightn't they be something more than just nerves? Might they be a dangerous sign of an adventurous, exalted spirit, twisted ever since childhood?'

'They were a mixture of many things.' The canon theologian tried to contain the exaltation which his friend had communicated to him and to speak with great calm and prudence. 'They were a mixture of many things. There was a treasure of feeling which could be turned in the direction of virtue, but there was danger, too. The previous evening the danger had been great' (he said this in ignorance of Don Alvaro's presence in Anita's box), 'and it was necessary to avoid any more attacks of that sort.'

The judge's wife had spoken of her invincible longings and of her desire to soar beyond the narrow confines of her old house – to feel more deeply and more intensely, to live for something other than vegetating like other women. She had also spoken of a universal love which was not ridiculous, however much it might be mocked by those who did not understand. She had even said that it would be hypocritical of her to affirm that she could find any true satisfaction of her desires in the limp, cool, prosaic, half-hearted affection of Víctor Quintanar, devoted to his plays, his collections, his friend Frillity, and his shotgun.

'It is all so full of peril,' added the canon after his summary of what Ana had said, 'that it verges on sin.'

'Yes, explained like this, as I have explained it, it does – but not as I feel it, not at all. Oh! I am sure that, as I feel it, none of what I have said is sinful. Feeling all these things must be dangerous, I don't deny that – but not sinful! Besides' (there was a change in her voice), 'in words it's ridiculous, it sounds like trite, foolish romanticism, I know – but it's not really like that, not at all!'

'But I do understand what you feel rather than what you say, my dear friend – you must believe me. I understand things as they are. But there is, just the same, a danger which verges on sin simply because it is a danger. Let me speak, Anita, and you will soon see how well we can understand each other. The danger verges on sin, I said – but I must add that it will be a manifest sin if all the energy of your ardent soul is not applied to an object worthy of it: worthy, Ana, of an honourable woman. If we allow these attacks to return without having prepared for them a virtuous task, a healthy occupation, they will make off down the easiest path, the path of vice, believe me, Anita. It is very good, very holy, that as a result of giving a child a coloured balloon you should think about God, and feel what you call the presence of God. Although there may be an element of pantheism in what you say it is not dangerous, since you are the person in question, and, in any case, I would make it my job to see that any such evil was nipped in the bud. But that is not what concerns us now. It is neither holy nor good, my dear friend, that on seeing a libertine in the cell of a nun – or the nun in the libertine's house and in his arms – the embrace of those sacrilegious lovers should lead you to devote yourself to thoughts of God. That is wrong. That is to scorn the natural ways of piety, to scorn healthy morality with selfish pride, attempting to arrive through abysses and mire and every kind of putrefaction at the place where the righteous arrive along very different paths. Forgive me for speaking with such severity. At this moment it is indispensable.'

The canon paused, to see if Ana had found the slope which he had placed before her too steep to climb.

She pondered her confessor's words, silent, solemn, recollected, sunk in her thoughts. She did not realize that his energy gratified her, that his opposition gave her great pleasure, and that she much preferred this powerful, indeed harsh, language to any amount of praise and flattery.

The canon continued, loosening the reins:

'It is necessary and urgent – most urgent – that we should put to good use your positive tendencies, your pious predisposition. I shall give it this name for the moment, because now is not the time to explain the degrees, the ways and the false ways of Grace, a highly delicate subject, full of danger. As I say, we must take advantage of your tendencies towards piety and contemplation – long-established tendencies, since you have felt them ever since childhood – for the benefit of virtue and by means of religious activities. Here you have the reason for many of the occupations of the Christian – the reason for public worship, which is more manifest, more ostentatious even, in our true religion than in the cold Protestant communions. You, Ana, need objects suggestive of the holy idea of God, occupations which will fill your soul with pious energy and satisfy your instincts of universal love, as you call them. All this, my child, can be achieved, satisfied and fulfilled in the life, apparently prosaic and even drab, as Doña Obdulia would say, of a devout woman, of a – religious fanatic, to use the ugly, scandalous expression. Yes, my dear friend' (the canon laughed as he said this), 'what you need, to assuage your thirst for universal love, is to become a religious fanatic. And now it's my turn to demand that you should understand me and not pay too much attention to the letter of what I say, ignoring the spirit. You should become a religious fanatic: that is to say, you should not be satisfied with calling yourself a church-goer and a Christian, while living like a pagan, believing all those banal commonplaces about the essential thing being not form but substance, about the details of worship and of discipline being meant for petty, mean spirits. No, my child, no. Everything is essential, form is substance, and it seems only natural that God should say to a woman who wants to love him, "Well now, my daughter, to remember me you don't need Zorrilla to have had the bright idea of depicting the love of a nun and a libertine. Come to my temple and there your senses will find all the incentive your soul needs to feel like praying, meditating and performing those acts of faith, hope and charity in which all worship of me consists." '

Hearing the canon theologian use this familiar, almost jocular language about such lofty, sublime matters, Ana felt both tears and smiles, and like Andromache[5] she laughed and wept together.

Night hurried on. The distant cathedral tower, spying on the couple through the rising mist, rang its bell three times as a warning. It considered that they had been talking quite long enough. But they did not hear the vigilant tower's signal.

Petra, in the shadows of the courtyard, was the one who said, to herself:

'A quarter to eight! And they still don't show any signs of stopping.'

The housemaid was burning with curiosity. She ventured a few steps on tiptoe towards the arbour, avoiding the dry leaves so as not to make any sound, but then, afraid she might be seen, she retreated into the courtyard, from where she could only hear a murmur, no distinct words. Then she heard Anselmo opening the hall door and the master climbing the stairs. Petra ran to meet him. If he asked for her mistress she was prepared to lie, say that she had gone up to the second floor, up to the attic – whatever came to mind – to carry out some household chore. For she was prepared to conceal the canon theologian's visit, although nobody had told her to, believing that this was a situation in which she should anticipate the wishes of her mistress and her mistress's friend, Don Fermín. 'Hadn't she been made to deliver letters *without any need for Don Víctor to know*? Well what need was there now for him to know that they had been chatting for more than an hour in the arbour – and in the dark?'

Quintanar did not inquire after his wife, which was nothing new – he often forgot her, especially when he had some project in hand. He requested a lamp for his study, sat at his desk and, pushing books and papers aside, placed upon it a package which he had been carrying under his arm. It contained a machine for charging rifle-cartridges. He had just wagered against Frillity that he could make so many dozen cartridges in an hour, and he had come home ready to put himself to the test. He had thoughts for nothing else. Petra brought the lamp. Quintanar glared at her with a look which was so utterly abstracted as to seem a searching one. The housemaid became flustered.

'Petra!'

'Yes sir?'

'Oh, nothing . . . Petra!'

'Yes sir?'

'Is that clock working?'

'Yes sir, you wound it up yesterday.'

'So the time is ten minutes to eight?'

'Yes sir.'

Petra was trembling – but she was still prepared to lie if she was asked about her mistress.

'Very well, you may go.'

Don Víctor proceeded to fill one cartridge after another at great speed.

The canon theologian had been expounding what he meant by the life of a *religious fanatic.*

'It was time for Ana to essay her first steps on the way of perfection;[6] the preliminaries could be considered concluded now. Even if most women went to church, to guild meetings and to the other centres of religious life in a routine manner which nullified the moral value of such pious practices, she could derive great benefit from them and find a worthy occupation for her soul in the same places and tasks. What had St Teresa been? A nun and a foundress of convents; yet how many nuns had never transcended the banal and commonplace? The life of a nun can become a mere routine, too, possess little merit in God's eyes and be inadequate to satisfy the desires of an ardent soul. Yet what vast worlds, what a universe of suns had been opened to St Teresa by the life of the cloister! The great work lies within ourselves, if we are capable of it. But we must search for this opportunity among the daily occupations of the righteous life. It was necessary for Anita to be, in future, a regular attender at religious ceremonies, hear more sermons and masses, go to novenas, become an active member of the Society of St Vincent de Paul, visit the sick and sit up with them, involve herself in the Mission for Catechesis. At first such occupations might seem wearisome, trivial, prosaic, and far removed from the path which leads to the life of pure piety; but by degrees she would acquire a taste for these humble activities and penetrate the mysterious charm of prayer and public worship, which may even appear to be a frivolous pastime as practised by tepid souls, by the mass of the faithful, who take only their senses with them when they go to church, but which is an edifying spectacle for the person who feels profound devotion.'

'The day will come – you will see,' said the canon, 'when you will not need Zorrilla, or any other poet under the sun, to make you weep tender tears and find your thoughts tripping on, as you say, until they are elevated to the holy idea of God. The Church, my dear friend, is sagacious indeed in finding the way to the heart! You will see, you will see! You will recognize our Mother's wisdom in many rites, ceremonies and splendours of worship which you now, perhaps, consider to be vapid and insignificant. Our feast-days! Such beauty, my beloved daughter! Christmas will come, for example, and you will use your powerful imagination to envisage the scenes of pure poetry of the birth of Jesus. What you had regarded as trite and commonplace carols will again be great poems, founts of tenderness, and you will weep as you think of Baby Jesus. And then you will tell me whether those tears are not sweeter and fresher than the tears which the good Don Juan Tenorio made you weep yesterday evening.

'There is no point', continued De Pas, 'in hearing sermons preached by all and sundry, in spite of the fact that the words of a humble village priest sometimes contain, in their own rude simplicity, treasures of truth, admirable laconic teaching, traces of profound, sincere philosophy and new parables worthy of the Bible. This does not often happen, however, and so it is advisable to restrict oneself to the sermons of orators of repute. Listen to the bishop, on the days when he wants to show what he can do. Listen to other good preachers. And, if it were not intolerably vain to do so, I would add: listen to me sometimes, on those occasions when it pleases the Lord that I should not explain my ideas altogether incompetently. For just as there are some things which cannot be said in the pulpit, things which require the confessional or an intimate conversation, there are others which call for the pulpit, and which it would be ridiculous to say face to face – for example part of what I want to say about those vague experiences of a divine presence which you believe you have had, experiences tainted by pantheism, my child, even though you do not realize it.'

The canon continued talking about his plans for the life of devotion to which his friend was now to dedicate herself body and soul. He concluded by treating with especial care the question of what she should read.

In particular, he recommended the lives of certain saints and the works of St Teresa and other mystics.

'It is sufficient to read her *Life* and that of St Jane Frances de Chantal[7] – reading between the lines, I mean – to enter on the life of perfection, not immediately, of course, but later. At the beginning there is great danger in the discouragement which is the result of comparing one's own life with the lives of the saints. It will be wretched indeed for you if you lose heart because you see that many acts which you have believed to be worthy of praise are sins for Teresa! It will make you ashamed to see that it was great vanity to believe yourself to be good long before you really were, and to take what the Saint calls voices of the devil for voices from God – but you should not linger over these passages. You should not make comparisons – you should continue to read and, when you have lived for some time under a healthy discipline, read the book again, and at each new reading you will be able to savour it better, and it will yield you more fruit.

'If we set ourselves the goal of becoming another St Teresa, that will be the end of everything! We would only see the infinite distance to be travelled and not even start out on the journey. How far we shall go is something which God will decide; the important thing now is to march onward.

'And, meanwhile, are we to wear a habit of serge, display a doleful face, fix our eyes on the ground and torture our husband with a domestic inquisition and a refusal to go to the promenade or have any dealings with the world? God forbid, Anita, God forbid. The peace of the home is not something to play with. And what about our health? The health of the body, what would become of that? Were we not concerned to try and get well again? Were we not talking a moment ago about the spirit and how to cure it? Well, the body needs fresh air and innocent pastimes, and all this must continue to the necessary degree and as circumstances indicate.'

A gust of cold air made the judge's wife shiver and caused a flurry of dry leaves at the entrance of the arbour. The canon sprang to his feet as if someone had pricked him and said with some trepidation:

'Goodness me! It must be very late. We have not noticed the time passing, talking away in here like this.'

'He did not want Don Víctor to find them at such an hour in the garden, alone in the arbour by the light of the stars.' But the canon kept this thought under his hat. He walked out of the arbour talking in a loud voice, but not a very loud one, making a show of not being afraid to make a noise, but afraid to do so none the less.

Ana followed him, lost in her thoughts, oblivious of the existence of husbands, and days, and nights, and hours, and places unsuited for talking alone with a handsome, well-built young man, even though he be a priest.

As if by mistake, the canon walked towards the courtyard door, although it would have been more natural to climb the stairs into the house and call on Quintanar in his room.

Petra was standing in the courtyard, like a sentry, in the place where she had received the canon.

'Has the master come home?' asked the judge's wife.

'Yes, ma'am,' replied her housemaid in a low voice, 'he is in his study.'

'Would you like to see him?' said Ana, turning to the canon.

Don Fermín replied:

'It would be a great pleasure . . .'

'They're shamming, shamming for my benefit!' thought Petra in anger.

'It would be a great pleasure – but it is very late. I should have been in the palace at eight o'clock, and it is nearly half past. I cannot stop. Please give him my best regards.'

'As you wish.'

'Besides, he must be absorbed in his work. I should not like to interrupt him. I shall leave this way. Good-night, madam, good-night.'

'They're shamming,' thought Petra again as she opened the hall door.

The canon theologian came close to the judge's wife and said in a hurried whisper:

'I'd forgotten to tell you. The most suitable place to – meet – is Doña Petronila's house. We'll talk about it another day.'

'Very well,' replied Ana.

'I've been thinking about it, it's the best place.'

'Yes, yes, you're right.'

Ana climbed the stairs and Don Fermín walked out into the porch. In the doorway he stopped, looked at Petra while he turned up his cloak collar, and saw her with her eyes fixed upon the ground and a large key in her hand, waiting for him to leave so as to lock the door. She looked the picture of secrecy. De Pas patted her shoulder and said with a smile:

'It's getting chilly, my girl.'

Petra looked at him face to face. She smiled as gracefully as she could, without abandoning her attitude of humility.

'Are you happy with your master and mistress?'

'Doña Ana is an angel.'

'She is indeed. Good-night, my child, good-night. Go indoors now, there's a draught here – and your face is flushed. You must be feeling hot.'

'You go out first, Father, don't worry about me.'

'Shut the door now, my child – you can shut the door.'

'No, Father, if I shut it you won't be able to see your way to the corner.'

'Many thanks. Good-night, good-night.'

'Good-night, Don Fermín.'

Petra said this in a hushed voice, poking her head out of the porch. She closed the door with the utmost care not to make any noise.

' "Don Fermín!" ' thought the canon. 'Why did the girl call me by my Christian name? What can she be imagining? All the better, though. Yes, all the better. It suits me for her to be well disposed towards me, like the other girl.'

The other girl was Teresina, his housemaid.

Petra went upstairs and presented herself in Doña Ana's boudoir without having been called.

'What do you want?' asked the mistress, who was wrapping herself in her shawl because she felt very cold.

'The master did not ask for you, ma'am. I did not tell him that Don Fermín was here.'

'Who?'

'Don Fermín.'

'Ah! Very well, very well – but why not? What does it matter?'

Petra bit her lip and turned away muttering:

'The proud creature! Does she think we haven't got eyes? Well, if I didn't want to – but I'm doing it for him.'

Yes, Petra was doing it for him, for the canon theologian, whom she wished to please at all costs. The sensual blonde had her plans.

Half an hour later Don Víctor Quintanar presented himself before his wife, his forehead and cheeks smeared with gunpowder.

He knew nothing of the canon theologian's nocturnal visit. 'He didn't ask any questions. Why tell him?'

The following morning, before sunrise, Frillity unlocked the back gate of the park and walked in. Quintanar's close friend was the dictator of that little nation of trees and bushes. On the days when the two men did not go hunting, Señor Crespo spent his time touring his *dominions*, as he called Quintanar's garden, pruning, grafting, planting or transplanting according to the season and other circumstances. Nobody else, not even the owner, was allowed to touch a single leaf. Frillity, and Frillity alone, was master. He made straight for the arbour, remembering that on the marble table, or on a bench – somewhere in there – he had left some seeds which were ready to be sent to a flower-show. He started searching, and on a rocking-chair he found a glove of purple silk among his seeds, which were scattered over the straw seat and the floor.

He uttered an early-morning oath, picked up the glove between two fingers and raised it to his eyes.

'Who the devil has been messing in here?' he inquired of the morning zephyrs.

He put the glove into his pocket, picked up those seeds which the wind had not blown away and sorted them with great care. They were the seeds of a most singular species of monochrome pansy, his own invention.

When he heard sounds in the house he called:

'Anselmo, Petra, Servanda, Petra!'

Petra appeared with her hair down, wearing a camisole and one of her mistress's old shawls, carelessly wrapped around her waist. She looked like the gold-tressed dawn-goddess. Frillity, in dudgeon, squared up to the goddess.

'Hey, you, you little minx, who's the damned bishop that comes in here at night to spoil all my seeds?'

'What? I can't hear you,' replied Petra from the courtyard.

'I went home yesterday as it was getting dark, leaving some seeds wrapped up in a piece of paper in the arbour – and now I find them all on the ground mixed up with the earth, and this canon's glove in a chair. Who came here last night?'

'Last night! You've been dreaming, Don Tomás.'

'God's fury! Last night I say . . .'

'Let me see the glove.'

'Here you are,' cried Frillity, hurling it at her.

'Well that's a good one! Ha, ha, ha – Lord! you and your canons. You know a lot about fashion, Don Tomás, I'm sure. Didn't you say it's a canon's glove?'

'Whose is it then?'

'It's my mistress's. Can't you see the hand – look how tiny. Unless there are *canonesses* now, too.'

'Do women wear purple gloves?'

'Well of course – with dresses of a certain colour.'

Frillity shrugged.

'But my seeds, my seeds, who has been throwing my seeds about?'

'The cat, I'll be bound – the little cat, Blackie. It must have taken the glove to the arbour, too – it's such a little magpie!'

A goldfinch warbled in Quintanar's aviary.

'The cat – Blackie!' murmured Frillity, shaking his head. 'The cat – my eye!'

A seraphic smile illuminated his face, and turning to Petra he pointed to the gallery windows.

'It's my finch! It's my finch! Can you hear? I'm sure of it. It's my finch! Your master said his canary would sing first. But can you hear it? Can you hear it? It's my finch singing, I lent it to him for a fortnight so that he could see it win – it's my finch!'

Frillity forgot the glove and the cat as he listened in raptures to the loud, clear, joyful chirruping of his beloved goldfinch.

Petra hid in her bosom of compact snow the canon theologian's purple glove.

XVIII

Dull grey clouds, as broad as the steppes, drove up from the west and were ripped open on the peaks of Mount Corfín. The rains poured from them on to Vetusta, sometimes cutting down aslant like furious whiplashes, like a biblical punishment, sometimes falling in a calm leisurely flow, in fine vertical threads. These clouds passed over, and others came, and others – the first clouds back again, it seemed, after going around the world, to be torn open on Corfín once more. The spongy earth was eaten away like the flesh on Job's bones;[1] a sluggish grey plume of mist was wafted over the sierra by the languid wind; the country extended, naked and frozen, into the distance, motionless like the corpse of a castaway shedding the water which has flung it ashore. Valley and mountain had a silent look of resignation and fatality, like stone being drilled by an eternal drip-drip-drip of water. Nature, lying dead, seemed to be waiting for its useless, motionless body to be dissolved. In the distance the cathedral tower stood out of the gloom like the mast of a sunken ship. The desolation of the countryside, its silent suffering, was resigned and poetic; but the sadness of the dingy city, its watery grime oozing from roofs and cracked walls, seemed base, repugnant and shrill, like the wailing of a beggar. It was irksome, inspiring not melancholy but a tedium of despair. Frillity preferred to get wet in the open country, and dragged Quintanar with him far from Vetusta to the deserted seaside meadows and marshes of Palomares and Roca Tajada. There they wearied hills[2] and flats chasing partridges and woodcocks in the thick of sylvan knolls,[3] and on stark plains pursuing dippers, sea-ducks, melancholy plaintive stone-curlews, clouds of starlings and dusky flocks of diligent lapwings. Don Víctor had his wife's permission for these long trips with his friend. They would leave at daybreak on the mail train, reach Roca Tajada an hour later, and at ten o'clock at night return to Vetusta in silence, laden with bouquets of feathers[4] and soaked to the skin. In the marshes at Palomares Don Víctor missed the theatre. 'If only the train left two hours earlier!' Frillity did not miss anything. His devotion to hunting, to a life in the open air, in the sad, sweet solitude of the country, was a deep devotion which had no rivals, but Quintanar's affections were divided between this hobby and his love for farces performed on stage. The theatre bored Frillity and made him catch colds. He lived in terror of draughts and only felt safe in the midst of the country, where there are no doors.

Crespo's vocation was well defined and deep-rooted: nature. Quintanar had grown old without ever discovering 'what was his destiny on earth', as he said, in the language of romantic times, of which there were still a few traces in his speech. The ex-magistrate had a spirit like pliable wax, which readily took a new shape, and just as readily changed it for another. He believed himself to be a man of spirit because at home he sometimes used imperious language (the language of the decrees issued by the municipal corporation), but in reality he was no more than clay with which people could do as they pleased. This explains why, although he was a brave man, he had never had an opportunity to demonstrate his valour in a struggle with a will opposed to his own. He maintained that in his house nothing but what he wanted was ever done, but he never noticed that what he wanted was always, in the end, something which others decided. If Ana Ozores had been a domineering woman, Don Víctor would have found himself occupying the sorry position of a slave, but, fortunately, the judge's wife left her worthy husband to his whims and fancies and was content to deny him any influence on her own tastes and interests. The programme of diversions, gaiety and noisy activity which Quintanar had trumpeted forth was being fulfilled only in those sections and at those times which met with Ana's approval. If she preferred to stay at home and go back to her dreams, Don Víctor – having promised and even sworn not to give way – gave way by slow degrees. He tried to make his retreat an honourable one; he pretended to be acceding to a compromise and believed that he had thereby saved his honour as a resolute man and the master of his home, even allowing himself the audacity of a little muttered grumble when nobody could hear. Even his servants imposed their will on his, although he did not suspect it, and had gone so far as to defeat him in the dining-room. As a good Aragonese he was a lover of highly spiced food, full-bodied wines, and classical abundance, but he had lost ground, little by little, and now ate much less, and put up with the dishes, more whimsical than succulent, which his wife liked. This was not because Ana imposed them on him, but because the cooks preferred to please the mistress, seeing her as a woman of strong will, and the master only as a preacher who bored them with sermons which they could not understand. Quintanar's lack of character was even reflected in his language. He spoke in the style of whichever newspaper or book he had just been reading. Some turns of phrase, inflexions of the voice and other features of his oratory, which might have been taken for signs of originality, were merely the vestiges of past interests and occupations. And so his speech was sometimes like a sentence delivered in the high court and his everyday conversation was larded with juridical technicalities, this being all that was left in him of the former magistrate. The contrast between his profession and his interests had helped in no small way to deprive him of both originality and determination. If he had been born to be anything it was, without doubt, to be a strolling player or, rather, an amateur actor. If society had been constituted in such a way that being an amateur actor were a career in which a man could earn a living, Quintanar would have been one until his dying day, and would have been able to take a part, as he put it, as well as any of those other leading men who tour provincial capitals like pedlars.

But Don Víctor had realized that an actor cannot live in Spain by his honourable labours unless he submits himself to the indignity of serving art to the public as a member of a company of professional players, and he had also realized that sooner or later he would have to *become a family man*. With some reluctance, therefore, he had entered upon a legal career. As luck would have it, and as his family's connections would also have it, he had risen rapidly, and had soon found himself to be a magistrate, and then had found himself to be the Chief Stipendiary Magistrate of the Royal Provincial Court of Granada, at an age when he still felt capable of playing the leading role in *The Mayor of Zalamea*[5] with all the energy which it requires. But the thorn was already lodged in his side; he was aware that the post of magistrate was delicate beyond measure, its responsibility great, but he 'was above all an artist'. He hated trials and loved the boards, but could not tread them *with dignity*. This was what twisted and tormented his spirit. If it had been licit for him to act, perhaps he would never have done anything else, but since this was barred to him by decorum and a multitude of other considerations he had tried to find alternative outlets for his urge to be something more than a wheel in the complicated machinery of judicial power. Thus he had become a huntsman, a botanist, an inventor, a cabinet-maker, a philosopher – everything that his friend Frillity and the winds of chance and caprice had wanted to make of him.

In the course of so many years of close friendship, Frillity had formed his dear Víctor in his image and after his likeness, so far as he was able. Quintanar would leave the unsuspected servitude of his home to enter the dictatorship – albeit an enlightened dictatorship – of Tomás Crespo, the apple of his eye, whom he was not sure that he did not love as much as his darling Anita. Their friendship had grown out of the passion which they shared for hunting. For the Aragonese gentleman, however, hunting had merely been an exercise for the primitive side of his nature. He hunted in ignorance of what happened inside partridges or hares or rabbits; but Frillity studied fauna and flora and meditated, like a philosopher of nature, while he was hunting. He was a man of few words – even fewer than usual when in the country – who seldom argued, preferring to give a laconic statement of his opinion, without trying to convince anybody. The influence of Frillity's naturalistic philosophy reached Quintanar's soul as a kind of alluvion. The ideas of that *good fellow*, whom most Vetustans considered to be *crack-brained*, a lunatic, were slowly and imperceptibly deposited on Quintanar's mind.

Frillity scorned the opinions of his fellow Vetustans and pitied them for their poverty of spirit. 'Humanity was evil – but it wasn't humanity's fault. Oidium consumed the grape, the maize-grub spoiled the maize plant, potatoes had their own disease, cows and pigs theirs; the oidium of the Vetustan was envy, his grub was ignorance – what fault of his was it?' Frillity pardoned all misconduct, forgave all sins, avoided contagion and tried to keep the few people whom he liked away from it. He visited few houses but many gardens, since his extensive knowledge of the cultivation of trees and flowers, and his practical ability, made him the arbiter of all the parks and gardens in town. He knew the Marquis de Corujedo's garden leaf by leaf, had planted trees in the Marquis de Vegallana's garden, and would even look into Doña Petronila's English garden now and then; but he did not know what Constantine the Great, the mother-bishop, looked like, had never set foot inside Doña Rufina's boudoir and only came across the Marquis de Corujedo in the Gentlemen's Club. He gave his orders to their gardeners. As soon as the winter rains began, after the ironical summer of St Martin, Vetusta felt like a prison to Frillity, and he only stayed within its bounds on days when its trees and flowers required him to do so.

Quintanar would follow him, half-asleep, encased in his hunting uniform, a rich source of amusement for Frillity, who wore the same clothes in the country and in town, and the same white shoes with their stout, studded soles. They would climb into a third-class carriage among cheerful villagers with fresh ruddy faces. Quintanar would slumber, his head knocking against the hard boards, while Frillity offered and accepted thick cigarettes and, more eloquent than in Vetusta, in a jovial and expansive mood, talked with the sons of the soil about today's harvests and yesterday's clouds. If the conversation degenerated and turned to lawsuits he would grimace and pay no further attention to it, sinking into the contemplation of the countryside, which was sorrowful now but which he loved always and knew like the back of his hand.

Ana envied her husband the good fortune to flee from Vetusta, to go and get soaked in the solitude of the country on hills and marshes far from those dingy red roofs which turned water falling from heaven into filth.

'Oh yes! she was prepared to try to save her soul, to search for the true path of virtue; but how much more receptive her spirit would have been to the grandeurs of religion in a setting worthier of such sublime poetry! How hard it was to admire creation and lift up one's heart to the idea of the Creator here in La Encimada, this morose place, soaked in damp to its very bones of worm-eaten wood and stone; with its narrow streets overrun with grass, which was joyful in the countryside but a symbol of abandonment here, and licked incessantly by the water which dribbled from roofs with a monotonous, measured, eternal plash on the sharp-edged cobble-stones below!'

The judge's wife did not understand how Visitación could come and go from house to house, as cheerful as ever, full of smiles, heedless of all the water and the mud in the gutter, not even seeming to realize that it was raining and that the sky was a shroud instead of the blue mantle which it was supposed to be. For Visita the weather was always the same – she never thought about it, and it was only of use to her as a topic of conversation when on courtesy visits.

The bank clerk's wife would dodge puddles and hop from stone to stone like a wagtail, revealing feet which were not badly shod, petticoats which were not very clean, and sometimes a little of a leg which was worthy of a better stocking. Water did not shut Obdulia up in her home, either, or paralyse her. She, too, cheerful and boisterous, would scamper from one doorway to another, defying the heaviest cloudbursts, guffawing if an indiscreet drop of rain fell on her warm, throbbing throat. It was a sight to behold her petticoats, as if they possessed the instincts of an ermine, cross those perilous expanses of mud and remain immaculate like drifts of open-worked snowflakes, as the patterned holland-cloth (the temptation of Bermúdez, the spiritual historian) rustled like windswept leaves.

Ana noticed with sorrow and almost with envy that, in the main, Vetustans resigned themselves without much difficulty to that submarine existence which lasted through a large part of the autumn, most of the winter and nearly all the spring. Each one looked for his or her own niche and seemed no less happy than Frillity when he was escaping with Don Víctor to plains by the sea to get soaked at his ease.

The harder it was raining the later the Marchioness de Vegallana rose from her bed. It was armoured against the fiercest attacks of cold and, snug in it, she savoured delights which she could not put into words as she read novels about journeys to the pole and bear-hunts, and others set in Russia, or north Germany at least. The contrast between the warmth in which she luxuriated and the freezing cold which the heroes of her novels had to suffer, between her delightful immobility and the long journeys which they made around the world, was the greatest pleasure which Doña Rufina could enjoy as each year drew to its close. Hearing the rain as it lashed her windows, and at the same time feeling sorry for a poor child lost in the snow – how delightful for a soul which was, in its own way, a tender one, like hers!

'I'm no sentimentalist,' she said to Don Saturnino Bermúdez, who listened with his head on one side and a smile stretched on pegs from ear to ear. 'I'm no sentimentalist, I mean to say I don't like people who gush, but reading about some things makes me feel well disposed – moved – and I weep. But I don't go making a show of it.'

'This is the gift of tears of which St Teresa speaks,[6] my Lady,' replied the historian, and he sighed as if unlocking the coffer of his own sentimental secrets.

The marquis did as cats do in January. He disappeared from Vetusta for days on end. He declared that he was going to make preparations for the elections, but his intimates had heard him say (in the secrecy of private gatherings, after a hearty meal, when the time came for confessions) that as far as he was concerned there was no better aphrodisiac than cold weather. 'Not even shellfish have the effect on me that rain and snow have.' And since all his amorous adventures took place in rural settings, the worthy Vegallana sallied forth to defy the elements, riding from village to village through mud, ice and snow in his travelling-carriage. And thus did the marquis make preparations for the elections, by going in search of votes for the distant future, to use the mischievous expression coined by Don Cayetano Ripamilán, who was always ready to pardon this kind of misdeed.

As soon as the weather turned wet the members of the marchioness's coterie saw the chance for which they had all been waiting. Those who enjoyed the enviable, and indeed envied, privilege of penetrating Doña Rufina's boudoir blessed the showers which gave them an excuse to enter that perfumed hothouse every evening. What were they to do otherwise? Where were they to go? In the fireplace the ancient forests of the marquis's dominions blazed; the feudal oaks burnt with a majestic crackle. But by their warmth olden legends were not recounted, as Trifón Cármenes assumed must happen in every stately hearth. Instead, there was gossip about everybody in town, new calumnies were invented and people flirted with all the unconcealed and prosaic sensualism which, according to Saturnino Bermúdez, 'was characteristic of the present historical moment, denuded of all the jewels of idealism and poetry'. The boudoir was not large and it was full of furniture, so the members of the coterie brushed against each other, touched each other, even pressed against each other if it could not be helped. Who had any thoughts for the rain?

In gatherings of the second class, of which there were many in Vetusta, the damp also stimulated gaiety. As people went to their customary niches, it was extraordinary to hear, for example, the racket made outside Visita's front door by 'those who favoured her once a week by honouring her rooms' (a sitting-room and a parlour) – to hear the guffaws and the jokes of her guests, sheltering under their umbrellas and shouting as they were showered by the great tin serpents above them. They all ignored the water, imagining the esoteric delights of lotto and charades which awaited them.

The devout element in Vetustan society (an expression taken from *El Lábaro*) turned to novenas as soon as the weather turned wet. The devout element was everybody in town once the bad weather came. Even the members of the Good Friday Club – wicked men who met during Passion Week to eat meat in a hostelry – attended church, although only to mock the preachers and look at the girls. Vetusta's religious fervour began with the Novena for the Souls of the Departed (which was not very popular) and the well-attended Novena to the Sacred Heart of Jesus, and did not come to an end until the most famous novena of them all had been performed, the Novena to Our Lady of Sorrows, and the Novena to the Mother of Beauteous Love (only a little less successful), in the merry month of May. But pious souls had many other opportunities to praise God and His holy saints during such notable solemnities as the festivals of Christmas and Lent, and especially during the Judges' Sermons, paid for by the Royal Provincial Court on every Friday during that time of holy meditation, as Trifón Cármenes called it.

The rains caused no small delay to the fulfilment of the plan for moral hygiene which Don Fermín had so delicately imposed on his dear friend. Ana hated the mud and the damp. The cold in the dirty wet streets attacked her nerves, and she seldom left the gloom of Ozores Mansion. She had been to confession twice more before the end of November, but she had not made up her mind to go to Doña Petronila's house, and the canon theologian did not dare remind her of their rendezvous there. Constantine the Great had already been informed by her beloved and admired Señor De Pas, who called more often now, that Doña Ana wished to help her in her holy labours and in the administration of the numerous pious works which she so wisely directed and financed.

'When is that angel most beauteous going to come?' the mother-bishop would ask. She always spoke in the language of novenas, loaded with abstract superlatives.

The holy ladies who acted as questors in the palace of Constantine the Great – the ladies of the conclave, as Ripamilán called them – waited with mystical longing and malicious curiosity for their new companion, who with her youth and beauty was going to bring such prestige to the pious and complicated enterprise of saving the world in Jesus and for Jesus – this, no less, being the goal of these sabre-rattling devotees, as militant as cavalrymen.

But Ana felt a vague, inexplicable repugnance to the idea of going to Doña Petronila's house. It seemed preferable to see the canon theologian in church, since it was there that she found the religious fervour she needed to confess her wicked thoughts and dangerous desires. The canon was becoming impatient. The judge's wife was not climbing the hill. She persisted in her perilous pantheistic aspirations (as he described them), she still maintained that the tender feelings awoken in her by profane spectacles were a form of piety, and she declared that reading holy books suggested thoughts which were probably heretical, or at least unlikely to lead to the deep faith which the canon demanded as an absolutely indispensable preparation for a firm step forward. At other times pious books made her fall into a melancholy somnolence, or a kind of intellectual paralysis which seemed like a form of stupidity. As for prayers, Ana said that reciting them by rote was a useless, soporific exercise which grated on her nerves; she would repeat them a hundred times so as to fix her attention on them, yet be overcome by nausea before she could manage even a little fervour. 'No, no, don't do that, there is nothing worse than praying in that way,' replied the canon. 'We will come to the question of prayer in due course, meanwhile your old way of praying is adequate.'

Although he feared the dangers of Ana's imagination, he believed that, in order not to lose any of the ground he had gained, he must permit her to abandon herself to those spontaneous bursts of sentimental piety, which she could not explain and which came at the most unexpected times, provoked by all sorts of events quite unrelated, it seemed, to religious ideas. His fear of her ardent spirit's natural ebullience had made him replace the mild plans which he had first proposed with those others expounded in the arbour, which were more like the ordinary discipline he imposed on his penitents. He now realized, however, that he must return to the gentle approach and allow his friend's instincts a greater share in the arduous task of winning for righteousness those treasures of feeling and lofty ideal-ism. This use of loose reins would delay his triumph, but it allowed him to present himself as a more congenial spirit, speaking the language of that vague romanticism which she believed to be sincere religiosity but which was, in fact, no more than disguised idolatry, according to him. No, he would not allow himself to be seduced by pantheistic ideas, even though they might look as attractive as those of his friend.

He did not doubt, however, that the beauty of worship would have a profound and healthy effect on a woman like Ana, once she was prepared to pay full attention to it, once her spirit had been made ready to succumb to mystical sensations by that nervous excitement about which the diligent confessor already knew too much.

When she again spoke about boredom, about the sorrow provoked by tedium and about the stupidity of water falling endlessly, he repeated, 'To church, my daughter, to church. Not to pray, just to be there, to dream there, to think there, listening to the music of the organ and of our excellent choir, smelling the incense of the high altar, feeling the warmth of the wax candles, looking at all the things there which shine and move, contemplating the lofty vaults, the slender columns, the delicate and mysteriously poetic pictures in the stained-glass windows.' This rhetoric, after the style of Chateaubriand,[7] was not to Don Fermín's taste, because he had always believed that to recommend religion for its external beauty was to offend the sanctity of Christian dogma. But he was a man who knew how to make the best of a bad bargain and adapt himself to the circumstances. Moreover (although this was something about which he preferred not to think), he was gratified by the hope that he might often find his friend in the cathedral and at meetings of the Society of St Vincent de Paul and the Mission for Catechesis, where she would see him triumphant, displaying his talent, his learning and his simple, natural elegance.

But the thought of leaving home became ever more repugnant to Anita. The damp horrified her, and kept her hunched-up and wrapped in a shawl by the side of the monumental fireplace in her doleful dining-room for hours and hours, by day and by night. Don Víctor did not stay long in the house. When he was not away hunting, he would come and go without a pause. He hardly stopped even in his study, for he had become somewhat afraid of it. Some of the machines which he was either inventing or perfecting had rebelled, bristling with the unexpected difficulties of rational mechanics. There upon the desk in the study, in all their dusty glory, stood diabolical contraptions of steel and wood, waiting in provisional postures for Don Víctor to undertake the serious study of mathematics, of all mathematics, which he had postponed because of the arrival of Perales's theatrical company. Meanwhile, somewhat ashamed in the presence of these mocking, ironical playthings, he avoided his study whenever he could, and did not even use it for letter-writing.

Moreover, his botanical, mineralogical and entomological collections lay in chaos, and his reluctance to undertake the arduous task of classifying so many plants and flies all over again helped to keep him away from home. He went to the Gentlemen's Club to argue and play at chess and often went visiting and searching for other ways to avoid the boredom of being shut up in the house. 'So much the better,' thought Ana, unintentionally. At first she had esteemed, respected and even loved her husband as much as she believed was necessary, but now he was becoming smaller in her eyes with every day that passed. Each time he presented himself before her he made havoc among her incipient plans for a pious life, her preparations for becoming, as soon as the weather should improve, a religious fanatic as the canon theologian had advised. So long as she thought of the abstract idea of a husband, all was well; she knew that her duty was to love him, cherish him, and obey him. But then Quintanar would appear, the bow of his black silk tie askew and under one ear, sprightly, restless, overflowing with insignificant notions, busy with some trivial concern, devoted heart and soul to matters which were the most paltry and worthy to be forgotten; and Ana, unable to help herself, would feel a pent-up rancour – irrational, yet invincible, and all the stronger for being hidden – which made her blame the entire universe for the absurdity of being united for ever with such a man. Quintanar would depart, leaving doors open behind him, giving capricious orders to be obeyed in his absence. Ana, alone once more, sitting in front of the morose fireplace with its smoky plaster figures, would try to resume her pious propaedeutics, her preparations for a virtuous life, only to find that the whole fabric of her sentimental religiosity had been submerged in vinegar, and that she regarded all her resignation as mere hypocrisy. 'Oh no, no! I can't be good! I don't know how to be good; I cannot forgive the weaknesses of others, or if I can I can't tolerate them. This man and this town fill my life with wretched prose, and, whatever Don Fermín may say, to soar one needs wings and air.' Sometimes she was so carried away by such thoughts that the image of Don Alvaro came before her again, inciting her to release the delightful, brilliant, poetic protest of the senses which the elegant dandy's eyes had placed in her heart on that memorable afternoon of All Saints' Day. But she would jump to her feet, pace about the dining-room with her head sunk in the shawl gathered tight to her body, walk around the oval table to the balcony window and press her forehead against the glass. Then she would leave the dining-room and walk through the dismal draw-ing-room and along galleries and passages to her boudoir and there, too, press her face to the window and stare with vacant eyes at the naked branches of the horse-chestnuts and at the proud eucalyptuses, with their covering of long, metallic, dull green leaves, shaking, tinkling. If the rain was not too heavy, Frillity would usually be somewhere below her (Quintanar was away from home longer than Frillity was away from the garden) and in the end Ana would see him. 'That man had been her only friend during her sorrowful youth, during her wretched servitude, and now she almost hated him. He had contrived her marriage, and now, without the slightest remorse or indeed any thoughts at all for his blunder, there he was devoting himself to his trees, pruning them without pity, grafting them as he pleased, without consulting them, not knowing whether they wanted to be cut and grafted like that. And to think that the man had once been intelligent and agreeable! Now he was just an agricultural machine, a lawn-mower, a pair of shears. Who could avoid being dehumanized by the life of Vetusta?'

If Frillity saw his beloved Ana behind the window, he would greet her with a smile. He would then bend down again over the earth, squash a snail, cut off an unwanted shoot, secure a stake and continue on his way, dragging his white shoes over the damp sand of the paths. Ana would watch his disappearance among the branches: the round hat of soft felt, always a grey one, the checked corduroy muffler eternally hanging around the neck, the brown shooting-jacket, and the trousers, neither loose nor tight, neither new nor old, embroidered with flowers of faded green and red wool on a black background.

The bank clerk's wife and the Young Marquis made frequent calls on Ana. Paco was astonished by her heroic resistance and unable to comprehend how his idol Don Alvaro could be taking so long to conquer a woman's will or, if her will was already conquered, to vanquish her virtue.

'She's in love with you, I'm sure of that,' said Paco to Mesía in the Gentlemen's Club late one evening, when only the professional night-birds remained there.

They were dining at a small pedestal-table covered with a fine white table-cloth, each with a half-bottle of claret by him. The moment of expansiveness and confidentiality was drawing close. A melancholy Mesía, suffering nostalgia for the infinite (which does affect unbelievers, in a way) was drooping his handsome, distinguished blond head and looking a little older than usual. He was eating and drinking in silence. Paco was talking with his mouth full – not, however, in an ill-mannered, but rather in an almost elegant way. His cheeks were bright red, and his eyes were aglow; his hat was on the back of his head.

'She's in love with you, I'm sure of that. But, with her, you aren't the man you are with other women – you almost seem to be frightened of her. You never want to come with me to her place, even though Don Víctor is never there – he's always out on the hills with that spiritualist Frillity.' (Paco believed that Frillity was a spiritualist, an opinion which was held by many Vetustans.)

'I can't make any progress at her house. She's a strange woman –
a hysterical woman. She has to be studied in depth.'

Alvaro did not want to confess that he considered himself defeated.
But he was convinced that Ana was in the canon theologian's power.
He did not welcome this kind of conversation and felt humiliated by
Paco's protection, which he himself had sought months earlier.
Without realizing what he was doing, the Young Marquis hurt Mesía
every time he spoke on the subject and proposed plans of attack and
ways of taking that stronghold by surprise. 'When had he, Alvaro
Mesía, ever needed help of this sort? When had he ever allowed
anybody to know how and when he conquered a woman? How this
lady was humiliating him! How Visita must be laughing at him, even
though she was hiding it! And Paco himself – what must he be
thinking? Ah, judge's wife, judge's wife, if I'm finally victorious – I'll
make you pay for all this!' But Mesía no longer expected victory; he
was fighting in desperation. It was in vain that he mounted his
handsome, pure-white Spanish thoroughbred whenever the weather
allowed, to ride through the Plaza Nueva again and again. Sometimes,
behind a window in the shadowed corner, he would see Quintanar's
wife, and she would acknowledge his presence with a tranquil,
amiable gesture; but the horse was not the talisman he had believed
it to be, for the scene of that first afternoon was never repeated. 'Yes,
it's as I feared, it was just a quarter of an hour which I was unable to
turn to my advantage.' He believed with unyielding faith that the
only recourse left to him was difficult beyond measure, almost
impossible – finding the opportunity for a direct, brutal attack to
coincide with another quarter of an hour. But this would not fulfil his
desires or satisfy his self-esteem, it would just be an ephemeral
pleasure and a revenge – and, besides, it was unspeakably difficult!
He had seldom dared call on her, and she did not receive him unless
Don Víctor was at home. But Quintanar would open his arms wide
and give him an effusive embrace, more and more enamoured, as he
put it, of the handsome dandy – what a majestic leading man the
splendid Don Alvaro would make in a comedy of manners! Since he
did not feel the call of the boards, why did he not become a deputy
in parliament? Mesía had been born to be something better than the
head of a dog; being a local party leader was small potatoes, it never
gave one any real power, in a second-class provincial capital. Why
did he not go to Madrid with a return to parliament in his pocket?

As Don Víctor asked these flattering questions, Don Alvaro bowed
his head and looked at Ana with a sorrowful face as if to say:

'It is because of you, because of my love for you, that I am still in
this miserable hole.'

'You are of the stuff ministers are made of.'

'Oh – Don Víctor, do not believe that I take any pleasure in such a
prospect. A minister! What for? I have no political ambitions. If I am

an activist in a certain party it is only to serve my country, for I find politics so disagreeable – full of farce, full of lies.'

'Certainly in the United States all politicians are rogues – but in Spain things are quite different. A man like you . . . My dear Don Alvaro, you would fly as high as a lark.'

Don Alvaro sighed and turned his gaze back towards the judge's wife. But he did still consider himself to be, above all, a political man. Going to Madrid was something he was leaving until later. For the moment he would remain in Vetusta manufacturing deputies, but as soon as he had softened the minister's wife a little more he would fly, he would fly – secure in the knowledge that he would not fall back to the ground. This was what he had planned. But Ana's resistance, which he had believed he would overcome in a few months if not in a few weeks, was another reason for postponing his move. How could he go to Madrid without having conquered this woman? And this woman now seemed unconquerable.

Since the evening of All Saints' Day – it made him ashamed to confess it to himself – he had not made the slightest progress. A whole week had gone by before he had managed to speak to Ana alone even for a moment, and then it was only to become still more convinced that her exultation on that happy afternoon had vanished, perhaps for ever.

Vistación was becoming more and more frantic. Her husband and her children had to eat their boiled chick-peas hard from re-heating and wash without towels because she had taken the cupboard-keys with her as usual and still not returned home. 'How could she go home when that wretched judge's wife refused to give in, and with stubborn heroism resisted the irresistible man?' The wretched bank clerk would twiddle his small, gummed moustache and in his soprano voice say to the multitude of his children, who were crying for their soup:

'Quiet, now, kiddies, mamma gets cross if we have lunch without her.'

And the soup would grow cold and finally Visitación would appear, out of breath, abstracted, and in a foul temper. She had come from Vegallana's house, where she had succeeded in making Ana and Alvaro talk for a moment alone, thanks to a coincidence – which she had created. But what sort of a conversation do you call that? He had come away from it biting his moustache and had said 'Leave me alone!' when she had made to rally him. 'Leave me alone!' – a sign that he wasn't making any progress. Visitación was assailed by a retrospective sense of shame as she remembered how soon she had given way and compared her own resistance with Ana's. Her cheeks burned with rage, with envy, with false, perverse modesty. Something in her conscience told her that the task which she had taken in hand was a despicable one, but she was in no state to listen to inner voices or to pieces of advice from moralizing dramas. That ignoble craving was a passion which became more intense every day; it had a pungent, bitter-sweet flavour which she now preferred to all the sweetmeats in the confectioner's shop. And as a passion it was something which recalled her youth – although, at the same time, it was like a symptom of old age. In short, she did not try to resist it, and by now believed herself to be capable of taking Ana by force and throwing her into the arms of her own former lover. At all events, in Visita's house nobody swept the floor or dusted the furniture or tidied the sitting-room or the kitchen; her home was far from being as bright as a new pin; and there were days when her husband could not find a shirt in the wardrobe and went to the bank wearing one of his wife's chemisettes which pretended, with only a modest degree of conviction, to be a sailor-collar.

But all Visita's diligence was to no avail. She, Paco, Mesía on his horse – nothing could overpower the judge's wife. It would be some consolation to be able to claim that her fortitude was simply indifference. But no, you could see it a mile away (according to all three of them), Ana was attracted to him. This was what most irritated them, in particular Visita. Don Alvaro refused to talk to her about this sorry affair, however much she encouraged him to do so. He only let off steam with Paco, and he did not often do even that.

Ana, meanwhile, believed that there was a plot against her, and this was a considerable help in her self-defence. She seldom went to Vegallana's house, in spite of Quintanar's tiresome, insufferable protests. He would repeat: 'What must they be saying, Anita, what must the marquis and marchioness be saying!'

So Don Alvaro was losing hope, but the canon theologian was not satisfied, either. The day of victory seemed remote. Ana's inertia kept presenting new obstacles for which he had not bargained. Moreover, his self-esteem was wounded. Whenever he had tried to arouse his friend's interest by telling her, either by way of an example or as a demonstration of familiarity, something of his private life, she had listened with an air of abstraction, as if all her thoughts were occupied by the selfish contemplation of her own worries and sorrows. What was more, this lady, who had spoken of great sacrifices and had said that she intended to live for the happiness of others, refused to break her habits by leaving home, stepping on mud and defying rain; she refused to rise early, putting forward as an excuse – as if this were something holy – the demands of health, the whims of her nerves. 'Rising early would be the death of me. The damp makes me feel as if there were an electric generator inside me.' This was humiliating for religion and depressing for Don Fermín. In other words, it was a bucket of cold water which chilled his soul and kept him awake at nights.

One afternoon De Pas entered his confessional in such a bad temper that Celedonio the acolyte saw him slam the door shut. Don Fermín had just come down from the belfry where, with the aid of his spyglass, he had been conducting one of his periodical examinations of the corners of houses and of gardens. He had seen the judge's wife strolling in her park, reading a book which must have been the life of St Jane Frances de Chantal – he himself had given it her. After five minutes Ana had tossed the book on to a bench in disdain.

'Oh! I don't like the look of that!' exclaimed the priest in the tower, but immediately repressed his anger, as though Ana could hear him. Two men appeared in the garden – Mesía and Quintanar. Don Alvaro shook Ana's hand, and she did not withdraw it as soon as she should have, 'even if only because *he* was watching!' Don Víctor went away and little by little the professional seducer and the lady disappeared among the trees in a turn of the path. At this point the canon theologian was seized by an impulse to hurl himself from the tower. He would have done so had he known that he would be able to fly. A little later Don Víctor, the stupid Don Víctor, turned up again. He had discarded his topcoat and was wearing a low-crowned hat and a light-coloured hunting-jacket. He was accompanied by Don Tomás Crespo, the man in the muffler. These two went off in search of the others, and the four of them presented themselves again before the lens of the spyglass, which was trembling in the canon's elegant white hands. Don Víctor was looking upwards, extending one arm, pointing to the clouds, and stamping his feet. Ana had disappeared again, she had gone into the house, leaving St Jane Frances forgotten upon the bench; but two minutes later she was back again with a shawl and a hat. The four of them left through the garden gate, unlocked by Frillity. They were going for a walk in the country!

When Don Fermín found himself enclosed within the four wooden walls of his confessional-box he compared himself to a criminal in the stocks.

On that day the canon theologian's spiritual daughters found him abstracted and impatient. They could hear him tossing and turning on his bench, and the great wooden contraption creaking. His penances were out of all proportion, enormous.

He waited in vain, held there by the wild hope that he might see the judge's wife appearing in the chapel, by chance, because of a sudden impulse – the reason did not matter so long as she appeared, which was what he wanted, what he needed. True, they had not agreed on any such meeting. Her next confession was a whole week off, why should she come? 'Just because she should, because he needed her to come, because he wanted to talk to her, tell her that she must mend her ways, that he was not some sack to be left leaning against a wall, that piety was not something to be played with, that edifying books are not tossed in disdain on to benches in the garden, and that one does not disappear at the drop of a hat among Frillity's trees in the company of a corrupt, materialistic and handsome man.' But no, Ana did not appear in the chapel. 'God knows where they can be. What sort of an outing was it? One of Don Víctor's foolish ideas, no doubt. He had raised an arm to point to the clouds, a gesture that seemed to be a kind of guarantee of good weather, and indeed it was a beautiful afternoon, one could be certain that it would not rain. But of what account was that? Was that a sufficient reason for going out into the countryside with the enemy? For Mesía was the enemy, yes, Don Fermín suspected him again. Yet the judge's wife had never accused herself of attraction to any one specific man. She had spoken of temptation in general and of lewd dreams, but she had never confessed that she loved any particular individual. And Ana, his sweet friend, never lied – still less in the tribunal of penance. But about whom did she dream? The canon recalled the delightful hypothesis which he had once cherished, and now this other opposing hypothesis presented itself and made him writhe inside the grated box: suppose she dreams about – that man?' He left the chapel in fury, hardly concealing the fact. He met Don Custodio in the retrochoir and did not return his greeting. He walked into the sacristy and threatened Turtle-dove with dismissal because the cat had dirtied the clothes-drawers again. He went on to the palace and the bishop suffered one of the severe reprimands which, in a sour, stinging, almost disrespectful voice, his vicar-general sometimes directed at him. The good Fortunato was in difficulties, he did not have the money to pay the tailor who had made new cassocks for his familiars. And the tailor, with the best manners in the world, now asked for the cash in squat letters covering a grubby piece of paper which the bishop held between his fingers. The tailor called the prelate 'Most Serene Highness'; but he wanted his money.

In a trembling voice, Fortunato asked De Pas for a loan. The canon theologian made this good shepherd who gave literal interpretations to biblical metaphors repeat his request over and over, and humiliated him a dozen times before he consented to lend him the money.

'What purpose had been served by the new cassocks? And, above all, why did Fortunato pay for them out of his own pocket? Knowing as he did that he was penniless – because he gave all his stipend away before he had even received it – why did he commit himself like this?' Fortunato confessed that he was like a spendthrift second lieutenant out of whose pay stoppages have to be made as if he were a common soldier. He said that he wanted to put this life of insolvency behind him:

'I don't know how much I owe your mother, Fermín, it must be a fortune, mustn't it?'

'Yes, my Lord, a fortune, but the worst aspect of the whole affair is not that you are ruining us, but that you are ruining yourself too, and the world knows it, and this brings discredit on the Church. Getting into debt for the sake of the poor! Cheating for charity! Come, now, in the name of the Lord, where is it to end? Christ said: give all that thou hast and follow me; but he did not say: give all that others have.'

'Wise words, my son, wise words, and if it weren't indecorous to do so I'd ask the Minister to stop my stipend, to see if that would make me mend my ways.'

Then De Pas went into the offices and gave the men there cause to remember his visit for a long time. He found fault with everything. He rummaged through files, discovered abuses, sent dust flying, threatened to suspend salaries, refused everything he could refuse, devised two or three punishments for village priests and, finally, as he walked out of the door, said that 'he was not giving a penny' to a subscription for the shipwrecked sailors of Palomares.

'But Father,' sobbed a poor white-bearded fisherman with his knitted pixie-cap in his hand, 'but Father, we're going to starve this year! This season we aren't making enough money to buy bread from our catches of fish!'

The canon theologian did not reply as he walked away thinking about Ana and Mesía. Half an hour later, as he promenaded alone in the Mall, striding along, forgetful of the rhythm of his normal gait, he heard some unknown voice repeating inside his skull: fish, fish!

'Why was he remembering the fish now?' And he shrugged his shoulders, irritated by this foolish obsession coming on top of all the other annoyances.

'It would crown it all if I were now to lose my reason.'

A week passed and at the appointed hour Anita presented herself on her knees before the grating of the confessional box.

After the absolution she dried a tear on her cheek, stood up, and went out into the porch. There she waited for the canon and, together, close to nightfall, they walked into Doña Petronila's house.

Constantine the Great was alone. She was going over the accounts of the Guild of the Mother of Beauteous Love, her large hazel eyes peeping out of the gold-framed lenses of her spectacles. She had a swarthy face, a bony forehead, bulging eyelids, eyebrows grey and bushy, like the great mop of wiry hair which covered her head, a round fleshy chin, a nose which was insignificant though well-proportioned, a large mouth and pale, thick lips. She was tall and broad-shouldered, and her long, immaculate widowhood seemed to have covered her with some kind of undergrowth of chastity which gave her the look of a virgin of great age. She wore a black Servite habit with a broad belt of patent leather, and there was a garish, ostentatious, silver coat of arms on her sleeve, lashed to her wrist (the wrist of a farm labourer) with bead-strings.

She was sitting at a bureau of black wood encrusted with gilded Chinese figures. She stood up, embraced the judge's wife and kissed the canon theologian's hand. After thanking them for their unexpected visit she begged to be allowed to finish sorting that tangle of numbers, and the lady and the priest found themselves alone in the murky sitting-room, decorated with dark green damask and grey and gold wallpaper. Ana sat on the sofa, the canon by her side on an armchair. The wooden balcony-shutters were ajar, letting narrow shafts of the light of the dying day into the room. Ana and De Pas could hardly see each other. From the parlour on their right came a plump white cat, its tail opulent and its curves elegant. It stalked up to the sofa, lifted its languid head, eyed the judge's wife, emitted a guttural moan, soft and kittenish, brushed its back in a familiar manner against the canon's soutane and wandered out into the passage in silence, as if it were walking on cotton wool. For a moment Ana fancied that the lily-white cat smelt of incense; it seemed, at all events, to be a symbol of Doña Petronila's domestic devotion. The house was pervaded by the silence of a padded coffin, the air was warm and lightly perfumed with something which smelt of wax and balm and maybe lavender. Ana felt drowsy, a pleasant yet somewhat alarming feeling; it was good to be there, but it gave one a vague fear of suffocation.

Doña Petronila was taking a long time to finish her accounts. A housemaid, also wearing a black habit, came into the room carrying an old brass lamp, which she placed upon a pedestal-table after saying 'Good-evening!' in the voice of a nun with a cold, without raising her eyes from the grey-and-green chequered felt carpet.

Ana and her confessor were alone again.

Interrupting a silence which had lasted for several minutes, the canon said in a voice which had much in common with the voice of the white cat:

'You cannot imagine, my dear, dear friend, how grateful I am to you for this decision.'

'If only you had spoken sooner.'

'I have spoken quite enough, you scoundrel.'

'But not as you did today, you had never told me that I was snubbing you by refusing to come here, and that these ladies knew it. It was raining so! You know that damp is the death of me, and wet streets horrify me. I'm ill – yes, Father, in spite of what Don Robustiano calls my good colour and fine flesh, I'm ill. Sometimes I imagine that deep down inside I'm just a heap of sand crumbling away. I don't know how to explain it. I feel my whole life cracking open. I'm breaking up inside. I'm losing heart, giving up. If you could see what I'm like inside, you'd feel sorry for me. But in spite of all that, if you had spoken earlier as you spoke today I would have come even if I'd had to swim here. Yes, Don Fermín, I'm no doubt full of all kinds of wickedness, but I'm not ungrateful. I know what I owe you, and I know I'll never be able to repay you. A voice, a voice in the empty desert where I was living – you can't imagine what that meant

– and your voice came at just the right time. I never had a mother, you know what my life has been like. I don't know how to be good, you're quite right, I don't want virtue unless it is pure poetry – and the poetry of virtue looks like prose to people who aren't virtuous. I know that's true. That's why I want you to be my guide. I shall come to this house, I shall copy these ladies, I shall busy myself with whatever task they give me. I shall do everything you tell me to, not out of submission, but out of self-interest, because I've shown that I can't order my own life; I prefer you to tell me what to do. I want to be a little girl again, I want to make a fresh start on my upbringing, be positive and stay so, have a constant inner impulse to urge me on, stop flitting to and fro as I am now. Besides, I need to be cured, sometimes I'm afraid of going mad. I've told you – some nights as I lie awake in bed I try to dispel my gloomy thoughts by thinking about God, about His presence. "If He is here, what does anything else matter?" This is what I say to myself, but it's no use, because, as I've told you, old ideas come back to life in my mind, like painful wounds which have never been allowed to heal – ideas of rebellion, irreligious arguments, stupid stubborn prejudices which I picked up sometime, I don't know when, which I vaguely remember hearing at home, when my father was alive. And sometimes I ask myself: might God be no more than this idea of mine, this aching weight which I think I feel on my brain each time I strive to demonstrate to myself the presence of God?'

'Anita, Anita – stop, stop, you're allowing yourself to be carried away! Yes, yes, we face danger, I can see that clearly now, great danger. But we shall be saved, I am certain of it; you are a good woman, the Lord is with you – and I would lay down my life to rid you of these idle fears. It is all part of your illness, it is flatulence, nerves – something of the sort. But that is purely physical, it has nothing to do with your soul. There is, however, a danger of contagion; yes, Anita, not for my sake but for your own you must begin a life of practical devotion. Good works, good works, my dear friend! This is a serious case, we need powerful medicine. If at times you feel repelled by certain words, certain actions of these good ladies, do not allow your imagination to carry you away, do not condemn them lightly; think well of other people, forgive them for their weaknesses and take no notice of appearances. And now, to talk about me for a moment – if only you could penetrate my soul, Anita! I shall certainly never be able to repay you for the wonderful decision which you have taken this afternoon.'

'You spoke so . . .!'

'I spoke from the soul.'

'I was behaving like an ungrateful woman, without realizing it.'

'But now – a new life, is that not so, my daughter?'

'Yes, yes, Father, a new life.'

They fell silent and looked at each other. Abandoning self-control, Don Fermín grasped Ana's hand, which had been resting upon a crochet-work cushion, pressed it between his own hands, and waved it to and fro. Ana felt her face aflame, but it seemed absurd to alarm herself. They both rose to their feet. Doña Petronila walked in, and De Pas, without releasing Ana's hand, said:

'Madam, you have come at precisely the right moment. You are a witness to the fact that the sheep has solemnly promised her shepherd never to stray from the fold chosen by her.'

Constantine the Great kissed Ana on the forehead.

The kiss was solemn and firm, but cold. It was as if Doña Petronila were imprinting Ana's brow with the stamp of a religious guild, after moistening it on a pad of ice.

XIX

Each year, as soon as March began, Don Robustiano Somoza diagnosed all his patients' illnesses as spring fever, although he had only the haziest notion of what he meant by this; but since the handsome doctor's principal mission was to console the afflicted, and since this climatological explanation usually satisfied them, he did not bother to search for another. Spring fever it was (according to Don Robustiano) which prostrated the judge's wife, who went to bed one night at the end of March uncontrollably clenching her teeth, and feeling as if her head were full of fireworks. As she awoke the next morning and emerged from dreams of ghosts, she realized that she was feverish.

Quintanar was hunting on the marshes at Palomares and would not be back until ten o'clock at night. Anselmo went to call the doctor, and Petra stationed herself like a faithful dog at the head of her mistress's bed. The cook, Servanda (a girl from a mountain village, new to the house), came and went in silence with cups of linden-tea, without making any attempt to conceal her indifference. It had been a long time since Anita had last been prompted by affectionate impulses towards Don Víctor, but now, in the afternoon and even more at dusk, she hid her face and wept as she thought about her absent husband. 'How she wished he were here! Only he could keep her company in the solitude of this, her latest illness.' It was in vain that the marchioness, Paco, Visitación and Ripamilán hurried to Ana's bedside as soon as they heard that she was ill. She received them all affably and smiled at them, but she was counting the minutes to ten o'clock. 'Her dear Quintanar! He was her true friend, her father, her mother, everything.' The marchioness did not stay long with her sick friend. She felt her forehead and said that it was nothing, that

Somoza was right, spring fever . . . spoke of sarsaparilla and hurriedly took her leave. Paco admired Ana's beauty in silence; her head, half buried in the soft white pillows, was, for him, like 'a jewel in its casket'. Visita observed that Ana now looked more than ever like the Madonna of the Chair. Fever had put light and fire into her eyes and red roses into her cheeks, and when she smiled she looked like a saint. Involuntarily, Paco thought 'that she was appetizing'. Like his mother he offered his services and left. In the passage he pinched Petra, who was bringing her mistress a glass of sugared water. Visita dropped her shawl upon her friend's bed and made ready to meddle, taking no notice of Petra's impertinent look. 'There was no trusting servants. Luckily she was there now to do whatever had to be done.'

'Apart from all that, you must admit that your dear Quintanar does some strange things. Taking it into his head to go hunting, and you in this state!'

'How could he tell?'

'But didn't you complain of not feeling well last night?'

'Frillity's to blame for everything.'

'If you go around with Frillity you'll end up as mad as he is. Isn't he the one who grafted bits of English cockerels on to Spanish ones?'

'Yes, yes, that's right.'

'The one who says that our forefathers were monkeys? He's the monkey, and a bad-mannered monkey at that. He doesn't even dress like a respectable person, my dear, I've never seen him with a shirt-collar on, or a topper.'

Somoza returned at eight o'clock that evening. In spite of 'spring fever' he was uneasy; he looked at his patient's tongue, felt her pulse, took a thermometer from his pocket, told her to put it under her arm, and observed the degrees. Then he turned as red as a cherry, scowled at Visita and, relying on guesswork, exclaimed in anger:

'We're in a bad way! There has been a great deal of chattering here. You have all been agitating her, haven't you? I can just see it – the place full of people, to be sure, full of talk!'

And then it was Visitación who felt her face aflame. Somoza had guessed right. He did not know medicine, but he knew Visita. The doctor wrote his prescription, censured Don Víctor for his untimely absence, and said that madness is catching and that Frillity knew as much about Darwinism as he himself knew about shoeing flies. He gave the judge's wife two tiny slaps on the face, enjoying the contact and, slamming doors behind him, departed, shouting that he would return early the following morning.

As Visitación, sitting at the foot of the bed, devoured a generous helping of jam, she affirmed, with her mouth full, that Somoza was about as much use as a poultice on a broken leg. The bank clerk's wife believed in household remedies and disparaged doctors. She had twice been pulled through the dangers of childbirth by a famous midwife who hadn't got any diploma or any need of one, so help her God. 'Still, everything in this world is a farce. Saying you're worse because we tried to take your mind off things! The animal! What does he know about women who are nervous and have lively imaginations! I'm sure if I hadn't been here you'd have been pining away all day long thinking about the most miserable things and brooding over your dear Quintanar's absence – "Why isn't he here? He's a good husband, though, but he isn't a little boy any more who can't think for himself" – and goodness knows what else, all the things that come into your head when you're alone and ill and you've got your reasons for complaining about somebody.'

Ana tried to avoid listening to Visita by thinking about something else – the only way to make the torture of her chatter bearable. At a quarter past ten Don Víctor, in large gaiters and a leather belt, with birds and hunting equipment streaming from him, entered the bedroom; behind him came Don Tomás Crespo, Frillity, in a crumpled grey hat, a checked muffler and white triple-soled shoes. Quintanar flung his raincoat to the floor, as Manrique flings his cape down in the first act of *The Troubadour*, leapt into his wife's arms and covered her forehead with kisses, forgetting that there were witnesses present.

'Oh yes! he was her father, her mother, her brother – the gentle strength of the familiar caress, the spiritual protection of domestic love. No, no, she wasn't alone in the world, her Quintanar belonged to her.' In silence she swore her husband eternal fidelity, in the long intense kiss with which she responded to his. Don Víctor's mustachios were like wet sweeping-brushes as he sprinkled his wife's forehead with the water which he had brought back on them from the marshes; but she did not feel any repugnance – indeed, she could see glints of gold and silver among those stiff bristles which looked like a brush made of straw, singed at both ends.

Don Víctor, too, was of opinion that 'it was nothing', but be that as it may he regretted with all his heart not having returned on the half-past-four train.

'You see, Crespo, if I had taken notice of my premonition . . . Yes, madam,' he added, addressing Visita, 'he can tell you. I felt – I know not why – that I should return home earlier today.'

'Oh yes, you can be sure of that, one does sometimes have forebodings,' cried the bank clerk's wife, making ready to relate three or four of her own.

'But Frillity here is to blame.'

Frillity shrugged and felt the sick woman's pulse; she squeezed his hand, forgiving him for everything. Don Víctor had indeed wanted to return early to Vetusta – so as not to miss the theatre. But one could not say so. Frillity, in silence, was able once again to deny the existence of supernatural messages. He had removed his hat, and his thick, forest-brown hair, cut the same length all over, looked like a bush or a piece of scrub. His eyes were closed and he was frowning; he was annoyed by the light and knocked against the furniture. He smelt of the hills, the mist of the marshes was still clinging to him and he seemed to be enveloped in the darkness and the freshness of the country. There was an air about him of the wild beast which has fallen into a trap, of the bat which has had the misfortune to be attracted by light into a house. As he stood beside a nervous, frightened, feverish Ana he was like a symbol of health attempting to infect the sick woman with its emanations.

When husband and wife were left alone, having at last persuaded Visita to renounce the idea of sacrificing herself by sitting up with her friend, Ana sought her husband's arms again and said in a voice in which her suppressed tears trembled:

'Don't go to bed yet, I'm feeling so nervous, I need you, stay here with me, for the Lord's sake, Quintanar.'

'Yes, my child, yes, most willingly.' And he drew the sheets around her shoulders, pink and as smooth as satin, with solicitous affection yet without giving them a glance. Ana soon noticed that her husband was worried.

'What's wrong? Are you afraid? You think I'm worse than they say, and you're trying to hide it.'

'No, my child, no – in the name of God – it is not that.'

'Yes, yes, I can see it is, but don't be frightened. I assure you I'll get over it, I know I will, you know what I'm like, sometimes I show the symptoms of some illness and then it all turns out to be nothing. But I am feeling very nervous, I keep fancying that the world is abandoning me, that I'm being left alone, alone, and I need you – but I'll get over it, it's only nerves.'

'Yes, my child, of course, nerves.'

Unable to restrain himself any longer he stood up, saying:

'My dear heart, I shall return, forthwith.'

He hurried out through the side-door.

'Hey!' he shouted in the passage; 'Petra, Servanda, Anselmo, anyone – did Don Tomás take the partridge?'

Anselmo inspected the dead birds, which had been deposited in the kitchen, and answered from a distance:

'Yes, sir – no partridges here!'

'God's fury! Begad! A curse on him! He is always up to this kind of trick! That partridge is mine, I killed it. I am certain that I shot it. He is such a vain fellow! Anselmo! Pay attention to what I am about to say to you. At daybreak tomorrow, do you understand? you are to proceed to Don Tomás's house and you are to request, on my behalf, with the utmost energy and seriousness, that he hand the partridge over to you, in whatever state it be, do you understand? Tell him that this is no joking matter, and that even if he has plucked it I demand that it be restored to me. *Suum cuique.*'[1]

Ana heard the shouts and at once forgave her husband for his innocent weakness. 'All hunters are like that,' she thought, with the benevolence lent her by incipient fever.

Don Víctor returned, and his wife's sweet, Christian smile restored him to calm, the partridge being unable to do so.

It was half past one before his wife *fell into the arms of Morpheus*, and *then and only then* could Don Víctor himself make ready to sleep.

Once he was in his shirt-sleeves at his bedside he started thinking that his deeply beloved Ana's illness was a serious setback. 'God knew, he was not alarmed, there was no danger. If there had been, he would have spotted it in her fear, in the pain which would have been torturing her; but there was no fear, no pain, therefore there was no danger. But there was a setback. To begin with, he could say goodbye to the theatre for many a day; and even though at the present time there was a company performing comic operas – a hybrid genre – none the less he had to confess that he was beginning to acquire a taste for the simple, gentle charms of the major comic operas, and during recent evenings had found a certain local colour in *Marina*, and period flavour in *The Blue Domino*, not to mention the thwarted love-affair in *The Oath*,[2] of exquisite beauty. But what about his trip with the governor of the province to inaugurate the Western Economical Railway? And his games of dominoes with the chief of the Engineers' Department? And the long walks which he needed for his digestion?' The prospect of not leaving home for many days horrified him. He went to bed in an angry mood. He put out the light; the darkness suggested remorse. 'He was an egotist, he was not thinking about his poor beloved wife but about his own comfort, his own caprices.' And as if to make amends, and to deceive himself, he heaved a large sigh and exclaimed: 'My poor, beloved Anita!'

And, satisfied, he slept.

Don Víctor awoke next morning with his head full of plans, as usual, but at once he remembered Ana and her fever, and his soul was filled with cowardly sorrow. 'God knows what it might be!' The medicines, those syrups he hated, his fear of getting the doses wrong, the terror with which any potion coloured green inspired him, making him think that it might be poisonous (despite his studies in physical chemistry, poison was always green or yellow as far as he was concerned), the blundering and the clumsiness of the servants, the hours of silence and tedium at the foot of the patient's bed, the inevitable worries, the need to hang on Somoza's every word and to talk to anyone who wanted to know about the development of the illness – all these vexations mounted up in Don Víctor's imagination, he spat his bile several times, and he rose from his bed full of self-pity. He repaired to his wife's bedroom and immediately forgot all his grievances. Ana was very ill, she had been delirious; the servants had been reluctant to awake him, but madam had spent a terrible night, according to Petra, who had sat up with her.

Somoza arrived at eight o'clock.

'What is it? What is wrong? Is it serious?'

Don Víctor wrung his hands and trembled as he asked these questions, in the patient's presence. She was half-asleep but she could hear every word.

The doctor made no reply. He wrote a prescription and walked into the boudoir.

'What is it? What is it?' repeated Quintanar in a hushed, quavering voice. 'What is it?'

Don Robustiano looked at him in contempt, abhorrence and indignation.

'What is it! What is it! That's soon asked.' Don Robustiano did not know what it was, but all the signs made it look like something serious. This is what he thought, but he said:

'It is the following: you must stay alert, take the utmost care, not leave your wife in the hands of servant girls or of Visitación, prattling away and agitating her. That is what it is.'

'But is it serious – is it something serious?'

'Psa – it is, and it isn't. No, it is not serious; science cannot say that it is serious; nor can science deny that it is so. But you don't understand such matters, my boy. Hepatitis? Maybe. Gastroenteritis perhaps. But certain deceptive reflex phenomena . . .'

'So it is not nerves? Not spring fever?'

'Nerves, my dear fellow, are always mixed up in these matters, and spring – blood – new sap – of course, they all play a part. But you cannot understand such matters.'

'No, sir, indeed I cannot. In my moments of leisure I have read a few books of medicine. I know Jaccoud[3] – but that class of book made me feel like . . . well, I felt nauseated and imagined that I could hear my blood circulating, and I thought that I was, well, something like the new Madrid waterworks, with pipes, sluices in my heart . . .'

'All right, all right. You needn't carry on with this nonsense just for *my* benefit. I shall come again this afternoon. If there is any change, let me know. Ah! don't put too many clothes on her bed, or let Visitación in – she only agitates her. Science categorically forbids that protectress of unqualified midwives to come poking her nose in here!'

Four days later Don Robustiano sent a young doctor, his protégé, as a replacement. He thought that the point had come at which he should stay away; for, as everyone knew, he could not attend dearly beloved friends when their illnesses reached a certain stage.

The replacement was a studious and intelligent young man. He declared that the illness was not serious but that it would be a protracted one and that the convalescence would be a difficult business. He did not like to refer to ailments by their imprecise common names, and used technical terms if he was pressed – not out of ridiculous pedantry but so as to fulfil his desire not to inform laymen about what they did not need to know and, truth to tell, could not know. As a result Ana believed she was dying. When she was told that she was on the mend her sufferings were even worse than in the times of greatest danger. On being told that she had spent six days in a stupor with intervals of exaltation and delirium, she was astonished that such a long martyrdom should have seemed so short.

Ana's illness left her exhausted, but even more than that, she felt over-excited, and seemed to be looking out at the world through glass. Everything was pale yellow. An infinity of dots and small circles of air, sometimes like bubbles, sometimes like dust and gossamer, floated in front of the objects around her. If she placed her arms upon the sheet and looked at her thin hands, etched with clusters of blue lines upon a matt white background, the thought suddenly came to her that the fingers did not depend upon her will, and it was hard work to decide to try to hide her hands. Ana's moments of worst anguish came when she started eating again: insipid, watery broth which Don Víctor cooled by puffing on it, puffing with faith and perserverance, demonstrating his concern and affection in the way he puffed. According to Quintanar the ideal broth was something never realized by the servant women of Vetusta. As he held forth on this subject Ana would feel a deadly sweat breaking out, which seemed to drain her little remaining strength, and even her will to live. She would close her eyes and lose all sensation of herself, both inside and out; even her sense of oneness vanished sometimes, and she saw herself split into a thousand fragments, but as horror started to overcome her it provoked a reaction strong enough to return her to her own self as to a safe harbour. She noticed that this recovery of her self-awareness was the cause of great suffering, but she almost enjoyed this pain, which was, after all, life – a proof that she was who she was. If Don Víctor was by Ana's side, talking, she would unintentionally follow the train of his thoughts. Much against her will, her attention would be attracted to his pronouncements and her mind would subject them to rigorous criticism, to a detailed analysis which hurt her. She could not stop herself from tearing her husband's absurdities to shreds and, as she did so, suffering indescribable torment in her brain.

The doctor seemed to be preoccupied with her body and heedless of the ineffable pains deep in the very core of her being, somewhere which was no doubt part of her body but which was so intimate that it seemed like her soul. Every day her abdomen had to be felt and questions asked about the lowest animal functions. Don Víctor did not trust his memory and, watch in hand, he kept a record in a notebook where, using seemly abbreviations and a gongoresque style,[4] he set down everything the doctor needed to know about these details.

So long as the gravity of Ana's illness gave cause for concern her loving husband had thoughts only for her, and did his duty like a saint. If at times his behaviour was tiresome, careless, or clumsy, he did not mean it to be so. Then he began to feel bored, to miss his normal life, and to exaggerate the number of hours he spent awake at night. So as to be able to bear his cross he decided to become interested in nursing, and was successful. Preparing potions, painting his wife's body with iodine, puffing on broth and skimming it, consulting his watch to count minutes and even seconds (an operation which he soon performed with a precision exasperating to Petra and Servanda), such activities became as entertaining as making fretwork Gothic portals. Don Víctor eagerly awaited the doctor each day: first, to make him say twenty times over that Ana was better, much better; and, second, to enjoy the cheerful conversation, remote from all the illnesses in the world, which followed the professional visit. Somoza's replacement, Benítez, was not a talkative man but he was amused by Quintanar, who soon professed a great affection for him. The contrast between, on the one hand, Don Víctor's humdrum, insignificant chores, the cramped bed-chamber with its oppressive atmosphere, in sum his monotonous life at home, and, on the other hand, current European affairs, the Russian War,[5] the open air, and the latest comic opera, enthralled him, and he always led their conversations towards topics which were fresh, momentous and eventful. He also liked to argue with Benítez and sound him out, as he put it. One of the problems which most concerned the master of the house was the plurality of inhabited worlds.[6] He believed that there were, indeed, people living on all the stars, God's generosity made it necessary; and he cited Flammarion, and the letters of Feijoo,[7] and the opinion of an English bishop whose name he did not remember, 'Mister what's his name' (because for Quintanar all Englishmen were called 'Mister').

Once the doctor declared that Ana's recovery would probably be steady, although slow, the joyful Quintanar would not permit any doubts about her uninterrupted journey in search of health. In his innocent yet resolute egotism he had tired of thinking about others and forgetting himself, he did not want his servitude to last a moment longer, and if Ana moaned he grimaced and even went so far as to talk in a bitter-sweet voice about patience and the need to behave oneself.

'Let us not act like children, Ana. You are better, what is bothering you now is a consequence of your weakness. Do not think about it, it is merely idle fear, fear does more harm than the illness itself.' And then, infallibly, he would repeat the saying about cholera and fear.[8]

He regarded the idea of a relapse or even a delay in Ana's return to

health as something subversive, a machination against his repose.
'He was not made of stone. He would not be able to stand it.'

No longer did he feel any pity for the patient – it was all nerves,
nothing but nerves – and he began to think exclusively about himself
again. He flitted in and out of Ana's bedroom, but seldom sat down
there, and even the record of medicines and other intimate details
began to irk him. The doctor had to give his orders to Petra. Quintanar
invented sophisms and even lies so as to stay away, in his study, in
the garden. 'How great were Art and Nature! In reality all was one,
and God was the author of everything.' And Don Víctor would inhale
the April zephyrs with voluptuous pleasure, gulping air by the
mouthful. He put his machines in order again, dreamed of new
inventions, and envied Frillity for his acclimatization of *Eucalyptus
globulus* in Vetusta.

Ana noticed her husband's absences. He left her alone for hours
and hours which only seemed to him like minutes. But when she felt
that she was drowning in boundless seas of sorrow, when she seemed
to be isolated from the world, abandoned without hope, she did not
call to Quintanar, although at such moments he was the only person
she remembered. She preferred to leave him undisturbed out in the
garden because if he came to her he hurt her with his garrulous and
absurd disdain for nervous suffering.

One leaden afternoon, which was the more desolate because it was
a spring afternoon and seemed like a winter one, she was sitting up
in bed alone amid massive walls of pillows. The back of her bedroom,
where her coats and a pair of trousers left there by Don Víctor were
poised in tragic postures, was already in darkness. Lacking all faith
in her doctor, she believed she had some incurable disease of which
she was ignorant, and which the medical men of Vetusta did not
understand. Suddenly an idea came into her head as if it were a bitter
taste in her brain: 'I am alone in the world.' And the world was lead-
coloured, or dirty yellow, or black, according to the time and the day.
The world was a remote, muffled, mournful murmur – senseless,
monotonous children's songs, and wheels clattering over cobble-
stones, making windows rattle and then fading into the distance like
the grumbling of rancorous waves. Life was a country dance performed by the sun revolving at speed around the earth, and this was
what each day was: nothing else. People entered and left her
bedchamber as if it were a stage in a theatre. They spoke with
assumed concern, but they thought about what was happening
outside, and their real selves were something different. It was all a
mask. 'Nobody loved anybody. That was the world and she was
alone.' She looked at her body and it was like earth. 'It was the
accomplice of all the others. It escaped from her, too, as soon as it
could; it was more like the world than it was like her; and it belonged
to the world more than it belonged to her.' 'I am my soul,' she

muttered to herself, and releasing her grip on the sheets she slipped down into the bed and lay there as the wall of pillows crumbled into ruin. She wept with her eyes closed. Life returned to her amid waves of tears. She heard the chiming of one of the clocks in the house. It was time for her medicine. That afternoon it was Quintanar's turn to attend to her, and he did not appear. Ana waited. She did not want to call him and she leaned towards the bedside table. On a book with green covers stood her tumbler. She took it and drank. And then, absently, she read on the spine of the voluminous book: *Works of St Teresa*, I.

She shuddered with a vague fear. She was assailed by the memory of the afternoon when as a girl she had read St Augustine in the arbour in Loreto and had heard supernatural voices exploding in her brain. She had lost the ingenuous faith of those days. 'It was a coincidence, a simple coincidence, that this mystical work was lying there at a time when her mind was full of sorrowful thoughts of abandonment, and that it was awaking compulsive ideas of piety – serious and profound ideas which warmed her soul – not imposed but revealed, and welcomed with all the embraces of her desires . . . But that didn't matter. Whether it was a message from heaven or not she would accept the lesson, turn the coincidence to good account, and understand the deep meaning of this lucky chance. Hadn't she been complaining of being alone, hadn't she almost fainted at the idea of her abandonment? Well, there in front of her were those golden letters: *Works of St Teresa*, I. Such eloquence in the title of a book! You're alone! Well, what about God?'

The thought of God was like a burning ember thrust into her heart, she was aflame with piety. Under the irresistible impulse of a self-evident, living, physical and overwhelming faith, she knelt upon the bed. A pallid figure, blinded by tears, her trembling hands clasped over her head, she exclaimed in the faltering tones of a sick, doting child:

'My Father! My Father! Lord! Lord! Dearly beloved God!'

She shivered and waves of dizziness surged to her head; she leaned against the cold stucco and fell senseless upon the counterpane of red damask.

In spite of Don Víctor's prohibition, Ana suffered a relapse, and the fears, the emergencies and the sleepless nights returned. The doctor again became an oracle, again the details of the bedchamber were arduous chores, the watch was a laconic dictator again.

Ana had terrible dreams at night. As day dawned and the pale, cowardly light filtered through the chinks between the shutters over the balcony windows and dragged itself across the floor, she awoke from her nightmares choking like a castaway on the sea-shore. She thought she could still feel the touch of coarse, salacious apparitions, covered with plague sores; smell the fetid emanations of their putrid flesh; breathe the cold, almost viscous atmosphere of the underground tunnels in which she had been imprisoned in her delirium. Fearful monsters dressed in rags, cackling and threatening to touch her with their festering wounds, had forced her to squeeze again and again through a narrow hole in the ground, an excruciating torture which made her believe that she was dying. One night she realized that the underground tunnels were the catacombs, according to the romantic descriptions of Chateaubriand and Wiseman,[9] but there were no virgins in white tunics – instead, repulsive emaciated spectres wearing golden chasubles, copes and clerical cloaks, like bats' wings to the touch, wandered along the damp, narrow, low-ceilinged passages. Ana would run, run, run, yet not be able to run as fast as she wanted, in her search for the narrow hole, for she preferred tearing her flesh upon it to suffering the stench and the touch of these repulsive ghosts; but when she reached the escape-hole some of the people there would ask her for kisses, others for gold, then she would hide her face and give out silver and copper coins as she heard guffawed prayers for the dead and felt on her face the filthy water which the hyssops were sucking up from puddles and sprinkling over her.

When she awoke she was bathed in cold sweat. Disgusted by her own body, she fancied that her bed smelt like the fetid fluids of the hyssops of her nightmare.

'Was she going to die? Were these repugnant dreams emanations from the grave, a foretaste of clay? And were these underground passages and the spectres in them a picture of hell? Hell! She had never thought at any length about it. For her, as for most of the faithful, it had merely been one of many unexamined beliefs. She had believed in hell as she had believed everything the Church told her to believe, because whenever her thoughts had become rebellious she had subdued them with an act of assumed faith, saying 'I believe blindly', mistaking the declaration and the determination to believe for belief itself. But it was different now. Hell was no longer a dogma lumped together with all the other dogmas, she had smelt it, tasted it. And she realized that until then she had not, in fact, believed in hell. Yes, yes, hell was a physical reality, or so it seemed – and why not? How vain was the shallow philosophy of rumbustious optimism, of abstract, easygoing spiritualism, lacking any awareness of the sad realities of life! Hell existed! And now she knew what it was – the corruption of matter, for souls corrupted by sin. And she had sinned, yes, yes, she had sinned. What a difference there was between the criteria with which she now judged her own transgressions and the world's judgement, so convenient previously for absolving herself of certain *indiscretions* which now weighed like lead on her heart!' She remembered the religious aphorisms and maxims which she had heard from the canon theologian without grasping their terrible severity; that profound, grim meaning which they seemed not to possess as they rustled from the soft and elegant lips of that impeccable clergyman.

The sun was already quite high in the sky, taking the chill off the morning with the tepid caresses of a Vetustan April. The other members of the household thought that Ana was still asleep or lying exhausted in her bed, and they did not come to open her balcony shutters or disturb her in any way. On those spring mornings, in the melancholy comfort of the bed which so often only inspired her with hatred, Ana felt the day developing. Life was beginning to stir again in her wasted body, ravaged like a battlefield; life was advancing over the terrain of its still uncertain victory. Her brain was recovering its own health, too – its control of the domain of logic – and her memory was firm again and no longer a torture, no longer confused by visions and other such absurdities.

Happy to be left alone and to be thought asleep or only half-awake, Ana conducted a new inquiry into the sins of which she wanted to accuse herself. Her memory was the officer on duty and her imagination was the public prosecutor. As health surged back into her body her terror disappeared, and she listened to the prosecutor's accusations with a growing and even tender curiosity. Her feelings of repugnance and horror were remote now, and the idea of hell faded from her mind, as the vibrations of a resounding bar die away; the transgressions which she remembered and which had been her life, her everyday reality, passed through her brain like food through a body, warming and strengthening her spirit; and although her remorse was not dulled, the account of her sins acquired more and more interest for her.

She remembered all the days which had followed her torpor during the relentless winter rains, the days when her spirit had started to emerge from its hibernation. And she found herself at the fiesta of St Blasius,[10] on the road to the Old Factory, that sunny afternoon when heaven seemed to be giving a party. The cathedral tower, up there on the apex of the hill of La Encimada, looked as if it were crowning some enormous monument, its lace-like open-work in dark stone standing out against the orange and violet background of a calm sky striped by long, narrow, wavy clouds poised over the abyss, waiting for the sun to go down so as to block off the horizon. Ana did not know why, but St Blasius heralded the spring. She was longing for those days which occur between endless spells of bad weather, days on which a little light appears, drawing vibrations of joy and brightness from the sleeping green fields of Vetusta: days which are better than April and May, for they are the happy anticipation of those months. Her doleful ideas had flown away like winter birds, and there, at the fiesta of St Blasius, she was surrounded by people, and was the object of all their attentions, and by her side was Don

Alvaro Mesía, in love with her, made miserable by so much love, resigned, treating her with disinterested affection, gentle and tender, hoping for nothing. The charm of his presence was rather like the charm of that day. In reality it was just another winter's day, nothing out of the ordinary; but with its tranquillity and the vague, tepid happiness of its atmosphere it gave her a delight which she savoured with ineffable pleasure.

Don Alvaro, too. She would never be his, never – that burning summer would never come, she would not even allow him to speak clearly or persist in his aspirations; but to have him at her side, to feel him loving her, adoring her – that she would permit herself. It was sweet, it was tender, it was a tranquil yet profound pleasure. She looked at him with flames in her eyes, flames which she extinguished as soon as they appeared, and she smiled at him like a goddess accepting a burnt offering – but a humble, maternal goddess, full of charity and grace if not of ardent love. And this was how she had spent the fiesta of St Blasius.

On that afternoon Mesía had recovered some of his hopes. His belief in the influence of his *physical attraction* had been restored, and he had decided to spend as much time as possible with Ana. He resorted to Don Víctor's blind friendship, even though this was an underhanded trick. In the Gentlemen's Club he would sit by his side, find the patience to watch him playing at dominoes or chess, and when the game came to an end take him by the arm and, since it was usually raining, promenade with him in the long room, the ballroom, dark, sad, and resounding with the steps of the five or six pairs of gentlemen who were pacing it from end to end, the fury of their heels registering a protest against the bad weather. There were some old members of the Gentlemen's Club who had walked far enough in the ballroom to have reached the moon. The two friends would promenade, and Mesía would probe deeper and deeper into the retired magistrate's soul, taking possession of its every corner.

Don Víctor began to believe that there were no longer any affairs in the whole world of any interest to Mesía but his own, and with no fears of boring his friend he kept him bound to his arm for entire afternoons, walking around the ballroom over its unsteady floorboards, coming to a halt at each interesting passage in his narration and whenever he had to consult him about some uncertainty. As Don Alvaro suffered this torture he was thinking about his revenge. His sense of propriety, or whatever it was, had long prevented him from setting out on this perfidious underground way, but now it could not be helped. Besides, 'The devil! There were more underhand tricks than that in the history of his amorous adventures!'

Don Víctor would come to a halt, release his confidant's arm, raise his head to look him in the face, and say:

'Look here, now that we are in the secrecy of . . . Well, relying upon your discretion – Frillity has his defects, too. I love him better than a brother, oh yes, but he – he underrates me, you can take my word for that. No, do not deny it, it is of no avail, I know him better than you do. He underrates me, he considers himself to be far superior. I do not deny that he possesses certain advantages. He knows more about arboriculture, he is better acquainted with the hunting-grounds, he is more dogged at his work – but to say that he is a better shot! For the Lord's sake! And what about our respective mechanical talents? He is butter-fingered and slow-witted.' Don Víctor, coming to a halt again, and bringing his mouth as close as he could to Mesía's ear, would add: 'This is the word for him: a routinist!'

Quintanar was inexhaustible when he was detailing his complaints and petty envy of his intimate friend Frillity. He felt dominated by him, and in these confidences he vented his pent-up, cowardly exasperation, which was good-natured at root. Mesía was a kind of emerging rival to Frillity, and Don Víctor found a certain malicious satisfaction in this incipient infidelity.

Don Alvaro would keep quiet and listen. Only when Don Víctor was discussing his own excellent marksmanship would Don Alvaro feel a little worried. It seemed impossible that there could be so much to say about a man as insignificant as Don Tomás Crespo, whom he believed to have been born mad.

As darkness closed in, with rain still falling, the servants would light two or three gas-lamps in the ballroom, and Quintanar would realize that this signal, and his weariness, which was drawing copious perspiration from his body, meant that he had been talking for a long time. He would be struck by remorse and pity for Mesía, and by heartfelt gratitude for his silence and his attention, and often invite him home for a glass of German beer.

His expression was:

'Shall we adjourn to the Plaza Nueva?'

Mesía would follow Don Víctor in silence.

A remarkable intuition told the ex-magistrate that taking his friend home was handsome payment for his attention. Why should Don Alvaro be so happy to follow him? If Quintanar had been asked this question he would have been unable to reply. But something told him that it did make Don Alvaro happy. He had observed it, without taking any notice of his observation at the time: yes, Mesía did like to go into the house in the corner of the Plaza Nueva.

Quintanar would take him into his study, his museum as he called it, and explain the workings of those intricate springs and pieces of wood – and, convinced of his friend's ignorance, unscrupulously deceive him. Where Don Alvaro drew the line was at the examination of the collections of plants and insects. It made him dizzy to fix his attention on so many useless pieces of rubbish in rapid succession. The only creature there with any appeal for Don Alvaro was a peacock which Frillity and his friend had stuffed. He would stroke its breast while Quintanar discoursed.

'Well, then,' Don Víctor would say, 'since you disparage my collections let us proceed into my den. Anselmo, beer in the den.'

The den was another museum: the arms and the theatrical costumes were kept there. A complete antique panoply, two modern ones, gleaming and finely embroidered, and shot-guns, pistols and blunderbusses of every epoch and size festooned the walls and the corners of the room. In chests and wardrobes, with all the loving care of a collector, Don Víctor kept the costumes which he had sported as an amateur actor in better times. If he became enthusiastic as he spoke of his wilted laurels he would open the chests and open the wardrobes, and silk, braid, feathers, beads and ribbons would pour on to the floor in a confusion of gaudy colours; and he would soon be lost in this sea of memories. Packed in straw in a large tin box, he kept and cherished like a priceless jewel an object which at first sight looked to Mesía like a snake. Yes, it lay coiled up in there and it was coloured dark green. There was nothing to fear. Taming wild beasts was not one of Don Víctor's hobbies. It was the chain which he had dragged behind him when playing the part of Segismundo in *Life is a Dream*, in the first act.

'Look, my dear friend, you are someone to whom I can say this. It is not immodesty. I recognize – how could I fail to recognize? – the superiority of Perales in the theatre of the old school; his Segismundo is a revelation, I concede that, it reveals the philosophy of the play better than mine; but I never liked the way he dragged his chain. He was like a dog with a tin can tied to its tail. I used to handle my chain with much more verisimilitude and naturalness. Believe me, I used to drag my chain as if I had never dragged anything else in my life. So much so that one evening, in Calatayud, this great quantity of iron was thrown on to the stage, as a symbol of my skill. The boards almost gave way. I conserve this chain as the finest memory of my ephemeral artistic life.'

Mesía was expecting Ana to appear and this helped him to endure his friend's conversation, but it often happened that she did not come into her husband's den, and then the beau had to make do with a bock of beer and the theatre of Calderón and Lope de Vega.

But at least he was in the house. By degrees he made bold to go there at all times of the day and, eventually, without having noticed what had happened, Ana regarded him as a familiar object when she found him by her side. Mesía was starting to be to the house what Frillity was to the garden.

This base, skulking approach should have irritated Ana, but it did not. She had to confess that she neither despised nor hated Don Alvaro, even though his intentions were wretched, even though he wanted to take advantage of Don Víctor's trustfulness. 'But suppose he didn't want to do anything of the sort? Suppose he was content to be near her, see and speak to her often, be her friend? She would soon see. If he overstepped the mark she was certain that she would be able to resist him, and even be bold enough to throw his base behaviour, his crime, in his teeth, and turn him from the house.'

As the days went by, Ana felt more and more reassured. 'No, he wasn't going to overstep the mark – all he did was admire her, love her in silence. Not a single dangerous word or audacious action, no question of waiting for opportunities or trying to create scenes – absolute uprightness, love which respects honour, passion which feeds by contemplating and breathing the atmosphere surrounding the loved one. The pleasure she was experiencing – this, too, she had to confess to herself – was the most intense pleasure she had ever enjoyed. Which wasn't saying much, for she had known so little pleasure!' Sensing Don Alvaro near her, certain that she was not in any danger, she would breathe with deep delight and surrender her spirit to a moral somnolence which made her feel as if she had taken opium. She compared this situation to the bliss of drifting in a calm, languid, shaded stream on a hot afternoon; the stream is bound for the abyss, one's body is drifting along with it – but one knows that one will be able to swim out of the current when danger approaches. A small effort, a couple of strokes, and one is out of it, on the bank. In her heart of hearts Ana knew that her behaviour was wrong, for she could not be sure of Don Alvaro's prudence. 'But wasn't she sure of herself? Yes, well, in that case, why not let him come to the house, contemplate her, be as full of loving kindness as a mother, as faithful as a dog? Besides, her husband gave the orders, not she. Did she go out in search of Mesía? No. Did she tell Quintanar to bring him home? No. Well, that was sufficient. If she behaved in any other way she would alarm her husband unnecessarily, instil unfounded suspicions into him, perhaps rob him for ever of his peace of mind. It would be best to say nothing, stay alert, and enjoy the cool flame of oblique passion. Its warmth was slight, but it was the hottest fire to which she had ever snuggled up.

'And the canon theologian wouldn't be told about it. What would be the point? There wasn't any sin involved. The opportunity to sin was there, but she wasn't looking for it.' Besides, since she was defending her virtue, she believed that it would be prudent to conceal from her confessor everything to do with specific personalities. 'If the danger grew she would speak of it. Until it did she would say nothing.'

It was at about this time that in the cathedral belfry the vicar-general saw through his spyglass the preparations for a trip into the country on which the judge's wife was accompanied by Mesía, Frillity and Quintanar. Nor was this their only trip of this sort. For as soon as Don Víctor glimpsed a sunbeam he would often take it into his head to make the best of the fine weather and abandon himself in the eating-stalls along the Castile road, or at Vistalegre on the road up Mount Corfín, in the company of the Vetustans dearest to him, to wit: his darling wife, Frillity and Don Alvaro. Poor Ripamilán was invited, too, but he said that unless they took him in a carriage . . . 'The spirit was willing, but bones have no spirit.'

They would climb the road and eat whatever they were given – whatever the astonished stall-holders provided: grilled chilli-sausages running with blood, fried bread, fried eggs, whatever there was. The bread was stale – so much the better! The wine was bad, it had caught the flavour of the pitch lining the wineskins – so much the better! This was what Quintanar liked, and here his taste coincided with his wife's, for she too was fond of these adventurous afternoon meals. They had a pungency which stimulated her appetite and awoke a childish gaiety in her. At these high places they would breathe as if they had never breathed before, and warm themselves in the rays of the sun with voluptuous languor, as if the sun were less beneficent in Vetusta, down below them.

Ana found that when she was on the mountainside, in this half-pastoral half-picaresque setting, surrounded like Don Quixote by muleteers, serving wenches and lords of castles, an instinct for the plastic arts and a new visual awareness were awoken in her. She noticed the shapes of trees, hens, ducks and pigs, she observed lines which were crying out for a pencil, she perceived more nuances of colour than ever before and she discovered artistic groupings of skilful and harmonious composition. In short, nature revealed itself to her as a poet and a painter in everything she saw and heard; in the shrewd retort of a village girl or an uncouth farm-hand, in the episodes of the life of the farmyard, in the way clouds were disposed, in the melancholy of a weary dusty mule, in the shadow of a tree, in the reflections in a puddle and, above all, in the hidden rhythm of phenomena, infinitely divisible, succeeding and overlapping each other and forming the dramatic plot of time with a harmony which is beyond the scope of our perceptive faculties and which we do not so much observe as divine. This new sense, of which Ana was only aware on these trips to the eating-stalls at Vistalegre, flooded her passive brain with visions and plunged her into a peaceful inertia; so much so, that she had to make a great effort just to bring her imagination into play. Often, though, she would be stirred from her naturalistic ecstasies by Mesía performing some attentive act, or Quintanar coming out with some untimely piece of good humour. Don Víctor believed that in the country, particularly if one is eating in the country, one should always play the fool; and, of course, it was necessary for somebody to dress up or, at least, change hats. He would search for a villager wearing the traditional cap of the region, borrow it and present himself before his audience with the floppy piece of black corduroy on his head. The audience would laugh, to humour him. They usually ate in the open air, contemplating Vetusta, a grey-brown huddle of houses below them. From where they were sitting the cathedral looked tiny, as if sunk in a well, or like some plaything of elegant construction; behind it was the smoke of the factories in the working-class suburb, the Campo del Sol and, beyond that, fields of green maize, meadows, woods of chestnut and oak, dark green hills and, in the far distance, mist blending with mountain-peaks. The four friends philosophized as they ate (sometimes with their fingers) underdone sausages, hard cheese, ham omelettes, whatever was provided. They spoke in a slow, offhand manner, their thoughts more profound than their words, gazing into the distance at memories, at the unknown, at vague dreams. They talked about the nature of the world, the nature of society, the nature of time, and about death, the other life, heaven, God. They evoked their childhood, those distant days about which their reminiscences coincided, and sentimentalism, as if emanating from the mist rolling down Corfín, engulfed the bucolic picnickers and their postprandial philosophy.

The breeze began to blow – it had a certain bite and it presented risks, but it was a pleasant sensation on the skin; a star started to twinkle; and the crescent moon (which reminded Don Víctor of the gold paper-knife presented to him in Granada) took on colour or, rather, light. The conversation, growing sluggish, turned to astronomy and ended at the concept of infinity; they emerged from it with a vague desire to listen to music. And then Quintanar remembered that *The Lightning-Flash* or *The Magyars*[11] was being performed that evening, and they broke camp and strolled back to sleepy Vetusta, letting the road's gentle slope carry them down. Frillity would give his arm to the judge's wife, who always asked him to do so; and a resigned Mesía, resolute in his intention to be prudent as long as necessary, would join Don Víctor, who was, perhaps, venturing to sing, in his own way, 'Spirto gentil' or 'Casta diva',[12] although he preferred to recite poetry, never forgetting to declare with Góngora:

> 'The villein leads them towards his cabin:
> The sun is sinking out of sight.
> His cabin chimney, gently smoking,
> Guides them home in the gathering night.'[13]

Toads sang in the meadows, the wind whispered among the naked boughs which, pregnant with new leaves, leaned over and happily knocked against each other. Ana, tranquil as she rested on the strong arm of her best friend, smelt the ineffable signs of spring in the air and talked with him about them. Crespo, happy, calm and peaceful, spoke in hushed tones, as if he did not wish to disturb his idol, the country, while it went to sleep. His words dropped like dew into

Ana's soul, and she could understand the calm adoration, the poetic yet unromantic worship which he devoted to nature (without using such words to describe it, of course). He offered no grand syntheses, or dissolving views, or pantheistic philosophy;[14] but rather details, the life-histories of birds, of plants, of clouds, of stars – in short, his own experience of nature, rich in lessons derived from minute and comprehensive observation. Frillity loved nature more like a husband than a lover, and more still like a mother. As he returned to Vetusta with Ana on his arm he became eloquent, speaking freely and at length, although always with deliberation. He purred with love for the countryside as he described it, and gratitude trembled on his lips as he heard someone else speak words of affection and interest about trees, birds and flowers. At such moments Ana was filled with envy for Frillity's existence, like that of an intelligent tree, and she leaned on him and almost rested her whole weight on him as if he were indeed some venerable oak. And the other man was walking behind her, she could sense him. Sometimes Don Alvaro spoke to Ana and she replied in an affable voice, as if to repay him for his prudence, his patience and his martyrdom. 'Because, to be sure, putting up with Quintanar for such a long time was martyrdom.'

Don Alvaro's sufferings were making him sweat. Don Víctor was hanging on to his arm, raising his eyes to heaven and amusing himself by finding similarities between the great dark clouds of the night and the most commonplace shapes on earth.

'Look, look, that cumulus is just like Ripamilán; imagine him with his shovel hat in his hand.'

'That black cirrhus looks like the buns bullfighters wear.'

When they reached the corner of the Plaza Nueva and Don Alvaro let Don Víctor pass in front of him to open the door with the latchkey, he held his clenched fist over the head of his unbearable friend. He did not deliver the blow – no, but 'He would, one day!'

'Oh!' he thought, 'I'm within my rights now! An eye for an eye.'

Thus Ana lived, less bored now if not happy, without any great remorse, but dissatisfied with herself. She neither allowed Don Alvaro to approach her or entertain any hopes fostered by her, nor rejected him with the absolute disdain which virtue, real virtue demanded. This half-and-half morality seemed to be what was most suited to weak human nature. 'Why should I believe myself to be stronger than I really am?'

Ana started to frequent the Vegallanas' house again. She was well received there; the bank clerk's wife covered her with kisses, talked to her about fashion, sent patterns to her house, and reminded her of visits which she had to return and on which Visita would accompany her, because Don Víctor refused to waste time on such formalities.

'No, no,' he would cry, 'I am no good at that kind of thing. Do not oblige me to talk about the weather, and how slovenly housemaids are nowadays, and how expensive food has become. Ask me to do anything rather than make courtesy visits!'

'I am an artist, such trivialities are not for me,' he would say to himself.

Visitación tried to force the world, the flesh and the devil down Ana's throat, into her eyes and through all her senses by the handful. The good weather assisted her.

The judge's wife did not take to these amusements with any great enthusiasm, but she preferred them to the sterile solitude in which she searched for pious thoughts – and found only sadness, profound tedium and the rancorous spirit of protest of her downtrodden flesh, which howled whenever it could. 'It was better to live like everybody else, let herself go, occupy her spirit with entertainments which were trivial and insipid, but at least passed the time away.'

She was in this state of mind when the canon theologian told her in the confessional that she was going astray, that he had seen her toss the life of St Jane Frances on to a turf-seat in disdain. That afternoon De Pas was more eloquent than ever. Ana realized that she was being ungrateful, not only to God but also to His apostle, who was all fire, luminous reason, tongue of gold, liquid gold. The priest's voice vibrated, his breath burned, and Ana thought she could hear stifled sobs. 'He had to be either followed or abandoned. He was not some accommodating chaplain serving grandees as a spiritual lackey; he was the father of her soul – the father, since no heed was paid to him as a brother. He had to be followed or left.' And he spoke of his own feelings, his illusions about her. 'Yes, Ana' – he did call her by her Christian name, she was certain of it – 'I dreamed of what our very first interview appeared to herald – a companion spirit, of the opposite sex, so that our complementary faculties might be conjoined in a harmonious union. I dreamed that Vetusta was no longer a cold prison, or a breeding-ground of petty envies which turn into venomous snakes, but the home of a pure, noble, delicate spirit; a spirit which, by the very act of coming in search of me to help it along the way of salvation was also, although unawares, leading me along that same path. I hoped that you were what was promised by what you told me, weeping, about your life, and what afterwards you yourself promised me a hundred times. But no, you do not trust me, you do not think that I am worthy to be your spiritual director and, to satisfy the longing for ideal love which you feel, it may be that you are already searching in the world for someone who understands you and is fit to be your confidant.'

'No, no,' Ana sobbed; but he continued speaking of his indignation, in an even sadder voice, with more and more warmth in his words and in his breath. And in the end came the reconciliation, and promises of a new life, a real reform, an effective change of habits.

Elated, she said, 'Would you like me to go with you this very day to Doña Petronila's house?' 'Yes, yes, that will be best,' he replied. And they went there together, neither of them thinking what they were doing.

On that afternoon the life of practical devotion began for the judge's wife. But there was little lasting force in her impulse, for it did not spring from piety but from gratitude, from the desire to please the man who was working so hard to save her and who was so eloquent and so able. On occasions, unable to raise her attention to things invisible, to pious contemplation, Ana would try to prepare for her mystical journey by thinking about the canon theologian. 'Oh what a great man! And how well he penetrated one's spirit, and how well he spoke of what seemed to be ineffable, of the underground ways of intentions, of the nuances of sentiment! And how much she owed him! Why should he take such an interest in a sinning woman who did not deserve it?' Tears would well in Ana's eyes, and she would weep with gratitude and admiration. Unable now to meditate about holy, pious matters, she would throw her shawl around her shoulders and hurry to the Society of St Vincent de Paul, or to the Society of the Sacred Heart, or to the Mission for Catechesis, or to mass – wherever there was something happening at that moment. But her faith was lukewarm; this was not the path to take her where she wanted to go. Besides, she knew herself; she knew that if she did give herself up to God she would do so with all her heart, but that so long as her devotion continued to be ostentatious and half-hearted, she herself would disparage it – and any strong, evil passion would easily destroy it.

But determined to avoid extremes, to be the same as everybody else, she persisted in following in the footsteps of all the other religious fanatics and, although it gave her no pleasure to do so, she joined all the guilds, and became a daughter or a sister, whatever she was asked to become, in all the pious societies of which she was invited to be a member.

She divided her time between the world and the Church, as did Doña Petronila, Olvido Páez, Obdulia and, after her own fashion, the marchioness. She was seen in Vegallana's house and at the Society of St Vincent, at El Vivero and at the Mission for Catechesis, at the theatre and at sermons. There were opportunities nearly every day for Don Fermín and Don Alvaro, in their respective circles, to talk to her, and there were days when both of them talked to her in the world and both also did so in church. There were even places where Ana was not sure whether she was present in the character of a religious woman or of a woman of society.

Yet neither De Pas nor Mesía was satisfied. Both expected to win, but the hour of victory was not coming any nearer for either.

'This woman', Don Alvaro would say, 'is worse than Troy.'

'The remedy has proved to be worse than the disease,' Don Fermín would think.

In the life of a religious fanatic Ana found a thousand and one details which repelled her, but she preferred not to pay any attention to them. She did not allow her spirit of contradiction to search out the shortcomings, the vulgarities, the wretchedness in this noisy, exterior devotion. She did not want to criticize; she did not even want to see.

She compared herself to the corpse of the Cid, led forth to defeat the Moors:[15] it wasn't her, it was her body they were taking from church to church.

A profound, pent-up restlessness started to burrow into her soul again, and she came to expect another period of inner struggles, of aridity and rebellion.

One night, after hearing a soporific sermon, she walked into her boudoir feeling almost ashamed to have spent two hours in church like a stone – hearing, without either piety or indignation, without any pity even, miserable monotonous absurdities – watching ceremonies which had nothing to say to her soul.

'Oh, no, no,' she thought as she undressed, 'I can't carry on like this.'

And shaking her head and extending her arms towards the ceiling she added aloud, to lend more solemnity to her protest: 'Let me be either saved or lost, but not blotted out in this idiotic life! Anything rather than being like all those women!'

A few days later she fell sick.

As the memory of her apathy and of her cowardly and indolent transactions with the world passed through the mind of the weak, convalescing Ana in scenes which, thanks to the new blood flowing through her body, were alive and theatrical, she felt a remorse which she was pleased to believe to be intense and biting. 'Oh! what a difference between the moral torpor of a few weeks earlier and her conscience's power of penetration now, as she lay helpless, unable to lift the counterpane with her hand, yet with enough strength in her will to lift from herself the overwhelming, leaden weight of sin!'

'This really was a firm decision! She was going to be good, good, belong to God, to God alone; the canon theologian would soon see. He would be her living, flesh-and-blood teacher; and she would have one other: the holy doctor of the Church, the divine Teresa of Jesus, who was there, by her bed, full of love, waiting to give her the treasures of her spirit.'

During the early days of her second convalescence, Ana, flouting the doctor's orders, tried to read that beloved book, taking it up as a child takes up a sweetmeat.

But she could not read. The letters jumped, exploded, hid, turned over, changed colour, her head whirled. 'She would come back to it later.' She left the book on her bedside table, and with a delight in which there was a large measure of sensuality, she amused herself by imagining that the days were passing by and that she was recovering her physical energy; she saw herself in the garden, in the arbour, or in the thick of the spinney reading, feasting on her St Teresa. 'How many things St Teresa was going to tell her now which she had not been capable of understanding when her reading was inattentive, mechanical, joyless!'

Ana's impatience was a stronger incentive than the doctor's orders and before she left her bed, when she was a little stronger and allowed to sit up amid the cushions again, she made a fresh attempt at reading and found the letters to be firm, still, compact; the white paper was not a bottomless abyss now, but a smooth, consistent surface. She read; she read whenever she could. As soon as she was left alone – and she was left alone for long periods – her eyes were riveted on the mystical pages of the saint from Ávila, and nothing, except tears of tenderness, disturbed the communion of two souls across three centuries.

XX

Don Pompeyo Guimarán, the late president of the Free Fraternity and a native of Vetusta, was of Portuguese stock. Don Saturnino Bermúdez, the historian and ethnographer, who divided all his friends into Celts, Iberians and Celtiberians after merely observing their facial angles or, at most, feeling their skulls, affirmed that there was still much of the Lusitanian about Don Pompeyo – not exactly in his skull, however, but in his abdomen. Don Pompeyo would neither deny nor confirm it; the passing years and his sedentary life had left him with something of a corporation, to be sure, but not much; and he held himself bolt upright, because he believed that 'he who is upright in spirit – for want of a better word – should also be upright in body'. But as regards national and racial traits he declared himself to be neutral. Which was to say that he was indifferent to the question, since he considered a Portuguese to be as much a Spaniard as a man from Castile or Extremadura. So whenever Don Pompeyo was addressed on this matter he concluded with a warm defence of Iberian union, a union which should begin with art, industry and commerce, and later enter into politics. Besides, of what concern to Don Pompeyo were such accidents of birth? His intelligence travelled in loftier regions. In this world, however, he was principally an altruist – a strange word which, it must be confessed, he had not encountered until, after a philosophical disputation in which he was defeated, his offended self-esteem made him read the works of Comte.

There he found that all men are either egotists or altruists; being a good-natured person, he declared himself to be an altruist for life; and, indeed, he did spend his life meddling in other people's business.

He owned a little property, most of it bought from the state after the confiscations,[1] and on the income he lived with his wife and four daughters of marrying age. He had soup, chick-peas and meat[2] for luncheon every day, every five years he had a new frock-coat made, and every three he bought a top hat, lamenting the demands of fashion, because the discarded hat was still in good condition. This he called his *aurea mediocritas*. He could have worked in an office, but, 'What office? In this country there is never a government worthy of the name!' He accepted all the unpaid posts offered him, because he was always at the disposal of his fellow citizens, especially when it was a matter of allotting them their due portions of something. In spite of all Don Pompeyo's modesty and parsimony, malicious people attributed his extreme liberalism, his unbelief, and his scorn for religion and the clergy to the provenance of the land which he owned. 'Of course,' said devout ladies as they chatted in small groups at the Society of St Vincent de Paul, and ultramontanists in the editorial offices of *El Lábaro*, 'of course, since he owes everything he possesses to those ghastly liberals and their impious depredations! How can he fail to hate the clergy, if he's devouring Church property?' To this Don Pompeyo, were he not 'secure in the sanctuary of his conscience' and scornful of such gossip, would have replied that Don Leandro Lobezno – the frock-coated bishop, the Prester John of Vetusta, the seraphic president of Catholic Youth – was a millionaire thanks to the confiscated lands which one of his uncles had bought and he had inherited. But, no, Don Pompeyo did not reply. He abhorred fanaticism but he forgave fanatics.

'Was he not a philosopher? God knew, he was.' When he asserted that God knew, he was using a conventional expression, as he said, which escaped from his lips against his will. For, truth to tell, Don Pompeyo Guimarán did not believe in God. There is no need to conceal the fact. It was common knowledge. Don Pompeyo was the atheist of Vetusta. 'The only one!' he would proclaim on those rare occasions when he could open his heart to a friend. And although, as he said 'the only one!', he affected profound grief for the blindness in which, according to him, his fellow citizens were living, it was not difficult to observe that this phrase contained more pride and satisfaction than true sorrow at the lack of a propaganda. He gave an example of atheism on all sides, but nobody followed it.

This particular plant could not be acclimatized in Vetusta. He was the only specimen: sturdy, unyielding, to be sure, but the only one. Don Pompeyo felt full of remorse when he caught himself hoping that the rational, saving doctrine, as he called it, would never spread. Everybody called him the Atheist, but experience had convinced even the most pious Vetustans that he did not bite. 'He is the lion enamoured of a maiden,'[3] said Gloucester elegantly; 'a wild beast without teeth.' The most refractory devotees walked past the Atheist without uttering a single curse: he was like an old, blind, muzzled domesticated bear ambling through the streets for the amusement of children – there was a nasty smell about him, but that was all. Nevertheless, there had several times been plans to give him a real fright in order to force him either to be converted or to leave town. This was something which depended on the apostolic zeal of the bishops and there was even one (he later became a cardinal) who had serious thoughts of excommunicating Don Pompeyo.[4] When the Atheist received the news, in the Gentlemen's Club, which at that time he still frequented, an angelical smile spread over his face. Thus the Greek must have smiled as he said, 'Strike but hear.'[5] Don Pompeyo's mouth watered, the very thought of excommunication made his soul tingle. What greater ambition could he cherish? Without delay he considered how to assume a moral posture worthy of the circumstances. No histrionics, no protests. He was content to say, 'The bishop has no right to excommunicate a man who does not communicate, but I welcome the excommunication – indeed, I couldn't care less about it.'

His wife and four daughters had very different thoughts on the subject. It was in vain that he attempted to hide the fact that a thunderbolt was threatening to shatter their tranquil home. Don Pompeyo's house became a sea of tears. Women fainted, Doña Gertrudis took to her bed and the unhappy Guimarán felt terrible remorse. He also felt unexpected weakness in his legs and his spirit. 'No question of being converted! Never! But his dear Gertrudis, his dear girls!' The unfortunate man wept and, turning towards the bishop's palace, he shook his fists and shouted between sighs and sobs, 'Those sons of aberration and blindness have got me bound hand and foot! How wretched I am! But they are more deserving of pity, they who are blind to the midday light and the sun of Justice.' Not even at such bitter moments did he insult the bishop and the rest of the higher clergy. In the end he had to compromise and tolerate something the mere thought of which had infuriated him at first: his daughters *moving in the matter* and his friends bringing their connections into play to persuade the bishop to put his thunderbolt back into his pocket. This was achieved, not without some difficulty, but without Don Pompeyo having to recant. Guimarán's atheism was hushed up and he kept his own counsel. In time, however, he renewed his attack, tireless in his propagandism which, in his heart of hearts, he hoped would not bear fruit, so that he should not forfeit the pleasure of being the only specimen of that precious species. He waged his major battles in the Gentlemen's Club where he spent half the day (though he later left it, for powerful motives). But in the main, Vetustans were not very fond of theology, and did not like to talk, either ill or well, about *spiritual concerns*. Progessives were content to attack the clergy and tell scandalous jokes in which the principal roles were played by priests and their housekeepers. Certain extremely orthodox conservatives were also pleased to take part in these agreeable conversations. If they thought they had gone too far and feared that people might have doubts about their pure faith they would add, once the scandalous gossip was finished, 'Of course, these are the exceptions.' 'All rules have their exceptions,' Don Frutos the American would say. 'The exception proves the rule,' Ronzal the deputy would add. And someone would even state, 'One must distinguish between a religion and its ministers.' 'They are men, just like us.' The progressives would present objections, upholding the solidarity of the dogma and the priest, and then Don Pompeyo would have to take sides with the reactionaries, up to a certain point, and say, 'Let us not confuse one thing with another, gentlemen, the very roots are diseased. The clergy is neither good nor evil, it is as it has to be.' But on hearing this everybody would oppose him, some for defending the clergy and others for attacking the dogma. He was so right to say that he was utterly alone, that he was unique. From these arguments, which he sought and provoked every day, he affirmed that 'his spirit – for want of a better word – emerged full of bitterness' (which was untrue, as his guilty feelings made clear to him), full of bitterness because nobody ever thought in Vetusta, people merely vegetated. Plenty of intrigues, plenty of petty politicking, plenty of material interests (though not even these were properly understood) – but no philosophy, no elevation of the mind to ideal regions. There were one or two scholars, various canonists, a few jurists, but not a single thinker. There was not a thinker in town – apart from himself. 'But gentlemen,' he would cry after he had taken coffee, sitting near the ombre-room, 'if there is ever any talk here about the grave questions regarding the immortality of the soul, which naturally I deny, or regarding Providence, which I also deny, you either take it all as a joke – as a gag, to use your own word – or concern yourselves exclusively with the utilitarian, egotistic aspects of the matter: whether Ronzal will be immortal, whether Don Frutos prefers annihilation to a future life with no memory of the present. Of what consequence, gentlemen, is what Don Frutos wants or what Ronzal prefers? That is not the question. The question is', and he checked off the points on his fingers, 'whether God does or does not exist; whether, supposing that he does exist, he ever thinks about wretched humanity; whether . . .'

'Hush! Silence!' the cry would come from the ombre-room; and Don Pompeyo would lower his voice, and the whole group would creep away from the ombre-players, full of respect and obedience,

convinced that their game was much more serious than Don Pompeyo's theologizing – more practical, more reputable. 'Look here,'
whispered Ronzal, who had not yet become wise, 'I believe everything
the Church believes and confesses, but really all that stuff about
heaven being eternal contemplation of the Deity – what a bore that
would be, man!' 'So what?' objected the American, Don Frutos, in
hushed tones, fearful of another warning from the ombre-players. 'So
what? I'd be happy to spend eternity twiddling my thumbs. I've
worked enough in this world. It'd be much worse if it was what they
say that guy Alan Cardgame[6] says, or whatever the devil his name is!
Well – that . . .' Poor Don Frutos could not explain it. 'What it boiled
down to was that when we died we went off to another star, and from
there to another one, to have a hell of a time earning our living all
over again.' The prospect of going to Venus or Mars, and there
searching for Negroes in Africa[7] and buying and selling them behind
the back of the law, seemed preposterous to Redondo and reduced
him to distraction. 'I'd prefer annihilation, as the Atheist says!' he
concluded, wiping from his brow the copious perspiration provoked
by this intellectual effort, so foreign to his habits. It was with this
question of immortality that Don Pompeyo made breaches in the
citadel of the members' faith, but they always concluded by repairing
the breaches with the customary reservations. 'God is supreme, of
course. There are experts in the Church who know all the answers.'

At all events, they were growing tired of Don Pompeyo and his
theologizing. They left him alone. The ombre-players complained
about him to the committee. He would have to move to another table
and, indeed, another room if he wished to continue preaching
atheism.

'This is the state of free thought in Vetusta!' said Guimarán to
himself, with a mixture of sorrow and pride.

The occupants of the billiards room did not want to know about
rational theology, either. Don Pompeyo, a more and more solitary
and taciturn figure, would spend hours standing with his legs apart
before the small carambole table (as Jeremiah might have stood in a
square in Jerusalem),[8] contemplating those deluded fools who wasted
the precious hours of their fleeting existence watching three ivory
balls either hitting or failing to hit each other. Sometimes the butt of
a cue would collide with Don Pompeyo's abdomen.

'Forgive me, Señor Guimarán.'

'You are forgiven, young man,' the thinker would reply, scratching
his beard with profound, tragic irony, smiling, and shaking his head
to imply that the world had gone to the dogs.

Bored with such superficiality he would go up to the *chamber of
crime* to observe the followers of fortune. There he heard God being
mentioned continually – in terms, however, which he did not
consider to be at all philosophical.

'You're right, Don Pompeyo!' one of the profligates would cry as he lost his last peseta. 'You're right, there's no such thing as Providence!'

'Stop being silly, young man, and do not confuse one thing with another!'

And Don Pompeyo would leave the Gentlemen's Club in fury. 'It was a place to avoid.'

When the September Revolution broke out, Guimarán had hopes that free-thinking might blossom. But his hopes were dashed. All that happened was that people started speaking ill of the clergy! A Philosophical Society was founded – and it turned into a society of spiritualists. Its president was a student from Madrid who amused himself by driving a few cobblers and tailors crazy; in the end, the Church was the victor, because the unhappy artisans began to see visions and cried out for confession, repenting of their errors with all their souls. That was all, that was what the religious revolution had been reduced to in Vetusta – unless one counted the group of men who publicly ate meat every Good Friday.

Don Pompeyo did not believe in God, but he did believe in Justice. By being imagined with a capital J it took on a certain divine air for him and, although he did not realize it, he was an idolator of this abstract word. For the sake of Justice he would have submitted to being chopped up into small pieces.

'Justice obliged him to recognize that the present Bishop of Vetusta, Don Fortunato Camoirán, was a person to be respected, a virtuous, worthy man; mistaken, mistaken through and through, but worthy. He had an ideal, and so Don Pompeyo respected him.'

Don Pompeyo did not read; he meditated. After Comte's works (which he could not finish) he did not look at any more new books and, to tell the truth, did not possess any. But he meditated.

Sometimes he argued with Frillity, whom he did not like, but in whom he recognized *the makings of a free-thinker*, in spite of his lack of an education. 'The fellow is a pantheist!' Don Pompeyo would say with disdain. 'He worships nature, animals, and in particular trees. Besides, he is not a philosopher, for he is unwilling to think about matters of great import and only studies trifles. He is full of himself because after a hundred thousand ridiculous attempts he acclimatized a eucalyptus tree in Vetusta. So what? Which metaphysical problem is solved by *Eucalyptus globulus*? Apart from that, I recognize that he has integrity, and that he is knowledgeable – however much his famous Darwinism . . . and that crazy notion of grafting English cockerels . . .'

Guimarán was defeated by Frillity several times in their polemics. Frillity was a fervent apostle of evolution and thought it absurd, ridiculous even, to claim to be disgusted by the idea of animal ancestry. Although Don Pompeyo was attracted to this theory, with its powerful and delicious tang of heresy and atheism, he could not bring himself to decide that he was the descendant of a hundred and one orang-utangs. He would smile as if he were being tickled, but could not make up his mind either to agree or to disagree.

'My ultimate affirmation is my doubt. It is uphill work to accept all this.' But his atheism remained firm. In order to deny God with the constancy and energy with which Don Pompeyo denied Him it was not necessary to read much, or perform experiments, or become some chemical cook. 'My reason tells me that there is no God: there is only Justice!'

As Don Pompeyo made these affirmations Frillity would regard him with a benevolent smile; and with gentle mockery, in which there was a portion of charity, he would ask:

'But are you so certain, Señor Guimarán, that there is no God?'

'Yes, my dear sir! My principles are firm! Firm! Do you understand? And I do not need to pore over great tomes and rummage around in the guts of Christians and animals to arrive at my categorical conclusion. If this science of yours with all its retorts and protoplasm and other such trash leads only to doubt, you can keep the science from your books wherever you like, for I have no need of it!'

The honourable Guimarán turned on his heel and stalked away in fury, his soul full of rancour and passing envy; and Frillity continued to smile and to shake his head.

If he was asked what he thought of the Atheist, he said:

'Who, Don Pompeyo? He's a good man. He can't tell a hawk from a handsaw, but his heart's in the right place.'

Guimarán finally swore (this was bound to happen, sooner or later) never again to set foot in the Gentlemen's Club. 'What they have done to me there is something which nobody has the right to do to any of God's creatures.'

His style was sprinkled with the phrases and idioms of a Christian, but as soon as he uttered one he protested against 'these metaphors and solecisms of language'.

What they had done to him was to celebrate the twenty-fifth anniversary of the exaltation of Pius IX to the papacy[9] by hanging out the gala-day drapery and the gas-lamps with which the façade was illuminated on solemn occasions.

Don Pompeyo addressed himself to the committee on official notepaper, citing regulations which, in his opinion, 'prohibited such signs of jubilation on the part of a body which, by virtue of being a society for recreation, should not, nay could not, profess any specific positive religion'.

As the servants hung drapery over the ballroom balconies, Don Pompeyo stood there shouting, gesticulating his indignation and invoking religious tolerance, freedom of worship, and even the session in the tennis court.[10]

'But look here,' said Ronzal, longing to hit him, 'what does it matter to you if the Gentlemen's Club drapes its balconies and illuminates its façade? What has the Holiness of Pius IX ever done to you?'

'What has the Holiness . . .? I shall tell you what he's done, my good sir, I shall tell you. I may say I used to like Pius IX. I recognized in him a man of good faith. But infallibility has placed between us a wall of ice, a chasm which cannot be spanned. A man who is infallible! Do you understand that, Ronzal?'

'Yes, sir, perfectly. It's as clear as . . .'

'Explain it to me then.'

'Make no mistake, Señor Guimarán, if you want examinations, you'd better remember that I won't have anyone pulling my leg!'

'Neither your limbs nor anyone else's are under discussion here, but your ability to prove infalli . . .'

'Infalliblety?'

'Yes, sir. Infallibility. In - fal - li - bi - li . . .'

'You listen here, Señor Don Pompeyo, your grey hairs won't protect you from me! And if you're laughing at me, I shall make it a personal matter!'

'What do you mean, a personal matter? Are you infallible, too?'

'Señor Guimarán!'

'In short, my dear sir . . .'

'Yes, to reassume . . .'

'I hereby take my name off the books.'

'Well, I couldn't care less!'

Ronzal did not demonstrate the reasons for infallibility, but Don Pompeyo did take his name off the books.

And so he lost this refuge of his idle hours, which were many, and wandered like a lost soul from one café to another until, after some years, he came across Don Santos Barinaga in the Restaurant and Café de la Paz, where every night this implacable enemy of the canon theologian prepared to die a bad death by drinking a brandy which almost tasted as if it had been made from grapes.

They became friends – close friends after a while. Don Santos had always been a good Catholic and, moreover, he lived on the Church, for he sold articles of worship.

But ever since the monopoly, ill-disguised as competition, of La Cruz Roja had started to reduce him to ruin, the citadel of his faith had become more and more unsteady – and his legs unsteadier still. He began, as many others like him have begun, by denying priestly virtue. But (this is not known to have happened with other heresiarchs) his scorn for men in holy orders coincided with his excessive fondness for alcohol, in its various shapes and forms.

Guimarán did not find it difficult to make a proselyte of Don Santos. With each new day and each new drink, impiety made more progress in him, until he came to believe that Jesus Christ was merely a constellation. Don Pompeyo had gleaned this piece of nonsense from an old book which he had bought at the fair. Guimarán had the cold impiety of the philosopher; Barinaga the rancour of the sectarian, the wrath of the apostate.

Whenever the worthy shopkeeper thought that his denials were taking him too far, he would hide his fear by standing up, glass in hand, and proclaiming in solemn tones: 'At all events, if I am wrong, if I am blaspheming, the responsibility lies with that scoundrel – with that candle-filcher – with that accursed Don Fermín!'

The Café de la Paz was large and cold. The dim yellow gaslight seemed to fill the room with smoke, although what in fact made the atmosphere heavy was the smoke from cigars and cooking-stoves. When the two friends held their conversations they were the only customers; the waiters in their black jackets and white aprons snoozed in the corners. A grey-brown cat walked to and fro between the bar counter and Don Santos's table; it would stand looking at him but then, convinced that all he said was nonsense, would yawn and turn away again.

With great satisfaction Guimarán watched the progress of impiety in this passionate spirit. Don Santos had not achieved atheism, 'but this was a degree of philosophical perfection which was perhaps beyond the capabilities of a former vendor of chalices and patens'. Don Pompeyo was content to extirpate all the roots and shoots of positive religion. He did not like to see his friend becoming more and more absorbed in brandy and other spirits, but if Don Santos did not drink he was like a fish out of water and could not understand the first thing about theological principles. So he had to be allowed to drink.

At half past ten the two friends departed. Don Pompeyo gave Don Santos his arm and walked with him until they were some distance from the café, for otherwise he would go back there alone. At the corner of an alley-way they took their leave of each other with a long handshake and Guimarán, serene and satisfied, returned to his tranquil home where his loving wife and four adoring daughters awaited him.

Don Santos, his mind and his eyes befogged, was left alone to do battle with the hallucinations of alcohol. His step faltered and his sense of shame, deprived now of its only support, struggled, in vain, to enable him to achieve a decorous bearing and gait. A zigzag motion convulsed the sick man's body; every step was a triumph; his head wobbled upon his shoulders. And from his throat, like the cooing of a turtle-dove, came stifled cries of protest – a monotonous, inarticulate protest which bespoke an obsession or, rather, a hatred, which his mania had hammered into his brain. To all the stains on the walls and all the shadows cast by the lamp-posts he growled the history of his ruin, and there was not a stone along his path but knew the scandalous tale of the canon theologian's fortune.

Barinaga acquired his apostasy from Don Pompeyo, and Don Pompeyo contracted Barinaga's hatred for the canon theologian and Dōna Paula. 'Such unworthy trafficking was scandalous indeed!' The two old men became trumpets of the canon's dishonour. Don Santos often disturbed the peace at night. The intervention of the night-watch was ineffective and the drunkard would hammer on the door of La Cruz Roja with his fists, his stick and even his feet. The proprietor of the establishment complained to the authorities, the scandal grew, the canon's enemies fomented discord and the cry arose on all sides, 'What is the meaning of this? Are they going to have Don Santos arrested on top of ruining him? Would the authorities dare to perpetrate such victimization?'

In the chapter house, Gloucester spoke into canons' ears of collective discredit, of what the Church – and particularly the cathedral – was forfeiting as a result of all these tumultuations'. The beneficiary Don Custodio supported Señor Mourelo.

'And if only that were the worst of it!' Gloucester would add.

And the second volume of the gossiping would commence.

'What was even worse was that rightly or wrongly, but not without some justification, to judge from appearances, it was being said that the canon theologian wanted to seduce – and was already on the way to seducing – no less a personage than the judge's wife.'

'Come, come, that cannot be!' the vicar-choral cried. 'She has become a saint. Ever since her illness, ever since she was at death's door, her life has been exemplary. If she was a virtuous lady before, like many others, she is a perfect Christian now. She is a little thinner, a little paler, but most beautiful, most beautiful – I mean she is edifying, she is a saint – yes, indeed, a saint.'

'My dear sir, I want facts – the public does not trust saintliness, it trusts facts.'

And Gloucester cited a large number of facts: the frequency of Ana Ozores's confessions, the length of the vicar-general's visits to her house, her visits to Doña Petronila's house. . . .

'So what? What can those visits signify? Are you suggesting that Doña Petronila lends herself . . .?'

'My dear sir, I am not suggesting anything. I am citing facts and repeating what the public says. The scandal is growing.'

This was true, thanks to Gloucester himself, Don Custodio and other members of the chapter, certain of the employees in the diocesan curia and, among laymen, Foja and Don Alvaro (the latter working in secret, and restricting his gossip to the simony and despotism of which the canon was accused). In the Gentlemen's Club Don Santos was the sole subject of conversation. They all affirmed that they had seen him kicking the door of La Cruz Roja and screaming defiance at the canon. Factions grew up, some demanding the intervention of the authorities, others supporting Barinaga's right to kick.

The Pug scurried to and fro, spying on all sides, and visited the vicar-general's house two or three times every day to report on the gossip to his chief, Doña Paula, who paid him well.

Don Fermín's mother lived in constant anxiety, but she did not lose heart. 'He was determined to ruin himself; but she was there, ready to save him.' It was vital to make frequent calls on the bishop and ensure that the gossip or slander or whatever it was did not reach his ears. Doña Paula spent a great part of the day and night in the palace. Her lieutenant, Ursula – the bishop's housekeeper – had orders not to allow any suspicious person into her master's room; his familiars, men devoted to Doña Paula – men made by her – had received the same command. The canon, too, spied and kept watch. He disliked doing so, but his instincts of self-preservation made him a partner in his mother's schemes.

Doña Paula and Don Fermín seldom spoke to each other now, for their self-defence had become a matter of tacit consent and they employed the same system of resistance without entering into communication about it. She was annoyed. 'Her son was deceiving her, ruining her. As far as she was concerned Ana Ozores, the blessed judge's wife, was already Fermo's kept-miss. That was the weak spot where the rope was going to break; that was where the boat was leaking. If there was so much talk now about the abuses of the diocesan curia, and about La Cruz Roja and Don Santos, it was only because that other business, the most scandalous one, the skirts business, had brought all the rest back to light.' Thus thought Doña Paula. 'All the rest is old hat, nobody was paying any attention to that ancient worn-out gossip, but now with this new scandal, with the business of that cunning little two-faced trollop, it's being stirred up again, it's becoming important again, and all these little things mount up. If Fortunato finds anything out or believes any of it we're dished.' The proprietor of La Cruz Roja was now forbidden to hear the blows which the drunkard Don Santos delivered on the door every night and there were no more thoughts of requesting help from the authorities. Instead, the night-watch was bribed to prevent noise at all costs. But this new tactic, too, was ineffective, for many neighbours waited each night, full of malicious curiosity, for the time when the disturbance was due, and came out on to their balconies to watch the scene.

But Doña Paula also had to keep track of her son's movements.

The Pug had seen the judge's wife and the canon theologian entering Doña Petronila's house together at nightfall. And Doña Paula knew. But Don Custodio had also seen them and he had told Gloucester and the two of them had told all Vetusta.

There was now an audience in the Café de la Paz to hear Don

Pompeyo and Don Santos curse all positive religions and, in particular, the vicar-general of Vetusta, as Señor Guimarán always called De Pas. The story of the altar-slabs, Don Santos's ruin, and the canon theologian's millions of pesetas in the bank was circulating among the lower orders, and had even led some workers in the Old Factory to talk of hanging the clergy *en masse*. This they called 'making a clean sweep'. Carlist workers, among whom the canon had some allies, were in a quandary, for although they respected him as a priest they feared him as a wealthy man – and they had their suspicions. The masses were not gossiping about the *skirts business*, however. There had been talk during the Revolution about whether Don Fermín had his little adventures in the poor quarters, but none of the people living there remembered such tales now. The workers who had directed revolutionary propaganda in those days had died, or grown old, or gone away, or become disillusioned with *the cause*, and the new generation was anticlerical only in fits and starts, being fonder of the bar than of the political club. All the talk now was of social revolution; priests, it was said, were no better and no worse than the rest of the bourgeoisie. Fanaticism was bad, but *capital* was worse. In the poor suburbs, then, the propaganda against cassocks had ceased, and the canon theologian had come to be more scorned than hated there. But the scandal of Don Santos the crucifix-man (as they called him), two or three acts of despotism in the diocesan curia, the fortune which it cost to get married (as if it had not cost the same before), and the story of the shares in the bank rekindled old hatreds, and now there was talk of hanging the vicar-general and all the rest of the black-coats.

The person who derived most pleasure from this propaganda of infamy – apart from Gloucester, who believed it to be all his own work – was Don Alvaro Mesía. By now he hated the canon theologian with all his heart. 'He was the first man – and a man in skirts, too! – who had crossed his path, the first rival who had contended with him for a quarry – and it looked as if he would win!' 'Maybe he had won already. Maybe the subtle, corrosive operations in the confessional had proved more effective than his own prudent system, his months-long siege, from which, according to all the rules, must ensue the surrender of the strongest fortress. I've raised the siege, but how do I know that he hasn't mined his way in?' The great Vetustan dandy sweated with anguish as he remembered his sufferings at the hands of Don Víctor, who, in only a few months of close friendship had, he calculated, declaimed to him the entire theatre of Calderón, Lope de Vega, Tirso de Molina, Rojas, Moreto and Alarcón. And to what end? 'For the devil to make the woman fall ill, feel afraid of dying, and change from being amiable, impressionable and complaisant (which was the first step) to being shy, prudish and mystical – mystical with a vengeance. And who had made her go like that? The canon theologian – there could be no doubt about it. Just when he had been making ready for the scene of the declaration of love, which would have been followed without delay by the scene of the personal attack, just when approaching spring had been promising valuable help – the woman had gone and caught a fever.' 'Madam is not receiving any visitors,' and he could not see her for a fortnight. He was allowed into her boudoir to ask her how she was – but not into her bedroom. He called daily, but he might just as well not have gone, for he wasn't allowed to see her. And, how infuriating, the canon – he saw it with his own two eyes – sailed straight in and was left alone with her! 'It wasn't a fair fight.' During those few days when Ana was convalescing, before her relapse, he too was allowed into her bedroom two or three times, but he was never able to speak to her alone. What happened afterwards was the saddest part of it all – what happened when her second attack gradually gave way to health. Ana received him in her boudoir. What a reception! His first impression was that she was quite thin, and as white as a corpse. 'Very beautiful, certainly, very beautiful – but in the romantic style. He didn't fight with women whose flesh and whose blood were in that state. She had given herself to God. That was obvious enough! She hardly ate at all! She couldn't lift an arm without getting tired.' Don Alvaro calculated, furious with impatience, how long *that organism* would take to acquire the strength necessary for it once again to feel sensual impulses, which were his living faith and his hope. It would take a long, long time, and in the meanwhile there was nothing useful he could do. 'And the canon was doing as he liked with her – stuffing her enfeebled brain with celestial visions. Ana was a different woman. She never looked at him now, and the few words with which she replied to his affectionate, concerned inquiries were courteous and affable, but cold – as if they had been shaped to a pattern. Sometimes he wondered whether the canon had dictated them to her.'

One day Ana was eating her lunch in the presence of her husband, Don Alvaro and De Pas. Each mouthful brought tears to her eyes. The canon was of the opinion that she should not force herself to eat. With some warmth, Mesía took up the defence of compulsory feeding:

'On the contrary, I am of the opinion – by the canon's leave – that the most important consideration is that she should feel well again, and soon, to prevent anaemia from gaining control of her organism.'

'Oh, my friend,' replied the canon, with an amiable smile, 'anaemia, as you must know better than I, can occur in spite of food. Moreover, to feed is not necessarily to nourish.'

'Well – by the canon's leave – I would recommend raw meat, a great deal of meat prepared in the English manner.'

'He was in a hurry, he would have given blood from one of his arms to see it running through those veins which he imagined to be exhausted. Life, strength at any cost for that woman!' Don Alvaro even spoke one day about transfusions. 'Science had made much progress in this matter.'

Somoza agreed, nodding his head and saying:

'Much progress! Indeed! Oh, yes, science! Indeed! Transfusion! Of course!' He was a little afraid of Don Alvaro's medical knowledge. That man who went to Paris and came back with those white hats and quoted Claude Bernard and Pasteur must know more than he did about modern medicine – because he himself did not read books, he did not have the time.

But the judge's wife was recovering her health. Blood was returning to her body, even though only by slow degrees; her muscles were becoming stronger and her flesh was rounding out; but her coldness and reserve were not disappearing. Don Víctor's behaviour towards his dear Don Alvaro never changed, the confidences accompanied by beer continued; but Ana did not appear. If Don Alvaro made bold to ask about her, Don Víctor pretended not to hear, or changed the subject; but if Don Alvaro insisted, Don Víctor sighed, shrugged his shoulders, and said:

'Leave her be. She must be praying.'

'Praying! But so much prayer could kill her.'

'No – it . . . she is not praying. That is to say – mental prayer. I do not know. Whims of hers. One has to leave her be.'

And he sighed again. Yes, one had to leave her be. But when Don Alvaro was alone he would tear his elegant blond hair – who would have believed it! – call himself an animal, a brute, a dumb creature (as if they were not all one and the same thing) and say: 'I have behaved like some lovesick adolescent! Timidity has been my undoing. I should have made the personal attack that night I came across her in the dark – or that afternoon in the arbour.'

But he had not made his attack and now there was nothing to be done about it. One day when he held out his hand to Ana she went to the extreme of not shaking it – with the special quick dexterity of a woman she found an excuse and did not give him her hand. He was not to touch those soft fingers again. What was more, he hardly even saw her.

'Oh, that this should be happening to him – to Don Alvaro Mesía! The ridicule of it all! The things Visita must be saying, Obdulia must be saying, Ronzal must be saying, everybody must be saying!'

'They must be saying that he had been beaten by a priest. It demanded vengeance! Yes, but that was easier said than done.' When Don Alvaro pictured the canon theologian, dressed in a frock-coat, coming to a duel to which he had challenged him, he could not help but shudder. And he remembered the trial of muscular strength in which the canon had defeated him in front of Ana. The valour which he felt when confronted by a cassock, because of his assumption that priests were forced by their meekness not to return blows, disappeared when he thought of Don Fermín's fists. 'There was no way out of this mess. All he could do was help Foja, Gloucester and the other enemies of his ecclesiastical tyranny to destroy him.'

In the afternoon, as Don Alvaro promenaded in the Mall – where priests and magistrates were beginning to be left in peace and comfort once more, because the hubbub of the world was departing for the shade of the leafy trees in the Esplanade – he often passed the vicar-general, and they greeted each other with deep bows. But the layman felt humiliated, and a slight blush rose to his cheeks. He imagined that everybody in the Mall was looking at them and comparing them and finding the priest, the victor, to be stronger, abler, more elegant. Don Fermín was the same as ever: arrogant in his humility, which was more a form of courtesy than a Christian virtue. Smiling, well proportioned, harmonious in all his movements as he walked along with an emphatic, rhythmical swish of his voluminous cloak, he defied all the gossip with imperturbable composure. The three most strapping members of the cathedral chapter often met in the Mall: the vicar-choral, tall and corpulent; the minister's cousin, better proportioned, slimmer, but a tall man too; and Don Fermín, the most elegant of the three, and not much shorter than the vicar-choral. They wore many yards of gleaming, immaculate black cloth, like unshakeable pillars of the Church draped in mourning. And, in spite of the sadness of their dress and the solemnity of their bearing, Don Alvaro could divine in the group a certain powerful seductiveness. Those priests enjoyed the prestige of the Church, the prestige of their gracefulness, the prestige of their talent and the prestige of their health, their strength and their flesh, which had developed as much as it had liked. He pictured three beautiful, well-built nuns, talented and graceful besides, promenading in the Mall – and he was certain that all the men would ogle them. Well, it must be the same vice versa. Indeed, in the greetings which the ladies who were still in the Mall dedicated to the three strapping young men from the cathedral – to those three towers of David[11] – the president of the Gentlemen's Club thought he could see hidden desires, unconscious declarations of intense, unnatural lust.

Every day Don Alvaro's superstition about the confessional was greater, every day more powerful the influence which he believed the priest to exercise over the woman who confesses her sins to him. As he looked at the ladies coming and going, some elegant and wearing luxurious clothes, others in mourning or in humble habits, but all of them, in their different ways, determined to look attractive and doing all they could to succeed, he imagined secret, invisible threads from skirt to skirt, from cassock to dress, from priest to woman.

In short, Don Alvaro was jealous, envious, and furious. His secret materialism was more radical than ever. 'No, no – force and matter,[12] that's all there is,' he thought.

Were it not the case that progressive parties are never in power, or are in power only for brief periods, he would have declared himself to be a demagogue and an enemy of the religion of the state.

He went to the extreme of proposing at a committee-meeting in the Gentlemen's Club that, in future, holidays of a religious nature should not be celebrated by draping and illuminating the balconies. Ronzal opposed the motion, but Mesía imposed it and it was accepted. Don Pompeyo Guimarán had triumphed after all!

Don Alvaro wanted the Atheist to return to the Gentlemen's Club because the men who were determined to disgrace the canon theologian needed this reinforcement. Foja and Joaquinito Orgaz, the leaders of the band of gossipers, proposed to Don Alvaro that a subcommittee be sent to bring Don Pompeyo back to the Gentlemen's Club, 'which he never should have left'. Guimarán's restoration would be celebrated with a hearty supper. At first Paco, the Young Marquis, who believed that, as a good aristocrat, he ought to be religious in form, at least, opposed the plans of Foja and Orgaz. But whereas Mesía, his friend and idol, wanted the fellow back in the club to help him to discredit the vicar-general, and whereas the beano to be held that night was really going to be great fun, he sentenced himself to assist the vicar-general's enemies, and joined the subcommittee which went to fetch Don Pompeyo.

Its members were the ex-mayor Señor Foja, Paco Vegallana and Joaquín Orgaz.

Señor Guimarán received them in his study, full of newspapers and cheap plaster busts representing, with various degrees of success, Voltaire, Rousseau, Dante, Franklin and Torquato Tasso, who stood in that order upon the cornice of a bookcase crammed with old books.

When he was at home Don Pompeyo wore a blue-and-white dressing-gown, patterned like a draughts-board. He welcomed the members of the subcommittee with the amiability which distinguished him, but was unable to conceal his surprise.

'Why could these gentlemen have come? Did they want to play some prank on him? He did not think so.' At all events, seeing the son of the Marquis de Vegallana there flooded his soul with joy, even though he did not like to admit it.

When Foja told him the purpose of the visit, he had to stand up to conceal his emotion. He felt his waistcoat-buckle snapping open on his back.

'Gentlemen,' he at last managed to utter in a trembling voice, 'were it not for the fact that a solemn oath obliges me to remain in the ostracism which I voluntarily imposed on myself so many years ago (or, rather, which fanaticism and injustice imposed upon me), were this not the case I would be highly delighted to return to the bosom of the society of which I was the founder together with six or seven of my friends. And how could it be otherwise, gentlemen, for I spent the happiest days of my life there in conversations both profitable and enjoyable with the most cultured section of the population of this town? It was the seat of tolerance; and the persons – the personages – in whom the roots are most firmly planted of certain ideas which are, when all is said and done, venerable, because they are professed with sincerity, and are ancestral to a certain extent, necessitated by race – those very personages, amongst whom I count the father of this cultured young man, my good friend and schoolmate the Excelentísimo Marquis de Vegallana, respected my opinions, as I respected theirs. I shall never be able to express sufficient gratitude for your present action. But my principal objective has been attained: freedom of thought shines again in the Gentlemen's Club. My aspiration has been realized. And now, as for me, gentlemen, I have to declare that I cannot break a solemn vow, an oath, and I shall not accompany you, although I would very much like to do so.'

The subcommittee insisted, seeing in Don Pompeyo's face that they were going to have their way.

Foja presented a weighty argument.

'You say, Señor Don Pompeyo, that you would like to come with us, to be restored to the Gentlemen's Club.'

'With all my heart! That is the right word – restored.'

'That only your oath holds you back.'

'Correct, the solemn oath nevermore to set foot there.'

'Solemn oath my eye! Forgive me for expressing myself in this way. The man who swears an oath makes God his witness, but you do not believe in God – therefore you cannot swear oaths.'

'Exactly,' said Joaquinito Orgaz, 'that's all A1, and P and Q,' and he stood up to execute a Flamenco pirouette.

Joaquín believed that in the house of a professional atheist – in other words, a madman – manners were dispensable.

Don Pompeyo stood staring at Orgaz, astonished by his impudence, while he considered Foja's argument.

He could find no answer to it.

In the end he said:

'True, oaths – I cannot swear oaths. But metaphorically . . . Besides, I can give my word of honour.'

'But on that occasion, my dear friend, you did not give your word of honour. You *swore* never to set foot in the club again. All Vetusta remembers your words.'

Don Pompeyo's head swam when he heard that all Vetusta remembered his words.

But he continued to uphold his refusal, although with waning conviction.

Foja winked at the Young Marquis, who took up the attack. Guimarán could resist no longer, and surrendered.

Vegallana's son – the son of the most important aristocrat in town

– had come to beg him to return to the Gentlemen's Club! Oh, that was too much. No longer could he defend the fortress of his decision.

'After all,' said he, 'the mere fact that the legislation which I invoked has been re-established, makes it possible for my feet to tread those floors without tarnishing . . .'

'Of course you can tread 'em. That's settled then. Put your frock-coat on, dinner's waiting.'

'What dinner?'

'It has been agreed by the victorious party, by those who request your presence in the club, to hold a banquet in your honour, and a dozen friends are going to have dinner together.'

Don Pompeyo did not know whether he should accept. But they would not listen to his modest protestations and he hurried away in a flutter to don his frock-coat and his top hat. He was bedazzled. He felt as though he were bathing in rose-water.

The Young Marquis's presence was the main cause of Don Pompeyo's joy. 'The aristocracy was something, after all, something more than a mere word – it was a historical element, an element of positive grandeur. It was possible for there to be a nobility and there to be no God – who could doubt it?'

An hour later, in the dining-room in the Gentlemen's Club – a hall on the second floor, not far from the gambling-room – Don Pompeyo Guimarán took his seat at the head of the table, Don Alvaro Mesía sat opposite him and then, in delightful confusion, heedless of priorities, sat Paco Vegallana, the Orgazes, father and son, Foja, Don Frutos Redondo, who attended all dinners regardless of which religious or political party was holding them, Captain Bedoya, Colonel Fulgosio, who had once been exiled for his republicanism and was famous for his bad temper and his good swordsmanship, a certain Juanito Reseco, who wrote for the Madrid newspapers and from time to time returned to Vetusta, his home town, to put on airs, a banker, and various young habitués of Don Alvaro's box, nocturnal members of the club.

Don Pompeyo seldom ate in restaurants and, since his relationships with the great of the earth were not intimate, he rarely saw a well-laid table. And so the cheap provincial pomp of the club's dining-room seemed to him worthy of Belshazzar. The glossy damask table-cloth; the thick, heavy plates, matt white with gilt edges; the napkins, shaped like tents and thrust into large, stemmed glasses; the rows of wineglasses arranged in order of size; the porcelain shells displaying wet olives, bumptious gherkins, red peppers like scarlet tongues, and other hors-d'œuvres; the grave, aristocratic claret bottles, guarding their aromatic contents like a secret; the reflections of the light as it was splintered in the winebottles and in the empty glasses and on the shiny cutlery of alloyed silver; the centre-piece out of which grew a bouquet of artificial flowers, with a guard of honour consisting of two cylindrical vases, decorated with Chinese paintings, out of which grew crude imitations of unknown plants (they reminded Don Pompeyo of the blond, tow-like hair of a certain artiste in an equestrian circus); the cigar boxes, some of scented wood and others of brass; the cumbersome, ostentatious cruet-stands, laden with oil and vinegar and more spices than a boat from the east – every detail helped to dazzle the worthy atheist, who sat smiling and spellbound as he contemplated the bright, cheerful, fresh, lively, promising picture presented by the table, still orderly, correct, and intact.

The meal began quietly, everyone making an effort to tell jokes. Joaquinito poked fun at the service and talked about Fornos – and La Taurina and El Puerto,[13] where meals were served with all the Flamenco trimmings.

Everyone ate heartily, except Don Pompeyo, whose throat was tight with emotion. During the second course he began to be tormented by a worry. 'I am', he thought, 'inescapably committed to proposing a toast. I must improvise a speech.' And he did not enjoy another mouthful. All the talk around him was meaningless noise. He smiled right and left, he replied in monosyllables, but he was thinking about his toast. His ears turned into flaming coals and from time to time he was attacked by nausea and trembling of the legs – in short, he was having a bad time of it. He expected events to follow a certain course. Don Alvaro would speak first and sing the praises of the constancy with which he, Don Pompeyo, had upheld the holy idea of freedom of thought, and would then promise on behalf of the committee that the Gentlemen's Club would never espouse any religion, thus setting an example which the state ought to follow. Then Foja, the Young Marquis and others would speak, expressing the same ideas, and, finally, he, Guimarán, would have to rise to his feet, in order to recapitulate.

As he mechanically ate and drank he prepared his harangue, without ever advancing beyond the preamble, which should be original without affectation, and modest without false humility. 'These young men should have warned me yesterday – then I would have had time.'

When the champagne arrived the conversation took a turn which the Atheist had not anticipated and which could not lead it towards the serious considerations appropriate to this solemn occasion. The conversation turned to women. Almost all the diners said they wished they could go back to their years of sweet illusion, not because of the sweet illusion itself but because of the secret powers in which, according to them, it originated. They all, including the young men, declared that they had reached the sad age at which love exists only in the mind and is pure imagination. Only Paco, frank and noble, confessed that he felt better than ever, even though he had lived it up as much as anybody else.

One of the men who shared Don Alvaro's box in the theatre, a fifty-year-old Don Juan, Señor Palma, the banker, lamented the fact that youth is not eternal and, standing with his empty glass in his hand and his eyes full of tears, expounded his philosophical system, which was heart-rendingly pessimistic, according to Captain Bedoya. Señor Palma was interrupted several times, the conversation moved on to higher things, and Guimarán condescended to pay attention to it. They were talking about the other life, and about morality, which was relative, in the opinion of the majority.

Foja, his face pale and contorted, maintained in a trembling voice that there was no such thing as morality, of any sort whatever – and he, too, came to his feet. He said that man was a creature of habit and that every individual was concerned simply to look after number one.

'*Homo homini lupus*,'[14] Captain Bedoya pointed out.

Colonel Fulgosio directed a respectful look at him and approved his proposition without understanding it.

'The struggle for life,' said Joaquinito Orgaz, in real earnest.

'Everything is matter,' added Foja, who only expounded his philosophical opinions when he was drunk.

'Force and matter,' said Orgaz senior, who had heard his son say so.

'Matter and money,' corrected Juanito Reseco in a shrill, strident voice charged with an irony which Orgaz senior could not appreciate.

'That's right,' cried Palma, the orator, and he continued toasting all the excellences of nature which he missed in his miserable, incurably anaemic body.

The conversation turned back to love and women, and the confessions began, coinciding with the coffee and the liqueurs, the heart's cork-screw. The names and honour of many women were dragged over the cigar ash, the breadcrumbs, and the stains of sauce and wine. 'There was no need for them to keep anything back, they were alone there, they were all as one man.' Mesía said little, which was his custom in such situations. He was afraid of these expansive conversations in which one takes any Tom, Dick or Harry for a friend and gives away secrets which afterwards one wants, in vain, to take back. While the others related shabby, humdrum adventures, Mesía, with his attention fastened on his own thoughts, his elbow resting on the table and his chin resting on his hand, smoked a good cigar, kissing the tobacco with affection and voluptuous calmness. His eyes, alive and moist, gleaming with reflections of light and with the electric glow of wine, were fixed on the ceiling. The other figures around the table were vulgar ones. There was no dignity in their drunkenness, nor was there any elegance in their unrestrained postures. But Mesía was looking handsome. The shapeliness and harmony of his well built, graceful person were more evident than ever. The after-effects of gluttony had not tinged his fine face with coarse colours but had imbued it with a certain half-melancholic half-lascivious spirituality. Here was a man of vice, but he was a priest, not a victim: he was in control of his drunkenness, a civilized, gentlemanly, discreet drunkenness. Don Alvaro, sitting alone among those poor devils, daydreamed and was moved by his dreams. During these moments he believed himself to be truly in love, and both believed and felt himself to be an attractive man. Although he was a sensualist, the devil! he thought, sensuality has its romantic side too. A *clair de lune* is a *clair de lune* even if the moon is a lump of old iron, a shoe of one of the sun's horses.

And through his memory and his imagination passed remembrances of nights of love, some of them murky and far from poetic – but many, many nights of love. He felt the urge to speak, to recount his exploits. This was a new experience. He had never felt such an urge until the judge's wife had humiliated him with her resistance.

He intervened in the hubbub two or three times to pronounce his opinion, so rich in experience of matters of love. Everyone turned towards him and was silent. And he spoke – uncontrollably, to satisfy a secret need to rehabilitate himself by telling his tale. The master spoke. He removed his elbow from the table and placed his forearms there, his hands crossed and his cigar, its ash an inch long, gripped between his fingers. He put his head a little to one side with an air of Bacchic mysticism and, with his eyes raised to the light of the chandelier, he began his confession in a soft, cool, slow voice to which his friends listened amid the silence of a church. Those who were some distance away sat up to listen, leaning on the table or their neighbours' shoulders. In a wretched way the scene recalled Leonardo da Vinci's *Last Supper*.

The audience's profound attention and the interest revealed in looks and open mouths flattered and indeed seduced the Don Juan of Vetusta, and he spoke as he might have spoken upon the breast of a friend. Joaquín Orgaz and the Young Marquis listened to their master with all the absorption of devoted sectarians. This was the word of wisdom.

Some of the adventures were romantic, perilous, full of audacity and good fortune, but most of them were proof of the weakness of woman, of all women. Some showed how necessary it was to forget one's scruples. And many of them demonstrated the success of perseverance, cunning and sudden attacks.

From time to time the hush was interrupted by boisterous bursts of laughter – whenever a comic adventure amused the audience and aroused it from its unhealthy, corrosive stupor. Those tapeworms of the soul, envy and lust, snaked together amid the general admiration. Dry eyes gleamed.

The seducer's art was laid out upon the table-cloth, by now wrinkled and soiled. It was an appropriate amphitheatre for the corpse of carnal love.

Mesía revealed his inner being, not so much to gratify his audience as to listen to himself and persuade himself that he was still the man he used to be.

'The ways of love were nearly always full of trickery, and anybody who thought otherwise was a dreamer. Now and again a woman had thrown herself into his arms, maddened by pure love, but there were not many adventures of that sort. If women were not in heat from time to time, there would not be many victories; few women surrender out of pure love. The moment of opportunity is more important than the months of preparation. Indeed, the preparation should be directed towards the opportunity.'

The time came for Don Alvaro to tell how he had conquered the daughter of an honest master-gunsmith who watched over the honour of his home like an Argus. Angelina had a mother, a father, a grandmother, brothers and sisters. She was as innocent as the child unborn. Mesía began by seducing her family. His mode of entry into his victims' houses depended upon the life which was led in them. Here he played at hide-and-seek with the children and made paper birds for them, played at dominoes with their grandmother, acted as a winding-frame for their mother, listened with patience and feigned interest to their father's socialist and humanitarian lucubrations, and captivated them all. He became the indispensable guest, the shoulder to cry on, the counsellor, the finest ornament in the house. He filled the house with his handsome presence. He was gentle, affectionate and as indulgent as a doting father, looked after their domestic interests as if they were his own, and even made peace between master and servant. And so he edged his way into their hearts. His arousal of Angelina (or whoever it was, for he had enjoyed many such adventures) began furtively. Little by little, by the side of the round table with a large cloth over it and a brazier under it, or on the balcony as night fell – whenever and wherever he could – he came close to his victim, pressed his body against hers, filled her with desire for him, for his proud, manly, winning beauty. He spoke of love as if he were joking, in a tone of paternal protection which seemed like innocence itself. And one day, or one night, during a picnic in the country, or after Christmas dinner, while the rest of the family laughed together, carefree and happy, Angelina's passion came to boiling-point, the moment of opportunity arrived, and dishonour entered the house – and the intimate friend, everybody's favourite, left, never to return.

Listening to Don Alvaro, the men could imagine themselves present at those tender, tranquil scenes of close friendship, expansive and trustful. As the seducer recalled them, his face, gestures, smiles and voice reflected his gentle kindness, his good-natured, affectionate manner, his straightforward, familiar, noble frankness, his usefulness about the house – all the skills and qualities which gave him the victory in such contests.

'On other occasions, my friends, I had to resort to violence. To renounce a victory which can be achieved with one's fists, sweating like a pig, being scratched and kicked, is to be a platonist, it's something genteel people do. The real Don Juan of our own times, and perhaps of all times, achieves his victories however he can: he is a romantic, a gentleman, a man of honour if it suits him; but coarse, crude, shameless, violent if need be.'

Don Alvaro would never forget a combat which had lasted three nights, and from which the loser had emerged with more glory than the winner. The setting was a granary, a wooden construction supported on four stone columns, like those houses which stand on tree-trunks over water, and the huts of some primitive peoples. In the granary slept Ramona, a country lass, and by the side of her creaky wooden bed, painted red and blue, lay the maize harvest in a crumbly heap which reached the ceiling.

This was the scene of the battle. As if Don Alvaro were reliving it all, he described the darkness of the night, the difficulties of the climb, the barking of the dog and the squeaking of the window as, standing on the platform around the granary, he forced the bolt; then the moaning of the flimsy bed, the grumbling of the mattress stuffed with noisy maize leaves, and the silent, yet energetic and indeed brutal, protest of the girl, who defended herself with her fists, her feet, her teeth, arousing a savage, intense, invincible lust which he had never felt before.

'There were moments, gentlemen, when, like Caesar in Munda,[15] I fought for my life. Ramona was a dark-haired girl, her flesh – my prey – was firm and smooth, and those arms which I desired to feel wrapped around my body in passionate ecstasy showed me their might as they tortured my own arms, pinned down and helpless. My desire was made all the more powerful by an incentive which was more piquant than pepper: I knew that Ramona was enjoying the fight – enjoying it madly. For she was certain that I could not overcome her by force; in a way she was in love with the young gentleman, above all because of his audacity; and such scenes of silent gymnastic love were not new to her. Not a word did she speak as she wrestled with me, bit me with delight, bruised me with voluptuous barbarity, and derived savage pleasure from the martyrdom of my senses, which were in contact with their prey yet felt dominated by it. The bed gave way, we rolled over the floor and we came to the pile of maize. And then the moon shone. Its rays entered through the window, which I had left open, and I saw my robust country lass standing with one leg buried in the golden grains and her other knee riveted on my chest. She was threatening me with a dry measure, an enormous wooden box covered with sheets of iron, and gave me the choice between flight and death. I fled through the window and jumped as best I could from the platform into the alley-way, and, though all my strength had been drained, I had to engage in another struggle – with the dog.' A pause. 'But the following night I returned.' The dog barked less insistently. The window was not shut – the bolt was broken. Ramona was not asleep, but waiting for me. As soon as she was aware of my presence she gave me a tremendous punch on the face. That did not deter me. We started to struggle again and the same incidents ensued: we rolled over the floor, we were buried in maize and I swallowed a deal of grains. And I was not victorious that night, either. I left after we had made a truce, with the promise of a future victory for me. But on the third night I had to fight yet again. She had deceived me. The prize cost me a fresh battle, and I had to claim it in unspeakable discomfort, because of the crumbly, curious, tiresome, prying maize. Ramona, her resistance overcome at last, complained of it too. Forgetful of everything, we sank into the maize, and if it weren't for the rule that in good literature comedy must not end in tragedy, that restless mound would have been the burying-place of Alvaro and Ramona, suffocated by one of our humblest cereals.'

Applause and laughter drowned the narrator's voice. Don Alvaro, exhilarated, went on to dazzle his audience with the contrast of romantic adventures in which he played the role of a knight of the round table.

While all this was happening Don Pompeyo Guimarán forgot his preamble, fascinated in spite of himself by the erotic adventures of the frivolous president of the Gentlemen's Club. Paco Vegallana had made the Atheist take, unawares, more wine than that which is authorized by Justice. He was not drunk, but he did feel queasy, and in spite of himself he quite enjoyed listening to descriptions of scandalous scenes which on any other occasion would have filled him with indignation.

Tired and somewhat repentant of having spoken so freely, Mesía brought his confessions to an end and, turning to Don Pompeyo, invited him to address the gathering.

'Don Pompeyo,' he said, and he stood up, swaying, thus showing that if the wine had not intoxicated him, his recollections had. 'Don Pompeyo, since this is the time for great revelations, you must now reveal to us the deepest recesses of your soul.'

'The deepest recesses of my soul, gentlemen,' interrupted the Atheist, 'are here on the surface for all to see.'

'Bravo! Bravo!' cried the diners. Glasses were knocked over and broken.

'I propose', cried Juanito Reseco, standing on a chair, 'that, in view of that stroke of genius, all formalities between him and us be dropped henceforth.'

'Agreed! Hear, hear!'

'Well then,' continued Juanito. 'O thou, Pompeyo, pompous Pompeyo, I bring thee bad tidings. You think you're the only atheist in Vetusta.'

'Sir!'

'Well, I'm an atheist, too – *anch'io son pittore*.[16] But you're a progressive atheist, a fanatical atheist, an upside-down theologian. You spend your life looking at heaven – but with your head bent over, peering between your legs. And although there's an apparent contradiction between being upside down and having your feet on the ground, it can all be reconciled – or, as cheap philosophers say, the antinomy can be resolved – if we remember that it doesn't fall to everybody to be a biped.'

'Sir – I fail to understand this philosophical gibberish. Before you were born I had been an atheist for years, and if what you are proposing is to insult my grey hairs and my steadfastness . . .'

'I said, my dear Pompeyo, that you're an upside-down theologian, because, you know, in the civilized world nobody talks about God any more, either to defend or to attack him. The question whether God does or does not exist has not been resolved – it has been dissolved. You can't understand that, but just listen to what I'm going to say – it's important to you: you, the fanatic of denial, will die in the bosom of the church, which you should never have left. *Amen dico vobis*.'[17]

And Juanito fell under the table.

His speech had made everyone indignant except Mesía, who extended a hand towards him, exclaiming –

'Forgive him, for he has drunk much!'[18]

'This Juanito fellow', said the colonel to Don Frutos the American, 'seems to me to be a great pedant.'

'He's a hungry beggar who's prouder than a pig with two tails.'

The talk turned back to religion. Don Frutos expounded his beliefs with a word here and another there, making islands and continents of red wine upon the table-cloth and gazing at his companions with eyes which implored them to finish his sentences for him.

Don Frutos insisted he had a hunch that his soul was immortal, that there was another world – apart from America – another, better world where souls who hadn't committed highway robbery went. Besides, God was merciful – he pretended not to see. And, of course, Don Frutos wanted to go to that better world carrying with him the memory of the bad life spent in this one – it wouldn't be much fun otherwise!

'Why should Don Frutos want to remember what an ignoramus

he's been on the face of the earth?' whispered Foja into the ear of Orgaz senior.

'If, gentlemen,' cried Joaquín, 'there's no Flamenco in the great beyond, or if they adulterate it there, I renounce the other world!'

And he grasped a pillar and bounded on to the table, beginning a Flamenco dance, with classical perfection. The little doctor did not lack encouragement and hands clapped as he sang in the hoarse, melancholy voice of the streets of Madrid:

> 'Frascuelo in his
> Sto-o-o-ockings, mamma,
> A sight that's something
> Sho-o-o-ocking, mamma.'[19]

Don Pompeyo could feel himself shivering. Such degradation! As he meditated he saw two Orgaz juniors on the table.

'They have intoxicated me with their heresies – I mean with their blasphemies,' he said to the Young Marquis, who was silent, thinking that it was all very dull without women.

Joaquín cried:

'Here's one to the health of Don Pompeyo.'

And he began an impious, brutal ditty about a holy image.

'Halt there, sir!' exclaimed the indignant Guimarán when he heard the last line but one. 'My health has no need of such obscenities – and what you are doing with these indecorous blasphemies is to favour the cause of the clergy, and play into their hands. Let me tell you, you inexperienced, precocious youth, that there have been many positive religions in the history of the world, and one day people have believed one thing and the next day another, but something with which cultured peoples have never dispensed, either now or in antiquity, is good manners, the respect which we all owe each other.'

'Well said, well said!' exclaimed everybody, including Joaquín.

'And I am tired of being taken for an iconoclast. Yes, I am an iconoclast, but an iconoclast of vice, an apostle of virtue, and a heresiarch of the darkness which envelops the mind and the heart of humanity.'

'Bravo! Bravo!'

'And in case anybody thinks that I can fraternalize with scandal, ally myself with impudence, and participate in an orgy, I indignantly protest that I am here for a very different reason. I believe that the time has come for serious talk.'

'Exactly so,' Foja interrupted, 'Señor Guimarán has spoken like a book, though he never reads them – but that doesn't matter, he has spoken like the book of his conscience, as he puts it. We are come together here, gentlemen, to celebrate Señor Guimarán's return home, so to speak – his return to the Gentlemen's Club. But ah! my fellow deputies, why has Señor Guimarán returned to the Gentlemen's

Club? That is a question, in the words of Blunderbuss, whom I am sorry not to see among us.' (Applause and laughter.) 'Well, he has returned because we have emancipated ourselves from the repugnant governance of fanaticism; and he has returned in order to found a society whose inaugural session you are now holding, possibly without realizing it. This society which, needless to say, will not be called a temperance society, proposes to persecute pharisees, tear masks off hypocrites, and wrench from the social body of Vetusta the mystical leeches which are sucking its blood.' (Clamorous applause. But Paco does not applaud, and he thinks what he had been thinking before: that what is missing is girls.) 'Gentlemen – let us declare war on the clergy who are usurpers, invaders, inquisitors; war on that part of the clergy which trafficks with holy objects, which uses underground passages to slide its octopus-tentacles into the coffers of La Cruz Roja . . .'

'Now you've put your finger on it!'

'The clergy which condemns worthy tradesmen, which condemns fathers, to the consumption of hunger; the clergy which breaks up families and sinks the virgins of the Lord in filthy sewers, misnamed cells, and considers that it gives them to Jesus by giving them to death.' (Frantic applause.) 'Let us all swear to be trumpets of this scandal and to make it acquire such proportions and reach such ears that the ruin of our common enemy becomes a reality. Because nobody, gentlemen, respects as I do the parish clergy, the honourable, poor, humble clergy – but the higher clergy – death to it – and, above all, death to the vicar-general, the . . .'

'Death to him! Death to him!' replied a few of the men: Joaquín Orgaz, two or three other inebriated diners, and the colonel, who was not drunk but did want the vicar-general to die.

By the time they rose from table day was breaking. They had spoken a great deal more. The vicar-general's life history, in the version of the scandalous legend, had been related in its entirety. All of them, including even the most prudent, had agreed that it was vital to found, with all due solemnity, the society proposed by Foja. It had been resolved to meet for dinner once a month and make intensive propaganda against the canon theologian. As they left in groups they said to each other in hushed tones:

'This has all been cooked up by Mesía, Don Fermín is his rival and he wants to ruin him, destroy him.'

'But which one is going to get the cat to wet its feet?'

'What cat?'

'*Its* feet or *her* feet?'

'The canon theologian.'

'Alvaro.'

'Or both of them.'

'Or neither.'

'Well,' asserted Foja, 'it's not for me to crown the king . . .'

'I merely help my master,'[20] concluded the choir.

Mesía, Paco Vegallana and Joaquín Orgaz accompanied Don Pompeyo home. It was a mild, cheerful, blushing June morning. There was a foretaste of the rays of the sun in the bright colours of the clouds in the east. The men's footsteps echoed in the streets of La Encimada as if they were walking over a huge echoing coffin and although it was not cold they had all turned up their collars. Don Pompeyo was in a taciturn mood. He opened his door with his latchkey, entered in silence and a little later was in bed with his eyes shut so as not to see the accusing light as it filtered in through the cracks around the closed shutters. Going to bed by day was a revolution which upset Guimarán so much that he doubted whether the laws of the world were still the same. As he shut his eyes he felt that his normally motionless bed was also rebelling – rising and falling beneath him. Soon he thought he was at sea, shut up in his cabin, a victim of seasickness in the midst of a storm.

He rose at midday and refused to talk to his wife and daughters about the dinner, the blessed dinner. He promised himself never again to let such a thing happen; but a few hours later, in the Gentlemen's Club, where he was received with a show of affection and jubilation, he gave a solemn undertaking to relapse into his old ways – to attend the monthly beanos at which an account would be given of the work of the *innominate society* which he had founded *inter pocula*.[21]

The Pug – whose information came from a waiter in the club's dining-room – told Doña Paula what had been said during the inaugural dinner, and about the aspirations of the men who had attended it. When De Pas heard from his mother that there had been cries of 'Death to the Vicar-General!' he shrugged, stood up, and left the house.

'The boy's gone daft. I don't know what's wrong with him, he doesn't seem to be living in this world at all. Oh, the damned judge's wife! The little trollop has got him spellbound!'

The following month the second session of the Innominate Society was celebrated. Wine flowed, the usual people became tipsy, and an account was given of the propaganda work. Foja informed the meeting that he had come to a secret understanding with the archdeacon, Don Custodio, and others of the vicar-general's capitular enemies (Foja's words). Many new scandals had come to light and both ecclesiastical and secular elements, agreed on the necessity to free Vetusta from the common enemy, were plotting the ruin of this monster. They would soon be able to place in the bishop's hands the proof of the multifarious abuses of which Don Fermín De Pas was accused. The worst abuse of all, which would make the bishop explode, was his indecorous abuse of the confessional. Shocking allegations were being made. The event would tell.

Don Alvaro proposed that the monthly dinners should be suspended until the autumn and requested that the closest secrecy be maintained. Moreover, he regretted that he had to deprive himself of the pleasure of attending the meetings in future. He would remain there in spirit but, for powerful reasons which he begged the members to respect, he would refrain from attending their delightful banquets.

A fortnight later, one afternoon in the middle of July, the president of the Gentlemen's Club entered Ozores Mansion. He had come to say goodbye. Don Víctor received him in his study. The master of the house was in his shirt-sleeves, as he always was during the summer, even if he was not feeling warm. For him this season and this light dress were inseparable. When Quintanar saw Don Alvaro he sighed, put a black book down on the desk, extended both hands towards him, and exclaimed:

'Oh my dear, dear Mesía! You ingrate! How long it is since you last came.'

'I have come to say goodbye. I am going on a tour of the provinces, then to the spa at Sobrón, and by mid-August I shall be in Palomares, as usual.'

'So until September . . .'

'We shall not meet again until the end of September.'

Don Alvaro spoke in a loud voice, as if he wanted to be heard throughout the house.

Don Víctor regretted Don Alvaro's departure. He sighed. 'This was yet another set-back, yet another cause for sadness.'

Don Alvaro noticed that his friend was less talkative than usual, and that he was not gesticulating with his normal vigour.

'Have you been ill?'

'Pooh! Who! Me! Out of the question! What, do I not look well? Tell me frankly – do I not look well? Pale, perhaps? Pale?'

'No, no, nothing like that. But you seem to be less cheerful, somewhat worried – I don't quite know . . .'

Don Víctor sighed again. After a pause he asked, in a plaintive tone:

'Have you read this?'

'What is it?'

'Kempis, the *Imitation of Christ*.'[22]

'What? you! you too . . . ?'

'It is a book that puts one out of humour. It makes one think about such things – things that had never occurred to one before. It matters not. Life, at all events, is very sad. Look, everything is ephemeral. You are going away from us. The marquis and the marchioness are going. Visita is going. Ripamilán has already gone. Within a fortnight Vetusta will be left deserted; and in La Colonia not a single soul remains. All the best people in La Encimada are going. Only the poor remain – the day-labourers – and we. We are not going away this year. A whole summer in Vetusta, how sad! The grass in the Esplanade will look like an esparto-mat – not a soul to be seen there, nothing but dogs and policemen in the streets. I prefer the winter with all its storms and eternal rains. I do not know: the cold revitalizes me. In sum, happy you who are going away.'

Don Víctor sighed again.

'I shall call my wife. You would like to take your leave of her, would you not? Naturally.'

'Oh, no – if she is occupied, do not disturb her.'

'Of course I shall call her. Occupied – she is always occupied – and unoccupied . . . I simply do not know . . . Whims of hers.'

He left the room. Don Alvaro picked up the book. It was a new one, but the first hundred pages were well-worn and full of slips of paper. He had never read it. He looked at it as if it were a box of explosives and put it back on the desk, with some fear and taking certain precautions.

Ana came into the study, wearing Carmelite garb. She was still pale, but she had put on a little weight. Mesía's heart pounded and his throat tightened, much to his dismay.

This woman was arousing pent-up anger mixed with intense, painful desire. He gazed at her as an explorer gazes at an island or a continent from whose shore a storm has swept him, maybe for ever, before he has been able to set foot on it. 'How could he tell whether this woman would ever be his?' His pride did not renounce her. But other voices said, 'Renounce the judge's wife for good.' Events would tell. But it was painful to postpone, yet again – and God knew until when – all hopes, all plans of conquest.

He would have liked to observe some sign of emotion on Ana's face when he told her that he was going away and did not know when he would return. But she heard the news with an abstracted air, and not a muscle moved in her face.

'This summer', she said, 'we are staying in Vetusta. I cannot bathe and the doctor has told me that sea air might do me more harm than good at the moment.'

'Vetusta becomes very sad in the summer.'

'No – I do not think so.'

Don Víctor left them alone.

Audaciously, Don Alvaro fixed his eyes on Ana's face, and she raised her large, gentle, tranquil eyes and looked without any fear at the seducer, at the temptation of years and years. He realized that he was losing his aplomb and feared that he was about to say or do something outrageous. Unable to help himself he stood up before her.

'Are you leaving already?'

'If I threw myself at her feet now, what would happen?' Don Alvaro asked himself. Not knowing what he was doing, he held out his gloved hand and said, as he trembled there:

'Anita – if there is anything I can do for you in the provinces . . .'

'I hope you have a very enjoyable time, Alvaro,' she replied without a trace of irony. But he imagined that she was mocking his ridiculous clumsiness, his stupid fear – and he was assailed by a vehement desire to strangle her. The hand of the judge's wife was steady, cool, dry, as it touched Mesía's hand.

That fine figure of a man left the room, bumping first into the stuffed peacock and then into the door. In the passage he said goodbye to his friend Quintanar.

The judge's wife took a crucifix from her bosom and placed her lips upon its warm yellow ivory, while her eyes, brimming with tears, searched among the grey clouds for the blue sky.

XXI

Ana lay in her bed reading the forty chapters of the *Life of St Teresa Written by Herself*, taking care not to let her husband know what she was doing.

This was during her long convalescence, interrupted by numerous fainting fits, nervous crises and other emergencies. Don Víctor, whose remorse during his wife's relapse had made him promise that until she was safe and sound he would never leave her side, broke his promise as soon as he thought she was out of danger. One day he ventured to take a stroll to the Gentlemen's Club; then he went there to peruse the newspapers; next he went to play at chess, and 'everyone knows what a slow game that is'. In the end he stayed away from home all afternoon without offering any excuses. His house felt like a prison. 'The weather was becoming hot,' for the calendar was Don Víctor's canon where the temperature was concerned, 'and everyone knew that he could not work in his study once he began to be molested by perspiration. He needed the open air, walks in abundance, nature.'

The marchioness, Visitación, Obdulia, Doña Petronila and other lady-friends who had kept Ana company during the bad weather now visited her every two or three days, and their visits were brief ones. There was a beautiful sun, blue days, cloudless skies, and one had to make the most of the good weather. This was the time of year when Vetusta became a little more lively: the theatre, bustling promenades with bands playing, outsiders, an exhibition of minerals. Even Petra asked her mistress one afternoon for permission to go and see an arch which had been built of coal.

Ana spent hour after hour in the solitude of her vast old house. As she lay in bed she could hear distant noises coming from the streets, but they were so muffled that they seemed like creations of her own senses. Servanda was downstairs in the kitchen, and sometimes Petra was with her. Anselmo sat in the courtyard, whistling and stroking an angora cat, his only friend.

The judge's wife felt even lonelier in such company. Those indifferent, silent servants, respectful but unaffectionate, made her miss the presence of compassionate people. She disliked Petra – she feared her, not knowing why. To make herself a little calmer when she was assailed by nervous anguish she would ask her maid:

'Is Don Tomás in the garden?'

If he was, Ana knew that there was protection near at hand, and calmed down. Crespo came up once every afternoon. He seldom sat with her, however – he spent five minutes in the boudoir pacing between the balcony and the door, then took his leave with an affectionate grunt.

It was vexatious to be left alone during moments of weakness when her frenzied nerves tormented her with grief and despair. Yet when she was calm, particularly after sleeping for a few hours or enjoying a meal, she found a subtle, almost sensual pleasure in her solitude. Her boudoir balcony overlooked the garden and if she sat up in bed she could see, behind the window-panes, tree-tops glittering with their new leaves, smooth, fresh, rustling. The chirruping of birds and the rays of a bright, powerful, joyful sun spoke to her of the life outside, of nature being reborn, with hopes of health and happiness for everybody.

'She, too, was going to be reborn, brought back to life – but to such a different world! How unlike the old Ana she was going to be! She was preparing a life of sacrifice for herself, uninterrupted by wicked thoughts or rancorous, pent-up rebelliousness: a life of good works, of love for all creatures and, therefore, of love for her husband – love in God and for the sake of God.' But in the meantime, so long as she could not move from her prison of pain, her soul soared and followed from afar the ethereal yet simple spirit of the saint who loved Christ.

Ana was living on passion. She had her idol and was happy even in the midst of her nervous frights, the pangs in her sickly flesh, and all the wretchedness of the human clay of which she was unfortunate enough to be made. Reading made her dizzy sometimes, so that she could not see the letters and had to close her eyes, lean back upon the pillows and let herself faint away. But as soon as she regained consciousness she would, at the risk of another attack, continue reading, feasting on the pages through which on previous occasions her inattentive spirit, vainly considering itself to be religious, had wandered without seeing what was there, experiencing only tedium, thinking that the visions of a sixteenth-century mystic could not edify her apprehensive, delicate, sad soul.

Ana's weakness had sharpened and excited her faculties, so that with both her reason and her feeling she penetrated the most hidden recesses of the mystical soul which spoke on that rough paper, dirty white, with its blurred, dense print. She was astonished that the whole world was not converted, that all humanity did not ceaselessly sing the praises of the saint from Avila. 'Oh, the blessed, gentle, sad, tender Fray Luis de León[1] was right: as St Teresa wrote, her hand was guided by the Holy Spirit, and so she inflames the heart of anyone who savours her writings.'

'Yes, Ana's heart was truly on fire. There would be no more idols on earth. She was going to love God, love God through the saint – her adored heroine of so many exploits of the spirit, so many victories over the flesh.'

Thinking about St Teresa she sometimes felt an intense desire to have lived in her times; or otherwise, what heavenly delight if the saint were alive today! Ana would have searched her out in the most remote corner of the world, but first she would have written a letter of burning love and admiration. In obedience to the canon theologian's prudent advice, she was not in the habit of turning her flights of religious elation into mental prayer; for her disjointed, confused, pagan upbringing had given strange forms to her sincere piety, and still revealed itself, so many years later, in touches of fickleness and incoherence.

She sought for similarities, even though they might be remote ones, between St Teresa's life and her own, trying to apply to the circumstances in which she found herself the mystic's thoughts about the vicissitudes of existence.

The spirit of imitation was taking hold of Ana; she did not realize how presumptuous she was being.

The saint's piety had been strengthened by the *Third Abecedary* by Francisco de Osuna,[2] and Ana sent Petra to look for it in the bookshops. The *Third Abecedary* was nowhere to be found, nor did the canon theologian have a copy of it. But Ana enjoyed better fortune as to confessors. Teresa had spent twenty years searching for one suitable to her needs, and even then she did not find him. Ana remembered her beloved canon theologian, and wept tears of tenderness. 'What a great man he was, and how much she was in his debt! Who but he had sown that piety in her soul?'

As soon as she could leave her bed, one of her first concerns was to write him a letter about which she had often dreamed. It was a whim of her convalescence. She wrote it without Quintanar knowing, for he had forbidden her *to bother her head with any preoccupations whatsoever.*

De Pas made frequent calls, and was delighted with the progress which was being made in her by piety of the purest kind. But she wanted to write to him, for there were certain profound, intimate things which she did not dare say to him; besides, she *could* not say them; and, even if it had been possible, rhetoric – which she would have to use, because great thoughts call for great words – seemed mannered and false in conversation.

The letter, on three sheets of notepaper, was taken to the canon's house by Petra, and was received by a smiling Teresina, paler and thinner than she had been months previously, but happier. The canon theologian locked himself into his study to read it. When his mother called him to luncheon, he appeared with eyes shining and cheeks aflame. Doña Paula looked at Fermín and Teresina in turn and shrugged her shoulders when neither the maid, who was coming and going with plates and dishes, nor her son, who was staring absently at the table-cloth and mechanically nibbling at his food, could see her. Teresina belonged to the master now; she said nothing to her mistress about the letters which she handed him. Petra brought them, giving a special knock on the door; Teresa went downstairs to open it; they kissed each other silently on both cheeks like young ladies, whispered together, laughed noiselessly, and gave each other a few pinches. Petra, recognizing a certain superiority in her friend, flattered her and praised her black hair, her eyes – the eyes of a Lady of Dolours – her complexion, and her other enviable qualities. Teresina promised Petra future favours, and they took their leave of each other with further kisses.

'Who was it?' Doña Paula would ask.

It was always a beggar or some other poor person – the truth was never told. Yet Doña Paula did not doubt her housemaid's loyalty. One day, examining the contents of Teresina's trunk in her absence, she had found jewellery worth at least five hundred pesetas.[3] She had smiled, both pleased and envious. 'Yes, it must be worth five hundred pesetas. That was too much – it was scandalous. If it wasn't indecorous to do so – if it wasn't embarrassing – she'd demand to be allowed to pay people as they deserved, without any pointless extravagance. The discovery pleased her, for when all was said and done this was all her own work; but the five hundred pesetas pained her – they were hers, too.'

Early in the morning of the day after the canon received Ana's letter, he left home, walked to the Esplanade, and looked for a secluded corner in the surrounding gardens. With no witnesses other than birds crazy with joy and flowers performing their toilette and washing in dew, he reread those sheets of paper on which Ana had sent him her heart, dissolved in mystical rhetoric. He could already recite some paragraphs – the ones which he found the most interesting and gratifying – almost word for word. His heart was flooded with happiness and he felt as though he had been turned back into a little boy on that rosy morning at the end of May, cool and cloudy, before the sun had torn open the canvas, white with a pink tinge, which stretched into the distance eastward.

The canon stood up, peered over the box-hedge which encircled his hiding-place and, seeing that he was alone – alone for certain – he took it into his head to add his own voice to the idle yet harmonious chatter of the birds hopping from branch to branch above him, by reading, in tones even sweeter and more melodious than theirs, the words of spiritual beauty which the judge's wife had written.

'I possess the gift of tears[4] now,' the canon read, as if to inform the goldfinches, sparrows, robins and other inhabitants of the branches. 'Now I weep, my dear friend, for something other than my own afflictions; I weep with love, and my soul is full of the presence of the Lord, Whom you and the beloved saint have taught me to know. Have no fears that sloth will ever again keep me at home, forgetful of my salvation; I know now that lukewarmness is death, I have read what our beloved Mother and Teacher says about her own sins: "I was careless of venial sins, and this was my undoing." *I* was careless even of mortal sins and, although you warned me of the danger, I long remained blind. But God sent me my illness in time (it was in time, wasn't it, my dear brother?) and in the nightmares of my fever I saw Hell, and I saw it as our saint saw it – a hole of anguish, into which my body was squeezed, to suffer indescribable torment. And my flesh, creeping with horror, was caressed by the loathsome sores of phantoms – devils dressed in mockery as priests, with chasubles and copes. I have already spoken to you about all this. Yet my piety, which I believe to be true piety now, was not born solely of terror, but also of love for God, and of a vehement desire to follow my immortal model – at a distance of millions and millions of leagues, of course. And now that I am telling you everything, I would like you to know that my resolution to become a good woman is due in a very, very large part to my determination not to be unthankful. St Teresa waited unsuccessfully for many years to find someone who could guide her as she wished; but I, a weaker woman, was sooner succoured by God when He sent me the man whom I would like to call my father but who prefers me to call him my brother. Yes, my brother – my dearly beloved brother. It fills me with joy to address you thus – here, now, certain of secrecy, far from profane ears whose understanding of such an expression would be contaminated by their own despicable impurity. How fortunate, how very fortunate am I, who as soon as I decided to become a good woman found someone to help me! And how long I took to understand you! But my brother, my beloved elder brother forgives me, doesn't he? And if you need proof – if you want me to do penance – only say so, command me, and I shall obey, you will see. But it does not surprise me that for so long I should have desired what the saint says that she, too, desired: 'to reconcile a spiritual life with sensual pleasures, tastes and amusements'. That is all finished now. You will tell me where to go; I shall follow blindly. And I love the idea of that affectionate mutual trust about which you spoke the other day when I was recovering from a paroxysm; I want that to be as my brother described it. And here, too, we shall follow the example not only of the German or Swedish monk and nun[5] about whom you told me but also of Teresa of Jesus, who, as you know, with good words and even, I believe, happy jests – and with the purest intentions – succeeded in turning a friend, a priest, away from vice. I well remember what she says. The priest, her confessor, was very fond of her, but sacrilegious love was his undoing: a woman had bewitched him by trickery, hanging an idol from his neck; and the evil did not cease until the Saint was able, thanks to her confessor's fondness for her, to persuade him to give her the charm, the idol which was the pledge of his infamous love. As you know, she threw it into the river, and the priest stopped sinning and later died free of such a great evil. Friendships of this kind are a great help in life, which without them is a desert, and anyone who entertains suspicions about them is a blackguard who cannot comprehend them because he is incapable of a proper understanding of something which is so good and such a great help in the salvation of the weak. In our case, of course, it is not the confessor but the penitent who is weak. There are no charms hanging from your neck, nor are there any idols for us to throw into the river. I am the sinner here, although no man has done to me the evil which that woman did to the bewitched priest. I have loved only my husband, and you know how I love him, not with the passion which takes from God something which belongs to Him, but with the gentle affection and the tender care which are due to a husband. In this respect I have made much improvement, for Fray Luis de León has shown me in his *Perfect Wife*[6] that one's obligations vary according to one's state; my husband deserves more than I used to give him, but following the wise poet's and your own counsel I now take more care to cherish my Quintanar and to love him as you know I can. By the way, I am going to begin a project to convert him, by little and little, and make him read holy books instead of mendacious plays. I am bound to achieve something, for he is docile and you will help me. In this, too, I shall be imitating our Holy Doctor, who took great pains to make her good father even more pious than he was already.'

The canon theologian did not speak these last sentences aloud, for he had sat down again and was reading to himself. Although he was somewhat jealous of St Teresa, with whom he could see that his friend was in love, he was happy, and his joy shone in his eyes, his cheeks and his lips. 'This was living, all the rest was merely vegetating. Ana was everything of which he had dreamed, everything which that secret voice had told him she was when she first came to his confessional.' The canon was still keeping hidden from himself the fact that the ideal passion which brother and sister had declared to each other could well turn into sexual passion. He did not want to think about that, he did not want to be frightened by his conscience or worried by any kind of danger. He only wanted to relish the joy flowing into his soul.

When he read 'my beloved elder brother' his heart leaped high and he was seized by painful pleasure, by mortal delight[7] – the most powerful emotion he had ever experienced. Well then, this was enough, this was the fact, the reality, what need was there to give it a name? What mattered was the thing, not the name. Besides, regardless of how it all might end, he was convinced that what he now felt for Ana had nothing to do with the coarse satisfaction of certain appetites – appetites which were not tormenting him. As the canon pondered in this way he heard, on the other side of the bush against which he was leaning, a boy's voice reciting in the singsong manner learned at school: 'Veritas in re est res ipsa, veritas in intellectu . . .'[8] It was a seminarist in his first year of philosophical studies, revising the first lesson in his textbook, Balmes. The canon walked away unseen, thinking about the years when he, too, had learned that 'the truth in the thing is the thing itself'. The thing itself mattered very little to him now – as did the truth, and everything else – for he wanted only to sink his soul in this unnamed passion which made him forget the whole world, his own ambition, his mother's sordid trickery, of which he was the agent, the calumnies, his enemies' intrigues, his shameful memories – everything, everything except this bond between two souls, his friendship with Ana Ozores. For how many years had they been neighbours without knowing each other, without suspecting what destiny had in store for them! Yes, destiny, thought the canon, he did not want to say 'Providence'; no theology, no more of those headaches which had turned his adolescence and early manhood into a desert peopled only by ghosts, the fears of a madman, apocalyptic figures. He had had enough of all that, for ever. None of that, or of what had followed: the blindness of the senses, the brutishness of base passions, satisfied in secret – that was shameful, above all because of the secrecy, the hypocrisy, the shadows which had enveloped it. But now – without fear, without scruples, without mental torment – present joy! this joy which he was relishing on a May morning, with June not far off, happy to be alive, in love with the country and the birds, longing to drink dew, smell the garlands of roses in the branches of the trees, open their swelling buds and bite their stamens, tucked up tight in cradles of petals. The canon picked a rose-bud, with some fear that he might be seen. The cool touch of the dew covering this little egg gave him a childish pleasure; it smelt of youth and freshness, but this did not satisfy his desires, his longing to bite it and enjoy its taste and contemplate the mysteries of nature hidden under its layers of satin.

Lost among paths covered by trees, he walked downhill towards Vetusta humming a song and tossing the rose-bud again and again high into the air. Every now and then it left a petal floating there until, when only the wrinkled, unformed ones at its centre remained, he put it into his mouth and bit it with a strange appetite – with a refined sensuality of which he himself was unaware.

He arrived at the cathedral and walked into the choir. Turtle-dove was sweeping the floor. Don Fermín spoke to him with caresses in his voice. He had to make amends to him for so many things! All those capricious reprimands which he had made the dog-catcher suffer! Now he flattered him and praised his zeal and love for the cathedral. Turtle-dove, astonished and grateful, was all polite words and compliments. De Pas walked over to the lectern, turned the pages of the large books of prayer, and even sol-faed a little in a quiet voice, reading the square notes with sides a full centimetre long. All was well. The organs above him stretched forth their pipes in dazzling vertical and horizontal lines, like two suns, face to face. Golden angels played violins under the vault, to which the organs' plateresque reliefs climbed, and through the pointed windows and the rose windows behind the choir and high in the aisles light flowed into the cathedral, separating into tones of red, blue, green and yellow.

On one side St Christopher[9] smiled through a span-wide red mouth – divided in two by the shadow cast by a lead – at the Christ-child supporting a green globe on His yellow hand. In front of him the canon saw a crib, which was also criss-crossed by dark lines. Jesus, in His orange cradle of hay, smiled at the mule and the ox. Don Fermín looked at it all as if he were seeing it for the first time. It was agreeably cool in the cathedral, and the smell of damp mingling with the smell of wax seemed delicate, symbolic in some mysterious way, voluptuous even. On that morning his performance of his duties in the choir was exemplary, and he regretted that it was not his turn to be hebdomadary, so as to show his paces. Gloucester, seeing him so cheerful and talkative, amiable both to friends and to secret enemies, said to himself, 'He's shamming! Well this simonist isn't going to get the better of me at pretence!' And he was all amiability, courtesy and flattering jests. 'Two could play at that game.'

'Have you noticed', said Don Custodio as they walked out of the cathedral, 'how pleased the vicar-general looks today?'

Gloucester replied into the beneficiary's ear:

'There's not an ounce of shame left in him, he is snapping his fingers at the world.'

'Something extraordinary must have happened.'

'To which crime are you alluding?'

'Adultery.'

'Mmm – I believe that the time is not quite ripe. None the less, it cannot be for any lack of trying – which makes it the same crime.'[10]

It displeased Gloucester to think of the canon theologian as the conqueror of the judge's wife. A simple question of envy. But it suited his purposes to presume that De Pas was her conqueror, so as to have something new to add to the long list of sins attributed to the enemy.

At eleven o'clock Don Fermín remembered that there was a meeting of the Holy Mission for the Catechesis of Girls. He was the director of this pious educational establishment, which met in the crossing of the church of St Mary the White. He was in the right mood for the meeting. Full of joy, he entered that happy temple, with its flamboyant decorations in spongy white stone. In the middle of the church was a portable platform of pine planks. On one side of this platform were three rows of backless benches, and in front of them stood a table covered with old wax-stained damask, an elbow-chair upholstered in red corduroy at its head, and around it various stools whose seats were made of the same material. The elbow-chair was for the canon theologian, the stools were for the catechists and the benches were for the girls, aged between seven and fourteen, who were learning Christian doctrine and some liturgy, sacred history, and hymns.

When De Pas entered the church there was a murmuring on the benches, like a gust of wind blowing over tree-tops.

The well-loved leader took holy water, crossed himself, and climbed the steps to the platform, radiant with evangelical joy, caressing one hand with the other. Finding an eight-year-old girl on her feet as he passed along he took her into a gentle grip and, as he gazed at the vaulting and bit his lower lip, he pressed her blonde head to his body and squeezed a pink ear, careful not to hurt it.

'A little bird has told me that Doña Rufinita refuses to be a good girl, and causes disturbances in church, and upsets the choir when it is singing!'

General laughter. The girls laugh with all their hearts, and the church's white vaults, shining with the light which enters through broad, unstained windows, resound with the echoes of their joy.

Everything the canon says provokes laughter, it is all a joke. Both the children and the priests feel at home. Scattered about the church are a few devout women praying devout prayers; and nobody pays any attention to them. These noisy scenes are also witnessed by a few young beaux (chickens scarcely out of their shells), whose loves are sitting on the benches on the platform. The catechists, all young men, look askance at those adolescents who come to church with profane intentions.

The canon theologian does not sit in the chair at the head of the table. He prefers to stroll about the platform, swerving now this way, now that, bowing like a palm-tree in a breeze, and every so often approaching the joyful benches to give a cheek a gentle slap or to whisper a secret into the ear of a little angel in skirts, thus exciting all the girls' curiosity and giving rise to a joke with a moral or religious lesson. The catechists, too, happy, graceful and vivacious, come and go, rebuke their pupils with honeyed words and paternal smiles, wend their various ways among the benches and intermingle their voluminous black cloaks with short frocks of bright colours and snow-white stockings clinging to womanly legs not yet officially recognized as such by the use of long dresses. In the first row, never still for a moment on its hard planks, are girls between eight and ten years of age. Most of them are sexless – indeed, their faces and figures are almost mannish – but some of them have premature curves which they cannot conceal, being dressed as innocents, and which make them feel a vague, unconscious shame. Looking at these signs of budding womanhood, Don Fermín remembered the rose-bud which he had been chewing – of which a crinkled fragment could still be seen between his lips. On the next bench sat the girls of twelve and thirteen summers, proud of their appearance, full of themselves; and behind them the young misses approaching fifteen, some of them the cream of Vetustan beauty, nearly all of them initiated into the legendary mysteries of flirtation, many of them close to the natural transformation which evidences their sex, and two or three of them – small, pale, sturdy – women already, although still dressed as girls, with pensive eyes charged with disguised knowingness. The girls moved almost like ballet-dancers as they rose, formed groups on the platform, fell into circles as each lesson and hymn began and, after it, broke apart again. As the catechists, in the midst of all this fresh youth, directed the orderly whirls and swirls, they inhaled spiritual aromas of quintessential voluptuousness with a kind of moral shudder which brought fire to their cheeks and eyes and produced in their robust natures effects similar to those of kirsch or absinthe.

The canon was in his element among those roses which belonged to him and not, like those in the Esplanade, to the municipal corporation. He took delight in the perusal of those two or three pairs of knowing eyes and derived a more subtle pleasure from fondling the hair of younger angels. After the hymns came the time for speeches, in which the voices of some of the girls revealed better than their bodies the physiological mysteries which they were experiencing. A young woman of fifteen – fourteen officially – came forward and, standing by the table, recited with assurance a philippic, somewhat tempered by the euphemisms of Jesuitical rhetoric, against modern materialists, who denied the immortality of the soul. She was blonde, her skin was marble-white, her features were perfect with the exception of her upturned chin; she had the body of a woman, and her tight-fitting skirt marked the outline of powerful, solid thighs, strangely enticing with their harmonious curves. She had pale blue eyes, and there was a disagreeable, vibrant ring in her voice, of hieratic monotony – an expression of the almost unconscious fanaticism of a soul being groomed for the convent. The blonde beauty with the arms of a Greek statue did not have any clear understanding of what she was saying, but she sensed the general meaning of her harangue and gave it all the appropriate tones of intolerance and pride. Indeed, she herself was a statue of pride and intolerance: a most beautiful statue. The other girls, the catechists, and the few people scattered about the nave listened to her in astonishment, their thoughts devoted not to what she was saying but to the beauty of her body and the imposing tones of her metallic voice. What was speaking there was the blind obedience of woman: the symbol of sentimental fanaticism, the initiation of the eternal feminine into eternal idolatry. The canon theologian's face was serious again, his mouth was open, his pupils were as sharp as needles. He was devouring with his gaze that arrogant amazon of religion, who was skilfully being formed by nature outside, and by him inside, in her soul. Yes, this dazzling fanaticism was his own work, this blonde was the pearl in his museum of devotees – a pearl which was still in the workshop. When that grey dress (which did not cover her rather long yet shapely feet, and revealed a couple of inches of the legs of a handsome, mature woman) reached the ground, the marvel of his studio would be brought to light, the public would admire it; and the Church would keep it for itself.

Sacred history was the responsibility of a plump, dark-haired girl with delicate features and a sweet, timid, nervous expression. She pressed her bodice against the budding breasts behind it, as if they were something of which to be ashamed, thinking less about her speech than about the fact that the boys looking up at her could see her legs, for which her skirt provided inadequate covering in spite of all the efforts of her instinctive modesty. She could not finish the history of the Maccabees. She felt a lump in her throat, her ears buzzed, the right side of her head suddenly went cold and her skin turned white. She was ill with shame and had to leave the church. But the assurance of other precocious orators obliterated the memory of the unfortunate, embarrassing scene of the pusillanimous girl who had run away in tears. The canon, too, revived spirits with moral jokes and half-funny half-mystical fables. The girls split their sides, rocking to and fro on the benches; and both laymen and catechists could see flashes of white lightning which the girls, in their indiscretion, revealed beneath their skirts, many of them not thinking about what they were doing, others not thinking about anything else.

When Don Fermín left the church of St Mary the White his mouth was watering with sticky saliva. All those sensations, which had caught him by surprise, reminded him of years long past. He did not like this; it betrayed levity. 'Damned girls!' he thought. But at least what was happening proved that he was still young, and that he was not disguising necessity as virtue when he made himself the promise to be platonic, platonic for ever (or at least for an indefinite period) in his relationship with his faithful, beloved friend. As his thoughts turned back to the judge's wife, that vague, piquant longing which he had felt on leaving church became a powerful, well-defined desire to see her and thank her for her letter with the most effective eloquence of which he was capable.

He found sufficient strength to restrain his longing and delay his call until the afternoon. His mother spoke about the gossiping, as she always did, and he shrugged his shoulders. He heard Doña Paula's hard, dry voice predicting, in an attempt to frighten him, the cataclysm of his fortune and the ruination of his honour as if she were talking about the geological cataclysms of Noah's times. He regarded the vicar-general about whom the public complained as another man. 'Ambition, simony, pride, meanness, scandal! What had it all to do with him? Why were they persecuting that poor Don Fermín now that he was dead and buried? Don Fermín was a different man now, a man who scorned his neighbours and did not even take the trouble to hate them. He lived for his ennobling, redeeming passion. But if they insisted on harassing him they would make him lose his patience and then he'd really give them something to be scandalized about.' The canon theologian was delighted to find such a man inside himself, stronger than ever, ready for any contingency, and in love with life, which has these intense, overpowering emotions in store for its favourites. Reality was acquiring a new meaning for him – it was more real. He recalled the philosophers with their doubts and the theologians with their dreams, and was sorry for them. The former denying the existence of the world, the latter volatilizing it – no more than pitiable idlers, the lot of them. 'Philosophy was a way of yawning. Life was what he was experiencing – he who was, now, at the very heart of activity and of feeling. A woman whose soul and whose body were of dazzling beauty, who in an hour of confession had made him see new worlds, now called him her beloved elder brother, and gave herself to him, to be led along the paths and trails of passionate, poetic mysticism. It was fortunate that he could handle any situation. He would know how to be a mystic, to whatever extent was necessary, would know how to lose himself in the clouds, without forgetting this earth.' He remembered that, years earlier, he had thought of becoming a novelist, of writing a truly Christian *Sybil*[11] and a modern *Fabiola*,[12] but had renounced the idea, not because he had felt unequipped for the task but because he had found it hurtful to strain his imagination. 'Novels were better lived.'

Such were the canon's thoughts as he tapped his knife on a bread-crust while his mother recounted Gloucester's intrigues and the machinations of the conspirators in the Gentlemen's Club.

He escaped from home at the earliest opportunity, promising to go and sound the bishop. He bent his steps towards the Plaza Nueva.

The large old house in the murky corner seemed to be surrounded by an aureola.

Ana and Don Víctor received him in the dining-room. He was a close friend of the family now. During Ana's two illnesses he had rendered Don Víctor many small services and, although Don Víctor did not like him, he was grateful. But having always been on the Crown's side in its tussles with the Church he was already beginning to entertain suspicions about the influence of the priesthood in his own home. He suspected imperialism. 'The clergy was absorptive.' Above all, Don Fermín had been something of a Jesuit. 'A Jesuit! Casuistry! Paraguay![13] *Caveant consules!*'[14] Not only gratitude but courtesy – the supreme law – placed Don Víctor under the obligation to behave in the most gentlemanly manner towards the canon; yet at the same time he was somewhat cold. His coldness was such, however, that the canon did not notice it. He was aware that the master of the house was in his way, that was all.

Ana – affectionate and still languorous – had shaken her confessor's hand and he, not realizing what he was doing, had prolonged the contact as much as he could. Don Víctor left them at about six o'clock. He was expected in the civil governor's offices for a meeting of cattle-farmers. The meeting concerned a plan to acquire foreign bulls. But Don Víctor was principally concerned to have himself elected vice-vicepresident and to claim for Frillity the position of first secretary. 'Frillity had sworn to refuse the job, but that did not signify. At all events, to be elected was an honour for them, however much that barbarian Tomás might deny it.' Quintanar could rely upon the governor's support. He left.

The judge's wife smiled at Don Fermín and said:

'You must be thinking that I'm mad. Why write when we can talk every day? I couldn't help it. I'm so happy! And I owe so much of my happiness to you! I tried to restrain my impulse but I couldn't. Sometimes I rebuke myself when I think that I rob God of many of my thoughts so as to dedicate them to the man whom He chose to save me.'

The canon felt as if he were choking. Ana was speaking precisely as he had so often made her speak in the stories he told himself as he went to sleep.

He did not hesitate to describe everything he had felt and thought since he had read her letter. 'The world was an uninhabitable desert, without a friend like Ana. For souls in love with the Infinite, living the everyday life of Vetusta was like locking oneself up with a brazier in a tiny room. It was suicide by suffocation. But after opening that window which gave a view of heaven, there was nothing more to fear.'

The judge's wife talked about St Teresa with all the enthusiasm of an idolatress; and the canon approved her admiration, but with less warmth than when he spoke of themselves, of their friendship, and of the pure piety which he could now discern in her. Don Fermín was jealous of the saint from Ávila.

What was more, his friend seemed excessively inclined to indulge in mystical speculation. He feared that she might fall into an ecstasy, something which always brought nervous complications with it; and it was necessary to avoid being blamed for her falling ill again – a likely event if she continued along this perilous path. He recommended pious activities. 'In her present state and in the times in which she was living, pure contemplation had to give way in large part to good works. If she could not now bestir herself to rub shoulders with the world it was because she was, after all, still convalescing, but when her full vigour returned she would stop being frightened by the prospect of action, of coming and going – of devoting herself to the work of piety in which she had been invited to participate.'

From that day onwards the canon theologian exerted as much influence as he could upon that spirit, which he now dominated, in an attempt to tear it away from contemplation and attract it towards the active life. 'If she went soaring too high she would forget him – for he was a finite being, after all. St Teresa had said – and Ana never forgot it – that she had "a kind of light, a sense that everything which comes to an end is not worthy of much esteem", and since Don Fermín was going to come to an end he was horrified by the idea that this might make Ana think little of him.'

His fear would not have been an empty one had events continued in the same vein as during the first few months. In spite of Ana's great love for her confessor she forgot him, as she forgot all the things of this world, for many hours on end.

Locked into her bedchamber or her boudoir – which was now something of an oratory – without any need of external stimuli, lost in the solitude of her soul, kneeling or sitting on the tiger-skin at the foot of her bed, with her eyes almost always closed, she luxuriated in voluptuous contentment as she imagined the world drowning in divine essence, devastated by it. She saw God with such clarity that on occasions she felt a vehement desire to stand up, run to her balcony and preach to the world and reveal the truth which was so palpable to her. At such moments it was hard to recognize the reality of her fellow creatures. 'How small they were! How frail! How much of them was mere appearance! The only part of them worth anything did not belong to them at all – it belonged to God, it was a loan. Happiness! Pain! Mere words; how could one appraise them or even distinguish them, when they lasted such a short time – no time at all?' Ana recalled the life of certain tiny flies which were born each morning on river-banks, took off and flew over the water, and died as they flew, to be eaten by fish which could depend upon this food every day. Life was like that for all creatures – a sunbeam through which one flits, to return to the shadows. These thoughts, which once used to torment her, now made her happy: for to live was to be without God, and to die was to be reborn in Him, renouncing oneself.

And then it was as if her very bowels were melting inside her. Something was crackling and sparkling in there – liquid fire, evaporating her – and soon all she could feel was a pure, vague idea, abhorring all resolution and rejoicing in its own simplicity. She prolonged these states as long as she could. She was horrified by movement, variety, life.

At such moments Don Víctor often poked his head, in its gold-tasselled smoking-cap, around the side-door, which he opened with great caution, noiselessly. Anita did not hear him. Somewhat alarmed, with the feelings which he imagined he would have on entering a room in which a corpse was laid out, he tiptoed away, full of superstitious respect. There were two things in life which terrified him: magnetism and ecstasy. No electricity or mysticism for him! One day he had slapped the face of a buffoon who, in the physics laboratory at the university, had seized him by the frock-coat and forced him into an electric current. Don Víctor had felt the shock, but, without delay, crack! he had cuffed the joker. He was also frightened by magnetism, in which he believed (although, according to him, this science was still in its infancy); and as for seeing the Divine Majesty, or even imagining Him, he thought that the emotion would be too much. 'I have no need of that to believe in Providence. A good thunderstorm is sufficient to make me recognize the existence of another world and a Supreme Judge. He who is not convinced by a lightning-flash is not convinced by anything.'

'But he had respected his wife's rapturous religiosity ever since he had observed that it was genuine.'

He would arrive home, give a gentle knock on the door, climb the stairs trying to stop his boots from squeaking, and ask Petra in a whisper and with a tone of sorrowful mystery in his voice:

'What of madam? Where is she?'

As if he were asking, how is the patient progressing? He behaved in this way all over the house, as if somebody were dying. For reasons unknown even to himself, Don Víctor regarded his wife's mysticism as some kind of acute headache. The most important consideration was that there should be no noise. If Anselmo's cat was mewing in the courtyard, Don Víctor would become furious and, contriving not to raise his voice, would cry in muffled, guttural tones:

'Hey! that cat! either keep it quiet or kill it!'

He would enter his study and resume work on his machines and his collections. Sometimes he had to use a hammer, a saw or a plane. How could he avoid making noise? The hammer, in particular, thundered throughout the house. Before using it Quintanar covered it with black flannel, as if it were a catafalque; and the muffled blows had a dull, mournful, fateful resonance, which filled him with melancholy. The canaries, goldfinches and starlings in his aviary also made too much noise, and were locked away to prevent their profane canticles from reaching Ana's boudoir-oratory.

Don Víctor became so accustomed to speaking in a low voice that even when he was strolling in the garden with Frillity each word he spoke was a faint, rustling whisper.

'Heavens, man, anyone would think you had a mute on,' Crespo would say, nettled.

Quintanar consulted him about Ana's state.

'What do you think about it?'

'Well, it's her own look-out. She must know what she's doing.'

'I believe, Tomás, speaking *inter nos*, that Anita will become a saint, unless God does something to prevent it. Sometimes she frightens me. If you could see her eyes when she is lost in thought! It would be an honour for the family – undoubtedly, but – it has its troublesome side. Above all, I am no good at this sort of thing. The supernatural makes me feel frightened. Do you think she is visited by apparitions?'

Frillity allowed himself the liberty of not replying to his friend's nonsense, as he deemed it.

He, too, thought about Anita. He often saw her from the garden – in her boudoir, sitting, kneeling, or standing with her face and hands pressed to her balcony window, looking up at the sky. She seldom noticed him. She always used to wave to him before, but not now. Ana's trouble was an illness, and a serious one, although he couldn't classify it. It was as if a tree began to produce flowers, and more and more flowers, using up all its sap in the process, and it became thinner and thinner, and ever more flowers appeared on it. Then its roots, its trunk, its boughs and branches all dried up, and the flowers became more and more beautiful and fell to the ground together with the dead wood, and on the ground, on the ground, unless there was a miracle, they withered, rotted, and turned into mud like everything else. Ana's illness was like that. As for contagion – that must have been the cause – he attributed it to the canon theologian. He remembered the purple glove. He had not thought about it for a long time but one day it had occurred to him to ask Ana whether ladies wore gloves of purple silk, and she had laughed. Therefore it was a canon's glove. Ripamilán seldom wore gloves. The only other likely canon was the canon theologian, for he was the only one clever enough to put all those ideas into Ana's head. The glove belonged to the canon theologian, without any doubt. And Petra had a finger in the pie, she was an accessory after the fact. What fact? That was the question. Ana couldn't be doing anything wrong. She was a virtuous woman. But virtue was relative, like everything else, and Anita was made of flesh and blood, after all. Frillity was not afraid of the present but of the future, of what might happen. He saw not a misdeed but a danger. He had heard some of the gossip circulating in Vetusta, even though nobody dared cast doubt upon the Quintanars' honour in his presence, for he was regarded as a brother to Don Víctor. 'At all events he would remain alert.' And he continued watching over Don Víctor's trees and over his honour, 'which was possibly in danger'.

Petra had no clearer picture of what was happening. Indeed, she was bewildered and considered her mistress's behaviour to be that of a lunatic. 'What was all that holiness in aid of? Who did she think she was kidding? Oh! if it weren't for her wanting to keep the canon theologian happy she wouldn't stay a moment longer in the service of that hypocrite who used her as a secret messenger and never gave her a tip or told her anything about what she was up to, or even gave her a friendly look unless you counted that idiotic holier-than-thou look that she took everyone in with.'

Petra often locked herself into her own room. Hanging on a nail at the head of her wooden bed she kept a travelling bag, old and dirty. In it, under lock and key, were her savings, certain articles of value which she had filched, and some compromising papers. From this bag she would often take the canon theologian's purple glove, of which she had not spoken to anybody. It was proof of something – she did not know what, but she sensed that somehow, sometime, that glove might be of great value to her.

'And what did the glove prove about her mistress and all her holiness? That she was a hypocrite. If it weren't for the canon theologian!'

The Vegallanas and their friends were astonished. The marquis believed in Ana's holiness. The marchioness, however, shrugged her shoulders; she feared for the girl's mind. Visitación was furious. 'All her plans dashed to the ground! Ana was holding out! The woman wasn't made of clay, after all, as she herself was!' Obdulia Fandiño did not envy the holiness of her friend, the judge's wife, but she did envy the stir she caused, all the talk about her throughout the town. She, the young widow, had never been such a sensation in even the most scandalous dress as Ana was with her religious habit and her cant. 'How backward, how terribly backward was that wretched hole!'

In the meantime, Ana was recovering her appetite, and health was flowing back into her. Her dreams were chaste, or at least she thought they were – they were free of any human burthen, as Ripamilán would say – but they were sweet, pleasurable dreams. As she lay half-asleep, in particular at day-break, she would feel palpitations deep inside her body, an agreeable tingling sensation; on other occasions it was as if a stream of milk and honey were flowing through her veins, and she imagined that her sense of taste – intense and exquisite – had moved to her breast, no, lower down, she didn't know where, not in her stomach, of course not, but not in her heart either, somewhere between the two. As she awoke each morning, she was smiling at the light. Her first thought, without fail, would be for the Lord. She would hear the cries of the birds in the garden and find mystical meaning in them, for her early-morning piety was of an optimistic nature. The world was good, God delighted in His work. The notion of the finite seemed more and more solid every day and it was less difficult to recognize its reality. Material phenomena possessed the ineffable poetry of a drawing again, their plastic qualities were a kind of demonstration of the well-being of matter, a proof of the solidity of the universe, and Ana felt at ease in the midst of life. She thought of the harmonies of the world and saw that everything was good, after its kind.[15] The idea of God, the profound, intense emotion produced by a manifest divine presence, did not lose any splendour or fade away, but she no longer saw God as sitting in sublime solitude but as reigning, full of love, over the chorus of planets, over His infinite creation. Ana sometimes forgot to read St Teresa at night. She was still in love with this sublime doctor of the Church, but the saint expressed certain opinions which Ana preferred to disregard, because they were in conflict with her own ideas; 'after all, three centuries hadn't passed by in vain'. She began to have a better understanding of what the canon meant when he spoke about pious activities.

'He's right,' she would say to herself, 'I can't spend all my life delighting selfishly in God like this. I need to work still harder at mental prayer and contemplation so as to see further into that region of light which only the soul can penetrate – but what about my brothers and sisters? Charity requires us to think about others. I can leave home now – I can leave home and live and sacrifice myself for my neighbour. I'm strong now, God has allowed it.'

While Ana was still weak the canon forbade her to kneel in bed to say her morning prayers. But as soon as she felt beneficent strength in her muscles – the body's self-esteem, as it were – she delighted to stretch her arms and legs, where pale roses were beginning to appear and life was beginning to pulse again. Ana would rouse herself and kneel – a white figure gently rocked by the mattress – and pray on the warm sheets, her rounded knees, with skin as smooth as satin, sunk into the welcoming softness. She would pray and, at times, in the enthusiasm of her religious fervour, would bring her face close to the crucifix leaning over the head of her bed and kiss its wounds as she wept a sea of tears. She thought of these sweet tears as the honey which flowed through her body, now streaming from her eyes in an inexhaustible torrent. When she was better, and stronger, she shunned the indolence of her bed, sprang from it to the floor and prayed on the tiger-skin. But she wanted something even harder and she pushed the skin aside and knelt on the moquette-carpet. It made her think of hair-shirts, and she desired to wear one, feeling fire in her flesh, which thirsted after this unknown pain; but the canon had forbidden all such delightful torment.

The first goal towards which Ana tried to direct her ardent charity was the conversion of her husband. St Teresa had worked for her own father's piety. He had been an excellent Christian, but she had wanted him to be more pious still. Ana decided to use all her zeal to win for God the soul of her own Don Víctor, 'who was her father, too, when all was said and done'.

Gentleness, sweetness, eloquence, caresses were the means – all perfectly licit ones – which she employed with masterly skill. It was some time before Quintanar realized that his Anita, his beloved Anita, was trying to convert him. At the beginning he only noticed that she was becoming more communicative and affectionate at all times, whereas previously this had only happened after nervous attacks and separations, and during her illnesses. 'She wanted to argue with him so as to pass the time away, did she? She was very welcome; he loved a good argument.' And he would uphold the thesis opposite to hers, so as to keep the discussion lively. But oh dear! she soon turned it all into a personal matter. Soon it was not a question of whether Christ had redeemed all the Humanities distributed over the planets at one fell swoop or by going from star to star to suffer death by crucifixion on each one of them; it was a question of whether Don Víctor only confessed once in a blue moon, and whether he often missed mass (which he did). 'Besides, the books with which he fed his spirit were vain ones: plays – futile, dangerous lies.'

'You have never read lives of saints, have you?'

'Yes, my child, oh yes – and mystery plays too.'

'I don't mean *that*. Look, Quintanar, I'm talking about the *Golden Legend*,[16] and the *Christian Year* by Croiset,[17] for example.'

'Do you know something, my child? I prefer books of meditation.'

'Well take Kempis, the *Imitation of Christ* – read and meditate.'

And she made him read it.

The combination of Kempis, Ana, the heat, which was beginning to annoy the worthy magistrate, and the ban on bathing put him out of humour. Before he went to sleep he read not Calderón but Job and that blessed Kempis. 'That devilish monk – or whatever he was – made the most extraordinary statements! Of course he was most certainly right, no doubt about that, for the world, seen in its true light, was indeed a dross-heap. He personally could not complain – there had been no terrible disappointments or great vexations in *his* life, apart from the very considerable vexation of not being an actor, but as a general thesis it was indeed true to say that the world had gone to the dogs. And besides, this business of growing old, which fell to his lot as it did to everybody else's, was a most serious inconvenience. He did not want to think about death, because it made him ill to do so, and God did not command us to fall sick. As for death – well, he had a kind of – vague, wild hope that he might not die. Medicine is making such progress! And besides, one can die without suffering great pain, however much Frillity might deny it.' But he did not want to think about death. Little by little, however, Kempis blackened Don Víctor's soul, and he came to scorn things for their ephemerality. One afternoon, in his park, he contemplated Frillity, who was squatting at his feet and planting bulbs, absorbed in the operation.

'A fine philosopher was Frillity!' Don Víctor regarded him from the heights of his borrowed pessimism, and both scorned and pitied him. 'Planting bulbs! Did St Alphonsus Liguori not prohibit the planting of trees in general and even the building of houses, which time destroyed and turned back into clay? Well then, why plant bulbs, when the world was a mere breath, nothing?

'Agreed, but this business of always being put out by everything was not very amusing. What was he going to do for an entire summer twiddling his thumbs without any baths or fun and games in the waters of Termasaltas?

'What a pretty kettle of fish it all was! And the worst part was still unresolved: the question whether he was going to be saved or not. This was a serious matter. He had a feeling that he was going to be saved, but the holy writers made it all look so difficult that he was beginning to be disturbed by certain doubts. What if he had not been sufficiently good throughout his life? One had to bear that in mind, but, O Lord! he did not want any headaches. When he had been arranging his retirement, justified by a fictional illness, he had found it very hard work putting his papers in order and asking people to speak a good word for him; and retirement was merely a temporal matter. So the salvation of the soul, eternal retirement so to speak, what a deal of effort, paperwork, and people to speak a good word for him *that* was going to require! He would have to place himself in his wife's hands, so that she could be of help in such an arduous business.'

The judge's wife soon realized that Don Víctor was placing himself in her care. Although she would have liked him to show purer piety, she had to be content with the attrition of which he gave manifest signs. And she did not scruple to make him a little more frightened than he already was by reminding him of the torments of hell, even though resorting to terror was repugnant to her. Quintanar maintained with great insistence that the fire in question was not material but symbolic.

'It is not of faith,' he would repeat, 'in my opinion, to believe that such fire is physical, material; it is a symbol, the symbol of remorse.'

It made him feel a little calmer to think that he was going to be roasted with symbols if the worst came to the worst and he did not achieve salvation, as he so earnestly desired.

The first time Ana made the effort to leave home, it was to take Don Víctor to church. They both went to confess with the canon theologian.

As Don Víctor took the communion he was tormented by the idea that he had not confessed a considerable peccadillo. He harboured doubts concerning papal infallibility.

Canon Döllinger[18] – of whom Don Víctor only knew that he existed and had been separated from the Church – captivated him with his tenacity, which reminded him of the tenacity of his homeland, Aragon, the noblest and stubbornest kingdom in the universe.

For the judge's wife the days slipped softly by.

The canon theologian, her master, and Don Víctor, her disciple, were her companions in a life which might have seemed dull and monotonous but was, beneath the surface, full of excitement. She still found ineffable delight in mental prayer. God was no less lovable as the Father of His creatures, as the Director of the great 'fabric of immense architecture',[19] than as a pure Idea to be contemplated. 'Besides,' thought Anita, 'to aspire so soon to a direct vision of the Deity would be a proud pretension, I still have many more steps to take, many mansions[20] to pass through. I shall arrive in due course, if the Lord so wishes. But now I must do as the canon says – now that strength is returning to my body, I must put it to good use in pious activity, the hygiene of the spirit, as he says. Idleness would turn me back to sin, as it did to St Teresa herself. If there was such grave danger in it for her, what must it contain for me!'

On the few occasions when Don Alvaro dared visit Ana she received him without any discomposure, calm in his presence and calm after he left. She tried to exclude him from her thoughts, for she knew that his memory was a wound in her spirit which would sting if it were touched. She found the courage to be cold to him, parry his attempts to increase his familiarity, refuse to shake his hand – anything, even watch him taking his leave. But when she saw him stumble away, knocking against the furniture, blind with love and grief in her opinion, infinite pity flooded her soul, and she shook with fear. A sigh heaved her bosom and weak flesh knocked against a dull yellow ivory crucifix, the gift of the canon theologian.

Ana kissed the image and turned her eyes back to heaven.

'O Jesus, Jesus: you can't have a rival. It would be infamous, disgusting.'

And she remembered Jesus's wrath when He appeared before St Teresa, who had forgotten Him.

'I would be deceiving both God and the canon theologian if I thought about that man for a single instant, even if only to pity him . . . Oh, what a hypocrite, what a wretched pharisee I would be if I did such a thing! How romantic – in the most ridiculous and repugnant way imaginable – I would be if after so much piety, which I believed to be profound, indeed to be my life's vocation, a forbidden passion were to come back and entwine itself around my heart, my flesh, or whatever . . .! No, No! Ridiculous, villainous, infamous, shameful and criminal! A thousand times no! I would rather die, die, Lord, than ever again fall prey to those thoughts which besmirch the soul, nailing its wings to the muddy ground.'

But when she awoke on the morning after Don Alvaro's departure she was thinking about him. 'He was no longer in Vetusta. So much the better. The terrible temptation was turning its back on her, fleeing in defeat. So much the better. It was a special favour granted her by God.'

That afternoon she went down into the garden at the time when Don Alvaro had said goodbye on the previous day.

'Twenty-four hours had passed by already.' On other occasions, days and days had elapsed without her seeing him, and the separation had seemed perfectly tolerable, even short. But these twenty-four hours were different – they had been counted in minutes – which is how hours are usually counted. 'Very well, the normal, regular thing – what must be, now and for ever – was precisely that: not seeing him. Twenty-four hours and then another twenty-four, and so on – throughout life.'

It was hot. Not even under the dense canopy of the horse-chestnuts, laden with broad leaves and white plumes, could Ana breathe a little cool air. Her thoughts tried to take off and soar to heaven, but the heat – thirty degrees, in Vetusta a great deal of heat – melted their wings and they fell back to the ground, which she imagined was burning.

And, to prevent Ana from taking it into her head to soar again all afternoon, into the garden came Visitación Olías de Cuervo, whom the summer suited down to the ground for it allowed her to sport calico dresses which were both fanciful and cheap. Visitación, happy and vaporous, burst in like a whirlwind; to see her coming made one want to shut one's eyes. A porter had tried to hug her in the street. The adventure, for all its absurdity, had rejuvenated her, bringing sparks to her small eyes, and 'there! now *she* felt like giving people hugs too'. She gave the judge's wife a hug, smothered her with kisses, and after telling her about the porter and his *comic sketch* suddenly cried:

'By the way, my dear, hasn't Víctor told you about Alvaro?'

Visita was holding Ana by the wrists; she wanted to feel her friend's pulse.

She riveted her tiny eyes on Ana's eyes and repeated:

'Don't you know about Alvaro?'

The pulse quickened – Visita felt it quickening with great satisfaction. 'Don't come to me with stories of saintliness,' she thought. '*Pulvy says*, as the proverb goes.'

'What about Alvaro? He's gone away? I know he has.'

'No, it's not that.'

'What? He *hasn't* gone away?'

Another quickening of the pulse, according to Visita.

'Yes, my dear – yes, he went all right, but just wait till I tell you *how* he went. You know he had that affair with the wife of that fellow who is or was a minister, I don't remember which one, well you know who I mean, that fellow who comes to the baths at Palomares.'

'Yes, yes, I know.'

'Well then, this morning, half Vetusta saw it, when Mesía was going to catch the train to Madrid, the mail-train, the up-train – are you with me? – he came across the minister's wife, who's very pretty by the way, in the middle of the platform. Just imagine! You see she was on the down-train to Palomares, where she's bought a kind of villa or something, I don't know what the devil it is exactly. Well then, just fancy, our Alvarito, instead of catching the up-train, the Madrid train, catches the down-train, gives his servant orders to collect the luggage and be quick about it, and gets into the reserved carriage the minister's wife's travelling in, a saloon car with a bed and all the rest of it. And her husband wasn't with her, of course, just her, two servants and the *enfants*, as Obdulia says. Just imagine! It just so happened that absolutely everybody was at the station this morning – and they were flabbergasted. It's going a bit far, even for Alvaro. But what of her? what do you think of her? Well, I'm coming to that, to these scandalous fine ladies from Madrid. And this one's renowned for her virtue, phew! I should say so, the most highly virtuous wife of the Minister of Grace and Refinement. O Lord, what the devil do they call that kind of minister?'[21]

Ana remembered very well what they called that 'kind of minister' but she would not say. She could tell that she was going pale, because of a death-like chill rising to her face; she turned away and, dissembling as much as she was able, leaned against a tree. She pretended to be amusing herself by tracing lines on the tree-trunk and, to change the subject, asked after one of Visita's children, who was ill.

But Visita was an old soldier, as she and the marchioness put it (or, to put it in another way, nobody pulled the wool over her eyes). She saw that Ana was upset and with great joy confirmed to herself the theory of *pulvy says* – that is to say, of universal ash.

'Ana's jealous, therefore she's in love. There's no smoke without fire.'

A short time later she said goodbye. She had told her piece of news, she knew what she wanted now and there was no time to be wasted. She had to go somewhere else to do another good deed of the same type. She went away like a stormy sea on the wane. The paths were left bare behind her, as if they had been swept. Her broom, of starched petticoats and sized calico, left a trail of wavy parallel lines on the sand.

Ana was afraid. The temptation, the old temptation of Don Alvaro, had seemed like something new; and she imagined for a moment that the ache which she had felt on hearing about the minister's wife was deeper in her body than her other woes. It was an ache which dazed her and cried out from inside her to be cured. For the first time since her illness she felt the old rebelliousness in her soul.

'Oh, no, she didn't want to start all over again. She belonged to Jesus, she had sworn it. But the enemy was strong – much stronger than she had thought. On other occasions she had defied the danger but now she quailed before it. Previously, the temptation had been made beautiful by the contrast, by the dramatic beauty of the struggle, by the pleasure of victory, but now it was just fearsome. In the wake of temptation there was now not only unknown, forbidden pleasure, with its own special seductive charm for the imagination; there was punishment too – the wrath of God, hell. Everything had changed. Her new religious vocation, her serious pact with Jesus, provided a more powerful constraint than those all too tenuous bonds of former days, the outcome of a feeling of obligation vaguely acknowledged by her conscience, without any thoughts for divine punishment. Previously she would not sin because of her self-respect, because of her gratitude – simply because she would not. But now sin was something more than repugnant adultery – it was mockery, blasphemy, jeering at Jesus – and it was hell. If she fell into the bonds of temptation, who would console her when remorse finally came? How could she call out to Jesus again? How think about Teresa, who had never fallen? No, she wouldn't call out to her, she preferred to die in despair, alone. But what after that? Hell, that tremendous truth, sublime in its boundless evil.'

'You'll win, my God, you'll win,' she exclaimed aloud, talking to the small pink clouds, a copy in the sky of the waves on a calm sea.

That night the judge's wife wept tears from the very depths of her being as she knelt upon the tiger-skin with her face buried in the bed, her arms outstretched above her head, her hands clasped together.

During the next few days the canon theologian noticed with great joy that Ana was turning her piety in the direction he wanted. 'Less contemplation, and more devotion, more pious works and more external worship, which keeps the imagination occupied.'

With an enthusiasm which eddied and swirled and attracted others,[22] Ana devoted herself to active piety, to charitable works, to teaching, to propaganda – to all the practices of the complicated, pettifogging devotion which was the predominant kind in Vetusta. All these excesses – as she had previously considered them to be –

she now found justifiable, in the way that lovers account for the nonsense they talk when they are alone together.

'Wasn't there in human love a ridiculous, infantile vocabulary, meaningless for outsiders? Yes, there was – she couldn't say so from her own experience, but she had read about it, and her heart confirmed what she had read. Well, then, love of God could also have childish, trivial aspects, which might seem absurd to cold, indifferent souls.' She could even understand why Doña Petronila, alias Constantine the Great, was so fond of using litaneutical superlatives.

The judge's wife ventured to talk to the canon in a familiar and tender tone, using words with a new, secret meaning and a style of what one might call pious humour. What was more, Ana took the liberty of concerning herself with her confessor's purely temporal interests. She would not allow him to do anything which might impair his health or expose him to the risk of catching so much as a common cold. 'It would be a fine thing for you to go and die now! All this, my dear sir, is simply selfishness on my part – there's no cause for either God or you to be grateful.'

These words and the accompanying smiles filled the canon with such ineffable bliss that he spent a week thinking about it. 'Yes, ineffable bliss. He could not understand it. He had never suspected that such joy was possible in this confounded world. At thirty-six years of age, when he thought that there was nothing more that anyone could teach him, a young, innocent, inexperienced lady had come to show him a new universe where a mere smile, a word which was like a poem set to music – the music of the way the word was spoken – was enough to put one among angels, rejoicing as if in Paradise, not wanting anything else, not thinking about anything else. Rejoicing, rejoicing, rejoicing!'

It never occurred to him to reflect on his situation. Was it sinful? Was this the kind of love which was forbidden to a priest? Neither for better nor for worse did Don Fermín remember these questions. It would have been the worse for the questions, had he remembered them.

'You never talk about yourself!' Ana said in reproachful tones one morning in August, in her garden, as she stroked his mouth and eyes with a large, powerfully perfumed blush-rose. They were alone. They had come to a tacit agreement that such demonstrations of friendship were perfectly innocent. They were two pure angels who had no bodies. Ana was so certain that the flesh did not play any part in their friendship that it was she who took each new liberty, each new step on the slippery ground of intimacy between man and woman.

The canon theologian, his face covered with the dew from the flower, and his heart even more refreshed, replied:

'Talk about myself? Why do that? My position in the Church militant means that half my life is in the hands of calumny, hatred and envy, for them to devour it and do with it as they please. I am persecuted, traps are set for me, there are even secret societies whose object is – as my enemies phrase it – to topple me from what they call power. It's all so wretched, Ana, and I despise it. I assure you that all my thoughts are for the other half of my life – the half which I bring with me here and which lives in the sweet peace of faith, and in the company of noble, saintly souls, such as that of a lady – whom you know well – and whose true worth you do not appreciate.'

The canon smiled like an angel as he savoured the perfume of the blush-rose, which he had gently taken from Ana's hands.

She became serious and demanded an explanation. 'He was persecuted, he was slandered, he had enemies – and he had said nothing about it to his friend. Now that was a fine way to carry on!' She had heard some gossip a long time before, but it had all been very vague. As far as she could tell, Don Fermín was accused of such crude vices, such wretched crimes, that the very coarseness of the calumny made it so implausible as to be almost inoffensive.

The judge's wife had scorned and even forgotten the rumours which had reached her ears from time to time. But since the canon himself was now complaining and hinting that the persecution was hurtful to him, she had to know more, try to console his harassed heart, find effective cures, succour the righteous man who was being persecuted – and who was not only a righteous man but her spiritual father, her elder brother, her soul brother, her beacon of mystical light, her guide on the path to heaven.

The canon considered that August morning to be one of the happiest mornings of his life. Ana made him talk and tell her everything. He spoke eloquently, using his lively, powerful and expert imagination to improvise one of the novels which he would have written if more serious occupations had not stolen his time away. They sat in the arbour. First Don Fermín said with a smile that now *he* wanted to confess himself to *her*. 'Did she believe that he was perfect? That there were no passions beneath the cassock? Oh yes! – unfortunately it was only too true that there were.' His confession was like the confessions of many authors who, instead of writing about their sins, seize the opportunity to paint themselves as heroes, putting the blame for their misfortunes on the world and retaining for themselves a few minor failings so as to have something to confess.

From the canon's confidences Ana concluded that he was, just as she had thought, a great man whose only sins had been a certain vague melancholy as a youth and a noble, elevated ambition as an adult. But that ambition had disappeared in the face of another grander, purer one: the ambition to save good souls – hers, for example. When Ana heard this she closed her eyes to hold back her tears, and swore in silence that she would devote herself to making this man happy – a man to whom she owed so much, who was showing himself to be such a great man, and who would rather live near her, so as to guide her along the path of virtue, than be a bishop, a cardinal, or even the Pope. 'And people slandered him! And he had enemies! And there had been a time when they had tried to ridicule him because she was still given over to the vanities of the world in spite of being his spiritual daughter! They would soon see, they would soon see!

'What could be finer than this ideal passion, this urge to do good works, this self-denial to which she proposed to devote herself so as to fight the temptation, more and more fearful, of the memory of Mesía – away in Palomares, in love with the minister's wife?'

De Pas did not know where it was all going to end.

Ana admired him, cared for him, he might almost say adored him – and as a result the danger was increasing daily. 'Although his passion had nothing to do with base lasciviousness – he was sure of that – and was not profane love, and indeed neither had a name nor needed one, nobody could tell where it might lead. He was certain that the slightest hint of the flesh, intrusive and fearsome, would anger and repel the judge's wife; and then he would lose the almost supernatural prestige which he enjoyed in her eyes. Besides, supposing that it did all end in a sacrilegious, adulterous affair – wretchedly sacrilegious in the light of its beginnings – that would be the end of its charm! He knew well enough how it would be. Brutish madness lasting for a few months; then an aftertaste of remorse mixed with self-abhorrence. He would consider himself despicable, base, intolerable, and, after that, there would be anger and pride, and vulgar ambition and hurricanes in the diocesan curia. No, no. His relationship with the judge's wife must be different. At any cost he must prevent it from degenerating into the mere satisfaction of carnal desire. And the judge's wife would change her tune if it did, claiming that she had been deceived. He was certain that she would.'

After a pause, the canon theologian thought:

'And if all else fails, time will tell.'

Don Víctor was becoming sadder every day. On one hand, the grief of his attrition, his fear of not being saved in spite of being so good – that is to say, of not having done anybody any harm – and on the other, the heat, the never-ending perspiration, the sleepless nights, the solitude of Vetusta, the brown grass in the Esplanade, the lack of entertainment. 'In addition to all that, the fact that nobody understood him. Frillity was a lump of stucco. Where spiritual affairs were concerned one knew that one could expect no help from him. He neither stifled in the summer nor became dispirited in the winter, he was a clod. Nor were Ana and the canon theologian discomforted in the slightest by the Vetustan summer, by that sadness in the streets and promenades!' Don Víctor went to the Gentlemen's Club, but there was hardly a soul to be seen. Just the occasional magistrate who had not gone on holiday, playing at billiards with one of the servants; Trifón Cármenes in the reading-room, perusing old copies of *L'Illustration*; and in the ombre-room not a single member. All that remained was dominoes, which he disliked because of the noise of the pieces and the necessity to be everlastingly performing calculations. His opponent at chess was away at the baths. 'Of course! *Everybody* was at the baths.' During previous summers spent at the seaside, Don Víctor had never bathed more than two or three times, but now he missed the coolness of the waves every day. In the Gentlemen's Club he read the newspapers from La Costa. Concerts by night in the open air, picnics in the country, regattas – they spoke of all these things. So many people! So much music! The theatre, the circus! Boats, great English steamships – and the sea, the immense sea. That was the way to enjoy oneself! Don Víctor sighed and returned home.

'Madam was not at home.'

But Kempis was. Lying open, on the bedside table. Unable to resist his impulse he took up the book, after removing his alpaca tailcoat; he took it and read. 'Back again to fear! Back to sadness, to spiritual lassitude. The world was indeed a place of wretchedness, as the book said – especially in the summer. Vetusta was a dying town. Even the green of the trees, a welcome sight in the spring after their nakedness throughout the winter, was tedious now. One almost wished for the leafless branch with its clearer outline.' The sadness and boredom might even make him go in seriously for painting.

Ana would return home, contented. 'So much the better – at least someone was having a good time. He was not an egotist.

'But what did his wife find so attractive about the solitude of Vetusta? Besides, was not Kempis lying there, for all to see, proving as clearly as two and two are four that in this world there is never any cause to be happy? True, his dear Anita was happy for higher reasons. He could not attain such a degree of piety as hers. He feared God and recognized His greatness, of course! God had made the stars, the sea, in short, everything! But having recognized this Infinite Power he, Víctor Quintanar, was still bored in that deserted town, without any theatre, without any promenades, without any sea, without any regattas, without any of the things of this world. If it weren't for his birds . . . !'

Ana threw herself into a life of incessant activity, trying, with frequent success, to forget what she called her temptation. It was becoming more and more fearsome, and the more she feared it the stronger it became. But she took refuge in piety and, with ardent charity and apostolic zeal, visited the poor, crowded into hovels and caves, to bring them the consolations of religion for the spirit and alms for the body. Although she was often accompanied by Doña Petronila Rianzares or one of the ladies in her conclave, she sometimes went alone. Among all the tasks imposed on her by the life of devotion, this was the one she liked best.

The summer stole away large parts of those pious armies, the Guild of the Sacred Heart of Jesus, the Guild of the Court of Mary, the Holy Mission for Catechesis, the Society of St Vincent de Paul, and the like. Many ladies went to the baths or the country. But the nucleus remained – the numerous and important group of illustrious devotees surrounding Doña Petronila. During the warm months there was a decrease in alms-giving, but there was, nevertheless, a great deal of talk in the guilds, as preparations were made for the autumn and winter feast-days, and a little gossip about the absent ladies. The judge's wife never took part in these conventicles but she forgave them as a small failing, 'which she, burdened with other more serious defects, had no right to censure'.

Don Fermín and Doña Ana saw each other every day, sometimes in Ozores Mansion, sometimes at the Mission for Catechesis, or in the cathedral, or at the Society of St Vincent; but most frequently in Doña Petronila's house. The mother-bishop was always busy and left her two friends alone in the murky sitting-room as (by their leave) she went away to continue putting her accounts in order – or to do whatever it was that was occupying her.

Vetusta belonged to them. The solitude of the summer seemed to give them possession of the town, and they took their time over their farewells in the cathedral porch, without fear of being seen, as if the emptiness of the cathedral extended throughout Vetusta. Anita found life more tolerable than in winter. In this particular, as least, she and her husband did not understand each other.

Don Fermín would have liked this season never to end, and the absent Vetustans to stay away for good. His mother had gone to Matalerejo to collect rents and prepare for the harvest (the interest on money scattered throughout the mountains). Teresina was the mistress now. Cheerful all day long, active and solicitous, she filled the canon theologian's house with religious songs to which she lent – not quite knowing what she was doing – a profane sense, an air of street ballads. This cheerful tone was made all the more piquant by the contrast with her face, which was the face of a Lady of Dolours. Teresina had taken on a little colour, and her eyes – ringed by slight shadows so that the pupils were full of a tender and mysterious darkness – were more profound and more beautiful than ever. Master and maid were happy. Freedom was like a taste of heaven. They both did as they pleased: since Doña Paula was away from home, there was no need to give explanations to anybody. Nothing was wanting.

The master was provided with everything at the right time and in the right place, as usual. He could live without the mistress now.

The canon theologian came and went without fear of insidious interrogations. For once it did not matter if he returned home late. Everything, everything was smiling at him. If only the summer were eternal! Even his enemies had abated the force of their calumny. There was less gossip now, for many of the slanderers were away on holiday, and those who remained lacked an audience. Don Santos Barinaga was ill and stayed indoors. Only Foja – who, for reasons of economy, never took a holiday – attempted to keep the sacred flame of gossip burning in the Gentlemen's Club among four or five bored members who spent half an hour there each day drinking coffee. In short, it was a suspension of hostilities. 'Don Fermín welcomed it. He was prepared to fight, if fight he must, but he preferred peace. Especially now, when he had other things to do, things better and sweeter than hating and hounding wretches who were worthy only of scorn and pity.'

The happiness which De Pas savoured as a gastronome savours food; the freedom, the voluptuous relaxation of his robust body; the vague dreams of nameless love; the delicious reality of seeing the judge's wife at all hours of the day and seeing himself in her eyes and hearing from her lips the sweet, sweet words of a mysterious and indeed almost mystical friendship: it all made him wish that the sun would stop again, that time would not pass by. That August, so sad for Don Víctor, was the happiest time of Don Fermín's life.

When, sitting in his study early in the morning, he heard Teresina singing 'Santo fuerte'[23] while she washed the pavement outside – as if that holy hymn were some common fandango – he was tempted to sing too. He did not sing, but he rose to his feet and walked into the passage.

'Teresina! Chocolate!' he cried happily, rubbing his hands together.

And he went into the dining-room.

A little later his maid came with his breakfast in a gleaming china cup decorated with golden posies. She closed the door behind her, approached the table, placed the breakfast service upon it, spread the master's napkin before him and waited motionless at his side.

Don Fermín smiled and dipped a sponge finger into the hot chocolate. Teresina brought her face close to her master, moving her body away from the table as she did so, and parted her delicate, scarlet lips. Then, with a comical gesture, she stuck out her moist red tongue rather more than was necessary, and upon it Don Fermín placed the sponge finger. The servant girl bit into it with teeth of pearl, and the master ate the other half.

This was what happened every morning.

XXII

The Archdeacon Don Restituto Mourelo returned from the baths at Termasaltas refreshed, joyful and majestic, ready to open another campaign, which he hoped would be the final, decisive one, 'against the despotism of the simoniacal and lascivious and avaricious enemy of the Church who, holding the will of the bishop in his grasp, had subjugated the diocese'. With this periphrasis the diplomatic Gloucester alluded to the vicar-general.

The news, which De Pas was given one morning in the choir, was his first vexation that summer.

'Gloucester has arrived.'

'He did not fear him – neither him nor anyone else – but he was so tired of fighting and hating!'

Mourelo found many other refreshed gossips, as well as the gossips left upon deposit in Vetusta, all of them no less anxious than he was to open fire at the common enemy. They were burning in the holy enthusiasm of slander. Those who had returned from stays in the mountains and in fishing villages were hungry for tales and tittle-tattle, having acquired a new appetite for gossip from the solitude of the country. Who was there to slander in those mountains and valleys of the province? 'Their beloved Vetusta! Oh, there is nothing to match the centres of civilization for flaying one's neighbour in comfort. In villages people speak ill of the doctor, the chemist, the priest, the mayor; but how could they, the Vetustans, the inhabitants of the capital of the province, be content with such trivialities?' 'Civis romanus sum!'[1] said Mourelo. 'I require gossip worthy of me. Let us with our tongues crush colossuses – not the likes of the doctor of Termasaltas.'

Foja and all the others who had stayed behind were also longing for the return of those who had gone away, to tell them the latest news and comment on it with them. When those who had gone on holiday began to reappear, Vetusta started to come to life again in its cathedral chapter, religious guilds, clubs, streets and promenades. False friendships, worn so thin as to be unbearable during the communal boredom of an endless winter, were renewed. The people who came back found the people who had stayed behind to be witty and talented, and vice versa, and everybody laughed at everybody else's jokes and saucy remarks. By slow degrees the circles of gossip became lively again and the fires of calumny were rekindled, so that the last to arrive, the stragglers, found a paradise awaiting them. 'Such wit, such subtle shrewdness, such perspicacity! Oh, the cleverness of the Vetustans!'

That year the canon theologian was the sole victim of the bacchanalia of slander.

'Don Santos Barinaga, the commercial rival of La Cruz Roja, the victim of the illegal and scandalous monopoly of Doña Paula and her son, poor Don Santos was dying, according to Don Robustiano Somoza, the doctor to the aristocracy, whose ideas were not open to suspicion.'

'And what do you think he's dying of?' asked Foja of a group of gossips in front of the cathedral after midday mass.

'I suppose he is dying of drink,' replied Ripamilán.

'No, sir, he's dying of hunger.'

'Brandy is killing him.'

'Hunger.'

Don Robustiano joined the group and science spoke:

'I am not accusing anybody. Science does not accuse anybody; it has a different mission. I do not deny that chronic alcoholism plays a part in Barinaga's illness, but its effects could, without doubt, have been levitated by an adequate diet. Besides, poor Don Santos hasn't enough money nowadays even to get tipsy, his poverty is such that he can't drink. And although you people cannot understand this, science declares that deprivation of alcohol is precipitating that man's demise – even though his illness is caused by the abuse of alcohol.'

'How can that be, my dear fellow?' asked the archpriest.

'Come on, explain yourself,' said Foja.

Don Robustiano smiled and, full of pity, shook his head and condescended to explain his statement. 'It might astonish them to hear it, but although Don Santos was dying of alcohol poisoning he needed more alcohol in order to rub on for a few months longer. Drink was killing him, but he would die sooner without it.'

'But Don Robustiano, how can that be?'

'You will soon see, Señor Foja. Do you know Todd?'

'Who?'

'Todd.'

'No, sir.'

'Then stop talking. Do you know what the hypothermal power of alcohol is? You don't, so keep quiet. Do you know what goes with the diaphoretic power of the said alcohol? You don't, so shut your mouth. Do you deny the haemostatic action of alcohol, identified by Campbell and Chevrière? You would be wrong to deny it, if we are referring to its internal use, I mean. So you don't know the first thing about the subject.'

'Well that's why I'm asking. But listen to me, sir: regardless of all you know and all Señor Todd says, your blessed science has no right to slander Don Santos Barinaga. The poor man has enough to contend with, being starved and harried to death, without you coming along and, just because you've read, God knows where and how fast, some magazine article about brandy, thinking you've got the authority to insult my good friend and call him, in technical terms, an old soak.'

'Easy there!' cried Ripamilán. 'In this question I am in agreement with science and Señor Somoza, its legitimate representative. I don't know whether one nail drives out another in medicine, or whether taking a hair of the dog that bit you is an effective remedy, but Don Santos is the personification of a barrel, and there is more spirit of wine in his body than blood in his veins. He is a fuse saturated with alcohol – just strike a light and you will see.'

'I do not need any help from the Church, Señor Ripamilán, to confute this fusty old progressive. Science – which is, in short, my religion – is more than enough for that.'

Turning to Foja the doctor added:

'And now, you superannuated decurion, just listen to me. Do you know about the action of alcohol on the phlegmasiae of drinkers? Don't tell a lie, you know nothing about it.'

'Go to blazes, you hospital humbug! If anybody's telling lies it's you! Well! Look at the bee that's got into the doctor's bonnet now, making himself out to be a scholar. No fool like an old fool.'

'Let's have less insults and more facts.'

'Less clowning and more common sense.'

'I, Sir Militiaman, am a man of science; and you are a pickled 1812 liberal.[2] Chomel recognizes, and anyone who isn't dead from the neck up recognizes, that in illnesses caused by drink the administration of spirits is indispensable.'

'But I reject your minor premise, Sir Blockhead!'

'There aren't any majors or minors in medicine – or court cards or plain cards, you old sharper.'

'Your minor premise is that Barinaga is a drunkard.'

'So if you deny the – prodromes of the disease . . .'

Don Robustiano coloured, realizing that he had made another blunder.

'I'm not talking about hippodromes – or hippopotamuses for that matter. I am defending an absent friend.'

'A word in conclusion. Do you deny that if a drunkard is completely deprived of alcohol, it is most likely that there will ensue an alarming decline, a veritable collapse?'

'Look here, you pedant, if you continue to shatter my ear-drums with your verbiage, I am going to quote fifty thousand Latin verses and maxims and leave you open-mouthed. You don't believe me? Just listen then –

> Ordine confectu, quisque libellus habet:
> quis, quid, coram quo, quo jure petatur et a quo.
> Cultus disparitas, vis, ordo, ligamen, honestas. . . .[3]

Ripamilán writhed with laughter as Somoza shouted in fury: collapse – phlegmasia – cardiopathy – and the ex-mayor did not pay attention but went on reciting a jumble of Latin words:

'Masculine is *fustis axis,*
turris, caulis, sanguis, collis,
piscis, vermis, callis, follis . . .⁴

The doctor and the money-lender were on the point of coming to blows. It was not possible to establish what Don Santos was dying of, but within half an hour the word was going around Vetusta that – because of the vicar-general – Foja and Somoza had struck and challenged each other, and that Ripamilán himself might have received a punch or two.

For some days the valetudinarian Barinaga, who was indeed wasting away in dire poverty, was eclipsed by an event of the most extreme gravity, according to Gloucester and Foja and their factions. 'Carraspique's daughter, Sister Teresa, was on her death-bed in the noisome retreat of the Salesian sisters, in the cell which was, according to Somoza, a convenience, not to say the very opposite.'

No sooner said than done. Rosa Carraspique in the world, Sister Teresa in the convent, she died of tuberculosis according to Somoza, of caseous phthisis according to the nuns' doctor, who was a dualist on the subject of phthisis.

But, whatever the truth might have been about the girl's lungs, something about which none of the vicar-general's enemies had any doubt was that he was to blame for her death.

Doña Paula and Don Alvaro arrived in Vetusta on the same day – the day when another angel flew to heaven according to Trifoncito Cármenes, who was still a romantic in spite of all Don Cayetano's advice.

One of Vetusta's liberal newspapers, *El Alerta,* published these two articles, one after the other, which put Don Fermín into a fiendish temper:

'*Welcome.* – Returning from his summer travels, the illustrious leader of the Dynastic Liberal Party of Vetusta, the Ilustrísimo Señor Don Alvaro Mesía, has arrived in this city. The numerous friends who have called to pay their respects to our distinguished collaborator say that he comes prepared to pursue his campaign of level-headed liberal propaganda in both the political and the moral and canonical and religious fields. He can count upon our support to overcome the traditional obstacles placed in the way of true progress by a theocratic despotism with which all Vetusta is fed to the back teeth, to use a common expression.'

'*R.I.P.* – Señorita Doña Rosa Carraspique y Somoza, the daughter of the well-known ultramontane capitalist, Don Francisco de Assisi Carraspique, a professed nun with the name of Sister Teresa, has died in her cell in the Salesian convent. We would have to say a great deal if we wished to echo all the comments to which this inopinate tragedy has given rise. We will only say that, in the opinion of the most reputable medical practitioners, no small part has been played in this much-lamented loss by the lack of hygienic conditions in the wretched building inhabited by the Salesian sisters. But, moreover, it occurs to us to ask: Is it very hygienic for *certain rodents* to insinuate themselves into the bosom of a family in order by little and little, with their deleterious and *pseudo-religious* influence, to undermine the peace of the home, the tranquillity of consciences?

'If all the unexaggeratedly liberal elements in our cultured capital city do not join forces to combat the powerful hierocratic tyrant who is oppressing us, we shall soon all be victims of the vilest, most blatant fanaticism. – R.I.P.'

Ripamilán, without the canon theologian's knowledge, took the ill-advised decision to pick up his pen and publish in *El Lábaro* an unsigned article defending his friend, the Salesian sisters, and grammar – which had also been maltreated by the progressive newspaper, according to Ripamilán. 'Leaving aside the fact', he wrote, 'that we do not know whether the professed nun is Señor Carraspique or his daughter, will the fiddle-faddle article-writer pray tell me . . . ?'

The 'fiddle-faddle' betrayed the archpriest. It was his humorous style, and everybody recognized it.

In Vetusta, printed insults and gossip always attracted a great deal of attention. It was in vain for Trifón Cármenes to publish odes and elegies, for no one read them, but the most insignificant article which might be a little vexatious to some resident was read and commented on for days and days. The regular subscribers could think of no better entertainment than a full-blooded journalistic skirmish, complete with a firing of notes and statements.

So the scandal grew, and for a long time nobody talked about anything other than the canon theologian's deleterious influence and Sister Teresa's death.

'This tragedy lies at his door.'

'He's a spiritual vampire, sucking our daughters' blood.'

'Yes, it's a kind of blood-tax we're paying to fanaticism.'

'It's like the tribute of a hundred maidens.'[5]

De Pas would have liked to be able to scorn such nonsense, such absurdity, but in spite of himself he was irritated by it. At first he thought that 'his noble, sublime passion would raise him a hundred cubits above all that wretchedness', but no, the stormy sea of false public indignation did splash his soul, it did reach up to his nameless ecstasy; and his resulting anger often chased the purest ideas, the most tender and pleasant impressions, from his brain. He went into towering rages, and was increasingly irritated by his inability to control them. Besides, the harm he was suffering was real enough, the absurdity of the fools' accusations did not make them any less potent or fearsome. He noticed that his power was tottering, that the efforts of so very many wretches were undermining it. In many houses he began to encounter a certain reserve. Some liberal gentlemen's wives stopped confessing with him, and even Fortunato, the bishop (whom De Pas had eating out of his hand) made bold to look at him with eyes which were cold and fraught with questions that pierced his own eyes like steel nails.

The season for taking strolls in the Mall came round again and, as Don Fermín promenaded his humble arrogance and his handsome figure, like some brawny mystic, he observed that his progress was no longer a triumphal march, a path of glory. In the greetings, looks and whispers which he left behind him like a wake, even in the way people stepped aside to let him pass, he was aware of a certain harshness and prickliness, a widespread, pent-up hostility – something like fear, about to display its own peculiar, insolent bravery.

At home sat Doña Paula, scowling, silent, distrustful, preparing for a storm, taking in the sails (that is to say, the money), realizing whatever she could, collecting debts, possessed by a feverish anxiety to be rid of the goods in La Cruz Roja. 'Anyone would think that they were making ready to wind up their affairs. What was the purpose of it all?' But Doña Paula did not give any explanations. 'She knew what she had to make up her mind to. Her son, her Fermo, had gone to the dogs, that shrew the judge's wife, that sanctimonious humbug living in mortal sin, had blinded him, maddened him. God only knew what was going on in Ozores Mansion! What a scandal! That woman, with all her wiles, was going to take everything away from them. Doña Paula must be prepared. Oh, maybe she was going to be thrown out of Vetusta, but she wouldn't go without carrying off half the town between her teeth.' This was why she was biting with a fury which frightened even her son.

Fermo, the master, sat alone in his study thinking, like a Faustus of the Church. 'I am alone, alone. Not even my mother comforts me. What am I to do? Give myself over with all my soul to this strong, noble passion. Ana, Ana – there is nothing else in this world for me! She is alone too, she needs me too. Together we are strong enough to defeat all these fools and villains.'

Pale – almost yellow – restless, agitated, De Pas would go to his mystical friend, who was becoming more and more beautiful, and healthy and majestic. Her figure was full, robust and harmonious; her sweetness was like an aureola surrounding her. Health, purified by a certain idealistic unction, had returned to the body – a body as splendid as that of some proud trans-Tiberine woman[6] – of that model for madonnas.

As soon as Don Alvaro Mesía returned from Palomares, Don Víctor Quintanar renewed his close friendship with him, and the canon soon noticed that the convert was rebelling. Although Don Víctor still believed himself to be a profoundly religious man, he made suspicious distinctions between religion and the clergy, between Catholicism and ultramontanism. 'I am as good a Catholic as the next man' was his favourite expression whenever he voiced a heresy. He took it upon himself to interpret texts from the Old and New Testaments in his own way, and even made so bold as to declare, in front of priests and ladies, that every virtuous man is a minister of God, that an age-old forest is the most suitable temple for pure religion, that Jesus Christ was a liberal, and other such nonsense. What was worst of all was not this, however, but that Ana and Don Fermín were aware of a certain coolness in Quintanar whenever he saw them together, and that the canon had to pretend not to notice certain half-concealed slights.

Don Alvaro only went to Ozores Mansion on brief and infrequent courtesy visits. Why was this? asked Don Víctor. His friend hinted that it was because Ana was loath to receive him and he did not like to be a nuisance. Besides, he was not the only person who was staying away. Paco himself, who in former times had been in and out of the house all day long, seldom appeared there now. Visitación's calls, too, were few and far between, those of the marchioness had almost ceased, and it was the same story with all Ana's old friends. The canon theologian and only the canon theologian: that worthy had created a vacuum around the judge's wife. She was happy, she seemed not to miss anybody, but Don Víctor was different: he wanted companionship, conversation, pleasant company.

He still confessed and took the communion every other month, but Kempis lay among profane books, covered with dust. He was still afraid of hell, 'but he was unwilling to deprive himself completely of the positive advantages offered by his brief existence on the face of the earth'. 'And, in particular, he was unwilling to have fanaticism taking possession of his house.' Don Víctor paid serious attention to the advice offered by Mesía in the Gentlemen's Club in an attempt to incite him to action; he was always making ready to follow it in practice – but he did not dare do so. His audacity only ran to pulling a vinegarish face from time to time (once in a blue moon) at the enemy, but since the canon pretended not to understand these mimicked innuendoes nothing was gained by them.

Don Víctor now recognized – but without admitting it to anybody – that he was a less resolute man than he had thought. 'No, he did not have the strength to oppose the Jesuitism which had invaded his home. Oh yes – he had been quite right to hesitate before allowing De Pas to take possession of his wife's spirit! Yes – when all was said and done the man had been a Jesuit.' Quintanar ended up comparing the vicar-general's power in Ozores Mansion to the Jesuits' former power in Paraguay. 'Yes, my house is a second Paraguay.' And every day he felt less able to oppose this pernicious influence. All he could do was pull faces and stay away from home.

This only had the effect of making his wife and the canon agree to meet less often in her house and more often elsewhere. 'It was better to talk in Doña Petronila's house. Why trouble poor Don Víctor? Since pernicious friends were again leading him astray and poisoning his soul with malevolent insinuations, with crude, impious suspicions, it was better to leave him in peace, remove from his gaze the innocent, yet for him disagreeable, sight of two soul brothers united by a strong bond in the most poetic piety and idealism.'

In Doña Petronila's house, in the sitting-room with its shutters left discreetly ajar and its grey felt carpet, the two soul friends spent hours and hours talking about spiritual interests, as Doña Petronila called them. There was no witness other than the white cat, which was growing fatter and fatter. It prowled back and forth and rubbed its side against the judge's wife's skirts and the canon theologian's cloak with more familiarity every day.

Anita noticed an attractive pallor in Don Fermín's face, large dark rings around his eyes and a weariness in his voice and breathing which worried her.

She begged him to take care of himself, in the tones of a loving mother pleading with a precious son to take medicine. He replied, smiling, and his eyes aflame, 'that there was nothing wrong with him, it was just idle fear on her part, she should not worry about his wretched body'.

On some days there were embarrassing pauses in their conversations, silences which were interminable, and as vexatious as a tireless talker.

Each was keeping something back from the other. They were both convinced that they knew every hidden recess of each other's souls, yet neither could stop thinking about a certain guilty secret.

The canon suffered whenever Ana spoke about his declining health. 'If she knew . . . !'

Resolved that his friendship 'with that beautiful angel' should not have an unfortunate ending in a gross, physical affair which would only bring him remorse and repugnant aftertastes, and certain that Ana put all the sincerity of a pure soul into their pious bond, and that to defile her – always supposing such a thing to be possible – would deprive it of its greatest charm, the canon, who by now was living exclusively on this refined passion which, according to him, had no name, was fighting against formidable temptations. He only managed to resist the sudden, furious rebellions of his flesh with the aid of shameful truces which he regarded as a kind of infidelity. It was in vain for him to think: of what concern is it to my dear Doña Ana how my body, this hulking body of a hunter from the mountains, lives when I leave her side? She does not ask me for anything to do with my body. My soul is all hers, and my soul is not involved when, far from her, I satisfy appetites which she herself unwittingly stimulates.

It was in vain for him to think all this, because he felt the pangs of acute remorse every time that Ana, solicitous, tender and smiling, implored him, wringing her hands, to take good care of himself and not to give all his time to work and penance.

'Suppose you go and die: what would become of me?'

'It is horrible, horrible,' thought the canon, 'to pass for a saint in her eyes and to be in reality a wretched body of clay living as clay must live. It does not hurt me to deceive others, but her! And it cannot be helped.' He tried to find consolation in the thought that it was all because of her – it was because of her that he was again feeling the powerful passions of his youth, passions which he had believed dead, and it was because of her, because of his respect for her purity, that he was wallowing in the mire of former times. But this idea did not console him, did not deaden his remorse.

There were times when Teresina was sad, afraid that she had lost her power over the master. This was when the canon's conscience was clear and he could sit with Ana untormented by remorse. But by degrees the torture of temptation would return and its attacks would be even more terrible – and, of course, more dangerous – than the attacks of remorse. Ana's chastity and innocence, her sincere piety, the faith with which she believed in their spiritual friendship, unsullied by sin, were all incentives for Don Fermín's passion and increased the danger; for she was not afraid that anything sinful might happen, and in this carefree state did not notice that her familiarity, her affectionate solicitude, her tender intimacy, indeed everything she said and did was fuel which she was throwing on to the flames. And, to avoid greater evils, De Pas would again take precautions, which were Teresina's joy and what she proudly believed to be her victory.

Ana, too, had a secret. Her piety was sincere, her desire to be saved was unwavering, her determination to ascend from one mansion to another (in the words of the saint from Avila)[7] was serious, but temptation became more fearsome every day. The more horrifying the sin of thinking about Don Alvaro seemed, the more pleasure she derived from it. She no longer doubted that this man meant perdition for her, but neither could she doubt that everything in her that was worldly, carnal, frail and mortal was in love with him. She would not now have dared, as in former times, to look him in the face, let him stay at her side for hours and hours, show him that his presence did not affect her. No, now she must flee from him, from his shadow, from his memory; for he was the devil, Jesus's powerful enemy. It could not be helped, she must flee from him; this was true humility, it had all been senseless pride before. To Grace, and to Grace alone, she owed the fact that she was still pure; she had to confess that left to her own devices she would succumb; if the Lord were to loosen His grip for a moment Don Alvaro could tighten his, and take his prey. For all these reasons she would not even see him. But she could not help thinking about him. She cast such thoughts away from her with all her strength, but they always returned. What horrible remorse! What would Jesus think? And what would the canon theologian think – if he knew? Her senses' inclination to delight in Mesía's memory as soon as they were given half a chance disgusted her as something vile and despicable. Why Mesía? The remorse which infidelity to Jesus awoke in her was full of terror and profound sadness, but it was enveloped in a vague idealism which attenuated it; yet the remorse awoken by infidelity to her soul friend, to her elder brother, to Don Fermín, was of the sort which gives rise to self-disgust, to the incomparable torment of having to despise oneself. Besides, Anita did not dare confess these things to him, for that would do him great harm and destroy the charm of their pure, ideal relationship. Once again she resorted to sophisms in order not to say anything in her confessions about this weakness. 'She did not want it to happen.' Whenever she was in command of her own thoughts she kept sinful images out of them, she avoided Don Alvaro, and was not, therefore, sinning voluntarily. Was there such a thing as involuntary sin? One day she spoke about this question to Don Fermín, without telling him that it concerned her personally. He replied that the question was a complex one – and cited various authors. Ana later remembered that one of them was Pascal, in his *Provincial Letters*.[8] She possessed this book and she read it – and thought she would go mad. 'Oh, being good was a question of talent as well. She was bewildered by so many distinctions and so much subtlety.' But she still said nothing to her friend about her dreadful temptation. She found a powerful weapon against it in the ardent charity with which she devoted herself to defending and comforting De Pas when his enemies let loose their hurricanes of slander, which she believed to be false through and through.

Ana was possessed with the idea of sacrificing herself to save the man to whom she owed the redemption of her spirit. This idea was like a powerful, overwhelming passion, and she welcomed it as a way to satisfy her hunger for love – love directed at a tangible object, something finite, a fellow creature. 'Yes, yes,' she thought, 'I shall fight my inclination towards evil by loving this good, this sacrifice, this self-denial. I am ready to die for this man, if need be.' But she could not discover a way to put her intentions into practice. She sought, but did not find, an opportunity to sacrifice herself for the canon. What could she do to abate the violence of the calumny? Nothing. Nothing as yet. But she did not lose hope, perhaps some way would present itself of exercising for the benefit of that poor martyr the self-denial upon which she was resolved. But until that moment came all she could do was console him. She was so successful that he had to make titanic efforts to restrain himself from showing his gratitude by kneeling before her and kissing her small, elegant, well-shod feet.

In the meantime Foja, Mourelo, Don Custodio, Guimarán, El Alerta and, behind the scenes, Don Alvaro and Visitación Olías de Cuervo, were also working like Titans – to destroy the mountain which lay over them: the power of the canon theologian.

Sister Teresa's death was a blow which made the canon totter in that lofty place which his enemies imagined him to occupy, and even overshadowed poor Don Santos Barinaga for a time. After a few weeks, though, this victim again began to shine in his halo, and Vetusta solicitously redirected its false piety and feigned amiability towards him, like an uncaring stepmother playing out the farce of being a second mother. For, in truth, the life or death of Don Santos was of little consequence to most Vetustans. Nobody had offered a hand to help him out of his poverty, and people even continued to call him a drunkard; yet everyone was indignant with the vicar-general, everyone cursed the man responsible for so much misfortune, and everyone felt satisfied, believing, or pretending to believe, that the indignation and the curses would keep Charity happy.

'Oh! in these times of ours,' Foja shouted in the Gentlemen's Club, 'in these times, slandered by the enemies of progress – in these so-called materialistic, corrupt times – nobody can insult with impunity the philanthropic sentiments of the people without a unanimous voice being raised to protest in the name of outraged humanity. Poor Don Santos Barinaga, the victim of the scandalous monopoly of La Cruz Roja, is dying of hunger in the deserted warehouses where once shone sacred vessels, patens and pyxes, lamps and candlesticks, together with a hundred and one other articles of worship. He is dying in that corner and he is dying of hunger, gentlemen, through the fault of the simonist whom we all know; he is dying, yes, he will die. But the man who employs tricks to make a mockery of our commercial law and the laws of the Church, engaging in trade although he is a priest; the man who is starving poor citizen Barinaga to death – that man will not rejoice in his works for long, because the tide of public indignation is rising, rising – and finally it will swallow the hated tyrant!'

In spite of this speech and other similar ones, it did not occur to Foja to send Don Santos a hen so that some broth could be made for him.

All the other theoretical defenders of the ruined tradesman behaved in the same way. They proclaimed with one voice that he was dying of hunger, but not one of them took him a piece of bread. Only a few even went to see him. Foja would enter the house and immediately go away again, it being sufficient for his purposes to ensure that the poor old fellow was still sick and destitute. He would hurry off to heap abuse upon *that man,* believing this was the way to serve the good cause of progress and solidary humanity.[9]

The well-established reputation of a heretic which the worthy Don Santos had made his own in recent times kept many pious souls, who would have been pleased to help him, away from his house.

Only the Vincentian ladies made bold to approach the old fellow's bed to offer him the material comforts of their society and the spiritual comforts of the Church.

They did so in vain.

'Fortunately,' said Don Pompeyo Guimarán as he described the incident, 'fortunately I was there to forestall any indignities.'

Don Santos had granted his friend Don Pompeyo full powers to repulse in his name the slightest suggestion of fanaticism.

Guimarán was well pleased to be given 'that important, delicate mission, which required great reserves of energy and deep-rooted conviction'.

The envoys of the Society of St Vincent de Paul – Doña Petronila and the beneficiary Don Custodio – betook themselves to the cold bare cubbyhole in which lay the victim of chronic alcoholism. Barinaga's daughter – the pallid dried-up devotee – received them downstairs in the empty shop, whimpering. The three talked in whispers. Don Custodio spoke words saturated with soft whistling sounds (in imitation of the canon theologian) into his spiritual daughter's ear, consoling her, and she raised her tear-filled eyes and fixed them on the eyes of the honeyed priest, like a woman settling down in a place which she knows and frequents. Then all tiptoed upstairs, ready to attempt an attack on the enemy.

'So Don Pompeyo is with him, is he?' Don Custodio asked on the way up.

'Yes, he never leaves the house nowadays. My father casts me from his side and cries out for that addle-pated old heretic.'

Don Pompeyo Guimarán heard a man's voice. It sounded like the voice of a priest. He prepared his defence, and attempted to assume an attitude worthy of a free-thinker who is convinced of his beliefs, yet prudent beyond measure. He clasped his hands behind his back and began to stride around the humble sitting-room, making its worm-eaten old chestnut floor· creak and squeak. In the adjacent bedroom, which had no door and was divided off by a dirty red calico curtain, the invalid's frequent moans and laboured breathing could be heard.

'Who is it?' asked Don Santos in a feeble voice in which there was no more energy than that lent it by impotent anger.

'I believe that they have arrived, but do not be afraid. I am here with you. You keep quiet, it is bad for you to become irritated. I am more than a match for these people.'

The enemy entered the room. Although it came in peace, and

although Don Pompeyo had resolved to be so very prudent, as soon as Doña Petronila opened her mouth he held out a hand and interrupted her:

'You must excuse me, madam, and this worthy Catholic priest must also excuse me – you have come on a fool's errand. Conditional alms are not accepted here.'

'What do you mean, conditional?' asked Don Custodio with the utmost courtesy.

'Don't you lose your temper with me, my friend – I do not believe *that* to be your mission on earth. As you can see, *I* am speaking in a perfectly calm manner.'

'But I do not think I have said anything . . .'

'You said "What do you mean, conditional?" and nobody comes rough-riding over me, and I don't mind whether he wears trousers or skirts. I do not hate the clergy systematically, but I do demand good manners from cultured persons.'

'Sir, we have not come here to argue, we have come to exercise charity.'

'Conditional charity.'

'Conditional – tommy-rot!' cried Doña Petronila, who did not see the necessity for such consideration when dealing with a mad atheist. She added, 'You have no authority in this house. This young lady is Don Santos's daughter and it is with her and with him that we wish to speak. We have come to make a spontaneous offering of the comforts which our society can give.'

'With the indignity of a retractation as the condition – yes, I know. Don Santos has delegated to me all the powers of his religious autonomy, and in his name, and with the utmost courtesy, I command you to withdraw.'

And Don Pompeyo extended an arm towards the door and stood admiring his own outstretched limb, and his own energy.

But he had to lower his arm because Doña Petronila replied that she was not prepared to take orders from a busybody.

'You, madam, are the busybodies here. Nobody has asked you to come, nobody wants you; the only charity accepted here is that which does not ask for letters of communion.'

'But we aren't asking for any letters . . .'

'Don't you come to me, priest, with sophisms from a seminary. Modern philosophy has demonstrated that scholasticism is a tissue of puerilities, and I know very well what you people are seeking. You want to buy my friend's deep-rooted convictions with a plate of lentils; pay a bowl of broth for confessing a dogma, a penny for apostasy – this is an indignity!'

'But sir . . . !'

'To conclude, Sir Priest: Don Santos is prepared to die without confessing or taking the communion. He does not recognize the faith of his forefathers. These are his irrevocable conditions. Well, then, at this price do you agree to attend to him, look after him, give him the food and medicine he requires?'

'But my dear sir . . .'

'Ah! *your* sir – just as I said! You see, you can't discomfit me with your scholasticism!'

'All that and much more besides,' said Constantine the Great, 'is something which we wish to discuss with the person concerned.'

'No you won't.'

'Yes we will.'

'Madam, with all due respect to your sex, I am prepared to hurl you both downstairs if you insist on your insolent attack.'

And Don Pompeyo placed himself in front of the calico curtain, to bar the mother-bishop's way.

'Who is it? Who is it?' came Barinaga's hoarse, panting cry from behind it.

'The Vincentians,' replied Guimarán.

'Thunder and lightning! Get out of my house! Haven't you got a broom handy, Don Pompeyo? Open fire on them – infamous creatures – and isn't there a priest among them, too?'

'Yes, sir, there is.'

'It must be the canon theologian, the robber, the candle-filcher, the man who fleeced me – and now he's come to crow over me, I suppose. Oh if I could just get out of bed . . . ! But why aren't you giving them a good hiding? Get out of my house! Justice – is there no justice left in the world? Is there no justice for the poor?'

'Calm yourself, it isn't the canon theologian.'

'Yes it is, yes it is – I know it is. Don't you know he's the ringleader, the president of the Vincentians? Come in here, just you come in here, you bandit – and I'll show you a weapon I've got, good for bashing your brain-box in.'

'Hush, hush, my friend, I am more than a match for these people, whom I shall send away in a courteous fashion.'

'No, no, if it's the vicar-general let him in, I want to kill him myself. Who's that snivelling?'

'Your daughter.'

'Ah, the great hypocrite – if I could just get out of bed, the little trollop! Starving her father to death, making his broth out of rosary-beads and hair from her head, sweeping the dust from the sitting-room up his nose, going to mass at dawn and coming back at lunch-time – the wretch. If I could just get out of bed!'

'Father, for the Lord's sake, for the sake of Our Lady of Beauteous Love, calm yourself. Doña Petronila is here, a priest is here.'

'It must be your precious Don Custodio – the one who stole you from me – the flash man of the cathedral chapter. Ah, you little tart, if I ever catch you two together . . . !'

'My God, my God, we must leave this house!' cried Doña Petronila, hurrying towards the stairs.

But they could not leave as soon as they wished, because Don Santos's daughter fainted. They carried her down into the shop to deliver her from her father's insults and furious screams. Don Pompeyo was left in possession of the field, and he resumed his pacing of it. After a while he went into the kitchen to skim Don Santos's miserable broth.

'The only charity there was his charity. True, he could not be too generous to his sick friend, because his own large family hardly had enough, but he would not lack solicitude and attention.'

A little later he returned, blowing on a pale, steaming liquid in which coal-dust floated.

He made Don Santos drink it; he supported his shaking head and would not let him hold the cup in his fleshless hand, which was also shaking.

So Don Pompeyo remained undisputed master of the field, thinking only about how to ensure the triumph of his ideas, to which end it was necessary to keep guard by the sick man's side for as long as possible and thus prevent his daughter from smuggling clerical elements into his room.

Guimarán rose early each morning and hurried to Barinaga's house, where he stayed until it was time for his supper; a *physical necessity* to which he attended in the twinkling of an eye, rushing the servant girl, his wife and his daughters through the meal.

'Come on, come on – less chatter, bring the soup. People are waiting for me.'

He finished his supper, collected crusts of bread, a little sugar and other left-overs from the table, put them into his pocket and hurried away.

Some nights he strode into his house shouting:

'Quick! Quick! My slippers and my flask of anisette, I'm sitting up with Don Santos tonight.'

And Don Pompeyo's wife sighed and brought him his Swiss carpet slippers and his flask of anisette, and the master of the house went away.

Foja, Orgaz senior, Orgaz junior, Gloucester ('as a private individual, not as a priest'), Don Alvaro Mesía, the members of the free-thinking club who solemnly ate meat in public every Good Friday, some of the men who attended the secret dinners in the Gentlemen's Club, the editorial staff of *El Alerta*, and many of the vicar-general's other enemies visited Don Santos from time to time. They all expressed sympathy for him in his dire poverty and protested about it with ill-concealed rage. 'Oh, the man who had reduced Señor Barinaga to such a state was indeed a wretch, he deserved public execration.' But that was all they did. Hardly anyone ventured to leave alms, 'not wanting to offend the invalid's susceptibilities'. There were many offers to sit up with him – if it should prove necessary.

Don Pompeyo received the visits as if he were the master of the house. Celestina had to tolerate this state of affairs because it was what her father demanded.

'He's my only child – you unnatural daughter – my only father – my only friend. You're the one who's in the way here. Monster! Pharisee!' the dying drunkard shouted from his bedroom.

There were heavy frosts at the end of November, and Don Santos's condition deteriorated.

On the first day of December Celestina, with the approbation of Don Custodio, decided to launch the final attack to make her father receive the sacraments.

When, at about eight o'clock in the morning, Don Pompeyo Guimarán walked in, blowing his fingers, she stopped him in the cold, deserted, rat-infested shop.

She tried all the shifts known to her: she begged, she implored, she knelt, wringing her hands, she wept. Then she demanded, she threatened, she insulted. But all to no avail.

'You must talk to your father,' was Guimarán's sole reply. 'I am merely fulfilling his will.'

In desperation Celestina went to her father's bed and, on her knees, wept again, her face buried in the thin straw mattress; while Don Santos repeated in a slow, weak voice, in which there was a certain majesty composed of pain, madness, abjection and wretchedness:

'Leave my presence forthwith, Pharisee! As God's in heaven I abominate you and all your black-coats. Away with the lot of you. Nobody's to enter the shop, they'll carry off every single pyx – and paten. That lamp, Sir Bandit! And you, child of perdition, stop hiding that sacrament under your apron. Get out!'

'Father, father, for pity's sake – receive the holy sacraments!'

'They've stolen them all – and the lamps – and you helped them, you're their accomplice. To prison with her!'

'Father, sir, out of pity for your daughter – the sacraments – take them! Please take them!'

'No, I will not. Let's be reasonable. A consignment of sacraments – what for? If I take it, it will only be left rotting in the shop. The vicar-general forbids them to buy anything here. Poor village priests – what can they do? Poor wretches! They're afraid of him, afraid of him. The villain! Poor wretches!'

And Don Santos sat up as best he could, dropped his head on to his breast, and wept in silence.

Every so often he repeated:

'Poor wretches!'

Celestina left his bedroom, sobbing.

'Her father had gone off his head. Now he couldn't confess, unless he recovered his reason – by some miracle.'

'He cannot, he should not, he will not!' exclaimed Don Pompeyo, his arms crossed, inflexible, prepared not to be moved by others' grief.

Early in the morning of Conception Day, Somoza the doctor said that Don Santos would die at dusk.

His reason kept leaving him, and a vivid impression was needed to stimulate the limited amount of thought of which he was still capable. The arrival of Don Robustiano – that is to say, the arrival of science – made Don Santos turn his attention to the outside world for a while. At midday Celestina announced that Señor Carraspique wanted to see him. This unexpected honour roused the dying man again. Carraspique walked in without greeting Don Pompeyo – who remained at the bedroom door with his arms crossed, as always – and stationed himself at the head of Barinaga's bed. He was accompanied by a clergyman: the parish priest, an old man with a pleasant face and a sweet voice who spoke with a strong local accent. Carraspique had once lent Don Santos money and he still exercised some authority over him. They had not been on speaking terms for years, but they still esteemed each other in spite of their ideological differences and the coolness which time had put between them. Barinaga, on his best behaviour, and using a cultured language which was not often on his lips, refused to entertain the requests of the illustrious Carlist and sincere believer, Don Francisco Carraspique.

'It is all quite useless. The Church has ruined me. I do not want to have anything to do with the Church. I believe in God. I believe in Jesus Christ – who was – a great man – but I do not want to confess, Señor Carraspique, and I am sorry to disappoint you. Apart from all that – I am sure – that this trouble of mine – could be cured or, at least, be – be . . . with brandy. Believe me, I am dying of a lack of liquids, both gaseous and solid.'

Don Santos raised his head a little and recognized the parish priest.

'Don Antero, you here, too. I am glad. Now you will be able to attest publicly – as a scribe of the spirit, so to speak – to what I am about to say – and this is my last will and testament: I, Santos Barinaga, am dying – of a lack of sufficiently alcoholic liquids. I am dying – of what – what the doctor calls – the caps – or the claps.[10] Secondly . . .'

He stopped; his cough was choking him. Making another effort and clutching the torn dirty sheet to his chin, he went on –

'Item: I am dying of a lack of tobacco. Furthermore – I am dying – of a lack of food – wholesome food. And the people to blame for this are a gentleman, the canon theologian, and a lady, my own daughter.'

'Come, Don Santos,' the priest made bold to say, 'don't make poor

Celestina suffer, now. Let's talk about something else. You're not dying, not at all. You'll soon be better again. This afternoon, I give you my word, I'm going to bring you all you need – but first we must talk alone for a short while. And then, then you'll receive the Bread of the soul.'

'The bread of the body!' the dying man shrieked, making a supreme effort, beside himself with rage. 'The bread of the body is what I need! So help me God I am dying of hunger! Yes, the bread of the body – I am dying of hunger! Hunger!'

These were his last rational words. He became delirious shortly afterwards. Celestina wept at the foot of the bed. The priest, Don Antero, his arms crossed, paced about the wretched room, making the floor creak and squeak. Guimarán, his arms also crossed, stood in the doorway, admiring what he called the death of a righteous man.

Carraspique had hurried off to the palace. He arrived and told all. The bishop was praying before an image of the Virgin, and when he heard that Don Santos had refused to confess and receive the Lord, he raised his clasped hands and in a voice tender and tearful and majestic he exclaimed:

'Oh my Mother, Mother of God, enlighten that unhappy man!'

The good Fortunato was pale; his fleshy lower lip quivered as he stammered his private prayers.

The canon theologian strode about the red damask-lined room with his hands clasped behind his back.

Carraspique, dressed in deep mourning for his daughter, looked at the canon through tearful eyes.

'Don Fermín is suffering,' thought poor Don Francisco, and against his will, with great remorse, he was glad and rejoiced in the pleasure of revenge 'which was irrational, unjust, whatever one liked to call it, but he did rejoice as he thought of his dead daughter'.

Yes indeed; Don Fermín was suffering. 'This shopkeeper's stupid behaviour was yet another complication.'

De Pas was no longer the man who had felt romantic remorse on that moonlit night as he saw Don Santos dragging his degradation and his wretchedness through the gutter. Now he was simply an egotist, living for his passion alone. He hated anything which might spoil the nameless ecstasy which Ana's presence gave him; he loved anything which might provide a solution to the terrible conflict – more terrible every day – between his repressed senses and the pure eternity of his passion. Nothing else in the world existed for him. 'And now Don Santos was dying scandalously, dying like a dog. The old drunk would have to be buried in that filthy, forsaken pit behind the cemetery, used for civil burials;[11] and *he* would be blamed for it, and all Vetusta would be at his throat.' The buzz of mutiny could already be heard. The Pug kept coming to tell him that Don Santos's shop and the street outside were crowded with his enemies, that people talking in groups were calling him a murderer (he made the Pug tell him the truth without any beating about the bush), a murderer and a robber. As the canon reached this point in his thoughts he stamped on the floor, unable to help himself. Carraspique jumped. The bishop, emerging from his oratory, his hands clasped, approached his vicar-general.

'For God's sake, Fermo, for God's sake I implore you to let me . . .'

'What?'

'Go myself: go to see that man. I want to see him myself. He will obey me. I shall persuade him. Let a coach be brought if you don't want me to be seen, a trap, a cart, whatever you like. I am going to see him – yes, I'm going to see him.'

'Madness, my Lord, sheer madness!' roared the vicar-general, shaking his head.

'But Fermo, a soul is being lost!'

'You must not leave this building. The bishop going to see an inveterate heretic! Absurd!'

'For that very reason, Fermo . . .'

'Come now! Come now! *Les Misérables*, always the same farce. It's the scene with the conventionalist[12] now, isn't it? Don Santos is an insolent drunkard who would most certainly have the nerve to spit at the bishop, and Don Pompeyo would argue with His Lordship about whether or not God exists. You must not even think of it. It would be absurd to go!'

There were a few moments of silence. Carraspique, the only witness of the scene, trembled and in his terror admired the canon theologian's power and energy.

'It was true; he had His Lordship eating out of his hand.' Don Fermín continued:

'Besides, going there would serve no purpose whatsoever. Señor Carraspique himself has said so. Barinaga has lost consciousness, has he not? It is too late, there is nothing to be achieved there. The man is already dead, to all intents and purposes.'

Encouraged by his pious desire to save Don Santos, Carraspique ventured, in timorous tones:

'None the less, perhaps . . . There are many cases . . .'

'Cases of what?' demanded the canon. His look and his voice were like razors. 'Cases of what?' he repeated, since the other man did not reply.

'The sick man might come out of his delirium and regain his reason.'

'Do not believe it. Besides, that priest is there – Don Antero is there, to deal with such a contingency. His Lordship cannot, shall not, leave this building!'

And he did not leave it.

The man who was coming and going, incessantly, was the Pug, Campillo. He spoke in secret to Don Fermín and went back into the streets to collect rumours and spy on the enemy, which was gathered menacingly in the steep, narrow lane – the Calle de los Canónigos, one of the ugliest and most aristocratic in La Encimada – where Don Santos lived, almost directly in front of the canon's house.

By nightfall it was impossible to walk past Barinaga's dismal, bare shop without being elbowed and jostled. His friends – whose numbers had grown prodigiously in the course of a few hours – blocked the pavement from the shop-front to the gutter, in groups which whispered, mingled, divided.

Foja was there, and so were Orgaz senior, Orgaz junior and some of the other members of the Gentlemen's Club who attended the monthly dinners at which plots were hatched against the vicar-general. The ex-mayor, hurrying in and out of Don Santos's house, was as busy as a bee. Each time he came down with news he was surrounded by friends.

'He is expiring.'

'But is he still conscious?'

'He is indeed, the same as you and me.' It was a lie. Barinaga was talking as he died, but he did not know what he was saying and his speech was incoherent. He confused his hatred of the vicar-general with his complaints against his daughter. Sometimes he lamented his lot like King Lear; sometimes he swore like a trooper.

'And tell me, Señor Foja, are there any priests up there? They say that the canon theologian himself has come.'

'The canon theologian? That would crown it all! That would be adding sarcasm to the ... the ... No, *he* won't come. The priest upstairs is Don Antero, the parish priest. He's a good soul, poor fellow – a fanatic worthy of compassion – and he thinks he's doing his duty, but he might as well be talking to a brick wall. Don Santos was a man with deep-rooted convictions.'

'Was? Has he died already, then?' asked someone who had just arrived.

'No, sir, he has not died. I say was, because he is by now more out of this world than in it.'

'Don Pompeyo, too, has shown great energy, so they say.'

'Yes.'

'But it's easier when you're healthy.'

'And since he's not the one in danger ...'

'He'll die tonight.'

'The doctor hasn't been back.'

'Somoza was certain he'd die this afternoon.'

'Well that's why he hasn't been back, because he was wrong.'

'The priest says he'll last until tomorrow.'

'And he's dying of hunger.'

'He said so himself, so they say.'

'Yes, sir, those were his last lucid words,' Foja observed, contradicting himself.

'They say he said: "The bread of the body is what I need, so help me God I am dying of hunger!"'

A laugh escaped from Orgaz junior's lips and he tried to stifle it in the lapel of his cloak.

'Yes, you laugh, young man, this is a fine joking matter, I'm sure.'

'Heavens man – it's not the moribund I'm laughing at, it's the drollery of what he said.'

' "The profound lesson" you should have called it. He is dying of hunger, that is a fact. He is given a consecrated wafer, something I respect and venerate, but he is not given a bread roll.' Thus spake a schoolmaster persecuted by the enemies of liberalism – and by hunger.

'I am as good a Catholic as the next man,' said a master-gunsmith who worked in the Old Factory and had a long, grey, fuzzy goatee beard, a Christian socialist in his way. 'I am as good a Catholic as the next man, but in my opinion the canon theologian ought to be dragged to that lamppost forthwith and hung there to see the funeral procession setting off.'

'The truth is, gentlemen,' Foja observed, 'that if Don Santos dies outside the bosom of the Church, like a Jew, it is the vicar-general's fault.'

'No two ways about it.'

'Evidently.'

'Who could doubt it?'

'And tell me, Señor Foja, he won't be buried in consecrated ground, will he?'

'I believe not, the canons are as clear as crystal; what I mean to say is that the synod is categorical.' And he coloured a little, because he had not the faintest idea whether the canons were as clear as crystal, nor did he know whether the synod was even discussing the matter.

'So he's going to be buried like a dog!'

'That's the least of it,' said the master-gunsmith, 'all earth is holy – hallowed by the labour of man.'

'Besides, once you're dead . . .'

'Not so fast, gentlemen, not so fast,' Foja interrupted, not wanting to lose the opportunity to attack the canon theologian with the weapon which had just been placed in his hands. 'Such matters cannot be judged philosophically. Philosophically speaking it is clear that one does not mind where one is buried. But what about one's family? And society? And honour? You all know that the part of our *municipal* cemetery' (emphasizing the word) 'assigned to non-Catholic corpses, so to speak . . .'

Orgaz junior smirked.

'Yes, I know, young man, I know that I am guilty of a slight lapse. But you are much too literal-minded.'

The group of earnest progressives and socialists looked at the impertinent little doctor *en masse* and with contempt.

And the Christian socialist said:

'There is far too much literal-mindedness in this country as it is. The letter killeth, young sir, and, as I have said a thousand times, one thing of which we have more than enough in Spain is orators.'

'Well you're no mean speaker yourself, Señor Parcerisa; remember the Political Club before it folded.'

And Orgaz junior slapped the factory worker on the back.

Parcerisa smiled with satisfaction.

The conversation wandered. There was an argument about whether the municipal corporation was being energetic enough in its struggle with the bishop for control of the cemetery.

Meanwhile, clergymen and other friends who had come to see the sick man or his daughter were thronging the stairs. Don Pompeyo had ordered that Celestina be taken to her room, and there she received the priests and pious ladies who came to console her. The only people allowed by Guimarán into the sitting-room were the strong-minded, or, at least, those who, if not as strong-minded as he (for it would not have been easy to find any such), were in favour of allowing a dying man 'to expire within whichever confession he wishes, or indeed without any religion at all if he sees fit'.

'A glorious death!' Don Pompeyo whispered to the vicar-general's enemies when they came at the last moment to sympathize with Barinaga in his wretched plight. 'A glorious death! Such resolution! Such firmness! Even the death of Socrates pales in comparison – because nobody told Socrates to confess.'

As the people on their way to the stairs or coming back from them walked through the deserted shop, they ran their eyes over the empty shelves and the dust-covered shop-window, boarded up with ancient, rickety planks.

Upon the chocolate-coloured counter an oil-lamp shed a feeble light upon the dismal room, whose bareness made the visitors feel cold. The empty shelves could be regarded as a representation of Don Santos's stomach. He had sold the last of his stock, which had lain there covered in dust for years and years, to a village shopkeeper for next to nothing, and on the proceeds he had lived and drunk during the latter part of his life. Now rats gnawed the shelves of the shop and consumption gnawed the bowels of the shopkeeper.

He died at dawn.

The mist from Mount Corfín was still asleep on the roofs and in the streets of Vetusta. It was a mild, damp morning. Ash-coloured light filtered into the bedroom through the cracks in the shutters like sticky, dirty dust. Don Pompeyo had spent the night by the side of the dying man, alone, completely alone – for a lap-dog on its last legs, which never left the house, did not count. Guimarán opened the balcony windows wide; a gust of humid wind shook the calico curtain, and the dismal light of the leaden day fell upon the pallid warm corpse.

At eight o'clock Celestina was taken from the mourning house and at ten the body, in its plain, narrow, pine coffin, was deposited on the counter of the empty shop. No priest, no pious lady appeared there again.

'So much the better,' said Don Pompeyo, as busy as a bee.

'We don't want any ravens poking around here!' exclaimed Foja, as busy as another bee.

'We must organize a demonstration,' the ex-mayor, standing at the corpse's feet, declared to a large gathering of sympathizers and other enemies of the canon theologian. 'We must organize a demonstration, and since the government will not allow us any other kind, let's make the most of this opportunity. Moreover, this is iniquitous: the poor old man died of hunger, murdered by the sacrilegious monopolizers of La Cruz Roja. And, just to add to all the shame and dishonour, he is now denied an honourable Christian burial, and will have to be interred among the rubble behind that wall they built at the back of the cemetery – in the dung-heap assigned to civil burials by those infamous . . .'

'Starved to death and buried like a dog!' exclaimed the schoolmaster who was persecuted for his ideas.

'This calls for a really loud protest!'

'Yes, yes!'

'This is iniquitous!'

'This calls for a demonstration!'

Many of the conspirators looked like officers of the diocesan curia. These were friends of the archdeacon, the implacable Mourelo, who was plotting in the shadows.

'Now then. Señor Sousa, you write the stop-press column in El Alerta – you must delay today's edition a little, to leave time to insert something . . .'

'Yes, sir, I'm off to the printing-office right away, and with as much energy as the law – the damned press law – allows, I'm going to compose a note calling upon all liberals, friends of justice, et cetera . . . Don't you worry, Señor Foja.'

'Entitle the note: Civil Burial.'

'Yes sir, I shall.'

'In big letters.'

'As big as houses – you'll see.'

'It can serve as a notification to all liberals.'

'Will the people from the Factory come?'

'They most certainly will!' exclaimed Parcerisa. 'I'm going there at once to rouse them. This is something the government can't stop us from doing.'

'So long as there aren't any disturbances.'

The funeral took place a little before dusk, this being the only time at which the factory workers could attend.

It was raining. The water fell in fine, languid, diagonal threads. Umbrellas covered the street.

The canon theologian, spying on events from behind his study windows, saw a mass of black and brown. Suddenly, like a warrior raised in triumph upon his pavis, a long narrow black-covered coffin appeared on high, leaning forwards as it emerged from the shop and then stopping as if wondering what to do next. Don Santos was leaving home for the last time. He seemed to be wondering whether to defy the water or to go back indoors. He came out, and the coffin was lost from sight in the sea of dark silk and calico. Between the rails of the balcony above the door the head of a dirty black poodle appeared. The canon looked at it in terror. The dog stretched its neck, tried to look into the street, and pricked up its ears. It barked at the coffin and the umbrellas, and went back into hiding. It had been forgotten by everybody and left in the sitting-room by Don Pompeyo when he had locked up.

Guimarán, wearing a black frock-coat, was chief mourner.

Many factory workers, a few retail traders, and some shoemakers and tailors walked in ranks in front of the coffin, saying paternosters.

Guimarán had proposed that not a word should be uttered.

'The great Barinaga – that martyr for ideas – belonged to no Christian confession when he died, so it is contradictory . . .'

'Wait a minute,' Foja had retorted, with a grimace. 'Let us not be intransigent; let us not go to extremes. The whole thing will be more effective if prayers are recited.'

'It isn't an anti-Catholic demonstration,' the schoolmaster had observed.

'No – it's anticlerical,' another proven liberal had said.

'The vicar-general's the target,' a smooth-chinned member of Gloucester's secret police had stated.

It had, then, been agreed that prayers would be recited; and so they were. At the end of each prayer Parcerisa intoned: *Requiescat in pace.*

And the men in the ranks, carrying lighted candles, replied: *Requiescat in pace.*

Don Pompeyo liked neither the Latin nor the candles, but he had to compromise.

'The whole thing was self-contradictory, but Vetusta was not yet ready for a true civil burial.'

The poor women collecting water from public fountains, the shoe-binders and seamstresses promenading in the Calle del Comercio and the Boulevard, dragging their ill-shod feet through the mud, and the servant girls with baskets on their arms going to buy supper, crowded around the funeral procession as it passed; and by a large majority they condemned the effrontery of burying 'a Christian' (a synonym for 'a man') without priests. But certain well-built although badly turned-out girls praised the idea in loud voices.

One of them shouted –

'That's the way – put them pittance-merchants in a huff!'

This indiscreet remark provoked a retort from an opponent.

'Clear off, you crowd of Jews!' exclaimed a woman of the town, thumping her acquaintances – bricklayers' labourers and stone-cutters – on the back with her clog.

Behind the coffin walked a few representatives of the weaker sex, but, according to the girls with baskets and the women at the fountains, these were 'hussies'.

'Hey there, you little tart!'

'Where are you off to now, you whores?'

And Don Pompeyo's female sympathizers shrieked with laughter, thus showing how shallow-rooted were their convictions. Night was approaching, the cemetery was still a long way off, and the pace had to be quickened.

The rain started to fall vertically, in larger drops, the umbrellas resounded with its lugubrious drumming and water poured from all their ribs. Windows packed with curious faces were opened and shut.

The spectacle was, in the main, regarded with mocking curiosity and some scorn. 'But for that very reason the vicar-general's crime was even more despicable. That poor man Don Santos had died like a dog, and it was the vicar-general's fault; he had renounced religion, and it was the vicar-general's fault; he had died of hunger and without the sacraments, and it was the vicar-general's fault.'

'And now the revolutionaries, always ready to turn everything to their own advantage, were making the most of the opportunity to play another of their tricks.'

'And it's all the vicar-general's fault.'

'It's wrong to tighten the screws too much.'

'That man is the ruin of us all.'

These were the comments in the balcony windows, and after the windows were shut the criticism continued indoors. De Pas lost many friends that evening.

Nobody knew how it happened, but it soon became a commonplace (that is to say, a self-evident truth for Vetustans) that 'Barinaga had died like a dog and it was the canon theologian's fault'. Don Fermín's few remaining friends realized that it would be impossible, for a few days at least, to fight against this unjust yet widespread affirmation.

The procession left La Colonia and its high street, now a quagmire a kilometre long, and began to climb the hill to the cemetery. Once more the rain poured down slantwise upon the mourners, and the wind blew it under their umbrellas. They were lashed by water. A black cloud with the form of a monstrous bird covered the city, hurling the furious downpour upon the funeral procession. It seemed to be casting them out of Vetusta, hissing at them through the mouth of the wind at their backs.

The hill was taken at a lively pace. The percaline with which the wretched coffin was draped had split in two or three places and the white flesh of the wood could be seen running with water. The men bearing the corpse were shaking it to and fro. Their weariness and a certain unconscious superstition had caused them to lose much of the respect due to the dead man. All the candles had gone out and were dripping water instead of wax. The people in the ranks were talking in loud voices.

'Get a move on!' was heard at every turn.

Some people went so far as to crack jokes about the storm. The mourners close to the body were more circumspect, but everyone agreed that the pace must be quickened.

The fury of the elements had aroused many silent worries.

Don Pompeyo's feet were drenched, and he knew that the damp was bad for him – it attacked his nerves and made him lose heart.

'God doesn't exist, of course,' he was thinking, 'but if he did exist anyone would think he had sent these devilish downpours to scourge us.'

They reached the top of the hill. The cemetery wall stood out against the leaden sky like a black band marking the horizon. Nothing could be seen clearly. The cypresses behind the wall were swaying. They looked like ghosts whispering into each other's ears, hatching some plot against the impertinent people on their way to disturb the peace of the graveyard.

The cortège came to a halt at the gate. Its entrance was barred. Certain formalities had been overlooked, and a malevolent grave-digger – and behind him, perhaps, a malevolent chaplain – was finding obstacles in the regulations.

'Where's Foja?' cried Don Pompeyo, who did not feel strong enough to wage yet another battle against clerical obscurantism.

Foja was nowhere to be found. Nobody had seen him in the procession.

Don Pompeyo felt his spirits drooping. 'I'm all alone, that Bragga-dochio has left me alone.'

But he gathered strength from despair and, with the help of the general indignation, prevailed over the gravedigger. The procession entered the cemetery – not through its main gate but through a breach in the wall which surrounded the small, filthy yard, overgrown with nettles and gorse, in which people who died outside the Catholic Church were buried. There had been very few such people. The gravedigger could only recall three or four burials of this sort.

The mourners departed without ceremony; the wind lashed them away with whips of ice-cold water.

Don Pompeyo Guimarán was the last to leave the graveyard. 'It was his duty to be last.'

Night had closed in. Don Pompeyo stopped, alone – utterly alone – on top of the hill. 'Twenty paces behind him stood the cemetery wall. Behind the cemetery wall lay his unfortunate friend – deserted, and so soon forgotten by everyone. There he lay, a mere couple of inches underground, separated by a wall which was a dishonour from all the other Vetustans who had lived and died; lost, like the skeleton of some wretched nag, among nettles, gorse and mud. Dogs and cats could get into the civil cemetery through the breach in its wall. The place was exposed to every kind of profanation. And there lay Don Santos, the good Barinaga, who once had sold patens and monstrances, and who had believed in them – once upon a time. And it was all his own work . . . the work of Don Pompeyo Guimarán. He, in the Restaurant and Café de la Paz, was the one who had started to demolish the citadel of that poor shopkeeper's faith!'

A shudder ran through Guimarán's body. He buttoned up his frock-coat. 'Coming without his cloak was another unwise thing to have done.'

And then he realized that he could no longer feel the rain. 'It must have stopped.' Over Vetusta, amid great areas of darkness, pale lights shone – the stars; in the darkness of the city he could see symmetrical red dots – the street lamps.

Guimarán shivered again; he could feel that his feet were wet and he quickened his step. What was more, he imagined that he was being followed; that from time to time a light finger touched the skirts of his frock-coat and the hair on the back of his neck. . . . And since he was alone, quite certainly alone, he had no objections to breaking out into a nimble trot downhill, with his umbrella under his arm.

'No, God doesn't exist,' he was thinking, 'but if he did, I'd be in a pretty pickle.'

Further down the hill –

'And in any case, the prospect of being buried for certain – inescapably – in that dung-heap up there – isn't a very amusing prospect.'

On he ran, shivering from time to time.

That night Don Pompeyo was feverish.

'Just as he had said: the damp!'

And he was delirious.

'He dreamed that he was made of stone and mortar and had a breach in his belly and through it cats and dogs went in and out, as well as the occasional little demon with a tail.'

XXIII

Tecum principium in die virtutis tuae in splendoribus sanctorum, ex utero ante luciferum genui te.[1]

The judge's wife read these words without fully understanding them. The translation in her book of devotion said: 'Thine shall be the princedom and the sovereignty in the day of thy power and in the midst of the light which shall shine in thy saints: I have engendered thee in my bowels before the birth of the star of the morning.'

Further on, with her eyes riveted to the book, Ana read: *Dominus dixit ad me: Filius meus es tu, ego hodie genui te. Alleluia.*[2]

Yes, yes, Alleluia! Alleluia! her heart cried, and the organ, as if it understood what her heart wanted, let out merry mischievous impish notes which filled the dark spaces of the cathedral, rose to the vault and struggled to get outside, to soar to heaven and soak the world in playful music. The organ was singing:

> *In a boat full of flowers,*
> *O Mary of Sorrows,*
> *I'm off to Havana*
> *Tomorrow, tomorrow,*

but suddenly it changed its tune and cried –

> *I've never seen the priest's house*
> *Looking like it does today . . .*

and forgetting its manners it interrupted itself and sang –

> *And up with Manolillo,*
> *And down with Manolé,*
> *The last time they conscripted,*
> *I kept the men away;*
> *But if I can the next time*
> *Is something I can't say.*
> *So up with Manolillo,*
> *Manolillo Manolé.*

And all this because one thousand eight hundred and seventy-odd years previously Baby Jesus had been born in the stable in Bethlehem. Of what concern was it to the organ? Yet it seemed to be mad with joy – going off its head and pouring from those conical tubes, from those pipes and trumpets, streams of notes like little lights, illuminating souls.

The cathedral was dark. Here and there an oil-lamp with a reflector, hanging from a nail on a pillar, interrupted the gloom, which returned a little further on. The lamps were scattered throughout nave, aisles and retrochoir and, together with the candles on the high altar and in the choir, shining on high in the distance like stars, they provided the only light in the cathedral. But the joyful music bouncing from pillar to chapel and from floor to vaults seemed to fill it with dawn sunshine. Dawn, however, was many hours away. Midnight mass was starting.

To express the Christian joy of this sublime moment the organ was recalling traditional tunes of the region and songs which popular caprice had made fashionable during recent years. Ana's soul was quivering with tender happy religious emotion and brimming over with universal charity: love for all men and all creatures – for the birds, for the beasts, for the grasses of the field, for the worms of the earth, for the waves of the sea, for the sighs of the air. 'It was perfectly plain, religion couldn't be more simple or more clear: God was in heaven, loving and reigning over His wonderful work, the universe; the Son of God had been born on earth and this honour, this proof of God's love, made everybody happier and nobler. It didn't matter that so many centuries had gone by, love didn't worry about time, it was as true now as in the days of the apostles that God had come into the world – the reason for all his creatures to be joyful hadn't changed. So the organist was quite right to declare these humble tunes, which brought happiness to ordinary people and which Vetustan girls sang at their boisterous open-air dances, to be worthy of the cathedral. Ana regarded these reminiscences of ephemeral songs – forgotten puffs of air – as a delicate act of charity on the part of the musician. Remembering what was humblest, paltriest, a gust of wind which had gone away, and dignifying profane emotions – love and youthful happiness – by making their songs resound in church, as an offering at the feet of Jesus . . . all this was beautiful, and the religion which permitted it was maternal, loving, artistic.

'There were no barriers in that place, at that moment, between the church and the world. Nature was pouring in through the cathedral door; and in the organ music there were reminiscences of the summer, of joyful fiestas in the country, of sailors' songs by the side of the sea; and there was the smell of thyme and of honeysuckle, and the smell of the beach, and the wild elusive smell of the woods, and prevailing over them all a mystical perfume, of ineffable poetry, which brought tears to the eyes.' Staying up late was upsetting her nerves. When her thoughts soared they were soon lost; when they expanded they faded into nothingness. She leaned her head against the baroque belly of a new stone altar, the main altar in the chapel where she knelt, buried in shadow. She was hardly thinking now; she was only feeling.

At either end of the high railing of gilded brass which separated the chancel from the crossing there were gaps for two iron pulpits of the most delicate workmanship. One golden eagle with wings outstretched was for the Epistle, and another for the Gospel. In the pulpit to the left of the chancel Ana saw Gloucester's figure appear, as always twisted yet arrogant; his sumptuous brocaded chasuble flashed in the light of the processional candles in the hands of the acolytes accompanying him. As soon as the organ was quiet the archdeacon, in the manner of someone determined to interrupt a joke and introduce a serious note, read the Epistle of St Paul the Apostle to Titus, chapter 2,[3] giving it a meaning which it does not possess. Gloucester enjoyed holding the public's attention, and he read in a slow voice, emphasizing the word-endings in *-us*, *-i* and *-is*. From his tone of voice one might have thought that St Paul's Epistle was his own work – a little piece he had scribbled once. As soon as the presumptuous archdeacon had finished, and taking as much notice of him as if he had been talking to a brick wall, the organ burst out laughing, let out all its stops and again flooded the cathedral with streams of joyful song; its bellows seemed to be blowing in a forge from which sparks of boisterous music flew; now it was playing like the bagpipes of the region, imitating the municipal piper's crude, faulty renderings of the toast from *La Traviata* and the Miserere from *Il Trovatore*. Finally, when Ripamilán poked his sprightly little head over the handrail of the other pulpit to sing the Gospel, the organist set to work on 'La mandilona':[4]

> So now you're just as glad as you could wish,
> *Jellyfish,*
> *Jellyfish,*
> *Jellyfish.*

The Carlists and liberals packed into the crossing welcomed this piece of good humour with whispers and stifled laughter, and in their reaction the judge's wife saw a sign of universal peace. At that moment, she thought, with everybody united before everybody's God as He was born, political differences were forgotten trivialities.

Ripamilán could not help smiling while, with a struggle, he placed upon the wings of the eagle the book from which he was to read the Gospel according to St Luke.

The archdeacon stood waiting on the stairs of his pulpit with his forearms crossed in front of him. Keeping guard by his side were two acolytes holding processional candles. Celedonio was one of them.

'*Secuentia Sancti Evangelii secundum Lucaaam!*' Ripamilán sang, half-asleep; taking advantage of the plainsong, he yawned on the last note.

'*In illo tempore . . .!*' he continued. In those days there went out a decree that all the world should be enrolled. It was the doing of Caesar Augustus, who was very keen on statistics. 'This enrolling was made by Cyrenius, who was later governor of Syria.' Ripamilán was falling asleep over Cyrenius, but when he reached the enrolling of Joseph he livened up, imagining the holy couple on the road to Bethlehem. 'And so it was that while they were there the days were accomplished when she should be delivered; and she brought forth her firstborn son and wrapped him in swaddling clothes and laid him in a manger.'

Ripamilán was reading slowly now, hoping that his audience might listen. When he reached the shepherds keeping watch over their flock by night he remembered his love of eclogues and felt deeply moved.

The judge's wife, following the simple, sublime story in her book of devotion, was even more affected. 'Baby Jesus! Baby Jesus! Now she could appreciate all the grandeur of that gentle poetic religion which began in a cradle and ended on a cross. Blessed God! Such sweetness flowing through her soul, such a taste of honey in her heart – or somewhere a little below it, more towards the middle of her body! And Ripamilán up there, that little old man describing the birth as if he had just come away from it! Ripamilán, too, was beautiful, in his way.'

In the meantime the congregation was becoming impatient, its stock of good manners was running out and, in the corners of the cathedral, jokers were beginning to make people laugh. In the retrochoir, the darkest part of the cathedral, young gentlemen hidden in chapels and in the shadows of pillars were amusing themselves by rolling over the marble draughts-board of the floor copper coins whose profane tinkling awoke the covetousness of the little ones. Bands of street arabs who, all eyes, had been awaiting this traditional profanation ran out and made the faithful laugh as they fell upon each successive coin in a bundle of flesh and rags, shoving each other, trampling on each other, biting each other, fighting over a farthing.

But the patrol came and the bundle of street arabs broke up, each running off in a different direction. In charge of the patrol was the canon theologian, wearing a rochet and a choir-cope; in his hands, which were crossed in front of him, he held his biretta. He was flanked by two acolytes each bearing a wax candle and stepping with solemn tread. The patrol was walking around the nave, the aisles and the retrochoir, keeping watch to prevent the worst abuses. The darkness of the cathedral, the excesses of the classical Christmas Eve collation, and the lack of respect which was believed to be a traditional feature of midnight mass, all helped to make such precautions necessary.

There was another kind of profanation which the patrol could not prevent. The congregation was huddled together below the pulpits in the crossing, pressing up against each other and against the altar-rails and the two barriers running from these to the choir. The few who preferred comfort to the human warmth of that mass of flesh were much at their ease in other parts of the cathedral. Everyone is equal in church, and so all classes, ages and conditions mingled in the crossing. Obdulia Fandiño stood hearing mass with her book of devotion upon the shoulder of Pedro, the Vegallanas' chef, while on the back of her neck she could feel the breath of Pepe Ronzal, who could not and perhaps did not want to prevent those behind him from pushing. For Obdulia this was what religion was all about –

pressing up against each other, squeezing each other, without any distinctions of class or sex, during those solemn ceremonies with which the Church commemorates important events about which she – Obdulia – had only the haziest of notions. Visitación was in the crossing, too, poking her head between the altar-rails. Near her Paco Vegallana was pretending to fight against the anonymous force which, like a surging sea, thrust him on to his cousin Edelmira. This girl, as red as a cherry, her eyes fastened on a picture of St Joseph in her book of devotion, and her soul hanging on her cousin's every movement, was trying to escape from the barrier, where she was at risk of being crushed by human waves imitating, in the gloom of the cathedral, the waves of the sea as they beat against a rock in its own black shadow. All the *youthful elements* of which *El Lábaro* spoke in its chronicle of the tiny *great world* of Vetusta were there, in the cathedral crossing, listening half-asleep to the organ, digesting their Christmas Eve collation, seeing small lights, feeling the shivers of fatigue and the urges of the flesh. Sleepiness was bringing with it impious absurdities, ideas which were profanations, and which were thrust aside so as to attend to the venial sins of immediate reality. Looks and smiles – if distance did not allow anything else – threaded their way to and fro as best they could through the dense forest of human heads. There was much coughing, not all of it innocent. These young ladies and gentlemen would have been happy to remain until daybreak in this soporific stillness, this nightmare-darkness. Obdulia was thinking (she only ever *said* this to her most intimate friends, of course) that gallivanting (what Joaquín Orgaz called *making eyes*), always an agreeable activity, was even more so in church, because there it had *cachet*. And for the widow the things with *cachet* were the best things.

'The immorality manifested by that agglomeration of bad Christians' was the subject of the thoughts of Don Pompeyo Guimarán who, not yet fully recovered from a fever, had consented to dine in the Gentlemen's Club with Don Alvaro, Orgaz, Foja and other birds of the night, and had come on with them to midnight mass.

'Yes, it weighed heavy on his fuddled conscience – yet there he was, in the cathedral. They had made him tipsy with a sweet liqueur which was turning his stomach, a liqueur which had converted his insides into something like a perfumery – ugh! how revolting! and then they had made him eat more than he should and in the end drink everything available. When he made ready to return home, if one of those gentlemen would be so kind as to accompany him – oh! could anyone imagine a more tedious and offensive trick? – they had all ended up in the middle of the cathedral, where he had not set foot for many a year. He had protested, he had attempted to leave, but they had not permitted him to do so – and he did not dare try to find his way home alone, and it was cold outside.'

'Gentlemen,' he muttered to Don Alvaro and Orgaz, 'I wish to make it quite clear that it is only under protest, and impelled by main force – the force of your intoxication – that I remain in this place.'

'Splendid, my dear fellow, splendid.'

'I wish to make it quite clear that this is not an abdication ...'

'Oh no – no one could possibly take it for an – abdication.'

'Or a profanation. I respect all religions, even though I do not profess any of them. What will the world say if it discovers that I have come here with a crowd of professional drunkards? I recognize that Turtle-dove has every right to kick or whip me out of the cathedral.'

'Yes, dear fellow, we know,' Foja managed to stammer. 'In a nutshell: Don Pompeyo admits that he is like – a dog at mass.'

'An exact comparison – that is correct, my position here is that of a dog. Besides, this is repugnant. Listen to that organist, in all probability as drunk as you are: he is turning the temple of the Lord, so to speak, into a cheap dance – into an orgy. Gentlemen, what *do* we believe in – the birth of Christ or the resuscitation of the god Pan?'

'Pam poom pim poom! I am the general! Boom boom!'

This was sung in a low voice by Joaquín Orgaz as he beat a tattoo upon Guimarán's head. And the little doctor hurried out of the dark chapel in which this scene was enacted, to look for a needle in a haystack, as he put it – that is, to look for Obdulia in the crowd. He found her, sandwiched between Paco's chef and the formidable Ronzal. Joaquín turned on his heel and hurried back to Don Pompeyo.

Only a high railing separated the chapel in which the judge's wife was hearing mass from the chapel in which the night-birds from the Gentlemen's Club were lurking. Ana could hear Orgaz dissuading the atheist from leaving the cathedral. But people were not recognizable by sight from one chapel to the next, only shadowy outlines were visible.

When the patrol passed by, however, everything changed. In the flickering yellow light of the acolytes' candles Anita could see both the canon theologian's arrogant figure and the graceful well-formed figure of Don Alvaro who, with his eyes almost shut, his head bowed, half-asleep, and holding on to the railing between the two chapels, seemed to be attending to the service with all the recollection of a sincere Christian.

The canon saw the judge's wife and Don Alvaro, side by side almost, although the railing was between them. His biretta shook in his hands and he had to make a great effort to continue in the procession, which at that moment seemed ridiculous.

Mesía did not see the canon theologian or the judge's wife or anybody. He was asleep on his feet and he was drunk. But since he never made any scandal when he was in this state, nobody suspected anything.

Ana could still see Don Alvaro even after the patrol, with its sleepy lights, had gone past. She could see him in her mind's eye, and she imagined him dressed in red, in very tight-fitting, very smart clothes. She did not know whether the clothes were of an operatic Mephistopheles or an elegant huntsman, but her enemy was handsome, very handsome. 'And there he was close to her, behind that railing – he had only to walk a few steps to touch her!' The organ was saying goodbye to the faithful with the craziest tunes in its repertoire, among them a song which Ana had first heard by Mesía's side at the fiesta of St Blasius earlier in the year. She closed her eyes, which had filled with tears. 'Look how temptation was attacking her now! She was becoming soft and sentimental, memories were returning, with all their special authority – always sacred, sweet, dear . . . What had happened at the fiesta of St Blasius? Nothing, and yet recalling that afternoon (it was the organist's fault) Ana could see Don Alvaro by her side, dying of love, struck dumb with respect, and could see herself happy in the depths of her soul – oh yes, yes! in the depths of her soul, or of her body, or of hell – depths not reached by the gentle conversations about mysticism and brotherhood which she still enjoyed with the canon who had just walked past with his hands crossed in front of him, surrounded by acolytes.'

By the time Ana tried to shake these untimely and sinful images from her head the cathedral was emptying. She felt cold and almost afraid of the shadow of the confessional against which she was leaning. She realized that she was about to fall asleep, and so she stood up and walked out.

The organ was silent, like a drunkard asleep after disturbing everyone with his racket. The lights were being turned out.

In the porch Ana met the canon theologian.

He was pale – she saw him by the light of a match which someone lit near by. When the porch was dark again he approached her and, in a sweet voice in which there was a note of complaint, asked:

'Did you enjoy yourself in mass?'

'Enjoy myself in mass?'

'I mean, did you enjoy – the music they played – the hymns they sang?'

Ana realized that her confessor did not know what he was saying.

They were walking out of the porch. In the street there were a few groups of stragglers. They had to separate.

'Good-night, good-night!' said the canon in a bad-tempered voice, almost an irate one.

Without another word he turned his collar up and strode away towards his home.

Ana wanted to follow him. She had annoyed him, although she did not know how. What had she done? She had thought about the enemy, rejoiced in hateful remembrances. But how could Don Fermín know? And striding away like that! Profound compassion and a gratitude which was like love invaded her soul. 'Oh! why couldn't she run after that man, call out to him, comfort him – prove that she hadn't changed, that she wasn't turning her back on him like so many other women? Yes: they were turning their backs on him – on the saint, the man of genius, the martyr to piety; the women who had fought over him were turning their backs on him, and why? Because of vile calumnies. She would never do such a thing, she believed in him, she'd follow him blindly to the end of the world; she knew that he, and St Teresa, had saved her from hell.' But she couldn't run after him to tell him all this. 'To begin with, what would Petra think – standing there by her side, silent, smiling, more disagreeable every day – and more obliging – and more unbearable!'

While the canon theologian and Ana had been talking, Petra had discreetly moved two paces away. When she saw the canon turn up his cloak-collar with such a flourish, and stride off into the night, she thought, 'They're having a tiff,' and she smiled.

The judge's wife walked towards the Plaza Nueva. She was half-asleep – almost intoxicated with sleep and music and fancies. Hardly knowing how she had arrived there she found herself in her porch thinking about Baby Jesus in his cradle, in a porch in Bethlehem. She imagined the scene as it was represented in a crib which she had seen early that night.

When she was alone in her boudoir she let down her hair in front of the mirror, and it fell over her shoulders.

'It was true, she did look like the Virgin, like the Madonna of the Chair – but the child was missing,' and with her arms crossed she sat contemplating herself for a few seconds.

Sometimes she was afraid of going mad. Her piety would suddenly desert her and she would be overcome by an invincible lethargy which stopped her trying to find in prayer or in religious books a remedy for the dryness of her soul. She seldom meditated now. If she paused to evoke religious thoughts, to contemplate sacred abstractions, what came before her was not God but Mesía.

'She had believed that the Ana who fluctuated between despair and hope, between rebelliousness and resignation, had died – but it was not so; she was still there, inside her; subjugated, yes, persecuted, cowering in a corner, but not dead. Just as St John the Baptist cried out from the underground tank in which Herod kept him prisoner, so the rebellious Ana, the sinner in thought, was crying out from the depths of her own body, and the captive cries could be heard throughout her brain. That forbidden Ana was a kind of tapeworm eating away all the good intentions of the devout Ana, the canon theologian's humble, affectionate sister.

'Baby Jesus! That image excited such sweet emotions! But why should evoking it have resulted in torture for her brain?'

Her need to love a child, a vague, tender longing, was awaking, yet again. Ana saw herself in her boudoir in the midst of a solitude which frightened her and made her feel cold. A child, a child would have put an end to the anguished struggles of her idle spirit, which was searching far from the natural centre of life – the home – for the satisfaction of her longing for love, for something to assuage her thirst for self-sacrifice!

Ana was hardly aware of what she was doing as she left her boudoir, walked through the drawing-room, in the dark as usual, along a passage, through the dining-room, along the gallery, and crept up to Quintanar's bedroom door. It was ajar and she could see light in the chink. Her husband was not asleep – she could hear murmured words.

'Who can he be talking to?' Ana brought her face to the line of light and saw Don Víctor sitting on his bed. From the waist down he was covered with bedclothes, and the rest of his body was wrapped in a red flannel jacket. Because of a respectable superstition he never wore sleeping-caps; although he was incapable of suspecting his dear Ana of the slightest misdemeanour, a certain literary prejudice made him avoid them – he said that the point on the end of the sleeping-cap attracted the attributes of conjugal infidelity. But that night he had felt cold and, not possessing any cotton or linen caps, had donned the green smoking-cap with a long golden tassel which he wore in the daytime. Ana saw and heard Quintanar, dressed in these grotesque clothes, reading aloud by the light of a candle in a flexible support fastened to the wall.

But her husband was not merely reading, he was declaiming. Half-afraid that he might have gone mad, Ana saw him, full of enthusiasm, holding aloft a hand in whose tremulous grip was an enormous sword with a splendid convoluted cross-guard. Don Víctor was reading with emphasis and brandishing the gleaming steel as if he were knighting the familiar spirit of the cloak-and-dagger theatre.

Given the situation in which Quintanar believed himself to be, cutting the air with cold steel was a very understandable and indeed noble action. He was engaged in defending with beautiful seventeenth-century verses a lady whose brother was trying to unmask and kill her, and he was swearing in *quintillas*[5] that, being a gentleman, he would sooner be chopped up into little pieces than permit such an atrocity.

But since the judge's wife knew none of this, her heart sank to her feet when she considered that this man sitting in his bed at two o'clock in the morning, wearing a cap and a flannel jacket, and flailing the air, was her husband; the only person in this world with a right to her caresses and her love – with a right to give her the delights which she believed motherhood to contain and for which she was aching, thanks to the stable in Bethlehem and other such reminders.

She had come to her husband's room to talk with him, if he was awake, to talk about midnight mass, sitting beside him on his bed. Poor Ana wanted to rid herself of those thoughts which were driving her crazy, and those contradictory feelings of exalted piety and disgruntled rebellion of the flesh; she wanted sweet words, cordial intimacy, family warmth – and something more, although she was vaguely ashamed about it. She wanted... she didn't know what it was, but she had a right to it – and instead she found her husband declaiming and looking like a jack-in-the-box. A wave of indignation rose to her face and coloured it fiery red. She decided not to enter her husband's theatre and took a step backwards. But her dressing-gown disturbed something on the floor, and he called out in alarm:

'Who is it?'

Ana did not reply.

'Who is it?' repeated Don Víctor, in an agitated voice, for he had frightened himself a little with his blustering verses.

After a pause he said somewhat more calmly:

'Petra! Petra! Is that you, Petra?'

A suspicion crossed Ana's mind, a suspicion which seemed grotesque. It was as if the temptation persecuting her were now assuming another form:

'Might the man be her housemaid's lover?'

'Anselmo! Anselmo!' added Don Víctor in the same gentle, familiar voice.

And Ana tiptoed away, ashamed of many things – of her suspicion, of her vague, ridiculous desire, of her husband, of herself.

'What a preposterous trip through rooms and passages, in the dark, at two o'clock in the morning, in search of the impossible, a grotesque farce, a comic absurdity – comic, yet so bitter for her!' As she felt her way around the objects in the drawing-room she thought, involuntarily as usual, 'If by some miracle, by some miracle of love, Alvaro were to appear here, now, in this darkness, and hold me, his arms tight around my waist, and say to me: you are my love – what could I do, unhappy wretch, weak flesh, but surrender, lose myself in his arms.' 'Yes, I'd surrender!' everything inside her cried. Almost fainting, she felt for the damask sofa and stretched out upon it half-naked and wept, for how long she did not know.

The clock in the dining-room chimed and brought Ana out of her feverish somnolence. Shivering with cold, she felt her way to her boudoir, her hair loose over her shoulders, and her dressing-gown open. The sperm-candle, reflected in the mirror, was flickering low, on the point of going out, and Ana saw herself as a beautiful ghost floating against the dark background of her bedroom. She smiled at her own reflection with a bitterness which seemed demoniacal. She was afraid of herself, and ran to take refuge in her bedroom where, standing on the tiger-skin, she slipped off the garments which she did not wear in bed. In a corner of the room Petra had left the whisks with which she cleaned those pieces of furniture that were in need of this discipline. Telling herself that she was drunk (but not knowing how it could have happened), catching glimpses amidst cambric of her own satin flesh, Ana sprang to the corner, grasped the whisks with their lashes of black wool and without pity whipped her useless beauty once, twice, ten times. But since this, too, was ridiculous she flung the prosaic disciplines aside and leaped into her bed like a bacchante; yet the pleasurable coldness of the sheets with their hint of dampness only heightened her rage, and she sank her teeth into the pillow. In order to escape from herself she tried to stop thinking, and half an hour later she fell asleep.

At eight o'clock that morning Ana was walking alone past the canon theologian's house. Why had she come here? This was not the way to the cathedral. A vague hope of meeting Don Fermín, of seeing him in his balcony, a hope of something which she could not define, had made her go along the Calle de los Canónigos. She did not find what she was looking for. She made her way to the cathedral and sat on the edge of the low wooden platform which covered the stone floor in the crossing. With her head resting on the ice-cold gilded central barrier she heard mass from a distance, and then recited interminable prayers and day-dreamed until the divine office was over. She saw her friend walking towards the choir and gave him an affectionate smile, charged with that tenderness which seared deep into his body like fire. He did not smile, but his look was intense, brief but eloquent: it accused, complained, questioned, forgave, said thank you. And he walked on. He entered the choir and went to his corner. When the canonical hours finished he left the choir, bowed to the altar, and walked to the sacristy; a little later the judge's wife saw him again, without his rochet, mozetta and cope, now wearing his cloak and holding his hat in his hand. Again they exchanged looks. This time they both smiled. Five minutes later Ana stood up. Without a word or even a sign they had agreed to meet. Soon they were both in Doña Petronila Rianzares's sitting-room, together with many ladies and three priests. The cream of what *El Alerta* called the clerical element of the town was gathered there. The ladies, most of them of respectable appearance, and some of them young and pretty, were celebrating the birth of Our Lord Jesus Christ with evangelical joy, as if He had come into the world exclusively for them and a few other distinguished persons. They thought of the Nativity of Our Lord as some kind of family party. Doña Petronila, in an ancient, ill-made mantelet of black satin, was receiving her devout world as if today were her birthday. All was smiles, handshakes, mutual praise and sonorous laughter reflecting the inner contentment of souls in a state of grace. The canon theologian was received in triumph. Such courtesy! Such consideration! Within the hour he had to be in the cathedral, in the pulpit, preaching one of the special sermons which it was his particular duty to deliver, but nevertheless he had first come to wish his friend Doña Petronila Happy Christmas! 'What a man! What an angel! What a word-spinner! What a luminary!'

The disrepute of Don Fermín had not reached Doña Petronila's circle. Nobody there doubted or questioned his virtue. Whether any of those present dared slander the saint outside that venerable sitting-room was something which nobody knew or wanted to know. But in Constantine the Great's house nobody would make bold to entertain suspicions about the holiness of the Chrysostom of Vetusta.

Ana and Don Fermín could only be alone together for a short time, in Doña Petronila's boudoir. She found them there. But smiling and waving from the door she said:

'No, don't worry. I was only coming for some papers. They can wait until later.'

Ana was going to call out – 'it wasn't a secret – why was she going away?' – but a look from the canon stopped her.

'Leave her be,' he said in the imperative tone which Ana always liked to hear. This was what she wanted – she wanted him to command, to be in charge of her and of her actions.

Ana turned to face the canon, who was standing by the balcony, and smiled at him as a little earlier she had smiled in the cathedral. Her smile asked him to forgive her; and blessed him.

Don Fermín was pale, his voice trembled, and he was thinner than in the summer, Anita thought.

'I am so tired!' he said, sighing with profound sorrow.

He dropped into an easy chair and Ana went to sit by his side.

'I am so lonely!'

'Lonely? I don't understand.'

'My mother worships me, I know – but she is not like me. She does her best for me, but her way is no longer my way – you know all about that, Ana.'

'But why are you lonely? What about – other people?'

'Other people are not my mother. They do not belong to me. What's wrong, Ana? Are you feeling ill? What is it? Wait, I'll call.'

'No, no, you mustn't. Just a shiver – a tremble. It's gone now – nothing at all.'

'Are you going to have an attack?'

'No, the attacks begin with different symptoms. Don't worry, don't worry. It's the cold – the damp – nothing.'

They fell silent.

De Pas could see that Ana was struggling not to cry.

'What is happening? I must know everything, I have a right – I believe I have a right.'

Ana fell on her knees at the feet of her elder brother and sobbed:

'Yes, you will know everything, but not here. In church. Tomorrow – early tomorrow morning.'

'No, no. Today, this afternoon!'

He rose to his feet. Ana's face was hidden in her hands and she did not see him lift his clenched fists to his eyes. He strode twice around the boudoir and then back to her; she was still on her knees, sobbing, trying not to cry aloud.

'*Now*, Ana – tell me now, here. There's still time.'

'No, not here. You must go – you'll be late.'

'But what is this – what is happening? For pity's sake, madam, show some compassion, Ana – can't you see I'm shaking like a leaf? I'm not a toy to be played with . . . What's happening, what must I fear? Yesterday, that man was drunk. He and others walked past my house, at three o'clock in the morning. Orgaz was shouting to him: "Alvaro! Alvaro! This is where your rival lives." That was what he said, your rival – the calumny has gone that far!'

Ana looked at Fermín in horror. She seemed not to understand him.

'Yes, madam, they resent our friendship, they want to separate us, and they might succeed: throw mud between us – and there's an end to it.'

It was the first time that he had spoken to Ana in this way. In their conversations they had never mentioned the danger, the calumny. He had thought about it often enough, but it did not suit his plans to say to her: I am a man, you are a woman, the world is evil-minded. But now, unable to help himself, he had said: *your rival*, emphasizing the words – even though they might frighten her.

'Yes, yes, he too was a man, he could be a rival for her love, why not?' He did not recognize himself. He was pacing about the boudoir like a wild beast in a cage; he realized that he was capable of saying all the things which his excited passion and his wounded self-esteem were prompting him to say. Afterwards he would regret having spoken – but that did not matter, now he must get things off his chest. 'Oh! he was not the man he used to be.'

Ana rose to her feet, waited for Don Fermín to reach the other end of the room, and said:

'You haven't understood me. I'm the one who's alone, you're the ungrateful one. Perhaps your mother loves you better than I do, but she doesn't owe you as much. I have sworn to God to die for you if need be. Everybody is slandering you, persecuting you – and I hate everybody and I am throwing myself at your feet to tell you my closest secrets. I didn't know what sacrifice I could make for you. Now I do know. You have revealed it to me. People gossip about my honour – the wretches! I hadn't suspected that anyone could gossip about that – but still, let them gossip. I will not be separated from the martyr who is being persecuted and slandered – just as if he were being stoned. I want the stones that bruise you to bruise me too. I shall be at your feet until you die. Now I know what I am good for! Now I know what I was born for! For this – kneeling at the feet of the martyr who is being killed by calumny.'

'Hush! Hush, Anita, she's coming.'

The canon theologian, with cheeks as red as coals of fire, strode back to the judge's wife, clasped her hands, and said in a hoarse voice, choking with passion:

'Ana, Ana! This afternoon without fail. And now, to the cathedral – by the altar of the Immaculate Conception, in front of the pulpit.'

'I'll see you this afternoon, but don't worry. Nearly everything I had to tell you I've told you already.'

'But that man . . .!'

'That man is nothing to me.'

Doña Petronila's voice had sounded out as the canon warned Ana of her arrival. She was speaking some distance away:

'The canon theologian is coming at once, yes at once, he's in my boudoir alone, looking over his sermon, I expect.'

As Doña Petronila walked into the room Ana was turning around to hide from her friend the confusion which he would have read on her face, had he not been obliged to look at the lady of the house, who cried:

'Come on, get ready, get ready. They're waiting for you – I believe mass has started.'

The canon theologian left through the bedroom door, at which the mistress of the house had appeared.

Constantine the Great contemplated the judge's wife and, taking her head between her hands, gave her a noisy kiss on the forehead. Then she said: 'This Rose of Jericho[6] is most beauteous today!'

'To the cathedral, to the cathedral!' the people in the sitting-room were crying.

Ana and the mother-bishop walked into the nave as De Pas climbed with majestic tread to the pulpit in which at the beginning of the day Ripamilán had sung the Gospel according to St Luke.

They found a place at the foot of the altar of the Immaculate Conception.

'There's a perfect view from here,' said Doña Petronila.

Leaning towards Ana she added in a quiet, honeyed voice:

'Just look, that apostle of the Gentiles[7] is really most handsome today! What a rochet! It looks like foam. In the name of the Father, the Son, and the Holy Ghost . . .'

XXIV

'But what if he insists?'

'He's very weak-willed – if we stand firm he'll give in.'

'And if he doesn't give in, if he puts his foot down?'

'But why should he?'

'Because he's like that. I don't know who can have put it into his head, but he says I'll make him look ridiculous if I don't go. And he alludes to us, he speaks of "the man who is to blame for all this" – he says that he isn't the master of his own house, that it's being governed from outside, that the marchioness is beginning to behave rather coldly towards us because we have snubbed her so often – and I don't know what else!'

'Well, if he does insist, we shall have to go to the blessed ball. We mustn't annoy him. After all, he is who he is. And that other man – is he still with him all the time? Are they still such cronies?'

'You know he never brings him home.'

'Is it a dress ball?'

'I think so.'

'Are low-necked gowns obligatory?'

'Mmm, no. "Dress ball" only refers to the men. The women wear what they like. Some of them go buttoned right up.'

'We will go – buttoned up, won't we?'

'Yes, of course. When do I see you in the cathedral again? The day after tomorrow? Well, the day after tomorrow I'll go to the chapel in the gown I'll be wearing to the ball.'

'How can you do that?'

'By . . . it's just one of the wiles of woman, you busybody. The bodice and the skirt are separate and, since I intend to wear dark colours, I can go to confess in the bodice – and we shall see the neckline when the mantilla is removed. And then we shall be satisfied.'

'I hope so.'

Don Fermín was satisfied with the gown, although he was not pleased that *we* were going to the ball. By bringing his eyes close to the grating of the confessional he could catch a glimpse of the gown and see that it had quite a high neck and only revealed a small angle of flesh where there was hardly room for the cross of diamonds which Ana was also wearing, so that he could appraise the effect of the ensemble.

So the judge's wife went to the ball in the Gentlemen's Club for, as she had anticipated, Don Víctor insisted 'that she must go – and go she did'.

The ex-magistrate's truly extraordinary show of energy made him think, as he and his wife climbed the stairs in the blackened old building which was the quarters of the Gentlemen's Club, that he would have made rather a good dictator. 'What he lacked was not character but a stage. Just ask his wife, who against her will was there on the stairs with him, hanging on to his arm, beautiful beyond words, almost happy, in spite of all the confessors in the world. We were no longer in Paraguay. Jesuits trying their tricks on him!'

It was Carnival Monday. On the previous day there had been a heated discussion in the Gentlemen's Club about whether it should throw its doors open to the general public that year. It was a long-established custom that a ball – but never a fancy-dress ball – should be given on Carnival Monday by this aristocratic circle (as it was called in *El Alerta*, the members of whose editorial staff were never invited, because they insisted on going in morning coats).

'Why shouldn't this year be like any other?' asked Ronzal, who had just had a dress coat made in Madrid.

'Because the carnival's very dull this year, thanks to the missioners – that's why,' retorted Foja, who had been put on the committee by the president, Don Alvaro.

'The fact is', said the latter, 'that we would be running the risk of being humiliated. Nearly all the young ladies who are *comme il faut* are given over body and soul to the Jesuits. I believe that many of them are even wearing hair shirts under their vests.'

'How awful!' exclaimed Don Víctor, who was not a committee member but had come to the meeting so as not to be separated from Mesía.

'Yes, sir, hair shirts,' Foja affirmed. 'The canon theologian isn't up to that, my friend. He hasn't managed to make *his* spiritual daughters wear hair shirts and other such devilish inventions.'

'Only because he hasn't tried,' Ronzal retorted.

Don Alvaro saw that Quintanar was blushing. Foja's comment had upset him. 'Yes, Foja was alluding to his wife when he mentioned the canon theologian, the gibe was directed at him.'

'The fact is', continued the ex-mayor, 'that we would be running the risk of being humiliated, as the president so rightly says. The cream of conservancy – the women that liven these things up – won't come. I know them like the back of my hand. At the moment they're amusing themselves by playing at saints – they're all mystics now. You whip my back and I'll whip yours, ha, ha, ha!'

'I have an idea,' said Mesía. 'Let's see how the land lies. Let those members who are in with the top families find out whether the girls are coming or not. If *they* come, all the other women will play follow-my-leader, as usual, and come too, for certain – *malgré* all the Jesuits and discalced friars in the world.'

'Splendid! Splendid!'

'That's that then; let's set to work.'

Each committee member offered to bring all the women he could.

Don Víctor, piqued by another of Foja's gibes could not restrain himself:

'I, gentlemen, guarantee to bring my wife. She will not dance but she will help to fill the place.'

'Oh, she would be a wonderful acquisition!' a member said. 'If Doña Ana comes, that will set an excellent example, because after living in seclusion for so long . . . Oh! it will set an excellent example.'

'Precisely. Put the word around that the judge's wife is coming and the place will be packed with all the best people.'

'Señor Quintanar,' said the ex-mayor, 'you will be declared a Glorious Son of the Gentlemen's Club – if you do manage to bring your wife, that is.'

'Yes, sir, indeed she will come! In my house, Señor Foja, my slightest hint is a binding decree.'

Don Víctor went home cursing the hour in which he had taken it into his head to go to the committee meeting.

'Why had he offered to do something which he was not going to be able to accomplish?'

'None the less, one's word was one's word.'

Quintanar had not read Kempis for some time now, and no longer had horrifying thoughts of hell. All that remained of his ephemeral piety was the conviction that good works as well as faith were necessary for salvation, and the habit of crossing himself when he rose from his bed in the morning, when he left home, when he went to sleep, and so on. He had gone back to Calderón and Lope de Vega with more enthusiasm than ever. He would shut himself into his study or his bedroom and recite long relations, as he called them, from the most famous plays, almost always with his sword in his hand. His wife had discovered him doing so on the night of Christmas Eve, although he never knew it. On that evening he had enjoyed a hearty supper, and had then thought to celebrate the Birth of Christ in his own way.

Even though his own religiosity had dissipated, or at least hidden itself in remote recesses of his soul where he could not find it, he respected other people's piety.

'Nevertheless,' he said to himself, gathering courage for his attack, 'my wife is no longer a budding saint. I respect her piety, as I always have, but it no longer frightens me, for now she is just a devout woman like many others. She blows hot and cold: novenas, masses, the guild, the Blessed Sacrament – but she has desisted from shutting herself away for ages and scaring the wits out of me, as if there were a lightning-conductor in the house. Well then, I shall pluck up my courage and tell her.'

And he told her. He told her after luncheon. To the great surprise of the energetic husband 'who was unwilling for his house to become another Paraguay' (an allusion which Ana did not understand), she did not offer as determined a resistance as he had expected, and soon surrendered. He put it all down to his own energy. 'She realizes that I am not going to give way, so she does not persist in opposing me.'

When Ana consulted the canon theologian in Doña Petronila's house she had already given her consent, but she intended to withdraw it if he said *non possumus*.

In the end everything was settled, except Ana's conscience. 'Why had she agreed after a weak resistance? Why was she going to the ball? To obey her husband, of course; but why did she obey him now whereas she was certain that months earlier she would not have obeyed him?'

She did not know; she did not want to know; she did not want to torture herself any more.

'The ball and Ana Ozores – what had they to do with each other? What did it matter to her – the sister of Don Fermín the saint and martyr – whether the dull girls of Vetusta danced in the long, narrow ballroom of the Gentlemen's Club? Not in the slightest.'

These were Ana's thoughts while her housemaid combed her hair and she herself positioned the cross of diamonds against the white background of the angle of flesh revealed by her dark, high-necked bodice.

Ronzal, one of the members of the committee receiving the ladies, hurried to offer the judge's wife his arm as soon as she appeared in the hall with her husband. Which arm? 'The right arm – the right arm, of course,' he thought. Great was his distress when he saw Paco Vegallana giving Olvido Páez, who entered at the same time, not his right but his left arm. At all events, Blunderbuss strode in glory into the ballroom with his partner of the moment. He had sufficient time, however, to participate in Ana's triumph. Conversations were suspended, looks were fastened on the Italian woman's daughter. There was a murmur of astonishment:

'The judge's wife!'
'The judge's wife!'
'Who'd have imagined it!'
'Poor Don Fermín!'
'And how beautiful!'
'But how plainly dressed!'
(This exclamation came from Obdulia.)
'How plainly dressed, but how beautiful!'
'The Madonna of the Chair.'
'The Venus of Melons, as Blunderbuss says.'
(This comment came from Joaquín Orgaz.)

The circle of the nobility opened to welcome into its bosom the prodigal daughter of Society, to use the Baron de la Barque's apt expression. *In illo tempore*[1] this gentleman had been deeply in love with Anita, in spite of his lady the baroness and their daughters.

The Marchioness de Vegallana, still wearing electric blue, rose from her walnut-backed chair of crimson satin and embraced her darling Anita, who was not to mind her doing so.

'My child, thank God, I thought this was going to be snub number one hundred and one.'

The marchioness had also insisted that Ana must go to the ball and to the dinner 'which the *élite* was going to enjoy *en petit comité'*. All these gallicisms had been imported by Mesía.

'But how divine, Ana, how divine!' Rudesinda, the baron's eldest daughter, said in a nasal voice. According to Don Saturnino Bermúdez, Rudesinda was an ogival beauty. And she did indeed look rather like a Gothic turret, although certain curves in the region of her bust, and in particular in her neck, made the marchioness see her as 'a chess knight'.

She and her two sisters were known by the lower orders as 'The Three Disgraces', and her father, the Baron de la Barque, had been dubbed the 'Baron of the Floating Debt' – an allusion to his title and his many creditors.

This family, worthy of a better income, spent a large part of each year in Madrid, and when the *girls* – the youngest of them twenty-six – were before the public gaze in Vetusta they pretended to be hiding their contempt for everything around them. They sought refuge in the aristocratic circle, to which Visitación and Obdulia, who were related to the nobility, had been granted the special privilege of belonging. The civil governor and his family were also considered part of the aristocracy. The young women of the middle classes took their revenge for the ill-concealed disdain of the baron's daughters by counting the bones on their chests and on those of other aristocratic young ladies. As it happened, nearly all the noble girls of Vetusta were thin.

Ana sat by the side of the Marchioness de Vegallana, the only person in the group whom she liked. The orchestra was announcing a rigadoon.

And its threat was not a vain one. Within two minutes those violins and violas, clarinets and flutes, accompanied in their laborious harmonic gestation by an Érard piano, began to fill the air with their chords, as Trifón Cármenes – who had ventured to ask the baron's second daughter 'if he might have the honour' – promised himself to say in the following day's edition of *El Lábaro*. Fabiolita, as she was called, pulled a face, but a sign from her father obliged her to let Trifón have the honour, although she resolved that if he dared speak to her she would reply only in monosyllables. The Baron of the Floating Debt, unlike his daughter, believed in the power of the periodical press. Before this young couple, in all his splendour, stood Ronzal, the gallant Blunderbuss, the member of the Provincial Standing Committee and of the committee of the Gentlemen's Club.

The shirt-front which Ronzal was sporting could not have shone more than it did. He was proud of that shirt-front, of that dress coat from Madrid, and of those boots without heels – the latest fashion, the height of *chic*, as people were beginning to say in Vetusta. But he was not so satisfied with his knowledge of, and proficiency in, the art of Terpsichore (another expression which Trifón proposed to use in his report). By Blunderbuss's side was his partner, Olvido Páez, who was not even looking at him. But he was not thinking about this; he was thinking that, as far as he could see – rather late in the day – he had to lead the dance: his *vis-à-vis* was Trifón, and Trifón had started to go into action. Blunderbuss was sweating before he had any cause to do so. Every so often he stuck the fingers of his right hand between his shirt-collar and what he called *this here neck* whenever he 'bet his head' on anything. He regarded this gesture as a very elegant one – and, above all, it was a great help in an emergency. While the Páez girl suggested with her air of melancholy and boredom that her kingdom was not of this world and that Ronzal had gone too far in daring to invite her to dance, the deputy was concentrating with all his five senses on not making any mistakes, on not treading on any gowns or toes, and on slavishly imitating all Trifón's comings and goings and genuflexions. Cármenes was a bad poet, but he possessed a profound knowledge of the rigadoon. Ronzal was full of envy. As the Páez girl and the baron's daughter passed by each other's side they exchanged discreet smiles as if to say: 'God's will be done!' or else, 'What a pair of clowns has fallen to our lot!' But Ronzal was blind to all this, he was thinking about his shirt-front, his shirt-collar, and the trains of the ladies' gowns. On his right danced Joaquín Orgaz, who was talking ceaselessly to his partner, a very rich and very languid American girl. Since the ballroom was narrow and Vetustan customs were somewhat casual, the dancers sat down on the nearest chair as soon as they had a breathing-space. Ronzal, who could not sit down, because all the nearby chairs were occupied, was thinking that this was a corrupt practice – as indeed it was. The Páez girl and the baron's daughter could hardly stand, and dropped on to their chairs as if each figure in the rigadoon were a journey around the world.

After the rigadoon came a waltz. Ronzal retired to smoke a cigarette. He did not dance the waltz; he had never been able to master it. All the doors in the ballroom were crammed with members who had no dress coats. In Vetusta a dress coat presupposed a *certain position*, and many young blades imagined that it needed the fortune of a Monte-Cristo[2] to acquire one.

And, thus, since it was a dress ball, the flower of Vetustan youth was left standing at the door. Some of them pretended to scorn the ridiculous pleasure of spinning around the room like a top and getting nowhere; others made a show of Bohemianism, of scepticism, of anything which, in their opinion, was incompatible with dress coats. And a few, being more ingenuous, confessed the penury of their budget, cursed social requirements – and kept themselves ready for the 'last minute'. For at the last minute all the men danced, in spite of Ronzal – men in frock-coats, men in morning coats, even men in jackets. 'It was only fair!'

Saturnino Bermúdez, who owned a dress coat, and a dress hat, and all the dress which was necessary, arrived at the ballroom a little late. He stopped at the door – and he trembled. He could not help himself. Entering halls on solemn days made him feel as if he were about to plunge into the ocean. And indeed anyone would have said that this man standing in the doorway believed himself to be on the sea-shore. Don Saturn replied with courteous smiles to the gibes of the envious dress-coatless onlookers, who said:

'Come on, man, in you go, be brave.'

'In a minute – wait – just a minute . . .'

He makes his gloves tight on his hands, and he straightens the knot of his tie, and he checks that his pocket handkerchief is in the right place – and he, too, runs two fingers around the neckband of his dress shirt. Finally, one, two – and at two he tidies his hair with his fingers, forgetting that it is cropped like that of a recruit. After this automatic gesture, frequent in those who are about to dive – in he goes! Saturn enters the ballroom, saluting right and left and, although his purpose seems to be to discover who is there, in *the deepest recesses of his soul* he well knows that what he is really trying to find is a chair or a corner of a divan which can be his harbour in this hazardous navigation through the seas of the *great world*. But little by little he becomes accustomed to the water, or to the ballroom, and soon he is at his ease, and dances and passes compliments in such lengthy and complicated sentences that no lady wishes to receive them.

At first, Ana felt sleepy. It was twelve o'clock. She only paid attention to what was happening before her eyes. She did not want to think. On entering the Gentlemen's Club she had said to herself: 'Will Don Alvaro come to greet me?' And she had felt afraid and tempted to pretend to be ill so as to return home. But that thought had gone away. Alvaro had still not appeared. The marchioness was chattering like a magpie. Ana was smiling in reply. Suddenly Visitación appeared wearing a dress of organdie smothered with artificial flowers. It was a very low-necked dress indeed.

'My dear girl, what a scandalous dress,' said the marchioness, nibbling Visita's face as she kissed it, in an attempt to stifle her own laughter.

Visita looked, as best she could, at where Doña Rufina had looked, and replied without the slightest embarrassment:

'Oh, I don't think so! But it wouldn't be surprising, because I haven't even had time to look in the mirror. Those devilish children! And their father – no energy at all, and not the faintest idea how to take them in! I simply *couldn't* get rid of them. But Ana, what's this? You here? But my dearest darling, what's this? Has the Pope published a bull or something?'

By the time she said this the bank clerk's wife was in front of Ana, leaning backwards and opening her arms; the ladies' knees were touching.

Half an hour later Visita, partly hidden behind the curtain in a balcony, was telling Ana a story. Ana was facing her friend's corner and listening attentively.

The ball became livelier. The backbiting and the absurd mistrust which characterize the cold, irrational etiquette adopted by nobles and plebeians when they have to rub shoulders gave way to other vices and passions. The Páez girl no longer saw Ronzal as a coarse man, but as a man. Even the baron's daughters were becoming human. And the middle-class girls were forgetting the bones displayed by the noble girls, because they were joining in the general gaiety and devoting themselves to the ball with invincible zeal, as if they longed to drink, in that perfumed atmosphere (excessively perfumed, perhaps) the unknown liqueur which would satisfy their vague desires. Poorly dressed girls, if they were pretty, no longer seemed to be poorly dressed, and there were no more thoughts about the queen of the ball, the best gown, or the finest jewels. For youth was in search of youth, love was in the air: looks of fire, languid smiles anticipating the impossible, dramatic jealousy lending the whole a certain grandeur. Even the most retiring girls, and even the girls who were as stiff as jack-in-the-boxes, made men think about the women underneath their commonplace dresses and their artificial, brusque best behaviour.

At two o'clock in the morning, during an interval, Ana rose from her chair for the first time and consented to take a walk around the ballroom. Visita walked by her side, silent, thoughtful, and satisfied with what she had just done. She had told Ana the story of Don Alvaro's life from the beginning of the previous summer until that day. Fire shot from the eyes and the cheeks of the bank clerk's wife as she savoured the triumph of her eloquence. Ana could ill conceal the vivid, profound impression which her friend's words had left. 'Don Alvaro had conquered the virtue of the minister's wife, he had been her lover throughout the summer in Palomares . . . and then he had tricked her, he hadn't followed her to Madrid.' That, in a nutshell, was the story. Ana remembered its end word for word:

'When Alvaro told me all about it,' Visita had said, 'I asked him (you know we're very close), well then, I asked him: "But look, my dear, why the devil did you leave the woman if she's as beautiful, as influential and as clever as you say she is? Why not follow her to Madrid?" And Alvaro replied very sadly, you know the face he pulls when he speaks like this, he replied: "Bah – the summer's quite sufficient for mere affairs. Winter is for true love. Besides, the minister's wife, as you call her, couldn't achieve for me what I wanted, in spite of all her charms. She couldn't make me forget . . . something that's no concern of yours." And after sighing in that special way of his, you know what I mean, he added: "Leave Vetusta? Oh, no, not that." And then, my dear – on my word of honour – he twitched, just as if he were shivering. "Look," he said after a moment, trying to smile, "I was offered a district, a safe seat, a priceless" – or did he say priestless? – "sinecure, an appetizing morsel . . . but no, no, I'm bound by a chain – and instead of biting it I kiss it." And he wrung my hand, and went away so I shouldn't see him crying, I think.'

This was the substance of Visita's confidences. Ana greeted people right and left and talked to friends, but she thought only about Don Alvaro's confession. 'Its credibility was vouched by the effect of her appearance in the Gentlemen's Club. At this very moment, while she strolled along, she could hear the sweet murmur – the sweetest murmur there was – of subdued praise, of amazed admiration, of sincere, discreet gallantry. Why shouldn't Don Alvaro be as deeply in love as Visita's story suggested?'

'Hey, listen,' said the bank clerk's wife, suddenly turning to face Ana, 'who do you think the chain is?'

'What chain?' asked Ana in a trembling voice.

'Oh, the chain binding Mesía – the woman who's made him fall truly in love. The bitch! I only hope she's made to pay for it. But who can she be?'

'I don't know.'

'Would you dare ask him?'

'God forbid.'

'She must be a married woman.'

'Good heavens!'

'Look, I'm going to sit him next to you, let's see if he dares tell you after dinner. You ask him yourself.'

'Visitación! You are out of your mind.'

'Ha, ha, ha! Here he comes, here he comes. Tell me all about it later.'

Visita released Ana's arm and disappeared among the groups of people blocking the narrow ballroom.

Standing in front of her, Ana saw Don Alvaro on the arm of Quintanar, his inseparable friend.

Mesía's dress coat, tie, shirt-front, waistcoat, trousers and opera-hat were not like those of the other men. Ana noticed this unintentionally, hardly thinking about it, but it was the first thing she noticed. Now she saw all the other men walking about the room, including Don Víctor, as servants in formal dress; they were all waiters, the only gentleman was Mesía. He was good-looking however he dressed, but he looked best of all in a dress suit. He was a handsome man wherever he went, dominating everybody with his proud figure; but there, at the ball, standing beneath that cut-glass chandelier and almost touching it with his head, he was more elegant, more dashing, more graceful than anywhere else. The ball, alive and burning with concealed yet intense voluptuousness, was the ideal background for that figure which she, poor Ana, had so often seen in her dreams.

All this passed through Ana's mind while Mesía, without hiding the emotion which was turning him pale, made a graceful bow and timidly held out his hand.

Sooner than she wished she felt her fingers held in the fingers of her enemy, her tempter. The fine leather of her glove made the sensation at the same time smoother and more penetrating: it flowed like a cool, pulsing stream deep into her body. Her ears buzzed and the ball was transformed into something new and unknown, something irresistibly beautiful, satanically seductive. She was afraid she might faint. Not knowing how it had happened, she found herself hanging on to Mesía's arm, surrounded by a whirl of coloured skirts and black cloth, hearing in the distance the catarrhal caterwauling of the violins and the baying of the brass, sensuous music in her ears; she realized that she was being taken from the ballroom. The marchioness was shouting, Obdulia was guffawing, she could hear the nasal voice of one of the baron's daughters; and the first flourishes of the waltz were left behind them.

'Where were they taking her?' To dinner.

'To dinner, my child,' Quintanar said into her ear. 'And for the Lord's sake, Anita, do not entertain the idea of refusing – it would be a slight!'

The Marchioness de Vegallana and the Baron de la Barque, and their coteries, and Pepe Ronzal, dined in the reading-room. It was all Blunderbuss's work. Invite him, Mesía had said, and his satisfied vanity will inspire him to work wonders. And indeed Ronzal, abusing his power as a committee member, had appropriated all the best things in the restaurant, taken the reading-room by storm, removed newspapers from the table and put table-cloths in their place, locked the door, and told the waiters to enter by a side-door near the bookcase; thus allowing the cream of the Vetustan aristocracy to dine there with its protégés and close friends. Obdulia made it her task from the beginning to reward Blunderbuss for his industry and zeal, and he was beside himself with joy. All the ladies congratulated him on his energy in locking the room and on the taste with which the table was laid. His animal eyes sparkled, but they did not move. Obdulia sat him by her side. Ronzal was a happy man that night!

Ana found herself sitting between the marchioness and Don Alvaro.

On the other side of the table Don Víctor, a little merry, was pretending to woo Visitación – reciting verses by his adored poets and repeating with the insistence of a hammer:

> 'But have I sinned so wretchedly
> By loving, wild and ingrate foe?
> By God, I wish that – but stay, no:
> For more than myself I love thee.'[3]

'For the sake of God and the eleven thousand virgins – won't you be quiet, Quintanar?' demanded the marchioness.

But he continued declaiming for his dear Visitación:

> 'And so, my lady, thou seest me
> Without myself, or God, or thee:
> Without thee, for thou art not mine . . .'[4]

Visitación covered his mouth with her hands.

'You're scandalous, scandalous!' she cried.

The daughters of the Floating Debt smiled and glanced at each other as if to say: 'Fine society the marchioness moves in!'

The marquis said to the Baron de la Barque:

'Since this is an informal dinner . . .!'

'Oh precisely, precisely!'

And the baron went to sit by the side of a large unaccompanied aristocratic lady.

Paco had his cousin Edelmira with him in Vetusta again, and 'he was spooning her for all he was worth'. His mother did not approve, because it was nasty to deceive one's own cousin.

Joaquín Orgaz had promised to sing some Flamenco at dessert.

The dinner was brief but excellent – highly flavoured dishes, good claret, good champagne: in short, as the marquis said, first of all the sea and pepper, and then fantasy and alcohol.

They all, including the *baronesses*, laughed at the *plebs*, still dancing outside, who had to be content with the ice-creams served on the billiard tables.

From time to time somebody would knock on the door.

'Who's that?' Ronzal would shout, with his much-praised energy.

'My overcoat – a coffee-coloured one – my overcoat's in there.'

'Ha ha ha!' replied the people in the reading-room.

'Wow – haven't things hotted up!' said Joaquín Orgaz to one of the baron's daughters, who smiled and looked at the ceiling.

'Yes, things have "hotted up" – but nobody is infringing the rules of Vetustan propriety,' said the marquis to the baron – by now as red as a tomato, and drawing closer and closer to the large lady.

The marchioness was feeling sleepy, but even so she was enjoying the fun.

'This is how life should always be,' she said to Saturnino, who had made up his mind to get drunk so as not to be out of place. 'This hole of a town is getting terribly dull. Isn't it, my young fellow?'

'Deci – ded – ly – dull.' Saturn gulped down a glass of champagne, delighted to have been called a young fellow.

The marchioness had the foolish idea, arising perhaps from the mists of drowsiness, of staring at Bermúdez long and hard with a look which she knew would have turned any man's head, *in illo tempore.*

'Why don't you get married?' she asked, serious and melancholic, it seemed.

Bermúdez stared back at the illustrious lady and for a moment forgot her fifty years. He sighed, the champagne rushed up to his nose, he coughed, his face turned blue as he half-choked, and the marchioness had to slap him on the back.

By the time he had recovered, her eyes were shut, and she only opened them from time to time to look at the judge's wife and Mesía.

The senile idyll about which Bermúdez had dreamed for an instant was shattered – in spite of the fact that he had already thought of Ninon de Lenclos[5] as a justification in the eyes of the world for his relationship with Doña Rufina!

Meanwhile, Don Alvaro was telling Ana the story which she had already heard from Visita, although in a very different form.

Ana had not been able to help but ask him if he had spent an enjoyable summer.

The question had given Mesía the chance for which he had been waiting.

He *turned on the charm*, which required little effort, because with each day that passed she found more demoniacal charm in him, even when he was not with her.

The noise, the lights, the bustle, the piquant food, the wine, the coffee and the atmosphere, all conspired to weaken her resolution and arouse feelings of languor and sensuality. Ana believed that she was about to succumb to moral asphyxia. In spite of herself, she derived intense delight from these trivial pleasures, from the seductive charm of dining at a ball – which had long since lost its magic for everybody else. More than any of them she was feeling the effects of the tainted atmosphere of romantic, aristocratic lasciviousness – and yet she was the one who had to fight against temptation. All her senses were pervaded by that strange mixture of irritation and smoothness which is the effect of new leather on the sense of touch. Everything reached deep into her body, everything was new to her. In the bouquet of the wine, in the taste of the Gruyère cheese, in the sparks thrown out by the champagne, in reflections in eyes, even in the contrast between Ronzal's black hair and his light-brown forehead – in everything Ana found beauty, mysterious attraction, a quality all its own, an expression of love.

'Ana's very red-faced tonight!' Paco said in a low voice to Visitación.
'Of course – that's partly because Alvaro's next to her.'

'And the other reason?'

'The other reason is her husband's tomfoolery – he's giving me such a headache.'

Indeed, Don Víctor was unbearable with his verses, however good they might have been.

As soon as Alvaro saw the judge's wife in the ballroom he felt what he called his 'hunch'. That look on her face, that sudden pallor told him that the night was his, that the time had come to take a risk.

He had never really renounced the idea of conquering that fortress.

Of course not! But realizing that so long as what he called 'erotic mysticism' (he reached even this extreme of coarseness in his private thoughts) reigned in Ana's heart he was not going to be able to make the slightest progress, he had broken camp and withdrawn to wait for a better opportunity. Besides, he had always expected his absence, his feigned indifference and the story of his affair with the minister's wife to prepare the ground for him.

'Always assuming, of course,' he concluded, 'that the fortress hasn't already surrendered to our militant churchman. If the canon theologian is the master here, then I can't expect anything for myself – besides, the victory would be deprived of much of its merit.'

He had not sought for the opportunity but he was now being presented with it: Ana had been placed by his side. He had the intuition that he should advance – go on, then, advance! First he must find out about the other man: was the canon theologian now in command?

When he told his story he had to make some alterations to the historical truth, because the judge's wife ('she was so backward') could not be told about an affair with a married woman, just like that; but he gave her to understand, as best he could, that he had disdained the passion of a woman coveted by many men, because – because – for his mother's son mere affairs were no longer even an agreeable pastime, now that love had fallen on to his soul like a punishment.

While Mesía expressed these sentiments and others like them, all taken from cheap novels, Anita's face showed him that the canon theologian was not the master of her heart. But since there are many other organs in the human anatomy, Mesía was not yet satisfied, for he thought, 'Even supposing that Ana is in love with me, I still need to know whether her weak flesh has sought a substitute.'

No, Don Alvaro did not harbour any illusions. This crude, materialistic modesty was forced on him by his philosophy, which seemed a more and more solid one as time went by.

Ana noticed that Don Alvaro's foot was brushing against hers and sometimes pressing it. She did not remember when this contact had begun, but on first noticing it she felt a fear like that which went with her most violent nervous attacks, mixed with a physical pleasure which was so intense that she could not recall anything like it in her life. The fear – the terror – was like that which had gripped her on the night when she had seen Mesía walking along the Calle de Traslacerca, near her garden gate; but the pleasure was new, utterly new, and so strong that it bound her with iron chains to what she was already condemning as a crime, a fall, perdition.

Don Alvaro spoke covertly of love, with good-natured, familiar melancholy and tender, gentle, insinuating passion. He recalled a thousand incidents without any apparent importance which Ana also remembered. She did not talk – but she listened. Their feet, too, continued their own dialogue; a poetic dialogue no doubt, in spite of the calf-skin separating them, for the intensity of the sensation enhanced the lowly, prosaic contact.

As soon as Ana found the strength to separate her body from the pleasure of brushing against Don Alvaro, another greater peril loomed: the ballroom music could be heard in the distance.

'Let's dance, let's dance!' cried Paco, Edelmira, Obdulia and Ronzal.

This was paradise for Blunderbuss – this dance which he called clandestine, right there in the club, among the best people, far from the common middle-classes.

The door was opened a little so that the music could be heard better, the table was pushed into a corner and the improvised dance began. The couples were jammed together and could hardly move.

Don Víctor shouted:

'Come on Ana, dance! Seize her, Alvaro.'

The worthy Quintanar would not abdicate his dictatorship. Don Alvaro offered his arm to Ana, who tried to find the courage to refuse, but failed.

She had almost forgotten how to dance the polka. Mesía was lifting her off her feet, as if he were abducting her. He could feel that firm, burning body, with its gentle curves, trembling in his hands.

Ana was silent, she could not see, she could not hear, all she could do was feel a pleasure which was like fire; this intense irresistible delight terrified her; she let herself be carried on like a dead body or the victim of a disaster; it seemed as if something inside her had snapped – virtue, or faith, or shame; she was lost, she vaguely thought.

In his imagination the president of the Gentlemen's Club was caressing that treasure of physical beauty which he held in his arms. 'She's mine! That canon must be a coward! She's mine. This is the first embrace the poor woman has ever enjoyed.' It was a dissembled, hypocritical, diplomatic embrace – but for Anita it was an embrace!

'Don't Alvaro and Ana look dull!' said Obdulia to her partner, Ronzal.

Mesía noticed that Ana's head was falling upon the spotless, shining shirt-front which Blunderbuss so admired. He stopped, put his head on one side to look at her, and saw that she had fainted. On her pale cheeks there were two tears, and another two had dropped upon the starched cloth of his shirt-front. General alarm. The clandestine dance is suspended, Don Víctor is in a daze, he begs his wife to come round – water and perfumes are brought. Somoza arrives, he feels Ana's pulse, he prescribes – a coach. It is agreed that Visita and Quintanar should take the lady home, well wrapped, in the marchioness's berlin. And they do so. As soon as Ana recovers, making profuse apologies for having interrupted the party, Don Víctor, in deep dudgeon and no longer afraid, swathes her body in furs, muffles her face, bids the amiable company farewell and departs with the bank-clerk's wife to take Ana to bed.

'The smoke, the heat, the novelty, dancing the polka straight after dinner, the lights! It could have been anything – it was of no importance. The party could continue.' It continued. The people in the ballroom knew: 'The judge's wife had had one of her attacks.' 'She had been forced to dance.' But the incident was soon forgotten as they commented on the conduct of those ladies and gentlemen who shut themselves into the reading-room to dine and dance as if the Gentlemen's Club did not belong to everybody.

At six o'clock in the morning, as Paco took his leave of Mesía at the door of the Gentlemen's Club with a handshake, he exclaimed:

'Bravo! At last – what?'

It was some time before Mesía replied. He buttoned his tailored, cherry-coloured topcoat up to the collar, tied a white silk scarf around his neck and at length said:

'Hmm. We shall see.'

He arrived at his hotel. The door was locked and he clapped for the night-watch, who took a long time to come; but instead of rebuking him, as he usually did, he gave him two slaps on the back and a silver coin.

'The young gentleman is happy today! Been at the ball, eh?'

'At the ball, Señor Roque.'

As Don Alvaro prepared for bed, and placed a warm flannel undergarment on a hanger, he murmured, as if he were talking to the bed while he turned down the sheet:

'It's a pity this campaign finds me – not quite so young as I used to be!'

XXV

Next morning in the cathedral, in the presence of the canon theologian, Gloucester described the events at the ball in pitiless detail. 'The aristocracy had shut itself into a room – the reading-room – to dine and dance, and Doña Ana Ozores, the selfsame judge's wife – none other – had fainted in the arms of Señor Don Alvaro Mesía.'

The canon theologian, who had not slept that night, and had been awaiting news of Ana in a fever of impatience, spun on his heel like a recruit. It was the first time that Gloucester's dagger – his tongue – had penetrated Don Fermín's heart. His face pale, his chin trembling until he stilled it by biting his lower lip, he looked at his enemy in astonishment and with an expression of pain which filled the archdeacon's soul with joy. The look said, 'you've won, yes, now you've won, now your poison has got into my guts'. De Pas was thinking that wretches like Mourelo, however weak, foolish and despicable they might appear to be, possess a formidable power in their wickedness. 'This toad, this rotting cassock, could stab a man like that!' Don Fermín remembered his mother: his mother had never betrayed him, his mother belonged to him, she was his own flesh and blood; Ana, the other woman, was a stranger, a foreign body in his heart.

Hardly even trying to hide his pain – the coldest, the deepest, the most inconsolable pain he could remember – De Pas left the sacristy and walked around the cathedral with a hesitant step. He could not find the door; he did not know where to go; he had been drained of all resolution. When he noticed that some of the faithful were watching him he fell on his knees before a chapel altar, and meditated on what he should do. Go to Ana's house? Absurd. Especially so soon. But his loneliness horrified him. He felt afraid of open spaces, he needed a refuge, everything was hostile. 'His mother, his beloved mother.' He left the cathedral and hurried home. Doña Paula was sweeping the dining-room floor. A black calico scarf bound her thick hard silver hair like a turban.

'Have you been to prayers?'

'Yes, mother.'

Doña Paula continued sweeping.

Don Fermín paced around the table and around his mother. 'Here was his only possible consolation, here was the lap on which he could weep, here the only true sympathy, here the only person to whom he could communicate his grief. The poison which was killing him would be but a noxious poison if his mother drew it out of him into herself. The desire to share his pain with her was squeezing his throat, as if he were in his death throes – but he could not, he could not speak. It was cruel of his mother not to divine her son's torture.

She was looking at him as everybody else looked at him, as the people he had met in the street had looked at him, not knowing that he was dying of despair. And he could not speak!'

'What's up with you, my lad? What are you doing here? Your new clothes are getting all covered with dust.'

Don Fermín walked out of the dining-room and into his study. Teresina was making the master's bed. She did not hear him come in because she was shaking the mattress and her ears were filled with the swish of the maize-leaves with which it was stuffed. As if he were fleeing from something, the master walked out of his study. He left home. He came to Doña Petronila Rianzares's house. 'Madam was at mass.' He paced about her sitting-room as he waited, sometimes holding one hand in the other behind his back, sometimes crossing them in front of him. The plump, spotless cat came in and greeted its friend with the beginnings of a moan. And it wound its sinuous body about his ankles. 'The cat seemed to know about the betrayal.' The sofa in which Ana always sat was calling to him with the voice of memory. At one end there was a loose spring and the cloth was wrinkled; this was her place. De Pas dropped into the easy chair by the side of the loose cloth. He closed his eyes, and his spirit was overcome by a weariness of living which made him feel as if he were asleep or about to fall asleep. He wished he could stop time. Now he hoped that Doña Petronila would return late. He was afraid to do anything, he was afraid to take any decisions – they would only make things worse. Death was in his soul. Distant memories teemed in his brain as if making ready to perform the *danse macabre* or the deliriums of a dying man. He caught the smell of a large rose which Ana was pressing to the lips of her dear friend, her elder brother; the music of her words mingled with the aroma of the flower in a mystical composition. 'Oh, yes, that was love, and good love, too.[1] He was a lover; love wasn't all lust – it was also this grief of disillusionment, this sudden loneliness, this bitter-sweet pain, capable of redeeming the gravest sin. Duty, priesthood, vows, chastity – it all sounded hollow now, like words in a play. He had been deceived, his soul had been trampled underfoot: this was the truth, these were the facts, this wasn't something invented by old bishops. The world, the world, was teaching him this lesson. Ana was his, this was the supreme law of justice. She, she herself had sworn it; it was not known for what purpose she was his, but his she was.' The canon jumped to his feet. Time was flying, the fact hit him like a slap on the face. Maybe those two were conspiring with time against him; perhaps they were together at that very moment. 'Infamous, infamous woman! And she had gone to his chapel to show him the cross of diamonds, to let him see the gown in which she was going to dishonour him – yes, dishonour him. He was the master, the husband, the spiritual husband – Don Víctor was just an idiot, incapable of looking after his own or others' honour. Such was Woman!'

He stepped into the passage and cried:

'Has Doña Petronila returned yet?'

'She's ringing now,' someone replied.

And in she came, but Don Fermín cut short her greetings:

'She must be brought here immediately.'

'Who – Ana?'

'Yes. Immediately.'

Don Fermín resumed his pacing; he did not want to talk. Doña Petronila, his slave, disappeared into her boudoir without another word.

Half an hour later the bell rang; Constantine the Great herself went to the door. There stood the judge's wife.

'What's the matter?'

'Don Fermín – in the sitting-room.'

'Ah! I'm so glad.'

The judge's wife entered, and Doña Petronila disappeared in the direction of the kitchen at the opposite end of the house. 'If anyone calls, I'm not at home,' she said to the housemaid as she went into the oratory near her bedroom.

The judge's wife looked more beautiful than ever . . . mysterious fire in her eyes, and in her cheeks that colour of enthusiasm which the canon had seen during their intimate spiritual conversations. An aureola of new glory seemed to surround that woman, that beloved figure which in such a small space encompassed everything of any value in life – the infinite, complete world of his unique passion.

'What is this?' he said in a voice suddenly hoarse, standing in the middle of the sitting-room as if rooted there.

'What I myself wanted – to see you straight away. I'm going mad. Last night I thought I was dying – yesterday – today – I don't know when – I'm going mad.'

She was choking.

De Pas felt a pity which seemed shameful.

'I know everything. I don't need to be told any tales.'

'What is everything?'

'What happened yesterday, or today. The ball, the dinner – what is the meaning of this, Ana, what is the meaning of this?'

'The ball! The dinner! It isn't *that*. They made me drink too much. I don't know . . . but it isn't that. I feel afraid, here, Fermín, in my head. Won't people have pity on me? Somebody have pity on me! I haven't got a mother. I'm alone.'

'It was true, she hadn't got a mother, as he had; she was more alone than he.' Don Fermín's love felt the ineffable pity which only love can feel; he came close to the judge's wife, he took her hands in his.

'Tell me, tell me – what happened? They said . . . but what

happened? Tell me!' he commanded in a trembling, anguished voice.

Ana told him, between sobs, what she could tell him about her fear, her torment, her agony, her hours of fever. 'When she found herself in bed a thousand horrifying visions assailed her amid confused memories of the ball. She thought she was falling back into those black pits of delirium where she had languished during the sorrowful nights of her illness. And then she was horrified by the wrong which she had done . . .' The canon flushed dark and Ana stopped and corrected herself: 'the wrong – that is to say, not having been good enough'. Her illness had been a lesson which, however, she had soon forgotten. That morning when, lying in her bed, she had felt the same weakness, the sensation that she was falling apart inside, turning into dust – and that life itself was fading away in her delirium – her conscience had seen, as by the light of a flare, horrors of shame, of punishment, the mirror of her own wretchedness, the reflection of the miserable mire in the human soul – and then madness, certain madness, a sudden, obstinate, painful, horrifying doubt about everything. God, God Himself was no more than a fixed idea, a mania, like something moving about her brain and nibbling at it, or like the ticking of a clock – like the insect which makes walls click and is known as the death-watch.

'Oh yes, I was mad,' Anita continued, frightened still. 'I was mad for an hour. What am I saying, an hour? A century. All I wanted was health, rest, a clear awareness of myself. But oh no! God, dear God – I – everything, we were all disappearing. Everything was dust inside me!'

And staring in terror at the carpet Ana saw a confused image of her fearsome memories.

De Pas was silent. For a moment he, too, felt the chill sensation of terror. Madness passed through his imagination like a wave of dizziness.

'If she were to go mad!' His face flushed purple. First he had imagined the disappearance, within Ana's head – her head of musical grace – of what he loved beneath her beauty: her soul, her mind; and then he had thought of her untouched external beauty, and of sating his love without fear of witnesses, alone, alone with a body he adored.

'I want to be saved, saved!' Ana suddenly cried, returning to reality. 'I want to go back to our sweet, tranquil summer, yes, our tranquil summer, and to our endless talk about God, about heaven, about the soul in love with thoughts of what is up there above us. Yes, I want my brother to save me, Teresa to illuminate me, the mirror of her life not to darken in my eyes, God to caress my soul. Fermín, this is my confession – here – the place doesn't matter, anywhere – my confession . . .'

'That is what I want, Ana. To know – to know everything. I am suffering too, I too thought I was dying, when I came – sitting over there – where we used to talk about heaven, and about ourselves. Ana, I am made of flesh and blood, too; I need a soul sister, but a faithful one, not a treacherous one. Yes, I thought I was dying.'

'And it was because of me – I was to blame, wasn't I? You thought I was being treacherous, I was lying to you, I was stained with sin?'

'Yes, yes – you must tell me everything – soon.'

'No, no.'

'Yes – yes.'

'No, that isn't what I mean – yes, I will tell you everything – but what is everything? Nothing. I mean, it wasn't my fault – they forced me to go. No, it wasn't *that*. I don't know how, I don't know why I gave in. And among them, there is a very evil woman.'

'No, don't blame others. The facts, I want to know the facts. I'll tell you the facts; I know them.'

'But what facts?'

'That man – Mesía. Ana, what happened between you and that man?'

Ana gathered her strength and concentrated on reality, on what she was being asked; now she was struggling with her confessor, fighting to protect her own interest, which was to hide her deepest thoughts. 'After all, this wasn't a confessional-box. Besides, it was charitable to lie, to hide at least the worst part.'

'I don't love him,' was the first thing she could say after she managed to recover her self-control. Now she was not thinking about her madness – she was thinking about how to defend her secret.

'But last night – this morning – I don't know what the time was – what happened?'

'I danced with him. It was Quintanar – Quintanar told me to . . .'

'No excuses, Ana! That isn't the way to confess.'

Ana looked around. This wasn't the chapel, thank God. This sophism, worthy of a hypocrite, was an innocent one in Ana. She was certain that a superior duty was ordering her to lie. 'Tell the canon theologian that she was in love with Mesía? She would rather tell her husband!'

'I danced with him because my husband wanted me to do so. They made me drink. I felt ill, I was dizzy, I fainted and I was taken home.'

'You fainted – in that man's arms?'

'In that man's . . . ! Fermín!'

'All right. That's what I heard. Let everyone hear! I mean – while you were dancing with him.'

'I can't remember, perhaps . . .'

'Such infamy!'

'Fermín, for the Lord's sake, Fermín!'

Ana stepped back.

'Silence! No need to shout, no need for histrionics – I don't eat people, why be so afraid? I frighten you, do I? Why? I – what can I do? Who am I? What power have I got? My power is spiritual. And last night you did not believe in God.'

'In my God! Fermín, for pity's sake . . .'

'That's what you said. Yes, that's the way. Without God I'm nothing. Without God you can go wherever you like, Ana. This has all finished. I've been made to look ridiculous, all Vetusta is laughing aloud at me. Mesía scorns me, he'll spit upon me as soon as he sees me. The spiritual father is a poor devil. All because I am what I am! The wretch! He insults me because I'm not free!'

The canon shook inside his soutane, as if he were bound in chains, and struck the sofa a herculean blow with his fist.

He rubbed his hands over his forehead and tried to come to his senses; he called for his cloak; he looked for his shovel hat, forced himself not to say anything else, fumbled for the door and left without turning his head.

He thought Ana would follow him, call him, start crying. But he soon realized that he was alone. He reached the porch. He stopped and listened. No, nobody was calling him. Once in the street he looked up at the balcony windows. None of them opened. 'There weren't even any eyes following him. That woman was staying in there. It was all true. She was deceiving him; she was a woman. But not any woman! She was his woman! The woman he loved with all his soul! Yes, yes, with all his soul! That was how he had loved her. But women couldn't understand that – the purest of them wanted something else.' And hundreds of enormities passed through his memory. All the carnality which had accumulated there during many years as a confessor. His conscience reminded him of Teresina. Teresina pale and smiling, and saying inside his brain, 'And what about you?' 'I am a man,' he replied. And he quickened his step. 'I loved her for my soul.' 'And her body, you loved that too,' said Teresina in his brain, 'her body, too, remember?' 'Yes, yes – but I was waiting – I would have waited until death rather than lose her. Because I loved all of her. She is my woman – the woman I love with all my body and soul. And she stayed behind, far away now, lost for ever!'

Ana had stood watching the canon theologian leave without finding the courage to stop him or the strength to call out to him. She had heard an idea inside her head, near her ears – word for word: 'This canon is in love with me!' 'Yes, in love as a man, not with the mystical, idealistic, seraphic love which she had imagined. He was jealous, he was dying of jealousy. He wasn't her elder brother, her soul brother, he was a man hiding passions – love, jealousy, anger – under his soutane. She was loved by a canon!' Ana shuddered as if she had felt the touch of something cold and slimy. That travesty of love made her smile to herself with a bitterness which came to her mouth from deep in her body. Her father, Don Carlos the free-thinker, suddenly appeared before her, in his shirt-sleeves, in Loreto, by a table, arguing with a priest and some other cronies, all atheists or progressives. Ana could remember phrases spoken by her father and the other gentlemen as if she had just heard them: 'The clergy was a corruptor of consciences, the priest was the same as other men, ecclesiastical celibacy was a mask.' All these asseverations, which she had heard without understanding them, came back into her memory with a clear, precise meaning, like lessons learned from experience. They wanted to corrupt her! That house – that silence – that Doña Petronila. Ana was disgusted and ashamed, and she hurried to the door. She left without saying goodbye. At home, Don Víctor was deafening the world with hammer-blows. He was building a model bridge which he intended to show at the exhibition to be held during the fiestas of St Matthew.[2] No longer did he cover his hammer with flannel; oh no, iron struck iron, there was a blood-curdling racket. 'He was the master there, the fact that his wife had attended the ball was proof of it. Paraguay was all over and done with, no more mysticism; a prudent piety inherited from our forefathers was more than enough. Apart from that: activity, industry and art – plenty of plays, plenty of hunting and plenty of hammering. Crash crash crash boom! Long live life!' Thus thought Don Víctor, with his tartan dressing-gown girt about him, hammering away as if his life depended upon it in his new workshop, a small room on the ground floor with a door giving on to the courtyard. The sun came in as far as Quintanar's feet, striking sparks from the beads and the golden ribbons on his semi-Turkish slippers. The carpenter was whistling; the song-thrush – the finest song-thrush in the province – which Quintanar carried with him from one room to another, was also whistling in its cage hanging on a piece of wire. Ana contemplated her husband in silence. 'He was her father! She loved him as she had loved her father! He even resembled Don Carlos in some ways. That February sun, a promise of spring; that fresh atmosphere, an invitation to activity and movement; that hammering, that whistling, those tiny wispy clouds crossing the blue square framed by the eaves of the courtyard roof – it was all edifying. It was her home, she was queen in it, the peace in it was her peace!' As Don Víctor put down his hammer and went to pick up his saw he caught sight of his wife.

In silence they smiled at each other. 'The sun rejuvenated Quintanar. And he was an excellent carpenter. His inventions might tend towards the fantastic, his mechanics might be a little idealistic, but he could do what he liked with a piece of wood. And he was such a neat workman!'

Ana praised her husband's workmanship.

This encouraged him; he coloured with satisfaction and promised her a sewing-box by the following week. 'All of it, all of it my own work.'

For a moment the judge's wife forgot the disillusionment which she had suffered that morning. When she remembered it again she found that Don Fermín was no longer a wicked man, but a pitiable one. Still, it was absurd of him to fall in love, being a canon. Ana had often imagined all the combinations possible in romantic love – except this one. 'One could conceive of the sacrilegious love of a priest in an opera – but a real prebendary in purple bands!' Her sense of honour also protested, with instinctive repugnance. 'But De Pas was worthy of pity. It was Doña Petronila who was unforgivable. If Ana ever spoke to the canon theologian again – as was likely, because after all they ought to explain things to each other – it wouldn't be in that old woman's house. What had she been trying to do? Who did she think Ana Ozores was?'

Don Víctor returned from a stroll a little later, happily singing excerpts from comic operas, and suddenly suggested to his wife that they should accept the marchioness's invitation to coffee after lunch, so as to go to promenade together and see the people in their carnival dress.

'Oh, no, Quintanar! I've had enough fun and games, enough of the carnival. I don't want any more parties – I'm tired. That ball last night upset me. No more, please – no more. Didn't I obey you yesterday? Isn't that enough for you?'

'All right, my child, all right – I shall not insist.'

Don Víctor fell silent, as some of his joy disappeared. He did not venture to make further use of that energy which God had given him. 'There was no need to tighten the screws too much.'

But, of course, he himself went to have coffee and to promenade.

Ana was left alone. Through the open balcony window in her boudoir came the sound of the distant music in the Esplanade, where the carnival was being celebrated. That indistinct music, coming and going in gusts like the wind, filled her soul with sorrow. She thought about Mesía, the tempter, and she thought about the canon theologian, in love, jealous, defenceless. Her compassion was infinite now. After all, it was he who had opened her soul to the light of religion and virtue. Ana thought about her faith, cracked and broken as if it had been attacked by an earthquake. The canon theologian and faith were too closely bound together in her spirit for her disillusion not to damage her beliefs. Besides, she had always loved more than she had believed. Don Fermín had tried to imbue her with the fear of God and of the Church, and with a vague, dreamy spirituality – but of dogmas he had spoken little. Ana realized that her imagination had exerted more influence upon her piety than was advisable, as far as the firmness of that edifice was concerned. Far distant now were the days of supposed mysticism, of contemplation. She had been ill then, and

St Teresa, and her own weakness and sorrow, had made her soul burn with visions of pure idealism. But when her health had returned, an active, unthinking piety had triumphed; the canon had eclipsed the saint, and there had been more talk about their 'tender brotherhood in virtue' than about God Himself. She could see it all now. Don Fermín wanted her for himself.

'It had all been a kind of preparation. For what?'

'Oh, Mesía was nobler, he fought without a visor, exposing his breast, declaring when he was going to strike his blows. He hadn't abused his friendship with Don Víctor, he hadn't refused to take no for an answer. But they both loved her!' Ana found tender if not intense consolation in this thought. 'She couldn't give in to either man. Certainly, she could not and would not give in to the canon theologian. She owed him eternal gratitude, but anything more would be a hideous absurdity. Disgusting. A fine thing it would be to start out on worldly love at nearly thirty years of age – and with a priest!' Ana's face fired up with shame and anger. 'But can that man have been expecting me to . . . ? Never!'

The judge's wife spent many days as she had spent that afternoon. The same ideas, in a thousand different combinations, crossed her excited brain.

Whenever she sensed Mesía's presence in her desires, she shunned it in shame. She was also ashamed that the memory of the ball and, in particular, the memory of touching him did not stir her to painful remorse. 'But no, it didn't. She regarded it all as a dream; she didn't believe herself to have been responsible, clearly responsible for what had happened that night. They had made her drunk with words, with lights, with vanity, with noise, with champagne. But she would be a wretch if she allowed Don Alvaro to continue enticing her. She would not allow herself to be deceived by the sophism which temptation shouted into her ears: after all, Don Alvaro isn't a canon, if you shun him you run the risk of falling into the other man's arms. Lies, cried integrity. I'm not going to give in to either of them. I love Don Fermín with my soul – in spite of his love for me, which perhaps he can't overcome just as I can't overcome Mesía's influence on my senses. But I'm quite sure I don't love the canon in any blameworthy way. Yes – quite sure. I must shun the canon, of course, but there's even more need for me to shun Don Alvaro. His passion's illicit, too, even though it's not repugnant and sacrilegious like the other man's. I shall shun both of them!'

Her only refuge was her home: Don Víctor with his Frillity and with all the lumber in his museum of manias; Don Víctor complete with the Spanish theatre of the Golden Age.

'But home had its own poetry, too.' Ana tried her best to find it. If she had children they would have given her so many things to do! How delightful that would have been! But there weren't any children in her home. And it wouldn't do any good to go and adopt an orphan. Regardless of all that, Ana began to work at home with enthusiasm, and to look after Don Víctor with diligence. Within a week she realized that this was the greatest hypocrisy of all. The household tasks were soon done. Why pretend that she was satisfied by an inadequate, insignificant activity which did not keep her mind occupied for so long as half an hour? Don Víctor was heartily grateful for Ana's domestic solicitude, but as far as he was concerned he would have preferred things to have continued as before. He was the only person who could sew a button as he liked a button to be sewn; to clean his study was to martyr him; it was useless to make his bed with exquisite care because he was, in any case, going to unmake it, shaking the pillows and turning down the sheets as he liked them to be turned down. When Ana left the housework to be done in the old way again, Don Víctor was heartily grateful for this, too, and breathed freely once more. 'His beloved wife's interference was worthy of eternal gratitude – but annoying for him. A fool knows more in his own house than a wise man in another's.'

Don Alvaro was not in a hurry. 'This time he was certain.' But he did not want to *brusquer une attaque*. The theory of the *quarter of an hour* was an incomplete theory. There was something in it, but in certain cases the only person who could discover a woman's quarter of an hour was a good clockmaker. He intended to wait until Lent was over. After all, this was a religion-besotted woman who was going to fast and not eat meat. A bad business. Easter offered the best opportunity. After the resurrection of Our Lord Jesus Christ the world seems happier and its pleasures seem more permissible; spring, well-advanced by then, does its bit to help; the fiestas, to which he would make Don Víctor take his wife, would be another spur to her desire. 'Yes, Easter was the time to measure swords.'

'Besides, he wanted to prepare for the campaign, being in a somewhat feeble state. The summer in Palomares had led to a kind of bankruptcy of his health. The minister's wife had loved much.[3] These excesses of defeated women were always in direct ratio to the square of the distance: the further the woman was from vice, the more excessive she was when she fell. If the judge's wife fell she was going to be very excessive indeed.' And Mesía prepared himself. He read books about hygiene, he did physical exercises, he went for frequent rides. And he refused to accompany Paco on his cheap adventures, paid for on the spot. 'The devil sick of flesh would be a monk,' Paco said. Don Alvaro smiled, and went early to bed. He rose early, too. At dawn the Esplanade was already a place of perfume, freshness and song. Birds hopped from branch to branch making their nests ready for the April eggs; they were like decorators hanging out the drapery for the spring fiestas, up in the lofty trees which surrounded and covered the broad paths and turned them into great halls. March was beginning with all the heat of June; early in the morning there was already a scorching sun. That advanced spring, a frequent phenomenon in Vetusta, was one of nature's jokes; for winter always returned – winter at its worst, with cold days, frost and rain, interminable rain. But Don Alvaro took advantage of the interval of light and heat, which was no less agreeable to him for being ephemeral; he was not one of those people who measure happiness by its duration. In any event, he did not believe in happiness, a metaphysical concept in his opinion; he believed in pleasure, which cannot be gauged in terms of time. One morning, in the main hall of the Esplanade, which was empty because few people trusted the early spring, Don Alvaro saw the shape of a priest in the distance. He was tall, his movements were stately. It was the canon theologian. They were alone in the promenade and had to cross, for they were walking towards each other on the same side. They greeted each other without speaking. Don Alvaro was a little frightened or, at least, a little apprehensive that he might be frightened. 'If this man,' he thought, 'in love with the judge's wife, and spurned by her, were suddenly to go mad on seeing me, believing me to be his rival, and were to hurl himself at me, punching and pummelling – here, alone . . .' Mesía remembered the scene of the swing in Vegallana's garden.

And when the canon theologian saw Don Alvaro he thought: 'If I were to throw myself upon this man and – as I could, as I am certain I could – were to drag him over the ground and trample his head and his guts under foot . . . !' And he was frightened of himself. He had read that in nervous people images and fears of this kind can provoke the corresponding actions. He remembered a certain murderer in the tales of Edgar Allan Poe.[4] The canon's look was insolent, provocative. As he greeted Mesía his eyes said: 'Take that! there's a good slap on the face for you.' But the greeting and the look of Mesía replied: 'God be with you, I don't understand a word of what you're trying to say.'

Each man continued on his way, but on the following morning neither returned to the Esplanade. They had gone there to accomplish opposite goals. The canon went for long walks in order to consume useless energy; Mesía in order to regain lost energy which he hoped he would be needing before very long. After that morning each went to out-of-the-way places for his walks, fearing another encounter.

But soon they both had to stay at home.

For, of course, winter returned with all its rigour, laughing heartily at those gullible souls who had believed themselves to be in the middle of spring. The birds hid in their holes and corners. The blossoming trees suffered the fury of the weather like damsels dressed up to the nines who on a day in the country, in their gay calico and their showy, delicate trimmings of silk and tulle, are surprised by a squall of rain, out in the open, without anywhere to shelter, without so much as an umbrella. The little white and pink flowers of the fruit-trees fell dead upon the mire, ripped to pieces by hail. Everything was set back; the attempt at an early spring had been unsuccessful and so everything had to start again – noses to the grindstone.

This happened in the middle of Lent. The result was that Vetusta gave itself to its devotions with redoubled fervour. The Jesuit missioners had passed through the town like another hailstorm; the flowers of love and joy planted by the carnival had been destroyed, beaten down by force of penance, thanks to Father Maroto, a retired artilleryman who preached gunshot and struck the fear of God into his listeners, and Father Goberna, a mellifluous French priest who pronounced Spanish with his throat and his nose, talked about *Gomoggha*, and cited the splendours of Nineveh and Babylon – lost for ever, here today and gone tomorrow – as proof of the paltriness of all things human. Vetusta was a cowed city. The rains and the Jesuits, between them, had made it sad, apprehensive, crestfallen. The general aspect of nature – grey, dissolved in puddles and mud – was an invitation not so much to remember the brevity of existence as to recognize the worthlessness of the world. It seemed as if everything was going to be liquefied. The universe, to judge from Vetusta and its environs, was less an ephemeral dream than a lengthy nightmare, full of images of dirt and stickiness. Father Goberna, who knew how to bring local colour into his sermons, did not say in Vetusta that we are but dust; he said that we are but mud. Dust in Vetusta? If only God would send some.

The bad weather took Anita Ozores's calm, languid resignation away from her. When the unrelenting rain returned, so did her sudden fears, the protests of her will, and those thistles pricking her soul. But now there was no canon theologian to help her!

She felt lonelier and more abandoned every day, and was already beginning to think that she had been unfair to the canon in thinking so badly of him and letting him flee from her in despair with those suspicions plunged into his heart like poisoned arrows. 'Why hadn't she been more affected by that disillusionment, that profanation of a disinterested, ideal, pure friendship? Perhaps because being loved, regardless of who the lover was, could never be an unwelcome experience for her, even if she did have to spurn and indeed revile the love. Perhaps because she knew that it was in her own power to bring an end to their estrangement. Couldn't she – perhaps the very next time she needed spiritual consolation – run to the confessional and persuade her confessor that she was not what he imagined her to be? And maybe she ought to do so as soon as possible. Why should De Pas think that what hadn't happened had happened? Yes, she must tell him the truth – that is to say, the truth about what hadn't happened. Don Alvaro hadn't managed to make Ana Ozores bestow any favours on him, this was the truth.'

But before she went to find the canon theologian she wanted to strengthen her spirit by herself. She could feel her faith wavering, the banal sophisms of Don Carlos the free-thinker returning again and again to torment her. She would begin by doubting the virtue of the priest and soon find herself doubting the Church and many of its dogmas. Then she would hurry to church. Skipping over puddles and defying showers she would go from one church to the next, from one novena to another, and linger in some cold empty nave, sitting in a pew to meditate. The cough of an old man praying in an unseen chapel echoed and re-echoed in the vault; the steps of an irreverent acolyte resounded on an altar platform; the noises of the streets of Vetusta reached her ears as a faint hum which enhanced the quiet of the church. Ana begged the solitude and the languid stillness to give her something like inspiration, or some kind of perfume of piety which, she thought, should emanate from those holy walls and from the altars, displaying in the white light of day their saints of plaster and varnished wood, worn down, it seemed, by the friction of prayers and the smoke from candles. Those images were reminiscent of the decorations in a theatre seen by daylight, and of actors in the street, out of the splendour of the footlights. But Anita did not think about that now. She was here to search for her faith, which was crumbling away. 'Why? What had the Church to do with the canon theologian? Wasn't it possible for that gentleman to have fallen in love with her – and for all the Church's teachings still to be true? Of course it was. She prayed that she might believe it. Oh, but it would be bad if the test didn't show the canon to be innocent. If he, her elder brother, were no more than a hypocrite, she would have to admit that Don Carlos – her father, after all – had been right about many things. Yes, yes, her father, the father she had mourned with heartfelt tears, who had said that religion was man's internal homage to God, to a God we could not imagine, who was not as positive religions said He was, but much better, much greater! Her father had spoken all these heresies!' And she prayed, prayed, because it no longer did any good to meditate. A voice inside her, severe and a little pedantic, shouted at the end of it all, 'But let's be quite clear about one thing: even if Don Carlos was right, even if God is greater, better than men could ever say or think or write in books, that doesn't mean to say that He overlooks sins of which our consciences will always accuse us. Don Alvaro will still be forbidden, whatever God is like. Evil is evil, regardless of other considerations. That's right,' the judge's wife said to herself, finding comfort in this decision, 'even if my faith does fail, I will continue to fight this passion of my senses, for it will still be wicked.'

She began to notice that the empty church did not inspire her with devotion; her brain, maybe ailing, drew up strange analogies, and those cold walls, those saints off duty between services, so to speak, reminded her of tired kings, tired monsters in fairgrounds, tired actors, tired politicians and all the other beings whose destiny it is to make a public spectacle of themselves for the gross material admiration of the foolish gaping multitude. The church without active worship, the church at rest, was like a theatre in the daytime. The sexton and the acolyte climbing up to the altar-piece, rubbing shoulders with the wooden image, placing candles in a symmetrical arrangement, consulting the laws of perspective, seemed like accomplices in some trick. In addition to all these sacrilegious fancies – the morbid temptations of a sickly spirit and the cause of so much inner strife – Ana suffered the torment of distraction. She began prayers but could not finish them; a phrase repeated on some pious inscription made her feel sick; the solitude of the church was peopled with a thousand images, little devils of distraction; its silence was a swarm of bees buzzing inside her. All this made her leave the empty church. She returned when services were being held: in the new piety which she was seeking her senses must play an important role. She sought the smell of incense, the splendours of the altar and the chasubles, the pulsing and the mysterious power of common prayer, the rustling of the *ora pro nobis* of the Catholic masses, the systematic tranquillity of the ceremonial, the gravity of the officiating priest, the mysteriousness of sacred canticles which seemed to float down from the clouds even though they only came from the choir, and the melodies of the organ, recalling in a moment all the warm, tender emotions of her former piety – that undefiled faith, a mixture of maternal caresses and mystical hopes.

The Novena to Our Lady of Sorrows[5] was of exceptional importance that year in Vetusta, if *El Lábaro* is to be believed.

Certainly St Isidore's Church, where the novena was performed, was decorated as it had never been decorated before, thanks to the seeds of artificial, lavish piety which Fathers Goberna and Maroto had left behind them. The church could not be festooned with blue and silver, nor could a cardboard construction imitating a fretwork gothic chapel be placed in front of the high-altar reredos, as during the Novena of the Immaculate Conception, but everything which was compatible with the Seven Sorrows of the Virgin was done. The effect was a majestic, sad, indeed lugubrious luxury. All was black and gold. The cathedral choir was transported *en masse* to the stalls of St Isidore's and reinforced by some straggling members of the last comic-opera company to have gone bankrupt in Vetusta. The sermons were entrusted to another Jesuit, Father Martínez, who came from afar and charged high fees. At the offertory table, set up against the screen at the main entrance, facing the high altar, alms were collected and holy books, medals and scapulars were sold by the noblest ladies, the prettiest ladies and the most meddlesome ladies.

Rain, boredom, piety and force of habit each brought its own contingent to the church, which was full to overflowing every afternoon. It could not have held a single Vetustan more.

The young laymen of the city, students most of them, were notable neither for excessive piety nor for premature irreligiousness; they simply did not think about certain things. There were both Carlists and liberals among them; but nearly all of them went to mass to look at the girls. Nor did they miss the novenas. Scattered throughout the chapels and corners of St Isidore's, with the ends of their cloaks tossed over their shoulders, and romantic or mischievous looks (according to disposition) on their faces, they *made eyes* at marriageable girls, who were more modest and better Christians than they, but no less eager for *relations*. While Father Martínez repeated for the hundredth time – and he had already made more than a thousand pesetas – that there is no sorrow like a mother's sorrow and, without the slightest sorrow on his own part, poured over the image dressed in mourning on the altar all the decayed rhetoric of his stale baroque oratory, sacrilegious love flew unseen to and fro through nave, aisles and chapels like a butterfly sent by the spring from the country to the town to announce the new joy.

To Ana, as she knelt near the sanctuary and recollected her spirit to immerse it in pure piety, the moanful mumbling in the pulpit sounded like the distant patter of the rain accompanied by the howls of the wind caught in doors. She was not listening to the Jesuit, she was listening to the eloquent silence of an act of manifest transcendence repeated throughout centuries and centuries in thousands and thousands of towns: collective piety, corporate devotion, the almost miraculous elevation of an entire people, prosaic and debased by poverty and ignorance, to ideal regions, to the adoration of the Absolute, in an act of prodigious concentration. As the judge's wife thought about these things she wished that the wave of piety would drag her with it, that she could be a molecule of its foam, or a particle of the dust being drawn by an unknown force through the desert of life towards a vaguely conceived ideal.

The voice of Father Martínez stopped, and the organ began to say in another and much better way what the de luxe orator had said. The organ seemed to take Mary's grief more to heart. Ana thought about Mary, about Rossini, about the first time she had heard his *Stabat Mater*,[6] when she was eighteen years old, in that same church. And after the organ had had its say, the faithful, like a well-rehearsed monster choir, sang the solemn repetitive choruses of hymns which came down from on high as if it were raining fresh flowers. Children were singing, old men were singing, women were singing. And Ana began to weep – she did not know why. At her side a poor boy, blond, pale and thin, about six years old, seated on the floor by the skirt of his mother, a woman covered with rags, was singing, his wide-open, unblinking eyes riveted on the Lady of Sorrows on the portable altar; he was singing, and suddenly, because of some mysterious association of ideas, he fell silent, turned his face to his mother, and said, 'Mother, give me a piece of bread!'

An old man by a confessional was singing, in a deep, sweet, quivering voice – oblivious of the exhausting toil forced on him by hunger, against all the rights of old age. All the people were singing, and the organ, like a father, was accompanying this choir and leading it through the ideal regions of ineffable consoling sorrow, the regions of music.

'And there are wretches', thought Ana, 'who want to do away with all this! Oh, no, no, not I! With you, holy Virgin, always with you, always at your feet. Being with those who are sad, that's the eternal religion, spending my life weeping for the sorrows of the world, loving amidst tears.' And she remembered the canon theologian. 'Oh how ungrateful, how cruel had been her behaviour towards that man! How sad, how lonely she had left him! Vetusta was insulting him, mocking him, scorning him, after raising him up on a throne of admiration, and she, she who owed him her honour, her religion, everything she valued most, was abandoning and forgetting him too. And why? Perhaps – almost certainly – because of idle fears prompted by vanity and by crude, coarse suspicion. Just because she had been bitten by that accursed maggot, sensual love, just because she had surrendered to Don Alvaro in her desires if not in reality – this was the truth – just because she was a sinner, must her soul brother, her beloved spiritual father be one too? What proof had she? Couldn't it all be idle fears, couldn't her vanity have made her imagine things? When had De Pas ever made any advances which could give her the slightest reason to suspect his purity? Hadn't they been alone together a thousand times, very close to each other, hadn't they touched each other, hadn't she, imprudently perhaps, ventured innocent caresses, soft nothings, which would have made any fire hidden in him burst forth? And he's been abandoned! They even make fun of him in the newspapers; even irreligious people are praising the missioners, to diminish his influence; fashion and calumny have cast him aside, and like the wretched multitude I too shout, crucify him, crucify him! What about the sacrifice I had promised? That great sacrifice I wanted to make, to pay that man what I owe him?'

At that moment the pious people stopped singing; there was a solemn silence; then coughs, a shuffling of shoes and clogs on the slippery stone floor – suppressed impatience. Near the main entrance the click clack could be heard of the coins with which Visitación and the marchioness knocked the collection plate as a reminder to forgetful charity. Doors creaked; there was a faint whispering in the air. In the choir violins and flutes showed signs of life, with muffled moans and sighs. Sheets of music rustled. A violin growled. Tin was tapped twice. Silence again. The *Stabat Mater* began.

Rossini's sublime music raised Ana's imagination to a pitch of excitement; from her irritated nerves came a decision which burst into being in her brain with all the compelling force of a mania. It was like a hallucination of her will. She could see the picture of her decision, as if she herself were there. 'Yes – she – she, Ana at the feet of the canon theologian, like Mary at the foot of the Cross. The canon theologian was being crucified, too, by calumny, by stupidity, by envy and by scorn and the people, his murderers, were turning their backs on him and leaving him there alone – and she – she – she was, too! Oh, no, to Calvary, to Calvary! To the foot of the cross of the man who was not her son but her father, her brother, the brother and father of her spirit.

'The Virgin was telling her yes, it was right, the decision was worthy of a Christian. Wherever there is a cross one can weep at its foot without thinking about what the man hanging on it was when he was alive; all the more reason to weep at the foot of the cross of a martyr. She was even feeling sorry for the bad robber.[7] How much sorrier she must feel for the canon theologian, who was not a robber at all – neither a good one nor a bad one!' The form that the sacrifice would take, the day, the occasion, everything was clear to her now: she swore not to turn back. This intense excitement was what she needed to continue living. If, later, tiredness, the relaxation of tensed fibres within her, filled her spirit with cowardliness, with prosaic worldly objections, with the fear of what people might say, she would not take any notice – she would go straight on to her goal without hesitating or deliberating any more. She would do what she had decided to do. And calm and sure of herself she turned her thoughts back to the Mother of Sorrows, throwing herself into the waves of the sad music with a suicidal impulse. Yes, she wanted to kill her doubt, her grief, her coldness, the influence of the stupid, circumspect world, always watching its step. She wanted to return to the fire of passion – for that was her element.

XXVI

After the day on which Don Pompeyo was chief mourner at Don Santos Barinaga's burial he never again enjoyed good health. The shivers which shook his body at the cemetery, and which recurred with increasing intensity during the illness that followed his soaking, came back every so often. Guimarán was always sad now; that Sun of Justice which the atheist worshipped suffered eclipses, and he found the spectacle of the wickedness all around him so disheartening that he began to have doubts about the unwavering progress of Humanity. 'Laurent[1] was right, we were far in advance of savages, but there were some fine scoundrels still left. And what about friendship? Friendship was a thing of the past.' Paquito Vegallana, Alvaro Mesía, Joaquinito Orgaz and the respectable, or apparently respectable, Señor Foja, who claimed to be such good friends, had made a fool of him, ridiculed him. They were a pack of libertines who met to gorge themselves and repudiate positive religion so as to win him over to their side and free their own minds from the fear of hell. Don Pompeyo severed all relations with these 'frivolous spirits' and never again set foot in the Gentlemen's Club. He took the decision on Christmas Day, when he discovered that word was going around Vetusta that he, Don Pompeyo Guimarán, the man who had more respect than anybody else for all creeds, although he did not believe in any of them, had profaned the cathedral by hearing Midnight Mass while drunk. It was even said that he had taken a bottle of anisette into the cathedral, under his cloak. 'Anisette! – he – Don Pompeyo!' He did not return to the Gentlemen's Club. 'Those infamous creatures who had made him drunk, or almost drunk, and had then forced him to enter the cathedral, were quite capable of having invented that calumny in an attempt to destroy him. For what authority could be retained by the atheism which became intoxicated in order to celebrate Christianity's feast-days, and attended services in the Holy Cathedral Church to blaspheme and stagger about its respectable aisles?

'Upon his soul – he had enough worries, with Barinaga's civil burial and the dislike which a great part of the town had consequently taken to the canon theologian!

'No, he did not want any more religious struggles. He was becoming a little too old for such enterprises. It was better to keep quiet, to live in peace with everybody.' He shuddered whenever he recalled Barinaga's death. 'Dying like a dog! And I have a wife and four daughters!'

He became a misanthrope. He always went out for his walk alone, at nightfall, and soon returned home.

One night his attention was attracted by a noise like that of a beehive, near the cathedral. He heard rockets. What was happening? The tower was illuminated with coloured glasses and Chinese lanterns. At its foot, in the narrow area at the cathedral entrance, which was paved with slippery stone and enclosed by strong, rough iron railings, he saw a swarming mass of people, like a heap of black maggots. From that human ferment emanated – like gas bubbles – shouts, laughter and a dull buzz reminiscent of the swish of the sea heard from a distance.

Don Pompeyo, whose teeth were chattering with cold and fever, stopped at the top of the Calle de la Rúa to contemplate that crowd, jammed together at the foot of the tower in such a confined space when it could have made itself comfortable by spreading out to

occupy the whole cathedral square. 'He knew what it was. The Roman
Catholics were celebrating some religious anniversary. But what a
way to celebrate! What a mockery!' Don Pompeyo walked towards the
cathedral and stood outside the railed area, watching. The best people
and the worst people in Vetusta were piled together there. Seamstresses, gunsmiths, the cream of the promenade in the Boulevard –
that great world of rags and tatters with its stench of poverty – was,
vociferous and insolent, rubbing shoulders with *elegant Vetusta*, the
Vetusta of the Mall and of the balls at the Gentlemen's Club; to crown
this – in Don Pompeyo's opinion – scandal, the gilded youth of the
Vetustan clergy, all those seminary licentiates as he malevolently
called them, were also there under the cloak of celebrating a religious
feast, packed and pressed, clerical garb and all, into that great sausage
of lascivious flesh, in the dark, with hardly any air to breathe, and
with no other amusement than the improper one of feeling the contact
of their fellow creatures, feeling the instinct of the flock or rather the
herd. Turning his eyes away 'from that fermenting corruption, from
that mindless mass of maggots', he raised them aloft and gazed up at
the steeple with its speck of red light at the top showing the way to
heaven. 'There's nothing Christian here', he thought, 'except that pile
of stones!'

He escaped from the cathedral, sad, apprehensive, doubting
Humanity, Justice, Progress – and clenching his teeth to prevent them
from chattering. He entered his house, asked for linden tea and went
to bed. When he was surrounded by his wife and daughters, covering
him with all the blankets in the house, this inveterate atheist felt
nervous tenderness, comforting warmth, and said to himself, 'There
is a religion, after all: the religion of the home.'

The following morning he awoke the entire household with his
bell. 'He felt ill. Somoza must be summoned.' Somoza said that it was
nothing. A week later he posed the arduous problem of what he called
'preparing the patient'. 'He had to be prepared.' What for? 'For a
good death.'

Two of Don Pompeyo's four daughters and their mother fainted.

The other two, being stronger, deliberated. Who was to bell the
cat? Who was to suggest to their father that he should receive the
sacraments?

His eldest daughter, Agapita, suggested it to him.

'Papa – dear, good, papa – surely you don't want to make me very
upset, above all make mamma upset – for she loves you so – and she's
so religious . . .'

'You don't have to say any more, dear Agapita,' said the sick man
in a feeble, tender, mellifluous voice. 'I know what you are asking me
to do. To confess. Very well, my child. Of course, of course. I have
been awaiting this moment for days. Doctor Somoza is an angel, and
he didn't want to give me a fright; but I realized that things were

going badly. I have been thinking a great deal about you all, and about what I could do to make you happy. I have only one request – that you call the canon theologian. I want Señor De Pas to hear my confession; I need him to hear me, and to forgive me.'

Agapita wept upon her father's scrawny breast. In the sitting-room Somoza and Guimarán's youngest daughter, Perpetua, had heard the dialogue. Half an hour later all Vetusta knew about the miracle. 'The Atheist had called for the canon theologian to help him to die a good death!'

Don Fermín was in bed. His mother, lying at its foot like a dog, growled as soon as she smelt an intruder. The canon was complaining of neuralgia; the slightest sound was like a kick on the head. Doña Paula had prohibited noise, all noise. The occupants of the house went about on tiptoe; indeed, they did their best to fly.

Teresina thought that the message from the Señoritas de Guimarán was important enough to merit an infringement of the general rule.

'A servant has come with a message from the Señora and Señoritas de Guimarán.'

'Guimarán!' said the canon, who was awake although his eyes were closed.

'Guimarán! You're mad,' said Doña Paula in a hushed voice.

'Yes, ma'am – Guimarán, Don Pompeyo, he's dying and he wants the master to go and confess him.'

Both mother and son jumped up. Doña Paula jumped to her feet, Don Fermín to a sitting position.

Guimarán's servant girl was summoned, and made to repeat the message.

She wept, and between sighs she described the family's sorrow and the consolation which hearing Don Pompeyo ask for the Holy Sacraments had brought them.

The canon theologian and Doña Paula consulted each other with their eyes. They understood each other's meaning.

'Won't it make you worse?'

'No. Say I'm coming immediately.'

'You can go, both of you. Say that the master is very ill, but first things are first and he's coming immediately.'

Mother and son were left alone.

'Do you think the scoundrel's playing a trick on us?'

'No, Mother, he's just a poor devil. It was bound to end like this. But I didn't know he was ill.'

De Pas was talking as he dressed. His mother helped him and looked in the bottom of a trunk for his warmest clothes.

'But Fermo, what if it makes you really ill – I mean seriously ill?'

'No – leave this in my hands. This cannot wait – and my head can. I must be there before the word gets around. Don't you understand?'

'Yes, of course, you're right.'

They fell silent.

The canon theologian stood up, supporting himself between the wall and his mother's shoulder.

When they reached his study, he sat down again.

'Shall we send for a carriage?'

'Yes, of course. That should have been done by now. Benito, here at the corner . . .'

Teresa appeared.

'A letter for the master.'

Doña Paula took it; she did not recognize the writing on the envelope.

Fermín did; it was Ana's writing – distorted, penned by a trembling hand.

'Who's it from?' asked Doña Paula when she saw her son going pale.

'I don't know. I'll look at it later. To the carriage now – to see Guimarán.'

He stood up, slipped the letter into an inside pocket and walked to the door with a steady step.

Although Doña Paul was suspicious, she did not dare insist this time. She felt sorry for that son of hers who, sick, sad, maybe desperate, was going out for her sake, to prolong the history of her greatness, of her profit; he was going out to rescue lost credit, in search of the kind of miracle that gets most talked about, the kind of miracle that's most telling and useful, a miracle of conversion. 'He was a hero. How he had suffered all through Lent!' She had guessed in the end that her son and the judge's wife weren't seeing each other any more; they'd had a tiff, it seemed. At first the mother's egotism had triumphed and she had rejoiced over the separation. She knew that her son would never sink so low as to seek a reconciliation, that he would sooner die in despair, like a dog, in that bed where he had finally fallen, after trying to walk off his suppressed rage throughout Vetusta by day and by night. But Fermo's taciturn despair, complicated by a mysterious ailment with an ugly look about it which might lead to madness, frightened his mother, who adored her son in her way. There were nights when, as she watched his grief, she thought of a thousand absurdities, of a mother's miracles, of going herself in search of the infamous woman who was to blame for it all, and cutting her throat, or dragging her back by her damned hair, back to the foot of that bed, to watch over him like her, to weep like her, to save her son at any cost, at the cost of reputation, of salvation, of everything, to save him or die with him . . . These absurd ideas, which Doña Paula's good sense soon dispelled, left her with a pent-up, concentrated anger and a vague notion of forming a strange plan, a plot to catch the judge's wife and make her submit to being used by Fermo for whatever he wanted – and then kill her or tear out her tongue.

The first days after the separation it had been the canon who, affecting indifference but always out of his mother's hearing, would ask Teresina: 'Have there been any messages, any letters for me?' But later Doña Paula – making sure first that her son was not there – often asked the housemaid, in a guttural strangled voice: 'Has anyone brought a message, or a note, for the master?'

No, nobody had brought anything. Lent had gone by, Passiontide had started, the first week was nearing its end – and still nothing came.

'It must be from her,' Doña Paula thought when she saw the note brought by Teresina. She felt both angry and pleased.

Hurricanes roared in the canon's ears. He was afraid he might fall. But he was determined to go. He promised himself that he would not read the letter to his mother, even though she beg it of him with outstretched arms. 'The letter belonged to him, to him alone.' The carriage arrived, a ramshackle old calash, drawn by two horses, one white and one black, both filthy and drooping with hunger.

Doña Paula, who had walked with her son to the porch, told the coachman in emphatic tones:

'Don Pompeyo Guimarán's house – you know . . .'

'Yes, yes.'

The carriage turned the corner. Don Fermín slid a window back and shouted:

'Go slowly – at a walking pace.'

He looked at the envelope.

He tore it open with trembling fingers and read the letters, in rose-coloured ink, hooked together, mingling into each other and jumping to and fro. He guessed rather than spelt out the characters as they evaporated before his weakened gaze.

Fermín, I need to see you. I want to beg your forgiveness and swear to you that I am worthy of your loving protection; God has seen fit to enlighten me again. The Virgin – I am certain of it – the Virgin wants me to seek you, to call out to you. I thought of going to your house myself, but I fear this might be indiscreet. I shall go none the less, in spite of everything, if it is true that you are ill and cannot leave home. Where can I talk to you? I am sure that you will not leave my letter unanswered, even if only out of charity. And if you do, I shall go to you. Your best friend, your slave, as I have sworn and shall demonstrate, ANA

De Pas stopped feeling his pains, he forgot all about them; he looked at the sky, it was darkening. In a fever of joy he grasped the coachman's blue overall. The man turned his head.

'What is it, master?'

'To the Plaza Nueva – the corner . . .'

'Yes, I know – but now?'

'Yes – now, and at full speed.'

The carriage continued at a walking pace.

'If Don Víctor is at home, which God forbid, it will be enough for Ana to look at me, to see me there. If he isn't – so much the better. In that case I shall speak, speak.'

Exhausted by so many efforts and surprises, Don Fermín dropped his head upon the threadbare blue rep of the seat; and in that dark corner of the carriage, his face hidden in his burning hands, he wept like a child, unashamed of those tears about which no one else would ever know.

Don Víctor was not at home.

The canon theologian stayed in Ozcres Mansion from seven o'clock until half past eight. When he left, the coachman was asleep in his seat. He had lit the lamps and settled down to wait, certain that he would be well paid for his sleep. Don Fermín walked into Don Pompeyo's house at a quarter to nine. The sitting-room was full of priests and devout laymen. All Guimarán's daughters stepped forward to greet the canon, whose face shone with a pallor which seemed supernatural. He gave the impression of being surrounded by an aureola.

Word had been sent three times to the canon theologian's house that he should come without delay. Don Pompeyo wanted to confess – to De Pas and only to De Pas. He said that the canon theologian was the only man to whom he wished to speak of his sins and declare his errors; that an inner voice was telling him with irresistible compulsion to call for the canon theologian and only the canon theologian.

Doña Paula replied that her son had left home at seven o'clock, in a carriage, as soon as word had come, and that he had gone straight to Guimarán's house. But since he did not arrive there, new messages were sent. Doña Paula was furious. What was her son up to now? What new madness was this?

In the end, there being no sign of the canon theologian, Guimarán's womenfolk called for the archdeacon, for Don Custodio, for the parish priest, and for any other clergyman who had ever spoken to their father. All to no avail. He wanted the canon theologian – his inner voice was shouting it at him. Gloucester stood by the death-bed, dying of envy and green with rage, yet still wearing his usual smile.

'But Señor Don Pompeyo, pray remember that we are all ministers of the Crucified – and so long as your conversion is sincere . . .'

'Yes, sir, it is sincere, I have never deceived anybody. I want to be restored to the Church, and die in its bosom, if it be God's will that I should die . . .'

'Oh, no, no . . .'

'That is my belief, too, but at all events, I want to return to the fold of my forefathers – but it must be with the help of Señor Don Fermín. I have powerful reasons for demanding this, the voice of my conscience.'

'Oh, most respectable, most respectable. But if the canon theologian does not come . . .'

'If he does not come, I shall confess with one of you – when I am in greater danger. In the meantime I want to wait for the canon theologian. I am resolved to wait for him.'

The parish priest was no more successful than the archdeacon. It goes without saying that Don Custodio achieved nothing. All these priests had been turned to ridicule, in Gloucester's opinion. The fact is that they did not know which way to turn.

'Do you think this is a plot?' said Mourelo into Don Custodio's ear.

After keeping everybody waiting so long, the canon theologian finally arrived.

Guimarán's daughters took him in triumph to their father.

De Pas looked like a saint descended from heaven. His handsome, strong face shone with the joy of a satisfied archangel and the youth of a robust yet fine-featured country lad: youth passionate and majestic. Guimarán shook the canon's gloved hand, but the canon could not bring his thoughts to bear on present reality, for he was still savouring the scene of tender reconciliation in which he had just played such an important role. 'Ana was his again: his slave! She had said so on her knees, weeping. And that project, that irrevocable intention to make all Vetusta see on a solemn occasion that the judge's wife was her confessor's slave, that she believed in him with blind faith . . . !' Remembering this, and all the other details of the conclusive proof which Ana had offered him, he felt his legs trembling; he was enervated by this joy which he called moral but which reached deep into his body like a breath of hot air blowing through his bones. He asked for a seat. He sat by the side of the sick man and for the first time he saw what was before him: a white, shrivelled face, all skin and bone, like light-coloured parchment. Guimarán's eyes were damp and shining as they gazed into the abysses of ideas among which his ailing brain was lost. They were like two windows out of which stared a speechless amazement.

The sick man and the confessor were left alone.

De Pas remembered his mother, the Jesuits, Barinaga, Gloucester, Mesía, Foja, the bishop; and he decided to make the most of this conversion which had come to hand, although it caused him some repugnance to do so. How much happiness in just one day! Ana and influence, both of which had been taken away from him, had returned together; Ana humbler than ever, influence with a certain supernatural aura. Yes, he was certain of it, he knew his Vetustans: one burial had made them scorn their tyrant, another burial was going to make them kneel at his feet – some of them fanaticized and the rest frightened, at least. While the canon spoke to Don Pompeyo about religion, about its sweet comforts, and about the need for a Church founded upon positive revelations, he was

preparing a detailed plan for turning his victory to good account . . .
Since the fool was delivering himself into his hands, let it not be
in vain. All the other fools – who believed that Guimarán was an
atheist because he was so wicked and so wise – would regard this
conquest as something of great importance, a gain of incalculable
value for the Church.

'The Atheist! Everybody considered him to be inoffensive,
yet most believed in his innate wickedness and his mysterious, diabolical superiority. And now this evil-doer – this devil –
was throwing himself at the feet of the spiritual lord of Vetusta.
Oh, what a splendid theatrical effect! No, *he* wasn't going to
be a fool, his mother was right, he must make the most of it.
And this was but a preparation for another yet more important
triumph. Hadn't it been said that even the judge's wife was
abandoning him? Well they'd soon see what the judge's wife was
doing.' Don Fermín was choking with pleasure and pride; his
passions were sticking in his throat. Don Pompeyo coughed, spat
phlegm, and murmured:

'You can believe me, Canon De Pas – it was a miracle – yes, a
miracle – I saw choirs of angels, I thought about Baby Jesus in his
little cradle – in the stable at Bethlehem – and I felt so tender – a –
paternal kind of feeling – I can't explain it . . . It's sublime, Don
Fermín – sublime – God in a cradle and me, blind – denying it all . . .
But what you say is true – I have spent my life thinking about God,
talking about Him – but back to front – I took everything back to
front . . .'

He continued his incoherent speech, interrupted by coughs and
sighs.

Then the canon theologian made him keep silence and listen.

Don Fermín spoke well and at length. If Don Pompeyo wanted to
obtain God's forgiveness he must, before he recovered, for doubtless he
would recover – and this was what he himself believed, too – give an
edifying example of piety. His conversion must be a solemn one, as
a warning to rogues and a healthy lesson to lukewarm believers.

'You can do the Church a great good now – having done it so much
harm in the past.'

'Just tell me – Don Fermín – I am the slave of your will – I want to
be forgiven by God and by you – you, whom I have offended so,
repeating calumnies. Believe me, it was not personal dislike, but
since my purpose was to combat fanaticism, the clergy in general –
besides, that was the only way to win Barinaga over. Oh, Barinaga!
Unhappy Don Santos! He must be in hell, mustn't he, Don Fermín?
Unhappy man! And I am to blame!'

'Who knows? The ways of God are inscrutable. And besides,
Barinaga can count upon God's infinite goodness. Who knows? What
is important now is to give a notable example of pure piety. This

lesson could bring many, many conversions in its wake. Ah, Don Pompeyo, you do not know how much our religion could gain from what you have done and what you are going to do!'

On the following morning all edified Vetusta prepared to accompany the Viaticum which was to be administered to Don Pompeyo in the afternoon. It was Palm Sunday. The air was saturated with religion.

'The vicar-general's stock is rising!' said furious Foja into Gloucester's ear when he met him by the cathedral entrance as he left mass.

'This is a plot!'

'Our fine Don Pompeyo's a complete idiot.'

'No, it's a plot.'

The fact was that the vicar-general's stock was rising much more than his enemies could imagine.

Just as it was not easy to explain why his discredit had been so great and so sudden, nobody now could fathom out how, in a few hours, opinion had turned back in his favour to such an extent that not a soul dared, in company, to recall his vices and sins; and the miraculous conversion which he had achieved was the sole topic of conversation.

It made no difference for Mourelo to shout on all sides: 'But it wasn't him, it was the Atheist's spontaneous impulse. That is what all these *esprits forts* do when their time comes.' Nobody paid any attention. 'Yes there had been a miracle, and the canon theologian was the one who had performed it.' No one doubted that. 'He was a great man, there was no getting away from it.' Doña Paula, through the agency of the Pug and other assistants, Doña Petronila, her conclave, Ripamilán, and even the bishop, who embraced the canon theologian in the cathedral soon after blessing the palms – all these and many others were enthusiastic propagandists of Don Fermín's fresh, new glory, his palmary victory over the hosts of Satan.

Foja, Mourelo and Don Custodio followed Mesía's advice, given to the former, and stopped trying to stem the surging tide of opinion, which was as favourable to Don Fermín as it could ever be.

'It was better to wait. The furore would come to an end in due course and then the whole town would see the miracle-monger Don Fermín De Pas in his true light again, in all his horrible nakedness.'

After Don Pompeyo had received the communion, with all the solemnity required by the circumstances, and with the family priest, Don Fermín, and Somoza, the doctor, standing at his bedside, all Vetusta, which had been waiting in the convert's house and at the doors, scattered throughout the city singing the praises of the unction with which death was being faced by the Atheist (who was now agreed by everyone to possess extraordinary talent and enormous wisdom) and celebrating the vicar-general's apostolic zeal, his tact, and his evangelical influence, which seemed almost magical, or miraculous.

When the religious ceremony was finished, there was a meeting of doctors. Somoza had made a mistake, as usual. Don Pompeyo was mortally ill, but he might last for many more days; he was still strong – one only had to hear him speak.

Somoza maintained his opinion with heroic energy. 'True, Señor Guimarán might last for a few more days than he had said, but science could only declare that death was imminent. The patient might last, of course; of course he might, but thanks to what? Undoubtedly to the moral influence of the sacraments. Not that he, Don Robustiano Somoza, above all a man of science, believed in the material efficacy of religion, but without falling into a fanaticism which ran contrary to all his convictions as a man of science, as he had already said, he could and did admit, having learned from experience, that the psychical influences the physical and vice versa, and that Don Pompeyo's sudden conversion could have originated a variation in the natural course of his illness – all of which was alien to medical science as such and in itself.'

Indeed, Don Pompeyo lasted until Holy Wednesday.

On the day of Guimarán's conversion Trifón Cármenes conceived the unhappy idea of devoting a literary page of *El Lábaro* to this momentous event. But it was necessary to wait for the sick man either to come out of danger or to go to glory. The latter eventuality was more probable, and more convenient for Cármenes, who ever since Palm Sunday had been on the point of finishing an extremely long poetic composition which sang the death of the Atheist happily restored to the faith of Christ. The elegiac ode, or simply the elegy – whatever it was, for Trifón did not know – began thus:

What telleth that funereal lament?

The poet scurried back and forth, from the mourning-house, as he was already calling it in his own mind, to the newspaper-office, from the newspaper-office to the mourning-house.

'How is he?' Trifón asked in hushed tones, in the porch.

The servant girl replied:

'Just about the same.'

Trifón hurried away, shut himself up with his elegy, and continued writing:

Oh, dreadful doubt, impious uncertainty!
Now standeth on the threshold cruël Fate,
Desisting not, nor pressing – patiently:
A fearful shade which silently doth wait.

A few hours went by and Trifón appeared at the dying man's house again. In a soft, mellifluous voice he asked:

'How is Don Pompeyo now?'

'A bit feverish.'

He returned to the newspaper-office at top speed, gasping for breath, 'he had to work hard, the gentleman might die and the poem be left without its final flourishes'. And he wrote with a *febrile hand*:

> Alas! 'Twas all in vain; for nutritor
> Heav'n's decree's fulfilled; inexorably . . .

Trifón did not know what 'nutritor' meant, that is to say he did not know exactly, but it sounded well.

Whenever Guimarán's servant girl replied that 'the master had had a better night' Cármenes winced, without realizing what he was doing, and experienced an unpleasant feeling rather like the one he had whenever he became convinced that a Madrid newspaper was not going to publish the verses he had submitted to it. He did not wish anyone any harm, but the fact was that now that the elegy was so far advanced Don Pompeyo would do him an extremely ill turn if he failed to die as soon as possible.

He died. He died on Holy Wednesday. The canon theologian and Trifón breathed again. Somoza breathed again too. All three of them would have looked ridiculous had the outcome been different. As for Cármenes, he concluded his verses:

> But weep him not. The tolling of the bronze
> Hymns of glory singeth; God's Holy Church
> Him gathered to Her bosom; the . . .

Poor Trifón's lines had a tendency to overlap.[2] He suffered from the same trouble in his toes.

The Atheist's burial was a rare solemnity. *The corpse of the deceased was accompanied to its final resting-place* by the civil and military authorities; by a delegation from the cathedral chapter led by the dean; by the Royal Provincial Court; by the university; and, in addition, by all those who piqued themselves on being good or bad Catholics. For the widow and daughters this public demonstration of sympathy was a special favour and consolation. The canon theologian was the chief family mourner. He was not related to the deceased, but he had snatched him from the clutches of the devil. According to Gloucester, who stayed in the chapter house, gossiping, 'this was not so much the burial of a Christian as the pagan apotheosis of the *pious, happy, triumphant vicar-general*'.[3] And, indeed, the people pointed him out to each other: 'That's him, that's him,' said the crowd, indicating the Apostle, the canon theologian. The stories of miracles which Doña Paula had spread among the impressionable, illiterate masses were enough to take the breath away. The bishop himself, in his most recent sermon to poor pious women, non-commissioned officers, servant girls and the like, had alluded to the triumph of that favourite son of the Church.

'There's nothing for it but to lie low and weather the storm,' said Foja.

The free-thinkers who ate meat in a hostelry every Good Friday were furious.

'That fellow Don Pompeyo has discredited us!'

'A fine free-thinker!'

'He was a chicken!'

'He died mad!'

'It was sorcery!'

'What do you mean sorcery? Morphine.'

'The clergy, miracles of the clergy . . .'

'They converted him with opium . . .'

'Physical weakness is enough to perform such miracles.'

'But more than that he was a nincompoop.'

Maundy Thursday came with a piece of news which was to make an epoch in the annals of Vetusta, annals which were being written with great deliberation by a teacher in the institute who was also the author of some notes on the Aragonese jig.

In Vegallana's house the news exploded like a bomb. The marchioness, all in black, returned with Visita from St Mary's Church, where they had been collecting alms. Obdulia Fandiño arrived, too, after collecting at St Peter's at the time when the officers from the garrison made their tour of the churches to view the specially decorated altars. These ladies gathered in the marchioness's boudoir and listened in astonishment to the solemn words of Doña Petronila Rianzares, who had taken a hundred pesetas at the offertory table in St Isidore's. The mother-bishop said:

'Yes, my Lady, there's no need to cross yourself so much, Anita is resolved to give this great example to the city and the world.'[4]

'But Quintanar – he won't agree to it.'

'He has already agreed – with a bad grace, of course. Ana made him understand that it was a sacred vow, and that stopping her from keeping her promise would be an act of despotism for which she would never forgive him.'

'And the poor old hen-pecked fellow gave his consent?' said Visita, red with indignation. 'What husbands – straight from the Isle of San Balandrán!'[5] she added, remembering her own husband.

The marchioness could not stop crossing herself. 'That wasn't piety, it wasn't religion; it was madness, sheer madness. Rational, enlightened, refined religion was her own sort – collecting alms for the hospital from corporations and private individuals at church doors, presenting embroidered banners to the parish church. But dressing up like a clown and making a spectacle of oneself . . . !'

'For God's sake, my Lady! Anyone who heard you would take you for a demagogue, a second Suñer.'[6]

'But what have I said?'

'Do you regard it as a mere trifle? Calling a penitent a clown?'

The marchioness shrugged her shoulders and crossed herself again. Obdulia's mouth was dry and her eyes were inflamed. She was possessed with immense curiosity and vague envy.

'Ana was going to make a spectacle of herself!' Exactly; that was it. What more could Obdulia have wanted than to make a spectacle of herself – to be looked at, contemplated by all Vetusta?

'And her dress? What's her dress like? Do you know?'

'Do you really think it likely that I don't know?' retorted Doña Petronila, proud of her knowledge of the entire affair. 'Ana will wear a long dark purple tunic of velvet with a *marron foncé* border . . .'

'*Marron foncé?*' Obdulia objected. 'That won't look very good – gold would be better.'

'What do you know about such things? I have taken personal charge of the dressmaker's work. Ana, too, is ignorant of these matters and she has asked me to take care of all these details.'

'And is the tunic a very full one?'

'Fairly full.'

'And has it a train?'

'No, it has a level hem.'

'And the footwear? Sandals?'

'Footwear! What footwear? Naked feet.'

'She's going barefoot!' cried the three ladies.

'Well of course, my dear children, that's the whole point. Ana has offered to go barefoot.'

'And what if it rains?'

'And what about all the stones?'

'But she's going to tear her skin to shreds.'

'The woman's mad.'

'But where has she seen anyone doing such devilish things?'

'For God's sake, my Lady, don't blaspheme! Devilish! – a vow like this, such a Christian example, of such edifying humility.'

'But what can have given her the idea of – that? Where has she ever seen a woman doing *that?*'

'She has certainly seen it in Saragossa and in others of the many towns she has visited. And even if she hadn't seen it, it would still be most meritorious of her to expose herself to the sarcasm of impious people and to the concealed mockery of pharisees – of both sexes – which is precisely what Our Lord did for us sinners.'

'Barefoot!' Obdulia repeated in astonishment. Her envy was swelling in her breast. 'Oh yes,' she thought, 'this has really got *cachet*. It rises above the commonplace, it's a *boutade*, it's something – exquisitely stylish.'

The marquis came in with Don Víctor hanging on to his arm.

Vegallana was consoling the wretched Quintanar, who could not hide his sorrow and dejection.

Doña Petronila took her leave before the afflicted ex-magistrate could apportion to this lady her share of the blame for an adventure which he regarded as a disaster.

'What's all this, Quintanar?' asked the marchioness with true interest and great curiosity.

'My Lady – my dear Rufina – this is – as the poet says – "They could not conquer me; but conquer me they did!" '[7]

'Leave poems out of it, dear fellow. Whoever put this notion into Ana's head?'

'Who do you expect? St Teresa, I mean – no – Paraguay.'

'Para . . . ?'

'No, not that. I know not what I say. I mean . . . Ladies, my wife is crazy. I do believe she is crazy. I have said so a thousand times. The fact is that just when I thought I had her under my control, just when I thought that mysticism and the vicar-general were waters passed away which cannot grind the mill – just when I had no doubts about my discretionary power in my own home – out of the blue, bang! My wife produces this effrontery, this procession.'

'But nobody has ever done such a thing in Vetusta.'

'Yes they have,' said the marquis. 'Every year Vinegar – you know, Don Belisario Zumarri, the bloodiest schoolmaster in town – walks in the Good Friday procession, dressed as a penitent and with a cross on his back.'

'But my Lord, do not compare my wife to Vinegar.'

'No, I'm not comparing . . .'

'But look – what I'm asking', Doña Rufina insisted, 'is when has Ana seen a *lady* in the burial procession, walking behind the urn, in a habit or whatever it's called of a penitent?'

'Yes, actually she has. We saw some in Saragossa, for example. But I am not so sure that they were really ladies.'

'And besides they wouldn't have gone barefoot,' said Obdulia.

'Barefoot! And my wife is to go barefoot? God's fury! That she will not do! Begad!'

It was no easy task to restrain Don Víctor's wrathful indignation. Once he was calmer he returned home, and between coming to another explanation with his wife and confining himself to a meaningful silence he chose to confine himself to silence – and to his study.

'He could not deceive himself. Ana's decision was irrevocable.'

Good Friday dawned with leaden skies. Very early, as soon as day broke, the canon theologian looked out of his balcony window to consult the clouds. 'Was it going to rain? He would have given years of his life for the sun to thrust that grey awning aside and illuminate his day of triumph, face to face, in the open. Two days of triumph!

On Wednesday the burial of the converted atheist, on Friday the burial of Christ, and at both of them he, Don Fermín, triumphant, covered with glory, Vetusta admiring, submissive, his enemies licking the dust, scattered, destroyed!'

Ana, too, looked at the sky early in the morning and, unable to help herself, thought: If only it would rain! She wished that it would rain and it filled her with remorse that she wished it. She was appalled by what she had done. 'I'm mad,' she thought, 'I take extreme decisions in moments of exaltation and then I have to carry them out with my courage sapped and exhausted and unable to make me want to do anything.' She remembered how, on her knees before the canon theologian, she had offered him that sacrifice, that solemn public proof of her adhesion to him, to the man being persecuted and slandered. That astounding project of self-mortification had occurred to her during the novena to Our Lady of Sorrows as she listened to Rossini's *Stabat Mater* and, with a heated imagination, conjured up the scene on Calvary, seeing Mary at her Son's feet, *dum pendebat filius*, as the poem said. As if by inspiration she had remembered seeing a woman in Saragossa dressed as a penitent, walking barefoot behind the glass urn which contained the recumbent image of the Lord; without stopping to think what she was doing she had decided and sworn to herself to walk in the same way, before the eyes of the whole town, through the streets of Vetusta behind the dead Christ, close to that canon who was also suffering death by crucifixion, slandered, scorned by everyone – and even by her. And now it couldn't be helped. After a not very determined opposition, Don Fermín had agreed, accepting Ana's chosen proof of spiritual fidelity. Doña Petronila, whom she had stopped regarding as a repugnant go-between in sacrilegious adventures, had offered to prepare the dress and all the details of the sacrifice. 'And now that the day had come, now that the hour was drawing near, she had to start doubting and fearing and wishing that the heavens would open and flood the world to stop this embarrassing procession!'

Ana also thought about Quintanar. 'She was doing it all for him, true; she had to cling on to piety so as to keep her honour – but weren't there other ways to be pious? Hadn't her promise been made in a fit of madness? Wasn't her husband going to look ridiculous, watching his wife dressed in purple walking barefoot through the mud in all the streets in La Encimada, making a spectacle of herself in front of the malice and the envy and all the deadly sins swarming on pavements and balconies and contemplating the *tableau vivant* which she was going to represent?' Ana tried to find the fire of enthusiasm, the frenzy of abnegation which had suggested the project to her a week before, but the enthusiasm and the frenzy did not return; she was not even supported by faith. She was overwhelmed with fear of the eyes of Vetusta, its open-mouthed malice; she no longer either believed or disbelieved; she did not think about God, or Christ, or Mary, or even the effectiveness of her sacrifice for restoring the canon theologian's reputation. She thought only about the scandalousness of her exhibition. 'Yes, it was a scandal. The housewife, the chaste spouse in Ana protested against the spectacle. She was not even certain that her abnegation was virtuous. Perhaps it was just brazen; the peace and the modesty of her home said so in solemn silence.' Ana was perspiring with anguish. 'What a promise to have made!'

It did not rain, but the sky's grey awning covered the town throughout the day. An hour before dusk the burial procession left St Isidore's Church.

'Here she comes, here she comes!' murmured the members of the Gentlemen's Club, packed into its balconies, elbowing each other, treading on each other's toes, crushing each other, tensing their neck muscles to get a better view of this strange spectacle, to gaze at the beautiful lady, the pearl of Vetusta, surrounded by priests and acolytes, walking barefoot and dressed as a penitent just like Vinegar, the brutal schoolmaster.

A wave of admiration preceded the burial cortège. Before the procession came to a street the lines of people packed tight along its pavements and the crowds in windows and balconies already knew that 'the judge's wife was looking very very pretty and pale, just like the Virgin at whose feet she was walking'. Nobody talked about anything else, nobody thought about anything else. Christ lying on His bed under glass, and His mother following Him in black, pierced by seven swords, did not merit the attention of the pious people of Vetusta. They waited in suspense for the judge's wife, then devoured her with their eyes. Facing the Gentlemen's Club, behind the drapery of crimson and gold in the balconies of the court-house, another ornate baroque palace of blackened stone, stood the civil governor's wife, the military governor's wife, the court president's wife, the marchioness, Visitación, Obdulia, the baron's womenfolk and many other female members of what the humble and envious middle class called the aristocracy. Obdulia was pale with emotion and dying of envy. 'The eyes of the whole town riveted on Ana's steps, her movements, her clothes, her colour, the look on her face! And she was barefoot! Her feet, naked and as white as white, admired and pitied by the immense crowd!' For Obdulia Fandiño this was the perfect ideal of coquetry. Her own naked shoulders, her ivory arms acting as a background for clinging black embroidered lace, her back with its vertiginous curves, her bosom, high and strong, exuberant and tempting, had never attracted in this way or in anything like this way the attention and the admiration of an entire town, however much she had displayed them in ballrooms, theatres, promenades – and processions. All that flesh – white, firm, full, suggestive, serious flesh – was made by circumstances to count for less than two bare feet which could only just be glimpsed from time to time under the penitent's purple velvet! 'And it's natural enough,' Obdulia went on thinking, 'all Vetusta's engrossed with those bare feet. Why? Because there's a tremendously distinguished *cachet* about the way they're being put on show, because – it's all a question of the setting.' 'When's she coming?' asked the widow, licking her lips, possessed by admiring envy, and conscious of the strange promptings of a kind of crazy, brutal lust, so absurd as to be inexplicable. Obdulia felt a – vague desire – to – to – to be a man.

The schoolmaster, Vinegar, Don Belisario, was a man indeed, a real man. It was his long-established and unfailing custom to dress up as a penitent on this solemn day – he who was the most terrible Herod of primary education on all the other days of the year. The children at his school, who hated him with all their hearts, were thronging in streets, squares and balconies to see *sir* walk past with his cardboard cross on his back and his crown of real thorns that really pricked, as you could tell from the movements of his eyebrows and the painful expression of the wrinkles on his forehead. It was the children's cordial desire that the thorns should pierce his skull. The burial of Christ was the vengeance of the entire school. In his anxiety to torment all the generations which passed through his hands, Vinegar enjoyed tormenting his generation, too, in his own person. But it was not only the urge to torture himself as he tortured every other mother's son that had inspired him with the devilish idea of crowning himself with thorns and giving the lambs in his pedagogical flock a treat; our old friend vanity also played a large part in this annual exhibition. The knowledge that once a year he, Vinegar, Don Belisario, was the object of general expectation filled his soul with glorious bliss. Nobody had ventured to follow his example; he was the only penitent in town and he had been calmly enjoying this privilege for many years.

Rather than vexing him, the rivalry of Doña Ana Ozores made him swell with pride. Prompted by the spur of the occasion he hurried to her as soon as he saw her coming out of St Isidore's, greeted her with great courtesy, and found ways to show that he was, above all, even on the way to Calvary with his cross on his back, a complete gentleman. Where there were puddles he walked through them, to keep the mud from the bare pearly feet of that illustrious lady, his companion. Ana was like a woman blinded – she could not hear or understand what was happening; but the grotesque presence of her unexpected companion made her blush, and she was attacked by a mad urge to start running. 'She had been deceived, she hadn't been told anything about that caricature by her side.' 'Oh, if she still had that spirit of sincere piety of former times this new mortification, this mockery, this saturation with ridicule would have gratified her, making her sacrifice still greater and giving her abnegation a sublime power.'

Like all the people, in particular the poor people, Vinegar admired the bare feet of the judge's wife. As for him – he was sporting a brilliant pair of patent-leather boots, begging the pardon of historical propriety. Vinegar knew only too well that patent-leather boots did not exist in the times of Augustus and that, even if they had existed, Jesus would not have worn them to Calvary. But he was just a godly man, a godly man who had no opportunity to show off all year long, and he had to be forgiven his little vanity – displaying his boots, which shone like mirrors, and which he only wore on this solemn day.

'Here they come, here they come!' repeated the gentlemen in their club and the ladies in the court-house when the procession was about to appear. 'This time it wasn't a false rumour, it was *them*, it was the burial procession.'

The people in the balconies stopped gossiping.

Their souls, in various degrees of wretchedness, peeped out of their eyes.

Not a single Vetustan was thinking about God.

Poor Don Pompeyo, the Atheist, was dead.

Instead of looking, like everybody else, in the direction of the narrow street where crosses and candles and doleful drooping banners were coming into sight, Visitación was observing Don Alvaro Mesía's face as he stood alone, it seemed, in the last balcony on the façade of the Gentlemen's Club, the corner balcony. All in black, his close-bodied frock-coat buttoned up to his chin, his face pale, Don Alvaro bit his Havana cigar from time to time, smiled every so often, and turned away now and again to reply to somebody who was speaking to him and whom Visita could not see.

It was Don Víctor Quintanar. The two friends had locked themselves into the office of the Gentlemen's Club at the request of the ex-magistrate, who wanted to see, without being seen, what he called the Calvary of his dignity. Behind Mesía, who threw a good shadow, Quintanar, trembling without knowing why, impatient and feverish, made ready to see as much as he could.

'Look here,' he said, 'if I had an Orsini bomb with me,[8] I would have no objection to throwing it at the canon theologian when he parades in triumph down there. The kidnapper!'

'Calm down, Don Víctor, calm down. This is the beginning of the end. I am certain that Ana is dying of shame. She has been turned into a fanatic, and that can't be helped now – but she will soon open her eyes. The excess of evil will supply its own remedy. That man has tried to tighten the screws too much; of course this is a great triumph for him – but in the end Ana is bound to realize that she has been made the tool of that man's pride.'

'That is right, a tool, an abject tool! He is parading her like a Roman victor with a slave – behind his chariot of glory.'

Don Víctor was in a tangle with these comparisons; but in his mind's eye he could see Don Fermín De Pas standing in a cardboard chariot in the middle of the procession, as he had seen the baritone come on to the stage at the Royal Theatre in Madrid one night when *Poliuto*[9] was performed.

Don Alvaro was not feigning his good humour. He was a little agitated, but he did not feel defeated; he trusted experience. 'That priest hadn't laid a finger on the judge's wife, he was sure of it.' He was smiling with all his heart, smiling at his thoughts and at his plans. 'Of course it jarred upon the nerves to witness that spectacle in which his rival was apparently vaunting his triumph in the Roman style, according to Don Víctor, but that priest hadn't laid a finger on her.'

Quintanar, in his hiding-place, peeping through the black balustrade of the balcony, saw a golden cross on the top of a pole bearing an ancient, venerable banner. He stood on his chair, taking care that he could not be seen from the street, and recognized Celedonio with a silver cross in his arms.

Mesía left his friend behind him and stepped into the middle of the balcony, an arrogant figure defying the looks of the priests passing below.

Doleful drums pulsated, determined to revive a grief which had been dead for nineteen centuries. To Don Víctor it sounded like a dirge, and he imagined that his wife was being taken to the scaffold.

The rolling of the drums reverberated in a monotonous silence.

Dusk had come early to the narrow street with its dark houses. The long lines of candles with yellow flames, looking like a broken rosary with golden beads, disappeared in the distance, up the street. In shop windows and balcony windows the moving flames were reflected, rising and falling in fantastic contortions, like shadows of light, in all the confusion of a witches' sabbath. The silent multitude, the noiseless steps, the blank faces of the collegians in white albs, lighting the dismal street with their candles, gave the scene a dream-like quality. They did not look like living beings, those seminarists dressed in black and white, some of them pale with dark rings around their eyes, others brown, almost black, and tousle-headed, nearly all of them frowning, obsessed with the fixed idea of their own boredom: religion-making machines, conscripts press-ganged by hunger and laziness. They were on their way to bury Christ as they would bury any Christian, without thinking about Him, just doing what they had to do. Forming long lines behind them came clergymen in cloaks, soldiers, shoemakers, tailors dressed like gentlemen, a few Carlists, and five or six town councillors also in gentlemen's clothes. There, too, walked Zapico, the ostensible owner of La Cruz Roja and the slave of Doña Paula. Christ lying on a bed of cambric was sweating drops of varnish. He looked as if He had died of consumption. In spite of the wretchedness of its execution the recumbent statue inspired religious respect because of the great ideals it symbolized. After so many centuries it still stood for a sublime sorrow. Behind it came Christ's Mother, tall, scraggy, wearing black, pallid like her Son, with the face of a corpse like her Son, too. Her look, the look of an idiot, was fixed on the cobblestones. The inexpert sculptor had unintentionally given the face an expression of speechless, shocked pain, of pain overflowing with suffering. Mary's breast was pierced by seven swords. But she did not give any sign that she could feel them; all she could feel was the death before her. She was swaying on her platform. This, too, was natural enough. From her lofty position she dominated the crowd, but she did not see it. The Mother of Jesus was not looking at the Vetustans. When the Lady of Sorrows was near Don Alvaro Mesía's feet he was afraid and stood back instead of kneeling down. The contrast between that image of infinite pain and his own thoughts, all profanation and lust, frightened even him. He had been thinking that after that act of madness which Ana was performing for her confessor, for De Pas, she was going to perform other greater ones for her lover, for Mesía.

And there was the judge's wife, on Vinegar's right, one pace ahead of him, at the feet of the mourning Virgin, behind the urn containing the dead Jesus. Ana, too, looked as if she were made of painted wood; her pallor was like white varnish, her eyes could not see. At each step she thought she would fall senseless. As her feet trod the stones and the mud they felt hot and painful. She tried to prevent them from appearing beneath her purple tunic, but at times they could be seen. For Ana, her naked feet were the nakedness of her whole body and soul. 'She was a madwoman who had fallen into a singular kind of prostitution! She did not know why, but she thought that after this promenade of shame there was no honour left in her home. Here was the foolish girl, the bluestocking, George Sand, the mystic, the prig, the madwoman, the shameless madwoman.' Not a single thought of piety came to her aid during the entire procession. Her thoughts gave her nothing but vinegar on that Calvary of her modesty. She even remembered passages from Fray Luis de León's *The Perfect Wife* which, in her opinion, condemned what she was doing. 'I was blinded by vanity, not piety,' she thought. 'My trouble is that I'm too fond of play-acting – I'm just like my husband.' When, now and again, she ventured to look back at the Virgin, she felt ice in her soul. 'The Mother of Jesus was not looking at her, she was not paying any heed to her; she was thinking about her own true pain. Mary was there because of her dead Son before her, but what was Ana doing there?'

According to the canon theologian, she was there to proclaim his glory. Although he was not the chief family mourner at this burial, as he had been on Wednesday, he was celebrating his fresh triumph with it. He was near Ana, almost by her side, in the line on the right among other canons. He was wearing a rochet, a mozetta and a cope, and he bore his extinguished candle as if it were a sceptre. 'He was the master. In spite of his enemies' slander he had converted the great atheist of Vetusta and made him die in the bosom of the Church; and now he was leading forth, as his prisoner in invisible chains, the lady who was most admired in all Vetusta for her beauty and her spiritual superiority. The judge's wife was edifying the whole town with her humility, with that sacrifice of weak flesh and of worldly prejudices, and it was because of him, it was due to him alone. Hadn't people been saying that the Jesuits had eclipsed him? That the missioners exercised more power over their spiritual daughters? Well here was proof to the contrary. The Jesuits made Vetustan virgins wear hair shirts? Well he bared the most select pair of feet in town and dragged them through the mire – there they were, showing now and then beneath that purple velvet, in the slime. Who was the stronger?' And after the promptings of pride came the flutterings of the heart in the hope of love. 'How would his relations with Ana be in the future?' He shivered. 'For the time being, great caution. It may be that when I let my jealousy show I frightened her and for that reason she took so long to come back to me. For the moment, caution, and then – time will tell.' De Pas could feel that what little of the clergyman he had left in his soul was disappearing. He compared himself to an empty sea shell tossed on to the sand by the waves. 'He was the shell of a priest.'

When they walked past the Gentlemen's Club and past Mesía's balcony, Ana was looking at the ground and did not see anybody. But Don Fermín raised his eyes and felt his look coming into collision with that of Don Alvaro, who flushed dark and stepped back – as he had when the Virgin had passed. The canon's look was haughty, provocative and sarcastic in its apparent humility and tenderness; it said *Vae victis!*[10] Mesía's look did not recognize the victory; it merely acknowledged a momentary advantage. It was discreet, mildly ironical, it did not say 'Thou has conquered, Galilean'[11] but 'Don't triumph before the victory'. De Pas realized, with anger in his heart, that the man in the balcony was not surrendering.

'She's looking most extraordinarily beautiful!' the ladies in the balconies of the court-house were saying.

'Extraordinarily beautiful!'

'It takes some courage, though.'

'But then she's a regular saint.'

'I think she's dying the death,' said Obdulia. 'How pale! How *low*! She looks like plaster.'

'I think she's dying of shame,' said Visita into the marchioness's ear.

Doña Rufina heaved a compassionate sigh, remarking:

'Going barefoot was an atrocious thing to do. She'll be a week in bed with her feet torn to tatters.'

The Baroness of the Floating Debt, living permanently in Vetusta now, ventured to say, with a shrug of the shoulders:

'People can say what they like, these extremes are inappropriate – in respectable people.'

The marquis supported the idea with great erudition.

'That's the sort of piety you'd expect from a trans-Tiberine woman.'[12]

'Exactly,' said the baroness, not remembering at that moment what a trans-Tiberine woman was.

After the procession had passed and the beauty and courage of the judge's wife had been contemplated and admired, gossip soon started in all the balconies along the processional route, as in the court-house balconies, and serious objections were found to that 'display of unprecedented audacity'.

In the Gentlemen's Club, Foja, at a good distance from Mesía and Don Víctor, heaped abuse upon the canon theologian and the judge's wife. 'The whole thing is despicable. All it does is egg the vicar-general on. What the judge's wife is doing will be paid for by the village priests. And besides, a woman's place is in the home.'

'Moreover,' added Joaquín Orgaz, 'this sort of thing lends itself to exaggeration and abuse. Next year we're going to see Obdulia Fandiño on Vinegar's arm, barefoot – and barelegged, too.'

The quip gave rise to hearty laughter.

But it was observed that Orgaz had only made it because he had not gained anything from his amorous advances, or at least had not gained enough.

The religious masses admired the lady's humility, without any objections or reservations. 'That really was what you'd call imitating Christ. Walking along, just like any ordinary person, by the side of Señor Vinegar the penitent, and going barefoot all around the town! She was a saint!'

As for Don Víctor: when the canon theologian and Ana were under his balcony he asked Mesía:

'Are they there?'

'Yes, there they go.'

And the husband craned his neck and poked his head out. He saw everything and jumped back.

'Infamous man! He is infamous! She has been fanaticized!'

He shuddered. At that instant the army band escorting the procession began to repeat a dead march.

Two tears slipped from poor Quintanar's eyes. When he heard the music he imagined that he was a widower, that this was the burial of his wife.

'Cheer up, Don Víctor,' said Mesía, turning to him and leaving the balcony. 'They have gone away now.'

'I do not want to look at her again. It pains me so!'

'Cheer up. All this will soon be over.'

And Mesía rested a hand on the old man's shoulder.

Don Víctor stood up, grateful and moved, and attempted to wrap his arms around his friend's breast and shoulders. In a solemn, sobbing voice he exclaimed:

'I swear it by my honoured name! Sooner than this, I would prefer to see her in the arms of a lover!'

'Yes, a thousand times yes,' he continued, 'find me a lover for her, seduce her for me, anything rather than seeing her in the arms of fanaticism!'

And he gripped, with warmth, the hand which Don Alvaro was holding out to him.

The dead march could be heard in the distance. The *chink chink* of the cymbals and the *boom boom* of the bass drum were an appropriate setting for Quintanar's grandiloquent words.

'What would become of man in these tempests of life if friendship did not offer the poor castaway a board on which to rest!'

'*Chink, chink, chink! Boom, boom, boom!*'

'Yes, my friend! Sooner seduced than fanaticized!'

'You can count upon my firm friendship, Don Víctor – a friend in need . . .'

'I know, Mesía, I know. Shut the window, that damned drum seems to be playing inside my head!'

XXVII

'Ten o'clock! Did you hear? the dining-room clock struck ten. Shall we go up to supper – what do you say?'

'Wait a little longer, wait until the cathedral clock chimes the hour.'

'The cathedral clock! But is it audible from here, lass? Can one really hear the clock in the tower? Don't forget it's a good half league away.'

'Yes, one can hear it; on calm nights like this one certainly can. Haven't you ever noticed? Wait five minutes more and you'll hear the bells, sad and muffled by distance.'

'The fact is, it's a beautiful night.'

'Like an August night.'

'Whene'er I contemplate the sky,
Adorned with lights too plenteous to count,
And to this earth I turn mine eye . . .'[1]

Forgive me, my child; quite unintentionally I'm going back to my verses.'

'Why not? So much the better, Quintanar. They're very beautiful. "Serene Night", of course. It brings sweet tears to the eyes. When I was a girl and I was beginning to read poetry, he was my favourite author.'

The memory of Fray Luis de León passed like a cloud through Ana's mind, together with a flash of bitter melancholy. She shook her head and stood up:

'Give me your arm, Quintanar, let's go and take a stroll around the pear-tree gallery while her grace the cathedral tower makes up her mind to sing the hour.'

'With all my heart, *mia sposa cara.*'

The couple disappeared beneath the low vault of a gallery of French pear-trees on espaliers. Here and there the moon pierced the new foliage, scattering pools of light along the path.

'May is taking its leave with a splendid night,' said Ana, leaning heavily on her husband's arm.

'Of course, May ends today. June tomorrow. "June – the fisherman's boon." Do you like fishing? You know the River Soto, just after you go past La Pumarada de Chusquín.'

'Yes, I know – where Obdulia and Visita often bathe in the summer, before they go to the seaside.'

'Exactly, that's the place – well, the River Soto contains exquisite trout, so the marquis told me. Would you like me to write to Frillity and ask him to send two rods and all the accessories?'

'Yes, yes, splendid! We'll go fishing.'

Don Víctor, well pleased, gripped his wife's arm more firmly with his own, and grasped her hand like an operatic tenor. He sang:

'Lasciami, lasciami
oh lasciami partir . . .'[2]

He fell silent and came to a halt. A moonbeam illuminated the end of his nose. He looked at his wife and she looked back at him.

'Do you like *Les Huguenots*? Do you remember? How badly that tenor from Valladolid sang it! But listen – what an idea – a beautiful idea. Just imagine, in the middle of El Vivero – over there, by the lake, imagine Gayarre or Masini[3] singing in this still night, in this silence – and us here, under this vault – listening, listening. That is how operas ought to be sung. What do we lack now? Music, nothing but music. This beautiful scene – the breeze, the foliage, the moon – well, all this with the accompaniment of a good quartet – paradise!

Oh! the spoken drama, the spoken drama is not always as eloquent as the art of the muses. I'm all for song, for poetry accompanied by the lyre or the phorminx. Do you know what the phorminx was?'

Ana smiled and explained the Greek instrument to her worthy spouse.

'My dear girl, you're quite a scholar.'

Another cloud passed through Ana's mind.

The cathedral clock, half a league from El Vivero, struck ten measured, vibrant notes, filling the air with melancholy.

'It's true, you can hear it,' said Quintanar.

And after a silence (a comment on the time), he added:

'Shall we have supper now?'

'To supper!' cried Ana.

Releasing Don Víctor's arm and raising the skirts of her morning-gown a little she ran off and disappeared in the black tunnel. Quintanar followed, shouting:

'Wait, wait. You crazy girl, you might trip.'

When he came out into the moonlight, under the starry vault, he saw his beloved wife at the top of the marble stairway with her left hand resting on the gilt outer door and her right arm, a flower between its fingers, extended towards the moon.

'What do you think of it, Quintanar? What do you think of my moonlight tableau?'

'Magnificent! A magnificent statue. A most original thought. "Aurora implores Diana to hasten the course of the night." '

Ana applauded and entered the house. Don Víctor followed her, saying:

'My dear child! She's a different woman. Benítez has saved her. She's a different woman. My beloved child!'

They used the marchioness's dinner service for their meal. They both had a good appetite. Sometimes Ana spoke with her mouth full, leaning over towards Quintanar, who smiled, chewed with vigour, nodded his head and waved his knife.

'This house is happy even by night,' she said.

And she added:

'Here you are, peel this apple for me.'

' "Peel this apple, peel this apple . . ." where have I heard that? Oh, I know.'

And his laughter made his food go down the wrong way.

'What is it, my dear?'

'It's something from a comic opera[4] – a comic opera by an academician. It's all about the Marquise de Pompadour. A gentleman called Beltrand is looking for her, he comes across a village girl in a windmill – and naturally enough they sit down and have supper together – indeed they eat apples.'

'Like you and me.'

'Exactly. Well then, the village girl, naturally enough, picks up a knife.'

'To kill Beltrand . . .'

'No, to peel the apple.'

'That isn't very plausible.'

'Both Beltrand and the orchestra are of your opinion. The shock makes the orchestra bristle up, with tremolo shudders from all its violins and squeals from all its clarinets, and Beltrand, no less shocked, sings' (standing, and singing):

> 'Good heavens! she peels the apple:
> 'Tis the Marquise
> De Pompadour,
> De Pompadour!'

Ana burst out laughing. She laughed with all her heart at the academician's absurdity and her husband's wit. 'In truth, Quintanar seemed a different man.'

Petra served tea.

'Has Anselmo returned from Vetusta?' asked the master.

'Yes sir, an hour ago.'

'Has he brought the cartridges?'

'Yes sir.'

'And the canary seed?'

'Yes sir.'

'Well tell him that he's to go back to town very early tomorrow morning with a message for Señor Crespo. Wait – I'll go and tell him myself. No, I'll write a note, that will be best, won't it Ana? That Anselmo fellow is such a lout . . .'

The master left the dining-room.

As Petra cleared the table she said:

'If madam wants anything . . . I'm planning to go to Vetusta tomorrow too, at daybreak. I've got to go and see the ironing woman. So if you want me to take any messages – to the marchioness, or . . .'

'Yes, you can take two letters. I'll leave them on the boudoir table tonight and you can collect them tomorrow – without making any noise, so as not to wake us up.'

'Don't you worry about that, ma'am.'

An hour later Don Víctor was falling asleep in a spacious stuccoed bedroom which contained two beds. In the adjacent boudoir Ana was writing. Her pen seemed to whistle sweet music as it sped over the satiny paper.

'Don't be long, don't write too much – it could be harmful. You know what Benítez says.'

'Yes, I know. Be quiet, now, and go to sleep.'

First Ana wrote to her doctor, Somoza's replacement. Benítez, the young man of few words and much learning, observant and taciturn, had allowed the judge's wife to write, if it helped to pass the time away, at those hours of the day when the country offers nothing better to do. 'Write to me, for example, now and then, to keep me informed about those matters which you know are my concern. But if fears of yours make you feel ill don't go into details; a general account will be enough.'

Ana wrote:

. . . Good news. Nothing but good news. I'm not fearful any more. I don't see ants in the air any more, or bubbles, or any of those things; I can talk about those visions without being afraid that they'll come back. I feel capable of reading Maudsley and Luys[5] with all their diagrams of brains and other inside parts without being disgusted or afraid. I talk to Quintanar about my fear of madness as if it were some other person's mania. I'm certain of my health. Thank you, my friend; I owe it all to you. If you had not forbidden me to *philosophize* I would now explain why I am certain that it is to this life-plan which you imposed on me that I owe the ineffable happiness of my serene good health – this refined pleasure of living in a healthy atmosphere, with pure blood coursing through me – but no rhetoric, I remember how you dislike fine phrases. In short, I'm as fit as a fiddle, to use the expression you prefer. Your regimen is being observed with religious scrupulosity. Fear keeps the vineyard . . . I shall be a slave to hygiene. Anything rather than fall back into my old ways. I'm keeping up my diary, in which I don't allow myself the luxury of getting lost in *psychological speculations*, since you forbid them, too. I write a little every day – not much. As you see, I obey you absolutely. Goodbye for now. Don't delay your visit. Quintanar sends you his kind regards – snoring. He snores, it's a fact. *In those days* the judge's wife would have regarded this as one more misfortune, sent by *destiny* on purpose to test her. A husband who snores! How terrible. That's enough. I can see you grimacing. I'm sorry. No more chatter. Tell Frillity to come with you – or sooner. My husband can say what he likes, but if Crespo doesn't come to prepare my rod for me and persuade the trout to allow themselves to be caught it will be an utter failure. Goodbye again. The slave of your regimen,

ANITA OZORES DE QUINTANAR

After signing and sealing this letter Ana resumed another one which she had begun in the morning.

But now the pen did not speed over the paper, it kept stopping on the up-strokes.

The whim had taken her to imitate the handwriting of the letter to which she was replying and which lay before her.

. . . Don't complain about the brevity of my explanations. I have already told you, my dear friend, that Benítez forbids me to analyse things too much, to study the details of my own thinking – and I believe he is right. The mere thought of it – of sifting out my ideas – is quite enough to give me fears of feeling that horrible weakness in my brain again. Let's not talk about that any more. It's more than enough for me to write to you at all, because I'm forbidden to do so. But don't misunderstand me. What is forbidden is not writing to *you* in particular. Am I making myself clear now? What is forbidden is writing at length, to anyone, and especially about serious subjects.

You ask when we are going to return to Vetusta. I don't know, Fermín, I don't know.

You say that I am much better now. True. But orders are orders. Benítez is a resolute man, of few but well-chosen words, and he has promised to cure me if I obey him but to abandon me if I deceive him or ignore his commands. I'm determined to obey him. You yourself have always said that the most important thing is to be healthy.

I have become lukewarm, perhaps? No, Fermín, a thousand times no. I shall convince you of this when I return.

I do not pray very much? True. But perhaps it would be too much for my health. If I were to tell Quintanar or Benítez the harm it does me to repeat prayers, even though I'm well again . . . I only write about Don Víctor and the doctor? But what do you expect me to write about? I see nobody other than my husband, and Benítez has saved my life and perhaps my reason. I know you don't like me to speak of my fears of going mad. But it's a fact – I had such fears once, and I am speaking to you of them now so that you can help me to thank the doctor (about whom I talk so much) for my *intellectual salvation*. What good would I have been to my *soul brother* without a soul – or with a soul darkened by madness?

'This, that and the other are all a part of the past? No, no, no. That is not true. In due course everything will begin again. Except calling on Doña Petronila. Don't ask me why, but I'm resolved not to return to that woman's house. And that's all. I can't write any more. It's forbidden (again!). I have just finished supper. Your most faithful friend and grateful penitent,

ANA OZORES

P.S. It is obvious that I am in a good humour? You're right again. That's thanks to my good health. If I were in a bad humour and inclined to be suspicious, I would think that you are sorry that I am in a good humour, to judge by the tone in which you say it. Please excuse all my mistakes.

Anita read the letter. She crossed out some words but, after some thought, wrote them in again.

As she licked the envelope, moving her head from side to side, she shrugged her shoulders and muttered:

'He hasn't any cause to feel offended.'

She lay down in the cheerful white bed by the side of her husband's.

The old man always rose earlier than Ana, and went out into the garden to wait for her. At eight o'clock they drank chocolate together in the conservatory – which he called, with a certain emphatic pride, *la serre*.

'If only all this belonged to us!' Quintanar would sometimes think as he contemplated the exotic plants on the packed shelves and in the Etruscan and Japanese vases, of questionable authenticity.

But his wife did not think about the title deeds of El Vivero. She enjoyed nature, health, and the luxury which the Vegallanas had accumulated in their famous villa with no thoughts for anything other than enjoyment. For Ana, living there was like living in a bath which she believed to be beneficent.

Don Víctor walked out of the garden, crossed meadows, apple-orchards and maize-fields, looked among hovels for the way down to the river Soto, and explored its banks in search of the most suitable place to ensconce himself and start fishing, as soon as Anselmo returned with the necessary paraphernalia.

When it grew hot – and in the middle of the day the heat was considerable – Ana went up to her boudoir. After reading for a while, lying on her white bed, she sat at the rosewood escritoire and thumbed through her book of memoirs. Before beginning to write in it she always reread a few pages, skipping back and forth.

She read the first page, which she almost knew by heart, with an artist's love for her own work. In a swift, nervous hand, intelligible only to herself, it said:

'Memoirs! A diary! Why not? Benítez agrees to it.

' "*Memoirs of a Nobody*", a joker might say. But since nobody's going to read them, except me . . . It's ridiculous? Nonsense! It would be more ridiculous *not* to write (since it's an exercise which I like and which doesn't do me any harm, taken in moderation) just because if the *world* knew it would call me a prig, a bluestocking, or a romantic, to use Visita's word. Those fears of what people might say are a thing of the past, thank God. Good health has made me more independent. And anyway, what *can* people say, since nobody's going to read it? Not even Quintanar. He has never understood my hand when I write fast. I'm alone, completely alone. I'm talking to myself in absolute secrecy. I can laugh, cry, sing, talk to God, to the birds, to the healthy, fresh blood which I feel running through me. Let's begin with a hymn. Let's write poetry in prose. "Hail to thee, O health! To thee I owe my new ideas, this vigour in my soul, this casting aside of idle fears and thoughts of fiendish phantoms, the composure of my spirit, the calm for which I yearned . . ." The hymn is suspended because Quintanar is swearing that he's dying of hunger, and he's calling me down to the dining-room, with an olive in his mouth. I'm coming, I'm coming! Coming!'

. . . .

'El Vivero, 1 May.

'It's raining, it's five o'clock in the afternoon and it has been raining all day. *In illo tempore* this would have been enough to make me consider myself a woe-worn woman. I would have thought about the paltriness – and the dampness – of everything human, about universal boredom, etc., etc. But now I find it natural and even enjoyable that it should be raining. What is the water falling upon those hills, woods and meadows? Nature's *toilette*. Tomorrow the sun will make all that dripping greenery shine. And besides, here in the country the rain is music. While Quintanar takes his nap (a new custom) and snores (an old complaint, worthy of respect) I open the window and hear

> The pattering of the rain
> On the leaves above,
> The fluttering of the wings
> Of the turtle-dove

as it puffs itself up on the roof of the square dovecot and pops in and out of the little windows. There's something of the harem, or of the tenement house (depending on how you look at it), about that dovecot. Communal life with its hours of tedium, negligence, and public idleness is reflected in the postures of those doves – in their short steps, in the way they shake their wings. There are couples that come together out of habit, out of some sense of duty. They are bored, as if each were alone in the middle of a desert. Suddenly the male (I suppose it's the male) has an idea, a feeling of remorse, and improvises a passion which he is very far from feeling, and kisses the female, and walks around her, singing *coo-coo* and fluffing up his feathers. She, surprised, but without shaking off her torpor, responds with half-hearted caresses; and a little later – tired, sleepy, finding the languid pleasure of standing motionless, puffed-up, getting soaked, to be a more voluptuous experience than all their love-making – they return to their passivity, tranquil, without any rancour, without any illusions, without any complaints about their mutual indifference. What rational doves! Quintanar snores; I write. Stop! This will never do. I was becoming ironical, and irony always contains bile. Bitters stimulate the appetite – but it's better to have an appetite without any need of them.

. . . .

'It's still raining. No matter. The Flood itself couldn't even bring a look of impatience to my face today. The window's shut, the streams of water slipping down the glass obscure the landscape. Víctor has gone out with Frillity (the second visit of the worthy Crespo, the only great man I know personally). Beneath an umbrella belonging to Pinón de Pepa – the marquis's caretaker – and looking as if they were sheltering in a tent, they tramp the wood of oaks which my husband always calls age-old. They're going to try some chemical experiment or other, Frillity's invention, according to him. God keep them happy and their feet dry. Today I feel inclined for history, for recollections. I'm not afraid of them. Little more than five weeks have gone by and it all seems to belong to ancient history already.

'Those three days! I imagined I had been prostituted in a strange fashion' (here Ana's writing becomes almost indecipherable, even for herself). 'All Vetusta had seen me, with naked feet, in the middle of a procession, very nearly on Vinegar's arm! And then I had to sit motionless for three days in an easy chair, my feet burning with pains which shamed me! I called Somoza, who begged to be excused. His replacement Benítez came, cold and silent; but I realized that he was observing me closely when I wasn't looking at him. He must have thought I was going mad. He denies it and says that my state can be explained by my religious exaltation and by the exquisite moral sense of my decision to sacrifice myself for the good of the man whom I believed I had offended with my thoughts and my rebuffs. When Benítez makes up his mind to talk he is like a confessor, too. I have told him secrets of my inner life like someone describing the symptoms of an illness. When I was talking about these things I could see, in spite of his impassive face, that he was learning me by heart. The illness rose from my feet to my head. I had a fever, I was confined to bed, and I was seized by that terror – that panic terror of madness. This is something I don't want to talk about, not even to myself. I'll stop for today. Off to the piano to recall 'Casta diva' – with one finger.'

.   .   .   .

Ana skipped a few pages, where she had written the history of the days following the procession, which was to become famous in the annals of Vetusta. She believed that she had prostituted herself. All that religious publicity seemed like some Babylonian sacrifice – like giving herself up in the temple of Bel for a mysterious vigil.[6] Such humiliation! It had been like her days as a bluestocking – something ridiculous, as she herself had finally come to recognize. She did not dare set foot in the street, imagining that all the passers-by would mock her, and that all the gossip would be about her, that every group of chatterers would comment on her absurd behaviour. 'She had been ridiculous, she had behaved foolishly' – this fixed idea tormented her. She could not forget it, however hard she tried, for she was continually reminded of it by the pain in her feet, which were hot, burning with shame. Her feet had been public property, naked for a whole afternoon.

If she looked to religion and the canon theologian's protection for some consolation, her troubles grew even greater, because then she felt faith – vigorous, orthodox faith – melting within her soul. As for St Teresa, Ana had become incapable of reading her. Not reading her was better than suffering the torture of the irreverent analysis in which she could not prevent herself from indulging when she found herself face to face with her ideas and phrases. And the canon theologian? That intense compassion which had again thrown her at his feet no longer existed. Perhaps his triumphs had made him conceited. At all events, Ana had stopped feeling sorry for him. Instead, she saw him triumphant, maybe abusing his victory, humiliating the enemy; for now she could see clearly – or, at least, her vision was less clouded than it had been before. Perhaps she had been a tool in the hands of her elder brother. True, De Pas had not made any more pathetic gestures revealing jealousy or love or anything similar. Ana observed him with the looks of an inquisitor – about which she had some guilty feelings – but she could not find in him any symptoms of worldly passion. Was she a bad observer? Or was he a good dissembler? Or was there nothing to observe or dissemble? At all events, her old devotion did not return, her faith was crumbling away, and she was discovering in her own mind theories which she had heard, without understanding them, from her father.

A vague, poetic, easygoing, romantic pantheism – or rather a rustic deism like Rousseau's, sentimental and optimistic, although melancholy and somewhat uninviting; this was what Ana found inside herself now, and she was determined to regard it as pure Christian religion. She did not want to renounce her faith or even philosophize, for this, too, seemed ridiculous; but there was nothing she could do to prevent ideas, protests and criticisms from flocking into her mind and her heart. This was a new torment. In spite of everything, she still confessed regularly with Don Fermín. She kept up a routine fidelity, for she was afraid of her remorse if she failed in what she regarded as her duty to him. Above all, she feared that if she broke her religious relationship with him a reaction of pity would follow, a reaction of repentance and imaginary piety which would drag her into another crazy action such as the one she had taken on Good Friday. So many opposed ideas and feelings, her secluded life, and the awareness that something inside her was suffering and rebelling and threatening to explode, caused the nervous crises which Benítez treated as best he could.

Ana believed with all her soul that she was going mad. A moment of sentimental elation would be followed by a period of spiritual languor and moral apathy. It was horrifying to think that at such times virtue and vice, success and failure, good and evil were all the same to her. 'God was breaking up into little pieces in her brain,' as she phrased it; and she was alone in the world, and her will was weakening, and all this tormented her and made her panic. The extreme form of this torture was scorn for logic, doubt about the laws of thought and language, and finally the disappearance of her awareness of her own unity: she believed that her moral faculties were falling apart, that inside her there was nobody who was *she*, *Ana*, essentially, really – and after this came vertigo and the reaction of terror with its screams and its spasms.

For many days she forgot everything else, thinking only about her own health, horrified by the idea of madness and the fear of the unknown pain of a deranged mind. With all her soul she appealed for Benítez's help, and the beginning of her cure was this very longing to get well and her blind obedience of the doctor's orders.

Benítez spoke about food, exercise, and even baths, but for the major part of Ana's recovery he prescribed a change, diversion, the open air, happiness, tranquil emotions. To the country! to the country! was the cry. Ana and Quintanar (who had also been given a good fright) did not stop exclaiming from morning to night: To the country! To the country!

But where was this country? They did not possess a holiday villa in the province of Vetusta, but Don Víctor still owned properties in Aragon.

Urged by a sudden courageous impulse – much more heroically courageous than her husband could suppose – she ventured to suggest:

'Quintanar, what do you think of this idea? – going away to spend a few months, until winter . . .'

'Where?'

'To your homeland, to La Almunia de Don Godino.'

Don Víctor jumped.

'My child, for the Lord's sake! I am too old to have my poor bones rattled about like that. La Almunia . . . I should have been only too delighted, in other days, but now . . . ! I love my homeland, of course, my heart is Aragonese, and I say with the poet that the man is happy who has seen "No other river than that of his homeland",[7] but by now I am more a Vetustan than anything else, and another poet, the Prince of Esquilache, has also said:

> And every happy man's fatherland should
> Be not where he's born but where'er he would.[8]

La Almunia de Don Godino! Out of the question. And, besides, being separated from Frillity, from Don Alvaro, from the marquis and the marchioness, from Benítez – impossible!'

The idea was not considered again. At heart, Ana was happy to find how Vetustan the Aragonese gentleman had become.

She hid her happiness from herself, believing that she had done her duty.

But where were they going to spend those months in the country which Benítez demanded as an indispensable condition of Ana's return to health?

One day the question was being discussed in Vegallana's house. Quintanar, the marquis, the marchioness, Alvaro and Paco were present.

'The doctor demands', said the ex-magistrate, 'that whatever part of the country we visit bring together a set of circumstances which it is difficult to find in one place.'

'Tell us about them,' said the marquis.

'It must be near Vetusta so that Benítez can make frequent calls and Ana can be quickly taken back to town in an emergency; it must be comfortable and agreeable; it must offer cheerful views, be close to running water, fresh grass, cows' milk . . . Goodness only knows what else!'

Don Alvaro had an inspiration. He came close to Paco's ear and whispered:

'El Vivero!'

Paco guessed, and admired. 'Only a genius had such inspirations!'

Without thinking that he was seconding mephistophelian plans he said in a low voice:

'Papa, I don't know of any villa which satisfies Benítez's conditions but one – at our disposal.'

And with one voice, happy at their discovery, Paco and his parents cried:

'El Vivero!'

'Bravo, bravo, eureka!' repeated the marquis. 'Paco's right, El Vivero! You're going to El Vivero.'

The marchioness exclaimed:

'Such a charming idea! How pleasant! And we shall often see each other before we go to the seaside.'

Don Víctor protested.

'How can we go to El Vivero? What about you?'

'We aren't going this year.'

'Or we shall go much later.'

'And when we do go there'll be room for all of us.'

'I have slept there with twenty others, each in complete privacy,' Alvaro pointed out.

'Of course; it's like a convent.'

'Say no more, say no more.'

'What do you mean, say no more? What about my scruples?'

In spite of Don Víctor's scruples it was decreed that he, his wife and all the servants they chose to take with them should go to spend the months requested by Benítez at El Vivero, where they were to be the absolute masters . . . No, no, the marquis and the marchioness would not listen to any objections.

'They were relations, weren't they?'

'We are, indeed,' Quintanar had to admit, swelling with pride.

When Ana heard his news she realized that this was the very opposite of going to La Almunia de Don Godino. But she did not want to think about the possible dangers of the stay at El Vivero, for by now she hated any kind of serious thought. Without examining causes, she felt throughout that day the joy of a young girl whose deepest desires have been satisfied; and her pleasure was even more intense when she awoke the next morning with this thought in her mind: 'I'm going to El Vivero to live like a village girl, to run, breathe, put on weight – be happy – sun, running water, leaves – health,' and, like a perfumed taste or a musical accompaniment throwing its own charm over the prospect, there was a vague hope . . . of what, she did not care to think. But the whole world seemed happier, and the prospect of a stay at El Vivero gave her positive, fortifying pleasure, the pleasure one enjoys while illusions last. 'Benítez was making her young again.'

After the pages in her book of memoirs which told of all these things, Ana stopped at the page on which she had sketched her impressions on entering El Vivero one April day which was like a June one: cheerful, burning, cloudless.

She read the page with delight, enjoying not so much its style as the memories it evoked. It said:

'Rosemary and Carnation suddenly change direction, the landau turns silently, shaking us a little, we leave the Santianes road and the wheels bounce over the fresh gravel of the drive leading to El Vivero. The willows, like a rain of grasses suspended in mid-air, tickle us with the tips of their branches, which brush against our foreheads like hair waving in the wind. The great gate in the old wall swings open. The horses' hoofs strike sparks from the pavement in front of the *Old Palace*, shut and empty, and their clatter awakes echoes in the silence. Had it been my choice we would have stayed in that immense house, with its two towers of brown stone and its colonnades – but the carriage continues at a trot. The marquis, somewhat ostentatiously, made the road to the *habitable* part of El Vivero come this way, in front of the stately old mansion. The wheels are silent again, as if they had cloth covers; the horses' lively hoofs noiselessly pound the soft, smooth, white sand of the broad avenue, flanked by a marble parapet with flowerpots and rosettes containing exotic greenery.

'The *New House* smiles upon us and we stop in front of the coquettish canopy at its entrance; general silence for a moment. The sun speaks; we rejoice. The cleanliness, the correctness, the elegance seem to be the work of nature, and the foliage, the splendour of the greenery, the discreet whispering of the breeze, the beauty of the view, the graceful flight of thousands of birds, are like luxuries brought from afar; wealth and nature join forces here; the sun, a courtier of comfort, is brighter. How peculiar! I had never *seen* El Vivero until now, never really seen it – until now I had never understood this intimate harmony between luxury and the country. And this is how it ought to be. There ought to be corners of the earth where there's nothing ugly or poor or sad.

'Paco and his mother, who have come to give us possession of El Vivero, are having lunch with us, and in the evening, at dusk, they are going back to Vetusta.

'We're alone now. I explored the house. On the ground floor there's a drawing-room, a billiards room, a library, a sewing-gallery overlooking the garden and with windows all around, and the dining-room with access to the conservatory by a white marble staircase. What happiness! It's all glass, flowers, plants with gigantic leaves, brightly coloured, rare. What I like most is a caprice of the marquis's on the first floor: a glassed gallery going all round the building. I have walked around it twice as if I had never seen El Vivero before. Why is it that everything here seems newer, better, more elegant, more poetic? Quintanar's enthralled – and I do think he's a little envious.

. . . .

'An excellent life. Spring has come into my soul. I get up early. Baths give me strength and cheer my spirit. Lying in the bath with my hand on the tap I let the cool water relax me, and my drowsy imagination lingers over calm, gentle, shapely images. Then I shiver in the towel and I joyfully return to the warmth of my body, happy with the life which I feel running through my veins. My head is firm and I am never tormented by subtle, intricate ideas. I don't think much, and my few thoughts are all vague ones; the details of everyday life absorb all my attention. Benítez can feel satisfied. In this way health will return with more vigour. This is life: enjoying the sweet pleasure of vegetating in the sun.

. . . .

'And yet there are times when things seem to send out vibrations which tell of a hidden music of ideas and feelings. What is this hope of an unknown good? Sometimes I think of El Vivero as the setting for a play or a novel. And then the wood seems even more solitary, the old palace more solitary too. It's a pensive kind of solitude. Everything remains in a thoughtful silence, remembering the sounds of gaiety and pleasure which have rung out here, or making ready to echo with the noise of future parties. I repeat – this is all reminiscent of the setting for a play before it has started. The Vetustans who are lucky enough to be invited to El Vivero are the characters in the scenes performed here. Obdulia, Visita, Edelmira, Paco, Joaquinito, Alvaro and so many others have spoken here, sung, run, played, danced and above all laughed. And I can scent past joy – or is it future joy? Yes, Quintanar is right, this is paradise; what do we lack here? According to Quintanar, only music. Well, I'm not going to let *that* spoil everything. I'll run to the drawing-room to play "La donna é mobile" with my forefinger, my only musical finger. How common that is, according to Obdulia! A lady who can only play the piano with one finger!

. . . .

'Quintanar is happy. And he's so good! How he looks after me!

What a fuss he makes of me, how he pampers me! He's like a different man. He thinks more about me now than about fretwork. He spends entire days without touching a saw! There isn't a single human soul that hasn't some poetry deep inside it. His happiness is too rumbustious, but it's sincere. I couldn't live here without him. If I imagine him absent and picture myself here on my own I feel afraid and lonely. And then he doesn't bother me, then I enjoy his company.

. . . .

'Here in the country I even like Petra. She dresses like the local village girls, she sings with them in front of the Old Palace, she joins in the dancing and she plays the Jew's harp with great skill. Yesterday, as dusk fell, by the old gate, she was playing Vetustan airs, monotonous, sweet and sad, the steel tongue vibrating between her lips. Pepe, the caretaker, was singing Andalusian songs converted into Vetustan ones and Petra was twanging her plaintive *trump*, and I was feeling sweet tears in my breast and that vague hope brightened my spirit again. The sadder the tongue of the *trump* became, the more hope, the more happiness I felt inside me. All this is good health, just good health.

. . . .

'I have brought some of my father's books to El Vivero. I hadn't opened them for years. Quintanar always kept them on the highest shelves of his bookcases.

'What an effect they had on me! Between the leaves of an *Illustrated Mythology* I found blades of grass from Loreto – they crumbled into dust – and pieces of paper on which I recognized the scrawls I used to make as a child, and a sailor I had drawn – according to the title at his feet, he was *Germán*.

. . . .

'Benítez would probably condemn this urge to read, and forbid me to become excessively fond of books. Oh, I'm finding such new things in these books which I could hardly understand in Loreto! Gods, heroes, life in the open air, art as a religion, a heaven full of human passions, happiness in this world, no thoughts for sorrow or the uncertain future; in short a young, healthy people. I wish I knew how to draw, and thus give form to these images from mythology which are bombarding my brain.'

. . . .

After reading these and other pages Ana started writing her impressions of the previous few days. Don Víctor interrupted her with the news that he had pitched his tent on the river bank, in the coolest and most agreeable spot, near a dark patch in the water where there must, infallibly, be trout.

Fishing started that afternoon. The fish they caught were few, but much praised. Ana sat reading on her stool of white canvas with blue stripes, holding her rod in her left hand in a grip no tighter than was necessary to prevent the river from carrying it away.

And while on the banks of the River Soto, half a league from Vetusta, Ana in the company of her dear Quintanar allowed trout to escape, dying of laughter, her imagination was back in classical times and places, bathing in the Cephissus, breathing the perfumes of the roses of Tempe, flying to the Scamander, climbing the Taygetus and leaping from island to island, from Lesbos to the Cyclades, from Cyprus to Sicily . . .

Anita would be travelling with Bacchus through India or sailing with him on the prodigious boat from whose flower-laden mast hung bunches of grapes and twisted stems – and have to return with a jump to the prosaic bank of the Soto, summoned by the ex-magistrate, who was shouting:

'But look, lass, they're taking your bait!'

It did not matter: Ana was happy and so was Quintanar. 'He's like a different man!' she said to herself. 'She's like a different woman!' he thought.

Time flew. June became hotter and hotter. Vetusta in the summer is like Andalusia in the spring. Every day, in the cool of the morning, Ana strolled around the garden with Don Víctor, Pepe the caretaker and Petra, shaking cherry-laden boughs. They heaped the damp, gleaming corals into great baskets lined with fig-leaves, and with a singular, healthy, cheerful voluptuousness the judge's wife would run her delicate white hand over the cherries piled upon the green leaves, broad and patterned. The baskets were destined for Vetusta – for the marquis and sometimes for his friends. One morning Ana saw that Petra and Pepe were filling a hand-basket of white and coloured straw with the reddest fruit and went to help them. Suddenly she asked:

'Who's it for?'

'Don Alvaro,' replied Petra.

'Yes, I'm going to take it to his hotel myself,' added Pepe, smiling at the thought of the tip.

Ana felt her hand trembling on the cherries. Their touch was even smoother and more sensual now. And when nobody was looking, not thinking what she was doing, unable to help herself, like a schoolgirl in love, she kissed the white straw of the basket with a kiss of fire. And she kissed the cherries, and bit one of them, which she replaced, bearing the faint marks of two teeth, in the hand-basket.

Astonished by her own audacity, yet unashamed, she spent the whole day thinking about this adventure.

'This, too, was an effect of her good health!'

The night before St Peter's Day the canon theologian received a formal card from the Marquis de Vegallana inviting him to spend the following day, once he was free from his duties in the cathedral, at El Vivero in the company of its owners, its present occupiers the Señores de Quintanar, and many other good friends. El Vivero belonged to the rural parish of Santianes, whose church was dedicated to St Peter. Pepe the caretaker was the organizer of the parish fiesta that year, and he intended to spend the marquis's money like water, 'not wanting m'Lord to cut a poor figure'.

In a postscript to her last letter to her confessor Ana had written: 'The marquis has told me that he intends to invite you to the fiesta on St Peter's Day. We are the organizers. I assume that you will not fail to come. I would consider it an absolute slight.'

'No, I won't fail to go,' thought Don Fermín as he tossed and turned in his bed. 'I wish I had the courage to do so – to scorn you all, to forget everything – but I'm so tired of struggling with this damned obsession which always gets the better of me. Yes, since I'm bound to go in the end, since I'm certain that I shall finish up on the road to El Vivero, it's best to avoid the torture of another battle and surrender now. I shall go.'

He did not enjoy one hour of unbroken sleep all night long. But this was an old trouble by now. Ever since Anita 'had deceived him again' he had not known a single hour's peace.

Since the marquis had not invited him to make the journey in the Vegallanas' carriage – indicating, perhaps, a certain premeditated coldness which he pretended not to notice – he had to go in person to hire a berlin. He ordered it for ten o'clock prompt, outside the Mall. He went to the cathedral, but he was incapable of stopping there, and at half past nine he was already on the road to Santianes and El Vivero, pacing it from side to side, pale, restless, in a devilish temper.

'Why am I going? That other man is bound to be there. What am I going to do? Damn El Vivero!' The berlin was taking a long time to come. De Pas stamped his feet with impatience. Finally the dirty, ramshackle carriage arrived, travelling at a snail's pace.

'To El Vivero, at full speed!' cried Don Fermín, dropping like a stone upon the hard, creaking seat.

The coachman smiled and cracked his whip, the emaciated horse pranced along the road for two or three minutes and then, as if this were a frivolity unworthy of its years (which were many), it reverted to its former languid shamble. Nobody complained.

The canon remembered that a few weeks earlier, in the same berlin, or perhaps another carriage hired from the same firm, he had wept with joy, his soul full of hopes and plans which tingled in all his senses and deep in his body. Now a foreboding was telling him that everything was finished, that Ana was no longer his, that he was going to lose her, that this trip to El Vivero was ridiculous; that if Mesía was there, as he was almost bound to be, he would enjoy all the advantages. The vicar-general was wearing a flowing robe of fine alpaca with tiny buttons, its broad collar shaped like a bat's wings. His dress was reminiscent of that worn by Mephistopheles in the serenata act of *Faust*. [9] He had deliberated for a long time: what clothes would he wear? He was finding his soutane heavier every day and his cloak more and more of a burden. The long shovel hat was odious, yet an excessively short one was affected, ridiculous, the sort of thing Don Custodio wore. With the sides turned up the shovel hat was old-fashioned, but if they were not turned up it was unworthy of a vicar-general. Wear a frock-coat? *Vade retro!* No, a priest in a frock-coat must be either a village priest or a liberal priest. The canon theologian seldom had recourse to such attire. Oh, if only he could wear his hunting clothes, his close-fitting sheepskin jacket, his trousers of strong cloth tight on his thighs, his riding boots, his slouch hat – if he could do that, yes, he would have gone in mufti, and his vanity told him that he would not then have had to fear comparison with the handsome dandy whom he hated. No longer did Don Fermín hide this fact from himself. He did not name his passion, but he recognized all its rights and he was very far from feeling any remorse. 'He was a priest, a priest – a ridiculous being, with things at the stage which they had now reached.' He had realized that Ana was repelled by the canon as soon as the canon tried to show that he was a man as well. 'And yes, he was a man, by God he was a man, as much a man as that other fellow – more of a man: capable of crushing him in his arms, of hurling him as high as a rubber ball . . . !' He stopped thinking about his sadness and his anger. He was looking, with the gaze of an idiot, at features of the landscape, at the telegraph poles which passed by every so often. He had to close the windows because of the choking dust. The sun was wearying and scorching him; there were no curtains in the berlin. The journey seemed interminable. That half-league had stretched out to an indefinite degree. 'The marquis had behaved abominably, not offering him a place in his own carriage. But he could only blame himself, he shouldn't have accepted the invitation. Yet what else could he have done?'

He heard the crunch of horses' hoofs on fresh gravel behind the berlin. He looked out of the window to see who the riders were, and recognized Don Alvaro and Paco as they galloped past on two handsome white Spanish thoroughbreds.

They did not see him, for they were absorbed in the pleasure of riding and did not pay any attention to the wretched berlin crawling along the road. Incapable of noble emulation, the sorry hired hack continued shambling along in the certainty that there was no happiness to be found in this world at the end of a race. One is always in time for a bad meal: this was its complete philosophy. The coachman must have been the horse's disciple.

By the time the canon theologian reached El Vivero the guests had all left the house, and so had the Vegallanas and the Quintanars.

Petra came before him dressed as a village girl, coquettish and provocative. She was displaying golden curls. A long corduroy kerchief passed behind her neck, made an X over her chest, and had its ends tied together behind her waist over her sleeveless shirt of scarlet silk, embroidered with posies and pulled tight against her shapely body. She was wearing a full green flannel skirt over a red one which could be glimpsed above her cloth boots. She was looking beautiful and she knew it. She smiled at the canon and said:

'The master and mistress have gone to church.'

'I imagined as much, my child, but I am dying of thirst and . . .'

The canon walked into the arbour and the make-believe village girl served him a delicious refreshing drink which she had skilfully improvised.

'God bless you, Petrica.'

They talked.

They talked about the life led there by her master and her mistress.

Petra said that Doña Ana was like a different woman: how happy! how playful! No more shutting herself up for hours and hours in chapels, no more praying for centuries and centuries, no more reading St Teresa for ages and ages. Yes – she was a different woman. Her health? She was as strong as an ox.

'Has Paco come?' De Pas suddenly asked.

'Yes, sir, about a quarter of an hour ago. He and Don Alvaro came on horses, at a gallop. They had a drink, like yourself, and they hurried off to church – I think they hadn't heard mass yet and wanted to catch the one at the fiesta.'

Loud explosions of sky-rockets sounded in the east.

'That's the elevation,' said the housemaid.

She was observing the canon's impatience out of the corner of her eye. He said:

'The church is near here, I believe – in that direction, through the wood?'

'Yes sir, but there are three paths that cross and you might end up in the river instead . . . If you want to go I'll take you. There's nothing for me to do in the house at the moment.'

'If you would be so kind.'

Petra set forth, in front of the canon theologian. They left the garden through a wicket-gate and walked into the wood of great ilexes and rugged, twisted oaks. The wood extended over the sides and top of a hill, the highest part being also the densest. As they climbed a steep slope Don Fermín could see the rainbow formed by the hems of Petra's flannel skirts, which she was not attempting to hide, as well as a little of her elaborately embroidered white petticoat and silk lace stockings – a piece of refined coquetry which made the costume less authentic, but which for this very reason lent it an attractive piquancy.

'Isn't it hot, Don Fermín!' she said, mopping her brow with a handkerchief of cheap cambric.

'Very hot, my dear girl, very hot,' replied the canon, unbuttoning his accursed robe, and puffing.

'But I bet you *never* get tired. I've heard that up in Matalerejo you run like a deer over the mountainsides.'

'Who has told you that?'

'Oh, Teresina.'

'You're friends, eh?'

'Close friends.'

Silence. They were both meditating. The canon resumed the dialogue.

'Believe you me: to look at me you might not think so, but I'm a villager, too – you ought to see me playing skittles.'

Petra stopped and turned to look at Don Fermín, who was pretending to hurl an oaken ball along a concave skittle-alley.

The housemaid laughed and, walking on, said:

'Yes, you're a strong man all right and you don't need to tell me so. Anyone can see that.'

They fell silent again.

Sky-rockets exploded once more, close now, on the other side of the hill, and then the screech of the bagpipe and the tabor's trembling timbre came filtering through the foliage, muted by distance.

The pipe's message reached deep into the bodies of the vicar-general and Petra, both villagers. Again they looked at each other and smiled.

'They'll be on their way back by now,' said Petra, stopping once more.

'Are we too late?'

'Yes, sir, the party'll go along the bottom path and by the time we reach the church they'll be back at El Vivero.'

'So . . .'

'So we'd better go back too. Oh, Don Fermín, you must forgive me for this walk – this trouble!'

'No, my child, not at all – on the contrary. It's pleasant here – in this shade, but I'm a bit tired and by your leave – among those roots over there, on that fresh green pile of new-mown grass – well, I'm going to sit down for a while.'

Petra, not daring to sit down but not wishing to abandon her post, looked at the ground, blushing, made catlike movements, and started to wring a corner of her apron.

'Tired? Bah!' she made bold to say. 'A youngster like you . . .'

The pipe and drum filled the green vaults with torrents of sound, now joyful, now melancholy, but always pervaded with pastoral perfumes and pleasant remembrances.

The canon theologian chewed long rough grasses and meditated, with a bitter smile on his lips. 'The ironies of fortune! The fruit which was offering itself to him, which was ready to fall into his mouth, there in front of him, he scorned – and the unattainable fruit he coveted, and the more unattainable it became, the more he coveted it. None the less, to make his situation at El Vivero a less ridiculous one it seemed a good idea to do what he was thinking of doing. Besides, it suited his plans to have the judge's wife's housemaid on his side – to make her his, completely his.'

'Petra.'

'Sir?' she cried, pretending to be frightened.

'Do you think standing there is going to make you grow taller? Surely you're well enough developed already. Come now, don't be silly. If you aren't in a hurry, come and sit down. Anyway, I'd like to ask you a few little questions . . .'

'As you wish, Don Fermín. Nobody will come this way, for sure: not many people go to church through the wood, and anyway, the ones that do, go by the bottom path – scarcely a soul comes up here. But if you want to talk in comfort, a bit higher up the hill there's a hut people call the woodcutter's cabin. It's very cool and there are some very comfy chairs in it.'

'That sounds ideal. We shall be more at ease talking there. Let's go.'

They climbed in silence. The wood became denser. The pipe and drum sounded far in the distance, like music imagined rather than heard.

When they reached the woodcutter's cabin Petra dropped on to the grass at some distance from Don Fermín, and, as red as her underskirt, ventured to look him in the face with serious eyes which were full of meaning.

The canon theologian sat in the hut.

They talked.

Don Fermín had good reason to fear the moment when he met the party, as Petra had called it. When, half an hour later, he walked alone into the garden through the wicket-gate, what first met his eyes was the judge's wife in the dry well, which was crammed full of hay, and by her side Don Alvaro, defending both himself and her against the attacks of Obdulia, Visita, Edelmira, Paco, Joaquín and Don Víctor, who were hurling upon them all the hay which they could steal in handfuls from a small stack in the nearby orchard belonging to Pepe the caretaker.

From the first-floor gallery the marquis was crying:

'Hey, you lunatics! I'll set the dogs on you, you're ruining Pepe's hay. What will his cows have for their supper? Lunatics!' Pepe, standing near the well, in his Sunday best and a black tie which he had deemed worthy of a fiesta organizer, let them all do just as they liked, scratching his head and smiling with delight.

'Don't you worry, m'Lord, you let the young ladies and gentlemen gambol about, I can rake up the hay afterwards. No harm done.'

The judge's wife, her head covered with hay and her eyes half-closed, did not see the canon theologian until the game was over and she scrambled out of the well, with the help of Don Alvaro and the other revellers.

It did not shame her to have been seen by her confessor in such a situation. She greeted him with boisterous amiability and hurried away with Obdulia, Visita and Edelmira to run around the garden pursued by Paco, Joaquín, Don Alvaro and Don Víctor.

The marquis took charge of the canon theologian and bore him off to the drawing-room. This was occupied by the marchioness, the civil governor's wife, the baroness and her eldest daughter (who did not wish to run about with *those crazy people*), the baron, Ripamilán, Bermúdez (who did not wish to run about, either), Ana's doctor Benítez, and various other illustrious Vetustans.

'You see, my dear Vicar-General,' said Vegallana, 'the fiesta has split up into two parties. Pepe's the organizer and he's invited all the priests hereabouts, fourteen of them unless I'm much mistaken. I asked them to come here to have lunch with us, but some of them are uncouth characters and I realized they'd prefer not to have to mix with fine ladies and gentlemen from the city – so a table's been laid for them in the Old Palace, and I'm going to eat with them there. I suggested to Ripamilán that he might go with me, but he doesn't want to. If you were so kind as to accompany me, those worthy parish priests would consider themselves honoured to an infinite degree – since you are the Vicar-General.'

It was unavoidable. He had to eat with the marquis and the priests in the Old Palace.

Petra made it her job to take charge of the servants at the *village table*. She was still dressed in local costume, still ruddy-faced. The curls on her forehead flashed sparks of gold, and her eyes (lively, eloquent eyes, full of a malicious joy which stole the hearts of the villagers and of some of the rural priests) flashed sparks of fire.

When coffee was served Don Fermín could restrain himself no longer. He made his escape as best he could and returned to the New House, where the merry-making had degenerated into a veritable uproar. When the canon walked in, Don Víctor (with the traditional pointed cap of the region on his head) was singing a duet with a rejuvenated Ripamilán. They were standing by the piano, which was being played after a fashion by Don Alvaro, who had a cigar in his mouth, shook his body to and fro, and opened and closed his gleaming smoke-blinded eyes.

The ladies had left. The marchioness, the civil governor's wife and the baroness were strolling in the garden; the girls – Obdulia, Visita, Ana, Edelmira, and the baron's daughter – were running through the wood.

Their cries could be heard from the glassed gallery. The screams and guffaws of Obdulia, Visita and Edelmira were directed at the men.

This, at least, was Joaquín's belief, and he proposed to Paco that they leave the concert being performed by Quintanar and Don Cayetano, and run after the girls.

'Wait a while,' said Paco, who delighted in Ripamilán's ancient songs, and was beginning sometimes to tire of his cousin.

When Quintanar and the archpriest became hoarse (which soon happened), the piano was abandoned and Orgaz's desires were fulfilled. He, Paco, Mesía and Bermúdez left the house and ran into the wood. 'They couldn't hear the girls' cries now.' 'Had they hidden?' 'That must be it.'

'Each one go a different way to look for them.'

'Splendid! Splendid!'

The four men scattered and it was not long before they had lost sight of each other.

As soon as Bermúdez found that he was alone he sat himself upon the grass. A solitary encounter with one of those young ladies in a dense wood of age-old oaks was a situation which demanded a special type of oratory, of which he did not feel capable. And yet how delightful an intimate conversation with Obdulia or with Ana upon the verdant carpet might prove to be!

The canon theologian was obliged to remain with Ripamilán, Don Víctor, the civil governor, Benítez and other grave gentlemen. Benítez was a young man, but he preferred to digest his food in a seated position and smoking a good cigar.

Don Víctor approached the doctor in a balcony window, and De Pas could hear their conversation.

'Oh! you cannot imagine how much I owe you.'

'Me, Don Víctor?'

'Yes, you. Ana is a different woman. Such happiness, such health, such an appetite! No more brooding, exaggerated devotion, apprehension, nerves, lunatic behaviour – like that procession . . . Oh, whenever I remember it, it sets my . . . well, that is all over and done with. She herself is ashamed of what happened. She has become convinced that saintliness does not belong to our times. This is the age of enlightenment, not the age of saints. Are you not of the same opinion, Doctor Benítez?'

'Yes, sir,' said the doctor, smiling and puffing on his cigar.

'So you believe that my wife is completely cured? Radically cured?'

'My dear friend, Doña Ana was never ill. I told you so a hundred times. The cure for her trouble was simply a change in her way of life. But it was never an illness – so she can't be said, strictly speaking, to be cured. Besides, this exultant happiness itself, this optimism, this systematic forgetting of former fears is simply the other side of the same coin.'

'What? You alarm me.'

'You have no reason to be alarmed. Doña Ana is like that, a woman of extremes. Vivacious. Excitable. She needs plenty of activity, something to stimulate her – she needs . . .'

Benítez chewed his cigar and looked at Don Víctor with a mysterious expression of pity mixed with mockery; the old man opened his eyes wide.

'What does she need?'

'What I have said. A strong stimulus, something to engage her attention in a – forceful way; some activity on a grand scale. In short, as I have said, she is inclined by temperament to go to extremes. Yesterday she was a mystic, in love with heaven; today she eats heartily, she goes for walks in the open air among trees and flowers, she's in love with life, with joyful life, and with nature, and with her mania for health.'

'You are right. The poor thing talks of nothing but health.'

'Poor thing! Why do you call her that?'

'Why? Because of her extremes – because of those stimuli you say she needs.'

'And what does that matter? Her temperament demands them.'

'So you believe that she was religious, exaggeratedly religious because – it may be that somebody was exerting a certain influence upon her spirit?'

'Exactly. It's very probable.'

In his usual thoughtless fashion, Don Víctor was chattering without any fear of being overheard, blind to the canon theologian who, pretending to read a newspaper and now and again to pay attention to Ripamilán, was making every effort not to miss a single word of the dialogue in the balcony.

'So the change in Anita is due to – another influence? Her passion for the country, for happiness, for diversions is due to a new influence?'

'Yes, sir. There's a medical aphorism: *ubi irritatio ibi fluxus.*'[10]

'Precisely! *Ubi irritatio* . . . exactly, *ibi fluxus*! I am convinced! But this new influence – where is it? I can see the other one, the clergy, Jesuitry . . . but what about this one? Who represents this new influence – this new *irritatio*, as one might say?'

'Well, it's clear enough. We do. The new regimen, hygiene, El

Vivero, you, me, wholesome food, milk, air, hay, the whiff of the cattle-shed, the morning breeze, and so on.'

'Enough, enough, I understand perfectly: hygiene, milk, the smell of cows – magnificent! So Ana is saved!'

'Yes sir.'

'Because this new extreme cannot lead to anything untoward – can it?'

Benítez spat out a piece of his cigar which he had bitten off, and replied with the same smile as before:

'No, no.'

'Holy St Barbara!'[11] cried Quintanar shutting his eyes and jumping to his feet.

And after the dazzling lightning-flash a roll of thunder shook the walls. All conversations stopped, everybody stood up. Ripamilán and Don Víctor had turned pale. They were two courageous men who always started to tremble as soon as they heard thunder.

Although Ripamilán had been somewhat deaf for several years he heard the discharge clearly, and he already felt unwell. He was not quite at home enough at El Vivero to ask for a mattress with which to cover his head, as he did in his own house.

All the guests except the two frightened men went to the balcony windows to look at the rain. It was pouring down. At the end of the garden the marchioness and the ladies accompanying her could be seen sheltering under the cupola of the belvedere which dominated the landscape, near a corner of the wall.

'What about the youngsters?' asked Ripamilán, frightened to death and pretending that he was afraid for the others' sake.

The youngsters were the people who had gone out into the wood.

'Yes indeed! What became of them? Somebody must go and look for them. They will get soaked!' exclaimed Quintanar, remembering his wife, deeply repentant for not having said something sooner.

The canon theologian was thinking of nothing else, but he kept silence. He had been suffering all afternoon like a soul in purgatory, but never so much as now. 'Those people in the wood – and it was raining cats and dogs on them. The things that Don Alvaro's gallantry must be obliging him to do at that moment!'

'It is necessary to go to look for them,' said the civil governor.

'Umbrellas must be taken to them.'

'And the point is, the marchioness has been caught down there by the rain and she's in no position to . . .'

'And the marquis is stuck with his priests in the Old Palace and he can't come and tell the servants . . .'

There was a long deliberation about what was to be done.

'The castaways must be saved,' said the baron, as a joke.

The canon theologian, who had left the drawing-room, appeared with two large rustic umbrellas, green and made of calico. He offered one of them to Don Víctor, saying:

'Come on, Quintanar, you're a huntsman and so am I. To the wood! To the wood!'

The canon glared at the husband and insulted him with those needle-like pupils, calling him idiotic and spineless – and worse names besides.

'Bravo, bravo!' cried the gentlemen, happy to applaud the heroism of others.

A formidable thunderclap, simultaneous with its lightning-flash, exploded over the house and turned the most valiant men pale.

'Come on, come on, hurry up!' cried the canon, whose pallor was not caused by the storm. The thunder sounded to him like someone roaring with laughter at his bad luck, like the very devil taunting him and mocking him and his wretched condition as a priest.

'But Don Fermín,' Quintanar ventured: 'precisely because I am a huntsman I am aware of the dangers. Trees attract lightning. There are bay-trees up there, too, and bay-trees attract electricity. If they were pines it would not be so bad! But bay-trees . . .'

'What do you mean? That those people can be struck by lightning for all you care? Don't you realize that Doña Ana's with them?'

'Yes, that is true, but could Pepe not go with another servant – with Anselmo? You will get your robe wet, and your soutane . . .'

'To the wood, Don Víctor, to the wood!' roared the vicar-general.

His fearsome cry was drowned by a thunderclap still more horrific than the previous ones.

'Look, gentlemen,' shouted Ripamilán, who was hiding in a bedroom. 'You need not worry, the youngsters must be under cover.'

'What?'

'Yes, Fermín, so don't be alarmed. Under cover – in the woodcutter's cabin. You didn't know about it – it's a rustic hut made of turf and reeds up there in the thick of the wood . . .'

The canon theologian did not want to hear any more. He left with one umbrella under his arm, dropping the other at Don Víctor's feet.

This worthy picked up the instrument of defence, which in his mind he called a shield, and followed 'that madman the canon theologian' without a word, unable to understand why he was so determined that they, and not the servants, should go and look for his wife.

The gentlemen in the drawing-room did not understand it, either, and smiled with discreet and scarcely perceptible archness as they said that the canon theologian's behaviour was a mystery.

'Don Víctor's right,' the baron asserted. 'Why couldn't the servants have gone?'

'Besides,' said the civil governor, 'he seems to be trying to show us all up – especially you, with your daughter up there.'

The thunder which burst at that moment seemed to Ripamilán to have hurled a hundred thunderbolts into the house.

Fear was general by now.

'Come, come, gentlemen,' cried the archpriest from the bedroom, 'time for prayers. By your leave I'm going to pray. *In nomine Patris . . .*'

XXVIII

'Where do you two think you're going?' cried the marchioness from the belvedere to the canon theologian and Don Víctor as they ran one after the other through the wood, some twenty paces apart, soaked to the skin, with water pouring from the brims of their hats and all the folds of their clothes.

'To hell! How should I know where this man is taking me!' the furious Don Víctor shouted, not very loud, struggling to open his umbrella as it collided with branches and became ensnared in brambles.

The marchioness continued vociferating and gesturing, but Don Víctor could no longer understand her and Don Fermín could not even hear her.

'One moment, my good man. Wait, let us deliberate; let us devise a plan! Where are you taking me?'

But it seemed that the good man could not hear Quintanar, either, for he strode up the hill, not looking back for a moment.

From branch to branch and from tree-trunk to tree-trunk spider-threads stretched up and down and in all directions, and into the ex-magistrate's eyes and mouth they all went. He shook the gossamer off and spat it out in fury and disgust.

'This is like being in the middle of an enormous loom!' he cried. The threads held him like ropes, and as he tried to avoid them he stumbled, slipped, and fell on his knees blaspheming, uncharacteristically.

'What a childish idea to come into the woods to play. There is nothing here but spiders and thorns. Don Fermín, wait for me – for the sake of the eleven thousand virgins – I am lost and I keep falling.'

The answer was a thunderclap which frightened him back on to his knees.

He did not dare blaspheme again.

'Don Fermín! Don Fermín! Wait for me, in the name of humanity!'

Don Fermín stopped, turned, looked down with pity, concealing his rage, and said the least unpleasant thing which came to mind:

'Nobody would take you for a huntsman.'

'I am a fine-weather huntsman, my friend, but this is the Flood, and it is a bombardment – and my stomach is full of spiders – and anyway I prefer heroic actions which are of some utility. As Baglivi said, *Nisi utile est id quod facimus, stulta est gloria.* [1] Where are we going, pray? Tell me if you know.'

'To look for Doña Ana, who must be getting – soaked.'

'Soaked – fiddlesticks! Do you take them for idiots? They are under cover, for certain. Do you imagine that they are playing the spider-catcher and swimming around the forest, like us? Besides, have they not feet of their own? Do they not know the way back? You will say that we are taking umbrellas to them – and of what use are umbrellas here?'

The canon theologian coloured. It was true, umbrellas were useless in the wood.

'Do as you please,' he said. 'I am going on.'

'You seem to be trying to show me up,' said Don Víctor, somewhat nettled, struggling after him.

'No, sir.'

'Yes, sir, this, this is – outpoping the Pope. I consider that my wife is of greater concern to me than to any other man. And forgive me for speaking thus, but, to be frank with you, this is pure quixotry.'

Quintanar realized that he was insulting the canon, but he was furious and he was not disposed to retract.

Don Fermín's first impulse was to bring the handle of his umbrella down upon the head of that man, whom he regarded as an imbecile, but for a multitude of reasons he restrained himself and climbed on in silence.

He had other work to do; he heard all the insults as a castaway might hear insults shouted at him from land. Two ideas were fastened in his brain with nails of fire: one said *Ubi irritatio ibi fluxus;* the other, they must be in the woodcutter's cabin! He did not believe in a Providence which makes use of fortuities, of theatrical coincidences, to teach men lessons, but he was superstitious enough to link his memories of the morning, of his walk and his talk with Petra, with those other coarse rustic scenes in which he feared he was going to see the judge's wife involved.

'*Ubi irritatio ibi fluxus!*' he was thinking; 'it's true, it's true. I've been blind – a woman can't stop being a woman, the purest of them is still a woman, and I've been a fool from the very beginning. And now it's too late. I've lost her. And that infamous man . . .'

He started running up the hill.

'The man's gone mad!' thought Quintanar as he followed him, some twenty paces behind again, his tongue hanging out of his mouth.

The canon theologian tried to find his bearings and remember which way he had come down from the woodcutter's cabin a few hours earlier. He kept losing his way, mistaking the landmarks, coming and going, and Don Víctor followed him, beating off spiders as if they were lions and disentangling himself from their webs as if they were chains.

'It will be best to take the steepest way up, the hut is at the very top – but there is a large level area up there, it will be no easy job to find the place.'

De Pas stopped. As if Don Víctor had not uttered a word he said in a tender imploring voice and with a friendly look:

'Señor Quintanar, if we want to find them we shall have to separate. Be so kind as to go up that way, to the right.'

Don Víctor refused, but the canon insisted and, with covert allusions to his companion's fear, he succeeded in piquing his self-esteem again and making him turn right.

As soon as De Pas was alone he ran uphill as fast as his legs would carry him, crashing into tree-trunks and brambles, fallen boughs and hanging branches. He was blind with passion. His heart, bursting with jealousy and anger, told him that he was going to surprise Don Alvaro and the judge's wife speaking love, at the very least. 'Why? Wasn't it likely that Paco, Joaquín, Visita, Obdulia and the others who had gone into the wood were still with them?' No, no, cried his foreboding. And it reasoned: Don Alvaro knows all about such adventures, he will have made the most of the opportunity, he will have contrived to be left alone with her. Paco and Joaquín will not have put any obstacles in his way – indeed they will have cooperated with him so as to be left with Obdulia and Edelmira. Visitación will have helped them. Bermúdez is an idiot – they are alone, they must be. And again he ran as fast as he could, bumping into trees, hauling along his immense robe, as heavy as lead with all the water which it had soaked up, and his soutane, torn and plastered with mud and wet cobwebs. Like Don Víctor he had fine, sticky, intrusive threads clinging to his mouth and eyes.

He came to the highest and thickest part of the wood. The thunderclaps were still formidable, but more distant. He had come the wrong way; the hut was not here. He turned right and blundered on, wresting aside the hundreds of vicious, spiky plants in his way. At last he saw the hut between some branches. There was somebody inside it, moving . . . He ran like a madman, not knowing what he would do if he found what he expected to find – ready to kill if necessary – blind . . .

'Hang it all! What a fright you gave me,' cried Don Víctor, sitting on a rustic bench and wringing a torrent of clear water from his soft felt hat.

'They aren't here!' said the canon theologian, not thinking about the suspicions which might be aroused by his look, his behaviour and his trembling voice, all of which proclaimed passion, jealousy, and the indignation – absurd in him – of an outraged husband.

But Don Víctor was worried, too, and not without reason.

'Look what I have found,' he said, and he inserted two fingers into his pocket and drew from it a garter of red silk with a silver buckle.

'What is that?' asked De Pas, unable to hide his perturbation.

'One of my wife's garters!' replied Don Víctor, not showing any husbandly anxiety – merely surprised at the strangeness of his discovery.

'One of your wife's garters!'

The canon theologian's mouth gaped with astonishment at the stupidity of this man who still did not suspect anything.

'That is to say,' continued Quintanar, 'a garter which used to belong to my wife, but which I have good reason to believe is no longer hers. I know that they do not fit her now – now that she has put on weight, with country air, milk, et cetera; so she has given them to her maid, to Petra. So this garter belongs to Petra. Petra has been here. This is what worries me. What has been the purpose of Petra's coming here and losing her garters? It is for this reason that I am worried, and so I have deemed it opportune to furnish you with this explanation. For, after all, she belongs to my household, she is in my service, and her honour is of concern to me. And I am quite certain of it: this is Petra's garter.'

Don Fermín was red with shame – he could feel that he was. This whole affair, which might have been tragic, had turned into a ridiculous comic escapade; and his remorse at the grotesqueness of it all began to pierce his brain with stabs of migraine. It was fortunate that, as De Pas could see, Don Víctor was in no state to notice others' shame, being absorbed in his own; he, too, had turned bright red. The canon realized that the ex-magistrate's way of recognizing his wife's garters was devious indeed.

Quintanar, too, was both jealous and abashed. De Pas could not know how far, in his weakness, he had gone, and he was saying to himself, 'No doubt this priest, nasty-minded like the rest of them, is imagining all sorts of scenes which have not taken place.'

The fact was that Don Víctor had – in the end, and up to a point – yielded to Petra's advances.

But remembering what he owed his wife, what he owed himself, what he owed his years, and a number of other debts – and above all because of that fatality which had never permitted him to carry a certain kind of enterprise to its natural conclusion – he had turned his back on *that way of perdition*, ever since the day when an attempted seduction had been frustrated by the maid's feigned modesty. 'In sum, he had not conquered his servant girl's charms, but in the course of those preliminary – and indeed final – amorous addresses he had been able to acquire the conviction that his wife had given Petra the garters which he, a loving spouse, had given his wife.'

'But why had he loosed his tongue in front of the canon theologian?'

'He could not understand it. His jealousy, if that was what it could be called, had made him speak. But apart from that, in his heart of hearts he despised that sensual blonde girl and it was only in a moment of excitation – of the mind, that he had been capable of . . .'

The storm was far away by now. Water was still gushing from the trees, but the sky was beginning to turn blue.

For the sake of saying something, Don Víctor said:

'This will be repeated tonight, you will see. There is some more bad weather on its way, down there – look, between those branches.'

'We had better return before it starts to rain again,' said De Pas, wishing the earth would swallow him.

Now they feared each other.

They descended the hill in silence, thinking about Petra's garter.

Before they reached the garden they met Pepe the caretaker, who called from a distance, through the wood:

'Don Víctor, Don Víctor. Hey, Don Víctor – over here.'

'What is it? Have they returned? Is there anything wrong?'

'Wrong? No, sir, the young gentlemen and the young ladies were safe and sound in the house before you could have been half-way into the wood. They hardly got wet at all. I went on my lady's orders to look for them as soon as it started to rain. I drove the cart straight to the Calle de Arreo and took the tarpaulin with me – I knew that Señor Paco would be there, that's the shortest road back, and Chinto's house is there, just a stone's throw away. I found all the young ladies in Chinto's house, they'd hardly got wet at all – when it's starting to rain, being in the wood is like being under cover. So they're all back in the house, dying laughing, all except Señora Doña Ana, who's afraid for you, sir – and for the priest here.'

'But why did the marchioness not tell us . . . ?'

'Well for sure my lady says she shouted to you, and you didn't take any notice, she was telling you I'd gone with the cart.'

Pepe laughed loud and long.

'Quite a joke, ha, ha, ha! Poor dears, what a sorry sight you are – especially the priest here, he looks as if he's on his way to Calvary, begging your pardon for the likeness, he's as wet as a drowned rat. My word, what a state he's got that robe of his into, and his cassock's sopping wet too.'

Pepe was right. De Pas and Don Víctor contemplated each other, and each looked to the other like a shipwrecked sailor.

'Hurry up, hurry up, you poor innocents, the wet might get into your bones and give you the rheumatics.'

'It has already got there, Pepe, it has already got there.'

'Señora Ana has some warm clothes ready for you, sir, and I expect there'll be something for the priest here, too. If there isn't, I've got a fine shirt that's fit for a princess.'

Instead of entering the garden by the wicket-gate through which they had left, the canon theologian walked around the outside of the wall to the coach-house, where he ordered his wretched hired berlin to be brought out.

Don Víctor was so deep in thought that he did not even see the canon leaving him.

The canon met the marquis, who did not want to let him go home in such a state:

'But you'll catch pneumonia. Change your clothes. There must be some clothes for you.'

De Pas could not be persuaded.

'Pray say goodbye to the marchioness on my behalf. I shall be home in no time.'

And he left El Vivero, not as fast as he would have liked, but at a false trot which turned by degrees into a leisurely walk.

'Use your whip on the creature, man,' screamed Don Fermín at the coachman. 'Can't you see I'm soaked to the skin and I want to get home fast?'

The coachman, seeing prospects of a tip, delivered two tremendous blows upon the back of the nag, which was thus made to pay for the wrath which had been stored in the vicar-general's breast for so many hours. They were blows which he would have been happy to deliver upon Mesía's face.

By the time the wretched, ramshackle vehicle reached the first houses on the outskirts of Vetusta, night was falling and, as Don Víctor had predicted, threatening another storm. The sky was covered with grey clouds which were slowly turning black. Sheets of lightning could be seen above the horizon, to the north and west, and from time to time thunder hummed and rolled in the distance.

Don Fermín's soul was choked with disgust and self-contempt. A fine day's work! A fine day's work! He was not even left with the consolation of feeling sorry for himself; he deserved every bit of it; the world was just as the confessional showed it, a heap of trash; great, noble passions were dreams, illusions, masks for vice. He himself was proof of that, feeling full of angelical love, yet falling again and again into the crudest kind of liaison and satisfying his basest appetites like any wretch. After all, Teresina belonged to his own household, but Petra belonged to another's, to Ana's. No longer did he make excuses for himself by recourse to Machiavellian sophistry – by saying that it suited his plans to have the servant girl on his side. 'I could have achieved the same result with a few coins of gold.' 'And what about Don Víctor? Another wretch, and a fool, too, who deserves every bit of the evil coming to him, as I deserve it, as Ana deserves it, as the whole world deserves it, one great pool of mire. Oh, that lightning ought to burn the whole world up if justice is to be done once for all!'

What was most annoying of all was to find that his conscience included him in its general contempt. 'Everything was base, petty, disgusting – and he was no exception.'

'And then, those words of the doctor. *Ubi irritatio* . . . in other words, Ana was going to fall into Don Alvaro's arms. Her fall was inevitable! All the mysticism, all the talk about elder brothers and soul brothers – of what use had it been? A farce, hypocrisy, thoughtless hypocrisy, like his own hypocrisy, like that of the entire universe.'

The canon's teeth were chattering. The cold made him think of his clothes; his clothes made him think of his mother.

'More trouble! What is she going to say when she sees me looking like this? I'll have to invent a lie. Bah! One more lie, what does it matter? And all those people back there, doing just as they please. They can do whatever obscene things they like with her in front of her idiot of a husband if they choose. Oh, who's the real husband here? Who's being offended here? I am! I – who can feel it coming, who can foresee it, who can smell it in the air – not he, who can't see it under his very nose.'

The canon thought of throwing himself from the carriage, running as fast as he could back to El Vivero and surprising 'what his foreboding told him was happening, what had perhaps not happened in the wood but must be happening in the house, among those men dissembling their drunkenness, and their accomplices, those lascivious, wild women.'

A thunderclap booming over Vetusta accompanied the canon's wrath.

'That's right! That's right!' he roared as he opened the carriage door and stepped out in front of his house. 'Thunderbolts – they're the only solution!'

The thunderbolts for which he called were awaiting him upstairs, ready to fall upon his own head.

When he retired that night he was thinking that he had never had such a formidable quarrel with his mother or seen her displaying larger lard-poultices on her temples.

As he fell asleep the last idea still persecuting him was the idea whose stabbing gave him the worst torture – the idea of his ridicule.

'What grotesque adventures – what horrible comic irony, all day long! And the blame for it all lay with the odious soutane, the repugnant soutane.'

The canon theologian's last thoughts were curses. In spite of everything, he slept, exhausted by his exertions.

At El Vivero the guests had put a good face on foul weather. In the Old Palace the village priests, the marquis and some other Vetustan worthies played at ombre first and later at monte – to which the country clergy referred by the euphemistic title of 'the saint's game'² – and in the New House all the ladies and gentlemen who had intended to run about the fields at the fiesta enjoyed themselves as best they could, with dancing and singing and the playing of the piano and of hide-and-seek throughout the house. This was the whole point of going to El Vivero, everyone knew that. Visitación, Obdulia and Edelmira had the greatest knowledge of out-of-the-way corners, side-doors and the other requirements of the children's games to which all these merry-makers devoted themselves without pausing to think how far from childhood some of them were.

Don Víctor was received in triumph: burlesque triumph. Some people, Visita and Paco among them, wanted to crown him, but he preferred to hurry to his room and change his clothes.

His wife went to help him.

'What about Don Fermín?' she asked.

'Your precious Don Fermín is a blunderhead, my child, and forgive me for saying so,' was Quintanar's ill-humoured reply as he changed his socks.

He told his wife everything that had happened, except the discovery of the garter.

Ana agreed that De Pas had taken gallantry to a ridiculous extreme, especially ridiculous in a priest.

'To whom is my wife of greater concern – to him or to me?' he kept repeating, as the supreme argument against the canon theologian.

'Yes,' Ana thought, 'Alvaro is right – that man is jealous, with the jealousy of a lover. What he did today was very rash – I must shun him, Alvaro's right.'

Mesía and Paco had ridden out to El Vivero several times recently. Mesía had found the judge's wife to be in an expansive, happy, trusting mood, and without uttering a word of love he had succeeded in making her listen to his advice, which he swore to be principally concerned with hygiene.

'Mysticism is a form of nervous over-excitement.'

Ana agreed, still frightened by the memory of her fears.

'Besides, the canon theologian is no mystic. The kindest way to think of him is as a man who wants to win ladies of consequence over to his side, so as to extend his influence.'

By the time Don Alvaro ventured to say this, his confidences had become very intimate indeed.

They did not talk of love. With some difficulty Don Alvaro maintained his respectful attitude towards the judge's wife, not laying so much as a finger on her. She was grateful and, as in former times, she tried not to think, and to forget the dangers of their friendship. She was more successful than she had been before.

'My health', she said to herself, 'demands that I be like all the other women. I must put an end to my brooding and my excessive, quixotic projects; I want peace, I want tranquillity. I shall be like all the other women. My honour won't suffer, but if I trouble myself with scruples I'll be back on the path to madness, to all those horrible fears.'

She shuddered as she remembered the misery and terror which she had suffered.

Passion – less clamorous than formerly, more furtive – continued to undermine her; to the few flutters of her conscience it replied with sophisms.

When Quintanar described the canon theologian's rash actions, Ana felt something like hatred for a moment. 'What? Her own confessor was compromising her? If Víctor were a different man, mightn't he have suspected either Don Alvaro or the canon himself? For wasn't it clear that it was simply jealousy on his part? That capped it all! How horrible! How disgusting! A love affair with a priest!'

And the image of Don Alvaro came before her, more agreeable, elegant, alive and fresh than ever. 'After all, it was permitted by natural and social laws – or at least it was less repugnant, less ridiculous; no, it certainly wasn't ridiculous at all – but a canon . . .'

The sin of loving a Mesía seemed hardly to be a sin at all, especially if it enabled her to avoid the love of a canon theologian. 'But what sort of woman can that priest have imagined her to be?'

The judge's wife did not remember 'elder brothers' or 'soul brothers' now, or the fuel which, without meaning any harm and without a trace of coquetry, she had thrown on the fire which was now making her feel so ashamed. Her own reborn passion – inviting, triumphant, about to erupt – suggested one sophism after another to make the canon's behaviour seem repugnant, odious and criminal, and that of Mesía noble and chivalrous.

That day Mesía had shown that he adored her – in the grass-filled well, earlier in the churchyard, in the village lanes as they walked in the procession behind the pipe and drum, in the wood, travelling together afterwards in the cart, where she had been forced to sit almost in his lap, later in the drawing-room – everywhere, all day long, he had shown that he adored her, 'but he had not told her, out of respect, and precisely because he loved her so much'.

Comparing one course of action with the other Anita found the priest's to have been abominable.

And she could not wait to tell Don Alvaro.

As soon as she could do so without being overheard, she said in a confidential tone, which was like a taste of heaven for the dandy:

'What do you think of the canon theologian's behaviour?'

What could he think of it? Abominable! Just as he had told her – she could not trust the man . . .

'Yes, Ana, he's in love with you, madly in love – I could see that a long time ago, because – because . . .'

And Alvaro smiled a smile which said everything. It was accom-

panied by sweet music which the judge's wife thought she could
hear deep in her body – music pouring from his eyes and his mouth,
'she couldn't explain it, but this was a much more potent delight than
any afforded by mysticism!'

While Ana talked with Alvaro as with another soul brother, night
was falling and in the distance the thunder and lightning which
surprised Don Fermín on his return to Vetusta were beginning to roll
and flash. Ana and Alvaro were alone, leaning on the handrail in a
corner of the glassed gallery which went around the first floor of the
house. Downstairs in the drawing-room most of the guests were
making ready to return to Vetusta; others preferred to accept the
hospitality which the marquis and marchioness offered them at El
Vivero for the night. All was noise, movement, confused orders,
jokes, indecision; some people declared that they would stay but
suddenly decided to go, others took a seat in a carriage but then
returned to the house, preferring 'to sleep there, even if they had to
sleep on the floor'. Ripamilán accepted with alacrity the bed offered
by the marchioness 'for him alone'.

'The storm's beginning again and I'm not prepared to play games
with electricity. I know that a moving carriage attracts lightning. I'm
staying, I'm staying.'

The baronesses decided to defy the storm and, although the baron
would rather have stayed, he had to follow his womenfolk. The civil
governor stepped into the carriage, too, but his wife remained with
the Vegallanas. Bermúdez returned to Vetusta; Visitación, Obdulia,
Edelmira, Paco and Mesía stayed behind.

While these arduous matters were resolved downstairs with
much shouting and coming and going, Edelmira, Obdulia, Visita,
Paco and Joaquín ran around the first-floor gallery like lunatics.
Visitación was tipsy, not so much from drinking as from rampaging. Obdulia said that her head was splitting: she had drunk much
more than Visita, but the whirl of the dance and the intense
emotions of hide-and-seek kept her on her feet with sheer excitement. Edelmira, who had by now mastered the art of having fun
in the Vegallana style, was as red as a poppy, noisily laughing and
playing. Her gaiety was agreeable and catching. Paco was pinching
her without mercy and she was tearing at Paco's arms; Joaquín
Orgaz, who that afternoon had made some progress in Obdulia's
ever ephemeral affections, was also pinching. There were races,
collisions, shouts, squeezes, leaps, scares, surprises. As Ana and
Alvaro talked by an open window, not worrying about the rain
splashing their faces or the lightning-flashes rending the distant
black sky before their eyes, the others, in the darkness of the
narrow corridor, were playing a children's game known in Vetusta
as 'Hunt the Truncheon', which consists in the hiding of a
handkerchief converted into a whip and the search for it aided by

those well-known directions, warm and cold. The one who finds it runs after the others whipping them until they reach the safety of the *den*. This innocent game gave rise to a multiplicity of delightful incidents among the players, who were the very opposite of innocent. Often two hands, one a woman's and the other a man's, would feel for the truncheon in the same hole, as people ran away they would bump into one another, and historical truth requires that it be owned, however unlikely it might appear, that these *youngsters* running like lunatics in a throng around the narrow gallery, fleeing from the whip, often fell upon the floor in a heap of confusion as their backs were flogged by the knotted handkerchief.

As the judge's wife heard below her the chatter and the bustle of farewells and preparations for the journey, and behind her the racket of the people running along the gallery, and up in the sky from time to time the roar of thunder – not noticing the drops of water on her face most of the time, delighting in their coolness when she did – she listened, for the first time in her life, to a declaration of love, passionate yet respectful and discreet. It was pure idealism, full of the reservations and euphemisms which her circumstances and condition required and which only increased its charm, irresistible for this woman of nearly thirty years of age who was experiencing the emotions of a fifteen-year-old girl.

She had not the courage or even the desire to tell Don Alvaro to stop, control himself, remember who she was. 'He was remembering that well enough, controlling himself well enough – considering how strong he said his feelings were, and really must be.'

All her soul said, 'No, no, I don't want him to stop, I want him to talk for ever.' Ana, her cheeks aflame, with the president of the Gentlemen's Club speaking close by her, did not remember that she was a married woman, or that she had been a mystic, or even that the world contained such people as husbands and canon theologians. She could feel herself falling into an abyss of flowers. She was falling, yes indeed – but she was falling into heaven.

The only matter for which she still had any thoughts, apart from what was happening to her, was the comparison between the delight which she was enjoying and the pleasure afforded by religious meditation. The latter involved painful effort, cold abstraction and something which one had to admit was unhealthy, a morbid exaltation; in what was happening now she was passive, there was no effort, there was no coldness, there was nothing but pleasure, health, strength, no abstraction, no need to imagine something absent, just positive, tangible, immediate delight, joy without reservation, giving rise only to the hope that it would last for ever. 'No, this was not the path to madness.'

Don Alvaro was eloquent. He asked for nothing, not even a reply. What was more, he was weeping (without weeping, of course) 'with pure gratitude, just because she was listening to him'. 'He had kept quiet for so long! There were thousands of prejudices, millions of obstacles opposing his happiness? He knew that well enough, but he asked only for pity, and the joy of being allowed to speak, and being heard and not dismissed as a common, foolish libertine, which was what the stupid common herd had tried to make him out to be.'

It had always pleased Ana to hear the common people called stupid; for her it was a sign of spiritual distinction to scorn the common people, the Vetustans. Perhaps it was a defect which she had inherited from her father. In order to be distinguished in her own mind from the believing masses she needed to have recourse to the now widespread theory of the idiotic common herd, human bestiality, and so on.

Fortunately Don Alvaro knew how to work this lever. He was capable, if need were, of disparaging the midday sun itself if it opposed his passions. 'It was all prejudice, petty-mindedness. But had he any right to expect Ana to agree with his ideas and scorn the malicious and coarse fancies of the common herd? Oh, no, he well knew that the *letter* was against it. In short, what was he? A man talking of love to a woman who, in men's eyes, belonged to another. He was well aware of that, oh yes, he wasn't demanding that Ana should rise above all the traditions, laws, customs, commonplaces and routines which condemned him. In this world there were of course many women, inferior to none in point of virtue, who knew in what spirit to take the letter of the moral law which condemned his love. But could he ask Ana, who had been brought up by fanatics and had spent her youth in a town like Vetusta – could he ask her to condescend to encourage his passion by giving him hope? Oh, no, he knew only too well that he couldn't – it was enough that she was hearing him. How many years without consenting to hear him! And how he had suffered! But still, it was better not to think about that now. His grief had been infinite, infinite, but the happiness of this moment made up for it all. Ana was quiet, she was listening – to what greater joy could he aspire.'

There was a flash of lightning and Ana saw Alvaro's eyes shining and wet with tears.

His cheeks were wet, too. She did not stop to think that it might be the water which was falling from the sky.

'This man was weeping – the handsomest man she had ever seen, the companion of her dreams, the man who should have been the companion of her life!

'But why had he spoken of gratitude? Just because she didn't interrupt him? If he knew – if he knew that she *couldn't* speak!'

Ana felt a purely physical pleasure in that place deep inside her which was neither her stomach nor her heart, but somewhere between the two. Yes, her pleasure was purely physical, but its intensity made it magnificent, sublime. 'When one's joy was so great one must have a right to it.'

Considering that the mine was sufficiently charged, Alvaro begged Ana to say something – to say if he was forgiven for his declaration, if he was regarded with distaste, if he had made a fool of himself, if he was being laughed at . . . Recoiling from the fiery touch of his arm, pouting like a little girl yet without a trace of coquetry, shrinking like a small wild animal which has been wounded, she uttered a moan – a deep, guttural, whimpering moan, the death-rattle of virtue in that hitherto solitary spirit.

She left Alvaro, called out to Visita, gave her a nervous embrace and, at last able to speak again, said:

'What are you playing at, you madcaps?'

'We've stopped playing. We were playing at "Hunt the Truncheon", but now Paco and Edelmira are over there in the corner on the other side arguing about which of them is stronger. Come on, come and see what a fine pair of fists Edelmira's got.'

The rest of the merry-makers were crowding together in a corner on the darkest side of the gallery. Edelmira and Paco, standing back to back (in the way local country dances are sometimes performed, especially in the theatre), were engaged in a trial of strength. Paco was finding it hard work to withstand the violent shoving of his cousin who, with a relish which only she – and the devil – could understand, was embedding herself in his flesh, softer than her own, determined to beat him by forcing him to step forward. At length Edelmira won, and Paco, hissed by the spectators, proposed that they push face to face, with their hands on each other's shoulders. This time Paco won.

Joaquín proposed the same struggle to Obdulia; Visita ventured to test her strength against the judge's wife. Joaquín and Ana were the victors. Don Alvaro, left without an opponent, remembered the scene of the swing, when the accursed De Pas had beaten him. 'But now he'd got the man under his foot.'

'Brain is better than brawn.'

The physical exercises continued. The pattering of the rain, the flashes of lightning, the distant thunderclaps, the enveloping darkness, the after-effects of the meal, the narrowness of the corridor – it all encouraged them, and plunged them into a peasant-like hilarity, into brutish games of surreptitious lust, which the influence of their upbringing led them sometimes to moderate. But then there would be a renewal of the pinching, the shouting and the punching of men's heads by women's fists. Ana had never witnessed such scenes. She and Don Alvaro did not take an active part in the fun and games at first, but in the end an occasional pinch – not from him – came her way, and he too was pinched several times, by Obdulia and Visita. Before she knew what was happening she realized that his back was pressed against hers in the mêlée. As soon as she became aware of this delightful contact with its own special flavour she tried to avoid it, but it returned again and again. She felt strange, utterly new emotions, an alarming restlessness, sudden choking sensations, and a kind of thirst throughout her body which made her oblivious to everything except that dark corner where people were singing, laughing, leaping. She only remembered – and this she remembered in detail – Mesía's declaration of love, like distant music, sweet and tender.

Exhausted by their exertions, their shows of strength and their collisions, by so much vain stimulation, Paco and Joaquín first, and then Edelmira, Obdulia and Visita, stopped running and *fooling about*. Serious now, with the melancholy caused by fatigue, they contemplated the moon standing over the horizon like a lantern on the battlefield of the clouds, which lay about the sky, torn to shreds.

Paco sang parts of *La Favorite* and *La Sonnambula*,[3] in a tolerable baritone. Joaquín came out with some fandangos (as he phrased it), in a sad voice which contrasted with his eyes, gleaming with joy and riveted on the eyes of Obdulia. For she had decided to bestow the prize of her favours – not, however, the ultimate favour – upon Flamenco that night. Fortunately, Joaquín was content with his *proxime accessit*.

Don Víctor, who was getting bored downstairs, heard 'Spirto gentil'[4] being sung and came up. Music was his latest hobby. Singing operas, in his own way, and hearing them sung by people who were better *harmonists* than he, was his new delight. If all this was done by the light of the moon, his joy was complete.

Standing in a group, breathing the cool night air, contemplating the moon as it advanced across its vault capriciously tearing shreds of clouds into even smaller pieces, they sang together or by turns and spoke in hushed voices as if out of respect for the majesty of nature as it slept, its body and its soul overcome by languor.

Don Víctor was even more sentimental than the others. He approached Mesía and succeeded in engaging him in a private conversation; since he found his friend more attentive than ever, more cordial, more affectionate, it was not long before he had bared his soul.

When all the others had long since tired of the moon and operas and fandangos, Don Víctor, having enjoyed a hearty lunch and an afternoon snack accompanied by generous quantities of wine, was still baring his bosom to Mesía, who gave him all his attention – silent, irreproachable attention.

'Look here,' the old man said, 'I cannot exactly explain it, but, without believing myself to be a Don Juan, I must say that I have always been fortunate in my amorous enterprises. Seldom have the women with whom I have ventured to be audacious thought amiss of my forwardness. But I must tell the whole truth. I do not know why it is – if it is because of some tepidity or bashfulness in my character, or coolness in my blood, or for whatever reason it be – the greater part of my adventures have not progressed beyond the halfway stage. I do not possess the gift of constancy.'

'It is indispensable.'

'Yes, I can see that, but I do not possess it. My passions are will-o'-the-wisps. In my time I have had more than ten women at the point of surrender – yet very few of them, perhaps even none of them, can I claim to have made mine, really mine. I do not have to look far to find an example.'

In the bosom of friendship, and confident that Mesía would keep as silent as the grave about his revelations, Don Víctor told him about the persecution of which he had been the victim, about Petra's wanton provocation. He confessed that after resisting for a long time, indeed for years, like a saint – in a moment of blindness he had dared all. But no, it had been the same story all over again; it had sufficed for the girl to put up the resistance which feigned modesty required of her, to make him grow cold just when he was certain of victory, and desist from his foolish enterprise, contenting himself with minor favours and an exact knowledge of that beauty which he was never to enjoy.

Rambling on, he ended by describing the discovery of the garter, although he did not say that it had once belonged to his wife. He thought it a weakness unworthy of a man of the world to make gifts of garters to his wife. He asked for Mesía's advice regarding his future behaviour towards Petra.

'Should I dismiss her?'

'Are you jealous?'

'No, sir, I am no dog in the manger – although I must confess that it was somewhat displeasing at first to discover that proof of her incontinence.'

'But are you certain that the garter belongs to Petra?'

'Ah, yes, I am absolutely certain.'

Quintanar went on talking and talking, without showing any signs of stopping.

In the bedroom in which Ana and Don Víctor slept there was a window giving on to the gallery where the two friends were talking.

Ana threw the window open and called to her husband:

'But Víctor, aren't you coming to bed tonight?'

The two friends turned around.

Quintanar's eyes were inflamed and his cheeks were glowing. His confidences had rejuvenated him.

'But what is the time, my child?'

'Very late. You know that out here in the country we retire early.

The Vegallanas have retired already. The marchioness has just called Edelmira, who's sleeping in her room.'

'One of mamma's stupid ideas,' said Paco, in great dudgeon, appearing at the end of the gallery. Edelmira would rather have slept with Obdulia, naturally, and now Doña Rufina was making her sleep in *her* bedroom. 'Stupid. One of mamma's silly ideas.'

'Obdulia's in no state to sleep with anyone,' said Visita, emerging from the room next to Ana's.

'What's wrong with her?'

'I think she's tight – drunk with noise, fatigue, wine even, thousands of things, I don't know, I'm sure. Anyway, she's in bed groaning and she says that nobody's sleeping with her, she wants to be alone. I'm going to her, I'm going to put my bed next to hers. Good-night.'

And she grasped the judge's wife by her shoulders, whispered into her ear, covered her face with noisy kisses and ran to her own room after making a grimace of derisive commiseration at Joaquinito Orgaz, who was wandering about the corridors, his head bowed, sunk in gloom.

'Come on, come on, you can see everyone's going to bed. Víctor, come to bed.'

Ana smiled, looking fresh and beautiful in her simple dressing-gown.

'What about you two?' said Quintanar.

'We two', replied Paco, 'haven't got a bed to sleep in, because the civil governor's precious wife has taken it into her head to feel frightened of the thunder and to stay here for the night.'

'So . . . ?' asked Ana with a smile.

'So we're sleeping on sofas.'

'Dear, dear. Well, good-night.'

'Wait a minute, silly, look what a lovely night – let's stay here and talk a little.'

'I am not sleepy. Paco is right, let us talk,' said Don Víctor, who had entered his room and donned his slippers and his gold-tasselled smoking-cap.

'Talk? No, sir, to bed.'

Ana, unintentionally coquettish, made a graceful, provocative move to close the windows and the shutters.

Mesía's look was an appeal to wait a while.

And so, talking in confidential tones, commenting on the day's events, on the fun and the games, they stayed there by the light of the moon for another hour; Ana and her husband in their room, Paco, Joaquín and Alvaro in the gallery.

Don Víctor was in the seventh heaven. Seeing his Anita cheerful, expansive, and seeing there, too, close to his bed, those young friends in whose company he felt young as well – what joy could be greater? There was not the slightest shadow of suspicion in the soul of the noble ex-magistrate. All was still in the house, everyone else was asleep, and only in that corner of the gallery, by the open window, was there a soft sound of whispering voices. Now and then two or three people spoke at once, but always in hushed tones which seemed to add interest and intimacy to what they were saying. Sometimes Ana avoided Don Alvaro's looks. He was smoking, with one elbow resting close to Ana's elbows on the handrail. On other more frequent occasions their eyes would meet and with growing eloquence speak love, without anyone being able to prevent it.

From time to time Alvaro cast sidelong glances, envious and covetous, into the bedroom. Ana surprised some of these hurried looks and felt sorry for the amorous beau, not taking his indiscreet curiosity amiss.

Don Víctor did not show any signs of putting an end to the chatter and Ana thought it incumbent on her to say:

'Come, come – good-night, Víctor, to bed.'

And she shut the window in Alvaro's and the youngsters' faces. Paco and Joaquín disappeared into the darkness of the corridor. Quintanar was already at the far end of the bedroom in his shirt-sleeves with his back to the window. Don Alvaro did not move. He saw the judge's wife behind the glass, slowly closing the wooden shutters. She was between them, in the rectangle of light, gazing at him seriously, tenderly – and when only a chink remained she gave him a smiling, playful look. She opened the shutters a little, and he could see her whole face again.

'Good-night, good-night, sound sleep to you,' said Ana, behind the glass, and she slammed and bolted the shutters.

Many other fiestas like the fiesta on St Peter's Day were held near El Vivero during the month of July. The Vegallanas and their friends went to nearly all of them. Quintanar and his wife would wait in the villa for the people from Vetusta, and they would all set off, sometimes on foot and sometimes in carriages. They would tour picturesque villages, listen to the songs, monotonous but always pleasant, sweet and melancholy, to which the villagers danced, and return at nightfall, munching hazel-nuts and singing, among peasants and frolicsome country girls. Landlords and tenants would mingle in a mixture which moved Don Víctor, who said: 'Look here: if equality and fraternity could be achieved, there could be nothing better or more poetic in this life.'

Mesía and Paco did not miss any of these trips, and went to see the judge's wife every three or four days as well. Sometimes after lunch, at about four o'clock, Ana and Quintanar would walk out to the Santianes road to await their friends. Solitude was becoming burdensome to Don Víctor, and he welcomed these visits with all his soul. When Ana espied in the distance, at the far end of the long, narrow ribbon of road, the shapes of the two powerful white horses, she felt a pleasure which seemed childish, and a nervous longing which grew as the shapes came closer and the figures of horses and riders were clearer.

Neither Paco nor Visitación dared talk to Don Alvaro about his amorous pretensions. They left him to himself, knowing, from the Don Juan's radiant look, that he expected victory, that he was perhaps on the verge of it; and they realized that modesty, or rather shame, demanded absolute silence. Don Alvaro was grateful to his accomplices for their 'delicacy', and he kept quiet, too, tranquil and satisfied.

At the end of the month the general dispersion commenced. All those who were not absolutely penniless, and many of those who were, departed from the city in quest of cool beaches.

Don Víctor, beside himself with joy, left El Vivero with his wife and Petra, and installed himself in the best port in the province, La Costa – a flourishing town, richer than Vetusta, a centre for coastal traffic, and very fashionably dressed. He usually spent the month of August in Palomares, however, where Visita, Obdulia and sometimes the Vegallanas and Mesía also went.

'It is two years since I last had a summer holiday!' he said, as happy as a little boy.

His wife preferred La Costa to Palomares because the canon theologian had begged her not to go to the seaside and, if the doctor ordered her to go, to stay away from Palomares at least. Ana did not want to cross her confessor, so she compromised.

'We're going to La Costa,' she said in her reply to Don Fermín's letter. The canon had the worst possible opinion of the moral effects of all the watering-places on the north coast of Spain, in particular of Palomares. Most of his penitents came back from this fishing town with their consciences overflowing with peccadilloes which almost made him smile but which, committed by the judge's wife, would not have amused him at all.

Don Fermín realized that his influence was diminishing, that Ana's faith was cooling and that her distrust was growing. Since the idea of losing his Ana frightened him, and tortured his pride and his jealousy, he tried to make the best of a bad bargain, pretended not to notice anything and held up his tottering spiritual power 'with props of tolerance and buttresses of patience'. He vented his anger on the bishop and in the diocesan curia. His power there was becoming ever greater, his tyranny ever crueller. The advantages which Don Alvaro was gaining over him in Ana's heart were being paid for by the parish clergy, by that clergy for which Foja said he had such great respect.

Ana, too, preferred this *modus vivendi*; she did not want to fall back into her old ways; she was afraid that if she broke all relations with the vicar-general her compassion and remorse and fear would return to molest her and in the end make her ill again.

'I know myself,' she thought. 'I know that I do, after all, feel a certain affection for him and that if I broke our friendship an unbearable voice would always be shouting at me in his favour. It's better like this. Since he's hiding his feelings and pretending not to notice the change, and since he isn't complaining as he did at first, let's leave things as they are. I want peace, peace, no more battles inside me.'

Don Alvaro had hinted, in the confidential tone of voice which he had adopted since his declaration of love, that it would not be a good idea to irritate Don Fermín, whom he believed to be always capable of mischief of one sort or another. Although Alvaro did not dare to be very explicit in this matter, Ana understood what her friend, her new brother, meant, and she approved of his prudence.

All this made it possible for the vicar-general to venture to insinuate his wish, which in former times he would have decreed without giving any reasons.

Ana went to La Costa. For the sake of appearances Mesía spent five days in Palomares, moved on to San Sebastian, and on Assumption Day[5] presented himself in La Costa, in a boat from Bilbao, new and gleaming.

Don Víctor always enjoyed a few weeks in a hotel. He had installed himself in the most luxurious, bustling and noisy hotel in town, on the quayside. Mesía went to stay there too, at the request of his friend the ex-magistrate.

Twenty days later the three of them returned to Vetusta together. Benítez congratulated Ana on her notable improvement. Her health really was guaranteed now: What a colour! What fine forms! How solidly robust she looked!

Don Víctor was as pleased as Punch. 'Oh, the sea, there is nothing to compare with the sea, and the table d'hôte, and the bathhouse, and the promenades on the quayside, and the open-air concerts, and the theatres and circuses!' How happy Quintanar was with life! His wife was a pearl: the pearl of the province, as she had always been, but now she was his, completely his, and her humour had turned cheerful and active, like the humour which God had granted him.

'And me? What? What about me, Doctor Benítez?'

'Magnificent, magnificent, too, looking like a mere chicken again.'

'Yes indeed!'

'And this old tortoise here? This tortoise that's beginning to get a bit long in the tooth – what about him?' And he slapped Mesía's back. 'Now *he* is looking like a youngster, to be sure.'

Turning to Frillity, for Frillity was present, haggard and miserable, Quintanar added:

'But you are fast on your way to Old Street. After putting on all those airs about your hygienic life, like that of some age-old tree. No, you will not live to any great age, you fogy.'

And he hugged Frillity and slapped him on the back, too, so that he should not feel jealous of Mesía. Quintanar was a happy man and he wanted everybody connected with him to be happy too – his wife, his servants and his friends, even mere acquaintances, everybody.

If Mesía asked him, as a joke, 'How's Kempis? What does Kempis have to say about it all?', he replied: 'Who? Kempis be blowed! I am going to set to work on the house. I shall whitewash the courtyard and the passages, paper the dining-room, and scrape the façade. You will see how handsome the yellow stone looks once we have scraped it. I want no darkness, no blackness, no sadness.'

Mesía had persuaded the judge's wife that Don Víctor was best regarded as a father. She had always been inclined to think so.

But none the less she owed him her honour. In spite of all their intimacy, and in spite of her love, implicitly confessed, Ana could say that Don Alvaro had never placed his lips upon that skin about whose touch he must doubtless dream.

Mesía was not in a hurry. 'She wasn't like other married women, she had to be conquered like a virgin. After all, he was her first love, and brutal attacks would scare her, rob her of all her illusions. Besides, he was also being rejuvenated by this situation of platonic love, of sweet intimacy, in which not only his tongue, but the eyes and the smiles (and everything else which was silent and not immodest or coarse) of both of them spoke love.

'And in any case, the summer always left him a bit languid and run-down.' With the frivolity which is affected by practical materialists and nevertheless comes naturally to them, he calculated that by winter he would be feeling as strong as a horse and she would be as meek and docile as a lamb. 'Besides, if he did something outrageous he might ruin the whole show or at least delay events and give them a less piquant and spicy turn than they had at present. Time would tell, time would tell – and it wouldn't be long now.'

In the meantime, life was delightful. The mature Don Juan who, as he himself said, *était déjà sur le retour*, felt transformed by Anita's youth and her dreamy yet vehement passion. Don Alvaro could not remember ever having desired a woman, or enjoyed platonic love (as he called all unconsummated love), as much as he did now.

The judge's wife was happy as she fell: she could feel the dizziness of the fall in her stomach. And if on some mornings she awoke not to happy thoughts but to doleful ones, mixed with a little bile – something like remorse – she soon cured herself with the new system of naturalistic metaphysics which she had at last unwittingly created for herself so as to satisfy her invincible desire to carry all the events of her life into the regions of abstraction and generality.

But even Ana, with her inclination to brood, had little time to do so. Life was all amusement, trips, happy meals, visits to the theatre, promenades. The Vegallanas and the Quintanars had developed a kind of life in common, in which Obdulia, Visita, Alvaro, Joaquín and a few other close friends also participated.

They often went to El Vivero, and there they ran in the wood, around the glassed gallery, through the garden, along the river bank. They all seemed to be accomplices. Obdulia and Visita adored the judge's wife, were the slaves of her caprices, smothered her with kisses; they swore that they were happy just to see her so sociable, so much more human. And not a single roguish allusion, or indiscreet question, or inopportune surprise. Nobody referred to the danger of which only Quintanar was ignorant. Often, when a storm like that of St Peter's Day broke over El Vivero, the whole party stayed the night. Ana frequently found herself touching Alvaro, pressed up against him in carriages, theatre-boxes, ballrooms, woods. She did not seek the contact, but she did not avoid the situations which gave rise to it, either.

One November day – one of the few fine days in St Martin's summer – they went on the year's last trip to El Vivero.

Their gaiety was intense, nervous. For those youngsters – as Ripamilán, who was also a member of the expedition, in spite of his years, still called them – the Vegallanas' villa held the pleasantest memories of their merry games, and they bade a sorrowful farewell to this corner of the springs and autumns of their lives. They wanted to savour the very last drop of mad gaiety in the freedom of the country and the secret, piquant confidences of the wood. Never had Visita played the little girl with a better appearance of good faith, or Obdulia allowed Joaquín to go further with his foolery, to use her euphemistic vocabulary; Edelmira and Paco made peace after a week of enmity; even the old men sang, danced a minuet and ran through the wood; Don Víctor was full of mischief and fell into the river when he tried to jump across it at a point where it was narrow.

When, in the morning, Alvaro handed Ana into the carriage, they both found that the contact made new impressions on their skin and in their blood. The previous night Alvaro had said that he wanted to die. He was not asking for anything, but he wanted to die. During the drive from Vetusta to El Vivero Ana said only this, in a quiet voice, into Alvaro's ear: 'Today is the last day.'

After lunch all the lovers of El Vivero were worried by the thought that the afternoon was going to be a very short one. Joaquín and Obdulia knew that all the world was their homeland,[6] 'but there was nowhere quite like El Vivero!' Edelmira and Paco, too, sighed for their hiding-holes in the villa, which they were very soon going to leave behind. Before the last outburst of madness, the last races through the wood and the last merry-making, there was a quarter of an hour of melancholy – of tiredness mixed with sadness. The afternoon was going to be a short one, and it was the last afternoon. Visita sat at the piano and played the polka from *Salacia*, a fantastic and spectacular ballet which was being performed in Vetusta. Salacia, the daughter of the sea, brought her sisters out of the ocean and, for unknown reasons, also brought Bacchantes out of the wings to dance an infernal dance on the beach. Ana remembered the impression that polka had made on her senses. 'The Bacchantes! Asia, their thyrsi; Bacchus's tiger-skin.' Ana, with her own knowledge of these mythological reminiscences, had soon stopped seeing the shoddy scenery and the prosaic ballerinas (not all of them well-formed) and had transported herself from the theatre of Vetusta to the Orient, where her half-educated imagination pictured mysterious woods and frenzied Bacchantes running through them, maddened by strident music and by drinking at their perpetual orgy in the open air. The Bacchante! The fanatic of nature, drunk with all the games of her lusty, wild life; ceaseless, boundless, fearless pleasure; racing through open fields, leaping across chasms, plunging into the delightful unknown, into the strange perils of abysses and luxuriant, treacherous boughs and branches. While Visita gave her clumsy rendering of the humble polka from *Salacia* – music good to the extent that it was borrowed – the judge's wife let all the phantoms of her books, her dreams and her excited passion dance in her brain.

She suddenly took it into her head to look at a copy of *L'Illustration* on an occasional table. 'The last flower' said the title of an engraving on which she fastened her gaze. In a garden, in autumn, a beautiful woman, about thirty years old, was in raptures as she smelt and pressed to her face a flower – the last flower.

'Come on, come on, off to the woods!' cried Obdulia from the garden. 'To the woods, to the woods! To say goodbye to the trees.'

Visitación pounded the keys, forcing her polka to a rapid conclusion, and slammed the piano shut.

'To the woods! To the woods!' came the cry from upstairs and downstairs.

And out they went through the wicket-gate to say goodbye to oaks, ilexes, hawthorns, brambles, ferns and fresh green autumn grass.

That night the party continued in Vetusta, a farewell party for good weather; winter was coming, the flood was on its way. A dinner was improvised for all the ladies and gentlemen. By midnight, after dancing and singing and rampaging, many of them already had good appetites. Lunch had been taken early, and some of them had only sampled sweetmeats and drunk wine. Since the night was so calm and warm that it seemed like early September, they dined in the new conservatory, large, high, comfortable, built to the Parisian pattern and used that day for the first time. Don Alvaro, who knew about such matters, said that it resembled, on a smaller scale, Princess Mathilde's conservatory.[7] How Obdulia envied that piece of information! And she swelled with pride! A man who had been her lover could talk about Princess Mathilde's *serre!*

They dined, then, in the conservatory. In the Yellow Salon, where the appearance of a few fresh guests had enabled them to dance after returning to Vetusta, the sperm-candles in the candelabra were flickering out in the draught from an open balcony window: the servants had only extinguished the cut-glass chandelier. The chairs were in disorder; upon the carpet lay two or three books, pieces of paper, mud from El Vivero, flower-petals, and a begonia-stem like a length of old brocade. The salon looked tired. The figures in the marchioness's elegant, provocative, coloured prints laughed in their awkward, mannered postures of false gracefulness. Everything there was licentious; the disordered furniture, poised in strange positions, seemed to be rebelling and threatening to tell even the deaf what it knew and had kept to itself for so many years. The sofa with its broad yellow seat, more prudent and experienced than the rest, kept its place and was silent.

A gust of wind extinguished the last candles lighting the deserted scene. The cathedral clock struck twelve. The salon door opened and two figures entered, their footsteps muffled by the carpet. The only light was that which filtered in feebly from outside, from the new moon and a new street lamp in front of the marquis's house, which the recently elected municipal corporation had decided thus to flatter. When the door was opened, the distant sounds of the servants in the kitchen could be heard: laughter and the humming of a guitar being played gingerly, with a certain respect for the master and mistress. These sounds mingled with other duller ones from the garden – the noise of the dinner in the conservatory, which reached the salon like the murmur of a distant, busy suburb.

The two figures were Mesía and Quintanar. The latter, intoxicated by his own confidences, was pursuing his intimate friend with the story of the amorous adventures of his youth in La Almunia de Don Godino.

Don Alvaro dropped on to the sofa, both sleepy and dreamy. He was not listening to Don Víctor, he was listening to the voice of his burning, brutal desire, which cried: 'Today, today, now, here, right here!'

Meanwhile, the ex-magistrate, who regarded the shadows in the salon and the discreet light of the street lamp and of the quarter moon as a most appropriate setting for the confession of his erotic escapades, continued his story, from time to time declaring his refrain:

'But what an ill-starred man am I! Do you think that I finally made her mine? No sir! However incredible it might appear! As usual, all my constancy, resolution, and enthusiasm deserted me – and yet again, my friend, was the cup dashed from my lips. I know not why. It is always the same story – at the critical moment my courage, I might almost say my desire, deserts me.'

Once when Don Víctor repeated this refrain Mesía happened to listen. He heard about cups being dashed from lips, and being deserted by courage – and with supreme resolution, almost with anger, thought:

'Without realizing what he's doing, this idiot is shaming me. He's asking for it, and he's going to get it. Tonight's the night. And if possible, right here.'

A little later, even Don Víctor having tired of his confessions, the two friends returned to the dinner-table, at which reigned the sweet fraternity of the happy digestion of a splendid meal. Anita was not there.

Alvaro left without being seen, or at least without anybody stopping to think whether he had left, and returned to the house. There was still a racket in the kitchen, but elsewhere all was silence. He went back to the salon. No one there. 'Impossible.' He entered the marchioness's boudoir. He could not see any human shape among the shadows in the room. Nothing but chairs. No female form upon any of them. 'Impossible.' With that faith in his hunches which was his only religion he searched further in the darkness and came to the balcony window, which was ajar.

'Ana!'

XXIX

'On Christmas Day you must come to eat the turkey with us. I have been sent one from León, stuffed with walnuts. It will be exquisite. And I have been sent some wine from my homeland, a Valdiñón so full-bodied you can chew it.'

Mesía kept his promise, and on Christmas Day he had luncheon in Ozores Mansion. The dining-room was now lined with blue-and-gold checked wallpaper. The great Churrigueresque chimney-piece had been retained, complete with its plaster mermaids, undulating and full-bosomed. Don Víctor had contented himself with applying paint of, as he called it, a discreet light grey to all those cornices, scrolls, casements, acanthuses and other foliage.

At dessert the master of the house became thoughtful. With furtive glances he followed Petra's comings and goings as she waited at table. After coffee Don Alvaro could see that his friend was impatient. Since the summer, when they had both stayed in the hotel in La Costa, Don Víctor had acquired the habit of having Don Alvaro as his table-companion. He found him more talkative and agreeable at table than anywhere else, and often invited him to luncheon. But on other occasions, after chatting for as long as he felt like chatting, Quintanar would leave the table, walk around the garden, and go to dress, singing all the time – and thus leave Anita and his friend alone together for half an hour or more. And now – no, he wasn't moving. Ana and Alvaro looked at each other, and their looks asked what could be the reason for this novelty.

Ana bent down to retrieve a napkin from the floor, and Don Víctor made Mesía a sign which said: 'She's in the way. If she left, we could talk.'

Mesía shrugged.

Ana raised her head smiling at Don Alvaro and he, without Quintana seeing, indicated the door with one movement of his eyes.

Ana left.

'Thank God!' said her husband, with a deep breath. 'I thought the girl was never going.'

He did not remember that he was always the one who went.

'Now we can talk.'

'I'm listening,' replied Alvaro in a calm voice, puffing on his Havana so as to obscure his face, it being his habit to put up smoke-screens when it suited him.

'What's got into the man now?' he thought, with a vague anxiety which he could not understand.

Don Víctor brought his chair up close, and began to talk in the voice which he used for great revelations.

'At the present time,' he said, 'everything smiles upon me. I am happy in my home and I play no part whatsoever in public life. I no longer fear the absorptive invasion of the Church, whose deleterious influence . . . but it is my belief that this girl Petra is planning some kind of trouble for me.'

Mesía signalled surprise.

'What do you mean? Have you fallen back into your old ways?'

'I have and I have not. I mean to say, there have been approaches – explanations – truces – promises to respect what the great strumpet does not want anyone to respect – in sum, she is piqued because I prefer the tranquillity of my home, the purity of my bed – of my *thorum*, so to speak – to the enjoyment of ephemeral pleasures. Do you understand me? She pretends that her agitation is a defence of her honour – which, in short, nobody in this house dares seriously to threaten – and what in reality vexes her is my coolness.'

'But what's she doing? Out with it!'

'Look, Alvaro, I would not upset my dear Anita for anything in the world. She is a pattern of wifely virtues now. She has always been a good woman – although formerly she did have her little quirks, as you may remember . . .'

'Yes, yes – come to the point.'

'But now the poor dear coincides with me in all my tastes. This way, say I, and this way she goes. She has even recovered from that rather uncivilized exaltation, that excessive love of bucolic delights, that exclusive preoccupation with health in the open air, with exercise – in sum, with hygiene. Every extremity is a fault, and Benítez informed me that Ana's complete recovery would be assured when she was seen to be less concerned with her bodily health – without reverting, needless to say, to the exaggerated, lunatic care of her soul. That was worst of all!'

'But you still haven't told me . . .'

'I am coming to that. Ana is now in a state of equilibrium which is a guarantee of that good health for which we have been sighing for so long. She no longer suffers from her nerves, that is to say she no longer gives us any frights; she never has any whimsical notions about saintliness or fills my house with cassocks. In short, she is a different woman, and I am unwilling – at any price – to forfeit the peace which I now enjoy. But Petra can, and I believe wishes to, jeopardize us.'

'Come now, what's she up to?'

'She is jeopardizing the peace of this house. I fear that she wishes to dominate us by taking advantage of my false position, false beyond words – I confess it. Do you not realize that it would be a terrible blow for Ana if any revelation were made by that hypocritical little whore?'

'But what is happening, sir? Tell me, clearly and quickly!' cried Mesía, beside himself with impatience, and much more interested in the matter than his friend could imagine.

'Hush, Alvaro, hush. What is happening? A great deal. Petra knows that I wish, at all costs, to avoid giving my wife any shocks, because I fear that a nervous attack could ruin everything and make her fall back into her old ways. Disillusionment, the discovery of my minimal infidelity, would most certainly start her brooding and scorning the world again. Then she would seek consolation in religion and the canon theologian would be back in a trice. Anything rather than that! It is necessary at all costs to prevent Ana from discovering that I, in a moment of intellectual and sensual blindness, was capable of soliciting the favours of that *scortum*, as Don Saturnino calls them.'

'But how can Ana discover anything? After all, nothing has happened for her to discover.'

'Yes it has, and what little has happened is sufficient to plunge a dagger into the poor dear's heart. I know her – if Petra reveals what has happened, my wife will imagine all the rest, all that has not happened.'

'But what about Petra? Come on – has she said anything? Has she threatened to tell . . . ?'

'That is the question. Her address is overweening, she is insolent, she will not work, she refuses to be reprimanded, and she aspires to an equal footing which is preposterous . . .'

'Preposterous . . .'

'And towards whom do you think that the infamous creature's behaviour is most haughty, most proud, and most insolent? Towards me? That would appear to be natural. But no, sir – towards Ana . . . ! Towards Ana, astonishing as it might seem!'

Don Alvaro replied from the cloud of smoke in which he was enveloped:

'That's understandable enough – she's trying to blackmail you. Jealousy, perhaps?'

'That is my opinion. "Suffer your wife to be insulted by the woman whom you attempted to make your concubine – or I shall reveal all." This, in a nutshell, is the sly little harlot's behaviour. Well, then, some advice, a solution, what am I to do? Suffer in silence? Preposterous. Besides, Anita's patience might come to an end. She has only tolerated it all for so long thanks to there still remaining a great deal in her from those times when she was almost a saint. But if she takes offence, if she becomes suspicious, if . . . woe is me!'

'Calm down, man, calm down.'

'What shall we do, Alvaro, what shall we do?'

'It's very simple.'

'Simple!'

'Yes – throw Petra out.'

Don Víctor jumped in his chair.

'That would be cutting the Gordian . . .'

'Well there's no other solution. Throw her out.'

Don Víctor expounded the difficulties and the dangers of the remedy, but Don Alvaro promised to smooth them all over for him. He knew how to deal with such people. Luckily it happened that in the hotel where he had been treated like a favourite child for so many years there was a vacancy for a serving-maid. Petra was ideal for the job. The offer would flatter her, he would make it himself, and if she refused it (something he did not anticipate) he would find a way to threaten her into . . .' Don Víctor left everything in the hands of his friend and set off for the Gentlemen's Club, in a somewhat calmer frame of mind.

'So you are staying here to prepare the ground – what?'

'Yes, my dear fellow – to fix everything.'

As soon as Don Víctor had slammed the door at the top of the stairs Ana entered the dining-room, in some alarm. She was about to speak but then Petra came in for the coffee service, and Ana pretended to be reading *El Lábaro*. The maid left and Ana said:

'What is it, Alvaro?'

'Just this, my dear: you have no more excuses for trying to keep me away at night.'

'I don't understand.'

'Petra's leaving: no more spies.'

'Petra? Petra's leaving?'

'Yes, he's given me the job of dismissing her. He says she's insolent and behaves badly to you.'

'My God! Has he noticed . . . ?'

'Yes, but don't be frightened, you silly girl. It won't do any harm – not the way he's taken it.'

Mesía explained himself. In fact he had already told Ana everything, and much more besides. Thanks to Don Alvaro's calumnies, poor Don Víctor's hesitant overtures were, in his wife's eyes, consummated crimes. But Ana did not attribute Petra's insolence to this. She feared that the girl had discovered her affair with Mesía and that her pride and the unwavering defiance in her looks and smiles expressed a threat to reveal the secret to Don Víctor.

'So you see it wasn't what you feared, you little worrier. It's very possible, indeed probable, that the poor girl doesn't suspect anything and that her forwardness is merely a threat to her master.'

Ana coloured. It was all so repugnant. 'The husband to whom she had sacrificed the best years of her life wasn't just an eccentric, a man she considered cold and shallow. He also chased housemaids along passages by night, surprised them in their rooms, looked at their garters! How disgusting! She wasn't jealous, how could she be jealous? She was disgusted, and overcome by a kind of retrospective remorse for having sacrificed her life to such a man. Yes, her life – her youth.

'It had been wrong of Alvaro to show her such wretchedness, to betray Quintanar however unworthy he was, and above all to embarrass her with the old man's ridiculous, repugnant adventures.' But since she was determined to remove all blame from her Mesía, from her lord and master, from the man to whom she had given her body and her soul for the rest of her life, she hastened to forgive him, considering that he had done it out of love, to free his Ana's mind from all the scruples and respect which might tie her to the old man who had turned the best years of her life into a desert of sorrow.

'Nor was she pleased to see Alvaro involved in domestic concerns such as the dismissal of housemaids – still less to find that he was such an expert at them. It was all so base and prosaic as to be repugnant, but how could it be helped? Alvaro was doing it for her sake, to enjoy in tranquillity the happiness which had cost him so many years of martyrdom.'

Ana tried to convert into shining stars of pure beauty these and all the other blemishes which her hateful spirit of analysis – the path to madness in her opinion – had made her recently discover in Mesía. Whenever the idea of losing Don Alvaro seized her she shuddered in horror, as she had shuddered in former times whenever she had been afraid of losing Jesus.

The first words of love which the defeated Ana dared murmur, in a tender, passionate voice, into her conqueror's ear, not on the day of her surrender but much later, were a plea for an oath of constancy:

'For ever, Alvaro, for ever, swear it. If it isn't for ever this is a disgrace – a wicked, villainous crime.'

Mesía swore, and went on swearing day after day, an eternity of love.

The idea of being alone *after it all* seemed more horrific to the judge's wife than the idea of hell had once seemed to her.

With love one could live anywhere, anyhow, thinking of nothing save love itself. Without love – back would come those black ghosts which she sometimes felt stirring deep inside her head as if they were appearing on a distant horizon like the first shadows of an eternal empty night of terror. Ana sensed that the end of love – this powerful, this overwhelming passion which she was enjoying for the first time in her life – would be the beginning of madness.

'Yes, Alvaro, if you left me I would certainly go mad. I'm afraid of my own brain when I'm not with you, when I'm not thinking about you. When I'm with you I only think about loving you.'

She said all these things in her lover's arms as she enjoyed his love, free now from the shyness which had been a considerable vexation for Mesía, but which had disappeared and had not left any pretence in its place. Ana gave herself to love and enjoyed it with all the vehemence of her temperament – with a kind of furore which Mesía privately and coarsely called 'stored-up hunger'.

During the first month she astounded him. At the beginning he cursed her fear, her ignorance and her scruples (absurd in a married woman of thirty according to the philosophy of the president of the Gentlemen's Club) but he soon found the cup of his desires running over to such an extent that 'another aspect' of this affair began to worry him. He had never been happier. He wanted to satisfy his self-esteem, which had been dealt a few blows as he grew older? Well Ana, the most beautiful woman in Vetusta, adored him; she adored him for his own qualities, for his person, for his body, for his physical attraction. Often when he was in a talkative mood she would cover his mouth with her hand and say in ecstasies of love, 'Don't speak.' Mesía did not take it amiss; he, too, recognized that it was better to keep quiet, to receive Ana's adoration of his manly beauty in silence. He wanted to satisfy caprices of his sated flesh, to enjoy delicate delights of the senses? Well, Ana's very ignorance and the strength of her passion and the circumstances of her former life and the conditions of her temperament and of her beauty provided him with all these subtle joys. He was jaded and weary, but he was still a good fighting cock, capable of fearlessly dying of pleasure. Yet although Mesía was so happy, he was uneasy too.

'You are looking unwell,' said Somoza.

'Be careful, now,' repeated Visitación.

He himself noticed that his face was losing the youthful look which it had recovered during those months of healthy living, exercise and abstinence – his prudent preparation for the decisive attack on the fortress of Ana's honour.

Yes, he could feel a creaking inside his body from time to time. There was something eating away at him in there. What he feared was not illness and old age themselves, no; he was a good soldier of love, a hero of pleasure, he would know how to die on the battlefield. He was uneasy for a different reason. Dying was one thing; but inexorably declining in front of Ana was quite another. It would be horrible: ridiculous and infamous. Yes, he would be breaking his oath if he grew old and weak. He shuddered as he remembered past periods of his life when temporary shortcomings, produced by excesses of pleasure, had made him resort to embarrassing stratagems which it was fun to describe amid guffaws of laughter late at night in the Gentlemen's Club to Paco, Joaquín and other night-birds – fun to describe once the whole thing was over and done with, and one's vigour had returned, and comic tricks were no longer needed. But such stratagems were, in reality, just as despicable as the devices used by proud poor people to hide their poverty. This shamming of youth, virility and constancy in physical love reminded Don Alvaro of the resources of ostentatious beggary described by Quevedo in *The Great Skinflint*.[1] He himself had been a Great Skinflint of love more than once, after periods as a spendthrift, but he couldn't play the old tricks now. 'No, he would rather run away, or shoot himself. Ana, poor Ana, had a right to eternal, inexhaustible youth.' But these gloomy thoughts, these fears of encroaching age, seldom assailed him; usually he was left free to enjoy undismayed this love affair which he regarded as the greatest glory of his life. He thought that there could be no one on the face of the earth (apart from the president of the Gentlemen's Club of Vetusta) more worthy of adoration than his Ana – docile now, and frantic with love, just as he had expected even in the days when the distance between them had been greatest. Don Alvaro did not own that there had been a time when he had abandoned all hope of conquering the judge's wife. His conquest was so complete now!

This was never more evident than when he had to wage the great battle to shift the scene of their adulterous love to Ozores Mansion. Ana refused, wept, implored, 'No, no, not that, Alvaro, for God's sake no, never.' For many days she resisted her lover's appeals and complaints that his enjoyment of their love was so infrequent, fleeting and uncomfortable. Usually they met in Vegallana's house; their caresses were furtive and hurried; the relaxed enjoyment of hours and hours of voluptuous intimacy could only be achieved by seeking a rendezvous less subject to alarms, interruptions and the need to dissemble. Alvaro promised to look for a love-nest, but Ana said that she would not go there, and he himself had to confess that it would be difficult to find a safe love-nest anywhere in a backward town like Vetusta. Besides, any place which he could find was bound to become repugnant to her in the end, and since her imagination was so strong, her repugnance for the place might lead to repugnance for adultery itself. There was no alternative but to take refuge in Ozores Mansion. There they would be safer, more tranquil, and more comfortable than anywhere else. Although Alvaro could understand Ana's scruples, he resolved to overcome them – and he was successful. The obstacles of a purely moral order, her mystical scruples, as Alvaro privately called them in an expression which was as inapposite as it was obscene, were overcome with the aid of passion; but the physical inconveniences, the precautions recommended by fear, presented weightier difficulties. It occurred to Don Alvaro that, unless he had one of the servants – preferably the housemaid – on his side, everything would be very difficult, if not impossible. He did not dare mention his idea to Anita, however, because she was always so chary of Petra, so full of ill-concealed dislike for her and, apart from that, he realized that she was too new to this kind of adventure to be cynical enough to seek the support of domestics – particularly when she knew that her husband was pursuing them.

Another solution would be to conquer the servant girl without letting her mistress know. Didn't Petra look like a frolicsome sort of wench? Didn't the incident of the garter, and other incidents of which he had heard, prove that it would be a simple matter to enlist her support? Yes. And no sooner said than done. In the absence of Ana and Don Víctor, behind doors, in passages, wherever he could, Don Alvaro began the attack on Petra, who surrendered much sooner than he had expected. But there was one grave inconvenience. The girl took it into her head to be, or pretend to be, disinterested – to prefer wild games of love to money, and to offer her services (with the most discreet half-words and good works) in exchange for an affection which Mesía was in no position to squander. 'Poor Ana, ignorant of all these complications!' But Don Alvaro did not know as much as he thought he knew. He did not know, for example, why Petra could allow herself the luxury of giving him good service without a thought for self-interest, with no other payment than the love which he could no longer waste. Petra was no enemy of filthy lucre, nor was the ambition to improve her lot and even her sphere (as she had learned to say) a feeble passion in her soul, which was greedy through and through. But this was not what she wanted from Mesía. She wanted him because he was a strong, handsome man; she wanted him because he gave her the opportunity to mock her mistress, whom she hated 'for being hypocritical, for being pretty, and for being proud'; she wanted him because of her vanity. As for giving him her services, this too suited her purposes, because it satisfied what was perhaps her favourite passion apart from lust – vindictiveness. By protecting the love affair of Mesía and Ana she was avenging herself upon 'that idiot Don Víctor' who went in for putting girls into compromising situations yet knew no more about it all than the Pope in Rome himself. She was also avenging herself upon the judge's wife who, thanks to her, was falling, falling into a bottomless pit and was – although the great hypocrite did not know it – in the power of her servant girl, who could, whenever it suited her, reveal everything. She had her mistress in her claws, what more could she want? For a few hours every night the honour and perhaps the life of her master hung from a thread which she held; if she wanted, if she felt like it, crash! everything smashed to pulp – the whole world ablaze. And as if this were not a pleasure, indeed a glorious delight, but a burden of hard work, the handsomest man in Vetusta was paying for her services with the love of a gentleman – the sort of love which she had always relished most, because of her powerful instinct of snobbery. On top of all this the perverse girl was savouring another revenge still more succulent than the others. What about the canon theologian, then? The canon theologian had tried to take her in, he had made love to her; she had surrendered in the belief that she was going straight into the position which she most envied in all Vetusta – Teresina's position. Petra knew how well Doña Paula married all her housemaids. Teresina was soon to become a fine lady by marrying a good-looking man who was one of her master's land-agents, and she had told Petra of things which she had not been able to observe or even guess – she had opened her eyes and made her mouth water. Petra realized that the canon theologian's house was the surest path to marriage and to becoming a lady, or, at least, very nearly one. The time had come. After the fiesta on St Peter's Day she believed that it was now a question of weeks, of biding her time just a little more; Teresina would soon leave for a good marriage and she would take Teresina's place. But this did not happen. The canon theologian did not make any more passes at Petra and when he spoke to her it was not about matters of interest to her but – the shame of it! – to buy her services as a spy. True, he did promise that in the near future she would take Teresina's place, with all the advantages that Teresina was enjoying and was going to enjoy, but still, she had been deceived – or had deceived herself, but the proud blonde was not willing to acknowledge this truth. She had believed that the canon had been Doña Ana's lover for a long time, and in her vanity had interpreted the scene in the wood at El Vivero as a victory for her own beauty, which, she thought, had made him fall into the sin of inconstancy. Petra had believed that Don Fermín had turned from loving her mistress to loving her. She had seen plenty of caprices of that sort. When Petra became convinced that, in spite of all his pretence, he was madly in love with the judge's wife, and furiously jealous, and that he had never been her lover or anything like it – and also that he had only wanted Petra herself as a tool – anger, envy, pride and lust all reared up like rattlesnakes inside her. For the time being she quietened them, hid her feelings and contented herself with the satisfaction of her avarice alone. She accepted the canon's proposals. She would start work in Don Fermín's house on the day when it became necessary for her to leave Ozores Mansion, but meanwhile she would render him her services and be well paid for them, better paid than she could have imagined. The canon would be informed of everything that happened: whether Doña Ana received any visitors, who entered the house when Don Víctor was not there, or stayed after he had left . . .

Petra promised to tell him everything. She pretended not to remember certain promises of another kind which Don Fermín had let slip as he improvised in the heat of the moment on that blessed morning at El Vivero, so shameful to him now. When he found Petra so ready to serve him for money he was even sorrier that he had approached her by the contemptible, absurd, ridiculous path of seduction. That adventure, which made him think of the adventures of former times, embarrassed him because it undermined the framework of sophisms with which he justified his passion for the judge's wife. 'My love, pure beyond measure, excuses everything.' 'But can such a love be reconciled with adventures like the one in the wood? Of course not,' said his conscience. Petra disgusted him now. But he had no alternative but to make use of her.

Petra was happy in this life of complicated intrigues which she alone could unravel. For the time being Mesía was the man whom she served loyally. He paid her with love, although he was rather remiss with his payments, and she helped him as much as she could, because by helping him she was also satisfying her own desires: ruining the mistress, getting her under her thumb, and making bloody mockery of that idiot the master and of the damned canon. The astute girl reserved the right to sell Don Alvaro later and help her master,[2] the man who paid money, the man who was going to make her into a fine lady – Don Fermín. When would this be? Time would tell. If Don Alvaro didn't behave himself the moment might come, the opportunity arise; if she grew tired or if Teresina left and it became advisable to hurry to take her place for fear that another girl might get there first – in that case, too, it might be a good idea to light the fuse. Meanwhile, Petra only gave Don Fermín vague information, enough to keep him on tenterhooks and make his life into that of a furious madman who also has to suffer the torture of hiding his fury from the world in general and from his mother in particular.

So while Don Alvaro might well say, 'Poor Ana, she knows nothing about all this!' Petra could exclaim, 'Poor Don Alvaro, he doesn't know the first thing about what matters so much to him!'

The president of the Gentlemen's Club of Vetusta had no objection to deceiving the judge's wife. It was, he believed, only right to respect the scruples of this novice adulteress who could not bring herself to take Petra as an accomplice. But it was also quite fair for him, without telling Ana – indeed, pretending to distrust her housemaid, too – to make use of her services, which were invaluable in the circumstances. The problem was – how to enter Ana's bedroom by her balcony every night? This was easily said, but doing it presented serious difficulties. Where was her boudoir balcony? Over the park. Which was the way into the park? Through the gate. But who had the keys to the gate? Frillity had one of them; Alvaro could forget about that one. And the other key? Don Víctor's. It could be taken from him, but Petra said that she would not go that far – getting keys mixed up in the affair would make it all too risky and might compromise her. The best idea would be for Don Alvaro to climb the wall – he had good long legs. In this way the show would be more convincing; if Doña Ana was certain that Don Alvaro climbed the wall she was less likely to suspect that he had an accomplice inside the house. Crossing the garden, and climbing the grille on the ground-floor window and the iron railing of the balcony itself would be easy work for such a well-built fellow.

Don Alvaro could do all this without any direct, immediate help from Petra; so it was not difficult for Doña Ana to believe everything her lover told her about his labours to reach her room. It was Petra's job to keep watch, to prevent Don Alvaro's being caught on his way in or out, and to contrive to make Doña Ana think that she herself had been in no position at any time to notice the presence of a lover. The housemaid also had to give the cry of alarm if necessary, and to be a timekeeper. Petra's service involved many of the responsibilities of a station-master. Don Alvaro knew (because Don Víctor had confessed it to him) that as soon as the season started he and Frillity went hunting much earlier than Ana thought. It had once been Petra's task to awaken the master (because Anselmo, a heavy sleeper, had so often failed in his duty). Frillity would come to the garden at the agreed time, bark – and Don Víctor would soon appear. But Frillity had begun to complain that sometimes his barks awakened neither the master nor the housemaid and that he was often made to wait for a long time. To avoid quarrels and delays it had been settled that Frillity and Don Víctor should meet at an agreed time without any barking. For safety's sake Don Víctor had bought an alarm clock which made a noise like an earthquake, and with the aid of this automatic warning-device, as he called it, he was able to present himself at the appointed hour. Almost every morning Quintanar and Crespo appeared in the park at the same time. The train which bore them to the marshes and woods of Palomares left Vetusta a little later this year and they did not need to rise before daybreak.

Don Alvaro had to know all this so as not to run the risk of meeting Frillity or Don Víctor himself on the way out. The latter, not knowing what he was doing, told Alvaro about his times of departure, and Petra told him all the other details. So he had nothing to fear. Climbing the wall presented some difficulties, but one night he set to work on its outside in the deserted Calle de Traslacerca, and by moving stones and scraping away mortar he constructed two or three well-concealed steps near the corner. He also made some openings in the wall, disguised as cracks and chinks, to grip as he climbed it. So the principal obstacle was overcome. On the inside it was child's play. An old barrel, placed against the wall as if someone happened to have left it there, and the remains of an espalier were enough to make a ladder, which nobody could notice, to enable Don Alvaro to climb up or down the wall on the park side with all the speed which circumstances might dictate. Don Alvaro compared his disguised ladder to the pictures on matchboxes bearing the well-known legend, 'Where is the shepherdess?' Where was the ladder? Once you had seen it you could see nothing else, but until it was pointed out it was invisible.

Only the hardest part remained now: persuading the judge's wife to open her window to him. Since she could not be told of his guarantees of security inside the house, he had little or nothing with which to counter her arguments about the probable suspicions of the disagreeable Petra. But in the end, having won the major battle, he won the lesser one as well: he made Ana realize that it was impossible, and even perhaps ridiculous, to refuse to allow into her bedroom a man to whom she had given herself. The purity of the marriage-bed – or rather the ex-marriage-bed – was important, of course, but wasn't the purity of the wife more important still? These sophisms, and passion, and Mesía's perseverance gave him his victory, and although he could not calm Ana's trepidation – every sound caused her to think that Petra was spying on them – he did often make her forget everything and enjoy the delirium of love in which he knew how to plunge her, as if he were enveloping her in a cloud of opium-smoke.

And so the days passed by. Ana was astonished that she was capable, so soon after her fall, of receiving a man in her own bedroom – she who had struggled for so many years before she did fall.

On Christmas afternoon, after clearing away the coffee service, Petra left Ozores Mansion and went to the canon theologian's house.

Doña Paula received her. They were good friends now. The canon's mother knew how close Teresina and Petra were, and Teresina had told her that Fermín wanted Petra as a replacement on that day in the near future when she was to leave with her prize of a marriage and a position as a land-agent for the *vicars-general*. Doña Paula, who only needed half-words – and often not even these – to understand what was happening, wanted (following her usual policy) to satisfy her son's desires in a seemly, decorous way, by anticipating them. She had decided to take the initiative and herself offer Petra the post which she so coveted. The proposal was made that afternoon. Teresina would be leaving any day now. Petra accepted without hesitation, trembling with delight. Until she was back in Ozores Mansion it did not occur to her to think that this happy event brought with it disaster for many others, and up to a point harm even to herself. No more love with Don Alvaro, love which was becoming scarcer and scarcer, more and more meanly rationed by the charming libertine, whose tips waxed as his caresses waned – but the love of a gentleman all the same, love which filled her with pride. What should she do? There could be no doubt about it – be prudent, snap up the coveted fruit, hurry to comforts of the canon theologian's house. Doing this meant lighting the fuse; it meant snapping the thread which she held in her hand and from which hung the honour, the tranquillity, maybe the lives of various people. As Petra thought about this she shrugged her shoulders. She imagined that she could see the judge's wife falling and being smashed to pulp, the canon theologian falling and being smashed to pulp, Don Víctor falling and ending up as mincemeat, and even Don Alvaro rolling over the ground split into smithereens. It didn't matter. The time had come. If she missed her chance of getting Teresina's job, another girl might take it and that would be the end of her hopes of being a lady. There was nothing for it but to move into the post straight away. But in that case she'd have to tell the canon everything. Once she'd left the house she couldn't be a spy any longer, or help her paymaster to open the eyes of that fool Don Víctor – who, naturally, would want to avenge himself and punish the guilty (which must be what the canon wanted to happen, since he couldn't go and challenge Don Alvaro himself, in his clerical cloak and all). Petra knew about such matters because she read *feuilletons* (the collections in *Las Novedades*,[3] which Doña Anuncia had left in the attic); she knew very well who challenged whom if the love affair of a married lady was discovered. The challenger is the husband, not a spurned would-be lover, especially if he's a priest. There was no doubt about it, the canon theologian needed her to be in Ozores Mansion at the critical moment. If she left earlier and couldn't be of any use to him he might throw her out of his house for it. She must act fast. *What* was she going to do? Something treacherous, of course, but exactly what . . . ?

These were Petra's thoughts as she went into the dining-room at nightfall to make the lamp ready. Someone grasped her around the waist and kissed the back of her neck.

'It was the other man. Poor thing, little did he know what was in store for him!'

After Don Alvaro's conversation with Ana he had told her to go away and had remained in the dining-room to 'make an attack' on Petra and propose between caresses – the caresses which he regarded with growing regret – that she change masters. It was not true that there was a vacancy in the hotel, but he was in charge there and a vacancy would be created. With all the diplomacy available to a man who believed himself to be above all a politician – but who was in reality a professional seducer – he offered the maid the new position, 'which would be great fun and highly lucrative'. Don Víctor was afraid of her, so was Doña Ana, and Don Alvaro would be better served if she agreed to leave the house.

'You see, dear girl, you've been behaving badly, treating your mistress with pride and insolence. This, which is unpleasant enough in itself, has alarmed her by making her think that you know something and are taking advantage of your secret; it has also alarmed him, and now he's afraid that you're going to let the cat out of the bag. Moreover, it's damaging to me, as you can understand, because, you see, if she's frightened, distrustful – I'm the one who pays. I don't need you in this house any more, because now I can come and go without a guide – and in my home, in the hotel you can be of use to us. Besides . . .'

Besides, Don Alvaro knew that he could no longer pay Petra for her services with love, because it was becoming more and more vital to economize; but if the girl were taken to the hotel, other guests who were hungry for this kind of morsel would keep her happy, and only money would be required from him. Petra was by now a nuisance in Ozores Mansion, for many reasons which he could not explain to her.

'Sir,' said Petra, who in spite of her recent decision felt her pride cut to the quick, 'you needn't go to such lengths to persuade me that I'd better get out of this house.'

'No, dear girl, of course, if you take it amiss I shan't insist.'

'But sir, you haven't given me time to explain. I want to go away, that's just it – but as for going to the hotel, no sir. It's one thing for a girl to have her whims and be good-natured, do you see what I mean? and it's quite another thing to be handed over to a fellow's friends, and shuttled to and fro, and . . .'

'But Petrica, it isn't that at all, it's all for your own good.'

Don Alvaro was lowering his voice and Petra was raising hers.

But the astute girl, who was well able to control herself if it was for her own good, did so and, changing her tone and manner, asked to be forgiven, hid her anger and said that everything was fine, that she herself was going to ask to be paid off, and that she would go away quite happily, not to the hotel but to another house: a chance which had come her way but which she couldn't say any more about at the moment. Apart from all that, no hard feelings, and if Don Alvaro ever needed her he just had to say the word, because she'd got a soft spot for him, she couldn't deny that; as for holding her tongue, she'd keep as quiet as a mouse. She'd done what she'd done out of fondness for one party, she'd got no cause to hide it, and out of pity for another, married to an old doter, so feeble and barmy you just had to feel sorry for him.

So Petra deceived Mesía once again. She even allowed some fresh caresses of gratitude which he swore to himself would be the last ones, for reasons of economy – about which he was by now obsessed.

That night in the Gentlemen's Club Don Víctor learned that on the following day Petra was going to ask to be paid off – she was going to leave. How marvellous! Quintanar blew like a bellows and hugged his friend. 'He owed him something more important than life itself: the tranquillity of his hearth and home.'

Don Fermín was working in his study, writing by the monotonous white light of the cloudy morning, his feet wrapped in his mother's old shawl. He heard a sound, looked up and saw Doña Paula in the doorway, looking pale – even paler than usual.

'What is it, Mother?'

'That Petra girl is here – Quintanar's maid. She wants to talk to you.'

'Talk to me! So early? What is the time?'

'Nine o'clock. She says it's urgent. She seems alarmed – her voice is shaky.'

The canon theologian turned the same colour as his mother and, mechanically standing up, said:

'Send her in, send her in.'

Doña Paula turned and walked into the passage. But first she caressed her son with a look of motherly pity.

'Go in,' she said to Petra who, dressed in black, stood waiting with her head bowed upon her breast.

Doña Paula's eyes were trying to ferret out the servant girl's secret. What could it be? She hesitated for a moment, almost making up her mind to ask – but restrained herself and again said:

'Go on, my child – in you go.'

' "My child",' thought Petra, 'she wants me here. I'm set up for life.'

'What is it?' cried the canon, hurrying to the servant girl, as if in an attempt to waylay her news.

Petra saw that they were alone, and burst into tears.

Don Fermín made a grimace of impatience which Petra did not see, because her eyes were lowered. The canon tried to speak but he could not; he felt the grip of iron hands on his throat, and in his spine and legs violent shudders and a cold, continuous quivering.

'Quick! What's up?' he was finally able to ask.

With much moaning, Petra said that she needed him to hear her confession, that she didn't know whether what she was about to do was a good work or a sin, that she wanted to serve him, serve her master, serve God, because after all religion meant looking after your neighbour's interests as well, but – she was afraid, she didn't know whether she should . . .

'Speak up! Speak up! Speak up I say, now. What is it, Petra? What is it?' Don Fermín placed a hand on the desk behind him for support, taking care not to be seen. There was a pause. 'Speak up, for God's sake!'

'In confession?'

'Petra, speak up, now!'

'Sir, I have promised to tell you . . . everything . . .'

'Yes, everything, speak up.'

'But now I don't know . . . I don't know whether I should . . .'

Don Fermín ran to the door, locked it and, hurrying back, his face contorted, gripped the servant girl's arm and screamed:

'Stop shamming, speak up or I'll tear the words out of your throat!'

Petra gazed up at him, feigning humility and fear. 'She wanted to see the look on the canon's face when he heard that his fine lady-friend was doing the dirty on him.'

'Without beating about the bush, Petra said that she had seen, with her own eyes, what she never would have credited. Her master's best friend, that man Don Alvaro, who never left Don Víctor's side by day, climbed the balcony into her mistress's room by night and didn't leave until daybreak. She had seen him one night, thinking she must be dreaming – she had started keeping a look-out, hoping to dispel certain suspicions – but oh! it was true, it was true. That wicked man had perverted her mistress, a saint – Don Fermín had been right to feel afraid!'

Petra continued talking, but he had not been hearing her for some time.

As soon as Don Fermín realized what the sensual blonde had come to tell him, before he heard the crude phrases with which she described the Vetustan Don Juan's assault on Ozores Mansion, he turned on his heel as if about to collapse, took two wavering steps towards the balcony, and leaned his forehead against the window. He seemed to be looking out, but his eyes were closed.

He heard Petra talking without following the sense of her chatter. He was annoyed by the sound of her shrill, whimpering voice, not the words she was speaking; he wanted to tell her to keep quiet, but he could not: he could not talk, he could not move.

Petra talked for as long as she liked. When she fell silent, all that could be heard were muffled sounds from outside: the wheels of a carriage in the distance, the cries of a pedlar proclaiming his wares: pocket-handkerchiefs and fine lace.

The canon theologian was thinking that the ice-cold glass pressing against his forehead felt like a knife gouging out his brains, and he was thinking, too, that his mother, by sticking his head into a cassock, had made him so unhappy, so wretched, that he was the only person in the world deserving of pity. The commonplace, false, obscene idea of comparing the clergyman to the eunuch was also infiltrating his brain with the damp of the icy window. 'Yes, he was like a eunuch in love, something to be laughed at, so ridiculous as to be repugnant. His wife, Ana – for she was his wife, his real wife, not before God, not before men, but before the two of them, before him especially, before his love, before his iron will, before all the tenderness of his soul – Ana, his soul sister, his woman, his wife, his humble wife, had deceived him, dishonoured him, just like any other woman. Thirsty for blood, he longed to throttle that blackguard, to squeeze all the breath out of him – certain of being able to do so, certain of vanquishing him, trampling and grinding him under foot, breaking him into little pieces, into dust, into wind. But his feet were bound with an ignominious length of rag, he was like a convict, like a goat, like a nag in a field; he, a wretched priest, a mockery of a man disguised as a sexless being, had to keep silence, bite his lip, his hands, his soul, all of himself, and not even touch that other man, that blackguard, that coward who was spitting in his face because his hands were tied. What was holding him back? The whole world. Twenty centuries of religion, millions of blind, indolent spirits who, since it did not affect them, could not see the absurdity of it all – calling it grandeur, abnegation, virtue when it was torture, unjust, barbarous, foolish, and above all cruel, cruel. Hundreds of popes, dozens of councils, thousands of towns, millions of stones in cathedrals and crosses and convents – all history, all civilization, a world of lead, were pressing down on him, on his arms, on his legs, they were his shackles. Ana had devoted her soul to him, and she had devoted the fidelity of a superhuman love to him, and now she was deceiving him as if he were a mere coarse, carnal, idiotic husband. She was leaving him and throwing herself into the arms of a wretched fop, a fool, a pinchbeck dandy, a man of plaster – a hollow statue! And the world could not even feel sorry for him; his mother, who thought she adored him, could not give him any consolation either, the consolation of her arms and her tears. If he were dying his mother would be at his feet tearing her hair and weeping in despair, but this, which was much worse than dying, much worse than being damned to hell, did not prompt his mother to a tear or an embrace or despair or even a look. He could not say anything, she could not guess, she must not guess. There was only one supreme duty, pretence – silence, not a single complaint, not a single move! He wanted to run out in search of the traitors and kill them, did he? Well, silence – he must not move a finger, must not set foot in the street. Soon he would – to prayers, to prayers! Maybe to say mass, to receive God!' The canon heard demoniacal laughter inside his body; yes, the devil had laughed at him, in his own bowels – and that deep guffaw, with roots in his belly and his chest, was choking him, suffocating him!

He punched the balcony window open and the cold damp air brought distant reality back to him. He heard the discreet cough of Petra, waiting behind him with her eyes riveted on his neck.

He shut the window and turned and looked with the eyes of an idiot at the blonde, who was wiping abject tears away. 'Didn't he need a tool to fight with, to do harm with? This was the only tool he had.'

Petra stood there silent and motionless, waiting to serve her master.

Watching the canon suffer was a source of intense delight, but she wanted more, she wanted to continue her work – to be ordered to pierce that proud fine lady her mistress's soul with all the needles which she had just buried in the flesh of the mad priest.

A slow, dull, hoarse voice, which did not seem to be in the study – the voice of a ventriloquist – asked:

'What about you, what do you intend to do, now?'

'Me? Leave that house, sir.' 'He won't be frank?' thought Petra, 'well then let him suffer, he'll come looking for me wherever I want him to.' 'Leave that house, sir,' she repeated. 'What else can I do? I don't want to further my master's shame by keeping quiet, there's nothing I can do about it, but I can go away from that house.'

'And you – you aren't concerned about Don Víctor's honour? Is this the way you repay the man whose bread you have eaten for so many years?'

'But sir, what can I do for him?'

'If you leave, nothing.'

'Well, they're throwing me out.'

'They?'

'Yes, they. Yesterday Don Alvaro, who's the one in charge there – because the master's blind, he sees everything through Don Alvaro's eyes – Don Alvaro kicked me out of the house. I've got to go today. He offered me a job in his hotel, but I'd rather be left in the street.'

'You shall come to this house, Petra,' said the cavernous voice, making vain efforts to sound kind.

Petra wept again. 'How could she ever repay such charity . . . ?'

This tender scene facilitated the treaty. Each relented a little, and by degrees they entered into an infamous pact, a vile and repugnant intrigue. At the beginning they feigned propriety and foisted sacred concerns into the affair, but later they forgot such formulae: in the end the canon theologian undertook to set the girl up for life and fulfil her ambitions; she undertook to place Quintanar's shame before his eyes, making it so plain and palpable to him that if there was any manly blood in his veins he would have to punish the traitors, as they deserved.

When their conversation drew to its close they were talking like two accomplices in a difficult crime. The canon spoke few words – except when it was a question of elucidating their plot. 'How was Petra going to make that fool Quintanar see his own shame? Simply tell him? She couldn't do that. Anonymous letters? They were risky.' 'What! No sir, nothing like that, he will see it for himself,' repeated Petra, all her pretence forgotten, with the quiet pleasure of an artist.

Here were two passionate criminals, with no witnesses of their ignominy; each could only see his own vengeance, and was blind to the other's crime and the shamefulness of their pact.

When Petra left the canon theologian's house he sensed a new man[4] inside himself: the man who kills for vengeance, the criminal, the man blinded by passion, 'the murderer, yes, the murderer; the girl was his weapon, he was the murderer. And he was not repentant, no. The wretches must die, die a hundred times over.' 'What would Don Víctor do? Which of his old plays would he remember, to take consummate revenge for the outrage? Would he start by killing her? Or would he go for him first?'

On the following day, 27 December, Don Víctor and Frillity were to take the train to Roca Tajada at eight fifty so as to reach the Palomares marshes by about half past nine. This was rather late in the day to commence the persecution of ducks and stone-curlews, but the railway company could not be expected to run a special train for huntsmen. This season, then, they rose less early than usual. Every hunting-day Quintanar set his alarm clock to wake him with its terrifying racket at eight o'clock sharp. In the twinkling of an eye he dressed, washed and went out into the garden, where he might have to wait two or three minutes for Frillity, if he was not there already. The time occupied by these activities and the walk to the station was just enough to enable them to arrive a few minutes before the departure of the mixed train.

From a deep, sweet sleep, of the kind which he did not often enjoy, Quintanar awoke that morning with a more violent start than usual, dazed by the shrill clangour of his alarm, a rapid, ear-rending, metallic death-rattle. With a great effort he overcame his lethargy, yawned several times, and decided to rise from his bed, not without a protest from his curled-up body at being made to stir so early in the morning. His lethargy and sleepiness told him that it must be earlier than on other days, that the alarm clock was a shameless liar, and that the real time could not be the one which it indicated or anything like it. The huntsman took no notice of this sophistry and, with much yawning and stretching of arms, directed his steps to the wash-basin and plunged his head into cold water. This was Don Víctor's reply to the suggestions of the wretched flesh, which wanted to return to the idleness of the sheets.

Once his ideas were clearer he was able impartially to recognize that his lethargy had not complained without good reason. 'It must indeed be considerably earlier than the clock indicated. Nevertheless he was certain that it did not gain, and that he had wound it up and set it with his own hand the previous morning. And yet it must be earlier than that. It could not be eight o'clock yet, or even seven, his sleepiness told him so as it returned in spite of his ablutions; the faint daylight told him so, too, with greater authority.' 'Sunrise today must be at seven-thirty, give or take a minute. Well, the sun has not risen yet, that is beyond doubt. True, the thick fog and the heavy ash-grey clouds covering the sky make the morning a dark one, but it matters not, the sun has not risen yet, everything is too dark, it cannot even be seven o'clock yet.' He could not consult his pocket watch because on the previous day when he had tried to wind it up he had found the mainspring broken.

'It will be best to call.'

He stole out into the passage in his slippers.

'Petra! Petra!' he said, trying to shout without making any noise.

'Petra, Petra! The devil! How can she answer when she no longer lives here? Habit, blessed habit – man is a creature of habit.'

Don Víctor sighed. He was overjoyed to find himself free of that witness and semi-victim of his weakness, and yet now he remembered that it was in vain for him to call 'Petra!' he felt a peculiar poetic melancholy. 'Strange are the workings of the human heart!'

'Servanda! Servanda! Anselmo! Anselmo!'

There was no reply.

'It is very early, without any doubt. It is not even time for the servants to get up. But in that case . . . who has put my clock forward? Two timepieces spoilt in two days! Misfortunes never come singly.'

Don Víctor started doubting again. Might not the servants have failed to awaken? Might not the dimness of the light be caused by the density of the clouds? Why distrust the clock when nobody could have tampered with it? And who could have any interest in putting it forward? Who would dare play such a joke on him? Quintanar changed his mind, and thinking that it might well be eight o'clock, he dressed quickly, picked up his flask of anisette and swallowed a draught, as was his custom whenever he was going hunting (for he was a mortal enemy of hot chocolate) and, throwing his knapsack, full of choice cold meats, on his back, descended to the garden by the stairs leading from the passage, on tiptoe as always, so as not to disturb the silence of the house. 'He would see to the servants when he returned. The sluggards! Now there was no time to be lost. Frillity must already be in the park waiting impatiently.'

'Well now, if indeed it is eight o'clock I have never seen a darker day in my life. And yet the fog is not very dense – no – nor is the sky very thick with cloud. I do not understand it.'

Quintanar reached the arbour, the meeting-place. Another strange thing! Frillity was not there. Might he be strolling around the park? Don Víctor slung his shotgun over his back and walked out of the arbour.

The cathedral clock struck three strokes like three yawns.

Don Víctor stopped to think, rested the butt of his shotgun on the damp sand of the path, and exclaimed:

'Someone did put it forward! But who? Is it a quarter to eight or a quarter to seven? This darkness!'

He felt a strange anguish, not knowing why; 'he too suffered from nerves, apparently.' For reasons which he could not fathom, he was worried and vexed by his uncertainty. 'What uncertainty? He had been muddled earlier, such light was impossible at eight o'clock, it was a quarter to seven, this was the morning twilight, now he was certain of it. But in that case who had put his clock forward by more than a hour? Who – and why? And above all why was this trivial incident affecting him so? What was this foreboding? Why was he thinking that he was about to fall ill?'

He had started walking again, towards the house, which he could glimpse between the leafless branches of the trees, packed close together in this part of the garden. He heard a sound like that of a window being eased open, took two steps forward between the tree-trunks which impeded his view and saw that one of the balcony windows in his house was being closed and that a man who seemed to be very tall was letting himself down, holding on to the railings, feeling with his feet for the grille over the ground-floor window and then jumping from it to a pile of earth.

'It was Anita's balcony.'

The man turned up the lapels of a scarlet cloak and, avoiding the sandy paths by leaping from one flower-bed to another and then running in great strides over the grass, reached the corner of the wall by the Calle de Traslacerca. There he jumped on to a half-rotten barrel leaning against the wall and, using some pieces of wood nailed there – the remains of an old espalier – as a ladder, was able, thanks to a very long pair of legs, to reach the top of the wall, on which he sat astride.

Don Víctor had followed the man's movements from a distance, standing among the trees, and he had slipped the safety catch of his shotgun without thinking, by instinct, as if he were hunting; but he had not taken aim. 'First he wanted to know who he was.' He was not content to guess.

In spite of the dim dawn light the owner of the park could no longer entertain any doubts about the man's identity once he was sitting astride the wall.

'It's Alvaro!' thought Don Víctor, lifting his gun to his face.

Mesía was sitting still, looking into the lane, with his head on one side, concerned only to find the stones and cracks which he used as steps in his descent.

'It's Alvaro!' thought Don Víctor again, with his friend's head at the end of the barrel of his shotgun.

'He himself was standing among trees. Even if the man on the wall looked towards the park he would not see him. He could wait, he could reflect, there was time enough, it was a simple shot; as soon as the man started to let himself down . . . then.

'But he was taking years, centuries to do so. One could not go on living like this. With a shotgun-barrel weighing a ton, a world of lead, and the cold eating one's body and soul, one could not live. It would have been better to be at the other end of the barrel, up there on the wall. Yes, yes, he would have changed places. Even though the man was going to die.

'It was Alvaro, and he hadn't a minute more to live! Would he fall into the park or into the lane?'

He did not fall. Without any haste or agitation he let himself down into the lane; he was used to the climb, and already knew every stone in the wall. Don Víctor watched him disappear without changing his aim and without daring to move the finger which lay across the trigger. Mesía was down in the lane now, and his friend was aiming at the sky.

'Wretch! I should have killed him!' cried Don Víctor when it was too late, and as if he were feeling the pangs of conscience he hurried to the park gate, opened it, and ran towards the corner of the wall where his enemy had climbed down. There was nobody to be seen. Quintanar approached the wall, and in its stones and cracks he could see the *stairway of his dishonour*.[5]

'Yes, now he could see it clearly, now he could see nothing else. Yet how many times had he walked past it without suspecting that it was the way into his wife's bedroom!' He went back into the park and examined the wall on that side. The half-rotten barrel standing by the wall – as if someone happened to have left it there – together with the remains of the broken espalier formed another ladder; he saw it twenty times every day and until now he had never noticed what it was: a ladder! He regarded it as a symbol of his own life. It was easy enough to find in his life all the signs of his dishonour, the steps of treachery: feigning friendship, and bearing with all his plays and confidences, and turning him against the canon theologian – it had all been another ladder and he had never seen it, and now he could see nothing else.

'What about Ana? Ana! She was up there, in the house, in her bed; he had her in his power, he could kill her, he should kill her. Since he had spared *his* life – for a few hours, only for a few hours – why not start with her? Yes, yes, in a minute, in a minute, he was resolved on it, it was perfectly clear, he had to kill, who could doubt it? But first – first he wanted to meditate, he needed to calculate – yes, the consequences of the crime, because after all it was a crime. They were infamous wretches, deceiving a husband, deceiving a friend, but he was going to be a murderer – worthy to be excused, oh yes indeed – but a murderer none the less.'

He sat down on a stone bench. But he stood up straight away. The cold of the seat had penetrated his bones. In his body there was a strange lethargy, a physical self-concern which seemed unworthy of himself and of the circumstances. He was very cold and very sleepy. Much against his will, he was thinking about this with perfect clarity, while the ideas relating to his misfortune, his dishonour and his shame were unmanageable, eluding him, mingling together and refusing to be ordered in the form of a rational argument.

He walked into the arbour and sat in a rocking-chair. He could see the window out of which Don Alvaro had climbed.

The cathedral clock struck seven.

The sound of the bell brought sad reality back into Quintanar's muddled head. 'Someone had put his clock forward. Who? Petra – of course, Petra. It had been her revenge. Oh! a consummate revenge indeed. Now it seemed absurd to have taken the dim light of the early dawn for a cloudy day. And if Petra had not put his clock forward or he had not believed it, perhaps he would never have known about the horrible misfortune – the misfortune which had destroyed his happiness. The lethargy of misfortune and suffering, together with the lethargy of his body, which was crying out for warm sheets and soft mattresses, numbed Don Víctor's spirit, and he did not want to move, or feel, or think, or even live. The idea of activity filled him with horror. Oh, if only time would stop! But no, it did not stop; it ran on, dragging him with it; and it shouted at him: move yourself, do something, do your duty; now's the time to keep all those promises, kill, burn, vociferate, tell the world about your vengeance, say goodbye to tranquillity for ever, find energy in the depths of your drowsiness, from your yawns wrest apostrophes to your outraged honour, play your part, it's your turn now, it's not Perales performing now, it's you, it's not Calderón inventing affairs of honour, it's life, it's your damned bad luck, it's the wretched world which used to seem so happy, made for amusement and for reciting verses! Go on, go on, rush off, up the stairs, kill the lady, then challenge her lover and kill him too! It's the only way. And all the time unable to stir hand or foot, longing to sleep, hating being awake and exposed to such wretchedness, so much misfortune – misfortune which would last for ever and ever!

'But now his turn had come. This was his own cloak-and-dagger drama. They existed in life, too. But how unpleasant they were, how horrible! How could all that treachery and death and hatred be so entertaining in verse and in the theatre? How wicked man was! Why should one enjoy such sorrow when others were suffering it, if it was so painful when it came one's own way? And he, the wretch, the despicable creature, the coward, was philosophizing – and his honour still unavenged! A start had to be made, time was flying! More torture! The ordering of the performance, the ordering of the plot! Where would he begin, what would he say, what would he do, how would he kill her, how would he search him out?'

The cathedral clock struck half past seven.

Quintanar jumped to his feet.

'Half an hour! Half an hour in a minute; and I failed to hear the quarter.'

'And Frillity is going to come, and I still have not decided . . .'

Don Víctor was perfectly aware that his will was inert – that he could not decide anything. He despised himself with all his heart, but more heartfelt still was his consolation as he realized that he lacked the courage to kill anybody, so soon.

'Either I go upstairs and kill her now, before Tomás arrives, or I do not kill her today.'

He dropped back into the rocking-chair. His nervous tension had been eased by the relaxation of his spirit as it stopped trying to fight against the impotence of his will; his feelings regained some of their vigour, and for the first time the sheer pain of the betrayal stabbed him with enough force to bring tears to his eyes.

He cried like an old man; he remembered that he was an old man. This idea had never occurred to him. His temperament had deceived him, shamming an endless youth; misfortune, attacking him so suddenly, had, like a shower of rain, washed all the dye out of the grey hairs of his spirit.

'Oh, yes, he was an old man, a poor old man, and he was being deceived and mocked. He was reaching the age when he would need a companion in life, a staff on which to lean – and the staff had fallen to pieces in his hands, his companion had betrayed him, he was going to be alone, alone; he had been abandoned by his wife and his friend.'

Grief and self-pity brought other ideas to his mind – ideas more natural and opportune than those aroused, amid the fantasies of fever and of sleepiness, by false indignation inspired by romantic readings and opposed by lethargy, self-concern and weakness of character.

He had stopped feeling jealous, he had stopped feeling ashamed and dishonoured, no longer was he thinking about other people's opinions or the ridicule to which he was going to be exposed. He was thinking about treachery and feeling the pain of deceit – the treachery and the deceit of his dear Ana, to whom he had given his honour, his life, everything. Oh, now he realized that his fondness for her was deeper than he had thought; now he loved her more than ever, but he knew that his was not the love of a lover, or the love of a loving husband, but the love of a dear friend, and the love of a father – yes, of a father who was kind and indulgent and needed care and attention!

'Kill her! That was soon said, but kill her! Bah – actors are quick to kill, poets too, because they do not kill – but an honourable person, a Christian does not kill the people to whom he is tied by all the bonds of affection and habit, so soon, or without dying of grief himself. His dear Ana was like a daughter. And he felt his dishonour as a father would feel it; he wanted to punish, he wanted to avenge himself – but killing was too much. No, he would not have the heart today or tomorrow or ever, why deceive himself? The man who kills is the man who is blinded, the man who hates: he was not blind, he did not hate, he was sad to death, drowning in icy tears. The wound was a harrowing one, he realized what an ingrate she had been, but he did not hate her, he did not want to kill her and he would not be able to kill her. The man he *would* kill; Alvaro had to die. But face to face, in a duel, and not with a bullet, no, he would kill him with a sword, that was nobler, worthier. Frillity must be put in charge of everything. But when? Now? As soon as he came? No – he could not bring himself to tell Frillity about it, not so soon. After talking to someone about such a shameful discovery there could be no turning back – that is to say, no changing one's plans, no postponing or modifying the vengeance. As soon as someone else found out about it, it would be necessary to act with speed and violence; the world, ideas of honour demanded it; he was a deceived husband. She would have to be put into a convent. And he himself, he would return to his homeland, if Mesía did not kill him. He would hide himself away in La Almunia de Don Godino.'

At this point the unhappy man remembered that months earlier Ana had proposed a trip there. 'If he had agreed, perhaps this misfortune would have been avoided – this irreparable misfortune! Yes, irreparable, who could doubt it?

'And Petra! Curse the girl! It is she who is responsible for my great misfortune, it is she who has thrown me into this black pit of sorrow from which I shall never emerge even if I kill everybody in the world, even if I cut Mesía to pieces and bury poor Ana alive! Oh, Ana is going to be very unhappy too!'

The cathedral clock struck eight. 'Eight o'clock! I should be waking up now – and I would know nothing.'

This thought shamed him. A word exploded in his brain – the obscene word used by foul-mouthed people to refer to husbands who condone their own dishonour. Anger flared again in his breast and blasted his tender grief away. 'Revenge! Revenge!' he cried to himself. 'Or else I am a wretch, a despicable wretch.'

He heard footsteps on the sand, looked up, and saw Frillity at his side.

'Hullo! We appear to have risen early today,' said Crespo, who liked to be first.

'Let's go,' replied Don Víctor, coming to his feet and hanging his shotgun from his shoulder.

Frillity's presence had disconcerted him. He summoned all his fortitude to reach a sudden decision. At last he made up his mind. He would keep silence, dissemble, go hunting. 'Out on the marshes, alone, lying in wait, throughout that sorrowful day which was going to be such a long one too, he would meditate – and on their way back, yes, on their way back, by then perhaps he would have formed his plan, and he would consult Tomás and tell him to go and issue the challenge, if this emerged as the proper thing to do. For the time being – keep silence, dissemble. It was not something to be let out lightly. The discovery which he owed to Petra should not be revealed without very good cause. Frillity could be told everything – in due course.'

They left the park. Quintanar locked the gate. Crespo walked on in front. Don Víctor gazed back into the garden towards the house, which looked so different now. 'What was he doing? Was postponing his revenge the act of a coward? No, because they suspected nothing, they would not escape, there was no fear of that. Silence and dissimulation, that was what was needed now. And deep reflection. Whatever he chose to do was going to be so grave!' It was anguish to think of the immense responsibility of what he would soon have to do. The realization that upon his will, always fickle, impressionable and weak, such important events and the entire futures of various people would hang, filled him with a silent, desperate panic. He felt an urge to call out to Frillity, tell him everything, place everything in his hands. 'Frillity was a dreamer, but when it came to the point he had more common sense, he was more practical. What should he do?'

For the moment, follow Tomás to the station. And keep silence. There would be plenty of time to talk.

It was still an ash-grey morning. More and more dark clouds were emerging, like cloth from a loom, from the peaks and plateaux of Mount Corfín, falling upon the sierra, dragging themselves over it, slipping down towards Vetusta, and filling the air with silent grey sadness.

'It isn't cold,' Frillity observed as they reached the station. He was not wearing a topcoat, only his checked muffler. But he always said that his shooting-jacket was as tough as the hide of a proboscidean: neither bullets nor catarrh could penetrate it.

Yet Quintanar, swathed in a heavy greatcoat, had to clench his teeth to stop them from chattering.

'No, it is not very cold!' he said, for fear of giving himself away.

'Luckily Tomás is a sleep-walker who never notices whether others have smiles or sour looks on their faces. My face must be pale, contorted – but this egotist is blind to all that.'

They climbed into a third-class carriage. Frillity found some old acquaintances on his bench. They were two stock-farmers on their way back from Castile; having spent the night in Vetusta, they were returning to the warmth of their homes in a country village. As if grief and friends drowning in grief did not exist, cheerful with that insulting joy inspired in him by the frost on the coldest mornings of the year, Crespo rubbed his hands together and talked about the price of cattle and the advantages of the *métayage* system. He was never half as loquacious in Vetusta. It seemed that as the train drew further and further from the dirty red-brown roofs of the sad city, sunk in sleep and fog, Frillity's soul waxed greater and greater, and his lungs of steel breathed more and more freely.

'Sitting there, blind and full of untimely chatter and cheer, the man did not suspect that his friend, his best friend, had been tempted to jump out on to the platform when the train set off, and then to hurl himself out of the window on to the track and run, run as fast as he could back to Vetusta, enter Ozores Mansion, and stab an infamous woman in the breast, over and over.'

This had been Don Víctor's intention. He had felt himself dying of shame and anger for the infamous adulterers and for himself, too, when he had noticed that the train was moving off and taking him away from the scene of the crime, of his dishonour, and of his necessary revenge.

'I am a wretch, I am a wretch!' cried Quintanar to himself as the train flew along and Vetusta was left far in the distance; so far that behind hillocks and bare trees all that could be seen now was the cathedral tower, like a black pennant standing out against the white background of Mount Corfín, which was surrounded by mist and lit by the cool sun's slanting rays.

'I am fleeing from my dishonour. Instead of expunging the offence I flee from it – my behaviour is indescribable, oh – no it is not! 'And bang! the name which the poor old man believed applicable to his own behaviour exploded like a sky-rocket in his brain.

'I am a ——, I am a ——!' and he said it in full and in such a loud voice that it seemed impossible that everyone in the carriage should not hear him.

'But the train was fleeing from Vetusta, whistling – whistling at him, and he lacked the courage to throw himself out and return to town – twelve hours would elapse before he saw Ozores Mansion again, he was postponing his revenge by more than twelve hours!'

They went through a tunnel and nothing was left of Vetusta or the country surrounding it. This was a different landscape. They were behind the sierra now, and monotonous dark-red hills stretched forth on their left like great symmetrical waves, shutting out the horizon. The sky was dark on that side, and the clouds were low, like great bags of dirty clothes unravelling upon the hills in the distance. On the right, empty maize-fields showed their earth, black with damp; at intervals among these blotches of bare soil there were areas of low woodland and apple orchards of doleful aspect with leafless trees whose tapering branches looked like hands of skeletons. On this side the sky promised to clear; the mist made the high, slender clouds look paler, and they were beginning to break up. Towards the sea a milky band of uniform colour and thickness lay over the horizon. Above the chestnut groves – looking like ruined buildings, and displaying what, only a few weeks earlier, had been the mysteries of their foliage – and above the woods of oak, and above the bare fields and the doleful apple orchards, flocks of cormorants flew every so often in V-shaped phalanxes towards the sea, like castaways of the mist, sometimes silent and sometimes moaning lugubrious caws, muffled, like underground laments.

As Frillity talked about the advisability of replacing maize-farming by a more intensive form of cultivation, Don Víctor, his head resting on the hard boards of the third-class carriage, gazed at the grey sky and saw a phalanx of cormorants pass by in the mist, in that desert of air. Now they were like grains of printer's sand, now something imagined rather than seen, now nothing.

'Lugarejo, stopping for two minutes!' cried a fast, hoarse voice.

Don Víctor leaned out of the window. The station, a dismal hut covered with chocolate-coloured paint and looking as cold as death, was almost within his reach. Sitting in a window above the door was a fair-haired woman of about thirty suckling a baby.

'She is the station-master's wife. They live in this desert. Fortunate people,' thought Quintanar.

The station-master walked by. He looked like a beggar. He was a young man – he seemed younger than the woman in the window.

'They love each other, no doubt. Or at least she is faithful to him.'

After this conjecture Don Víctor dropped back into his place. He closed his eyes and hid his face with one hand as best he could. The train started moving. The ringing of iron and the clatter of wood and the constant vibration had the effect of a lullaby. Not thinking what he was doing, Quintanar fitted the rhythm of the heavy creaking wheels to a march often chirruped by his song-thrush, that song-thrush which was the pride and joy of the house. Then he fitted the train's rhythm to a certain polka – and then he fell asleep.

Half an hour later they arrived at the station where they had to alight and start walking along the road to the marshes of Palomares.

Don Víctor awoke with a start, thanks to a tap on the shoulder from Frillity.

He had been dreaming a thousand disconnected absurdities. Dressed as a canon in choir clothes, he was marrying his own wife to Don Alvaro in the parish church near El Vivero. And Don Alvaro was wearing priest's clothes too, in spite of his moustache and goatee beard. Afterwards the three of them started to perform the piano scene from *The Barber of Seville*, and he himself stepped forward to the footlights to sing in a cracked voice:

'Quando la mia Rosina . . .'[6]

at which the audience in the stalls cawed at him as one man. The stalls were full of cormorants opening their beaks wide and writhing their necks in serpent-coils. 'A nightmare,' thought Quintanar, still half-asleep, as he set off down the Palomares road. They were at Roca Tajada, and on their right Mount Areo rose sheer above them, split by the gorge along which they were walking. In the gorge there was only room for the narrow road and the River Abroño. Half-way along the two changed sides, the road crossing the river on a bridge of white stone.

After breakfast in Roca Tajada, in the tavern owned by Matiella, tobacconist and bricklayer, and a great friend of Frillity's, the two huntsmen left the road, cut across muddy meadows full of tall dark-green grass, and came back at length to the banks of the Abroño, much wider here, bordered by sand and rushes, and crinkled by the green waves sent up it by the nearby sea.

They crossed the river in a ferry-boat and started to climb a hill crowned by a village of white houses set among apple-trees and bay-trees, spreading umbrella-pines and slim poplars. The green of the pines and bay-trees, and of orange-trees in gardens, above the lighter green of the meadows, gently sloping and as clearly defined as if someone had cut them out with a pair of scissors, brightened the hilltop beneath the milky sky and between the white house-walls, which seemed to absorb all the diffuse, cloud-filtered daylight. The two friends climbed on up the skirt of the hill, which was like the first step of a great stairway, and the earth became firmer, the grass lighter in colour and scantier. Frillity stopped, turned, and contemplated Mount Areo in front of him, the meandering river below, and the sea, a blue band with white flecks which could be glimpsed between the hills. It seemed to be on a higher plane than the river, like a dark wall climbing towards the clouds.

Quintanar sat on a rock which jutted out of the meadow. From the direction of the mountain, crossing the river at a great height, came a flock of water-ouzels. When they were within range Frillity fired both barrels of his shotgun, but luck was against him and he only succeeded in scattering the dense ranks of birds.

'Shoot, you fool!' he shouted in fury.

Quintanar stood, aimed and fired. Four water-ouzels fell wounded by the pellets which, as he remembered at that moment, should have been in the brains of his treacherous friend, the infamous Don Alvaro.

'Yes, that shot should have been for Alvaro. The innocent water-ouzels were falling in pairs and the thief of his honour was still alive.' And how strange! When he had stood in the park aiming at Mesía's head he had not remembered that the cartridge was only charged with pellets. He had supposed that it contained buckshot or slugs.

Much against his will, and in spite of the misfortune weighing upon him, the huntsman experienced the pleasure of vanity satisfied. 'Frillity had fired both barrels and hit not a thing; he had fired one only and – four. Yes, four, there they were, bleeding upon the meadow, mingling the drops of red with the white frost on the grass.'

Half an hour later Frillity took his revenge by killing a superb sea-duck. Quintanar, out of caprice, killed a cormorant, which he left where it fell.

They hunted until twelve o'clock, the time to have their cold meat. Frillity's dogs were bored. This kind of hunt, in which they played minor roles, was beneath them. They yawned and were reluctant to obey their master's voice.

After eating his cold meat and taking a few draughts of wine, Don Víctor felt his grief with redoubled intensity. Everything became clear to him; the full significance of his discovery earlier in the morning appeared before him like a classical treatise on history. What had happened, what was going to happen – he could see it all, as in a panorama. And he felt an urge to speak and a longing to cry. Why did he not open his heart to his bosom friend, his true friend, his only friend? But he did not open it to him. 'It was not yet time.'

They separated to pursue a flock of lapwings which was flying from meadow to meadow, always on the alert. These creatures were inedible, but Frillity had declared war on them, because they mocked huntsmen with a kind of irony or sarcasm which seemed almost rational. They would wait, pretend to be off guard, dissemble their watchfulness, and when Frillity, hiding behind a hedge, was about to fire – the devils would take to wing, screaming like witches surprised in a sabbath. So he pursued them, tenacious and angry.

They separated. If the lapwings went one way when they left the meadow which was covered and stained black by them they would be met by Frillity's shotgun; if they went the other way Don Víctor would fire at them.

He was alone on a hillock which dominated the valley. The sun had not been able to dissipate the mist, but it could be made out behind a white awning, as if it were a theatrical moon painted with oil on paper. In the distance the winter birds of ill omen screamed and appeared beneath the clouds, flying out of range, fearless of the huntsmen, but sad, tired of life, as Quintanar supposed.

'The countryside looked melancholic. Winter was a kind of nakedness. But in spite of everything, how beautiful was nature! How tranquil its repose! It was man, it was man who had engendered hatred, treachery, conventional laws which bound the heart to misfortune!' The philosophy of Frillity, that agricultural thinker who despised society with its false principles, its prejudices, its extremes and its violence, appeared now to Quintanar, whose well-filled body was begging him for a nap, as the one true philosophy, the only eternal wisdom. 'Vetusta over there, behind mountains and more mountains, what was it compared to the wide world? Nothing; a dot. And all the cities, and all the holes where man, that ant, built dwelling-places – what were they compared to the virgin forests, the deserts, the mountain ranges, the vast seas? Nothing. And the laws of honour, all the prejudices of social life – what were they beside the great, unchanging, natural laws obeyed by the stars in heaven, the waves in the sea, the fire in the earth, the sap circulating in plants?'

For a moment Quintanar was seized with an intense desire to grow roots and branches and be covered with moss like one of those age-old oaks which he could see crowning the peaks of Mount Areo. 'Vegetating was much better than living.'

He heard a distant shot and then the racket made by the lapwings as they took off, cackling and screeching. He watched them as they passed over his head. He did not stir. Let them go to the devil. He was thinking about Thomas à Kempis. Yes, Kempis, whom he had forgotten, was right: the cross was everywhere. 'Settle and order everything', said the wise ascetic, 'according to your own views and wishes, yet whether you like it or not you will always be made to suffer; you will always find a cross.'

He also remembered: 'Sometimes it will seem as if God has abandoned you, and sometimes you will be mortified by your neighbour; what is more, you will often be a burden to yourself.'[7]

'Yes, my neighbour is mortifying me, and I am a burden to myself – I am hurting myself so much that my very soul is bleeding. I do not know what I should do, or even what I should think. Anita is deceiving me, she is an infamous woman – but what about me? Do I not deceive her? What right had I to join my coldness, the coldness of a boring, scatter-brained old man, with the ardour and the dreams of her romantic, excitable youth? And why did I adduce the rights of my age so as not to serve as a soldier of matrimony – and then try to be a smuggler of adultery? Does it cease to be adultery when committed by a man – whatever the law may say?'

It infuriated him to find himself in such a philosophical mood, but he could not help it. He realized that his meditations were distancing him from his revenge, that in his heart he no longer wanted to avenge himself, that he only wanted to punish like a just judge and save his honour. And this itself irritated him. Then his tender self-pity returned, the vision of a solitary old age. The stone-curlews in the grey sky wailed like someone reciting Kempis in an unknown tongue.

'Yes, sorrow was universal, the whole world was putrefaction and humanity was the most putrid part of it all.'

And he always came back to the conclusion that he did not know what he should do, or even what he should think, or even what he should feel.

'In any event, cloak-and-dagger dramas were a tissue of shameless lies. The world was not what they said it was, one does not transfix one's neighbour after giving him time only to recite a few lines of poetry. Honourable Christian men do not kill so often or so fast.'

That night, in the train, when they were returning to Vetusta alone in a second-class carriage, for fear of the cold in the third-class ones, Frillity was looking at the sad landscape by the light of the moon, which on this occasion had proved stronger than the sun and had broken up the clouds, when he heard an explosive sigh behind him. He turned his head, saying:

'What's up, man? You've seemed worried and gloomy all day long. What's up?'

The ceiling-lamp, which served for two compartments, hardly pierced the shadows in their coffin-like carriage.

Frillity could not see Don Víctor's face, but he suddenly heard him crying like a small boy and felt his strong white head leaning on his own friendly shoulder. The poor old man was resting there with love and trust, and weighing as much as a man dropping dead. It was like the abdication of all his thought and initiative.

'Tomás, I need your advice. Great is my misfortune. Listen . . .'

XXX

'And now take great care. Don't you do anything rash!'

'Aren't you coming in?'

'No, no. I'm in a hurry, I've got work to do.'

'You are leaving me alone – now!'

'I'll come back later if you like – but it would be better if you went straight to bed. I'll be here early tomorrow morning.'

'Mind you, I have not said that I agree to do as you say.'

'Very well, very well. Good-night.'

'Wait, wait, don't leave me alone – yet. I have not said that I agree.

Perhaps – I might have second thoughts and decide to follow the opposite course of action.'

'But for the moment, Víctor, be prudent, hide your feelings. That is, if you don't want to run the risk of another misfortune. You know what I mean.'

'Yes, yes! Benítez believes that a fright, a shock . . .'

'Could kill her.'

'She is sick!'

'Yes, sicker than you think.'

'She is sick! And a fright, a shock – could kill her.'

'That's right – it could kill her.'

'And I must go in, and keep all this rancour to myself, swallow all this bile, and dissemble, and talk to her, so that she does not suspect anything, or become frightened – or fall down dead at my feet.'

'Yes, Víctor, yes, that's what you must do.'

'But you have to admit, Tomás, that it is easier said than done. And, you must comprehend why that door-knocker fills me with dread, and realize that I have good reasons for being as unwilling to touch it as if it were made of molten iron.'

Frillity made no reply.

Having walked from the station, they were standing in the porch of Ozores Mansion, where the gilt lamp hanging from the ceiling shed here and there some hardly perceptible light.

Quintanar could not find the courage to enter his house. He did not want to knock on the door. 'It would open and she would come to greet him, she would have the impudence to smile as usual, perhaps to bring her forehead close to his lips for him to kiss. And he would have to smile, and kiss, and keep silence – and retire to his bed in as serene a manner as on any other night. Tomás ought to comprehend that it was too much to ask.'

What was more, Frillity's revelations about Ana's health had hit the poor ex-magistrate like a pile-driver on the head. 'That gaiety, that exaltation, which had led her to crime, to the infamy of betrayal, was an illness! Ana might suddenly die, at any time; any great shock, whether painful or joyful – but particularly if painful – could kill her in a matter of hours.' This had been Frillity's reply to Víctor's narration. We'll shoot Mesía, he had said, if that will give you any consolation, but we must wait, avoid scandal, above all avoid the fright, the shock which your wife would receive if you were to burst into her bedroom as husbands do in the theatre. Ana was guilty according to both divine and human law, but not so guilty, in Frillity's opinion, that she deserved to die.

This moved Don Víctor to interject:

'Who wants to kill her? That is not what I want!'

But Frillity replied:

'Yes that *is* what you want, if you tell her that you know all. What has to be done is a matter for further consideration. I'm not saying that you must forgive her, or that forgiving her is the only solution – but you must admit that it is a possible solution.'

'To forgive her would be to condone my dishonour.'

'I'm not so sure about that. You're a Christian, aren't you?'

'Yes, with all my heart, more and more so every day. Seeing no other refuge for my soul than religion . . .'

'Well now, if you're a Christian I'm not so sure that you oughtn't to forgive her. But we haven't come to that yet. We're still talking about the need not to remove the possibility of forgiveness before discovering whether it is suitable, by dealing your wife a mortal blow – as you would if you burst into her room and cried: "Death to the unfaithful wife!" for her to reply: "Lord have mercy on me!" and drop down dead. I don't know if she'd say "Lord have mercy on me", but I'm certain that she would drop dead. And, as you can see, before we kill her we must find out if we have any right to do so.'

'No, I have no right, my conscience tells me . . .'

'It tells you the truth. And I have no right to advise you to do anything tragic. When I married you to her – because it was I who married you, Víctor, remember – I thought I was making you both happy.'

'And you did not seem to be wrong. You did make me happy. And Ana – for more than ten years you seemed to have made her happy, too.'

'Yes, so it seemed, but she was keeping her feelings to herself. Life is short, she was a good wife for ten years. That isn't something to be sniffed at.'

'Look here, Frillity, your philosophy is not well suited to comfort a husband in my situation. I already know everything you can tell me, and much more besides. That is no comfort.'

'And I don't think there is any comfort for you in your situation, except time, and slow, lengthy thought. But we aren't concerned with you now, we're concerned with her. You're determined to cut Mesía to pieces with a foil or a sword? Very well, but we have to see when and how it's to be done. We must keep calm. Knowing what you now know about Ana's illness – a secret which Benítez made me promise to keep and which I'm breaking now because of the urgency of the situation – knowing that such a revelation could be a death-blow to her . . .'

'But is it not worse for her to do what she is doing than to know that I know? How can you be so sure that she will not reject me and try to run away with the man?'

'Víctor, don't be such a fool! The man is a coxcomb. All he did was wait for the fruit to ripen and fall. She isn't in love with Mesía. As soon as she realizes he's a coward who deserts her rather than fight for her, she will reject him, curse him – and her remorse will turn her back to you, whom she has always loved.'

'Has always loved!'

'Yes, more than a father. What better proof do you want than everything that has happened? Why did she turn mystical? And the poor thing must have suffered other attacks, too, I believe, from another direction, from – but still, we won't talk about that. Why did she resist as much as no doubt she did? Because she loved you – because she loves you – she loves you very much.'

'And she betrays me!'

'She betrays you! She betrays you! But we won't talk about that – you've already said you don't want any of my philosophizing. The point is that if you make a great scene in there by playing the outraged husband, it will be followed by another scene – a burial scene.'

'I must say you have a fine way of putting things!'

'It's the truth. A complete drama. But if, after all, you're so enraged, if you're so blind, if you can't listen to reason or to your conscience, which is speaking clearly enough – then knock on the door, climb the stairs, go on the rampage, burn the house down. But you don't have to go that far, because you only need frighten her with your news to make her fall flat on her back and burst one of those things inside her which you don't believe in, but which are as necessary to life as wires are to the telegraph. If you are furious, if you can't restrain yourself, you too will have an excuse, whatever you do.' (A pause.) 'But if not, Quintanar, it would be unforgivable.'

Crespo said the last words in a solemn, grave, vibrant voice which made his friend shudder.

It was after this dialogue, part of which took place as they walked home from the station and the rest in the porch, that Quintanar went to the door to lift the knocker and Frillity exclaimed:

'And now take great care. Don't you do anything rash!'

Frillity was in a hurry, he wanted to rush off in search of Don Alvaro and warn him that Quintanar knew about his treachery – which would prevent his assailing the park again that night and keeping his rendezvous if, as was to be supposed, he had one. Crespo thought that it would not have occurred to Don Víctor – as many other things did not occur to him – that the scene of the previous night would be repeated this night, for it must be an old custom by now. Don Alvaro, who had not seen his victim when he was being stalked by him in the park, might come back to play his usual game, Quintanar might catch him, and then it would be impossible to avert a tragedy. Besides, Frillity was convinced that Don Alvaro would flee from Vetusta as soon as he was told that Quintanar intended to challenge him to a duel. He had reason to believe that the Don Juan was a coward.

'But Víctor refused to let him go!'

At last, having again promised to dissemble, to conceal his grief or his wrath or whatever it was – but only for the night – the worthy retired magistrate knocked on the door with the same energetic concise rap with which he used to make the courtyard echo when the house had been an honourable one and the head of the family a respected and maybe beloved man.

'Good-night, good-night, I'll see you early tomorrow morning!' said Frillity, shaking his arm free of the quivering hand which held it.

'The egotist!' thought Don Víctor when he was left alone. 'He is the only person in the world who loves me – and he is an egotist!'

The door opened. He hesitated for a moment – he fancied he could feel a draught of ice-cold air from the courtyard.

He entered, and as he turned back towards the porch to close the door he saw a tall black ghost come gliding in. It approached him step by step through the gloomy porch and removed its hat – a shovel hat.

'My dear Don Víctor!' pronounced a trembling, honeyed voice.

'What! You? It's you – Don Fermín!' A cold shudder, like the start of a fainting fit, ran through the ex-magistrate's body as he added, trying to speak in a calm voice, 'To what do I owe – at this time of night – the honour? What is it? Some misfortune?'

'But doesn't the man know anything?' thought De Pas, who looked like a disinterred corpse.

He examined Don Víctor by the light of the lamp above the staircase and saw that his features were disfigured. Don Víctor saw the canon's face so pale, with such a look in his eyes, that he felt a vague, superstitious fear of him, the fear of unknown evil. The canon theologian did not speak again; he only shook Quintanar's hand and invited him with a gesture both graceful and energetic to proceed upstairs.

'But what is it?' repeated Don Víctor in hushed tones when they reached the first landing.

'Have you been hunting?' the other man replied in a feeble voice.

'Yes, sir, with Crespo – but what has happened? It is so long since . . . and at this time of night.'

'To your study, to your study. There is no cause for alarm. To your study.'

Anselmo lit the corridors of the mansion for his master, who was followed by the canon.

'He doesn't ask about Ana,' thought De Pas.

'Madam did not hear you knock, she is in her boudoir – would you like me to call her, sir?' asked Anselmo.

'Eh? No, no, leave her there. I mean – if the canon theologian wants to talk to me alone . . .' and the master of the house turned back.

'Very well, yes, your study – let us go to your study.'

By the time they reached it, Quintanar's shivers were clearly visible. 'What was the man going to say? What had he come for?'

Anselmo lit two candles.

'Anselmo, if madam asks for me, say that I shall come directly – that I am busy, that she is to wait in her room. Is that not right? Do you not wish us to be alone?'

The canon theologian assented with a movement of his head, his eyes riveted on the doorway through which Anselmo was leaving the room.

'He was there now, he had to say something now – what was he going to say? What a predicament! He had to say something, but not an idea, not the faintest idea came to enlighten his mind; he had no notion at all what it might be in his interest to say. How could he speak without first asking what Don Víctor knew? For this was the question – what he could say depended upon what the other man knew. But no, that was no good, he would have to begin by explaining himself. What a quandary!' The canon theologian felt as if he had been caught by Don Víctor in his study stealing the silver holders in which the candles were burning.

Quintanar's teeth were chattering and his eyes were wide with astonishment and dancing with questions.

'What do you want?' asked those shining pupils.

'One had to say something.'

'Could you find – somewhere – a little water?' said Don Fermín, who was choking, his tongue stuck to his palate.

Don Víctor looked for some water and found it in a glass on his bedside table. It was full of dust and had a vile taste. Don Fermín would not have been surprised had it tasted of vinegar. He was on Calvary. He had come because he had not been able to control himself, knowing that he must come, do something, see what was happening, promote his revenge. But now he did not know what to do. 'There he was, at nearly ten o'clock at night, in the study of the husband of the woman who was deceiving them both. What was he doing there? What was he going to say?' All the stations of that day of Passion flashed through the canon's excited memory. As he drank the glass of water and wiped his pale, compressed lips, the emotions of that day passed through his brain like a bitter purgative through his body.

He was feverish when he awoke in the morning. He called to his mother in alarm and then, unable to explain the cause of his illness to her, pretended to be well, got up, and left the house. The streets and the people in them glowed with the yellow gleam of distant candles. Footsteps and voices sounded muffled, solid bodies seemed hollow, everything had the brittleness of a dream. The universal indifference reflected brutal cruelty and stony selfishness: why did all the Vetustans talk about thousands of subjects which were of no concern to him, and nobody notice his grief or feel sorrow for him or join him in cursing the traitors and punishing them? He left the streets for the Summer Promenade, which was doleful now, with its cold bare trees and its damp sand patterned by the marks of flowing water. Furiously he strode about as if he were trying to rip his soutane open with his knees; that soutane in which he kept entangling his legs – a joke played on him by fate, fancy dress hanging from his neck.

'He, he himself was the husband, not that idiot who still had not killed anybody (and it was midday already) – although he must have known all ever since seven o'clock. The laws of the world, what a farce! Don Víctor had the right to avenge himself, but not the wish; *he* had the wish, the need to kill and devour what he killed, but not the right. He was a priest, a canon, a prebendary. Fate never stopped mocking him, laughing at him from all sides.' At that moment his head contained an entire mythology of scoffing divinities, all conspiring against the wretched canon theologian of Vetusta.

His soutane, flailed by his vigorous legs, was saying *swish, swish, swish*, like a chinking chain which refuses to be broken.

Without knowing how it had happened, De Pas found himself walking past Don Alvaro Mesía's hotel. 'Mesía was in there. If, as De Pas feared, Don Víctor had not prevented Mesía from leaving Ozores Park, if nothing had happened, then the man was lying calmly in his bed up there, resting from his pleasures. He could go up, enter his room, and smother him with his own pillows. And that was what he ought to do; if he did not do it he was a coward, afraid of his mother, the world, justice, afraid of scandal, the new experience of being a known criminal, held back by the inertia of everyday life with its lack of great adventures . . . a coward. A man of courage would go on up, kill. And if the world, the fools of Vetusta, and his mother and the bishop and the Pope asked why, he would scream his answer, from the pulpit if need were: You idiots; why do I kill? Because my wife has been stolen from me, because my wife has deceived me, because I respected that infamous woman's body so as not to lose her soul, and she, a prostitute like all women, steals her soul from me because I did not take her body as well. I kill both of them because I did not remember what I heard her doctor say, I did not remember that *ubi irritatio ibi fluxus*, I did not remember to be as coarse with her as with other women, I did not remember that her divine flesh was human flesh. I was afraid of her chastity and her chastity did the dirty on me; I thought that hers was a saintly body and her corrupt body is poisoning my very soul. I kill because she deceived me, because her eyes gazed into my eyes and called me elder brother, soul brother, in time with her lips, which said the same things with a smile; I kill because I should kill, I kill because I can kill, because I am strong, because I am a man – because I am a beast!'

But he did not kill. He approached the porter's lodge and asked for the Bishop of Nauplia, who was passing through Vetusta.

'He has gone out,' De Pas was told.

Blind to what he was doing, he took out a card, folded it, and left it with the porter.

He returned to his house, said that he was not at home to anybody, locked himself in his study, and paced it as if it were a cage.

He sat down and covered two sheets of paper with writing. It was a letter to the judge's wife. He read what he had written and tore it to shreds. He started pacing again, and again he wrote and tore and dug his finger-nails into his head.

In these letters the canon wept, wailed, cursed, implored, roared, cooed. Sometimes the narrow, tortuous trickles of fine ink were like a pipe through which poured all the filth in his soul; pride, wrath, lust beguiled and repressed and excited gushed along it like thick liquid putrescence. At such times his passion spoke with the dull guttural gurgle of sewage in a drain. At other times his fanciful idealism moaned like a turtle-dove; without rancour, as in an elegy, he recalled the days of their gentle, tender, intimate friendship – their smiles which had vouched for their spirits' eternal faithfulness, their plans to meet in heaven, their fervent promises, their sweet closeness. He recalled summer mornings amid flowers and dew, mystical hopes and delightful conversation, present happiness comparable only to future happiness. But the moaning of the turtle-dove was interrupted by the wind howling and shaking the branches, the hurricane roared again, thunder exploded and cruel, coarse sarcasm tore into the paper like a lightning-flash into a black sky. 'And look at the person for whom Ana was abandoning the salvation of her soul, the company of the saints, and the friendship of a faithful, trusting heart! A pinchbeck Don Juan, a village dandy, an occasional Parisian, a pretty bust, a stupid Narcissus, a plaster egotist, a soul so superficial, hollow and dull that even in hell it would not be welcomed!' 'But he understood the cause of her love; it was foul lust, she had fallen in love with flabby flesh – and still worse, with the craft of the tailor, the handiwork of the ironer, the skill of the shoemaker, the good looks of a horse, the nonsense of a reputation, the scandals of a libertine, caprice, idleness, dust, air. Hypocrite, hypocrite, lascivious woman, irremediably damned to hell because you are vile, and unworthy, and deceitful, and false, and . . .' and it was here that, furious with himself, he ripped the paper up, enraged because he could not write to insult, to kill, to tear limb from limb, without using words which insulted, killed, tore limb from limb. 'It could not be sent in an envelope to a woman, however much she deserved it. No, it was nobler to take a dagger from its sheath and strike with it than to strike with those letters of poison hidden in a perfumed envelope.'

But then he would write again, trying to control himself, and in the end his indignation and the frankness which his passion forced upon him would burst out on another side, and it was he himself who was hypocritical, lascivious, treacherous. 'Yes, yes,' he wrote, 'I would not admit it, but I wanted you for myself. I was not even conscious of it, just as I breathe without thinking about breathing, but in my guts I wanted to make you mine, show you that love, our love, must come first, show you that everything else was lies, children's play, useless chat, show you that all that mattered was for you to love me and above all for me to love you, and for us to run away if we had to, and for me to throw off my mask and my black clothes and be myself, far from here where I cannot. Yes, Anita, yes, I am a man, didn't you know? Is that why you deceived me? Well look here, I can smash your lover with a single blow. He's frightened of me, if you want to know, frightened just to see me looking at him; if he met me in some deserted spot, alone face to face, he would run away. I am your husband, you have promised me so in a hundred different ways; your precious Don Víctor is nobody, look how he doesn't complain. I am your master, you swore it. I had command of your soul, and that is what counts; you are mine, all of you, more than anything else because I love you as your wretched Vetustan and your Aragonese cannot love you, what do they know, Anita, of all those things which you and I know? Yes, you knew them too – and you forgot them, for a lump of flabby flesh, licked and licked again by all the fallen women in town. You kiss the flesh of orgies, the lips which have slobbered over all the suppurating sores of adultery, over all the open wounds of rape, over . . .'

Don Fermín tore this letter up, too, into shreds ten times smaller than the others. The pieces of paper missed the basket, and the floor looked as if it were covered with snow. Over these ruins of his artistic indignation the canon paced in fury, wishing that he had something more succulent to offer his anger and his vengeance than ink and cold, silent paper.

He went out again and paced up and down the colonnade in the Plaza Nueva, in front of Ozores Mansion.

'What had happened? Had Don Víctor discovered anything? No, if anything had happened, people would know by now. Don Víctor would have fired his shotgun at Don Alvaro, or they would be arranging a duel, and people would know. Nobody knew anything, therefore nothing had happened.'

Two, three times, as night was falling, the canon theologian entered the dark porch of the great house in the corner of the square. He wanted to discover something, spy for sounds – but he did not dare knock. 'Why had he come? Who was calling him to this house where in former times his advice had been valued so highly, and he had been so respected and even loved? Nobody was calling him. He

should not enter.' 'Besides,' he thought as he walked away, 'I don't
know what I would do if I were to find myself face to face with her.
Even if that unworthy husband forgives her, because he has milk in
his veins instead of blood, I – I do not forgive her, and if I had her in
my hands or even within their reach, God only knows what I would
do. No, I must not go into that house; it would be the ruin of me, the
ruin of them all.'

He returned to his own house.

Doña Paula came into his study. They talked about the shop and
the palace and many other things, but nothing was said about what
so worried both mother and son.

'That is something about which we cannot speak,' thought he.

'That's something we can't speak about, not even alone,' thought
she.

Mother knew all. She had bought the secret from Petra.

Thanks to her secret police service and to what she had been able
to observe for herself, she had already discovered that her son had
lost his power over the judge's wife. Doña Paula, who had cursed
that woman because she believed Fermo loved her, now hated her
because she too was hurt by the scorn, the mockery and the deceit.
Scorning her son, leaving him for a wilting dandy like Don Alvaro!
Motherly pride danced with rage inside Doña Paula. 'There was
nobody in the whole world better than her son. It was a sin to fall in
love with him, because he was a priest, but it was an even bigger sin
to cheat him, stick those thorns into his soul. And to think that there
wasn't any way to take revenge! No, there wasn't.' What Doña Paula
most feared was that her son might not be able to bear his jealousy
and his rage, and commit some scandalous crime.

It drove her to despair that she could not give him any comfort or
advice.

She had thought of a way to punish the infamous couple and in
particular the faded dandy: divulging the crime, spreading the news
of the execrable adultery, and thus rousing the Don Quixote in Don
Víctor and making him sally forth, with his lance at the ready, to kill
Don Alvaro.

'But not a word could she say to Fermo.'

Doña Paula came and went, talked about a thousand things, took
note of her son's face, his pallor, his hoarse voice, his trembling
hands, his pacing to and fro in the study.

'She would give anything to be able to suggest his revenge! Yes,
that beloved son of hers deserved to have all those thorns pulled out
of his soul. He had been such a good son! He had been so skilful at
defending and increasing his prestige in the face of all the attacks on
it!' Once Doña Paula had seen that 'there wasn't going to be an
outburst of scandal', that Fermín was showing incomparable discretion and caution in his strange relationship with the judge's wife,

she had forgiven him everything and stopped bothering him with her reprimands. After her son's triumph over impiety in the person of Don Pompeyo Guimarán – after that glorious conversion – she had admired him with renewed fervour and tried to help him to satisfy his intimate desires, always with the circumspection required by what she regarded as decency.

No, they could not speak about the subject which was of such concern to them both, and at last Doña Paula left Don Fermín alone. She went up to her room and resolved to stay awake there and spy on her son's movements; she could just hear him pacing about downstairs.

Don Fermín locked his study door as soon as he was alone. He was restless, he still had a fever. Nonsensical plans occurred to him, tragic crimes, but he rejected them immediately. 'He was bound hand and foot.' The atrocities which came to his mind might have been sublime, if committed by another man; committed by him they seemed grotesque, ridiculous.

But his soutane was burning him. The maniac notion that he was wearing fancy dress had become an intolerable obsession. Not knowing what he was doing and unable to control himself he ran to a wardrobe and took out the hunting clothes which he had often worn in Matalerejo to pursue wild beasts over the mountainsides. In the space of two minutes the priest was transformed into a powerful, well-built highlander whose handsome physique was shown to advantage in those brown clothes tight on his strong and still youthful body of natural virile elegance. He looked at himself in the mirror. 'There stood a man.' The judge's wife had never seen him looking like that.

'In the wardrobe there was a hunting-knife.'

He found it and hung it from his black leather belt. Its blade glinted; its cutting edge, marked by rays of light, seemed to be in harmony with his passion. He perceived a kind of music in the suggestive blade.

'He could go out, it was night now, dark night, there would be few people in the streets, nobody would recognize him in those clothes of a huntsman from the mountains. He could go and wait for Don Alvaro in the Calle de Traslacerca, at the corner where Petra said she had seen him climbing the wall. If Don Víctor had not discovered anything, or even if he had and Don Alvaro did not know, he would come back again, as perhaps he did every night – and he, Don Fermín, could be waiting for him at the foot of the wall, in the lane, in the dark, and make him fight, beat him, knock him down, kill him. That was what the knife was good for!'

Doña Paula moved overhead; boards creaked in the ceiling.

As if his mother's ideas had seeped through the wood into his brain he thought:

'But no, this is all nonsense. I cannot murder the infamous creature with a dagger. I do not possess that kind of courage. These are foolish notions from novels. Why think about what I am never going to do? I have no alternative but to use the courage and the romantic, chivalresque notions of Don Víctor. I shall put the knife away, my tongue must be my sword.'

Don Fermín took off his brown hunting-jacket, removed his broad-brimmed hat, unbuckled his black belt, put clothes and knife away in the wardrobe, and donned his soutane and his cloak, as if they were a suit of armour. 'Yes, that was his coat of mail – that was his fighting equipment.'

'Now is the time. I must go to see him now. If the great idiot went to Palomares to hunt, he must have returned or be about to return, for the train arrives about now. I shall go to his house.'

He walked into the passage.

'If my mother waylays me I shall tell her that a sick man is waiting for me, that he wants me to hear his confession without delay.'

When Doña Paula heard her son in the passage she duly came hurrying down the stairs.

'Where are you going?'

He told his lie.

And she pretended to believe it and let him go on his way, because she could tell from his face, his voice, and everything about him that he was not blind with passion, that he was not going to make a scandal.

'Perhaps the same idea had occurred to him as to her.'

So Don Fermín De Pas arrived at Ozores Mansion, saw Don Tomás Crespo disappearing into the square, entered the porch, decided to greet Don Víctor, who was opening the door, and went upstairs with him. He was ready to talk to him, interrogate him, advise him, suggest his necessary revenge – but he did not know how to begin.

When he finished drinking the water which tasted of dust he still did not know what he was going to say.

Quintanar's eyes were still wide with astonishment and dancing with questions, and Don Fermín spoke:

'My dear friend, I am torn between the desire to satisfy your impatience and the fear of making the wrong approach to a subject which is thorny and, unhappily, however much one might temper one's expression, disagreeable to broach.'

'Pray come to the point, sir.'

'The time of my visit, the fact that I have but seldom called at this house in recent months, all this must contribute . . .'

'Yes, sir, it does, but pray continue. What is it, Don Fermín? By God's nails!'

'I, too, must speak of God, and of His nails, and of His thorns, and of the Cross . . .'

'For pity's sake . . .'

'Don Víctor, before I speak I must ask you to tell me about your state of mind.'

'What do you mean?'

'You are pale, visibly worried, labouring under the burden of some great sorrow, it seems. I noticed it as I came in, by the light of the lamp over the stairs.'

'And you, too – are . . .'

Quintanar's voice trembled.

'Well, that is what I want to know. For if you are aware of the cause of my visit, in part at least, I can avoid the pain of entering upon the most vexatious preliminaries of a matter . . .'

'But what is it all about? For the sake of the eleven thousand virgins!'

'Señor Quintanar, you are a good Christian and I am a priest; if you have anything that you wish to say – if you need any advice . . . I have come to speak to you, too – about something I know, as a priest, but the conscience of the person who told me of it requires, precisely, that I take this step first.'

Don Víctor jumped to his feet.

The canon theologian felt well pleased with himself, because he had started to see clearly. Now he knew which way to take.

'A person who tells you to come to my house at this time of night?'

'Don Víctor, you must confess whether you know anything about the subject of the greatest concern to you, and whether this knowledge is the cause of the discomposure which is reflected on your face. This is where I must start.'

'Yes, sir, today I know something which I did not know yesterday – and which is of the greatest concern to me, yes indeed! greater than life itself. But if you do not speak more clearly, I do not know whether I should . . . whether I can . . .'

'Yes, now I can speak more clearly.'

'You were saying, a person . . .'

'A person who has furthered a crime which is prejudicial to you has come repentant to the tribunal of penance, to confess her shameful complicity; and to tell me that she had felt herself accused by her conscience and that, as a peremptory means of reparation, she had made it possible for you to discover that infamy. But fearing fresh misfortunes, because of the blundering manner in which she had acted, she hurried to tell me what had happened, in the hope that further crimes might be avoided – for, after all, any violent action would be a crime; any bloody revenge . . .'

Don Fermín stopped the flow of his talk and kept silence as a mark of respect for Don Víctor's grief. The old man had dropped upon a sofa and was pressing his head between his hands.

'Petra – was it Petra?' he asked in the special tone of voice of the man who already knows the answer to his question.

'The unhappy girl did not at first realize that her conduct might be the cause of even more havoc. And that is why I have come, Don Víctor, to prevent it if I am not too late. In the name of the Crucified, Don Víctor, what has been happening here?'

'Nothing – but there is still time!' replied the deceived husband, on his feet again, his fists clenched, ashamed, as if he had found himself standing in the middle of the square in his night-shirt; furious that nothing had happened there, no crime of which he should have been the author, as was demanded by the laws of honour – and of the theatre. 'Nothing, nothing – but something is going to happen, blood is going to be spilt! And you know about it? That woman has divulged my dishonour? It was revenge, not repentance: revenge, but it does not much signify. What does signify is that the world knows! O wretched Quintanar! Woe is me!'

The poor old man dropped back into the sofa. He was beginning to feel that intense drowsiness which had dispirited him in the morning.

'The world knows,' Don Víctor had declared, and these words suggested another useful lie to Don Fermín.

But first he said:

'Don Víctor, I am not surprised that in your grief you have neither the time nor the strength for reflection, but I did not say that the world knows. I am not the world, I am a confessor.'

'But can you believe that Petra has not told . . . ?'

'Petra has not. But, unhappily . . .'

'Besides, what signifies now is my honour, not whether the world knows or not. At all events, it will soon know of my revenge and be able to inform itself of everything else.'

He began to pace around his study.

De Pas also stood up.

'Unhappily,' he continued, 'slander took hold some time ago of certain rumours, of appearances . . .'

Don Víctor roared:

'My God! What is this? This too? The world is saying . . . ? All Vetusta is talking?'

He dug his finger-nails into his head, tearing his grey hair.

While Don Víctor devoted himself to his theatrical outbursts of grief and shame, Don Fermín spoke at length on the subject. 'Yes, unhappily, for some months now, ever since the summer or maybe even earlier, people had been gossiping about the familiarity and the frequency of Don Alvaro's visits to Ozores Mansion. This was the worst aspect of the matter, apart from the misfortune itself. It was the worst aspect because the canon, who knew how passionate were Don Víctor's ideas concerning honour, feared that, obeying impulses which were pardonable although not just, and deaf to the voice of religion, he might hurl himself into a terrible and violent vengeance, directed especially against Don Alvaro, whose crime could not have been more repugnant and worthy of punishment. But although as a man, and indeed a man of experience, Don Fermín could well comprehend the vehement anger which must be dominating Don Víctor, and although he understood, and even excused to a certain extent, his desire for a rapid and terrible vengeance – although this was his reaction as a man, none the less as the priest of a religion of peace and forgiveness he had to recommend and encourage, in so far as he was able, leniency and the procedure recommended by morality for such cases.' Don Víctor, with his face hidden in his hands, made signs of protest, shaking his head as if he were trying to wrench it from his body.

'But what would or could Quintanar say that De Pas could not understand? Yes, yes, regarding the affair from the point of view of the world, blood must be spilt. And not just to satisfy the desire for revenge but even to live in society in what the world calls a decorous manner, it was necessary, according to social laws, according to the exigencies of contemporary customs and ideas, for Don Víctor to go in search of Mesía, challenge him to a duel, and kill him if he could – or, if he caught him red-handed, committing the crime or immediately before or after it, put him to death there and then, with rapid justice. This had been the reaction of various illustrious heroes, wonders of the world sung and praised in poems and tragedies. All this he knew very well.' Indeed, the canon employed such eloquence and warmth in the exposition of 'the factors which, from the world's point of view, recommended bloodshed' that afterwards, when he remembered that it was his duty to defend the opposite cause, the cause of charity, forgiveness and love for one's neighbour, burial of grievances and acceptance of the Cross, he seemed, wearied by his earlier efforts, to be a different man, his language became laboured, and he uttered in a cold voice the commonplaces of the sermon of a village priest. Don Víctor did not penetrate the canon's scheme, but he felt the effects of his perfidy. 'Yes,' thought the ex-magistrate, as the canon theologian enumerated once more the sacrifice of self-esteem, honour and much else besides which religion demanded of the good Christian who had been deceived by his wife, 'yes, I have been blind, my behaviour has been despicable, I should have killed Mesía with a hail of pellets when he was on the wall, or else run to his hotel and made him fight me to the death, immediately. The world knows everything, all Vetusta considers me a – a – a . . .' and he started almost up to the ceiling as, in his brain, he heard himself saying the shameful word.

And then the cold, feeble phrases with which the canon theologian advised him to forgive and forget sounded hollow, like empty rhetoric. 'That holy man had no idea what an outrage of that kind was – or what the demands of society were.'

In order that the priest should leave him alone and stop wearying him with his dull sermons, lacking any life or unction, he pretended to submit. He agreed not to do anything foolish, to meditate and to attempt to harmonize the demands of his honour with whatever was required of him by religion.

At this Don Fermín became alarmed, thinking he had lost ground, and returned to the charge. He painted in bright colours the contempt which the world pours upon the husband who forgives such a crime, and is believed by evil-minded people to condone it.

As Don Víctor listened to the canon theologian he thought he must be the most contemptible man in the world if he did not do something to make everybody sit up and take notice. 'Oh yes, as soon as possible – as soon as day dawned he would make his move, he would send two seconds to Don Alvaro. Don Alvaro must be killed.'

Don Fermín saw the passionate wrath written on the magistrate's face and became calm again. 'Yes, that was his man, the weapon was ready, the cannon from which he was going to fire his mortal hatred was loaded to the muzzle.'

Don Víctor did not speak. He was growling in a corner.

'There was nothing further to be done there.' The canon theologian took his leave. But as he was walking through the door he span on his heel and with a solemn gesture and great deliberation, like a priest in an opera, he exclaimed:

'I demand, as the man who was, and I believe still is, your spiritual father, I demand in the name of God that if, tonight, you were to surprise some new crime – if that infamous wretch, who is unaware that you know all, were to return tonight – I realize that it is a great deal to ask – but there is never any excuse for murder in the eyes of God, even though there may be in the eyes of the world. Prevent the man from coming here, by all means, but – no bloodshed, Don Víctor, no bloodshed, in the name of the Crucified and the blood He spilt for us!'

'Of course,' thought Don Víctor when he was left by himself, 'of course! And I, idiot and fool that I am, had not thought of it? The man will return tonight. And I, so as not to give her a mortal shock, was going to allow again – again . . .! And I had not even thought about it!'

The door opened and the judge's wife walked in.

She was pale, she was wearing a white *peignoir*, and she made no sound as she walked. Her eyes seemed larger than ever and they were fixed in a gaze which brought shudders to the spine. At least Don Víctor shuddered, and he stepped back in terror, as if in the presence of a ghost. His first thoughts were not for this woman's treachery but for the great danger to which her life was exposed if she were assailed by a strong emotion. She did not look like his wife, she looked like La Traviata in the scene in which she dies singing. The poor old man felt superstitious compassion; that vaporous being which had suddenly appeared before him in silence, walking with the step of a ghost, was something which at that moment he both loved with the love of a father who is afraid for his daughter's life and feared as if it had come from the other world. 'How easy it would be to murder the poor sick child with a word – the poor sick child who was perhaps not responsible for her crime! Oh, no, her he would not kill – not with a dagger, nor with a bullet, nor with thunderous words.'

'Who was it?' asked Ana in a calm voice.

'The canon theologian,' replied Don Víctor, supposing that his wife already knew the answer to her question.

Ana became flustered.

'What did he want – at this time of night?' she asked, hiding her fears.

'What did he want? Political matters. The trouble between the bishop and the civil governor – the business of the elections, which is urgent; in sum, political matters.'

The judge's wife did not insist. She left the room without approaching her husband, nor did he go to her to deposit upon her forehead the kiss with which they always took their leave of each other at night.

Quintanar breathed again when he found himself alone. 'So far so good. He had not given himself away. Anita could not have suspected anything. His conscience was clear, a sign that he had acted aright so far.'

He called for tea, which was his supper on the days when he went hunting and had cold meat for lunch, he ordered the servants to bed, and at half past eleven he tiptoed in his slippers through the gloom – yet without bumping into anything – down into the park, armed with his shotgun. He had loaded it with buckshot.

'Oh yes! The canon theologian, quite unintentionally, had suggested a good idea to him. No bloodshed, eh? Oh, if Don Alvaro returned tonight – he would die! And never mind the consequences. Ana could be filled with terror, she could drop down dead, they could arrest him. No matter what – if Alvaro returned, he would die.' Just as a little earlier Don Víctor's conscience had been clear because he had suppressed his anger in Ana's presence, now he felt pleased with himself because of his decision to kill the thief of his honour if he returned.

The night was dark, the cold intense. He had no alternative but to return to his room for his cloak, thus running the risk of making noise or giving the man time to come and climb the balcony in his absence – but he could not remain there without a cloak, he would be frozen. He hurried to fetch his cloak and, muffled in it, returned to his sentry-post in the arbour, whence he could see the hazy outline of the wall against the black sky and would also be able to see the boudoir window if it were opened to allow Don Alvaro to enter.

He heard the clock strike twelve, one, two – not three, for he must have dozed off, although he denied it to himself. At four he could not bear the cold or resist his need to sleep any longer; delirious, without any awareness of himself or the world around him, bumping into everything, he went up to his room, groped for his bed, undressed mechanically, wrapped himself in the sheets, and a deep, feverish sleep, full of burning ghosts and pitiful monsters, fell upon him.

On the following afternoon, at coffee-time, Mesía, Ronzal, Captain Bedoya and Colonel Fulgosio did not make their usual appearance in the Gentlemen's Club.

Note having duly been taken of which by Foja, the ex-mayor, he exclaimed in mysterious tones:

'Gentlemen, when I say there's a nigger in . . .'

'What nigger?' asked Don Frutos Redondo, the American.

They were – as they always were at this hour – in the room next to the red parlour, or ombre-room.

All the gentlemen surrounded Foja, who added:

'Observe that neither Ronzal nor the captain nor the colonel have come today. I always feared the worst. There's no smoke . . .'

'What smoke?' asked Orgaz senior, who knew a little about the matter.

Orgaz junior, who always gave himself the air of a man who knew a great deal about everything, said:

'No, gentlemen, I tell you there's nothing in it.'

'Well, by your leave, I know that great things are afoot. I know it on good authority. By now Quintanar must have sent his seconds to Don Alvaro.'

'Seconds! Why?' asked Redondo.

'Bah! Don't try to come the little innocent over me. You know only too well why. And, in truth, it was a scandalous state of affairs.'

Joaquín Orgaz defended Don Alvaro.

But Foja was not attacking Mesía, he was attacking Don Víctor for condoning such a disgraceful situation for so long.

'But how can you say he was condoning it? He didn't know a thing. And if he's challenging the man now, it must be because he's found him out at last.'

'Or because he has grown tired of putting up with it.'

'Or perhaps he isn't challenging him at all.'

Discussion of the same subject continued all afternoon. At nightfall Ronzal arrived. At first nobody dared question him, but Foja grew tired of being prudent, patted Blunderbuss on the back and asked:

'Are you one of the seconds?'

'Seconds in what?' said Ronzal with a scowl and a mysterious air, like a man prudent beyond words erecting a wall of ice so as to repel an indiscreet approach.

'One of the seconds in the duel to the death between Mesía and Quintanar.'

'But who told you? In the name . . . I mean – I don't know – I deny it. You are a fool and an idle prattler. Do you think that such serious matters are fit to be talked about in the club?'

'Do you see? Just as I said,' cried Foja in triumph, taking no notice of the insults.

Ronzal denied it and refused to say anything, but it was plain to see that it cost him a great effort to do so.

He kept looking at the clock, and he asked Joaquinito Orgaz, taking him aside but speaking in such a way that all the others could hear:

'Do you know if Don Pedro the horse-breaker has still got any of those sabres . . . ?'

He concluded the sentence in a low voice.

Orgaz did not know. Ronzal grimaced and left the club.

'Good-night, gentlemen.'

'Do you see? Just as I said. There's going to be a duel.'

The gentlemen opened a continuous sitting. The servants lit the gas-lamps, and the afternoon session ran on into the evening one. Some members went away for supper and returned later. By eight o'clock nobody in the club was talking about anything other than the duel. The billiards-players abandoned their cues and came to the hall of lies in search of news; even the men upstairs, in the chamber of crime, who had played on throughout revolutions without appearing to notice that anything was amiss, sent their emissaries down to discover what was happening.

In Vetusta a challenge was one of the most extraordinary occurrences imaginable. At rare intervals young gentlemen would slap each other's faces in the Mall or some other public place, but that was as far as their arguments ever went. Insults never had any consequences. There had never been a shooting-gallery in Vetusta. Years earlier a retired major had tried to earn his living by teaching the art of the sabre. The Young Marquis, Orgaz junior and senior, Ronzal and a few others had begun with great eagerness to allow themselves to be beaten with large sticks, but they had soon tired of it and the major had then been obliged to earn his living by requesting small loans.

Vetustans could only remember two challenges which had reached the duelling-ground. In one of them, many years earlier, Mesía had been involved; Frillity had been one of his opponent's seconds and the only Vetustan to witness the incident.

He had never been persuaded to say what had happened but the fact was that neither Mesía nor his opponent had been confined to bed for a single day after the duel.

The other duel had been between a financial secretary and a cashier, and it had been provoked by the cash-box – whether you dipped your fingers into it, or I mine. Whoever first drew blood would be the victor. The cashier had been scratched on the neck, because the financial secretary had aimed horizontal sabre-blows in the hope of beheading his opponent. And in the annals of Vetusta there were no other challenges which had reached the duelling-ground.

That night, to pass the time away while news came in, there was a lengthy discussion about the legitimacy of this barbarous custom which we had inherited from the Middle Ages.

Orgaz senior, who was something of a scholar although he earned his living as a secretary, affirmed that the duel was a relic of the ordeal.

Don Frutos said that was as may be, but all the ordeals in the world weren't going to make him fight a duel. If he was offended he'd go see the judge, and if there was nothing doing there he'd settle things with a cudgel. 'Being killed by some smart swordsman who's never had to work for his living – my mother's son will never stand for that.'

'None the less,' Orgaz senior said, 'there are certain circumstances – honour, society. Fígaro,[1] you will remember, condemns duelling and yet confesses that he would fight a duel himself if he had to.'

'But I'm not some third-rate barber, sir,' cried Don Frutos, 'I've got something to lose.'

They had to explain who Fígaro was, but even then Don Frutos, sweating from so much argument and vociferation, yelled that in any case anyone who challenged him would get smashed to pulp.

'Well,' said the ex-mayor, 'I stick to justice, a criminal action – the law is categorical.'

'Well,' exclaimed Orgaz senior, coming to his feet and speaking in solemn trembling tones, 'I don't take any notice of that. If the man who challenges me is a skilled swordsman I force him to accept the following conditions for the duel.' (General attention.) 'Two paces apart' (he measures two long strides and places himself in front of Don Frutos, who becomes very serious and draws himself bolt upright), 'one loaded pistol and one unloaded.' (Orgaz pales at the idea that it could happen just as he is describing it.) 'One, two, three' (he claps his hands three times), 'bang! God save whoever He sends the bullet to! That's how I would fight a duel. It isn't a question of skill, it's a question of courage.'

'Bravo, bravo! Hear, hear!' cried a large part of the gathering, as if it were listening to the speech for the first time.

Whenever there was a discussion about duels, Foja, Don Frutos, Orgaz and the other gentlemen said what they said on that day.

It was in vain that the members of the club waited for news. Neither Ronzal nor Fulgosio nor Bedoya appeared there in the course of the evening. It was said that these gentlemen, together with Frillity, were the seconds.

This was true. Crespo had exhorted everyone involved in the sad affair to absolute secrecy, and yet – nobody knew how it had happened, but Ronzal was suspected – the truthful rumour sped around Vetusta. In fact both Ronzal and Petra had been indiscreet. Petra, impelled by revenge and spite, had talked, she had told friends all about her former mistress, 'Why had she left that house? Because . . .' Blunderbuss, puffed up with pride by the honour of being taken into Quintanar's confidence, had been unable to resist the temptation to let his secret slip out. The result was that in all Vetusta nobody was talking about anything else.

The civil governor said in his house that no one must speak about the matter there, for a clear contradiction existed between his duty as an authority and his duty as a gentleman, and he had to turn a deaf ear and a blind eye – and would turn them.

That day went by, and the following day, and still nothing was known.

'Was all the talk about a duel just moonshine?' asked Foja in the Gentlemen's Club.

And then Joaquinito Orgaz finally burst. He knew everything, thanks to the Young Marquis.

'No, no, it was no joke, it was for real. A duel to the death.'

But the seconds had behaved badly. They were incompetent, in spite of all the pretensions of Colonel Fulgosio, who claimed to have the code of honour at his fingertips; and no arms appeared. At first there had been talk of sabres, but no duelling-sabres appeared. Either there were no sabres of this sort in Vetusta or those who owned them were unwilling to lend them. They had fallen back on pistols, but no suitable pistols had appeared, either. 'I think,' Joaquinito added, 'and so does Paco, that this is incredible and that Frillity is trying to stretch things out, in the hope that he might persuade Mesía to leave Vetusta.'

'How unworthy!' Foja cried.

'Well, that was the original solution. It seems – at least this is what they say – that the night after Don Víctor discovered his dishonour, Frillity went to see Mesía and asked him to leave town as soon as possible. Mesía told Paco all about it.'

'Yes, yes, what else?'

'Oh, Mesía naturally objected. He said that Quintanar and all Vetusta might put his departure down to fear. But Frillity's got some influence over Alvaro and he made him give his word of honour that he'd catch the Madrid train the next day. Apparently Quintanar had Alvaro's life in his hands: he could have shot him dead and didn't. And Frillity harped on all this and on the rights of an outraged husband to get Mesía to run away. "It wouldn't be cowardice," he says he said, "it would be doing yourself justice. You deserve death for your treachery, but I am commuting your sentence to exile." '

'That's what Frillity said?'

'That's what he said.'

'Well I never!'

'He's on very close terms with Alvaro, and Alvaro's got a lot of respect for him.'

'Yes, yes, what else?'

'Oh, Alvaro gave him his word. But the following day, yesterday morning, when our Don Juan was packing his bags to leave, Frillity and Ronzal turned up with a challenge. Apparently Don Víctor had called Frillity very early and had made him find Blunderbuss and go with him to challenge Mesía. Frillity had no alternative but to obey Quintanar, because when Quintanar found out that Mesía was planning to escape he threatened to follow him to the end of the world and call him a coward in the newspapers and in the streets – he was furious.'

'Of course, all those plays!'

'And so Frillity had to tell Alvaro to forget his promise and find some seconds.'

'And what did Mesía do?'

'Naturally he dropped his journey and looked around for seconds. He wanted me to be one' (a lie) 'but then, since I'm so friendly with both of them – well, others were looked for, but didn't turn up. Only Fulgosio, who's always happy to be involved in this kind of to-do, and Bedoya, who's a soldier, after all.'

In the main, Joaquinito was well informed. The Young Marquis had gone to see Mesía in his hotel, and had heard all about the affair.

But one detail that Mesía had not mentioned was that he was in great dread: that he was as horrified by the idea of standing in front of Don Víctor with a sword or a pistol in his hand as he was happy to find broken the relationship which would have exhausted what little health he had left and made him look ridiculous in Ana's eyes.

He accepted Frillity's original proposal with alacrity.

'Of course! He ought to go, what right had he to try to kill the man who had spared his life that very morning and whose honour he had stolen? He would go. On the following day, without fail, he would catch the train.'

This was the reply anticipated by Frillity, who knew what to expect from Alvaro's courage.

For he had been a witness of the mysterious duel mentioned by the members of the Gentlemen's Club. Because of a woman, Don Alvaro had been challenged to single combat by an outsider; all the seconds had come from the garrison except Frillity, the only Vetustan present. The duel had been fought with sabres, in a clearing on Montico Hill, a little before nightfall. There, in shirt-sleeves, stood Mesía and his opponent (Frillity remembered it all as if it had happened on the previous day) with their sabres in their hands, both of them pale and shivering with cold and fear. The overcast sky threatened to engulf them in torrents of rain. The two combatants looked at the clouds and Frillity knew what they were hoping for. The single combat commenced and at the first clash of steel there was a crash of thunder and enormous drops of rain began to fall. Mesía and his opponent shook like the branches of the trees as they were buffeted by the wind. So heavy was the downpour that the seconds suspended the duel. It was not resumed. 'They hadn't gone there to fight the elements.'[2] So Mesía emerged safe and sound from his ordeal, and Crespo gave him an implicit assurance that he would not tell anyone about the ridiculous episode or about the cowardice of the Don Juan of Vetusta.

Remembering all this, Frillity treated Mesía like a dog on that memorable night when he told him to go away. But Joaquín Orgaz was right; on the following day Frillity had to inform Mesía that he could forget his promise. Now he should not go. Quintanar was resolved on a duel – he came from Aragon, and would not change his mind.

'I don't know who can have brought about this change in him. Last night he seemed more or less reconciled to a peaceful solution, he was content for you to disappear; yet today, when I went to see him, I found Señor Ronzal by his bedside.'

Ronzal bowed.

Mesía had been packing his underwear into a large trunk. He stopped, his face white.

'So . . .'

'So you must find some seconds.'

It had vexed Frillity to find that, without consulting him, Don Víctor had summoned Ronzal. Quintanar believed in the energy of the deputy for Pernueces and knew that he disliked Mesía. According to the ex-magistrate, he would make a good second. A mistake, according to Frillity.

And, worst of all, Quintanar could not be dissuaded.

'This is not to be postponed by so much as a single day! Since my dishonour has been made public, let its reparation be so too, and terrible and rapid besides.'

'But you've got a fever, you're ill.'

'It matters not. Indeed, so much the better. If you two do not challenge that man, I shall leave my bed and go myself in search of other seconds.'

They had no choice.

With a bad grace, and hiding his dread as best he could, Mesía looked for his two seconds.

It was agreed that the duel would be fought with sabres. But no usable sabres appeared. And difficulties arose about certain other details. A day passed.

The next morning it was agreed that they would fight with pistols. And then Don Víctor formed his plan. He was happy that pistols had finally been chosen.

But no duelling-pistols appeared, either.

Another day passed.

On the following afternoon Don Víctor left his bed after spending sixty hours in it and being feverish for a whole day, impatient at times, anguished at others, but always hiding his feelings in the presence of Ana, who cared for him with diligence.

During those long hours in bed the weakness which had followed the fever had been accompanied by fits of melancholy and religio-philosophical meditation. Don Víctor had felt his spirits failing, not because of concern for his own life, which he did not believe to be in much danger from Don Alvaro, but from fear of remorse. So when he heard that pistols had been decided upon, he resolved not to kill his opponent. 'He would lame him, firing at his legs. He was not likely to be hit by the man, shooting at twenty paces – that could only happen by accident.'

Ana did not suspect anything (for Mesía had kept his word, given to Frillity, that he would write to her saying that he had to go away on a brief but extremely urgent electioneering trip) or, at least, Ana did not suspect that the lives of her husband and her lover were at stake when Don Víctor and Frillity walked out of the park-gate at the time when they always left to go hunting.

Ronzal was waiting in the Calle de Traslacerca. It was a raw morning and the frost on the grass looked like a light fall of snow.

A carriage was waiting on the Santianes road. Inside sat Benítez, Ana's doctor. When Don Víctor saw him he paled, but he showed no other signs of emotion.

After a drive in which hardly a word was spoken they reached the wall of El Vivero. They stepped out of the carriage, walked around the outside of the marquis's estate and entered the oak-wood in which months earlier Don Víctor had searched for his wife with the help of the canon theologian. 'How many things were clear to him now which he had not understood then!' It mattered not. Of the fury which had made havoc in his heart after Don Fermín's nocturnal visit only burnt-out remains were left now. No longer did he hate Don Alvaro, no longer did he think that life was impossible until that man was dead, for philosophy and religion had triumphed in his soul. He was resolved not to kill.

They reached the highest part of the wood, where there was an area of flat ground and a clearing with sufficient room to measure more than thirty paces. These were the conditions which were finally agreed: the two men would stand twenty-five paces apart, each being allowed to advance five and to take aim in the intervals between the three handclaps, intervals which would, however, be very brief ones. The truth of the matter was that Colonel Fulgosio had never been present at a duel fought with pistols (even though he affirmed that he had witnessed plenty of them), Ronzal and Bedoya had never been involved in any kind of duel, Frillity had only seen Mesía's frustrated combat – and so the conditions had been copied by the colonel from a French novel which Bedoya had lent him. The only original aspect of it all was that Fulgosio, swearing that his soldierly honour did not allow him to authorize a sham duel, declared that a pistol-duel, at such a distance, firing on command without taking aim, between two novices – for Mesía was also a novice in pistol-duels – might just as well be fought with guns loaded with cotton wool.

Bedoya remembered that Don Víctor was a good shot, but he did not dare present objections to his own colleague. There were no observations from the opposing party, either.

When Don Víctor and his followers reached the duelling ground, the flat hilltop, they found it empty. Fifteen minutes later among the naked trees appeared Don Alvaro, his seconds, and Don Robustiano Somoza. Mesía was looking handsome; his face was white and he wore an elegant, immaculate, buttoned-up black suit.

Tears sprang to Don Víctor's eyes when he saw his enemy. He would have been happy to shout, I forgive him! I forgive him! like Jesus on the cross. Quintanar was not afraid, but sheer sadness was sapping all his strength, 'how bitter were the ironies of fortune! He, he was going to shoot at that handsome fellow who would have made Ana happy had he won her love ten years earlier! – and then he, Quintanar, would have been a carefree man in the High Court or at La Almunia de Don Godino! The whole business of fighting to the death was absurd. But he had no alternative. The proof of it was that he was being summoned and having the cold pistol placed in his hand.'

Frillity, looking calm because his sense of dignity demanded it, but fearing an accident – fearing that Mesía might find the courage to fire and, also by accident, might hit Víctor – squeezed his friend's hand when he left him at his post of honour.

Seconds and doctors betook themselves a good distance away, for they all feared a stray bullet.

Don Alvaro thought about God, much against his will. This increased his dread; he remembered that he had only experienced such piety during serious illnesses, in the loneliness of his bachelor-bed.

Frillity was astonished by the man's bravery.

Mesía himself could hardly understand how he had brought himself to be there.

As he pondered over this and attempted to aim at Don Víctor without seeing him, without seeing anything, without the strength to pull the trigger, he heard three rapid handclaps and a bang. Quintanar's bullet scorched the dandy's close-fitting trousers.

Mesía suddenly felt strange strength in his heart; it was a robust heart and the blood boiled inside it. His instinct of self-preservation sprang into life. 'He had to defend himself. If the man fired again he was going to be killed; his opponent was Don Víctor, the great huntsman!'

Mesía took five paces forward and aimed. He felt as brave as any man in the world. It was one of his hunches! His hand was steady. He believed he had Don Víctor's head on top of the barrel of his pistol. Gently he squeezed the cold trigger. He thought he had fired the pistol. 'No, he wasn't the one who had fired, it had been his hunch.'

Don Víctor Quintanar was dragging himself over the frosty grass and biting the ground.

Mesía's bullet had entered his bladder, which was full.

This was what the doctors discovered later in the New House, to which the still body of the worthy magistrate was taken as best it could be. Don Víctor lay on the same bed where months earlier he had slept the sweet sleep of a child.

The bed was surrounded by the two doctors, Frillity, who had frozen tears in his eyes, a stupefied Ronzal, and a remorseful Colonel Fulgosio. Bedoya had accompanied Mesía, who was to catch the Madrid train a few hours later – and three days later than Frillity had intended.

In the next room Pepe, the Vegallanas' caretaker, stood open-mouthed in sorrow and astonishment, awaiting orders. He saw Frillity come out, shaking his fists at heaven in the belief that he was alone.

'What's the news, sir? How is the poor lamb?'

Frillity looked at Pepe as if he did not know him, and as if talking to himself he said:

'A full bladder. Peritonitis – of some kind or other. That's what they say.'

'What, sir?'

'No matter – he's going to die!'

Frillity went off to a parlour where the blinds were drawn, to weep alone.

A little later Pepe saw Colonel Fulgosio come out of the room followed by Somoza.

'What about taking him to Vetusta?' the soldier was asking.

'Impossible! Out of the question! What good would it do? He will die this afternoon, for certain.'

Somoza was nearly always wrong, saying his patients would die sooner than they did.

This time he was wrong, too, but he gave his patient longer to live than did Don Alvaro's bullet.

Quintanar died at eleven o'clock in the morning.

The month of May was worthy of its name that year in Vetusta. A rare occurrence!

The eternal clouds of Mount Corfín had discharged all their humours in March and April. The Vetustans came out of doors as Noah's raven[3] might have come out of the Ark, and they could all understand why it had not returned. After two months under water it was so good to see blue skies, breathe fresh air and walk in green meadows spattered with primroses which looked like sparks from the sun!

All Vetusta was out walking.

But Frillity could not persuade Ana to set foot out of doors.

'This is suicide, my child. You know what Benítez said: exercise is indispensable, those nerves of yours won't keep quiet until they're taken outside to get some air and see the sun – come on, Anita, for God's sake, be reasonable, take pity on yourself. We'll go out very early, at daybreak, if you like; the Esplanade is so beautiful at that time of the morning! Or else at nightfall, to breathe fresh air, along one of the roads. For God's sake, my child – you're going to fall ill again!'

'No, I'm not going out,' and Ana moved her head from side to side like a blind woman. 'Please, Don Tomás, don't torture me, don't torture me by insisting so. I'll go out later. I don't know when. The very idea horrifies me now. Oh no, please, no! Please leave me be.'

She pressed her hands together and became more and more agitated, and Frillity had to keep quiet.

Ana had hovered between life and death for a week, had lain in bed for a month until she was out of danger, and had convalesced for two more months, suffering from nervous attacks which had taken strange forms and each of which had seemed like a new illness.

Frillity had told her that Quintanar was wounded, in the marshes at Palomares, that his shotgun had gone off by accident. . . . But Ana, alarmed and guessing the truth, had demanded to be taken to Palomares without delay.

'That's impossible, there aren't any trains until tomorrow.'

'Well a carriage then, a carriage. You're deceiving me; if it were true you'd be at Víctor's side.'

Frillity explained his presence in Vetusta as best he could.

White lies were useless, and Ana made ready to hasten off alone to Víctor. She had to be told a part of the truth: the death of her husband. She wanted to see his body, but she could not move; she fainted, and recovered consciousness in bed. For two days Frillity thought that

Ana believed the misfortune to have been caused by a hunting accident, as he had told her. But she believed the truth. Mesía's absence and Víctor's death explained everything.

One afternoon, three days after the catastrophe, in the absence of Frillity, Anselmo handed his mistress a letter in which Don Alvaro, from Madrid, explained his disappearance and his silence.

When, at nightfall, Crespo entered Ana's bedroom he called to her two, three times in vain. Alarmed, he cried out for a lamp and saw his friend lying on her back as if she were dead, and upon the sheet Mesía's perfumed letter.

A little later, while Benítez brought the judge's wife back to life with anti-spasmodics and prescribed new medicines to combat new perils, complications of the nervous system, Frillity sat in the boudoir reading the letter sent by the man whom, in his own mind, he called the cowardly murderer. After reading the repulsive piece of paper he crumpled it up in his fists, the fists of a farmer, and said in a hoarse voice:

'Idiot! Villain! Pig! Idiot!'

On that piece of paper which smelt of prostitutes Mesía spoke in untimely romantic phrases of his crime, of Quintanar's death, of the blindness of passion. 'He had fled because . . .'

'Because you were afraid of justice and of me, too, you coward!' Frillity muttered.

'He had fled because his remorse had dragged him far from her. But love was telling him to return. Should he return? Did Ana believe he should return? Or should they come together somewhere else – in Madrid, for example?' Everything was false, cold, foolish in that letter written by an egotist incapable of true love for others, and no less incapable of behaving with dignity in the circumstances in which fate and his crimes had placed him.

Ana had not been able to finish reading the letter. She had fallen back upon her pillow as if dying when she saw in that pool of mire the categorical confirmation of all her suspicions; and she could not think about the pettiness of the wretched spirit housed in the graceful body which she had thought she loved, and which her senses had indeed loved in their way. It was not until much later that she thought about this.

In the delirium of the long and serious illness desperately combated by Benítez, Ana's brain was tormented by remorse mixed with the absurd visions of fever.

Again she was afraid of dying, again she was panic-stricken at the prospect of madness, at the terrible dread of losing her reason and knowing that she had lost it, and again this terror which was far worse than fear made her try to rest and follow the orders of her doctor, always cold, always faithful, always attentive, always intelligent.

She spent entire days without a thought for her adultery or for Quintanar. This was at the beginning of her recovery, when her weak body started to feel the love of life, to which it clung like a castaway weary from the struggle against the dark bitter waves of death.

Nourishment and renewed strength revived the phantom of sin. How manifest was her crime! She was damned. That was as clear as the day. But sometimes when Ana meditated on her crime, on her double crime – and above all on Quintanar's death – her remorse, which was something solid in her conscience, a palpable evil, and an evident, defined reason for despair, became confused, as if fog were drifting in front of her, confused with a vague terror much more dreadful than the fear of hell: the terror of madness. Then she could not see her crime so clearly; someone was arguing inside her, inventing sophisms to which there were no answers and which did not relieve the pain of remorse but which did make her doubt everything, doubt whether there were such things as justice, crime, piety, God, logic, soul . . . Ana. 'No, there is nothing,' said the torment in her brain. 'There is nothing but an interplay of pains, a clash of contradictions which can make you suffer for ever. There's no reason why there should be any limits to this torture of your spirit, which doubts everything, which doubts even itself, but which doesn't doubt pain, for this alone reaches into your centre of feeling, that place about which nobody knows anything except that it suffers, yes, since you suffer.'

These logomachies of the sick woman's inner voice were evident truths for her, because everything it said was prompted by what she was experiencing. This is what she thought because it was what she observed inside herself, and she came to believe only in her own pain.

It was a kind of consolation – like breathing pure air, feeling firm ground beneath her feet, coming back into the light – to emerge from this chaos of pain and return to the clarity of life, logic and the order and solidity of the world, even if this also meant returning to the remembrance of an infamous adultery and a deceived husband, struck down by the bullet of a wretched coward who fled from a corpse and had not fled from crime.

And this pleasure, this selfish satisfaction, which she could not avoid, which she felt in spite of the repugnance it caused her to feel it, brought fresh remorse.

She surprised a confused sense of well-being inside herself when logic was working with some efficiency, and when she believed in moral laws and saw that she was a criminal, clearly a criminal, according to principles which her reason respected. This was horrible, but at least it meant that she was standing on firm ground instead of that shifting mass of absurdities, the whims of her mind – instead of that kind of inner earthquake which was the worst thing that it was possible for her feelings to convey to her brain.

Ana explained all this to Benítez as best she could, avoiding references to her remorse.

But he could understand both what she was saying and what she was keeping to herself, and declared that for the moment her principal duty was to free herself from the danger of death.

'Do you want to commit suicide?'

'Oh, no, not that!'

'Well if we aren't going to commit suicide we must take care of our body. And yet again, bodily health requires the exact opposite of what you are doing. You, madam, believe that it is your duty to torture yourself by recalling and loving what has been – and hating what should not have been. All this would be very well if you had strength enough to bear such a hurly-burly in your mind. You have not. You need oblivion, peace, inner silence, conversation with the world and with the new spring which has come to help us to live. I promise you that the day when I see you out of all danger, safe and sound, I shall say, if you like: Anita, now you are healthy enough to start to torture yourself.'

Frillity spoke to the same effect.

And nobody else spoke, because Anselmo hardly knew how to speak, Servanda came and went like a walking statue, and no other Vetustans had set foot in Ozores Mansion since Don Víctor's death.

They would not set foot there. Vetusta the noble was scandalized, horrified. Behind looks of hypocritical compunction the worthy Vetustans concealed from each other the intimate pleasure which that great scandal, just like a novel, gave them, something to interrupt the eternal monotony of the sad city. Very few of them showed that they were pleased about what had happened. It was a scandal! Adultery, discovered! A duel! A husband, an ex-magistrate of the Provincial Court, killed by a pistol bullet in the bladder! In Vetusta there had never been any shooting, not even in times of revolution. The conquest of the inalienable rights of man had not cost anybody there so much as a rifle-cartridge. Mesía's bullet, for which the judge's wife was to blame, broke the peaceful tradition of silent, well-mannered, prudent crime. Many illustrious ladies of La Encimada and La Colonia were known to be deceiving, or to have deceived, or to be about to deceive their respective husbands – but without any shooting! The envy which hitherto had disguised itself as admiration now came out into the open, displaying all its yellow flesh. And it became clear that the judge's wife's beauty and virtuous reputation were secretly envied not only by Visitación Olías and Obdulia Fandiño and the Baroness of the Floating Debt, but also by the civil governor's wife and the Páez girl and Señora de Carraspique and Señora de Rianzares and the marchioness's servant girls and the servant girls of the entire aristocracy, and all the middle classes and even working-class women; and also – who would have thought it possible! – by the marchioness herself, Doña Rufina, that lady who was so liberal and who absolved herself with such magnanimity of the peccadilloes of her youth, and of other more recent ones.

All the women of Vetusta spoke ill of Ana Ozores, and she was even envied and flayed by many men with souls like those of the women. In the chapter house Gloucester and, by his side, Don Custodio spoke of scandal, hypocrisy, immorality, Babylonian perversions; in the Gentlemen's Club Ronzal, Foja, Orgaz senior and Orgaz junior scooped up mud with both hands and poured it upon the dead honour of the poor widow, buried between four walls.

A few hours after the catastrophe became known in town, Obdulia Fandiño swept out of her house wearing her largest hat and her most clinging skirt and her most rustling petticoats, to breathe the air of slander, to catch a whiff of scandal, to savour the after-taste of crime being passed from mouth to mouth like a bon-bon which everybody was licking, careful to hide the pleasure afforded by its sticky sweetness.

'Do you see?' said Obdulia's looks of triumph. 'All we women are the same.'

But her lips said:

'Poor Ana. Lost beyond hope! How can she find the face to present herself in public now? She was so romantic! She had to make even something like that end up in gunfire and shooting, so that everyone should find out about it.'

'Do you remember her little walk on Good Friday?' asked the baron.

'Yes – just compare. Who would have thought it!'

'I would!' exclaimed the marchioness. 'I never liked the look of that immodesty – going along showing her naked feet. *Malorum signum.*'

'Yes, *malorum signum*,' repeated the baroness, as if she were saying *et cum spiritu tuo.*

'And, above all, the scandal!' added Doña Rufina with indignation, after a pause.

'The scandal!' repeated the choir.

'The imprudence, the clumsiness!'

'Yes! Yes!'

'Poor Don Víctor!'

'Yes, poor man, and God forgive him – but he deserved it.'

'Every bit of it.'

'Really, to have such a close friendship . . .'

'Was scandalous.'

'It was . . .'

'Nauseating!'

Thus spake the Marquis de Vegallana, all of whose illegitimate children lived in remote country villages.

Obdulia witnessed these conversations as if they signalled the triumph of her own reputation. She had never caused such scandal. All Vetusta knew about Obdulia – but she had never caused any scandal.

Yes, yes, the scandal was the worst of it, but that disastrous duel was another complication. Mesía had run away and was living in Madrid. There was already talk of his renewed affair with the minister's wife from Palomares. Vetusta had lost two of its most important personages – all because of Ana and her blundering.

Vetusta punished her by breaking off all relations. Nobody went to see her, not even the Young Marquis, who had thought of going along to pick up the inheritance left him by Mesía.

The formula for the rupture, for the *cordon sanitaire*, was:

'She must be isolated! Have absolutely nothing to do with the Italian dancer's daughter!'

The honour of having resuscitated this expression belonged to the Baroness de la Barque.

If Ripamilán could have left his house he would not have respected the great world's cruel resolution. But poor Don Cayetano had gone to his bed never to rise from it again. There he lived, always contented, for two years more.

He ended his pilgrimage on earth singing and reciting poems by Villegas.[4]

So the judge's wife did not have to shut the door of Ozores Mansion in anybody's face, as she had promised herself to do. She was known to be very ill, but even the most charitable Vetustans confined themselves to asking the servants and Benítez after the patient, whom they called 'that unfortunate woman'.

Ana preferred to be left alone and would have demanded to be left alone had Vetusta not anticipated her desires. But when, during her convalescence, she again thought about the world around her and about the future, she felt the ice on every side and tasted the bitter taste of universal wickedness. 'She was abandoned by everybody! She deserved it, but still, how wicked were all those Vetustans whom she had always scorned, even when they had flattered her and fawned on her!'

Quintanar's widow decided to follow Benítez's advice as far as she could. She gave the least possible thought to her remorse, her loneliness, and her sad future, black through and through.

As soon as she was strong enough she started crocheting and knitting and attempting with an iron will to find some interest in these occupations.

She hated all books now, of whatever sort they might be, for thinking only made her remember her misfortunes and she must therefore try to avoid using her mind. Sometimes she was successful. At such times she imagined that the best part of her soul was asleep, but that there was enough of her spirit left awake to make her as much of a woman as all the others.

Now she could understand those eternal afternoons which Anselmo spent in the courtyard, squatting and stroking the cat. Just being alive, keeping quiet, doing no more than feeling well and letting the hours slip by – this was something, maybe it was the best thing. It must be the path to death. And Ana was walking this path unafraid. No, death did not frighten her. Indeed, what she most wanted was to die without losing herself among the crazy imaginings of her enfeebled brain.

When Benítez visited Ana during these sad, silent, calm spells, she would ask him, smiling like a woman on her death-bed:

'Are you pleased with me?'

And with another cold sad smile the doctor would reply:

'Well, Ana, I am pleased that you are being obedient.'

But when he was alone with Crespo he would say:

'I don't like the look of Ana.'

'I often find her in a very tranquil state.'

'That, precisely, is why I don't like the look of her. She must be made to amuse herself.'

Frillity decided to make her amuse herself.

This was why he begged her to walk out with him when May came – that cloudless, warm, dry, smiling May so seldom enjoyed in Vetusta.

But since he was unsuccessful, since Anita implored him, clasping her hands, to be left alone and quiet in her house, Crespo determined to amuse her there.

'If only he could arouse in her a fondness for trees and flowers!'

He couldn't lose anything by trying.

To humour him, Ana smiled and listened with her eyes fixed on his face, and went down into the park for practical lessons. Frillity became enthusiastic, and one afternoon he related the history of his great triumph, the acclimatization in Vetusta of *Eucalyptus globulus*.

During his friend's illness, having no faith in the zeal of Anselmo and Servanda, he had installed himself in Ozores Mansion, without asking for permission to do so. He had moved from the inn where he had slept since 1860 to the ground floor of the great house. Ana's boudoir and bedroom were above the room chosen by Frillity. There, making as little fuss as possible, and without disturbing anybody, he had installed himself to watch over the judge's wife and go to her if she was in the slightest danger, continuing to eat at the inn, but sleeping in Ozores Mansion.

Ana had remained ignorant of this until one day, when she was convalescing, she complained of her loneliness. She confessed that she sometimes felt afraid at night. And turning as red as a tomato the worthy Frillity made her the timid revelation that more than a month and a half earlier he had taken the liberty of coming to sleep in the room under hers and ordering the servants not to say anything to their mistress.

Once she knew this, Anita felt less lonely during her sorrowful nights. Now that his presence was no longer a secret, Frillity took care to cough so that Ana should hear him, as if to say, 'Don't be afraid, I'm down here.'

But since malice is omniscient, Vetusta also found out about Frillity's move. It was said that he had gone to live as a lodger in Ana's house, in that noble pile Ozores Mansion.

And some said:

'It must be an act of charity. The poor woman must be hard up, and with Frillity's help she will be able to rub along.'

The great world counted on its fingers the money which Anita could have been left. 'She couldn't have been left anything to speak of.'

'She hasn't got any income of her own.'

'Her husband's income from his property in Aragon doesn't belong to her.'[5]

'She can't have applied for her widow's pension.'

'That would be ignominious!'

'Yes indeed! Claiming a widow's pension – she, the cause of the worthy magistrate's death!'

'It would be despicable.'

'Despicable.'

'And it isn't right for her to be living in Ozores Mansion.'

'Of course not, because although her husband gave it to her, so they say, he bought it from Ana's aunts – and not with money earned since the marriage but with the proceeds of the sale of some lands in La Almunia de Don Godino.'

'Be all that as it may, she should not be living in that house.'

'So nobody knows what she's living on.'

'She's living on what I've just said – Frillity staying in the house and paying through the nose.'

'That's right, because he's a crackbrain without any scruples – but he's a decent sort.'

'Decent – relatively speaking,' said the marquis, who was acquiring a severe morality and a temper as black as coal, as his gout became more bothersome.

Remembering the participle which had been so effective on another occasion, he summarized with the words:

'At all events, for him to be living under the same roof which shelters his best friend's unfaithful widow is – is nauseating!'

Nobody dared deny it.

All the scruples which exercised the Vegallana coterie had also tormented the judge's wife. As soon as she felt strong enough to go out into the garden she summoned courage to tell Frillity what had been torturing her for some time.

'I would like to leave this house. This house, strictly speaking, does not belong to me. It belongs to Víctor's heirs – to his sister Doña Paquita, who has children, and . . .'

Frillity was furious. What was the meaning of this? He had already arranged everything. He had written to Doña Paquita in Saragossa, and she was satisfied with the property at La Aluminia de Don Godino. 'It was more than enough for her. The house belonged to Ana both legally and morally.'

Ana surrendered, because she no longer had enough energy to oppose a strong will.

She was more resolute in refusing to sign the documents which Frillity presented to her when he suggested that she apply for her widow's pension.

'Not that, not that, Don Tomás. I'd sooner starve!'

Indeed, hunger and bleak, oppressive poverty faced the widow if she did not claim her rights.

Ana said that she preferred to apply for the orphan's allowance due to her as the daughter of a soldier.

'You can forget about that. It can't be worth anything. I don't know if it would be possible, anyway.'

Frillity forged Ana's signature, not without a blush. A few months later he presented her with the first instalment of her widow's pension.

Her need was such, it being impossible to find elsewhere enough money to live, that after weeping and refusing a hundred times she accepted the wretched pension and henceforth signed the documents herself.

Both Benítez and Frillity saw unhappy symptoms in this behaviour. 'Her will is dying,' thought Crespo. 'In former times she would have preferred to go begging. Now she gives in, to avoid having to struggle.'

Tears rolled down his cheeks.

'If only I were rich – but I'm not, I'm so poor.'

'And', he added, 'of course it isn't shameful to collect that pittance. It seems so to her – but it isn't. That money belongs to her.'

This was Ana's life.

Once she was out of danger Benítez made fewer calls on her.

Servanda and Anselmo were faithful. Perhaps they were fond of their mistress, but they were incapable of showing it. They served and obeyed her like shadows. The cat was better company.

Frillity was her constant friend, her companion in sadness.

He spoke little.

But it comforted her to think, 'Frillity's here.'

By slow degrees good health again took possession of Ana's beautiful body.

And with some pangs of conscience she began to feel a new interest in life and a desire to be active. The day came when it was no longer enough to vegetate by Frillity's side, watching him sow seeds and plant seedlings in the garden and listening to his apologies for the eucalyptus.

She had promised herself not to leave home. But it was now beginning to seem like a narrow, cramped prison.

One morning she awoke thinking that she had not fulfilled her religious obligations that year. And now she could leave her gloomy old house to go to mass. Yes, in future she would go to mass, wearing a thick veil, very early in the morning, in the Chapel of the Victory, which was near her house.

She would also go to confession.

Neither full of faith nor empty of it, in the habit of not thinking about those mighty matters which turned her crazy, Anita Ozores resumed her religious practices, swearing that she would never again be overcome by that false mysticism which now filled her with shame. 'The vision of God, St Teresa . . . all that had passed away never to return. She was no longer tortured by the terror of hell, although she considered herself damned because of her crime; nor was she comforted by those outbursts of ideal love which in former times had given her clear revelations of the divine and the supernatural.'

Now there was none of that; just the need to flee from pain and thought. But that mechanical piety, praying and hearing mass like all the other women, seemed right, it seemed to be the kind of religion which was compatible with the apathy in her soul. What was more, although she did not realize it, this commonplace religion (as she called it in her own mind) gave her an excuse to break her promise never to leave the house.

October came, and one afternoon when the south wind was blowing, languid and warm, Ana, dressed all in black, with her veil drawn over her face, left Ozores Mansion and walked into the silent, solitary cathedral. The divine office had finished.

A few canons and beneficiaries were in their confessionals scattered in the side-chapels and between the columns in the apsidal retrochoir.

How long it was since she had last been here!

Like a woman returning to her mother-country Ana felt tender tears in her eyes. But how sad was everything the cathedral was telling her as it spoke with its vaults, its columns, its glass, its nave, its aisles, its chapels – as it spoke to Ana's memory with everything it contained!

Its singular smell, unlike all others – a fresh smell, intimate and voluptuous – reached into her soul. It was like silent music which could find its way into the heart without passing through the ears.

'Oh, if only faith would be reborn! If only she could weep like Mary Magdalene at the feet of Jesus!'

For the first time after so long she heard in her head that explosion which always seemed like a supernatural voice, and deep inside her body she felt that upsurge of tenderness which rose to her throat and threatened delightful strangulation. Tears welled to her eyes and without another thought she walked into the dark chapel where the canon theologian had so often spoken to her of heaven and of love between souls.

'What had brought her here? She did not know. She had been going to confess with any available priest and without knowing how it had happened she now found herself within a couple of paces of the confessional of her elder brother, her soul brother, slandered by everybody because of her, slandered by her, too, when, prompted by the sophisms of that foul passion which had blinded her, she had imagined that his affection was carnal love, love like that of the infamous Alvaro, whereas maybe it was a pure sentiment which her own foulness had prevented her from understanding.

'Resuming their friendship – was it just a dream? Was the impulse which had cast her into that chapel a voice from on high or a whim caused by her hysteria, by that accursed illness which was sometimes her most intimate desires and thoughts – was sometimes Ana herself?' With all her heart she begged God, Whom at that moment she thought she could see, that the voice should have been His, that the canon theologian should be the soul brother in whom she had believed for so long, and not the lascivious philanderer portrayed by the infamous Mesía. Ana prayed with fervour as she had prayed in times of impassioned piety; she believed it possible to come back out of the limbo of that spiritual somnolence, which was worse than hell itself, to faith and to the love of God and of life. She believed that she could save herself by clinging to the ledge of that sacred box which knew so many of her dreams and sorrows.

The dim light from the aisle and the mysterious yellow gleams of the lamp in the chapel mingled on the anaemic face of the Christ on the altar, as always sad and pale, its life concentrated in those glass eyes which reflected an unchanging eternal idea. The chapel was occupied by four or five black shapes. A pious woman was whispering in the confessional, making a sound like the droning of flies as they wander through the air on a summer day.

The canon theologian was in his usual place.

As soon as the judge's wife came into the chapel he recognized her, in spite of her veil. He had been listening with scant attention to the penitent's chatter and looking in the direction of the railing at the entrance; suddenly that familiar beloved shape appeared, as in a dream. Her figure, every part of her outline, her genuflexion before the altar, other signs which only he could remember and recognize, cried like an explosion inside his brain:

'It's Ana!'

The pious woman behind the grating was still mumbling her sins. The canon could not hear her, he could only hear the roaring of his passion.

When the pious woman fell silent the priest returned to reality, and absolved her of her sins like a blessing-machine, and with the same hand beckoned another woman to the grating.

Ana had decided to go to the grating too, lift her veil before the network of oblique laths, and through those holes beg for the forgiveness of God and of her soul brother, and if forgiveness was not possible beg for penance without forgiveness, beg for the return of her faith, lost or sleeping or broken, she did not know which, beg for her faith even if it brought the dread of hell back with it. She wanted to weep there, where she had wept so often, sometimes with bitterness, sometimes smiling with pleasure between her tears; she wanted to rediscover the canon theologian of those days when she had believed him to be an emissary of God. She wanted faith, she wanted charity – and afterwards the punishment of her sins, if she deserved any more punishment than that darkness and that faintness of soul.

Every so often a rasping noise came from the confessional, as if its bones were creaking.

The canon theologian gave another absolution and beckoned to another pious woman. The chapel was emptying. Four or five silent absolved black shapes left at intervals. At last, the judge's wife, upon the altar platform, was left alone with the vicar-general, inside his confessional.

It was late now. The cathedral was empty. Night was beginning in it.

Ana, hardly able to breathe, awaited the sign calling her to the grating.

But the confessional was silent. The hand did not appear and the wood no longer creaked.

The wooden Jesus, with its glossy stare and its pale lips slightly parted, seemed to be overcome by terror, as if it were awaiting some imminent tragic scene.

Confronted by this silence, Ana felt a strange dread.

Seconds, long minutes went by, and still the hand did not beckon. The judge's wife rose from her knees with the nervous courage which came to her in great crises, and she ventured a step towards the confessional.

And the dark box creaked loud, and from its centre sprang a tall black figure. By the light of the lamp Ana saw a pale face and eyes which stung like fire, staring in bewilderment like the eyes of the Christ on the altar.

The canon theologian stretched out an arm and stepped towards the judge's wife, as if to murder her. In horror she backed away until she stumbled against the altar platform. She tried to cry out, call for help, but she could not speak. She fell to the boards where she sat with her mouth agape, her eyes filled with fear and her hands held out towards her enemy. Her terror told her that he was about to kill her.

The canon theologian stopped, lowered his arms and held them in front of his body, one wrist over the other. He could not talk; nor did he wish to talk. His whole body was shaking, again he stretched his arms towards Ana, he took another step forwards – and then digging his finger-nails into his neck he turned on his heel as if he were going to collapse, and on weak, wavering legs stumbled out of the chapel. When he was in the retrochoir he gathered strength from despair, and although he could see nothing he managed not to bump into the columns; he reached the sacristy without falling or even staggering.

Overcome by terror Ana fell forwards upon the black-and-white marble floor, unconscious.

The cathedral was empty. The shadows of the columns and of the vaults were glooming together, leaving it in darkness.

Celedonio, the tall, scrawny, effeminate acolyte, in his short, filthy cassock, was shuffling from chapel to chapel, locking gates and rattling his bunch of keys.

He came to the canon theologian's chapel and slammed the gate.

After locking it he fancied that he had heard something inside the chapel. He pressed his face to the railing and peered in, scanning the gloom. He thought he could see under the lamp a shadow larger than the one usually there.

He redoubled his attention and heard a murmur, something like a feeble moan, like a sigh.

He opened the gate, walked in, and recognized the judge's wife, lying there unconscious.

A wretched desire stirred in Celedonio: a perversion of his perverted lust. To enjoy a strange pleasure, or perhaps to discover whether he would enjoy it, he bent over and brought his vile face close to the face of the judge's wife and kissed her mouth.

Ana returned to life, overcome by nausea and tearing at the mists of delirium.

For she thought that she had felt on her lips the cold and slimy belly of a toad.

NOTES

I

1 (p. 22) *Wamba*. A bell named after a Visigoth king of Spain, who reigned from 672 to 680.

2 (p. 29) *the age of thirty*. Thirty is the youngest age at which a man can be made canon theologian.

3 (p. 32) *the September Revolution*. For this and other historical references see the Introduction to this translation.

4 (p. 33) *distributive injustice*. One of the two categories into which Aristotle divided justice was 'distributive justice'.

5 (p. 33) *Ecbatana*. A city in ancient Persia, said to have contained a palace surrounded by seven concentric walls of different colours.

6 (p. 34) *Amerigo Vespuccis*. Men who had emigrated to America and returned to Spain with fortunes. Amerigo Vespucci (1451–1512), an Italian adventurer, gave his name to the New World.

7 (p. 35) *King Bermudo*. King of Asturias (788–91).

8 (p. 35) *King Fruela*. King of Asturias (757–68).

9 (p. 35) *epanadiplosis*. A rhetorical figure: a phrase which begins and ends with the same word.

10 (p. 35) *sunt lacrymae rerum*. Virgil, *Aeneid*, I, 462 (Saturnino, too clever by half, misspells *lacrimae*): 'There are tears for our miseries.' In Spain these words have often been believed to mean 'Even objects join us in our sorrow'; Saturnino seems to share this misconception.

11 (p. 37) *Carmelite garb*. Many devout Spanish lay women wore a modified form of religious habit.

12 (p. 40) *rigadoon*. An old-fashioned dance even in late nineteenth-century Spain. Waltzes and polkas had become popular in the course of the century, although they were considered to be unseemly and even indecent by some people.

13 (p. 40) *'Casta diva'*. The well-known aria from *Norma* (1831) by Vicenzo Bellini. Norma prays to the moon for peace between Gaul and Rome.

14 (p. 40) *'Spirto gentil'*. Another popular aria, from *La Favorite* (1840) by Gaetano Donizetti. Fernando sings of his ideal love for Leonora.

15 (p. 40) *'Santo fuerte'*. A Spanish setting of the Trisagion: 'Sanctus Deus, Sanctus fortis, Sanctus immortalis, miserere nobis.' In the Roman Catholic Church it is sung during the Veneration of the Cross on Good Friday.

16 (p. 41) *Memento homo*. Saturnino remembers the words pronounced by priests on Ash Wednesday, 'Memento homo quia pulvis es et in pulverem reverteris', which recall the words spoken by God to Adam after original sin (Genesis 3:19).

17 (p. 41) *the new man*. See, for example, 3 John 3, and the Epistles of Paul.

18 (p. 41) *the soul grows older*. Lucretius, in Book III of *De rerum natura* (see note 10 to Chapter IX), argues that the soul ages and perishes with the body.

19 (p. 42) *the proverbial Tostado*. Alonso de Madrigal, Bishop of Avila (1400–54), 'El Tostado', famous for his erudition and scholarly productiveness.

20 (p. 42) *Lovelace*. The libertine hero of Samuel Richardson's novel *Clarissa* (1747–8).

II

1 (p. 48) *A whiff of . . .* Don Cayetano seems to be quoting from a translation of Mozart's *Don Giovanni*. In Act I, Scene 2, Giovanni exclaims as Doña Elvira enters, 'Zitto! mi pare sentir odor di femina!'

2 (p. 49) *Garcilaso . . . Meléndez Valdés . . . Inarco Celenio*. Garcilaso de la Vega (1503–36) renovated the Spanish poetic tradition by the use of Italian models. Juan Meléndez Valdés (1754–1817) and Inarco Celenio (pseudonym of Nicolás Fernández de Moratín, 1737–80) were two prominent Spanish poets of the eighteenth century, much influenced by French classicism.

3 (p. 49) *Bilbilis*. Roman Calatayud, Don Cayetano's home town in Aragon.

4 (p. 49) *laudatores temporis acti*. Horace,

Ars poetica, 173: 'inclined to praise times gone by'.

5 (p. 50) *versate manu.* Horace, *Ars poetica,* 268–9: 'Vos exemplaria Graeca/Nocturna versate manu, versate diurna' ('Thumb well by night and day Greek models').

6 (p. 50) *basil-bush.* Don Cayetano misquotes the first two lines of *Cantilena VII* by Esteban Manuel de Villegas (1589–1669), a famous Spanish imitator of the classics.

7 (p. 51) *vita proba est.* Martial, *Epigrammata,* I, 5: 'The pages which I have written are lascivious, but my life is chaste.'

8 (p. 52) *Les Enfants d'Édouard.* Manuel Bretón de los Herreros's play *Los hijos de Eduardo* (1835) was a Spanish adaptation of the French play (1833), which was in turn based upon Shakespeare's *Richard III.*

9 (p. 53) *the sixth commandment.* 'Thou shalt not commit adultery.' More bluntly in Spanish catechisms, 'No fornicar.' The numbering of the Commandments is different in the *Book of Common Prayer,* and for Anglicans this is the seventh commandment.

10 (p. 54) *Don Rodrigo Calderón.* A notorious intriguer at the court of Philip III. He was toppled from his high position, tortured and executed in 1621.

11 (p. 60) *Berruguete.* Alonso Berruguete (1480–1561), famous painter and sculptor. Palma Artela and Grijalte are fictional inventions, although their names seem to have been suggested by those of Balsameda and Giralte, minor sculptors who worked on the cathedral of Oviedo.

12 (p. 61) *Veremundo.* A latinization of 'Bermudo' (see Chapter I, note 7).

13 (p. 62) *Churrigueresque.* A late and ornate development of Spanish baroque architecture, named after the sculptor and architect José Churriguera (1650–1725).

III

1 (p. 71) *Ecco ridente in cielo.* The serenade at the beginning of Rossini's *The Barber of Seville* (1816). 'Lindoro' (really Count Almaviva) sings to the young Rosina, who is destined, however, to marry her guardian Bartolo, a feeble-minded old fogy. Lindoro later succeeds in capturing Rosina's heart and after much intrigue involving Figaro, the barber, they marry.

The reader is reminded of the parallels between Rosina and Ana at the end of the novel, when Don Víctor identifies himself with Bartolo (Chapter XXIX, note 6).

2 (p. 73) *Pylades.* In Greek legend the inseparable friend of Orestes.

3 (p. 76) *Justice Without Revenge. El castigo sin venganza* is one of the 'honour plays' written by the founder of the Spanish theatre of the Golden Age, Félix Lope de Vega Carpio (1562–1635). Honour was an important theme in the Spanish theatre of the seventeenth century although not, as Don Víctor thinks, the only or even the most important one.

4 (p. 76) *The Physician of His Own Honour. El médico de su honra* by Pedro Calderón de la Barca (1600–81).

5 (p. 77) *décimas. Décimas* (stanzas of ten octosyllabic lines rhyming ABBAACC-DDC), like the other verse forms mentioned a little later, *redondillas* (stanzas of four lines rhyming ABBA) and *quintillas* (stanzas of five lines rhyming ABABA, AABBA, etc.), were considered by Golden Age playwrights to be particularly suitable for dramatic monologues.

6 (p. 78) *Nimrod.* The 'mighty hunter before the Lord' (Genesis 10:9).

IV

1 (p. 79) *Vauban's art.* Sébastien le Prestre de Vauban (1633–1707) was a celebrated French military engineer.

2 (p. 79) *Capua.* A principal town of ancient Italy, proverbial in Roman times for luxury and dissipation.

3 (p. 81) *Spanish Englishwoman. La española inglesa* is one of Cervantes's *novelas ejemplares,* or exemplary tales.

4 (p. 82) *Saint-Simonian.* The school founded by Henri de Saint-Simon (1760–1825) held that the state should be the sole proprietor and should be governed by a scientific meritocracy.

5 (p. 83) *Poussin.* Nicolas Poussin (1594–1665), French painter.

6 (p. 84) *Ramayana.* The ancient Indian epic, 48,000 lines long.

7 (p. 88) *an omnilateral and harmonic education.* Characteristic jargon of the *krausistas,* the Spanish followers of the German idealist philosopher Karl Christian Friedrich Krause (1781–1832).

8 (p. 89) *'Oh, procul . . .!'* Don Carlos misquotes Virgil, *Aeneid*, VI, 258: 'Procul, o procul este, profani' ('Hence, o hence, ye that are uninitiated').

9 (p. 89) *Theocritus, Bion and Moschus.* Ancient Greek bucolic poets.

10 (p. 92) *'Tolle, lege'.* St Augustine, *Confessions*, VIII, xii: 'Take and read.'

11 (p. 93) *The Genius of Christianity. Génie du christianisme, ou beautés de la religion chrétienne* (1802, first translated into Spanish in 1806) was Chateaubriand's exaltation of Christianity on aesthetic grounds, much praised for its exquisite style.

12 (p. 93) *The Martyrs.* Chateaubriand's prose epic *Les Martyrs, ou le triomphe de la religion chrétienne* (1809, first translated into Spanish in 1816). It is set in the third century. Eudore, a young Greek Christian, loves a pagan girl, Cymodocée, the daughter of the priest Demodocus. Eudore tells her the story of his life: he had become a soldier and a libertine but later repented and regained his faith. Cymodocée falls in love with Eudore and becomes a Christian. The lovers are separated but meet again in Rome, where Eudore is condemned to the lions. They die together in the arena.

13 (p. 93) *Spanish Parnassus. El parnaso español* (nine volumes, 1768–78), an anthology of Spanish poetry edited by Juan José López de Sedano. This and other poems attributed in it to Fray Luis de León, the sixteenth-century religious poet, are now considered not to be his work.

14 (p. 94) *St John of the Cross.* The sixteenth-century Spanish mystic's *Cántico espiritual* is not a mere 'poetic version' of the Song of Songs but an intense and powerful evocation of mystical experience with the help of some of the imagery from the Song of Songs.

jungen Werthers (1774) was much translated and very popular in Spain in the early nineteenth century.

5 (p. 115) *bandit chiefs.* Ripamilán is thinking about *Don Juan Tenorio* (1844) by José Zorrilla y Moral (1817–93) and *El trovador* (1836) by Antonio García Gutiérrez (1813–84). In Chapter XVI Ana goes to a performance of the former play.

6 (p. 115) *Maidens Choosing. El sí de las niñas* (1805) was a popular comedy by Leandro Fernández de Moratín (1760–1828), in which the heroine rejects an arranged marriage and chooses her own husband.

7 (p. 116) *Carlos Latorre.* Generally hailed as the greatest Spanish actor of his time (1799–1851).

8 (p. 117) *Sancho Ortiz and Don Gutierre Alonso.* The protagonists of the Golden Age plays *La estrella de Sevilla* (then attributed to Lope de Vega) and *El médico de su honra* (by Calderón).

9 (p. 118) *Manriques or Tenorios.* Ripamilán is referring to the protagonists of the two Romantic plays to which he has alluded a little earlier (see note 5 above).

10 (p. 118) *Matanzas.* A port in Cuba, then still a Spanish colony.

11 (p. 119) *Ethelwina. Etelvina o Historia de la baronesa de Castle Acre* (1805?), a novel by an anonymous author, presented as a translation from an English original.

12 (p. 120) *La Almunia de Don Godino.* Víctor's home town in Aragon.

13 (p. 120) *aurea mediocritas.* Horace, *Odes*, II, 10, 5.

14 (p. 121) *her aunts.* A presiding magistrate was not allowed to serve in a province where any of his relations resided.

15 (p. 123) *Jealousy the Greatest Monster . . . El mayor monstruo los celos*, another Calderonian honour play.

V

1 (p. 106) *the Scottish school.* The school of common-sense philosophy founded by Thomas Reid (1710–96). It rejected sceptical empiricism.

2 (p. 107) *a Vespucci.* See note 6 to Chapter I.

3 (p. 108) *Las Novedades.* One of the principal Spanish daily newspapers of the time, of liberal tendencies.

4 (p. 109) *Werther.* Goethe's famous sentimental love-story *Die Leiden des*

VI

1 (p. 124) *the ombre-room.* Ombre is a card-game of the whist family, of Spanish origin although popular in England in the eighteenth century. It is a game for four players but, since the dealer does not take part in the actual play, only three of them are involved in it at any one time. One player attempts to defeat the other two, who work together; if he fails he is said to be given *codille. Sans prendre*

is the term for playing without drawing cards from stock.

2 (p. 124) *toga virilis*. The *toga praetexta* was worn by Roman males until they reached maturity, when they put on the *toga virilis*.

3 (p. 124) *the chamber of crime*. Gaming (the playing for money of games in which skill is not involved) was prohibited in Spain.

4 (p. 125) *monte*. The forbidden game played upstairs, in the 'chamber of crime': a card-game of chance, played for high stakes.

5 (p. 126) *temple . . . rivers of blood*. An ironical echo of biblical passages such as Psalms 79: 1–3, Matthew 23: 34–5 and 1 Corinthians 3: 17.

6 (p. 126) *Sagunto . . . Covadonga . . . 1808*. The town of Sagunto, in eastern Spain, is known for the long and noble resistance of its inhabitants against Hannibal during the Second Punic War (219–218 B.C.). Pelayo the Goth and his Asturian followers – said to be the only inhabitants of the Iberian peninsula not to fall to the invading Moors – are supposed to have taken refuge in the cave of Covadonga and used it as the base for the Christian reconquest of the peninsula. In 1808 there were several popular uprisings in Spain against the country's French rulers, giving rise to the Peninsular War and the departure of the French.

7 (p. 127) *Alcubilla*. The common name for the monumental *Diccionario de la administración española* (five volumes, 1858–62, with subsequent yearly supplements) by Marcelo Martínez Alcubilla.

8 (p. 128) *Metz*. Metz capitulated in 1870.

9 (p. 130) *Farneses or Spinolas*. Alexander Farnese (1545–92) was a famous Italian military commander who served Philip II and became governor-general of the Netherlands. Ambrose Spinola (1569–1630) was another Italian general, who distinguished himself in the service of Spain in the Netherlands and in Lombardy.

10 (p. 131) *Risum teneatis*. Horace, *Ars poetica*, 5. 'Could you contain your laughter?'

11 (p. 133) *Flórez Estrada*. Alvaro Flórez Estrada (1769–1853), influential Spanish political economist.

12 (p. 134) *Zamacois, Luján, the younger Romea*. Ricardo Zamacois (1850–88),

Juan José Luján (1831–89), and Julián Romea y Parra (1848–1903).

13 (p. 135) *Bell of Huesca*. According to Spanish legend, King Ramiro II of Aragón, wanting in 1136 to teach rebellious nobles a lesson, told them that with their aid he was going to make a bell which would be heard throughout the kingdom. He had fifteen of them secretly beheaded in the city of Huesca and brought the others to see the heads arranged in a circle, with one hanging from a rope in the middle. A painting of the scene by José Casado del Alisal (1832–86) was well known. But it is more likely that Alas was thinking of *La campana de Huesca* (1852) by Antonio Cánovas del Castillo (1828–97). After writing this novel Cánovas became the leader of the moderate conservatives, and the creator of the *turno pacífico*. Alas expressed contempt for him in the essay *Cánovas y su tiempo* (1887). Cánovas, the Spanish President when *La Regenta* was written, was a notorious Don Juan, and it has been suggested that Alvaro Mesía was modelled upon him.

14 (p. 136) *et nihil humani . . .* Terence, *Heauton timorumenos*, I, i, 25: 'Homo sum; humani nil a me alienum puto' ('I am a man; I count nothing human indifferent to me'; a much misquoted saying).

15 (p. 138) *Pigault-Lebrun and Paul de Kock*. Charles Antoine Guillaume Pigault-Lebrun (1753–1835), and Paul de Kock (1793–1871), popular and prolific French novelists.

VII

1 (p. 141) *turby and torby*. 'Urbi et orbi' is the motto on the gates of the Vatican and the formula appended to papal rescripts.

2 (p. 142) *the Zouave*. The Zouaves were French infantry soldiers (originally Algerians) famous, especially after the Crimean War, for their bizarre uniforms and their bravery. The reference here could be to the statue of a Zouave on the Pont d'Alma in Paris, or to the painting of a Zouave, well known in Spain at the time, by F. W. Topham (1808–77), or to the comic opera about a Zouave (1859) by Cristóbal Oudrid.

3 (p. 142) *plaster-on*. *Plastron* is the French word.

4 (p. 145) *Montes de Toledo*. Mountains

in the province of Toledo, until the late nineteenth century densely wooded. They had the reputation of being a hiding-place for thieves and outlaws.

5 (p. 147) *Dictionary of Authorities*. Not, of course, 'the authorities' in Ronzal's sense. The *Diccionario de autoridades* was a six-volume dictionary published between 1726 and 1739 by the Real Academia Española (founded in 1714 on the model of the French academies).

6 (p. 148) *the Great Siege of Vienna. El gran cerco de Viena* is the absurd play written by Don Eleuterio Crispín de Andorra, a character in *La comedia nueva* (1792) by Leandro Fernández de Moratín.

7 (p. 148) *Pauperum tabernas, regumque turris.* Horace, *Odes*, I, iv, 13–14: 'Pallida Mors aequo pulsat pede pauperum tabernas/Regumque turris' ('Pale Death with impartial foot knocks at the doors of poor men's hovels and kings' palaces').

8 (p. 150) *History of Prostitution. Histoire de la prostitution chez tous les peuples du monde, depuis l'antiquité la plus reculée jusqu'd nos jours* (six volumes, 1851–61).

9 (p. 150) *The Lady of the Camellias. La Dame aux camélias* (1848), popular novel by Alexandre Dumas the younger.

10 (p. 152) *dosimetric love.* Dosimetry was a branch of medicine developed in the 1880s. The *Oxford English Dictionary* defines it as 'the employment of simple and active remedies in doses that are mathematically defined and administered according to certain rules'.

11 (p. 155) *a virtuous woman.* Proverbs 31: 10.

12 (p. 156) *Marguerite Gautier.* The protagonist of *La Dame aux camélias.*

VIII

1 (p. 158) *his Mentor, his nymph Egeria.* Mentor was the friend of Ulysses and the teacher and adviser of Telemachus. Egeria was a prophetic nymph, the wife and adviser of the second Roman king, Numa.

2 (p. 158) *Pythoness.* The priestess of Apollo at Delphi, who delivered the oracles.

3 (p. 158) *Wandering Jew.* The Jew who, according to legend, insulted Christ

when he was on his way to Calvary and was condemned to wander over the face of the earth until Judgement Day.

4 (p. 159) *German philosophy.* The idealism of Schelling, Fichte, Hegel, Krause, etc., as opposed to French positivism.

5 (p. 159) *distingue tempora.* 'Distingue tempora et concordabis iura' ('distinguish the times and you will bring the laws into agreement'). A legal axiom which states that in order to reconcile different rulings about the same subject one must take account of their historical circumstances.

6 (p. 159) *post hoc ergo propter hoc.* 'After this, therefore because of this.' A formula descriptive of the fallacy that one event is necessarily the cause of another which follows it.

7 (p. 160) *the sixth commandment.* See Chapter II, note 9.

8 (p. 160) *Regency.* That of Philip of Orléans (1715–23).

9 (p. 160) *Espartero.* Baldomero Espartero was Regent of Spain between 1841 and 1843.

10 (p. 161) *Cenceño.* The obscure local artist one of whose works is the object of Saturnino Bermúdez's admiration in Chapter I.

11 (p. 161) *anacreontic song.* Anacreon was a Greek poet who wrote bacchanalian and amatory verse.

12 (p. 162) *Videor meliora.* Ovid, *Metamorphoses*, VII, 20–1, misquoted by Saturnino. 'Video meliora, proboque:/ Deteriora sequor' ('I see and approve better things, but follow worse').

13 (p. 163) *in extremis.* 'In the last moments of life.'

14 (p. 165) *so tender and happy . . . when God willed it . . . for his joy discover'd.* References to the famous sonnet by Garcilaso de la Vega: 'Oh dulces prendas por mi mal halladas,/dulces y alegres cuando Dios quería . . . !'

15 (p. 166) *Henry II furniture.* French furniture of the sixteenth century.

16 (p. 166) *the horse-riding king.* Francis I of France (1494–1547), father of Henry II (1519–59). Hunting was his ruling passion.

17 (p. 167) *The Mohicans. Les Mohicans de Paris* (nineteen volumes, 1854–5), detective stories by Alexandre Dumas the elder.

18 (p. 171) *flatus vocis.* Literally 'breaths of the voice'. The expression originated in the medieval philosophical

debate about whether universals exist merely as conceptions of the mind (Nominalism) or have a substantial existence of their own (Realism). The Nominalist Roscellinus (d. c. 1125) is reported to have stated that universals are no more than 'flatus vocis', 'verbal breathing'. The marquis's use of the expression is not, however, an unlikely touch of erudition on his part. 'Flatus vocis' became in Spain a proverbial expression for empty verbosity.

19 (p. 173) *la donna è mobile*. Verdi, *Rigoletto* (1851), Act III, Scene 2.

20 (p. 174) *They too were painters*. Correggio (1494–1534), the celebrated Italian painter, is supposed to have exclaimed 'Anch'io son pittore!' upon first seeing Raphael's *St Cecilia*.

21 (p. 174) *antinomies of love*. Kant's 'antinomies of reason' are contradictions between conclusions which seem equally logical.

22 (p. 178) *Madonna of the Chair*. Raphael's painting of a seated Virgin with her Child in the Palazzo Pitti, Florence. It is the most famous of Raphael's many Madonnas. In it the Virgin is portrayed as a wistful yet voluptuous Latin beauty with her head bowed over her Child, whom she holds in a protective embrace. It might seem strange that there is no detailed physical description of the heroine of *La Regenta*. In fact, it would have been superfluous, for the close resemblance between her and this Madonna is noticed by many different characters.

IX

1 (p. 188) *the new man*. See Chapter I, note 17.

2 (p. 190) *the rattles*. Ana is thinking of Tenebrae, 'the special form of Mattins and Lauds provided for the last three days of Holy Week. Until 1955 it was sung by anticipation on the three preceding evenings. The name (lit. darkness) probably derived from the ceremony of extinguishing the lights in church one by one during the service. The only light was provided by a set of fifteen (since the later Middle Ages) candles fitted on a "hearse" (a triangular frame on a stand) placed before the altar; one candle was extinguished at the end of each Psalm until only that at the apex remained; this

was hidden behind the altar at the end of the Benedictus (signifying Christ's death)' (*The Oxford Dictionary of the Christian Church*). Until relatively recent times it was the custom in northern Spain for all the children in church to produce racketed rattles at this point and swing them with great vigour and enthusiasm, an action which signified the earthquake after Christ's death.

3 (p. 191) *Calle del Triunfo de 1836*. On 19 October 1836 the government forces in Oviedo won a notable victory against a Carlist army.

4 (p. 193) *an Andalusian lad with a northern accent*. In the late nineteenth century it was becoming fashionable among certain young men in Madrid to ape the manners and accent of the south of Spain (Joaquinito Orgaz is the main representative in the novel of this new Flamenco cult). Young men in the northern provincial cities were, in turn, starting to imitate the Madrid imitation.

5 (p. 194) *putty shoe*. The lad is probably referring to the cakes known as *petits choux*.

6 (p. 199) *Hamadan*. Formerly Ecbatana (see Chapter I, note 5).

7 (p. 199) *Büchner's Force and Matter*. *Kraft und Stoff* (1855) was the major work of the German philosopher and physician Friedrich Karl Christian Büchner (1824–99). It became a textbook of materialism. It asserted that since all nature is physical there is no God, no final cause, no immortality, no free will and no soul; and that mind, like any other physical fact, is simply a movement of matter.

8 (p. 199) *Flammarion*. Camille Flammarion (1842–1925), the popular writer about astronomy, best known for his *Astronomie populaire* (1880). He also had philosophical interests, expressed in *La Pluralité des mondes habités* (1862) and *Dieu dans la nature* (1866). For a time he was an enthusiastic spiritualist.

9 (p. 199) *Moleschott, Virchow and Vogt*. Jacob Moleschott (1822–93) was a Dutch physiologist and philosopher. In his *Kreislauf des Lebens* (1852) he expounded the theory that life is metabolism, a perpetual circulation of matter from the inorganic to the organic world and back again. Matter consequently rules man, and there is no vital force or soul. His aphorisms

were well known: 'Without matter no force, without force no matter', and 'No phosphorus no thought'. Rudolf Virchow (1821–1902) was a German pathologist and politician, one of the foremost men of science of his time and the father of modern pathology. He had progressive liberal and democratic views. He published many books on pathology, anthropology and political and social subjects. Karl Christolph Vogt (1817–1895) was a German naturalist and geologist. Apart from technical works he gave some *Lectures on Man and His Place in Creation and in the History of the Earth* (English version, 1864), materialistic and anti-metaphysical. He declared that: 'Thought stands in the same relation to the brain as the bile to the liver or urine to the kidneys.'

10 (p. 199) *De rerum natura.* Lucretius (*c.* 98–55 B.C.) expounded his epicurean and materialistic philosophy in this didactic poem. Everything can be explained, he declares, in terms of elemental atoms, the atom being the only eternal and immutable substance. The world, therefore, was created not by gods but by the movement of atoms; men should abandon their fear of the gods and of eternal punishment.

11 (p. 202) *natura naturans.* An ironical misuse of an old theological and philosophical concept, much discussed by the scholastics and by later philosophers such as Giordano Bruno and Spinoza. It refers to nature which creates or which exists in itself and is created by itself as opposed to *natura naturata*, the nature created by God or which follows from the necessity of the nature of God.

12 (p. 203) *Calvo.* Rafael Calvo (1824–88), a famous Spanish actor, renowned especially for his interpretation of the Golden Age theatre.

13 (p. 203) *Life is a Dream. La vida es sueño*, Calderón's famous play.

X

1 (p. 203) *languishing hillocks.* A reference to the poem 'A las ruinas de Itálica', by Rodrigo Caro (1573–1647), which begins: 'Estos, Fabio, ¡ ay dolor! que ves ahora / campos de soledad, mustio collado, / fueron un tiempo Itálica famosa' ('Alas, Fabio, these fields of loneliness, this languishing hillock, which you now see, were once

the famous Italica'). Italica was a Roman city near Seville.

2 (p. 204) *'Wild hippogryph, that flyest with the wind ...'* The famous first words of *La vida es sueño*: 'Hipogrifo violento / que corriste parejas con el viento.'

3 (p. 205) *Darro.* The rivers Ebro and Genil run through the cities of Saragossa and Granada. The Darro is a tributary of the Genil. The Romantic play *El trobador* (see Chapter V, note 5) is set on the banks of the Ebro.

4 (p. 205) *Generalife ... Albaicín.* The Generalife is a beautiful Moorish palace in Granada, near the Alhambra. The Albaicín was a picturesque but poor gipsy quarter.

5 (p. 207) *Achilles, the son of Peleus.* In the tenth year of the siege of Troy, Agamemnon took for himself Achilles' favourite slave-girl, Briseis. Achilles withdrew in wrath to his tent, where he consoled himself with music and singing, and refused to take any further part in the war.

6 (p. 209) *serene night.* 'Noche serena' is the title of a well-known poem by Fray Luis de León (1537–91), the first lines of which are quoted by Don Víctor Quintanar at the beginning of Chapter XXVII. Its theme is the harmony of the heavens, conceived in Platonic and Pythagorean terms.

7 (p. 209) *Pylades.* See Chapter III, note 2.

8 (p. 212) *Me, and opportunity!* One of the mottoes of Philip II of Spain is said to have been 'El tiempo y yo, para otros dos' ('Time and I – a match for any other two').

9 (p. 213) *as the Cid had done.* According to legend, the Cid, after dying during a battle against Moors, was strapped and propped in his saddle by his followers. When his horse appeared with its ghostly mount, the Moors fled in terror.

10 (p. 215) *almost breaking the law to do so.* See Chapter V, note 14.

11 (p. 216) *Jovellanos.* Gaspar Melchor de Jovellanos (1744–1811), the Spanish political thinker and man of letters.

12 (p. 216) *Benavides ... Carvajal.* Characters in *La prudencia en la mujer* by Tirso de Molina (1571–1648). The speeches quoted are from Act I, Scene 3.

13 (p. 217) *Segismundo.* The protagonist of *La vida es sueño*, at the beginning of the play a man who has been turned

into a beast as a result of many years of imprisonment by his father, the king. When Segismundo is released one of his first actions is to hurl a servant who annoys him from a balcony.

XI

1 (p. 219) *three thousand pesetas.* Equivalent to approximately £125 in the late 1870s. At that time, working men earned between two and three pesetas a day.

2 (p. 219) *when the government refused to pay us.* The Spanish Constitution of 1845 made the state responsible for the finances of the Church. When liberals were in power the ecclesiastical budget was often reduced to a minimum.

3 (p. 219) *habit of St Rita.* See Chapter I, note 11.

4 (p. 219) *Scottish school.* See Chapter V, note 1.

5 (p. 219) *Stoa . . . Academy.* The Stoa was the gallery on the north side of the market-place in Athens, where the followers of Zeno of Citium (the stoics) met. The Academy was a garden near Athens where Plato taught.

6 (p. 221) *Sir Fierabras.* The Saracen giant who stole the relics of Christ in Rome (and was subsequently defeated and converted by Oliver).

7 (p. 222) *Montes de Toledo.* See Chapter VII, note 4.

8 (p. 222) *Luis Candelas.* A notorious bandit of the nineteenth century.

9 (p. 223) *Thalia.* The eighth of the Muses. She presided over comedy and idyllic poetry. Thalia was also one of the three Graces, the patroness of festive meetings.

10 (p. 226) *treasure . . . fields.* Matthew 13: 44: 'Again, the kingdom of God is like unto a treasure hid in a field; the which when a man hath found, he hideth, and for joy thereof goeth and selleth all that he hath, and buyeth that field.'

11 (p. 227) *the Bernesga.* The river which runs through the city of León.

12 (p. 228) *Dupanloup.* Félix Antoine Philibert Dupanloup (1802–78), the Bishop of Orléans, was the chief spokesman for liberal Roman Catholics, and opposed the dogma of papal infallibility.

13 (p. 232) *Renan.* A slight anachronism, as Gonzalo Sobejano points out in his edition: the story is *Une Idylle monacale au XIIIᵉ siècle: Christine de Stommeln,* first published under the title *La Bienheureuse Christine de Stommeln, béguine* in 1879, a little after the action of the novel.

14 (p. 232) *Luther . . . Abelard.* After the break with Rome, Martin Luther, a monk, married Catherine von Bora, a nun. Peter Abelard's case is less serious in the eyes of De Pas because after his marriage with Héloïse his love for her became (perforce) purely spiritual, and it was then that they both entered monastic orders.

15 (p. 232) *King of Babylon.* Nebuchadnezzar, punished by God for pride: 'and he was driven from men, and did eat grass as oxen, and his body was wet with the dew of heaven, till his hairs were grown like eagles' feathers, and his nails like birds' claws' (Daniel 4: 33).

16 (p. 238) *first-fruits.* A payment, usually representing the amount of the first year's income, made by each new holder of an ecclesiastical benefice to some superior, who in this case should be the bishop.

17 (p. 239) *the fall of Solomon.* The destruction (after his death) of all that, thanks to his God-given wisdom, he had created; the punishment for his excessive and uncontrolled fondness for women.

18 (p. 242) *vir bonus.* One of the maxims of Cato the Censor, a man renowned for his strict morality, who stated that the orator is the 'vir bonus dicendi peritus' ('the good man who is skilled in speaking'). Quintilian uses it as his starting-point for the *Institutio oratoria.*

XII

1 (p. 244) *an Érard grand piano.* Érard pianos, made in Paris, were often splendid, even sumptuous pieces of furniture. They have a characteristic happy, jingling tone.

2 (p. 246) *Panurge's sheep.* In Rabelais's *Pantagruel* Panurge becomes annoyed with a sheep-merchant and throws one of his animals into the sea. All the others run after it. The expression became proverbial in Spain for people who blindly follow a leader.

3 (p. 247) *the fox and the stork.* One of Aesop's fables. 'A stork which had arrived from foreign parts received an

invitation to dinner from a fox, who served her with clear soup on a smooth slab of marble, so that the hungry bird could not taste a drop of it. Returning the invitation, the stork produced a flagon filled with pap, into which she stuck her bill and had a good meal, while her guest was tormented with hunger.' (*Fables of Aesop*, translated by S. A. Handsford, Penguin Classics.)

4 (p. 248) *Vade retro!* 'Get thee behind me': Jesus's words to Peter after the latter had tried to persuade Him not to allow Himself to be killed (Matthew 16: 23).

5 (p. 253) *Judith . . . careers*. An interesting choice of heroines: four beautiful Old Testament women who used their charms and guile to dominate and deceive weak-willed men. Judith delivered the Jews by using trickery to gain access to their persecutor the Assyrian general Holofernes, beguiling him, making him drunk and cutting off his head (Book of Judith). Esther became the wife of Xerxes I of Persia (not mentioning that she was a Jewess) and turned him against his grand vizier, Haman, who wished to exterminate the Jews and found himself exterminated instead, together with large numbers of his alleged followers (Book of Esther). Delilah was the well-known betrayer of Samson to the Philistines (Judges 16). Rebecca put her son Jacob up to his elaborate and successful ruse to go to his father Isaac disguised as his elder brother Esau, obtain his father's blessing under false pretences, and thus deprive his brother of his birthright (Genesis 27).

6 (p. 256) *the bishop in Les Misérables*. The kind and generous Mgr Bienvenu Myriel, a character in the novel by Victor Hugo (1862).

7 (p. 257) *non serviam*. The words of Lucifer, the fallen angel: 'I will not serve.'

8 (p. 258) *Strauss . . . Göttingen*. David Friedrich Strauss (1808–74) was one of the most progressive German Protestant theologians of the nineteenth century. His denial of the historical foundation of all supernatural elements in the Gospels roused a storm of indignation. The universities of Tübingen and Göttingen were centres of German Protestant theology.

9 (p. 258) *the crazy Genevan philosopher*. Jean-Jacques Rousseau (1712–78).

10 (p. 258) *Risum teneatis*. See Chapter VI, note 10.

11 (p. 261) *The Characters*. Les Caractères (1688) by Jean de la Bruyère, aphoristic pen-portraits of contemporaries.

12 (p. 261) *The Art of Thinking*. El criterio (1845), the shortest and most practical major work by Jaime Luciano Balmes (1810–48), the leading Spanish conservative and Roman Catholic philosopher of his times.

13 (p. 262) *Bastiat*. Frédéric Bastiat (1801–50), French economist, advocate of free trade and opponent of socialism. He held that human interests, when left to themselves, tend to harmonious combination and to the general good.

14 (p. 263) *exempt diocese*. A diocese not subject to a bishop, but directly under the Holy See.

15 (p. 264) *Holy God . . .* The Trisagion (see Chapter I, note 15).

16 (p. 264) *O come . . .* A popular Spanish Marian hymn.

17 (p. 272) *General Dispensation Agency*. The 'Agencia de Preces', a government office (part of the Department of State) through which dispensations, indults, indulgences and other papal favours had to be obtained. It was attacked by the clergy as one of the most obvious examples of the much-resented interference of the state bureaucracy in religious affairs.

18 (p. 275) *Henao y Muñoz*. Manuel Henao y Muñoz (1828–91) wrote a book entitled not *El evangelio del pueblo* but *El libro del pueblo* (1868). Páez's confusion of titles is understandable: *The People's Book* is a moralizing work written in simple, exhortative language.

XIII

1 (p. 281) *The Antonelli of Vestusta*. A dubious compliment but a telling and accurate comparison. Giacomo Antonelli (1806–76) was an Italian cardinal who wielded great power under Pius IX as cardinal secretary of state, virtually becoming the temporal ruler of Rome. An extreme reactionary, he displayed consummate duplicity in all his activities, acquired a considerable personal fortune by dubious means, and had an unscrupulous, grasping and sinister personality (according to the *Encyclopaedia Britannica*, 13th ed.).

By his friends, however, he was loaded with praise.

2 (p. 294) *Feuillet*. Octave Feuillet (1821–90), French writer of idealistic and sentimental novels.

3 (p. 294) *Balmes*. See Chapter XII, note 12.

4 (p. 298) *non erat his locus*. Horace, *Ars poetica*, 19. 'This was not the place.'

XIV

1 (p. 311) *Rege Carolo III*. Charles III ruled from 1759 until 1788.

2 (p. 321) *turns . . . pacific*. For the *turno pacífico*, see the Introduction.

3 (p. 322) *serene night*. See Chapter X, note 6.

XV

1 (p. 332) *for Christ's sake*. Matthew 19: 29: 'And every one that hath forsaken houses, or brethren, or sisters, or father, or mother, or wife, or children, or lands, for my name's sake, shall receive an hundredfold, and shall inherit everlasting life.'

2 (p. 334) *no other river than that of their homeland*. A quotation, 'no habían visto más río que el de su patria', from an unidentified poem.

3 (p. 338) *the foolishness of the Cross*. A concept expounded by Paul in 1 Corinthians 1 and by Erasmus in *The Praise of Folly*.

4 (p. 341) *astri d'or*. *Faust* (1859), by Charles Gounod, Act III.

5 (p. 342) *chrysology*. The science of gold or wealth.

6 (p. 345) *Don Simon Magus . . . Torquemada . . . Calomarde*. Simon Magus was a sorcerer who professed Christianity and was baptized, and tried to obtain spiritual powers from the apostles for money. Tomás de Torquemada was the notorious inquisitor-general of Spain from 1484 until 1498. Francisco Tadeo Calomarde (1773–1842) was a minister under the reactionary and repressive Ferdinand VII, and an enthusiastic persecutor of liberals.

7 (p. 345) *Philip II*. The king of Spain from 1556 until 1598, a zealous Roman Catholic and ardent persecutor of heretics.

XVI

1 (p. 352) *the centre of the soul*. A reference to the last line of a sonnet by Bartolomé Leonardo de Argensola (1562–1631): 'Ciego, ¿ es la tierra el centro de las almas?'

2 (p. 352) *how lonely do remain the dead*. A commonplace of the time, which started life in a poem by Gustavo Adolfo Bécquer (1836–70): '¡Dios mío, qué solos / se quedan los muertos!'

3 (p. 352) *tercets and silvas of all things*. Silvas are eleven- and seven-syllable lines combined and rhymed as the poet pleases, although no poet apart from Trifón Cármenes is known to have grouped them in tercets.

4 (p. 356) *pulvy says*. See Chapter I, note 16.

5 (p. 359) *Lot's daughters*. Lot's two daughters made him drunk and lay with him, so as to preserve his seed (Genesis 19: 30–8).

6 (p. 360) *Deus, in adjutorium meum intende*. Psalms 69: 1: 'Save me, O God.' It continues: '. . . for the waters are come in unto my soul. I sink in deep mire, where there is no standing: I am come into deep waters, where the floods overflow me. I am weary of my crying: my throat is dried: mine eyes fail while I wait for my God. They that hate me without a cause are more than the hairs of mine head: they that would destroy me, being mine enemies wrongfully, are mighty. . . .'

7 (p. 364) *wild . . . wind*. See Chapter X, note 2.

8 (p. 364) *Don Juan Tenorio*. A major, popular work of the Spanish Romantic drama, by José Zorrilla y Moral (1817–93). It was first performed in 1844. It became customary to perform it on All Saints' Day, probably because of its finale in a cemetery. In this chapter of *La Regenta* frequent reference is made to its complicated story (set in and near Seville in 1545–50), which can be summarized as follows. *Part One, Act One*: Don Juan Tenorio and Don Luis Mejía meet by appointment to see which has managed to make more mischief in a year; Don Juan wins with a score of one hundred and four (thirty-two murders and seventy-two seductions) to Don Luis's seventy-nine (twenty-three and fifty-six). Don Luis objects that no novices from nunneries appear in his opponent's list of victims, and Don Juan

retorts by wagering that he will now complete his triumph by seducing not only a novice but also the woman whom Don Luis is to marry the following day, Doña Ana de Pantoja. Don Juan's father Don Diego Tenorio has arranged a marriage between his son and Doña Inés, the daughter of the Commander of Ulloa. She has hitherto lived in a nunnery, preparing to take the veil. But Don Diego and the commander, suspicious of Don Juan's behaviour, have come to witness his meeting with Don Luis, disguised in masks (it is carnival time). The commander, horrified at what he has heard, confronts Don Juan and withdraws his consent to the marriage; Don Juan retorts that Doña Inés will do very well as the novice to be seduced. Don Diego upbraids his son, while refusing to reveal his own identity. Don Juan tears the mask from his father's face. *Act Two:* Don Luis arranges with Doña Ana to be allowed into her house at an agreed time, in order to protect her against Don Juan's attack, but Don Juan tells his servant Ciutti to seize Don Luis and lock him up, while he himself impersonates Don Luis and seduces Doña Ana. *Act Three:* Don Juan has bribed Doña Inés's old servant Brígida to help him. Doña Inés has only once caught a glimpse of Don Juan, but thanks to Brígida's praises he now has a mysterious, almost magical fascination for her. Brígida smuggles a love-letter from Don Juan to her mistress in the convent and as soon as Doña Inés has read it she finds Don Juan himself standing before her. She faints and Don Juan carries her away. *Act Four:* Don Juan has taken Doña Inés to his estate outside Seville. Doña Inés, believing that Don Juan exerts some irresistible influence over her, declares her love for him and begs him to love her. Don Juan now loves Doña Inés. The commander arrives on the scene to rescue his daughter and kill her abductor, but Don Juan throws himself at his feet, begging for the hand of Doña Inés and saying that she has made him repent and is his last chance to live a good life and save his soul. But the commander refuses to believe him, and Don Luis Mejía (who has also come for his enemy and has overheard the conversation) mocks him for his unmanly behaviour. Don Juan is forced against

his will to fight and kill them both, and flee. *Part Two*, consisting of three acts, is of less concern to readers of *La Regenta*. Don Juan returns to Seville after five years abroad and, after a multiplicity of spectacular supernatural occurrences in the cemetery where all his victims are buried, the ghost of Doña Inés (who has died of a broken heart) brings about his last-gasp repentance and salvation, by the power of love.

9 (p. 366) *Diego Marsilla . . . Doña Isabel de Segura.* Characters in *Los amantes de Teruel* (1837) by Juan Eugenio Hartzenbusch.

10 (p. 369) *lucent region.* An echo of the poem by Fray Luis de León (1537–91), 'De la vida del cielo', in which heaven is described as a 'región luciente'.

11 (p. 370) *Manrique.* Don Frutos refers to *El trovador* (1836) by Antonio García Gutiérrez.

12 (p. 372) *music is the noise that bothers me least.* A saying attributed to Napoleon.

13 (p. 372) *Castelar.* Emilio Castelar (1832–99), Spanish conservative leader and an orator fond of florid rhetoric.

14 (p. 374) *Disdain's Reward Disdain. El desdén por el desdén* by Agustín Moreto (1618–69). The quoted lines are from Act II, Scene 2.

15 (p. 377) *Dumas and Sardou.* Alexandre Dumas the younger (1824–95) and Victorien Sardou (1831–1908) were prominent French post-romantic dramatists.

16 (p. 379) *Don Juan . . . nobility.* Lines from the speech (often parodied) in which Doña Inés begs Don Juan to love her.

XVII

1 (p. 385) *Taparelli.* Luigi Taparelli (1793–1862), Italian Jesuit economist.

2 (p. 386) *the promise in the gospels.* Matthew 18: 4: 'Whomsoever therefore shall humble himself as this little child, the same is greatest in the kingdom of heaven.' Also Luke 18: 14: '. . . every one that exalteth himself shall be abased; and he that humbleth himself shall be exalted.'

3 (p. 387) *persecuted for his virtues.* 'Blessed are those which are persecuted for righteousness' sake; for theirs is the kingdom of heaven' (Matthew 5: 10).

4 (p. 390) *Archpriest of Hita, and Tirso de Molina.* Juan Ruiz, the Archpriest of Hita, finished his famous fictional autobiography, *El libro de buen amor,* in 1343. Amorous adventures, narrated with relish, form a large part of it. The dramatist Tirso de Molina (1571–1648) explored feminine psychology in many of his plays. His *El burlador de Sevilla* presented Don Juan to the world.

5 (p. 394) *Andromache.* Hector's wife, who 'smiled with tears in her eyes' when saying goodbye to her husband (*Iliad,* VI, 484).

6 (p. 396) *the way of perfection. El camino de perfección* is a book about the religious life by the mystic St Teresa of Jesus (1515–82).

7 (p. 397) *St Jane Frances de Chantal.* Foundress of the Order of the Visitation, for young girls and widows unable to endure the severe ascetic life of the ordinary religious house (1572–1641). St Teresa, on the other hand, insisted on the importance of strict asceticism.

XVIII

1 (p. 401) *the flesh on Job's bones.* Job 19: 20: 'My bone cleaveth to my skin and to my flesh, and I am escaped with the skin of my teeth.'

2 (p. 402) *they wearied hills.* A reference to the First Eclogue of Garcilaso de la Vega (see Chapter II, note 2). One of the activities in which Garcilaso suggests that the Viceroy of Naples, to whom the poem is dedicated, might be engaged, is hunting: 'agora, de cuidados enojosos / y de negocios libre, por ventura / andes a caça, el monte fatigando / en ardiente ginette que apressura / el curso tras los ciervos temorosos / que en vano su morir van dilatando' (ll. 15–20: 'you may, perhaps, free from tiresome worries and affairs, be hunting, wearying the hills, an ardent horseman galloping after the timorous deer, who try in vain to postpone their deaths').

3 (p. 402) *sylvan knolls.* 'Los altozanos nemorosos': another reference to Golden Age literature. St John of the Cross refers in his 'Cántico espiritual' (see above, Chapter IV, note 14) to 'los valles solitarios nemorosos'.

4 (p. 402) *bouquets of feathers.* In his soliloquy in Act I of *La vida es sueño* Segismundo talks of a bird as 'flor de pluma, o ramillete con alas' ('a flower of feathers, or a bouquet with wings').

5 (p. 403) *The Mayor of Zalamea. El alcalde de Zalamea.* Both Lope de Vega and Calderón wrote plays with this title.

6 (p. 406) *the gift of tears of which St Teresa speaks.* In her *Vida,* St Teresa says that tears, which bring strength and consolation, are a gift from God.

7 (p. 409) *Chateaubriand.* See Chapter IV, note 11.

XIX

1 (p. 423) *Suum cuique.* 'To each his own': Cicero, *De officiis,* I, 5.

2 (p. 424) *Marina . . . The Blue Domino . . . The Oath. Marina, El dominó azul* and *El juramento,* three well-known *zarzuelas* of the 1850s. The *zarzuela* is the Spanish comic opera.

3 (p. 425) *Jaccoud.* François Jaccoud (1830–1913) a Swiss doctor and author of books on medicine, such as *Traité de pathologie interne* (1872).

4 (p. 427) *gongoresque style.* The poems of Luis de Góngora y Argote (1561–1627) are renowned for their use of such rhetorical figures as euphemism and periphrasis.

5 (p. 427) *the Russian War.* The war between Russia and Turkey, April 1877 to January 1878.

6 (p. 427) *the plurality of inhabited worlds.* This is the title of a book by Flammarion (see Chapter IX, note 8).

7 (p. 427) *Feijoo.* The Spanish scholar Benito Jerónimo Feijoo y Montenegro (1676–1764), in whose *Cartas eruditas* (1742–60) there are several discussions of this question.

8 (p. 427) *the saying about cholera and fear.* The reference is to some untraced saying, no doubt common during the Spanish cholera epidemic of 1885 (which was at its height when this chapter was being written), and analogous to the saying to be found in Captain Marryat's *Peter Simple,* ch. 29: 'Fear kills more people than the yellow fever.'

9 (p. 430) *Chateaubriand and Wiseman.* The references are to the well-known description in *Les Martyrs,* book V (see above, Chapter IV, note 12) and to part II, chs. II–IV of Cardinal Wiseman's novel *Fabiola; or, The Church of the Catacombs* (1854). In Ana's dreams this literary vision of the catacombs is combined with an equally literary vision of hell, that of St Teresa (*Vida,* XXXII):

a hole into which the sinner is forced to squeeze, and claustrophobic tunnels full of repulsive vermin, filthy water and a foul smell.

10 (p. 431) *the fiesta of St Blasius.* Held on the third of February.

11 (p. 437) *The Lightning-Flash . . . The Magyars.* Two more *zarzuelas* of the 1850s.

12 (p. 437) *'Spirto gentil' . . . 'Casta diva'.* Don Víctor's musical tastes coincide with those of Saturnino Bermúdez (see Chapter I, notes 13 and 14).

13 (p. 437) *The villein . . . night.* From Góngora's ballad *Angélica y Medoro.*

14 (p. 438) *grand syntheses . . . dissolving views . . . pantheistic philosophy.* Slighting references to the complicated idealism of the *krausistas* (see Chapter IV, note 7).

15 (p. 441) *the corpse of the Cid, led forth to defeat the Moors.* See Chapter X, note 9.

XX

1 (p. 443) *the confiscations.* Liberal governments in the nineteenth century had freed much Church land from mortmain.

2 (p. 443) *soup, chick-peas and meat.* The typical Spanish middle-class lunch of the time.

3 (p. 444) *the lion enamoured of a maiden.* A reference to the fable by Aesop: 'A lion fell in love with a farmer's daughter and wooed her. The farmer could not bear to give his girl in marriage to a wild beast; yet he dared not refuse. So he evaded the difficulty by telling the importunate suitor that, while he quite approved of him as a husband for his daughter, he could not give her to him unless he would pull out his teeth and cut off his claws, because the girl was afraid of them. The lion was so much in love that he readily submitted to these sacrifices. But when he presented himself again, the farmer treated him with contempt and cudgelled him off the premises.' (*Fables of Aesop,* translated by S. A. Handsford, Penguin Classics.)

4 (p. 444) *excommunicating Don Pompeyo.* It is not easy to realize how intransigent the Spanish Church was a hundred years ago. The following, the work of the Bishop of Minorca in 1876, may help: 'We renew and reiterate our sentence of the highest order of excommunication against heretics of every sort, kind and description, against their pupils or adopted children, against their fathers, mothers, preceptors and all who sit at meat with them. We fully excommunicate all who aid or look kindly on them; we excommunicate the domestic servants of all heretics; we excommunicate each and every person or persons who dare to let a house to a heretic or Protestant for school or services, and every one who gives money, or makes a loan, or leaves a legacy to such persons; we excommunicate every one who lives on terms of friendship with such a heretic, and every one who dares to say or write one word in their defence. The clergy of my diocese are commanded to read this out on three successive Sundays during Divine Service and to take good care that all its injunctions shall be carried out to the letter.' (Quoted in *The Annual Register,* 1876, p. 201.)

5 (p. 444) *'Strike but hear.'* The words of the Athenian soldier and statesman Themistocles when threatened by the Spartan Euribiades, according to Plutarch in his *Life of Themistocles,* ch. XI.

6 (p. 446) *Alan Cardgame.* Allan Kardec, the pseudonym of the French spiritualist Hyppolite Léon Rivail (1803–69), who promulgated the doctrine of successive reincarnations with intervals of spirit life.

7 (p. 446) *searching for Negroes in Africa.* The slave trade was legally abolished in the Spanish colonies in 1820, but in practice it continued throughout much of the nineteenth century. Slavery itself was abolished in Cuba (where Redondo made his fortune) in 1880.

square in Jerusalem. The prophet Jeremiah denounced the sins of Judah, in particular their idolatry, and proclaimed their punishment – the destruction of Jerusalem. He was misunderstood and treated with ingratitude by his own people.

9 (p. 448) *the twenty-fifth anniversary of the exaltation of Pius IX to the papacy.* The year 1871.

10 (p. 448) *the session in the tennis court.* The meeting in Versailles of the third estate to swear not to separate before having established the constitution of the kingdom (20 June 1789).

11 (p. 456) *three towers of David.* Song of Songs 4: 4. The bridegroom addresses the bride: 'Thy neck is like the tower of David builded for an armoury, whereon there hang a thousand bucklers, all

shields of mighty men.' In the Litany of the Blessed Virgin, the latter is called 'Turris Davidica, Turris Eburnea'.

12 (p. 456) *force and matter*. See Chapter IX, note 7.

13 (p. 460) *Fornos ... La Taurina ... El Puerto*. Fornos was (and is) a fashionable Madrid restaurant. The other two restaurants are probably Alas's inventions.

14 (p. 461) *Homo homini lupus*. Plautus, *Asinaria*, Act II, Scene 4, line 88: 'Lupus est homo homini, non homo' ('man is a wolf, not a man, towards man').

15 (p. 464) *Munda*. The city in southern Spain (now Montilla) where Julius Caesar defeated the two sons of Pompey in 45 B.C.

16 (p. 466) *anch'io son pittore*. See Chapter VIII, note 20.

17 (p. 466) *Amen dico vobis*. 'Verily, verily, I say unto you.'

18 (p. 466) *Forgive him, for he has drunk much*. Jesus said of Mary Magdalene, 'Her sins, which are many, are forgiven, for she loved much' (Luke 7: 47); and, on the cross, of his persecutors, 'Father, forgive them; for they know not what they do' (Luke 23: 34).

19 (p. 467) *Frascuelo*. The famous bullfighter Salvador Sánchez Povedano (1842–98). The traditional bullfighter's garb reveals his stockinged lower leg.

20 (p. 469) *it's not for me ... help my master*. Words attributed to the French knight Bertrand du Guesclin, who helped Henry of Trastamar to kill his half-brother Peter I of Castile (Peter the Cruel) in 1369 and gain the crown. They characterize the mercenary man who feigns impartiality. They are quoted in the ballad about this incident, 'El fratricidio', by the Spanish romantic poet El Duque de Rivas (1791–1865).

21 (p. 469) *inter pocula*. 'In his cups.'

22 (p. 470) *Kempis, The Imitation of Christ*. The famous manual of spiritual devotion, which tells the Christian how to seek perfection by taking Christ as his model.

XXI

1 (p. 474) *Fray Luis de León*. The famous religious poet edited St Teresa's works in 1588.

2 (p. 474) *the Third Abecedary by Francisco de Osuna*. The third part of this Fran-

ciscan theologian's *Abecedario espiritual* appeared in 1527.

3 (p. 475) *five hundred pesetas*. Equivalent to a little over £20 in the late 1870s. See Chapter XI, note 1.

4 (p. 476) *gift of tears*. See Chapter XVIII, note 6.

5 (p. 477) *the German or Swedish monk and nun*. See Chapter XI, note 13.

6 (p. 477) *Perfect Wife*. *La perfecta casada* (1583).

7 (p. 478) *by painful pleasure, by mortal delight*. Characteristic paradoxical language of Spanish mysticism.

8 (p. 478) *Veritas ... intellectu*. 'The truth in the thing is the thing itself; the truth in the mind (is the understanding of the thing as it is in itself).' J. Balmes, *Curso de filosofía elemental: Lógica*. Ch. 1. See above, Chapter XII, note 12.

9 (p. 479) *St Christopher*. Legend represents this saint as 'a powerful giant who earned his living by carrying travellers across a river, and on one occasion numbered among his passengers a small child who caused him to bow beneath his burden, since the child was none other than the Christ and His weight that of the whole world' (*Oxford Dictionary of the Christian Church*). The saint's image was placed opposite the south door of churches, in the belief that it would safeguard the passer-by from accident. St Christopher is the patron of travellers.

10 (p. 479) *... the same crime*. Matthew 5: 28: 'But I say unto you, that whosoever looketh on a woman to lust after her hath committed adultery with her already in his heart.'

11 (p. 483) *Sybil*. *Sybil, or The Two Nations* (1845), a novel by Benjamin Disraeli.

12 (p. 483) *Fabiola*. *Fabiola; or, The Church of the Catacombs* (1854), the best-selling novel by Cardinal Wiseman, translated into ten languages.

13 (p. 484) *Paraguay*. A country in which the Company of Jesus exerted a huge influence in the seventeenth and eighteenth centuries.

14 (p. 484) *Caveant consules*. 'Caveant consules ne quid respublica detrimenti capiat' ('Let the consuls take care that the republic suffers no harm') was the formula with which the Roman senate declared a state of emergency and gave the consuls full powers.

15 (p. 489) *after its kind*. References to Genesis 1 in this paragraph imply a

parallel in Ana's mind between the Creation and her own return to life after illness.

16 (p. 490) *the Golden Legend*. A once popular manual consisting mainly of lives of the saints and short treatises about the Christian festivals, drawn up by Jacob of Voragine between 1255 and 1266 with the purpose of fostering piety.

17 (p. 490) *the Christian Year by Croiset*. *L'Année chrétienne, ou exercises de piété pour tous les dimanches et les fêtes mobiles de l'année*, five volumes, 1712–20, by Jean Croiset (a French Jesuit). It was first translated into Spanish in 1753. Another, augmented Spanish edition, in twelve volumes, was published between 1878 and 1883.

18 (p. 492) *Canon Döllinger*. Johann Joseph Ignaz von Döllinger (1799–1890), a Bavarian Church historian and liberal Roman Catholic, was excommunicated in 1871 for rejecting the doctrine of papal infallibility.

19 (p. 492) *'fabric of immense architecture'*. A reminiscence of the first lines of the poem 'El siglo de oro' by Lope de Vega: 'Fábrica fue la inmensa arquitectura / deste mundo inferior que el hombre imita' ('The immense architecture of this inferior world was a building imitated by man').

20 (p. 492) *mansions*. St Teresa's *Interior Castle* (*Castillo interior*) describes the life of the mystic as a progress from one mansion (*morada*) to another.

21 (p. 494) *that kind of minister*. He was called the Minister of Grace and Justice ('Ministro de Gracia y Justicia').

22 (p. 495) *enthusiasm . . . others*. Probably a quotation, from an unidentified source.

23 (p. 501) *'Santo fuerte'*. See Chapter I, note 15.

XXII

1 (p. 502) *Civis romanus sum*. Cicero, *In verrem*, v, lvii, 147: 'I am a Roman citizen', the expression of the Roman's conviction that he could not be exposed to indignity.

2 (p. 504) *pickled 1812 liberal*. In 1812 a Spanish constitution, on Jacobin lines, was published.

3 (p. 504) *Ordine . . . honestas*. Part of a description of a brief learnt by rote from some legal textbook.

4 (p. 505) *Masculine . . . follis*. Quoted from Raimundo de Miguel, *Gramática*

hispano–latina teórico–práctica (14th ed., Madrid, 1875, p. 18). This was a much-used school textbook, in which Latin grammar was expounded in lengthy doggerel verse.

5 (p. 506) *the tribute of a hundred maidens*. It is a widespread belief in Spain that in many Spanish towns the Moorish invaders of the Middle Ages obliged the inhabitants to provide them from time to time with one hundred virgins.

6 (p. 507) *trans-Tiberine woman*. A woman from Trans Tiberim, the part of Rome on the right bank of the Tiber. Women from this region were said to be powerful, beautiful and proud, yet uncivilized.

7 (p. 510) *the saint from Avila*. See Chapter XXI, note 20.

8 (p. 511) *Pascal . . . Provincial Letters*. In his *Lettres écrites à un provincial* (1656–7) Blaise Pascal attacked the Jesuit theories of grace and moral theology, and Jesuit casuistry in general, opposing to it the rigorous morality of the Jansenists.

9 (p. 513) *solidary humanity*. Krausista jargon (see Chapter IV, note 7).

10 (p. 518) *the claps*. A collapse.

11 (p. 519) *civil burials*. Adjoining many Spanish cemeteries there is an unconsecrated graveyard for those who die outside the Roman Catholic Church. Such graveyards, being seldom used or visited, are neglected and overgrown.

12 (p. 520) *the conventionalist*. The bishop in this novel (see above, Chapter XII, note 6) visits a dying conventionalist.

XXIII

1 (p. 529) *Tecum . . . genui te*. Psalms 110: 3. Ana is right to be confused. The texts and interpretations of this obscure verse differ greatly. The Authorized Version says: 'Thy people shall be willing in the day of thy power, in the beauties of holiness from the womb of the morning: thou hast the dew of thy youth.'

2 (p. 529) *Dominus . . . Alleluia*. Psalms 2: 7: 'The Lord hath said unto me, Thou art my son; this day have I begotten thee.'

3 (p. 531) *Titus, chapter 2*. Paul advises Titus to teach young people of both sexes sobriety, purity and discretion, and to practise what he preaches.

4 (p. 531) *'La mandilona'*. This song has not been traced, but the context

indicates that it was popular during the Second Carlist War (1874–6).

5 (p. 537) *quintillas*. See Chapter III, note 5.

6 (p. 542) *Rose of Jericho*. A plant native to the sandy deserts of south-west Asia and north-east Africa. Once it has developed its fruits it dries up, becomes detached from the ground, and is rolled over the desert by the wind. As soon as it is exposed to moisture it revives and grows and flowers again. It is a symbol of the Virgin Mary.

7 (p. 542) *apostle of the Gentiles*. The title traditionally given to St Paul.

XXIV

1 (p. 546) *in illo tempore*. The first words of the description of the Nativity in Luke 2 (sung by Ripamilán during midnight mass in Chapter XXIII): 'In those days.'

2 (p. 548) *the fortune of a Monte-Cristo*. The protagonist of *Le Comte de Monte-Cristo* (1844), by Alexandre Dumas the elder, discovers a vast hidden treasure which he uses to help his friends and take revenge on his enemies.

3 (p. 553) *But have . . . I love thee. Las paredes oyen*, by Juan Ruiz de Alarcón (1580–1639), Act I, Scene 6.

4 (p. 553) *And so . . . thou art not mine. El castigo sin venganza*, by Lope de Vega, Act II, ll. 1916–20.

5 (p. 554) *Ninon de Lenclos*. Frenchwoman of society (1615–1705) who had a long succession of distinguished lovers, and whose lively sexual activity lasted well into old age.

XXV

1 (p. 559) *good love, too*. At the beginning of *The Book of Good Love* (*El libro de buen amor* – see Chapter XVII, note 4) Juan Ruiz claims that by 'good love' he means pure Christian love, but in his playful, ironical, ambiguous poem the term often seems to refer to sexual love.

2 (p. 564) *the fiestas of St Matthew*. The major annual fiestas of Vetusta/Oviedo, held in September.

3 (p. 567) *had loved much*. See Chapter XX, note 18.

4 (p. 568) *Edgar Allan Poe*. Possibly the narrator in *The Tell-Tale Heart*, an obsessive, mad murderer.

5 (p. 571) *Novena to Our Lady of Sorrows*.

Beginning on the fifth Thursday in Lent.

6 (p. 572) *Stabat Mater*. A hymn of unknown date descriptive of the sorrows of the Virgin at the foot of the Cross. Among the many musical settings is that of Rossini, composed in 1832–9.

7 (p. 574) *the bad robber*. The one who, crucified with Christ and another robber, railed at Him; the other robber rebuked him and was promised by Christ that he would go to heaven (Luke 23: 39–43).

XXVI

1 (p. 574) *Laurent*. François Laurent (1810–87), Belgian historian and jurisconsult, and advocate of liberal and anticlerical policies. His chief work was *Études sur l'histoire de l'humanité* (eighteen volumes, 1855–70).

2 (p. 585) *a tendency to overlap*. Such overlapping lines were a commonplace of the jargon of late nineteenth-century subromantic Spanish poetry.

3 (p. 585) *pious, happy, triumphant vicar-general*. An echo of the line (about the Roman emperor Trajan) 'pío, felice, triunfador Trajano' from the poem 'A las ruinas de Itálica' by Rodrigo Haro (1573–1647).

4 (p. 586) *to the city and the world*. Papal language (see Chapter VII, note 1).

5 (p. 586) *the Isle of San Balandrán*. In the anti-feminist satirical *zarzuela La isla de San Balandrán* by José Picón and Cristóbal Oudrid (first performance 1862) the men on this island are feeble creatures who do women's work.

6 (p. 587) *Suñer*. F. Suñer y Capdevila (1826–98) was a federal deputy and a notorious outspoken atheist.

7 (p. 588) *They could not . . . they did*. José Echegaray, *Haroldo el Normando*, Act III, Scene 10. An anachronism: this play was written in 1881, three years after Don Víctor quotes from it.

8 (p. 592) *Orsini bomb*. In 1857 the Italian liberal revolutionist Felice Orsini and his accomplices threw three bombs at the carriage of Napoleon III in Paris. The assassination attempt was unsuccessful and Orsini was executed in 1858.

9 (p. 593) *Poliuto*. Opera (1839) by Gaetano Donizetti.

10 (p. 595) *Vae victis*. Livy, *History*, V, xlviii, 9: 'Woe to the vanquished.' The words of the chief of the Celtic Gauls,

Brennus, after his annihilation of the Roman army and occupation and sack of Rome in 390.

11 (p. 595) *Thou hast conquered, Galilean.* Said to have been the last words of Julian the Apostate, the anti-Christian Roman Emperor who was assassinated in 363.

12 (p. 596) *a trans-Tiberine woman.* See Chapter XXII, note 6.

XXVII

1 (p. 598) *Whene'er . . . turn mine eye.* The first lines of Luis de León's poem 'Noche serena' (see Chapter X, note 6).

2 (p. 598) *Lasciami . . . partir.* Quintanar misquotes the duet of Raoul de Nangis and Valentine in Act III of *Les Huguenots* (1836), the opera by Giacomo Meyerbeer.

3 (p. 598) *Gayarre . . . Masini.* Julián Gayarre (1843–90), a Spanish singer, and Angelo Masini (1845–1908), an Italian singer, both of international repute.

4 (p. 599) *a comic opera.* The zarzuela *Beltrán y la Pompadour*, by the member of the Real Academia Española, Manuel Cañete (1822–91).

5 (p. 601) *Maudsley and Luys.* Henry Maudsley (1835–1918), English alienist, and Jules Luys (1828–97), French alienist.

6 (p. 605) *Babylonian sacrifice . . . mysterious vigil.* Ana is thinking of a Babylonian custom described by Herodotus (I, 199; translated by G. C. Macaulay): 'Now the most shameful of the customs of the Babylonians is as follows: – Every woman of the country must sit down in the precincts of the temple of Aphrodite once in her life and have commerce with a man who is a stranger . . . in the sacred enclosure of Aphrodite sit great numbers of women with a wreath of cord about their heads; some come and others go; and there are passages in straight lines going between the women in every direction, through which the strangers pass by and make their choice. Here when a woman takes her seat she does not depart again to her house until one of the strangers has thrown a silver coin into her lap and has had commerce with her outside the temple, and after throwing it he must say these words only: "I demand thee in the name of the goddess Mylitta": now Mylitta is the name given by the Assyrians to Aphrodite: and the silver

coin may be of any value; whatever it is she will not refuse it, for that is not lawful for her, seeing that this coin is made sacred by the act: and she follows the man who has first thrown, and does not reject any: and after that she departs to her house, having acquitted herself of her duty to the goddess. . . . So then as many as have attained to beauty and stature are speedily released, but those of them who are unshapely remain there much time, not being able to fulfil the law; for some of them remain even as long as three or four years.' Ana's mistaken belief that the scene of this religious prostitution was the temple of Bel is explicable if we assume that she has read the much briefer account of it in the apocryphal Epistle of Jeremiah (v. 43), which gives that impression.

7 (p. 607) *No other river than that of his homeland.* See Chapter XV, note 2.

8 (p. 607) *And every . . . where'er he would.* 'Jacob y Raquel', 431–2, by Francisco de Borja y Aragón, príncipe de Esquilache (1581–1658), a minor Spanish poet of the Golden Age.

9 (p. 614) *Faust.* The fourth act of *Faust* (1859) by Charles Gounod.

10 (p. 620) *ubi irritatio ibi fluxus.* 'Where there is a stimulus there is a flux.'

11 (p. 621) *St Barbara.* A saint traditionally invoked against thunder and lightning.

XXVIII

1 (p. 624) *Nisi utile . . . gloria.* 'If what we do is not useful, the glory is vain.' Giorgio Baglivi (1669–1707) was an eminent Italian doctor.

2 (p. 629) *the saint's game.* For Asturians the saint ('santina') is the Virgin of Covadonga, whose shrine is in the Asturian mountains ('monte').

3 (p. 636) *La Favorite and La Sonnambula.* Operas by Gaetano Donizetti (1840) and Vincenzo Bellini (1831).

4 (p. 636) *'Spirto gentil'.* See Chapter I, note 14.

5 (p. 641) *Assumption Day.* 15 August.

6 (p. 643) *all the world was their homeland.* An echo of the classical sententia found, for example, in Aulus Gellius, *Noctes atticae*, III, 15: 'forti viro omnis locus est patria' ('all the world is a strong man's homeland').

7 (p. 644) *Princess Mathilde's conservatory.* Mathilde Bonaparte (1820–1904), the

niece of Napoleon I, presided over a famous salon.

XXIX

1 (p. 652) *The Great Skinflint*. The picaresque novel *Historia de la vida del buscón* (1626) by Francisco de Quevedo y Villegas.
2 (p. 655) *help her master*. See Chapter XX, note 20.
3 (p. 658) *Las Novedades*. See Chapter V, note 3.
4 (p. 664) *a new man*. A grotesque parody of the New Testament concept (see Chapter I, note 17).
5 (p. 667) *the stairway of his dishonour*. An echo of the titles of some Golden Age honour plays, notably Calderón's *El pintor de su deshonra*.
6 (p. 674) *'Quando la mia Rosina'*. In the piano scene in the second and final act of Rossini's *The Barber of Seville* (see above, Chapter III, note 1), Lindoro has come into Bartolo's house to be with Rosina, in the guise of a piano teacher. He accompanies the senile Bartolo, who sings: 'Quando mi sei vicina, / amabile Rosina, / l'aria dicea Giannina, / ma io dico Rosina. /

Quando mi sei vicina, / amabile Rosina, / il cor mi brilla in petto, / io ballo il minuetto.'
7 (p. 676) *Settle and order . . . to yourself*. *The Imitation of Christ*, bk ii, ch. xii.

XXX

1 (p. 696) *Fígaro*. The pseudonym of the Spanish satirist Mariano José de Larra (1809–37).
2 (p. 699) *to fight the elements*. After the defeat of the Spanish Armada, Philip II is reported to have said: 'I sent my ships to fight against men, not against God's winds and His waves.'
3 (p. 703) *Noah's raven*. The first bird sent out of the Ark, before the dove (Genesis 8: 7).
4 (p. 708) *Villegas*. See Chapter II, note 6.
5 (p. 710) *Her husband's income . . . doesn't belong to her*. In Spanish law a widow only has a right to money acquired by her husband since the marriage and to property acquired with such money. She has no claims, for example, on that part of his estate which he inherited; this goes to his nearest blood-relations.